I0763463

GREATSHADOW • HUSH • WITCHBREAKER
CINDER • GREATSHADOW: ORIGINS

DRAGON APOCALYPSE

THE COMPLETE COLLECTION

Cover art by Julie Dillon

First Printing

The author may be contacted at
james@jamesmaxey.net

Greatshadow: Origins originally published in
Blood and Devotion 2010

Greatshadow originally published by Solaris Books 2012

Hush originally published by Solaris Books 2012

Witchbreaker originally published by Solaris Books 2012

Cinder originally published by author 2016

ISBN-13: 978-1-7325537-3-6

Table of Contents

GREATSHADOW

BOOK ONE OF THE DRAGON APOCALYPSE

Truth is hard.
Truth is harsh.
Truth is all that matters.
It is stark and beautiful
and complete.

1 - BONE-HANDLED KNIFE

WHEN INFIDEL GRABBED me by the seat of my pants and charged toward the window, I didn't protest. Partly this was due to the speed of her action, but mostly due to my inebriation from the sacramental wine we'd stolen. Plus, it wasn't the first time I'd been defenestrated by her. Of course, this window was five hundred feet up, in a lava-pygmy temple carved into the sheer cliff face of a volcano.

In my semi-drunken haze, I admired the view as I departed the temple, surveying the landscape around me. The night sky was bright orange as the bubbling caldera above reflected against belching steam. Far below, the dark, vine-covered canopy of trees draped like a casually tossed blanket down slopes stretching to the moonlit ocean. A lovely tropical night, one might even call it serene, save for the steady pulse of war drums and the nerve-jangling pygmy battle cry. It's difficult to relax with angry hordes of waist-high men barking in unison, "Yik-yik-yik-yik-yik!"

I reached the apex of my arc and began to fall. A deafening, high-pitched shriek drowned out the pygmies.

I don't know why I was screaming. If experience was any guide, Infidel had aimed me toward a bushy looking patch of forest. While my brain had faith in her, my vocal cords had doubts. I quickly saw that my brain was correct as I fell toward a living net of blood-tangle vines. I threw my hands over my eyes. My leather gauntlets spared my face from the worst of the thorns as I punched into the canopy, the vines popping and snapping beneath my weight. I bounced from branch to branch on the trees below. Even with my leather armor, the beating was as bad as anything I'd ever received at the hands of a mean-spirited bouncer.

Seconds later I jerked to a stop, completely tangled. I spread my fingers and found my face inches above a jagged obsidian boulder. The sobering realization I'd just escaped a messy death negated the effects of the stolen wine. I reached for the steel flask in my back pocket and took a quick gulp to restore myself. As much as I wanted to hang in the vines until my nerves calmed, I knew the pygmies wouldn't need long to find me. I reached for my bone-handled hunting knife and chopped at the tendrils, my body lurching, until I dropped onto the boulder and tumbled to the ground.

I looked up at the hole I'd punched in the canopy. Far above, a dark speck shot from the window through which my hasty exit had been facilitated. The speck quickly took on the shape of a woman as she hurtled toward the gap in the trees.

Infidel was laughing. She had both hands wrapped around the dragon-skull, hugging it to her chest like an oversized watermelon. Her long blonde hair trailed out behind her. She wore the loose-fitting white blouse and navy breeches from her recent stint as a mercenary in the pirate wars. She was barefoot, the soles of her feet black as coal. The orange light caught the string of yellow beads around her throat, a necklace of human molars that she'd kept as a diary of sorts while she'd served aboard the *Freewind*.

If she'd been aiming for the hole I'd left in the vines she missed, overshooting by several yards. I lost sight of her, but heard curses and grunts as she bounced from branch to branch, the blood-tangle snapping as it slowed her fall.

I managed to find my feet as she stumbled out of the darkness. Her blouse and breeches had been torn in a dozen places, but there wasn't a scratch on her enchanted skin. She had blood red flowers jutting from her hair and thorny vines draped over her shoulders. She held the dragon skull above her head one-handed, as if it was carved from balsa. With her other hand, she used her cutlass as a machete. Her lips were pressed together tightly as she spotted me.

"Are you okay?" she asked.

"Nothing's broken," I said, my voice trembling. I took another swig from the flask. "Your aim's still good."

She giggled. "I'm glad you're fine, because I'm looking forward to teasing you for the next ten years about that scream. Even I can't hit a note that high."

I held a finger to my lips and whispered, "You can laugh later. The pygmies won't be far behind."

"We've got a good head start," she said, looking up at the temple. She plucked a few flowers from her hair and flicked them away. "You worry too much.

For most of my life, I've earned a reputation as a man who doesn't worry enough. It's only around Infidel that I play the role of responsible adult. She's been magicked up to be as strong as ten men, with skin as tough as dragon hide. Her supernatural gifts have left her fearless, an aspect of her personality that draws me like a moth to a flame. Like many a moth, I sometimes get singed.

She held the dragon skull toward me, admiring it in the dim light. "The Black Swan's going to slip in her own drool when she gets a look at this."

Since I was presently in hock for a life-endangering sum of money to the Black Swan, I hoped that would be the case. Blood-houses throughout the Shining Lands pay handsomely for dragon bones. A single knuckle can be worth its weight in gold. An entire skull, complete with lower jaw and all the teeth, was a fortune so large that adjectives fail me. It would cover my debt and, more importantly, once more restore my line of credit at the bar. The cheap river-pygmy hooch I'd been swilling since the Black Swan cut me off was unbefitting of a connoisseur of fine spirits.

I whispered, "Let's get going. The pygmies know this jungle better than we do and –"

There was a tapping sound, like raindrops hitting a leaf. Infidel looked over her shoulder, stretching out her long, slender leg. Three porcupine quills were caught in the torn fabric of her pants. Suddenly, the air around her was thick with flying quills, some tangling in her hair, some bouncing off her impervious forehead. My own armor sprouted a dozen of the missiles. None made it through the leather, which was good. Lava-pygmies tip their darts with poison.

"Follow me!" Infidel shouted, slicing at a wall of vines with her cutlass and leaping through, the dragon-skull balanced on her shoulder. She could have stayed and fought without risk. By running she was protecting both me and the pygmies. We'd come here to rob them, not kill them.

I ran as fast as I could, slashing out with my bone-handled knife to better clear the path. In the darkness, I focused on Infidel's bright hair bobbing before me like a ghost. The pitter-patter of pygmy feet echoed in the canopy. Darts tapped across my shoulder blades as they continued to fire.

I kept falling farther behind. I was only a week away from my fiftieth birthday, too old for this profession. Once this was over, I swore to find a safer, more gentlemanly way of earning a living. My breath came in ragged gasps. A stabbing pain ran up my side. I could barely raise my knife to chop away the remnant vines Infidel left in her wake. I felt sure that if I pulled off my boots, sweat would pour out like stale beer from a pitcher.

I wiped the perspiration from my eyes. When I pulled my hand away, Infidel was gone. I kept running. The darkness in front of me had an Infidel-sized hole torn from it. Beyond I could see the rolling clouds of the eerie orange sky. There was a bass rumble ahead, a sound like a waterfall. I skid to a halt on the lip of a cliff and looked down into a deep scar in the earth. Infidel dangled from a mass of roots just beneath my feet. She still had the dragon skull, but her cutlass was nowhere to be seen.

"I know where we are!" she yelled, her voice nearly drowned out by the rushing water beneath her.

I knew as well: the southeast slope of the volcano is cut through by a whitewater river that cascades all the way to the sea.

"We're practically home!" she shouted.

I was of a different opinion. Many years ago, a palm-reader in Commonground told me I'd die of drowning. More poetically, she'd told me, "The sea will swallow your bones." It had been one reason I hadn't joined Infidel on the *Freewind*. I extend my caution by never imbibing anything watery enough for a fish to live in.

"Jump!" Infidel yelled.

"Let's weigh our options!" I shouted back.

Arguing proved pointless. Infidel pulled herself up on the thick root she held, clamping onto it with her teeth. With her now free hand, she punched the cliff wall. The root-draped stone beneath me crumbled.

As I dropped, Infidel grabbed me by the shoulder, pulling me toward her. She wrapped her arm around me, pressing me tight against her unbreakable body. Her breasts flattened against my back as she spooned me, curling us into a ball with her powerful legs. Her breath was hot against my neck. We fell through darkness, weightless.

I couldn't breathe. Partially because Infidel's arm across my belly was as gentle as a python, but, even more, because I so often dream of Infidel's embrace. She'd been a mere teen when I met her; I, a worn-out drunk twice her age. I'd watched as she'd ripped the arm off a bold warrior two feet taller than her who'd pawed her lithe body as she'd stood at the bar of the *Black Swan*. I wasn't the only man to witness this that quickly decided an attempt at seduction wasn't worth the risk.

I was, however, the only one who bought her a cider that evening and told her tales of the ruined cities hidden in the jungle. I've always been quick to make friends. Fate's brought me many fortunes over the years, and I've spent those fortunes making sure the patrons of the *Black Swan* never go thirsty. Yet I've never had a friend quite so true as Infidel. Her lightness balances my darkness; her recklessness makes the ongoing foolishness of my life look like sage wisdom. The two of us laugh together freely, and trust each other with our lives. I'm the one person who would never betray her for the obscenely large bounty on her head. She's the one person who never abandons me when my money runs out and I'm suddenly begging for drinks.

Never once in ten years of friendship has a night passed in which I didn't fantasize about her touch. I've never spoken a word of my secret passion. She means too much to me. It's not my arm I fear losing; it's her company. Our time together is so much sweeter than our time apart.

As dreamlike as her embrace might be, there was the unfortunate reality that we were hurtling toward a dark, raging river. With a horrible jolt, Infidel's shoulder cracked a boulder. We bounced into the torrent and her grip loosened. I inhaled, a bad move since my head was under water. We slammed into another rock and I slipped from her grasp. My face popped above the surface for a second and I coughed, water spraying from my lips. I sucked a cupful of air and croaked, weakly, "Infidel!"

She didn't answer as I bobbed along, careening from rock to rock. In moments of panic the mind can latch onto the most trivial details, and I noticed I'd lost my knife. Infidel either misplaced or broke her weapons on a daily basis, but I'd carried this knife for forty years; it had been a gift from my grandfather. For a fleeting second, finding the knife felt like a priority. Then, from the thunder ahead, I realized that I was about to be swept over a waterfall and my new priority became not to do so. I clawed desperately at boulders, but my hands had no strength. I still could only gulp small mouthfuls of air. The rocks pummeled me like the fists of giants. The knife-sharp pain that had torn my gut while running sliced me from groin to gullet. The water pushed me under and I went numb.

They say that drowning men see their lives pass before them. I could only see the fortuneteller, an old woman with dark eyes, her ears sporting gold rings and thick tufts of gray hair. Her voice crackled like dry leaves as she traced the line of my palm and told me how I'd meet my end.

Of course, she'd told Caleb the Crusher he'd die by hanging and he'd been the man whose arm Infidel had torn off on her first night in Commonground. You have to question the skills of a diviner who misses such a fate.

I slammed into a rock face first. Stars danced before me, changing to snowflakes as they showered down in the darkness. I found myself standing before Aurora, the ice-ogress who serves as the main muscle at the *Black Swan*. She was discussing the small matter of my bar tab. In the three months Infidel had been at sea, I'd been a little freer with my purse than usual. When I confessed that I had no money, Aurora had pointed out that a man was never completely without assets. Artfully butchered, human flesh could pass for pork; only a few coins per pound, but for a grown man that added up. I assured her that once Infidel returned, my fortunes would improve. She gave me thirty days. It was thirty-two days later when Infidel got back. Unfortunately, the *Freewind* had been on the losing side of the pirate wars. This was in no way Infidel's fault, but it meant that she'd not received the bonus promised to her in the event of victory. Given the way the Black Swan calculated interest, the handful of coins Infidel had been paid failed to dent my debt. Thus, not for the first time in my life, I was off to plunder the ancient tombs and temples of the Vanished Kingdom.

As I plunged over the lip of the waterfall, I took some small measure of comfort that my corpse would be sufficiently mangled that Aurora couldn't even sell it as dog food.

The drop proved to be the shortest distance I'd fallen that evening, a trifling fifty-foot plunge into a broad pool. The water at the base of the fall roiled. In the turbulence, I couldn't even guess which direction was up. The shallow gulps of air I'd gotten bobbing in the river were exhausted in seconds. My leather armor was heavy as steel plates. The pounding water pinned me. Yet, the pain and pressure felt distant. The water was warm, heated by the volcano, almost pleasant. The polished gravel beneath me was as comfortable as a feather bed. I went limp, all my weariness flowing from me like bubbles from my lips. There were worse ways to die.

As I was about to discover.

Just as I was on the verge of sleep and surrender, a strong hand grabbed my hair. Infidel tugged me above the surface and flung me across her left shoulder like a sack of sodden potatoes. She still carried the dragon skull, her fist shoved inside the base. She waded through knee-deep water as I draped across her back, my eyes at the level of her heart-shaped buttocks. Water poured from my lips, but I couldn't muster the will to inhale.

Infidel laid me on a beach of black sand, dropping the skull beside me, then straightened, shaking her head to get the hair from her eyes. She looked as soggy as a drowned rat; her torn pirate blouse hung from her arms like flaps of skin on a once-fat man. Her hair was plastered to her scalp, knotted so horribly that she needed a razor more than a comb. At some point, her necklace of molars must have snapped. The only evidence it had ever been there was a single tooth wedged between her hip and the top of her broad belt. Despite her sorry condition, her waterlogged clothes revealed the magnificent paradox of her body, the sleek and sultry curves that sat atop angular, iron muscles.

I spotted something amiss on her flawless form. A dark red stain glistened atop her left shoulder. I sucked in a spoonful of air, the effort making me tremble, and whispered, "You're bleeding."

She frowned as she followed my gaze to the crimson circle that seeped out across her blouse in ever-lightening shades of pink. Her eyes grew wide. In the adventures we'd shared, I'd only seen her bleed three times. Once, No-Face had caught her square in the mouth with his ball and chain, producing a split lip. He'd hit her by accident and she didn't hold grudges, which was the only reason he was still alive. The same couldn't be said for the bounty hunter who'd gone after her with a shadow sword. He'd crisscrossed her arms with a dozen cuts before she wrestled the blade away. They'd had to carry out what was left of him in buckets. And, of course, there had been the tussle with that mechanical tiger with the diamond-tipped claws. The only scars on her otherwise flawless legs had come from that fight.

Her face turned pale as she pushed the remnants of her pirate blouse down her shoulder, revealing streaks of red across her ivory skin. She wiped away the blood with her fingers, leaving behind smooth, unblemished flesh.

She looked back at me, her face turning whiter still.

I looked down. I understood why I couldn't breathe.

The good news was, I'd found my knife.

The bone-handle jutted from the waist of my leather armor. Eight inches of honed steel were lodged in my gut. I couldn't feel a thing, but blood pulsed from the wound with every fading heartbeat.

Infidel dropped to her knees. I looked up at her, her face so bright as the world around me darkened. I took in another teaspoon of air and mumbled, "Tell the f-fortuneteller… I want… my m-money back."

Infidel frowned, then just as quickly grinned. "You faker," she giggled. "It's nothing more than a scratch." She grabbed the edge of my vest with both hands. The thick leather tore like tissue paper in her superhuman grasp.

Her jaw went slack.

It was something more than a scratch.

Her gaze met mine once more, and for the first time ever I saw tears gleaming in her eyes, her lovely eyes, a pale blue-gray, the ephemeral color sometimes found on the horizon of the ocean, where you can no longer tell where the sky ends and the water begins.

I couldn't let my final words to her be some joke, some quip that hid the great secret truth of my life. I managed to swallow another mouthful of air and whispered, "I… have always… l-loved you."

"Stagger," she whispered back, eyes closing, tears rolling down her cheeks. "Oh, Stagger."

I closed my eyes as well, unable to spare the strength to keep them open. My heartbeat fluttered in my ears, faint and failing. I hoped I could die at peace now; I'd confessed what I should have revealed ten years before. And yet... and yet there was one thing more. One last secret haunting me as I slipped toward my final rest. My blood turned cold as the guilt of my only betrayal of Infidel's trust pulsed through me.

I mouthed the words, my voice barely audible, "I... didn't lose... the m-map. I... s-sold it... to the... the... f-fishmon—" my voice failed. I tried to breathe but couldn't. My body refused to obey, save for my eyes, which opened once more.

Infidel's face was inches from my own. Her lips were puckered. I had the distinct impression she was about to kiss me. Then her eyes snapped open. She jerked upward as my final words sank in.

"You did *what?*" she asked.

I tried to answer, but it was no use. My body was done for. I couldn't even close my eyes. Her lips moved, but I couldn't hear what she said. Her words were lost beneath the roar of waves from a distant, invisible ocean. Behind her, I could see the bright orange faces of lava-pygmies as they emerged from the forest, holding spears tipped with glassy black rock above their heads, preparing to strike. I couldn't warn her. I couldn't do anything except drift upward. Whatever essence there may be of a man that is separate from his body had come loose as my heart went silent. I found myself floating, a shapeless, formless thing, a fog composed of memories and broken dreams, cut free from my flesh.

I looked down though non-existent eyes at the scene beneath me. Spears were bouncing off Infidel's back. She rose with a snarl, yanking the bone-handled knife from my belly. Normally, I love to watch Infidel in combat. She fights like the unholy union of a bobcat and a ballerina, a whirlwind of blades and laughter that traces the landscape around her with long and looping arcs of blood.

But I paid little mind as she raced toward the first pygmy and delivered a kick that sent him flying above the treetops. Instead, I looked down at the sorry, sodden thing that I'd once thought of as me. I hadn't made it to fifty, but the mask of wrinkles around my eyes could have belonged to a man twice that age. My cheeks and chin were speckled with scraggly white stubble; I couldn't grow a decent beard on a bet. My shoulder-length hair was streaked through with gray. My pony-tail did nothing to hide the scaly bald patch at the back of my skull. I was tall, and in my better days my torso had been shaped like a V, with broad shoulders and a narrow waist. Until this moment, I always pictured myself with that body, and never accepted that the bottom of the V had gotten lost beneath an O, a big, oval jug of jiggling fat that must inevitably attach itself to a man who loved his liquor as much as I did.

With my eyeless vision, I could see the truth of who I'd been: a fat, half-bald old drunk who'd been vain enough to fantasize that a woman whom the gods must surely envy might one day love him.

As my consciousness expanded, ever wider, ever thinner, I was dimly aware that I'd miss that man.

Then, I had no awareness at all.

Or, more accurately, I had awareness, but no will, no ability to guide my perceptions or ponder the scenes I saw. I was spread through all things. I was present in the dark depths of the ocean, floating beside hideous fish with lantern eyes and jaws like bear-traps. I was present in the jungle, slithering among the branches crawling with snakes and toads and beetles, all in rainbow hues brighter than gemstones. I was present in the bars of Commonground, where battle-weary veterans of the pirate wars stumbled along the uneven boardwalks as whores called out for their company. I could feel all the lust and loneliness of their moments, all the sorrowful joy that spills into the universe when two strangers touch in intimacy.

And, far, far above the squalid city, I was present in the clouds, looking out upon a night sky full of glittering diamonds, keenly aware of every point of light. The sky shimmered with distant suns and unseen planets. I could hear the murmur of countless voices, the indecipherable echoes of life on worlds too numerous to number. What was left of my mind shrugged and surrendered, unable to absorb the infinite majesty of a creation in which my life had been of no consequence at all.

It was into this vastness that I would disappear. The final spark of my consciousness calmly dissipated. Like a stream of stinking urine spreading into the ocean, I was absorbed once more into the Great Incomprehensible All.

Then, blood pulsed within my non-existent heart.

There was another pulse, then another, and I began to feel as if I once more had veins and arteries, as if I once more had lungs. The atoms of my awareness raced back from the ocean, from the forest, from the sky, coalescing into a specter above my still very dead corpse. Where I'd been only a formless mass of thought, I could now look down at ghostly fingers, wraith-like toes, and a phantom wang. I was hanging naked above the shell of my body. I reached down to touch it, but my ghost hands found no purchase in the dead flesh. Yet, I was definitely me again. Something had halted the dispersal of my soul.

Around my body, the ground was wet with blood. Far more blood, I knew, than had ever pumped through my heart. I quickly spotted the severed limbs and mangled torsos of half a dozen pygmies. I felt a shiver of guilt that I'd brought this fate upon them. I spun around, searching for Infidel.

She looked as if she'd been doused with buckets of tomato juice. She had a pygmy dangling in her grasp, a chief judging from his feathered head-dress. She had my bone-handled knife pressed against his throat.

"Call them off!" she growled, as more pygmies emerged from the trees. "Leave us alone and no one else gets hurt!"

The chief responded by spitting in her eye. Two seconds later, his head was separated from his shoulders.

As his blood flowed across the bone-handled knife, life flowed back into me. I inhaled, my ghost lungs filling, and shouted, "Infidel!"

She didn't react. She was too lost in her anger to hear me as she charged the newest round of warriors, a dozen spearmen clustered in a frightened clump at the edge of the clearing.

I grabbed at her arm as she raced past me. My fingers passed right through her skin.

"Infidel!" I screamed again.

She didn't even blink as she crashed into the wall of spears, splintering them. The wide-eyed pygmies turned in unison to flee. She gave chase for only a yard or so, then, either in frustration or as a warning, she punched the nearest tree, splintering the trunk.

The tree groaned, then toppled, as Infidel lowered into a half crouch and scanned the area, her eyes as intense as a cat searching a bush for a bird.

Infidel remained alert for several minutes as her panting breath returned to normal. At last, she relaxed, straightening up. The pygmies had taken the hint. She twisted her head in a slow arc, her bones popping as the tension in her neck and shoulders slackened. Her lips parted slightly as she took a deep breath. Looking at my body, her shoulders sagged.

She walked toward my corpse, her arms limp at her sides, my bone-handled knife barely dangling in her grasp. When she reached my remains, she stared down, breathing slowly. The music of frogs and insects began to hum and strum as the violence of the moment before was swept away by the unceasing flow of time.

She shoved my knife into her broad leather belt and knelt before my body. Placing her arms beneath my knees and shoulders, she lifted me. I twisted my ghostly form to occupy the space of my corpse, trying to feel her hands upon my dead flesh, to no avail. I could no more grasp my body than I could grasp the wind.

She carried my cadaver into the calm end of the pool, walking ever deeper until I was submerged. She ducked her whole body beneath the water. I didn't know what she was doing. I was mystified, unable to read the blank mask of her face. She bobbed back above water to breathe. The blood from the battle washed from her cheeks. As the water carried off the gore that caked my grandfather's knife, my ghostly body faded from my sight. I was no longer dispersing into nothingness, or allness, but was instead simply invisible, intangible, a memory of a man haunting the woman he once loved, his soul somehow bound to the blade that had killed him.

Beneath the water, she undressed me, peeling away my torn armor, still studded with pygmy darts. She washed the blood and mud and sand from my pale skin, her fingers gently tracing the lines of my face. She calmly worked the tangles from my hair, then let my body drift in the still water as she ducked back beneath and pulled off the shreds of her own clothes, scrubbing her skin, her hair spreading through the water like a halo as she patiently pulled out bits of vines from the numerous knots. Twenty minutes later, she carried my now clean corpse from the water. She was naked save for the thick black belt that sat upon her angular hips. The blade of my knife pressed against the smooth arc that traced where her belly met her hip, the tip resting near the thick blonde curls of her pubic hair.

She laid me gently on the black sand and sat beside me, her legs folded beneath her. I looked as if I was sleeping. The hole from which my life had drained was just a ragged flap an inch or two across, not so fearsome. She folded my arms over my chest, cupping the uppermost hand in her slender fingers. Free of blood, her skin gleamed like marble.

She sat for a long time, her lips twitching. Sometimes, she looked on the verge of tears. In other moments, I was certain she was about to curse and beat my battered corpse with her fists. In the end, her lips curled upwards, as the faintest hint of a smile managed to claw its way up from beneath grief and guilt and rage.

She shook her head gently as she looked into my face. As the jungle crescendo grew with the approaching daylight, and songbirds lent their voices to the drone of bugs and frogs, she swallowed deeply.

"You old fool," she whispered. "I loved you too."

2 - THAT DAMNED MAP

INFIDEL BURIED ME on a high bluff overlooking the sea. She'd carried me here wrapped in a colorful cloth she stole from the lava-pygmy village not far from the base of the falls. She'd met no opposition. It would be a long time before members of that tribe would come anywhere near her. The village emptied out as she'd walked into it. She could have robbed them blind, except, of course, they didn't have much to steal. The village was nothing but stick huts with dirt floors, with a few scrawny chickens the only livestock. It brought home the magnitude of my sins.

When the monks who raised me had had taught me about hell, they'd painted vivid pictures of barren landscapes in which the damned are tormented by horned devils. I never feared it. But, if I'd been told that I'd linger on after death, forever confronted by the people I'd hurt the most... maybe I would have tried to be a better person.

After making my shroud, Infidel had fashioned an impromptu sarong from the remaining cloth. The fabric had a crimson base looped through with green lines and yellow circles. The yellow circle motif could be found all through the ruins of the Vanished Kingdom. My grandfather had speculated that the yellow circle represented Glorious, the primal dragon of the sun, who had been worshipped as a god in ancient times. I don't know if the pygmies gave the same symbolic value to it, or just liked the design. The festive pattern was remarkably inappropriate for wrapping a corpse, but Infidel valued practicality over propriety. Despite its failings as a shroud, I thought the cloth looked good on her. She normally didn't wear vivid colors; she especially disliked bright greens for some reason.

She'd spent much of the day following the river to the sea. Given the rugged terrain, she made better time with me as a limp corpse across her shoulder than if I'd still been alive. Her endurance matched her strength. Even with my weight, plus the dragon skull, she never stopped to rest or eat.

By the end of the day she'd reached my final resting spot. I don't know if she'd planned to bury me here. Perhaps she intended to take me all the way to Commonground, to have me outfitted for a proper coffin by one of the city's numerous undertakers. Unfortunately, after a single day in the jungle heat, I was beginning to spoil. Dark, foul-smelling fluid stained my shroud, and by the time we reached the bluff the fabric would go black with flies faster than Infidel could shoo them away.

Infidel placed me at the foot of a shaggy, wind-blown tree as the sun set behind us. Shadows danced on the waves as she rested. A cool, steady breeze blew up from the sea, drinking up the sweat beaded on her face. Her hair danced around her eyes as she stared out at the darkening sky, watching the stars flicker to life above the water.

At last, she began to dig. She had no tools other than her bare hands and my old knife. The soil was sandy, covered with a layer of scraggly grass. She worked through the night, digging until she had a pit deeper than she was tall. She lowered my body into the ground with a look of utter weariness, then proceeded to cover me with the mounds of damp earth heaped on both sides of the hole. She finished just before dawn, running her hands over the sandy grave as if she was smoothing out the wrinkles on a sheet.

She thrust the bone-handled knife into the soil above my head, where it stood like the world's smallest tombstone. I felt a flutter of panic. Would she leave the blade there? My spirit was now tied to the knife. For my soul to remain anchored here so close to my body was, I suppose, appropriate. Yet, I no longer felt any connection to the rotting meat six feet below. I wanted to remain with Infidel.

I had no lips with which to speak, so I merely thought the words, *Keep the knife. Keep the knife*. I suddenly understood what the monks had tried to teach me about the fierce urgency of prayer. *Keep the knife. Keep the knife. Keep the knife.*

She sat down, resting her hands on her knees as she glanced at the yellowed handle. The humble bone gleamed like precious ivory, polished and oiled by a lifetime spent in my sweaty hands. *Take it,* I prayed. *Take it.* Her face was lined with deep furrows around her lips as she frowned. She looked as if she was about to cry, but, always when she was on the verge, she'd swallow. Her fists would go tight, then the moment would pass. Her eyes turned away from the tiny tombstone. I sensed that my prayers would go unanswered. Still, as long as she still lingered by my grave, there was hope.

At last the sun came up. The water danced with colors to rival the sarong still draped around her shoulders. Gulls wheeled in the air above the cliff, calling out to one another. Clouds drifted leisurely overhead, white as lambs in a distant field. I wanted to tell her that she'd done a good job. My bones had to rest somewhere. This was a fine choice, a grave any ghost could be proud of. As much as I wished to continue to journey by her side, I knew my time had passed. If I was now a prisoner to eternity, this peaceful, sun-drenched bluff would be an acceptable jail.

By my count, Infidel had been awake for almost forty hours. Her endurance was superhuman, but not infinite. Her head sagged as she watched the endless dance of the waves. At last, she stretched out on the white sand of my grave. She used her arm as a pillow, and her fingers brushed against the handle of the knife. She looked at it again, her eyes bloodshot and bleary. She snatched the knife free of the soil, clutching it to her invulnerable breast like a doll. Then, with a shudder, she gave herself to sleep.

She slept fitfully through the day, undraping the cloth of her sarong and using it as a blanket pulled over her head to block out the light. As someone who'd shared campsites with Infidel, I knew she talked in her sleep. Mumbled, more accurately. Many a night I've lain awake and tried to make sense of her slurred half-words. Usually, I can't interpret them. But, as she turned from one side to the other, three unmistakable syllables escaped her lips: "So sorry."

She thinks she killed me. She thinks that as we fell toward the river, she was the one who drove the knife into my gut.

Perhaps.

I wish I could tell her that I don't blame her. She shouldn't ignore the fact that we were out robbing that temple because I was the one in debt, because I'm the one who needs to buy the company of crowds, because I'm the sucker who can't resist a good sob story from any down-on-his-luck bum who begs me for a few spare coins and winds up with my entire purse.

Of course, I wouldn't have been in debt when she got back from the pirate wars if I'd sold the map for even a fraction of what it was worth.

That damned map.

A year ago, Infidel had hunted down a fallen Wanderer by the name of Hurricane. Wanderers have a longstanding pact with Abyss, the primal dragon of the sea, that prevents them from ever drowning as long as they spend their lives without touching dry land. Their behavior is guided by ancient and elaborate laws; transgress these laws and a Wanderer can find himself put ashore on some distant desert island. Hurricane had suffered that fate, due to acts of piracy against fellow Wanderers. But, he didn't live out his days on his island prison. He'd built a raft, fled to the Isle of Fire, and resumed his piracy. The Wanderers placed a bounty on his head, a price large enough to catch Infidel's eye.

Finding Hurricane was no great challenge. He'd set up camp in a sea cave on the western side of the island. Infidel made swift work of his crew, and took Hurricane out with a single punch. We were searching his treasure chest when we found the map in a hidden compartment at the bottom. Even before we opened the thing, we knew it was something special. It was embroidered onto metallic cloth spun from threads of gold far finer than silk. The fabric made a musical sound as we unrolled it, like tiny guitar strings plinking. The map showed the central volcano of the Isle of Fire and plotted out several key buildings from the Vanished Kingdom. I knew this area well, both from my own explorations and my grandfather's detailed surveys. At the building I call the Shattered Palace, the map marked a tunnel leading into the volcano. Depending on how you held the map to the light, different layers were revealed; there were tunnels beneath tunnels. Someone had used ordinary ink to trace out some of the pathways, and there were notes near these paths, written in a code I couldn't decipher. I could only scratch my head as I turned the map from side to side, pondering the different images. Beneath the overlapping layers I spotted an 'X', and two words written in old-tongue that were perfectly clear.

Greatshadow. Treasure.

Greatshadow is the primal dragon who lives in the central volcano of this island. I've never seen Greatshadow, but my grandfather wrote that he'd been on the island once when the dragon was awake. He said that the big lizard had a wingspan half a mile wide. The heat of Greatshadow's breath will turn iron armor into hot white syrup dripping off the blackened bones of any knight foolish enough to face him. Like all dragons, Greatshadow has an eye for gems and precious metal. What he does with them, I can't even guess. It's not as if he strolls down to the *Black Swan* from time to time to buy a round. Still, he's been hoarding riches during the rise and fall and rise of at least two civilizations. If a man could sneak into that treasure vault for even five minutes, he could snatch up enough wealth to carry him through a dozen lifetimes.

While I deciphered the map, I was thinking out loud, pitching my thoughts and theories to Infidel. Almost instantly, I regretted it. I could hear the wheels turning in her mind. We'd been tomb-raiding together for a long time. Why not go after the ultimate treasure?

Here's why: Greatshadow isn't just another monster. He's the living embodiment of fire. He may be wrapped in scaly hide, but he's fundamentally an elemental being, a sentient force of nature. A fraction of his intelligence is present in every flame. You can't kill something like this with just a strong arm and sharp sword.

Infidel is tough, but her skills as a thief tend toward the smash and grab. There was no way she could reach Greatshadow's treasure without confronting the dragon, and, if it came to that, good as she was, Greatshadow would win.

So, at my first convenient opportunity, I 'lost' the map.

This was really the only time I've ever deceived her, other than the daily, ongoing, unspoken lie that I wanted nothing more of her than friendship. It's weighed heavily on my conscious for the last year, mainly because she'd accepted my lame explanation of how I'd lost the map down a privy hole on the docks in Commonground. She'd reacted to my story with her easy-come, easy-go shrug and never mentioned it again. Maybe she'd known all along the adventure was too big for her. If so, that makes my lie even worse. If she could have been dissuaded from the lair by simple reason, we could have sold the map for a small fortune, perhaps even a large one. I didn't need to betray her trust. We could have been living it up in Commonground rather than out robbing pygmies with the same foolish bravery of young boys throwing rocks at a hornet nest.

She turns again in her slumber, moaning softly.

I'm sorry, I pray to her. *So, so sorry.*

INFIDEL RETURNED TO Commonground the following day, making good time as she bounded along the shore. In open terrain, she's fast as a jack-rabbit, using her super-strong legs to propel herself in skips that cover a dozen yards a stride. Around mid-morning she found the wreck of a ship; it couldn't have been more than a few weeks old. She didn't take long to explore it, but did manage to pull a damp, sand covered yard of canvas from the wreckage. She wrapped the dragon-skull in this – a wise precaution. Even with Infidel's reputation, Commonground is full of thieves who would be tempted by the sight. It's a lawless city, a bad place to call home. Of course, there's not a lot of choice in addresses when you live on the Isle of Fire. Commonground is the only real city on the island.

Actually, there are a couple of things wrong with that statement.

For starters, the city isn't on the island, but out in the bay. The whole place is up on stilts. Plus, it's not really a city in the ordinary sense of the word. It's a collection of docks. It's like a city that exists entirely of streets where the homes come and go on a daily basis. Wanderers gather here, taking refuge in the sheltered bay. On any given day you can find a hundred or so of their ships at the port, and several thousand of their ilk milling about. Of course, the Wanderers don't live in Commonground. They stay only a little while, then move on, replaced by the crews of other ships.

The only permanent residents of Commonground are people who've come there due to the lawless nature of the place. The Wanderers don't impose their codes on outsiders; they care nothing of the actions of others as long as it doesn't harm them. So, over the years, Commonground has become a haven to men and women not welcome in the more civilized parts of the world. Along the docks you'll find barges housing bars and brothels and blood-houses. These draw visitors from distant ports, mainly young, hedonistic men escaping the chains of morality that confine them in places like the Silver City. Also drawn to the place are criminals who've fled their homelands to seek out the one place on earth where no one ever asks about your past. It's taboo even to ask a person's real name in Commonground. Everyone goes by nicknames. It wasn't like my mother looked at me in the crib and said, "I bet he'll be a drunkard. Let's call him Stagger."

Commonground is just a lousy name. As noted, there's no ground at all. And you'd be hard pressed to find anyone who's common.

A few hours after she'd plundered the wreckage for the canvas, Infidel reached one of the boardwalks leading out into the bay. She strode purposely through the maze of docks, ignoring gawkers as she passed. The sight of her in the colorful sarong was turning heads. Infidel normally dressed in a more masculine fashion, often wearing leather armor even though she didn't need it.

Not that there were that many people out to gawk at her. The late afternoon sun was unbearable. The docks didn't really come to life until darkness fell. The algae green water of the bay was as smooth as jade in the windless heat. Fortunately, the tide was in. When the tide was out, a strong sea wind was the only protection against the raw sewage and fish-rot stench. With the water high, the stink wasn't so bad, though I was left to ponder why I could smell at all, since I no longer had a nose. Of course, I was seeing without eyes, and hearing without ears. If I wound up near whiskey, would I be able to taste it?

Of course, the best place to put that to the test was exactly where Infidel was heading. Near the heart of Commonground, Infidel reached the largest barge anchored at the docks – the *Black Swan*. This was a saloon and gambling house that catered to the high rollers from the Silver Isles. Wealthy men could visit the *Black Swan* with little fear for their safety. Thieves knew that messing with a guest of the barge could result in a visit from the Three Goons. Not many people would risk that for a bag of gold. A dragon skull on the other hand…

Infidel stepped through the door of the bar, pausing as her eyes adjusted to the shadows. The bar was decorated with a level of opulence that stumbled across the fine line separating good taste from garishness. The walls were lined with dark, polished teak; large paintings of scantily clad goddesses hung on the walls. The various gaming tables sported crisp velvet surfaces. Only a single poker table was fully occupied. Everyone else was likely sleeping in the well-furnished rooms above. The main room was at least twenty degrees cooler than the air outside. Behind the bar at the far end of the room was the reason why.

A first timer to the bar might mistake the creature who stood there as male, given the broad shoulders and looming height. Few people have ever seen an ice-ogre of either sex. Aurora's nine feet tall, with pale blue skin mottled with patches of white, like a sky full of clouds. She's bald save for a tuft of dark blue hair in a knot at the tip of her scalp. Tusks jut up from her lower jaws, reaching to her eyebrows. Her clothes offer no hint of her gender; she always wears a long sleeved, walrus-skin coat that hangs down to her ankles. Aurora exhaled as she spotted Infidel, her breath coming out in a fog. The ogress is in charge of security at the *Black Swan*. While most of Infidel's visits are peaceful, she's been known, occasionally, to cause a bit of property damage.

"Where's your shadow?" Aurora asked, squinting at the doorway behind Infidel. Crystals of frost on her cheeks sparkled like diamonds.

"My shadow?" Infidel asked, walking toward the bar.

"Stagger," said Aurora. "I never see you without him hang-dogging behind."

"Stagger's dead," said Infidel, placing the sack onto the bar. There was no emotion as she spoke the words.

"Oh," said Aurora. She shook her head slowly. "I'll miss him. Most drunks think they're funny and charming. He really was, sometimes."

"He was more than just a drunk," said Infidel.

"No offense," said Aurora, in a tone that sounded as if she had, indeed, meant no offense.

Infidel looked directly into Aurora's eyes. She knew about Aurora's threat to sell my body for meat; Aurora probably knew she knew. Of course, Aurora was just the enforcer. If Infidel had come here looking for revenge, she'd be looking for the woman who really called the shots.

"I need to see the Black Swan," said Infidel.

Aurora crossed her arms, her biceps bulging beneath the walrus leather. She and Infidel had never lit into one another; Infidel probably had an edge, but Aurora wasn't going to be a pushover. Her strength was supplemented by a formidable array of ice magic; for a tropical town, Commonground has a surprising number of residents who've lost limbs to frostbite. "The Black Swan has a busy schedule," Aurora said. "I'll see if I can work you into her calendar."

"I need to see her now," said Infidel.

Aurora shook her head. "She'll see you when she wants to see you."

"She'll want to see me now," said Infidel, pulling the canvas away from the dragon skull. All the people at the poker table suddenly placed their cards face down and stared at the bar. Whatever stakes they were playing for, a dragon skull would trump it.

The ice-ogress let loose an appreciative whistle as she eyed the priceless object. "The lower jaw and everything," she said, reaching out to touch it.

Infidel caught her by the wrist. Aurora tried to pull back, but Infidel held her arm immobile. I had my answer as to who was strongest. Then, Aurora grinned, and Infidel grimaced as her whole arm turned blue.

"Hold me too long and you'll lose those fingers," said Aurora, coolly.

"No one touches the skull but me and the Black Swan," Infidel said, through chattering teeth.

Aurora nodded. Infidel released her wrist.

"Given the nature of this transaction, I'll see if the boss is available," said Aurora, drawing her arm back. Infidel rubbed her frosted fingers as the ice-ogress vanished behind a red silk curtain at one end of the bar.

I sincerely hoped the Black Swan wasn't available. Whatever Infidel was planning to do, it couldn't be good.

As Infidel waited, a tall man in chain mail peeled away from the shadows in the far corner. He was broad-shouldered, his hair cropped short, his face rugged, probably handsome once, before his nose had been broken one too many times. His proboscis perched over his lips like a scaly red vulture. His hands were large and rough, his knuckles thick with calluses. I'd never seen him before. Perhaps this was some new enforcer that the Black Swan had hired, though more likely he was employed by one of the clients as private muscle. The man's gaze kept darting between the dragon skull and Infidel's bosom, accented as it was by the sarong.

"That's a mighty expensive thing for a little lady to be carrying," Vulture-nose said, easing up to the bar. "Seems like you could use a little security."

There was a commotion at the poker table. Everyone was standing up and stuffing their chips into their pockets. One by one, they bolted for the door.

Infidel gave him a sideways glance and said, with remarkable restraint, "Go away."

The big fellow grinned. "Aw, don't be like that. For a pretty gal like yourself, I wouldn't have to work for money. We could work out things out in trade. You scratch my back, I scratch yours."

To demonstrate what he had in mind, the doomed man placed one of his meaty paws on the small of Infidel's bare back. His hand was nearly as large as her slender waist as he began to gently rub her.

It's easy to rub Infidel the wrong way.

When Aurora poked her head back into the room a second later, Infidel was in exactly the same pose as when she'd left. Above her was a hole about a yard across. Sunlight filtered down. A naked man in the room directly above sat up in his bed, looking up at the hole that had suddenly appeared in his ceiling. He looked down at the matching hole in the floor. He rubbed his eyes, perhaps not certain if he was awake. A single boot tumbled from the sky, landing with a *thump* on the floor next to Infidel.

"Some guy knocked a hole in your ceiling," she said. "You should be more careful who you let in this joint."

Aurora grimaced. "The Black Swan will see you now."

THE SALON WAS dark save for a red glow from the glass window of the cast iron stove. A ceramic crock of potpourri simmered on the stove, filling the room with a cloying floral perfume and a level of humidity worse than anything out in the jungle. Despite the heat, the Black Swan had a shawl of black feathers draped across her silk dress; save for its ebony hue her gown looked like something she might have worn at her wedding. Like a bride, a lace veil concealed her face. Her hands were wrinkled claws, speckled with dark brown liver spots, her long nails painted to match her wardrobe.

In a city of outlaws who would rob their own grandmother, the rise of the Black Swan as its most powerful denizen was something of a mystery. It seemed improbable that this frail old woman commanded the respect of ogres and half-seeds, but Aurora kept her head bowed as she approached the leather couch where the Black Swan lounged and said, in a reverent hush, "Madam, Infidel has come to discuss a matter of commerce."

"Thank you, Aurora," said the Black Swan. Her scratchy, dry voice made me imagine that, should she cough, dust would come out.

The old woman turned her head toward Infidel, then motioned her to have a seat on the padded leather chair across from the couch. As Infidel sat down, the Black Swan said, "Aurora informs me your lover has passed away."

"He wasn't my lover," said Infidel, somewhat over-emphatically, I thought.

"I see. I had assumed –"

"You assumed wrong," Infidel snapped. "Stagger was my friend. With the life I've led, I needed a friend more than I ever needed a lover."

"Ah, friendship," said the Black Swan. "It's a commodity I find sorely overrated. You cannot pay someone to be your friend; they may pretend to be so, but you would always know the truth. In my experience, if a thing cannot be purchased, it has no true value."

"Or it may have the greatest value of all," said Infidel.

"Your naiveté is charming." The Black Swan shifted on her couch. A handful of downy black feathers drifted to the floor. "Though, perhaps I've underestimated your judgment if you didn't take that old drunkard as a lover. You must have known that when the desire for alcohol gripped him, he would have gladly walked over any of his so-called friends to reach a bottle. Even you, my dear."

If I'd still had teeth, I would have ground them.

Infidel pressed her lips together. I was surprised at how calm she seemed. She said, "I haven't come to discuss my personal life. I've come to pay off Stagger's debts."

The Black Swan tilted her head. "This is most honorable of you."

"Honor has nothing to do with it," said Infidel. "I want to clear the balance sheets once and for all. I know you think of Stagger and me as a team; I don't want the money he owed you to influence any business we may undertake."

The Black Swan nodded. "The skull will cover Stagger's debt, and more. I will arrange an auction. Aurora will deliver the balance of the proceeds to you."

"Keep them," said Infidel. "I want to open my own account to make use of your services."

Aurora raised an eyebrow, obviously surprised by this news. The Black Swan's face showed no reaction.

"I want to hire the Three Goons," said Infidel.

Aurora's other eyebrow shot up.

"This is… most unusual," said the Black Swan.

"Is it?" asked Infidel. "They're hired muscle. People purchase their services every day."

"Despite your many limitations, my dear, you are hardly lacking in muscle. Why would you possibly need their help?"

"I've got a robbery in mind. A smash-and-grab with a payoff that will make this dragon skull look like a hunk of tin. As good as I am, I'll need backup. The Three Goons can get the job done."

"Undoubtedly," said the Black Swan. "Alas, I cannot give you what you ask for. Another client recently engaged the Three Goons in an open contract. I don't know when they will be available."

"I'll buy out the contract," said Infidel. "Just name the price."

"My dear, I admire your ambition, but you cannot possibly match the resources of this client. For all practical purposes, their purse is infinitely deep."

"Who is it?" Infidel asked. "I'll talk to them. Make them an offer."

"You know that is a confidential matter."

Infidel frowned as she crossed her arms. Negotiations weren't Infidel's strong suit. I used to handle this sort of business.

The Black Swan said, "Perhaps there are others who could serve your needs? Commonground is thick with mercenaries. Post a bill and you'll have a hundred men standing in line for the job within an hour."

Which was true, but the Three Goons were worth a lot more than a hundred men. Remember No-Face? The only man who ever gave Infidel a split lip? He's one of the goons. And he's not the one that most people are afraid of.

Infidel's hands balled into fists. Aurora tensed up. Infidel's eyes narrowed as thoughts danced in her mind. She still hadn't given up. "You've tried to hire me before," she said. "I'll work for you for the next year. Take any job you give me. At the end of the year, you give me the Goons, no questions asked."

The Black Swan nodded, smiling faintly. I quickly sensed this was a bittersweet smile. She wanted to accept Infidel's offer, but couldn't. "Tempting. Quite tempting. There are men who would pay a lifetime of wages to use you for a night."

The color drained from Infidel's cheeks.

"My darling, you don't think I would waste a year of your service on fighting, do you? As you note, I already have access to the finest mercenaries on the island. I have a high priestess for my chief enforcer. Why shouldn't I have a princess for a whore?"

Aurora scowled deeply. It took me a second to realize that she had to be the priestess. It seems I wasn't the only one with a religious background that never got discussed. But I was even more intrigued that the Black Swan referred to Infidel as a princess. What did she mean?

Infidel jumped to her feet. Snow began to fall in the room as the temperature dropped to single digits. A sheen of ice glistened on Aurora's clenched fists, with icicles growing down like spiky claws.

"That wasn't what I was offering," Infidel said, her voice trembling as she tried to control her temper. "Don't twist my words!"

"You should be more careful with what you say, my dear," said the Black Swan. "You've offered a binding contract. Alas, I cannot act upon it. My word is my bond. My previous contract for the Three Goons is sacrosanct. Your virtue - such as it may be - is safe."

Infidel stared at the Black Swan, then cast one more glance at Aurora, now encased in a shell of ice that resembled armor. Infidel unclenched her fists, her shoulders sagging. I could sense she wasn't afraid of Aurora; she just knew that she wouldn't get what she wanted by hitting anyone in this room. She turned toward the door, then glanced back. "I want the balance of the skull in diamonds."

"Of course, my dear," said the Black Swan. "I've often thought you'd look good in jewelry. This new fashion of yours is a step forward, but could benefit from a few simple adornments."

Apparently, the Black Swan had never seen one of Infidel's molar necklaces.

The poker players were back at their table as Infidel stalked across the main room. The hole in the ceiling already had planks laid across it. As Infidel reached the door, Aurora called out to her.

"Hey," she said.

Infidel paused at the door, but didn't look back.

"I... I wanted to say that the Black Swan was wrong about Stagger," said Aurora. "He'd do a lot of things for a bottle. But he'd never sell out a friend. And everyone could tell you were much more than a friend to him."

Infidel sighed, shaking her head.

"Not everyone," she whispered, as she stepped outside.

3 - RIPPER

I FELT SENTIMENTAL as Infidel climbed from the creaking gangplank onto my old boat. She grabbed at rigging and rails as she moved across the slanted deck. I've lived my life askew - the mud-locked boat sits at a ten-degree tilt. An objective man would describe the place as a hovel. To me, the place was the closest thing I've ever had to home.

If you witnessed my vagabond lifestyle, you'd never suspect that not so long ago my family was wealthy. My great-grandfather was the famous - or perhaps infamous - Ambitious Merchant. Merchant is a family name stretching back generations, and it's common for followers of the Church of the Book to name their children after desirable virtues. Seldom has a man been more suitably monikered. Ambitious made a fortune in the slave trade, with Commonground as his base. The river-pygmies have enslaved forest-pygmies for centuries, but it was my ancestor who realized that these squat, muscular men could be sold as a commodity to the mines on the Isle of Storm. The trade goes on to this day, though my family no longer has any role in it.

The so-called pirate wars had more to do with the slave trade than with actual piracy. Many Wanderers regard slaves as just another cargo, which doesn't seem to mesh with their claims to hold freedom as the highest virtue. A band of radical Wanderers had taken a stand against the slave trade, going so far as to raid ships and free the captives. For this, they were branded as pirates and wound up with every navy in the world united against them. Infidel had signed on to a losing cause from the start.

While I've never gone so far as to take up arms to oppose the slave trade, I've always had a gut dislike of the practice and have never been shy about sharing my views. The business corrupts everyone, especially the river-pygmies. They think of forest-pygmies as animals, when anyone can see they're the same race, just of differing hues. Each of the three major pygmy tribes dye their skin with jungle berries: forest-pygmies are green, river-pygmies blue, lava-pygmies orange. Wash them off with vinegar and they're all fish-belly white. My grandfather, Judicious Merchant, son of Ambitious, discovered that the bitter dyes were an effective mosquito repellent, which is why I remember him with dark green skin.

Judicious had been trained to take up the family business until he made the mistake of actually talking to the pygmies. They told him tales of the Vanished Kingdom, a once great nation on this island, its monuments now buried beneath roots and vines. My grandfather burned through a great deal of the family wealth with his elaborate expeditions into the jungle. Judicious bore a son by a forest-pygmy woman; this was my father, Studious Merchant. As a teen, Studious aided his father by traveling to the Monastery of the Book, home of the world's most extensive library. He went to these archives to read everything that had ever been written about the Vanished Kingdom. But, while he was there, he grew to love the prayerful, contemplative life of the monks and joined their order. As a monk, father had his flaws. My existence is testimony to his difficulty with the vow of celibacy.

I'm told my mother was a prostitute who abandoned me on the monastery's doorstep. I've never even learned her name. I was raised in an orphanage run by the monks. My father taught there, but barely acknowledged me. Every three or four years, my grandfather, Judicious, would visit and tell me stories about his jungle adventures. He said that when I was old enough, he'd take me with him. I never saw him after my tenth birthday, when he'd given me the knife. I eventually reached Commonground on my own when I was seventeen, but no one had seen my grandfather in years. The jungle had swallowed him long ago.

My grandfather had owned the sailboat Infidel now stood upon; in his day, it was quite a vessel. As years passed with my grandfather absent from Commonground, the boat had been looted. Pretty much everything that hadn't been nailed down had been stripped, along with a fair share of stuff that had been nailed down. The husk was still anchored at the docks when I got to town, and no one protested when I moved in.

Infidel pushed aside the torn curtain that led into the small shack I'd built from cast-off lumber. She found the duffel bag of clothes she kept stashed in the rafters and tossed her sarong onto the floor. I'd never seen her naked when I was alive, but this was the second time since I'd died I'd gotten to see her full glory. Yet, her nudity didn't provoke lust. All my ordinary desires seem muted. Since dying, I haven't felt hungry or sleepy. Of greater interest is that I haven't felt thirsty. Perhaps I should be relieved. My afterlife truly would be hell if I were tormented by desires I had no hope of slaking. Still, it seems wasteful to finally look at Infidel's body and feel only dispassionate appreciation of her symmetry.

She pulled on a pair of canvas breeches, but frowned as she looked through her various blouses. Many were blood-stained and torn; she always was hard on clothes. She pitched aside the duffel and picked up one of my old shirts from the back of a chair, holding it to her face to sniff it. At first, I thought she must have found the scent unpleasant; her eyes began to water. Then, she hugged the shirt to her chest as she closed her eyes tightly. After a moment, she composed herself, slipping the shirt on, rolling up the too-long sleeves and cinching up the dangling shirt tails with her thick leather belt. She dug around under the bunk and found an old pair of boots she'd left here. In the jungle, she normally went barefoot. However, the boardwalks of Commonground were littered with things no sane person would want squishing between their toes. She shoved my bone-handled knife into the boot sheath, then rooted under the bed until she produced the scabbard that held my old saber.

For the first time in two days, she ate, raiding my pantry for dried herring wrapped in seaweed and a jar of pickled peppers. She washed it all down with the ceramic jug of rotgut I kept by the bed. Infidel rarely drank anything stronger than cider, but she chugged down the hard liquor like it was cool water. Afterward, she wiped her mouth on her sleeve and belched.

Usually, my shack felt cramped with the two of us. Now that it was just her, the place looked larger than it used to. Infidel scanned the room, her eyes surveying the clutter. There were books everywhere. Like my father, I'm an avid reader. A muddied pair of my boots sat next to the door. The oil-cloth coat I wore during the rainy season was still slumped on the floor next to them.

But the dominant feature of the room were all the empty bottles - wine, cider, ale, whiskey. Somewhere in the world was a glassblower who earned a living due to my habits, though the bastard had never bothered to write me a thank-you note.

This mound of mildewed books and dirty bottles was all the evidence left that I'd once been alive. Whatever the quirks of my sundry ancestors, at least they'd all successfully reproduced. I'd died childless. The only legacy I left the world amounted to little more than litter.

THE SUN HAD set by the time Infidel departed my shack. The tide was flowing back out to sea. She wrinkled her nose as the stench of the muck wafted around her. She wound her way through the maze of gangplanks and piers, heading west. I knew where she was going. I had, after all, managed to choke out most of the word 'fishmonger' in my feeble dying effort to shed my guilt.

Bigsby was a rarity in Commonground, a man who made his living in an honest profession. Bigsby did brisk business selling barrels of dried and pickled fish to Wanderer ships and supplying the more upscale establishments, like the *Black Swan*, with fresh oysters and rock lobsters to serve their clientele. Of course, Bigsby wouldn't live in Commonground if there wasn't something wrong with him. In his case, it's physical. Bigsby is a dwarf, barely four feet tall, with the torso of a normal man but stubby legs and arms. He spends much of his time haggling with river-pygmies, buying their daily catch. Perhaps he came to Commonground to feel tall.

I'd sold Bigsby the Greatshadow map for a handful of coins. I'd been quite casual about it. I told him the map had belonged to my grandfather, but was a fraud that he could probably sell as a historical curiosity. My conscience had been assuaged because I knew that Bigsby wasn't likely to raise a band of adventurers to go after the fortune. Nor would he drunkenly boast in one of the local bars about his treasure map. He was a quiet, timid man, who survived in this rough city by keeping - please pardon the expression - a low profile. If Bigsby did sell the map, he'd do it discreetly.

The fishmonger rarely went out at night. He was up at dawn every day to buy the night's catch. As Infidel came within sight of his warehouse on the western edge of the bay, all the windows were dark. I guessed he'd gone to bed. Then I noticed a single dim light in one window, no brighter than a candle. As I focused on the window, I thought I could hear muffled voices. But the voices fell silent as Infidel stepped onto the gangplank leading to Bigsby's door. The plank squeaked; the candlelight went dark.

As Infidel neared the door, I noticed that something was off. Specifically, the door was off its hinges. It was merely leaning in the frame, the wood around the lock and hinges freshly splintered. Infidel didn't notice this detail. Instead, she paused a few feet away and kicked, cracking the door in twain. The halves fell into the room, clattering loudly as Infidel stomped inside.

The door that Infidel had entered led to the room that served as Bigsby's office. Bigsby sat on short stool next to an empty pickle barrel he used as a desk. He was scribbling in the ledger he used to record the day's trades. An extinguished candle sat beside the ledger, a plume of pale smoke rising from it.

He stared at Infidel, slack-jawed. His face was covered with sweat; dark stains seeped from beneath his armpits. He looked terrified, but this wasn't fresh terror. His clothes had been soaked before Infidel had kicked in the door.

"C-can I-I-I... can I help you?"

"I'm here for my map," said Infidel.

"Y-y-yuh-yuh... uh... huh?" All the blood was gone from Bigsby's face, apparently taking with it the capacity for coherent speech.

Infidel stalked forward. She slammed her fist on the barrel, which all but vaporized in a spray of splinters. She reached for Bigsby.

"I don't... I don't... I don't..." Bigsby's voice fluttered as her hands slowly neared. I thought he was about to faint.

As her hands reached his throat, Infidel sighed. Her mouth relaxed from its menacing snarl as she stared down at Bigsby's frightened face.

She stepped back and crossed her arms.

"Look," she said. "I'm having a bad day. Let's pretend I didn't just kick in your door and start over. Stagger gave you a map. I want it back. It's rightfully mine; I killed the last guy who owned it."

Bigsby wiped sweat from his eyes as he contemplated this bit of mercenary logic.

Infidel continued: "I'm willing to pay a reward for the map. We'll call it a finder's fee."

Bigsby swallowed hard. His eyes kept darting from Infidel toward the door on the side wall. I'd been in this shop a hundred times; there was nothing behind that door except for a small porch and stairs leading down to the dock where he traded with the pygmies. Was he thinking of making a run for it?

As I looked at the door, I felt a strange sensation, like the hair on my neck rising, if I'd still had hair, or a neck. I could barely hear a faint, distant buzz. I watched Bigsby's eyes. He wasn't thinking of running. He was afraid of whatever was lurking on the porch.

He whispered, not looking Infidel in the face, "I'm sorry, b-but I don't know anything about a m-map."

"We both know you're lying," said Infidel, cracking her knuckles. "I'm trying to be nice, but I'm prepared to be nasty. Don't be stupid."

The Bigsby I knew wasn't stupid. Nor was he all that brave. Which made his next move all the more shocking. On the short stool, he barely came up to Infidel's waist. This meant that the hilt of my bone-handled knife, sitting in the boot-sheath, was at the level of his bent knee, on which his hand rested. It took only a fraction of a second for his hand to dart out and grab the knife. He thrust it upward into Infidel's belly, shouting, "I'm sick and tired of being bullied!"

The knife had the expected effect, ripping a button from my old shirt as it slid along her impervious skin.

She reached down and hooked two fingers into Bigsby's nostrils and lifted him to eye level. Bigsby raised his hands to grab at her fingers, a dumb move considering he had a knife in his hands. He cut a gash across his cheek, nearly blinding himself. The blade tumbled from his fingers, landing upright in the floor as Infidel growled, "And I'm sick and tired of your little game!"

I barely paid attention to her words. There was a line of blood along the edge of the knife. As it slowly rolled down, forming a red bead, I once again had the sensation of a heartbeat. I waved my phantom fingers before my face as they materialized. I sucked in a ghost-breath, savoring the sensation.

"If you like to play games so much, let's play one called 'hotter, colder,'" Infidel said as she spun Bigsby around like a fish on a gaff. He squealed from the pain. "When I get closer to the map, you call out 'hotter!' When I move away from it, say, 'colder!'"

Bigsby's eyes flicked once more to the door to the porch.

"Outside, huh? Through that door?" she said. She didn't wait for his answer.

He didn't say 'hotter' or "colder" as she reached for the doorknob. Instead, he jabbered, "No, no, no, no, no, no, no, no, no!"

My foggy guts knotted as she touched the doorknob.

She yanked the door open and stared into the burlap covered crotch of a man who had to be a dozen feet tall. Only his legs and lower torso could be seen. The rest of his body was above the level of the doorframe. An impossibly large hand with nine fingers clamped over Infidel's face. Bigsby tumbled from her grasp. The giant jerked Infidel from her feet and flung her far out over the dark waters of the bay. I could hear her curses fade off into the distance, until at last there was a faint, faraway splash.

Bigsby curled into a fetal position where he fell, his hands clamped over his bleeding nose. A hunchback suddenly stuck his head into the room from behind the giant. His whole body was concealed beneath a tattered gray cloak; his head hung so low beneath the misshapen lump of his back that it was nearly even with his waist. He supported his ill-distributed weight with a gnarled staff, grasped with equally gnarled fingers. His hands were wrapped tightly in filthy brown gauze; not a single inch of flesh was visible. Beneath his hood, his face was concealed by a burlap sack; blood red eyes peered through two holes. The inhuman eyes made my ghost-skin crawl. I moved in closer for a better look, trying to fathom what manner of creature this might be. The hunchback cast a baleful glare toward me.

Though he didn't say anything, I heard a voice whisper, "This is none of your concern, blood-ghost." Invisible hands grasped my limbs and pushed me back. They lost their strength as they reached the bone-handled knife, but I couldn't move any closer. I was frightened by this stranger and scared for Infidel, yet also weirdly excited. He saw me?

"Can you hear me?" I asked.

The hooded man turned his head to look at Bigsby, ignoring my question. But, the way he held his body, it looked like he was choosing to ignore me; I was certain he'd heard my words.

"Pull yourself together," said the hunchback, staring down at Bigsby. "She won't be bothering you again. Patch has disposed of her."

Patch, apparently, was the giant. At the sound of his name, the creature squatted in the doorway. He proved to be far more misshapen than the hunchback. All his features were twice the normal size. His arms were bare and his biceps looked like they were woven from at least three different sets of arms; long, dark-threaded stitches held his patchwork flesh together. His face was almost impossible to look at. The left half and right half of his face were different shades, and the scalp and brow were a different tone entirely. He'd plainly been sewn together from the skin of more than one man.

When Bigsby remained in his fetal ball, the hunchback turned to the giant and said, "Carry him."

Patch stretched his long arm through the doorway and scooped the dwarf up in his enormous grasp, cradling him to his chest like an infant. The tall man's eyes were dead and lifeless. His mouth hung in a limp gape that gave no hint of expression. His lips and gray tongue were bone dry; he didn't look as if he were breathing.

Patch started to rise, placing his free hand on the railing of the porch to steady himself. Suddenly, Infidel dropped from the sky, straight down, as if she'd been hanging from the moon. An aura of water droplets enveloped her as she drove her boots into the back of the giant's neck. The brute dropped Bigsby, who bounced inside the doorway, as the porch collapsed beneath the giant's weight.

The hunchback slowly shook his head as he looked at the empty doorway where his monster had just stood. He grumbled, "One must admire her persistence."

From below, there was a rapid series of loud, wet smacks, the sound that a sledgehammer makes when it hits a cow between the eyes.

With the hunchback's attention focused elsewhere, I felt free to move again. I peered down onto the docks, where Infidel was raining blow after blow onto the giant's gut. The huge man didn't seem to feel it. He rose to one knee, his dead eyes gazing in her approximate direction. His right fist pumped out like a piston and Infidel flew off as if she'd been shot from a bow, smacking into the thick pilings that supported the nearby pier. The logs cracked, but halted Infidel's flight. Her arms flailed like a rag-doll as she dropped face first into the tar-black mud that covered this area at ebb tide.

"Infidel!" I screamed as I stared down into the muck.

The hunchback winced. I was shouting only inches from his ear.

"You *can* hear me," I said.

He glared at me. Then, he turned, hobbling across the room, his staff clacking on the wooden floor. He reached the knife. My vaporous fingers failed to halt his wrist as he snatched it up. He studied the knife for a long moment. I could definitely see that his eyes weren't human. They looked more like the eyes of a snake, with vertical slits. What skin I could see around the eyes was dark red and scaly.

"It is not the role of the dead to be inquisitive," he scolded. He lifted his crooked fingers to the blade and drew the bandages that covered them along the thin remnant of blood. My ghost body faded once more. He tilted his head to where I'd last stood. "But it may be that I can find other uses for you."

He tucked the knife into a pocket hidden in the folds of his cloak, then walked back to the door. Suddenly, the whole room shuddered. The pots and pans in the kitchen next door clattered as they fell from their ceiling hooks.

The hunchback was nearly thrown from his feet, staggering until he reached the wall, where he regained his balance. He peered once more out the open door.

Infidel was tricky to see in the darkness, as she was now black as ink, the twin specks of her eyes the only clean spots left on her. She was perched in the center of the giant's shoulders, pounding his head with rapid fire blows. The sewn together scalp had come apart, revealing bones held together with thick copper wires. The beast groped around, awkwardly fumbling, until he found her leg. He snatched her free and slammed her into the dock with his full strength. The building shuddered from the shockwave. The giant tried to pick Infidel up again, but she grabbed the edge of the dock with her iron grasp and his fingers slipped from her mud-slicked leg.

She spun around, eyes narrowed as he tried once more to grab her, this time aiming for her head. As his arm closed in on her face, she clamped his wrist with both hands, then kicked both legs into the pit of his arm. She stretched out, her body straight as a board. With a sound like a branch breaking, the arm snapped free of the shoulder and she fell back to the deck with the severed limb. The giant stumbled backwards, off balance. No blood came from his wound.

Infidel rolled, rising to her knees, shaking her head slowly. Her body shuddered as she took a deep breath. She seemed not to notice that the patchwork man had regained his footing. He lumbered toward her, his remaining hand outstretched.

At the last second, she sprung up with a growl, swinging his liberated arm back over her head, two-handed, like an axe. Her growl turned into a grunt as she swung the limb, smashing it directly into his face. The blow knocked Patch from his feet and he fell to the dock on his back. Infidel sneered as she stomped down on his left ankle, pulverizing the bones.

Infidel lighted on the center of his chest, digging her fingers into the folds of sewn together flesh, ripping it open. She made short work of his rib cage, bones and wires flying into the night. The creature possessed no internal organs. Where his heart should have been, there was only a small golden box secured by silver rods. The giant's remaining hand grabbed her by the hair as she reached into his chest cavity and tore the box free. She popped it between her fingers, the lid flying open. It was difficult to see clearly, but what looked like a large, white mosquito buzzed up from the open container. It was at least two inches long and glowed with an internal fire. It shot upward, like a shooting star in reverse, then vanished among its brethren in the sparkling firmament.

The giant no longer moved. Infidel made certain it never would again, as she snapped every bone and dried up muscle that she touched, tossing the fragments out into the bay. In a matter of minutes, the beast was completely disassembled; all that remained were the shredded remnants of his impossibly large pants.

She turned her face toward the doorway, twenty feet above. The hunchback met her gaze. Without warning, she leapt.

The hunchback calmly stepped aside as she flew into the room. She nearly tripped over Bigsby, who was still curled up on the floor, whimpering. Skidding to a halt in her muddy boots, Infidel whipped around. A trail of black mud splattered the walls like paint, stinking of dead fish and rotten eggs. She quickly spotted the hunchback, who held an open palm toward her.

"You seek the map," he said. "It's not here. Calm yourself, and I will tell you all you wish to know."

Infidel straightened up from her fighting crouch. She was still seething. The hunchback held his ground as she moved toward him. I was certain the creature had misplayed his hand. She paused before him, reaching out to grab his cloak. But, instead of yanking the hunchback off his feet, she wiped her muddy face, using the gray tatters of his cape like a towel. Ordinarily, these dingy rags were the last thing anyone would use for cleaning, but after you've rolled in Commonground muck, pretty much everything is more sanitary than you are.

I was heartbroken when she dropped the edge of the cloak. She was bleeding, her own blood this time. Her right eyebrow sported a gash at least an inch long. There was a knot just above this big as a hen's egg. Her nose was bleeding from both nostrils. When she spoke, I could see blood pooling around her gums.

"I'm listening," she said.

"Bigsby sold the map to a man named Ivory Blade. You know him."

Infidel nodded. "He's King Brightmoon's top spy."

"Correct. The king was quick to recognize the importance of the map. Even now, a ship of his warriors is under sail, heading for the Isle of Fire."

I suddenly put two and two together. I knew why the Black Swan hadn't been free to give Infidel the Three Goons.

The hunchback continued: "Blade has been recruiting local talent to aid in the quest. I intended to offer the services of Patch. Now, I intend to offer you."

"I'm not yours to offer," said Infidel.

"You need not play coy," said the hunchback. "We share a mutual goal. We each have our reasons for wanting to reach Greatshadow's lair. The simplest path forward is to assist the king's team. He's assembled the finest warriors at his command, masters of both physical and spiritual warfare. Earlier this evening, you sought to hire the Three Goons. You'll still be able to fight by their side; you just won't have to pay their wages."

Infidel shook her head as she walked away from the hunchback. "I'm not really a team player. I could get along with the Goons for a couple of weeks, but put me together with a bunch of knights and priests and I kill someone."

"Indeed," said the hunchback. "You're perfectly suited to such a task."

Infidel toed around the shattered slivers of barrel that littered the floor.

"You see a knife around here?" she asked. I saw she'd also lost my saber; it was probably out in the middle of the bay.

The hunchback produced the blade from his pocket and held it toward her.

"This knife belonged to your friend," he said. "You think of it as your last link to him."

She scowled as she snatched the knife from his grasp. "What are you, some kind of mind-reader?"

"Yes," he said. "Your thoughts are not a secret from me, Infidel. I could deceive you and not reveal this fact. But, I want you to know that I am not without my talents. If we form a partnership, we each have something to gain."

Infidel kicked most of the muck off her leg, then slid the knife back into her boot. Dark sludge bubbled up around the hilt as it sank into the sheath. "Thanks, but no thanks. I'm not looking for any new friends."

"I'm not offering friendship, Infidel. Only an alliance."

She stared at him. "It seems unfair that you know my name, while you get to remain a mystery. Who the hell are you?"

The hunchback chuckled. "Who indeed? As difficult as it may be to believe, I've lived my life without a name. I was cast out to die at birth."

"How tragic. But you still must have a name." Infidel said. "A relic like you can't have made it this far without someone calling you something."

"And yet, it is so."

"Well, today's your lucky day. From now on, you'll be called 'Lumpy.'"

The hunchback cocked his head, unsure if she was joking. I was pretty sure she wasn't. Infidel didn't like her own nickname much and compensated by sticking others with bad ones. After her debut at the *Black Swan*, people called her Ripper and she liked it. Then, a month later, she'd been sitting at the bar when a wild-eyed man in a black robe burst through the door, shouted, "Infidel!" then broke his knife stabbing her in the back. The name might not have stuck, except the scene repeated itself about nine times over the next year. Everyone at the bar started calling her Infidel and eventually I made the switch as well. She's never volunteered what she did to piss off the fanatics and I've never asked. The rule is, what happens outside Commonground, stays outside Commonground.

The hunchback rubbed his chin as he contemplated his need for a sobriquet. "You called me a relic. This will suffice."

"Relic?" she said with a smirk. She thought it was a lousy name.

The hunchback nodded.

"Well, Relic, it's nice meeting you, but it's been a long day and I've got a headache like you wouldn't believe."

"I believe you," said Relic. "I feel your pain."

"Whatever," she said, heading toward the door with a dismissive wave. "Have fun on your dragon hunt."

"Lord Tower is leading the quest," said Relic.

Infidel froze in her tracks. Her eyes widened. I wasn't surprised she knew who Lord Tower was; he was easily the most famous knight in the Shining Lands. Still, what did that matter to her?

Relic said, "He's carrying a weapon that can actually slay Greatshadow."

"Which one?" she asked, not looking back. "The Gloryhammer?"

"Something much, much more dangerous."

Infidel pondered this, shook her head, then kept walking.

"After Tower slays the dragon, your job will be to kill the knight."

Infidel spun on her heels. She eyed Bigsby, who'd uncurled sufficiently from his fetal ball to stare at her. "Go fix me a tub of boiling water," she said. "And find me soap. Lots and lots of soap."

Bigsby nodded as he stood, then scampered off.

Infidel leaned against the wall. She spat a gob of pink spittle into the middle of the floor.

"I'm not promising anything," she said. "But let's hear your plan."

4 - GOONS

FOR THE THIRD time since I croaked, I watched Infidel strip off her ruined clothes, dropping the tar-black rags into a growing pile of goop. The candle-lit tub of steaming water before her filled the air with a pale haze. I was intrigued that Bigsby had such fancy private quarters. The fishmonger may not have flashed his wealth around in public, but his bathroom was opulent to the point of stupidity. Did a bath brush with a gilded handle scrub his back better than a plain wooden one? Even his toothbrush was studded with gems. And why did he need all these bejeweled bottles of perfumes and ointments? As Infidel moved around the room, my consciousness floated through a black lacquer cabinet decorated with inlaid mother of pearl. Even though it was dark in there, I thought I spotted an ivory wig stand sporting a curly blond wig. What a very odd thing for a bachelor like Bigsby to have spent money on.

I did, however, admire his bathtub, a long, deep vessel carved from a single block of polished black marble. It was large enough that I, with my lanky frame, could have stretched out comfortably. Bigsby must be able to swim in it. Infidel sank beneath the surface, resting there a moment as the muck that still clung to her hands, face, and hair began to dissolve. She reached for a bar of bright white lye soap and the bath brush. The steamy air grew foul with the low-tide stench, cut through with the burning fumes of the lye. The bathwater quickly turned dark gray; I could no longer see her clearly through the haze.

Perhaps I've never seen her clearly. The truth is, while I've known Infidel all these years, I know so little about her. I've kept few secrets from her. I've talked about growing up in the monastery, and about my convoluted family history. I've freely shared by innermost thoughts on politics, religion, and the human condition. She, in return, has revealed that her favorite color is black (despite my insistence that black isn't a color), that she likes dogs more than cats, and that she hates carrots. Everything else I know about her, I've learned by observation. She's obviously from the Silver City; her speech has become much rougher and more colloquial over the years, but she still has traces of the accent and a vocabulary that hints of good breeding. It's not unusual to meet young men from wealthy families visiting Commonground, seeking vices they can't find at home. But most women in Commonground are usually coming from the other end of the economic scale. It's hard to imagine what she was looking for when she came here - or what she was running from.

After Infidel finished her bath, she spent time examining her wounds in the foggy mirror. It wasn't just her face that had taken a beating from Patch; her whole body was mottled with dark blue bruises, fading to yellow. I wondered how long it would take her to heal. The few times I'd seen her injured, she recovered much faster than a normal person. Why? She made no secret she'd been enchanted, but by whom, and for what purpose? Why hadn't I pried deeper about these things when I'd had the chance? I'd always hoped that, one day, she'd open up to me and tell me of her life before Commonground.

"It's not the role of the dead to be inquisitive," Relic had said.

I felt like proving him wrong. I'd messed up my chance to learn Infidel's secrets while I was alive. Perhaps, in death, I had a new opportunity to unravel her mysteries. It seemed unethical, perhaps, to spy on her unseen and unsuspected. On the other hand, did I even have a choice in the matter? I suspected that by being around her at all times, a lot more than her naked body was going to be revealed.

Bigsby had left a small pile of fresh clothes for Infidel. They were decidedly more feminine than anything I'd ever seen her wear. Lacy underwear, a short black leather skirt, a black silk blouse with a low neck. Again, it seemed strange he'd just had these lying around. Bigsby wasn't married and I'd never seen him consort with whores. The clothes hung horribly on Infidel, both too big and too short, but would have fit a pot-bellied dwarf just fine.

I dropped the line of thought before I had a picture in my head I wouldn't be able to get rid of.

WHEN YOU'RE UP on the slopes of Tanakiki, (the central volcano, which translates from lava-pygmy as 'the Farting Dragon') you see that the

Commonground bay must once have been a volcanic caldera. The water is almost a perfect circle three miles across, with a gap several hundred yards wide at the far end open to the sea. Twin arcs of land lead out to the gap. The southern arc is mostly low, rolling dunes surrounded by marshes. The northern arc is rockier, and the ocean beyond is unimaginably deep. There's a place out near the tip called the Old Temple. It's a long stretch of hexagonal basalt columns bunched tightly together; there's some debate as to whether it's a natural formation or man-made. I've poked around out there a time or two and don't have a strong opinion, other than the place is damn spooky. The rock is black as coal, but etched with white rings of salt left by evaporating seawater. Nothing grows there, not even lichen. Pygmy lore says that Greatshadow once landed here to drink from the sea, then pissed on his rocky perch, poisoning the ground.

It was still a few hours before dawn when Relic led Infidel out to the Old Temple. Her skin was pink in the moonlight, raw from the lye soap and vigorous scrubbing. She looked ridiculous in the clothes Bigsby had provided. The outfit could have come from a whore's wardrobe, but the scowl on Infidel's face would likely discourage any customers. She was barefoot again. My knife was stuck into the waistband of her skirt.

Bigsby had been dispatched by Relic on an errand. I'd missed the specifics while Infidel was bathing, but apparently the dwarf was supposed to bring someone out to the Old Temple to meet with Infidel.

Relic no longer seemed to be aware of me. With my knife free of blood, I was unable to shout at him. He may have been able to read the minds of the living, but the dead lay outside his awareness, as long as they weren't drunk on blood. Still, he knew I was haunting the knife. I couldn't help but wonder what other uses he had in mind for me. If he talked to me again, what was I going to say? Should I try to use him to convey messages to Infidel? Tell her I was haunting her? Would that make her feel better, or worse?

Infidel leaned against one of the basalt columns, gently kneading the knot on her forehead. After she'd been mauled by the iron tiger, she told me that it was interesting to be hurt. She'd been fascinated by her scabs for days. She acted like she'd made it through her entire childhood without so much as a scratch.

A fog started to gather, masking the edges of the salt-crusted platform on which we waited. The lanterns aboard the ships at Commonground faded as the mist thickened. The damp night turned decidedly cold. Infidel folded her arms across her chest, tucking her hands into her armpits for warmth.

Relic looked toward the thickest clump of fog and said, "There's no point in hiding. You've come this far; you won't turn back."

The fog swirled as a dark shadow moved through it, then parted as Aurora stepped onto the basalt platform. I don't remember ever seeing the ogress outside the *Black Swan*. Bigsby emerged from the fog right behind her. I wondered what he'd said to her to convince her to leave the bar.

Aurora glowered at the hunchback. She was easily twice as tall as him. She said, "The dwarf gave me your message. How did you learn my true name?"

Relic chuckled. "I plucked it from your mind, Aksarna. I have the gift, and the curse, of hearing the thoughts of others."

"Do you have the gift of an iron neck?" Aurora asked as her eyes narrowed. "Since you know of my past, you leave me little choice but to strangle you."

Infidel spoke up. "The Black Swan knows your past and you don't strangle her. Give ol' Lumpy here five minutes."

Aurora looked at Infidel, pausing for a second to study her odd attire and bruised face. "What's your role in this, *princess?*"

"I think I'm auditioning for the villain.".

"Infidel has agreed to kill the king's men once they've slain Greatshadow," said Relic.

"You know about the mission?" asked Aurora.

Relic tapped his brow with a gnarled finger.

"Right, right. Mind-reader," said the ogress. "Fine. Why have you dragged me out here?"

"Ivory Blade negotiated with you to hire the Three Goons," said Relic. "We need you to arrange for him to hire us as well."

"You've already confessed that you're planning to kill the king's men. As of now, that includes the Goons. I'm no traitor."

"You've been accused of treason in the past. I've come to offer you a chance to clear your name."

Aurora shook her head. "It doesn't matter what you offer me. My loyalty lies with the Black Swan. I could never betray her."

"You have deeper, older loyalties, Aksarna."

"Don't call me that," said Aurora. "Aksarna died long ago. Commonground and the Black Swan are all I have now."

"You didn't die," said Relic. "You failed. The difference is significant. The dead are devoid of hope, but the fallen may dream of redemption. I know you are haunted by the possibility that you could one day return to Qikiqtabruk with the Jagged Heart, restoring the temple and erasing your shame."

"The Jagged Heart was destroyed," said Aurora. "My soul was bound to it. My spirit died when the tip was shattered. It's only my stubborn body that carries on."

"Wrong, wrong, and wrong," said Relic. "The Jagged Heart was never so much as scratched. Your soul was never bound to it, despite the teachings of your religion. You may have loved it so much that if felt like a part of you, but this attachment was emotional, not supernatural."

"I know what I saw."

Relic shook his head. "The eyes are the easiest sense to deceive. The weapon was switched in the moments it was out of your sight; the raiders masked the true shard with dream magic. When you reached the raiders, they brandished a duplicate. It is this you saw shattered."

Aurora clenched her jaw. She placed her giant hands over her left breast as her eyes grew moist. "You know nothing. I *felt* it shatter. You can never understand."

"Cling to this falsehood if you wish," said Relic. "But the Jagged Heart still exists. It's carried by Lord Tower on his quest. With it, he'll slay Greatshadow."

Infidel rapped her knuckles on the basalt column, a sound like a hammer striking brick. "Sorry to interrupt, but what the hell are you two talking about? What's the Jagged Heart and why is it any more likely to kill Greatshadow than, say, a pointy stick?"

Aurora contemplated her question. The sea mist beaded on her leather coat, running down in rivulets, pooling at her feet. At last, she said, "The Jagged Heart was a ceremonial harpoon. As High Priestess, I would use it to hunt the spirit whales in the Great Sea Above. The shaft is carved from the tusk of a narwhale; the blade itself is a knife sharp fragment of pure ice taken from the shattered heart of Hush, the primal dragon of cold. In shape, the blade resembles the heart from a deck of cards."

"A fragment of Hush's heart?" Infidel asked. "I thought that Verdant was the only primal dragon ever to be slain."

"Hush didn't truly become a primal dragon until her heart was broken. It was only then that the elemental cold filled the vacant space inside her. My people revere Hush; our land rests upon her slumbering back. In exchange for our worship, the dragon grants her followers magical gifts."

"Back to the topic at hand, Tower is seriously going to try to kill Greatshadow with a harpoon made of ice?" Infidel rolled her eyes. "This is going to last, what, five seconds inside the volcano?"

"The Jagged Heart can negate any heat it encounters. Cold is the true condition of all existence; heat is merely a local aberration. If the Heart still exists, it's the perfect weapon to destroy Greatshadow. Of course, someone would need to carry it within striking distance of the dragon. That's a nearly impossible task."

"'Nearly impossible' is semantically the same as 'possible,'" said Relic. "With Lord Tower involved, it's probable. He wears the Armor of Faith. It will shield him from Greatshadow's powers."

Infidel nodded. "Yeah, I guess that would work."

Now it was Aurora's turn to look puzzled. "Armor of Faith?"

"It looks like a suit of plate armor," said Infidel. "It encases Tower completely and is filled with a lot of gears and ratchets that enhance his strength. Pretty much nothing can penetrate it."

"Greatshadow's breath melts armor," said Aurora.

"If it's metal. But this armor is made of prayer. The Church of the Book has a team of monks whose sole job is to pray Tower's armor into existence. One monk does nothing but pray for the helmet, another prays for the greaves, another guy prays for the shoulder pads, and so on. Every single gear and rivet on this thing has a monk - actually a whole squad of monks - whose only spiritual duty is to maintain their unceasing faith that the armor can't be so much as scratched."

Aurora nodded slowly. "Very well. Let's suppose the armor works. Tower can reach Greatshadow and slay his body. Then what? This is a primal dragon, the very spirit of fire. There's a little of Greatshadow's essence in all flame. You need to extinguish every fire in the world at once to truly kill him. If you overlooked a single flickering candle, he could eventually weave a new body and seek vengeance."

"This is why Lord Tower doesn't travel alone," said Relic. "The Voice of the Book has issued a Writ of Judgment. A Truthspeaker will read this writ aloud before Greatshadow's spirit, slaying it."

Aurora stroked her chin, rubbing the bulges where her tusks anchored in her jaw. "I still can't believe they have the Jagged Heart. Maybe they're the ones fooled by a replica."

"But you would know when you saw it," said Relic. "And you *can* see it again. Arrange for Infidel and myself to be hired as mercenaries on the quest, and when we kill Lord Tower, we'll return the harpoon to you."

Aurora shook her head. "I see no reason to trust you with this task. I owe the Black Swan my life, but it's my sacred duty to recover the Jagged Heart. I'll resign my position with the Black Swan and petition Lord Tower to join his team on my own. You may attempt the same. I won't speak against you."

Relic glared at her. I could tell he hadn't considered the possibility that Aurora would take a more direct path toward recovering the artifact.

Aurora seemed unconcerned by Relic's baleful gaze. She looked over at Infidel.

"First the sarong, now a skirt. What's with your wardrobe lately?"

Infidel shrugged. "Once I have Greatshadow's treasure, I'll hire a team of tailors to follow me around. Until then, I'm getting by with whatever's handy."

"Why are you so confident you can kill Lord Tower? If he's good enough to take down a primal dragon, I don't see how an undisciplined brawler like you will stand a chance."

Infidel chuckled. "Armor or not, I've thought of a thousand different ways of killing Tower. He'll be dead before he knows what hit him."

"A thousand?" asked Aurora, sounding amused. "What's your grudge against the knight?"

"It's kind of a long story," said Infidel, raising her hand and pinching about a half inch of air between her thumb and forefinger, "but I once got *this* close to marrying the bastard."

TO MY GREAT frustration, Aurora didn't ask to hear the long story, not even a short version of it. Her devotion to the unwritten rules of Commonground was admirable to a fault.

Relic dismissed Bigsby, telling him his services were no longer needed, as he and Infidel set off for the *Black Swan*. Aurora walked alone, a few hundred feet ahead. Relic, despite his bent form and hobbling gait, proved to be rather spry, keeping up with Infidel's tireless pace with no sign of effort.

The sun was rising by the time we reached the docks. The daylight revealed a half dozen corpses floating in the brine. It was a rare night in Commonground that didn't yield a few murder victims. Bleary-eyed river-pygmies in dugout canoes poled their ways under the docks, gathering the bodies. Commonground bred strange industries. Pulling the right corpse out of the drink could be the equivalent of winning a lottery. Any given body might turn out to be an outlaw with a price on his head, payable dead or alive. Or, you might recover the corpse of a wayward son of a wealthy family and demand a ransom to return the remains for proper burial. In contrast, my career of looting temples and ruins seemed like honest work.

As Relic and Infidel approached the *Black Swan* barge, I noticed that the stream of clients leaving the bar was a bit heavier than usual. It was like the place was emptying out completely. Patrons grumbled as they walked past us, luggage in hand. Some of them were standing around, looking lost as they stared at empty boat slips. It dawned on me that only half the ordinary number of ships were docked this morning. What was going on?

Waiting at the front door of the *Black Swan*, arms crossed, were the Three Goons, looking stern. When Aurora walked up to them, No-Face moved to intercept her as Menagerie locked the front door. We were still too far away to hear what the Goons said, but not too far away to hear Aurora's loud and astonished reply: "What do you mean, I'm fired?"

Hearing this, Infidel launched herself into the air, covering the distance with a single bound. She landed beside Aurora, not wanting to miss any juicy details, as Menagerie said, "The Black Swan no longer requires your services. This establishment is closed until further notice."

"You're joking," said Aurora.

Menagerie shook his head. Reeker chewed a toothpick as he stared at Aurora, obviously amused by her confusion. No-Face slowly tossed the iron ball he carried back and forth between his beefy hands, his attention focused tightly on Aurora, no doubt hoping she'd make trouble. It was almost breakfast time. It was a rare day when the Goons didn't beat up someone before breakfast.

Here's a quick primer on the Goons: I've mentioned No-Face a couple of times. He's got a flap of scarred skin that hangs down from where a normal man's eyebrows should be, covering his face like a curtain. There's a tiny gap on the left side of the flesh-mask where a single pale eye peers out. Perhaps because his eyesight is iffy, he tends to strike anything that moves when he's in combat, which is why he pegged Infidel that one time. He's bald, his whole scalp covered with pale, shiny scars from the countless brawls he's been in. They say he was sold as a baby to a traveling circus for display as a freak, but by the time he was eight he was big and mean enough to take up pit-fighting. Now, he's seven feet tall, but manages to look squat due to the thickness of his muscles. The only armor he wears is a chain-mail vest; his only weapon is a fifty pound iron ball at the end of a long chain that he keeps rolled around his forearm. I've heard he feeds himself by pounding his victims into pulp with the ball, then sucking the remains under his flap into whatever mouth is hidden there.

Next on the goon roster is Reeker, a half-seed. Half-seeding is a variant of blood magic, suppressed by the church but never wiped out. Women who wish to get pregnant visit blood-houses to acquire specially prepared animal semen to, shall we say, supplement contributions from their husbands. In theory, the mix of animal and human sperm produces children with desirable qualities. A half-seed bull child will be strong and willful. A half-seed panther, agile and silent. No one knows if Reeker's mother meant to purchase skunk juice, or if she got burned by an unscrupulous blood-house. The product was a man who can emit odors at will from every bodily orifice. The stench can bring even the toughest fighter to his knees. When Reeker's not actively shooting out stink clouds, he's still got a wet-dog whiff to him that makes you envy No-Face's lack of nose.

Unlike No-Face, Reeker doesn't have a scar on him. No one ever gets close enough to land a punch. He's learned to spit a gob of the worse smelling phlegm you can imagine up to twenty feet, and he's more than happy to cut a gagging man's throat to put him out of his misery. Reeker matches his dastardly combat style with a personality that's all leers and crude jokes. Yet, for reasons I've never understood, he's popular with women, even women who aren't whores. He's got a dumpy physique and, at 5'9", looks tiny next to the other Goons. Maybe it's his hair. Above a pasty, round face, he's got a thick, wavy, black mane that any woman would envy, sporting two snow-white streaks running back from his temples.

The final goon is Menagerie. He's about six four and skinny as a rail. He's normally dressed in a loin cloth and sandals, showing off the animal tattoos covering him from the crown of his shaved head to the little gaps between his toes. Most of the animals are predators. He's got lions, tigers, bears, ohmis (a jungle viper), sharks, and eagles. Being tattooed in Commonground rarely earns you a second glance, though Menagerie has taken his skin art further than the average sailor. What makes Menagerie stand out is that his tattoos are alive, inked in the blood of the various beasts and infused with their spirits. Stare at them long enough and you'll swear they're breathing. No one has ever actually seen one move, but one day the shark will be on his right shoulder, the next day on his left thigh, like it's swimming around. That's a neat trick, but it's not what makes him dangerous. Menagerie's a shape-shifter. He can surrender his body to any of these spirits, taking on their forms in the blink of an eye. The people he fights face off with a tall, skinny, unarmed man, and two seconds later they've had their hand bitten off by an alligator, their guts raked by a tiger, and have a rattlesnake clamped down on their jugular.

Remember I told you that No-Face wasn't the Goon people were really afraid of? Menagerie is the Goon people are really afraid of.

Back to the confrontation: Aurora clenched her fists. "Stand aside. What you're saying makes no sense."

Menagerie shook his head. "We both know that everything the Black Swan does makes sense, even if we mere mortals are blind to the logic."

Reeker spit out his toothpick. "Heh. Maybe the bar ain't profitable now that Stagger's pushing daisies."

If it was possible to die from a mean look, Reeker would have joined me in the afterlife from the glare Infidel gave him. No-Face found the crack funny, judging from the muffled, farting, "hur hur hur," that filtered from beneath his face flap.

Menagerie raised his hand. Reeker looked instantly chagrined. No-Face's spooky chuckle went silent.

"I apologize for the insensitivity of my colleagues," the tattooed man said to Infidel. "Stagger was a beloved brother in the larger family of Commonground. I, for one, shall miss him."

"Yeah," said Reeker. "I kind of liked the guy. There going to be a funeral? I'll send flowers."

"The funeral was private," said Infidel. "And I don't want to talk about Stagger any more. I want to talk about the dragon hunt you boys are going on. I want in."

"As do I," said Relic, hobbling up beside the women.

Menagerie looked down at the hunchback. "Who the hell are you?"

"Infidel calls me Relic. This will serve."

"Uh-huh," said Menagerie. "I can't help but notice that you look, um… less than formidable. While I can't confirm the existence of any upcoming dragon hunts, may I ask what, exactly, would you bring to the table?"

"Knowledge," said Relic. "I've survived Greatshadow's lair before. My experience may provide the difference between success and failure."

"Is that so?" said Menagerie.

The hunchback nodded.

"Be that as it may, I am not in charge of hiring for any missions that may or may not be occurring soon," said Menagerie. "The Black Swan may have been conducting transactions of this nature, but to reiterate, she's now closed to all business."

Aurora clenched her fists. "Menagerie, who do you think you're fooling? You know I know all about the mission. Get the hell out of my way. I'm talking to the Black Swan." She stepped forward, looking ready to push the mercenaries aside.

Reeker spit a gob of pale-green phlegm toward her eyes. The wad crackled as it froze inches from her skin, bouncing harmlessly off her cheek, its foul payload neutralized. She punched out with an ice-gauntleted fist, sending the skunk-man flying toward the edge of the dock. He landed on his feet with inches to spare, but momentum was against him. He stumbled backward and vanished over the edge with a splash.

No-Face swung his chain-draped fist and caught Aurora beneath the chin, hard enough that the frost coating her face flew off in a spray. She went down, landing flat on her back, as snow danced in the air where she'd just stood. She started to rise, but before she could sit up, Menagerie leapt toward her, taking the form of a huge, black-horned ram. His head smashed into Aurora's tusks with a loud, sharp *crack*. Aurora's arms flopped to her side as she stared up into the pale morning sky, cross-eyed and dazed.

Infidel grinned. This was her, oh-good-there's-a-fight-and-I-was-wanting-to-hit-someone grin. She punched No-Face right where his mouth should have been. He staggered backward, stopping when his back slammed into the locked door of the *Black Swan*. Infidel kicked him in the gut, shattering the wood behind him, knocking him inside.

Infidel spun to face Menagerie, who'd leapt into the air as a ram. In the span of a heartbeat, his body flowed into a fifteen-foot-long shark, his mouth stretched wide enough to clamp onto Infidel's face. She raised both hands, shielding herself with her forearms as the toothy jaws snapped shut. There was a loud *crunch*. Bright fragments of white teeth showered onto the docks. For half a second, the shark hung there, clamped onto Infidel's unbreakable arms. Infidel head-butted the shark in the snout. The big fish flew off, and Menagerie was once again human as he landed ass-first on the dock, blood streaming from his nose.

"Ouch," he said, spitting out broken teeth.

Infidel loomed over him, fists clenched. "Had enough?"

From inside the jagged hole that No-Face had left in the door, there was a confused grunt.

Menagerie looked toward the hole. His face went slack. Infidel turned toward the noise as well. Her brow furrowed as her eyes adjusted to the shadows before her. Aurora rose up on her knees, shaking her head. When she finally followed the others' gazes, she whispered, "This is unexpected."

The main room of the bar was completely transformed. All the gaming tables were gone, as were the paintings on the wall. No-Face was sitting up, rubbing his skin-flap, dust swirling around him. "Whuduhfuh?" he mumbled as he looked around.

Cobwebs clung to every corner of the room. The grime was so thick on the floor that No-Face had left a little dust-angel where he'd fallen. Behind the bar, the shelves were empty, save for dirt. There was no evidence that the place had been a thriving business full of people only moments before.

Menagerie stepped into the room. Aurora and Infidel followed.

Menagerie muttered something to himself I couldn't quite catch, save for the word 'time.'

"Oh no," said Aurora, who'd apparently caught what he was saying. "She was too old to go back more than a day or two. She'd never survive a longer trip. She —"

"You aren't blind, Aurora," said Menagerie.

"Is this a private conversation, or would you care to fill me in on what's happened?" asked Infidel.

Relic hobbled into the room. "They won't betray the Black Swan's secret. I, however, am not bound by their oaths of loyalty. The Black Swan owes her power and influence to a rather tragic curse. She —"

"Guys!" shouted Reeker as he rushed into the room, water streaming from his clothes. "You gotta come look at this."

The whole building shuddered as he spoke. The air took on the stench of rotten eggs, but Reeker didn't seem to be the source of the odor.

Menagerie furrowed his brow. "Did the barge just hit bottom?"

"All the water's draining out of the bay!" said Reeker, waving his arms for emphasis.

"Luhguptaruh," said No-Face.

"Good idea," said Menagerie. "To the roof!"

Before he finished speaking, where the man had stood there was an owl gliding forward. He flapped his wings once and shot toward the cobwebbed spiral staircase in the far corner of the room, vanishing as he tilted his wings and flew up to the second floor.

No-Face and Reeker followed without hesitation.

Aurora grabbed Infidel by the arm. "You took my side," she said. "Thank you."

"What?" asked Infidel.

"In the fight with the Goons. You defended me when I was down."

Infidel shrugged. "It was three against one. I always side with the underdog. It's nothing."

Aurora nodded. "Still, I owe you one."

Relic sighed as he hobbled across the room toward the staircase.

"You women can bond another time," he grumbled. "Right now, we should follow the owl."

5 -All Must Burn!

THE ROOF OF the *Black Swan* was a broad, flat deck with four large stained-glass dome skylights and a sixty foot mast that jutted up from the middle, with smaller masts fore and aft. It had been many years since the bar had actually been moved with sails; the masts now served mainly as flag poles to fly the barge's banner, a field of pure white with a black swan in the center. Menagerie stood in the crows nest atop the tallest mast, peering out at the bay, his hand raised to shield his eyes from the morning sun. Infidel leapt, grabbing the rigging, and in seconds reached his side.

Ignoring the main reason we'd come out here, her gaze was instead drawn to Menagerie's face. It took me half a second to understand why it was so interesting at this particular moment.

"You have your teeth back," she said.

"Owls don't have teeth, so when I changed back, I grew new ones," said Menagerie. "Can we focus on the problem at hand?"

The water was flowing out from the bay so swiftly that fish were left flopping in the mud. The *Black Swan* was anchored in water ordinarily twenty feet deep at its lowest, but it now sat flat on the bottom, the whole structure shuddering as it slowly sunk into the muck. As far as the eye could see boats were stranded across the bay, except, I noted, the ships of Wanderers. These had been the ships that had gone missing during the night. They were now far out at the mouth of the bay, dozens of them, riding on a ridge of water that bunched up near the gap leading to open water.

"You ever see anything like this?" Infidel asked.

Menagerie shook his head; he was the oldest of the Goons, a resident of Commonground for over forty years. He pointed toward the bright blue forms of river-pygmies running out on the mud flats, snatching up the stranded fish. "Maybe they know what's going on."

But before Infidel could leap down to speak to a pygmy, a mountain of bright blue-green water rose from the sea just beyond the Wanderer's ships. It kept rising, as other bulges formed around it. It vaguely resembled, from a distance, an enormous sea-turtle, assuming one could grow to be several miles wide.

Suddenly, the impossibility that this was a giant turtle changed into reality as the beast's eyes snapped open. Its vast maw yawned wide, a mouth several hundred yards across. The Wanderer ships were pulled toward it by a fierce suction. Yet, these expert seafarers proved the match of the turbulent white water, guiding their schooners across the ship-studded waves as agilely as a river pygmy steering a canoe through the pilings of Commonground. In moments, all the vessels had ridden the flow of water into the mouth of the great beast.

"It's Abyss," said Menagerie, his voice hushed in awe.

Abyss is the primal dragon of the sea. His consciousness spreads through every wave and ripple in the world's vast ocean. Due to his pact with the Wanderers, he's one of the few dragons who still intervenes in human affairs. Most of the primal dragons don't even notice mankind, anymore than an earthquake notices the cities it topples, or a tornado notices the villages it smashes to splinters. To witness a primal dragon personify itself, taking on at least an echo of its original form, was something few men would ever see in their lives.

With the last of the Wanderers swallowed, Abyss closed his mouth and spun, heading back toward the open ocean. The mound of water that had been heaped up by his arrival collapsed, sending a wave fifty feet high surging back into the emptied bay.

"Brace yourselves!" Menagerie shouted, before changing into an eagle and launching himself into the air. He could barely be heard as the roar of the water reached us, a thundering wall of sound that made the timbers of the *Black Swan* tremble. The tidal wave hit the far end of the docks, sending boards and pilings flying high into the air. The boats of slavers, pirates, and pleasure seekers splintered as the rushing water crushed them.

The wave hit the *Black Swan*. The barge was solidly built, but still the timbers cracked and snapped as the water lifted it, spinning it sideways, carrying it up over the docks and gangplanks, crushing everything in its path. Infidel clung to the railing of the crow's nest; the mast groaned, but didn't topple. The barge began to bob in the relatively smoother water behind the crest of the wave. The tsunami kept moving, reaching the normal boundaries of the shore, then beyond, carrying debris and corpses up over the marshes, into the forests.

Infidel looked down as the barge settled on the remains of docks and boats trapped beneath it. Relic was nowhere to be seen. No-Face had wrapped his ball and chain around the mast and was still on his feet, completely drenched. Reeker dangled in his hammy grasp, his normally well-groomed mane now tangled with a mass of brown seaweed. Aurora stood on the water next to the barge, seemingly walking on the waves, until the current calmed and revealed an ice floe beneath her.

The ogress shouted to the eagle circling overhead, "This is what she saw! This is why she went back!"

Infidel shouted down, "Would someone tell me what the hell is going on?"

Relic cleared his throat. Infidel spun around. He was standing right behind her. I never saw him climb the rigging, though, admittedly, my attention had been focused elsewhere. His rags were drenched; steam rose from them as if they'd been soaked in boiling wash-water rather than the tepid waters of the bay. He smelled vaguely of brimstone as he said, "On the day that the Black Swan was to be married, her groom was killed in a horseback accident. It was a senseless, pointless, random tragedy; the world is full of such moments.

Unknown to her fiancé, the Black Swan was a Weaver, a member of a secret sect of witches with the power to rend the fabric of reality and knit it back into something more to their liking. Yet, even Weavers lack the power to restore life to the dead. In her grief, the Black Swan sought out Avaris, Queen of Weavers, and asked her for a boon. She wished for the power to go back in time so that she might avoid these random tragedies."

Infidel looked around at the devastated mishmash of broken ships and crushed docks that had once been Commonground. "She didn't do a very good job of stopping this."

"I didn't say she could stop tragedies," said Relic. "I said she could avoid them; the Black Swan isn't here. She's lived through this tidal wave, then traveled back in time to abandon the barge and relocate elsewhere before the destruction occurred."

The eagle lighted gently onto the rail of the crow's nest. Then, in a twinkling, Menagerie stood next to Relic.

"How do you know this?" he asked.

Relic shrugged. "Is it important? You know it's the truth. You and Aurora have experienced the time shifts enough to recognize them and remember them. I know what's happening due to… certain talents."

Menagerie scowled. "Who are you again?"

"The only name I've ever been given is Relic."

Infidel said, "You've also been called Lum —"

"Relic," said Relic.

Menagerie looked down as Aurora formed a staircase of ice to walk back onto the deck of the barge. The water was swirling all around; the mast swayed as the barge bumped along the bottom.

"She was too old," Aurora called out, looking around at the wreckage. "She'll never survive going back."

Infidel shook her head. "Has everyone but me lost their minds? You're seriously expecting me to believe the Black Swan is some kind of time-traveler?"

"Yes, but only in one direction. She can jump backwards in her own timeline to pivotal moments. She moves forward in time at the same speed as the rest of us," said Menagerie, apparently no longer seeing a reason to protect the secret. "Her curse is that, when she goes back in time, she doesn't regain her youth. If she lived through an event at age forty that she could have changed by making a different decision at age twenty, she can go back to that event, but she'll go back as a forty year old, not a twenty year old. Only twenty-nine years have passed since the Black Swan was born, but physically, she's almost 120. The husband she loved so dearly rejected her, disgusted that she turned into old crone while he was still a youth. The Black Swan only cares about wealth now; everything else she regards as impermanent."

"A fat lot of good all her money will do her if she's dead," said Infidel.

Menagerie shrugged. "So far, her money has allowed her to purchase the potions needed to keep her alive. I'm in no position to disapprove of her priorities. I've made a sizable fortune from the Black Swan's business acumen."

"Really?" said Infidel. "The only thing you seem to own is that loincloth."

"Even a Goon may have a family," said Menagerie. "My loved ones are very comfortable."

By now, the bay was slowly starting to return to a normal level, as the water flowed back from the forest. The air smelled horrible, like every outhouse in the world had been overturned at once. All over the place, men were climbing out the water, clinging to overturned boats and the few strips of dock that had somehow survived.

Aurora shouted up, "There are people trapped in all this rubble. I'm going to help who I can."

Menagerie nodded. "A wise suggestion. We should all help out. We can... can...." His voice trailed off as his eyes were drawn toward the mouth of the bay. Seven large ships were sailing through the rocky gap. Their sails were a pale blue white, catching the morning sun like silver. Flags fluttered from the pinnacles, showing a green dragon against a sky-blue field.

Infidel followed his gaze toward the ships.

"It's King Brightmoon's fleet," she said.

"Some of it, at least," said Menagerie. "Rather bold of them, just sailing in during broad daylight. Aren't they worried that Greatshadow might notice?"

Suddenly, the sky darkened. Everyone looked up, back toward the peak of Tanakiki. A mile high jet of solid black smoke mushroomed up into the air, swiftly turning day into night. Bright red sparks shot through the atmosphere as the rim of the caldera crumpled, sending a white-orange river of molten lava spilling toward the bay. Trees exploded into flame ahead of the lava as a shimmering wave of heat spread outward.

The smoke and cinders swirled until they took on the shape of a dragon, spreading mile-long wings of black smoke. Two smaller dragons shot out of the folds of the wings, flying toward the bay. Smaller, in this case, is a relative term. These were huge beasts, a hundred yards long tip to tail, with glowing red scales edged in black. Their wings were larger than the mainsails of the king's ships. They had long tails that ended in tufts of flame. They looked as if they swam through the air, surfing the wind as they sailed down the slopes, aiming toward the king's ships.

Greatshadow himself remained in the caldera, a beast composed of flame and smoke, who roared, in a language I'd never heard yet instantly understood: "ALL MUST BURN!"

"He noticed," said Infidel.

These were the first living dragons I'd ever seen, even though I've handled a lot of dragon bones in my time, and seen more than a few depictions of the beasts carved onto walls or woven into tapestries. Dragons used to be numerous, until the Church of the Book nearly wiped them all out.

The survivors are the primal dragons. These beasts were so fluent in elemental magic that they eventually became the elements themselves.

Of course, if there are no more ordinary dragons, I had to wonder just what the hell was flying toward us. The creatures looked exactly like they did in the books in the monastery; big serpents, with a long neck and serpentine tail, and a short, thick, pot-bellied torso with four legs a bit too small in proportion to the rest of its form. What it lacked in legs, it more than made up for in wings. The wings were easily as wide as the body was long, huge membranes of drum-taut flesh that reminded me of the limbs of jungle bats.

Smoke trailed from their nostrils as they passed overhead. They were at least a quarter mile up, but the furnace-like heat of their bodies washed over the remnants of the *Black Swan* as they beat their wings in a powerful downstroke. In seconds, they were at the mouth of the bay, facing the king's ships. Their jaws gaped open and their pot bellies swelled as they inhaled uncounted gallons of air. At last, they breathed out.

Infidel shielded her eyes as a second sun formed where the jets of flame shooting from the twin dragons overlapped. As the light faded, all seven of the king's ships were aflame. At this distance, the men were little more than insects throwing themselves into the sea, trailing smoke as they fell.

The dragons spun around. Again, they sucked in air and breathed flame, the light of their assault casting long stark shadows on the roof of the *Black Swan*. When the light faded, little remained of the ships. The sea itself was boiling where the boats had been mere seconds before.

Satisfied with their work on the fleet, the dragons split, making a more leisurely approach toward what remained of Commonground. Along the way, they spit fire at the few boats and canoes that were afloat out in the bay. The distant screams of frying men carried over the water.

One of the dragons turned its serpent face toward the *Black Swan*.

"Uh oh," said Infidel.

"Goons!" Menagerie shouted to No-Face and Reeker on the roof below. "Let's teach these oversized garden snakes some manners. Maneuver nine!"

"Rurh!" said No-Face, grabbing up a shattered roof beam.

Reeker looked pale as he shouted to Menagerie, "You're joking, right?"

No-Face handled the twenty-foot beam, thick as a grown man's thigh, like it was no heavier than a piece of kindling. The big man slapped the beam down at the edge of the roof, with about six feet hanging out, pointing straight toward the advancing dragon. Reeker held up his hands as No-Face approached him.

"C'mon, guy, I mean, you can't really —"

No-Face grabbed him by his shirt and spun him around, sitting him squarely on the end of the beam that sat upon the roof. Reeker swallowed hard. "Boys, it's been good knowing ya," he whispered.

"Guh," said No-Face, nodding.

"On the count of three!" Menagerie shouted. "Three!" He threw himself from the crow,s nest. When he was over the point where the broken beam jutted into space, he changed again, taking the form of a hippopotamus.

Like most hippos who discover themselves to be sixty feet up in the air, he dropped like a stone. He hit the edge of the plank with all four of his fat, round feet expertly placed for leverage. Reeker shot into the sky, his hands clasped before him, his eyes tightly closed. His lips were moving, though I couldn't hear him. It looked for all the world like he was praying.

The goons' aim was perfection; there was a reason why they were the best paid mercenaries in Commonground. The dragon dove toward the *Black Swan*, opening its mouth to fill its great bellow lungs with air. What it got, instead, was a damp skunk-man slapping against the roof of its mouth. Instinctively, the beast clamped its jaws shut. Instantly, a cloud of yellow-green fumes shot out from between its long, jagged teeth. Its eyes grew wide.

The creature veered away from the *Black Swan*, whipping its head back and forth, coughing violently, unable to breathe deeply enough to ignite its flames. Reeker clung to the beast's tongue, hugging it with his arms and legs like it was a greased pole. Slowly, he slipped toward the tip. His entire form was hazy, as the most powerful stenches he could summon poured out of every pore. The dragon began to convulse, its nervous system overwhelmed by the chemical assault. With a final, frantic jerk of its neck, it sent Reeker flying. Before it could recover, it slammed into the waters of the bay, hard, vanishing beneath the surface in a violent boil.

Reeker shrieked like a teenage girl as he sailed through the air before he, too, hit the surface of the water, bouncing once, twice, thrice like a skimming stone before he sank, leaving an oily film.

"One down," said Relic, casting his gaze toward the beast's twin, who was still burning ships at the other edge of the bay. "Unfortunately, we're running out of Goons."

Reeker still hadn't surfaced, nor was there any sign of a hippo thrashing about in the waters below. No-Face had run to the edge of the barge and was looking down into the water, shouting out, "Munuh! Rukuh!"

Infidel cracked her knuckles. "We don't need no stinkin' Goons."

Below, there was a loud crash. I hadn't seen Aurora in over a minute, but now her head was sticking up from a trap door in the roof. She climbed out, bearing a large wooden harpoon, nearly twice as tall as she was, with a long coil of rope looped around her shoulders.

"I've hunted whales bigger than these things," she shouted, as she met Infidel's gaze.

"Fire-breathing, flying whales?" asked Infidel.

"You wouldn't believe," Aurora said.

The ogress spun around as the remaining dragon roared angrily and shot toward the barge, apparently aware of the loss of its twin. Aurora dropped the coil of rope to the deck and drew back with the harpoon. "For honor!" she cried as she hurled the weapon toward the approaching beast.

The harpoon never even got close. The coil snagged on a ragged board and the weapon jerked to a sudden halt not fifty feet overhead. The dragon inhaled deeply as it plunged straight toward Aurora. Aurora crouched down, covering her head with her hands as the dragon exhaled, shooting out a jet of flame, engulfing the ice-ogress. The dragon's momentum carried it toward the mast upon which Infidel was perched. The flames instantly disintegrated the lower half of the mast. Infidel jumped from the crow's nest, grabbing Relic by the cloak and hurling him out toward the bay. She dropped down, hands open wide, as the dragon's scaly back flashed beneath her. She grabbed hold of scales near the beast's tail. The dragon reacted with the speed of thought, whipping the end of its tail down to shatter more beams on the roof of the *Black Swan*. The jolt knocked Infidel free. She bounced across the deck, flying off the edge, until a long length of chain whipped out and lassoed her ankle. No-Face jerked her back onto the roof, if it could still be called a roof. Little was left but a pile of broken boards and timbers, and half of these were on fire.

Aurora was still alive. She was crouched behind a wall of cracked and melting ice, fighting to untangle the snagged rope of the harpoon.

Infidel leapt to where the harpoon had fallen. It jutted up from the boards of the deck. She snatched it free, spinning around, racing toward Aurora, splintering the snagged board that had caught the rope. She wordlessly snatched the freshly coiled rope from Aurora's hands and jumped over the edge, flying from the *Black Swan* toward a still intact piling. She landed on this and leapt again, giving chase to the retreating dragon, who now spun slowly over the area where the other dragon had fallen. The sea still boiled furiously. The dragon again cried out; this time the thunderous roar had an edge of grief to it. The beast turned its head upward, flapping its mighty wings as it steered back toward the distant volcano. The whole south slope was aflame now, the forests forming the world's largest bonfire as the pyroclastic flow slipped through the once lush jungles.

Infidel landed on a final piling before deciding she was close enough. She dropped the coil into the water, wrapping the last few inches around her wrist. The beast was low over the waves, the down beat of its wings brushing the surface. She reared back with the harpoon, the weapon comically long compared to her. When she let it fly, it flashed through the air more swiftly than an arrow. The dragon grunted as the harpoon buried itself in its flank, but didn't look back. It flapped its wings again and flew higher, as the rope trailed behind it. Infidel grabbed hold with both hands as she was snapped into the air. She clambered up the rope like a monkey on a vine. The dragon tilted its head back, aware of her weight. It sucked in air and exhaled a long cone of flame, engulfing Infidel. For a second, she couldn't be seen at all in the conflagration. Then, her hand reached out of the flame, grasping onto the hind-claw of the dragon just as the rope disintegrated.

The flames faded, revealing Infidel clasped by a single hand onto the middle nail of the dragon's hind-claw. Her clothes were mostly burned away; her skin was flushed red, like she had sun-burn. It broke my heart to see that her long, flowing tresses were mostly gone, singed down to a frizzled mess. Her eyes were set in a look of determination.

The dragon wasn't impressed. It flexed its claw forward, bending its head toward her to bite away the unwelcome passenger. As it opened its jaws, Infidel swung her body back and forth, dangling from the claw. The creature's mouth glowed with the fading remnants of its flame. I saw a flash of light as the well-honed blade of my bone-handled knife was revealed in Infidel's free hand. She swung forward, leaping into the beast's open jaws, clearing its teeth. The creature's mouth clamped shut.

Suddenly, I was alive again. Not ghost alive; I was physically whole once more, popping into existence inches above the dragon's snout. Unlike my previous manifestations, this time the laws of gravity applied. I slammed into the dragon's scales, sliding down its snout, scraping my restored flesh on its raspy hide. I cut my hands trying to grab hold. The scales were like flakes of razor sharp volcanic glass. I screamed as I left a trail of blood down its snout, but caught myself at last, my foot coming to rest on the ridge of its nostrils.

My stomach twisted as the beast lurched through the air. The ground seemed impossibly distant. I felt certain I'd been restored to life only to face a second death. But… why? How had this happened?

Suddenly, Infidel's fist burst through the skin only a few feet down the snout from the dragon's eyes, my bone-handled knife firmly in her grasp. The dragon's blood bubbled on the surface of the blade, quickly boiling off now that it was exposed to air. Infidel's whole arm tore through the skin, followed by a shoulder, then her bloodied head burst through. The blood boiled on her skin as well as the knife. The creature shuddered, then went limp in the air; whatever Infidel had done to it had apparently been too much to withstand. The beast's snout tilted down. I could see water far below; at some point, we'd come back out over the bay. I was thrown free of the beast's nose, my naked, bleeding body tumbling in the air. As I spun, I looked back toward Infidel, who was gawking at me, her eyes wide.

"Infidel!" I shouted, straining my hand toward her.

"Stagger?" she whispered.

Then, the last of the fresh blood vaporized from the knife, leaving only a crust of black gore. The wind once more passed straight through me. I was suspended in mid-air, no longer in the grip of gravity. Light passed through my vaporous fingers.

"Stagger!" Infidel cried, her eyes frantic as they searched the air where she'd last seen me.

Then the dragon hit the water and I plunged beneath as well, my ghost still tethered to the knife. The sea was black as ink, full of the stirred up silt from the tidal wave. My vision was all but useless, unable to make sense of the images that flashed past me. The dragon's hide seemed to be crumbling, breaking apart into bits of black and red gravel. For half a second, I saw a flash of Infidel's torso. There was something long and ropelike wrapped around it, covered with cup-sized suckers. The water roiled as an eye the size of a dinner plate flashed past me, glowing with golden phosphorescence.

Then, suddenly, Infidel and my knife were back above the surface of the water. She was wrapped in the tentacle of an enormous squid, at least sixty foot long. A second tentacle held the soggy, sputtering form of Reeker.

Infidel raised her knife to stab at the tentacle that held her, but stopped herself before she thrust the blade down. The dragon blood had been washed off by her plunge into the bay. As the last bit of pink water ran down the handle, I faded once more, invisible even to myself.

The squid's tentacles gingerly placed Infidel onto the wrecked roof of the *Black Swan*. She was, yet again, buck naked save for a ring of ruined leather that had once been the too-short skirt. Aurora rushed to her side, snatching up the half-charred flag of the barge and draping it over Infidel's bare shoulders before Reeker had recovered enough to ogle her.

"That was really damn impressive," Aurora said. "But… who was up there with you?"

"What?" asked Infidel, running her fingers through what was left of her hair. The longest bits were only a few inches long.

"For a second, I thought I saw someone else clamped onto the dragon's snout with you. Were my eyes playing tricks?"

Infidel turned pale. "I thought I saw… I thought…" her voice trailed off. "It was just some poor sailor. He… he fell."

Menagerie dragged himself up onto the roof, human once more. The squid tattoo that had once been dark black upon his neck had faded to a barely visible gray-blue outline.

He collapsed against what was left of the mast, staring up toward the still bubbling volcano, "I guess the king's dragon hunt has been cancelled."

Infidel shook her head as she, too, looked at the raging mountain. "I don't think so. Greatshadow has just been suckered. Those ships were decoys; I'll stake my life on it."

"You're probably right," said Reeker, wringing water from his hair. He looked at Menagerie. "So, anyway, I quit. I'm done with dragons. Infidel can be the third goon."

"You aren't quitting," said Menagerie. "You signed the contract." He tapped at a section of cursive text on the left cheek of his buttocks. "Didn't you read all the terms? You're in this until Greatshadow's dead, or you are."

Reeker sighed, then muttered something underneath his breath.

"Hur hur hur," said No-Face.

Infidel laughed as she contemplated Menagerie's skinny ass. "I guess that's one way of discouraging people from studying the fine print."

6 - INNOCENT

MY OLD SAILBOAT had come to rest in the tangled branches of a mangrove thicket half a mile away. The gaping holes in the hull would never allow it to return to the bay, but as a tree house it possessed a certain charm. Menagerie had spotted it in the aftermath of the dragon strike, as he'd flitted over the area in his vulture form, surveying the damage. He'd quickly singled out the most likely places to look for survivors, then he and the other Goons had set forth to help who they could.

Infidel was never afraid to lend a hand to anyone in need, but she declined to take part in the rescue mission. I couldn't blame her; she looked completely wiped out after her fight with the dragon. She found Relic's gnarled staff among the shattered planks of the *Black Swan* and used it for support as she limped across the rubble in search of my boat. She was sweating, her face pale and feverish. Her invulnerable skin didn't burn, but, like anyone, when she got overheated, she could feel sick. It didn't help that the sun had come out with a fury, its tropical rays turning the humid atmosphere over the churned up bay into a pressure cooker.

At mid-day, while Infidel still searched through the mangroves, I noticed the Wanderer ships returning. They sailed back into the bay in droves, once again forming a boat city, held together by ropes and ladders instead of docks and gangplanks. River-pygmies were now thick in the bay as well, an entire flotilla of canoes searching among the shattered ships and buildings.

The eruption of the volcano had finally subsided. The once verdant southern slope of the mountain was black now, cloaked with smoke and steam. A shower of fine charcoal ash rained down on the bay, coating every surface.

Infidel was grimy as a miner by the time she found my boat. The once white flag she was wrapped in was now mostly gray. She was all alone as she climbed into the branches. I wondered if Relic had possibly survived. No one had seen the hunchback since she'd tossed him from the crow's nest.

My place was even more of a trash heap than usual. The piles of books had all toppled. The towers of bottles and jugs had turned into a carpet of broken glass. Infidel dug through the rubble until she'd found the thin cotton mat that served as my bed. She yanked it free of the debris and tossed it onto the deck outside. She located a few stained blankets and draped them in the branches, forming an umbrella to provide shade and shield her from the drifting ash.

She toppled onto the bed face first, her body completely slack. She lay motionless for half a minute until she raised her hand to the back of her neck, running her palm along the uneven stubble of her scalp. She groaned, a sound mixing weariness, frustration, and despair.

Then, she fell silent. After five minutes, I could hear her muffled snores. She slept like a corpse, her slumber undisturbed by the tossing, turning, and mumbling that normally characterized it. Hours passed; eventually the long day drew to an end and still she slept, without a single muscle twitching.

The ash rain had finally stopped and the stars were slowly emerging when there was a loud *crunch* in the debris beneath the boat. Infidel didn't stir as the sound repeated itself; something large and heavy was walking around.

Someone called out, "Infidel?"

Infidel remained face down and immobile, her voice muffled as she replied, "Mwuh?"

"Infidel, it's Aurora. Where are you?"

Infidel rolled over on her side.

"Go away," she said, without opening her eyes. Her voice was feeble and scratchy.

"I want to talk," said Aurora. "I brought you some food."

Infidel's unbruised eye cracked open slightly.

"Monkey?" she asked, the faintest glimmer of hope in her voice. River-pygmies sold monkey meat stuck on bamboo reeds, deep fried and served with a chili sauce. Infidel loved the stuff, though I'd never cared for it.

"Sea beans, some whale jerky, and a coconut," said Aurora.

Infidel rolled over on her back, her brow furrowed. She seemed to be caught in an internal debate, weighing her hunger against her desire not to have company. At last, she sighed. "Come on up."

She scooted into a seated position against a mangrove branch, tugging the flag she was wrapped in like a towel higher up her breasts as Aurora climbed onto the boat. Despite the devastation of the day, the night was coming to life with the chirps of frogs and birds. Off in the distance, a troop of apes howled as they scrambled through the canopy. The air was still thick with the smell of putrid water mixed with smoke. All along the slope of the volcano, remnant blazes danced. I felt a sense of longing, looking up at the mountain. It was impossible to say what ancient ruins had been wiped out by the eruption. On the other hand, the forest fires no doubt cleared away the tangles of vines that hid many a lost wonder. I wished I could go up on the slope later this week to scope out the newly revealed terrain.

Aurora sat down on the deck, cross-legged, dropping a large canvas bag in front of her. "I found you some more clothes. I have to say, that idea about a team of tailors following you around sounds like a good idea."

Infidel shrugged. "There aren't many people in the world with skin tougher than their clothing. I can be hell on a pair of pants."

"How did your skin get to be so tough?"

"You aren't supposed to ask stuff like that in Commonground," said Infidel.

"I'm not sure there is a Commonground anymore," said Aurora, glancing back out over the bay.

"Fair enough." Infidel dug into the bag and found the coconut. She cracked it in her bare hands, holding the nut to her lips as the milk began to run out. She gulped down the pale white fluid then wiped her mouth, sitting the coconut aside as she dug back into the bag, pulling out a slender plank of purple meat as long as her forearm.

"Whale jerky, huh? I guess I shouldn't be surprised. Even in a city by the bay, there aren't that many people who keep harpoons in their room."

Aurora nodded. "Whales are central to life on Qikiqtabruk. We eat their flesh, drink their blood, make cheese from their milk —"

"What?"

"What what?"

"Milk? Whales are fish. They don't have teats. How can they have milk?"

"Whales aren't fish. They breathe air like you or me. And, they suckle their young on milk. If you kill a mother whale while she's still nursing, you can harvest barrels of cream. The cheese we make from it is a great delicacy. As high priestess, I would always be given the first batch after a hunt."

"High priestess sounds like nice work if you can get it," said Infidel. "I take it the Jagged Heart was used on the whale hunts?"

"Indirectly. Before each hunt, I would summon the ghosts of whales we'd slain on the previous hunt and vanquish the spirits, so that they couldn't do evil against the ogres going out to hunt. The spirit meat was also essential provision for the dead of our people on their journey into the Great Sea Above. The Jagged Heart also had the power to open a pathway into the afterlife where I could commune with our ancestors. It's pale light would guide us as we sailed from the dragon's jaws into the Great Sea Above."

Infidel rolled her eyes.

"What?" asked Aurora.

"Nothing." She said, as she chomped down on the sheet of meat and tore off a mouthful. She chewed with her mouth open as she said, "Hmm. Not bad. Not fishy at all. I hope you got the spirit of this one; I'd hate for an angry whale ghost to give me indigestion."

Aurora frowned. "You aren't terribly respectful of other people's beliefs."

Infidel shrugged. "I'm not even terribly respectful of my own beliefs. Anyway, why should you care what people think of your religion? It certainly didn't do you much good. Banished by your own people for losing a harpoon."

Aurora's eyes narrowed. I thought she was about to scold Infidel, but then her expression softened. "I wasn't banished. I was executed. I was wrapped in chains and taken to an iceberg. My people chiseled a hole in the ice, then buried me in it. My own brother, Tarpok, filled the hole with water so that it would refreeze. Cold cannot harm me, and my people can survive for days without breathing if we don't struggle. Still, I was left to drift in my frozen tomb, completely trapped, doomed to eventually suffocate or starve."

"You obviously escaped."

"The Black Swan rescued me. I don't know if it was by pure chance, or due to her ability to travel back in time, but she found me after I'd been adrift for little more than a week. I was near death when she freed me. I had no will to live, but she nursed me back to health anyway. She told me that, since I was dead to my people, I could make a new life with her in Commonground. I hope she's survived. I searched the ruins of the barge and found no sign of her. I don't know what to do if she's gone forever."

"She'll be okay. She strikes me as a survivor," said Infidel, who'd by now had found the sea beans. Sea beans aren't actual beans; they're a puffy weed that grows in marshes. They taste like asparagus soaked in saltwater. They make my mouth pucker, but Infidel likes their crisp snap. "You were going to quit working for the Black Swan anyway. What do you care?"

"As priestess, my whole life was devoted to serving others. Without service, I have no purpose. I didn't always approve of the Black Swan's actions. If she had any greater goal for her life other than accumulating wealth, I never learned of it. Yet, serving her gave structure to my days. I know I was only another employee to her, but she was my world."

Infidel rooted around in the sack once again and pulled out a jug with a cork in it, looking at it skeptically. "What's this?"

"Fresh water," said Aurora. "I don't drink spirits."

Infidel popped the cork and chugged down several cupfuls. "Mmm. I needed that. After a big fight, I'm always thirsty for days."

"It must take a lot of energy, to do the things you do," said Aurora. "There aren't many people who can say they've killed a dragon."

Infidel shrugged. "Yeah. It takes a lot out of me. But, not as much as you might think. My strength is more magic than muscles."

"What is the source of your magic?" asked Aurora.

Infidel stared at her, obviously annoyed by the question. Then, to my surprise, she flashed her what-the-hell grin. "Okay," she said. "You know that there used to be a primal dragon of the forest named Verdant. He was killed, like, a thousand years ago by the first Knight of the Book, the original King Brightmoon."

Aurora nodded. "I'm familiar with the legend."

"It's not legend, it's history," said Infidel. "Brightmoon killed Verdant, who had been weakened by the decimation of the forests near his lair. The blood of the beast was drained and dried, forming a dark green powder. A gilded casket of this blood was kept at the Brightmoon Cathedral. When Knights of the Book are initiated, they're given a spoonful of the stuff, dissolved in wine. It grants them a small measure of the dragon's strength and toughness."

"Blood magic," said Aurora. "I thought the church disapproved of such things."

"The Church is just a wealth of contradictions," said Infidel. "They preach peace, then raise armies of violent tempered men to impose it. They sing the virtues of forgiveness and mercy, but build torture chambers to focus the faith of those who've gone astray. Dabbling in blood magic is a sin for you and me, but priests don't have to play by the same rules. Since they decree what is and isn't a sin, a priest could eat babies and pick his teeth with the bones and still be praised for his rectitude."

"I'm starting to see how you earned the name 'Infidel.'"

Infidel shook her head. "The church doesn't give a damn about my opinions. It's my actions that put me on the naughty list. When I was fifteen, I stole their casket of dragon blood. Knights had been gobbling down this stuff for centuries, so it was almost gone, but there was still about a pound of it caked up in the corners. I went at it with my fingernails and polished off everything that was left. At first, I didn't think anything had happened to me. When the priest came to get me from the inner sanctum, he found me crouched down over the empty casket, blood caked around my lips and under my finger nails. The sleeves of my wedding gown were green with —"

"Wait," said Aurora, holding up her hand. "Wedding gown? Is this part of the story about you once being engaged to Lord Tower?"

Infidel pressed her lips tightly together, as if contemplating whether to say more. After several long seconds, she said, "Engaged isn't the right word. It implies that he asked me to marry him and I said yes. The truth isn't so pretty. I was sold to him."

Aurora raised her eyebrows.

"My birth name was Innocent Brightmoon. I was the king's third daughter, but the first to survive to breeding age."

"A princess," said Aurora.

"It's not as good a job as it sounds," said Infidel. "'Princess' is just a fancy label for a high-priced slave-whore. My wedding to the first born male heir of the Tower family had been arranged before I was born. The Towers were immensely wealthy; there were all sorts of political and economic reasons that the Tower and Brightmoon lines were fated to mingle. My father had decided that his first eligible daughter would marry the first eligible son of the Tower family, and that was that. No one ever asked my opinion on the matter."

"Still..." said Aurora. "You were born into luxury. Life couldn't have been all bad."

"Couldn't it?" Infidel asked. She sighed. "I guess, from the outside, it looked like I was living a life of wealth. But, it wasn't my wealth, or my life. I was little more than a doll, a pretty thing to be dressed in gowns and decorate my father's court. I was never allowed to make a single decision. I lived in a palace where court dinners were held, with meals literally fit for a king, and all I'd be given to eat would be a meager salad. I wasn't allowed to taste dessert because my wedding gown had been designed before I was even conceived, and it was important that my waist be slender enough that I might get mistaken for a wasp. I never wore shackles, but I was a prisoner all the same."

Aurora nodded. "So you decided to run away."

"I wish I could say my actions were that deliberate. My education, such as it was, didn't teach me much about making good choices. When my wedding day finally came, I could barely think. I felt like a caged rat; my mind was darting all over the place, looking for any escape, but I found nothing."

"You must have really hated the young Lord Tower."

Infidel made a gagging noise. "Hated doesn't begin to cover it. He's such a sanctimonious idiot; he can't fart without running to the nearest priest to offer repentance. He believes every lie the church has ever crafted. You wouldn't believe his awkward, ritualistic attempts to court me. I could tell he really had no choice in this matter either. If he'd been a little rebellious about it, who knows? Maybe I might have liked him. I mean, he was good-looking, and he was always winning jousting tournaments, so he wasn't without a certain physical charm. But, his attempts to write love poems were cringe inducing. They sounded like sermons! 'Praise the creator who this day has blessed me with the bounty of your chaste lips, blah blah bluhhh.'" She stuck out her tongue. "We never even held hands."

Somehow, my ghost heart felt lighter to learn this. Since hearing she'd been engaged to Lord Tower, I'd assumed that she must have loved him once. I was jealous, though, obviously, there was no rational basis for this. I found myself annoyed that she was spilling her guts so freely to Aurora. I'd been her closest companion for ages. Why had she never shared this with me? Worse, why had I never had the courage to ask?

Infidel continued her story, "Anyway, it was my wedding day. There's this ten minute ritual before the ceremony where the bride goes to the inner sanctum to pray in private; there's not even a priest present. The inner sanctum was where they kept the casket of dragon blood. The second the priest closed the door, my eyes fixed on it. It was locked, but it was also a thousand freakin' years old. I had it cracked open in about thirty seconds. And, like I said, when the high priest came back into the sanctuary, I was coated in the stuff. I'd gobbled it down like it was all the ice cream and cake that I'd been denied since I was a toddler."

Aurora chuckled softly. "You must have been a sight in your bloodied gown."

"To this day, I still don't like wearing green," said Infidel, with a small shudder. "I get bad flashbacks of looking down at the green coating my arms. The priest stared at me for about half a minute, just dumbfounded, then clenched his fists and came out me, shouting, 'What have you done? What have you done?' Even though I'd never hit anyone in my life, I gave him a backhanded slap to shut him up. And… um… and… and his face sort of caved in. After that, I kind of… I kind of snapped. I launched out of the inner sanctum and tore through anyone in my way. I jumped out a stained glass window and kept running. I killed… I killed a lot of people on my way out of town. There might have been a puppy that got squished as well. I… my memory's fuzzy, and I don't like to think about it anyway. I was completely drunk on the blood. It's one reason I seldom drink now. I don't like feeling out-of-control. Anyway, long story short, I wandered around the islands for a couple of years getting my head straight before winding up in Commonground. It's been a while since any of the church's assassins came after me, but I'm guessing I'm still public enemy number one."

"Which makes it strange that you want to sign on to the king's dragon hunt," said Aurora. "Won't Tower recognize you?"

Infidel shrugged. "Who knows? I was just a girl back then. I have boobs now." She ran her hands along her ruined hair. "And, you know, a different hair cut."

"Father Ver is with him," said Aurora.

Infidel pressed her lips together tightly. If I'd still had arms, I would have hugged her to console her. I knew what she was thinking. A few extra curves and a dragon-induced haircut weren't going to fool the church's best Truthspeaker. I had personal experience with Father Ver's powers. Infidel was screwed.

"Why do you want to go on this quest any way?" asked Aurora. "It can't be the treasure. You've never been obsessed with money."

Infidel drew her knees up to her chest, resting her chin on her arms as she stared out over the dark bay. Boat lanterns twinkled like stars across the water.

"Maybe I'm tired," she whispered.

"Maybe?"

"Screw it," she said, raising her chin. "I *am* tired. I mean, I've had fun. Stagger led me on some wild adventures. I've had experiences I couldn't even imagine when I was fifteen. My life hasn't been boring. But..." Her voice trailed off as she shook her head.

"But?"

"But maybe I'd like boring." She took a deep, weary breath. "Maybe I'd enjoy sleeping in a real bed at night, and wearing clean clothes every day. Maybe I'd like to walk down a street where I'm not looking over my shoulder wondering who's about to jump me with a shadow blade. Maybe I'd like to meet a stranger and not instantly start thinking about how I'm going to kill him if things turn ugly. Maybe thirty-year-old Infidel doesn't want to live her life trapped by choices made by fifteen-year-old Innocent."

Her eyes were narrowed as she spoke. She sounded so angry. I'd never suspected. What kind of friend had I been that I'd missed this?

She finally relaxed and said, softly, "The closest I ever came to feeling normal was when I hung out with Stagger. This is... this is crazy. But I used to imagine me and him getting out of here, finding some little village where no one knew who the hell we were, and settling down. Maybe find a little peace and quiet and normal."

I'd dreamed that too. Why hadn't I told her?

"Why didn't you tell him?" asked Aurora.

"We... we...." She cradled her head in her hands. Her voice cracked as she said, "There are things that are wrong with me."

"Stagger was wild about you. You have a crazy streak, sure, but anyone could see that he loved you."

Infidel closed her eyes and clenched her fists. She looked as sad as when she'd sat at my grave. She was silent for a long time. Finally, she relaxed her hands, and sniffed. She whispered, "Normal couples can... they can do stuff. Intimate stuff. And I wanted that. I wanted that so badly."

I wanted that! I wanted that so much it hurt. Why didn't I have the courage to tell her? If I'd still had lungs, I would have cursed the sky for my cowardice.

"I'm guessing Stagger would have been okay with, um, intimacy," said Aurora, with what might have been a grin, though her tusks made it hard to tell.

Infidel shuddered. "My strength makes touching things tricky. I try to slap a man, and I smash his face in. It took me years to learn to pick up a glass without breaking it. I'm more dangerous than people know."

"You seem to have it under control."

"I could have held his hand without crushing it, sure. Maybe even kissed him without breaking his teeth. But… but *all* my muscles are supernaturally powerful. Even ones… even ones I don't always have full control over."

"Oh," said Aurora. Then, she said, "Ooooh," in a way that made it clear she understood what Infidel was getting at.

Suddenly, I understood as well. Ordinary coupling could have left me maimed and mangled, if not outright dead.

"So…" said Aurora. "You're a thirty year old virgin."

Infidel shrugged. "I'll die one, I guess. I'm never going to know anything like love. But, at least when I hung out with Stagger, I felt… I felt happy."

I'd been happy too. And, even with my fantasies of shared sexual bliss crushed by Infidel's physical realities, I still would gladly have gone with her to that quiet little village and lived out my days beside her. I'd loved her without even so much as a kiss for years. I could have accepted anything to make her happy.

"And now you're unhappy," said Aurora. "So what? The plan is to go get yourself killed by Greatshadow?"

"No," said Infidel, sounding deadly serious. "The plan is to go get myself rich. Not pirate booty rich, not ancient artifact rich, but filthy, filthy, filthy rich. Because if there's one thing I learned growing up in my father's court, it's that if you're filthy rich everyone will bend over backwards to tell you you're clean. If I show up in my father's court with sole possession of Greatshadow's treasure, I'm confident I'll have a full pardon in my hands inside of ten minutes. The church might not be happy about this, but I'm betting after I donate funds to build a few new cathedrals, they'll come around. I'll be rich with my own money, not my father's. I'll be free to live where and how I wish. I'll have my own palace with silk sheets on a bed so fluffy you'd think it's stuffed with clouds. Every day I'll take a hot bath while musicians serenade me and I'll get out of the water and put on clean freakin' underwear. And when I walk into my own damn dining room, people are going to run up to me with trays full of goddamn cake!"

Aurora nodded slowly, contemplating the dream. "And this is going to make you happy?"

Infidel shrugged. "I'm not shooting for happy. I'm aiming for comfortable and fat."

"You'll achieve more than this," said a voice from the branches above. Infidel jumped to her feet. Aurora jerked her head up as a sheen of ice grew across her clenched fists. It was Relic. How the hunchback had climbed into the branches without us hearing him I don't know. It seemed like a bit of a stretch that this could have been where Infidel had thrown him.

Relic peered down at the two women. His eyes glowed faintly golden in the darkness. He said, "You shall be beloved by all mankind, princess. You will be the champion who slew Greatshadow. For centuries men have perished due to the unpredictable malevolence of fire. Castles, hovels, entire towns have been reduced to cinders with no warning, killing young and old alike. Once Greatshadow is dead, fire will be a trusted tool of mankind, fully tamed, a danger no more. Children will sing songs about you a thousand years hence, just as they sing the tale of how the first Brightmoon vanquished the dragon of the forest. As for seeking the forgiveness of the Church of the Book, remember you won't just return with the dragon's treasure. You can also return with barrels of fresh blood, replacing the dwindling holy relic you stole.

You can claim you were driven by divine visions to renew the blood. One day you'll be regarded as a saint."

Infidel looked up the slope of the mountain, toward the glowing caldera. "And maybe one day I'll sprout wings and fly. Because if there's a Truthspeaker on this quest, then I'm never going to be part of this dragon hunt."

"Assuming there's still a hunt," Aurora said. "The Truthspeaker's charred bones are probably at the bottom of the bay with the rest of the king's fleet."

"Nah," said Infidel. "My father's a jerk, but not an idiot. He sent those ships in to give the dragon a chance to feel like he'd finished off the threat before it even reached shore. It had to be a distraction. Tower and his team are already on the island."

Relic nodded. "I concur. It's only a matter of time before they contact the Three Goons. We must prepare for this moment."

"Prepare how?" asked Infidel.

"You will need a disguise that Lord Tower cannot see through," said Relic. "I have just the persona in mind."

"Forget Tower. How am I supposed to fool a Truthspeaker?"

Relic's glowing eyes twinkled as he chuckled. "That, my dear, will be far easier than you may think. Few are as easy to deceive as those most confident of the truth." Then he cast his gaze toward Aurora. "The deception will require your cooperation, as well as the silence of the Three Goons."

Aurora nodded. "If you promise to help me recover the Jagged Heart, I pledge to keep my mouth shut. As for the Goons, they've been hired as muscle; there's no clause requiring them to disclose everything they know. We can buy their silence with a non-competing contract for these sub-rights."

"I vow that recovering the Heart for you will be my second goal, though ensuring that Greatshadow dies remains my top priority. If you accept this, then we have a deal," said Relic. He held out his gnarled hand. Aurora placed her giant hand upon it. Infidel lay her smaller hand against the ogress's knuckles.

Infidel said, "Excellent. It looks like we've got it all worked out for me to join a group of men sworn to kill me so we can face off with a dragon that melts stone with his breath." She grinned. "And Stagger used to complain that I never planned ahead."

7 -SUCH CRUEL THINGS

AT DAWN THE harbor rang with a cacophony of sledgehammers and saws as the Wanderers salvaged useful lumber from the shattered remains of Commonground. Along the shores, river-pygmies gathered up scraps of wood too splintered to be of use and heaped them onto bonfires. Nearby, the bodies of dead brethren were stacked into muddy blue piles. I always found it odd that the river-pygmies cremate their dead; a water burial would seem more appropriate. I need only glance up the blackened slope of the mountain to understand the origins of the custom. Greatshadow could wipe out the pygmy tribes at any time for any reason. They pygmies believed that, as long as they let fire consume their bodies when they were done with them, Greatshadow would leave them alone most of the time. Whether Greatshadow was even aware of this bargain I can't guess.

Once or twice during the night, pygmies had come poking around the trees beneath the boat. I've no doubt they would have climbed aboard if Aurora hadn't stuck her head over to investigate the noise. Her big, tusked face had sent would-be scavengers scurrying back into the darkness.

Relic left at sunrise. I'd watched as he scrambled down through the branches of the trees then dashed off through the debris-threaded thickets, agile as a cat. His crippled routine was obviously just a disguise. I have to say that he'd sounded like he knew a thing or two about disguises when he spent the better part of the night explaining his ideas for how to hide Infidel's identity. He had wanted her to wear a suit of full plate armor, including a bucket-style helmet that would conceal her features. Infidel had vetoed this; she liked her comfort and full freedom of movement. Helmets got in the way of her peripheral vision. After a few hours of circular discussions, Relic had thrown his hands into the air and announced that he'd thought of the perfect disguise, but couldn't share it. It would be a surprise, he said, as he scurried out to gather whatever supplies he had in mind.

I still felt like they were wasting their time. With Father Ver among the king's men, Infidel would be discovered in seconds. My upbringing in the monastery had left me keenly aware of the power of Truthspeakers, and Father Ver was a legend. He was the most powerful Truthspeaker the Church of the Book had ever produced, as I knew all too well.

To appreciate the power of Truthspeakers, you need to know a little bit about the Church of the Book. High in the mountains of Raitingu, what the Wanderers call the Isle of Storm, there's a temple built into the bedrock of the world's tallest mountain. Within this temple is a chamber carved from pure white quartz. Here, on a pedestal of gold, sits the One True Book. The book is roughly five feet long, three feet across, and two feet thick. It's bound in leather black as a moonless night; it's said that if you stare at the cover, you can see stars twinkling in the void. In contrast, the pages are snowy white, thin as onion skin. The priests calculate that the book contains 7,777 pages.

Within this book, the Divine Author has written the history of the world, from the moment of creation to the final day of judgment. My life, your life, the lives of the dead and yet to be born, are recorded in minute detail on these holy pages. The One True Book is the final authority on all that has been, all that is, and all that will be.

Having access to this document would seem to give the Church of the Book a certain advantage over everyone else, save for one tiny detail: the book is far too sacred to ever be sullied by human hands. All men are too corrupted by lies to risk opening the book and actually reading it. The pure light of sacred truth would melt the flesh from the bones of anyone deluded enough to think himself worthy of sullying the pages with his unworthy gaze.

It's taught that, one day, a Golden Child will arise, a perfect being uncorrupted by lies, who will open the book and read out the final account. The world we live in is built from four fundamental and opposing forces: spirit, matter, lies, and truth. As the book is read, all falsehood will be banished; all matter will be cleansed, all spirit will be purified. The world we know will be wiped away and replaced with the world as it always should have been, with a trinity of unified forces: truth, spirit, and substance.

Until the day of that Final Account, all that we know of the contents of the Book have been learned through prayer. Truthspeakers spend years on their knees in the temple, their faces pressed to the floor, weeping, sweating, laughing, screaming as they plead with the Divine Author to reveal even a few lines of sacred truth to them. After years of effort, the Truthspeakers go out into the world to spread the received revelations.

The Truthspeakers gain certain gifts as a result of their devotion. The most powerful Truthspeakers can see the falsehoods of the world and correct it. For instance, if it's raining and a pious Truthspeaker understands that the One True Book foretold that the day would be sunny, he simply tells the sky it's supposed to be blue. The clouds will part and the sun will come out. This may be hyperbole; I've never personally witnessed a Truthspeaker pull off such a feat. But, I have witnessed another magical gift. It's impossible to lie to a Truthspeaker. Believe me, I've tried.

The monks run a vineyard where they produce the sacramental wine used in certain church rites. The wine isn't intended to be used recreationally, but when I had my first sip at age ten, I appreciated the warmth that spread through me as I swallowed, and wanted more. By age twelve I'd sneak out at night to the pitch dark wine cellars to finish off entire bottles, luxuriating in the mellow heat that spread through my body and washed over my mind in a soothing wave. I'd lie on the frigid stone floor in the darkness and dream of using grandfather's bone-handled knife to hack away vines from ancient statues in steaming tropical jungles.

Alas, the monks kept meticulous track of their inventory. A Truthspeaker was brought in to investigate the missing gallons. I'd heard from other orphans that you can fool a Truthspeaker if you can fool yourself. You couldn't lie, but truth wasn't always black and white. I was certain I'd be asked if I'd stolen the wine, and, technically, I hadn't. The wine didn't belong to any one person. It was property of the Church, and I was a member of the Church. It was no more a theft than for me to share the wine than it was to drink water from the communal well. I trusted I could slip through this loophole if the Truthspeaker interrogated me.

I remember the moment that I'd been brought into the room where Father Ver waited. He was middle-aged then, his close-cropped dark hair speckled with gray at the temples. His skin was pale from spending most of his life in a cave. There was a large callous in the center of his forehead from decades spent rubbing it against the floor. His eyes were sunk back into his skull, hidden in shadows. The interrogation room was lit by a single candle which sat on the table between us. The light flickered like twin stars in the void of his eyes.

Despite his stern expression, I walked into the room with a confident swagger. I sat down and faced him, unafraid to meet his gaze. I waited for him to speak to me. Seconds passed and he said nothing. I slid back in my chair, prepared to wait him out, but turned my face away. It was uncomfortable to look at someone so directly without saying anything. As the seconds passed into minutes, I'd glance at him and always find his eyes locked on my face. I began to fidget. I could feel his stare boring into me. I started sweating. My palms were clammy as I wiped away the moisture on my brow. I trembled as I worried he might mistake my discomfort for evidence of guilt. Which was absurd, I reminded myself, since I hadn't stolen anything. I wanted to tell him this, but my tongue had grown thick in my mouth. If my rubbery limbs had possessed the strength, I would have fled the room. Instead, some horrible internal magnet kept pulling my gaze toward his. I felt as if my face wasn't truly my own, but was instead a mask I'd all but forgotten I was wearing. The Truthspeaker's eyes were peeling back that mask to reveal the sinner beneath.

After what felt like hours, he spoke, in a low, gravelly voice, "You are the wine thief."

I collapsed to the floor, my tongue leaping to life: "Yes! Oh yes! Yes! It's true! I stole the wine!"

Hot tears erupted from my eyes as I wept, my body wracked with sobs. I was vaguely aware of Father Ver rising and walking around the desk.

"You will stop crying," he said, standing before me.

Instantly, I stopped. It was like he'd reached in and flicked some unseen switch that commanded my tears. I reached out and hugged his ankles, groveling as I pressed my cheeks against his sandal-clad feet. "Forgive me," I whispered. "Forgive me."

"You will stand," he said.

Though my body felt hollow, gutted by guilt and shame, my muscles moved to obey his words and I rose.

Father Ver frowned. "There's a weakness in you," he said. "Unfounded hope is the source. Your grandfather paid you a visit two years ago."

"Y-yes," I said, sniffling.

"He filled your head with tales of vanished kingdoms, pygmy tribes, and lost treasures. Seductive visions for a boy your age. You've turned your eyes from the path of righteousness and now dream of life outside this monastery."

I wiped snot onto my sleeve and said, "My g-grandfather is going to t-take me with him next time."

"We both know this isn't true," said Father Ver.

I swallowed hard.

"If your grandfather wanted you, he could have taken you on his last visit. You aren't our property, boy. We'd welcome one less mouth to feed. The truth is plain; Judicious Merchant loves the jungle more than he loves you."

I wiped my cheeks and whispered, "He... he said the jungle is too dangerous for a child."

"Do the pygmies not have children? In any case, your grandfather is a free man, still in possession of remnants of your family fortune. He need not live in a jungle like a savage. He could have raised you in comfort on some modest country estate. His actions show what he truly loves in this world. It isn't you."

I dropped to my knees, doubled over, feeling as if I'd been kicked in the gut.

"Your thirst for wine comes from your love of falsehood. In your intoxication, it's easy to feel as if the dreams you cling to are real. It's time to let go of your childish embrace of fantasy. Truth will never be found digging among the ruins of failed civilizations. Truth is revealed through prayer and obedience to the church. The great adventure for any man lies not in exploring the ruins of distant jungles, but in navigating the ruins of his own soul. Your soul in particular is a treacherous labyrinth. Your father, mother, and grandfather all live, yet you are an orphan. What a heavy burden, to be so unloved. I understand why your dreams seem more attractive than your piteous reality."

I dug my nails into my palms, trying to make the pain blot out the words. I sniffled. "H-how can... how can you say such cruel things?"

"It is a measure of your weakness that you mistake truth for cruelty," said Father Ver. "Within the One True Book, your life has already been written. I know nothing of your future; there is too much contained within the Book for one man to study it all. I have no certainty of your eventual fate, but slaking your blasphemous thirst with sacramental wine is a poor omen. My informed speculation is that one day you'll die drunk on some distant shore, leaving your bones to rot in an unmarked grave."

He walked to the door and rang a small bell to summon the monks. He didn't look at me as he said, "If I were the sole arbiter of your fate, you would be hung. A boy who is a thief will almost certainly grow into a man who is something worse. Alas, the brothers will sanction no punishment more severe than flogging. You will receive ten lashes a day with a braided leather whip for the next seven days."

My mouth went dry as I thought of the pain I would endure.

"I know you are afraid of what's to come," he said, his voice softening ever so slightly. "Look at me."

I turned my face toward him as he untied the knot that held his simple robes at the waist. He shrugged the heavy cloth from his shoulders. He turned, revealing his bare back. He was more muscular than I'd suspected. There was no fat on him; his muscles looked wiry and powerful beneath his white skin. I squinted in the candle light. Quickly, I understood what he was showing me. His back was crisscrossed with scars and countless fresh scabs.

"When the whip touches you, pain flashes through your mind like a light," he said. "Follow this light. It will lead you to truth. Pleasure leads only to falsehood; pain guides men to what is real. Truth is hard. Truth is harsh. *Truth is all that matters.* It is stark and beautiful and complete. Embrace your pain, child, and you may yet live a righteous life."

He pulled his robes back up his shoulders. "Should you not heed my words, pray we do not cross paths again," he said. "When next we meet, I will not show such mercy."

He left, and I listened to this feet pad away down the stone hall. I was all alone, his words echoing in my ears. All I could feel was gratitude. Father Ver had given me a precious second chance. I didn't fear the punishment to come; I was eager for it, ready for the whip to beat away my weakness and bring me to the same state of grace as this holy man.

I didn't find enlightenment in my floggings. The instant the whip touched me I found only hurt and humiliation and a festering distrust for all things labeled holy. I returned to wine theft within the year. When I finally fled the monastery, it was with a belly full of sacramental wine and the contents of the poor box jingling in my pockets.

RELIC HAD TOLD Infidel to wait for his return, but nothing was holding her at the boat beyond her own weariness. As the heat of the day settled over the bay, she was wide awake. Aurora's cold compresses had helped reduce her lumps and bruises. She looked like her old self as she finished off the last of the whale jerky. She and Aurora cracked crude jokes as they speculated as to what, exactly, Relic might be. There are nineteen sentient species in the Shining Lands; toss in the more popular half-seeds and there were roughly fifty different types of humanoid that could be hiding under that cloak.

There was no reason to limit the speculation to the earthly realms. Aurora's belief in a Great Sea Above was hardly the only auxiliary reality one could believe in. The Church of the Book believed there were two further realms of existence. Heaven was populated by true men, glorious creatures who had reached the final perfection after passing through the trials of life. Hell was populated by sinners and worse things. There were demons whose very existence was a lie the universe had been tricked into accepting. Only when the Golden Child read the One True Book would these false creatures be eradicated.

Of course, I take these teachings with a grain of salt. The Vanished Kingdom is proof that men lived long before the Church of the Book. I'm sure that these men believed in the stone idols they worshipped, gods whose names are now completely forgotten. If ancient men had been mistaken about their beliefs, why should modern men be any different?

All my life, I assumed that I'd finally discover the answers to these philosophical questions once I was dead. What a gyp that I have more questions now than ever. Still, when I think of the scaly flesh that surrounds Relic's eyes, I can't help but think of how closely he resembles the drawings of demons from the books of my youth.

After her meal, Infidel got dressed in the clothes Aurora had found. Though the tan britches and striped shirt were tailored for a man, I thought she looked fantastic. Her sculpted perfection makes her enticing even in peasant clothing, her features unadorned by make-up or jewelry. Royalty breeds for beauty. I can only imagine that, dressed in lacy gowns in a palace, her face framed by pearls and gold, she must be breathtaking.

Aurora created a mirror of ice for Infidel to use to fix what was left of her hair. She had little choice but to crop what was left, trimming away the frizzled ends. While I'd always liked her long silver tresses, I had to admit this new style had a certain charm. It highlighted the graceful lines of her smooth, slender neck, and drew attention to her enigmatic gray eyes.

I wondered where she would go after she was done with her hair; I was certain she wouldn't simply wait for Relic. Then, fate provided her with a destination. Far out at the mouth of the harbor, dark shapes appeared, a long line of humps rising and falling in the water. At first, I thought it was an enormous serpent, but as it drew closer I could see that it was, in fact, a pod of a dozen whales, enormous blue gray beasts big as ships. Long strands of woven seaweed trailed from elaborate harnesses that hung over their broad, flat faces. A crew of mermen swam beside them, urging them on, prodding the slower ones with tridents, and trumpeting long, low commands through horns fashioned from giant conch shells.

Behind it all, towed by the mighty sea beasts, was an enormous barge, waves breaking against its squat frame. From the center of the barge a single mast thrust into the air, sporting a banner of white and the silhouette of a black swan.

Aurora rose, shielding her eyes, staring at the barge like it was an apparition. The new arrival looked much like the old *Black Swan* barge, only larger and obviously newer. It now rose three stories instead of two. One by one, the whales were set free of their harnesses as momentum and tides carried the vessel forward. The mermen exceeded even the Wanderers in their understanding of water currents. The barge came to a halt mere feet from a newly built dock the Wanderers had finished only hours before. A crew of men leapt from the barge to lash it into place. Anchors splashed all around the vessel, sinking down to the mud. The *Black Swan* had come home.

Aurora jumped down from the boat, quickly clearing the tangled mangroves and reaching the mudflats. The ground crackled as she froze a long, rock-hard path across the mire. Infidel leapt to follow her, slipping the second she hit the icy mud. She grimaced as she waved her arms for balance, looking around for a less slippery path. She jumped toward a river pygmy canoe floating about twenty feet out in shallow water. The two pygmies currently occupying the canoe toppled into the bay as Infidel landed in the center of the craft. The canoe spun, capsizing as the lip sank beneath the water, but Infidel had already kicked off again, flying toward a slanted piling that jutted from the water. She barely touched down before she sprang again, leap-frogging her way toward her destination. When she reached the *Black Swan*, she leaned against a wall, crossing her arms. She looked nonchalant as Aurora climbed up onto the dock.

"What took you so long?" she asked.

Aurora didn't respond, racing past Infidel toward the main door of the new *Black Swan*. There were no guards in place to stop the ogress from bursting through the door. The main room had more gambling tables than the old one, and the whole place smelled of pine varnish. It hadn't yet acquired the funk of ten-thousand cigar smoking men and the heavily perfumed women who clung to their arms. Infidel followed as Aurora vaulted over the bar and down the hall beyond. At the end of the passage she looked ready to throw her shoulder against the door there.

Before she could make a move, the door opened.

The thick, cloying scent of potpourri poured out into the hallway. Aurora stepped into the dimly lit room with Infidel at her heels. The room was little changed. If not for the smell of freshly finished carpentry, it would be easy to mistake the Black Swan's new chamber for her old one.

The Black Swan herself was stretched on the couch. In front of her, there was now a low table covered with a long semi-circle of engraved letters, painted white against the black finish of the wood. It was a simple alphabet, plus the numbers 0 through 9, and a few common marks of punctuation. The only actual words were a 'YES' at one end and a 'NO' at the other.

"Mistress," said Aurora, sounding joyful. "You're still alive!"

The Black Swan said nothing. One of her bony hands unfolded from her chest and pointed toward the 'NO.'

Infidel sucked in her breath. I followed her eyes to the Black Swan's wrist. It wasn't merely bony; it was actual bone. Beneath her black veil, I could see an eyeless skull, white as chalk.

"Oh, mistress," whispered Aurora.

The Black Swan moved her finger across the board with a surprising rapidity; she seemed much faster now that she was freed from her withered muscles.

"My work is too important to be slowed by death," she spelled.

Infidel stepped back toward the doorway. She looked… spooked. I'd never seen her react like this.

The Black Swan nodded toward her and spelled, "You need not fear me."

Infidel squared her shoulders. She put on her brave face, but I could hear a hint of discomfort in her voice as she said, "I'm not afraid. If you give me any problems, you won't be the first undead I've taken apart this week."

The Black Swan nodded.

"How did you do this?" Aurora whispered. "Why?"

The skeletal hand tapped out. "My great work is not yet finished."

Aurora furrowed her brow. "Your great work? What great work? I've never known you to want anything other than money."

The Black Swan tapped the 'YES.'

"People say you can't take it with you," said Infidel. "Guess you proved them wrong."

'YES.'

Then, she spelled out, "Priests tell us the world is built of matter, spirit, truth, and lies. There is a fifth force, most powerful of all. Money."

Infidel looked skeptical. "I've known more than my fair share of rich people. Money hasn't kept their skeletons animated after they croak."

"They didn't know how to spend it," the Black Swan tapped. "With every journey into the future, my wealth grows exponentially. My purse strings entangle all the world's kings. The future rests upon my decisions."

"Really?" said Infidel. "Because with that kind of power, you'd think you'd choose to be something other than a bag of bones stuck in a dark, smelly room."

Before the Black Swan could respond, Aurora asked, "Menagerie told me I was fired. Why?"

"You cannot serve two masters. You have chosen to recover the Jagged Heart and return to your people. I have arranged a contract with Ivory Blade on your behalf. We will not meet again after this day."

Infidel stepped closer. "Then it's true. Tower has the Jagged Heart."

The Black Swan's hand remained motionless as her empty eyes gazed at Infidel. At last, she shrugged.

"You mean you don't know, or won't tell us?" asked Infidel.

The Black Swan shook her head, the vertebrae in her neck creaking. "In my most recent trip to the future, I was unable to learn whether or not the Jagged Heart endures. All that is certain of is that twelve of the world's greatest warriors set out to slay Greatshadow. They failed. Only two survived." She nodded toward Infidel. "I learned this from your daughter."

Infidel's eyebrows shot up. "My daughter?"

"Given her birth date, you may be pregnant now. If not, the child will be conceived within the month."

"Umm… no. No, I can assure you that's not possible. Whoever you met in the future, she wasn't my kid."

The Black Swan shrugged, then once more began tapping out a message. "The resemblance leads me to think otherwise, but no matter. I've returned to ensure that the future I lived through doesn't come to pass. Your daughter died soon after I met her. Everyone died. Everyone."

Aurora gave Infidel a puzzled glance.

"What do you mean, everyone?" she asked.

The room grew quiet save for the tapping of bone on wood. "All humanity is destroyed when the primal dragons rise as one to wipe out civilization in the span of a day."

"That's impossible," said Aurora. "Hush would never take part in such destruction."

"She does," tapped the Black Swan.

"Why?"

"The dragons judge mankind for their sins; none are found worthy of forgiveness."

Infidel looked pale. "Do… do we cause this? Does our quest to kill Greatshadow cause this destruction?"

The Black Swan shook her head. "The world carries on twenty years after the assault on Greatshadow."

"The primal dragons think of time differently than we do," said Aurora. "If there's a risk that Lord Tower is going to trigger some kind of dragon apocalypse, we need to stop him."

The Black Swan's skeletal hand lingered over the board, edging toward the 'YES.' Then, her fingers returned to the letters to tap, "Rather than stop him, ensure he succeeds. We must hope the primal dragons will be weakened if Greatshadow is no longer among their ranks."

"Hope?" said Infidel. "If you're trying to change the future, shouldn't we be going on more than hunches?"

The Black Swan shrugged and sank back onto the couch, growing very still.

"So, what, your plan boils down to guessing what we should do?" asked Infidel.

The Black Swan didn't move.

Aurora put her hand on Infidel's shoulder. "Don't drive yourself crazy. I try to ignore any hints she tells me about the future. The more she tells you about tomorrow, the more she changes today, and pretty soon hunches and guesses are all you have. The best thing to do is make the choices you would make anyway. Try to pretend you're in charge of your own fate, not a puppet following someone else's script."

Infidel nodded as they left the room. "Yeah. Sure. I've never worried what the Black Swan thought before now. I guess there's no reason to change that."

They went back outside, blinking in the light. Aurora said, "I'm still going on the quest, but if you want to back out, I understand. I mean, if you're pregnant..."

"I'm not pregnant!" snapped Infidel. "It's not possible. It's never going to be possible. Without Stagger, I wouldn't want it to be possible."

"You two never fooled around even a little? You can get pregnant just by -"

"No!" Infidel threw her hands up in the air. "This is crazy." She gave a dismissive wave toward the Black Swan. "Forget her. All I know is I woke up this morning planning to kill Greatshadow. Nothing I've heard today has changed my mind."

"What about the Truthspeaker?"

Infidel clenched her fists. "If he messes with me, he won't be the first priest I've killed."

Aurora nodded as they walked down the rebuilt dock. "For what it's worth, I don't believe the Truthspeaker's powers will affect me. Our faiths don't overlap even a little. The whole truth and lies as foundations of reality, that's just dumb. The world is obviously a flux of heat, light, cold, and darkness." She blew out rings of fog. "The evidence is right before your eyes."

"Whatever," said Infidel. "I'll let the two of you debate religion. I just want to get on with this dragon hunt. The quicker I get my hands on that treasure, the faster I can build my palace and hire my cake servants."

"There are simpler ways to get cake," said Aurora.

They reached the edge of the dock. Once it had led all the way to shore; now, crooked pilings were all that remained.

"There are simpler ways to get back to the boat," said Infidel, looking out over the water. "But simple isn't always entertaining."

Without warning, the grabbed Aurora by the hips and hefted her up, holding the oversized woman directly over her head. Aurora let out a yelp as Infidel leapt, flying out over the topsy-turvy pilings, alighting every third or fourth post before skipping on again. They reached the mangroves in under a minute and practically flew the last dozen yards to the boat. The old boards creaked as Infidel landed and planted the ogress on the deck feet first.

"Don't do that again!" Aurora growled as Infidel giggled.

"What?" said Infidel. "You don't like short cuts?"

Aurora sighed. "I'm not as invulnerable as you. One misstep on your part could have broken my neck, for no reason other than you wanting to show off. You're reckless, *princess*. Perhaps this was charming when you were fifteen, but it's not a quality I want in an ally when we face Greatshadow."

"I was just having a little fun."

"Children have fun. A warrior needs discipline."

"I'm living backwards. I was disciplined as a child so I'm having fun as an adult."

Aurora didn't look persuaded by the reasoning. Before she could argue, someone cleared his throat from inside the tilted doorway to the cabin. Both women turned to see Relic squeezing from the opening, a large canvas bag slung over his shoulder.

"I told you to wait for me," he grumbled. "Speed is of the essence. Ivory Blade has contacted the Three Goons. We need to prepare your disguise and the dye takes several hours to set properly."

He dropped the sack to the deck. Things within it clattered loudly, as metal hit metal.

"There's dye involved?" said Infidel, squatting down over the sack. "I like my hair blonde."

"It's not your hair we'll be dying," said Relic.

Infidel opened the sack and pulled out various objects. She paused to study what looked like two shoulder caps for a suit of plate armor. They were formed of half-inch steel and polished to almost a mirror finish. Only, as shoulder plates, they weren't very practical; the two halves were joined together by a single link of chain. And, the plates were too rounded. No one had shoulders this circular. Infidel looked puzzled as she turned the metal cups over and over in her hand.

"What the hell is this?" she asked.

Aurora chuckled. "It looks like a plate-steel bra."

Relic was very quiet.

Both women stared at him.

He stared back.

"No freakin' way," said Infidel.

"This would be easier if you'd wear a helmet," said Relic. "If not, we must choose attire that ensures none of the king's men will be staring at your face."

I expected Infidel to fling the armored lingerie into the bay. To my surprise, she shrugged. "What the hell," she said. "It's about time I had an outfit that doesn't get ripped to shreds every five minutes. But if there are chain mail panties in here, I'm drawing a line."

It turned out that there weren't any chain mail panties, which provoked a mixed reaction within me. As unfair as it was for me to have such thoughts, I would have been relieved to see a full-blown, padlocked, cast-iron chastity belt. Infidel might have shrugged off the talk of pregnancy, but I was a little worried. My poor mortal frame might not have been up to the task of fathering a child with Infidel, but the king's men were more than mere mortals. Lord Tower could fly, Father Ver can change reality with his voice, and Ivory Blade supposedly can move faster than the human eye can follow. Who knew who else might along for the trip? What if someone among the heroes matched Infidel in strength and stamina? What if what the Black Swan said about an impending pregnancy was true?

8 - War Doll

THE SUN WAS directly overhead as we rode the churning waves toward the pirate cave. Was it only coincidence that Tower's party had set up camp in the very place where all this had begun with the discovery of the map? I hadn't told Bigsby the truth of where I acquired it, so he hadn't passed on the information. Perhaps Ivory Blade had researched the map further and other sources had led him here.

The cave was located on the western side of the Isle of Fire, a stark landscape of steep, rocky cliffs scoured by ceaseless wind. The waters here are turbulent but deep; a ship can sail within inches of the cliffs if her captain is crazy enough to risk the swirling currents. The cave we aimed for wasn't the only one along this coast line. The area was riddled with old lava tubes exposed by the churning sea.

Most of the caves hold nothing but bird nests; indeed, the sky above was full of feathered creatures in every hue of the rainbow, from tiny finches no larger than my thumb to albatrosses with wingspans longer than my bar tab. The pirate cave was right at sea level. The tides here can rise and fall twenty feet, and when the tide is low the opening of the cave is a long, narrow slash amid jagged stones, just wide enough to sail a good-sized schooner through. Within lies an underground lagoon nearly a mile across, ringed by a pebble beach polished smooth by the waves. It was a safe, sheltered haven, assuming the captain was skilled enough to thread the needle.

Fortunately, Infidel, Aurora, and Relic were in a small rowboat that could navigate the gap with ease, even with the rising tide. Infidel manned both oars, and her iron muscles proved more than a match for the swirling currents. She aimed the boat for the gap and rowed confidently over the waves, shooting into the cavern swiftly enough to leave a wake. Gulls cried as they dove at the churned up water.

The last time I'd been here, the room had been full of torches and lanterns. Now, the shore was lined with bright glorystones, rare gems purported to be fragments of the sun itself. Glorystones were far more expensive than diamonds, and there were more in this cave than I could count. Reflected on the dark water of the lagoon, they looked like stars. We'd definitely arrived at a camp outfitted by a king.

As my eyes searched the shadows beyond the shore, I was surprised at how empty the cave looked. When we'd come here to fight pirates, the noise in this place had been deafening, as the voices of a hundred rowdy men echoed through the chamber. The air had been foul with the smoke of fires fueled by dried guano, not to mention the stink left from using the lagoon as a toilet. Today, the air was clean and cool; everything was quiet. Off in the distance I spotted a few modest canvas tents, shelter enough for a dozen men perhaps, if they were friendly.

The only boat was a single-mast skiff that I recognized as belonging to the Black Swan. No-Face was standing near the boat, his arms crossed, his feet planted wide, looking ready to smite anyone who came too close. Reeker was in the boat, stretched out on the folded sail, snoozing, using a backpack as a pillow. Menagerie sat beneath a glorystone lantern, reading a book. The faded letters on the leather-bound tome could barely be made out: *The Vanished Kingdom,* by Judicious Merchant. My grandfather had published his discoveries years before I was born. With it, I had retraced his steps on the island, or at least attempted to. Sadly, I found most of his directions convoluted and his cartography rather cryptic. Some of the most interesting places he claimed to have explored I've never found. I can't say if he embellished his adventures, or was simply rotten at drawing maps.

Menagerie had beaten us here even though he'd remained behind the other Goons to assist Infidel with her disguise. He'd requested an eye-popping sum of money for his services as an artist; in what he claimed was pure coincidence, it was equal to the value of the dragon skull once my bar debt was paid. Infidel hadn't haggled. Menagerie had sent the other Goons on their way, promising he'd catch up to them. What might take No-Face a full day to row Menagerie could cover in mere hours as an eagle. As for whether the tattooed man's artistry had produced a passable disguise, I wasn't the best judge. I'd spent enough time staring at Infidel's face to know its subtle lines no matter what color it was dyed. And I still didn't understand how any amount of coloring and cleavage was going to hide her identity from Father Ver.

Aurora jumped from the boat and helped pull it up onto the stony beach. Relic hobbled out, placing a hand on his back as if it pained him to have sat so many hours. I could hear his bones popping as he craned his neck from side to side.

As Infidel stepped out of the boat, No-Face rattled the chain around his arm, waking Reeker. Menagerie set down his book and shouted, "Halt!"

"It's okay, guys, they're with me," said Aurora.

Menagerie marched within inches of her and stared up into her tusked face. He shouted, "It is not okay! This is a secure area. What the hell are you doing bringing unauthorized personnel? What's wrong with you?"

Aurora thrust her finger into Menagerie's chest. "Back off. I have every right to be here and these two are my guests. If you have a problem —"

Before she could finish her sentence, a voice beyond the Goons shouted, "Yes, we have a problem!"

Further up the rocky slope, a ghostly white figure strode swiftly towards us. This was Ivory Blade; I recognized him from his occasional visits to the *Black Swan*, though I'd never actually met him. Blade was the king's top spy, though I wondered how good a spy he could have been since everyone knew it. On the other hand, Blade is a six-foot three albino. He doesn't exactly blend into the shadows. Hiding in plain sight might be the best strategy available. He was certainly an eye-catching figure, dressed in stark white leather armor. This was the famed Immaculate Attire, crafted for Alabaster Brightmoon, the Warrior Queen, nearly three centuries earlier. Since the armor fit him like a full body glove, I can only assume that Alabastar Brightmoon was rather tall for a woman, or else some enchantment allowed the armor to adapt to the form of its wearer. The leather truly did look immaculate, without a single scrape or scuff.

The fact that Blade's armor was unmarred might have been evidence that his reputation as a master swordsman was deserved. I've heard he can draw his sword, kill a man, wipe the blade and return it to his scabbard more swiftly than the eye can follow. He certainly possessed an air of confidence as he marched up to Aurora.

"I'm reporting for duty," Aurora said, addressing Ivory Blade over the heads of the Goons. "The Black Swan has provided the appropriate contracts."

"For you," Blade growled. "Who are these two?" His pink eyes narrowed as he stared at Relic and Infidel. "Or perhaps I should ask, what are these two?"

Relic bowed. He spoke in a raspy, trembling voice, "Long ago, I was called Urthric. Alas, the men for whom that name had meaning have long since passed away. Today, I am known only as Relic."

"Relic showed up after the attack on Commonground," said Aurora. "I wouldn't ordinarily risk the safety of a mission with a last second recruit, especially one I can't vouch for. Still, I think his story is worth listening to. Hear him out; if you don't think he'll be useful, I'll personally snap his neck."

Blade sneered as he looked down at Relic. "What can this decrepit fool possibly have to offer us?"

I found it interesting that Blade's attention was so fixed on Relic. Infidel was standing only inches behind the ragged man, not moving or making a sound, but she was hardly invisible. Given her garb, I expected at least a little gawking.

"I may be decrepit," said Relic, "but I'm no fool. I'm the most important person you can hire for this mission."

Blade smirked. "Truly?"

As Blade spoke, a woman stepped out from behind him; only, it wasn't so much a woman as the absence of a woman. It was a bubble of air the shape of a naked female wielding a sword in each hand. No one else reacted as she silently tiptoed around the Goons, pausing to study Aurora, then moving to study Infidel up close. She placed her face only inches from Infidel's eyes. Infidel didn't even blink; the woman was apparently invisible to all but my ghostly gaze.

Relic said, "My tale is difficult to believe, yet I know you have a Truthspeaker among you. Bring me to him, so he may judge the veracity of my words."

"Why don't you try your story on me first?" said Blade.

Relic nodded. "Very well. I am the sole survivor of the Vanished Kingdom. When I was young, a great nation had tamed this island. From shore to shore the land supported vibrant cities. Our harbors sheltered armadas of trade ships that brought treasures from the far reaches of the world. Truly, it was a golden age."

Blade smirked. "I'll give you credit for imagination. But, assuming you are thirty centuries old, how does this make you an asset for our mission?"

"This quest has been set in motion by the discovery of a map. I am the author of this document. I was an engineer for the king during the construction of what is now referred to as the Shattered Palace."

Blade studied the ragged figure before him with a more critical eye. Even I was taking another look at Relic. Was he telling the truth?

"How is it that you have survived all these years?" Blade asked.

"Modern men are not the only ones to have gods," said Relic. "The gods in those days were far more active in the affairs of this world. They would travel the kingdoms, disguised as men, granting favors to those who were kind, curses to those who were cruel. The god I met gave me eternal life; alas, he was not so kind as to grant me eternal youth."

Blade rubbed his chin, contemplating Relic's words. The invisible woman now stood beside Relic, staring at his burlap-covered face. Blade gave the slightest nod and the woman raised her hands to grab the cloth, no doubt to pull it away.

Relic said, "It would be unwise for your companion to touch me."

The woman halted. Blade looked impressed. "You can see the Whisper?"

Relic nodded. "I've learned many arcane arts during the endless parade of centuries."

"So you know a little magic," said Blade. The Whisper's hands still lingered only inches from the hood. She looked to Blade for further cues. "I still don't see why we shouldn't just pull your mask off to see what you truly are."

"An understandable desire," said Relic. "Alas, long ago, I contracted a disease that causes flesh to wither and rot. It cannot kill me due to my curse, but it has disfigured me horribly. I'm not contagious as long as my scabs are closed. Much of my garb is adhered to my skin. Tearing it free could expose others to the illness."

"I see," said Blade, as the Whisper backed away. "That certainly makes the thought of sharing a camp with you appealing."

"I'm a difficult companion. But my knowledge outweighs the risks. Currently you have a map. With me, you shall have a living atlas."

Blade finally turned his gaze toward Infidel, who stood quietly on the shore. "And who… or what… is that?"

Menagerie grinned ever so slightly at Blade's confusion. Infidel couldn't be tattooed; no needle could penetrate her skin. Still, Menagerie knew a thing or two about pygmy dyes. From scalp to toe, Infidel's skin was now a pale silver-blue, looking more like metal than flesh. Her limbs were concealed beneath skin-tight leather armor, though her torso was mostly bare save for the shiny steel bra. Her face was also naked, though bold black dyes created the illusion of a mask around her eyes. Menagerie had assured Relic the pigments would last for weeks without streaking or smearing.

"This is my War Doll," said Relic. "As an educated man, you may know that the engineers of the Vanished Kingdom have no peers in today's world. We crafted clockwork animals that mimicked life in every way, only with skeletons of steel instead of fragile bone, muscles of wire instead of meat, and veins pumping oil instead of water."

Infidel stared silently at Blade. The greatest flaw of her disguise was that to play the role of a machine, she would need to remain mute and keep her face passive. A quiet, unexpressive Infidel was impossible for me to imagine.

Relic continued: "The men of my time were as blood-thirsty as the people of today. We constructed machines in the likeness of men to fight as gladiators in our arenas."

Blade furrowed his brow. "I would hardly call this the likeness of a man."

"We were lustful as well as blood-thirsty," said Relic. "It pleased the king to watch women in mortal combat. The War Doll, and others like her, were far more resilient than a true woman. Her performances could entertain the king for hours on end."

Blade looked skeptical. But he wasn't the one who gave voice to doubt. Instead, it was Menagerie who said, "I'm not buying it. This is obviously just a painted woman. You can see her breathing!"

Relic placed his hand on the small of Infidel's back and pushed her forward. "The engines within the War Doll produce heat. She inhales and exhales air to maintain an optimal operating temperature. When she's active, she will appear to sweat; this is partially for cooling and partially aesthetics. She's been designed to mimic life in the finest detail."

"This is the biggest load of garbage I've ever heard," said Menagerie.

"You have the power to ensure our veracity," said Relic, ignoring Menagerie and addressing Blade. "Bring us to the Truthspeaker."

"We don't need to waste his time," said Menagerie. He reached over to Ivory Blade and drew the dagger the albino carried on his belt. Before anyone could blink, Menagerie threw the blade with a grunt. The tip struck Infidel directly at the base of her throat, in what should have been a killing blow. The dagger bounced off, landing on the pebbles before her. She continued to stare impassively, not displaying the slightest discomfort.

Relic clapped his hands. "Demonstrate your strength."

Infidel leaned over and picked up the blade. She thrust the edge into her mouth, clamping down on it with her pearly teeth, then biting through the steel before dropping the dagger. She spit out a half-moon fragment of metal. It clattered on the pebbles beside the damaged blade.

Menagerie stared, slack-jawed.

"What is your opinion now?" asked Relic.

Menagerie cleared his throat and crossed his arms. "I'm not getting paid to offer opinions. I'll shut up."

The Whisper knelt and picked up the dagger and the wedge that had been bitten from it. She returned it to Blade, who sighed as he tapped the matching pieces together. "This was my favorite dagger," he said, sadly. He gave Menagerie a stern look. "This will come out of your pay."

"I insist on it," said the tattooed man.

Blade gave Infidel one more long stare, before looking down at Relic. "I'll probably regret this, but you've earned your audience with Father Ver."

Blade led us further back into the cave, toward a broad circle of sunlight. A section of the roof had collapsed, leaving a large shaft to the sky. Blood tangle vines hung from above, their leaves swaying in the wind. The rise and fall of the lagoon turned the cave into a bellows, with air flowing in and out through the shaft in gushes. The breeze and the sunlight made this area of the cavern less dank. It was here that the king's men had made their camp.

I watched as the Whisper slipped into one of the tents to alert Father Ver. She moved with such grace that the tent flap showed only the slightest flutter. Still, since it had moved, I deduced she wasn't intangible. That ruled out the chance she might possibly be another ghost.

Blade led us to the center of the circle and motioned that we should wait. Reeker wandered over to a large boulder at the edge of the sunlight. He reached into his jacket and produced a cigar as thick as Aurora's index finger. He flicked a match against the rough stone. The tip sputtered to life - then was just as quickly extinguished as the Whisper leaned down from the top of the boulder and snuffed the match between her fingers.

"What are you doing?" Ivory Blade cried as he ran toward Reeker.

"Catching a quick smoke?" Reeker said, looking at his dead match with puzzlement.

"That is entirely the wrong answer!" Blade yanked the cigar from the skunk-man's grasp. "Didn't you read your contract?"

"Maybe."

"I apologize for the lapse," Menagerie said as he approached. He raised his hand and slapped the offending Goon on the top of his head with a good solid, *THWACK!*

Reeker cringed, whining, "Watch the hair, boss."

"I read every last line of the contract to you," said Menagerie. "You have no excuse."

"My mind wanders sometimes," said Reeker. "There's a no smoking clause?"

"Fire of any kind is forbidden," said Blade. "Greatshadow's spirit is present in all flame. There will be no campfires, no torches, no lanterns, and, yes, no smoking! Striking a match opens Greatshadow's eye and invites him to stare at us."

"That's a little paranoid," said Reeker. "I thought the no-fire clause meant something big enough to cook on. There must be a million candles burning right now. You think the dragon pays attention to what he sees through all of them? You think he even notices a match that gets lit for a couple of seconds?"

"This isn't subject to debate," said Blade. "We've arrived safely on this island by adhering to strict discipline in our avoidance of fire. I won't tolerate any further lapses."

"There won't be any," said Menagerie. "The contract says no fire. We'll comply. Right, Reeker?"

"Sure, boss," said the skunk-man, frowning as he tossed the cigar into the dark reaches of the cave.

Like everyone else, Aurora had been focused on the confrontation. As it wound down, she turned toward the center of the circle. She jumped back, startled.

Father Ver was standing mere feet behind her, staring at her massive frame. Despite the years, I recognized him instantly. His dark eyes were still set deep in a face that resembled a skull wrapped in old, crinkled parchment. He was completely bald save for bushy white eyebrows and tufts of hair just behind his ears. While his face had grown more skeletal, his body still looked robust. He stood straight as a board in his ink-black robes.

He said, with a glance toward Blade, "This... *creature*... is the best muscle you could hire?"

Blade nodded. "Aurora comes with the highest recommendation."

"She's an ice-ogress," Father Ver said, in a weary tone that made it sound as if he thought that Blade had somehow missed this fact. "Of what use can she be in the tropics?"

Aurora raised her fist as an ice gauntlet formed around it. "Actually, the jungle enhances my powers. Ice magic depends on moisture. The atmosphere of my homeland was arid; here, water is plentiful. Spells that take minutes back home can be cast in seconds. Plus, though you wouldn't know it from the heat outside, it *is* nearly the winter solstice, the time of year when my powers are at their peak."

"I asked my question of Blade, not of you, ogress," said Father Ver. He turned once more to the albino. "The Whisper says you need my powers."

"These two," said Blade, nodding toward Infidel and Relic. "They showed up uninvited. Aurora vouches for them, but —"

The Truthspeaker raised his hand as he glared at Relic and asked, "Who are you and why are you here?"

Relic stared directly into the Father Ver's eyes as he said, "I was once known as Urthric," before launching into his tale of being a survivor of the Vanished Kingdom and the author of the map.

During Relic's monologue, Father Ver gave no reaction beyond his default scowl. Finally, Relic finished. Father Ver continued to glare down into the hunchback's face. I noticed the Whisper slip up next to Ivory Blade. She stood on her tiptoes and placed her lips to his ear. As she spoke so softly only he could hear, I noticed that she ran her hand along Blade's face and hair in a gesture that told me their relationship was more than simply teammates.

"Oh, right," said Blade. "You should also know the hunchback is afflicted with a potentially contagious flesh-eating disease."

"This information would be important only if we were considering allowing him to join our mission," said Father Ver.

"So he's lying?"

"He speaks the truth, or believes he does," said Father Ver. "It doesn't matter. I recommend we kill him and dismantle this abomination." He gave Infidel only the barest glance as he spoke. Again, I couldn't help but suspect there was something odd going on with the way the king's men were ignoring her.

Blade leaned back against the boulder, scratching his chin as he thought. The Whisper wrapped her arms around him and began to plant soft, silent kisses along the side of neck. Blade's voice remained steady despite this as he said, "If he's telling the truth, killing him seems short-sighted. Physically, he's no asset, but the War Doll offsets this liability."

"I don't understand why the king feels we need to hire mercenaries," grumbled Father Ver. "It shows a lack of faith."

"I'm not going to second guess the king. And, now that we're actually on the mission, the decision of who we hire isn't mine to make. Tower will have to decide."

Menagerie asked, "Where is Lord Tower anyway? Isn't it time we meet the man leading this mission?"

"Tower can only carry one other adult with him when he flies," said Blade. "He'll be back soon enough with the final members of the team."

"Flies?" asked Menagerie. "He can turn into a bird as well?"

"No. Flight is a power granted by the Gloryhammer."

"What's a hammer got to do with flying?" asked Reeker.

"Kumuk yuh fuh wut wuh," said No-Face.

"Just try it," said Reeker.

Before anyone else could ask for a translation, a shadow flickered across the cavern floor. I'd never met Lord Tower, but there was no mistaking the identity of the man who descended slowly through the shaft toward us. He was covered in plate armor polished to a mirror finish; Aurora raised her hand to shield her eyes from the glare. He had his right arm thrust straight out, grasping the Gloryhammer. The sacred artifact was a sledgehammer carved from a single glorystone, blazing with a bright white intensity.

Tower's right arm was wrapped around a slender figure; at first, I thought it was a woman, but as he drew closer to us I could see it was a man. He had black hair gathered into a pony-tail, and priestly robes of the same style as Father Ver's, only bright red. His arms were tightly wrapped around Tower's torso, his eyes wide with terror as he gazed at the ground. Of course, the look of fear wasn't the first thing I noticed about his face. I couldn't help but wonder why he had a large letter 'D' tattooed onto his forehead in blood-red ink.

The terrified man wasn't Lord Tower's only passenger. There was also a bored-looking boy standing on Lord Tower's left boot. He balanced there on one foot, with one hand gripping Tower's belt, looking quite relaxed as Tower descended. The boy looked no older than ten. His head was shaved; he wore no shirt, only a pair of white cotton britches. He was heavily tanned, the shade of a loaf of bread fresh from an oven. The boy hopped from Tower's boot with the ground still ten feet away, dropping to a silent touchdown on the gravel. Tower's metal boots came to rest seconds later with a loud *CLANK*. The man in the red robes fell to the rocky ground, groveling at the knight's feet. It took a second to realize he wasn't showing gratitude to Lord Tower but was, instead, kissing the ground.

Tower's face was hidden behind his steel faceplate. His eyes could barely be seen through twin slits in the mirrored surface. He surveyed everyone in the room; glancing quickly at Reeker and Menagerie, pausing at No-Face. I detected a slight shudder before he moved on to Aurora. His eyes narrowed; she returned his gaze without flinching. He then sized up Relic and, apparently judging him harmless, turned his attention to Infidel.

His eyes lingered on the metal bra longer than necessary. Infidel didn't move a muscle. He raised his eyes to her face. Again, his gaze lingered for longer than it should have.

He said, finally, "I see we have… guests."

"Trespassers," said Father Ver.

"Applicants," said Blade. "Who did quite admirably on their interview, I thought."

The sun-tanned boy had been studying everyone as well. He said, "The hunchback and the painted woman are seeking to join our mission?"

"Correct," said Blade. "I think they could prove valuable."

"All they prove is that someone has already compromised our mission," said Father Ver. "Killing them will set an example to those who might seek to betray us." He looked directly at the man in the red robes as he spoke.

I found it curious that Blade and Father Ver were addressing the boy instead of Lord Tower, the supposed leader of this mission. Just who was this kid?

The boy walked up to Relic. "You appear too old and feeble to make the journey."

Unlike Father Ver, the child spoke in a neutral, observational tone, with no hint of scorn or disdain.

"Hiring only my body would be a poor investment," Relic said. "It is my knowledge that will be of value."

"Your knowledge is of little use if you cannot survive the tests before us."

"I assure you, I will be alive long after everyone in this room has returned to dust. As for my diminished physicality, the War Doll more than compensates. She is the ultimate fighting machine; no one in this room is her match."

"That," said the boy, cracking his knuckles, "sounds like a challenge." He clasped his hands together prayerfully and bowed toward Relic. "I accept."

9 - THE GOLDEN CHILD

RELIC TILTED HIS head quizzically. "Are you challenging the War Doll?"

"Yes," said the child. Despite the fact that he was well-muscled for his age, the boy didn't look like a fighter. Most boys of a combative nature were covered with scabs and scars, but this kid didn't look like he'd ever even been scratched. Despite his modest attire, his gray eyes hinted at a royal lineage. Perhaps, if he'd been in fights before, it had been against opponents who understood the political advantages of not landing a punch.

"I mean no disrespect, but you don't understand the danger," said Relic. "The War Doll is a finely tuned killing machine. Her bones are solid steel; her artificial skin is impervious to the sharpest blade. Her mesh-cable muscles can crush a man's skull like an eggshell."

The boy responded with a serene smile. "You're lying. Your companion is a woman with painted skin, not a machine. Your dire warnings are nothing but a bluff. Isn't that right, Father Ver?"

The Truthspeaker frowned. "The hunchback believes he is telling the truth."

The boy furrowed his brow. "There is an aura of magic around you, creature. Somehow, you are fooling Father Ver."

"No magic could conceal the truth from a servant of the Divine Author, could it?" Relic replied.

The boy frowned as he continued to study Relic and Infidel. Finally, he said, "If your 'War Doll' can simply knock me from my feet, we shall consider that a victory. I'll acknowledge that she's not a painted woman, despite the plain evidence of my senses."

"And if you knock her from her feet?" asked Relic.

"She is welcome to continue the fight," said the boy. "My intention is to prove that she's a fraud. I shall do so by breaking the woman's bones until she confesses, proving that there's no steel within her."

"Fierce little bastard, ain't he?" Reeker said with a chuckle.

"You will hold your blasphemous tongue!" shouted the Truthspeaker.

Reeker opened his jaw so wide I worried his cheeks would tear. He thrust both hands toward his mouth and grabbed his tongue in a death grip.

"This is the Golden Child," said Ivory Blade, glaring at the skunk-man. "He is the culmination of generations of pious men and women who have faithfully adhered to the teachings of the One True Book. He is the perfect blend of body, spirit, and truth, untainted by falsehood."

Father Ver placed his hand upon Blade's shoulders. "Be careful with your words," he counseled. "While there is evidence that Numinous Pilgrim is the Golden Child, we do not have the final proof. Perhaps one day he shall be the Omega Reader; first he must conclude the seventeen sacred tests."

Numinous? I felt sympathy for the boy. His name was even worse than the one I'd been stuck with as a baby. Menagerie apparently found the name amusing as well, since he looked as if he was fighting back a laugh.

The Truthspeaker glowered as he saw the look on Menagerie's face. "Do you have something to say, mercenary?"

The tattooed man gave Reeker a sideways glance. His fellow Goon was still wrestling with his tongue. "I'm good," said Menagerie.

"Now that you know who I am," said Numinous, "you know it is futile to attempt to deceive me."

"Of course," said Relic. "I wouldn't want a person of your sacred esteem to doubt my claim. I accept your challenge."

Infidel, standing beside Relic, casually placed a hand upon his shoulder. There was a faint crunching sound.

"If you'll excuse me," said Relic, speaking through clenched teeth, "I will require only a moment to fine tune the War Doll before battle."

He hobbled toward the shadows, with Infidel clamped to his shoulder. Once they were out of earshot, she leaned close and whispered, "Are you out of your mind? I can't fight a little boy!"

Relic nodded. His voice was barely audible as he said, "From the mind of Ivory Blade, I've learned that Numinous has already completed twelve of the seventeen sacred tests. If the boy truly is the Omega Reader, all our planning may be for naught. Your fear may be justified."

"Fear? I'm not… look, I just won't beat up a kid. I only fight people bigger than me."

"You've fought pygmies," said Relic. "You've slaughtered them and stacked their bodies like firewood."

Infidel frowned.

Relic continued, "I know you don't wish to be a bully. But if you fail to beat Numinous, we shall be exposed."

Infidel glanced back toward the circle of light. The Golden Child stared into the shadows as if he could see them clearly. "He's so skinny. I'm worried I'll break him."

"Break him if you can," said Relic. "The Golden Child's senses are uncluttered by falsehood. He can hear your heart beating. He can smell your sweat. He alone can expose you."

"What about Lord Tower?" asked Infidel. "Have we fooled him? I thought I saw something in his eyes. I don't know if it was recognition, or… or something else."

Relic shook his head. "While he wears his armor, I cannot read his thoughts, let alone manipulate them."

Infidel cocked her head. "You manipulate thoughts?"

"To a degree," said Relic. "I'm no puppet-master, controlling the actions of others. But, I have the power to subtly guide the focus of men. Our ruse would crumble if Father Ver thought to ask you the truth of your identity. Fortunately, I've managed to keep his attention fixed upon me. Even though he can see you, he's too distracted to focus on you. The same is true of Blade. Alas, Numinous and Tower are beyond the reach of my powers."

"I wondered why I was being ignored in this outfit," said Infidel.

"Back to the matter at hand: you need only knock Numinous from his feet to silence him. He's given his word and dare not go back on it. If he is the true Omega Reader, he must never make a false promise."

"I don't think knocking him down is a real problem," she said, clenching her fists. "This is going to be my shortest fight ever."

Relic shook his head. "Don't be overly confident."

"C'mon. Let's get this over with."

They headed back toward the sunlit circle.

"The War Doll is ready," Relic announced as they returned.

Lord Tower's eyes narrowed as he looked at Infidel. She had a sword on one hip, a mace on the other, and still had my knife in her boot. The knight held up his gleaming gauntlet and said, "There's no need to shed blood. Your gladiator must relinquish her weapons."

"As you wish," said Relic.

"This is an unnecessary precaution," said Numinous. "Even if she was armed with the Gloryhammer, she could not harm me."

Infidel's face was passive as she handed Relic her weapons. I felt a shiver pass down my non-existent spine as he grasped the hilt of the knife.

The king's men and the goons retreated to the edge of the sunlit circle, forming an impromptu arena. I noticed that Reeker had finally let go of his tongue; apparently the Truthspeaker's command wasn't permanent. The boy stood in the center of the circle, his stance loose, his arms dangling. His eyes were fixed on Infidel's face. She stopped about six feet away and raised her fists, planting her feet in a boxer's stance.

Seconds passed into moments as the two studied each other. Infidel bobbed back and forth as she waited for the boy to make his move. I could tell she still worried about hurting the kid. With his placid face, Numinous looked more like a bored observer of the fight than a participant.

Infidel was the first to lose patience. She jumped toward the boy, kicking out, her foot aimed at his gut. Numinous stepped aside fluidly, placing one hand on her ankle, another behind her knee as she flew into the space where he'd just stood. With an ear-splitting cry of "Yiaiiah!" he spun her in the air, slamming her face-down into the gravel. Before she could pick herself up, he leapt into the air, shouted, "Hiaaayah!" and landed with his full weight on the back of her neck, burying her head deeper into the small stones. He bounced off, landing gracefully. He looked down at Infidel with a smug expression. Infidel didn't move a muscle.

"That didn't take long," Ivory Blade said from the edge of the circle.

"It's not over," said Numinous. "She's still conscious."

As he said this, Infidel's fists closed around big handfuls of gravel. In a flash, she sat up and whipped her arms toward the Golden Child, letting the gravel fly in a dangerous hail of stone shrapnel. Yet before the gravel had even left her fingers, Numinous dove toward her. His body twisted as he spun through the stony cloud, avoiding every last piece. The gravel sparked as it struck the boulders beyond.

Infidel was still sitting with her arms out when the boy reached her. His leg blurred as he kicked her three times in the throat with cries of "Hyia! Hyia! Hyia!" She went down, flat on her back, her arms limp. The boy landed, hopping on a single foot. His placid expression was replaced by an unmistakable frown. He winced as he placed weight on his kicking-foot.

Infidel sat back up, rubbing her wind-pipe. "Son of a bitch," she muttered.

Among the king's men, there was a simultaneous furrowing of brows.

Relic cleared his throat. "The War Doll has been programmed to utter simple phrases to simulate pain or frustration. The old kings demanded this verisimilitude."

The boy wasn't distracted by the conversation at the edge of the arena. His eyes were locked on Infidel as she rose. The kicks to the throat might have decapitated an ordinary woman. Right about now, the Golden Child was probably starting to wonder about the possibility of steel bones after all.

Infidel made it back to her feet. She took a deep breath, steadying herself. She leaned forward slightly and the boy danced back. Even with a sore foot, he was still as nimble as a cat. Maybe he was going to have a hard time breaking Infidel, but she faced an equally tough challenge in knocking him down.

Infidel lunged toward the boy. Instead of aiming a blow at the child, she raised both fists above her head, then dropped to her knees, delivering a powerful two-fisted strike to the ground. Gravel flew into the air in a wave. I gave the cave roof a worried glance as the shock toppled boulders and popped tent pegs. Numinous merely lifted his feet into the air as the destructive energy passed beneath him. When he landed, he somersaulted toward Infidel. She rose, punching out, and he used her outstretched arm as a springboard. He landed behind her and shouted, "Hyuh!" as he kicked into the bend of her knees. Infidel's legs folded beneath her, but before she hit the ground, the boy unleashed a whirlwind of blows—"Hyi! Hyun! Haih! Yah! Huu!"—as he aimed precise strikes at nerves in her spine, elbows, and shoulders.

Infidel sucked in air as her face twisted in pain. She rolled to her back as the Golden Child dropped toward her, sinking both knees into her gut just beneath her ribs, then rolling forward and cuffing both ears simultaneously as he shouted, "Kiii!" His momentum carried him out of Infidel's reach as she flayed her arms uselessly in the air.

"I've seen enough," said Lord Tower, raising his hand. "The War Doll has failed the test."

Relic sighed. "Centuries of wear have cost the War Doll some of its former prowess. Still, you must admit, it has withstood the best the boy can throw at it without breaking."

I prayed that he was right, that Infidel wasn't broken, but I wasn't sure. Her eyes were unfocused as her legs uselessly pushed at the gravel. Her arms were splayed to her side, fingers twitching.

The Golden Child paced in a circle around his victim.

"The fight continues!" he cried, his voice a fierce growl. "She has yet to cry out for mercy! I won't rest until she confesses her ruse!"

"Your holy urchin is a sadist," Aurora said, from across the sunlit arena.

"He has an unwavering passion for truth," said Father Ver.

"Nonetheless," said Lord Tower, "The fight is over. We should —"

He never got to complete his sentence. The Golden Child leapt into the air above Infidel, spinning like a top, as he unleashed an ear-piercing battle-cry. Gone was the placidity that had gripped his features earlier. Blood-lust blazed in his eyes.

Then, to everyone's surprise, Infidel moved, grabbing a fist-sized rock in her right hand, a slightly larger one in her left. She swung her arms together as the boy dropped toward her, his feet aimed at her belly. Numinous tucked up his legs and the rocks passed beneath his toes. The stones collided with a *BANG* that raised everyone's hands to their ears. The rocks were pulverized, concealing Infidel and the boy inside a cloud of smoky gray dust.

From inside the haze there was a sharp high-pitched shout of "Aiigh!" It took a fraction of a second to realize that this wasn't another war cry. Numinous trailed dust as he shot skyward, a good fifty feet up the shaft, both hands grasping his crotch. Infidel sprang up as the boy reached his apex. The Golden Child's eyes went wide as he spun his body, trying to avoid landing in Infidel's grasp, but, as I knew all too well, no amount of arm-flapping and desperate kicking can change the trajectory of a falling body.

Infidel lifted an arm and grabbed the boy by the ankle, then swung him in an overhead arc to plant his face in the gravel.

"The fight is over!" shouted Lord Tower, jumping toward the combatants.

"The hell it is," growled Infidel, whipping the boy up again, painting the gravel before her with a line of bright blood.

"The War Doll is programmed to taunt its enemies," Relic said, though I don't know if anyone was listening. Everyone's eyes were wide with horror as Infidel spun the boy's limp body around overhead and flung him. The child smashed into the stone wall above the Truthspeaker. The boy bounced off, completely limp, as the Whisper dove to catch him. She lowered his battered body gently to the ground. He was bleeding from both ears. His arms were bent at odd angles, as if they had too many joints.

Everyone was paralyzed as they stared, slack-jawed, at the bloodied child. Ivory Blade was the first to recover his senses. He whirled around, drawing his sword, as he shouted, "You've broken our Golden Child!" He leapt toward Relic, the tip of his sword aimed for the hunchback's eyes.

Lord Tower reached out his gauntleted hand and caught the albino swordsman in mid-strike. The sword sliced the air six inches away from Relic's hood.

"Let me go!" Blade cried out.

Father Ver turned from Numinous and shouted, "You will calm yourself!"

Instantly, the look of rage vanished from Blade's features. He straightened his clothes as Tower set him back on the ground.

"The boy is not the Omega Reader," said Father Ver, coolly. "He failed the thirteenth test; he faced an ancient monster, and could not defeat it."

"But —" said Blade.

"The truth is before your very eyes. The boy misjudged his opponent; the true Omega Reader would never deceive himself so. This boy was just the latest in a long string of false hopes." Father Ver glanced at the fallen boy with a look that was half pity, half contempt. "Numinous was poisoned by arrogance. This is one of the most insidious forms of self-deception."

Infidel wasn't paying any attention to the conversation. Instead, she moved slowly toward the boy, her eyes full of guilt. Relic intercepted her, taking her by the arm as he said to Tower, "Aurora has some skill as a healer. Let her look at the boy; perhaps his life can be saved."

I doubted that Aurora was up to the task. Barely a minute had passed and both the boy's arms were swelling up, turning purple from where bone had punched through muscle. His body trembled as he sank deeper into shock. A cold compress on the forehead wasn't going to fix this.

However, the question of what Aurora could do was rendered moot as the man in red robes stepped toward Lord Tower. "You threatened to cut off my hands if I touched your precious Golden Child," he said. "Now that he's failed you, do you mind if I save his life?"

The knight nodded. "Do what you can, Deceiver."

I suddenly had an explanation for why this man had a big 'D' tattooed on his forehead. I had thought that Deceivers were only bogey-monsters that monks used to frighten orphans. A fundamental tenant of the Church of the Book was that truth was truth; there was nothing subjective under the sun. The reality recorded in the One True Book was the only reality, inviolate, inflexible.

Deceivers, on the other hand, believed that nothing at all is true, not even the experience of our own senses. Everything we assume about reality - that the sky is blue, that grass is green, that snow is cold and fire is hot - is merely a shared delusion, constantly reinforced by people desperately clinging to the illusion of stability in a world where nothing is absolute. The One True Book was merely a work of fiction in the Deceiver's world view. The Deceivers thought of themselves as shared authors of this fiction and, as such, were free to edit reality to their liking. They were the greatest enemies of the church. What was one doing here, alive? I couldn't believe Father Ver hadn't slit his throat the second they met.

The Whisper recoiled as the Deceiver knelt beside the boy, stepping back several feet, as if she didn't want to risk breathing the same air.

"Can you help him?" asked Aurora, as she knelt down next to the Deceiver.

"I possess the power to heal any injury," the Deceiver said, running his hand along the boy's arm. "Though I believe we were all mistaken in thinking the boy was seriously harmed. Wipe the blood away, and he's suffered little more than a few scratches and bruises."

And, indeed, as the Deceiver wiped the blood and grit from the boy's limbs, the flesh no longer looked so distorted. Perhaps it had only been a trick of the light that had made the wounds looks so serious before.

"He's just had the wind knocked out of him," the Deceiver said, cradling the boy's face, pushing back the eyelids to look at the dilated pupils. "He'll come out of it any minute."

Everyone had fallen silent as they watched the Deceiver tend to the fallen boy. The only sound was a faint rasping noise. The sound was coming from the Truthspeaker, grinding his teeth. His eyes were narrowed into slits as he watched the Deceiver restore the boy to health. Finally, he could stand no more.

"Get your unholy hands off him!" He jumped forward, his robes flying as he kicked the kneeling man in the head. "I would rather see the boy die than be tainted by your filthy lies!"

Numinous, still unconscious, gasped as his left arm twisted once more, obviously broken. Yet, the boy still looked better than he had before. The Deceiver lay beside the boy, glaring at Father Ver with naked hatred as he rubbed the sandal-print on the side of his jaw.

Tower grabbed Father Ver by the nape of his neck and hauled him back before he could kick the Deceiver again. "Control yourself," he said. "Zetetic is using his power for good, as promised."

"Promises mean nothing to his kind!" Father Ver shouted. His spittle flecked Tower's faceplate. "He swore only to use his power to alter his own form, but already he has broken this vow by altering the boy's body!"

Zetetic, the Deceiver said, "Technically, I gave myself the power to heal. The boy's body wasn't altered, only restored, until you meddled."

Father Ver went bug-eyed. He once more lunged toward his enemy, but Lord Tower held him back. "His presence is an abomination! The king is mad to include him on this quest!"

Tower sighed. "If the king is mad, so be it. He's still the king and it's our duty to obey him. I forbid you to strike Zetetic again."

"There are greater authorities than the king," Father Ver growled. "You cannot honestly expect me to simply stand and bear witness to such blasphemy!"

"You could always close your eyes," Zetetic said.

Father Ver sputtered a string of meaningless syllables as his rage stripped him of coherent speech.

"Get back to work," the knight said to Zetetic as he lifted the Truthspeaker from his feet and carried him back several yards.

The Deceiver looked at the boy and shrugged sadly. "I've done all I can. Father Ver has aborted the newborn reality we created where the boy was cured. Still, I think it persisted long enough to save the boy's life."

Aurora still knelt beside the unconscious child, probing his arm tenderly with her beefy fingers. She looked up and said, "I can set the arm in a splint. For a boy this age, the bone will heal in a matter of weeks."

Father Ver turned away in disgust. He grumbled to Tower, "At the command of an earthly king we ally ourselves with liars, ogres, and rogues. What does it matter if our quest succeeds when we corrupt our very souls in the journey?"

"The primal dragons are the enemy of all mankind," said the knight, resting the Gloryhammer on his shoulder. "If I must be damned in order that the world can be free of their tyranny, I shall pay the price. You, of all people, understand the importance of our mission."

Father Ver's shoulders sagged. His voice trembled as he whispered. "Very well. But the boy must remain behind. If he isn't the Omega Reader, we have no business endangering a child."

Tower nodded. "I concur."

Father Ver gave Relic a rueful glance. "The hunchback doesn't believe he's lying, but I still don't trust him or his whorish toy. Given all they know of our quest, I must advise you to destroy them."

Blade stepped over to the conversation.

"I second that opinion," he said. "I was impressed with the War Doll's strength, but now that I've seen its savagery, I fear it's a danger to us all."

"Thank you for your counsel. However, since we can't have pack animals on this mission, it seems wasteful to destroy the War Doll. It would make a good substitute for a mule." Tower looked up the shaft. The sun was no longer directly overhead, and the shadows in the cave grew deeper. "Our emotions run high at the moment. We won't be ready to leave until morning. I'll make my decision then."

Despite the fact that he was the subject of the ongoing conversation, no one was paying attention to Relic. He walked to the wall where the Golden Child had hit. There was a spattering of blood dripping down the stone. Casually, he reached out and dabbed the gore with a rag-covered finger. Then, since he still carried Infidel's weaponry, he drew the bone-handled knife from its scabbard and ran his blood-damp finger along the steel.

My ghost lungs gasped for air as I materialized once more. I was fainter than my previous incarnations; I could see through my ghostly fingers to the bones of fog beneath.

He spoke to me in his soundless voice: *It seems I have need of you after all, Blood-Ghost.*

I looked down at my body, on the verge of tears from the joy of seeing myself again. As a thought-fog, my emotions are muted; now that I once more felt ephemeral blood pulsing in my veins, I was terrified at the thought of having the knife cleaned once more.

Obey me, and I will see that the knife is never bare of blood.

"What would you have me do?" I asked.

The king's men are a dangerous lot. While the boy is no longer a threat, I cannot read the mind of Lord Tower while he wears his armor. Were he the only one immune to my powers, I would have few fears. But the Whisper's thoughts are dim; the harder I concentrate on them, the fainter they become.

"Is she a ghost?"

Doubtful. Your thoughts are clear to me. Blade may know her true nature but I've yet to find her origins among his thoughts. What worries me even more is the Deceiver. His mind is unlike anything I've encountered. His true thoughts are buried beneath veils of hallucinations. I risk my very sanity probing him.

"What am I supposed to do about this?"

You will be my spy. In your phantom form, you aren't tethered as tightly to the knife. You may wander, listening in on conversations I will not be privy to. Have a care, however. Should Father Ver suspect your presence, he has the power to banish you forever to the spirit world.

I furrowed my brow, confused. "Aren't I already in the spirit world?"

Obviously not. You are a spirit in the material world.

Actually, that was kind of obvious. But, if there was a spirit world, what was it like? Why hadn't I gone there?

I will help you reach the spirit world at the proper time should you assist me.

"Maybe I don't want to go. I'd rather stay here. I'll help you only if you promise to let me speak to Infidel."

A fair bargain. I will grant this if you serve me well. Have a care, however. You may desire to speak to the woman, but the feeling may not be mutual. The living seldom wish to be confronted by the dead.

I clenched my jaw as I thought over his offer. If I refused to cooperate, he could just wipe the blood from the blade and banish me once more. But, while he had the power, perhaps, to grant me what I wanted, I had to wonder what he wanted, beyond my immediate services as a spy. Aside from a desire to kill Greatshadow, I knew nothing of his plans or purpose.

Relic's eyes glimmered. *You are wise to be suspicious of me, Blood-Ghost. Yet, my motives are simple. I hate Greatshadow with every fiber of my being. The world can hold no joy for me as long as he lives. Tower would sacrifice his soul. I would sacrifice this, and more, for the pleasure of watching Greatshadow die.*

"And then what?" I asked. "You take his treasure?"

Relic gave a low, soft chuckle that chilled my vaporous guts. *Then, my dear Blood-Ghost, I take the world.*

10 - FLAWED VESSELS

THAT EVENING, EVERYONE dined on hardtack and dried beef; I would have expected an expedition backed by a king to have food fit for one, but apparently all the funds had gone into buying glorystones and Goons. Tower still had his helmet on as Blade handed him his rations. I waited for him to pull off his helmet to eat, but instead he retreated into his tent.

"Guess he's too good to eat with us," Aurora said as she sat cross-legged on the ground by the Three Goons.

"I heard he never takes off that tin-can because his face is covered with scars," said Reeker.

"Boo hoo hoo," No-Face answered. For once I didn't need any translation.

Relic came over to the circle of mercenaries. "Perhaps he has other reasons for hiding his face. Most warriors, in my experience, are eager to show off their battle scars."

"It ain't battle scars," said Reeker. "According to what I heard, about fifteen years ago on his wedding day, one of Tower's enemies launched a sneak attack. Half the chapel got knocked down by a catapult and a fire broke out. Tower kept running back into the conflagration, saving the lives of a dozen people even though he was getting all burnt up himself. But he never pulled out the one person he was searching for: his bride. Now, when he sees his scars, he thinks of her."

"A tragic tale," said Relic.

"A stupid tale," said Reeker. "Ain't no dame worth risking your life for. They're like stray cats; one gets killed, two more show up the next day."

"Tower must not have felt that way," said Menagerie. "My sources say he's still unmarried."

"Maybe that's just proof he sees things my way now," said Reeker.

"Mubuh huh duug guh buhn uf," said No-Face.

"Maybe we should stop gossiping about the man who's paying our wages," said Menagerie. "Don't forget they have an invisible spy."

Infidel was several yards away from the ring of dining Goons. She was standing with her back to the others, looking into the shadows of the cave. I moved in front of her and waived my ephemeral hand before her eyes, though I knew it was futile. Her face was completely blank, with no hint of a reaction to Reeker's tale. Save for the occasional blink, she really looked like nothing more than a statue.

THE FOLLOWING MORNING, Tower announced his decision: "Relic and his War Doll can join the expedition. We'll use the War Doll chiefly to carry gear. Aurora will also have pack duty as punishment for revealing our location."

Reeker raised his hand. "We're going to hike to the dragon's lair? The caldera's, like, fifty miles away. Can't you fly us?"

Tower shook his head. "The Gloryhammer glows most brightly when I'm in the air. Flying low over the ocean in mid-day wasn't a problem, since the glare of the sun upon the waves masks the weapon's radiance. Short bursts of flight to help us over obstacles are probably safe, but I don't dare risk making a dozen long trips back and forth over the jungle canopy. Greatshadow would surely spot us."

"So he spots us and comes down to kill us," said Reeker. "We fight him on the slopes instead of in the volcano. What's the big deal?"

Ivory Blade nodded toward Lord Tower. "If I may?"

Tower nodded back.

"First," said Blade, "Our mission is more than to simply kill the dragon's body. We must also slay his spirit and forever sever his intelligence from the element of fire. This can only be done in his lair. Second, you're being paid to do what we tell you to, not to question our commander's decisions before we even leave the base."

Reeker looked as if he were going to say something back, until he spotted Menagerie glaring at him. He crossed his arms and gave a subservient nod.

Aurora apparently was undeterred from asking questions. "What will happen to the boy? He still needs medical attention."

Numinous was sitting near the main tent, gazing toward Lord Tower with a look that bordered on hatred. He'd been furious when he'd been told earlier that he was no longer taking part in the mission. Gone was the placid, supremely confident Golden Child of the day before. In his place was an ill-tempered ten-year old boy who'd always gotten his way until now. I felt sympathy for the kid. Every day of his life until today, he'd been surrounded by adults who treated him like he was the salvation of the world. Now, the adults had decided he was nobody important. That can't be easy to swallow.

Tower said, "Numinous may not be the Omega Reader, but he is still exceptionally educated and trained. Despite his injuries, he's able to fend for himself until we return. He can use this time alone to reflect on whether life in the priesthood will suit his future, or perhaps a more martial life as a knight will be his calling. When this mission is over, I will ensure that his education continues for a new, more suitable, role."

This answer seemed to satisfy Aurora, though not Numinous, who rose and went back into the tent.

"If there are no more questions, we shall begin. First, allow Father Ver to bless our mission with a prayer."

Father Ver's left eyebrow shot up. He looked surprised by the request, which I found curious. A man in his position was no doubt asked to lead prayers a dozen times a day.

The look of surprise was quickly wiped away by his omnipresent scowl. He stepped forward into the middle of the circle and looked up the shaft of sunlight spilling into the cavern. He then looked down at his hands, bony and wrinkled, covered with age spots. He cleared his throat.

"The question before us," he said, in what sounded more like a sermon than a prayer, "is one of predestination."

Tower, Relic, Ivory Blade, and even Zetetic, the Deceiver, all nodded reverently as he began. The Goons and Aurora just looked bored. The Whisper, apparently, wasn't all that religious. She slipped in up behind Blade as the priest spoke and began to kiss him gently on the nape of the neck.

"The future was written long before we were born. We know in our hearts that the Divine Author would not have written a story in which the wicked are allowed to triumph and the righteous meet endless defeat. In the end, good shall triumph over evil."

I gave a little ghost-yawn. I'd heard this generic prattle about the inevitable victory of good ten times a day growing up.

"There can be no doubt that Greatshadow embodies evil. No honest man has ever stared into a flame without perceiving the malignant intelligence behind it, the predator spirit that waits to pounce upon the weak and unwary. The Divine Author has left no room for doubt as to the identity of the villain of our tale. The only question that remains is: Are we good enough to be the heroes? Do we undertake this mission in complete honesty regarding our motivations? Do we seek to vanquish evil purely because it is our duty, or have the seeds of our defeat already been planted in falsehoods buried deep inside our hearts? Will our tale not be one of triumph, but of instruction, a warning against vanity, or greed, or lust?"

It may have been my imagination, but Ivory Blade looked chastened by these words. He hung his head low, his lips pressed tightly together, even as the Whisper gave him a comforting hug. Tower's shoulders also sagged a little as Father Ver spoke.

The only person who looked inspired by Father Ver was Zetetic, who was grinning broadly.

Father Ver concluded by looking back up the shaft and switching from sermon to something more like a prayer. "We ask, oh Author of Our Fates, that even if we are flawed vessels, you still will use us as vessels of your will. Help us, oh Lord, to bring the world one page closer to its perfect ending. Your will is our will. Amen."

"Amen," echoed Tower. Then he raised his head and said, "Relic, get your War Doll loaded. We'll use it to cart our gear up the cliff, with Aurora's help. I'll ferry the other's one by one. As long as I don't rise above the tree line, this flight shouldn't draw attention."

Tower grabbed Ver by the arm and pulled the cleric to his chest. "You first," he said, sounding somewhat terse. The holy man didn't have time to say a word before the knight launched skyward.

Follow them! Relic screamed in my mind. *If they have a private conversation, I want to know the details.*

I looked at him and said, "Maybe you didn't notice that they're flying?"

And perhaps you haven't noticed that gravity no longer holds you to this earth?

I had noticed that, but I'd still been hovering at pretty much the same eye-level I'd been at when I was alive. In my ghostly form, I could wander around where I wanted to just by thinking. Did it work the same way going up?

I moved toward the shaft and spotted Tower high overhead. I furrowed my brow as I willed myself to follow him. Then – *whoosh!* – not only did I fly, I flew fast, shooting up along the rugged cliffs to reach the knight and the cleric in a matter of seconds. The terrain atop the cliff was still a fairly steep slope, but had soil enough to support trees and shrubs in a nearly uniform canopy of green. Tower punched through the foliage into the shadowy forest beyond. There were huge boulders among the trees. Tower landed on one, releasing Father Ver, before asking, in a voice that was almost a shout, "What was that?"

Father Ver looked undaunted by the anger in the knight's tone. "You are unhappy with my prayer."

"I wanted an invocation to our inevitable success, not some admonition that we might be too vain or lustful or whatever to defeat the dragon. Where's your faith?"

"Faith is a crutch for the spiritually weak," Father Ver said. "It's something used by women, children, and the feeble-minded unprepared to handle truth. I've never thought of you in this category."

"You've been unpleasant company since this expedition was announced," said Tower. "I've always looked up to you and respected you, Father. I can't understand your sudden embrace of pessimism."

Father Ver closed his eyes and rubbed the thick callous on his forehead. "Truthfulness often precludes optimism. You of all men should understand this."

"And you, of all men, should understand that the righteous always defeat the wicked. It is the only conclusion that will satisfy the Divine Author."

Ver shook his head. "You're a warrior, not a priest. You overstep your bounds when you claim insight into the mind of our creator."

"I'm only repeating what you've taught!"

"You are only repeating the teachings you find convenient to remember," said Ver. "You remember that good triumphs over evil in the end. But you fail to recall that we may not be at the end. The One True Book is a very thick document. There may yet be centuries, even eons, before the final victory. In the intervening time, the outcome of any given battle can never truly be known."

Tower sighed. "Fine. You're technically correct. We may not actually know how this particular story ends. But I'd appreciate it if you would be a little more inspirational, to help motivate the troops."

"What troops?" asked Father Ver. "There are eleven of us. The Goons aren't believers in the Book, nor are the ogress and the hunchback. Blade and the Whisper walk a middle path and are not so pure as you may wish to believe, though they are saints compared to Zetetic, who twists all truths he encounters into lies. The only one among us whom my words may truly inspire is you."

Tower crossed his arms, tapping his gauntleted fingers on his iron biceps with little clanking sounds. His feet were hovering a few inches above the ground. He shook his head slowly. "Perhaps I need the inspiration."

"What you need is to know yourself," said the priest. "Are you honest regarding your reasons for leading this mission?"

"I seek only to defeat evil and improve the lives of my fellow men. You would know if I was lying."

"I would know if you were lying to me. I cannot know if you're lying to yourself."

"You think I have some other motive? What? Treasure? I'm already wealthy. Fame? Glory? The streets of the Silver City are lined with statues erected in honor of my previous victories. It matters not at all if they erect another."

"So you say."

"Such is the truth," said Lord Tower. "Years have passed since I first saw my image carved in stone. Any pride I once felt has passed as I've aged. A statue is an empty legacy to leave the world. My only goal now is to leave the world a better place than what I inherited. The death of Greatshadow is a step toward that goal."

"Very well. Even if your motives are pure, you must know your chosen allies are motivated by nothing other than greed."

"True. But I need not share the same motives as an ally in order to achieve a common goal. I've had years of battle experience to learn this truth. Still, I understand it must be difficult for you. This mission is forcing you into alliances with men you wouldn't normally associate with."

"You're being too polite," said Ver. "I would normally order these scoundrels and heretics flogged, imprisoned, or hanged."

"Understood. Now, try to understand that I've fought beside rough men and unbelievers in previous battles," said Tower. "Against some foes, power is more important than purity. We could lead an army of ten thousand pilgrims up these slopes and Greatshadow could kill them in a matter of seconds by unleashing an inferno. These scoundrels and heretics are survivors. I'm confident we've assembled the perfect team to defeat Greatshadow. I want you to feel this confidence also."

Ver pressed his lips tightly together. "If I believed this to be a doomed enterprise, I wouldn't have accepted your invitation to join. I'm not blind to the difference between principals and truth. I respect the power of the team you've assembled. We stand a good chance of success. But I cannot pretend that victory is certain."

"I suppose I'll have to settle for that," said Tower.

"Yes, you shall. Go get the others," said Ver, with a dismissive wave. "They'll wonder what's keeping you."

Tower nodded, then shot back over the cliff side. I started to follow him, but was distracted by something I spotted out on the water. I raised my hand to shield my eyes from the sun, though, alas, it proved pointless, since the rays passed right through my spectral skin. As I got used to the light after the shade of the trees, there was no mistaking I was looking at a clipper ship, still a mile out, but heading toward the cliffs at a breakneck pace.

A few seconds later, I spotted Tower rising back up from the cave, now with Zetetic in tow. Tower sat the red-robed figure on a boulder facing Father Ver, then swung back out to grab another passenger.

"Nice little prayer you gave down there, Ver," said Zetetic. "Did I detect a little bit of a guilty conscience in all that talk about whether you're good enough for this mission? After all, given what you've done to me...."

"You've suffered nothing you haven't earned," said Father Ver. "Count each breath you draw as a blessing from the Divine Author. If I were the master of your fate, your bones would have long since been picked over by ravens."

"No doubt. But, since a higher authority than you has seen to it I'm along for this journey, could you maybe try to be more courteous? Or at least try not to kick me in the head any more?" He rubbed the side of his skull for emphasis.

"I can make no such promise," said Father Ver.

Zetetic shrugged. "I can't be blamed for asking."

No-Face was next up, followed by Reeker and Menagerie in the form of a parrot. I might not have recognized Menagerie among the other parrots flitting through the trees if not for his voice: "Looks like trouble," the bird said, as it landed on No-Face's shoulder. It pointed seaward with a wing.

By now, the ship had gotten much closer and seemed to be heading directly for the pirate cave below.

"Suh hurs," said No-Face.

I squinted. He was right. It was the *Seahorse*, a pirate ship. I could even see Captain Stallion on the deck, in case there had been any doubt. Stallion is a distinctive figure. He looks like a half-seed, but is really just a man's torso jammed onto the body of a donkey, though he tells everyone his equine parts are prize-winning stallion. He got this way after a badly thought out double-cross of a Weaver, who have a flair for this sort of magic.

"This is inconvenient timing," said Tower, glancing down. "He's heading straight for the cave. So much for the thought of leaving Numinous behind."

"We could just kill Stallion and his crew," said Menagerie. "We'll be glad to do it for no charge, as long as we don't have to split the bounty for his head with you."

While Tower pondered this offer, I drifted back down toward the cave. The *Seahorse* was moving toward the entrance at a speed that no sane sailor would risk. Captain Stallion wasn't known for being timid. I passed Infidel and Aurora on the way down. They were climbing the cliffs, lugging large bales of gear from ledge to ledge. Relic was nowhere to be seen. I slipped back into the cave just as the *Seahorse* reached the mouth. Numinous, Ivory Blade, and the Whisper were still inside. The *Seahorse* carried at least fifty men, battle-hardened cut-throats who would give even the Goons a run for their money. Whatever Tower decided, I hope he decided it fast.

Within the cave, Ivory Blade stood on the shore, watching the pirates set anchor in the cove. Numinous came out of the sole tent remaining in the camp. A handful of glorystone lanterns were still scattered about the place. It took the pirates all of ten seconds to notice the precious rocks. The *Seahorse* leaned starboard as the entire crew rushed to the rails to look at the glowing gems.

Captain Stallion leapt from the deck, his pirate hat flying off as he sailed across the water to land in the shallows, splashing onto the shore with a few more jumps. He had a saber drawn as he eyed Ivory Blade.

"Well, well, well!" Stallion shouted. "Look who we have here! Mister Ivory Blade! The deal-breaking, cowardly dog who I swore would walk the plank if ever we met again!"

"Didn't know you were the type to hold a grudge, Stallion," said Blade.

A dozen men jumped from the ship, swimming ashore quickly, blades in their teeth, to stand beside their captain. Stallion said, "A grudge?" he pranced closer to the albino. His donkey body left him a little taller. While Blade was a figure of composure, every hair in place, Stallion looked as if he'd gone feral. His long hair was tangled and matted around his sunburnt-face. His clothing was half-rotten on his back. "A grudge is weak beer, Mr. Blade. My feelings for you have been distilled into a brew of pure hatred. Whatever happens from this day forward, I'll die a happy man to have finally learned if your entrails are the same spook white as the rest of your unholy flesh."

"Don't make any hasty decisions until you hear what I have to say," said Blade.

"I'll not be listening to your lying tongue ever again!" cried Stallion. He turned to his men and cried, "Kill him!"

In the blink of an eye, the dozen men that surrounded him fell to the ground, grasping their slit throats, as the silhouetted form of the Whisper danced silently through their midst. She ended her dance by slicing up with her sword and chopping Stallion's blade in twain four inches above the hilt. The impact made no sound; what was her sword made of?

Stallion frowned as he looked at his abbreviated weapon. He glanced around at the dying men surrounding him. Then, he grinned broadly. "Blade! Old friend! Can't you recognize a little joke?"

"Only when dead pirates are the punchline," said Blade, still with his arms crossed. "Shall we discuss business now?"

"What do you have in mind?"

"I'd like to hire you as a shuttle service. We have a boy here who's far from home. You can return him to the Silver City."

"Ah," said Stallion. "That could be a problem. A man such as yourself has perhaps heard of the small matter that your own king has placed a sizable price on my head?"

"Among other body parts," said Blade. "Which is why, as payment for your services, King Brightmoon himself shall grant a pardon for your crimes. I can give you a letter of safe passage that all members of his navy will respect."

"His pardon would carry no weight with the Wanderers. Or the Stormguard, for that matter."

"No. But it will open an entire archipelago of ports where you could legally dock. Any number of towns where you could trot the streets a free man. And, the king recently lost several ships. Perhaps he'd find a position for you and the *Seahorse* in his navy."

"I seem to recall similar promises being made five years ago, when I handled the small matter of bringing you the Book of the Abyss."

"If it had been the genuine article and not a blatant forgery, all promises would have been kept."

Stallion ran a hand along his tangled mane. "Aye, it was a piss-poor forgery. I knew you'd discover it sooner or later."

"It was sooner," said Blade.

Stallion chuckled. "This boy must be precious to you, that he'd bring a king's pardon."

"Indeed. And if a person of a mercenary nature were to try to hold the boy against his will and seek a ransom, I can give you my solemn vow that his corpse would be rendered into glue."

"I'm sure. Fortunately, I can't imagine a person of a mercenary nature wanting a treasure greater than the king's pardon... especially if these glorystones are thrown into the agreement."

Blade shrugged. "Why not? We're leaving them behind anyway."

"Very well, sir. We have a deal."

The albino and the pseudo-centaur sealed their verbal contract with a handshake.

Blade said, "I was certain you were still a reasonable man, despite the haircut."

"Aye," said Stallion. "It's been many years since I've docked in a port with a barber I'd trust with a razor."

"A shave and a haircut will make you feel like a new man," said Blade. He glanced back over his shoulder and shouted, "Numinous."

Numinous was already standing behind him.

"I've heard every word of this transaction," he said. "I approve. The thought of waiting endless weeks in this cave in solitude held little appeal to me."

"He's got a busted arm," said Stallion, studying Numinous. "Is there a bonus for being a floating hospital?"

"The bonus is that if you stop trying to haggle on an already closed deal, I won't sever your testicles and hang them from your earrings."

"That is an excellent bonus," said Stallion, nodding.

Later, after the letter of safe passage had been written, Blade left the pirate cave, following the same path that Aurora and Infidel had taken. Tower met him at the first ledge.

"I was waiting in the shaft the whole time, listening," said the knight carrying them skyward. "It seemed as if you had the situation in hand. But, are you certain you can trust him with Numinous?"

"Stallion wants that pardon. He wanted it five years ago. Other pirates can slip into towns in disguise from time to time to spend their ill-gotten gains. Stallion doesn't have that option. He's got to be the most recognizable pirate in the world. Just as I'm probably the most recognizable secret agent in the world. We understand each other."

The reached the top of the cliff. Blade sat down on a rock and the Whisper slipped behind him and wrapped her arms around his neck. Tower hadn't carried her up. Could she fly? Or was she just as fast at climbing as she was at cutting throats?

11 - EVERYTHING THAT CAN BE IMAGINED IS TRUE

TOWER HADN'T BEEN joking about using the War Doll as a mule. After the gear was all brought up from the camp, they began to test how much weight she could carry, piling more and more tents, rations, and tools upon her shoulders until the mound was almost comical. Infidel bore it all with mechanical stoicism. After a certain point, the roped-together pile on her shoulders was so large it risked getting tangled by branches as they walked, so they gave the rest of the gear to Aurora before reaching the limits of the War Doll's strength. I wasn't surprised. Infidel was probably strong enough to carry all the gear and the rest of the party as well, along with an actual mule if we'd had one.

Of course, pack animals were out of the question. The part of Greatshadow that was still a big hungry lizard had a taste for livestock. Paintings and sculpture from the Vanished Kingdom showed that cows, horses, and oxen had once had a home here. After Greatshadow rose to power, he stripped the land of any mammals larger than pygmies. It's rumored that the pygmies' bitter dyes protect them; more likely, Greatshadow doesn't hunt pygmies for the same reason that men don't hunt mice. The meat you get isn't worth the effort.

I floated next to Relic as we set off into the jungle. I said, "The Black Swan was a bit off. She said a dozen adventurers would join the hunt for Greatshadow. With Numinous down, there's only eleven."

Perhaps she's counting you, said Relic.

"Was she? She can see me?"

Relic shrugged. *I could read her thoughts before she became undead. Now, her thoughts are lost to me.*

"Eleven against Greatshadow doesn't seem like good odds," I said.

The king has chosen quality over quantity. As to whether the king has chosen well, we shall see.

Progress up the slopes was frustratingly slow. The terrain was steep and rugged, dotted with boulders as big as houses all tangled with tenacious vines. No-Face was armed with a machete and turned loose on the foliage, but we still barely covered a mile by mid-day. Despite the thick canopy above us, the sun directly overhead soon raised the temperature from sweltering to unbearable. As we paused for No-Face to chop away a particularly nasty tangle, Father Ver leaned wearily against a tree, looking pale. His heavy clerical robes were better suited to a chilly mountain monastery than the tropics. Aurora, taking pity, approached him. She cupped her oversize hands and, within seconds, crafted a bowl of ice, filled to the rim with cool water drawn from the soggy air.

"Have a drink," she said.

Father Ver wrinkled his nose at the offering. "I must decline," he said. "I'm certain you mean well, but it would be a sin to drink water created by your pagan magic."

"I didn't create the water. I just gathered it. But, suit yourself." She turned around, only to find Reeker standing just behind her. He took the cup from her hands without asking and gulped it, rivulets running down his chest.

I didn't notice if Aurora took offense at this because from the corner of my eye I caught a glimpse of the Whisper giving a canteen to Ivory Blade. As Blade drank the water, the Whisper unbuttoned the top few clasps of his armor and folded back a flap of white leather to expose the skin around his collarbones. Then, in a move that probably warmed him rather than cooled him, she leaned her invisible face to his chest and began to lick at his sweat. I looked around, feeling squeamish about witnessing such an intimate act.

After a few more hours of hacking, we eventually made it through the worst of the vines into the denser jungle beyond. It's counterintuitive, but the deeper you go into a jungle, the easier the going becomes. The canopy above is so thick with plants growing on other plants that most of the available sunlight gets captured long before it reaches the ground, creating a semi-permanent twilight in which only a few hardy, broad-leafed plants grow. You might expect the ground to be covered by fallen leaves and branches, but the soil is constantly scoured by ants and beetles that make short work of anything that hits the jungle floor.

With most of the machete work behind us, Menagerie took the lead, scouting ahead of the party as a panther. Ivory Blade and the Whisper followed, then Lord Tower, Father Ver, and No-Face. No-Face, when not on machete duty, was assigned as Father Ver's bodyguard. Despite his deformity, No-Face wasn't a half-seed, nor did he openly dabble in blood magic. Apparently, this made him acceptable to walk within an arm's length of the holy man.

Reeker and Zetetic were next. Reeker was the Deceiver's bodyguard, or perhaps just his guard, period, since he had orders from Lord Tower to give the Deceiver a snoot full of skunk juice at the first sign of anything suspicious. I had to wonder why the Deceiver was part of this team, if he couldn't be trusted.

Relic took my private musings and turned them into a prompt for a telepathic exposition.

The Deceiver is immensely powerful. He is the master of falsehoods, and the things that are false in this world far outnumber the things that are true. Zetetic may be the greatest threat Greatshadow faces, assuming he can find the courage to stand up to the dragon. He's definitely not undertaking this quest out of choice.

"How can you know that?" I asked. "I thought you couldn't read his mind."

His mind is labyrinth of hallucination that protects his innermost thoughts, but I am slowly navigating that labyrinth. I've learned that he blames his presence here on the Black Swan. She paid a substantial fee to persuade King Brightmoon of the importance of including him.

I scratched my ghostly scalp as I contemplated this. It was difficult to wrap my head around the idea that the Black Swan had already witnessed the next twenty years. I wondered what else she'd changed on this mission, beside including Zetetic and Aurora? I glanced back at the ogress, who was bringing up the rear along with Infidel. One thing conspicuously absent from the mountains of gear upon their backs was a harpoon. From the way Aurora had described it, the shaft of the harpoon was over fifteen feet long. It plainly wasn't with the gear, and Tower wasn't carrying it either. Could it have been broken down into something smaller?

I spent most of my time drifting near the two women, mostly because of my craving for Infidel's company, but also because of the circle of chilled air that surrounded Aurora. Even as a ghost, the jungle heat was unpleasant. Still, being a traveling ghost wasn't all bad. On my trips through the jungle while I was alive, I was normally too exhausted by hiking to enjoy the scenery. In my weightless, ogre-cooled comfort zone, I had time to appreciate the rich tapestry we walked through. If everything around us was the work of the

Divine Author, he had a sense of playfulness when it came to the colors surrounding us. Translucent pink salamanders the size of bananas crawled over dark jade leaves big enough to use as a tent. Parrots and parakeets the color of lemons and oranges flitted between chocolate-brown tree trunks, devouring iridescent copper beetles and finger-length ants red as chili peppers. Orchids blossomed in every nook and cranny, flowers I'd only seen in botany books - yellow and black tipsy tigers, snow-white wedding gloves, pale purple danglers. The breeze was a heady mix of their perfumes; though, little by little, the floral aroma was getting drowned out by the low tide stench of Reeker as he and the Deceiver slowed their pace to skirt the bubble of cool air surrounding Aurora.

"Allow me to apologize for Father Ver," said the Deceiver, looking back at Aurora with a friendly smile. "His church teaches that ogres and mermen and the like are false beings, existing as sort of a shared dream that will all be wiped away when the world finally awakes to the truth. I pity him for the limits of his worldview. I personally am happy to be in the company of someone who knows ice magic."

Aurora gave him a suspicious look. Even a compliment felt dangerous coming from the man. Still, I wondered if I was giving him a fair shake. I distrusted Deceivers mainly because the church had drilled into my brain from an early age that heretics like Zetetic were the incarnation of evil. That same church harbored a supply of knife-wielding maniacs dedicated to stabbing the woman I loved. Perhaps I needed to keep an open mind.

"I've always been fascinated by the magic of your people," Zetetic continued. "It's based on completely different theories of reality than those that are taught by the Church of the Book. Since Father Ver believes he is in possession of the sole path to truth, your mere presence is a threat to him. The undeniable evidence that your magic works undermines everything he believes. No wonder he hates you."

Aurora shrugged. "I don't care what he thinks."

"A healthy attitude," said Zetetic. Then he turned toward Relic, who was hobbling along near Infidel. "The ruins of the Vanished Kingdom are filled with idols of gods long since forgotten. I'd love to learn more about who these gods were, and what the men of your time believed."

Relic shrugged. "The men of my time were no different than the men of today. There was no one great, universal truth accepted by all. In the end, it mattered little who or what was worshipped. Time wiped away both the just and unjust. The followers of the dog-god vanished from the world just as completely as the followers of the snake-god. The temples where a thousand men gathered to sing the praises of their makers are now hidden beneath roots and rocks. I cannot help but think that, no matter what men believe to be true, over a long enough time scale, it will be proven false."

Zetetic smiled. "Just because an idea is eventually false doesn't mean it wasn't true once. We Deceivers are smeared as believing that the world is created from shared lies. It's more accurate, however, to say that the world is composed of contradictory truths."

"How can truths be contradictory?" asked Aurora. "Things either are, or they aren't. It can't be both night and day at the same time."

"It can if the world is a sphere," said Zetetic. "In your homeland it is always winter; here it is always summer. If I could travel instantly between the two physical spaces and ask the season, I would receive two contrary yet true answers. People are limited to thinking that their immediate experiences represent all that is real. The Church of the Book believes one model of reality, while weavers, blood magicians, and somnomancers all are certain that they are in sole possession of the actual truth of the world. You can't blame people for thinking that these competing ideas can't all be correct. But, what if reality is large enough to accommodate everything? What if we live in a world where all truth is local? What if, on the grand scale, everything that can be imagined is true?"

"Remind me not to ask you any more questions," grumbled Aurora.

"I'm merely trying to pass the time with some intellectually stimulating conversation."

"The only thing I need stimulated is my spine," said Aurora, with a hint of strain in her voice. She shifted the oversize pack she hauled to redistribute the weight to her left shoulder. "What the hell does Tower have in the packs? Anvils?"

"If your load is heavy, perhaps I could be of assistance."

Aurora gave the Deceiver's slender form a quizzical look. "What? You'll tell me some lie about the gear? Convince me that it's lighter?"

Reeker suddenly became much more alert.

"Uh-uh," he said, grabbing Zetetic by the arm and pulling him a yard further up the trail from the ogress. "If you try to use your powers, I'm supposed to give you a full blast of juice."

Zetetic frowned. "You wound me, sir. I was merely offering aide to a member of the fairer sex. Have you no sense of chivalry?"

Aurora snorted. "He's the wrong guy to ask that question."

The faintest trace of a snicker flickered over Infidel's face.

"Reeker's the worst womanizer I've ever seen," said Aurora. "He's slept with every whore in Commonground without paying a dime. Treats them like something you'd scrape off a boot, and still they line up outside the bar waiting for him."

Reeker didn't look offended by this summary of his character. Instead, he slicked back the white streak in his hair and said, "Aurora, honey, I'd be happy to show you what the women are so hungry for."

Zetetic stroked his chin as he studied the skunk-man. "I suspect his secret is musk."

Reeker cut him a sideways glance.

Zetetic wasn't deterred, "Most mammals use scent to convey sexual signals. With his control of aromas, perhaps Reeker is seducing women on a primal level with odors they aren't consciously aware of."

Reeker poked the Deceiver in the chest. "You don't know nothing! Women like me for my good looks and charm."

Zetetic held up his palms. "I meant no offense. However, since I lack your striking features and erudite manners, I'm left with only simple kindness with which to befriend women. This is why I'd like to help Aurora."

"No magic!" said Reeker, again with a finger-poke.

"I don't really do magic," said Zetetic. "I only tell lies. What have you to fear from a mere liar?"

"I'm not afraid of you," said Reeker. "But you're lying in saying you're a liar. Or not a liar. Or not lying about… I mean, you're not telling the truth in… what I'm saying is…." He furrowed his brow as he got lost ever deeper in the thicket of the sentence he was attempting to construct.

"You're trying to say I'm lying about being merely a liar," said Zetetic. "That's an astute observation. Any man can tell a lie. I know how to make the universe believe it."

Suddenly, for no apparent reason, Relic gasped loudly. His staff fell from his gnarled hand as he collapsed to the ground, completely limp.

"My head is not a safe place to eavesdrop," Zetetic said, sneering down. Then, while Reeker was looking at the fallen hunchback, the Deceiver casually placed a hand on Aurora's pack. His gaze met the ogress's eyes as he said, in a matter-of-fact tone, "I'm big enough to lift this pack with one hand."

Reeker spun around and spat, sending a gob of yellow goo toward Zetetic's face. Only, by the time the spit had crossed the five-foot gap between them, Zetetic's face was replaced by a giant ankle, and Aurora was jerked from her feet.

Everyone looked up through the hole that had suddenly been punched in the canopy. Zetetic was now two-hundred feet tall, holding the pack by a single finger looped under a rope. Aurora dangled beneath the pack, looking no bigger than a rat.

"I do believe I've remembered another appointment," Zetetic said, laughing, his voice booming like thunder. He flicked his arm toward the ocean, sending Aurora and her pack flying in a long arc down the slope.

Infidel knelt next to Relic. She whispered, "You alright?"

Relic sucked air through clenched teeth, then said, "His thoughts... like razors... my mind... is bleeding...."

Infidel shrugged off the shoulder straps of her pack, letting it drop to the ground in a clatter. She cracked her knuckles and looked up with the same eager grin she always brought to fights where she could beat up someone bigger. Her face fell into shadow as Zetetic's sandaled foot flew down toward her and Relic. Infidel whirled around, kicking, catching Relic in the gut and launching him out of the stomp-zone. She crouched to jump away but was too late. The giant foot slammed into her with a shudder that shook the whole mountain.

Zetetic jumped, knocking over trees, flying down the slope a good fifty yards before crashing back to earth, waving his arms to maintain his balance on the uneven terrain. Off in the distance, perhaps a half mile away, I caught a glimpse of Aurora and her pack tumbling head over heels, on the verge of vanishing once more into the canopy. Then, in a sudden flash of light, her downward arc was intercepted by the shining silver form of Lord Tower, catching the ogress in his outstretched arms. Her pack tore loose at the impact, sending a spray of camping gear out over the treetops.

As difficult as it was to tear my eyes from this spectacle, I turned back to Infidel, who was splayed out in the center of a giant footprint. With a grunt, she popped her face up from the earth. She spat out a mouthful of black jungle dirt as she sat up, rubbing her eyes.

Satisfied she wasn't hurt, I turned my attention back toward the Deceiver. He had leapt again. His robes were tattered below his knees, shredded by the ancient trees he pushed aside like tall brush. Long streamers of blood-tangle vines trailed behind him as he fled down the mountain.

Lord Tower had circled around and now shot like an arrow toward the Deceiver's chin, the Gloryhammer blazing like a second sun in his outstretched arm. Aurora hugged his chest for dear life, in a death-grip that probably would have crushed anyone not encased in enchanted armor. Yet, before the knight could strike, Zetetic swung out with his tree-sized right arm and back-handed the knight in mid-air, sending him shooting back toward the ocean, looking like a spiraling comet as Aurora left a trail of bright snow in their wake.

Infidel rose back to her feet just in time to see Father Ver fly past, his hands locked onto the hide of a large tiger that effortlessly carried the old man. I followed as they caromed down the mountainside, leaping from rock to log, covering the quarter-mile to the giant's ankles in a span of seconds. The Truthspeaker cupped both hands around his mouth and shouted, "You will go no further!"

The Deceiver smirked as he spun away from the Truthspeaker's voice. His smirk changed to a frown, however, as his feet remained firmly planted on the ground. He raised his hands, feeling the air before him as if it were an invisible wall.

"You are no giant! You are a vile fabricator who will turn and face me at your true size!"

Zetetic's face contorted as his limbs jerked. "Graaah!" he cried out as he began to shrink, swinging his arms before him as if swatting at unseen bees. "Graaah! Naayaaah!"

With each second that passed he shed size, dropping to fifty feet, twenty, ten, and then he was only a man again, face to face with a panting tiger and a very angry cleric.

Zetetic held up his hands and gave a sheepish grin. "You can't blame a fellow for trying."

Father Ver had a different opinion, which he expressed by leaping off the tiger and planting his bony fist squarely in the center of the Deceiver's mouth. Zetetic spun from the blow, falling to his hands and knees.

He spat out blood and growled, "You bast —"

Father Ver silenced him by kicking him in the throat. The Deceiver fell to his back, his arms flopped out to his sides. Father Ver dropped with his knees, straddling the Deceiver's chest as he pummeled the man's face.

"Blasphemer!" Father Ver screamed. "Accursed malignancy! May your filthy name be erased from the Book!"

Zetetic raised his hands to block the blows, but the priest simply knocked them aside and continued to rain down punishment. Menagerie changed from tiger back to human and leaned against a fallen tree, his arms crossed as he watched the whirl of violence. Reeker and No-Face reached the area a moment later, saying nothing as they stared at the beating unfolding before them.

The Deceiver's arms fell limp. He'd never gotten in a single blow. Father Ver's fists trailed blood as he cut his knuckles pounding his victim's teeth. The Deceiver's pale face began to resemble a scary clown, as bright red blood painted his cheeks with a lopsided grin.

Ivory Blade and the Whisper suddenly bounded into the triangle formed by the goons. Blade grabbed the Truthspeaker by the shoulders and tried to pull him off the fallen man.

"You're going to kill him!" he growled, as he tugged at the cleric's robes. With the Whisper's help he pulled the elderly man back to his feet. Blade grabbed Father Ver by the collar and said, "Calm yourself. You don't need to sink to his level."

"You will take your freakish hands off me," Father Ver said, his voice a low hiss.

Blade snapped both hands into the air, his fingers spread in a gesture of surrender.

"Now you will go away!"

Blade spun on his heels and bounded off up the trail, running at breakneck speed, quickly disappearing among the trees. The Whisper looked after her fleeing lover for a few seconds, slack-jawed with surprise, before she shot off in pursuit.

Father Ver looked back down on his bloodied victim. Blood bubbled from the Deceivers nostrils as his breath came out in gurgles. The Truthspeaker knelt beside his victim. Zetetic flinched as his hand approached. The Truthspeaker grabbed the Deceiver's chin and turned his barely focused gaze to meet his own, then asked, "Where is it?"

Zetetic looked back with sad puppy eyes.

"Don't pretend you don't know," Father Ver said. "You wouldn't have dared this without the sketchbook. You will hand it over."

Zetetic's hands reached into the folds of his red robes and producing a small leather-bound notebook, barely six inches tall. The cover had no words on it, but it was scuffed and scratched, the parchment pages within looking dog-eared and folded over. Father Ver snatched the book away.

"Your wicked imagination exceeds my ability to think of prohibitions," said Father Ver. "Let us keep this simple. I gave my word to the king that I will not kill you. I've made no vow that would prohibit me from cutting out your blasphemous tongue. Attempt to escape again and I swear you will never utter another lie."

The Deceiver glared at Father Ver with a mix of hatred and terror, then nodded slowly, indicating he understood. Father Ver let go of the man's chin and wiped his gore-drenched hands on his victim's red robes, looking disgusted. He glanced toward the sky as Lord Tower drifted down toward them. Aurora was still clamped onto his chest; her hair had come undone from its top knot and lay against her scalp in a chaotic tangle.

She looked a bit wobbly as Tower set her on the ground.

"You believed his lie, ogress," grumbled Father Ver, without looking at her. "Your pagan faith makes you an easy target for his falsehoods. If he speaks to you again, feel free to break his jaw."

Before Aurora could reply, Lord Tower looked down at the semi-conscious Deceiver and said, "Why would he try something like this? Even if he'd reached the sea, we could have stopped him at any time."

"Not without this," said Father Ver, holding up the small book.

Tower reached both hands to his hip, popping open a compartment in his armor exactly the right size to hold the book. He stared silently at the emptiness within. "By the sacred quill," he mumbled. "How did...? When could he...?"

"The Deceiver fails to respect reality itself," Father Ver said. "It would have been a simple matter for him to become a master pickpocket." The priest cast a glance toward Reeker. "You were supposed to keep this from happening."

Reeker shrugged. "He caught me by surprise."

"Of course it was a surprise!" Father Ver shouted, throwing his hands into the air. "Did you think he would be considerate enough to send you a detailed letter explaining his plan? Are all half-seeds half-wits as well?"

Reeker's eyes flashed with anger as he drew back his shoulders and pressed his lips into a pucker. Menagerie nodded toward No-Face. The giant man's hand clamped over the skunk-man's mouth.

Menagerie said, "This is twice I've had to apologize for my colleague's behavior. I assure you, there will not be a third incident. For now, he's going to go help gather up what gear we can find from Aurora's pack. He won't grumble while he's doing it. Right?"

No-Face lowered his hand. Reeker swallowed his pride and whatever else he might have been holding in his mouth, then said, "Sure, boss." Then, to Father Ver, "Won't happen again."

Lord Tower scanned the tree tops, paying no attention to Infidel and Relic as they joined the rest of the party. Relic was limping more than usual; his whole body was wracked with tremors. Infidel was holding his arm, supporting him.

Lord Tower sighed. "Since we aren't under attack right now, maybe Greatshadow didn't notice this incident. Perhaps the worst that has come from this is that our supplies are scattered halfway back to the sea. We're going to lose the rest of the day gathering them." He looked at Menagerie. "I need more than just Reeker on the job. You'll all help recover the gear."

Menagerie nodded. "We're on it. I can work the tree tops as a monkey."

Tower turned to Father Ver. "While Zetetic's stunt has cost us time, it's also proof that he has skills no one else brings to the mission. Help him get cleaned up and stitch his wounds."

Father Ver's left eye began to twitch. He looked as if he was about to explode, but he said, softly, "As you wish."

Lord Tower looked down at the Deceiver, who had managed to sit up. The beaten man probed his bloodied mouth with his fingers, wincing as he pulled out a broken molar. The knight said, "Before you fell into heresy, you earned renown as a scholar. Some priests tell me you were the smartest man they'd ever met. How can you be dumb enough to pull a stunt like this? Even if you'd escaped with the book, you would not be free. Should ten days pass without word from me, the monk's will initiate the X sanction. You understand the consequences?"

The Deceiver nodded. His wet voice whistled as he said, "I undershtand the damned conshequencesh."

Tower turned back to the others. "Let's get busy. Goons, gather gear. Blade, I need you to... to..." His voice trailed off as he looked around the clearing. He turned to Father Ver and asked, "Where are Blade and the Whisper?"

12 - SOMNOMANCER

"I CAN FOLLOW their scent," said Menagerie, shifting into the form of a wolf. His voice was a yelping growl as he said, "I'll take the War Doll for back up, assuming it can act independently. It's the only one with a chance to keep up with me."

"Agreed," said Relic, his voice still weak.

"There's no need for a search party. Blade won't run forever," said Father Ver. He didn't sound apologetic for having caused the problem. "Once he trips, or runs into something, he'll return to his senses."

"Given Blade's agility, he might run a long time," said Lord Tower, as he rose into the sky. "With the thickness of this canopy, I'll never spot him from the air. Menagerie's plan is a sensible one. I'll help gather gear while they're gone."

Stay with me, Blood-Ghost, thought Relic. *I dare not look into the Deceiver's mind again. You must watch him with complete vigilance.*

The Deceiver didn't look as if he was going start mischief anytime soon. Father Ver knelt before him, examining the man's torn face. Zetetic was oddly passive as the priest reached out to touch a gash on his upper lip. "This will require stitches," Ver said. "It will hurt."

Menagerie sniffed the ground, then bounded up the trail at breakneck speed with Infidel at his heels. Or rather, his paws. I looked at Relic and said, "I go where she goes." I spun around before he could answer and surrendered myself to the tug of the knife in her boot sheath. My ghostly feet lifted from the ground and I flew after them far more swiftly than I could have run.

A mile up the trail, the wolf slowed to sniff the ground next to a shallow stream. The vegetation here thickened again due to the presence of the water, and I searched the dense foliage in vain for any sign of Blade. Infidel caught up a few seconds later, panting heavily. Even with her strength, running a mile uphill in the furnace-like heat was no easy task.

"I thought you might like a chance to talk," said Menagerie in his wolf-yips. "It's got to be killing you keeping quiet around those assholes."

"It's not all that tough," Infidel said. "It's not like I'm eager to chat with any of them."

"I find Father Ver moderately entertaining," said Menagerie, pausing to take a few laps from the stream. "Have you noticed that he and the Deceiver seem to have exactly the same power? They both say things that aren't true and make them come true."

"Actually," said Infidel, "The Deceiver's power is less creepy. He says things that change himself. The Truthspeaker says things to change others."

"Creepy or not, I could have laughed my ass off when Reeker had to hold his tongue. I went into the wrong line of business with blood magic. I'd trade all my tattoos for the ability to shut Reeker up whenever I wanted to."

"I thought you guys were friends," said Infidel.

The wolf shrugged. "I'm not in a career where it pays to have friends. The people I grow close to have a depressing tendency to die. Reeker and No-Face are my companions chiefly because they've proven themselves as survivors."

Infidel pressed her lips tightly together and swallowed hard.

"You okay?" asked Menagerie.

"Just thinking about Stagger," said Infidel. "He'd still be alive if he hadn't been my friend."

"You can't blame yourself," said Menagerie.

"Can't I?" said Infidel with a feeble grin. "I'd trade Greatshadow's treasure for the chance to go back and do things differently. Sometimes I forget that he's gone, and feel like I'm going to look back over my shoulder and find him standing there, giving me a reassuring smile."

"I'm here!" I shouted, waving my arms. "I'm here!"

"You'll always have his memory, at least."

"Maybe I don't want the memories," she said. "Because, when I do turn around, and see that he's not there, it feels like hands grab my heart and squeeze, and squeeze, and squeeze."

She closed her eyes and clenched her fists, drawing a long, slow, breath.

"It helps some, pretending to be a machine," she said. "To think there's only a mechanical pump in my chest, not a heart. I'd pay any price for a head full of gears instead of memories."

Menagerie sat down, scratching behind his ear with a paw. He took a moment to let Infidel compose herself before he said, "I know it's trite, but time does make the pain go away."

Infidel shook her head. "When I think about the Black Swan in her cobwebbed wedding dress, I wonder if that's true."

"You've never lost anyone close to you before?"

"Stagger's the only one who ever got close," she said. "My mother died when I was thirteen. I was told I should mourn her, but I didn't really feel anything. I was raised by servants; my mother was just this pretty china doll who decorated my father's palace. She barely ever spoke to me. I can't remember the sound of her voice."

"My mother was my world," said Menagerie.

"Was? She passed away?"

"She's still alive. I just don't see her."

"But you used to be close?"

Menagerie looked up and down the trail, as if making sure no one else was listening. Finally, he said, "My mother was a prostitute, sold by her parents to a brothel when she was eleven. She was fourteen when she gave birth to me, and I was swiftly followed by two baby sisters. She gave us the best life she could; stashing away a few coins here and there in the hope that she might one day purchase her freedom and raise us in a better home. From the age I first understood what was going on, I dreamed of having enough money to make her dream come true. I joined a street gang when I was seven and began shoplifting and picking pockets. I committed my first murder at age nine. Got involved in blood magic not long after; by age thirteen, I was running my own gang, and earned enough to send my sisters off to a boarding school. By the time I was sixteen I bought my mother's freedom and set her up in a house with servants."

"That's very noble of you," said Infidel.

The wolf let out a series of low barks that it took me a second to recognize as a bitter chuckle. "Noble is not a label often applied to me. The evidence is before your eyes; I've surrendered to blood magic so completely, I'm no longer fully human. I've killed hundreds of men, too many to count, and am incapable of remorse. My sisters are both married to respectable men and have large families, but I've not seen them in twenty years. I send them the fortunes I earn so that they may live like royalty in the heart of the Silver City, in homes surrounded by high walls and armed guards, specifically to protect them from men like me."

As he finished, he tilted his head. He raised his nose and sniffed the air.

"Blood," he said.

"Whose?" asked Infidel. "Blade's?"

Menagerie leapt across the stream and raised his ears, cocking his head from side to side.

"Do you hear something?" she asked.

"Someone running?" Menagerie said, but he sounded confused. "It might be Blade, except —"

Suddenly, a green-skinned midget shot out from the undergrowth and splashed into the stream. He was naked save for a gourd cod-piece, and bleeding profusely from his neck. He slid to a halt as he saw Menagerie and Infidel. He opened his mouth to scream but only gurgles escaped his lips. His eyes rolled up into his head and he fell face first into the water as blood loss won out over panic.

"Quickly," said Menagerie, leaping into the hole the pygmy had left in the greenery. He bounded along the blood trail, panting as he leapt over logs and boulders. Infidel chased after him, pulling out her long sword to use as a machete. They ran no more than a quarter mile before anguished cries reached them, the sound of men dying.

In their haste, the wolf and Infidel raced right past a cluster of knotted vines laced through with palm fronds. I paused to study it; I knew this sign. It marked the edge of a forest-pygmy clan line. It announced to other pygmies that this area was off limits to all but members of a single extended family. My pygmy knot literacy wasn't fluent, but I think this clan called themselves the Jawa Fruit.

Since the others were well ahead now, I again surrendered myself to the tug of the knife and flew to join Infidel, flowing through trees and rocks as if they weren't even there.

I caught up in seconds. Infidel and Menagerie had stopped. I couldn't see past them at first. I did notice, however, that the ground around them was slick with blood. Beyond them, I could hear more screaming.

"This will come out of our pay for sure," Menagerie grumbled.

I moved to see what he was looking at. I wished I hadn't.

Ivory Blade was slumped up against a rock. At least, what was left of him was. His head was missing from his shoulders. There was a heavy log hanging from vines, swaying back and forth. One end was wet with blood, and worse things. Remnants of white-haired scalp were pressed into the grain of the wood. Infidel had triggered one of these traps by accident a few years ago. Trip over the wrong vine, and suddenly a log swings down like a hammer. Infidel had escaped her trap with a minor headache. Ivory Blade, alas, had popped like a balloon. Despite the gore coating every nearby surface, Blade's Immaculate Attire was still spotless.

"Whisper must be taking revenge," said Menagerie as he tilted his ears toward the screams coming from further upslope. "Sounds like she's tearing through some pygmies."

"Déjà vu," said Infidel. "Still... it's not really their fault. That damned Truthspeaker caused this."

"She'll get to him next," said a voice behind me.

I turned around and there, like a pillar of fog, stood Ivory Blade.

Blade looked down at his wispy form. Blood from his corpse was trickling down the stony ground to form a little pool, and he rose from this pool like steam. He looked at me with sad eyes, shaking his head. "How ironic. As a somnomancer, I always assumed I'd die in my sleep."

"You can see me?" I asked.

"Can you see me?" he asked.

We both nodded. Infidel had no reaction at all to the words being spoken mere inches behind her, but Menagerie turned his head slightly, his ears twitching.

"Hear something?" Infidel asked.

"I... don't think so. Dog ears are so sensitive, they play tricks on me. I'm picking up faint voices, but they must be coming from miles away."

"She's free now," Blade said, his voice trembling. "She was my dream while I was alive. Now, she'll be the world's nightmare."

"What? Who? What's going on?"

"The Whisper," he said, holding his ghostly hands toward the sky, watching the light filter through his ethereal skin. "I died with a heart full of rage. She'll be trapped in this emotion. She'll kill and kill and nothing will ever slake her anger."

"Let's start over," I said. "I'm not following you. I mean, I understand she'll be angry, but —"

"Whisper was my wildest dream, brought back from the land of sleep by my experimentation in somnomancy. Dream magic." he said, his voice sounding choked and tight. "She's a dream creature who pretended to be human to make me happy. She became the living embodiment of my lust and vanity. I've walked in the shadows for so long I grew to love the darkness. Now..." he frowned, the saddest face I've ever seen. "Now I will have nothing but darkness."

He shuddered and the wispy edges of his body began to blur.

"Don't surrender!" I shouted, offering him my hand. "You can stay behind if you hold on to something hard enough."

If he heard me, he didn't respond. The tower of mist no longer looked like a man; then, it didn't even look like mist. All that was left was the pool of blood where he'd stood and the light and shadows of the forest dancing upon it.

I dropped to my knees before the pool of blood. I was desperate to bring him back; until this moment, I hadn't known that I could talk with other ghosts. I plunged my hand into the gore. "Come back," I cried out. "Come back, please!"

Nothing happened. Though my condition was no different than what it had been a moment before, I suddenly felt desperately lonely, like a fallen Wanderer left on a desert island. I was surrounded by the living, but was not a part of them. Were there other ghosts in the world? Or was I the only soul who'd failed to move on? Was I just as much a failure at dying as I had been at living?

I lifted my hand from the blood, expecting it to come away clean. Instead, it was coated red, the warm fluid running down my naked arm. Yet, the drops that fell didn't ripple in the pool below. It wasn't real. It was ghost blood. I smeared it between my fingers and it faded away.

Suddenly, there was a loud canine yelp; I turned and found that Infidel and Menagerie had pressed ahead toward the fight up-trail. Now, a gutted wolf was hurling through the air straight toward me. It tumbled in mid-flight, trailing loops of blue-gray intestine. The wolf crashed into a tree with a sickening wet-meat slap. Menagerie shifted back to human form as he slid to the ground, still gutted. His eyes were glassy as he stared at the gore in his lap. I noticed two bloody prints on his shoulders, about the size of a woman's hands. Infidel?

I flew to her side, tugged by the knife. She stood on a vine-draped stone platform, all that remained of some lost temple. She was surrounded by dead forest-pygmies, but, this time, she wasn't the person who had killed them.

Instead, that was the work of the Whisper. My ghost skin crawled as I saw her. She was no longer an empty hole in space, as she had been when I'd seen her earlier. She was now a creature of flesh, though it wasn't human flesh. Her skin looked as if it had been carved from onyx; her eyes and lips and nails were gems of dazzling ruby. In her left hand was the hilt of a sword, the blade nothing more than a jagged stump. Despite her mineral skin, she moved fluidly as she lunged toward Infidel.

I noticed that fragments of a broken sword lay at Infidel's feet. She was looking down, confused by where the metal had come from. She didn't seem to see the stone demon about to strike her.

The Whisper caught Infidel beneath the chin with a two-handed upper cut that lifted her from her feet and made her lose her grip on her long sword. Infidel fell on her butt as her sword spun in the air. The Whisper caught the sword with a fluid back-swipe, lifted it over her head, then chopped down with a vicious grunt, attempting to cleave Infidel in half. The sword snapped as it crashed into Infidel's skull.

"Ow!" Infidel said, raising her hands to her scalp. She drew her fingers away. No blood.

The Whisper leaned back, howling, shaking her clenched fists at the sky in frustration.

"Leave her alone!" I shouted.

The stone woman spun around, her eyes narrowed into slits as she glared at me.

"She's done nothing to you!" I shouted. "It's the Truthspeaker who you should be pissed off at."

The Whisper growled and leapt toward me. I felt no fear, certain her hands would pass through my ghostly form. Instead, I sucked in air as her ice cold fingers grabbed me by the throat and jerked me from my feet.

She licked my cheek with a tongue rough as sandstone. She whispered in my ear, "A spirit untainted by matter! What a delightful treat! We dream-dwellers feast upon souls, which are too often made foul by the filth of the bodies they cling to. Once I've choked down the Truthspeaker and the others, I'll come back for you as dessert."

She tossed me aside like I weighed no more than a kitten; I suppose, in hindsight, that I don't even weigh that. Then, she bounded from the platform, darting back down the trail. I was very happy at that instant not to be Father Ver. My cheek burned where she'd licked it. It wasn't all that good to be me, either. What had I done to deserve this?

My eyes were caught by movement. Menagerie raised a trembling hand to his neck and touched the jellyfish outlined there. He collapsed into a puddle of quivering, glassy snot. I don't know what he'd thought he'd been reaching for, but I doubted this was it. Then, a heartbeat later, he was once more back in his human form. His guts were back inside his body. There was no sign he'd ever been injured other than the dazed look on his features.

Meanwhile, Infidel was back on her feet, the bone-handled knife in her hand, spinning around, thrusting the blade toward any stray sound. As much as I wanted to stay with her, I did some cold calculations and realized that if I didn't want to become nightmare chow, I needed to get back to Relic and warn him of what was coming down the mountain. He'd been aware of the Whisper earlier; apparently he could see dream-women as easily as ghosts.

I leaned in Relic's direction, picturing him in my mind. *Go!* I thought, and I went. I shot back down the mountain, flashing through trees and blood tangle vine, moving in a straight line unencumbered by the tortuous terrain of the volcanic slope.

I whipped to a stop inches from Relic's burlap covered face.

"Relic!" I shouted.

He winced. *So. The disobedient dead man returns.*

"The Whisper! Nightmare! Kill us all! Dessert!"

Relic sighed. *Calm yourself, Blood-Ghost. You need not try to form sentences. If you will still the turmoil of your thoughts, I will pluck what you wish to tell me from your mind.*

I surrendered all attempts at speaking a coherent warning and allowed the memories of the past five minutes to wash through my mind.

"A nightmare loose in the material realm," said Relic. "This is bad. This is very bad."

Relic looked around. Everyone able-bodied was off in the jungle collecting the scattered gear. Father Ver and Zetetic were left sitting in the center of an enormous footprint.

Relic hobbled toward Father Ver. "Sir, if I may interrupt, you are in great and imminent danger."

Father Ver looked up. He had finished stitching together the Deceiver's torn lips. Despite his hatred for the man, I couldn't help but notice he'd done a clean and competent job. The priest asked, "What are you babbling about?"

"Ivory Blade is dead," said Relic. "The dream-lover he crafted is on her way to take revenge against you. I suggest you call Lord Tower back from his work."

Father Ver stood and looked toward the sky. The knight was nowhere to be seen. He looked at Relic skeptically. He was used to only being told the truth, but I could see he didn't trust Relic. He said, "If there is a danger —"

He never finished his sentence. There was a sudden crash from a nearby bush. A spray of leaves flew out as the Whisper leapt. She cast no shadow; no doubt I was the only person who could see her as she flew with hands outstretched toward the Truthspeaker's neck. Her mouth opened wide, revealing diamond teeth, then wider still, far beyond a human jaw-span, as she prepared to bite out the Truthspeaker's throat.

Relic moved with a speed that proved he wasn't as crippled as he pretended, striking out with his staff, catching the Truthspeaker at the back of the knees. Father Ver was knocked from his feet as the Whisper flew through the space where his throat had just been. She thrust her leg down, catching the priest dead in the center of his face with her stony knee. He gave a sharp cry of pain as he went down hard, blood streaming from his nose.

The Whisper tumbled like an acrobat as she hit the ground, rolling to her feet, spinning around, prepared to leap again at her fallen opponent. Before she left the ground, a small brown bat flitted over the tree tops, diving right for her face. She swung her hand to knock it away, but the bat changed in mid-slap into a water buffalo. The beast dug his horn into her jaw as he slammed into her. They both bounced and rolled into the brush beyond the edge of the clearing.

Clever, thought Relic. *As a bat, he could see her.*

Suddenly, the water buffalo went flying up through the canopy. The Whisper was apparently at least as strong as Infidel, and just as tough if she'd survived a blow like that. Seconds later, she staggered out of the brush, trailing vines. There was enough greenery enveloping her that you could make out her form. She paused a second to tear away the vegetation. She turned back toward Father Ver, only to find that Reeker had run out of the forest to stand between her and the priest.

He sucked in a lungful of air as she dropped the last of the vines. She stepped toward him, a sneer on her ruby lips. Reeker exhaled, a billowy greenish fog that rolled through the air before him, spreading quickly to cover the space where she stood. She was faintly visible as the miasma clung to her. A tendril of the cloud reached me and I quickly retreated. It stank like awful, eye-watering, fetid cheese, after it had been eaten, half-digested, and vomited back up.

Reeker stood with his hands on his hips, looking pleased with his work. His eyes widened as her hand thrust out of the cloud and she jerked his face close to her own.

"A good trick," she said, "assuming I needed to breathe."

The Whisper flung the skunk-man skyward. She stepped from the cloud, coated with pale green droplets of condensation like jade on her onyx skin. Her gaze lowered once more to the Truthspeaker, who by now had risen to his hands and knees. She stepped toward him, only to be intercepted by an iron ball at the end of a chain that caught her in the gut. She folded over, carried backward by the momentum of the blow. No-Face charged out of the brush to pounce on top of the Whisper as she hit the ground. Straddling her, he pounded her face with a chain-draped fist, striking sparks. He struck again, but she opened her jaws to reveal her diamond teeth. She bit down on his fist as he struck.

"Haurrg!" No-Face howled as he jerked his hand away. She'd bitten straight through the chain. His little finger and a fair chunk of the side of his hand were missing. She slapped him where his ear should have been, knocking him off her. He writhed as he clamped his good hand over his mangled fingers. Blood spurted between his knuckles.

The Whisper stood and chuckled as she looked at Father Ver. "Is that the best you have to defend you?" She stalked toward the Truthspeaker. "If you'd like, I'll wait around and finish off the ogress and the knight as well, crushing your hopes one by one. You're going to die, Truthspeaker. There is absolutely nothing you can do about it."

"There is no need to wait," Father Ver said, kneeling before her.

The Whisper raised both hands above her head, knitting her fingers together, then swung with all her might to bash in the priest's skull.

Father Ver lifted his right hand and caught the blow, stopping it with no more effort than he might have spent to catch a drifting leaf. He looked at her with a look of utter calmness and said, "I do not fear you. You are nothing but a dream, and your dreamer is dead."

And then she wasn't there. The stink mist that had clung to her hung in the air for a fraction of a second, then dispersed in the breeze.

A shadow grew on the ground as Lord Tower dropped from the sky, cradling Reeker in his arms. He landed with a *clang,* spinning around swiftly to survey the scene. No-Face still writhed on the ground. Father Ver was on his knees with a bloody nose and a placid look in his eyes.

"What attacked you?" Lord Tower asked.

"Nothing," said Father Ver.

I could see Lord Tower's eyes narrow through the slits in his faceplate. "This is a lot of damage for nothing."

Father Ver nodded. "This nothing mistakenly believed it was something. We won't be bothered further by it. We've lost both Blade and the Whisper, by the way."

"What? How did… how…." he paused, sniffing the air. "By the sacred quill, what is this wretched odor?"

"The scent of victory," said Father Ver. "Without the half-seed's miasma clinging to her, I wouldn't have seen the Whisper about to strike."

"Wait," said Tower. "The Whisper did this?"

Father Ver nodded. "It is good that we culled her out this early. Blade endangered us all with his reckless dabbling in dream magic. Our chances are improved without him." There was no hint of remorse that he'd caused Blade's death with his ill-thought command.

No-Face sat up, cradling his injured hand. "Yurga bunnah juh!"

"He's right," buzzed a hummingbird that hovered into the clearing. The bird flitted closer to Lord Tower, and suddenly Menagerie stood before the knight. The contrast between the two couldn't have been more striking; the tattooed man in nothing but a loin cloth facing the knight encased scalp to sole in spotless armor. "You came here with a team of six and you're three down before we've even gotten close to the dragon. We're professionals; we don't like to work for amateurs."

"That's enough of your insolence," growled Father Ver.

Menagerie opened his mouth to speak, but no sound came out.

Lord Tower said, "Your concerns are noted, but matter little. I've taken a sacred vow to complete this mission. You are free to retreat if you wish, but I must carry on until the dragon is dead, or I am."

Menagerie took a deep breath then said, in a respectful tone, "You have something better than a vow from us. You have a contract. We'll continue on as long as you do."

Tower looked up the slope. "I spotted a stream a short distance from here. We'll make camp there while we continue to gather our gear and tend our wounded. If Blade is dead, we have a burial to perform. Tomorrow we'll press on."

"We're right on the edge of forest-pygmy territory," I said to Relic. "They'll be out for blood after what the Whisper did to them. We should retreat back to the cave."

We have nothing to fear, thought Relic. *Even with these setbacks, we still have the power to kill any pygmy that dares to threaten us.*

"You're right. We'll slaughter them when the come to drive us out, which they will. I've seen enough dead pygmies lately. Let's retreat."

I had no idea you were so tender-hearted, Blood-Ghost. Very well. Relic turned to Lord Tower he said, "I believe we are on the edge of forest-pygmy territory. It would be wise to go back to the cave. We can be assured of our safety there."

Lord Tower shook his head. "We've paid dearly to cover even this small amount of ground. I won't give up the progress we've made."

Relic nodded. "As you wish."

"Where is your War Doll?" Tower asked. "Have we lost her - I mean it - as well?"

I didn't wait for Relic to answer. It struck me that Infidel should have been back by now. I tuned myself to the knife and mentally leaned in its direction, flying to it in the speed of thought.

I found myself once more upon the vine draped platform where I'd left her. She was surrounded by forest-pygmies, easily a hundred of them. To my relief, they weren't fighting her. Instead, they were gathering up the dead. A dozen of them stood around Infidel, holding her at bay with pointy sticks. I knew that Infidel could have easily fought her way out of the situation, but instead she just stood there with her hands in the air.

"Look," she explained, in a calm voice. "I didn't do this. I've got no grudge against you. Just put down the sticks. You're only going to hurt yourself."

"Ugamadebasda!" the lead pygmy shouted. "Ugamadebasda!" Every forest-pygmy tribe had its own dialect; I could understand most east-slope pygmies, but these west-slope pygmies slurred all the syllables of a sentence together into a single word, which made it tricky to follow. Still, from the general tone I gathered he was saying, "Shut up and keep your hands up."

"I don't speak the lingo, guys," said Infidel. "I do know a little river-pygmy. Nanda chaka? Gratan doy bro?" Her accent was atrocious. She probably meant to ask if anyone knew river-pygmy, but instead she was asking if anyone had a canoe in their mouth. It didn't matter; the forest-pygmies didn't seem to understand her anyway.

She sighed. "I'm not getting of here without hurting a lot of you, am I?"

"I think there's been enough hurting here today," said a man's voice from high in the trees above. The speaker used the crisp, finely enunciated syllables of a Silver Isle accent; it could have been Lord Tower speaking, except the voice wasn't as deep or forceful. "Are you responsible for this slaughter?"

"Not me," said Infidel. "There was this invisible woman who went crazy and, uh… hell, that's just not believable at all is it?"

"Not terribly," said the voice above.

Infidel shrugged. "If I was any good at lying, I'd make up something. But, there really was an invisible woman. She cracked a few swords over my head as well. I'm not here to hurt anyone."

The branches above rustled. Suddenly, a patch of green, the color of moss, lowered down toward the platform on a slowly descending loop of vine. It was no pygmy. It was an elderly man of normal stature, wearing only the same gourd cod-piece as the pygmies, his skin dyed green. He was all bones and skin, his flesh covering his thin limbs like aged leather. His hair was a few long green strands braided down the back of his scalp. His eyes were a sharp and penetrating blue.

"Who are you?" he asked, as his vine brought him to the platform.

"Who are you?" Infidel answered.

The old man scowled, then cocked his head, as if he was searching for some bit of information just beyond his grasp. "It's been a while since anyone asked that question. The jawa fruit tribe calls me Tenoba. It means old long gourd. Among your people, my name… my name was…"

He paused, trying to remember how to say the words. It didn't matter. I knew what he was about to say before he said it.

A light flickered in his ancient eyes. "My name," he said, "was Judicious Merchant."

13 - ENOUGH

I WAS TOO stunned by my grandfather being alive to closely follow the swirl of activity that unfolded. A wounded pygmy at the edge of the platform verified that they had, indeed, been attacked by something invisible, and confirmed that Infidel hadn't hurt anyone. Forest-pygmy scouts were rushing up, telling about the fight further down slope, and how a group of long-men had killed the invisible assassin. I would have focused more on what they were saying, but I was too busy doing math in my head. My father had me when he was twenty-three. Judicious had been twenty-five when he sired Studious. So… that meant the man standing before me was 98.

For a man two years shy of a century, he looked pretty good. He still had all his teeth, for starters, even if they were the same jade hue as the rest of him. When he moved, he was as fluid as a jungle cat, without a hint of the stiffness or weakness that hampered most people his age. There wasn't an ounce of fat on him; his wrinkled leather skin sat atop wiry muscles so sharply defined you could have taught an anatomy class using them. Of course, I was seeing more of that anatomy than I truly wanted to. It's one thing to discover your long lost grandfather is still alive. It's another thing entirely to learn he's a grass-colored nudist with his privates stuffed into a dried fruit.

"I knew your grandson, Stagger," said Infidel.

Grandpa frowned.

"His real name was Abstemious Merchant."

I winced on hearing my birth name. I must have been really drunk to have told her. Abstemious means someone with control of his appetites… perhaps my father's lapse on his vow of celibacy inspired the choice. Stuck with this moniker, it was only a matter of time before I became an incurable drunkard.

My grandfather frowned even deeper. "I'm sorry," he said. "I've had seven wives. My children have produced scores of grandchildren. I'm afraid the name isn't triggering any memories."

The words were like a slap in the face. I'd revered this man. I lived on the Isle of Fire in imitation of his greatness. He didn't even remember my name?

Infidel produced the bone-handled knife. "You gave him this when he was ten."

My grandfather took the blade, sliding it in and out of the sheath. He scowled as he saw the dried blood smeared along the metal. "He didn't take care of it. It's dirty."

"He took great care of it," said Infidel. "He kept it clean and sharp for forty years. If it's dirty, it's my fault."

"Hmm." Suddenly, a light flickered in his blue eyes. "I remember this knife. The handle was carved from the tibia of a dragon."

Or so he thought. He'd told me this when he gave me the knife, but one of the monks who specialized in the study of anatomy had assured me the bone was merely that of a bull. But, what if the monk had been wrong? If the hilt truly was dragon-bone, could the magic that infused dragons explain how my spirit had become ensnared by the knife?

As Judicious turned the knife over in his hands, he nodded slowly, as if he were accepting the memories flooding back to him. "I had a son who became a monk. Studious, I think? He had a bastard child raised in an orphanage. That was Abstemious?"

"Yes."

Grandfather grinned. "I recall him now. Bright kid. Voracious reader. He became a monk?"

"He became you," said Infidel. "Or, at least his dream of you. He was an explorer, a scholar, and a storyteller. No one knew more than him about the ruins of the Vanished Kingdom. He lived in your old boat in Commonground."

"I notice you're speaking in the past tense."

Infidel nodded.

Grandfather sighed. "I outlive many of my relatives." He looked down the slope, in the direction of Tower's party. "I suppose, if you're friends of the family, I should show a little hospitality. Go tell your companions they're welcome to stay the night in our huts."

"I'm not sure they'll take you up on the offer," said Infidel. "The leader of the party is kind of snooty."

"Still, extend the offer."

Infidel nodded. "If they accept, you need to know that I'm pretending to be a machine. I don't talk around them."

"Ah," said Grandfather. "I wondered why you were dyed silver. I thought it might be some new fashion. You fooled me, by the way. When I first saw you from the trees, I mistook you for one of the ancient engines, and wondered how you were still intact. You reminded me of a mechanical dancer I once excavated. A lovely, wondrous thing, though I never found her head. The clockwork that used to drive her had long-since corroded, but I'm still left breathless by the cleverness of the men who once lived on this island."

THE PYGMY HUTS were better described as tree houses. I'd never been in one before, though I'd caught sight of them often enough. The floor of the forest can be a quiet place; the real action is unfolding high above in the canopy.

Here, the forest-pygmies had woven together seemingly endless ropes from blood-tangle vines and strung them together in a complex network of swinging bridges. Houses were built with floors of dense netting spread from branch to branch, with roofs of still living vines and branches woven together overhead. The floors seemed solid enough when the pygmies flitted across them, but once Lord Tower began to carry the party up to the huts, the platforms sagged ominously beneath the weight. The floor weavers had probably never planned for someone as large as Aurora to visit. No-Face swiftly moved toward the thick trunk of the tree that formed one corner of a large communal area and wrapped his chain around it, with his good arm still coiled in the links. It was hard to read the mood of a man who didn't have expressions, but I got the distinct impression he didn't like heights.

The forest-pygmies seemed especially wary of Aurora. None dared look directly at her, though behind her there was a crowd of small green people pointing and gawking.

"The blue tint of your skin makes them think you're some sort of oddly sized river-pygmy," Grandfather said. "The river-pygmies work with the slavers, so they're wary."

Aurora took a seat near the edge of the netting, looking out over the lush forest. She didn't seem bothered by the sagging floor or the drop off. "Since I left the north, I've gotten used to people being cautious around me," she said. "At home, I was a runt and a weakling. If not for being born with the mark of a shaman, I doubt they would have fed me as a child."

Zetetic stayed as close to the center of the floor as possible. I remembered his reaction when he'd first arrived in the cave. Apparently, No-Face wasn't alone in his acrophobia. Yet, though Zetetic clung to the woven floor with white-knuckles, his voice was curiously enthusiastic as he said, "Mr. Merchant, I've read everything you ever wrote about the Vanished Kingdom. The world lost quite a scholar when you vanished."

Father Ver glowered as Zetetic spoke, ready to pounce if the Deceiver attempted anything. Reeker also kept his gaze fixed on the man, no doubt intent not to be taken by surprise again.

My grandfather seemed unaware of the tension in the air. He dismissed Zetetic's compliment with a shrug. "The world lost nothing. I've come to understand that scholarship has very little to do with actual knowledge. In the world I grew up in, knowledge was something found chiefly in books. It was information that gets passed on as scribbled marks on paper. When I first started exploring this land, I wrote down everything I learned, because that seemed like a validation. It was as if nothing I was doing mattered until I committed it to paper."

"It's the echo of the divine that makes you feel this," said Lord Tower. He had never actually landed on the platform; instead, he was hovering a few inches above the netting, perhaps worried about adding his weight to the already strained vines. "When we write, we imitate, in our own pale way, the original act of creation."

Grandfather chuckled. "You're my guests, so I'll say this as respectfully as possible: books aren't real. I mean, yes, books as physical objects exist, but they contain no reality or truth within them."

"Have a care," said Father Ver. "Your words venture dangerously close to the heresy of the Deceivers."

"No," said Grandfather. "The Deceivers think that everything is a lie. Reality itself is a fiction, which clever men are free to rewrite."

"Actually —" said Zetetic.

Grandfather kept talking, ignoring the interruption. "The Deceivers are wrong, as is the Church of the Book. Neither accept the obvious truth: the only thing that defines the world is the world itself. Reality is the tree we sit in; it's the sun on your face, the evening breeze, the bitter burst of jawa fruit on the tongue. The things we write in books are only daydreams and memories, mental constructs pleasant and useful, but not real. By the time a man writes of an experience, that experience is forever gone. The past vaporizes behind us; the future is devoured voraciously by the present. It is only in the now that we are alive. The physical world surrounding us is the only truth." He looked out over the green mountain, toward the azure sea. "It is... enough."

"Bah," said Father Ver with a dismissive wave. "These are the pointless musings of the spiritually weak. The here-and-now is but a trap; the pleasure of the moment seduces men from contemplation of larger truths. Feeble-minded youth sometimes fall prey to the desire to glamorize the now, but I'm disappointed a man of your advanced age has made this error. Look around you, old man. You live in a bug-infested tree, among primatives who don't even know how to make clothing. Without accepting a greater spiritual truth, man can be nothing more than another beast."

Grandfather smiled as he looked at the leaves above him. He lifted up his skinny arm and snatched a bright green katydid from the nearest branch. The insect was perfectly blended with its surroundings, but my grandfather seemed to have spotted it effortlessly. "You call them bugs," he said. He popped the leggy creature into his mouth and crunched down. "We call them snacks."

During this philosophical debate, a stream of pygmy women had been flowing onto the vine platform across the rope bridges, carrying dark green leaves the size of dinner trays. And, dinner trays were precisely what they were. A buffet was laid out on the floor; bright blue jawa fruit adorned one leaf, plump white maggots writhed on another. There were speckled eggs the size of grapes, dark red snails the size of oranges, and at least a dozen kinds of nuts, half of which I didn't recognize. One leaf held what looked like raw meat, chopped and ground to a paste. Nothing looked cooked.

"There's no formality here. Dig in," said Grandfather, snatching up a snail and a jawa fruit. "Since we live in trees, we don't built fires." He squeezed the fruit and the bright blue juice sluiced through his fingers and into the snail shell. "Fortunately, jawa juice is acidic enough that it effectively cooks most meat. Your *civilized* guts won't suffer."

Father Ver looked aghast as Grandfather sucked the snail out of its shell, giving it a tug as the last of the meat fought to hold onto its casing. The coil of pale flesh smacked into his lips before it disappeared into his mouth. Grandfather lay back on the floor-net, looking up at the sun-dappled branches. "Eat meat while it still has life in it. Keep fruit in your belly and sun on your skin. Sleep when you are tired and drink when you are thirsty. This is all a man needs to enjoy a long life."

"There are elderly among the civilized as well," said Father Ver. "Your recipe for life will not keep you alive a single day longer than the span the Divine Author has recorded for you in the book."

Grandfather scratched the dark green pubic hair around his gourd, seemingly unconcerned that anyone was watching. "You are free to think what you wish. I wouldn't trade my life for the wealth of a king. I live in the eternal moment, while a civilized man worries only about tomorrow, or longs for yesterday."

While Grandfather and the Truthspeaker sparred, Menagerie dug into the food with gusto, not bothering with the fruits, just tearing into the raw meat directly. Reeker was more dainty, picking through the nuts and berries and less wriggly-looking insects. He carried a leaf full of food over to No-Face, who squeezed the fruits and bugs into a colorful mush, which he slurped loudly from his palm into a fold beneath his face-flap.

The Deceiver went straight for the nastiest looking dish, a sort of chopped spider salad laced with bright green chilies. He washed it down with a freshly opened coconut, the pale milk spilling down the corners of his damaged mouth.

"Doesn't the spice hurt the cuts in your mouth?" Reeker asked, still keeping a close eye on the man.

Zetetic shrugged. "I've learned to enjoy pain. Plus, I've always had a sense of adventure in my diet. In my travels, I've been delighted by the different attitudes regarding what one is supposed to put in one's mouth. One man's spoiled milk is another man's cheese. Some men hunt with dogs, others eat them in stews. What half the world believes is true about food, the other half thinks is false. It's left me with an open mind and a daring stomach. I'll put anything in my mouth at least once."

Neither Lord Tower nor Father Ver made any move toward the dishes.

"Aren't you hungry?" asked Grandfather.

"We have our own provisions," Tower answered. "It would be a sin for me to partake in this food. Your people live in such poverty."

Infidel's eyes kept flickering toward the buffet. All the earlier excitement had probably built up her appetite, but she did an admirable job of just standing at attention, her face devoid of obvious longing.

"I assume you'll see she gets fed later," I said to Relic, who had a fist-full of maggots.

Of course, he answered, as he shoved one of the plump larvae into the shadows beneath his hood. *We have all the details planned out. You need not worry for her comfort.*

Meanwhile, Grandfather had responded to Lord Tower. "Poverty? What poverty? None among us are hungry. We all have a safe place to sleep in the company of our family. There is not a single physical need we go without."

"You dwell in spiritual poverty, separated from the Church," said Father Ver.

Zetetic said, with a mouthful of spiders, "Why do you have to be such a jerk, Ver? Show a little graciousness for a fellow who's giving us a roof to sleep under." He glanced up at the leaves. "So to speak."

"I'm not bothered by his attitude," said Grandfather, as Father Ver eyed the Deceiver with a murderous gaze. "It's nice to be reminded of all I left behind. Which I suppose leads to the question, why are you here? You didn't come looking for me. You're too heavily armed for tomb raiding. Are you going after Greatshadow?"

"Yes," said Lord Tower. "King Brightmoon has decided to rid the world of his tyranny."

"I don't think tyranny is the word you're looking for," said Grandfather.

"I chose the word with precision," said Tower. "The dragon has crushed every attempt to colonize this island. He's shown nothing but hatred toward humanity. We must destroy him now, before he one day destroys the world."

Grandfather smiled softly. He said, "If he hates humanity so much, why does our tribe live in peace in his very shadow? Presumably, he could kill us at any time. He could daily scour the slopes of this island with lava. Nothing at all could grow here. It would be as dead as the Silver Isle."

"You know nothing of the Silver Isle, sir," said Tower. "I've flown from shore to shore; there is no inch of it I have not witnessed. It's a lovely, green land, an emerald jewel amid the vast dark sea."

"Green, yes," said Grandfather. "Green with crops and orchards, grape arbors and olive groves. The hills are lush with grass, planted so that cattle may graze. Well-tended oak trees still decorate the gardens of wealthy men. But, at no point when you flew over the island did you find a forest, or any wild thing. Men murdered the Silver Isle, then decorated the corpse with flowers. It doesn't compare to the untamed beauty of the Isle of Fire."

"We are of a different opinion," said Tower.

"Again, I must disagree. I have an opinion. You have narrow-minded dogma." Grandfather paused for a second to squeeze jawa juice into a second snail. "Greatshadow is no tyrant. Is the sun a tyrant when drought kills crops in the field? Is the stream a tyrant when it overruns its banks and floods a village? Greatshadow is merely an aspect of nature, the embodiment of fire. You civilized men need fire to cook your meals and forge your swords. You bring it into your homes to survive the winter, and your fields would be unmanageable if you didn't burn them at the start of each planting season. To wage war against the natural world is madness."

"Nonsense," said Lord Tower, speaking calmly. Unlike Father Ver, he didn't seem angered by Grandfather's bluntness. "It isn't waging war against a stream to build a dam to control flooding. We don't wound the earth by digging into it with plows. As you must know, there was once a primal dragon of the forest. The church defeated him after a long struggle, banishing his spirit. Yet, all around you is evidence that trees have endured. We didn't wage war against the forest; we waged war against an unholy spirit that had laid an unjust claim to an elemental force. The same is true of Greatshadow. When he is gone, we'll still have flames in our foundries and candles in our homes. They'll simply be free of his all-watching eye."

"You're not the first to come this way, you know," said Grandfather. "Every generation sends a team of men against the beast. Every generation fails."

"You've met previous parties?" Zetetic asked. "Do you know the fate of the Castlebridge expedition?"

Grandfather nodded. "I believe you are referring to the two-hundred soldiers who hacked their way up the mountain almost twenty years ago."

Zetetic nodded. "My father was with the expedition. We know the Wanderers delivered them safely to landfall. After this, they simply vanished from the face of the earth."

"Into the face of the earth is more accurate," said Grandfather. "Their ashes are no doubt well-mingled with the soil by now. Lava-pygmies witnessed it all. Greatshadow sent out his avatars as they were halfway up the slope. All flesh was burned away. The armor they wore turned to slag amid a field of blackened glass. It was a horrible scar upon the earth for all of a month; the jungle has long since swallowed all evidence of their passing."

"He attacked Commonground with two of these avatars," said Menagerie. "They were enough to get the job done, but I still wonder, does he have limits? Could he have created a dozen if he wished? If he animates these forms with his spirit, does his spirit weaken as he divides himself? No magic comes without a price. Blood magic costs a man his humanity, dream magic withers men's souls, the Deceivers pay for their powers with their sanity." Zetetic opened his mouth to dispute this, but Menagerie finished by saying, "Elemental magic can't be an exception. The dragon must have some weakness."

"True," said Grandfather. "For the primal dragons, the price they pay for their elemental magic seems to be their sense of identity. A dragon's mind is no more infinite than a man's mind. Rott, the primal dragon of decay, spread his essence so thinly that he hasn't been seen to manifest himself in a body for centuries. No one knows if he even remembers that he was once a dragon. However, Greatshadow has avoided this fate. He maintains his original body, feasting, sleeping, and fornicating; his sense of identity is in no real danger."

"Fornicating?" Zetetic asked, with a raised eyebrow. "Wouldn't this require another dragon?"

"You've already witnessed his ability to create avatars."

"But they're part of him. Wouldn't they...?"

Grandfather shrugged. "According to pygmy lore, he can create avatars with female aspects. I assume he enjoys the act of mating from both his original body and his second form."

Zetetic's face brightened. "That seems to be a fantastically practical —"

"Perversion!" snapped Father Ver. "All the more reason to kill the depraved beast."

"Just because you don't let yourself have any fun is no reason to be angry with the dragon," said Zetetic.

"Let him be angry if he wishes," said Grandfather. "It won't matter to Greatshadow. You've witnessed his power. I'm sure you wouldn't have come to this island if you didn't have some tricks up your sleeve. A flying knight, a shapeshifter, an ice-ogress; I admire Brightmoon's imagination in assembling this team. But, in the end, if you continue toward the dragon's lair, you will die. Even if ice-magic and enchanted armor can protect you from the heat of Greatshadow's breath, he's still in possession of claws harder than diamond that can shred steel like tissue paper."

"My armor is made of something more enduring than steel," said Lord Tower.

"So what if it is?" said Grandfather. "Odds are, you won't even face the dragon. Greatshadow has had centuries to perfect his magic. It's said he's populated his lair with guardians summoned from abstract realms. The most powerful magical artifacts that survive from the Vanished Kingdom are his to command; you cannot even imagine the forces he may throw against you. And while you may enter his lair in possession of some secret plan to beat the beast, it will all be for naught. The pygmies say that Greatshadow's mind spreads so completely through his lair that a visitor's thoughts will become the dragon's thoughts. First, he will strip your mind of all its secrets. Then, he will pour his mind into your bodies, and you will dance for him like puppets on strings."

The Goons and Aurora looked sobered by this recitation of the challenges before them. Relic, of course, remained an enigma beneath his rags. Zetetic's mouth was puckered with pain, but that was probably from the hot peppers. Lord Tower's eyes looked unconcerned; perhaps he already knew all the dangers they faced.

Father Ver's lips were turned up into something almost resembling a smile.

Zetetic took note. "Perhaps I'm not the only one here who enjoys pain."

Father Ver shook his head. "I'm merely thinking that the beast has had centuries to become overconfident. Think of Numinous, brought low by a mere decade in which to grow arrogant. No doubt, the beast's soul is rotten to the core from believing his own lies. Perhaps we've reached the page in the One True Book where he falls before the greater truth."

"Amen," said Tower, slapping the Gloryhammer against his gauntleted palm with a true-believer's fervor.

No one else echoed his sentiment. Instead, everyone sat quietly, staring down at their food as they contemplated their fates. The only sound was the *slup, slup, slup* of No-Face eating.

14 - Heart to Heart

THAT NIGHT, AS everyone else slept spread out on woven platforms across the tree village, Infidel stepped down onto a thick branch. Relic stirred from his sleep and held out a leather sack the size of a saddlebag. She took the bag and climbed down the vine-draped trunk in silence. When she reached the ground, she followed a trail to the nearby stream, then followed this to a large pool. Looking around to make certain no one was watching, she shed her clothes and plunged in. Her body gleamed beneath the water's surface like a silver-skinned fish darting about. She surfaced with a gasp, rubbing her face, ridding herself of the sweat of the day. Whatever dye Menagerie had used wasn't smeared by her fingers. Now that she was wet, the illusion that her skin was metal was especially strong.

After only a moment in the pool, she rose from the water and opened the sack, producing a rolled up towel. Wrapped within it were fresh jawa fruits and several of the snails. She gobbled them down as she dried her hair. Mosquitoes crawled over her arms and legs, denting their noses on her impenetrable skin. She paid no attention to them as she finished off the snails in record time. She wiped her mouth then leaned over the pool, looking at her faint reflection in the still water. Her face went slack as she studied herself. Her eyes had a distant focus, as if she wasn't watching her reflection but was, instead, lost in memory.

She looked, if you will forgive the expression, haunted.

Was I causing psychic harm by sticking around? Did she sense me watching her and feel guilt? Should I leave and spare her any further pain? Could I leave if I tried?

My musings were cut short by Relic's voice in my head.

Return to me.

"I'm busy," I said.

Return to me!

The command felt like a thousand fishhooks tearing into my brain. He reeled me in as I flopped about. Fortunately, my agony was short lived, halting the second I stood before him. He was curled up on the netting, completely still; to anyone else he would have looked asleep. I saw the bone-handled knife clutched securely in his gnarled claw.

"I don't like being pushed around," I said.

We have our bargain.

"Do we? I agreed to watch Tower and the others. I don't remember signing on to be your slave."

And yet, you aren't watching Tower.

"He's probably asleep," I said.

I am certain he is not. He and Father Ver are outside the range of my mental powers, but I can still hear the murmurs of their voices on the night breeze. Go and listen to their conversation.

He shoved me with his mind out into the open air beside the central tree house. Tower and Father Ver slept separated from the rest of the rabble on a platform a good fifty yards distant. Apparently, Relic's telepathy didn't extend terribly far. The knight and the cleric had hung sheets of canvas for privacy. A glorystone cast their shadows on the cloth walls. I misted straight through the canvas into their room. To my surprise, Tower had shed his armor. For some reason, I'd expected him to sleep in it. If they monks could pray that the armor be invulnerable in battle, couldn't they also make it pillow soft come bedtime?

Out of his armor, Tower looked... ordinary. Not average, by any means, but nothing like the iron-clad warrior feared by evil-doers everywhere. Rumors of terrible scars proved unfounded. The few nicks and divots around his eyes and lips testified he'd taken a few hits over the years, but the scars were hardly disfiguring. If anything, they gave character to a face so symmetrical it was boring. He had a square jaw and a nose that jutted from his face at a perfect 30 degree angle. His black hair was cut in a bowl style that would have been unflattering on almost any other head. Here, it served to draw attention to the sharp lines of his cheek bones and his pale gray eyes. The only person I'd ever met who shared this eye color was Infidel.

Save for stray silver hairs, he had the appearance of a man in his early thirties, though, if I understood the chronology of Infidel's life, he must be closer to my age.

He was dressed in a simple linen shirt and tight-fitting cotton pants that showed off his muscular legs. He was kneeling by the side of the platform, his head bowed to touch the floor. I drew closer just in time to hear his whispered prayers come to an end. He closed his supplication to the Divine Author with, "... and grant me the wisdom to tell lust from love, desire from devotion. Amen."

It seemed like a prayer most men would find handy, though I was a little surprised lust was high on Lord Tower's list of concerns. He rose, a little closer to the edge of the sagging platform than most men would find comfortable. Perhaps he spent so much time flying with the Gloryhammer he'd lost all fear of heights. I wondered where the legendary weapon was. Or the armor; it should have made quite a pile once it was off him. Not to mention the Immaculate Attire, which they'd removed before they buried Blade. For that matter, where was the Jagged Heart? There still was no evidence that Tower had the harpoon.

Father Ver was sitting nearby, also kneeling, his head beaded with sweat. He was stripped from the waist up, his robes bunched around his hips. Before him lay a two-foot-long braid of leather. I drifted around behind him and saw bright red welts raised among the constellation of scabs along his back.

Tower pulled a small leather notebook from the waistband of his pants. This was the book Zetetic had taken. As he flipped through the pages, he said, softly, "There's no point in blaming yourself. Blade was the one who chose to dabble in dream magic. You couldn't have known."

"We both know that isn't true," Father Ver said, closing his eyes. "I could have known." His voice sounded wet and raspy, as if he'd been crying. "I've made too many bad bargains. My pursuit of the greater good has forced me to accept the unacceptable. Ten thousand years of lashings can never erase the harm I've done to my soul by agreeing to these compromises."

"The Divine Author would not have given you these trials if he did not feel you could endure them," said Tower. "I need you, Ver. You're the wisest man I've ever known. I wouldn't have accepted this mission without you on the team. But you'll be of no use to me if you're too paralyzed by guilt to do the job."

"I have no guilt," said Father Ver. "Undeserved guilt is a form of self-deception. Instead I feel shame, regret, and anger."

"Well, try to work on those," said Tower dismissively, looking away from the holy man and gazing out of the jungle. "I'm going to go get a little fresh air."

Without warning he pitched forward and dropped off the edge. We were a hundred feet up. He hadn't struck me as suicidal. I drifted over the lip of the platform. A light suddenly sparked below, casting shadows upward. I looked down and saw the Gloryhammer in Tower's right hand; the small notebook was still in his left. His forearm bulged as he gripped the glowing weapon and shot off through the trees, deftly avoiding vines and trunks. I followed, though I didn't need to follow far. A knot formed in the pit of my stomach as I realized where he was heading. The night went dark again as his feet touched down and the Gloryhammer suddenly disappeared. I blinked as I caught up to him. What had he done with the hammer? Could he simply summon it at will? He stuck the notebook back into the waistband of his britches.

The mystery of the missing hammer was the least of my concerns. Tower had flown directly to the pool, landing barely five yards in front of Infidel, who still perched on the rock, buck naked. Her eyes were wide with shock. She had one arm across her breasts and the towel draped over her lap. Tower dropped to one knee before her and bowed deeply.

"Princess Innocent," he said, in a voice just above a whisper. "Praise be to the Divine Author that you are still alive."

"Ummm..." said Infidel. She furrowed her brow. "Hmm."

"I presume you wear this disguise because you fear retribution from the church," he said. "You have nothing to fear, my princess. The king has long since used his influence to revoke the sentence of death placed upon you in absentia. Given the unmistakable perfection of your lineage, the Voice of the Book agreed that a proper trial was in order before any punishment is decided."

Infidel bit her lower lip. She opened her mouth as if to say something, then closed it again. I couldn't tell if she was still maintaining the ruse that she was a machine, or if she just didn't know what to say.

Tower continued: "When you disappeared on our wedding day, I suspected you were kidnapped by one of my political enemies. My investigation eventually led to Lord Claypot. He possessed some magic that confounded the Truthspeakers, but I had him tortured until he confessed the plot. Alas, he expired before I learned the full details of the events of that fateful day fourteen years, seven months, and nine days ago."

Infidel continued to silently stare at the knight.

"I did discover that you had escaped, but were in hiding because you feared retribution from the small segment of fanatics within the Church of the Book who blame you for the destruction. I assure you, I will protect you from them with all my powers. You were a pure and chaste young woman untainted by any hint of wickedness. I'm certain of your innocence and trust you have the best of reasons for not returning home after you escaped from your captors."

"Well, yeah," she said, rolling her eyes. "Like, this 'pure and chaste young woman' crap. What the hell? If my father's spies are even halfway competent, you have to know I support myself primarily by killing people for money. Don't you think, maybe, just maybe, I don't exactly fit the definition of pure?"

"I, too, have killed men," said Tower. "Yet, my heart is pure. Motives matter when judging actions. You've done what you must to survive."

"Motives?" Infidel shook her head sadly. "You idiot. My number one motive was to get away from you!"

"Bu... but... but..." Tower's face fell as her words sank in.

"Turn around," said Infidel. "Did you have to wait until I was naked to have this little heart to heart?"

Tower turned around. "I didn't know you'd be naked. Since I knew you were in the area, I had the Gloryhammer guide me to you. It was poor timing that you are unrobed. I promise I haven't seen anything. I kept my eyes toward the ground."

"'I promise I haven't seen anything,'" Infidel said in a mocking tone. She jumped from the rock and grabbed her pants. "By the sacred quill! You're still the same simpering bore. I wouldn't expect you to know this, but some women are actually flattered by the idea that men want to look at them. When we were engaged, I couldn't even get eye contact. You acted like holding my hand before marriage might get us sent to hell! I used to have nightmares that you'd show up in our wedding bed with full plate armor, a blind-fold, and a pair of tongs."

She pulled up her pants, buttoning them hastily, getting one of the buttons out of order, so that the leather sat on her hips at an odd angle. She turned around and found the steel bra she'd been wearing, pulling free the cotton slip inside. "If you've known since the damned cave who I really was, you should have said something so I could get out of this damned metal bra. My nipples are killing me!"

She spun back to face him, preparing to pull on the slip, and jumped slightly when she found Tower standing only inches from her. He was staring at her with fire in his eyes.

"You dreamed..." he said, breathing heavily, "of our wedding night? Don't you think I had such dreams as well?"

She didn't get a chance to answer. He suddenly grabbed her by both arms and pressed his mouth to hers. Her eyes bulged as he pulled her to him, pressing her still naked breasts against his chest. He worked his lips against hers for a long moment. I watched in gruesome anticipation, certain that at any moment Infidel would decapitate this lustful fool. But, to my growing horror, she didn't move a muscle. She let him kiss her for five seconds, ten, a minute, as her eyes stayed wide open. Finally, she pushed him away, with frustrating gentleness.

"Ooookay," she said, pausing to wipe her lips with the back of her hand. "Let's stop for a minute. I've spent fifteen years avoiding assassins sent after me by the Church of the Book. I'm telling you point blank that I found you boring beyond all imagination when we were engaged. Can you understand I might be a little confused that you show up fifteen years later finally wanting to kiss?"

"I want much more than a kiss," Tower growled, pulling her against his chest once again. He looked down into her eyes. "When you were young, I found you utterly uninteresting. I was a battle-hardened warrior who'd traveled the world. You were a spoiled child, completely ignorant of life beyond the palace gates. You did nothing to stir my baser passions. But you...

you are no longer sweet, virginal, Innocent. You're a warrior with blood on her hands. Indeed, not just on your hands… you have a dragon's blood pumping in your very veins. Having witnessed your strength, I know that rumor that you consumed Verdant's blood must be true."

"You know I could crush your head like an eggshell?"

"Yes! Whatever the reasons for your actions, you are now the perfect match for my passion! I am a man of fiery needs. You will find no plate mail or tongs in our wedding chamber. There will only be an endless bed covered in the finest silk, upon which we will crawl and scream and bite and scratch! We shall smother each other with our lust! The earth will tremble as I hammer you with my —"

"Whoah!" said Infidel, raising a finger to his lips. "Calm down."

He closed his lips over her finger and shut his eyes. He let loose a moan of pleasure as he sucked her slender digit.

"Nnyarg!" I cried out, gripping my ghost hair, tugging with all my might. This was the most horrible thing I'd seen in my entire life - you know what I mean - and there was nothing I could do to stop it. Nor could I turn away. My traitorous eyes remained fixed on the lustful display. Tower ran his hands along Infidel's bare back as he embraced her tightly. Why wasn't she stopping this?

"Wow," she said, pulling her finger free, then pushing him with her other hand. She spun around, swiftly pulling on her slip. "So… wow. Wow. I, uh, I really don't know what to say, Tower."

"What is there to say?" I shouted at her. "Tear his lips off!"

"Just say that you want to surrender to me," said Tower, coming up behind her, wrapping his arms around her waist. "Say that you long for me with all your heart —" he lowered his lips to her ear and finished in a whispered growl "- and all your body."

He blew gently on her ear. She shivered, gently raising her hands to his, before peeling them away and putting a little space between them.

She didn't look at him as she said, "It's funny you should show up now."

"It's destiny. All things unfold according to the One True Book. We parted so that we each could grow, to become the perfect match for the other."

"Yeah," she said, crossing her arms. "I mean, no. I mean, look, I don't know what I mean. Lately, I've spent a fair amount of time thinking of how to get back to a life of royalty. Then, boom, here you are, telling me you can make it happen. And, I have to say, if I'd seen this level of interest from you fifteen years ago, maybe things might have played out differently. But you can't just show up and start slobbering all over me. What the hell ever happened to courtship?"

Tower dropped to his knees once more. He grabbed her hand, cupping it with both palms in a prayerful pose and said, "If it's courtship you desire, I promise you romance beyond your imagination. I shall fly to the moon and carve your portrait to decorate the night sky. I shall part the sea and pluck pearls from the depths. I will search every corner of the world for flowers and perfumes and silks to adorn your bedroom. You will wear a wedding dress spun from pure gold, beaded with priceless gems from Greatshadow's treasure. The entire world will —"

"I get the idea," said Infidel, again silencing him with a finger on his lips, then snatching the finger back as his lips parted. "How about cake? Would you go get me a slice of cake?"

"For you, my love, anything," he vowed.

"Make it chocolate."

Ten seconds of silence passed as she looked down at him. Tower furrowed his brow. "Right now?"

"Why not now?"

"We... um... we're in the middle of a jungle. The nearest town is Commonground and it's in ruins. At top speed, I would need a full day to fly back to the Silver Isle to find a baker."

"So... no cake."

Tower frowned. Then, he said, in utter seriousness. "If... if you demand it, I will go."

She shrugged. "I guess I can wait."

"Thank you," he said.

She leaned back against a tree and took a second to fix her miss-buttoned pants. "So you saw right through my disguise. What about the Father Ver?"

"I don't know why he accepts that you are a machine. It doesn't matter, in the end. If he suspected the truth, he'd have already ordered that I apprehend you and secure you until a trial could be held."

"Would you?"

Tower looked like he wished he'd left for the cake.

His features sagged as he looked to the ground.

"I would have no choice but to obey Ver's direct command," he said. "Even without his powers."

Infidel placed a hand on his shoulder. "You know, I kind of like that. I mean, five minutes ago you were a lust-crazed teenager. Now, you're a knight with a sense of duty and honor. Somewhere between these extremes is my idea of a pretty good man."

"No!" I shouted. "No, no, no, no, no!"

The faintest ghost of a smile flickered across her lips as he gently kissed the back of her hand.

"Thank you for understanding," he said.

She shrugged. "No problem."

I spun around, growling, and found the nearest tree. I attempted to slam my head into it, but wound up staring at a family of possums dwelling in its rotted out center.

I took a deep, phantom breath and calmed myself. With any luck, Greatshadow would swallow him.

TOWER FLEW OFF as Infidel continued dressing. She paused as she found the boot sheath empty. She started pacing as she chewed on her fingernails. She reached the finger that Lord Tower had sucked on and regarded it with an expression half curiosity, half disgust. You can guess which half of the expression I appreciated.

At last she muttered, "Did it fall out in the tree?" She started back toward the village. She hadn't gone but a few dozen feet before she froze, turning her head toward a rustling sound from a nearby thicket. I poked my head through the screen of leaves and found myself face to face with Aurora squatting on the ground with her pants around her ankles. I quickly jerked my head back. Infidel took note of the wisps of fog drifting across the ground. Aurora had trouble with stealth in humid climates.

"Aurora?" Infidel whispered.

There was a rapid rustle from the other side of the bushes. "Infidel?"

They each poked their heads around the leafy wall and grinned.

"I'm glad to see you," said Aurora. "I need to gripe to someone. This whole mission is turning into a big, stinking pile of yellow snow."

"You don't know the half of it," said Infidel.

"I'm not even sure what I'm doing here," said Aurora. "I thought I'd feel the Jagged Heart's presence. I don't. Tower plainly isn't carting it around with him, and it wasn't in the gear. If he doesn't have it, I'm wasting my time."

"The Black Swan wanted you on the mission," said Infidel. "She must have seen something in the future that made her think you needed to be here."

"She's not always right. The whole point of her going back in time is to change the future. Sometimes, little things she does wipe out whole events she was counting on. She went back quite a ways to order a new barge built. What if some guy she hired to build it would have otherwise joined the raiders that stole the Jagged Heart? Maybe it never wound up in Tower's possession."

"I'll ask Tower about it when I see him again," said Infidel.

"Ah ah ah!" Aurora wagged her finger. "You're a machine around him. You cart gear, not pump knights for information."

"Funny you should mention pumping," said Infidel.

"How so?"

"Because Tower just caught me bathing at the stream and confessed that he knows who I am. He says he wants to take me back, clear my name, and go ahead with the marriage. I'm suddenly really glad the Black Swan didn't tell me who the father of my daughter would be."

Aurora's jaw opened slowly, until her tusks were almost pointing straight out. She snapped out of her shock and said, "I, uh, thought you couldn't… I mean, there's still some, um, issues. Of crushing. Accidentally. Certain important parts."

"We only have to do it once," said Infidel.

I jammed my fingers into my ears to keep from hearing more. It didn't work.

"And if he's not any good, maybe I won't have any, you know, involuntary muscle spasms."

I screamed, "La-la-la-la-la!"

She continued, "I mean, it's not like I'd actually feel anything for him. It wouldn't be like it would have been with Stagger."

I stopped la-la-ing and lowered my fingers.

Infidel swallowed hard. "If Stagger were still around, I would have head-butted him when he kissed me."

"Stagger?" Aurora looked confused. "Why would you head-butt him?"

"No! Tower!"

Aurora's brow knotted with bewilderment.

Infidel looked up toward the tree village, then said in a hushed voice, "Tower kissed me."

"You're joking."

Infidel raised her hand and resumed biting her nails.

"You're not joking."

Infidel shook her head.

Aurora crossed her arms, tapping her beefy fingers on her biceps.

"So," she asked, casually. "Was he any good?"

Infidel rolled her eyes. "It… it was… I really have nothing to judge by. I've never been kissed before."

"You've never kissed? For a battle hardened mercenary who wears necklaces of human teeth, you've lived kind of a sheltered life."

Infidel threw up her hands. "What's the point of me kissing anyone? I mean, what's it going to lead to? Look, I've made it this far without any kind of intimacy. I've been perfectly content without it. I mean it. Who needs it?"

Aurora smirked. "In my experience, when people say, 'I mean it,' they don't mean it."

Infidel folded her arms across her chest. "Fine. Maybe, just maybe... maybe I'm curious. Maybe this is one of those choices made by fifteen-year-old Innocent that I'm not so sure about any more. I mean... this is going to sound stupid... but... I ... well, there was this thing he did, when he, um, sucked, uh, my finger and..."

Aurora's eyebrows shot up.

"And... I dunno. I could feel his tongue. It was, like, soft. Warm. I thought it would be slimy, but it felt clean. It was... I don't know. It wasn't nice. I mean, I didn't want it to happen. But... it wasn't unpleasant, either. I felt... this is stupid."

"What?"

"There was like... like a spark. Like, a voice in my head going, 'He's sucking your finger! What a pervert!' and... I... I guess I'm just... curious. About perversions."

Aurora laughed.

"It's not funny," said Infidel.

Aurora shook her head and wiped a tear from her cheek. "No," she said, gasping for air. "I know. It's not. I haven't seen another female of my species for twenty years. I'm not going to judge anyone for feeling sexually frustrated. The dreams I've had..."

"You mean male," said Infidel.

"Hmm?"

"You said you hadn't seen another female. It wouldn't do you any good if you had."

"Ah," said Aurora. She pressed her lips together. "This is awkward. You see, uh, the priesthood, it's all female, and, um, sexual release is a big part of fertility ceremonies, so, we spend a lot of time engaged in —"

"I don't think I need to hear more," said Infidel, holding up her hands.

I sort of hoped Aurora would at least finish her sentence. I was to be disappointed. She changed the subject back to the issue at hand.

"So, you've got a sex-crazed ex-boy friend in charge of the dragon hunt. What about the Truthspeaker?"

"He hasn't seen through the disguise. Relic said he's distracting the priest. Don't ask me to explain, I still haven't figured out all of that weirdo's powers. But, anyway, if the priest finds me out, apparently he has orders to capture me instead of killing me outright."

"That's good, I guess."

"Not really. If the Truthspeaker gives me grief, I'll probably twist his head off. I'm not sure that Tower's going to be quite as forgiving after that. And, if I twist Tower's head off, I'm suddenly short on candidates to father my daughter."

"Do you want a child?" asked Aurora.

"Until the Black Swan mentioned it, I hadn't wasted any time thinking about motherhood," said Infidel. "Now... I mean, if it's, you know, fate... then maybe I wouldn't be terrible at it."

Aurora looked skeptical.

"I know," said Infidel, shaking her head. "I mean, it's hard to imagine making the jump from bounty-hunter and tomb-looter to breast-feeder and diaper-changer. The person I've been would be a lousy mother. But, the whole purpose of this dragon hunt, for me, is to make a new life. And there are... there are nurturing instincts I have that I've never really explored. I just... maybe I should keep an open mind."

Aurora nodded, but didn't ask any follow-up questions. Instead she said, "Speaking of the dragon hunt, it's worth noting that of twelve would-be dragon slayers, the three we've lost have all been put out of action by other team members."

"Technically, Blade was killed by a pygmy deadfall."

"Blade was killed by the damn Truthspeaker," grumbled Aurora.

Infidel nodded. "What's your point?"

"My point is that our dragon hunt is going to be over before it even begins if we kill each other before Greatshadow gets a shot."

"We won't all kill each other," said Infidel. "I've got your back. You've got mine. And I think we can count on the Goons to side with us."

"Don't fool yourself," said Aurora. "Menagerie's willing to mess around with stuff that's not spelled out in his contract, like keeping your secret, but if it comes down to a fight between us and the Truthspeaker, he's being paid to protect the priest."

Infidel nodded. "At least you and I are a team," she said.

"Sure," said Aurora. "As long as you don't try to protect the future father of your child if he does have the sacred harpoon."

Infidel nodded, but she was no longer looking directly at the ogress. Her gaze was once more unfocused; I could practically hear her thoughts churning. As Aurora turned away, Infidel stared off into the distance.

Straight at me. Straight through me.

Haunted.

15 -SIZZLE

I'D HEARD ALL I could stomach about finger-sucking and motherhood, so I decided to get back to the job and watch Lord Tower. I floated up to his tree house. While I hesitate to say that anything about being dead is fun, freedom from gravity is not without advantages. I drifted through his floor and found him flat on his back, eyes wide open, staring at the leaves above him. He looked as if he was unlikely to get any sleep, and not just because Father Ver was snoring. Tower didn't look all that happy for a man who had just kissed the woman he'd obsessed about for fifteen years.

"Forgive me," he whispered, as tears welled in his eyes. "Forgive me."

He swallowed down his emotions with a loud, snotty snort, then turned onto his side, hugging the thin blanket draped over him.

I sighed. I hated the guy, but I understood what he was going through. What if I'd thrown myself at Infidel years ago and confessed everything I felt for her? She'd said a lot of nice things about me since my death, but what if she'd reacted with the same lukewarm confusion Tower had received? I wouldn't have gotten any sleep either.

Angry for feeling any sympathy and rapidly tiring of the Truthspeaker's snoring, I drifted back toward Relic to tell him about the encounter. With any luck, he was fast asleep and I'd wake him.

As I air-walked back across the gap to the main platform, my eye was caught by movement on the tree where the Goons were staying. I moved closer. In the shadows, I could make out Menagerie. He had a row of small glass vials laid out before him as he studied the faint outline of a bat on his inner thigh. A drop of black ink glistened on a needle held in his right hand. His lips were pressed tightly together as he jabbed the bat in rapid, repeated motions. On his left forearm, a tiger glistened with fresh black ink. I was curious how he'd ever reach the faded wolf tattoos on small of his back, but I didn't get the chance to find out.

As Menagerie concentrated, oblivious to the world around him, I noticed Reeker peek at him from beneath his blanket. Deciding that Menagerie wasn't watching, Reeker rolled slowly to the edge of the platform and carefully lowered himself down to the woven vine ladder.

If he hadn't been so quiet, I'd have assumed he was going down to use the bathroom. But, he kept looking over his shoulder and was taking care not to make a sound. He'd never struck me as someone who worried about disturbing other people's sleep. Suspicious, I drifted closer to him, though not too close. Even though my sense of smell was muted as a ghost, I knew to keep several arm lengths between us.

Reeker reached the forest floor and stealthily crept toward the edge of the village. He went to the far side of a huge tree trunk and pressed his back to the bark. He took one more look around, then crouched and pulled out a small leather pouch, placing it on his knee. Quickly he produced a small rectangle of paper, flattened it out, then placed a large pinch of tobacco in the center. He glanced off to his right, then his left, as he rolled the paper into an untidy tube.

Finally, satisfied that he was truly alone, he pulled a wooden match out of the pouch. He ignited the tip with a quick flick of his thumbnail. A brief breath of sulfur scented the air. He brought the tiny flame to the cigarette and puffed once, twice, three times, firing it to a bright cherry ember.

He shook the match to snuff it. The small fire kept burning.

He shook it again, harder. Still, it didn't go out.

He frowned, staring at the miniscule blaze as it sputtered down the wooden dowel, nearing his finger and thumb. He reached out with his free hand and closed his forefinger and thumb upon the feeble flare to be done with it.

He screamed. A sizzle sounded from his fingers as white tendrils of smoke spun into the air. A yellow-orange flame danced over his hairy knuckles. He waved his hand frantically, crying, "Yowowowow!" as the fire grew brighter.

Now, his sleeve was on fire. He dropped and rolled on the forest floor. The ground was damp, but his efforts only stoked the flames to greater heights. In a matter of seconds, his clothes were engulfed. His screams grew ever louder.

With a sudden *whoosh*, Lord Tower shot from the sky. He was fully enveloped in his armor; there was no way he'd had time to put it on in any ordinary way. The Gloryhammer turned night into day as the knight flashed toward Reeker. He grabbed the flailing skunk-man by the ankle, then streaked off in the direction of the stream. I followed at the speed of thought as he threw Reeker into the pool where Infidel had bathed. Reeker vanished beneath the surface with a loud hiss and a mushroom cloud of steam.

Tower spun around. There were flames dancing on the forest floor where Reeker had rolled. They flared higher and higher, the ground crackling and whistling as dampness boiled away. Tower gripped his Gloryhammer with both hands as the flames took on a decidedly serpentine form. At first, I thought a vine was on fire, curling from the heat. Then, I realized I was looking at a dragon - a small drake, no taller than a man, made of pure flame. It reared up on its blazing legs and sucked in air. Tower charged as the beast spewed a cone of flame. The fire engulfed the knight as he swung his enchanted hammer with a grunt. The weapon went right through the flame-beast.

"I'm on it!" shouted Aurora, running toward the conflagration with her hands outstretched. Snowflakes the size of saucers began to fall, vaporizing as they hit the beast with a staccato *sss sss sss*. Aurora was iced up and took a swing at the fire-dragon with her frozen gauntlet. She spun around, off balance, as her punch failed to connect. There was nothing solid about the beast to hit.

The fire seemed to laugh as it blazed brighter. Aurora raised her arm to cover her eyes as she stumbled back, her armor cracking.

Suddenly, Infidel dropped straight down toward the drake, holding an outstretched blanket. The fluttering edges engulfed the small dragon as she landed, dimming the light. The beast screamed as sparks swirled around the edges.

Off to one corner, there was a tiny remnant of flame curling around a small twig, no bigger than a cockroach. It leapt to a stick and flashed into a tiny dragon the size of a mouse, then leapt again toward a fallen branch to grow as big as a cat.

Tower charged toward it, trying to stomp it beneath his gleaming boots, but the fire-cat darted away, burning leaves and twigs as it grew to the size of a dog. Aurora pointed both hands at the ground and the forest debris it needed to grow was suddenly coated in ice. The creature darted back toward Infidel, stretching its neck out to nip the edge of the blanket. Infidel jumped back with a yelp as the cloth flared; in the blink of an eye, the creature was man-sized once more.

"You guys are a frickin' joke," grumbled a voice from the shadows. The creature craned its blazing neck to discover Zetetic standing directly behind it, hiking up his tattered robes. The Deceiver grumbled, "I can piss out a fire no bigger than this."

The creature roared toward him, reaching out with claws of flame.

The Deceiver began to pee.

The creature hissed, drawing back. It writhed as stream of urine spattered the ground where it stood. The flames flickered and danced, reaching for new fuel, but the Deceiver kept a steady aim and soon the ground around it was drenched. Fifteen seconds later, the flame flickered out and the last pale red ember went black.

Aurora demurely covered her eyes as Zetetic stuffed his manhood back into the briefs he wore beneath his robe.

"Good job," said Tower, his eyes on the Deceiver's face. "Fast thinking."

"I'm sure it seemed fast to *you*," said Zetetic. He dropped to one knee, studying the blackened ground. His eyes flickered over it like he was reading a map. He reached out and picked up a twisted black twig a few inches in length, right where Reeker had first been standing. He studied it closely, then asked, "Which idiot lit the match?"

"The half-seed!" exclaimed Lord Tower. He turned and bounded through the forest, his armor clanging. Up above, there were a hundred voices jabbering; we'd probably awakened every pygmy in a five mile radius.

Tower leapt into the pool with a splash, fishing around in the waist deep water with his gauntlets. He jerked upright suddenly, pulling a limp, blackened form back into the air.

Reeker wasn't moving. His hair was completely burned away; his scalp was raw and red, with charred black flesh peeling away from the bone in places. Tower laid him on the stone by the pool. He pressed on the skunk-man's chest, forcing out a fountain of water.

Menagerie rushed onto the scene, with No-Face trailing behind him. He didn't pause to ask what had happened. He pushed Tower aside and dropped his ear to his friend's chest. His brow knitted as he listened. Then, he jerked his head away and placed his mouth on Reeker's lips. Reeker's belly rose as Menagerie blew breath into him.

"Gluh," said No-Face, sadly.

Menagerie continued to work, breathing in air, then pushing it out, pausing between breathes to listen to the chest.

"Is there a heartbeat?" Aurora asked.

Menagerie shook his head.

"I can't believe he's dead," said Aurora, sounding sadder than I would have expected.

The Deceiver looked down at Reeker's charred form and said, "Why not? He's not breathing, there's no heartbeat, his skin looks like charcoal. It's not a difficult diagnosis."

Menagerie looked at the Deceiver as if he was ready to pounce on the man. Then, his body slackened and he said, in a soft voice, "Fix him. Please."

The Deceiver shook his head. "The Truthspeakers stripped me of the power to raise the dead. I'm sorry."

Menagerie ground his teeth together and clenched his fists, his anger rising. But instead of attacking Zetetic, he looked down at the fallen Goon.

"You moron," he said, his voice trembling.

"That's a fine good-bye," said Reeker's voice from the pool. I looked toward the rippling water and found a bilious yellow vapor rising, coalescing into the familiar form of Reeker. The pale spirit lingered for a few seconds as it looked down on the scene.

"Reeker! It's me! Stagger!"

Reeker's eye widened as he saw me. I drifted closer. His naked, barefoot ghost seemed shorter than he had been alive. There had been whispers that he wore lifts in his boots; apparently these rumors were true.

"Stagger?" he asked. "What are you doing here? You're dead!"

"So are you," I said. "I'm haunting Infidel. Well, technically, I'm haunting a knife. If you pick something and focus on it, you might be able to stick around."

He looked down at his burnt body. "Why would I want to stick around?" he said. "Look at what's left of me. It's going to hurt like hell popping back inside."

"I meant you can stay here as a ghost."

Reeker laughed. "How pathetic would that be? Life was fun because my body was fun. I could eat, drink, and fool around. Can a ghost do any of that?"

"No. But it beats just fading out to nothing, doesn't it?"

"What? You don't believe in heaven?" Reeker asked.

"You do?"

"Sure. Like a *Black Swan* barge in the sky. I'll just keep on eating, drinking, and sleeping around, only there I won't get bossed around by tattooed shapeshifters. And in heaven, all my friends will have, you know, faces." He looked on No-Face with a look of unconcealed disdain.

The giant man was standing over Reeker's body, shuddering, tears rolling over his blank features from his one visible eye, as he gurgled, "Guh huh huh huh. Guh huh huh huh."

"The big baby," Reeker said.

"Kind of a cold thing to say about the only man crying over your death."

Reeker shrugged. "Remember that little calico cat that used to hang around the bar? No-Face cried like a little girl when it got run over by that cart. Him crying over me is nothing special."

I had an epiphany as I looked into Reeker's remorseless face.

"I never liked you," I said.

"What a disappointment," he said with a sneer. "You were the biggest loser in Commonground. You had the most gorgeous girl on the island giving you goo-goo eyes and you never had the guts to sneak a kiss. You acted like you were smart, reading all those damn books, but what did you ever do that was important? You wasted your life."

I ground my ghost teeth, sorry I'd called out to his wraith.

Reeker glanced up at the tree houses. A hundred dark faces looked down at us. Among them was the tall, thin form of my grandfather. "Must run in the family. Hard to get less ambitious than living up a tree like a damn squirrel."

Before I could think of a retort, he turned his eyes toward the stars and drifted upward. "I've stuck around long enough. There are women waiting in the next world. I can hear them calling to me now." His phantom body remained intact as he rose, not dissipating the way Blade had. He cast one last glimpse down at his battered, broken body.

"Damn," he said, as he cleared the trees. "I was one handsome devil."

Meanwhile, Relic and Father Ver had joined the others at the pool. The assembled dragon-slayers glanced at one another.

"This is insane," said Zetetic, the first to state the obvious. "The dragon knows we're here. Let's call this off and try again some other century."

"Maybe he does know we're here," said Tower. "But does he know who we are? If he knows the danger we pose, why such a feeble attack?"

Relic nodded. "I concur. This was merely a test to see what he was up against. If he was worried by what he'd seen, lava would now be flowing down the slope toward us."

"We've lost a third of the party without reaching his lair," Zetetic said to Tower. "How many of us will have to die before you call this off?"

"All of us," said Tower. "We have a duty."

"*You* have a duty," snapped Zetetic. "What's in it for the rest of us?"

"Munuh," said No-Face.

"Money was going to be my answer too," said Menagerie.

"Was it worth losing a friend?"

"Reeker broke the contract; he paid the price." Menagerie's face was hard as he said, "The next Goon I recruit won't be such a pain in the ass."

"That's a very mercenary attitude," said the Deceiver.

"Is that surprising?" asked Aurora. "We're mercenaries."

Zetetic looked at Relic. "Fine. So Tower and Ver are here for duty, and the other's are here for money. What are you after?"

Relic pulled back his hunched shoulders and said, in a firm voice, "I'm surprised a man of your learning has to ask. Greatshadow's hoard is more than a collection of gold and gems. The greatest treasures of the Vanished Kingdom may be found amid his trove. There are scrolls containing plays that no man has seen performed in centuries, sculptures that once adorned the gardens of kings, and paintings and carvings that show the long forgotten world of my youth. I would pay any price to look once more upon these arts."

"You sound almost like you mean this," I said.

I thought it would sound plausible. It's simpler to say this than to reveal my true motive.

"Which is?"

Hatred. Pure and simple hatred of the beast. Every moment that he survives torments my very soul.

"Fine," said Zetetic. "Let me set you all straight on the real reason we're here. The Isle of Fire is the largest wild plot of land left in the world. It's covered in virgin timber, beneath which lies rich volcanic soils begging to be cultivated. The island has fresh water rivers and deep harbors perfect for cities. The king isn't trying to rid the world of some great evil by slaying Greatshadow. He's trying to expand his empire. Are you willing to die for that? Because I think that the greedy dreams of an already rich king are a lousy thing to die for."

"The king's motives are of no importance," said the Truthspeaker. "It matters only that you obey. Remember the X sanction."

Zetetic looked at Aurora, Menagerie, and No-Face. "Don't any of you wonder what he's talking about? Do any of you care what kind of monsters are paying your salaries?"

"Enlighten us," said Menagerie.

"I told you the Truthspeaker's stripped me of the power to raise the dead," said Zetetic. "When *I* do it, apparently, it's 'evil.'" He formed little quote marks with his fingers as he spoke the word. "But the Church is rife with hypocrisy when it comes to necromancy. I was captured a year ago. I didn't go down easy. I killed… what? Fifty knights?"

"Forty-three," said Lord Tower, tersely.

"They wasted no time when I was captured. I was bound and gagged and given a trial that lasted less than an hour. Ten minutes after my conviction, I was marched to the gallows where a noose was placed around my neck. Father Ver himself gave the order to hang me. I still have nightmares about the trapdoor swinging open beneath my feet."

"Apparently, you survived," said Aurora.

"No," said Zetetic. "I died."

Aurora furrowed her brow.

"King Brightmoon knew of my powers, and how useful those powers might be if he commanded them. So, he paid the church a bribe. He had the monks who pray Tower's armor into existence pray that my heart would once more start beating. I awoke from death to learn I'll stay alive only as long as they keep praying. Tower can send an order through his little magic book at any time for them to stop. That's the X sanction. Tower and Ver act all high and mighty and righteous, but they aren't above enslaving the unwilling dead if it will help the king expand his empire."

Father Ver said, "You are no slave, Deceiver. You're merely employed. Your wages are paid in heartbeats."

Zetetic looked at Aurora with a desperate look in his eyes. "I've no choice but to obey these bastards. But you and the others are free to resist!"

Aurora shrugged. "The Goons and I work for the Black Swan. We aren't all that shocked by a boss motivated by greed."

Zetetic shut up, a moderate pout upon his face. I suspect his feelings ran deeper, but his stitched lips prevented him from showing a full-fledged frown.

As interesting as learning what the X sanction was, I was more intrigued by the idea that Tower could communicate with the monks through his book. The notebook had been the only thing in Tower's hand when he stepped off the platform, then two seconds later he'd had the Gloryhammer in his grasp.

Did the notebook contain some kind of portal spell? Maybe the Jagged Heart was still at the monastery, and could be sent to Tower when he was ready for it.

Before I could ponder the puzzle further, Grandfather lowered himself down from the trees on a looped vine. He stopped with his penis-gourd at eye-level and said, "You've worn out your welcome, long-men." Our packs and gear rained to the ground around us as the pygmies tossed them from the platform. "Leave at once. Return to the sea. You may not pass through our territory."

"We'll go where we wish," said Father Ver. "Should your kinsmen threaten us, we'll meet any attack with deadly force. You have no —"

Lord Tower raised his gauntlet, motioning for the Truthspeaker to stop speaking. "You were gracious to show us hospitality," he said to Grandfather. "We won't cause you any further bother. We're here to fight the dragon, not fellow men, pagans though you may be. We'll find another path."

The knight cast his gaze toward Relic. "It seems we must put your knowledge of this island to a test after all."

Relic nodded. "I know a way."

"Do you?" I asked.

Not really, he thought back at me.

I smiled. For the first time since I died, I finally felt useful. All these years of poking around the island were going to prove valuable after all.

"It looks like I've finally got the upper hand," I said. "I know how to get to the lair from here while avoiding Jawa Fruit territory."

And what is the price of this information? asked Relic.

I pressed my lips together, feeling horrible about what I was going to say. But... what choice did I have? "I'll keep spying on Tower. And in return... in return, you'll tell me what Infidel's thinking. I have to know. Is she really interested in him? Is there any danger at all that he'll win her over?"

Relic's eyes glowed in the shadows of his hood. *A fair price. And what will you ask if you find that she does feel attraction?*

I clenched my fists and said, "Nothing you're not already planning to do. Tower was never going to come out of Greatshadow's lair alive."

16 - OMENS

TO EVERYONE'S ASTONISHMENT, nobody died during the next week. I'll take credit. Having been turned away from Jawa Fruit territory, I had Relic guide the party along the cliffs to reach the north slope. This was the harshest terrain on the island; I knew it well, since the ruins of the Vanished Kingdom here had been left relatively untouched by previous generations of tomb raiders. Treasure seekers have a tendency to look for the easy score; if they had the taste for actual work, there were more reliable careers available. So, most of the explorers stuck to the relative ease of the southern and eastern slopes, as I had done early in my career. It was only after I'd forged a friendship with a woman who could toss half-ton rocks around like bales of hay that the northern slope had opened up to me. Some of my most profitable discoveries had been made here.

There were no navigable rivers on this side of the island, just cascading streams, so there were no river-pygmies. The few trees that clung to the rocky slopes were gnarled and stunted, unsuitable for forest-pygmies. That left only lava-pygmies to worry about, but since the Shattered Palace sat near the dead center of their territory, I didn't see anything we could do to avoid them.

As luck would have it, in the chaos that followed Infidel meeting my grandfather, she'd never bothered to clean the bone-handled knife. Relic had returned it to her and I was still free to move about. I felt like a child opening gift-wrapped presents, flitting from ruin to ruin as the others slogged slowly along narrow tracks that would give a mountain goat vertigo. The men of the Vanished Kingdom had regarded this rugged landscape as a spiritual place, carving countless small temples directly into the steep rock faces.

On my last trip through the area, I'd spotted some dark spots high up a jutting cliff that looked more like windows than natural cave openings. Infidel had been willing to risk the climb, but we'd spotted it near the end of our trip and our packs were already bulging, so we'd decided to save it for another day. As Tower's party crept along the yard-wide lip of rock that led beneath the windows, I could see from Infidel's expression that she remembered the place. I felt a pang of regret over this and a thousand other plans we'd made that we never got around to doing.

I fixed my eyes upon the windows and lifted toward them, as if carried by the updrafts that swept across the slope. I drifted inside, eager to discover if we'd passed up some priceless treasure.

Even before I went in, I saw clues that this wasn't an old temple. I'd looked at enough weathered rock over the years to tell the difference between stones dressed centuries ago and relatively fresh work. These windows looked no more than a few decades old, which meant they were likely the work of lava-pygmies. Once inside, the truth was even more evident, since the ceiling was low, only about five feet high, black with soot from a fire pit lined with stones. The fire pit was still warm and the gritty floor was covered with fresh footprints. At the back of the cave was a tunnel leading deeper into the mountain.

The whole volcano was honeycombed with these passages, carved by lava-pygmies with obsidian pick-axes. Despite all the work the little orange men put into digging these tunnels and caves, they didn't actually live underground. They used these tunnels mainly for religious rituals. For forest-pygmies and river-pygmies, Greatshadow was *a* god, but for lava-pygmies, Greatshadow was *the* god. These tunnels normally led to pools of lava where sacrifices would be made.

When I first discovered these areas, my instinct was to back out. For one thing, exploring them meant crawling for hours, which was rough on the knees. Plus, you never knew when you'd turn a corner and find yourself face to face with a band of pygmies armed with poison darts and a sense of righteous indignation.

Once I started exploring with Infidel, the balance of power had shifted enough that lava-pygmy temples had become targets. While the lava-pygmies lived in the same relative poverty as the rest of the islanders, their sacred sites were often decorated with a commodity too valuable to ignore: dragon bones.

In theory, there were no dragons left other than the primal dragons. A scrap of dragon hide or a single dragon tooth were exceedingly rare in the rest of the world. Yet, somehow lava pygmies always had dragon bones aplenty, along with hides that looked like they could have been tanned the week before. In *The Vanished Kingdom*, Grandfather had argued that these were the remains of ancient dragons, mummified and preserved by the dry, hot air inside the volcanic chambers. I'd never liked the theory. I'd spent enough time around the volcano to know that it might be hot, but it definitely wasn't dry.

Things rotted in a heartbeat in these areas.

I may have been given a key to the mystery when the two dragons attacked Commonground. Maybe the remains came from Greatshadow's avatars once his spirit no longer animated them. Yet, when they'd been killed, their bodies had turned into slag and stone. No bones or hide had been recovered.

Since the party was creeping along the narrow path at a pace somewhere between snail and turtle, I decided I'd probe the tunnel a little deeper. The narrow passage was pitch black, yet my ghost eyes proved worthy to the task. In the absence of true light, the walls glowed with a soft, pale luminance. I wondered if the eerie illumination was some spiritual energy I had been unaware of when I was alive.

I followed the winding passageway long enough to get bored. Just as I decided to turn back I heard faint whispers ahead. I willed myself more swiftly along the corridor, in pursuit of the sound. The feeble, colorless spirit light gave way to a red glow. The dank tunnel air began to stink of smoke and rotten meat. I floated out of the narrow passage into a relatively large room, a rough circle twenty feet across, with a ceiling high enough that I was able to stand up straight again, assuming standing means anything when your feet can't actually touch the floor.

A dozen pygmies were gathered near a jagged crack in the floor, casting long shadows from a dull red glow. Lava bubbled at the bottom of the crack. A shaman dressed in feathers was tossing sticks into the hole, where they exploded into bright flares. The smoke had the sweetness of eucalyptus.

They pygmies jabbered excitedly; I think they were discussing the patterns of the smoke, reading them for omens. My lava-pygmy vocabulary wasn't all it could be. The only phrase I ever heard directly from lava-pygmies was "Yik! Yik! Yik!" which loosely translates as, "It's a long-man! Kill him!" Still, as best as I could piece together, the shaman was telling the men that the fire-giver had once again blessed them. The pygmies were standing shoulder to shoulder in a circle, looking down at something other than the smoking lava. I peered over the short wall they created and gasped.

A dragon lay before them.

Unlike the beasts that had attacked Commonground, there was no question this creature was flesh and blood. It was quite dead; its burst belly revealed entrails writhing with white maggots. The pygmies leaned down and began cutting into the scaly hide with obsidian knives. I'd used these blades before. They didn't hold an edge well, but when they were fresh, there wasn't anything sharper.

The pygmies peeled the flesh away from the skull. I winced as I saw that the left half of the skull was bashed in. That would certainly hurt its market value.

In size, the dragon wasn't much bigger than a goat. Its leathery wings had already been hacked off and were folded up along the edges of the lava pit. The snout had a bony horn similar to ones that baby lizards have to help chop themselves free of their eggshells.

Off to one side, a team of three shaman dressed in parrot feathers were scraping bright red scales from the hide into a large stone bowl. One of them grabbed a stone pestle and started grinding up the jewel-like scales. All three men spit frequently into the bowl, until it turned into a dark orange paste.

I'd always wondered what lava-pygmies used to dye their skins. Mystery solved.

Sadly, the dragon was decayed well past the stage where it had anything that could be called blood. I remembered my brief return to corporeality when Infidel had hacked into the dragon in Commonground, and my ability to touch Ivory Blade's ghost-blood. What would happen if I could put my hands onto some fresh dragon blood?

Hoping that Relic might have some insight on the matter, I surrendered to the ever present tug of the bone-handled knife. A second later, I shot out into bright sunlight and hot, gusty winds, where the others still inched along the rugged path.

I flitted down to Relic. "I just saw a dragon. Not a flame drake like Reeker let loose, but an actual corpse that was probably alive as little as a week ago."

Relic nodded. *I see it in your mind.*

"I thought all ordinary dragons were dead."

And that is all you saw. A dead dragon.

"Yeah, but freshly dead. Well, not fresh, but recent."

Relic didn't respond as he kept hobbling along the path.

"If human blood can restore my ghostly body, could dragon blood bring me back to life?"

Relic shook his head.

"But when Infidel —"

Regaining corporeality isn't the same as regaining life.

"I had a heartbeat. I was breathing. I was solid enough to get cut by the dragon's scales. If it wasn't exactly life, it was still better than what I've got right now."

Relic dismissed my reasoning with a wave of his gnarled hand. *Dragon blood possesses more life energy than human blood, but it is far more volatile. Human blood will dry on the knife, sustaining your phantom form indefinitely. Dragon blood will vaporize in seconds. The illusion of life will be powerful during those seconds, but it will be unsustainable.*

"In theory, if I had a herd of dragons to stab, I might stay alive for a long time."

Relic rolled his eyes.

"What's wrong with this idea?" I asked. "That baby dragon can't be the only one. It must have parents, uncles, aunts, cousins. I mean, what are the odds that I just happened to stumble on the very last one of its kind?"

I admire your reasoning, but it is deeply flawed. The dragon you saw had but one parent: Greatshadow.

"This wasn't like the slag or fire dragons we've seen. It had entrails. It was meaty enough to rot."

Judicious provided you with the solution to the puzzle.

I scratched my ethereal scalp. What was he talking about?

Greatshadow is among the more physical of the primal dragons. Just as he hungers for meat, he also still possesses sexual urges, and has the magical abilities needed to satisfy these instincts.

"You mean Grandfather wasn't joking when the he said that Greatshadow can make extra bodies with female aspects?"

Judicious also told you that the primal dragons pay for the vast scope of their powers with a loss of identity. The female bodies Greatshadow creates sometimes become so confused they believe themselves to be true dragons, separate from Greatshadow. They unconsciously use the magical energy that sustains them to shape their bodies further, to the point that mating with Greatshadow is capable of producing fertilized eggs.

"That is just disturbing."

Greatshadow isn't pleased by the consequences either. Some females are wily enough to conceal the eggs; once or twice a decade, an egg actually hatches and a new dragon is born. Despite being born with a portion of Greatshadow's own memory and intelligence due to their inherited telepathy, they never survive long. Greatshadow eventually discovers them and kills them. Lava-pygmy shaman harvest the remains.

"How do you know all this?" I asked.

He again tapped his forehead. Maybe he'd read the thoughts of lava-pygmies. For all I knew, he'd read the thoughts of Greatshadow himself.

He looked up the slope and thought to me, *We are near. I smell it on the air.*

He was right. In another mile we'd leave the worst of the cliffs behind and have a clear path along the relatively tame terrain leading to the Shattered Palace. It was still ten miles away, but once we were off these goat-tripping pathways, we'd make good progress.

I glanced back to Infidel, who'd fallen once more into her War Doll role. Her face was utterly blank as she inched along the narrow stone, the oversized pack balanced upon her shoulders. A single misstep and she'd be over the edge; it might be a mile before she stopped rolling. Of course, Tower would probably swoop in to save her.

"So… have you been keeping track of her thoughts? About Tower?"

Yes. Would you like to know her true feelings?

I stared at her for a long moment. When I'd been alive, I'd lacked the courage to ask about her feelings. Now, I was going to learn them in the most cowardly way possible.

I turned away from both Infidel and Relic. "Not yet," I said.

And maybe never. Because, if there was even a sliver of hope that I might be briefly reunited with her, I wanted to be able to look into her eyes without shame.

WE ARRIVED AT the Shattered Palace barely an hour from sunset. I hadn't visited these ruins in years; they hadn't gotten any less spooky in the intervening time. The entire area is surrounded by a stone wall that used to be sixty feet tall, but most of it has collapsed into overgrown mounds. A few lone towers still stand, leaning at precarious angles, the stones held together by their corsets of vines. Beyond this was the grand courtyard, a quarter mile of barren, pitch-black stone rumored to be cursed. The fine ghost-hairs of my arms rose as I followed Infidel across the ebony earth.

The palace itself had once been carved into the side of the mountain. In classic Vanished Kingdom style, it had been adorned with high, narrow pillars, large stone heads, and numerous windows and balconies. At some point in the distant past, the palace had collapsed in on itself. The columns were broken, the stone heads split in two, and the walls shattered into gravel. If you scrambled over the rubble, there were passages leading into the mountain, but these, too, were mostly filled with broken stone and more bat guano than any sane man would want to crawl through.

Of course, men who came this far into the jungle were seldom the model of mental health. In any tunnel, you could find evidence of previous explorers, lanterns with broken glass, block and tackles locked with rust, various spikes and pinions draped with the rotting remains of rope.

The sheer scale and scope of the ruins called out to any treasure hunter. I'd come here long before I met Infidel. I'd turned back when I found the crushed remains of an earlier explorer. There's a chance the guy had been someone I knew; the stench of the corpse, if corpse was the right word, was still relatively ripe. The reason I hesitate to use the word corpse is that it implies there was a body, and, really, what remained was best described as a smeared paste, vaguely man-shaped, coating a smooth stone wall. Whoever he'd been, he'd had a shovel, and whatever had smacked into him had caught the blade on the edge and folded it up like an accordion. After two days of wheezing in the ammonia rich air, slipping in the guano, the sight of the flattened body had dampened my curiosity and I turned back.

"This is a good place to set up camp," said Tower, touching down in the center of the courtyard.

"I respectfully disagree," said Relic. "Lava-pygmies conduct rituals here. If they find us on their sacred ground, we'll have to fight."

"They already know we're here," said Menagerie, in the form of an ocelot, scanning the mounds of stone surrounding the courtyard. "I've spotted a few dozen, but they seem wary. My gut tells me they'll keep their distance. They may not be as kind to the others."

"Others?" asked Tower.

"Explorers. Tomb looters. They have a camp about a half mile down the mountain. I can smell them."

Zetetic raised an eyebrow. "You can tell they're looters by the way they smell?"

"In this case, yes," said Menagerie. "I know these scents well. It's Hookhand and his Machete Quartet. They always fence their stuff at the *Black Swan*."

"Of all the people to survive the tidal wave," I said, giving Infidel a knowing look. Hookhand and I had a rivalry that ran back twenty years. More than once I'd gone off chasing the rumor of some newly discovered ruin to find the bastard had beaten me to it.

"I don't think the pygmies pose a serious threat," said Lord Tower, rising up to survey the area. "The walls may be in ruins, but they're still formidable barriers. To attack in mass, the pygmies would have to come through the gate. We'll simply post a watch there and frighten them away with a show of force if necessary. Aurora and Father Ver can start the night. No-Face and Menagerie will follow them. The War Doll and I will take the final shift to see us through until dawn."

Aurora winked at Infidel, though I don't think anyone else saw it. Infidel simply stared straight ahead, still playing the emotionless machine.

WITHOUT THE STEADY winds of the north slope to shield us, the mosquitoes came on strong that evening. Father Ver was particularly afflicted by the buzzing bloodsuckers. He was in a foul mood as he waited at the gate, his scowl lines and bald pate covered with red welts.

Aurora had little to fear from the insects. They froze stiff the second they touched her pale skin, tumbling into an ever growing pile around her.

"I can soothe those if you'd like," Aurora said as Father Ver scratched his face.

"I want no part of your pagan magic," said Father Ver. "Under any other circumstances, I would have already banished an abomination such as yourself."

Aurora leaned back against the stone pillar. "Is there something in your holy book that demands that you be nasty to people?"

"You don't qualify as people," said the Truthspeaker. "Ogres, along with pygmies, mermen, and the shadowfolk, are merely distorted reflections of true humanity, lies given substance by the false beliefs of fools. When the Omega Reader opens the One True Book, your kind will vanish from this world like a nightmare fading from a waking mind."

"Whatever," said Aurora. "You know, I hope I'm around when your book is finally opened. It would be priceless to watch your face fall as you discover everything you believe is wrong."

Father Ver didn't respond.

Aurora kept talking: "You Truthspeakers spend the majority of your life hidden in a remote temple, purposefully set apart from the real world, so that you can be brainwashed into a 'truth' that has nothing to do with reality." Aurora looked up at the sky. There were very few stars shining through the tropical humidity. "I come from a land where truth is stark and tangible, a landscape white as paper for as far as the eye can see. You quickly come to grips with what is real, or you die. Spend a single week out on the tundra, old man, then come back and tell me if you still believe reality is found in some book."

Father Ver slapped a mosquito on the back of his hand. "I find discussions with unreal beings tedious. Let us pass the guard shift without further attempts at conversation."

Aurora said, "I'd be fine with that, except we're going to be fighting for our lives together against Greatshadow. Among my people, it's important to know the mind of the person you're standing shoulder to shoulder with. If you and I must be allies, shouldn't we make at least some small attempt to be friends?"

"My mind is no great mystery," said Father Ver. "I've come here to make a stand for what is good; against an evil as strong as Greatshadow, I grudgingly agree to stand shoulder to shoulder with monsters. I don't like you, ogre, and will never be your friend. But, in battle, know that I will surrender my life to save yours should victory demand it. You do not need my friendship. You have something far more valuable: my sacred word."

Aurora nodded slightly, then returned to her star-gazing, letting the rest of their shift pass in silence. And though Father Ver never acknowledged it, let alone thanked her, the air around the gate was cold and dry, as frost covered mosquitoes fell like snowflakes around them.

"MUH HUHN HURS," moaned No-Face, rubbing his bandaged hand as he leaned against the stone gate and peered out into the darkness.

Menagerie sat cross-legged on the ground, his hands resting lightly on his knees. He said, "I know your hand hurts. Talking about it won't make it feel better. Listen."

No-Face tilted his head. The forest was cacophonous with life; frogs, bugs, and night-birds shouting with all their power to catch the attention of potential mates. It took a moment's concentration to pick out a distant, dull, *doom, doom, doom.*

"Guh?"

"War drums. They say the Death Angel has returned."

No-Face pointed a finger at his own chest.

"Don't flatter yourself. They mean Infidel. Apparently she did something to piss them off."

No-Face chuckled, low and gravelly, then said, "Muhbuh shuh fuhd. Huh huh huh."

"Yeah, right."

They both fell silent, listening to the bass pulse beneath the thrumming ocean of sound.

Menagerie craned his neck, following the bouncing signals. He allowed himself a slight smile. "The Cracked Earth tribe reports a bad omen. The goat they tossed into the lava screamed three times before it died. Attacking tonight would bring certain disaster."

"Grah," said No-Face, his shoulder's sagging.

"Don't sound so disappointed. You'll see plenty of action. We won't have Reeker around for wide area control. I'm already out of blood for some of my big cats. I need you to fight smart."

No-Face wrapped his chain around his damaged hand, then spun around and punched the stone beside him, sending out a spray of sparks. The sharp crack of the blow momentarily silenced the nearest wildlife, leaving only the throb of the drums, which suddenly quickened their pace. No-Face lowered his hand, his one eye gleaming with satisfaction at the dinner-plate-sized crater he'd made in the solid rock.

"Gut duh jub dum muh wah!"

"Fine then," Menagerie said, shaking his head. "Fight the way you always fight."

The bugs began to buzz again as the two men fell into silence. Soon the drums vanished once more beneath the sonic waves of life.

"Duhm," said No-Face, rubbing his knuckles. "Muh Rukuh."

"I know," said Menagerie, staring into the darkness. "I miss him too."

SINCE WE'D LEFT the Jawa Fruit tribe, Tower had barely made eye contact with Infidel. When I spied on him at night, his prayers had been especially heavy with the whole "wisdom to know lust from love" theme. With any luck, he'd decide to just forget Infidel and find some nice girl whose life wasn't an affront to all he held holy.

The two of them walked up to relieve the Goons. Lord Tower was fully dressed in his armor; I couldn't see his face. Infidel strolled behind him, biting her lower lip. Her expression could have been nervousness… or it could have been anticipation.

"You hear the war drums?" Menagerie asked as Tower reached the gates.

"No," said Tower.

"The pygmies aren't happy we're here. But, the Cracked Earth tribe is refusing to take part in an attack tonight. Bad omens."

"Excellent," said Tower. "We won't be here tomorrow night. I see no reason for unnecessary bloodshed."

"Hukhuh," said No-Face.

"He's right," said Menagerie. "They aren't going to attack Hookhand either. With your permission, we'll slip down to their camp and finish them off."

Tower cocked his head. "Why would we want to do that?"

Menagerie looked genuinely startled by the question. "We're going to be too busy fighting the dragon to secure any treasures we might find along the way. We don't want Hookhand to slip in behind us and start looting before we even have time to make an inventory."

"They don't even know we're here," said Tower.

"Which makes this the perfect time to take them by surprise," said Menagerie, grinding his fist into his palm.

"I'm not going to order innocent men be put to death simply because they had the misfortune of camping near us."

"Innocent?" Menagerie stared at the knight in shock. "You don't earn a name like Hookhand and the Machete Quartet by being good citizens. We need to —"

"I've heard your concerns," Tower said. "I've made my decision. If Hookhand bothers us, we'll deal with him. For now, get some rest."

Menagerie opened his mouth to argue further, then caught himself. He said, tersely, "Yes sir," then headed back to the sleeping area with No-Face close behind, rattling his chain.

Once they were several yards away, Tower pulled off his helmet. He produced the small leather bound book from his hip compartment, opened it to a blank page, and tapped his helmet against it. There was a bubble of light, a sound like ripping paper, and the helmet was gone. The blank page now had a drawing of a helmet upon it.

"That's damn convenient," said Infidel, her eyes wide as she looked at the book. Her expression changed to a frown as she rubbed her jaw. "Man, it feels weird to talk after being quiet for so long." She pursed her lips, licking them. "The words tickle my mouth."

"I have something else to tickle your mouth," said Tower, leaning forward, his eyes closed, his lips puckered.

He kissed only air. She stepped backwards at the last second.

"Careful," said Infidel, glancing back toward camp. "The Goons aren't in bed yet. You don't want them to see anything."

"Let them see," said Tower, stepping toward her, grabbing her by the arms. "Soon, I shall declare my love to the entire world!"

"Soon, maybe, but not now," said Infidel. "We don't want to get Father Ver all riled up."

Tower's grip loosened on her arms at the mention of the holy man. His eyes locked on hers in a look of fierce confidence. "Since last we spoke, I have searched my soul. You asked if I would obey Father Ver if he ordered that I arrest you. At the time, I was greatly troubled by the question. Now, I have no doubt. I would fight to the death to protect you, even against Father Ver. My love for you is greater than blind obedience to authority."

"Ooooh," said Infidel. "That kind of attitude will get you put on the naughty list. Believe me, I know."

"Let it be so. I would suffer the torments of hell for a single night in your arms, my love," he said, his voice low and serious.

Infidel pushed his hands off her arms and turned her back to him. "Let's hope it doesn't come to that. I mean, I'm flattered. Really, it's a very nice thing to say. But, I hate to think I just lugged a half ton of gear across a million miles of goat trails for nothing. We've got a dragon to hunt. After we kill it, we can start discussing, you know, romantic stuff. For now, we need to stay focused on the task at hand. Like… well, for instance, I was wondering if you had, I don't know, any sort of special weapon to use against Greatshadow? I mean, your hammer didn't even make a dent in that little fire lizard we fought."

Tower smiled. "We would not undertake this quest if the proper weapon for the job hadn't fallen into our hands. Have you heard of the Jagged Heart?"

"Nope. Never. Tell me about it," said Infidel.

"The Jagged Heart was a weapon revered by the frost-ogres. It's a harpoon tipped with a fragment of the shattered heart of Hush, the primal dragon of cold. Once, she was in love with Greatshadow, but she betrayed his trust in an affair with Glorious, the primal dragon of the sun. After Glorious went on to reject her, Greatshadow spurned her as well. Hush's heart broke into a thousand shards, the largest of which was turned into a harpoon by the ice ogres."

"Sound's painful. Must not have been fatal, however. Hush is still a power up north."

"As elemental creatures, primal dragons obey different physical rules. Hush endures, but her bitterness still chills much of the world."

"And this Jagged Heart is pretty powerful, huh?"

"It's cold is such that it extinguishes any heat or flame. Anything it touches shatters, be it steel or dragon hide."

"Anything? How about your armor?"

"My armor could resist the cold. It's composed of prayer and faith rather than base matter. As long as the monk's maintain their vigilance, I'm immune from all harm."

Infidel leaned close, placing a hand on his chest. "So… nothing can break through it? Nothing at all?" She ran her fingers along his breastplate. "Oh," she said, her eyes widening. "It doesn't feel like metal. It's warm. And sort of… silky." She breathed on it, then rubbed her finger. "I notice it doesn't show fingerprints, either."

"You may touch it as much as you desire," said Tower, his voice purring. "It will always maintain its pristine condition."

Infidel pulled her hand away. "So, uh, the Jagged Heart's a harpoon? Those are pretty big. You obviously aren't carrying it. I guess that book stores more than just your armor?"

"Yes," said Tower. "It's filled with many types of equipment. And, on the final page, anything I write is instantly duplicated in a matching book in the monastery. They may also add items to their book for my use."

"And that's how you'd trigger the X sanction?" she asked.

He nodded.

"Don't you think it's creepy that we're working with someone who's kinda, sorta dead? I mean, I never got along with my father, but I didn't think he'd get involved with necromancy. I especially didn't think the church would go along with something like this."

"The needs of a king and the needs of the church don't always overlap," said Tower. He looked toward the faint glow of the caldera. It had been especially calm ever since the eruption. "Of course, sometimes they do. The church hates all primal dragons. The king wants this island for its natural wealth." He waved his gauntleted hand toward the forest. "Think of the navy that can be built with such an endless supply of large trees. We've long ago exhausted all useful timber on the Silver Isle, and now the forests on the Isle of Apes are producing fewer and fewer large trees. Anywhere the king searches for new resources, he finds primal dragons standing in the way. But, plans have now been set in motion to rid the world not just of Greatshadow, but of all the dragons. In the not so distant future, King Brightmoon will face no barriers at all in his quest to expand our great civilization."

"Hmm," said Infidel, running her hands along the seams of his chest plate, tracing the joints lightly with her fingernails. "I suppose ruling the world does excuse a little necromancy."

Tower stared deeply into Infidel's eyes. "And you, my lovely princess, *you* are the last surviving link to the bloodline of your father. Our children will have the sole claim to inherit the crown. Think of it, my darling: the product of my seed and your womb will hold dominion over the earth!"

Infidel met his gaze and said, "This is quite a vision."

"A grand vision," said Tower. "And a true one. I believe with all my heart that our story is the central narrative of the One True Book. Our life and love are the very core of history. It is destiny. Our destiny."

Infidel turned her back to him. "You'll pardon me if I need some time to think about this. This is quite a lot to swallow."

"Would it help if you had something sweet and cream-filled to swallow first?" Tower asked.

At first I assumed this was the worst sexual innuendo I'd ever heard, but Tower surprised me by turning to a new page in the book and tapping it. Instantly the night air was cut through by the scent of vanilla. Infidel's nose twitched as she peaked back over her shoulder. Her face lit up with a huge grin as she spun around.

Tower was holding a silver plate on which set the tallest slice of cake I'd ever seen. The dessert was composed of seven inch thick layers of golden cake separated by velvety frosting as white as fresh snow. The whole plate was dusted with confectioner's sugar and delicate daisy petals composed of frosting. As Infidel stared at the pastry, I felt a surge of delight to see her smiling so after such a long period of sadness, then a surge of jealousy that I wasn't responsible for her joy.

"I wrote the monks and asked them to hire the finest bakers. They placed the result into my book only hours ago. Enjoy!"

Tower produced a fork as he spoke, but it was too late. Infidel had already snatched up the confection with her fingers and was shoving into her mouth. She might have been raised in a palace, but she'd had fifteen years in Commonground to shed any table manners. I hoped that Tower might be turned off by the sight of such messy hunger.

Instead, his own eyes as he stared at her frosted covered lips told of a deeper hunger still.

17 - THRONE

THE WAR DRUMS ended at dawn. Silver mist covered the black stones of the courtyard as the sunbeams seeped through the trees. The dragon-hunters woke to a breakfast of dried sausages and bananas.

Father Ver unrolled the golden map on a section of lichen-covered column. Everyone gathered around, chewing their sausages as they looked at the gleaming scroll.

Aurora was the first to break the silence. "So this is really going to happen. We're going face to face with Greatshadow."

Lord Tower nodded. "We've paid a steep price to come this far. Yet, when I look around this courtyard, I'm certain we shall succeed. Never before has the dragon faced a band of adventurers with our combined power."

"It isn't power that will guarantee our victory," said Father Ver. "It's the rightness of our cause. We're the champions of truth, pitting ourselves against the living embodiment of falsehood. We must not fail."

Zetetic opened his mouth, inhaling to speak.

Ver cut him off with a raised hand. "We know your thoughts on the matter."

"Not all of them," said the Deceiver. "You've dragged me back from the grave for this mission. That's an admission that you can't do this without me. I'd like to name my terms."

"You'll do what we tell you," said Father Ver, "or you will die."

"You admit I do have a choice," said Zetetic.

"You won't disobey," said Tower. "You've proven your instincts for self-preservation."

"Which is why I'm not thrilled about being drafted for this suicide mission. But, let's pretend for a moment that there's one chance in a million we'll beat Greatshadow. Our goal, while unlikely, isn't impossible. Assuming we come out of this alive, I have certain demands."

"You're in no position to issue demands," grumbled Father Ver.

Tower said, "I'd like to hear them."

Father Ver raised his eyebrows. Even the Deceiver looked surprised.

Tower said, "Believe it or not, Zetetic, I'd prefer you were a willing member of this party. If there is something you want that we can provide, tell us."

Zetetic looked off balance, as if he hadn't expected Tower to actually listen. He cleared his throat. "Very well. Of all the reasons I've heard for doing this, Relic's motive is the only one that makes sense to me. Look around you. We're standing in the middle of a fallen civilization once more advanced than our own. Within Greatshadow's lair, we'll find artifacts of these people. Our understanding of the world could be forever changed by what we learn of their science, their religion, and their art."

"The fact that their civilization failed is evidence that they had nothing of value to offer us," said Father Ver.

"Nonetheless, if we do survive this, I don't want to see the artifacts simply looted. I'll promise my willing cooperation on one condition: I get to review each item we recover for cultural, historical, and magical significance. I don't want to unearth these treasures merely so that the king can use the jewels to decorate his toilet."

"We cannot grant this," said Father Ver, wasting no time to consider the offer. "We shall bring in monks to catalog the treasure. The mercenaries will be compensated according to their contracts, and what remains will be divided between the church and the king."

"The church and the king are wealthy enough," said Zetetic. "The king will get the island and its natural wealth. The church will grow as it boasts of an evil vanquished. The only treasure I seek is knowledge. I've traveled the world, driven by my hunger to learn more. I've explored palaces beneath the waves, and studied in cities built upon clouds. Greatshadow's hoard is a doorway to a new land: the distant past."

Father Ver shook his head. "We know all we need to of the Vanished Kingdom. These poor men followed mistaken religions. Time has erased their failed gods from memory. Should any idols of these false faiths be found, we must destroy them so that no weak-minded men can be led astray."

"Your church claims to honor truth above all," said Zetetic. "Yet you seek to erase the truth of earlier times. We should document and study —"

"Enough!" Lord Tower slapped the Gloryhammer into his gauntleted palm. "Father Ver, the Church will remain the final arbiter in distributing the treasure. However, I find no problem with granting the Deceiver what he's asked for: not control of the treasure, but the opportunity to study it. We must catalog the treasure anyway. Zetetic may oversee this work."

"This had better not slow down our pay," said Menagerie.

"It won't," said Tower.

"I'm surprised you're capitulating on this, Tower," said Zetetic.

"Surprised or not, I'm giving you my word," said the knight. "I want you to fight with your full heart. I want you" — he glanced around the gathering — "all of you, to understand the importance of our mission. As Reeker's death reminds us, Greatshadow's malignant intelligence spies upon mankind through every candle, waiting for any moment of carelessness to strike. After we slay the dragon, mankind need never fear fire again." He looked around the tangled jungle and shook his head. "A once great kingdom, buried beneath a hostile wilderness. Such a waste, and Greatshadow is to blame. Here, life is brutal and short; the civilized concepts of mercy, compassion, and justice have failed to take hold against these twisted roots. These noble ideas are what we are truly fighting for. When Greatshadow falls, we shall tame this land. The world will no longer have any place where the wicked may hide from the righteous."

"I appreciate the attempt at inspiring us," said Aurora. "What I'm not hearing is how we're going to actually kill the dragon. Your hammer couldn't even touch the fire-drake."

"The drake was nothing but flame. Greatshadow has a body."

"True. But he's not just a body. Assuming we can kill the big lizard part of him, how do we touch his spirit?"

I knew she was digging for information about the Jagged Heart, but Tower didn't give her any satisfaction. "An excellent question," he said. "We will launch our assault on the beast from the ancient temple that lies below." He tapped a star-shaped chamber on the map.

"Why's that going to make any difference?" asked Menagerie.

Zetetic said, "Despite Ver's insistence that his religion has all the answers, all temples are imbued by the collective energies of their worshippers with special properties. The veil between the material and immaterial is especially thin in these places. Thanks to my metaphysical flexibility, I can manipulate the temple energies to open a door to the spirit world. Father Ver is in possession of a Writ of Judgment. I'll send him into the spirit world to confront Greatshadow's soul."

"He's that powerful?" Aurora asked.

Father Ver shook his head. "Even if I weren't reading the scroll, the sentence of death written upon it comes from the highest earthly power of the church, the Voice of the Book. The beast's soul will fade when confronted by his truthful verdict as frost retreats before sunlight."

Aurora looked dubious; frost sparkled on her cheeks as the morning brightened.

Lord Tower said, "With Greatshadow's soul destroyed, slaying the beast's body will be my duty."

"Buhuh pluh?" asked No-Face.

Menagerie nodded. "Your plan does seems a little… spare. What happens if the priest fails? What happens if the dragon fries you?"

Tower nodded. "If needed, I may also travel to the spirit realm, since I have a weapon that may harm the dragon's spirit. As for Greatshadow's body, you killed two dragons in Commonground. You're the back-up plan."

"I appreciate your confidence," said Menagerie.

Tower looked back at the map. "Of course, there are challenges before we reach the dragon. Most of this palace used to be above ground. Lava flows have covered much of it; earthquakes have wiped out entire sections of a complex that once covered two square miles. Previous explorers have wiggled through a maze of narrow tunnels to try to survey what they could. However, if the monks have interpreted the map correctly, the depression in the center of the courtyard was once a ceremonial well before it was filled with debris. We can dig straight down one hundred feet through the courtyard to reach deep passageways that may still be intact, then follow these to the temple."

Tower pointed at the spot in the courtyard where they'd have to dig.

Menagerie looked at the jumbled boulders than said, "I hope the Gloryhammer can turn into a Gloryshovel. Even though I have a mole tattoo, digging through a hundred feet of rock might take a while."

"We can be down below in ten minutes, if Father Ver doesn't screw with me," said Zetetic.

"Behave and he won't have to," said Tower. "Show us what you can do."

"Very well." Zetetic glanced at No-Face, their gazes locking for the briefest of seconds. "I possess the ability to move rocks through pure mental force."

He held his hands toward the rock pile, his brow furrowed. Everyone looked at the rocks, anticipating a show. Seconds passed, stretching into minutes. Father Ver turned his back to the Deceiver, scowling deeply. Still, nothing happened. Aurora shook her head. You could tell she didn't think Zetetic could do it.

No-Face kept staring. I floated over the boulder-filled pit. I held my ghost-breath, catching hint of a faint rumble below. Without warning, fist-sized stones beneath me began to dance, bouncing into the air a few inches at first, then a few feet. A stone the size of a watermelon stood on end, then slowly rose, wobbling, until suddenly it shot out in a long arc over the jungle, vanishing from sight. The ground trembled as stone after stone rose; chunks of rock as big as rowboats lurched heavenward. Waves of dust rolled over the courtyard as uncounted tons of stone sailed out of sight.

"Damn," I said, looking back at Relic. "I wish I'd known this guy back when I was looting these ruins. I mean, exploring. Exploring these ruins."

You could be exploring the ruins now, thought Relic. *You could confirm that this does, in fact, lead to an open passage.*

I slapped myself on my intangible forehead. What was I waiting for? I dove into the solid ground like it was a swimming pool. Instantly, I regretted it. It was one of the few moments since I'd died that I truly felt dead, cut off from light and air, surrounded by lifeless earth. It took all my willpower to continue sinking into the suffocating darkness. I couldn't help but think about my body, enshrouded by silent blackness, six-feet of sandy soil forever pressing down. I hadn't thought much about my old shell, but burial now struck me as a cruel thing to do to a body. Still, what was the alternative? Reeker hadn't made cremation look attractive. If I'd had a say in deciding my final resting place, I'd have asked that my corpse be placed inside a giant glass jar full of pure grain alcohol. Set me in the corner of the *Black Swan* and let life go on around me. Of course, if everyone did this, bars would be pretty overcrowded with pickled mummies. Worse, it'd waste an awful lot of booze.

I've no way of judging how far I sank before my head emerged into the hallway. It glowed with the same pale spirit light I'd found in the pygmy tunnels. Tile murals decorated both walls. Beneath thick layers of grime, once vivid colors depicted a procession of what I assumed to be royalty. The people portrayed were tall and slender, with bone-white skin, the color of pygmy flesh without dye. Both women and men were bare-breasted; both sexes wore bright green skirts rather than pants. The men's legs showed from the mid-thigh down, while the women were covered all the way to the ankle. Everyone portrayed wore copious amounts of jewelry; I peered closer, trying to figure out if the yellow gleam beneath the dust was actual gold or merely paint. I instinctively scraped at the grime but, of course, my nails passed right through.

The men were depicted with large jade rings in their noses and ears; the women had no piercings, but their hair was piled high on their heads and bound up in coils of gold. In the background of the mural were a dozen buildings ablaze with color; bright red and yellow flags decorated bamboo mansions, long since rotted away. Beyond the cityscape, the jungle looked much the same, the towering trees flecked with red. Blood-tangle vine must have been a nuisance even then.

The procession was accompanied by animals on leashes - tall dogs with wasp-thin waists, yellow and black tigers, and some big-ass preying mantises. I'd seen plenty of giant bugs in the jungle, but you could have put a saddle on these things.

I leaned closer, studying the legs of the insects. The joints were ringed with small dots, like rivets. They looked familiar. Then it hit me - the bugs were machines, like the mechanical tiger that had given Infidel a hard time. I examined a tiger in the mural: it, too, was plainly mechanical beneath its yellow and black paint. Could Infidel have fought this very same cat?

Before I could explore further, dust began to rain down from the walls as the surrounding earth groaned. Up ahead, shafts of light began to jab into the darkness as the fallen rubble was jerked skyward by the Deceiver's telekinesis. I squinted as I made my way through the dust toward the ever brightening light. The last of the rocks lifted, revealing a ragged hole in the roof. I peeked to see how high it was, but jumped back as a boa constrictor slithered through the hole, scanning the hallway with copper-colored eyes. Its tongue flicked in and out, tasting the air as its seemingly endless body flowed into the hall.

The serpent erupted into a sudden fit of coughing. After catching its breath, it twisted its head back up into the hole and shouted, "It'sss dusssty, but looksss sssafe!"

The shaft of sunlight suddenly grew a dozen times brighter. I retreated back, shielding my eyes, as Lord Tower landed with a clatter in the center of the hall, the Gloryhammer casting shadows out behind him. He raised the hammer over his head as he turned in a slow circle to study his surroundings. The gold glittering in the mosaic caught his eye and he wiped away the dust with gauntleted fingers. My hate for him deepened exponentially. It wasn't enough that got to kiss Infidel? He got to explore ruins more effectively as well?

"Paint?" asked the boa.

Tower flicked his right hand and the gauntlet of the faith armor sprouted razorblade fingernails. He delicately grabbed a single golden tile the size of an olive pit and twisted, popping it free. He rolled it in his palm, letting it catch the light.

"Sssolid gold," said the boa, its tongue flickering near the metal. He looked up and down the hall. "If the gemstones are also real, this hall alone is priceless. Once we melt down the metals and —"

"You'd do that?" Tower asked. As he spoke, ropes were dropping into the hole from above.

"Do what?" asked the boa. "Melt down the metalsss?"

"As much as I hate to side with Zetetic, it seems wasteful to destroy such a work of art," said Tower.

The boa's nostrils twitched. "I don't see how we'll spend the money otherwise. It would be difficult to carry an entire hallway back to Commonground."

Tower placed the gold tile back in place, carefully balancing it so that it wouldn't fall. He didn't say anything; perhaps he was shocked by Menagerie's attitude. I really couldn't claim any moral high ground. If I'd found this wall a year ago, I'd have chipped out the more valuable bits myself.

No-Face and the Deceiver were the next ones down. The Deceiver whistled as he looked at the murals.

No-Face chuckled, then said, "Wuh ruh!"

"Yeah," said the boa, "we're rich."

Zetetic moved toward the dusty wall. "I can clear this dust so we can get a better look." He sucked in a lungful of air, then exhaled, his breath swiftly turning into a gale force wind that blew the dirt from a ten foot section of the mural, sending everyone else into a sneezing fit. The Deceiver's eyes lit up like a child being offered candy. He leapt to the exposed artwork, tracing his fingers along a yellow circle near the top of the mosaic, a single piece of glazed ceramic nearly a yard across.

"A sun disk!" he said, excited. "It's rare to find these intact. Judicious Merchant said that he found so many shattered, he was certain that they'd been destroyed deliberately. He speculated that a new god arose in opposition to the sun god these disks represent."

"All it representsss to me isss money," said the boa. "Large artifacts bring good prices."

"How can you be so crass?" asked Zetetic. He looked at Tower. "This is precisely why we need to protect these treasures."

"Protect them for what?" asked the snake. "The world hasss carried on without them for thousandsss of yearsss. Who'sss harmed if thessse thingsss are sssold to the highessst bidder?"

"Tower, if the king wants to civilize this island, think of how much easier it will be to draw settlers if there are artistic wonders in place to delight them," said Zetetic.

"You'll draw more people once word essspreadssss of lossst gold to be found," said the boa.

Aurora and Father Ver were down now; Infidel followed a second later, with Relic clinging to her back.

Father Ver looked at the sun disk. He looked toward Tower, his eyes fixed on the Gloryhammer as he said, "May I?"

Tower handed over the magic weapon as casually as if the priest had asked him to pass him the salt at dinner.

With a grunt, the Truthspeaker swung the hammer, smashing it into the center of the ancient artifact. The disk rained to the floor in a hundred shards.

Father Ver tossed the hammer back to Tower. "The false idols of doomed men aren't treasure. They're physical blasphemy, fit only for destruction."

Zetetic stared at the shattered disk, slack-jawed. His face hardened as he turned his eyes toward the Truthspeaker. He lunged, hands reaching for the holy man's throat as he shouted, "You son of a —"

No-Face caught the Deceiver by the neck and threw him to the ground. He dropped his iron ball, letting the chain catch half an inch from Zetetic's face. The Deceiver flinched.

"I'll behave now," he said.

"Maybe he will," said Menagerie, his snake-eyes gleaming. "But I must protessst. That disssk was more valuable intact than broken. We're due a percentage of the treasure. I mussst insissst that we do not decreassse the value of the artifactsss we find."

"You're the one wanting to melt down the gold," said Tower, sounding exasperated.

"Whuh buh hukha?" asked No-Face.

"He'ssss right," said Menagerie. "We mussst refill the hole ssso that Hookhand cannot loot thisss hall while we're busy elsewhere."

Tower raised his hand and said, "This debate is over." He glared at Father Ver. "Leave the idols and artwork we pass unmolested." He turned to Menagerie. "You aren't owed a single coin until Greatshadow's dead. Once we've accomplished that mission, we'll secure the area. Until then, ignore any treasure we happen upon."

The boa turned his pointy face away and grumbled, "You're the bossss."

"Gruh," said No-Face, with a shrug. He looked down, then offered Zetetic an outstretched hand to help him back to his feet.

"Lord Tower, if I may offer guidance, this way leads to the King's Court." Relic pointed westward with his spindly arm. I noticed that his cloak was stirring in a slight breeze. Air was flowing around him, the dust in the sunlit circle rising up in a swirl.

Aurora held her hand toward the breeze. "It's hot as a furnace," she said.

"It will only get hotter as we descend," said Relic.

The air cooled as Aurora whispered a prayer. "No sense in being uncomfortable."

"Menagerie, you take point," said Tower. "Heat shouldn't bother you as a snake. Aurora, you're next. Keep cooling the air as it passes you. Deceiver, you and No-Face stay close behind her. Father Ver and myself will follow." He looked to Relic. "You and the War-Doll will watch our backs." He glanced down the corridor, holding his hammer high, his eyes searching the shadows. "Everyone stay alert. We've no idea what we might face down here."

"There's a damn dragon, for one thing," muttered Zetetic.

Tower nodded to Menagerie, still in his boa constrictor form. "Move out."

The giant serpent slithered off down the hall much faster than anything without legs should move. Aurora trotted after him and everyone fell into place behind her. I floated next to Relic and said, "So, have you really been here before?"

Does it matter? thought Relic.

"You said you hate Greatshadow. I thought if you really did come from the Vanished Kingdom, and Greatshadow destroyed civilization back then, it might explain your grudge."

A reasonable theory.

"But is it right?"

Relic shook his head. *Without the primal dragons, there would never have been a Vanished Kingdom. Humans lived as little more than animals before three thousand years ago. But, as the primal dragons merged with their various elemental forces, previously untamable aspects of nature suddenly possessed intelligence. Men had always prayed to gods; they adapted to pray and make offerings to dragons. Luckily for man, dragons respond well to flattery.*

"Then what did destroy this place?"

Men themselves. You saw Father Ver destroy the sun-disk. His is not the first religion ever to loathe other religions. In the final days of the Vanished Kingdom, a god called Nowowon rose in power. He was a god of destruction. You find his image throughout the kingdom carved in obsidian.

"I've found a lot of obsidian statues, but they're always of different creatures."

Nowowon had no fixed form. He took the shape of each follower's greatest fear. His followers hoped to avoid their own destruction by destroying the worshippers of other gods to appease him. In the end they wound up destroying themselves as the entire civilization collapsed; self-destruction gave Nowowon his greatest pleasure.

"And Greatshadow just moved into the ruins?"

Greatshadow was always present. No civilization can exist without the use of fire. In his earliest days as a primal dragon, Greatshadow enjoyed the respect given to him by humanity. But as the Vanished Kingdom aged and grew corrupt, Greatshadow grew increasingly disgusted with mankind. Once the Vanished Kingdom fell, Greatshadow decided he preferred the wilderness that surrounded him to the company of men. He's stopped every attempt to restore advanced civilizations on this island. The pygmies escape his notice by living in harmony with their surroundings.

I was intrigued by this news and had a dozen questions, but before I could ask them the passage we traveled opened into a huge, circular chamber a hundred yards across, ringed with columns. We all craned our necks as we entered, looking up at the high cone-shaped roof. A checkerboard pattern spiraled up the steep walls, producing a feeling of vertigo.

In the center of the chamber was a raised platform. Upon this sat a mirrored glass pyramid roughly ten feet along the base. Sitting upon this, perfectly balanced, was a cube of what looked to be black, seamless iron the same height. Perched atop this was an equally large sphere of polished jade, seemingly carved from a single block of stone. My ghost heart skipped a beat as I looked at it. I couldn't even begin to guess its value.

Finally, on top of these three, perfect solids, sat a throne of gold.

"Muh fuh uh," said No-Face, softly.

"It's magnificent," whispered Zetetic, sounding awed as he looked at the tower of geometric shapes. "I wonder what these objects must have meant?"

The boa constrictor rose up next to him, its eyes glazed. "I can tell you what the throne meant," he said. "The man who ssssssat upon that throne ruled the damn world."

Father Ver spat on the dusty floor. "The man who sat on that throne is dead. No one remembers his name."

As dazzled as I was by the wealth before me, Father Ver's words struck me. What did wealth mean if you could afford to build something like this, then vanish so completely from memory? The man who sat upon that throne had probably thought he was pretty important, but time had swept him away completely. Since everything a man might do with his life would be erased by time, perhaps my grandfather was right. Maybe the only sensible path was to live naked in a tree, eat fruit and bask in the sun. Not that this had been Father Ver's point at all.

Menagerie, however, had different feelings on the matter. He slithered across the room, his serpentine belly somehow finding purchase on the smooth surfaces of the pyramid.

"Don't climb it!" cried Zetetic. "It's precariously balanced!"

"Precarioussss my asssss," said Menagerie as he zipped up the cube and slid over the sphere to the throne. "There'sss an iron rod or sssomething ssstuck through the middle to hold everything in place."

He slid his chin on the throne itself. The boa pulled loop after loop of his body onto the seat. In a flicker, Menagerie's human form appeared on the throne. "I know you said the debate about treasure was over, but look at this! We have to take measures to protect our finds. We can't leave this here for Hookhand to just walk in and grab!"

"No one is going to grab it," said Tower. "The sheer weight will protect it from being stolen."

"Are you really willing to take that chance? If you come back tomorrow and it's gone, you'll hate yourself." Menagerie rubbed his hands along the golden arms of the throne.

"I assure you, I'll be able to sleep in peace," said Tower. "Come down at once and let's move on."

Menagerie ground his teeth, glaring at the knight. Then he said, tersely, "As you wish."

He clamped his hands around the armrest as he stood up, his feet on the jade sphere. As he rose, there was a loud click. From beneath the floor, there was a ticking sound, like the world's largest clock counting off seconds.

"That can't be good," said Zetetic.

Menagerie lifted his hands from the armrests. "Nobody panic. It's probably just —"

Before he could finish the sentence, the ticking stopped. The jade globe snapped open, a wedge widening into a giant mouth full of saw-edged green teeth. The mouth proved larger than the footprint of the throne. The golden chair dropped into the maw, carrying Menagerie with it.

The jaws clamped shut with a loud clang, biting right through the throne. The metal posts and backrest spun off through the air, flying twenty feet before clattering loudly on the floor. Menagerie's torso from the belly-button up tumbled through the air. His legs were completely gone. The sphere spun around to face the rest of the party with an eyeless face, as its mouth once more opened in a toothy smile.

18 - Devoured by the Monster

MENAGERIE'S TORSO BOUNCED once on the floor. His left hand flopped limply against a small squiggle tattooed behind his ear and he suddenly vanished. I blinked, wondering where he'd gone, but had no time to dwell on the matter.

The sphere, the cube, and the pyramid had all separated, hovering in the air, spinning to face new targets. The jade sphere shot toward No-Face as a deafening, high pitched scream erupted from within. With only inches to spare, the faceless mercenary leaped from the path of the green ball, leaving the toothy maw aimed at Father Ver. Yet as No-Face dodged, he let his iron ball and chain trail behind him. The giant mouth snapped down as the weapon passed through its mineral lips. Shards of jade sprayed out as the teeth snapped on the iron links. With a grunt, No-Face planted his feet and jerked the chain taut. The jade orb spun dizzily as it cut an arc, narrowly missing Father Ver. Infidel dropped her pack and leapt into the curving path of the spinning sphere, drawing back her fist.

A thunderclap echoed through the chamber as she landed her punch. The gleaming green stone shattered, sending sharp, fist-sized chunks in all directions. Chewed up bits of golden throne bounced on the marble floor. What must have been hundreds of concentric platinum hoops, in diameters from ten feet to smaller than a wedding ring, spilled out, rolling everywhere.

There was no sign of Menagerie's legs amid the rubble, though I didn't exactly spend a lot of time looking. My attention was drawn to the cube and the pyramid, which were hanging in the air, unseen motors within whining like a billion mosquitoes. Unlike the sphere, no mouths opened on these solids as they selected targets and launched forward.

The iron cube raced toward Infidel. She reared back to punch it, but the flying cube smashed her in mid-swing, flattening her against the face. The whining, buzzing noise within rose in pitch as it built speed, pushing her with it. With a shock wave that knocked Relic, Father Ver, and the Deceiver from their feet, the cube hammered into the chamber wall.

I thought of the flattened skeletons I'd found embedded in stone and felt sick. Any normal person would be nothing more than a smear of blood after such a blow. Yet, when the cube pulled back, Infidel looked intact; the marble panel behind her was shattered into gravel, and she was driven into the dense volcanic soil behind. She looked dazed, but was plainly alive.

The cube whirled and targeted Lord Tower, zipping in a straight line toward the knight. Tower was hovering an inch or two in the air. Steel spikes snapped out of the soles of his metal boots and he kicked down onto the marble floor, driving the spikes into the stone. The sphere hit him with an ear-splitting *WHANG*, driving him backward. Marble fragments flew as Tower's boot carved a long, ragged gouge in the floor. The pitch of the unseen engines grew ever louder, but the cube's speed was visibly diminishing. I wondered if Tower could actually stop it before they reached the wall.

My eyes were drawn elsewhere before I saw the outcome of Tower's braking action. Amidst the larger chunks of chewed up throne, I spotted what looked like a bit of brownish red intestine wriggling on a scrap of purple silk. I looked closer, in morbid fascination, wondering if Menagerie had been chewed up so completely by the inner workings of the sphere that this was all that was left. I stared closer and suddenly understood what I was seeing: Half an earthworm, pinched off at one end, writhing in pain.

Was there a second half to this worm amid the rubble? Could Menagerie be restored if we could join the two halves? I turned to find Relic to share my theory, but was distracted as the glass pyramid flashed past me.

Unlike the straight paths the sphere and cube had followed, the pyramid moved chaotically through the air, darting a few yards in one direction, then shooting off at a crisp angle without losing speed in defiance of all logic and physics. Its glass faces were cycling through colors, pale blues, bloody reds, banana-yellows. It rang with a sound like off-key chimes as it jerked through the air. No-Face chased after it, trying to shatter it with his ball and chain, but the pyramid would tumble aside before his blows connected, shooting off in some new random direction.

Aurora, meanwhile, was grabbing the fog that surrounded her, shaping and pressing the mist into her palm until she'd packed a ball of ice the size of a grapefruit. She hung back, studying the pyramid's lurching flight path, her eyes narrowed. Perhaps she figured out a pattern, or perhaps it was only luck, but when she reared back and flung the ice-ball, aiming to the left of the pyramid, her target obliged by darting left. The ice-ball hit the triangle face dead center, passing through the glass as if it wasn't even there. Instantly, the neighboring face flashed green as the ice-ball shot out. No-Face, still chasing the dancing pyramid, wound up getting punched right in the gut by the projectile. He stumbled, off-balance, clutching his belly.

"Sorry!" shouted Aurora. She turned her eyes away from the pyramid for only a second, but in that second all the faces turned black as it charged her. She looked up, raising an ice-covered fist as the pyramid overtook her. Instead of the crash of glass hitting ice, the collision unfolded with eerie silence as Aurora simply sank into the ebony surface. The pyramid tumbled as it passed over her, kissing the floor where she stood before shooting straight up, once more flashing through a spectrum of bright shades.

Aurora was gone.

Meanwhile, Lord Tower had finally won his contest of momentum against the cube. He now held it motionless in mid-air with a single hand holding the Gloryhammer across the cube face while his free hand popped open the compartment on his belt that held his magic notebook. The visor of his helmet lifted on its own as he awkwardly flipped through the book with one hand. Finding the page he wanted, he brought the book to his face and bit down on the edge, trapping a page open as he let go with his hand and brought his fingers to the long, skinny item sketched on the page. He drew his hand back, tugging a loop of leather from the paper, followed by a long shaft of narwhale tusk that he kept working out a few feet at a time, continually adjusting his grip. The bone-white shaft proved to be eighteen feet long, tipped with a gleaming heart-shaped blade of pinkish ice.

If this wasn't the Jagged Heart, it's hard to imagine what was.

Tower let the book tumble from his mouth. With a grunt, he pushed the iron cube away from him, tapping it with the Gloryhammer so that it flew back a half dozen yards. The iron block whined as it shot toward the knight once more. Tower brought the tip of the harpoon down, dropping the Gloryhammer to grasp the shaft with both hands.

The iron cube ground to a halt as the ice tip burrowed into its solid face, sinking nearly a foot. Cracks spread across the iron as the whining noise within changed to a growling grind. Tower twisted the shaft and the entire cube shattered. Fragments of springs and gears bounced all around him.

The knight didn't waste any time savoring his victory. Instead, he charged back across the room, his spiked iron boots shooting out sparks as he ran, the harpoon held like a lance. The glass pyramid flashed white on all faces as Tower neared, a bright, burning light nearly impossible to look at.

I turned away just as the light suddenly dimmed and a cacophony of breaking glass reached my ears. I looked back and saw that the pyramid was gone; all that remained was glassy dust scattered across the floor like snowflakes.

"Uhrurruh!" No-Face shouted, dropping to his hands and knees. He ran his fingers through the glass dust. "Uhrurruh!" he cried again.

Tower surveyed the scene. "Is everyone okay?" he asked.

"Aurora was inside the pyramid when you broke it," said Zetetic, now back on his feet. He nudged his boot around in the glassy remains, until he found a splinter the size of a man's thumb. He picked it up and looked at it closely. "She's gone forever, I fear."

"Nuh!" cried No-Face.

Tower, his faceplate still open, turned pale. "I didn't know."

"What could you have done differently if you had known?" asked Father Ver, still sitting on the floor. "You couldn't let the thing keep tumbling until it had swallowed us all."

No-Face stood up, his whole body trembling. He stared at the Lord Tower with his single, misshapen eye, his fists clenched. He screamed at the knight, "Yuh guhdum muhfugguh! Yuh kuh uhrurruh!"

"It was an accident," said Tower, lowering his faceplate.

Relic was back on his feet, wandering through the rubble that covered the floor. He pushed aside bits of shattered jade and chewed up gold with the tip of his staff. At last he leaned over and picked up a small, moist, wriggling bit of meat, then moved to the other half of the worm I'd spotted on the silk.

"Is this going to work?" I asked. "Can you read Menagerie's thoughts?"

Relic didn't answer me as he placed the two halves together, letting the bisected worms touch at their shared wound.

There was a rapid blur of motion, as the thin, squiggling worms gained mass and muscle. In the span of a heart beat, the worm was gone and Menagerie sat before us, restored once more. The speed of the recovery left me seeing double.

Only, I wasn't seeing double.

There were two Menageries, sitting facing each other, both the size of pygmies.

"What the hell?" they both asked in unison. Their voices were high-pitched squeaks as they asked, "How did… It wasn't supposed to work like…" They each reached out to touch the other, their fingertips tapping together in mirror symmetry.

Both reached for tattoos on their shins and suddenly two small bears were staring at one another. "Terrific," both bears said, in a resigned tone.

Father Ver walked toward the twin bears and looked down, his eyes narrowed. "You're to blame for this! You were ordered to ignore the treasure. You've cost us the ogress and the War-Doll by your disobedience.

Relic shook his head. "The War Doll is still functioning."

Infidel punctuated his sentence by tearing free of her stony outline, staggering onto the floor, still looking dazed.

The Truthspeaker continued to glare down at the small bears. "Disobey again and your contract will be terminated."

The Menageries shifted back into their twin, pint-sized human forms. They both placed their hands across their knees and sighed. They said in their stereo voices, "You don't need to threaten me. No one feels worse about this than I do. The sight of all that gold made me stupid."

"Muh fuh," said No-Face, looming over his fellow goon. "Nuh whoowa smuh guh?"

"Yeah, you're the smart goon now," the Menageries said, shaking their heads.

The faceless giant held out his hands. Menagerie took them, and let himselves be pulled back to their feet.

While this was happening, I'm certain that I'm the only one who noticed that the Deceiver had pulled out a piece of cloth and wrapped the largest shard of glass within it, stuffing it into his bag.

"Let's take an hour to rest," said Tower, sliding the harpoon back into the book. "There are prayers of penance I need to perform for having allowed a book to touch the ground. No-Face, you're bleeding; let Father Ver stitch you up." The big man's hands and knees were red with blood from where he's dug through the glass fragments searching for Aurora. Finally, Tower turned to Relic and said, "Make certain your War-Doll is still functioning. If you need more time for repairs, let me know."

"Of course," said Relic. He left the others and headed toward the shadows of the hall where we had first entered. Infidel sat there, crouched down out of sight of the others. She'd removed her shining steel bra, which was squashed flat. She was hammering the flattened plates back into cup shapes with her fists, using her knee caps as a guide.

"I'm sick of this," she grumbled softly as Relic approached.

"Patience. You may shed your disguise soon enough."

"I don't mean I'm sick of my disguise. I'm sick of this mission. Stagger and I goofed around in these ruins for a decade before he got killed. This team is dropping like flies. Maybe Aurora and I weren't always friends, but she deserved a better death than that."

Relic squatted down beside her. With his limbs hidden within the confines of his cloak, he looked more like a heap of rotting rags than a man. "We can't be certain that Aurora is dead. Her thoughts simply vanished when the pyramid swallowed her. Perhaps she was transported elsewhere."

I also had my doubts she was dead. Unlike Ivory Blade or Reeker, Aurora hadn't lingered behind as a ghost. Or would a human ghost and an ogre ghost go to the same afterlife? The Great Sea Above she'd described certainly was nothing like the church's version of heaven. Since the ghosts usually only lingered a moment, had I simply missed her in all the excitement?

Infidel tried the repaired cup on for size. It was still dented, but it did vaguely resemble the curve of her breast again. "The Black Swan said that only two people survived this quest and made it pretty clear I was one of them. Tower's probably the other survivor, given his bag of tricks. It doesn't bother you that your death has been foretold? Why don't you get out while you still can?"

"Whatever the Black Swan saw, she's already altered our fates. It's possible we'll all survive and the dragon will die."

Infidel didn't look at him as she worked on the second bra cup. Her lips were pursed tightly together for several seconds before she said, softly, "Or maybe we'll all die. Even me."

I put my ghostly hand on her shoulder, wanting to comfort her. I'd never heard such despair in her voice.

"I thought I was done with this," she said, hammering the metal on her knee.

I didn't think she was talking about the bra.

Relic nodded. "And now you are afraid again."

She picked up the cup-shaped steel and began to smooth it between her fingers. "I haven't felt like this since I left the palace. I used to be so timid and terrified. I never wanted to feel that way again."

I was surprised to find out she'd been afraid of anything as a child. It seemed counter-intuitive. As a princess, I would have guessed she'd been protected from everything.

"I was treated like a china doll," she said. "I wasn't allowed to play outside because I might fall and get scratched. I couldn't sit too near a window because the sun might burn my skin. I slept with armed guards stationed at my bed because my father was afraid of kidnappers. My whole family had tasters who sampled our food to make certain it wasn't poison. Being constantly reminded I was so fragile left me in a unending state of terror."

Relic nodded knowingly, but I had trouble imagining a fragile, frightened Infidel.

She sighed. "I wanted to do this treasure hunt as a quick smash and grab, making stuff up as we went along, the way Stagger and I always played it. Events never got out of control when we were together, because we never tried to control them. We just moved on whim and instinct, living fast and fearless. Now, Tower is talking about destiny and history, the Black Swan is playing with people's lives like they're pawns in some game, and it sounds like my father is already studying maps of this island figuring out where to build his new palace. I can't help feeling that all this planning has put things out of control. We're all going to die."

Relic rose up, stretching his back, sinews popping. His hunch disappeared as he rose to the height of an ordinary man. His body was still hidden by the tattered cloak. His eyes glowed like red embers in the shadow of his hood.

"Perhaps you're saying these things hoping I'll reassure you," he said, in a stern tone. "I need offer no comfort. All the strength you need to prevail pulses within your veins. You ceased to be a frightened little girl the second you devoured the blood of a primal dragon. A dragon soul shares your body now, a soul more powerful than the sniveling child you once were. Surrender yourself to the dragon inside and our victory is assured."

Infidel shook her head slowly as she tested the second cup. Satisfied, she worked silently with the link of chain that held the cups together, crimping the ends between her fingernails, then slipping the whole thing on from the back like a vest before pinching the final connecting link between the cups shut at the front.

She stood up. Relic, still standing straight, looked down upon her, a good head taller. She peered up into his glowing eyes. "Who the hell are you?" she asked.

"I'm the second survivor of this mission," he said.

"How can you know this? Are you a seer as well as a mind-reader?"

"No," said Relic, as his head lowered once more, returning his outline to his hunchbacked profile. "But you cannot imagine the trials I've endured to reach this moment. There is nothing left for me to fear. Not even Greatshadow."

"So tell me about the trials. Tell me who you are. Why should I keep listening to you?"

Relic shook his head. "I must remain an enigma until we achieve our goals. Greatshadow can pluck thoughts from the minds of others. If you knew my true identity, he might learn it as well. I'm the one enemy he should fear above all others… because he doesn't even know I exist."

"Why are you his enemy? Why do you hate the dragon so?"

Relic clenched his gnarled fist. "This too, must remain my secret. But know that my hatred for the beast is deep and righteous. Turning back is unthinkable. I cannot live any longer in a world that contains Greatshadow."

I rolled my eyes and said, "I'm really getting tired of your mumbo jumbo. Just answer her questions."

Relic ignored me.

Infidel shrugged. "Fine. I've lived with your mystery man act this long, I can put up with it for another day."

"And your fears? Can you put them behind you?"

She pulled back her shoulders and clenched her fists. "Dragons are cold-blooded. That's the only blood I've got now. So cold my heart's a block of ice, incapable of fear. Timid little Innocent has long since been devoured by the monster." She cracked her knuckles, as all emotion drained from her face. She looked like a machine once more. "Let's go kick Greatshadow's scaly ass."

19 - ROUGH TREATMENT

AFTER EVERYONE HAD rested, we pressed deeper into the palace complex. The rooms we passed through were mostly barren. After all this time, I suppose items made of wood or cloth would have turned to dust, but it was curious that there were no ordinary objects made of stone or ceramic, which would have endured. The emptiness hinted that the people who had dwelled here had time to pack before they abandoned the place. On the other hand, it was tough to ignore the gems and gold embedded in the countless mosaics. Certainly, if people had time to pack up their dinner plates and chamber pots, they would have taken their valuables as well.

With Aurora gone, everyone was sweating profusely. The narrow passageway we followed descended at a rather sharp angle and stretched for what must have been at least a mile. It made me wonder what the ancients had been digging for.

"It doesn't make sense," the Menageries grumbled. They were once more in their human forms, walking in mirror symmetry; as one miniature goon swung his left foot forward, the other moved his right.

"What doesn't make sense?" asked Tower.

"We're heading toward a temple, right? This doesn't seem like a good location to attract followers. Why put it so deep inside a mountain?"

"Muhskuh wuh thuh," said No-Face.

The Menageries chuckled, a sound like chattering chipmunks.

"What did he say?" I asked.

The mosquitoes were worse then, answered Relic.

"Obviously, they were a mining culture," said Zetetic. "You don't produce the gold and gemstones we've seen simply panning in streams. These people spent a lot of time underground."

Relic nodded. "There was spiritual significance to the depths as well. The trees sink their roots deep into the soil. The ancient's deduced that the earth was the origin of all life; the ground was regarded as sacred. Digging into the earth produced precious metals and priceless gems, further evidence that the divine dwelled beneath the surface. The deeper they dug, the greater the treasures produced. Temples were built as deep as possible so that the gods could better hear the prayers of the priests."

Father Ver shook his head. "How sad to live oblivious to the truth."

"A truth contained in a book your own church didn't discover until a mere thousand years ago," said Zetetic. "You have plain evidence men existed long before then. Does it strike you as unfair that your Divine Author condemned so many generations of men to ignorance by hiding the book?"

Father Ver started to answer, but Tower raised his gauntlet. "This is the wrong time and place to debate this. According to the map, we've reached the entrance to the temple." He glanced at Relic. "I assume you can verify this?"

Relic nodded. We were in a long narrow room filled with arches covered with pale blue tiles. At the end of the hall there was a circle of stone, nearly fifteen feet across. Relic pointed to the stone and said, "That stone rolls aside. Beyond is a spiral stairway built of human bones leading down seven hundred seventy seven steps. At the bottom is a natural cavern filled with gleaming crystals hundreds of feet tall; this was the most sacred spot in the kingdom."

I perked up. "If Zetetic is right, and the veil between the spirit world and the realm of the living is thin in temples, could I escape? Could I come back to life?"

Relic didn't look at me as he led the others toward the stone door. He replied mentally, saying, *You've already escaped the pull of the spirit world, Blood-Ghost. Abandon hope; you will never be alive again.*

"You know, you could sugar coat that a little. There's no need to be rude. You still need me as your spy, remember?"

For all the information you've so far gathered, I believe my circumstances would be materially unchanged without you.

I punched him in the back of the head with a phantom fist. It passed right through, but I felt a teeny bit better.

We reached the end of the hall. I'd seen this type of door before, a giant disk of stone sitting inside a matching groove. The ancients were marvelous engineers. Though the stone weighed several tons, no doubt it was so well balanced even a child could move it.

The disk was ringed with cup-sized indentations. Tower placed his hands into the holes, then flexed to roll the stone aside.

The door didn't budge. Maybe it wasn't that well balanced after all.

"It's locked," said Relic.

"I see," said Tower. "How do we unlock it?"

Relic ran his gnarled hand along the blue tiles that decorated the arch surrounding the stone. He found the one he was looking for and pressed it. It slid aside, revealing a shaft about six inches wide. He thrust his skinny arm into it. "There's a lever that releases the…" A muffled *SNAP* caused his sentence to go unfinished. He pulled out his hand, opening his fingers to reveal the rusty remains of an iron rod. He sighed. "Not all ancient artifacts are as well maintained as the War Doll."

He looked back over his shoulder and motioned that Infidel should step forward. She placed her hands into the same holes Tower had tried. The muscles of her back bulged in sculpted relief as she strained to move the door. Whatever mechanism held the stone resisted even her magnificent muscles.

"This looks like a job for a ghost," I said, poking my head into the wall to examine the lock mechanism. Unfortunately, I couldn't make heads or tails of the jumbled of rusted gears and levers embedded in the wall. I drifted through the door completely, into the stairwell on the other side. I discovered that it no longer contained a staircase; the seven hundred seventy seven steps of bone must have crumbled to dust, though I could see the spiral holes in the wall where they'd once been anchored. Far below, in what must have been the temple, there was an eerie orange light that looked like boiling lava. The heat was unbearable.

I poked my head back through the door to tell Relic that it looked like the temple had been claimed by the volcano. I flinched when I found the Gloryhammer flying toward my face. Fortunately, it passed straight through my nose and sank into the two foot-thick slab of stone I was ghosting through. Shards of rock flew everywhere as cracks spread across the surface. I drifted aside as Tower brought the hammer around once more, delivering a second blow. The door crumbled. He kicked aside shattered rock and looked down the shaft on the other side.

"There are no stairs," he said. "I do see a green glow far below."

Green? I looked back down, and found that the previously orange light was, in fact, green. As I watched, the green broke apart into blue and yellow swirls, which were washed away by waves of purple. If this was lava, it was like no lava I'd ever seen.

"Missing stairs are no problem," said twin squeaky voices. A pair of squirrel-sized spider monkeys jumped to Tower's shoulders. "I'll check it out," they said, before leaping into the shaft, bouncing back and forth across the gaps in the stone where the bone stairs once stood.

Since stairs were optional for me as well, I decided I'd beat Menagerie to the bottom of the shaft. I dropped down, passing them, the heat growing in intensity as I descended. The disk of light at the bottom continued to change colors and patterns in a chaotic, unpredictable fashion.

My ghost skin tingled as my body emerged from the shaft. What I saw defied my understanding. Relic had said the temple was in a crystal cavern, but this didn't look like any cavern I'd ever been inside, and there wasn't a crystal in sight. Imagine, if you can, a large, turbulent cloud, ever changing as it drifts across the sky. Now imagine what it would look like if you were inside the cloud. The stone around me was an undulating, amorphous shape. The walls looked solid, despite their refusal to stand still or maintain a single color. The room was full of bones, no doubt the remnants of the stairwell. Fragments of skulls, femurs, and chalk white teeth were scattered in all directions, resting on the ceiling and walls as well as the floor, though if I wasn't looking at the round opening of the stairwell, I couldn't be certain what was a floor and what was a wall. I closed my eyes, since the shifting walls left me feeling seasick. It didn't help. I lost all sensation of what was up or down. My ghost form had only a tenuous connection with gravity at best, but here there was nothing at all to orient me. Fortunately, when I envisioned the bone-handled knife, I felt its familiar tug.

I turned my face in its direction, glancing back up the shaft. The spider monkeys had reached the opening to the room, staring at the chaos with wide eyes. Further up the shaft I saw a shadowy figure clambering down the walls like some human spider. As it drew nearer, I saw it was Zetetic.

The monkeys glanced up. Perhaps feeling a sense of obligation to be first into the room, they jumped, dropping lightly to the writhing stone. The monkeys stumbled as the stone shifted beneath them. Though they didn't sink, it looked as if they were riding waves. One of the monkeys managed to rise on all fours, his tail wrapped around a shimmering polka-dotted stalagmite, but was toppled a second later when the pillar sank back into the surface. The confused monkeys tapped the stone beneath them with their knuckles, then rubbed their tiny fists. The stone was hard, despite its fluid nature.

The Deceiver's head popped out of the shaft and looked around. He dropped onto the shifting floor and landed on his knees, giggling. "By the unanswerable questions! False matter!" He looked around, delight in his eyes. "I saw a nugget of it once, preserved inside an enchanted pearl in the palace of the mer-king. I had no idea that such a large volume of the stuff still existed!"

The monkeys had been carried by the shifting floor until one now stood perpendicular to Zetetic, while another was surfing a wave of stone fifty feet away. The monkey near Zetetic looked slightly green as it said, "What the hell is wrong with this place?" He rode the chaotic stone higher, until he was looking straight down on the Deceiver. "Shouldn't one of us be falling?"

The Deceiver shook his head. "Ignore your eyes. Think of down as whatever direction you point the soles of your feet." Zetetic rose on trembling legs, holding his hands out to steady himself. His eyes were closed. A few seconds later, he cautiously opened his eyes. He grinned as the monkey was carried back and forth on currents of stone. "Imagine you are perfectly stationary. You are the center of your world; let the room orbit around you. Everything's relative here."

The monkey responded by vomiting. The clear, frothy broth pooled around his feet. He closed his eyes and moaned, "Make it stop."

Zetetic shrugged. "I don't know what else to say to help you. Your body is made of true matter. It obeys the same physical rules it always has. You can control your physical response with simple willpower."

Menagerie was still two very sick little monkeys by the time No-Face, Relic, and Father Ver made it down the shaft on a rope ladder. No-Face and Relic were quickly toppled by the changing landscape. Father Ver managed to remain upright as he dropped from the shaft, frowning as he took in the bodies in motion around him. He responded by holding out his arms and turning around slowly. The stone in a ten foot disk beneath him flattened out and stopped moving.

He crossed his arms and said, in a firm tone, "I'm standing on the floor."

No-Face, who was directly overhead, suddenly plummeted onto the circle of motionless stone, landing at the Truthspeaker's feet. The monkey who'd been speaking with Zetetic leapt from his perch on the wall and landed on No-Face's chest. I had no idea where the second half of Menagerie had gotten to. It was impossible to estimate the size of the chamber. It seemed to stretch out for miles, but the rules of perspective were completely useless. Relic was just a little speck, seemingly a hundred yards away, then he reached out and tapped the edge of his staff onto the circle that Ver had calmed and suddenly he was close enough to touch, crawling onto the island and collapsing next to No-Face.

Zetetic didn't seem bothered by the sudden emergence of a floor. He continued to ride the shifting stone, as surefooted as a forest-pygmy on a swaying vine. "Fighting it is only going to make you more disoriented."

"Fighting falsehood is my sworn duty," said Father Ver. "The truth of what has happened here is plain. The pagans corrupted the true matter of the cavern, infecting it with falseness, which has flourished in isolation. In the beginning, before the Divine Author dipped the sacred quill in the holy ink, matter was devoid of such truths as width and length and breadth. By worshipping false gods, the ancient priests weakened the walls surrounding them. The stone has gone feral."

"This is going to shock you," said Zetetic, "but I concur. We're surrounded by the original stuff of creation, matter unshaped by mind. With practice, we could mold it to anything we can imagine. This is the greatest treasure we've yet discovered, far more valuable than gold, and you're wasting it by turning it into mere rock."

"Stone must learn to respect the truth that it is stone," said Father Ver, striding forward, calming more of the undulating rock into smooth gray solidity. Soon, he had an oblong island fifty feet long and a few yards wide frozen into rather mundane looking granite.

Relic pulled himself back to his feet and said, "At least there is no question that we have found the perfect location to attack the dragon's spirit. In a place like this, we should have little difficulty ripping the veil between the physical and the spiritual worlds."

Looking around, I realized that everyone was present and accounted for except Tower and Infidel. I flew back up the shaft, homing in on the bone-handled knife. I cut a path through stone and emerged in the hall where I found Tower with his helmet removed, on his knees before Infidel, holding her hand. He was kissing her knuckles.

"My love, before I go below to face the dragon, there is something I must give you."

"Great!" she said. "I hope it's chocolate this time."

Tower brought a gauntlet to his breastplate, directly above his heart, and pressed a small panel there. A tiny door slid open and something glowing fell into his palm.

My eyes bulged as he slipped a dazzling ring studded with diamonds and glorystones onto Infidel's finger. Infidel's mouth fell open slightly, but she made no sound.

"I've carried this over my heart since the day you vanished. I always knew the moment would come when I would have another chance to give it to you."

"Um," said Infidel. "Why now?"

"I've won every battle I've ever fought, my love. Still, I can't underestimate the danger that waits below. It may be that I shall perish. But I would die a happy man if I knew this ring was on your finger, testament to all the world of our eternal love, my princess."

"Ah," she said. "Hmm. Uh, it doesn't really go with my disguise, you know? Father Ver might figure everything out if I go below flashing this around." She slid the ring from her finger.

"You won't be going below," said Tower. "The danger is too great. I want you to go back to the surface. I'll find you after the battle. I couldn't bear to see a single hair on your head singed by the dragon."

"It's a little late for that," she said, running her fingers through her spiky locks."

"That fact that you can jest is testimony to your courageous spirit," said Tower. "Still, I beg you…"

Infidel sighed. "Don't beg."

"But my love for you is —"

"You aren't in love, you idiot," she said, grabbing his gauntlet and dropping the ring into it. "At least, not with me. You don't even have a clue who I am."

"You're Princess Innocent, daughter of —"

"Stop," she said. "You know my family tree. You don't know me."

"But your lineage is part of who you are," said Tower. "Your royal breeding proves that you're a woman of beauty, grace, and wit, matchless in —"

"Please stop talking," she said. "You think I haven't heard this crap growing up? Being a princess means you stop being a real person. You're just an actress following a script written by history. In case you didn't notice, I tore up that script. I'm not sweet little Innocent anymore."

"Oh, I know this," he said, rising, looking down at her with a leer. "You've grown into a very, very naughty girl. You may even require a spank —"

"Try it and I will rip your arms off," she said, smiling sweetly.

He cocked his head, looking confused. "I'm sorry. Since you're wearing leather pants, I assumed you might enjoy such rough treatment."

Infidel sighed, powerfully enough to stir the dust in the room. She closed her eyes, rubbing them as she contemplated her next words. Finally, she said, "It's time to come clean. I'm not going to marry you. I don't like you. At least, not romantically. It's possible we could, I dunno, be friends. You seem like a decent guy who would probably make the right woman happy."

"Yes!" he said, squeezing her hand. "And you are that woman!"

"You're sure of that?"

"With all my heart."

"You know me that well?"

"I've known you since before I met you!"

"What's my favorite color?"

His face went blank. Then, he smiled softly and said, "I remember the green ribbons you wore in your hair. Green is your favorite color."

In fact, she hated green. She didn't enlighten him, however, hitting him quickly with a second question: "What's my favorite food?"

His face brightened. "Cake!"

"A good guess, but the correct answer is fried monkey."

He furrowed his brow, trying to figure out if she was joking. He waved his hand dismissively. "We have years to learn this trivia."

She shook her head. "I know I've been giving you mixed signals. You ran into me at a very confusing time. I'm still mourning the death of someone I truly loved, wondering how to move forward without him. Plus, I've been given some unexpected news about my future, and you seemed like you might, maybe, be a candidate for helping fulfill a little prophecy. Any daughter I had with you would at least have pretty eyes."

"Any son you had with me would some day be king!" Tower said. "Think of your destiny!"

"I don't really do destiny. I escaped from my father's plans for my future. The Black Swan told me something about my future that messed with my mind a little, but I really don't have any reason to take her seriously. I thought maybe you played some role in my future, but you care far more about potential kings that might fall out of my womb than you care about me as a person. I'm sorry, but I'm no longer interested."

"But... but... but..." said Tower, his voice trailing away.

"I should have told you this earlier, but Aurora thought you might have the Jagged Heart and I played along to find out if it was true. Now that she's gone, there's really no need to humor you."

Tower set his jaw as his eyes hardened into an angry stare. "Yes," he said, his voice low and trembling. "Yes, my princess, there *is* a need for you to humor me. You're still a fugitive, accused of crimes beyond imagining. I'm your sole path to forgiveness."

"Forgiveness is a vastly overrated commodity," she said. "Also, are you really trying to win me over with blackmail?"

Tower said nothing as he put his helmet back on.

"So, what, we fight now?" asked Infidel.

"Yes," said Tower. There was something strange about his voice. Was he crying? "Yes, we fight now. But not each other. Not yet. My first mission is to slay the dragon. Then... then I'll return to my sacred duty of smiting infidels." His shoulders sagged. "Flee if you wish. I won't pursue."

"Flee?" Infidel cracked her knuckles. "There's more proof you don't have a clue who I am."

Flashing a grin, she jumped down the shaft.

DOWN BELOW, THE Truthspeaker had carved out a hundred-foot circle of calm stone amid the chaotic false matter. The cavity seemed even larger than it had before, as if the false matter of the walls was retreating from the holy man. The heat was as horrible as ever; Father Ver's armpits were stained with dark circles of sweat. The second Menagerie spider monkey had rejoined the group; the two tiny primates were fanning one another with triangular wedges of shoulder bones to keep cool.

Infidel dropped from the shaft, landing on the stone island. She looked around, her eyes wide. I floated toward her, wondering if the veil between the spirit world and the material world was as thin at Zetetic claimed. I placed my lips by her ear and whispered, "Your favorite color is black, even though that isn't really a color. I could have answered the monkey question in my sleep. Tower might know your family tree back a dozen generations; I know ten thousand things that make you smile. And when you smile, I smile."

She didn't smile. She didn't respond at all, other than to look toward the shaft just as Lord Tower flew through the opening. He shot off sideways at blinding speed, slamming face first into a wall, sending out a rainbow spray of undulating false matter gravel. He rose on hands and knees, perpendicular to the others, and said, "By the sacred quill! What madness is this?"

A huge stalagmite grew beside him; he placed his hand upon it to try to rise. The stone fell away just as quickly revealing Zetetic, his hands behind his back, looking amused.

"You'll find it difficult to fly. If you're not in contact with a surface, up and down don't really exist. The Gloryhammer has no objective gravity to resist."

The steel spikes in Tower's boots sprung out and dug into the rock. He rose to his full height, using the Gloryhammer as an impromptu cane. He sounded nervous as he asked, "This cursed landscape is where we fight the dragon?"

"Not exactly," said Zetetic. "This is where I send the Truthspeaker into the spirit world, and open a tunnel for you to launch a sneak attack."

"When?" asked Tower.

"I can cast the spells at any time, but I assume you wish to pray or meditate or drink some holy water. Whatever it is the righteous do to prepare themselves for battle."

Tower looked toward Infidel. With his faceplate down, there was no way to tell what he was thinking. After a gaze that lingered long enough to make everyone uncomfortable, the knight said, "I'm as righteous at this moment as I'll ever be. Let's do this."

"Now?"

"Now."

Zetetic crossed his arms. "Is there some reason to rush? Maybe you feel ready to fight, but the rest of us are hot, tired, and hungry. Let's set up camp, rest a little, get some food in our bellies."

"Let's not talk about food right now," said Menagerie.

"Agreed," said Tower. "This is no fit place to make camp. The less time we linger, the better. Open the portal."

Zetetic grumbled something beneath his breath, then reached out to grab Tower's gauntlet. He turned toward the calm stone island where the Father Ver stood and towed the knight over the shifting stone to join the others.

"Maybe I'm not hungry," said Menagerie, "but I wouldn't mind a little rest before we face the dragon. What's the hurry?"

"Zetetic is no doubt gambling that more of you will die if we delay our mission," said Father Ver.

Zetetic pursed his lips tightly together.

Father Ver continued, "His powers draw on the beliefs of others. Tower and I offer him no fuel for his corrupt arts. If only the three of us had made it this far, he'd be powerless, since the Deceiver doesn't truly believe his own lies. And, if he were powerless, we'd be unable to open the doorways to the dragon. He imagines this would save his life."

"That's a pretty elaborate theory," said Zetetic.

"We both know it's the truth," said Father Ver.

"Whatever," said Zetetic, with a dismissive wave. He faced the monkeys and No-Face. "I want the two of you to give me your full attention."

The mercenaries turned their heads toward him with weary stares.

"I have… I have the power to open gateways that lead from this chamber to anywhere I wish, even the abstract realms."

The monkey's nodded simultaneously. No-Face, in his expressionless stare, also seemed convinced.

The only one who looked doubtful was Zetetic. He studied the ground at his feet, taking a deep breath, before stepping up to Tower. His face was mirrored in the knight's gleaming faceplate as he said, "I'm going to send you to Greatshadow's lair. So far, my mental shields haven't detected any of his telepathic probes. He won't know you're coming, but you only get one shot. Make it count. If you merely wound the dragon, you might condemn the entire world to burn."

Tower nodded. "I've prepared for this moment my whole life. Though some among us may doubt the purity of my intentions, I will not shirk from my duty… or my destiny."

Tower opened the compartment on his hip and pulled out his magic book, swapping the Gloryhammer for the Jagged Heart. The searing heat of the chamber instantly cooled from hellish to merely unbearable.

"Ready?" Zetetic asked again.

"Do it," said Tower.

Zetetic grabbed the knight by his biceps and jerked him from his feet, holding him overhead. He looked like he was getting ready to throw the knight, and, as it turns out, that was exactly the plan. With a grunt he hurled Lord Tower at the nearest wall. The stone swirled as Tower approached, forming a vortex, like the cone of air that forms when water drains from a tub. Tower shot down this ever-lengthening vortex, until he became little more than a speck, flying toward a pinpoint of bright white light.

"Your turn," said Zetetic, grabbing Father Ver by the arms. Their gazes met. The Deceiver's voice was little more than a whisper as he said, "You heard the speech. For the sake of mankind, *do not fuck this up!"*

He snatched the holy man from his feet, holding him overhead for a few seconds as his eyes studied the swirling stone, searching for the exact spot where the barrier between dimensions was at its weakest. Suddenly, his eyes brightened. He could see it. I could as well. At the edge of the platform, at a ninety-degree angle from the direction he'd tossed Lord Tower, a vortex of brilliant white light began to spin. I raised my hand to shield my eyes from the radiance, but no one else on the platform save for the Deceiver seemed aware of the light show. The vortex quickly grew, becoming a hole in the air several yards across. From the other side of the hole, I could hear the wail of a terrible wind, a sound that sent shudders through my soul, though, again, the others remained oblivious.

With all his muscles straining, Zetetic tossed the holy man toward the spirit door.

The Truthspeaker never reached the portal. Instead, in mid-flight, he was struck by a flying body that shot out from the vortex Tower had flown down. Father Ver landed on the stone platform face first, then flopped to his back unconscious, revealing a huge gash along his left eyebrow. His twitching legs kicked Zetetic in the ankle and the Deceiver went down as well, cursing as he landed on his butt.

At the far end of the platform, Lord Tower, or something that looked a lot like him, slid to a halt near Infidel's feet. She jumped back, landing on the shifting false matter, spreading her arms to keep her balance. The figure before Infidel wasn't Tower, but instead a statue of the knight carved from dull gray stone. The Jagged Heart was nowhere to be seen. Infidel stared at the statue with a confusion that rivaled my own as the fluid stone beneath her carried her away. She jumped to return to the island, but wound up even further away, thwarted by the room's meandering geometry.

Meanwhile, I heard the rattle of No-Face's chain, the familiar sound that always rang out when he readied himself for a fight. The twin monkeys were suddenly replaced by a pair of snarling wolverines. I looked to the stone vortex, squinting to make out the shadowy figure approaching.

The thing that stalked toward us was human in form, mostly. It was transparent, but not invisible, more like murky water than air, so that anything beyond appeared distorted. The fluid it was composed of had a slight brownish hue, like sewer water. It was carrying the Jagged Heart, but showed no signs of freezing.

As it walked toward us, it shouted, "O stone! Be not so!" It then shrieked with laughter, a high-pitched, slurred barking that reminded me of the forced, empty cackle of a drunken whore who hadn't truly understood her client's joke.

The unpleasant sounds of the liquid man before us were matched by a shrieking behind us. It was the Deceiver, looking at the approaching figure, crying out with terror until his lungs were emptied of the last drop of air.

Just as the Deceiver's voice faded out, the liquid man stepped from the vortex and placed his feet on the stable stone island. Now that he was closer, I recognized he was formed not of water, but of booze — whiskey judging from the smell. He was an impressive figure, as tall and muscular as Aurora had been.

"If you've got a straw handy, I can tackle this," I said to Relic.

He didn't find it funny.

This is the old god I spoke of! he thought back. *Nowowon, the god of destruction!*

"He sounds fun," I said.

Nowowon turned his liquid eyes toward me and said, in a solemn seriousness, "I lived, evil I."

This will not be fun for anyone. Nowowon had no match for cruelty among the old gods. He delighted in tormenting the dead as well as the living.

"Party pooper," I said.

"Party booby trap!" said Nowowon, licking his liquid lips. "Are we not drawn onward to new era?"

Behind us, Zetetic finished filling his lungs with air, and screamed again.

20 - RAW WAR

FOR A SUPPOSED god, Nowowon didn't impress me. Except for Zetetic freaking out, no one else showed any obvious panic. That may have been because not everyone was paying attention. Father Ver was unconscious from his face-plant and Infidel had her back to the action as her repeated leaps over the false matter kept carrying her random directions and distances. Relic stared at Nowowon with the same detached calmness he showed toward most events.

Menagerie in his wolverine bodies and No-Face with his swinging chain didn't look worried as they slowly circled the old god. I wondered what they saw? It made sense, in a completely senseless, magical way, that a god of destruction would appear to me as walking whiskey. Self-destruction no doubt had a special place in his heart. He was appearing to me as my greatest weakness. Maybe Menagerie was currently looking at a ten-foot tall guy made entirely of money. Whatever he was made of, he'd taken the Jagged Heart from Tower, so he wasn't going to be a pushover.

No-Face was first to strike, leaping forward with a noise half-war-cry, half-grunt: "HRUNN!" The iron ball sliced through the air and came down dead center of Nowowon's face, bouncing off without so much as leaving a scratch, at least from my point of view.

Nowowon met the blow with a thrust of the Jagged Heart, moving at blinding speed. No-Face didn't stand a chance; the harpoon impaled his rib cage, driving down into the stone beneath him until the icy blade was completely embedded, leaving only the shaft exposed. Blood bubbled around the wound, then froze, as the ball and chain slipped from his fingers. No-Face sank to his knees, pinned by the shaft, unable to fall completely. No ghost appeared; as horrific as the wound was, he wasn't dead yet.

The wolverines let loose angry howls as they launched themselves at the god, sinking their teeth into his throat. Nowowon grabbed them, then tossed them away, shouting, "Ooze zoo!"

As the beasts spun through the air, they began to break apart into dozens, if not hundreds of animals. Instead of two wolverines hitting the ground, the floor was suddenly covered with countless pint-sized creatures, no larger than they'd been depicted on the original tattoos. There were kitten-sized lions, wolves smaller than mice, and sharks no bigger than goldfish flopping on the floor.

As bad a development as this was, it was followed by something far worse as the miniature animals launched into a feeding frenzy. The lions leapt upon the sharks, the bug-sized boars were stomped by ankle-high elephants, and worm-like anacondas wrapped themselves around tiny eagles. Blood, fur, and feathers flew in a bloody whirlwind.

"Bad animals I slam in a dab," Nowowon laughed as he stomped over the surviving beastlets, smearing them to paste beneath his heel.

No-Face groaned as he writhed on the harpoon, sinking lower, until his trembling, outstretched fingers reached his fallen ball and chain. With a muffled groan, he flung the weapon, bouncing it off the old god's ear.

Nowowon stopped laughing as he paced back over to No-Face. He stared down at the impaled mercenary and growled, "Lived as a dog, reviled? Deliver god as a devil!"

He placed his thick fingers beneath No-Face's chin flap and gave a sudden yank. With a sickening slurp the tumorous mask tore away, revealing... nothing. A completely blank, unblemished mass of skin, unmarred by scars, devoid of mouth, nostrils, or even eyes, despite the fact he'd always had one showing.

"I know how the god's power works!" I shouted at Relic, hoping that my insight might be of some help. "No-Face was afraid there was nothing under his skin flap! Menagerie was afraid that there was nothing human left in him, that he was nothing but a mass of animals!"

Relic nodded. "And Tower feared that his only legacy to the world would be a statue. Nowowon destroys men with their greatest fears."

"I really hope your greatest fear is of something harmless, like squirrels," I said, as Nowowon stalked toward Relic.

Relic looked around the island; the Goons certainly looked dead, even if I hadn't seen their spirits. Zetetic was curled into a fetal ball, sucking on his fist, his face awash with tears and snot. Father Ver was unconscious, Tower was stoned, and Infidel was still leaping around like a drunken jackrabbit. Finally, Relic looked back at me. *Stall him while I mentally guide Infidel back across the shifting terrain.*

I felt his mental hands grab me and hold me in place as he beat a retreat for the edge of the island. I struggled to break free of his invisible grasp, and did so just as Nowowon reached me. The old god grabbed me by the throat and lifted me from my feet. He brought my face to his. I could see right through him; the whiskey fumes of his breath left me dizzy as his lips brushed my ears and whispered, "Murder for a jar of red rum?"

Though he asked it as a question, I was apparently not intended to answer. From nowhere he'd produced a glass pitcher full of what smelled like rum, but looked like blood. He pushed me to the ground, pinning my arms. He pinched my cheeks to force my lips open, then poured the alcoholic blood between my teeth.

The taste… the taste was heavenly. The booze played upon my tongue like a symphony, sweet and bitter, cool and burning, and with each precious drop I swallowed my heart beat stronger. I grew increasingly aware of the stone beneath me. I moved my legs, feeling my naked foot scrape along the cold stone, chilled as it was by the Jagged Heart embedded not twenty feet away. Goosebumps covered my skin as he freed my arms. I used both hands to grab the glass and sat up, still guzzling the precious fluid, fire burning in my veins. This bloody broth had brought me back to life!

Murder for a jar of red rum? The Black Swan had been right. I'd kill my own mother for more of this. I emptied the glass and ran my tongue around the inner rim, searching for the final molecules of goodness.

I rose, woozy, and held the glass out toward the old god.

"Thank you, sir, may I have another?"

Giggling, Nowowon pointed toward the Jagged Heart and said, "Red rum, sir, is murder."

I nodded, then stumbled toward No-Face's still body and the long harpoon that jutted from his chest. The sound of my feet slapping the stone was a wondrous thing. I nearly wept as my solid fingers closed around the cold shaft of the harpoon. Needles of ice ran up my bare arm, but even this sensation took my breath away. My breath! My breath! I heaved out great clouds of smoke as I strained to free the Jagged Heart from its sheath in No-Face's massive rib-cage, and the solid stone beneath.

The ground creaked as I withdrew the frozen weapon. No-Face's body slid down the narwhale tusk slowly. I placed my foot on his neck to pull the harpoon free. There was no question he was dead now. Maybe I had missed his departing spirit in all the excitement.

Or perhaps he'd lingered on until I'd removed the harpoon and, alive once more, I could no longer see ghosts. It wasn't a power I'd miss. Of course, who knew how long Nowowon's brew would restore me? I needed to guarantee a second glass. Who to kill? Who to kill to prolong this feeling? Zetetic, who was getting on my nerves with his rabbit-like shrieking? Father Ver, who I didn't like much, and who was an easy target in his slumber?

Relic?

Oh, definitely Relic.

I turned to face the man who'd been jerking me around like a puppet and discovered that he'd fallen into Nowowon's clutches. Nowowon was tearing away the hunchback's robes to reveal… a dragon?

I blinked. The blood rum was blurring my vision ever so slightly, but there was no mistaking what I was looking at. It was a baby dragon only a little larger than the dead one I'd seen in the hands of the lava-pygmy shamans. Unlike the earlier specimen, which had looked healthy save for, you know, being dead, this dragon was badly lamed. Its wings were tiny, twisted knots perched upon its back. Its legs were spindly and bent at odd angles, as if they'd been broken then mended without being set properly. The little dragon hung limp in Nowowon's grasp; the old god had the disfigured dragon's long spindly fingers splayed out in his palm and was bending them backwards until they snapped, one by one. Had Relic possessed a fear of dragons and been transformed into one by Nowowon? Or had he been a dragon all along, with a fear of being crippled?

"Maim? I? Him I am!" said Nowowon, giggling.

Then, from the corner of my eye, I saw Infidel fly back onto the platform with one final lucky leap, landing near the fallen statue of Tower. She picked up the stone knight by the ankles and charged at the old god. She didn't even glance in my direction. Was I still invisible? Or, was she just locked into combat tunnel vision?

With a savage growl she leapt, swinging the statue like a hammer. She struck Nowowon squarely on the top of his head, driving his skull down into his shoulders, forcing him to drop Relic, assuming that's who the dragon was. The blow also had the effect of sending a spider web of cracks across the surface of the statue. Bits of gravel flaked away, revealing gleaming armor beneath.

She raised her knight-club again and hammered the old god once more. Now shards of stone the size of saucers flaked away from the statue. Tower shuddered and broke completely free of his stony prison. The old god had been driven into the ground up to his knees, his head flat between his shoulders. Apparently, this wasn't fatal to a god; his arms were flailing about, trying to grab his assailant. Infidel, still in her battle rage, danced around his groping hands, and either didn't notice or didn't care that her weapon was alive once more. She again swung Tower overhead and chopped him down to smash the old god even flatter.

"Stop!" Tower cried out, as she raised him once more overhead.

Infidel looked up, confused.

Nowowon's hands found Infidel's ankles and jerked her from her feet. She hit the ground hard, as Tower fell on top of her with a loud crash.

I didn't know what horrors Nowowon might be ready to inflict upon Infidel and I didn't want to find out. I charged with the Jagged Heart, driving it into his body, which still appeared to be liquid despite the mangling Infidel had inflicted. I sank the weapon in until my fingers reached his fluid skin, and twisted.

In response, two fresh arms emerged from Nowowon's armpits and pulled aside his liquid breastbone, revealing his bashed-in face beneath. He still had his original arms clamped on Infidel's ankles. She was kicking, to no avail. Her fingers left small trenches in the stone as she tried to drag herself away. I'd never seen such fear and confusion in her eyes as she looked back over her shoulder and saw me.

"Stagger?" she asked, her voice trembling.

Having seen the fate of No-Face, Menagerie, and Relic, I didn't dare give Nowowon time to get creative with Infidel's weaknesses, whatever those might be. I yelled out, "Tower! Use the Gloryhammer on this thing!"

Tower scrambled to his feet, reaching for his magic book. The Armor of Faith had resisted Nowowon's powers, protecting him from full statuefication. Maybe the Gloryhammer would prove equally effective.

"I hope this hurts," I said, wriggling the harpoon around as the Gloryhammer burst into full radiance behind me.

A grin passed over Nowowon's liquid lips. "Won't lovers revolt now?"

"I don't need your help to save her!" Tower cried. The hair stood up on the back of my neck. I spun with all the speed I could muster, tearing the Jagged Heart free, as Tower swung the Gloryhammer not at the old god, but at me. With a speed that shocked both of us, I was able to raise the blade of the harpoon into the path of the enchanted hammer. There was a blinding flash, like the high noon sun dazzling on pure white snow. The force of the impact knocked the Jagged Heart from my fingers. Yet, as the light of the hammer spun off behind me, I realized my blocking action had not only spared my skull, it had knocked the Gloryhammer from the knight's grasp.

Infidel screamed, kicking uselessly as Nowowon's body restored itself, rising above us. He now had six arms; I had a very bad feeling in the pit of my stomach as I saw that one of these arms now grasped the Gloryhammer, and another the Jagged Heart.

Nowowon pinned Infidel's ankles to the ground as he flipped her over on her back. He placed the tip of the Jagged Heart against her sternum as he grew ever larger. The sweat that beaded on her torso instantly froze into little diamonds. He raised the Gloryhammer, ready to drive the world's biggest nail straight through her.

"I'll save you!" Tower cried, reaching for her left arm.

"I've got you," I yelled, grabbing her right hand.

We both pulled with all our might as Nowowon struck.

I lost my grip and had my breath knocked from me as I hit the ground, rolling. Nearby, I heard a loud crash as Tower's armored ass slammed into the rock. I rose on my hands and knees, looking at him. He was flat on his back, staring up at a young girl in a lacy white gown who stood before him. She had a silver tiara atop her brow, studded with emeralds. Green ribbons threaded through her platinum braids. There had still been some of Princess Innocent inside Infidel after all, it seemed.

Where Infidel had been pinned only a second before, there was now only her empty clothes.

It was then I noticed the tree trunk next to me. I gave it a closer look. It wasn't a tree trunk. It was a dark green shin, covered with thick, overlapping scales, like the hide of a rattlesnake.

I looked up. I was sitting between the legs of a woman at least twenty feet tall. Her feet and hands ended in three-clawed talons, sporting dagger-length claws black with dried gore. A long, thick crocodilian tail trust out from just above her buttocks. A fringe of dark green scales ran up her spine, to join with a mane of what looked like spiky vines.

I made a hasty retreat as the half-giantess, half-dragon reared back and roared, her voice causing the false matter of the cavern to ripple. Her jaws opened much further than an ordinary woman's should have, revealing a mouth full of glistening fangs.

Not that I'm complaining, but in a fair world, the knight in the enchanted armor would have gotten the enraged she-dragon to deal with, while the unarmed naked man got to face off with the little girl in the frilly dress.

Alas, as it turned out, neither of us had a chance to take any action at all. Perhaps a little worried about what he'd unleashed, Nowowon frowned at the giantess. "God damn mad dog," he growled, bringing the Gloryhammer around in a vicious back swing. He caught the dragon-woman in the side of her head, knocking her from her feet, sending her bouncing toward the swirling light of the spirit doorway. There was a loud sucking sound as her tail pointed straight as an arrow toward the gate. Her knife-like nails trailed sparks as the vortex to the spirit world sucked her toward its depths. Her face was a mask of rage, her eyes a bright, glowing green, as jade spittle foamed on her snarling lips. Then, as if understanding there was no escape, she smiled, casting her gaze toward young Princess Innocent. A long, slimy, serpentine tongue flicked from between her lips, flying across the gap toward the girl. The tongue wrapped around Innocent's forearm, then yanked her from her feet swiftly enough to pull her out of her white silk slippers. Innocent screamed at an octave that would have made bats wince as she was sucked into the spirit vortex in the wake of the dragon-lady.

With sickening suddenness, the screaming stopped. The doorway to the spirit world was gone.

Tower leapt at Nowowon, punching him hard in the knee. "Bring her back!"

"No sir! Prefer prison," chortled the old god, before smashing the knight in the head with the Gloryhammer. The metallic chime that rang out from the impact almost made my ears bleed. I could only imagine what it must have sounded like on the inside. Tower fell to his knees, holding his head, and Nowowon pushed him over with an oversized toe. He pinned the knight beneath his foot, then tossed the Jagged Heart so that it imbedded in the ground near my feet.

I didn't flinch. He wasn't trying to strike me.

I still owed him a murder.

"I need another drink to do this," I said, holding out my trembling hands. "All the excitement has left me shaky."

He nodded as he gave me a look of sympathy, an expression out of place on the features of a sadistic god of self-destruction. One of his free hands produced a second jar. "Regal lager," he said, offering it to me.

"Regal lager," I agreed, taking the crimson brew from him. I lifted it to my lips, inhaling one long, intoxicating sniff of the heady aroma. Never had I wanted a drink so badly.

But instead of drinking, I spun around, covered a dozen feet in three long strides, and dumped the ice-cold liquor on Father Ver's face.

The priest's eyes snapped open, his bloodied brow furrowed in confusion as he focused on me. "You're the boy who ran away after stealing the poor box," he said.

Considering that had been damn near forty years ago, I was more impressed than offended by the greeting. The bastard really was good at seeing truth.

"False god!" I said, pointing in Nowowon's direction. "Get him!"

"Was it a rat I saw?" asked Nowowon. He snapped his fingers. Instantly, my heart stopped. I moaned as my body faded back to its spectral form.

If Father Ver was bothered by my vanishing act, he showed no sign of it. He rose, wiped the blood from his eyes, then straightened his shoulders to look at the old god.

"No! It is opposition!" cried Nowowon, as he shrank back down to the height of an ordinary man. He brandished the Gloryhammer in both hands and growled, "Raw war!"

"War is not necessary," said Father Ver. "You'll drop the hammer. It isn't yours."

The Gloryhammer slipped from the old god's shaking fingers.

Father Ver walked toward Nowowon, stepping over the gibbering form of the Deceiver. He looked down on the man with contempt, but took pity as he said, "Your vision isn't real. You've been caught in a mental trap. Arise."

Zetetic's eyes opened. He pulled his drool-covered fist from his mouth and gave it a puzzled look.

Father Ver thrust an accusing finger at Nowowon.

"You do not belong here. You are a false being, and have no place in this world."

Nowowon walked backward toward the vortex of stone, looking at it nervously, as if he was considering making a break for it. But he sounded defiant as he looked back at the Truthspeaker and shouted, "Evil dogma! I am God, live!"

"We both know that isn't true," said Father Ver, as Tower crawled to retrieve the Gloryhammer. "I sense a summoning spell at work. Someone has trapped you here against your will. You faded from the memory of men long ago. There are no believers to sustain you."

"O no! O no! O no!" the old god screamed as he shrank before the force of the Truthspeaker's words.

"You're a fraud," said Father Ver, as the old god shrank to waist height.

"A perversion," he said, reducing Nowowon to the size of a house cat.

Father Ver looked down on the diminutive old god and crossed his arms. "You aren't even worth crushing beneath my sandal. You're a lie, and no one believes you any more."

Nowowon squealed as he shrank to the size of a mouse, then a cockroach, then a fly. Lord Tower's spiked metal boot suddenly slammed down, driving into the solid stone.

"I'm not wearing sandals," he said, casting the Truthspeaker a sideways glance.

Zetetic ran up, snatching the Jagged Heart from the ground. "Why is there a crippled baby dragon over there? Why is the spirit gate closed? What the hell happened? I thought the world had come to an end!"

"Why would you think that?" asked Tower.

"I threw you both through your gates. Greatshadow was ready for us. He killed you both and came into the chamber and killed the rest of us. I survived because I had told No-Face that fire couldn't burn me. But when I left this place, I found nothing but ash as far as the eye could see. I traveled the world, entirely alone, for decades without finding another survivor. Even the mermen and ice-ogres were gone. The primal dragons had joined together to strip the earth of all sentient life."

"You were trapped in a deception by the old god," said the small dragon, rising up on his misshapen legs with the help of his gnarled cane. This was definitely Relic's voice, and there was no mistaking this dragon's eyes were the same eyes I'd spied through the burlap hood. "Nowowon knew that you were vulnerable to assault with a highly detailed hallucination. You were trapped by what was essentially a lie."

"It lasted forty years!" said Zetetic, waving the Jagged Heart in Relic's face for emphasis. "And who the hell are you? Why is no-one telling me why there's a dragon here?"

He was answered with a deep voice that made the ground tremble.

"There's a dragon here because you woke me from my slumber."

Everyone turned to the vortex of stone.

A scaly head the size of a ship had squeezed through the hole. It was a deep, glowing red, the color of embers shimmering beneath a blanket of dark ash. Sulfurous smoke rose from the creature's nostrils. The dragon glared at us with eyes that burned like foundry furnaces, with a heat that caused Father Ver's robes to send up tendrils of white smoke from fifty feet away. All we could do was stare back, the moment frozen, as Greatshadow opened his enormous maw, revealing teeth like ivory stalactites and a tongue like a carpet of lava. Wind howled through me as Greatshadow sucked in air like a bellows.

21 - OILY BLACK SMOKE

AND THEN THERE was fire, a great red wave of flickering tendrils engulfing us in a flood of heat and light. Imagine a coal-fired oven, stoked to a cherry red, with a pot of oil boiling furiously upon it. Imagine plunging your head into this pot, the burning oil working its way into your nostrils and ear canals, into your tear ducts, searing every pore. My spectral teeth burned, my tongue scalded, and there was nothing to do but keep screaming, though I couldn't even hear my own voice. Once, I'd ridden out a hurricane in my small boat and the roar of the wind had been so loud it loosened my bowels. This devouring flame howled far louder, a crescendo appropriate for announcing the end of the world.

And the smell. As a veteran explorer of volcanoes, I knew all too well the brimstone stench and the peculiar acid tang of molten rock. Add to this the stink of vaporized hair and flesh crackling on the bone and you still cannot imagine the foulness of the atmosphere.

As suddenly as it had begun, the flame passed. The pain jangling my phantom nerves collapsed from incapacitating to merely agonizing. Blinking away the ghost tears in my scalded eyes, it appeared that little had changed. The four figures who'd been present before were still there: Relic, revealed as a dragon, was unharmed, save that his staff was but a heap of white ashes at his feet. He was standing where Infidel's clothes had been; they were completely gone. There was no sign of the bone-handled knife, though I still felt its tug… from Relic's mouth?

The Deceiver had survived as well, crouched down, hugging the Jagged Heart to his chest, its aura of supernatural cold sparing him from the flame. Tower, too, was untouched; his Armor of Faith gleamed even brighter, as if the flames had cleansed it of the dust and grime it had gathered on our journey. Somehow, Father Ver, standing just behind the knight, wasn't even singed even though his robes had burned away.

If fact, the only party member missing was No-Face's corpse. There wasn't even a pile of ash, just a small rivulet of serpentine liquid metal flowing where his ball and chain had once been.

Father Ver turned toward me. As I studied his face, I realized I could see Tower through him. I wasn't looking at a man. I was looking at a ghost.

The phantom glared at me and said, "You cannot be my guide."

"Nice to see you too," I said. "Look, you might be here for only a few seconds, so let's get to the point: it looks like you're still heading for the spirit world. When you get there, I need you to rescue Infidel. I mean, the War Doll."

"You mean Princess Innocent."

"You knew?"

He frowned deeply. "This was just one of many obvious truths I turned a blind eye toward with the goal of ridding the world of Greatshadow."

"But how could you know? Relic was reading your mind and said you were fooled."

"I sensed his mental probes instantly," Father Ver said. "It was a simple matter to command him to see in my mind whatever he wished to see."

I crossed my arms and shook my head, imitating the same pose of disapproval I had encountered so frequently in my youth. "So you not only kept quiet about things you knew weren't true, you actively took part in a deception. For shame."

"Your judgment matters to me not in the slightest," said Father Ver. "Tower was my friend. I would not deny him his chance to find his lost love. In the end, the Divine Author will deliver the final verdict on my choices. Let us hope… let us hope it was His intention to write a romance."

I opened my mouth to respond, but he looked heavenward, not caring whether I spoke to him or not. He spread his arms wide as his face was bathed in light from above. I looked to see its source, but there was nothing there.

"Ah," he said, in a tone, half joy, half sorrow. "So that's the truth of it."

He pressed his lips together in a wistful smile as the outline of his face wavered. Then he was gone, and all that was left were a few blackened teeth where he'd stood.

My attention returned to the danger at hand. I didn't want to be around if Greatshadow unleashed another inferno. Fortunately, while I had been chatting, Tower had sprung into action, leaping into the air and flying straight toward the dragon. In scale, it was like a bee diving toward a bear's nose. With both hands, he slammed the Gloryhammer into the center of Greatshadow's snout. Like a bear stung on the nose, Greatshadow winced and drew his head back. The false-matter tunnel warped and wobbled, allowing the impossibly large beast free movement as he retreated. Tower grabbed the rim of a scaly nostril with his razor-tipped left gauntlet, refusing to give the dragon a second of relief as he rained blow after blow on the creature's nose.

As Greatshadow departed, Relic spat the bone-handled knife from his mouth into his hand. It had been completely untouched by the flames. The misshapen little dragon shouted to the Deceiver, "We must give chase! Tower needs the Jagged Heart!"

"You're out of your mind!" shouted Zetetic. "I'd be dead if I wasn't carrying this. And why should I listen to you? You're a dragon!"

"A dragon maimed by Greatshadow," snarled Relic as he wiggled his stunted wings and limped toward the Deceiver. "A dragon whose sole purpose is to see his father suffer and die for the cruelties he's inflicted."

"Father? You're Greatshadow's son?"

"Possibly."

"How can you not be sure?"

"I'm definitely his offspring. But I'm uncertain if I'm his son or daughter. Since my genitals are internal and I've not yet matured, this remains —"

"Stop." Zetetic scrunched up his face and rubbed his closed eyes. "Just stop."

"You're uncomfortable discussing sexual biology?" asked Relic.

Zetetic sighed. "It's one of my favorite topics. But, maybe, right now isn't the best time to get into this?"

"Agreed. We must help Tower."

Tower was a fair distance away at this point, still maintaining his assault. There was little Greatshadow could do to remove his annoying assailant while he was in the tunnel, but the second he pulled his head free into the larger chamber beyond, a talon with claws longer than the Jagged Heart swatted Tower away.

The far end of the tunnel became a solid sheet of flame as Greatshadow tried a second time to melt the knight.

"Make yourself immune to flame," said Relic, grabbing Zetetic by the arm and tugging him.

"I can't!" cried the Deceiver, planting his feet wide to resist. "There's no one left to believe my lies! Your reptilian mind is useless to me!"

"Lie to Menagerie. He's still alive," said Relic.

"What?" I said.

"What?" said Zetetic.

"No shape-shifting blood magician would neglect to include a tick among his forms," said Relic. "I sense him now, dug in behind your knee. Nowowon's magic has robbed him of his humanity, but the Goon is an accomplished survivor."

Zetetic lifted the hem of his robe and bent over, using the Jagged Heart to balance himself as he twisted to see the back of his leg. Sure enough, there was a little black speck there. "Do ticks have ears? Can he hear me?"

Relic was silent as he stared at the bug.

He shook his head. "Unfortunately, his mental state has been greatly damaged. Perhaps he may recover once he has consumed sufficient blood, but, for now, your skepticism is justified. He'll be of no use to you."

"Do you have a second plan?" asked Zetetic.

"As a matter of fact," said Relic, running the sharp edge of the bone-handled knife along his palm. He sucked in air as a line of bright blood bubbled up.

I was floating near him, watching with interest, a bit off vertical amid the room's distorted landscape. I fell about a yard as I materialized, landing on the cracked black stone. I instantly leapt up with a yelp; the stone was hot as a furnace. I jumped closer to Zetetic and the Jagged Heart, and while my feet were spared a scalding, I became keenly aware of my nakedness and the possibility of losing toes and other more valued parts to frostbite. I hopped a few feet away, into a zone where the ground was more bearable.

"Stagger is a ghost haunting this knife. His soul manifests physically when the knife drinks the enchanted blood of dragons."

Zetetic furrowed his brow. Then he shrugged, and said, "I've seen crazier stuff. If I must work with a dead man, I'd rather not be confronted with his private bits. Luckily, I have the power to summon clothing from thin air."

Instantly, I was dressed in finery; a cream silk shirt tucked into black satin britches with calf high boots of soft leather. The whole thing was topped with a rather flamboyant red velvet cape.

"That's handy," I said. "Have you ever thought of earning a living as a tailor?"

"It wouldn't work. One limitation of my art is that I can never convince people of the same lie twice."

"There's no time for discussion!" said Relic. "We must get the harpoon to Tower. With every passing second, Greatshadow grows closer to victory."

Zetetic chewed his lower lip. He looked to be in genuine agony as he said, "Every fiber of my being is screaming I should run. But… Nowowon's little hallucination trap may not have worked the way Greatshadow would have wanted. We can't end this merely by wounding the beast, or even annoying him. Humanity may pay the ultimate price for our failure. I'm in."

"Wait," I said, grabbing Zetetic by the arm. "If you can't convince people of the same thing twice, how do we get to the spirit world? How do we kill Greatshadow's soul without Ver's scroll, and, more important to me, how do we rescue Infidel?"

"Who's Infidel?"

"The War Doll, formerly Princess Innocent Brightmoon," said Relic, holding the blade in his intact claw as he allowed drops of blood to drip one by one onto the bone-handled knife. His blood boiled and bubbled, etching the steel as it vaporized, but he timed his bleeding so that another drop had fallen before the first evaporated. "By now the dragon half of her nature has no doubt consumed the last remnants of her human self. She cannot be rescued. Killing Greatshadow's soul can be accomplished with the Jagged Heart; as Aurora revealed, it's been crafted to slay spirits. As for getting the harpoon to the spirit world, there is a magical item in Greatshadow's lair we can use."

"How do you know this?" I asked.

"Even in my egg, I could read minds. I was hatched with many of Greatshadow's memories. From the moment I first breathed air, I already had a full command of language and a deep understanding of his mystic arts."

"Precocious little scamp," said Zetetic. "Let's hope you know what you're talking about. Hurry!"

The two of them set off at a fast jog down the tunnel. I hung behind for a second, staring at the spot in the air where I'd last seen Infidel, and decided my only chance of seeing her again was to cast my lot with these two.

About a hundred yards down the tunnel, we were all knocked from our feet. A wave of lava swept into the far end of the passage, rushing toward us in a glowing river. Fortunately, since I was behind the Jagged Heart, I was spared from the heat, which rolled toward us as a shimmering wave, but stopped the second it reached the air around the enchanted weapon. The lava stopped flowing as well, freezing into a low wall about three feet tall. Behind it, the molten rock began to drain away, back into the chamber beyond.

I strained to see, missing my power to just float around and look at whatever interested me. As we climbed into the wall and rushed forward, with the ground cooling and crackling as we advanced, what I could catch a glimpse of interested me greatly. I saw Greatshadow stumbling, bleeding profusely from the side of his head, his blood coming out in great surges of liquid fire.

We arrived at a large ledge on the inner lip of a volcanic caldera open to the sky. Before us was a bubbling lake of magma stretching off as far as I could see, which wasn't all that far due to the haze of sulfurous smoke. Greatshadow had dropped to all fours, shaking his head to clear it. His eyes had a glassy look. His sheer size was almost impossible to comprehend; not even whales were this large. He was more like a landmass than a living being, though the muscles rippling beneath his crimson hide revealed the truth of his animal nature.

Above us, beyond the sulfur clouds, the sun blazed brightly. Only I quickly realized that it wasn't the sun; the light was moving far too swiftly across the sky. Suddenly the glowing object burst through the clouds. It was Lord Tower, blazing down with the speed of a shooting star. He slammed, hammer-first, into the dragon's head. The addition of speed turned Tower into something more dangerous than a bee - he was now like a bullet shot from the sling of an expert marksman, and his momentum was enough to drive his invulnerable armor deep into the dragon's skull.

The blow flattened Greatshadow, driving him down into the burning mire. He unleashed a low, mournful howl as he struggled to rise. Magma-like blood bubbled from a series of holes near the fringe of spikes along the ridge of his skull. His eyes seemed unfocused as his limbs jerked spastically.

"Plainly, we're not needed here at all," said Zetetic, turning back toward the tunnel.

"Die!" Relic shouted. It took me a second to realize he wasn't shouting at the Deceiver. Instead, he was shaking his bony fist at Greatshadow. "Your suffering is like wine to me! I drink in your agony as you die! Die! Die!"

Tower clawed back out of the hole he'd dug into Greatshadow, covered in flaming gore. He rose into the air, twirling, throwing off a halo of muck. When he stopped spinning he was clean again, his silver armor a dazzling light show reflecting the Gloryhammer, the lava, and Greatshadow's pulsing blood.

"Your final page has been written, Greatshadow!" Tower shouted, his voice echoing from the walls of rock surrounding the battlefield. "Your name shall vanish from the One True Book!" Tower shot into the air, vanishing into the haze as he rose toward heaven to summon speed.

"Do it!" screamed Relic. "Kill him! Kill him!"

The resentment I felt toward my own negligent father suddenly seemed rather mild.

Zetetic's retreat had halted only a few feet into the tunnel. He was looking back at Greatshadow. Apparently, the opportunity to witness the death of a primal dragon was overriding his desire to flee.

Greatshadow's glazed eyes suddenly focused on the ledge we stood on. With a voice like a rumbling earthquake he growled as he spotted Relic. "This was your doing!"

"Yes!" screamed Relic, spittle flying. "I've plotted your demise since the day you tossed my twisted body onto the volcano's slopes! Once you die, I shall become the new primal dragon of fire! No one will deny me my destiny!"

"Indeed?" said Greatshadow, his voice firm despite the fact he still flopped helplessly in the lava, unable to rise. "You've shielded your mind from me, but your dead companion has no mental defenses. I've just learned that the knight's armor is made of prayer."

He cast his gaze skyward as Tower reached his apex, the brightest object in all the heavens.

Relic's waving fist froze in mid-air. A sudden look of horror filled his reptilian eyes.

"The monks would be too disciplined to light a candle," he mumbled, sounding almost as if he was speaking to himself.

"I'm pretty sure none of them smoke," I said.

"They don't even cook there," said Zetetic. "All their food is prepared in a nearby village and brought to them daily."

"In that village, there is a bakery, with an oven that never grows cold," Greatshadow said, sinking deeper into the lava as the light shot back down toward him. Tower punched through the clouds, his speed so great that a thunderclap sounded in his wake. Yet, as impressive as his speed was, he suddenly had no target. Greatshadow vanished completely beneath the bubbling rock with little more than a ripple. Tower punched into the glowing surface, throwing up a white-hot splash of magma.

For ten seconds, everything was quiet.

Then, the Gloryhammer shot up into the air, pulling Lord Tower from his blazing bath. Tower spun to clear his armor then surveyed the lava beneath him, searching for his foe.

His foe found him first, as a flame-wreathed talon punched from the surface and snapped around the knight like a man snatching an annoying fly. Greatshadow rose from the syrupy rock with a growl and slammed his talon down on the stone ledge we stood on, knocking us all from our feet. Tower was pinned beneath the impossible bulk of the massive lizard as Greatshadow brought his head to the platform and said, in very satisfied tones: "Embers rise constantly from the furnace of this bakery. They dance above the chimney like turbulent stars. A few may travel far, holding their heat until they land. Sometimes, such embers set roofs aflame."

"Rrraahhhhg!" screamed Relic, as the bone-handled knife dropped from his talon. He fell to all fours and charged the larger dragon. He opened his jaws wide, to almost a perfect ninety-degree angle, before he sunk them into Greatshadow's knuckle.

He shook his head from side to side, tearing at flesh, though in scale, he was doing about as much damage to Greatshadow as Menagerie was doing to Zetetic. "Da! Da! Da!" he raged. I think he meant, "Die! Die! Die!" Though, considering the relationship, perhaps not.

"You annoy me," said Greatshadow, flicking Relic with his talon and sending him flying far across the lava.

Around this time, the last of Relic's blood bubbled away from the bone-handled knife and I faded from existence. I watched with despair as my hands once more turned to mist, though I was slightly intrigued that, for some reason, this time I wasn't naked. Zetetic's clothing had made the transition with me back to the ghost-zone I dwelled in.

Tower had grabbed one of Greatshadow's nails and was bending it back. He said, in booming, heroic tones, "You're bleeding, dragon. Your strength wanes with each heartbeat. Death is near!"

Tower was right. For the primal dragon of fire, Greatshadow didn't look so hot. He had big, gory holes on the side of his face, and his blood gushed out by the bucketful. His vital fluids no longer glowed like flame, but were now a thick brown-red stream that spilled down onto the knight's face, splattering across the platform. I looked to where the knife had fallen, to see if there was a chance any of the drops might hit it.

The knife was gone.

I spun around.

Zetetic was nowhere to be seen.

"Your allies… have abandoned you," said Greatshadow, his voice strained.

"A pure heart may face evil alone," said Tower, defiant, as the strength of the Armor of Faith snapped the nail he wrestled with. He reached out and sank spiky fingers into the stone and began to drag himself free of Greatshadow's weakening grasp.

"You aren't… alone," said Greatshadow. "Three hundred monks pray… for your victory."

"Which is why I cannot fail!"

"The monastery has a library with ten centuries full of ancient books, dry as kindling," said Greatshadow, as his eyelids drooped. "There is an open window. And now… there is fire."

"Die!" screamed Relic as he rose from the lava near Greatshadow's hips, climbing the dragon like a mountain, pausing every few feet to take a nip from his hide.

The prayer-driven gears within Tower's armor purred at a louder pitch as he finally kicked himself free of the dragon's failing grasp. He lifted the Gloryhammer above his head and shouted, "This ends now!"

At that moment, the metallic ring that covered the thumb on his left gauntlet vanished.

"One of the faithful… has abandoned his post," said Greatshadow. Suddenly, a bolt popped out of the plate covering Tower's left kneecap. "He is not alone in loving books more than duty."

Tower answered by swinging the Gloryhammer with all his might toward Greatshadow's mocking tongue. Greatshadow's front teeth splintered with a wet sound that made me cringe. The dragon drew in a shallow breath as his mouth closed around the Gloryhammer and Tower's hands.

The dragon's scaly cheeks puffed out as he exhaled. A jet of white flame shot thirty feet out from Tower's left kneecap, quickly fading into a stream of oily black smoke.

Greatshadow spit out the Gloryhammer and stared at the smoking husk of armor standing before him. With a creak, the armor tilted to the left, then toppled, landing with a clatter as it broke into scattered pieces. The interior was covered with soot half an inch thick.

Relic was now almost to Greatshadow's neck. The larger dragon grabbed the annoying assailant gingerly between two claws and placed him on the ledge amidst the scattered armor parts.

"Die! You must die!" screamed Relic.

"I sense I may have – in some fashion – offended you," said Greatshadow.

"You discovered me fresh from the egg and snapped my bones between your talons! You tossed my half-dead body from the caldera onto the slopes for the pygmies to scavenge! I was nothing but the unwelcome waste of your perversions, tossed away like trash! You will suffer! You will pay!"

Greatshadow rolled the tiny dragon between his talons, turning him to his back, taking a misshapen wing and snapping it once more. Relic screamed in agony as Greatshadow twisted the flesh back and forth, until a sharp bone punched through the surface.

"Little Brokenwing," said Greatshadow, tossing him onto the platform so that he bounced near the mouth of the tunnel. "Let the pain you feel at this moment linger. You have cost me dearly today. Nowowon required four centuries of incantations to properly enslave as my watchdog. You took him from me. I've worn my original body for thirty centuries, but the damage done by the knight may yet rob me of it. I saw your cowardly ally in possession of the Jagged Heart. You would dare bring *her* weapon to my lair, knowing what you know of our history?"

"I dare any price!" Relic hissed through clenched teeth. "Beginning with the pygmies who came to butcher my corpse, I've left a trail of death and destruction in my wake. My hate for you is a fire that can never be quenched!"

Greatshadow's mention of cowardly allies made me wonder where Zetetic had gone. Assuming he had the bone-handled knife, I felt for the familiar tug, and instantly found it. I flashed down the tunnel only a few yards. Zetetic was pressed to the wall, his face drained of all color; the red D tattooed on his forehead looked pink. He was shivering, and not just because he had both arms wrapped around the Jagged Heart, hugging it like a frightened child holding a doll. He had the bone-handled knife clutched in his right hand and what looked like a shard of glass in his left. He stared toward the opening of the ledge where Greatshadow busied himself with tormenting his overly ambitious offspring.

Greatshadow's blood seeped and bubbled across the stone like a dark river.

Setting his jaw, Zetetic leapt from the shadows, diving toward the stream of boiling ichor. He slapped the flat of the knife blade into the fluid. Instantly I was on my ass before him, meeting his frightened gaze. From the corner of my eye, I saw Greatshadow turning toward us, drawing a breath. The Jagged

Heart had saved Zetetic before, but the dragon was so close that Zetetic's long, frazzled ponytail fluttered as the beast inhaled. This blast was coming at point blank range.

With a voice squeaking with terror he gazed deeply into my eyes and announced, "I understand the interspatial geometry of the ancients!"

He snapped the gleaming glass in his left hand, which I now saw to be a mirror.

At that second, Greatshadow breathed, a great blinding gush of fire licking around me in all directions. Yet, I wasn't burned. The flames danced behind me, swirled above me, spun before me, but I remained safe in a bubble of cool air.

The conflagration died away. It seemed to me that Greatshadow, in his weakened state, had lost much of the power of his flame. He looked odd as I stared at him, distorted and wavy. Then I realized I was seeing him through a wall of pure ice at least a yard thick.

The wall of ice had materialized from the tip of the Jagged Heart. The Jagged Heart was being held by a humanoid figure nine feet tall, broad across the shoulders, wearing a long black walrus hide coat. I looked up and saw the mostly bald, blue-white scalp and the curve of ivory tusks. Never had I been so happy to see a woman whose last words to me had been a not so subtle threat of butchery.

Aurora looked down at me. As usual, her expression was one of utter coolness; she seemed unflustered that she'd just emerged from some unfathomable extra-dimensional prison to find herself face to face with a primal dragon. "I'll ask later what you're doing here," she said, shifting the shaft of the harpoon from her right hand to the left. "Right now, it's time for Greatshadow to meet someone who knows how to use this thing."

22 - Worst Nightmare

AURORA LUNGED, THE Jagged Heart held above her head, aiming for the gap between Greatshadow's eyes. The dragon pulled away, pressing down on the stone ledge with his massive claw. The volcanic rock cracked beneath his weight, creating a deep pit a yard wide just where Aurora's oversized boot should have landed. She fell as the ground between her and Greatshadow gave way.

Greatshadow plunged into the magma lake once more. I ran to the hole where Aurora had vanished. She'd dropped about twenty feet; her heels were balanced on a six-inch lip of stone. Fresh lava bubbled below her, fiery red.

I pulled off my cloak and dropped to my chest, my arms dangling over the edge to allow the hem to reach her.

"Climb up!" I shouted.

"Infidel thinks you're dead, you bastard!" Aurora said as she grabbed the thick velvet cloth. "Why the hell are you still alive? What on earth are you doing here? For that matter, what the hell am I doing here?"

Zetetic looked over the edge as Aurora began to climb up the cloak. My arms felt like they'd be pulled from their sockets. Zetetic said, "The pyramid trapped you in an interstitial realm where time doesn't exist as a dimension. I freed you."

"And while you're pondering that, you should know I'm a ghost, but turn solid when dragon blood gets on my knife," I explained, my voice strained as I struggled not to drop her. "I may dematerialize any second, so hurry."

Aurora furrowed her brow as she climbed. "I can't decide which of you is making less sense. Let me talk to someone sane. Where's Infidel?"

"The spirit realm," said Zetetic.

"She's dead?"

The Deceiver stroked his chin as he contemplated the question, then said, "I don't believe any existing word adequately describes her condition. She's been split into physically manifested dual aspects of her psyche then thrust bodily into a non-material realm of souls."

"You are not allowed to answer any more of my questions," Aurora grumbled as she grabbed the rocky ledge next to my shoulder with her sausage-sized fingers. My teeth chattered as she clambered over me back onto the relative safety of the ledge. "Where'd the damn dragon get off too?"

Relic crawled from the tunnel toward the bone-handled knife. He answered Aurora through teeth clenched with pain. "Greatshadow is bathing in magma to cauterize his wounds."

Aurora tensed as she saw the small dragon. She raised the Jagged Heart, looking ready to put him out of his misery.

"Wait!" said Zetetic, grabbing her arm. "He's a friend."

"I wouldn't go that far," I said.

"He's an enemy of our enemy," said Zetetic.

Relic reached the knife and moved it from the vaporizing dark brown pool it lay in, touching it to the sticky red blood coating his shoulder from his broken wing. The fresh fluid filled me with a surge of energy.

"So, can Greatshadow just wait us out?" I asked. "Could he stay under the magma forever?"

"Actually, no," said Relic. "Despite the fact my father dwells in a volcano, the elemental force he's merged with isn't magma, it's fire. His physical body and his internal flames both require air. He must surface soon."

Zetetic looked around. "Soon may not be soon enough," he said. "Tower's armor is disappearing piece by piece."

He was right. Tower's chest plate was still there, along with various nuts, bolts, and gears, but the bulk of the armor had vanished. As I watched, the hip compartment that held the magic book flickered, then turned to smoke, leaving the leather-bound volume within sitting on the barren ground. Zetetic tore off pieces of his robe and fashioned them into impromptu mittens, lifting the book.

"Technically, I'm not touching it," he said as he flipped through the book. He shook his head slowly as he studied the pages. "Not that having this will do me any good. Greatshadow is no doubt burning the monastery to the ground, killing everyone inside. When the last monk praying to keep my heart beating is slain I'll be dead, permanently this time."

"Greatshadow may have plucked that information from Stagger's mind," said Relic. "Perhaps he thinks if he waits long enough, he can face one less foe. Aurora is our best hope now. She can use the Jagged Heart to slay Greatshadow."

"This still doesn't make sense to me," I said. "Fire melts ice. Why is an icy fragment of Hush more powerful than a whole dragon?"

"Hush isn't the dragon of ice," said Aurora. "She's the dragon of cold."

"So?"

"To understand the true nature of reality, you need only look into the night sky. Darkness is the permanent state of things; light is merely a fleeting local phenomenon. The same is true of heat and fire. Flames can rage brightly for but a moment. Just as darkness will always win out over light, cold is the eternal backdrop that existed before fire, and will endure after. Flame can never win any permanent victory against cold."

"The true power of the weapon lies in more than simply its elemental chill," said Relic. "Greatshadow is the dragon who broke Hush's heart. Its frosty bitterness embodies the hatred Hush feels toward Greatshadow. It can, and will, slay him."

"I know a lot of dragon history, but I've never heard that," said Zetetic.

Before Relic could provide us with a history lesson, Greatshadow burst from the surface of the bubbling magma, his neck rising up fifty feet, a hundred, as he drew a deep breath into his mighty lungs. He was wreathed in fresh flames, his skin aglow with his newly stoked energies. The ground beneath us trembled as the lava pool began to rise.

Relic shook his head, looking as if he might be about to cry. "He's opened fresh lava vents beneath the surface! If the volcano erupts, we'll all perish!"

Aurora craned her neck up, drawing the harpoon back. Greatshadow spread his enormous wings, beating them in a powerful downstroke. Globs of molten rock rained around us as a foundry wind nearly swept us from our feet.

"His head's too far away!" Aurora shouted over the gale. "I can throw a harpoon a hundred yards on a good day, but not straight up!"

"You could if you were bigger!" Zetetic leapt in front of her. "Fortunately, I have the power to make you a giantess with an enchanted kiss!" He stood on his tiptoes, grabbed her cheeks, and mashed his puckered lips between her tusks.

A wall of flame shot down toward us as Greatshadow exhaled once more. As before, the flame was thwarted by a shield of ice as Aurora grew rapidly, doubling to sixteen feet, then thirty, as Zetetic grabbed Relic by the tail and dragged him back toward the tunnel.

I lingered behind for half a second to watch as Aurora topped out close to ninety feet tall. The Jagged Heart had grown with her, taller than any tree. Her long black coat flapped as she leaned back to throw, the hem catching me like a sail, knocking me from my feet. Flat on my back, I watched as she let the harpoon fly, aiming toward Greatshadow's open maw as the jet of flames died away.

The Jagged Heart flashed up like reverse lightning, trailing snow, entering the dragon's cavernous jaws and punching into the roof of his mouth. His head tilted sideways as he shrieked in pain. The bright, crystalline tip of the harpoon jutted from the top of his skull. His eyes rolled up, as if trying to focus on it.

Finally, Greatshadow shuddered, his body wracked with a death spasm. Zetetic ran from the tunnel and grabbed my hand, dragging me back toward relative safety as the dragon began to fall. Magma splashed up in a raging tidal wave as his body collapsed. Aurora, no longer in possession of the Jagged Heart, dropped to her hands and knees and tried to squeeze her massive bulk into the tunnel.

She was too late. The molten wave fell upon her and she screamed as her giant shoulders slammed into the tunnel entrance, plugging it, saving Zetetic, Relic, and myself from the magma bath.

I ran to her as the magic that had transformed her drained away. She returned to her normal size, inside a large cave that was a perfect negative outline of her body. The lava had hardened into solid stone on touching her, but not before it had burned away much of her skin. Her face had been spared, at least, and she was still alive as I dropped to my knees in front of her. "Hang on!" I screamed. "Zetetic can fix you!"

Her words were nothing but a whisper as she answered, "Th-the Heart… i-it must b-be returned…"

"Don't try to talk," I said.

"P-promise!" she said, straining to raise her voice. "T-take the Heart… take it… home."

"I promise," I said, taking her hands. "Now, hold still while…."

"Thank you," she sighed, as the last of her breath passed between her ivory tusks. Her eyes closed.

I pursed my lips together, fighting to keep from crying. She'd never intended to fight Greatshadow when this all began. She'd never done a thing to deserve this fate. I'd given my promise as a matter of convenience. It wouldn't have been right to argue with her. But looking at her now placid face I swore, somehow, someway, I'd keep my word to her.

Relic hobbled next to me, the bone-handled knife in his bleeding claw. "There is no time for mourning," said the small dragon. "Greatshadow's body is dead. We must act swiftly to kill his elemental spirit, before he can grow a new shell."

Zetetic wandered around the cave left by Aurora, staring up at specks of light that dotted the ceiling. He climbed a wall and thrust his fingers into one of the lights, which proved to be a hole in a paper-thin sheet of rock. He flaked it away in big handfuls, and soon had a large enough gap to climb through.

"Follow me," he said, as he wriggled out.

Relic leapt onto the wall and clambered after him. Despite his injuries and the obvious pain of every movement, the little dragon still seemed much stronger and faster than I was. I guess even a lamed dragon was a better physical specimen than an ordinary man. Or, at least in better shape than me. I was panting, my arms trembling, by the time I managed to drag myself through the hole. My legs were quivering as I walked out onto a freshly formed plain of soot-black rock still spiderwebbed with tendrils of bright red lava. The volcano seemed to have lost a great deal of its energy with Greatshadow gone. Still, I danced around, grateful I had boots. As long as I kept moving, the heat was merely blistering instead of crippling.

In the center of the rapidly cooling lava, amid rock that cracked and popped as it gave up its heat, was Greatshadow's enormous head and shoulders, frozen into the solidifying stone. One wing jutted into the air behind him like a giant black sail. The deep brick red of his scalp was now pink beneath a layer of thick frost. The Jagged Heart had returned to its normal size and lay upon his snout as if it had been dropped there by some hopelessly lost whaler.

Zetetic ran across the smoking plane, jumping over glowing cracks, scrambling up Greatshadow's scaly hide. Though it was entirely the wrong thing to be thinking about, I couldn't help but gawk at the sheer size of the dragon's skull as my internal booze calculator tried to figure out how many rounds I could buy at the *Black Swan* if I could somehow cash it in. A lot. A whole damn lot. Numbers weren't my strong suit.

Zetetic stood between the dragon's eyes as he snatched up the Jagged Heart. "Got it!" he shouted. "Now, we just need to get a warrior to the spirit world to finish off the dragon!"

Relic nodded, standing before the Greatshadow's toothy jaws, staring up at Zetetic. "Stagger will have to do."

"Have to do what?" I asked.

"Go to the spirit world to kill Greatshadow," said Zetetic, tossing the harpoon at me. I jumped back as the tip buried into the stone where I'd just stood.

"You almost killed me!" I shouted.

"I don't think that's possible," the Deceiver said. "You aren't alive, remember? No court would convict me."

I grabbed the harpoon and yanked it free. I held it toward Relic. "You're the one with the daddy-grudge. You do it."

"Nowowon has broken my claws. It's agonizing to hold this knife; I could never wield the harpoon effectively," said Relic. "And Zetetic is too cowardly to be trusted with the mission."

"I concur," said the Deceiver.

"I'm not exactly a prime physical specimen myself," I said, wiping sweat from my brow. "And I'll fight any man who says I'm not a yellow-bellied coward!"

"You may not need to fight the dragon yourself," said Zetetic. "The War-Doll – I mean, Infidel – is already in the spirit realm. The gate she passed through leads to the specific abstract reality where Greatshadow's soul resides. She did show a certain talent for violence. If she's somehow recovered from her psychic split, you could have her complete the mission."

My immediate thought was, screw the mission. Except for the whole end-of-the-world-by-fire thing, what did I care if Greatshadow's soul was killed? But the thought that I could be reunited with Infidel in the spirit world made my heart beat faster. I didn't want her to die, but, if she was already a spirit, I'd rather be on the other side with her than trapped here as a ghost.

"Okay," I said, holding the harpoon in a two-handed grasp. "You've made your case. How do I get to Infidel? Zetetic can't open another spirit gate. If there was a magic item here that could open the portal, isn't it buried under about a thousand feet of rock now?"

"Oh," said Relic. "That was a lie."

"Nice," said Zetetic.

"Then there's not some object here with the power to send me to the land of the dead?" I asked, confused.

"I wouldn't say that's true either," said Relic, walking toward me, wincing as he shifted the bone-handled knife around in his claw to grasp it by the hilt instead of the blade.

Before I understood his intention he stabbed me, the blade punching though my left nipple. In a second of time that dribbled by like molasses I felt the knife tear through my pectoral muscles, skim between my ribs, slice the edge of my left lung, and puncture my heart, halting it mid-beat.

The world went black.

I LIFTED MY throbbing head from my folded arms and looked around the bar at the *Black Swan*. I blinked my bleary eyes, attempting to focus in the dim light. The lanterns barely flickered behind soot-grimed crystal globes. A score of empty tankards were set out around me in a semi-circle of pewter and glass. My whole body was stiff and cold as I stretched, working out the kinks in my back.

I rubbed my sleep fogged eyes, then studied the bottles behind the bar, choosing what I'd drink next. I frowned when I realized all the bottles looked empty. Everything was covered with dust. Busty, one of the regular serving wenches, was at the far end of the bar, her back to me.

"I just had the worst nightmare," I said. My tongue felt thick in my mouth, covered with a dry, pasty scum. "Bring me a beer, would you, luv?"

She wouldn't. At least, she didn't. She just stood there, still as a statue. I got up from the stool and staggered toward her, keeping one hand on the bar for balance. I reached the end of the bar and suddenly sobered up.

Busty was nothing but a dusty skeleton, still standing upright, staring blankly ahead with empty sockets. Her frilly blouse hung like a sack, the generous bustline now dangling to reveal a desiccated breastbone. I spun around, surveying the silent room. There were a hundred people packed into every corner, all dead, their skeletons frozen in rough approximation of daily motion. Players gathered around a table, faded cards forever clasped in their bony fingers. A whore leaned on the shoulder of a client in a corner booth, her mummified cheeks stained with rouge, her dusty wig askew atop her skull.

"Hello?" I said, to the silent room.

No one answered.

However, as I strained to listen, in the distance I heard a long, low howl, like the baying of a wolf. I crept across the dusty floorboards to the door, looking out onto the familiar skyline of the Isle of Fire.

Only, it wasn't quite as I remembered. The boats surrounding me were all derelict husks, floating in water the color of red wine. A rotting, tilted pier ran toward the banks of the bay. The damage done by Greatshadow's attack on Commonground was nowhere to be seen. Instead, the slopes of the island were still covered with a thick jade canopy of trees, rising to a volcano from which plumes of stark white steam boiled heavenward. The sky was a light gray slate, devoid of a sun, or even clearly defined clouds. The island that lay before me seemed out of scale, smaller somehow.

I crouched down, startled, as the animalistic howl once more rolled over the bay. Wolves weren't native to the Isle of Fire, though they haunted the mountains near the monastery where I'd spent my childhood. I'd gone to sleep many a night pondering the meanings of their different songs; sometimes, they sang toward the moon to tell tales of loneliness and lost loves. Sometimes, their songs were almost joyous, a simple declaration of, "I'm alive! I'm here! And I'm a wolf!" That song was easy to distinguish from a harsher, more sinister war cry, when they howled to frighten prey, to startle them into running. This was that last type of howl.

I glanced back to the bar. The Jagged Heart was lying on the floor beside my stool. I looked down, surprised to find I was still wearing the finery Zetetic had conjured. To my greater surprise, I found the bone-handled knife jutting from my chest. I didn't feel a thing as I grasped the hilt and popped it free. No blood flowed from the wound.

"Relic?" I said, wondering if he could still hear me.

The only answer was the gentle lapping of the wine-dark sea.

Going back inside, I grabbed the Jagged Heart. I wondered how it had made the transition. I'd been holding it when I was stabbed, but when I first died, I'd passed over naked. Maybe the difference was that Relic hadn't stabbed a living man to dispatch to the ghost realms. He'd stabbed a materialized spirit. If I ever met the Divine Author, it seemed like a good thing to ask Him about over a pint of beer. Assuming the Divine Author drinks.

What am I saying? He's a writer. Of course He drinks.

Alas, He wasn't here at the moment, and my quick pillaging pass behind the bar showed that beer wasn't present either. If this were paradise, the sea outside would have been made of actual wine, but I suspected I would be in for an unpleasant surprise if I tested that. I was going to be doing this dragon hunt sober, damn it.

Back outside, I headed up the boardwalk toward the forest. Like the bar, it was eerily silent: no bugs buzzing, no bullfrogs bleating, no birds providing a serenade. I pushed through underbrush studded with fearsome thorns. The Jagged Heart proved better than a machete; vines and limbs studded with wooden needles froze solid as I touched them, snapping with only the slightest touch. Once I was through the brush, towering trees surrounded me, their smooth, perfectly formed trunks stretching high overhead into a curtain of unbroken green. It was dark as a moonless night, but my eyes soon adjusted to the dimness.

From high up the slope, the howl of the unseen beast once more rolled through the air. As the sound faded, I thought I could hear a *crunch, crunch, crunch* in the distance, the footsteps of something large creeping amongst the trees. I had a pretty good idea what might be making the noise.

Somewhere out in the darkness was the monster who'd lived inside the woman I'd loved.

I skulked up the slopes, holding the harpoon like a halberd, a weapon I had absolutely no experience with. Not that I had much experience with any weapons. Infidel had been my principal mode of defense, which was for the best. Given how often I'd been drunk when our fights broke out, if I'd tried handling anything sharp I'd probably eventually have stabbed myself.

I heard a *shuff, shuff, shuff* of something moving through the leaves and pressed up closely against an ancient tree trunk thick enough to hide an elephant. I peeked around, listening closely to see if the noise was drawing closer.

Shuff, shuff, shuff. It was right on the other side of the tree.

When I met the she-dragon, would I kill her? Could I? What if I tried to talk to her? Would she recognize me or just try to eat me?

Trusting that I would know what to do when the moment came, I grasped the harpoon and raced around the tree at top speed, which, thanks to my cape snagging on the trunk, wasn't all that fast. Still, it was fast enough to terrify the little girl in the lacy dress I found pressed up against the tree on the far side. Her eyes popped wide and her mouth gaped into an almost perfect 'O' as she filled her lungs, ready to scream. I dropped the Jagged Heart and jumped toward her, hands outstretched, knocking her to the ground as I clamped my hand over her mouth. Air gushed around my fingers as her muffled scream tickled my palm.

"Shhh!" I hissed, as quietly as I could manage. "Shhh! Do you want your other half to hear?"

Tears welled in her eyes as she shook her head, 'no.'

I couldn't believe how tiny she was, pinned beneath me. Infidel had actually been somewhat petite, I guess, but it was easy to forget this when she was juggling around bruisers and brutes. Princess Innocent was a whole lot shorter and her arms were thin as broomsticks. My hand practically covered her whole face.

"I'm going to let go," I whispered. "Don't scream."

She trembled as I pulled my hand free. I helped her stand, while I rose to my knees so we'd be on eye level.

"Are you all right?" I asked. Her dress was torn in a dozen places, and her cheeks were covered with scratches. Her long silver hair was a mess.

"Who are you?" she whispered.

"You don't remember?"

She shook her head.

I weighed my words carefully. I had dreamed, should I ever reunite with Infidel, I'd confess my love and kiss her hard enough to make us both dizzy. That seemed highly inappropriate now, given her reversion to such a young age. "I was... I was a friend. My name is Stagger."

"You smell bad," she said, scrunching up her nose.

No doubt I did. Growing up in a palace, Innocent had probably never met anyone who sweated.

"Have you seen your other half?" I asked. "Is she near?"

She furrowed her brow, looking confused.

"The she-dragon," I said. "She brought you here."

"She wants to eat me," said Innocent. "But I'm good at hiding."

Which was true enough. The princess had hidden inside Infidel all these years without me suspecting a thing.

As I thought this, an idea occurred to me. Innocent had been hiding inside Infidel. Could she do so again? What if... what if the way to join her two halves back together was simply to let the dragon once more devour the princess?

"The way you're looking at me scares me," said Innocent.

I pursed my lips as I pondered my options.

Whatever was showing on my face couldn't have been good, because Innocent suddenly burst into tears. She went limp, almost fainting, as she fell against my chest, sobbing. I wrapped my arms around her, stroking her hair.

"It's okay," I whispered. "It's okay. I'll protect you. I won't let the monster hurt you."

And that was that. The vile thought of feeding this little girl to the she-dragon was banished back to whatever dark pit in my brain it had crawled from. Some fatherly instinct welled within me and I knew with absolute certainty I'd willingly die to protect this girl.

"I'm s-so tired," she sobbed. "I've b-been running and running and running."

Again, this was true for Infidel as well. The whole time I'd known her, I'd thought of her as a fighter, but, in truth, she'd lived every moment on the run from her own past. How had I been so blind?

"You won't have to run any more," I whispered, setting my jaw firmly. "I'll fight the monster for you."

I hugged her for a long time, her face pressed against my chest, until her sobs died down to whimpers, then sniffles. I finally pulled away from her, still on my knees, my hands on her shoulders as I said, "Everything is going to be fine. I'm your friend, and I'll take care of you."

She didn't say anything. She didn't move. Her mouth hung half open as her eyes were fixed at a point in space somewhere over my shoulder.

I didn't have to turn around to know what was standing behind me.

23 - THE WORLD CAN WAIT

I DOVE ASIDE as a three-clawed foot stomped down where I'd stood, causing the earth to shudder. My flight was brought to a choking halt by the red velvet cape, caught beneath the she-dragon's heel. I should have dumped the cloak the second the damn thing had been inflicted on me. I fiddled with the collar for half a second before slicing the clasp open with the bone-handled knife. I dropped the blade as I scrambled toward the Jagged Heart. The ground was slippery with frost. I slid across ice-etched leaves, my hand outstretched. A giant claw punched into the soil in front of me, forming a scaly fence. I slammed into it, the harpoon only inches beyond my grasp.

The she-dragon leaned down, her jaws dripping sap-like spittle, the tangles of her hair dangling like vines. Bright yellow eyes stared into mine as she paused in reptilian concentration. Did she recognize me?

"Infidel!" I shouted. "It's me, Stagger!"

Her oversized fingers wrapped around my throat as she snatched me off the ground. Her nose was merely two holes flat against her face, like the nose of a snake. The emerald green scales that glittered around her eyes were weirdly beautiful, in a terrifying, inhuman way.

"I love you!" I shouted. "You loved me!"

The creature licked her lips, her eyes twinkling with the same delighted hunger I'd seen in Infidel's face when Tower had produced the cake. Her head tilted back as her jaws opened to an impossible angle. I flailed helplessly as she brought me toward her jagged teeth.

"Leave him alone!" a tiny voice shouted below my feet.

The she-dragon closed her mouth and looked down. From the corner of my eye, I glimpsed Princess Innocent with her hands on her hips.

"He's my friend and I won't let you hurt him," the princess shouted, a stern look in her eyes.

A low growl rumbled from the she-dragon's chest as she eyed the annoying creature.

The princess stomped her feet, obviously furious at the delay. "My daddy's the king and you have to do what I say! Put him down!"

"You really should listen to her," I squeaked.

The she-dragon responded by flinging me aside. I went flying above the canopy of trees, feeling profound déjà vu as I reached the apex of my flight and began to plummet toward the blood tangle vines far below. My re-entry was thoroughly unpleasant. If I'd truly been alive, it's possible it would even have been fatal, as I slammed into a tree trunk hard enough to knock off bark. But, just as the wound had been clean when I pulled the bone-handled knife from my ribs, the cuts and scrapes that crosshatched my arms beneath the shredded remains of my sleeves didn't ooze a single drop of blood.

I rose on rubbery legs as a high-pitched shriek of pain reached my ears. I struggled back up the slope, limping, my ankle twisted, though the pain I felt was muted by the same general gauziness that wreathed all my senses in death. Then, for no apparent reason, my ankle suddenly hurt like the devil. In fact, my entire body felt like I'd gone two rounds in a pit fight with No-Face. Blood bubbled up from my various cuts, though almost a minute had passed since the wounds had been inflicted.

A hundred yards ahead there was another ear-piercing scream, far louder than before.

"Infidel!" I shouted, hopping back up the slope with all the speed I could muster. "Infidel!"

At last I spotted the elephantine tree I'd hidden behind only a few minutes before. I moved to one side and saw the Jagged Heart still on the ground, near freshly fallen trees.

I hopped a little further, my heart growing cold as I realized how utterly silent the forest had become. The shrieking I'd heard earlier had stopped, and now the quietness was broken only by a wet, crunching sound, repeating every few seconds, a sound that I imagined might come from the jaws of a she-dragon devouring meat and gristle.

Braced for the worst, I stepped into the clearing.

Sitting atop one of the fallen trees, her face covered in bright green goo, was Princess Innocent. She lifted the bone-handled knife overhead and gave a solid punch down with both hands, planting it to the hilt in the tree trunk, creating the sound I'd heard. I wondered if, for some reason, my blood was pumping in my body because the knife blade was wet again, though with what looked like green slime instead of blood.

I then realized the tree trunk the princess was hacking into was covered in dark green scales and shaped like a woman. It wasn't sap coating the knife.

I sagged, resting my hands on my knees, catching my breath, as Princess Innocent placed her mouth against the fresh wound she'd gouged in the she-dragon and sucked up the oozing blood. With every mouthful, she grew a little larger. The gown she wore tightened, then split along the seams.

After a moment the princess sat back and wiped the bright green blood from her face. She had a woman's body now, over a foot taller than when she'd started her feast, with magnificent breasts I instantly recognized. Before me was the woman I'd known all these years, her silver hair long and gleaming, her skin pale beneath blood and shredded gown, completely free of pygmy dyes. Innocent looked like Infidel once more.

I smiled at the perfect logic of the magic unfolding before me. Infidel hadn't been created when a dragon devoured a princess. Infidel had been born when a princess devoured a dragon.

Infidel looked slightly drunk, oblivious to her surroundings as the dragon blood settled into her belly. Yet, as she surveyed the forest with her glazed eyes, her face broke into a giant grin as her gaze reached me. She cried, "Stagger!"

"Infidel!" I answered, throwing my arms open as I hobbled toward her.

She jumped from the corpse and bounded toward me like a sprightly gazelle. I flinched as she reached me, her arms wrapping around me, braced for significant damage to my ribs. However, her hug, while robust, seemed to have only ordinary strength behind it. I bent my face down to gaze at her in wonder, but instantly closed my eyes as she pressed her lips to mine. The green blood still on her cheeks smelled like papaya. Her sticky tongue slid between my teeth. I hugged her back with all my might and kissed her till we were both dizzy.

Not metaphorically dizzy, mind you, but actual stumble and collapse from lack of air dizzy. We fell, landing atop the red cape that lay over the leafy earth like a bed-spread. Only the impact of the ground made our lips pull apart. I was on top of her, staring down into her sea-gray eyes and all the words and wisdom and wonder that they contained. Her body beneath mine was hot as a furnace. Where our skin met through our tattered clothing, it was slippery from dragon blood and my own blood and a copious amount of sweat. Our breaths intermingled as we studied each others faces and for the span of several heartbeats it felt as if all was right with the universe.

Except, alas, it wasn't.

"As much as I hate to ruin this moment, the world might come to a fiery end if we don't go kill Greatshadow's spirit," I whispered.

"The world can wait," she replied, as she placed her hand in my tangled hair and drew my mouth to hers once more.

Fortunately, she'd left the bone-handled knife in the dragon's blood.

For the events which followed, it was useful to be in full, unmuted possession of all my senses, and to have a heart free to pump blood to wherever it was needed.

As we kissed, her gentle fingers slowly pulled away the damaged rags that had once been my shirt. My own fingers slipped into the strained seams of her gown and completed the tearing, freeing her from her silken confinement.

And then…

And then…

And then…

Shall I tell you how she looked, bare beneath me, the body of an angel wearing the grin of a devil, hungry for pleasure? Shall I tell you of the noises that came from deep within her, the guttural growls, the sibilant songs, the barely-voiced moans as my mouth fell against her skin? Shall I tell you how she tasted, all sweetness and salt, of the wine that was her sweat and spit and tears? Or how she smelled, like earth, like ocean, like sunlight, a symphony of aromas where every scent note built to a perfect crescendo?

And shall I tell you how she felt? Do I even possess the vocabulary to describe the smooth, slick landscape of her body, the warm terrain so full of curves and creases, the silken softness overlaying muscle and bone of breathtaking artfulness? Can I possibly find the vocabulary to describe the magic of feeling her heart beating as I pressed my lips against her throat, the steady *thump, thump, thump* a drum beating out a single message of *life, life, life,* so elegant and simple it moved me to tears?

No. No, I don't believe I can tell you of these things, and I don't believe that I should.

But they happened all the same.

SINCE I CANNOT tell you about the unspeakable wonder of the moments that followed my reunion with Infidel, allow me to fill you in on what was occurring back in the real world with Relic and Zetetic. While I wasn't personally witness to these events, I've since learned enough to reconstruct the moment: Zetetic and Relic had freed the Gloryhammer from where it was partially trapped beneath freshly cooling lava. I had wondered if the Gloryhammer would vanish like Tower's armor, but, apparently it was a far older creation, an enchanted weapon with a history dating back centuries, and Zetetic recounted this history to Relic with his usual enthusiasm for obscure magical lore.

As they spoke, Zetetic and Relic retreated to a perch atop Greatshadow's skull, which rose like a little island from the lava plane. They amused themselves for a time by pulling possessions out of Tower's sketchbook, including the Immaculate Attire, which Zetetic used as a seat on the still hot skull. Several more slices of cake in various flavors were also retrieved, which they devoured with gusto.

As daylight faded they passed the time speculating as to what was happening elsewhere. For instance, Zetetic put forth the theory the fire Greatshadow had started in the monastery must have been brought under control, even though the last bolts from Tower's armor had finally faded away. Some monks had survived, Zetetic argued, since his heart was still beating.

Relic chuckled lowly in response and said, "You never died."

"I was hanged," said Zetetic.

"Yes. But your neck didn't break. You suffocated and merely passed out."

"My neck was pure agony for a week after," said Zetetic. "It certainly felt broken."

"No doubt you'd injured some ligaments," said Relic. "But Father Ver knew the truth. When they hung you, the noose was designed to suffocate you without severing your spine. You passed out from asphyxiation, feeling as if you were dying. When you woke up, you were told of your death, though it had never occurred. No monks have ever had to pray to keep you alive. I snatched the truth from Ivory Blade's mind."

"Oh," said Zetetic, then burst out into raucous laughter.

"You're relieved you need not fear imminent death?"

Zetetic wiped a tear from his eye. "There's that. But I also appreciate the irony. How appropriate that I should be ensnared with a simple lie."

They both sat quietly for a while, listening to the crackle of the stone cooling around them, until Zetetic asked, "How are we going to know if Stagger succeeds?"

"We shall know when the world doesn't end," said Relic.

"It's not ending right now."

"That we know of," said Relic.

Zetetic nodded, pondering this. Then he said, "Do you think Stagger ever found the she-dragon or the princess?"

"Let us hope not," said Relic.

"Why?"

"Because the princess would distract him. He would probably try to protect her from danger, which means he might not do what is needed to slay Greatshadow."

"But maybe he'll find the she-dragon," said Zetetic.

Relic sighed. "In that case, the creature is probably chewing his flesh right now."

And, in a way, he was right, since as my reunion with Infidel unfolded, I became increasingly decorated with bite marks.

But I'm not telling you of such things, am I?

ONCE WE WERE too exhausted to continue the more athletic portion of our reunion, we wrapped our tenderized bodies in the red cloak, our limbs entangled as we slipped into a dreamy haze in which time lost all grip upon us. Infidel's face was pressed up against my chest, listening to my heartbeat. She was so still and quiet I thought she'd gone to sleep, until she whispered, "You smell nice."

I chuckled. "Innocent didn't think so."

"Innocent didn't know what was good for her. You, Stagger, are good for me. I was so lucky to know you."

"Why are you speaking in the past tense?" I asked.

"You're still dead, right? That wasn't just some bad dream?"

My mouth went dry. "It wasn't a dream," I whispered. "I am dead. But I never left you; I've been with you every moment, haunting the bone-handled knife. And now we can be together forever."

"Can we?" she asked, sounding skeptical.

"Can't we?" I asked. "I guess, honestly, I don't know. I don't understand how things work here in the spirit world. Maybe there will never be any ending here."

"But I don't belong here," she said. "I'm still alive. At least, I think I am. There's this... tug... inside me. I feel like my time here is limited. Eventually, I'll be drawn back to the real world."

"I understand," I said. "I wish I could come with you."

"I don't see why you can't, if I can take the knife back. Haunting the blade that killed you. That's kind of weird."

"This coming from a woman with a belly full of dragon's blood."

Infidel sat up, frowning as she noticed the tangled green ribbons in her long hair. As she worked to unknot them, she said, "The first time I swallowed Verdant's blood, it was dried up and concentrated. I could feel the power surging through my body. This time, it turned me back to my correct age, but I don't feel super-strong." She ran her fingers along a line of hickeys on her neck. "And I'm definitely not invulnerable."

"Maybe things work differently here. Hopefully you'll be back to your arm-ripping self when you get home."

She looked up the slope toward the caldera. "I wish I knew how to get home. The only path I can think of leads straight through Greatshadow. The dragon must know how to travel between the spirit world and the material world, or Zetetic wouldn't be worried."

"We still have the Jagged Heart," I said. "Even with just normal strength, we can take him."

She sighed as she pulled the last ribbon free from her hair and tossed it away. "That's so sad about Aurora," she said, referring to a conversation we'd had during an earlier pause.

I sat up and rubbed her back. "She was a good friend."

"She was my only friend," said Infidel. "Except you."

"I'll always be with you," I said.

She nodded gazing off into the distance. "Especially if the Black Swan is right."

"About what? The dragon apocalypse?"

Infidel rolled her eyes. "About us having a daughter."

Somehow, despite everything that we'd done together since our reunion, that possibility hadn't crossed my mind. Could I really impregnate Infidel? Did this half-alive, materialized phantom body of mine have that power?

"You're quiet," she said, as I grew lost in thought. "Don't you want her to be yours?"

I smiled as I lay back, pulling her down with me. "I want it so much, I think we should take at least one more run at increasing the odds."

And then there was another hour that I can't talk about.

"STAGGER MUST HAVE gotten the job done by now," said Zetetic. By now it had gotten really dark in the caldera. Outside the small circle of light cast by the Gloryhammer, ghostly flames flickered and danced above cracks in the ground, as gasses beneath the earth seeped free and ignited.

"I'm not so certain," said Relic. "I don't feel… a release."

"A release?"

"Like all dragons, I'm attuned to elemental forces. Greatshadow is still present in the flames surrounding us. He simply hasn't gathered the strength yet to control them."

"If he died, you could take over the element of flame? Just like that?"

Relic shrugged. "It would require time. How much is difficult to say."

"How long did it take Greatshadow to master the element?"

"Though I have many of his memories, I can't judge the time, since time as we know it wasn't invented when my father was young."

Zetetic looked perplexed.

"Before Glorious merged his spirit with the sun, the sun's path was more chaotic. Years and days had no fixed length. Glorious inadvertently gave birth to human civilization when he guided the sun into a fixed path, making seasons predictable and agriculture possible."

"Amazing," said Zetetic.

"Still, to answer your question as best I can, I expect it will take a decade or more to merge my soul with fire."

"A decade doesn't seem very long to achieve such power."

"To you, perhaps. I've only been alive a few months. A decade seems unbearably long."

Zetetic stroked his chin as he contemplated the small dragon. "You're an interesting infant, Relic."

"I don't want to be called Relic any more."

"Why not?"

"I used that name because I never was given another. But my father finally fulfilled this simple obligation, at least. He called me Brokenwing."

"So he did. Little Brokenwing."

"I won't be using the 'little,'" said the dragon, somewhat indignant.

"So, if Stagger fails, what are we going to do?" asked Zetetic.

Relic shook his head. "There's no point in asking. Stagger is our only hope."

Zetetic looked up into the darkness. "I wonder what's taking so long to get the job done?"

If I'd been there to answer, I'd have reminded him that at fifty, my body isn't quite as robust as it once was. It takes a little longer to get the job done.

AND EVEN LONGER to get the job done a third time. This dayless, nightless land provided few clues as to how much time had passed as we rested, utterly exhausted.

Infidel was using my hairy belly as a pillow, looking up at me with a dreamy gaze. Suddenly, her eyes widened.

"It's so obvious!" she said, jumping to her feet.

"What's obvious?"

"Dragon's blood! You come back to life when the knife touches dragon's blood. And, you came back to life when Nowowon gave you a drink of blood. So, to come back to life permanently, you need to drink dragon's blood!"

I sat up, scratching my head. "You think it's that easy?"

"Who's the brain in this operation?" she said, placing her hands on her hips.

"Um," I said, deciding to pretend I didn't understand the question. Anyway, what could it hurt? She scrambled toward the fallen body of her dragon-self.

"Ow, ow, ow!" she said as she crossed over the ground. "Lot's of sharp rocks under these leaves. I'm not used to being tender-footed."

"You want to wear my boots?" I asked, wrestling to put on what remained of my pants.

"I'd slip right out of those things," she said, scrambling onto the dragon corpse. "I'll wrap my feet in some cloth from the cape. Right now, you need to suck some dragon-blood."

She grabbed the bone-handled knife, struggling to free it. She gouged a new hole on the side of the hip. Gore the consistency and color of pea soup oozed out.

My lips were tender from Infidel's nibbles, but I heroically pressed them to the scaly hide of the corpse and sucked. The blood was sticky, as difficult to swallow as molasses, and the fruity flavor I had tasted on Infidel's tongue had a sourness when drank directly that grew more unbearable the longer it sat in my mouth. It took a few moments to force down a cup of the stuff.

"Ugg," I said, wiping my lips. "I'm used to putting bad things in my mouth, but this is fairly rotten."

"How do you feel?" she asked.

"Fantastic!" I said. "But I've felt that way ever since we've been back together. Just being able to talk to you again is more magical than dragon's blood."

"Maybe you won't notice any changes to your body until we get back to the real world," she said, studying my bruised frame with a critical eye.

"That's probably how it works," I said, hoping it was true.

She sat down on the she-dragon's log-like foot and began to cut the lower edges of my cape into strips with the knife. She wrapped her feet in the thick velvet, forming what could have passed as ballerina slippers. They looked surprisingly functional; Infidel had a lot of experience improvising with clothing. She took what remained of my shirt, tore off the shredded sleeves, and wore it like a tunic, cinching it at the waist with a belt made from the braided sleeve rags.

I dressed while she worked, slipping my boots back on. Since I was shirtless, I decided I'd wear what was left of the cape. I brushed off the twigs and leaves and noticed a snarl of long, tangled hair. I looked at it closer, unable to tell if it had come out of my scalp or hers, and finally decided it was a little of both. Inspired by the intertwined fibers, I wrapped the long strands around my little finger, tucking and twisting them until I formed a small braided ring. It barely fit on my little finger. I braided another, slightly larger. I finished my efforts just as she jumped down from the log.

I dropped to one knee before her and took her hand.

"I don't know if this counts, since there's no church, no priest, and, alas, no wedding cake. But, my parents never got married, and I want our daughter to grow up respectable. So, Infidel, with this ring, I thee wed, if you'll have me."

I paused before I slipped the smaller hair ring onto her finger, looking into her face. Her eyes were wet as she nodded and said, "I do."

The ring fit perfectly; the silver in her hair and the gray in mine even gave it a bit of sparkle. "It's not exactly gold and glorystone," I said.

"It's far more precious," she whispered, pulling me close. I handed her the larger ring. She slipped it onto my finger.

At this point, I should probably switch to another interlude in the material world, but, alas, there really wasn't anything interesting going on there. So I'll just skip ahead to the part where we got dressed again.

She finished binding up her slippers as I finished fixing the clasp on my cape. She tossed me the bone-handled knife, which I stuck in my belt, then went to grab the Jagged Heart.

"Wow," she said, lifting it, a bit off balance. "It's kind of heavy."

"Yeah," I said. "I should probably carry it. You carry the knife."

"Nah. Even if I don't have supernatural strength, I still have more experience jabbing holes in things than you do."

"Conceded."

She looked toward the caldera. "You're certain the world will be destroyed if we don't do this?"

"I'm not certain of anything. But Zetetic thinks it's a real possibility."

"Yeah, but he's, you know, a Deceiver. He's got the tattoo on his forehead and everything. What if he's tricking us into doing something awful?"

"I don't have an answer for that. But what's our alternative?"

She shrugged, but still didn't look eager to tramp up the slope.

"We have the best reason of all for doing this," I said. "Assuming you're pregnant, I don't want my daughter being born in the land of the dead. For her sake, we have to get you home safely, and we have to make sure that there's still a world left for us to raise her in."

Infidel nodded as she pressed her lips together in a look of grim determination.

"Let's go find this oversized iguana and get out of here," she said, marching up the slope, the harpoon resting on her shoulder like a soldier's pike.

THE PECULIAR GEOGRAPHY of this corner of the afterlife meant we didn't have far to go. Barely a hundred yards passed before we pushed through a wall of thorny brush onto a steep rocky ridge that led to the caldera. We advanced arm in arm, in part because it's the way lovers like to walk, and in part because we were each having trouble walking individually. My ankle still hurt like hell and Infidel was leaving bloody footprints from where thorns had punched through her satin shoes. Not to mention, we were both tender and chaffed and raw. In places.

As we limped our way past the lip of the caldera, we looked down over a field of black rock, dotted with vents of steam. In the center of this barren landscape there was what looked to be the remains of the world's largest bonfire, a half-mile-long hill of soot-covered coals and glowing embers wreathed in a skin of pale blue flames.

The bonfire crackled with sparks as we approached. There was a peculiar rumble, low and rhythmic, that I had difficulty identifying. Then, Infidel grabbed my shoulder and pulled my ear down to lip level. She whispered, softly, "Is that fire snoring?"

I nodded. Of course it was snoring. This was Greatshadow's spirit and it was asleep. Infidel always crashed into a corpse-like slumber after a tough battle. Greatshadow probably did the same.

Our eyes locked. Would it really be this easy? Did we just have to sneak up on an exhausted dragon and punch the Jagged Heart between his eyes?

Infidel placed her hand on the back of my neck. She tilted her face to meet mine and gave me a long, lingering kiss. In the aftermath I stared at her, moon-eyed. There was frost in her long platinum locks. Her breath came out as mist. And her eyes, her eyes glistened like deep and mysterious pools in a cavern as she said, softly, "Trust me."

I nodded. There was never any doubt. My fate, her fate, the fate of our daughter, the fate of all mankind: I surrendered them willingly into her hands.

She motioned for me to wait where we stood, a good fifty yards from the smoldering flames, as she lowered the harpoon to attack position and crept forward. I held my breath as she inched closer, my eyes flickering from her to the slumbering dragon. Now that I understood the true nature of the flaming hill before us, it was easy to make out the dragon's long neck and ship-sized head. Infidel was marching straight toward his mouth.

Thirty feet away, she knelt, placing the harpoon on the ground before her.

"Greatshadow," she said, in a very loud voice. "Wake up."

She didn't reach for the Jagged Heart as enormous eyes flickered open, great orbs glowing like furnaces, to focus on her with a hate-filled stare.

24 - WE FELL

"YOU'VE BEEN SENT to kill me," said Greatshadow, smoke rising from his jaws. His teeth looked like ash covered logs glowing with internal fires.

"Yes," said Infidel, still kneeling, her head bowed low. "But I'm not going to. I don't wish to hurt you."

"Yet you've brought the accursed Heart to my elemental realm. Merely looking upon it causes my soul to weaken. You must know the agony it brings me."

Infidel shook her head. "I'm sorry. I didn't personally bring the harpoon here, though I was told it could hurt you. I confess, however, I don't really understand why."

The ashen heap that was once the most feared dragon in the world turned his enormous head away, so that the Jagged Heart was no longer within his line of sight.

"It's a part of her," he sighed, his voice crackling like a campfire stirred by a breeze. "Long ago, before we dragons entangled our souls with the elements, we were mortal creatures. Like all beasts, the most important goal of our lives was to mate. Unlike other beasts, we dragons prided ourselves on the spiritual nature of our relationships. We weren't mere animals, slaves of our instincts and lusts. We based our coupling on refined courtship that insured that we were perfectly paired: mentally, spiritually, magically, and physically."

"I was told that you and Hush were lovers?"

Greatshadow shook his ragged head as cinders fell from his eyes like dark tears. "More than lovers. Alone, we were incomplete beings; together, we were one perfect soul. Her cold balanced my heat. My wrathful nature was calmed by her grace, while my brash and sudden passions could stir her cool and logical heart. When we lay entangled together in our coupling, staring into one another's eyes, there was no loneliness. We were a universe in total, beyond all cares. Or so I thought." Greatshadow swallowed hard as the ground trembled beneath my feet.

Infidel cast a glance back at me. I studied her face for some clue as to why she hadn't attacked. I longed for Relic's telepathy. I didn't know why she was taking this risk. And yet… and yet she gave me a slight nod, with her eyes locked on mine, and the message was plain. *Trust me.*

I nodded back, and waited.

Greatshadow's voice was almost a whisper as he said. "Our universe was not so complete as I thought. There was… another. As I stared into the eyes of Hush, she dreamed she was looking into the eyes of Glorious, the dragon who was to become the elemental partner of the sun. My flames, it seems, were not enough for Hush. Her cold, logical heart judged that Glorious would be her perfect mate. So, she abandoned me, and flew to him, to profess her love."

"I'm sorry," said Infidel.

"What is there to be sorry of?" Greatshadow growled. "It proved a great stroke of good fortune, at least for those of us who were to become the primal dragons. Glorious rejected Hush; he was on the verge of merging his spirit with the sun, and had no time for such trivia as love. In her anger, Hush struck Glorious, killing his body, which freed his soul to fully merge with the sun. Such was the violence of Hush's blow that fragments of solar material fell to earth."

"The glorystones," said Infidel.

Greatshadow nodded. "While I was not yet the dragon of fire, I studied all flame, and saw the blaze of the glorystones as they fell. I flew to investigate and found Hush standing over the mortal shell of Glorious. Hush tried to convince me that Glorious had attacked her, but my telepathy was superior and I saw the truth. My rage was so great that I felt my soul burst into flame; I became the elemental embodiment of wrath. My first act upon wielding this power was to lash out at Hush for her betrayal. Even then, her mastery of cold helped protect her from my physical assault, but the emotional pain of that moment forever altered her. Understanding the source of my primal rage, her heart literally froze when she realized she'd driven away the one dragon who truly loved her. As her ice-bound heart shattered into a thousand sharp shards, the unfathomable chill that filled the vacant spot within her soul triggered Hush's transformation into the primal dragon of cold."

"I'm sorry you've felt such pain," said Infidel.

Greatshadow let loose a low rumble that might have been a rueful chuckle. "We've become much greater beings as a result of her betrayal. Though I wonder, at times, if we aren't also something less."

He cast a baleful glare at the harpoon. "Just as everything I cherish eventually turns to ash, everything exposed to her cold heart will eventually wither and perish. Even I."

"If I knew how, I would remove it from this place to stop it from hurting you," said Infidel.

"I know," said Greatshadow. "I see your thoughts so plainly. You have not come here with hatred in your heart."

"No," she said. "I set out on this quest to find comfort for my own broken heart, not because I held any animosity toward you."

"You came to steal my treasure," he said.

"Yes."

"But you've decided you no longer want it."

Infidel touched the band of hair on her finger.

"Gold and glorystones are wealth, not treasure. I can see that I was surrounded by genuine treasures all along. I just had to learn how to recognize them."

"How sorrowful to find these truths only once you are in the realm of the dead," Greatshadow said.

"But I'm not dead." Infidel looked up to meet his gaze. "I arrived here by accident and I need to go back. You must possess the power to send me home. You have the ability to travel between the spiritual and physical worlds, or else Zetetic wouldn't be so worried."

"Traveling between the worlds comes at a cost," said Greatshadow.

"Name the price," she said. "Send us back and I promise that we'll never bother you again. I promise to take the Jagged Heart as far away from you as possible, and I promise to fight anyone who even whispers of making an attempt to kill you."

"You would kill my offspring? The one you call Relic?"

"Consider it done," she said, snapping her fingers.

Greatshadow pondered for a long moment. "No. Tell the pathetic broken-wing that I shall have my revenge at the time and place of my choosing. The thought of the sleepless nights the young one shall endure pleases me. A swift death shall not slake my smoldering rage."

"Consider the message delivered," she said. "Just send us back."

Greatshadow eyed the Jagged Heart. "You must take this weapon from this place. I cannot recover while its bitterness poisons the energies of this land."

She gingerly lifted the harpoon, making sure not to point the tip toward him.

"Some people are worried you'll destroy the world because of what we've done to you," she said, softly. "I could have killed you as you slept. I chose mercy instead."

"Mercy is not a quality often attributed to flame," growled Greatshadow.

"Is it not?" asked Infidel. "Many a wound has been cauterized by fire. Meat half-gone to rot becomes a safe meal once it's cooked. Men couldn't survive harsh winters without your help. There's more to flame than wrath and destruction."

"Too many men think this way," said Greatshadow, sounding indignant at what I thought had been a compliment. His eyes began to blaze as he said, "Men believe they've tamed me, trapping me in hearths to bake their bread and in foundries to forge their steel. They forget that I am a wild thing that won't remain in a cage. I've killed many men to remind others of this truth."

"Perhaps you need reminding, too," she said.

The dragon tilted his head in a quizzical look.

Infidel said, "The wind, the sea, the frozen wastes… these elements are used by men, but none are worthy of the partnership that man has formed with flame. Thanks to mankind, fire is everywhere. In the middle of the trackless ocean, fire can be found in lanterns aboard a ship. On the most frigid, snow-capped mountain, you'll find fires glowing on hearths. Right now, at this moment when you're at your weakest, men light candles, torches, and bonfires, all of which help restore you. There's far more fire in the world due to the actions of men than there would be without us. You may be a wild thing that doesn't wish to be tamed, but certainly, even the wildest beast enjoys being fed. We nourish you with coal from far beneath the earth, we cut down forests to fill our fireplaces, and sometimes we even offer you our dead."

Greatshadow nodded grudgingly. "You are wise, Princess Innocent, though you tell me a truth I already know. Even in my darkest moments of smoldering anger, I dare not destroy mankind. In a world without men, I would be very hungry indeed."

"I don't know that I'm wise," said Infidel. "I just think we're alike in some ways. We both hate anyone who tries to tame us, but understand we sometimes must do things we dislike in order to keep a full belly."

Greatshadow lifted his head high, sparks flying from his jaws as he roared, a sound like a blast furnace in great, puffing gusts. The noise nearly deafened me, but I felt no fear. It was obvious from the expression in his eyes that he was laughing.

"That a mere mortal thinks she is in any way like me is an amusing notion, Princess," said the dragon. "It's been many centuries since I laughed so freely. You've earned your passage home."

With these words, he extended his talon and used a long glowing claw to trace a large circle upon the ground before him. The stone inside that circle fell away, revealing a black pit, full of stars.

"The material world lies through this portal," said Greatshadow.

Infidel turned her head toward me and motioned with her eyes that I should join her. I ran up and clasped her hand, giving her a swift kiss. She dragged me closer to the ring of fire. Fortunately, the Jagged Heart shielded us from the heat. Hand in hand, we stared into the abyss.

"Is it safe to jump?" I asked.

"When have we ever worried about that?" she said with a grin, falling forward, her fingers wrapped in mine. She dangled on the edge for the barest instant as my weight held her. Then, in total confidence, I leaned forward and we tumbled into the darkness.

INFIDEL RELEASED THE Jagged Heart and it fell beside us in a lazy spin. We hugged each other tightly as we flew past stars, past moons and suns and comets. We tumbled though airless voids, hugging one another in terror, awe, and wonder. We were neither in the spirit realm nor the ordinary world of matter; we were two isolated souls, entangled, entwined, a whole and complete universe where seconds and hours had no meaning. Yet, despite our inability to measure time, our eternity of togetherness drew to a close as a great blue jewel of a world emerged from the void beneath us. We clung to each other as the world grew large enough for us to make out the shapes of landmasses beneath the wispy white oceans of clouds. We fell toward a small green speck amidst a vast blue sea, the wind tangling our hair as we slowly emerged from the abstract realms. Far below, we spotted a smoking caldera atop a high mountain that seemed to be the bulls-eye where we'd land.

We looked into each other's eyes. There was no hope of speaking amid the howl of the wind whipping past us. We both knew that Greatshadow had cared nothing for our safety by sending us back along this path. Dropping to earth was no problem for him; he had wings. It was going to take more than a net of vines to save us this time.

Despite this knowledge, all I felt looking into Infidel's face was joy that we would once more be together in the land of the living, however brief that experience might be.

She kissed me.

I kissed her back.

Her lips grew softer and softer until, suddenly, her lips were gone. My arms closed around empty air. I opened my eyes and she was still inches away, her eyes wide, searching. I raised my hand to her cheek and it passed right through, as if she was a ghost.

Or as if I was. Infidel had fully emerged into the physical realm, but I was left behind, still a phantom.

"Infidel!" I screamed, as she dropped away, feeling the full tug of gravity. The Jagged Heart flashed past me, following its parallel path. I hovered in mid-air, no longer touched by gravity. I felt for the spirit tether of the bone-handled knife to pull me closer to Infidel but didn't move at all. I looked down and saw the knife tucked in my belt. My link to the material world was trapped with me on the other side.

I gave chase with all the speed I could muster, drawing close enough that I could see genuine fear in Infidel's eyes as she tumbled toward the black caldera below. Even if Infidel had still been invulnerable, I don't know if she could have survived a landing on volcanic stone without a net of vines to cushion her.

Then, rising from the caldera in a pale blue mist, a humanoid shape flew to intercept Infidel a half mile above the ground. The foggy wraith reached out with ethereal fingers, stroking the shaft of the Jagged Heart. Light flashed from the tip of the harpoon, striking the stone below, and suddenly there was a hill of snow heaped a hundred feet tall, its base sizzling on the black rock. A second later, Infidel punched into the snow mound, leaving the perfect outline of her splayed limbs in the surface. The Jagged Heart dropped into the snow several yards distant, far enough away I didn't worry she'd been impaled.

The ghost of Aurora continued to drift upward, raising a hand in greeting as she saw me. "You can see why my people built a temple around the harpoon."

"Will she be alright?" I asked, staring down into the hole Infidel had left in the snow mountain. I couldn't see anything in the shadows. The whole pile was melting at a frightening pace, an ever-growing puddle boiling off at the edges.

"It was like she fell onto a mountain of feathers," said Aurora.

"I can't tell you how happy I am to see you. You've stuck around longer than the others did after they died," I said. "Does that mean I'll have some company from now on?"

She shook her head. "I couldn't leave until I saw the Jagged Heart had returned from the land of the dead. I assume your efforts were successful?"

I shrugged. "We'll need to wait a few weeks to find out if she's pregnant."

Aurora gave me a blank stare.

"Oh! You mean did we kill Greatshadow?"

She nodded.

"She let him live. He let us go."

She raised a blue eyebrow. "Why?"

I shrugged. "She had her reasons." I didn't want to admit that I didn't fully understand Infidel's choices. I hoped Aurora wouldn't ask any follow-up questions.

Aurora looked north. "It doesn't matter. The call of my ancestors is strong. I hear the songs they sing as they chase the ghost whales in the Great Sea Above. I want to join their hunt."

"Go," I said. "The Jagged Heart is in good hands. We'll see that it gets home."

Aurora gave me a smile that said, *I know,* then faded from my sight.

A half-mile below, Infidel climbed from a pile of slushy snow now only a few yards high. Her lips and fingertips were completely blue. She stumbled forward, dragging the Jagged Heart behind her, limping toward the circle of light atop the dragon skull where Zetetic and Relic waited. I flew toward Relic and said, "You're in big trouble."

He didn't respond.

"Hey!" I shouted, waving my fingers in front of him.

Nothing. Yet, I was still relatively solid, as a phantom goes. I could see my own fingers, and was pleased to see I was still wearing my braided wedding ring. I seemed to have my full phantom body; I even had the clothing Zetetic had dressed me in. Why couldn't Relic hear me? Or, maybe he could, and was just being spiteful?

Infidel climbed up onto the skull, her teeth chattering. She tossed the harpoon to Zetetic and said, "You. Carry this. Carry it over there, in fact. I'm freezing."

He nodded and backed up about ten feet, so that she was no longer in the range of the harpoon's aura of cold. He said, "You've changed since last we met. I like you with long hair. You could use a comb, though."

"I could use a jacket even more. Brrr." She leaned down and picked up the Immaculate Attire. "I wondered where this went." She slipped the pants and vest on and the magical leather adjusted to fit her. With her arms outstretched as she dressed, her eyes lingered for a moment on the braid of hair still on her finger. I wondered why it had made the transition while mine didn't?

Infidel didn't dwell on the ring for long, however. Instead, while she pulled on the boots that went with the armor, she eyed Relic (we didn't yet know he'd changed his name). "Your daddy is going to kill you one day. But he wants to build suspense first."

"Greatshadow's alive? How can he still be alive?"

"You're the mind reader. You already know why I did what I did."

His reptilian eyes narrowed into slits as he stared at her. "I... I can't read your thoughts."

She looked surprised.

"Oh no," said Relic, rising up. "I could feel it earlier. During his sadistic assault, his spirit moved within me, ripping my mind as he snapped my body. But, with no other minds near that I could look within, I didn't realize what he'd done. He's torn the part of my mind that senses the thoughts of others! I'm blind!"

"It won't matter once you're dead," said Infidel.

"Isn't it enough he crippled me physically?" Relic growled, as his eyes burned like cinders. "He had to cripple my mind as well?"

Zetetic cleared his throat. "You may not be as crippled as you think. One of my teachers was the world's foremost scholar on dragons. I could introduce you to him, if you'd like. He's studied dragon skeletons at every stage of development. Reptiles possess amazing powers of regeneration. He might know how to break your bones and reset them properly."

"That sounds painful," said Relic.

Zetetic shrugged. "Just a suggestion."

Relic nodded. "I will... consider the offer."

He looked back toward Infidel. "I don't suppose my father... that he... did he, by chance..."

"What?" she asked.

"Did he happen to mention my gender? Did he refer to me as 'my son' or 'my daughter?'"

"Um, no. He called you 'offspring.'"

Relic looked crushed by this news.

Infidel leaned over and picked up the Gloryhammer. She slung it over her shoulder. "This is mine now."

"Really?" asked Zetetic. "What gives you a claim to it?"

"The fact that I'll flatten anyone who tries to take it from me."

"I find your reasoning quite persuasive," said Zetetic.

Infidel's feet lifted from the ground a few wobbling inches. The light of the Gloryhammer gleamed on the silver trim of her new boots. "This hammer will come in handy. Flying will make getting to Aurora's homeland a lot faster."

"Why are you going there?" asked Zetetic.

"To return the Jagged Heart," she said. "Stagger told me that Aurora's dying words were a plea to see that the harpoon was returned to its rightful home. I intend to make this happen. I need to do this mission fast. I can't afford to spend a few months aboard a ship."

"Why not?" asked Zetetic.

"She thinks she's pregnant," said Relic.

"I thought you couldn't read minds," she said.

"I knew of the Black Swan's prophecy. I take it you reunited with Stagger?"

"I have the Jagged Heart, don't I?"

"But he remains in the realm of the dead?"

She frowned, looking down at the braided band on her finger. "He sort of... faded out on the way back. But... but I..." She swallowed hard. "He'll always be with me in my heart."

"I'm here," I whispered near her cheek. "I'll always be here."

"The bone-handled knife is gone?" asked Relic.

She looked a little pale as she nodded slowly.

"Then he's lost forever," said Relic.

Infidel rose a few feet higher in the air, looking straight overhead, toward the last place she saw me. "He trusted me," she said, her voice faint. Then, she looked down, her face firm with resolve. "And I'll spend every day of my life proving I deserve that trust. My leap-before-I-look days are behind me. I'm going to be a great mother."

"Says the woman who just made a spur of the moment decision to fly to the North Pole via enchanted mallet," said Zetetic.

"Just for that, I'm not giving you a ride out of this volcano."

"That's fine. I have the power to fly and I'm finally over my fear of heights," he said, as their gazes locked. He jumped into the air and stayed there. "You warmed up?"

"Warm enough," she said.

He tossed her the Jagged Heart, which she caught in one hand. Her flight grew wobbly as she rose another couple of yards in the air. "Thinking-ahead Infidel sure wishes she had Tower's little magic book to carry the harpoon," she said.

Zetetic shrugged as he rose to her level. "Too bad it got incinerated."

"No!" I shouted. "He has it!"

But, I hadn't mentioned this to Infidel, so she merely said, "I guess I can rig up some kind of sling."

Zetetic sank back down and offered a hand to Relic. "Can I offer you a ride?"

Relic sighed as he raised the claw that Nowowon had mangled least. "Any place in the world is safer than here."

I floated next to Infidel as the three of them rose like balloons toward the edge of the caldera. The shadows of the vast pit fell away as we reached the sky and found the sun rising on the eastern ocean. Pale golden rays danced over a shimmering sea, bathing the tree tops below with a radiance that made the dewy canopy look as if someone had spilled a bucket of glistening jewels.

And I finally got it. I understood what Infidel had meant when she said she'd already discovered Greatshadow's treasure. It was the island itself, the last wilderness, and I knew, with the same certainty that I knew that stone is hard and fire is hot and water is wet, that there would be no better place on the planet for our daughter to grow up.

"I'm dying to hear the details of what happened in the spirit realm," Zetetic said.

"What happened between Stagger and me is private, you creep," said Infidel, sounding genuinely offended.

Zetetic shook his head. "I mean, the details of your confrontation with Greatshadow. The Jagged Heart should have killed him. You got close enough for conversation; presumably you were close enough to strike. Why didn't you finish him? You've gambled the safety of the world by sparing him. What possible reason could have stayed your hand?"

"If I'd killed Greatshadow, all this would be gone," she said, her eyes scanning the jungle as they slowly flew down the slope at about the pace of a good jog, heading toward Commonground. "My father's men would come and set up lumber mills and mines. Before you know it, there would be farms everywhere. The priests would follow and build churches, and in a couple of years, this place would start to look civilized."

"Indeed," said Zetetic. "That was precisely the plan."

"Well, it wasn't my plan. I've spent the best years of my life here. I like the island as it is: untamed and untamable. I grew up in a world of castle walls and armed guards. Now that I've tasted freedom I'll never give it up. I want to raise my daughter in a world that still has a place where the wicked may hide from the righteous."

Zetetic slowed a bit. "Damn," he said, with a nod. "That's not a bad reason at all."

Infidel shrugged, with an expression that told me she didn't particularly care if he approved of her reasons or not. She flew on a little ways, until, suddenly, she looked back over her shoulder, her eyes wistful as she stared at the sky above the caldera, toward the spot where I'd vanished.

Then her distant gaze shifted, looking much closer, not quite to where I hovered, but not so far off either.

"You aren't in this alone," I said, with a reassuring smile.

I'm sure it was only a coincidence that, at that exact second, she smiled back.

HUSH

BOOK TWO OF THE DRAGON APOCALYPSE

From perfect cold,
dark and silent,
the world has flickered.
Now it sputters; soon it fades.
The hush of an unending winter night
is the only true eternity.

1 - A DANGEROUS SPLINTER

A PRINCESS, A SHAPE-SHIFTER, and a ghost walked into a bar.

The room fell silent as all eyes turned toward the princess. The bar was the *Black Swan*, the most prestigious saloon in Commonground. While the house wasn't as packed as it would be come midnight, scores of hardcore gamblers crowded around the poker tables. Ordinarily, you could march a two-headed tiger through the joint and the players wouldn't glance up from their cards. The gamblers made an exception for the princess, known in these parts as Infidel, who was much more dangerous than a tiger no matter how many heads it might have.

Infidel looked imposing as she stood in the doorway with the evening sun as her backdrop. She was a woman who wore her three decades well, with sculpted curves, generous platinum curls, and enigmatic gray eyes. The money-hungry men in the room wouldn't linger long on her face, however. Infidel wore the priceless Immaculate Attire crafted for Queen Alabaster Brightmoon nearly three centuries before. Formed from the hide of the last unicorn, the legendary armor, milky white, clung to Infidel's body like a second skin. Slung over her shoulder was another famed artifact of the Silver Isles, the Gloryhammer, glowing with a pale yellow light.

Despite her impressive armaments, it was Infidel's reputation that brought the room to a standstill. On her first night in this bar, ten years ago, she'd ripped the arm off a bruiser twice her size. The whole town soon learned that this young woman possessed magical strength and skin so tough that swords couldn't scratch her. Even as her fame grew, her beauty tempted many a fool to a place an unwelcome hand upon her. Commonground now possesses an unusually high population of one-armed sailors.

I say this as the biggest fool of all. My name is Abstemious Merchant, though everyone in Commonground called me Stagger. For ten years, I was Infidel's constant companion, moon-eyed in my adoration, but far too cowardly to confess my love. Yet, fate can be kind to fools and cowards. Beneath Infidel's white leather gauntlet, on her left hand, she wears a ring of woven gray hair. This is my hair. I wear a matching small braid of platinum-hued locks. These serve as our wedding bands, since at the time of our betrothal there were no jewelers handy.

Fate's kindness, you see, is balanced by a wicked sense of humor. In this unfolding joke, I'm the ghost. In death, as in life, I follow her everywhere.

As a phantom, I'm unseen and unheard. If I could have spoken to Infidel, I would have advised her to wear a cloak and cowl, despite the tropical heat. Wearing the Immaculate Attire in this city of thieves was like walking through a lion's den wearing a suit sewn from steaks. Worse, someone in this town wonder why she bothered to wear armor at all. If word spread that Infidel had lost her magical strength and invulnerability, her enemies would turn out in droves. Plus, as her husband, I wasn't thrilled with the way the skin-tight armor accented her breathtaking assets. For Immaculate Attire, the outfit certainly lent itself to dirty thoughts.

Infidel's silver trimmed boots clicked on the polished oak floor as she walked across the room. Ordinarily stone-faced poker players gawked and drooled, though I tried to assure myself they were hungering for the Gloryhammer in its refulgent splendor. Glorystones are fragments of the sun, rarer than diamonds and twice as hard. The Gloryhammer is literally priceless. All the gold in the world couldn't buy it. The Tower clan, a family of famous knights, had passed down the weapon for generations. Alas, the last surviving male of the line had recently been reduced to soot. Infidel now owned the hammer under the legal precedent of finders, keepers.

Infidel didn't look back at the gawking crowd as she arrived at the bar. Battle Ox was bartending. Battle was a half-seed, meaning his mother had visited a blood house to imbue her yet-to-be conceived child with animalistic traits. If the magic is done properly, a half-seed ox child should be big, strong, and tenacious. Do the magic wrong, and you get Battle Ox — a full-blown minotaur with horns wider than his considerably broad shoulders.

In the more civilized parts of the world an infant born with a bovine face would have been put to death as an abomination against nature. In Commonground, Battle's visage seldom merited a second glance. Despite the name inflicted by the pun-happy denizens of Commonground, Battle was a gentle vegetarian. While he would willingly eject a rowdy patron if the need arose, his true calling in life was drawing beers with perfect heads of foam. My mouth watered at the smell of the amber fluid.

Battle nodded at my wife. "A lot of people here won't be happy to see you back" he said, with his gruff, bass voice. "Odds were running ten to one that Greatshadow would fry you."

Infidel leaned on the bar. "How did anyone know we were going to slay the dragon? The mission was a secret."

Battle shrugged as he picked up a glass and a towel. "The Black Swan started taking bets on the outcome of your dragon hunt the second you left town. The volcano's been belching lava for the last week, so we figured Greatshadow's still alive."

"Maybe he is and maybe he isn't," she said. "The Black Swan will want the full details. Tell her I need to see her. Now."

Battle put down the glass he was cleaning. "You ever learn the word 'please?'"

"Don't mess with me. I've got one hour to get back to the *Freewind* and don't have time to waste. I've got something the Black Swan needs to see immediately."

Battle shook his furry head. "No can do. She's already in a meeting. Going to be a lot longer than an hour."

Infidel unclasped the top three buttons of her leather armor and peeled it back, showing the top of her cleavage. Battle's eyes bulged.

"You see this?" Infidel pointed to a black speck the size of an apple seed that nestled in the ampleness of her décolletage.

"Uh…," said Battle, his mouth hanging open.

"This is Menagerie. What's left of him."

Remember the shape-shifter who came into the bar with us? Menagerie used to be the most feared mercenary in Commonground. A blood-magician of unparalleled skill, Menagerie could turn into any of the scores of animals that used to decorate his tattooed flesh. Menagerie had barely survived our dragon hunt. Since shape-shifting into this tick, he'd yet to change back into a man. A telepath of our acquaintance informed us that Menagerie had been so traumatized by his brush with death that his mind was shattered.

Battle couldn't know any of this, of course, but Infidel didn't have to produce any further explanations. Men believe almost anything while they're looking at a woman's breasts.

"I'm the only one that can hear him since he's latched onto me," she said, while his eyes were fixed on her. "The Black Swan has a potion that will change him back to human, and he has to drink it within the next five minutes or he'll die. Do you want to tell the Black Swan she's lost her most valuable employee because you were too timid to interrupt a meeting?"

Battle frowned. No, no he did not want this, was the message I was seeing in his eyes. But he also looked as if he had his doubts. Infidel wasn't particularly gifted at lying. If Battle asked any follow-up questions, Infidel would be in trouble.

Fortunately, Battle was too cleavage-addled to notice any holes in her story. He grunted, "Wait here," then went through the curtain that covered the doorway behind the beer kegs, leaving Infidel alone. At least as alone as a woman can be with a brain-damaged shape-shifter sipping her blood and her disembodied husband hovering close behind.

Infidel turned around, leaning back against the bar.

Every eye in the house stared at her.

Even though the *Black Swan* was the classiest joint in Commonground, it was still a den where desperate men gathered to try to make an easy fortune. Their already questionable judgment was numbed further by generous tankards of booze. Ordinarily, order was maintained by the Swan's infamous hired muscle, the Three Goons. Even when the Goons weren't present, their reputation kept most people in line.

Of course, except for Menagerie, the Goons were now dead. If the patrons knew about the dragon hunt, did they also know that the bar's most feared enforcers weren't coming back?

Infidel reached over her shoulder and grabbed the Gloryhammer. Instantly, its enchantment kicked in. Her skin glowed faintly as she lifted off the floor ever so subtly. In addition to granting her flight, the hammer also enhanced her strength. The boost was nothing like her former arm-ripping power, but anyone looking at her had to be sizing up their odds of getting their skulls smashed.

The odds were too high even for this room full of hardened gamblers. One by one, everyone turned back at the cards in their hands. The roulette wheel spun, dice jiggled in cups, and in under a minute the saloon resumed its normal routine. Infidel slowly drifted back to the floor.

Then Hookhand and his Machete Quartet walked in from the street. If I had a heartbeat, it would have skipped. I had history with Hookhand. When I was alive, my primary revenue came from locating ruins in the jungle and salvaging lost treasures. Hookhand made his living by an uncanny knack for showing up just as I was climbing out of some god-forsaken tomb with a sack full of artifacts. I often traded my treasures in exchange for not being nailed to a tree and flayed. This arrangement lasted for years until Infidel started adventuring with me. In the intervening decade, there've been about seventeen different members of the Machete Quartet. Infidel normally doesn't let them suffer for too long. Hookhand hasn't been as lucky. When he first came to Commonground, he was known as Fairchild the Nimble. Now, he's got one eye, his nose is squashed against his cheek, and he walks with a prominent limp. He's got maybe six teeth left, and, of course, where he once had a right hand he now has a hook, a big nasty one, the sort you might use to gaff a large fish.

Despite a decade as Infidel's punching bag, Hookhand was a feared figure in the city. He recruits street urchins for his gang just after they hit puberty, when they're strong and agile enough to swing a machete like a dagger, but too young to have any fear of life and limb. Once they join the quartet they become Kid White, Kid Blue, Kid Green, and Kid Black, based on the color bandana they wear. Hookhand doesn't like to waste time memorizing names.

In theory, the black bandana is worn by the gang member with the most seniority, but I didn't recognize this kid. If I'd seen him before, I would have remembered; the boy was a half-seed, part hound-dog by the look of him. He had a nasty snout of ragged teeth, but any air of menace was diluted by his floppy ears.

"Well, well," said Hookhand as he spied Infidel. "If it ain't ol' Ripper herself. I see you killed the knight. Quite a prize, that hammer. Quite a prize indeed."

Infidel nodded. She leaned forward, resting her hand on the shaft of the Gloryhammer like it was a cane. She said, "Surprised to see you back in town. I thought you were up on the mountain, robbing pygmies."

"The volcano's been spitting lava ever since we saw you and your friends fly out. Looks like you made the dragon mad. I made the executive decision to place some distance between us and the caldera." Hookhand looked around the room. "Where are your friends?"

"Who are you talking about?" Infidel asked. "I don't have time for coyness."

"Zetetic the Deceiver. He was right by your side, carrying a baby dragon."

"Your eye's playing tricks on you." Infidel shook her head. "Never met the guy."

"Zetetic has a large red 'D' tattooed in the middle of his forehead. He's easy to recognize, even 200 feet in the air."

"Your depth perception isn't what it used to be," said Infidel.

"True enough." Hookhand slowly limped toward her. His gang spread out to the far ends of the bar. There was no way that Infidel could keep all four of them in her field of vision. Once that wouldn't have mattered; a machete would have bounced off her invulnerable hide. While the Immaculate Attire protected her body, at some point in the convoluted chain of ownership from Queen Alabaster Brightmoon to Infidel, the helmet had disappeared. Infidel's head and neck were completely vulnerable. But, Hookhand couldn't know this, could he?

Hookhand stopped about eight feet away. Infidel didn't look perturbed. Was this just for appearances, or was she overly confident?

"I want Zetetic," said Hookhand.

"You want to turn him in for the price on his head? Old news. He's working for the Church of the Book now. They don't want him dead any more."

"I thought you didn't know him," said Hookhand.

"I don't," said Infidel. "But you know I bounty hunt. I stay informed."

Zetetic had split company with Infidel shortly after getting back to Commonground. He'd promised Brokenwing, the only other survivor of our ill-fated dragon hunt, a visit with a former teacher who was the world's foremost authority on dragon anatomy. Since Brokenwing was a rather badly mangled young dragon, they'd departed on their quest with understandable alacrity.

"If you like to stay informed, here are a few facts for you," said Hookhand. "We saw eight people go into the Shattered Palace. You were part of a dragon hunt organized by Lord Tower and Father Ver."

Infidel laughed. "Father Ver's a Truthspeaker and Lord Tower's the most respected knight of the church. I, as my nickname implies, am a notorious infidel. A knight and a priest wouldn't be caught dead in my company."

"I think getting caught dead is precisely what happened," said Hookhand. "You were disguised as some kind of mechanical woman to fool them. It doesn't take a genius to figure out what happened. You and Zetetic betrayed the others. You're carrying Tower's hammer and dressed in armor that used to be worn by Ivory Blade. I didn't see Blade go into the Shattered Palace, but I'm guessing I'd find his corpse if I went poking around."

Blade had died a good week before we reached the dragon's lair. But, despite the fact that his conclusions were off, Hookhand had some surprisingly good intelligence. How did he know so much?

I studied his thugs closer. In addition to Kid Black being part blood-hound, Kid Green had distinctly hawkish features, including freakishly alert eyes and feathery sideburns. Kid Blue's overly long arms clued me in that he had some monkey blood. Kid White had jaguar in him, judging from his cat-eyes and the mottled patches in his close-cropped hair. A hound, a hawk, a monkey, and a jaguar would make damn good spies out in the jungle. By now, Kid Black, the dog-boy, and Kid White, the half-jaguar, were at opposite ends of the bar, machetes drawn.

Infidel retained her cool as she pressed a gauntleted fist into her palm and cracked her knuckles. The sound echoed around the room. Half the gamblers abandoned their chips and headed for the door. Infidel's brawls were hard on bystanders.

Infidel took the hammer in both hands and once more her skin went luminous. She said, "Lord Tower could fly. He had impenetrable armor made of solid prayer. If you take your accusations seriously, you might tell these children to get where I can see them. If I killed someone like Tower, what makes you think these kids stand a chance?"

"Tower wouldn't fight dirty," said Hookhand, snapping his fingers. The Machete Quartet lunged, but Infidel had anticipated the signal. The hammer flared to solar brightness as she shot up ten feet, snapping to a halt inches beneath a broad ceiling beam. Most of the machete blows that connected hit her boots, leaving little more than scuff marks that were swiftly erased by the armor's magic. Kid Blue, the monkey boy, reacted to Infidel's flight by dropping his machete and hooking his long, skinny fingers into the heel of her right boot. He used his momentum to swing his legs overhead, grabbing her belt with his toes, then flipping up to grab the shaft of the hammer with both hands. Kicking into her chest, he grunted as he tried to pull the weapon from her grasp. The speed and power of the assault caught Infidel off guard and she lost her grip with her left hand, though her right hand held on.

The monkey child placed a foot on Infidel's face as he struggled to twist the hammer away. Infidel responded by opening her mouth and sinking her pearly whites deep into Kid Blue's heel. A shudder ran along my intangible spine. Biting the bare foot of someone who'd been walking around the docks of Commonground was the most reckless thing I'd ever seen Infidel do, and I'd watched her dive headfirst into the jaws of a dragon. But, the tactic worked. Kid Blue shrieked as he let go of the hammer, dropping back down to the floor, where he landed on his outstretched hands and somersaulted back to his feet. Nimble little devil.

The jaguar kid was no slouch either. With Kid Blue clear, Kid White sprang, flat-footed, from the floor to the bar to the shelf of liquors behind, then shot toward Infidel like an arrow, with a savage swing of his machete. The chiming of the booze bottles as he kicked off caused Infidel to look over her shoulder and she spun in time to block the machete blow with the Gloryhammer. She jerked her knee up to connect a solid blow to the kid's chin. The half-seed was stunned and fell hard, landing spine-first on the back of a wooden chair, his body folding backward at an acute angle that made me wince.

Infidel pointed the hammer toward Hookhand. Her eyes were narrow slits of murder as she shot toward him. But in her rage she either didn't notice or didn't care that a slender tube of bamboo had appeared in his hand. He drew breath as he raised it to his lips. He blew so hard I thought his eye was going to pop out of his skull. A cloud of red powder caught Infidel right in the face as Hookhand dove to the side. Infidel gasped as she hit the cloud, then grunted as she slammed into the floor. Her armored shoulder took the brunt of the blow, but the impact was enough to topple chairs around the room. She bounced across the oak planks, losing her grip on the hammer. Her eyes were scrunched tightly together as she slid to a halt on her back.

As a ghost, my senses are muted, but even my nostrils burned from the cayenne cloud that hung in the air. Infidel's face was blood-red with the pepper. She tried to breathe but her throat closed after the barest gasp. Even when she'd had impenetrable skin, she couldn't have shrugged off an attack like this.

Kid Blue, the monkey child, sprang across the room and landed on Infidel's right hand, pinning it. Kids Black and Green followed suit, pinning her left arm and both legs, respectively. If she'd still been super-strong, she could have flicked them off like fleas. Now, her limbs trembled, but her weak spasms couldn't shake them.

The Gloryhammer hung in mid-air, where it had come to rest after bouncing off the floor. Hookhand snatched it with his good hand. His eye went wide as the hammer's power filled him. He tilted back his head and laughed. "At last! At last!"

His feet left the floor as he moved toward Infidel. "I've watched a lot of machetes bounce off that pretty head of yours," he said. "I've long dreamed of seeing your brains splattered across these planks. Considerate of you to deliver the perfect tool to get the job done."

Hookhand continued to drift toward her, approaching at a speed fairly described as lackadaisical. Was he trying to prolong the moment? Was flight with the hammer harder than Infidel made it look? Or was Hookhand still afraid of her?

"Hold her tight, boys," he said, pausing a few arm-lengths away.

"She's weak as a kitten, boss," said Kid Black, the dog-boy who trapped her left arm beneath his knee as he ran his hairy knuckles through her hair. She twisted her head away from his fingers, unable to open her eyes. She'd started breathing again, rapid shallow spasms that had to be filling her lungs with fire. Sweat poured from her brow and bright red snot ran from both nostrils; I couldn't tell if this was blood or cayenne. Any normal person would have been moved to either pity or revulsion by the sight, but Kid Black was staring at her with barely disguised lust. "Such pretty hair. So soft. So pretty, pretty soft."

"She won't be soft when she catches her breath," said Hookhand.

"She's weak now," said Kid Black, stroking her chin, then tracing his fingers down the ivory arc of her throat. The top buttons of her armor were still undone. "Weak and helpless."

"Just like a dog," snickered Kid Blue, the half-monkey. "Always looking for something to hump."

"I thought he was always looking for something to eat," said Kid Green, the falcon-child.

"She could be both," said Kid Black, folding the top of the leather breastplate down to reveal her pale cleavage. He lowered his long narrow face to her throat and licked at her sweat.

I screamed in my rage, my impotence to alter things in the living world stabbing at me like a knife.

Hookhand held back, his eye a little glassy as he watched Kid Black run his hairy hand along the top of Infidel's cleavage. Infidel's face was already scrunched up as much as humanly possible, and pinned as she was I couldn't tell if she was even aware of this assault.

"Wake up!" I screamed, my ghost voice hauntingly silent in the room. "Wake up! Wake up! Wake up!"

"Ow," said Kid Black, yanking his hand away.

"What?" asked Kid Green.

"Something bit me."

"Wake… up…," my voice trailed off as I saw that the tick on Infidel's breast had vanished.

Kid Black put the edge of his hand into his mouth to gnaw at the tiny parasite digging into him.

Then his head came apart.

Menagerie could change shape faster than the eye could follow. His powers flowed from blood magic; his human form had been covered scalp to toe in tattoos inked with the blood of the animals they represented. He'd been able to switch between these forms instantly, and even vast differences in sizes hadn't been a barrier to his magic. He'd been able to change from mouse to elephant as swiftly as he could between lion and tiger. I'd never before pondered what would happen if he'd entered a person's mouth the size of a tick, then turned into a full-sized blood-hound. As it happened, Menagerie's expanding body proved powerful enough to rip Kid Black's skull open from the inside out.

Kid Black flopped backward, his lower jaw missing, his upper jaw cracked open in such a way that I could see his brains. As his body hit the floor, his ghost was knocked loose. His spirit rose above his corporeal form, looking bewildered. Since dying, I've had the ability to see ghosts as they depart the mortal world, and occasionally converse with them. I felt like saying something particularly nasty to this spirit. I know this dog-boy was poor street trash, a freak, never standing a chance at a normal life, but any pity I might have felt had vanished the instant he started pawing my wife. Unable to summon sufficiently nasty curses from my normally abundant lexicon, I lifted my middle finger to his spirit as it flickered and faded.

The hound that had sprung fully formed from Kid Black's mouth growled as he faced Hookhand. Hookhand shook off his confusion about what he'd witnessed with remarkable speed and swung the hammer overhead, aiming for the dog's skull. The hound lunged forward, sinking his teeth into Hookhand's groin as the hammer splintered the floorboards.

Infidel's eyes jerked open, bloodshot and brimming with tears. Her blurry gaze fixed on Kid Blue, who was pinning down her right forearm with both his hands. The monkey child had his eyes on Hookhand, probably wondering where he was going to swing the hammer next, and failed to notice Infidel's left hand was now free.

Infidel reached for the scabbard on her hip. Two seconds later, a dagger was hilt deep in the center of the monkey-child's chest. He looked at her with sad eyes as he toppled over. His spirit stuck around no longer than the dog-boy's.

Infidel sat up, fixing her gaze on Kid Green, the half-seed falcon who pinned her legs. Sweat from her brow washed a fresh flood of cayenne into her eyes and once more her lids scrunched shut as she gasped in pain. Kid Green leapt up, bringing his machete overhead two handed, preparing to cleave her skull in half.

Hookhand continued swinging the Gloryhammer wildly. A sledgehammer is a remarkably inappropriate instrument for removing a dog from one's crotch. It is, however, a surprisingly effective tool for bashing in the head of your own henchman if you're not careful. The hammer connected with the falcon child's skull with a sound somewhere between a thud and a splash. The machete held by Kid Green flew into the air as he fell lifeless.

I watched with a sick feeling in the pit of my stomach as the tumbling machete fell toward Infidel's blinded face. Then a huge, three-fingered hand snatched the machete in mid-flight. It was Battle Ox. He turned with a snort toward Hookhand, who was floating now, using the power of the hammer as poorly as it could possibly be used, smashing furniture right and left with his all-powerful weapon as the hound dog between his legs twisted out of the path of every blow.

With a swift, precise chop of the machete, Battle lopped off Hookhand's remaining hand at the wrist. The hammer spun up to the chandelier, smashing the crystal, but Battle Ox's thick hide protected him from the rain of shards.

Hookhand wasn't so lucky. A finger-length dart of glass sank into his remaining eye. He fell to the ground, crying in pain, until Battle brought his whimpering to an end. Hookhand's ghost bubbled up from his corpse. Usually, spirits resembled the bodies that housed them, but Hookhand's spirit was small and gnarled, a scarred broken thing that stank of rot and despair. His pathetic yellow eyes fixed on me as his toothless mouth voiced my name. I lunged toward him and he shot downward, percolating through cracks in the floorboard, dragged to whatever hell awaited. The hound dog sensed that his opponent was no longer a threat and released his jaws. He loped back over toward Infidel.

Battle ran back to the bar and snatched up a bottle of whiskey. He pulled off the stopper as he approached Infidel. The hound leapt into his path, hackles raised, snarling.

"This is the only thing that's going to wash off that pepper," said Battle. "Water will make it burn worse."

"He's right," I said to Menagerie.

The hound went silent as I spoke, then stepped aside.

"Hold still," said Battle as he knelt, taking Infidel's chin in his massive hand. "This is going to feel worse for a minute, but it might save your eyes."

Infidel seemed to understand, growing calm as Battle tilted the bottle over her face, letting it come in a deluge that washed away most of the cayenne. He motioned for one of the barmaids to bring him a second bottle. The light in the room was dizzying as the Gloryhammer bounced around in the rafters, casting stark shadows. Battle's eyes narrowed as he studied Infidel's face. Infidel had a splinter of wood jammed into her cheek from her impact with the floor. A dozen small cuts speckled her face from where fragments of chandelier had hit her.

He washed away the remaining pepper with most of the second bottle. A barmaid handed him a dishtowel and he used it to wipe Infidel's face. She sat up and grabbed the towel, taking control of cleaning the last of the cayenne from the creases around her eyes. She let out a long sigh as she forced her eyes open and looked down into the towel, flecked with blood.

A few seconds of silence passed as she pulled the splinter from her cheek. It was, by any objective standard, a trivial wound. But, I could tell from Infidel's eyes that she understood that this splinter might be the most dangerous injury she'd ever received. Her secret was revealed. Given the speed rumors spread through the city, it was only a matter of hours before everyone learned she'd lost her powers.

"I thought you couldn't be cut," Battle said.

"You've seen me bleed before," Infidel whispered, her voice weak from pain. "That assassin with the shadow blade. The right magic can break my skin."

"The floor ain't magic," he said. Battle put the whiskey bottle into her hands and he helped her to her feet. A bare inch of fluid sloshed in the bottle. "Drink the rest of it."

"Can't," she said. "I might be pregnant. Maybe it's an old wives tale that whiskey will hurt the baby, but I'm not taking any chances."

"Damn!" said Battle, shaking his horns. "She did it to me again!"

"What?"

"The Black Swan. She bet me you'd have a baby this year. I mean, Stagger's dead. If he was still around, maybe, but I just can't believe it otherwise. Who—?"

"Stagger's the father," said Infidel as she managed to stand on her own. Her eyes were bloodshot, but worked well enough that she spotted the Gloryhammer bouncing around in the rafters.

"Help me grab that," she said to Battle. "The Black Swan's probably going to bill me for the damned chandelier. Better stop that thing before it floats behind the bar and takes out the inventory."

"Right," said Battle, grabbing her by the hips and lifting her overhead. She stretched her fingers as far as she could, barely touching the shaft of the hammer. Yet, the barest touch was all she needed to regain control. It slid fully into her grasp and she floated to the floor.

The hound dog came up to her and sat before her, its tongue hanging out.

"Whose dog?" she asked.

"Um, ain't that Menagerie?" Battle asked. "I saw him leap out of what was left of Kid Black's skull."

Infidel looked down at her chest, running her fingers along the red bump where the tick had once rested.

"Menagerie?" she asked the dog.

The dog said nothing. Menagerie had always been able to talk before, no matter what animal shape he'd worn.

"Menagerie?" I said. The dog tilted its head in my general direction, but said nothing. There was intelligence in his eyes, but dog level intelligence, none of the tactical genius that normally burned in the shape-shifter's visage.

"We'd better get him to the Black Swan fast," said Battle Ox. "She's working on the potion now."

"Riiiight," said Infidel, sounding confused. "Right, the potion."

She placed the whiskey on the bar as she followed Battle. I wasn't surprised she'd refused the drink. She hadn't drank much before. It's not so tough to give up something that you never enjoyed in the first place. But, I wondered, when Hookhand first showed up… were Infidel's taunts meant to scare him off? Or was she trying to provoke him? This was her first fight since losing her powers. Had she chosen an opponent she'd routinely beaten in the past to test her new combat style with the hammer and armor? Imagining Infidel going the next nine months without a brawl was a lot tougher than imagining her going nine months without a drink. Once word got out that she was vulnerable, was there any place in the world she'd be safe?

2 - OBSERVER OF DOOM

INFIDEL LIMPED AS she followed Battle Ox down the hall to the Black Swan's chamber. She was favoring the leg that had taken most of the machete blows. The Immaculate Attire couldn't be cut, but that didn't mean she couldn't be hurt. A machete might not be able to break her skin, but it was still like being whacked with an iron bar. It couldn't feel good.

The last time I'd seen the Black Swan she'd been nothing more than a skeleton. This hadn't slowed the old witch down much. Her spirit continued to animate her bones, though without a throat she'd been reduced to 'speaking' by pointing to letters on a board. The Black Swan claimed that death was too trivial an obstacle to stand in the way of her great mission. She says she's a time traveler, using her knowledge to accumulate wealth and power today so that she can prevent a 'dragon apocalypse' that she's lived through in the future.

I'm not sure I believe her. The Black Swan has a propensity for using manipulation and outright lies to gain the upper hand. But she'd also told us that Infidel would soon be pregnant, which seemed impossible at the time, since I was dead and Infidel wasn't open-minded to new suitors. What we could never have imagined was that Infidel's quest to kill Greatshadow would take her bodily into the spirit world, where we'd been able to reunite as the world's most star-crossed lovers. It was certainly plausible that Infidel was pregnant now, since in the ghost realms my spirit had been as functional as my old material body. On the other hand, when we left the spirit world together, Infidel had physically returned to the land of the breathing, while I'd faded back into ghosthood. If we'd conceived a daughter, as the Black Swan prophesied, would the unusual circumstances of her conception affect her?

Menagerie followed closely behind Infidel, looking and acting like an ordinary bloodhound, sniffing the floor as he walked. Shaking off his tick form hadn't repaired his shattered mind. Was there any flicker of his humanity left? His loyalty toward Infidel was a hopeful sign. During the dragon hunt, Menagerie and Infidel had formed a friendship. Perhaps the dog retained some human memories.

Battle pushed open the polished mahogany door to the Black Swan's chamber. He motioned Infidel inside but didn't follow us. The room had changed dramatically in the last two weeks. Then, the walls had been covered with tapestries and filled with antique bedroom furnishings. The place had reeked of potpourri, a concentrated floral miasma that hadn't quite masked the undercurrent of rot that hung in the air.

Now, the walls had been stripped down to the bare wood, and every last stick of furniture had been removed. Freed of its clutter, the Black Swan's chamber proved surprisingly spacious. My old sailboat could probably have fit in the space. At first glance, it looked as if someone might be testing that theory, since there was a white canvas sail covering the floor.

In the center of this canvas was a small cloaked figure kneeling before an iron sculpture. The sculpture drew my eye first. It was a shapely woman, slightly larger than life. It was cast iron, black as soot, highly articulated, so that there was a separate plate for each rib of the torso. Both arms were finished, ending in delicately formed hands sporting long, slender fingers, though the sharpened steel nails provided a detail of menace to a work of art that would otherwise have been noteworthy for its beauty. The face was mostly done, with separate plates for each cheek and a small nose that sat above intricately jointed steel lips. The eyes were closed and I noted the fine detail of the wire eyelashes. The top of the head wasn't finished, and as I drifted around I noticed that the back of the head was open. Sitting in the cavity of the dark steel was a stark white skull.

I looked down at the cloaked figure, whose hands were busy working on the right ankle. The left leg was finished, a sleek curvy gam that would have been the pride of any bride when her groom had hitched up her hem to remove her garter. A row of rivets ran up the back of each leg like the seam of a stocking. As I drifted lower to admire the workmanship, I confess that my eyes lingered a moment on the heart-shaped buttocks, so smoothly finished and perfectly formed that they looked soft, despite being formed of iron. The illusion of softness vanished, however, when one reached the unfinished right leg, which was nothing more than a jointed steel rod jutting from the hollow of the hip. Floating lower to better observe the sculptress (for, despite the cloak, it was apparent that the artist was female, given the slenderness of her form and her delicate fingers), I saw that she had no tools. Instead, she was shaping hard ingots of raw pig iron with her hands as if it was mere clay. Her fingers moved in a dizzying dance as they twisted and kneaded the metal, forming and fastening ankles to a feminine metal foot that sported razor toenails.

The sculptress completed the ankle by scraping away a bit of the iron rod of the leg and exposing a patch of pure bone. The lower half of the rod, apparently, enclosed a skeletal tibia and fibula. The Black Swan's leg bones, no doubt. The sculptress spun delicate silver wires to link the bone to the ankles, which sat like bracelets upon the foot.

"Wiggle your foot," the sculptress said, looking up.

The Black Swan lifted her skeletal right leg and twisted her foot from side to side. She wiggled her toes in an eerie approximation of life, though with the plates of the various pieces sliding silently across one another, her toes reminded me more of hard-shelled beetles than human flesh.

"Excellent," the sculptress said, guiding the Black Swan's foot back to the floor.

With her head tilted up, I could see the artist's face. Her most striking features were her eyes, a shocking emerald hue that was almost certainly the result of magical manipulation. Yet if she'd manipulated her eyes to be such gems, it made little sense that the rest of her features were, shall we say, less felicitous. Her age was difficult to judge; the right half of her face could have belonged to a teenage girl, but the left half of her face was slack and wrinkled, the flesh a pale gray as opposed to the rosy hue of her other cheek. Though her cloak concealed much of her scalp, she appeared to be completely bald, with her head speckled by large dark warts.

The sculptress rose, stretching her back. The sleeves of her robe slipped down, revealing that her left arm and hand were supported by an iron brace. She glanced back at Infidel. "I'll step outside so the two of you may talk."

The Black Swan's iron eyelids clicked open, revealing empty orbs of bone. There was a sucking sound within her chest, like a bellows drawing in air, followed by reedy musical notes, something like an accordion. The sculpted jaws jerked open and snapped shut as the overlapping plates of the steel lips sliced up the notes pouring from the mouth. The resulting sound was almost, but not quite, completely inhuman. Yet, however inferior the construct's vocal apparatus might have been when compared with a living human throat, I found, with grudging admiration, that I could understand individual words. "Stay and work, Sorrow. The princess and I have nothing to hide."

Infidel frowned. She, of course, had many things to hide, including the fact that she was a princess. But, she shrugged and said, "I can't stay to chat. I need the money you owe me for the dragon skull."

"You traded those funds to Menagerie," said the Black Swan. "You used them to purchase the silence of the Three Goons when you infiltrated Lord Tower's party in a disguise Menagerie helped to design."

"Fine," said Infidel. She nodded toward the dog. "This is Menagerie. Give him all the money he's owed. Since he's a bit impaired in the hand department for the time being, I'll carry it."

"This isn't Menagerie," said the Black Swan, turning her vacant gaze upon the hound. "This is merely a physical echo of his blood magic, a spell lingering on after the death of the spellcaster. Soon its magic will burn out and this soulless thing will vanish."

"Or you could help him," said Infidel. "He's worked for you for years. Use your magic to restore his memories."

"This isn't a question of memories. It's a question of soul. There's no spirit within this creature. It looks like a dog, but it isn't truly alive. Any funds due Menagerie will be sent to his family. As for this sad little pseudo-dog, I recommend you kill it swiftly and put an end to its miserable half-life. I owe it nothing."

"How about Aurora? Do you owe her anything?"

"She collected the last of her wages when she left my employment."

"I'm not talking about wages. I'm talking about the fact that she was your loyal companion. She's dead now, killed by Greatshadow. I'm in possession of the Jagged Heart, the sacred relic she died to defend. Stagger made a promise to return it to her homeland. I intend to keep this promise. I'm hoping you'll help."

The Black Swan shook her iron head in a smooth, mechanical motion. "Stagger could make no such promise. He's dead. You killed him."

"You of all people should know that being dead isn't the same as being done. Stagger's ghost has been following me. He's with us right now, I think. We were reunited in the spirit world." She rubbed her ring finger where the band of hair I'd woven for her sat. When we'd returned to the land of the living and my physical form faded back to nothingness, the ring of hair had remained intact. Why this should be, I don't know. Perhaps there's genuine magic in a wedding vow after all. "We were married there."

"Now you're merely a widow." The Black Swan sounded mocking with her squeaking, artificial voice. "And you're pregnant, as I foretold."

"On the assumption that I'm pregnant, I need to return the Jagged Heart as quickly as possible. I'd rather not be adventuring in some faraway land when I start dealing with morning sickness. But that doesn't kick in for about a month, right?"

"I'm uncertain. I was childless," the Black Swan said.

"A month. Six weeks," said the sculptress as she fastened the plates of the calf to the shin plate. "Not that I've had personal experience."

The Black Swan's empty orbs gazed toward the Gloryhammer. "My dear, I can't help but notice you're in possession of a magic artifact known to grant its owner the power of flight. Why do you need my help? You can simply fly to Aurora's home in Qikiqtabruk."

Infidel shook her head. "Flying isn't as easy as it looks. If I go too fast, I can't breathe. Even flying slow wears me out. Flying for an hour is like hanging from a branch for an hour. I'd rather not have my arms give out when I'm over the middle of the ocean. I need a ship, a very fast ship, if I'm going to complete this mission. As luck would have it, the *Freewind* is in port."

"The *Freewind?*" The Black Swan tilted her head and gave what might have been a look of skepticism, though her empty eye-sockets made it difficult to interpret her expression. "You can't seriously intend to seek passage aboard the most wanted pirate ship on the seas. Every navy on the planet is hunting the Romers."

"No navy can catch them," said Infidel. "The *Freewind* is the fastest ship in the Shining Lands. And we both know that the charge of piracy is bogus. Gale Romer is an honest woman who's been branded a pirate because of her opposition to slavery."

"She's scuttled entire ships and stolen their cargo."

"She's raided slave ships and released men from their chains," said Infidel, crossing her arms. "The fact that she's an outlaw is an indictment of the law, not of her."

The Black Swan nodded slowly. "Captain Romer's moral code isn't the issue. Whether the charges against her are just or unjust, you place yourself in danger by seeking passage on her vessel."

Infidel shrugged. "It's not like I'm safe anywhere. I'll take my chances with Captain Romer. She tells me the *Freewind* was chartered weeks ago by a single passenger; she's not at liberty to tell me whom. But, her employer didn't show up to depart this morning at the prearranged time. If they don't show up by sundown, the contract's broken. She says that if I'm there with money in hand when the sun sets she'll let me hire the ship."

"Very well. While I question your wisdom, I must admit that the *Freewind's* speed is unmatched. Since the Gloryhammer is of no use to you as transportation, I'll give you the money you need in trade."

Infidel laughed. "I'm in a hurry, but I'm not an idiot."

"What else do you have to offer me?"

"Information. You must be dying to know what happened with Greatshadow."

"I know the dragon is alive. You failed in your mission to kill him, placing the world in great peril when he seeks revenge."

"That's nowhere near accurate. I'll give you the complete story for the money."

"My dear, I employee the most gifted diviners from the furthest reaches of the known world. I personally have lived though the events of this day a dozen times in my efforts to avert the impending apocalypse. I know all I need to know of your dragon hunt."

Infidel crossed her arms. "You didn't know Stagger is still around."

"What does it matter if his spirit lingers? He's hardly the only ghost in this port. What's more, he can't endure for long if he has no anchor to the material world."

"I'm his anchor."

"This isn't accurate. The bone-handled knife was his anchor, but you lost this in the ghost lands."

Infidel furrowed her brow. Zetetic and Relic were the only other entities to know that my soul had become trapped in the dragon bone in the handle of my grandfather's hunting knife. Technically, we hadn't lost the knife. It was tucked into the belt of the pants I was wearing when we came back to the material world. It stayed in the ghost realms with me. The pants, too. I can take the knife out and hold it, despite the fact it's as much a phantom as I am now. What good an intangible knife does me I can't say. If I had some intangible toast perhaps I could butter it, assuming I had some intangible butter.

But I digress. The Black Swan continued scolding Infidel. "You also lost the battle against Greatshadow in the spirit realm. Lord Tower dealt Greatshadow's physical body a mortal blow with the Gloryhammer; Aurora slew the beast with the Jagged Heart, but was killed by the creature's death throes. Father Ver's mission was to kill Greatshadow's spirit before the beast could grow a new body. But, he died, so the mission fell to you. However, Greatshadow banished you back to the material world before you could strike the final blow. Have I missed any significant detail?"

A few. Greatshadow hadn't banished Infidel; he'd opened a portal for her after she spared his life in exchange for a promise not to seek revenge. Infidel had convinced the beast that the element of flame was well served by mankind. We cut down forests and hollow entire mountains of coal to feed Greatshadow's appetites. Were he to wipe us out, he'd be one hungry dragon. We left the spirit world with Greatshadow feeling a grudging appreciation of mankind rather than a deep blood lust for revenge. We count that as a win.

Infidel had a few bits of information the Black Swan hadn't hinted at. She knew that Relic had turned out to be Greatshadow's own child, an infant dragon named Brokenwing with genius level intelligence and an excess of ambition. And, she knew that Zetetic, the Deceiver, had also survived, and where he was heading next. Would she try to barter this information?

Infidel pressed her lips tightly together. With what looked like great reluctance, she said, "Fine. You've forced my hand. I do have one thing left to trade. Stagger's boat is stuffed with old books, maps, and notes detailing his explorations. Plenty of treasure seekers would pay through the nose for these documents. I'll trade you the entire collection for the *Freewind's* fee."

The Black Swan shook her head. "You can't seriously believe that a heap of mildewed notes scribbled by a notorious drunkard are worth anything."

"We both know they're worth a great deal. Stagger recovered hundreds of artifacts from the ruins of the Vanished Kingdom. He left behind hundreds more too big to carry. He documented his explorations carefully, just like his grandfather."

The sculptress looked up. "This Stagger… is he the grandson of Judicious Merchant?"

My grandfather was famous throughout the scholarly world for his masterwork, *The Vanished Kingdom*. The legend surrounding him and the book had only grown larger when he disappeared four decades ago, swallowed by the jungle-draped ruins he'd spent his life exploring. We'd recently discovered Judicious still alive, living in a treetop village with the Jawa Fruit tribe. Just shy of a century old, my grandfather spends his retirement lounging naked in the sun, attended by his countless pygmy offspring.

Infidel studied the sculptress for a second, her eyes lingering on the woman's withered face, before she answered, "Yes. Stagger was an explorer like Judicious."

The Black Swan released a single high-pitched accordion note. It took me a second to recognize the squeak was intended as a scoffing laugh. "Judicious Merchant was a scholar who braved the dangers of this island in search of knowledge. Stagger was a wastrel who exploited his grandfather's research to loot ancient treasures to slake his thirst for whiskey."

"Don't hold back, Swan," I said. "Say what you really thought of me." She'd been much more diplomatic when she'd haggled for some of the junk I looted. I mean artifacts I looted. I mean artifacts I rescued from their forgotten tombs and brought back so they could be properly studied.

"I want those papers," said the sculptress. "I'll pay for your use of the *Freewind*. I'm the mystery client who failed to show up. This project has taken longer than I'd anticipated. I fear I've lost track of time."

"Indeed," said the Black Swan. "I hope you don't plan to pass on the expense of your additional hours to me. I'm not to blame for your poor time management."

"I certainly believe you *are* to blame," said the cloaked woman. "You made me rework your breasts eleven times!"

"I remain unsatisfied," the Black Swan grumbled. "They don't look natural."

Given that they were cast iron, it was impossible to dispute this. On the other hand, I thought they looked like a reasonable approximation of boobs, about the size of grapefruits, nicely proportioned to her chest, with decorative floral rivets for nipples. Still, no matter how well sculpted in size or shape, they lacked a certain quality - Pillowiness? Jigglability? — that reduced their ability to stir lust.

The sculptress sighed and rubbed her eyes. She turned from the Black Swan and approached Infidel, extending her hand. "We've not been introduced. I'm Sorrow Stern."

"My friends call me Infidel," said Infidel, with a handshake.

Menagerie raised his left paw.

"How cute," said Sorrow, shaking the paw. "You've trained your dog well."

"I can't take credit. I can't even call him my dog. No matter what this old witch says, Menagerie's a person. Somehow, I've got to help him remember this."

"Hmm," said Sorrow, taking the dog's head between her hands and staring into his dark eyes. "The Black Swan's right. I sense only magic animating this creature, not a soul."

"Menagerie once told me he felt like his soul had been long ago devoured by all the animals that lived inside him. I'd be happy at this point if we can change him back into his human form. I think if he could see his human self in a mirror, it might jog his memory."

"I'm afraid I can't help. I've yet to master the art of sculpting living flesh."

"Wouldn't that be easier than sculpting solid iron?" asked Infidel.

"To the contrary," said Sorrow. "You're familiar with the teachings of the Church of the Book? The foundational belief that all of reality is formed of four base elements, matter, spirit, truth and lies?"

"I just spent a few weeks in the company of a Truthspeaker and a Deceiver. I've heard the subject debated, yes."

"I'm a materialist," said Sorrow. "By manipulating the proportions of truth and falsehood in matter, I'm able to shape it to my will. Iron is simple, being almost completely devoid of spirit. It possesses no internal conception of itself to resist alteration."

"I'm sure this is a fascinating subject," Infidel said, "But sundown is, like, ten minutes away. Let's talk about our deal."

"Of course. As I said, I'm the client who reserved the use of the *Freewind,* paying for passage both to and from the island with the advance given me by the Black Swan. There's no need for money to exchange hands. I'll simply write a letter informing Captain Romer that you're representing my interests and taking command of the charter. Supply her with whatever destination you wish. I'll be remaining on the Isle of Fire for some time, if Stagger's papers are as extensive as you say."

"You won't be disappointed."

"I'm sure I won't be," said Sorrow. She walked back to the Black Swan and knelt. On the floor lay a notebook covered with elaborate sketches of an iron woman. She turned to a fresh page and, using a razor freshly minted from raw iron, cut free a sheet of white parchment. She then ground the razor to dust between her fingers, allowing the black filings to sprinkle on the page. With a fingernail, she twirled the iron dust around, lining it into looping letters. I admired the crispness of her handwriting, and felt a stirring of familiarity as I watched the care with which she crossed her T's and dotted her I's. While the shape of her letters were softer and more rounded than my own handwriting, I recognized the same underlying rigidity that had been drilled into my penmanship by the monks at the orphanage in which I was raised. The whole authority of the Church of the Book rested upon the sacredness of the written word. Learning to write correctly akin to learning to pray. Sorrow's handwriting would have delighted any monk. Booze, a lack of piety, and general laziness had rendered my own once neat calligraphy somewhat less pleasing to the eye.

She finished the letter, rolled it up, and sealed it with a band of iron foil. She handed it to Infidel. "I'll finish my work this evening. I'll meet you at Stagger's boat in the morning so I can take possession of his papers."

"Agreed," said Infidel.

Infidel departed, limping on the leg that had taken the machete blow. I was nervous about her passing through town noticeably wounded, with visible cuts on her face. This isn't a good town to show weakness. But, once she was outside, she'd no doubt use the Gloryhammer to fly to the *Freewind*. Not exactly stealthy, but the skies of Commonground were safer than the gangplanks.

Since I knew where to find Infidel, I lingered behind. I had a hunch I wanted to follow up on. I moved my face before the Black Swan's vacant eyes.

"You can see me," I said.

Slowly, the hollow sockets filled with translucent fog, knitting into ghostly orbs that burned with a soft glow. The fog flowed over the iron cheeks and lips, growing denser, until I found myself staring at the face of a young woman rather than the mechanical mockery of one. The woman had thick black eyebrows and an angular nose a bit too large for her face. The iron lips didn't move; the bellows stayed silent. Yet, as the woman's ghost lips parted, a voice in my mind said, "I'm aware of you."

"I thought you might be. Your barbs seemed a little gratuitous if you didn't think I was around to suffer. Why didn't you tell Infidel I was here?"

"I don't wish to encourage her memory of you. The sooner she forgets you, the sooner she'll be free to master her own destiny."

"She's free now."

"No. She's undertaking a dangerous quest to fulfill a promise *you* made. It's an unnecessary risk and a pointless distraction."

"Distraction from what?"

"The dragon apocalypse! Have you failed to pay attention at all?"

"Greatshadow isn't angry at humanity. Infidel showed him mercy when he was at his weakest. He's promised not to seek revenge."

"And yet, again and again, I've lived through the day in which the primal dragons rise against humanity. I'll never be able to erase the memory of blizzards blasting even the southernmost islands, the sea rising to swallow whole cities, and mountains crumbling like sand castles as the earth shakes off mankind like an annoying flea."

"Tragic. But why must Infidel be the one who stops this?"

The Black Swan sighed. "Infidel's former power was derived from dragon blood flowing through her veins. She alone possessed the sheer physical might to perform the heroic undertakings required to spare mankind. Behind the scenes, I arranged that she would come to Commonground so that I might oversee her training. But instead of becoming a focused, highly skilled warrior under my command, she met you and was seduced by your slovenly ways. Now, she's an undisciplined brawler, though stripped of her powers she'll not remain one for long. Unfortunately, in the timelines where I had you killed, Infidel is corrupted by her rage and assassinated by the Church of the Book long before her powers mature to the point that she can slay Greatshadow."

"Well, she has no powers now," I said. "You'll need some new pawn for your game."

"True. Which is why I'm placing my hope in Sorrow." She motioned to the sculptress still shaping her thighs. "Unlike Infidel, her talents are meshed with a driving ambition and a grand vision. As Princess Innocent Brightmoon, Infidel's childhood was too sheltered and pampered to allow her to grow into a serious adult. Sorrow has been tempered by tragedy from an early age. Her hatred and bitterness that spurs her ever onward toward her goals of revenge."

"She seems nice enough."

"Nice is a word seldom used to describe Sorrow. And, unlike Infidel, she loathes men; foolish love will never distract her from her greater destiny."

I shrugged. "What you do with this woman is of no concern to me. I want you to leave Infidel alone. If you don't...." I let the thought trail off. I felt like I should be inserting a threat, but couldn't really think of one.

"Are you attempting to be menacing?" she asked.

"Maybe."

"You're failing at it. I've nothing to fear from you. You'll not linger in this world for much longer."

"You've managed to stick a long time. Why can't I?"

"I never surrendered my hold on my bones," she said. "I renew my energies by bathing my skeleton in blood. You performed a similar trick with your knife. But now that you've foolishly removed it from the mortal world, you're fated to fade away. All actions require energy, even the actions of a spirit. Currently, you're empowered by the dragon blood that the bone-handled knife drank in Greatshadow's realm. That magic may sustain you for some time. But, with no further source of blood, your energies will fade. One day you won't even have the power to remember your name. Soon after, you'll vanish from this world forever."

I ground my ghost teeth. Could I believe her? Where was the profit in lying to me? On the other hand, what was the profit in telling me the truth? "My actual bones aren't all that far from here. What if Sorrow builds me a new body like yours?"

"I think cast iron breasts would look even more ridiculous on you than they do on me."

"You know what I mean."

"Abandon hope, Stagger. Though I despised you in life, I'm not so hard-hearted I take pleasure as you suffer in death. You love Infidel, but her love for you will only lead to a tragic end. In the most probable future, Infidel will die on her journey to Qikiqtabruk. Your daughter will never be born. Do you wish to linger as an impotent observer to the doom of those you hold dearest? Move on, poor ghost, to the great unknown."

"I can't help but get the feeling you're manipulating me," I said. "You're taunting me so I'll do something. But what? Just tell me what you want. Maybe if you'd tried that with Infidel, she would have become the savior you wanted her to be. By trying to treat her like a puppet, you've gotten her strings all tangled."

"There is nothing more I need from you, Stagger. Return to your bones."

"You're not getting rid of me that easily."

She raised her ghostly hand and waved me away.

Suddenly, I was on a sandy bluff, overlooking the sea. This was where Infidel had buried my body. The sun was low against the water, almost gone. My grave of white sand had been somewhat flattened by wind and rain, but there was a man-sized bulge in the earth that hinted that bones lay beneath.

"Maybe you *can* get rid of me that easily," I said, scratching my ghost scalp. What now? Was Infidel really in danger? Or was the Black Swan trying to trick me into stopping her mission? If so, how? What could I do?

Impotent observer of doom. That didn't sound pleasant at all. But as long as that little band of hair was on Infidel's hand, there was at least some small part of me left in the world. Blood wasn't the only source of magic. I was determined to hold on powered by nothing but love.

3 - SERIOUS, HARD-WORKING PEOPLE

THE SKY REMAINED luminous as the sun vanished below the horizon, casting eerie shadows across the hill that held my grave. In the dimming light I stared at the ground, imagining my body six feet below. Not even a month had gone by. How much of me was recognizable underneath this mound of sand? I'd done a lot of digging around the island. In the jungle, a corpse might disappear inside a week in the dank and worm-ridden soil. Here, on a windswept hilltop, in salty sand baked daily beneath a tropical sun... perhaps my corpse had mummified. Certainly my bones were intact. Probably my teeth and nails and hair. The colorful shroud Infidel had fashioned from a stolen pygmy blanket might still be recognizable.

Why I found it comforting to think that I might be slowly turning into jerky instead of jelly I can't say. I suppose that as long as I have bones, I have hope. I've heard that on the island of Podredumbre, the natives dig up the skeletons of their ancestors on the winter solstice and bring them back into their homes for a feast in their honor. Perhaps one day that ritual would catch on here. In fact, winter solstice was only a few days away, though in the eternal summer of the Isle of Fire I doubt many of the residents of Commonground would even notice.

For a moment, I contemplated thrusting my head underground. I'd discovered while exploring the pygmy tunnels as a ghost that, in pitch darkness, I could see the faint aura given off by all material objects. Given that mirrors weren't any use to me now, it might be interesting to see my face once more.

Instead, I clenched my fists of fog and turned away, floating upward. Some things are best left unseen. Above me the boldest stars were starting to glow in the darkening sky. I drifted on the sultry wind that flowed down from the jungle slopes, the moist air infused with the redolence of a thousand species of orchids. I rose nearly a mile before I spotted Commonground, roughly twenty miles away. Even at this distance, the city sparkled with the lanterns of countless ships. The beaches around the bay blazed with funeral pyres. It had been weeks since Greatshadow attacked the city, but new corpses washed ashore with each tide.

I set off for Commonground at a leisurely pace, lost in thought, wondering if Infidel had done the right thing by sparing the dragon. I was shaken from my reverie by a faint high-pitched wail. I scanned the horizon. Was it some sort of bird? It sounded almost human, and was definitely getting louder.

Then, I spotted what looked like a man flashing toward me against the darkening sky. At first glance, it looked like Battle Ox tumbling head over heels through the firmament. As the flying figure hurtled closer, I saw it was instead a heavyset man dressed in a bear skin vest and wearing a horned helmet, a two-handed axe clamped in his sinewy hands. As he tumbled past, I saw that his beard was flecked with vomit as he shrieked at a much higher pitch than one would expect from such a bruiser. In his wake, he left a strong odor of piss. I had the distinct impression his flight was involuntary.

I could have given chase, but I was more interested in who'd launched the man into the atmosphere rather than where he was going to land. Ordinarily, if bodies flew this sort of distance, Infidel was involved.

Though Commonground was thick with ships, it didn't take long to spot the *Freewind*. A long, square-rigged clipper with three masts, the vessel possessed a distinctive burgundy hull. I've heard that the boards were soaked in red wine before it was assembled. This isn't a standard building practice among the Wanderers, and I've no idea what advantage it might have given the ship, but it certainly helps the boat stand out in a crowded harbor.

To my utter lack of surprise, the *Freewind* was under attack. While Commonground was a sanctuary city among the Wanderers, meaning that even the *Freewind* wouldn't be molested while at port, the attackers plainly weren't from around here and probably didn't understand the rules. Two long ships with figureheads carved to look like angry dragons had pinned the *Freewind* against the docks, rendering the ship's legendary speed moot. The attacking boats had hulls wrapped in what looked to be oily hides. At least a hundred burly men wearing bear skin vests and horned helmets swarmed from the boats, running along boarding planks or climbing the numerous grappling ropes that now draped the *Freewind*. They roared deafening battle cries at a pitch more dignified and manly than the shrieker who'd passed me seconds before. While I didn't understand the language, the raiders matched the description of a race of warriors from lands north of the Silver Isles who called themselves Skellings. The only thing I really knew about them was that they were supposedly cannibals. Since their homeland was two-thousand miles away, I doubted they'd come this far looking for dinner.

At first glance, the Skellings appeared to be attacking an empty ship, which made it embarrassing that they were failing to get on board. Those climbing ropes had the misfortune of having the knots slip free from their grappling hooks inches before they reached the railing. Those attempting to run up gangplanks were snatched from their feet by hurricane winds on a bay that was otherwise calm. The waters around the ships grew crowded with flailing bodies.

One of the grapplers, however, had managed to leap for the railing as his rope broke. I watched as he climbed aboard the all but empty deck. Suddenly, a child dropped out of the rigging, hands first, grabbing the warrior by his horned helmet. The Skelling staggered around, cursing, as the slender figure maintained a perfectly balanced handstand. As I drew closer, I saw that the mysterious gymnast was a girl, perhaps ten years old, with a very stern grimace on her face. She had curly black locks that spilled out from a wine-red beret that marked her as a member of the crew. Her agility at riding her unwilling mount was all the more remarkable for the fact that she was wearing a belt studded with lead sinkers that had to weigh at least fifty pounds.

After balancing on the Skelling for a few seconds, she dismounted with a summersault. The second her fingers left the helmet, the confused warrior shot into the air as if he'd been launched from a catapult. He vanished into the night so swiftly that he was gone from sight before the girl's feet even touched the deck. She bounced as if she had springs in her toes, with her hands stretched overhead. As if by magic, a rope swung toward her. She grabbed hold as it lifted her once more into the rigging.

Perhaps the phrase 'as if by magic' is a bit too coy, since I knew damn well that every member of the Romer family that owned the *Freewind* had been given magical powers as a gift for rescuing the mer-king's daughter. Though I normally avoided sea-travel, Infidel had done a stint aboard the *Freewind* as a sword-for-hire during the so-called Pirate Wars. The Romers were serious, hard-working people who neither drank, gambled, nor trafficked in stolen merchandise, which meant I didn't know them personally. Luckily, thanks to Infidel's tales, it wasn't hard to piece together who was who.

The girl had to be Poppy, the youngest Romer. The mermen had given her one of the stranger magical abilities I knew of. Basically, anything she pressed down on would spring into the air with a hundred times the force she'd applied to it. From what Infidel had told me, Poppy was ten years old, and something of a tomboy.

The ropes were being cooperative with Poppy and uncooperative with the Skellings thanks, no doubt, to another family member, Rigger. He was only seventeen and purportedly something of a worrywart. I'd likely find him at the wheel. I flew to the back of the boat and found what had to be him, along with two other family members. All had the same kinky black hair and red berets, along with sharp noses and blue eyes. Rigger had a narrow face adorned by an unflattering scraggle of beard. With his slender limbs he looked like a puppet, with a score of thick ropes wrapped around his arms and legs. He was drenched with sweat, his teeth clenched, as he drew upon his mer-gift, which was the ability to manipulate ropes with his mind. Ordinarily a ship the size of the *Freewind* would have required a crew of at least twenty, but Infidel told me that Rigger was capable of sailing the boat alone.

He wasn't alone in defending the boat, however. Standing beside him was a young woman holding a long spyglass pressed to her right eye. She was a bit younger than Rigger, perhaps fifteen, and was staring into the glass with the same sweaty intensity Rigger showed in manipulating the ropes. Perhaps the fact that she had the cover over the lens explained her effort. But even with the cap she was seeing something, since she shouted out, "Another grappling hook starboard! Three men on the rope!"

Rigger nodded. "Anyone else? Should I drop them?"

"Wait… there's a fourth climber getting on… now!" She looked pleased as the screams of men falling toward water reached the wheel. It was easy to deduce that this young woman was Sage, the clairvoyant of the Romer clan.

"The attacks are slowing down," shouted the third person at the wheel, an older woman with streaks of gray in her dark hair, her skin tan and deeply lined by a life at sea. This was Gale Romer, matriarch captain of the *Freewind*, and the reason the Skellings kept getting gusted off their gangplanks. Gale controlled winds, which helped explain the *Freewind's* reputation for speed. She looked at Sage and cried, "Give me a count of the dead!"

"Thirty-seven," said Sage. "Mako and Jetsam are making short work of them."

"How's Infidel doing against those ice-serpents?"

"Hard to say," Sage answered. "The Gloryhammer's so bright I can't see through the glare."

"What's that about Infidel?" I asked, forgetting I couldn't be heard.

Fortunately, I wasn't kept in suspense long. The hatch to the cargo hold was wide open and a bright beam of light shot up from the guts of the ship.

With a *whoosh*, Infidel flew from the hatch, completely enwrapped by what I can only describe as a python covered in thick silver fur. Three or four pythons, in fact, though it was difficult to tell where one snake ended and another began. Infidel had only one arm free of the tangle, but she had a death grip on the Gloryhammer as she rocketed into the sky, then dove, heading for the shore. I gave chase, unable to tell if she was in control of her flight or not. She flew directly for a large bonfire. In a flurry of sparks and flames, she dropped feet first into a pygmy funeral pyre, shielding her face by pressing it into the crook of her elbow. She stood there for only a second, protected by her armor as the serpents screamed. Their squealing voices were disturbingly similar to those of human babies as their oily fur ignited. Infidel leapt from the thick of the flames. The writhing serpents slipped from her torso to bunch around her legs. She rubbed her eyes and coughed for a few seconds, then spat out a gob of spit that looked like blood, though that might have been due to the firelight. Without waiting to catch her breath, she shot off like a comet. The burning serpents couldn't hold their grip against the acceleration and fell, crying as they tumbled.

In the blink of an eye, Infidel was back at the *Freewind*, barreling through a line of a dozen burly warriors struggling against the wind up a gangplank, tossing them like tenpins. The water below was thick with bodies. A boy maybe sixteen years old ran atop the waves, jumping and skipping over the reaching arms of drowning Skellings. He wore no armor and was armed with only a slender rapier, but his skill with it was, literally, eye-popping. This had to be Jetsam. He had the power to run on water as if it was solid earth, and from his relatively solid footing he was moving among the struggling barbarians and driving the tip of his blade into their brains. I'd seen my share of eye-gouging in Commonground, so I wasn't too horrified by Jetsam's battle tactics, but I was slightly put off by the fact that as he danced around the waves he was *singing*, a rollicking sea shanty I'd heard a time or two sung drunkenly in bars:

And all my enemies,
Will sleep beneath the seas
Around me waves turn red
As they sink down to their bed

While it was good to see a young man enjoying his work, I couldn't help but think his light-hearted manner wouldn't contribute to a long life span. Almost as quickly as I'd had that thought, a Skelling reached up from bobbing in the waves behind Jetsam to try to grab the young Romer by his leg.

I shouted out a warning, despite the futility. Then, with the Skelling's fingers mere inches from Jetsam's ankle, the sea boiled and a dark shape burst into the air. Before I could even understand what was happening, the Skelling's hand was gone and all that was left was a bloody stump. Meanwhile, the shark that had bitten it off continued to fly skyward. Only, it wasn't a shark. It was Mako, at nineteen, the eldest of the Romer children still calling the ship home. He was a large man in what looked like black cotton pajamas plastered to his skin. He was heavily muscled, with an angular face and a mouth twice as wide as it should be. His hair was long and perfectly straight, clinging to his muscular neck like a coat of black ink. From sheer momentum he'd thrown himself ten feet into the air. He twisted to face Jetsam as he fell back toward the water. "Pay attention!" he growled.

As the water swallowed his brother, Jetsam called out, "I saw him, Mako! I was about to take him by surprise!"

Mako's head thrust back to the surface. "This isn't play-fighting," he growled. "These fools want to kill you!"

"They can't touch me," said Jetsam. "I saw him coming, I swear. I've killed twice as many of these guys as you have tonight."

"We aren't keeping score," Mako grumbled as he sank back beneath the bloodied water once more.

"We would be if you were winning," said Jetsam.

Meanwhile, one of the Skelling dragonships had capsized, thanks to Infidel's aggressive hammer work. She, too, looked like she was enjoying herself. As the ship sank lower into the water, she eyed the remaining vessel. She started toward it, until a blond-haired man with no shirt popped up on the deck and held his right arm overhead with his thumb pointed upward.

"I've got their boss!" the man shouted toward the *Freewind*.

Gale appeared at the railing of the boat in seconds. "Good job!"

She gazed out over the water. Only a few stragglers remained. One by one, they vanished beneath the waves, as Mako's shadow flitted beneath the surface. Given that a crew of a half dozen teenagers had finished off a hundred heavily armed warriors without suffering a scratch, I could see how Jetsam might have developed his streak of cockiness.

Gale cast her gaze toward Infidel. "Friends of yours?"

"I've never seen them before in my life!" Infidel said. "I thought they were after you!"

"They're Skellings!" the shirtless blond man called out. "They conduct random raids for a living."

"I figured they were after the bounty on our heads," said Jetsam.

"A reasonable theory," said Gale. "*If* they weren't so far from their homeland."

"Luckily, I've got their warlord tied up," said Shirtless.

"How do you know he's their warlord?" Infidel asked, drifting nearer.

"It will be pretty obvious when you see him."

It bugged me that I didn't know who this blond guy was. Gale obviously knew him. He looked to be in his mid-twenties, and he might have been the first man in Commonground I'd ever seen without a single scar. His body was flawless, his muscles perfectly symmetrical beneath taut tan skin. He had a square jaw, sharp cheekbones and teeth so white it hurt to look at them. I instantly felt a gut dislike of the man, despite no longer having a gut.

His white cotton britches were practically painted onto his skin, and it was difficult not to notice an unusually large bulge along his inner thigh. Infidel stared at him, her mouth slightly agape. My gut dislike hardened to outright hatred.

Gale grabbed hold of a rope and swung to the Skelling's boat. I drifted overhead and saw a large warrior hog-tied on the deck. I had to admit that the blond guy was good at spotting warlords. His captive was completely bald and his face was riddled with scars. Around his neck he wore a chain of what, at first glance, might have been dried fruit, but on second glance were mummified human ears. His bear skin vest sported gold buttons, and he had gold earrings as well. His gray beard and mustache were braided together and reached down to his belly button. Gold trimmed his horn helmet, almost enough to call it a crown. He glared at his captors with utter hatred.

"Good work, Brand," said Gale, stepping forward and kissing the shirtless guy on the cheek. Gale was old enough to be the man's mother; indeed, Mako and Brand looked about the same age.

Brand flashed his brilliant teeth in a broad smile. "I couldn't have done it without your tactical brilliance, my captain."

Gale blushed as he batted his eyelashes at her.

Infidel cleared her throat as she floated to the deck. "I don't think we've met."

"Infidel," said Gale. "This is Brand. Brand, Infidel."

"You must be new," said Infidel, stretching out her white leather gauntlet for a handshake.

Brand grasped her offered hand by the fingers and bent to kiss it. "I was hired on the journey here," he said. "It's my pleasure to meet you."

"Brand is my new dry-man," said Gale.

"What happened to Boggy?" asked Infidel.

"Tiger shark got him when he went for a swim," said Gale.

"Guess he should have stayed dry," said Infidel.

Brand didn't look like a dry-man. Most members of this profession were older gentlemen noted for their soberness, with a reputation for stinginess rather than charm. Wanderers were a sea-faring race who'd long ago made a pact with Abyss, the primal dragon of the sea. As long as a Wanderer never set foot on land, Abyss promised that they would never drown. Most Wanderers lived their lives completely aboard ship. They would band their boats together in remote harbors like Commonground to form impromptu cities where they socialized with one another. To conduct business with the rest of the land-bound world, most Wanderer ships hired dry-men. Somehow, as I watched Gale eye her employee with a look of school-girl giddiness, I got the impression that Brand had been hired for talents other than his skill at haggling for supplies.

"Is everything okay now?" a girl's voice called out from the other ship.

I looked back and saw a hound dog with two paws balanced on the rails of the *Freewind*. Menagerie? He could talk again? Why did he sound like a girl?

Then, an actual girl walked up behind the dog. She had kinky hair like the other Romers, but red instead of black. I guessed her to be about thirteen years old. She looked worried as she gazed out over the corpse-filled water. "Did you get them all?"

This had to be Cinnamon. Infidel had said that Cinnamon was the most timid of the Romers. Perhaps it was because she had the least useful magical ability. I was told that she had the power to control other people's sense of taste. No doubt she'd been hiding below deck. The others probably didn't want her underfoot in battle.

"I kept your dog safe like you asked, Infidel," she called out.

"Appreciate it," Infidel said, with a salute.

Gale, meanwhile, had knelt before the captive warlord. She grabbed him by the beard and turned his face toward her.

"Why did you attack us?" she asked.

He responded by hocking up a gob and spitting in Gale's face.

The stink was powerful enough to wrinkle my nose in the spirit realm.

"Oh lord," gagged Infidel, covering her mouth.

Gale calmly wiped her cheek.

Brand stepped toward the far end of the boat. "How can anyone's breath smell so bad?"

Gale shrugged. "The main meat in a Skelling's diet is rotten fish soaked in lye. It has a distinctive aroma."

"I'd heard they were cannibals," said Brand.

"Don't believe everything you hear," said Gale. "The Skellings come from an island where nothing grows but grass and thistles. They don't have a lot of dietary options."

"I'd eat thistles before I'd eat rotten fish," said Brand.

"They eat thistles for breakfast," said Gale. "But I think we're getting sidetracked."

She turned her attention back to the warlord.

"Mako," she said, picking up his horned helmet from the deck.

Mako had slipped aboard when I wasn't looking. He stepped forward and took the helmet. Then he opened his jaws far wider than any man should be able to, revealing saw-rows of teeth. Without bothering to say grace he bit into the helmet and devoured it in a half dozen bites, horns and all. He spat out the golden bits into his palm. "No sense in wasting these."

The warlord's eyes grew rather large.

Gale tried her question again, this time slipping into a language I didn't understand. "Jabber jabber," she asked.

"Jabber *jabber*," the man growled in response. "Jabber jabber *jabber!*"

They went on like this for five minutes. The warlord's answers kept getting shorter and shorter. Gale paused for a moment and had Mako chew up the warlord's battle axe. The man looked distraught. I got the impression the weapon might have been a family heirloom.

The questioning resumed. Finally, the man answered with what turned into a monologue of utter gibberish that ran on for ten minutes.

Gale nodded, then stood from her squatting position, stretching her hands overhead to work the kinks from her back.

"What'd he say?" asked Infidel.

"It's a little convoluted," said Gale. "Apparently, they came here to set up an ambush. He says there's a two-hundred year old witch named Purity who's enslaved all their women and turned them into a brain-washed army. She's got a grudge against Ivory Blade, since he stole some kind of sacred harpoon, and she's heading to Commonground to capture him. They want to find him first to use as bait to get their women back. When they got into port, they saw Ivory Blade fly onto my boat. They sent the ice-serpents in to take him by surprise, then decided to raid the boat when they realized there were only a handful of men on board."

"Ah," said Infidel. "They must have mistaken me for Blade since I'm wearing his armor. And the harpoon this witch is after must be the Jagged Heart."

"So you know more about this than you've let on," said Gale.

"And yet I really don't," said Infidel. "Here's everything I know. Aurora told me that the harpoon was carved from the shattered remains of Hush's broken heart. Hush became the primal dragon of cold after her heart splintered into a thousand pieces when she was jilted by Glorious, the sun-dragon. The ice-ogres used the largest fragment of the heart as the tip of a harpoon that Aurora said was used to hunt ghost whales."

"Whales have ghosts?" asked Brand.

Infidel didn't answer him. She said, "Aurora said the harpoon had been stolen by raiders, but she didn't really describe them. Maybe it was this witch who took it. All I know is, Lord Tower had possession of the harpoon during our dragon hunt. It was the only weapon capable of killing Greatshadow."

"Wouldn't a harpoon tipped with ice melt once it got near a dragon made of fire?" asked Gale.

"Nope," said Infidel. "I'm not an authority on the pecking order of primal dragons, but apparently cold trumps fire when it comes to elemental forces. Aurora said that cold was the eternal backdrop of all creation, while heat and flame were merely flickering aberrations."

Gale sighed. "You're leaving out one little detail, aren't you?"

"What?"

"You now have the Jagged Heart. You're wearing Blade's armor and using Tower's hammer. I assume you stole the harpoon as well."

"I most certainly did not steal it. Aurora was the high priestess of the ice-ogres. She died recovering the harpoon since it was the most sacred relic of her people. I've made a promise to see that it gets returned to her homeland."

"When you said you wanted to book passage to Qikiqtabruk you didn't mention that you'd be transporting a treasure that an ancient witch was hunting. You're placing my family in danger by bringing it aboard."

"I swear I didn't know there was a witch looking for the harpoon," said Infidel. "But, look, does it really matter what kind of cargo I'm bringing aboard? Everyone here is being hunted by the Church of the Book, the Storm Guard, and the slaving Wanderers. What's one more enemy?"

"If you're my passenger, I have an obligation to defend you. I can't do that if you're keeping secrets."

"I don't need defending," said Infidel.

"Don't you?" Gale asked. "I've been too polite to mention it, but your face is covered with cuts and bruises. When you were last aboard my ship, swords bounced off your skin. You didn't bother with armor."

Infidel crossed her arms. "You Wanderers make a big deal out of privacy. I'll ask you to respect mine."

"Don't speak to me of respect. You're asking me to risk my family. It's easy to forget this here in the tropics, but the northern kingdoms are in the thick of winter. The coast of Qikiqtabruk is completely ice-locked. There will be no safe harbor."

"Aw, Ma, don't be like that," said Jetsam, who was no longer standing on the waves but was instead doing a breaststroke in the air above his mother. I'd forgotten that in addition to being able to walk on water, Jetsam could swim in air. "If we make another boring run between the Isle of Apes and Raitingu I'll go crazy. Let's go to Qikiqtabruk and fight some witches."

Mako stretched his lanky arms overhead to snatch his brother by the belt. He yanked Jetsam back down to the deck and said, "Speak to Mother with such disrespect again and I'll break your jaw."

"No jawbreaking, please!" said Infidel, looking embarrassed to be in the middle of a family dispute. "Look, the whole reason I'm hiring the *Freewind* is that I don't want to fight anybody. I want to get to up north as quickly as humanly possible, hand the harpoon to the first ice-ogre we meet, then get the hell out of there. If I liked cold weather even a little, I wouldn't live on the Isle of Fire."

"So what's your hurry?" asked Gale. "I'd be more open-minded about this mission if you waited until summer. The north sea isn't nearly as treacherous then."

Infidel bit her lower lip. She stared at Gale for several long seconds. Finally, she took a deep breath and said, "If you must know, I'm pregnant. I think. I want to get this over with as quickly as possible before my health won't permit such an adventure."

Gale chuckled, then dismissed Infidel's concerns with a wave of her hand. "You'll not be so fragile as you imagine. I first sailed the Sea of Wine when I was six months pregnant with Levi. You'll be fine if you wait until summer."

"Or," said Brand, stepping forward, "Or, we can accept the mission now, but for an extra fee."

"You've already admitted that Sorrow paid a large fee for you to carry her to any destination she wanted. Just because I'm choosing the destination doesn't mean you can change the price," said Infidel.

"We negotiated that price without full disclosure of the value of the cargo," said Brand. "Due to the need for additional security, our standard fee must be doubled."

Gale didn't look upset that Brand was launching into a negotiation to sail to a place that she'd just said was too dangerous to sail to. Wanderers were notorious hagglers; Gale probably voiced protests as an opening for negotiating a higher fee. Brand was now doing his job by double-teaming Infidel.

Infidel smirked. I could tell she was aware of the game being played. "Double is outrageous. I'll offer a five percent bonus if, but only if, we get attacked by… what was the witch's name again?"

"Purity," said Gale.

"Right. If Purity attacks, and if I can't handle things myself, you get a bonus. These Skellings took us by surprise, but out on open water, I could have sunk both vessels before they even got near."

Gale shook her head. "Five percent isn't a serious offer. Forty percent is the lowest I can go. The safety of my family is paramount. I'll not risk their lives for petty sums."

"And the fee should be paid whether or not we see combat," said Brand. "Sage is capable of spotting enemies long before they spot us, giving us an edge on evasion. This is a valuable service. We shouldn't be penalized for being good at our jobs."

"If she's so good, why didn't you see these Skellings coming?"

Gale frowned. "She took note of them. It's my own fault for not believing they would attack in Commonground. Here, all Wanderers are sworn to come to the defense of other Wanderers."

"And yet, they didn't," said Infidel.

Gale gave a weary sigh. "These damn slave wars are ripping the very foundations of Wanderer society to shreds. I've blood relatives on at least a dozen ships in this port. That none would come to our aid is a heavy burden. And further proof that defending you against attacks will be a burden that falls completely on my immediate family. A twenty-five percent bonus paid up front would be the absolute bare-bones sum I'd consider fair."

Before Infidel could make a counteroffer, I was distracted. Something was crawling on my right hand. The sensation of being touched was unnerving after my weeks of intangibility. I stretched out my arm and spied a large silver mosquito perched upon my knuckles. I froze, paralyzed by the strangeness of the moment. I was no entomologist, but could any bug be agile enough to alight upon something with no more substance than a cloud? It had to be an illusion that the mosquito was crawling on my hand. It must be flying in the spot my hand occupied, and I only imagined that I could feel it.

It was a fine theory. I might have convinced myself if the creature's wings had been moving.

Shaking off my paralysis, I brought my hand closer to my eyes. The mosquito wasn't a living insect, but was instead a finely constructed bit of jewelry, with a body of silver and legs of jointed copper wire. Its delicate wings were formed from gold leaf so thin it was translucent. The mosquito had glass eyes that served as tiny mirrors reflecting my ghostly visage as we stared at one another.

"I… I've seen you before," I whispered.

To my utter astonishment, my phantom breath fogged the delicate wings.

The mosquito didn't react.

I swallowed hard.

After I'd died, when Infidel had first returned to town, she'd fought an undead giant. The unliving thing had been sewn together out of multiple corpses, a patchwork monstrosity with inhuman strength in its misshapen limbs. The giant had given Infidel quite a beating, but she'd eventually pounded it to pulp using its own torn-off arm as a club. When she'd dismantled the torso, she'd found a small cage, and within that cage was a glowing mosquito. This one lacked the inner radiance, but how could it not be the same creature? How many magical mosquitoes could be flying around this town?

"Wh… what are you?" I asked. I felt certain that some higher intelligence gazed at me through those glass eyes.

The thing answered by doing a little dance back and forth. A tongue like a tiny corkscrew worked itself out of the construct's mouth. I shook my hand to throw the thing off, too late. The mosquito sank the corkscrew into my skin. My frantic hand waving failed to loosen it. I watched as a bead of ruby ichor rose around the tiny hole augured in my wraith flesh. I reached out with my other hand to tear the insect loose.

Before my fingers could close upon it, the mosquito placed its mouth against the small pearl of blood that sat upon my knuckle. Nearly microscopic jaws snapped open and a glass pipette thrust down into my ghost blood, drawing the bead up into its belly.

The jaws clicked shut. The noise was too faint to truly hear, but in my imagination it echoed like the lonely clang of dungeon doors. I recovered my wits sufficiently to flick it with my fingers. The blow tore the insect from my skin. As it tumbled, the tiny mosquito spread its wings and took flight. I was none the worse for wear, save for a small smear of blood where the creature had feasted. I watched it buzz a drunken path across the deck, unseen by the assembled Romers. I cast one last glance at Infidel. Though my instincts were to stay at her side I threw myself into the air, narrowing my eyes to concentrate on my ever-accelerating target. I didn't know why it wanted my blood or where it was going. Despite my normally inquisitive nature, I honestly didn't want to learn. I had to stop this thing.

4 - AN EXCEPTIONALLY UGLY BIRD

THE MOSQUITO DOVE over the edge of the railing. I gave chase as it flitted above the stinking tide. The bay of Commonground emits an open sewer aura under the best of conditions, but since the tsunami churned up the muck it's been especially gag inducing. The mosquito flew barely a foot above the water, darting around pilings and between boats and their anchor chains with an agility that might have shaken me if I'd been a bat or a bird. I ghosted through these obstacles as if they weren't even there.

The fact that this mystery bug had touched me meant that I could touch it back. I gave it a good swat with my right hand. It darted to avoid the blow, but the tip of my middle finger managed to clip its wing, sending into a tailspin as it neared the hull of a boat. To my chagrin, it passed straight through the tar-impregnated wood without leaving a scratch.

I flew into the ship's hold, spotting the mosquito easily in the pitch-black interior, despite the jumbled maze of barrels and crates. The thing glowed with an internal magic that my phantom eyes could easily track. Even if I hadn't been able to see it, I could have followed the high-pitched buzz of the mosquito's golden wings.

The mosquito zipped out of the hold, then shot strait up, disappearing though the pier above. I emerged onto a boardwalk crowded with bodies. Now that night had fallen, the denizens of the city were out in force. Cutthroats and whores stumbled groggily along the pier, searching for breakfast at a time when law-abiding men sought out supper. The area was crowded with ramshackle shacks slapped together by river pygmies, who cooked plantains, turtle eggs, and crabs on charcoal grills stoked to ruby heat. Dark amber rum with a whisper of coffee was the beverage of choice for this clientele, and I felt a pang of longing as I caught a whiff of this much cherished elixir.

I lingered for a fraction of a second, distracted by the aroma, and spotted faces of former friends among the crowd. Ol' Scummy Stone was sitting on a bench, drinking from a silver flask he'd won from me in a game of darts. Scummy was in his sixties and had survived for decades in this rough and tumble town using the same strategy I'd employed, which was to be obsequious enough that no one had reason to kill you, but not so pathetic that you aroused actual hatred. Further down the planks I saw Rose Thirteen; by this point she'd had twenty husbands, but her name had gotten locked down after she botched the job of poisoning husband thirteen and had to finish him off with a hatchet in the door of the Drunken Monkey Saloon. Her hair was streaked with gray now, but she still had the same lushness of figure that had caught so many men in her orbit. Despite her propensity toward murder, she was welcome company on a night of drinking, since she knew more dirty jokes than a sailor. She was also Commonground's only competent seamstress – she'd mended the pants I'd died in.

If the mosquito had meant to distract me by tracing a path through places and faces familiar to me, I'm vexed to confess that it succeeded. It had gained a hundred feet of distance as I paused to reminisce. I caught one last glimpse of the tiny beast as it zipped into Big Blue's Bug and Bun Barn at the end of the pier. I flew after it, but the second I entered the restaurant I lost focus. My mouth watered as I caught sight of plates full of yeasty fried dough stuffed with bananas and lemon spiders. Unfortunately, for a ghost, concentration equals movement. For the briefest second, the mosquito vanished from my mind and I found myself stalled in the middle of the bug barn, stirred to hunger.

It took only an instant to shake off my reverie and zoom out the back wall but it was too late. I couldn't spot the mosquito amid the chaos of lights and bodies, nor hear its faint buzz beneath all the laughter and shouts. Outwitted by an insect!

The creature had been heading due east when it first took flight. There wasn't much left in that direction. Once, Bigsby's fish house had been the central feature of that area, but the tidal wave had left nothing but slanted timbers thrusting up from the water. I wondered if Bigsby would rebuild, assuming he was even alive. Between the volcano erupting, the tidal wave, and the avatars of Greatshadow burning everything in sight, the population of Commonground wasn't what it used to be.

Flying over the barren water, I noticed a dim glow on the shore no more than a mile distant. This was no funeral pyre or bonfire; I guessed it to be the faint, flickering light of numerous candles.

Which, indeed, it was. Hundreds of slender tapers formed a large spiral in a circle of raked beach sand. I flew higher to better perceive the design and found myself mesmerized by the snail-shell shape, unable to turn away.

At the center of the whirl of light was a familiar figure. Sorrow Stern knelt on the beach, laying gnarled bits of driftwood together into a shape that bore a vague resemblance to a man. Its legs were splintery remnants of a mast split by lightning. Its arms were thick branches of dark teak, the fine grain looking almost like muscle beneath a thin coat of damp sand. For a head it possessed a large coconut still in its husk, given a jagged mouth by a machete chop and what could pass as eyes formed by two oval pecan shells. The twin iron nails that held the false eyes to the surface glinted like irises in the candlelight. To the sides of the head were curled tamarind seedpods that served as makeshift ears.

For the first time I saw Sorrow free of her hood. She'd stripped off her cloak and wore a bright red dress that left her shoulders bare. The garment looked more appropriate for a ballroom than a beach. She was smaller without the cloak, with a figure best described as girlish, but I found her age a mystery. The left half of her body was withered, the limbs supported by iron braces, but her right half looked young and strong. Her head was shaved, which added years to her appearance. Her scalp was dotted with dark studs, some of which flashed as they caught the candlelight. I found myself drawn in along the spiral, fascinated by the bumps on her head. They looked, for all the world, like the blunt heads of nails jutting up. There were half a dozen, one gold, another silver, another rusted iron, one green copper, one that might have been glass, and the last with the appearance of polished wood.

She stood, lifting her hand straight up as if she were reaching for me as I hovered overhead. I heard a buzz and the silver mosquito flashed toward her fingers, alighting gently on her outstretched palm. She knelt once more, opening the barrel chest of the driftwood man she'd built, revealing a small cage of golden wire. She opened a tiny door and the mosquito crawled inside.

"Wandering spirit, thou shall roam no more," said Sorrow, her voice deeper than what should have come from her slender throat. "By thy blood I bind thee to this body of wood. Thy soul shall be its soul."

She shut the door to the cage.

Long ago, before arriving in Commonground, I worked on a fishing vessel in the Green Straights, where swordfish are caught with hooks of tempered steel fed out on long weighted lines. I'd had the misfortune of running one of those hooks through my hand, the point slipping between the bones of my little finger and ring finger just beneath my knuckles. I'd been beaten by professionals during my years at the monastery but nothing quite prepared me for the pain as the weighted line played out and snatched me overboard.

That same pain now seized me in every pore. I felt invisible hooks slip into my mouth, scraping across tooth and tongue and bone. Hooks pierced my eyes and ears, slid into my neck bones, tangled in every rib. I thrashed against the unseen barbs that tormented me, beating the night air with my ghost limbs, to no avail. Fine silver threads appeared all around me, connecting my wraith-form to the driftwood man. With a sound like fingernails dragged along guitar strings, these lines went taut and reeled me in.

For a moment, everything went black.

When I opened my eyes again the world was painted in shades of amber. My limbs felt numb and heavy. I could barely turn my head... and yet, to my surprise, I did have a head to turn. I was a physical being once more, my body cold and stiff, but undeniably present. I raised an arm that felt weighted with iron and brought it to my face. With my monochromatic vision, I could make out the gnarled remnants of the base of a mangrove tree, with five finger-length roots jutting out. Such was the resemblance of the root to a hand that I imagined I could close the fingers into a fist, and, at the thought it happened. I felt the friction of finger against finger, felt the damp grit that coated the limb grinding into wooden flesh.

Sorrow loomed above me. Unlike the rest of my monochrome world, she looked crafted from a rainbow, a being of pure energy swirling within the translucent flesh of a woman. Her voice was thunderous in my seedpod ears:

"Ghost, you are bound to this body of wood. It was alive once, but devoid of spirit, as you were alive once, but are devoid of body. I give you dominion over this form for a time, till decay and entropy reduce this shell to dust, and the last spark of your animating spirit fades from this domain. Until you meet this final death, you are my property, and shall obey my commands."

I attempted to offer my opinion of her demands in the form of a string of artfully delivered curse words. No sound emerged from my coconut lips. Despite having a mouth, I discovered I had no tongue. I sat up, feeling clumsy and disoriented. My eyes had difficulty keeping the world on the level as I swayed first to the left, then the right. I had only a muted sense of proprioception. I stretched out my driftwood arms, fingers splayed, to steady myself on the sand.

It felt, I must confess, a good bit like being drunk. Had I really spent fortunes in pursuit of this sensation when I was alive? *This* had been my preferred state of existence, listing through the world like a ship with a damaged keel?

Perhaps I'd paid freely for this sensation in life, but in death I'd grown used to sobriety, and wanted it back. Still seated, I scraped out letters on the sand using my gnarled fingers.

P-L-E-A-S

I don't know what she thought I was about to ask, but Sorrow dropped to her knees before my wooden body and placed her lips upon the jagged gash of my new mouth. She sucked in air from my coconut and I felt dizzier than ever.

She broke off the kiss and stood, turning her back to me. Yet, due to the quirk of my new vision that saw her as radiant energy, I could see through her clothes, her skin, her ribs and lungs, all the way through to the other side, where her hands were busily knitting something dark and cold. It took me a second to understand it was a little doll made of twigs and grass. She brought it to her lips and breathed into it.

My own body suddenly felt warm.

She stood the tiny doll in the palm of her hand and said, "Rise."

I rose, feeling as if unseen hands had taken me by the arms to help me stand. The world was askew, with my head lopsided upon my shoulders, until she adjusted the head of the miniature and my own skull rolled to right the world. I glanced down at the letters I'd written; they seemed very far away. My new body was a good foot taller than my old one. Sorrow looked tiny as I loomed over her. But, despite our different statures, there was no question that she was the dominant entity in our new partnership.

"Those letters," she said, glancing at the sand. "Erase them."

I wanted with all my soul to disobey, but instead my left foot dragged across the letters, blotting out my pitiful attempt at communication.

"You remember how to write," she said, softly. "Perhaps you have other memories from your former life. I've no power to force you to forget them. But forget them you must, or your days will be agony."

I slowly shook my head. I could still say, "No," at least.

"Whoever you were, that person is dead," she said, sounding defiant. "You had your chance at life, and you had your chance to move on to the abstract realms when you passed away. It's your fault you've lingered and become fuel for my creation. I'm not to blame for the fate that has befallen you. I'm simply a weaver, a materialist who is able to sculpt lifeless matter into useful forms. Your soul no longer served a purpose; its energy was wasted on aimless wandering. I've done you no harm, ghost. Indeed, I've given you a gift; a few final days of purpose."

I again shook my head, "No." The grinding sound of my coconut skull swiveling on my wooden shoulders was unnerving.

She didn't look directly at my face as she said, "You've no choice. In the morning, I shall take possession of a large quantity of manuscripts. I don't trust the scoundrels of this port sufficiently to hire assistants to move them. You'll serve as my porter, as well as my bodyguard. Just as wood is tougher than muscle, so too are you stronger than a man, and impervious to pain. You'll make a formidable warrior if needed. Fortunately, I'm not one who behaves recklessly. With luck you'll never need to expend your energy in battle."

She walked off beyond the edge of my vision. I couldn't turn my head sufficiently to follow her. She returned a few minutes later with a bundle of clothing. "Get dressed. You won't pass for human, but in Commonground that's not such a rarity. In this garb, you'll draw less attention."

The paralysis that inflicted me vanished and I was able to take the clothes she offered. Unfortunately, my freedom of movement was decidedly limited. Any of the ordinary actions one might take while dressing seemed permissible, but when I wanted to wheel around and dash for the forest, my body proved deaf to my commands.

The clothing was surprisingly fresh and clean. Given my resemblance to a scarecrow, I'd expected nothing more than rags, but there was little evidence that these clothes had ever been worn before. Perhaps she was as adept at knitting cloth as she was at molding steel or shaping wood. The pants were heavy wool; they no doubt would have been hot and scratchy if I'd still had skin. The shirt was even rougher; fabrics aren't my specialty but I believe it was woven from jute, more suited for burlap bags than clothing, though given the splintery nature of my new joints perhaps the thick fabric was a good match. Heavy cloth gloves and sturdy leather boots hid the plainly inhuman nature of my limbs. The final touch was to cover my coconut skull with a tri-corn hat, matched with a large bandana hiding most of my face and neck. I imagined I looked a bit like a bandit in the get-up.

"You're rather dashing with that crimson bandana," Sorrow said, adjusting the way it rested on my cheeks, if a coconut had cheeks. I found myself curious about what other colors I might be wearing. With my amber vision, I'd thought all my clothing was shades of brown, but for all I knew she might have dressed me to rival a peacock.

"Follow," she said, and I followed.

WE PASSED THE night in one of the luxury suites aboard the *Black Swan*. I'd been in similar suites before. During the times in my life when I was blessed with money, I saw little reason to hoard it. "Seize the day!" was my motto, though in practice this usually meant, "grab the bottle!" The old *Black Swan* had been destroyed when Greatshadow attacked Commonground, and this new room was so clean and polished that the light of a single bedside lamp hurt my new eyes. Sorrow hadn't bothered to give my coconut face a nose, but when she hung her cloak in the closet the scent of fresh cedar was powerful enough I could taste it in my false mouth despite my lack of a tongue. Formerly, the rooms I'd stayed in had sported artwork with scantily clad pagan goddesses as a popular theme. Now, the paintings on the wall were all landscapes in muted colors. I suppose it was more tasteful, but also a little dull.

Sorrow placed me in the corner of the room and told me to sit. She returned to the door and sealed it shut by molding the frame to the wood of the door itself. She stripped down unselfconsciously before me, changing into a simple cotton nightgown. Again, I noted the health of the right half of her body, and the dark veins, wrinkles, and amber blotches of her left side. "You may not move tonight unless danger arises while I'm sleeping, in which case you are free to defend me. Remain alert; your senses may be dulled by your new encasement, but you have far less to distract you than you did in life. You've no need for sleep or food or water now; focus your attention on any noises from the hall."

She climbed into the bed of silk and was asleep in moments, the covers pulled almost to her chin despite the tropical heat. A veil of mosquito netting surrounded her bed, but I could see her easily enough, even in the darkness. Like Infidel, she proved to be a restless sleeper. All through the night, she tossed and mumbled.

I wondered how she had come to be named Sorrow. It seemed off-key for a nickname, since it was neither cruel nor funny, and it didn't strike me as the sort of name a person would willingly choose for herself. But it made little sense as a given name, either. What mother would wish such a label upon her daughter?

SORROW ROSE BEFORE dawn, lingering a while before a mirror as she ran her fingers around the dark, inflamed flesh surrounding one of the nails driven into her scalp. This was the nail that looked like it was carved from mahogany. To judge by her wincing, the wound felt as painful as it looked. She applied a bit of pressure and a bead of thick amber puss bubbled up. She wiped this away with a cotton ball soaked in alcohol as a deep frown once more lined her face. As she worked the last of the puss from the wound, she took a moment to drag her fingers around her scalp. Even in the dim candlelight, I could see a haze of stubble had arisen during the night. Her baldness was the product of a razor.

An hour later we were back outside, amidst a cacophony of hammers and saws. Commonground was busily being rebuilt by the river pygmies and the Wanderers, both of whom relied on the town as an economic hub.

I followed Sorrow to the shore and recognized the path she was walking toward a tangle of dense trees. Sitting in the upper branches of one particularly robust mangrove was what was left of a sailboat. The ground beneath the boat had been picked clean by river-pygmy scavengers, but despite the relative ease of climbing the gnarled and knotty trees, it looked as if the boat was unmolested. Even out of water, everyone would have recognized this as my boat. In life, I was hardly a fearsome enough figure to discourage looters. Infidel, however, had a reputation as someone who didn't trifle with thieves. She'd lived here a few days following Greatshadow's attack and had made it her home since returning from the hunt. Until word got out that she'd lost her powers, the place was safe.

"Climb," said Sorrow, as she hopped upon my back. Her arms wrapped around my neck in a way that would have choked me if I'd needed to breathe. I barely felt her weight upon me. Nor, I should note, did I much feel my own weight. The soggy driftwood had dried a good bit during the night and my limbs felt stronger and steadier than they had before. In one of the few civil conversations I'd ever had with Hookhand, he told me that when he'd first put on his hook it had been a lifeless weight strapped to the stump of his arm, but over time he felt as if the ghost of his hand had flowed into it, and that, impossible as it seemed, he'd been able to feel things with the cold iron.

While there was no mistaking my new body's crude sense of touch for the nuance of actual flesh, I found that there was some truth to Hookhand's story. My phantom fingers had flowed into the roots beneath my gloves and I could sense pressure as I grasped the branches, and feel the spiky bark digging into my wooden palms. My sense of hearing had improved during the night, and though I was hampered by my vision possessing a single hue, my ability to focus was improving.

I climbed over the railing of my boat. The vessel had been in poor repair for years, but a few weeks in the branches had warped and twisted the deck into a surface where not a single plank could be described as flat. It looked as if the whole thing could fall apart in a good stiff wind, though that was currently being tested, as the omnipresent sea breeze kept the whole structure swaying. Sorrow dropped from my back and called out, "Hello?"

There was no answer. She looked around, then crouched down to enter what remained of the cabin. I knelt to watch. I was never fastidious in my housekeeping, but the place was a disaster even by my slovenly standards. The boat had obviously flipped end over end when the tidal wave carried it here. Everything had been drenched as well, and what books I could see were coated with mold. My heart ached as I contemplated the ruined pages. Despite my early years in the monastery orphanage where I was taught to read and write, I've always considered myself an autodidact. I've stuffed my skull with information both trivial and profound without the guidance of any teachers other than these books. I mourned their death as much as I would have mourned the passing of a human friend.

I couldn't blame Infidel for the poor state of my belongings. Even if she'd emptied out the cabin and tried to salvage the books, the truth was most had mildewed long ago, as I tended to keep my reading material in tottering stacks by my bedside rather than safely arranged in glass cases. Perhaps it was the combination of my lax housekeeping and the tidal wave destruction that led Infidel to simply ignore this mess. She'd been sleeping in a hammock she'd strung in the branches above the deck, with a patch of sail stretched above serving as a roof.

Sorrow sighed. She grumbled, as much to the wind as to me, "My grandmother used to say one should never buy a pig in a poke. I'd imagined the grandson of Judicious Merchant would have taken better care of his writings."

I silently chuckled inside my driftwood cage, delighted at her consternation. For while I'd been a lackluster guardian of my reading materials, I was far more diligent with my own writing. Somewhere under all the clutter and debris was my grandfather's sea chest. It was tightly constructed from high quality cedar and utterly airtight. All my important papers were probably safe inside, but she had no way of knowing this. It was her own fault for not carving me a tongue, or even allowing me to write in the sand.

Sorrow cast her gaze upwards, shielding her eyes with her hand. Infidel was coming near, the Gloryhammer glowing like a second sun. A darker shape followed closely behind, flapping awkward, ungainly wings. Some sort of injured pelican?

Infidel covered the half mile that separated us in mere seconds, wisely choosing to land on a thick limb beside the boat rather than on the deck itself. She nodded in greeting toward Sorrow, then looked at me. "Who's this?"

"A little extra muscle," said Sorrow. "I haven't bothered to name him yet. I guess I'll call him Drifter."

"You can't just ask him his name?"

"He's the strong silent type. Very, very silent."

By now, the flapping shape that had followed Infidel caught up, lighting on the branch beside her. It was a creature I'd never seen before, with the body, legs, and ears of a hound-dog, but with wings, big webbed claws and a long, ungainly beak like a pelican. The overall appearance was comical, but also unnerving, for the creature's form was ever shifting, with the margin around his neck and chest where feathers transitioned into fur ebbing and flowing in slow, rippling waves.

"That's your, uh, man-dog?" asked Sorrow. "The shape-shifter? Menagerie?"

"Yeah," said Infidel. "This morning I found him on deck chewing on a freshly killed pelican. His face was coated with the blood. I was going to leave him at the ship, but when I jumped into the air to fly here, he turned into this and gave chase."

"Maybe the pelican blood gave him a new form?" Sorrow said.

"Maybe. But he also sucked my blood when he was a tick, so why didn't he change back into a human?"

"I'm not an authority on blood magic," said Sorrow. "But, I can see the auras of living things, and this creature has not even the faintest hint of a human aura. It doesn't possess the spiritual template to change into a man."

"Whatever," Infidel said. "Humans are vastly overrated in my book. I hope Menagerie gets better, but for now you have to admit it's kind of cool that I have a flying dog."

Sorrow shrugged and looked back into the cabin. "That's a very positive attitude. It would be equally accurate to say that you merely have the affection of an exceptionally ugly bird."

"There's no need to be nasty," said Infidel.

"Is there not?" said Sorrow. "I entered into this deal foolishly, I admit. The citizens of Commonground aren't famous for their honesty. There was something about your aura that led me to trust you. Most dishonest people have feeble and dirty auras. Yours was bright and clear; I thought that in this city of sin, I'd somehow stumbled upon a true innocent. Yet, rather than finding the organized collection of books and maps I thought I was purchasing, I find only rotting litter."

Infidel stepped gingerly onto the deck. "I didn't cheat you," she said, ducking into the cabin, motioning for Sorrow to follow.

Sorrow glanced at me and said, "Don't move," then followed.

Menagerie lingered behind, perched on the branch, staring at me, his head tilted.

Though I couldn't move my physical form, I tried to speak. A ghost voice tore from my ghost throat and echoed in my ghost ears, though the morning air was silent save for the chirping of birds and the distant stir of the waves.

"Menagerie!" I called to the dog-bird. "Can you hear me? Can you hear me?"

The dog furrowed his brow as it loped onto the deck. Its head became almost fully hound as it took the time to sniff me, then flowed back toward pelican as it sat on its haunches and looked up at my face.

"Can you hear me? Say something," I said.

He didn't say anything.

"Speak!" I said.

Nothing.

"Roll over!" I said, feeling bad that I was treating a man who had once been a brilliant mercenary as if he had only the intelligence to do canine tricks.

He kept staring. Did he not hear me? Did his dog form not understand that command? What other commands could I try? I couldn't tell him to heel or fetch since I was immobile. Telling him to sit was pointless since he was already sitting.

"Shake?" I said, rather tentatively since I couldn't move my arms.

Menagerie raised his right front leg with its webbed bird's foot. With his hound dog eyes, he looked heartbroken when I left him hanging.

5 - Sorrow Would Soon Know My Name

"BY THE SACRED quill," gasped Infidel as she dragged my sea chest out onto the deck. The thing was five feet long, three feet tall and wide, solidly constructed and stuffed to the brim. I'm surprised she could move it without her old powers. She collapsed against the railing and wiped her brow. "That wasn't fun."

"I'm learning not to believe everything I hear in Commonground," Sorrow said as she, too, emerged from the cabin.

"Look, don't get distracted by all the ruined books," said Infidel. "The real treasure's in this box."

"I was referring to the stories I'd heard of your strength," said Sorrow. "I'd been told you were as strong as a score of men, but even one man could have gotten that sea chest out of the cabin with less effort. I'd also heard that swords bounced off your skin, but your face certainly doesn't lend much credence to that claim."

"Oh," said Infidel, sliding her fingers along the thin brown scabs that lay upon her cheeks. "My powers, uh, only kick in when I'm fighting. I don't waste magic on moving furniture."

"I see," said Sorrow, kneeling in front of the chest. She contemplated the big brass lock on the front. "Do you have the key?"

"Sorry," Infidel said, shaking her head. She grabbed the Gloryhammer. "Stand back and I'll knock the lock off."

"That won't be needed. If you're willing to damage the lock to open the chest, there's no need for me to respect its integrity."

She grasped the padlock, squishing it between her fingers like a ball of clay. She twisted the metal and tugged it away from the chest, stretching it like taffy until it snapped.

"Looks like you've got some inhuman strength of your own there," said Infidel.

"Nonsense," said Sorrow. "My strength is unremarkable. As a materialist, I comprehend ordinary matter in a way that your untrained eyes cannot. You believe the illusion that the material world is made of solid objects. I see through this illusion."

"You sound like Zetetic," said Infidel. "In Greatshadow's lair, we encountered a room carved from false matter. It had no fixed form or color. He said this was the original state of all matter."

"I sound nothing like Zetetic," said Sorrow. "Though I never met the man, Deceivers believe all of reality to be a shared fiction, lacking objective truth. I don't dispute the reality of the material world; indeed, I study it and understand it. The key concept is that the things we think of as solid objects are composed of much tinier particles. If you could shrink to the size of a flea, the smooth surface of this lock would be revealed as a rugged landscape of boulders. Shrink to the size of a dust mote, and you would find that the boulders are built of individual grains. If you could become so small as to be invisible, you would find that these grains cling to one another like damp sand. Even a child on the beach can sculpt and mold damp sand using only their bare hands."

"But that lock wasn't made of sand," said Infidel.

Sorrow shrugged. "My analogy is difficult for the uninitiated to follow. The true nature of matter is so counterintuitive that our language lacks words to accurately describe it." She pulled her cloak back, revealing the scalp full of nails. "Even I couldn't learn the truth through mere language. I had to have reality driven into my brain directly. Every nail in my skull is made from a pure material form. These have been placed in contact with the portion of my mind that perceives the corresponding substance. The copper nail gives me command over copper, which was the primary component of this brass lock."

Infidel grimaced when she saw Sorrow's scalp. I was a little queasy myself, since the wooden nail that had been infected this morning was now even worse. Dark veins ran from the wound, which was now an ugly bruise, almost black, fading to lighter hues of amber at the edges.

"Most metals are simple," said Sorrow. "In their natural state they hold a faint echo of the primal spirit of Krag, the dragon of earth, but this spirit is driven out in the smelting process. Thus, they have no will to resist my magic. I recently expanded my repertoire to include wood. It's been 1000 years since Verdant, the primal dragon of the forest, last spread his spirit into trees, but even so, as once living material, wood possesses a cellular memory that can fight my manipulations. It's exhausting in both body and spirit to make use of it. However, it's worth the price since wood can be imbued with a persistent animating spirit, unlike iron or copper."

Infidel's brow wrinkled. "I'm not sure I'm following you. Are you saying *anyone* could bang a nail into her head and gain your powers?"

"With the right nail, in exactly the right place, to precisely the right depth," she said. "But not anyone. Only females are able to master the art. Feminine prowess in magic is a threat to the male assumption of superiority. Thus, the patriarchal powers-that-be label me a witch and a heretic. So be it. I wear their slurs as a badge of honor."

Infidel grinned. "I know where you're coming from. I hated it at first when people called me 'Infidel.' Now I've come to like it. I guess it was your enemies who named you Sorrow?"

As she spoke, Infidel repeatedly scratched the scabs on her face. It was almost impossible to look at Sorrow's scalp, with its festering wound and stubbled hair, and not feel itchy. If my own hands hadn't been paralyzed, I'd have been scratching my coconut dome.

Sorrow frowned. "I thought it was impolite in Commonground to inquire about the pasts of others."

Infidel shrugged. "Yeah, it is. But I'm curious. From your accent, you must be from the Silver Isle. Most girls there get named something churchy, like Faith, Hope, or Innocent. Sorrow isn't a name I've heard before."

"My father was especially, as you say, 'churchy.'" Sorrow looked down at the mass of copper in her hands. She'd wadded it up into a tight ball. "Have you heard of Judge Adamant Stern?"

Infidel raised an eyebrow. "The commander of the Judgment Fleet? The guy who hung his own mother?"

Sorrow nodded. "You know of him."

"Who doesn't?"

"Indeed. His story is well known. As his daughter, I've witnessed his infamy first hand. An accusation was made that his mother was a weaver… a witch. He had her head shaved, but found no nails. He did, however, find scars. My grandmother claimed these were childhood cuts and scrapes, but the letter of the law was that if her head weren't free of blemish, she was to be hung. I was nine years old at the time. My grandmother was everything to me. My mother had died giving birth to me… this is why my father named me Sorrow."

"Harsh," said Infidel.

"He never showed me kindness. He barely spoke to me, allowing my grandmother to raise me as if I were her own daughter. After he hung her, he left me in the care of the family maid to raise me as he pursued his career upon the seas. What he didn't know was that our maid was an actual weaver. She gave me my first nail, of silver. Not long after, she was discovered. She was tortured to death and confessed to converting me to the dark arts. But this I learned second-hand, since I was on a boat to the Isle of Grass by the time her head was being shaved by my father."

"The Isle of Grass? The *Freewind* was attacked by Skelling's earlier tonight."

"This far south?"

"Yeah. About a hundred of them. They used furry white pythons for attack dogs."

"Snow-wyrms. Despite their reptilian characteristics, they're actually a relative of otters. Why would they venture so far from home?"

"They said some witch named Purity had kidnapped their women and they'd come here to find her."

Sorrow's mouth fell open. Then her eyes narrowed as she said, skeptically, "So you know of my past. I would prefer you confront me directly with your questions rather than take such an oblique approach to your queries."

"What the hell are you talking about?" asked Infidel. "Wait? Are you Purity?"

"Don't be stupid." Sorrow rolled her eyes. "Purity was a weaver of great renown. It's said that her magic kept her alive for two hundred years."

"Hmm," said Infidel, studying Sorrow closely. "Your age *is* kind of hard to pin down."

Sorrow frowned. "If you must know, I'm only twenty-two. The left half of my body withered when I unsuccessfully tried to master bone-weaving. Unfortunately, I mistakenly inserted the bone into the portion of my brain meant to command wood. I've paid a terrible price for this failure."

"Tough break," said Infidel. "So, you're not a two-hundred year old witch. But from your reaction to her name, I'm guessing you know her."

"No," said Sorrow. "I know only her legend. She was originally a maiden dwelling on the north shore of the Silver Isle, until she was kidnapped by Skellings. She was brutally raped during her time in captivity, but eventually a drunken Skelling carelessly placed his sword by her bed as he prepared to abuse her. She killed him and a dozen other men on her escape. She nearly died upon the high seas in an open boat she'd stolen until she was rescued by a mysterious old woman with strange powers. This was the legendary witch Avaris; she took Purity under her wing and taught her all the arts of weaving. Purity returned to the northlands with her newfound powers intending to exact revenge upon the entire race."

"Avaris? I've heard that name before. The Black Swan supposedly learned to travel through time with her help."

"Yes," said Sorrow. "Time-weaving is one of the abstract arts, the highest class of witchcraft. I manipulate material objects, but dream of one day expanding my powers to the manipulation of abstract forces. Avaris is the only witch to have mastered all the material and abstract realms. If I could speak with her for even five minutes, I'm certain the knowledge I could gain would transform me."

Infidel nodded. "So, when you went to the Isle of Grass, you were looking for Purity. And, if you could, you'd like to learn a few things from Avaris?"

"I sense a hint of disapproval in your tone."

"History is a subject that bored me, but even I've heard stories about Avaris. She's one of the most evil women who ever lived. She used to eat children!"

"History is written by victors," said Sorrow. "Once, the weavers were a force to be reckoned with, willful females with powers rivaling those of gods. The men of this world couldn't tolerate the threat to their sovereignty, and used the Church of the Book to turn the world against the weavers and hunt them down. Unfortunately, men possess a greater stomach for bloodshed and brutality than most women. They ended the era of weavers through a campaign of violence. They now ensure the subservience of women through a phallocentric mythology that treats females as inferior beings."

Infidel cracked her knuckles. "I like to think I'm doing my small part to help women get back into the bloodshed and brutality business."

"I'm not content with playing a small part," Sorrow said, clenching her fists. "The world I was born into is fundamentally corrupt. The grand crimes committed against humanity are so audacious that all notions of right and wrong are upended. The rich and the powerful build their civilization upon the backs of the weak, justifying their cruelty and theft with a fictional moral code supposedly enshrined in a book that no man has read."

Infidel nodded. "Sister, you don't have to preach to me that civilization is screwed up. That's why I do everything I can to avoid it."

"I'm not content to run. I'm going to tear it all down." There was a hard determination to Sorrow's voice I found chilling. "I'm going to destroy the Church of the Book, topple the kingdoms of men, and establish a new golden age."

Infidel stared blankly at Sorrow for half a minute, uncertain what to say. Finally, she cleared her throat. "It's good to have goals."

"Yes," said Sorrow. "But I need more than goals. I need power, and I need allies. If you're truly aware of the unjust nature of the world, and even half deserving of your legend as warrior, why not join me in my battle?"

"Because it's a stupid battle," said Infidel.

"How can you be so blind?" asked Sorrow.

Infidel crossed her arms. "I think you're the one who might be missing her own contradictions. You think you're wise enough and smart enough to remake the world? Don't you see that anyone arrogant enough to think that is likely going to wind up making things worse?"

"I'd rather try to remake the world and fail than hide in this remote backwater and avoid the struggle for justice."

"If you think I avoid struggles on the Isle of Fire, you've got a lot to learn."

"You fight pointless battles against freaks and scoundrels. It's hardly a worthy struggle."

"There's a difference between battles and struggles," said Infidel. "Fighting is easy for me. My struggle has been to learn to love and trust after being raised in a life where these words had been stripped of meaning. My struggle now is to rise above a life where my main pursuit has been to amuse myself, and remake myself into a mother who can raise a child. I've lived most of my life stuck with the same attitudes and emotions I had when I was fifteen. My struggle is simply to grow up."

"Don't you owe your unborn child a chance to grow up in a better world?"

Infidel shrugged. "This world isn't so bad. Stagger used to take me up into the jungle, where we'd explore vine-draped ruins and eat fruit fresh straight from the tree. We'd make our beds under stars so bright and crisp it looked like the sky was full of glorystones. Civilization might have its problems, but the world… the world's all right."

"You're wasting your talents," Sorrow said.

"It sounds like you've got more powerful allies in mind anyway. What about Purity? Did you find her when you visited the Isle of Grass? Was she able to help you?"

"No," said Sorrow, sounding bitter. "I found only Purity's grave. Tales of an ageless witch who tormented the northern land proved only a myth."

"Those Skellings were pretty insistent that someone was stealing their women." Infidel stood up. The hammer glowed as she lifted slowly into the air. She drifted over to the long beam of what had once been the mast of my sailboat, now straddling the branches of three different trees. I noticed for the first time the long, skinny roll of canvas lashed to the mast. Odd. I hadn't had sails rigged on the boat since I owned it.

She untied the rope and the canvas dropped into her hands. I noticed that the white cloth sparkled like it was coated with diamond dust… or frost. She unrolled the canvas above the deck and the Jagged Heart dropped down, tip first into the wood. The harpoon stood like a second mast, carved from a spiraling narwhale horn.

"Purity is supposedly stealing their women to build an army because she's looking for this," said Infidel. "It's the Jagged Heart. Belonged to a friend of mine named Aurora. The Church of the Book stole it. I've made an oath to take it back."

"The ice ogres may not give you a warm reception," said Sorrow.

"I'm armed with a big hammer made of solid sunlight," said Infidel. "They won't give me any guff."

"I admire your confidence," said Sorrow. "But the northern realms are dangerous. Your quest may not be as simple as you think."

"I think it's a more realistic goal than wiping out the church and overthrowing all the kingdoms of the world."

Sorrow sighed, then turned back to my sea chest and opened it. I could taste the clean odor of cedar in the roof of my mouth as she gingerly lifted the lid.

The contents were mostly intact. From my limited view, it looked as if a bottle of squid ink had broken as the boat had tumbled, but the damage was mostly to the items packed on the right side of the chest where I kept blank parchment and writing material. Three quarters of the chest looked untouched by the spill, and this was the section where I'd stored a life's worth of maps and notes. Two life's worth, since at least half the material had been drafted by my grandfather, Judicious Merchant. Waves of nostalgia washed over me as Sorrow gingerly lifted papers from the chest. Her eyes grew wide with excitement.

"Marvelous," she whispered, as she unrolled a master map of the island. "Well worth my investment if it leads me to my quarry."

"You know, I've been almost every place Stagger's been," said Infidel. "You might save some time if you just ask me the location of whatever it is you're looking for."

"Perhaps. But you're unfamiliar with the witch nails in my scalp. You've never seen them before."

"So?"

"So I'm looking for more of them. Somewhere on this island, I believe I shall find the grave of Avaris."

"She's dead? I thought she was still out there handing out magic powers to mean girls like Purity and the Black Swan."

"Those leads have proven elusive," said Sorrow. "The Black Swan denies any connection to Avaris. But there's another oral tradition that says Avaris once had a palace here on the Isle of Fire where she commanded an army of witches until they were wiped out by the Church of the Book. According to legend, this island is home to a vast graveyard of weavers. My study of witch nails is hampered by the fact that there are so few weavers left. Much of the knowledge I seek has been lost. My hope is that I will discover nails in the skulls of old weavers that will provide a template for me to take my studies further."

"Hmm," said Infidel. "Can't say I've heard about a witch's graveyard."

Sorrow flipped through the notebook in her hand. "Did Stagger have any sort of indexing or organizational system?"

"Sure. If he thought it was important, he put it in the sea chest."

"This might take a while," Sorrow grumbled, as she looked at the reams of parchment.

"This might be a waste of time," said Infidel. "Stagger used to give me long, drunken lectures on pretty much every scrap of stone or bone we yanked out of the ground. He never said a thing about Avaris."

"He was older than you, correct? He'd explored the island before you met him."

"Yeah, but you didn't know him. Stagger was… uh… what's the word I want?"

"Loquacious," I offered, from my ghost cage.

"Chatty. Get a few pints in him and he wouldn't shut up. I've heard about every damn rock he ever turned over in this jungle." She sighed, placing her arms across her chest in a way that looked almost like she was trying to hug herself. "By the sacred quill, he used to bore me, but it was worth sitting through an hour of meandering drudgery for the five minutes of brilliant wit that would suddenly spill from him. He'd make me laugh till my face hurt." She shook her head. "Now, I even miss the boring lectures."

"I wish I could have met him," said Sorrow. "I've heard he was the best authority on the secrets of this island."

Again, I appreciated the irony that Sorrow had stripped herself of the chance to have what she really wanted, which was a conversation with me. Of course, I would have disappointed her. I'd never found the legendary witch's graveyard. I took a little delight in knowing that the woman who'd imprisoned me had wasted her money buying my papers. There was nothing in those notes or maps that would direct a person to Avaris.

Which isn't to say I didn't have some idea of where to look. I do know my history, after all. Supplement this with a little legend and rumor, and I knew where I'd start looking, based on three pieces of evidence.

Item One: The weavers had reached the peak of their collective powers 500 years ago, during the rein of King Glorified Brightmoon. Ol' Glory, as he was called, vowed to wipe out all the witches in his kingdom, and commissioned a blacksmith to craft a weapon up to the job… the Gloryhammer. He entrusted the weapon to one of his best knights, Stark Tower, ancestor of Infidel's former fiancé. As impressive as the Gloryhammer might be, Stark actually took his duties so seriously that he had an even more dangerous weapon commissioned, an ebony sword called the Witchbreaker. This blade was said to be forged from iron stolen from the gates of hell. Anyone killed by the blade was instantly banished to the pits.

As you might guess from someone who felt the need for such a weapon, Stark took a no-nonsense approach to his job, and eventually people started calling him Witchbreaker instead of the sword. According to legend, he killed over 10,000 witches. He was allowed to keep any valuables his victims might have had. If they had children, he had the legal authority to sell them into slavery. The Tower clan remains obscenely wealthy to this day.

Like any rich person, Stark liked to travel in comfort. When Avaris fled more civilized climes to set up shop on the Isle of Fire, it's said that Stark gave chase in nine ships filled with servants and building supplies and erected a castle for the duration of his stay.

Item two: The bay of Commonground is the only place on the island with a safe harbor for cargo ships carrying enough swag to equip a castle. Odds are excellent he would have built his home near the bay.

Item three: There are, in fact, several big stone ruins a few miles upriver from the bay that are sometimes called "the Knight's Castle." They're so close to Commonground, they're the first place every amateur treasure hunter strikes out for. I've done some poking around, but didn't waste much time because my grandfather's notes indicated he'd explored the place and found nothing. He also recognized, architecturally, that the walls were the work of middle period stone masons from the Silver Isle, not remnants of the Vanished Kingdom. He'd moved on to more fruitful targets deep in the jungle. But about a half-mile away from the Knight's Castle there are hundreds of earthen pits grandfather noted as possible burial sites. He never made any notes about digging them up. I did a few test digs, but they didn't strike me as particularly promising. There were no headstones. The fate of Stark Tower is unknown; there's at least six different legends of how, where, and when he died. But, if he'd been buried, he almost certainly would have had a stone monument. I'd assumed the unmarked graves had been for his servants and slaves. But what if it had been where he'd buried his prey?

I strained to move my wooden limbs. Not long ago, this would have been exactly the moment in my thought process where I charged into the jungle with a shovel, a dozen flasks of rum, and my invulnerable best friend. I sighed heavily, then rattled the invisible bars of my ghost cage and shouted out a common four-letter word for excrement.

This triggered Menagerie, who'd been perched on the rudder. He hopped over to me and raised his left paw toward my gloved hand.

"I didn't say 'shake,'" I grumbled.

Infidel had turned her head when Menagerie went into motion. Sorrow too glanced up from the pile of papers she had spread out before her.

"Looks like your dog wants to practice his tricks. Though why he's trying to shake hands with my golem I have no clue."

"Twenty-four hours ago whatever brains Menagerie had left had were squeezed into a tiny bug," said Infidel. "Cut him some slack."

Sorrow shrugged and looked to the sky. "No point in trying to make sense of this here."

"Golem?" said Infidel.

"Hmm?" asked Sorrow.

"You said Drifter is a golem?"

"Yes," Sorrow said.

"I took apart one of those a couple of weeks ago. It was made mostly of bone; Relic called it Patch. But, I had the impression he'd stolen Patch rather than making him. Was he your work?"

"If only," Sorrow said, shading her head. "My attempts at bone-weaving were where all my troubles began."

"I think your troubles might have started when you hammered nails into your skull in order to get back at your father," said Infidel. "But who am I to judge?"

Sorrow frowned deeply. "The avenues of the Silver City are lined with statues of men like the Witchbreaker, whom they praise for his wisdom and courage because it would be unseemly to openly recognize his true accomplishments, the mass slaughter of women who dared dream of a better world. I'd gladly drive a hundred nails in my head — a thousand — for the power to set things right."

"You've got a ways to go," said Infidel. I could tell she was counting the studs; I had as well. Sorrow had six.

Sorrow closed the lid of the sea chest. She looped a finger-thick strand of copper trough the clasp and closed it into a solid ring.

"You see only the physical nails," said Sorrow. "Each weaver must master seven physical elements. Iron, copper, and glass are the simplest arts. Gold and silver are also highly valued, as mastery of these materials provides a life of comfort. There are very few fragments of glorystone large enough to craft a nail from, but a weaver who did so would be welcomed in the court of any earthly king. There are over twenty potential materials to master, but it was my intention to round out my five minerals with two spiritual transitions — wood and bone."

Her voice grew quieter. "Since the church has been ruthless in its suppression, I had no one to guide me on my sixth nail, one of bone. I later discovered that the codex I'd stolen to guide me had been deliberately sabotaged by the church. The irony, of course, is that if I had mastered bone-weaving, I could cure my physical ailments. I'd be healthy again, free of this half-crippled body."

"Can't you get another bone nail?"

"Yes. But I dare not move forward without the guidance of a more experienced weaver."

Sorrow turned to me and said, "Carry this chest to the *Freewind.*"

"Why the *Freewind?*" asked Infidel.

"I've footed the bill for its services. I need a quiet place to rest and study Stagger's notes at my leisure. The master cabin isn't luxurious, but it will serve my purposes."

"You said I could have the ship! I've already got my stuff in the master cabin."

"I said you could direct the captain to sail you wherever you wished. You may still do so. I'm only using the master cabin as an isolated and safe place to study. I can return to the Isle of Fire once I've read these notes."

"Where am I supposed to bunk?"

"Where did you bunk when you were a mercenary during the Pirate Wars?"

"They'd set up bunks in the hold. But I wasn't pregnant then."

"I'm sure you'll find someplace comfortable to sleep," Sorrow said, with a dismissive wave of her hand.

By now, I'd picked up the sea chest. I'd never been able to lift it when it was full, but my wooden body flicked it from the deck as if it weighed no more than a pillow. I balanced it on my shoulder as I headed over the rail. The drunken feeling of the previous night was almost gone. The women's voices above me grew fainter as I climbed down the tree. Infidel sounded determined to keep possession of the cabin.

Eventually I couldn't hear their voices at all. Perhaps I was too far down the beach. Or perhaps Sorrow had won the argument. I knew she wouldn't back down; it was obvious to me that she was heading north in hopes of learning more about the mystery witch the Skellings were after. Infidel could be pretty stubborn, but she was debating a woman who practiced self-inflicted brain damage as a hobby. You can't win against crazy.

Two seconds later, Infidel flashed overhead, the Gloryhammer blazing before her, the Jagged Heart leaving a trail of snowflakes in her wake. Menagerie flapped past a moment later, so close I could probably have jumped up and grabbed his tail.

I had nothing to lose. I shouted out, "Heel!"

Menagerie spun in mid-air, tracing a long, gliding arc back to me. He landed on the black sand I trudged across and fell into a loping pace beside me. With all four paws on the ground, his bird-like elements slipped into his larger mass and he was almost full dog again, save for a few stray feathers in his fur.

"Good boy!" I shouted.

He looked at me as if awaiting another command. I've always been indifferent to dogs. On this island, I'm more used to eating them than befriending them. But this dog had a bright look in its eyes. I liked him. I'd never cared much for Menagerie as a man. He was too cold and, well, mercenary, which was a shame, since I know that Menagerie was an avid reader, and under different circumstances perhaps we could have discussed books.

Suddenly I wondered if I was in the presence of a dog who might remember the alphabet.

"Make an 's!'" I said, in that high-pitched, overly enthusiastic tone one uses when talking with dogs. "Make an 's' in the sand, boy!"

Menagerie ran a little ways ahead, paused as if sniffing the ground, then pushed out a serpentine squiggle. If I'd had freedom to do anything other than carry the sea chest, I would have jumped and clicked my heels. Unfortunately, I didn't even have the power to sway from my direct path toward the dock, so I stepped in the newly drawn letter. I couldn't even look back to see how much survived.

"Good dog!" I cried. "Now a 't!'" He did so. "An 'a!'" Unfortunately, I was walking fast enough that I couldn't see all the letters before I marched past them. I did see that the 'r'" at the end of my name looked almost like an 'n.'"

So my name was on the beach. Infidel was probably already back at the *Freewind*. Would Sorrow walk this way? Would she notice the letters? Would she think twice?

Despite my growing sense of futility, I called out five more letters before we reached the gangplank that led from the beach up onto the pier.

I turned at a ninety degree angle to ascend, and with what I hope was force of will but what might simply have been my body shifting to balance on the rickety boards, I glanced back down the beach. M-E-L-O-G – R-E-G-G-A-T-S, it read, upside down, or at least something to that effect.

Sorrow was nowhere to be seen.

But as I turned my gaze back to the docks, I held out the briefest glimmer of hope that Sorrow would soon know my name.

Which sounds a little ominous, now that I think of it.

6 - STAGGERMANCY

IF THE RESIDENTS of Commonground were fazed by a driftwood man walking among them, they managed to hide their astonishment behind masks of utter indifference. Of course, many of these masks of indifference were on men who owned actual masks, robbers and highwaymen who eyed the sea chest on my shoulders and pondered what it might contain. Fortunately, I was protected both by broad daylight and broad shoulders. My barrel-chested form no doubt discouraged the more cowardly thieves. The fact that I was accompanied by the world's ugliest dog may also have helped keep eyes from dwelling in my direction too long. I could hear Menagerie following at my heels, his webbed claws clicking as he loped along.

As I approached the far end of the pier, I spotted the *Freewind*. Brand stood alone on the deck, looking around furtively, as if making certain no one watched him. Seeing no eyes upon him (I was still some distance away), he waved toward some barrels on the dock. "Hurry," he called out, in a voice that was half shout, half whisper. A cloaked figure broke from behind the barrels and scurried up the gangplank to the ship. From the person's height, I assumed this was a pygmy, but the fine silk cloak might also have concealed a child or perhaps a petite adult woman. The cloak certainly looked like it belonged in a woman's wardrobe, as it was embroidered with lacy floral designs.

Brand guided the short woman toward the hold, looking over his shoulder to see if they'd been spotted. He didn't see anyone looking at him, but I did. The *Freewind*, like many ships, sported a figurehead carved to look like a shapely woman. And I swear that it wasn't a trick of the light that this figurehead twisted from her bolted-on position beneath the bowsprit and peered out across the deck, her eyes narrowed as she watched Brand and his guest.

By the time I reached the gangplank, Brand and his visitor had disappeared. The figurehead slipped back into her rightful position. I trudged onto a deserted ship. The command that had allowed me the freedom to walk here wore off as I reached the middle of the deck. I stood there still as a statue. Menagerie came around and sat before me, looking up as if he expected a new command.

There was a noise off to my left. Menagerie turned his head as I strained my peripheral vision to see Brand climbing the stairs from the cargo hold. He appeared lost in thought, a bit worried. He again looked around to make sure the deck was empty. When he spotted me, his eyes bulged.

Five seconds of comic discombobulation followed as he jumped backward at least a full yard while reaching for his sword. He whipped the blade free from its scabbard in what would have been a jaw-dropping display of reflexes if he hadn't then dropped the weapon when he landed on a thick coil of rope and failed to keep his feet under him. He tumbled backward, but used his momentum to keep rolling so that he was carried back onto his feet. The sword had fallen across the coiled rope and with a fluid motion he stomped the tip of his blade with the toe of his boot, causing the hilt to fly up to his waiting hand. He pointed the blade at me and shouted, "Halt!"

Of course, I was already halted.

This sank in a few seconds later, as Brand tightened the grip on his weapon and demanded, "Who are you?"

Who am I? I wanted to shout. *Who am I? I'm Abstemious Merchant, known throughout this bobbing metropolis as Stagger, grandson of Judicious Merchant, husband of Infidel, slayer of dragons! I'm an explorer of lost worlds, a scholar with a Brobdingnagian lexicon, and a connoisseur of fine spirits. That's who the hell I am!*

Unfortunately, lacking a tongue, I could only glare at him with my pecan peepers.

"Could you at least growl at this guy for me?" I asked Menagerie.

Menagerie wasn't looking at me. Instead, his eyes gazed skyward. Long shadows rapidly stretched out before us.

Infidel shouted from about the level of the mast, "You can put the sword away, Brand. The big guy's coming with us."

Infidel landed on the deck with a solid thump. The harpoon was attached to her back by rope, jutting up from between her shoulder blades like a flagpole. She had three bright red skewers of grilled meat in her left hand. She tore off a chunk and tossed it to Menagerie, who caught it in mid-air and swallowed it with a single gulp.

She studied the dog intently for half a minute as he stared at her, his eyes begging for more. She sighed. "Dang. I thought he might turn into a monkey. At least part of one."

She tossed Menagerie another chunk, then tore into a skewer herself.

"Where is everybody?" she asked, her mouth full.

"Gale took her family over to the *Aggressive* to meet with Captain Dare. He's traveled the northern realms and can provide advice on navigating the coast of Qikiqtabruk in the dead of winter."

"I thought that Sage handled all the navigation," said Infidel, with oily chili sauce glistening on her lips like blood.

"Sage's powers work best if she knows what she's looking for. A map can save her hours of blind searching."

Infidel took a swig from the silver flask of coconut milk tucked in her waistband. "Sorrow said she's also been up north, so maybe she can help guide us as well."

"Ah. Then Sorrow does exist," said Brand. "On the voyage here, she shut herself into the stateroom the second she came aboard and took all her meals there. I never caught even a glimpse of her. Poppy says she's an aged crone with one dead eye and an iron claw in place of a hand."

"That's about right," said Infidel. "Except she just looks old; she's about your age. A shame, given your taste in older women."

Brand grinned. "Experienced women, you mean. Skinny little naïfs whose greatest challenge in life has been to decide what color ribbons to put in their hair bore me. Even if they're halfway competent in bed, their post-coital conversations are unfailingly vapid."

"Careful," she said. "I used to be one of those skinny little naïfs."

"I don't believe you," said Brand. "I've heard that you single-handedly took out one of Greatshadow's avatars by jumping down his throat and punching his brains out from the inside. I'm guessing that in the sack you must be equally bold."

Infidel's cheeks flushed. "I, uh..., hmm. If you know about the dragons, you also know I can crush men's skulls like eggshells?"

"I've heard rumors."

"Well, skulls aren't my favorite part of a man's anatomy to crush," she said.

Brand laughed, but it sounded forced to me.

At this point, I heard Sorrow's limping gait on the gangplank. With the iron brace on her leg, she was anything but stealthy.

"Now you get to finally meet her," said Infidel pointing toward the approaching witch with her last monkey skewer.

Though my back was to her, I could feel Sorrow growing closer.

Infidel said, "Brand, this is Sorrow. Sorrow—"

Sorrow raised her hand to cut Infidel off. "I know who he is. He's the captain's gigolo."

Both Infidel and Brand looked taken aback by her directness. Sensing she'd broken some unwritten social code, Sorrow tried to explain herself. "I'm sorry if I come across as brusque. I've many things on my mind at the moment. I don't have time for pleasantries."

"I'm guessing you're not interested in post-coital conversation either?" asked Infidel.

Sorrow furrowed her brow. "Are you... propositioning me?"

"By the Divine Author, no!" Infidel laughed. "You're not my type."

"So what is your type?" asked Brand.

Infidel sighed. "Tall, dark, and deceased."

"I'll be in my cabin. Tell Captain Romer to see me there for her orders." Sorrow didn't look at me as she said, "Follow."

I followed. In desperation I called back to Menagerie, "Do something!"

But Menagerie didn't even turn his head. He was focused on the third skewer of monkey.

We went below deck, into the voluminous hold. The *Freewind* was small for a clipper, just under 200 feet long, but the hold seemed especially large because it was especially empty. Most ships that had been in port more than a week would already be filled with cargo. I could only deduce that the bounty placed upon the *Freewind* was bad for business. What reputable merchant would place his cargo on a ship that the world's most powerful navies had sworn to sink?

Toward the rear of the boat, beneath the poop-deck, was a walled off section divided by a narrow corridor. I followed Sorrow down this passageway. On each side were cabins filled with bunks. At the end of the hall was an oak door with brass hinges. It opened to reveal a small but tidy room, nearly thirty feet across but only about eight feet deep. I had to crouch to navigate beneath the broad ceiling beams. Sunlight spilled through portholes upon a bed large enough for two, a sturdy looking desk with an oil lantern hanging above it, and a table in the far corner with a large pitcher, a wash basin, and a chamber pot beneath. The room was spotless, smelling of furniture polish and fresh linens.

"Place your sea chest by the desk," said Sorrow as she closed the door.

I did so.

"Go beside the table and fold yourself as small as you can manage. I've no need of you for now."

I sat by the table, folded my legs up along my barrel chest and hugged them with my driftwood arms. I found my obedience distasteful and humiliating. I hadn't enjoyed being manipulated by Truthspeakers as a child; I certainly didn't find the experience any more pleasant as an adult.

Yet, in my misery, there were two tiny flickers of hope.

Flicker one: For better or worse, I was near Infidel. If Sorrow had decided to remain on the Isle of Fire while my wife sailed north, I'd have been inconsolable. Flicker two: She'd said, "*Your sea chest.* Had she meant only, "the sea chest that you carry?" Or had she seen my message on the beach and now knew my true identity?

I waited. My world narrowed to the slight band of gleaming wood floor directly before me. With my head folded down, the rest of the room was blocked by the brim of my hat. I listened. Sorrow busied herself with settling into the room and sorting through the contents of the sea chest. After a time, Captain Romer visited the cabin.

"I understand you wished to see me, madam?" said Gale.

"I want you to tell me everything you can about the Skellings who attacked," said Sorrow.

Sorrow listened intently, but I couldn't notice any details that Captain Romer added to the story that Infidel hadn't also covered. True, Infidel hadn't mentioned the sea-worthiness of the hide boats, and Gale went on about their construction at length, but I sensed that this wasn't information of interest to Sorrow.

The only follow-up questions Sorrow asked were about the witch.

"And the Skellings said that this witch was searching for the *Freewind?*"

"Not precisely. She's hunting for a magical artifact."

"Do you think there's a chance this ship will come under assault by her forces?" Sorrow asked.

"She might try," said Gale. "But on the high seas we can evade her. If you're truly concerned about avoiding her, I do have… options. May we speak in the fullest confidence?"

"Of course."

"When you hire the *Freewind,* you hire the fastest ship available for travel by sail. But, for an additional fee, there may be shortcuts that would trim our travel time and make us utterly untraceable."

"I know of these so-called *shortcuts,*" said Sorrow. "I'd rather take my chances with an elderly witch than risk my sanity in the abstract realms."

"Of course, madam. Quite wise of you."

I was a little taken aback by the way that Gale was taking such a subservient role with Sorrow. Wanderers are known for their independence and freedom loving nature. It seemed odd that the captain of a ship should be so obsequious. On the other hand, the one thing that Wanderer's loved as much as freedom was money. Sorrow was no-doubt well compensated for building the Black Swan a new body.

If the rest of the world was no longer eager to hire the *Freewind,* I suppose I couldn't begrudge Captain Romer for bending over backward to make her remaining customers happy, but at the same time it didn't sit well with me. I've never treated a person differently based on the size of their purse. It mattered nothing to me if you were rag-picker or royalty. If you could tell a good joke and willing to chuckle at my own attempts at wit, you were fit company to share a pint.

Perhaps it comes from having been raised by monks. Their vow of poverty took hold in me, even if their vows of faith, abstinence and chastity did not.

Sorrow concluded the conversation by giving orders about her meals. Captain Romer acknowledged these and left the cabin after thanking Sorrow for her business. Just as I learned a little bit about the captain by overhearing their conversation, I also think I learned a few things about Sorrow. It was easy to believe she'd been the daughter of a wealthy and powerful judge. I'm guessing she'd had a whole complement of cooks, maids, and butlers growing up. Perhaps she'd never been trained to be nice to the hired help.

Above, I could hear Gale shouting out commands and Rigger responding. I was near the porthole. Due to my stillness, my wooden ears caught a conversation that ensued as the sails rattled and flapped up the masts.

"I don't like setting sail with an empty hold." It was Mako's deep voice that carried these words to me. "You shouldn't have been so dismissive of Captain Dare's offer."

Gale's answer was much more difficult to hear. "It's not enough that Levi betrayed us? Now you question my judgment?"

"I'm not Levi," said Mako. "I'm just saying—"

"I know what you're saying. But Dare's splitting hairs. He won't take a cargo of slaves, but he'll gladly fill his hold with the shoddy food stocks the slavers purchase in order to feed their human chattel. We've sacrificed too much to engage in such compromises."

"By your logic, any cargo in the world is unacceptable," Mako said. "Most of the iron ore and the coal used to smelt it comes from mines worked by slaves. Are we never again to accept a load that includes steel? Every golden moon in the Shining Land is stamped with the image of a sovereign who supports the slave trade. Are we to refuse these coins for our future wages and be paid only through barter?"

Gale answered, but her words were lost as the ship groaned. The sails had caught the wind and the ship began to gently roll as she headed from the harbor. I wished I'd been above to see our departure. Clippers sport more sails than any other ship, making an impressive sight when all their canvas is unfurled. Plus, I welcome all opportunities to expand my vocabulary, and the sailors I've known over the years have filled my head with terms like spankers, flying jibs and mizzen topgallants. I'd enjoy the opportunity to finally make sense of all the terms and figure out which of the thirty plus sails was which.

Of course, from the sound of things above, I doubt that any of the Romers would have found the time to explain their jargon. A clipper this size normally set to sea with a minimum crew of twenty, and the Romers numbered seven, eight if you counted Brand. Even with their magical talents, I imagine they wouldn't welcome a lubber like me wandering around the deck.

Further shouts drifted through the porthole, enough to catch Sorrow's attention. She went to the small window near me and peered out.

"That didn't take long," she mumbled.

From the shouts above, I quickly deduced that the *Freewind* had been ambushed the second it sailed from the harbor onto the open ocean. Out here, the rules that made Commonground a sanctuary no longer applied. I wanted to ask questions about the nature of the assault, the number of ships, how close they were, etc. At the very least, I'd have liked to stand and look out the porthole. It was not to be. Instead, all I know is that the winds grew ever stronger. The sunlight through the portal brightened, and above the splashing of waves I heard a thunderous crack, like lightning splitting a tree trunk.

Sorrow chuckled. "Infidel's not half bad with that hammer."

There were further cracks. Finally, Sorrow turned away with a shrug. "That's that," she mumbled. The shouts from above had a decidedly celebratory tone. I had the feeling we weren't being chased any more.

Sorrow settled at her desk. She opened a page of a fresh notebook and a new bottle of ink. As I tuned out the noise above deck, I heard the faint scratching rhythm of her quill racing across paper, trapping thoughts into words.

Lulled by this familiar noise, I dropped into memory. Since becoming a ghost, I'd not slept or dreamed. I never grew weary. I had no eyelids to close if I wished to sleep. But now, my wooden body felt, well, wooden. Heavy. It possessed a gravity that weighed down my thoughts. I was lulled by the sound of waves washing against the hull as we swayed across the sea. The muffled shouts of Romers in the rigging sunk into my seedpod ears, sounding not of this moment, but of some long distant past. Murmurs layered beneath whispers lay beneath the pulse of water, like a heartbeat, my heartbeat, so familiar after such a long absence.

Thus, for the first time in death, I found myself perched upon the precipice of sleep…

…then, slowly, I drifted free. My ghost fingers slipped loose of my knot-root hands as if they were oversized gloves. My legs twitched and came loose of their wooden counterparts and it felt good to wiggle my toes freely once more. I craned my neck, pulling free of my coconut mask. I was loose! I rose, my spirit spilling from the boundaries of its wooden cage.

Then I stopped short.

Silver wires still jutted from my phantom flesh.

I grabbed them and tried to yank them free.

Something yanked back, hard and fast, and I was pulled into the wood, into the barrel chest, shrinking ever smaller until I was tiny enough to be fit into the golden cage, then smaller still as I passed into the belly of the silver mosquito.

Though I must have been no larger than a flea to fit in such a compact space, I felt whole. And, indeed, I still looked whole; the curved silver surface of the interior of the mosquito's belly reflected me perfectly. I looked just as I had when Infidel and I escaped the spirit realm after confronting Greatshadow. I was wearing the black boots and pants Zetetic had conjured for me, as well as the ridiculous red velvet cape, though it was now mostly in tatters. I was bare-chested; in the spirit world, I'd given my shirt to Infidel to replace her own shredded clothing.

I touched a jagged hole in my belly. This was my fatal wound, inflicted by my own knife.

And of course there was the knife.

I reached under the cape to my hip where the bone-handled knife was slipped into my belt. The knife was plain looking, simple, but elegant in its match of form and function. It had been my grandfather's hunting knife; the blade was eight inches long and sturdy, with a pattern in the metal almost like fingerprints where the steel had been folded in on itself a dozen times as a skilled blacksmith had worked in carbon to temper the edge. The hilt was a single length of yellowed bone; only after death had I learned this was dragon bone. The natural magical resonance of such beasts had trapped my soul within the weapon.

I was a ghost imprisoned in the belly of a jeweled mosquito. But how many ghosts had knives?

I rushed the wall, stabbing the silver. I laughed as my blade sank through the foil skin. Cutting through the mosquito's metallic hide was no more difficult than cutting through the hide of a wild boar, something well within the scope of the blade's intended purpose. In moments, I'd cut a flap in the side of the artificial insect. The mosquito didn't protest as I pushed my arm through, followed by my head and shoulders. In another moment, with quite a bit of kicking and struggle, I worked myself loose of my silver prison.

But, not quite free. I remained locked inside the golden cage. Worse, silver wires still hooked into my flesh. Tentatively, I grabbed the wire hooked into my left thigh. I took the knife and sliced the wire in twain.

Then screamed.

Then screamed some more.

It was the worst agony imaginable. It was as if a knife had been stabbed all the way into my thigh bone and was now twisting, digging at the marrow. I gritted my teeth to resist the pain, and tried to breathe deep breaths. In desperation, I retrieved the loose wire from the gilded floor and placed it back in contact with the length of silver line hanging from my leg. The metal ends flowed together. Instantly, the acute pain turned to welcome numbness.

I limped to the cage wall and slid down, my back to the bars as I struggled to catch my breath, until I remembered that I didn't need to breathe. I was acting purely on instinct. Calmness settled over me. I looked out beyond my gilded cage, to the barrel chest in which this strange artificial heart was suspended.

Hmmm.

It struck me as curious that, having bound my spirit to this mosquito, she'd then sealed the mosquito inside a cage. I walked back toward the insect. In relative size, it loomed over me like an elephant. Viewed at this scale, the craftmanship was even more remarkable. I could now see the tiny bolts that fastened the leg joints, and the tightly coiled iron springs, far finer than a human hair, that powered the gold foil wings. The facetted eyes were made of glass lenses flickering with rainbows as I walked around them, gathering up the silver lines in my hand.

Sorrow's powers were over gold, silver, iron, copper, glass, and wood. There was gold on the bars, the mosquito was largely silver, with iron springs and copper wings and glass eyes. The wood was the larger form, the golem itself.

What did it all mean?

This may seem like a curious statement from a ghost, but I've never thought much about the supernatural. Yes, my life was awash in magic. My best friend could jump over buildings, I'd been raised in a religion where I regularly witnessed men editing reality with their words, and I hung out on a daily basis with shape-shifters and ogres. I had no propensity toward skepticism, but I also never bothered to try to learn any magical arts. None even intrigued me. The art of truthspeaking I found morally reprehensible, the art of deceiving was difficult to unravel from the art of driving yourself insane, blood magic was an excellent avenue for contracting hideous parasitic diseases, and elemental magic was a good way to draw the unwelcome attention of dragons. I followed few rules in my unruly life, but "don't annoy dragons" was one I faithfully obeyed.

Zetetic had told Aurora he'd become a deceiver after studying forty different types of magic and finding all of them to be valid, even if the underlying premises contradicted each other. Aurora had protested that they couldn't all be true. Her fundamental assumptions about the structure of the universe were completely contrary to the fundamental assumptions of Father Ver, for instance. She'd said that some things must be false if other things were true, and asserted that it couldn't be both night and day at the same time.

"Unless the world is a sphere," Zetetic had answered.

He'd also said, "All truth is local."

I think Zetetic's point was that magic works because people believe it works. Magic flows from human faith. Maybe I wasn't well educated in existing systems of magic, but if all magical systems were just the product of the mind, could I create a new one? It wasn't as if I was completely ignorant of magical thinking. I'd spent years of my life with my nose wedged between the pages of books. I'd learned a lot of symbolism in my studies. Did my current prison have some symbolic significance?

The mosquito was obvious. It's a widespread belief that blood contains the soul. Ordinary mosquitoes drink blood, so spiritual mosquitoes drink spirit blood. As for the cage, well, a cage is a cage. It holds creatures against their will.

What about the materials? Gold was easy. It symbolized perfection and wealth, but also greed. Was I trapped by a golden cage because I was greedy? At first I shrugged off the notion. Money never meant a damn thing to me. But, were there other aspects of greed I was overlooking? Certainly, booze had been a weakness in life. I'd been more than willing to steal it, and when I wasn't stealing it directly, I was stealing other people's possessions and selling them to keep the precious elixirs flowing.

Of course, before I could ever escape my golden cage, I had the more immediate problem of losing these silver wires running through me. Silver commonly symbolized purity and innocence, but also sagacity and lies. Old men with silver hair are respected for their wisdom; smooth liars are said to have a silver tongue. The children of wealthy men are said to be born with silver spoons in their mouths.

It's impossible to think of wealthy men and not think of King Brightmoon, ruler of the Silver Isles. If he wasn't the wealthiest man alive, he was certainly in the top five. The moon is often associated with silver. The most common coin in the world was a small disk of silver ringed with gold, minted by the king's treasury, and commonly called a moon. Infidel, King Brightmoon's daughter, was named Innocent, and she has silver hair. I respect her for her purity and innocence, despite knowing that the woman I've grown to love is merely the adult mask of a damaged child.

Could the silver somehow represent her? Was I trapped here by my love for Infidel?

It seemed at once self-evidently true and also obviously false. I had no evidence the silver mosquito had been designed to capture me; I had the impression it had been looking for any old ghost it might find. I was probably over-thinking this.

But could over-thinking lead me toward a magical art?

All the magicians I'd ever known had spent their whole lives in the study of a single concept, elevating it in importance above all else. I've witnessed some pretty amazing results; Ivory Blade, for instance, and his somnomancy, rending the veil between the dream realms and our own to give life to nightmares. It was a little late for me to start studying dreams, or to seriously puzzle out the aspects of the various elements that bound me like some amateur alchemist. But I'd spent my whole damn life trying to understand myself.

If all truth was local, could I somehow understand myself so fully that I could alter my local truths and be free?

I chuckled ruefully.

"Great," I said, my voice tiny in the vastness of the wooden barrel. "I'm placing my hope in Staggermancy."

7 - SEA OF WINE

"WAKE!" COMMANDED SORROW.

I lifted my coconut head, feeling groggy. Had I been sleeping? Had my shrinking to explore the silver mosquito and golden cage been only a dream? The room was now dark. How long had I been out?

"Rise," said Sorrow, just as the ship shuddered strongly enough to throw her from her feet, slamming her into the oak door. The room had seemed immaculate before, but the impact was enough to raise dust hidden in the crooks and crevasses of the wooden beams and planks. Sorrow raised her hand to her mouth as she coughed. "We're under attack!"

I stood, trying to make sense of the noises coming from every direction. The whole Romer family was shouting at once. A dog bayed as if there was a full moon. The timbers of the ship groaned and popped. Above all this, I could hear a woman's voice shouting. It wasn't Captain Romer; whoever it was had a thick accent I couldn't quite place. The only words I was certain she'd shouted: "Ivory Blade!"

Sorrow braced herself against the door as she climbed back to her feet. "You're not to try to communicate with anyone. You're forbidden to write! Beyond these restrictions, take whatever actions are needed to defend this ship, its crew and its passengers!"

I nodded, acknowledging the command. I glanced toward the desk and the overturned bottle of ink. I clenched and unclenched my fingers. To be expressly forbidden to write must be the ultimate tonic for writer's block. If a quill had been thrust into my hand at that moment, I could have written volumes.

Sorrow threw herself onto the desk, stretching across it to reach her bed, tossing aside a pillow. She drew a yard long shaft of pitch-black iron from between the mattress and the wall.

"If we face who I believe we face, a sword will prove mightier than a pen. Fight with all the savagery you can muster. Infidel's life may be at stake."

She handed me the iron shaft and I saw that it was indeed a sword, no doubt forged by her own fingers and drawn to a razor-sharp double-edge.

"Make haste!" she cried.

I threw open the door and lumbered into the narrow hall. All the cabins were open and the Romer girls sat in their bunks, looking only half awake. The last door in the hall jerked open, revealing Captain Romer's quarters. Gale leapt into the hall, her tangled, sweaty hair fastened behind her neck with a scarlet ribbon. In the shadows of her cabin, I could see the blond hair of Brand bobbing as he struggled to pull on his boots.

Gale hadn't bothered with boots; she was barefoot in her cotton britches, and her billowy blouse was only tied together across her breasts. The captain bounded up the stairs to the deck in two leaps, drawing her cutlass. I gave chase, though my bulky form slowed me in the tight hall. I nearly fell as the ship lurched once more. The timbers didn't so much groan now as scream.

I emerged behind Captain Romer, who'd skidded to a stop on a deck slick with frost. It was night, as I'd guessed. Every lantern that hung in the rigging had gone dark, their flames extinguished beneath ice at least an inch thick that coated everything in sight. Of course, "in sight" was somewhat limited by the pale fog that hung in the air, narrowing the world to a circle about twenty feet around me. The only light came from Captain Romer's cutlass, which gave off an eerie phosphorescent glow.

Before us, on their knees, were the frozen bodies of Jetsam, Mako, and Rigger, Gale's three sons, their faces locked in silent screams beneath a sheen of ice. I'd seen this magic before. Aurora had frozen more than her share of unruly patrons at the Black Swan, and the magic seldom proved fatal. Victims of this spell were simply shocked into unconsciousness by the sudden blast of cold, then held upright by their rigid ice exoskeletons. As long as they were freed before they suffocated, the three Romers would likely survive.

I noticed that I could no longer hear Menagerie howling. I spotted a lump curled on the deck behind Mako's bulky form that might have been a frozen dog, though it was difficult to tell given the fog, the dim lighting, and the limits of my monochrome vision.

Continuing my scan of the scene, I saw that we were surrounded by at least two dozen women. At first they appeared to be frozen just as the Romer boys were, since they were coated in ice. But, at a second glance, I saw that the ice was instead shaped into armor and swords. They were plainly conscious, staring at us with narrowed eyes, their breath coming out in gusts of fog. Their lips and cheeks were very dark; beneath their semi-transparent armor none of them were clothed. It struck me as a rather uncomfortable way to go into battle. However, they weren't going into battle just yet, merely standing, ice blades at the ready, as if waiting for a command.

"Captain Romer, I presume?" said a woman's voice from just beyond the fog.

"What have you done to my sons?" Gale demanded.

"They are not yet dead," the voice answered. Slowly, from the fog directly before us, a trio of figures emerged. In the center was a woman also in ice armor, but unlike the others, her ice was pale white rather than clear, concealing her body. She wore a cloak of white fox pelts, and carried a sword made of jagged bubble-filled ice in the shape of a crescent moon. I realized instantly that I'd seen this particular ice before; it was the same substance that tipped the Jagged Heart.

Flanking the woman were two creatures like nothing I'd ever seen. My years of association with Menagerie had given me a decent knowledge of scores of beasts from lands I couldn't dream of. Somewhere in his travels he'd encountered rhinos and cobras and wolverines, or at least gotten hold of their blood. But given Menagerie's fondness for big, toothy predators, I can't believe he wouldn't have added the monsters before me to his arsenal if he knew about them. They looked like a cross between a gorilla and a grizzly bear, walking upright, with snow-white pelts, long arms ending in dagger-claws, and gaping jaws filled with fangs.

I was vaguely aware of the Romer sisters climbing the stairs behind me. Sage was clever enough to bring a lantern with her, which greatly improved the lighting, though not my sense of dread. The pale light made the riggings look ghostly.

Infidel hadn't put in an appearance yet. Had something happened to her? Or was she just taking her time getting dressed?

Captain Romer studied the woman in the white fox cloak. "Who are you? You obviously want something from us. State your demands."

"I'm known as Purity," the woman answered. "I've come for Ivory Blade."

Captain Romer frowned. "Ivory Blade isn't on this ship. He hasn't been a passenger of mine in three years, in fact."

"There's no time for your lies," said Purity. "Blade stole the Jagged Heart from us only months ago. He shielded himself from my seers with his somnomancy, but in his hunt for Greatshadow he's let down his guard. My most trusted seer has fixed her sightless gaze upon his armor, which is aboard this very ship. I've no quarrel with you or your family, Captain Romer. Give us Blade and we shall let you live. Defy us, and I shall command the ice sheet that has locked your ship within its unbreakable grasp to crush the hull of the *Freewind*. You're three hundred miles from the nearest shore, a long way for even a Wanderer to swim. Not that you'll have a chance to try. Long before your ship is torn apart my yetis and ice-maidens will finish off everyone aboard. Are you so loyal to Blade that you'd sacrifice your family?"

Captain Romer's face was completely neutral. She couldn't turn over Blade if she wanted to. But she also knew that the Jagged Heart was down below, wrapped inside a sail, and this was what Purity truly was looking for. The only reason to find Blade was to find the harpoon.

"Thank you for your offer," said Captain Romer. "You've made what I'm sure you feel is a fair bargain, trading my family and ship for a notorious spy who is doubtless guilty of the theft you're charging him with. I see only three small obstacles to making a deal with you."

"And these are?" asked Purity.

"First, Ivory Blade isn't aboard this ship. Second, were he aboard, it's against my code to traffic in human lives. And, third, you're mistaken in thinking the *Freewind* is trapped by ice."

Purity chuckled. "I understand your confusion. These are the tropics, after all. But the Ice-Moon Blade is a conduit for the elemental power of Hush. I could freeze a thousand earthly seas with its frigid touch."

"No doubt," said Captain Romer. "But the *Freewind* is known as the fastest ship upon the waves for a reason."

"What does your speed matter now?" asked Purity. "You've been taken by surprise. Don't you understand? Your ship is already icebound. The sea has been frozen for half a mile in every direction."

"No," said Captain Romer, kneeling. The ice sizzled as her sword of phosphors touched it, boiling away a saucer-sized hole to reveal the wooden deck. She placed her bare hand upon the burgundy wood. "You see, there is no ice upon the Sea of Wine."

Suddenly the sky was a violent amber-red, streaked with clouds, like a sunset seeping from every point on the horizon. The fog was gone and the chilly air banished by a blast furnace of hot, humid air. The ship rolled as it rose upon a wave and the sails above us snapped in the sudden breeze, cracking the ice that coated them. All around us the sea was full of blood dark swells topped with amber foam; the scent of wine filled my mouth, stirring old thirsts.

"We sail an abstract realm where Hush does not dwell," said Captain Romer, her eyes locked upon Purity. "Here's my bargain: Free my sons and surrender and I shall put you ashore upon a deserted isle when we return to the material world. Defy me, and I'll have you keelhauled in the Sea of Wine. Whatever hell you may believe in, this fate shall prove a hundred times worse."

"Hush," said Purity, which at first I took for a command, but then understood to be an invocation. The crescent-sword glowed like the moon and the temperature dropped noticeably as a beam of pale light flashed toward the captain. She jumped straight up, grabbing the riggings, sending a shower of melting ice down upon me as she flipped her legs up from the path of the ray. Instantly, my world dimmed as a thick sheet of ice formed on my body. I'm certain, had I been human, the shock of the cold would have incapacitated me. Instead, I simply punched myself in the face with a fist of roots and knocked the ice free.

The Romer girls joined their mother in the riggings as the ice-armored women lurched forward like zombies. It looked like the time for chatting was over and the time for hitting things had begun.

I've never been a brawler; usually, when a fight breaks out, I either hide behind Infidel or run for the nearest exit. But, after who knows how long of being trapped in this wooden body, I welcomed the opportunity to let out some frustrations. I was conflicted, however; I've enough chivalry in me to feel bad about hitting a woman, even though Purity was obviously the leader of the opposition. Fortunately, I was spared from my squeamishness by being pounced upon by one of the yetis. My barrel ribs cracked as he knocked me to the deck. His slathering jaws rushed toward my face, but I shoved my left arm between his teeth before his jaws could fully close. I felt pressure, but no pain. More importantly, though this beast likely outweighed me by half a ton, I was strong enough to push him back. Remembering that I had a sword in my free hand, I stabbed the beast in the side of its skull. The iron blade punched straight through the monster's temple and came out the other side. Its eyes rolled up in its head as it collapsed upon me.

Despite my strength, I had little leverage to push the beast off. Making things worse, as imposing as the yeti looked, its shaggy hair proved to be as soft as lamb's wool, and it apparently survived the artic cold by being built largely of blubber. On top of this, the deck was coated with ice, which completely robbed me of traction. At least half a minute passed as I fought to rid myself of the dead weight. When my head was at last free, I was confronted by a horrible site. Every last Romer daughter was frozen in the rigging, completely immobile. The second yeti had leapt into the rigging and was giving chase to Gale, who retreated ever higher, toward the crow's nest.

All around, the ice-armored women watched the battle above. Purity appeared displeased by their lack of initiative. "Mindless fools!" she shouted. "Don't just stand there! Go below! Bring me Ivory Blade!"

The woman nearest the hatch turned just in time to find a knife flying from below deck. The blade came to a sudden halt between her eyes. As she fell backward Brand jumped onto the deck, a leather belt with sheathes for a dozen throwing knives slung over his shoulder. He ducked and rolled with impressive speed as Purity shot a freezing moonbeam in his direction. He popped up to his feet six inches clear of the ray, and let loose with a carefully aimed blade, a thin one, almost a dart. The slender knife hit the gauntlet of ice Purity wore on her sword hand and slipped between the joints at her knuckles. She sucked in air as the Ice-Moon blade slipped from her grasp.

"Protect me!" she shouted as the women lunged to form a human wall between her and Brand. The others closed in on Brand, looking cautious, unsure who he'd next target with the blades he held in each hand. Then, from the hatch, came the last person on earth I expected to see. When the mane of silver-blonde hair first thrust above the deck, I thought Infidel had at last joined the fight. Instead, a dwarf waddled onto the deck, dressed in a wig and a feminine cape, wearing dark lipstick and heavy rouge. The dwarf wore plate armor, polished to a mirror gleam, and formed in such a way that the breast plate resembled actual breasts. Despite the female attire, I instantly recognized the new arrival's true identity: It was my old friend Bigsby, the fishmonger! He was armed with a mace, also polished to a silvery finish, which he brandished as he stepped between Brand and the advancing warriors.

"Back!" he shouted, in a falsetto pitch. "Lay down your arms or face the wrath of Princess Innocent Brightmoon, daughter of King Valiant Brightmoon, champion of the faithful!"

"You tell 'em, Sis," said Brand.

Then, a yeti hit the deck inches before Bigsby, knocking him off his feet. A flash of a second later, Captain Romer dropped onto the beast's chest, driving her phosphor blade deep into his gut. The beast yowled in pain, but wasn't dead. He snatched the captain by the nape of her neck and flung her skyward, on an arc that carried her out over the waves of wine. Brand again proved to have reflexes like a cat, as he grabbed a coil of rope and tossed it on a path that would intercept Gale. She grabbed at the rope as she fell past my line of sight. The line suddenly went taut.

Before Brand could reel the captain in, both he and Bigsby went rigid as a sheet of ice coated them. Purity was now holding the crescent blade in her left hand, which, in hindsight, was pretty much exactly what I'd have done if I'd been her. I finally managed to kick myself free of the dead yeti and rose to my feet. I was the sole defender left standing.

And then there was light. The sky that had once been sunsets in all directions suddenly had a single sun as Infidel shot up from the hold, racing high above the crow's nest to survey the scene.

"Am I too late for the festivities?" she shouted down. "This damn armor has, like, two hundred buckles."

"Ivory Blade!" Purity shouted, raising her weapon overhead. "You've taken what's rightfully mine!"

The enchanted blade glowed. I sensed she was about to fire a freeze ray at Infidel, who had never mastered ducking. So I grabbed Bigsby by his frozen arm and threw him. He caught Purity dead in the chest and she went down hard.

The yeti Gale had stabbed was back on his feet. He was bleeding profusely, but his injury hadn't taken him out. He turned to me with baleful eyes. I glanced down at his brother, who still had my sword jutting from his temple. Before I could bend to grab the blade, the yeti lunged toward me, jaws open wide, claws outstretched.

Then, with a flash of light and a loud *WHAP!* the yeti vanished. Infidel was standing in front of me and the yeti was a diminishing speck hurtling out over the waves. All the ice-maiden minions raised their hands to shield their eyes from the luminance of the Gloryhammer, which left them completely vulnerable as Infidel danced forward and began launching them over the sides of the boat one by one. A few landed near the ship. As they sunk beneath the waves, I swear they were laughing. It was a sound I knew well, the sound of my own laughter when I was completely besotted and everything tragic in the world was rendered comic.

I had no time to ponder the effects of the enchanted sea. Purity rose again, sword in hand once more. Having run out of dwarves to fling, I put aside my aversion to punching a woman. I charged across the deck, slush splashing beneath my oversized boots. The ice coating was melting in the warm air of the Sea of Wine; indeed, Mako was now almost free of ice, and I was certain I heard him groan as he fell to his knees. Bigsby had all his ice knocked off of him by the impact, and he was clearly awake, dragging himself toward his platinum wig. Not having retrieved my sword, I balled my gloved root into the tightest fist I could manage and let loose with a savage right hook, clocking Purity in the jaw. Her ice helmet proved sturdy, and didn't dent or crack from the impact. I'm certain I would have killed her otherwise. As it was, her eyes lost focus, the Ice-Moon Blade slipped from her hand, and she went down, limp.

I rubbed my knuckles, not because my hand hurt, but because I'd watched Infidel do the same gesture a thousand times and it seemed natural. I heard movement nearby and spun around. There was an ice-maiden charging toward me, sword brandished high overhead. I caught her in the gut with a solid kick that shattered her armor and she folded to her knees, vomiting on my boots.

I felt sick to my own stomach, despite, technically, not having one.

I glanced around the deck. All the intruders were down; Infidel and I were the only people left standing. Cinnamon, up in the riggings, began to slip from her frozen perch and Infidel flashed toward her, catching her just as she fell. In seconds, Infidel had peeled the remaining frozen Romers from the ropes and brought them to the deck. By now the ice that remained in the sails and riggings had turned into a rain. Water ran off the frozen figures on the deck in great rivulets. The air echoed with people sucking in gasps of air as the ice that covered their faces fell away.

I wanted to run to Infidel and hug her, to let her know I was still with her, but this lay beyond the scope of the freedom Sorrow had granted me. Fortunately, I was free to help protect the crew, so I knelt beside Mako and brushed off his remaining ice. He shivered uncontrollably, but seemed okay. I moved on to Brand. Within seconds, I'd freed his face and he sucked in air through chattering teeth.

"Everyone on this deck will survive," a female voice said behind me. "You must save my daughter."

I turned around. The nude woman who served as the figurehead for the ship had somehow crawled up from beneath the bowsprit to stand before me. Though, stand may not have been the right word since she didn't have feet. She was a ghostly form, floating, looking almost solid enough to touch from her breasts up, but with the rest of her composed of mist so fine it would likely have been invisible if the bright glow of the Gloryhammer hadn't made it shimmer.

"That horrible woman below told you not to talk," the figurehead said. "But you're not the only ghost upon this ship. I'm Jasmine Romer, Gale's mother, and the first captain of the *Freewind*. My spirit is now locked within these timbers. Unlike you, I've chosen my fate."

I was frustrated I couldn't ask for further details. Not that there was time for palaver.

"My daughter drowns within the Sea of Wine. You're her only hope. The inebriating spirits cannot harm your wooden form. Save her!"

I loped to the railing where Gale had gone over. The rope was now completely limp. I looked down. It's uncanny how, when collected into an ocean, wine can look just like blood.

"Where's your boss?" Infidel asked me as she helped Sage back to her feet. Sage was only fifteen, and had looked small when I saw her next to Rigger, but she was a good three inches taller than Infidel.

I wish I could have at least shrugged to answer Infidel's question. Sorrow hadn't cared enough about the outcome of the fight to help defend the ship in person.

I bent over the railing, listening. I could hear laughter, a drunken, high-pitched guffawing. I scanned the waves and spotted Captain Romer far out in front of the ship, not where I'd expected her to be at all.

"I'm bringing the ship back around!" Jasmine called out to me. "Prepare to jump!"

Gale's drunken laughter grew louder as we lurched across the waves. I pull up the slack rope that trailed in the water and wrapped the end around my wrist. As I did so, the captain's laughter suddenly died off. I looked down and saw only a single hand, stained amber, as it sank beneath the waves.

I leapt, leaving my tri-corn hat hanging in the air. I wondered if my wooden body floated. It was called 'driftwood' for a reason. Luckily, I didn't need to test my seaworthiness for long. I practically landed on top of Captain Romer, her body limp as I wrapped my free arm around her. The line around my wrist snapped taut and I wondered just how much force it would take to tear my arm free of my torso. Fortunately, Sorrow's handiwork proved suited to the task. My arm held, even when my body slammed into the hull of the ship.

Unfortunately, I was beneath the surface. Captain Romer's head bent backward as I gazed down upon her, her jaws slack, small bubbles rising from her lips. I'd heard that Wanderers had a pact with Abyss, the primal dragon of the sea, that guaranteed they'd never die from drowning, but his pact apparently didn't extend to – how had Sorrow worded it? – the *abstract* realms.

Far below, I saw a light; I think it was Gale's phosphorescent sword tumbling ever deeper, growing fainter. Then, for the most fleeting instant, I swear the sword came to rest upon something pitch black, undulating, serpentine, and vast. A sea monster? Whatever it was, the sword slid from its back and vanished into darkness. Whatever I'd glimpsed was free to move about without my ability to track it.

It was well past time to leave. Though it was utterly graceless, I placed Romer's limp belly against by crotch and wrapped my legs as tightly as possible around her hips. With both hands free, I dragged myself up the rope, in yard-long lunges. In seconds, I was above the surface. Instinctively, I tried to breathe. Captain Romer displayed no such instinct. As I made my way slowly to the deck, she didn't cough, or even twitch.

By the time I reached the rail, a half dozen arms reached over to grab at us. Mako and Brand both looked fully recovered from their ordeal, and as they lugged me over, Sage and Jetsam grabbed their mother and pried her free of my leg-lock. I saw that Menagerie was back on his feet, or paws at least, and Bigsby had recovered both his wits and his wig, and was currently tying Purity's arms behind her back. Infidel, I saw, had taken possession of the fallen Ice-Moon Blade. Her enchanted armory was growing rather impressive.

I found my way back to my feet and looked around for my hat. I spotted it near the bow. When I reached it, before I could bend over, the ghost of Jasmine Romer once more materialized and lifted the hat from the deck, offering it to me.

"Well done," she said.

I wanted to shake my head, but couldn't. I could make no attempt at communication due to Sorrow's command, but I was certain that Gale was dead.

"You're troubled, young spirit," she said, her voice growing soft. "You spotted it, didn't you?"

It? Was she talking about the sea monster?

"The beast that tracks us is Rott," she said with a sigh. "The dragon of entropy and decay. He passes freely between the material world and the abstract realms. He's the only truly universal elemental force."

If I'd been able to speak, I would have asked if there were a dragon of taxes. But, considering that her daughter was dead, I was grateful that my lack of voice spared her from my tasteless humor.

"Do not think that, by surviving the death of your body, you've cheated Rott for long. There is no true immortality. Things fall apart, even things that are only the memory of things. In the end, entropy will devour us all. We risk destruction any time we traverse this realm. But, for now, you've brought my daughter another day, at least."

As she said this, I heard coughing behind me. Captain Romer was flat on her back, her arms flailing limply as she spat up wine. Mako and Rigger flanked her, and Jetsam was at her feet. Suddenly, her eyes snapped open and she let loose a high-pitched shriek that devolved into laughter as she kicked Jetsam hard in the chest and let loose with twin uppercuts that caught Mako and Rigger beneath their chins. She sprang up as they went down. Though her motions were exaggerated and woozy, she landed on her feet and managed to snatch up a belaying pin from the pin rail. She brandished the improvised club as she shrieked, "I'll kill the lot of you!"

She let loose a fierce growl to give weight to her threat, but mid-way through her exhalation her growl changed into giggles.

"I'm on it!" shouted Infidel, flying across the deck in a single hop to land in front of the drunken captain. She said firmly, "Put the club down! You know who I am, right?"

"Infidel," Gale laughed, before unleashing a haymaker punch with the belaying pin. Infidel blocked the blow with the shaft of her hammer. Gale attempted a kick, but Infidel dodged by jumping a yard into the air and hanging there.

Suddenly a gust of wind howled across the deck, catching Infidel and throwing her back. She tried to spin in the air to take control of her flight, but succeeded only in turning her face toward the foremast as she raced toward it. With a sound like a butcher's mallet pounding a slab of tough meat, Infidel slammed into the wood. The Gloryhammer was left floating in the air as she dropped to the deck, blood pouring from her temple.

8 - INADEQUATE VESSELS

FOR THIRTY SECONDS, pandemonium reigned. Mako and Jetsam tackled their mother as she cursed, giggled, and got in a couple of good licks with the belaying pin before being dragged down by their weight. A dozen ropes snaked to snare her thrashing legs, until violent winds pushed them back. Cinnamon rushed forward, dodging her mother's kicks, crouching to place her hand on the bare skin of her mother's midriff. Gale's drunken giggles cut off in mid-breath, replaced by gagging. Her limbs went limp as all color drained from her face. Jetsam released his mother's arm and leapt skyward, kicking to gain altitude as she began to projectile vomit the wine she'd swallowed. Now too sick to command winds, Gale was quickly wrapped by Rigger's ropes. Even after she'd emptied her stomach, Gale continued to spit, trying to rid her mouth of whatever foul flavor Cinnamon had inflicted upon her.

Meanwhile, Bigsby jogged across the deck, holding his wig on with one hand, as he stretched his other hand toward the Gloryhammer, which hovered in mid-air six feet directly above Infidel's fallen form. "I claim the holy power that is my birthright!" he cried as he used Infidel's butt as a trampoline to leap for the hammer. Bigsby's jump was a good six inches short of his target. Please note that I do not, in anyway, place the blame on the springiness of my wife's derriere, which I assure you is more than adequate. He landed on the deck, hard, his plate armor clanging, and was pushed to his belly by a snarling dog with wings. Menagerie had finally recovered from his chill.

I moved toward Infidel, who lay limp and unconscious on the deck. I wanted to kneel and investigate her injuries, but this simple act lay outside the range of freedom that Sorrow had granted me. I couldn't even motion for one of the Romers to come to her aid.

To add further to the distractions that kept Infidel from getting help, one of the ice-maidens recovered her wits and leapt to her feet just then, grabbing Sage from behind. Sage looked curiously unworried as the ice-maiden pressed a sword against her throat and shouted, "Jabber jabber jabber!" This might have been a threat in her native tongue, but on this boat all it meant was, "I'm an idiot! Kill me!" Her request was carried out a heartbeat later by Brand, who sank one of his throwing knives deep into the orbit of her left eye.

Rigger neutralized the threat of further ice-maidens waking by having every rope in sight come to life and bind their hands and feet. His brow was furrowed in concentration, his lips pressed tightly together. Despite the heat and humidity of the Sea of Wine, his lips were nearly blue, and his limbs shook beneath his black uniform, soggy with icy water.

Sage shouted, "Poppy! Go get Rigger a blanket before he freezes to death!" She ran to Rigger's side. "We have to get him out of these freezing clothes."

"We're all drenched," said Poppy, who was also shivering. "Why aren't you telling him to get me a blanket?"

"If Rigger gets sick, the *Freewind's* all but crippled," said Sage. "The rest of us are expendable."

"No one's expendable," Mako said. He'd already pulled off his soaked shirt and boots and his muscular body had shaken off the effects of the cold. "Bring blankets for everyone, Poppy."

Meanwhile, Jetsam had also gotten over his chill, perhaps because of the exertion of swimming through the air around the now limp sails. He dove down from near the tip of the mainmast to land beside Bigsby. He dropped to his knees and grabbed the fallen dwarf by his cheeks.

"Who are you?" he demanded as he drew his dagger.

"Whoa, whoa, whoa," Brand shouted, holding up his hands. "It's okay. She's with me!"

"Only if she's a stowaway," Jetsam said, shaking his head. "We officially have two passengers aboard, and she's not one of them. And why are we saying she? She's plainly a he!" He snatched Bigsby's platinum locks and shook them before the dwarf's face.

"I am too a she!" Bigsby screamed, grabbing Jetsam's sinewy wrist and twisting to no avail. "I'm Princess Innocent Brightmoon!"

"It's true," said Brand. "She's my sister. I'm Prince Steadfast Brightmoon!"

"You're both mad," said Jetsam, rubbing Bigsby's makeup off with his sleeve.

Now it was Mako's turn to join in the confrontation. He grabbed Brand by the throat and pushed him against the mast. I noticed for the first time that Mako's hands had webs between his fingers. He pushed his toothy face inches from Brand's pale blue eyes and snarled, "You're no prince! You're nothing but carnival trash! Your looks and charm may have reduced my mother's wisdom to that of a teenage girl—"

"Hey!" shouted Sage. By now Poppy had returned with a heavy wool blanket, which Sage draped over Rigger's skinny shoulders.

Mako continued: "I took care to learn everything there was to know about you once you became our dryman. Before you turned up in Commonground, you traveled the Silver Isle as a member of the Slinger Carnival. You were the show's knife thrower."

Sage glanced at the dead ice-maiden who'd tried to take her hostage. "You've got to admit he's good at it."

"Not so good that he could survive on the income from his act. My sources say his true talent lay as a pick-pocket."

Brand gave a surprisingly natural looking smile for a man on the verge of having his windpipe crushed. "You only know I'm a pick-pocket because it was part of my act. I always returned what I stole. I'm no thief, and I'm not 'trash' simply because I traveled with a carnival. I joined them because I was searching for my long lost sister who had been magically transformed into a dwarf. Dwarves frequently seek employment with carnival freak shows. It seemed like a good place to look."

"I'll admit I've heard stranger stories," Jetsam said, spitting on his captive's face as he wiped away the last of the rouge and mascara. "But this can't be the lost princess. This is Bigsby, the Fishmonger! I recognize him now that he's not painted like a tart. He's lived in Commonground since before I was born!"

"No!" Bigsby sobbed. "I've always been Princess Innocent! I only appear to be an old, ugly dwarf due to a witch's curse!"

There was a loud sigh from the hatch. Sorrow's head was just above deck. "Witches get blamed for everything," she grumbled. She climbed the rest of the way up the stairs and looked around. Her brow furrowed at the sight of all the semi-nude women bound on the deck. "The missing Skelling women, I presume?" She nudged a yeti with her boot. "That pelt should bring a nice price."

"We've captured their leader, no thanks to you," said Mako, taking his eyes off Brand, but not his grip. "What was so important you couldn't help save the ship?"

"Excuse me?" Sorrow said. "It wasn't my job to fight them. You're getting paid to protect your passengers. I thought you Wanderers understood contracts."

"If these ice-maidens had killed us all, I'm sure that you could have waved the contract in their faces and made them understand the error of their ways," Mako said.

"But they didn't kill you all, or any of you, as far as I can tell. Anyway, your charge that I did nothing is baseless. Perhaps you failed to notice the seven foot tall wooden golem who fought by your side?" She knelt and yanked my sword from the yeti's skull. "Catch," she said as she tossed me the blade, and I caught.

She looked around at the sky.

"Would someone care to explain why we're no longer in the material world?"

"No," said Mako. Then, with his meaty hand still clamped on Brand's throat, he turned to Rigger and Sage. "We're trapped here until Mother recovers. The two of you keep your eyes peeled for any trouble. We've sent many an enemy to the Sea of Wine, and I'd hate for them to show up now."

"If they do show up, there's nothing we can do," said Rigger, shaking his head sadly. "Without Mother, there's no wind."

"If there's no wind, no ghost ships can come hunting us," said Sage, trying to sound positive.

"They could have row-boats," said Jetsam.

"I'm taking mother to her cabin," said Mako. "We can do nothing but wait for her to sober up." He turned toward Jetsam and Cinnamon who stood nearby. "Take Brand and the dwarf below and place them in manacles. Ordinarily I'd keelhaul a stowaway, but the dwarf is plainly insane. I'm not going to punish a man for losing his mind."

He tightened his grip on Brand's throat as he brought his face close and smiled. It was a smile from a nightmare, saw-toothed and twice as wide as it should have been. "As for you, I haven't figured out your game. I should just rip out your throat for helping conceal a stowaway."

"Ma will tan your hide if you kill her dryman without asking permission," Jetsam said as he guided the dwarf toward the hatch. "Remember how mad she got at Levi?"

"I'm not afraid of Ma," Mako said. "But I'll wait until she sobers up before deciding this scoundrel's fate."

He stepped back as Cinnamon moved forward and took Brand by the hand. Brand's mouth suddenly puckered.

"You'll go below and play nice or my sister will put a taste in your mouth that will have you cutting out your own tongue. Understood?"

Brand nodded.

Satisfied that Brand was neutralized, Mako walked toward Purity, unconscious on the deck where Bigsby had hog-tied her. "Rigger, since she's bound, use your power to guide her down to my cabin. Once Ma's tucked in, I'll see to it that this witch is stripped of her armor and properly disarmed."

"You'll do no such thing," said Sorrow.

Mako raised his eyebrows. "With my mother incapacitated, I'm captain. The safety of this ship is my responsibility."

"That is not in dispute, but I don't care for your tone. I fear that you mean to abuse this woman in her helpless state."

Mako's face twisted into a snarl. "Choose your words with care. I've won't stand here and take your baseless slander."

"And I'll not stand by as a defenseless female is stripped searched by a lone male, no matter what his reputation."

"I can help," said Sage. "Though I assure you she'd suffer no abuse if Mako were alone."

Sorrow nodded. "This is acceptable. But search her and bind her properly so that she doesn't lose any limbs to gangrene. Gag her so that she may not speak. Don't interrogate her until I can properly construct iron bands of negation to baffle any delayed magic she might seek to trigger with her words."

"Good call," said Sage. "There's something strange about her. Her internal light is all indigo."

"You can see auras?" Sorrow asked, sounding surprised.

"I see lots of stuff," said Sage, shrugging.

"How long will it take you to construct these bands?" grumbled Mako.

"As long as needed," said Sorrow, now kneeling next to Infidel. "It's not something that should be rushed. Something that must be rushed, however, is treatment of this woman's injuries. This wound on her temple requires stitches." She looked up at me. "Drifter, take her to my quarters. Bring the hammer. Its light will prove useful."

As the various Romers vanished down the stairs with their captives, I grabbed the Gloryhammer in my gloved hand. Not having any convenient place to carry it, I improvised and shoved it down the back of my shirt. I knelt and scooped Infidel into my arms. I lifted her as a groom lifts a bride across a threshold. Whatever romance the moment may have held was negated by the two-inch gash on the side of Infidel's head that gushed blood with every heartbeat. Praying that Sorrow could mend Infidel's wound, I stepped onto the staircase and descended once more into the dark hold.

SORROW'S LIPS WERE pressed tightly together as I arranged Infidel on the bed. Sorrow removed her cape and hung it on the back of the door, then pulled the front of my shirt open. The Gloryhammer along my spine was powerful enough to push beams of sunlight through the gaps in the barrel staves that formed my chest. The gore on Infidel's brow glistened from the illumination.

"Who knew you'd make such a convenient lantern?" Sorrow asked as she slid a towel under Infidel's head. She went to the table in the corner and washed her hands in the basin. She then brought over the pitcher of water and a second towel and began to clean Infidel's wound.

"As you may suspect, I've some experience tending to scalp injuries," she said. "They always look worse than they are."

It took only a moment to dab away the blood. Sorrow then produced a razor and scraped away a few fine hairs that extended down from Infidel's scalp. She swabbed the area with clear fluid from a small bottle - vodka, from the smell of it. Infidel's face clenched despite her unconscious state.

"This wound isn't so bad," said Sorrow. "But I must work fast. She may wake soon. Move one step to your left."

I did, as Sorrow turned Infidel's head so that the light fell directly on the gaping flesh. I wondered for a moment if I was seeing bone beneath the gash, but it was all just amber on amber to my wooden eyes. Sorrow produced a silver needle that looked too large for the task at hand. I expected her to thread the needle, but instead the metal came to life, wriggling like a serpent, stretching and tapering until it was as thin as a hair before plunging into Infidel's flesh. The silver filament rose and fell, rose and fell, moving through the torn skin as if it had a will of its own. In less time than it's taken me to tell it, it reached the end of the wound and tugged itself tight. Sorrow dabbed her handiwork with a fresh corner of the towel and wiped away what blood had bubbled up during the procedure. Now that the skin was clean, no further blood seeped through. Infidel's wound was neatly stitched together, the silver thread so fine as to almost be invisible.

Finished with her work, Sorrow turned back the bed's linens and commanded me to place Infidel beneath them. With her injury turned away from me, Infidel looked as if she was merely sleeping.

Going once more to the basin, Sorrow washed her hands. Without looking at me, she said, "You're forbidden to injure me or in any way seek to take revenge. Should anyone attempt to harm me, even Infidel, you're obligated to defend me."

I nodded.

Drying her hands, she crossed back to the desk. She lifted one of my notebooks, my favorite one, actually. I used a lot of different materials for writing. Parchment, made of old animal hide, is fine to write on, but thick, so you don't get many pages in a book. There's also papyrus. It's the cheapest writing surface available, just flattened reed mats woven together by river pygmies. It's a pain to write on and it falls apart with use, but you can buy more than you can carry for the cost of a pint of ale. And then there's paper; the Church of the Book manufactures this sacred material at a remote nunnery on the Isle of Apes. Supposedly it's made of ground up trees boiled in nun's urine impregnated with spices. This seems an unlikely recipe, though Wanderers who trade with the island tell me that the fumes from the nunnery make their eyes sting five miles out to sea, so who knows?

Paper is smooth, white as cotton, and thin enough that a book barely an inch thick can have a hundred flexible yet durable pages. Its main drawback is that it's expensive as hell. The only reason I own so many notebooks made from paper is that most knights and priests of the Church of the Book own them. A steady stream of these people have flowed to Commonground over the years to kill the woman I love. They'd failed in their quests, but succeeded in supplying me with excellent stationary.

The notebook on the desk had belonged to a church assassin who called himself Penumbra. He'd attacked Infidel with shadow swords, blades that could hurt her even when she was invulnerable. It had been a particular pleasure to loot his backpack and find this notebook. It was sturdy, bound in black leather, yet compact, just five inches across and seven inches tall. It had fit nicely in my jacket pocket, and except for ten pages of coded notes at the front that I'd never figured out, the rest of it was blank. When I'd gotten it, I'd been so enamored that I vowed I would write something special within its pages, an epic poem, perhaps, or my own authoritative history of the Vanished Kingdom that would replace my grandfather's famous book as the epitome of scholarship.

Seven years later, no pen of mine had ever marked the notebook, though Sorrow had filled another ten pages with her looping, elegant script. Turning beyond the last page she'd written anything on, Sorrow cut a blank sheet loose with the razor she'd used to shave Infidel's temple. She folded the paper into a long, tapered wedge, flattening it out, then turned toward me. It looked a bit like an origami snake that had been stepped on. She stood on tip-toes to place the paper sculpture between my gaping coconut jaws, then used silver thread to sew it into place, or so I assume. I couldn't see what she was doing, obviously, but the sound of a silver needle punching through paper and coconut husk has a rather distinctive rasp within the confines of a hollow skull.

When she was done, she stepped back and said, "You may now speak."

"Really?" I asked. If I'd had eyebrows, they would have shot up. I *could* speak! Sort of. "Is that me?" I said, cringing at hearing the words. "I sound… funny."

"Don't be ungrateful," said Sorrow. "You're making words without lungs, throat, palette, teeth, or lips. You've only a paper tongue that vibrates to approximate the noises you would have made in life. You should be amazed at the cleverness of my craftsmanship, not critical."

"I sound like a squirrel playing a kazoo," I protested, though no tone of protest came through. I could neither shout nor whisper; all the sounds coming from my paper tongue were of roughly the same volume, which wasn't terribly loud. On the other hand, if anyone had come aboard the *Black Swan* with a squirrel that played kazoo, I would have paid money to see it. Perhaps Sorrow was right; the fact that I could make recognizable words at all was a thing worthy of note. When had I become so jaded?

"I saw the letters on the beach. You're Stagger. These are your notes."

"Yes," I said, then nodded toward the bed. "And this is my wife. Will she be okay? Why hasn't she woke up?"

"Infidel was sound asleep when the ice-maidens attacked; I could hear her snoring in the cabin next door. Her body was already primed for slumber. It's too soon to worry."

"It's never too soon to worry," I said. "It's not just her I'm concerned about. According to the Black Swan, she's pregnant with my daughter."

"The Black Swan is a manipulator of the highest order," said Sorrow. "I would place no faith in what she says unless there's a written contract involved, and then you should read every last word of the fine print."

"Now that you know who I am, will you set me free?"

"You're valuable to me," said Sorrow. "I invested a tremendous amount of time and effort in creating a soul-catcher. I'm not prepared to throw that away. Besides, you were an unbound spirit when I found you. It was only a matter of time before you faded away to nothingness. You can last much longer now that you're embodied again."

"You said I would burn out."

"It's true. Your life energy isn't infinite. But this was true before you were captured as well. For now, it is to the benefit of both of us that you occupy this form."

I wasn't certain of this. I'd enjoyed my freedom as a ghost, the ability to flit around as I pleased, my thoughts instantly translating into movement. On the other hand, this new body did have a tongue. I desperately wanted to talk to Infidel.

"Fine," I said, crossing my arms. "Having a body again, even this clunky wooden one, isn't completely unwelcome. But from now on, I'm not your slave to boss around. I'll work with you as an equal partner."

She snorted. "You're in no way my equal, ghost. *You* are the echo of a drunken tomb-looter whose life's work amounts to a few pages of barely legible notes. *I* am a master of fundamental materials, driven to remake the world. A century from now, you will be completely forgotten, while I will be remembered as the woman who freed humankind from the authoritarian clutches of a wicked church and ushered in a new age of enlightenment and equality."

I laughed, or tried to. My paper tongue turned it more into the sound of sneezing.

"Are you amused?" asked Sorrow.

"For someone smart, you're ignorant of the word 'hubris.'"

"This would apply to me only if I felt confidence in excess of my capacity," said Sorrow. "I assure you, I never fail at my goals."

"You have a self-inflicted hole in your head that's killing you," I said.

She frowned. She looked ready to change the subject. Glancing back at the maps spread on the desk she asked, "Do you know where to find the Witch's Graveyard?"

"Maybe," I said. "There are folk legends and intriguing place names that provide clues. I can't make any guarantees, but give me half a day and a pick-axe once we're back in Commonground and I can probably root out the truth."

"You can draw me a map?" she said.

"Already drawn," I said, motioning toward the desk.

"Show me. You're free to move as you wish, though I do not release you from the command to save me from harm."

I walked to the pile of documents and pulled the corner of a sheet of parchment jutting out from beneath the stack. It had a purple ring on it from where I'd sat a bottle of wine while discussing the map with a potential buyer at the Black Swan. I tapped a roughly sketched rectangle next to the ring. "This place is called the Knight's Castle. It's a complex of stonework a few miles upriver from the bay. It's been picked over pretty thoroughly, but there is one noteworthy feature, several hundred yards off the main complex. It's overgrown with trees, but when I surveyed the land here" – I took a quill from the ink bottle and drew an X at the western edge of the castle – "there are several acres marked by evenly spaced, rectangular depressions. No head stones, but even without them, it looks exactly like a graveyard where all the coffins have disintegrated, letting the soil collapse down into the graves."

My 'X' looked a little barren. So I drew a circle around it, then jotted 'Witch Graveyard' above it. Those words looked lonely, so I wrote beneath them, 'Treasure!'

"The embellishment isn't necessary," said Sorrow.

"Sorry," I said. "Old habit. In the dry spells between finding actual relics, I supplemented my income by selling maps to treasure hunters from the Silver Isles. I saw a steady stream of barbers, barristers and haberdashers who'd run away from their boring lives and demanding wives to get rich quick by looting the Vanished Kingdom. Nearly all my customers got themselves killed during their first week in the jungle, so repeat business was lousy."

"Couldn't the hollow depressions be evidence the graves have been dug up?"

"There would be mounds next to the depressions. This is just gut instinct, but I don't think anyone's dug there because the area's kind of boring. Every year or two somebody stumbles over a vine-covered temple housing idols with jade eyes and golden earrings. The folks who built the Vanished Kingdom weren't noted for doing things small or subtle. Treasure hunters would rather hack away vines from a hundred mounds of boulders hoping to find an old temple than take a shovel to unmarked graves where everything has probably rotted."

"The nails I'm seeking wouldn't rot," said Sorrow.

"Why not? Bone rots. Wood rots. Iron rusts. I guess the gold and glass might survive a long time underground."

Sorrow gave my arguments a dismissive wave.

"You know little of the higher arts of weaving."

"I know damn little of the lower arts, for that matter. Considering that the church has pretty much wiped out your kind, I think I can be forgiven a little ignorance."

"While I've perfected the manipulation of the material world, within limits, there is self-evidently more to the known world than matter. This ship currently sails in one of the abstract realms."

"I know a little bit about abstract realms," I said. "They're like dream worlds, only shared. They form the foundation of somnomancy."

"I would dispute this," said Sorrow. "Somnomancy isn't a distinct magical art in my opinion. It's more akin to the reality manipulation of the Deceivers, only the somnomancer is being lied to by his unconscious mind. The abstract realms, on the other hand, are real, unless you believe we're dreaming now."

"Do you have any convincing evidence that we're not?"

"Don't try to play games with me. I've no patience for such things. My body weakens with the passage of each day; each heartbeat is like a grain of sand through an hourglass. I'm keenly aware that death waits for me if I don't reverse the damage to my body."

"And your plan to save yourself is… abstract nails?"

"Avaris is said to have possessed a nail of time. Imagine the power to being able to sculpt and mold seconds and moments to your will! I thought the Black Swan possessed it, but her skull was unblemished."

"What would such a nail look like? How would you even hammer it in?"

Sorrow sighed. "Sensible questions. I don't know. I'm hoping to gather clues from context when I finally discover the skull of an ancient witch."

"If I weren't a walking, talking pile of driftwood, I might be inclined to call you crazy."

"I'm not crazy," said Sorrow, clenching her right fist. "I'm mad. Mad at my father, mad at the church, and the damned Divine Author. I'm mad because I see the world as it truly is, not as the veil of convenient and comforting illusions everyone else embraces. I'm mad to be facing this fight alone."

I shrugged. "You could try being nicer to people. Commonground is full of people who have grudges against the church. Hell, a lot of people probably have grudges against your father personally. You could probably make some allies if you weren't so, uh…, um, intense."

"You were about to say 'bitchy.'"

"Maybe."

"My father is blunt, demanding and stubborn. People call him a great leader. When I display these same qualities, I'm dismissed as a bitch."

"Please note that I did avoid the word," said Stagger. "Twenty years ago, the execration would have crossed my tongue with barely a thought. But, I've heard Infidel called a bitch a thousand times, when her greatest sin has been that she is insufficiently fearful of men who enjoy being feared. If you must fuss at me, please focus on things I actually say."

"My apologies," said Sorrow. To my surprise, she sounded sincere. "Perhaps I'm overly defensive. I've survived as long as I have by being suspicious of everyone."

I sighed, though my paper tongue turned the sound into the buzz of fly wings. "I'm really not your enemy. I couldn't care less if you wish to wage war against the church. I live in Commonground because it's one of the few places on earth where the church has no power. Hell, that's pretty much why everyone who isn't a Wanderer or a pygmy comes to Commonground. A lot of them would probably cheer you on."

Sorrow's shoulders sagged as she shook her head. "In some circumstances, the enemy of an enemy can be a friend; for me, the enemies of my enemies almost always prove to be unreliable scoundrels who view me as an easy victim."

Part of me wanted to pat her on the back and say, "There, there." She sounded lonely and worn out, and I'm a man with an excess of empathy. On the other hand, given that she had enslaved me and showed no inclination toward releasing me, my empathy could only go so far.

She rubbed her eyes. "I need to sleep. It will be hours before Captain Romer has recovered from her excursion into the Sea of Wine. I'm interested in learning how we got here. I assume Mako knows more than he's telling."

"I have a few insights. I saw Captain Romer lean down, touch the bare wood of the deck, and announce we were sailing the Sea of Wine. I also know from talking to Wanderers in the past that the Sea of Wine is sort of a gateway to their afterlife. If she dies, do you think we'll be trapped here?"

"She won't die," said Sorrow. "And, don't think of our situation as trapped. We're in the safest place imaginable at the moment. We don't have to worry about assault by the Judgment Fleet, pirates, or Skellings while we're here. We're the only living thing upon these waves."

"But maybe not beneath them. I saw… something… lurking beneath the ship. A big, black serpent." I was hesitant to say all I knew. I didn't want to accidentally reveal the ghost of Jasmine Romer to Sorrow.

"Abyss, perhaps? The primal dragon of the sea has a pact to protect Wanderers."

"I don't think so. I've seen Abyss. He's more of a giant turtle. This thing was covered in big black snake scales."

"Hmm. That fits the description of Rott," said Sorrow. "It would be appropriate that the dragon of decay would dwell here. Wine is a product of rotting grapes, after all."

"That's a terrible thing to say about one of my favorite beverages."

"I appreciate wine not for its flavor but for its inspiration," she said. "Destruction is the precursor of creation. Perfectly good fruit when crushed and allowed to molder releases something new and precious. I wouldn't be eager to bring the kingdoms of the world to ruin if I didn't believe something far more vibrant would emerge."

"You're not going to be overthrowing anything if Rott gets a sudden whim to swallow this ship."

Sorrow shrugged. "If he does, he does. Some things are too big even for me to worry about. For now, it looks like Infidel will get to use the stateroom after all. I'll go sleep in her bunk."

"Where should I go?"

Sorrow shrugged again. "Stay by her side, if you wish. For now, I release you of all restrictions save the command to protect me."

She opened the door, took her cloak, and left.

I was alone with Infidel, who had turned onto her side, hugging her pillow. Her sleep now looked more natural than it had when she'd first been tucked in. I had renewed hope that she'd recover.

If I'd been a courageous man, I might have woken her.

Now that I had the freedom to speak to her, I knew that I couldn't. Between her quest and her pregnancy, she had enough worries without having to concern herself about my fate. And yet, there was still so much I wish I'd told her when I was alive.

I went to the desk, to the notebook with its neatly trimmed page cut to build my tongue. At least a hundred sheets of blank paper remained. This book had always looked so pristine and promising that any words I'd contemplated filling it with had seemed unworthy to stain its pages. Now, at last, I had a message deserving of its snow-white fibers.

I took the book and the bottle of ink and crouched as I left the cabin. The Romer men were arranging their captives in the hold. Many of the ice-maidens had been taken alive and we now had quite a cargo of prisoners.

Above deck, the sky was the same unchanging omnidirectional sunset. The waters had grown still, and the sails hung limp in the quiet air. The ice was nearly gone, leaving only a few puddles here and there.

I moved to the bow and sat cross-legged, placing the book before me. I steadied my ink and quill.

Dearest Infidel, I began. *It is a great injustice upon my part that I have spent so many years in your company, pen and paper always at hand, and somehow failed to write you a love letter. Fate has granted me the chance to atone for this oversight. Perhaps the Divine Author is a romantic after all.*

And so the words flowed, page after page, as I spoke of my hopes and confessed my regrets, and told her of my love. My normally opulent vocabulary faded as I wrote, as my language turned simple and sincere. Perhaps, in their simplicity, I even managed to capture some truth, though I fear that words will ever be inadequate vessels for the cargo of emotions. Yet on I wrote, undaunted, placing heart to paper in a setting that, while strange, was also familiar. In death as in life, I felt at home adrift on a Sea of Wine.

9 - THE VESTIBULE OF SELF-ABNEGATION

I HAD NO way to measure the time I spent writing. My body no longer possessed the natural rhythms of weariness or hunger, and the unnatural sky gave no hint of the passage of time. I filled twenty pages with my scratchings. My wooden fingers were numb instruments, leaving my clumsy cursive a mess of smears and smudges. The only saving grace was that, for the first time in memory, I wrote completely sober. My lines of script were attractively parallel, rather than undulating serpents that sometimes overlapped one another.

It's possible I could have kept writing until the book was filled. I'd moved on from singing the praises of Infidel's virtues and was now discussing the future, specifically our unborn daughter. Infidel and I came from a culture where women were regarded as inferior and subordinate. Infidel, born a princess, had less freedom than the most humble baker or candlestick maker in the Silver City. Men were allowed to own property; women were allowed to be property.

Commonground, for all its anarchistic freedom, was little better. While it's true that an exceptional woman like the Black Swan could become a powerful force, and strong women like Infidel and Aurora were essentially free to live as they wished, the reality was most women in Commonground survived as whores. The notable exceptions, of course, were the Wanderers. Of all the various societies throughout the long string of islands sometimes called the Shining Lands, only among the Wanderers was there a true sense of equality between the sexes. I suppose it rose both from their professed belief in individual freedom and the practical realities of their lives. They lived as close family units on boats. Even in traditional homes on land, women frequently are the true masters of a household, the ones whose decisions are treated as final by the children, while the men serve mainly as enforcers of the woman's decisions. On land, women are mostly trapped within their own houses, kept busy raising children and cooking meals, while men are free to roam about and engage in commerce and spend their relatively more plentiful free time plotting wars and forming governments. Among the Wanderers, the men are just as confined to the ships as the women, and when it's time to visit a neighbor, the whole household moves as one.

Yet I didn't want my daughter to become a Wanderer. Wanderers fancy themselves travelers and explorers, visiting a hundred ports a year, citizens of the world. In truth, they seldom stray more than a few hundred feet from their boats. Casting anchor in Commonground is a pale experience compared to exploring the jungles of the Isle of Fire. The view from a crow's nest is not the same as the view from atop a mountain. For all their vaunted freedom, the Wanderers were curiously self-imprisoned.

I wanted my daughter to be boundless. I wanted her to stride the world with the knowledge she was equal to anyone, able to freely look into the eyes of kings or paupers, without looking down upon either. Infidel had spent much of her adult life reacting to the fears drilled into her as a child. I made my life choices haunted by the shame I'd experienced as a boy abandoned by both of his still-living parents. When I looked at Sorrow, I could see her childhood bitterly seeping out of every pore. Could a human be raised free of fear, shame, or bitterness? Free of greed, pride, or privilege? Was I already dooming my daughter to failure by wishing such a utopian upbringing upon her?

My musings were shattered as a scream tore from the hatch.

"Hurry," a woman's voice said beside me. I looked up and once more found myself staring at the imposing naked breasts of the ghost of Jasmine Romer. "My daughter isn't in her right mind. She'll hurt herself, or others, if you don't stop her."

I closed the book mid-sentence without waiting for the ink to dry. I stood, just as Mako leapt up the stairs onto the deck, blood streaming from his nose.

He bent backward to avoid a dagger that flew by his head, then did a handspring back to the railing before bouncing into the rigging. His mother climbed to the deck half a second later, with Sage locked in a stranglehold beneath her right arm. Gale was wearing a modest cotton nightgown, white but blood spattered, and her hair, normally woven in a tight braid, hung loose around her face, showing the gray streaks within. Sage was a little taller than her mother, with an athletic build, but Gale had more experience as a brawler.

No matter how Sage twisted to escape, Gale kept her forearm tight across the girl's throat. I moved toward the fight, hoping I could keep Gale from killing her daughter.

Before I reached her, Gale let go of Sage, throwing her roughly against the mast. Sage sank to the deck, looking dazed. Gale cried, "I gave life to you all and I can take it! The next hand that touches me I'll cut off, I swear!"

Since she had no sword currently in hand, her words were probably bluff, but her half-strangled daughter and bloodied son looked hesitant to test her. I ran toward her, arms outstretched. She turned to face me. My wooden legs weren't built for stealth, but I leapt from 15 feet away with more than enough strength to fly the distance. With her well-honed reflexes she leapt from my path, but I clipped her legs with my outstretched arms and we both fell to the deck. My wooden fingers clamped onto her ankle. She pummeled me with her fists and scratched at my wooden face with her nails as she screamed, "It's hopeless! All hopeless! Let me die!"

I shifted my bulk to pin her legs. Tears streamed down her cheeks as her limbs lost strength, her frantic motions devolving into spastic tremors. "By the seven stars it's over! *All over.* Can't you see the doom that pursues us? Better to drown in the wine than to be chewed in the maw of such a beast!"

"What beast?" I asked, startling both her and myself with my squeaky, buzzing voice.

She sobbed. "It's no use. Oh, my vanity! I thought I could steer this ship between the teeth of destruction. I thought mine was the hand upon the wheel of destiny. But there is no wheel!" She choked as snot and mucus bubbled from her lips. "There is no wheel!"

Her face was drenched with sweat and mottled by dark red patches, as if stained by wine.

"She's completely mad," Sage said, rising on wobbly legs.

"It's delirium tremens," I said. "She's been poisoned by alcohol. She's hallucinating!"

"What can we do?"

Sadly, I knew. While I'd never been so far gone that I'd been unable to tell reality from dreams, I'd lived the last ten years of my life with a subtle tremor that seized my hands on those rare moments when I'd been completely sober. There was only one treatment.

"More wine," I said. "Or something stronger. It's her only hope."

"You want to cure her drunkenness with more drink?"

"It's the only thing that can help once you start seeing hallucinations!"

"What if she's not hallucinating?" asked Brand, who practically made me jump out of my wooden skin as he spoke only inches from my ear. His head had popped up from the hatch leading to the hold. "Can't you smell it? The air has shifted. The wine is being replaced by vinegar."

Mako growled as he glared at Brand, "Who freed you? You were in manacles just moments ago!"

"Please," said Brand, rubbing his wrists. "If you know about my circus past, you also know I did escape work. Plus, your mother likes to, um, play games. This wasn't the first time I've worn those shackles. Once you've seen the key, picking a lock is child's play."

Mako snatched the dagger his mother had thrown at him from the mast. "You insolent bastard! I'll kill you!"

But as he raised his arm to strike, a thick rope snaked down from above and caught his wrist. "Calm yourself, Mako," shouted Rigger, who'd been watching from the poop deck this whole time. "We lost Levi because he couldn't control his temper."

"I'd say that was more due to mother's temper," said Sage, brushing her hair from her eyes, stuffing the stray strands back beneath her red cap.

"You can talk about your family history some other time," said Brand, kneeling beside Gale and stroking her sweating brow. "Your mother is trapped deep in a thicket of despair. I can help her find her way back."

"She needs wine," I said.

"There are things better than wine for curing a damaged soul," said Brand, he picked up Gale. For a woman in her forties, she looked small and girlish cradled in his muscular arms. "Leave her to me."

Mako let loose an inhuman growl as he watched Brand carry Gale toward the hold. Mako bit the rope that held his arm, but another caught him just as swiftly. He cried, "Rigger, I'm going to kick your ass once I'm done killing this fool!"

"Grow up!" Sage said as she stepped directly underneath Mako. "You're always trying to solve problems by making threats."

"Because the rest of you idiots don't listen!" Mako thrashed as more ropes wrapped around him. "Have you all lost your senses? Mother's not in her right mind. She's seeing things! And you're going to let this bastard take advantage of her?"

Brand didn't react to these words as he carried Gale down the stairs.

Sage put her hands on her hips. "I haven't gone crazy and neither has mother. She's not hallucinating. Look behind the ship!"

Rigger swung Mako back to the stern and dropped him. Mako stared at the water in silence, his lips pressed tightly together. I moved to the back to see what he was staring at. Mere feet below the water was what appeared to be an oily black stain stretching out behind the *Freewind* for a mile or more. This dark shape was serpentine, a hundred yards across at its thickest point, and here and there small islands of tar broke above the waves along what would have been the serpent's spine.

Only, as the waves continued to wash in ever lightening shades of amber foam, the beast rose higher still and I could see I wasn't looking at the spine of an enormous serpent, but at the belly. The thing was obviously dead, but that didn't make it any less menacing. Its lifeless head was twisted sideways in the water, its toothy jaws opened in a giant V aimed straight at the *Freewind*. The gaping maw was more than wide enough to swallow the ship whole; any individual fang of the beast was as thick and long as our foremast. The waves pushed the jaws open and shut in a lazy, listless chew.

Sage pointed her spyglass at the thing, which I found odd given that the monster was pretty hard to miss with plain old eyesight. But, after a moment's study she said, "This thing is drifting faster than we are. We've got about ten minutes before it hits."

We all glanced up at what sails were set. Every canvas hung limp. There wasn't enough of a breeze to push a feather, let alone a ship. As I looked down from the sails, I discovered the whole Romer family was now above deck, as was Bigsby, once more wearing his wig. Sorrow in her cloak was coming up the stairs followed by Infidel, still in her armor, her bed-head hair a fright.

"Somebody want to fill me in on what's going on?" Infidel asked, sounding groggy. "The last thing I remember was trying to help Gale."

"How did mother hurt you?" Sage asked as she studied Infidel's brow. "I saw a cutlass break over your head at Half-Moon Bay without even leaving a scratch!"

Infidel sighed. "I need you to keep this a secret. But, right now, I'm not invulnerable. My strength is gone too."

"You knocked those ice-maidens half a mile out to sea," said Jetsam, scratching his head.

"All in the hammer," said Infidel.

"You should have told us," said Mako, sounding angry. He shoved his face inches from Infidel and said, "You assured us you wouldn't need protection! We trusted you!"

"The only injury I've suffered has been because your mother fights dirty, not because of our attackers," said Infidel. "Between my armor and my hammer, I can handle myself."

"Your armor might be a little more effective if you wore a helmet," said Jetsam.

Infidel nodded. "I hate helmets. Who wants to wear a steel bucket on their head when you live in the tropics? But, yeah, it's time I learn to like them."

"If we'd known you didn't have your powers, we could have taken extra steps to protect you," said Mako.

"I don't want anyone putting themselves in danger because of me."

Sorrow joined the conversation. "Aren't others in greater danger if they're depending on physical skills you no longer possess?" She punctuated her sentence by spitting. At first, I thought it was an act of contempt, but then she swatted the air before her face and said, "Excuse me, but a fly just flew into my mouth."

She hardly need have said it. Flies were everywhere now.

I buzzed in with my paper voice. "Sorrow, there's a sea serpent following the boat. It looks dead. But I think it might be–"

"Rott?" said Sorrow, half in surprise, half in excitement. She sprinted to the rail.

Jetsam was already at the back of the boat, floating in the air, kicking his legs slowly to hold his position above the rudder. He let out a long, low, whistle, interrupted by gagging. "By the southern stars, what a stench!"

I was about to join with the others at the back of the ship when I caught a motion from the corner of my eye. I turned and found the ghost of Jasmine Romer once more hovering above the bowsprit. She motioned me towards her.

"It's a pretty big coincidence that a primal dragon would show up at the same time we're attacked by Purity," I said.

"It is no coincidence for Rott to appear anywhere," said Jasmine. "The entropic force he represents is omnipresent."

"Maybe entropy is everywhere, but mile long dead snakes sure aren't. Something's causing him to show up here. Is Purity summoning him?"

"That's doubtful. Rott isn't like Hush or Abyss or even Greatshadow, who all maintain their intellect and personalities. The elemental force Rott commanded long ago consumed his very sense of self. He's essentially mindless, incapable of ordered thought. Only the barest flicker of animalistic hunger compels him to manifest. Bluntly, if he's here, he's come to feast."

"If he keeps turning the Sea of Wine into vinegar, we'll be in a real pickle," I said.

Jasmine wagged a ghostly finger in my face. "Don't make light of this! Though Rott isn't conscious of his actions, he can sense that the cosmic balance is off. Lives have been lost without their life force returning to the source. He hungers for this missing energy."

"What are you saying?"

"My body died, but my soul never left the world. The same is true of you."

"And your point is?"

"When Avaris helped prepare this boat to house my soul, she took precautions to hide my spirit from Rott's notice. I suspect that Sorrow, being inexperienced in her craft, has taken no such precautions. Just as a dead body emits a stench that draws vultures, the scent of your decaying soul has drawn the ultimate scavenger. Rott will consume this ship to feed his hunger."

"Oh," I said, raising my hand and running it along the back of my coconut scalp, as if I still had hair. "That's unfortunate. Why hasn't he bothered me before now?"

"Until now, your spirit dwelled on the material realm. Your soul is just one of thousands of lost spirits existing at any time. Rott feasts in the material world at his leisure. Here on the Sea of Wine, you're his sole focus."

"Then get out of here," I said. "Shift us back to the real world. Problem solved."

"Only my daughter can trigger this magic," said Jasmine. "Complicating matters further, it's now daylight in our home seas. We can only make the transit in the dead of night."

"So… what? You expect me to jump off the ship so this thing will leave the rest of you alone?"

Jasmine said nothing as she lowered her head.

"Oh," I said.

"I can think of no other reason Rott would manifest so aggressively. He's never before molested us within this realm."

As it happened, our conversation unfolded near where I'd been writing to Infidel. I barely had to walk a yard before leaning down to lift up the book. I clumsily ripped out the half-finished letter and folded it into a thick bundle. I tugged away the bandana that hid my hideous coconut skull and tied the letter within the cloth. Flies landed on my gloved fingers as I worked.

I took one look back at Jasmine. I sighed, or tried to. "The first time I died, it was just a dumb mistake." I shook my head. "I mean, it's something you might tell a seven-year-old: 'Don't run with a knife!'" I stared down at the bundled letter for a long time. "I guess it's appropriate that my death was careless, given how careless I was with my life. But you know… good things came of it. I'm going to have a daughter. I want to be there to watch her grow up."

"I understand," said Jasmine.

I looked back to the stern. Infidel was floating there, next to Jetsam, her eyes fixed on the doom that drifted toward us.

Even at this distance, I could hear that Jetsam was singing again, a little barroom ditty called 'The Death Song.'

"Oh you can die from scurvy,
And you can die from plague
You can croak when a rattlesnake
Bites you in the leg
You can die from shaving
From a thousand tiny cuts
Or go out in a world of pain
By a swift kick to the…"

Mako jumped up and grabbed his brother by the ankle, yanking him down.

"That's enough," he said.

Enough, I thought, though the thought had nothing to do with Jetsam's singing. Instead, the thought reflected a sense of peace that settled over me. Jasmine was asking me to die. But was this such a sacrifice considering I was already dead? I'd had my time in the world. I wanted more. But, deep down, I recognized the fundamental selfishness of this desire. Who was I, among the hordes of mankind, to dare ask for more than my allotted time? I'd gotten a lifetime. Wasn't that enough?

I said to Jasmine, "You seem to know more about being dead than I do. It caught me by surprise that there was something after life. What happens once I throw myself down Rott's throat? What follows death after death?"

"I've never had the courage to find out," said Jasmine, turning her face away, hugging herself.

I slowly walked to the back of the boat. Was I doing the right thing? If my life had ever caught the attention of a biographer, it's a sure bet he could have written my story without checking a thesaurus to find a synonym for 'self-sacrifice.' Maybe I could wait a little while longer, until the dragon was actually chewing on the timbers, just to make sure what I was about to do was really necessary.

Infidel's boots were a good two feet off the deck as she studied the approaching monster. Curiously, in life, whenever I dreamed of Infidel, I nearly always dreamed we were flying. It was natural to see her in this element. And in her white armor trimmed with silver it was a simple thing to imagine her in a wedding gown. She deserved a more regal ceremony than our shared vows in the midst of that shadowy jungle. Yet, those vows had been made, and I held them to be sacred. This was my bride, she wore my ring, she carried my child, and for her I would throw myself into the teeth of any monster.

And such a monster! Rott was fully at the surface now, a bloated corpse crawling with flies, riding so high upon the waves that its dead, flapping jaws opened to reveal a cavern more than large enough to swallow the *Freewind.* The sky was no longer sunset red, but mostly black as a million oil-black gulls, feathers falling from wings of bone, spiraled through the air in vast clouds to feast upon the corpse of their carrion master.

The Romers seemed paralyzed as they stared at the horrid thing less than a ship's length off the stern.

"The waves smell like pure vinegar now," said Cinnamon, wrinkling her nose.

"Should we… attack it? We have bows," said Mako. It was the first time I'd ever heard him sound doubtful.

"Even it wasn't already dead, that thing's the size of an island," said Rigger. "It wouldn't even notice."

"How can it notice anything? It has no eyes! Nothing but empty sockets!" said Jetsam.

"Something's drawing it to us," said Sorrow. "Something…" She turned toward me, her eyes full of understanding.

"Is there nothing we can do to… to discourage it?" asked Mako.

Rigger shook his head. "How do you discourage the dead?"

Taking this as my motto, I embraced my final moment with gusto. I walked to Infidel, whose head was conveniently at the level of my own thanks to her defiance of gravity. I spun her and gave her a powerful hug, taking care not to crush her. I pressed my coconut jaw against her cheek and tried to whisper, "I love you no matter what," though my kazoo voice bleated the words in such a graceless tone that the Divine Author alone knows what she might have heard. Then I thrust the folded letter into her grasp, leapt to the railing, and with a roguish tip of my tri-corn hat announced, "As I stand in the vestibule of self-abnegation, I wish to say that I have no regrets. Unfortunately, that would be the foulest lie. I fiercely regret my impending absence." I fixed my pecan eyes squarely on Infidel, who looked utterly confused by the erratic behavior of Sorrow's driftwood construct. I directed my final words to her alone: "If I had a thousand lives to give, I'd give them for you. My life was nothing but an empty glass until you filled it with the wine of your company. May the Divine Author guide his sacred quill to write the happy ending you deserve."

All the Romers were staring at me with mouths agape. I gave them a crisp salute, then turned and leapt toward the decaying beast. The jaws surged forward upon the waves as if driven by hunger. The tip of one of his teeth tore through my shirt as I fell into the chasm of his mouth. As Rott's wicked fangs closed behind me, it occurred to me that my farewell speech might have been more moving if I'd remembered to mention my name.

10 - BODIES IN MOTION

A WRIGGLING CARPET of worms covered the black, bloated tongue, which oozed pale puss as I tried to gain my balance. The tongue was a mass of muscular knots, stiff with rigor mortis, but my boots had trouble finding traction in the slime. The rotting skin covering the dead muscle peeled away as I slipped to my hands and knees. The putrescence that soaked into my gloves would certainly have cost me the contents of my stomach, if I'd had a stomach. I shook my hands to cleanse them, but succeeded only in splattering the awful ick across my face. I prayed to the divine author that my paper tongue was useful only for speech, and insensate to taste should a drop find its way past my ragged lips.

The vinegar swells pushed Rott's jaws to a lazy chew, slamming me against the boney mouth roof. Despite the unpleasantness of my surroundings, I felt strangely unthreatened. The beast was too dead to even swallow. Would I have to crawl down its gullet to meet my final end?

A sudden jolt toppled me. As I rolled over, I saw that the beast's snout had collided with the rudder of the *Freewind*. If I was to save the ship, it was apparently up to me to march into Rott's stomach. The dragon of entropy was also the dragon of indolence.

My gloves found purchase in the crack of a massive tooth. I pulled myself up and struggled to advance, inch by precious inch, through the cavernous mouth. In the dim shadows at the back of the gullet I saw shapes, vaguely human. I drew closer and found that the undulation of the waves had caused the beast to regurgitate the corpses of sailors. The dead men surged toward me as Rott's body rode a particularly energetic swell. The walking dead I could have faced bravely, but these were the half-digested dead, as listless and lifeless as their master. I let loose a buzzing scream. Even without brains to give the dead sailors purpose or muscles to drive their limbs, their advance was effective. I was knocked over by their collective weight, struggling helplessly as they dragged me down beneath their slimy, acid dripping forms. My left leg slipped deep beneath the tongue and with a sudden jolt I was limbless from the knee down, my wooden foot sliced free by the beast's closing teeth.

I had no time to dwell upon my own dissolution, however, for behind me there was a far louder crunch. I strained to look backward and found half the rudder of the *Freewind* splintered. Was my sacrifice in vain? Was the beast not to be satisfied until all the ship was in its bowels?

"I'm the one you want," I shouted, as the jaws clamped shut, plunging me into utter darkness. "I'm the lost soul you seek!"

There was a loud crash behind me. Light suddenly filled the mouth, bright as dawn. I pushed aside the liquefying décolletage of a decaying woman to see the source of the illumination. The teeth at the front of the mouth had been shattered. Standing in the gap was a goddess in pristine white armor, her hammer ablaze. She had a red bandana tied tightly over her mouth and nose to protect her from the stench as she swung her weapon in wide arcs, shattering columns of ivory thick as tree trunks to rid the beast of fangs. Yet her eyes weren't focused on the demolition. Instead, they searched the cavernous mouth, narrowing as she spotted the mound of corpses that even now dragged me down the gullet.

In a flash she reached me, planting her feet on either side of my shoulders as she pulverized the half-gelatinized bodies with roundhouse swings of the Gloryhammer.

"Infidel!" I cried as I grabbed her pristine white boot.

"Stagger!" she answered. "Is it truly you?"

"I'm the lost soul you seek," I said, in what would have been a sob if my tongue had been up to the task. "How did you know it was me? You haven't had time to read the letter!"

"'The vestibule of self-abnegation?' Please. Why didn't you say something earlier?"

"Sorrow didn't build me with a tongue. She just gave me the power of speech a few hours ago."

Satisfied that she'd cleared away the corpses, she grabbed my outstretched hand and pulled me, freeing my lower half from beneath the rotten tongue.

"Your leg," she said, looking pale.

"It doesn't hurt," I said. "Sorrow can make another."

"Not if I kill her first," she growled. "How could she do this to you?"

"I don't believe it was personal," I said, as Infidel helped me stand.

"Why did you jump into this damn thing's mouth?" she asked.

"Rott knows I should be dead. Sacrificing myself is the ship's only hope. You have to let me finish this."

"This thing can't chew without teeth," said Infidel, swinging her hammer to pulverize the fang nearest us.

"Look at the size of the jaws!" I protested. "It can swallow the ship whole!"

"If it can catch us," said Infidel, thrusting her hammer into the gap left by the missing tooth, then shooting skyward, dragging me to freedom. We arced back over the *Freewind*, my remaining boot clipping the crow's nest as she dropped toward the bow. There was a giant cleat there that held a rope as thick as a woman's arm. Infidel dropped me, then wrapped the rope over her shoulder and launched herself toward the sky once more. She grunted as the line went taut, having flown only a few feet beyond the tip of the jibboom. Her right arm, holding the Gloryhammer, was thrust straight before her. The rope was tight enough a man could have walked upon it.

With a squawking bark, Menagerie sank his teeth into the rope and began to flap his wings furiously.

The bow of the *Freewind* creaked as this single point of force created by the two aeronauts strained to move the ship through the undulating sea.

"It's as good an idea as any," shouted Jetsam, as he threw himself to hug the main mast then pushed his feet out behind him and began to vigorously kick against the air.

"That's the spirit!" shouted Mako. He turned to his siblings and shouted, "Throw anything you can overboard! Lighten the load! We'll outrun death itself!"

"You're mad!" snorted Rigger. "These three can't drag the ship no matter how hard they try. It's a simple matter of mass!"

He ducked as a barrel shot past his head, courtesy of Poppy, though I don't think she'd intentionally aimed for him.

"Given that you're floating on an enchanted ocean being pursued by a fundamental force of nature manifesting itself as an enormous snake, I admire your devotion to logic," Sorrow said to Rigger. "But if the Gloryhammer can move a person through the air, why can't it move a ship?"

But any sense of optimism that Sorrow might have been trying to build was demolished as the *Freewind* shook violently, knocking everyone off their feet. Rott's jaws had just flapped shut, trapping the entire rear of the boat.

"Rott's momentum was greater than our own," Rigger said, rising to his hands and knees. "You can't just stop a mass like that! You can't drag a ship forward on wishful thoughts!"

Despite Rigger's pessimism, the lifeless, limp jaws soon washed open and the *Freewind* limped forward another yard. We were moments away from doom, but moments do matter.

"Get every sail up," said Mako.

"There's no damn wind without mother!" screamed Rigger.

"He'll have a harder time washing us down his gullet if we're fully rigged," said Mako.

"Or if his jaws were frozen shut," I whispered.

"You're thinking of Purity's sword?" asked Sorrow, kneeling beside me to examine my missing leg.

"I'm thinking of the Jagged Heart!"

"Do you know how to activate its powers?" she asked, as she grabbed a belaying pin from the deck. She swiftly fashioned a peg leg from the wood to restore my mobility.

"Not a clue. But I watched Aurora summon a wall of ice thick enough to survive a direct blast of Greatshadow's breath using the harpoon. It's worth a try." I stood on my new peg leg, my arms outstretched for balance.

"The good part of your plan is, should you succeed, we'll get staved in by an iceberg instead of chewed to bits," grumbled Rigger.

His words were almost drowned out by ropes dancing through every block and tackle on the ship, raising all the sails in great, noisy flaps. Despite his dour attitude, Rigger was doing what he could.

Sage stood nearby, watching the sails unfurl. I felt a stir of optimism as I saw her black curls flicker in a breeze. But, as the yards of canvas settled into position, they hung limp. The only breeze had been that caused by the sails unfurling.

Sage shook her head sadly as she stared into her spyglass. "Two minutes," she said to Rigger. "If I'm calculating the undulations of the body on the currents correctly, we have two minutes before we get gnawed again. We have to gain some speed!"

"We've just enough time to puff our way out of this if we all take deep breaths," said Rigger, with mock cheerfulness.

Sage chewed her fingernails as her gaze shifted from her spyglass to the sails to the bow, where Infidel and Menagerie strained against the rope. Her eyes widened as she watched Menagerie's frantic flapping. Without warning she bolted across the deck, toward my fallen notebook and the bottle of ink that lay nearby. She didn't waste time locating a quill, but simply popped the stopper free and pressed the tip of her index finger to the bottle as she upended it. She smeared something quickly upon the page as she ran back to Rigger, still standing at the wheel.

"Wings!" she cried, holding the book open before him. "We need wings! You can make them!"

Rigger furrowed his brow as he tried to decipher his sister's strange babblings. The crude thing she'd scrawled on the page wasn't helping him understand her. I dragged myself up on my new leg, off balance as it was a good two inches shorter than its more carefully formed mate.

I limped toward the wheel, and saw that Sage had drawn what looked like a banana with two big ovals coming off it. Luckily, the fate of the ship didn't rest on my understanding her gist. At the instant when I was most completely baffled, Rigger's eyebrows raised up. "I've never tried anything like this!" he said, sounding excited. "It will destroy the sails and the rigging just to—"

"Try!" screamed Sage. "We don't even have a minute before it hits us again!"

Rigger let go of the wheel and threw his hands toward the mainsail, as if he were grabbing it in his mind. He gave a violent sideways tug with his hands and suddenly the ropes rigging the mainsail shattered the thick block and tackle housings that held them. The ropes flew in opposing directions, jerking the mainsail completely taut. With a sickening sound no sailor ever wants to hear, the mainsail ripped, splitting right down its center.

"Rigger!" Mako shouted, dropping the barrel he was throwing overboard and running toward his brother. "Have you lost your mind?"

Rigger didn't answer. His face contorted, turning red. His jaw clenched as if he were straining to lift an impossibly heavy weight. The ropes pulled the split mainsails toward opposite sides of the boat, the canvas taut as kites. The ropes stayed taut even as a wave rippled through them, unleashing a powerful flapping sound as Rigger threw his arms back.

The boat surged forward with enough momentum that I had to grab the wheel for balance.

The drawing suddenly made sense.

"Wings!" Sage shouted at Mako. "We've turned the mainsail into wings!"

Rigger brought his hands forward once more, the sails dancing like flags, until they caught air as Rigger spread his arms as if he were doing a breaststroke.

Behind us, the massive jaws were once more closing.

"Just one more yard!" screamed Sage

Rigger gave a third flap, then dropped to his knees. Behind us, Rott's jaws closed on empty air.

The wing-sails suddenly went limp, dropping into the water.

"I can't hold them any more," Rigger groaned as he fell on his side. "Without the aid of the pulleys, the weight is too much! I feel as if I've torn every muscle in my body."

"Cut those ropes and sails loose!" Sage shouted. "They'll cost us our speed."

Mako and Cinnamon drew swords and ran to the taut ropes hanging overboard.

"You did good, Rigger," said Sage, kneeling beside her trembling brother. "We're moving faster than we were, and bodies in motion want to stay in motion."

Indeed, we were moving forward, though barely at the speed of a good walk. Now that the ship had been given a nudge by the makeshift wings, the Gloryhammer's magic proved sufficient to maintain this momentum. Rott remained too close for comfort, and flies still covered the ship, but even without waiting for Sage's new calculations, I could see that we were putting precious inches between us and the dead thing at our tail.

"I command you to keep pulling!" a voice shouted from the front of the ship. "Know that the royal family salutes your courage!" It was Bigsby, posed heroically upon the bow, waving his fist at Infidel and Menagerie. "When I return home, my father will reward you handsomely for your heroism!"

But, instead of finding encouragement in the dwarf's words, Infidel shouted back, "My damn arm's about to come out of its socket! I can't do this much longer!"

Back at the main mast, Jetsam suddenly dropped to the deck. Dark circles of sweat stained his black shirt under the arms. "I'm spent," he whispered.

In truth, I doubted he'd added much to our speed.

Our gains were only temporary and I had the only plan that might maintain them. I headed for the hatch to retrieve the Jagged Heart. My idea was to weigh down Rott with so much ice that he couldn't move. What could it hurt to try?

But, before I could go down the hatch, I was met by a woman heading up the stairs. It was Gale Romer, her hair drenched in sweat and twisted back behind her ears in a crude bun held in place by a few pins. Stray strands were plastered to her neck, which sported a half dozen bite marks. Rather than the modest nightgown she'd worn when last I saw her, she wore Brand's white silk shirt, cinched around her waist by a braided leather whip. Her cheeks were flushed red, her lips swollen and dark.

The oversized shirt hung to the middle of her thighs and her legs were bare. For a woman almost my age, her limbs were rather shapely; I was particularly struck by the superb design of her feet and toes. The Divine Author was also an excellent architect, though it could be that my thoughts were pushed in this direction by my stumbling attempts at movement now that one of my 'feet' was no bigger around than a coat button.

Gale climbed onto deck and wasted little time accessing the situation. A strong wind filled the remaining sails and pushed us forward. "Mako, take the wheel!" she barked. "Where's Rigger! What happened to the mainsail?"

"Rigger's hurt!" shouted Sage, as she cradled her brother's head in her lap. "He pushed himself too hard and it's all my fault!"

"We're being pursued by Rott," Sorrow said to Gale. "I advise that you take us back to the material realm. Perhaps Abyss can intervene to halt his restless advance."

"And I advise you to go back to your quarters and wait," said Gale. "A full span of daylight must pass between our jumps. We can't make the journey back until nightfall."

"Six hours to go," said Brand, glancing down at a pocket watch as he emerged onto the deck. He was as sweaty as Gale, and his shirtless back was covered with scratch marks.

Suddenly, there was flapping overhead. I looked up to see Infidel and Menagerie coming toward me. "If we've got wind, I guess I'm done," she said.

Bigsby didn't approve of them quitting. He chased after them, shaking his fists, yelling, "I didn't tell you to stop!"

Gale casually stuck out a leg to trip Bigsby as he ran past. She pinned him beneath her foot as she said, "Anyone want to tell me how this dwarf got on board?"

"Ah, right," said Brand, running his hand through his hair. "You weren't really yourself when I made introductions. This is my, uh, my... sister. Princess Innocent Brightmoon."

I stopped paying attention. I'd already heard this conversation, and I happened to know that the true Princess Innocent Brightmoon was present and accounted for. As Infidel landed, I threw my arms around her. She hugged me back, though only for a brief instant. "Sorry," she said, turning her face away, her voice catching in her throat.

"Are you crying?"

"Gagging," she said. "You stink. Like, seriously. Some of that dragon goo has seeped into you."

Sorrow approached. "Indeed. I saw it - and smelled it - when I examined your leg. I'll continue to repair your physical form while I can, but I fear you may not last much more than another day or two. The wood I crafted you from is rotting at an accelerated pace. I can replace bits as they fall off, but as the last fragments of the original binding decay, so too, will the enchantment fail."

"Speaking of binding... ," said Infidel, dropping the shaft of the Gloryhammer into her gauntlet with a rather menacing *slap*. "What have you done to my husband, Sorrow?"

"In fairness, I didn't know he was your husband. He was merely a wandering spirit discovered at random by my soul-catcher. A lost soul was required to animate my golem. He didn't reveal his true identity until later."

"Because you wouldn't let me write!" I protested. "For that matter, you could have built me with a tongue."

"Conversations with lost souls are tedious affairs," Sorrow explained.

"Stop saying I was lost!" I said. "I was following Infidel."

"I knew it," Infidel said. "I could feel you beside me. I never had any doubt."

"The two of you should be grateful to me for making this brief reunion possible," said Sorrow, crossing her arms.

I began to peel off my clothes. They fell apart at the seams as I tugged on them. "Tossing these rags overboard will help with my general ripeness. I'll also dip back into the Sea of Wine to try to wash more of the stink off me; the wine didn't hurt me before. Maybe alcohol will slow my decay. That was my theory in life, at least."

"Cold also slows decay," said Sorrow. "We can use the Jagged Heart to chill you after you return from your bath. The cold shouldn't harm you. But let's not fool ourselves. We'll never completely remove Rott's curse. Decay was built into your body from the start." She looked down at her withered left hand. "Just like everyone else. Now that you two are reunited, I advise that you treat your remaining time together as brief."

Sorrow took one last glance at me as she turned away. Then, she whirled back around, her eyebrows raised as she examined the staves of my barrel chest. "By the thirteenth nail," she whispered, sounding dazed. But while her eyes were fixed and motionless, her hand was busily searching the folds of her cloak. She pulled out a small silver rod that melted in her grasp, flowing like mercury to coat her hand with a thin glove of precious metal. She gingerly probed my chest to wiggle free a black shard embedded in the boards. Her gauntlet instantly turned dark gray with tarnish.

"What is it?" I asked.

"A fragment of Rott's tooth," she whispered as she looked at the object, roughly the size and shape of a man's middle finger.

"Yeah. He snagged me as I first went in."

She produced a golden coin and coated the black shard with a thin layer of the precious metal. "Gold will seal it," she said. "It can withstand corruption better than any other metal."

"Funny," said Infidel. "I thought gold was the chief cause of corruption."

I almost asked what Sorrow intended to do with the shard, but decided I'd rather not know the answer.

"You should see to your bath," said Sorrow, not looking at me.

Infidel assisted as I tied a rope around myself and slipped down into the wine. The ship now moved at a good clip through the sea. The waves buffeted me, and I climbed out mere moments after I went in, lest the current tear me apart. As I inched my way back up the rope, I watched with morbid fascination as pale white worms writhed free of the wood of my limbs. The wine had left them drunk or poisoned. They fell away, vanishing into the burgundy beneath me, leaving me filled with tiny holes.

I made it back to the deck, utterly sodden.

"How do I smell now?" I asked, as the wine puddled around me.

"Just like you used to," said Infidel, as she wrapped me in her embrace.

II - I COULD OPEN THE DOOR

WE LAY IN the bed, my coconut skull resting on Infidel's outstretched arm. We'd been talking for hours with a lightness that might have struck others as curious given our greater circumstances. But, our marriage was built first and foremost on friendship. We'd loved each other chastely for over a decade, separated by my cowardice and Infidel's former powers. When she'd been as strong as a dragon, she'd been afraid to even hug me for fear of maiming me. My new wooden carcass was equally useless for intimacy. If our relationship had been built merely on lust, it couldn't have endured the strange barriers fate had constructed between us. Fortunately, deeper bonds held us together.

So it was ironic that we were talking about falling apart.

"Fixing your leg wasn't a problem. Why can't we do that when the rest of you rots away? Can't we just keep changing parts?" she asked, tracing my seed-pod ears with her fingers.

"I don't know," I buzzed, wishing I could whisper, or convey any tone at all. "Perhaps I'll continue being a ghost. Or perhaps I'll simply fade away."

She swallowed.

I said, "When I first... died, I, uh, I had an ... experience. It's tough to describe. I felt like I was part of the larger universe. I felt like my... my energy had been concentrated in my old body, and now that it had been cut loose I was... dissipating. Spreading out. Like I was everywhere at once, a tiny part of everything. It wasn't... it wasn't scary. I felt at peace. I felt connected to something bigger than myself."

"And you think that will happen again?" She stared up at the beams of the ceiling, then closed her eyes. "It doesn't sound so bad."

"No," I said. "But it doesn't sound even half as good as staying with you."

"I want you to be with me too," she said.

"But what if I can't? What if the next time I slip free from the world I don't come back?"

"Then I'll miss you and remember you," said Infidel, stoically. "We face the same future as every other marriage. The day comes when one of the spouses is no longer around. When brides and grooms say, 'Til in death we part,' they don't know if they are making a promise for fifty years or fifty seconds. We just… we just have a little more information than most people do."

This was another reason I loved her. Underneath her swaggering bravado, beneath the mask of her daredevil grin, Infidel was a person who understood her limits. She'd always accepted there were some fights too big for her. Unlike Sorrow, she'd never decided to avenge herself against the father who'd wronged her, or declare war on the church that pursued her. She'd merely declared herself done with their madness, and carved her life anew.

Infidel nudged aside a loose barrel slat on my chest and peered into the darkness.

"So it's costing you energy to animate this body?"

"That's what Sorrow says. I don't really feel any different."

"But you could be free if you weren't trapped inside that silver bug?"

"Actually, I've been able to slip out of the mosquito. Now I'm trapped by the golden cage that forms this body's heart."

Infidel stared into the center of my chest for several long seconds.

"I could open the door," she said.

I didn't hesitate for even a second. "The best moment of my life was the moment I opened my heart to you. Do it."

For a fleeting instant, I regretted the words. We were messing with magic neither of us understood. But it was too late to protest as her slender hand slipped into my hollow chest and found the cage. I heard a tiny *click* as the door opened.

Infidel carefully withdrew her fingers. "Did that do anything? Are you free?"

I didn't answer. Though I heard her, once more I had shrunk down within my enchanted body, becoming a tiny homunculus standing beside the silver mosquito, staring at the open door of the cage.

I walked to the lip. Through the slats I could see Infidel's chest pressed next to mine, her white and silver armor gleaming in the faint light cast by the Gloryhammer, which was floating the corner, draped with a sheet to soften its glow.

I stepped out of the cage.

Instantly, the silver wires that pierced my spiritual body fell free. I was once more a full sized phantom floating above the bed. The room seemed subtly different than the one I'd been in mere seconds before. For one thing, the room now possessed color. The bruise on Infidel's brow had a blue tint rimmed by a jaundiced yellow. The quilt we lay upon was a patchwork of a dozen faded green hues. The air in the room had been mostly dead to me before, but now smelled of wine, mixed with a shore at low-tide.

My wooden body lay completely limp. Infidel shook its shoulder. "Stagger?"

"I'm okay," I said. "I'm here." Of course, she didn't hear me.

"Stagger?" she asked again, staring desperately into my pecans as tears welled in her eyes.

Willingly, I flew back into the wooden body, shrinking as I approached the cage. I stepped through the open door and the silver wires snaked to life and jabbed into me once more. I turned and found the cage door remained open. Was I now able to come and go as I pleased?

For now, I was more focused on the coming than the going. I felt my life force move into every fiber of the rotting wood. My coconut skull shifted on my shoulders as I brought my gaze to hers.

"It's okay," I said. "I'm still here."

She hugged me tightly, as her tears came in earnest.

She regained her composure a moment later. "Good," she whispered. "Good. Because… I know you can't stay forever. But… but I don't want you to go yet."

Before I could tell her I wasn't planning on going anywhere, the door to our room swung open.

"I've finished preparing the bands of negation," Sorrow said, poking her head around the door. "Do you want to take part in the questioning?"

"Don't you knock?" Infidel asked, propped up on one elbow to look over me. "What if we'd been naked?"

"He *is* naked," said Sorrow. "Just come as you are. Gale says she'll be ready in fifteen minutes."

Infidel had never taken off her armor since the fight. We hoped that the magic that kept it immaculate would protect her from any lingering death juice that might seep from my pores. When I rose from the bed, I couldn't help but notice I left behind a faint outline of sawdust. There were tiny things with tiny jaws within me, grinding me down. This is true of all men, I suppose. I remember the same feeling from ten years ago when I'd first noticed how much hair I was leaving in my comb.

At the end of the hall, Sorrow stood in the main hold. Purity was tied to a simple wooden chair. The left side of her face was bruised where I'd clocked her. She'd been stripped of her armor and dressed in one of Gale's nightgowns. Her arms were bound behind her; her feet were tied to the legs of the chair. Surrounding her were several concentric circles of iron stretching out to a full five feet around her. I saw no signs of torture, but Purity stared at the floor with an empty gaze, as if all will had drained from her.

I was curious as to what was so important that Gale wasn't here already. It seemed like a good time to test my powers now that my heart cage was open. I leaned against the wall, crossing my arms as if I was merely waiting. Satisfied that my body was propped up sufficiently, I abandoned the cage.

It worked. I flew free once more, ghosting through the wall into what I thought was Gale's room. Only, instead of Gale's room, I found I was in the bunkroom that Mako, Rigger, and Jetsam shared. Mako and Jetsam stood together next to their bunks, their ears pressed to the wall.

I realized where I'd gotten turned around and flashed through the further wall and found Gale speaking to Brand. I'd obviously caught them in mid-conversation.

"— Unforgivable," she said. Gale was dressed once more in her captain's garb. Her long heavy coat looked uncomfortable in the sweltering confines of the room, but I had to admit she was an imposing figure in her full uniform. The padding gave her broad shoulders, adorned with gleaming brass buttons. Her buccaneer boots made her feet look heavy and solid, as if nothing in the world could push her over. Her hair was pulled back into a tight knot. Her eyes were hard and emotionless. She was standing with her hands behind her back, her posture rigid and formal.

Brand was seated on a low stool before her. He hung his head, looking like a scolded puppy.

"You're fired as my dryman," said Gale, in a calm tone.

"How about as your lover?" Brand said, managing a grin.

"Love was never part of our relationship. I've physical cravings. You satisfied them adequately, and were compensated for your trouble. It won't be difficult to replace you."

He shook his head. "I don't think you mean that."

"Are you saying you're a better judge of my true feelings than I am?"

"I think I might be, yeah," he said. "I mean, I knew when you first laid eyes on me that you wanted me for more than just my skills at haggling. But I didn't enter your bed because you offered me a job. I took one look at you and knew I was in the presence of a true woman, a creature of the world. I've looked into the eyes of many a young naïf and found them to be nothing but shallow pools. Your eyes were oceans, and I've loved swimming in your depths. I've come to know your soul, Gale."

Captain Roamer sighed. "Yesterday, I might have found such flattery charming. Now, it only adds to the evidence that you're nothing but a silver-tongued scoundrel. Bringing a stowaway onto my ship? What were you thinking? I'd have tossed you into the Sea of Wine already, but I can't help but be curious as to what your game is."

"Bigsby's my brother," Brand said, shrugging his shoulders. "I couldn't just leave him."

"Don't you mean sister?" Gale said sarcastically. "I'm not ignorant of Silver Isle politics. King Brightmoon has no son named Steadfast. And Bigsby's been selling fish in Commonground for longer than Princess Innocent has been missing. If you must lie, why lie so clumsily?"

Brand sighed. "Look, if I want to lie, I swear I can come up with a more plausible yarn than this one. I can't tell you what my game is because there is no game. I've just been reacting to events that even I find difficult to believe."

Gale crossed her arms. "Go on."

"Here's the simple truth," said Brand. "Bigsby is my brother, though we've never met before two days ago. My real name is Brand Cooper. I'm the son of Perfect Cooper, founder of the Cooper Barrel Works."

Gale looked skeptical. I was a little dubious myself. Cooper Barrel Works made half the barrels in the Shining Lands. Perfect Cooper was a very wealthy man.

"My father is quite old," said Brand. "Five years ago, he fell into a seizure while on the toilet. We found him barely alive. He survived, but was a changed man. He was too weak to walk for almost a year. He couldn't even talk for over a month, but when he did regain his powers of speech, he told me quite the tale."

Gale tilted her head. "And now I suppose you'll tell me a tale."

"My father has worked hard to live up to his name. He's famous throughout the realms because the quality of his product is unmatched. I was raised with this same eye toward perfection, trained in both body and mind to be flawless. But, in the grip of his malady, too weak to lift his limbs, Father confessed that he'd been a fool to demand perfection from mere human flesh. He told me of his greatest shame; almost thirty years before I'd been born, his first wife had given birth to his first son. Unfortunately, the child had been born with stunted limbs. His wife had died during the birth, and father had ordered the mid-wife to smother the baby. He couldn't bear the thought of the Cooper name being attached to a dwarf.

"The mid-wife vowed to follow his wishes and took the child from his home. Only, she had other plans for the baby. Circuses paid good money for freaks. In the months that followed, she carelessly displayed signs of newfound wealth. Father accused her of stealing from him. She confessed to having sold the infant."

"And you think Bigsby's that child?" asked Gale.

Brand nodded. "My father kept his secret for almost two decades. He remarried twice, but lost child after child to stillbirths. I thought I was the only child to have survived. But, on what he thought might be his deathbed, he told me his dark secret. He knew the name of the circus, and the date the child had been sold. He wanted me to find my missing brother and bring him home.

"Thus began my grand adventure. The circus my brother had been sold to had disbanded years before. The acts had all joined other outfits. It took me several years to follow all the leads. At first, I looked down upon the people I spoke too. I'd lived a sheltered life and been convinced of my superiority to vagabond performers. Eventually, I saw their world was far richer than the comfortable cage of my own upbringing. My father lived in luxury but had never been happy; the performers lived with hardship, yet had joyous hearts.

"I joined the circus. After I was accepted by my fellow performers, I finally learned the truth of my brother's whereabouts. He was called Bigsby, and he'd fled to Commonground after being accused of murder. I went to the docks to find passage to the Isle of Fire. Unfortunately, I didn't have a single coin in my pockets. I had a purse full of moons when I first left home, but as that money ran out, I discovered I could get by with charm alone. I heard rumors that your ship was in port to ferry a passenger to Commonground, but from what I knew of Wanderers, it was unlikely that mere charm would gain me passage. As fate would have it, I also heard that you needed a dryman and decided to take my chances. When we met, I knew I'd be setting sail with you. It was love at first sight."

"Merely lust," said Gale, crossing her arms. "Assuming I believe you, why does Bigsby think he's the princess? Why are you peddling this absurd lie?"

"I don't know. He suffered severe trauma when Greatshadow attacked Commonground. In his mind, the dwarf known as Bigsby is dead, and the princess has awakened to reclaim her birthright. When I called him Bigsby, he acted crazy. I mean, crazier. Like he was going to hurt himself. He stays relatively manageable as long as I play along with his fantasy. I'm hoping that he remembers his true identity before we return home."

"Why didn't you tell me this?"

"Events have their own momentum. You weren't aboard when I brought Bigsby back to the *Freewind*. I wasn't certain you'd welcome an unpaid passenger who was both a freak and insane. In retrospect, my hopes that he'd stay quiet and hidden until we made it back to the Silver Isles were perhaps naïve."

Gale sighed, rubbing her temples. "Perhaps. I wish you'd been honest. Things might have worked out differently. As it is… the best I can do is spare your lives. I'll put you off the ship at the next port."

"But—"

"This is mercy, Brand. It's more than I'd show anyone else in your circumstances."

"So you do still have feelings for me?" he asked.

"If I do, I assure you, they are not feelings you want me to give voice to. For now, be content that you're merely fired instead of facing sterner justice."

"I'm more than content," said Brand. "I'm joyous. I should never have accepted the job as your dryman."

Gale turned to leave. "Then we're of the same opinion."

He spoke before her hand fell on the wooden handle that opened the door. "Only if we both agree that there was something real between us. I should never have accepted your offer of employment since I knew when I saw you I wanted something more. The relationship of a boss to an employee is always going to be tainted by the power one holds over the other. To woo you properly, I must approach you as an equal."

"You aren't my equal," she sighed. "Despite your claims of inherited wealth, you're a penniless vagabond, while I am a ship's captain, responsible for my family and my business. Despite my ill turn of fortune due to these accursed slave wars, I'm respected as an honest woman. I've fought hard to ensure that my name means something in this world. I'm not certain I believe your story, but, if it's true, you've just admitted to pissing away your fathers money and amusing yourself among carnies rather that staying focused on your mission. You're irresponsible."

He shrugged, "Opposites attract."

Gale closed her eyes and took a deep breath. "I enjoyed you, Brand. It's been ten years since Rudder passed away. Oh, there was a man."

Brand nodded, though she couldn't see it.

She continued, "I've had no time for romance since he died. I've had quite a few Wanderer's court me – good men, good captains. But I'm too old to entangle my life with a man my age, with his own family and ship. I'm proud of the life I've made for myself; I've no interest in starting anew."

"You deserve to be proud," said Brand.

Gale shook her head. "I don't deserve anything. Nothing good can come of me thinking the world owes me some reward."

"The Gale Romer I know wouldn't indulge herself with pity."

Gale turned from the door to face him once more. "Pity has nothing to do with my feelings. Unlike you, I've experienced genuine love. Rudder was my life. Love wasn't merely sweet whispers or shared desire. We were bonded so strongly we felt like one being. We were two halves of the same whole. You can't know what losing him felt like."

"I don't pretend I can," said Brand. "But no matter who you were then, now, you're your own woman."

"Am I?" She crossed her arms. "My dryman at the time of Rudder's death was a man five years my senior named Hunter. We had a completely professional relationship. He would never have violated my trust. We worked together on running this ship side by side, day after day. We were the best of friends. And then… then one night, I was a little drunk on wine, and I decided we should be more than friends."

"You sound so guilty about it," said Brand. "But you were both adults. There's nothing to be ashamed of."

"In your eyes," she said. "We kept our relationship secret for a time, unsure how my children would react. But, you know I enjoy… I like…." Her voice trailed off.

"A little role-playing," said Brand.

Her cheeks flushed red. "We were in the galley. We thought all the children were above deck. Hunter had me pressed up against the pantry with my arms bound behind my back with my blouse. I was making mock protests as he explored my body. And then… and then Levi walked in."

"Your oldest son."

Gale nodded. "I… I know how it must have looked to Levi. But… he'd known Hunter for years. He should have trusted that Hunter was no rapist. Instead, he grabbed a butcher's knife from the block and plunged it into Hunter's back."

Brand rose from the stool and looked as if he were going to hug Gale. She pressed her right hand into his chest and forced him back down.

"I lost a son that day. I was so angry with Levi that he ran off. He now serves with the Stormguard. The Stormguard! My mortal enemies!"

Brand shrugged. "But this was before the Pirate Wars started. He wasn't betraying you then."

Gale gave a small, bitter laugh. "Oh Brand. Listen to me, still talking about Levi. He's dead to me. Dead." She gave him a stern look. "And he wasn't the point of my story at all."

"Then what was your point?" Brand asked.

"My point is that you're an attractive man who smells fantastic and happens to be a genius in the sack. I liked playing with you. But the only reason I've let you in my bed is that you aren't my equal. You're so obviously a toy. A trinket."

"A treasure?" Brand offered.

"A diversion. You're someone I could play with. Your presence might embarrass my children, but it didn't threaten them. They knew I wasn't taking you on as their new father."

"I'm not sure Mako felt that way."

"Mako's young. He's still trying to figure out how to project strength so that he can one day command his own ship. One day, he'll figure it out. Meanwhile, the rest of the Wanderer clans might hear that I was fooling around with you, but they wouldn't be gossiping about how families might get woven together and shipping interests merged. There are no political repercussions to bedding you. If you'd been my equal, Brand, I wouldn't have wanted you. I could only let you touch me because you were so inconsequential."

Brand's shoulders sagged. "You really are an expert with your tongue, aren't you?"

"You and the dwarf can bunk in the forecastle until we get back home. Keep out of my sight. The less I see you, the less I'll be inclined to change my mind about you."

"And take me back?" asked Brand.

"And keelhaul you," she said.

With this, she turned, and left her cabin.

In the hall, she met Mako, who was closing his door behind him. Mako grinned as he gave a nod of greeting. It was obvious from his satisfied expression that he'd heard every word. Gale scowled at him. If her eyes had been daggers, Mako would have bled.

12 - SOULS SNUFFED OUT

I FLEW BACK into my wooden body as the two Romers marched into the room. Without pausing for pleasantries, Mako grabbed Purity by the hair and pulled her head back so that she faced Gale. He tugged with such force that the front two legs of the wooden chair lifted up.

Purity's eyes remained dull as she stared at Captain Romer, who stood with her hands clasped behind her back, in the same formal posture she'd used when addressing Brand. A single whale-oil lantern above Purity's head lighted the room. The reflected flame danced in Gale's eyes.

"I threatened to keelhaul you in the Sea of Wine," said Gale, in a cool, firm tone. "I may yet. However, you've so far had the good luck not to inflict a single substantial injury on any member of my family. We've killed a dozen of your minions and captured the rest. Given the pathetic nature of your menace, if you cooperate and answer our questions, I'll spare your life."

Purity's unfocused eyes showed no hint of understanding.

Gale tried her speech again, switching to Skelling. The woman still didn't react.

"She has no reason to answer us," grumbled Mako as he let go of her hair. He came around and grabbed Purity by the chin and turned her gaze toward his. He pulled his lips back to reveal his toothy jaws. "She'll be more cooperative if you let me chew on her a bit. Maybe her left ear should go first?"

"Stand aside," said Sorrow, pushing Mako away. She crouched before the woman and looked deeply into her eyes. She shook her head slowly. "Something's wrong. I've seen this look before."

"Where?" said Gale.

"Among the Skellings. I told you I've traveled to the Isle of Grass. I barely survived my visit. Among the Skellings, women are treated as little more than cattle. There are no words in their language for romantic love. Marriage is indistinguishable from a master/slave relationship. I tried to help these women escape their oppressors, but couldn't. They'd endured such abuse that many of these women have literally had their souls snuffed out. They become empty shells, alive on an animalistic level, but devoid of free will."

"The other women we've imprisoned do seem unusually passive," said Gale.

"They're despondent in defeat," said Mako. "They were active enough when they were trying to chop our heads off."

I once more leaned against the wall and leapt from my body. All living things possess an internal light that my ghostly eyes can sense, though it's often so faint that I don't notice it in good lighting. Here in the dimly lit hold, everyone in the room possessed a spiritual aura save for our captive. Her body had barely more light than the chair she was tied to. Her aura was a faint, flickering indigo.

I flashed back into my wooden body just in time to catch it before it toppled over.

"I can verify this woman has no soul," I said.

"How can you know that?" asked Mako.

"My eyes are different than yours." I didn't want to hint to Sorrow that I could escape her cage at will.

"Soul or no soul, if she's willful enough to attack our ship, she's willful enough to avoid pain," said Mako, gnashing his teeth. "She *will* answer our questions."

Infidel interrupted. "Hey, what happened to her sword? I grabbed it off the deck earlier."

"We secured it while you were unconscious," said Mako.

"Bring it here," she said.

"You've no rightful claim to it," said Gale. "It was used in an unjust assault on this ship. By the code of the Wanderers, the sword is mine."

Infidel closed her eyes and sighed. "I'm not trying to take the damn sword. I've got a hunch. I'm the only person on this ship who regularly fights using a weapon crafted from the body of a primal dragon. When I use it, I feel… it's tough to describe, but it's like an energy flows into me. I can feel it all the way to my toes. And it's not just a physical thing. For lack of a better description, I feel it spiritually as well."

"What's your point?" asked Mako.

"Since the Ice-Moon Blade is part of Hush, what if it does something similar? What if… I don't know… it empowers Purity?"

Gale nodded toward Mako. "It's worth a shot. Bring it."

Mako left, muttering, his eyes narrowed. He returned moments later with the blade in his hand.

"I feel nothing when I hold the blade," he said, though his breath came out in a fog.

"You've a strong soul," I said. "Maybe its effects can only be felt by the weak."

"Careful," said Sorrow, taking the blade after coating her hands with silver to insulate herself. She knelt and placed the blade on the first band of negation. Nothing happened. Methodically, she moved the blade closer. The final band was only three inches from the captured woman's foot. As the barest edge of the blade crossed this threshold, frost suddenly painted the walls of the room.

The bound woman inhaled deeply, lifting her sagging head. Her irises, dark brown moments before, were now pale blue. She chuckled softly as her eyes fixed on Infidel.

"Ivory Blade," she said, smirking. "I never doubted you were on board."

Infidel stepped closer to Gale, so that Purity could better see her.

"People call me Infidel, not Ivory. If you really want to talk to Ivory, you're going to need a necromancer."

Purity pressed her lips tightly together, looking confused and disappointed.

"Why did you want Ivory Blade?" asked Gale.

"He stole the Jagged Heart from us! We cannot rest until it is recovered."

"The Jagged Heart didn't belong to you," said Infidel. "It belonged to the ice-ogres."

"It belonged to *Hush*," said Purity. "I'm her final prophet."

"Hush is a dragon, not a god," said Gale. "What use has she for prophets?"

"Hush isn't *a* god," said Purity. "She's *the* god. She's the great unifier, the secret truth beneath all of creation. She's eternal silence and eternal peace. It's my sacred duty to usher in her final reign."

"The ogres worship Hush as a goddess as well," said Infidel. "I was friends with the priestess you stole the Jagged Heart from. If you both worship the same god, why couldn't you just have asked politely to use the harpoon?"

"The ogres are unworthy, impure beings," said Purity, wrinkling her nose. "I tolerate them merely as pawns. They know nothing of Hush's true peace."

Gale shook her head. "If you value peace, why attack my ship unprovoked?"

"If you'd turned Ivory Blade over to us, no one would have been harmed."

"You do see the underlying flaw in that argument?" asked Infidel.

"I have only your word that Blade's dead," said Purity. "Assuming it's true, I would also assume that *you* are now my most likely lead to reclaiming the Jagged Heart."

Gale and Sorrow remained poker-faced. Infidel looked like she was about to say something, then didn't. She frowned slightly. If we'd been playing cards, this would be the moment I went all in.

Apparently I wasn't the only one good at reading her expressions.

"It's here?" Purity asked, as passion returned to her voice. She sat fully upright in the chair. "The Jagged Heart is aboard this ship?"

"No," said Infidel. "I don't know where it is. Blade was already dead when I took his armor."

"You're a terrible liar," said Purity.

"And you're tied to a chair while your followers are confined by manacles," said Gale. "Infidel isn't the one being questioned here. You are."

"Ask what you wish," said Purity. "Only the guilty have anything to hide."

"First, who are you really?" asked Sorrow. "Why does everyone call you Purity? Purity was an ancient witch, but I found her grave. She died ages ago."

"Ancient?" Purity chuckled. "Do I look ancient to you?"

Sorrow shook her head. "No. You're what? Thirty-five? Forty? And, if you were the real Purity, you wouldn't have needed the sword to do your ice magic. You'd have the power embedded in your skull. But I've felt your scalp. There's not a single nail in it."

The bound woman laughed.

"What so funny?" asked Sorrow.

"You and your ridiculous scalp, studded with nails. You truly believe these to be the source of your power?"

"I've empirical evidence that they work, yes."

"You know nothing of true magic," said Purity.

"Enlighten me," said Sorrow.

"True magic is passion. True magic is hatred and anger and the thirst for revenge. This is the power that binds me to this world two centuries after my first death."

Perhaps it was my imagination, but I thought Sorrow held her head a little higher upon hearing this definition of true magic.

Gale, on the other hand, looked exasperated. "Make up your mind. Are you after revenge or peace? You can't have both."

"Don't be foolish," said Purity. "Revenge fits peace like a hand fits a glove."

"If you've nothing to hide," said Sorrow, "tell us everything. If you don't use nails to gain your power, what is the source?"

"I've told you," said Purity. "Hatred binds me. When I was thirteen, Skellings attacked my village. I watched them disembowel my father while they raped my mother. Due to my youth and beauty, I was spared the worst of their violence. I was taken as a prize and presented to the Skelling overlord. His name was Gorg. He weighed three hundred pounds and smelled of rotten teeth. I was given to him on the eve of the winter solstice; it was considered good fortune for a Skelling warlord to deflower an innocent on that night. He was not gentle." Purity shook her head slowly, as if trying to fight back the memory.

"I'm sorry this fate befell you," said Sorrow. "I know all too well the cruelty of men. I intend to create a world where such things happen no more."

Purity's haunted expression changed to one of amusement. She chuckled softly. "You shall fail, little witch. Are you as blind as I was? Sheltered and protected, ignorant of the truth of the world?"

"My life has been anything but sheltered."

"Then release your dreams of a just world to the winds. They are of no more value than dust. The core of life is pain and violence. You can no more strip cruelty from the heart of man than you can peel thunder from lightning. I learned this truth well on the night Gorg tore my flesh with his violent lusts.

A weaker woman would have withered when faced with such a horrifying truth, to know that nothing compels the strong to have mercy upon the weak. I, on the other hand, embraced the truth. The world belongs to those strong enough to take it. I killed Gorg with his own dagger. I gouged his eyes from his fat face, then ran into the night, losing myself in the wild, frozen wastes of the Isle of Grass."

"I've experienced those wastes," said Sorrow. "You're lucky to have survived, especially during the winter solstice."

"But I didn't survive," said Purity. "I ran until I could no longer move my legs, then fell numb and senseless in the snow. My soul slipped loose of my body and I found myself alone, all alone, on an endless plain of ice. The sky above was bright with crisp stars. There was no wind. Never had I listened to such silence. I could see my lifeless body at my feet, the skin a pale blue white. I was draped in nothing but a bearskin blanket. My naked feet and hands had turned black. Frozen blood crusted my face, though I cannot say whether this was my blood, or Gorg's.

"I turned from my body and began to walk. That weak slab of meat and bone no longer felt important to me. I journeyed for a very long time. My feet left no trace upon the snow. The quiet absorbed my every thought. All the pain of life slowly faded from memory. Not just the abuse I'd suffered, but the tiny pains, the small day to day agonies that accompany a body, the pangs of hunger or thirst, the needle pricks of heat and cold. I was free. Truly free, in a world where all was black and white, where peace was the final solution. The one heartache I felt, the one pain, was to think that all the living world was denied such a heaven."

"No offense, but your afterlife sounds kind of boring," said Infidel. "I've been to a couple of dead lands counting the one we're in. Both had dragons, and definitely weren't dull."

"Ah," said Purity. "My afterlife had a dragon as well. Whether I walked for hours or years I cannot guess, but as I journeyed a shape rose on the horizon. As I grew closer I found a giant mountain of ice carved into a dragon. I entered through the mouth. Within this mountain there were tunnels. I explored them, drawn by a force I did not yet understand. In the center of the mountain, where a true dragon's heart would have been, I found an altar. Upon this altar was the Ice-Moon Blade. When I lifted it, my soul was pulled inside. Hush whispered to me. Then I woke.

"I was in a new body. It was springtime on the Isle of Grass, and the fields were covered in yellow flowers. In the placid melt-water of a nearby pool I saw that I was now a woman in her fifties. She was half lame and blind in her right eye as a result of beatings. I had only the faintest echo of her memories. She'd found the Ice-Moon Blade in a streambed where it had washed down from the glaciers. My spirit now filled a body whose original soul had withered long ago.

"I murdered her husband and his brothers, even her sons who treated her as no more than a slave. Eventually I was caught and killed. My soul once more retreated into the sword. What happened in the intervening gap I don't know, but a dozen years later a young woman, merely fourteen touched the blade. She'd suffered a miscarriage after being kicked in the belly by her father. I rode her for a long time, and killed many men as I mastered the true power of the Ice-Moon Blade. Eventually, that body fell. To this day, the Skellings call her grave my grave. Since then, nine different women have carried my soul."

"This one shall be your last," said Mako.

"Truly? Kill this body if you wish. Drag it in the Sea of Wine for all I care. My soul will always fly free and return to the blade."

Sorrow looked at me. "Looks like you aren't the only bodiless soul aboard. Maybe Rott wasn't after you. A two hundred year old soul is probably a tastier meal."

Purity shook her head. "Do you seek to intimidate me with talk of the dragon of decay? I'm the prophet of Hush. Her power is greater than that of entropy. She is timeless. She existed before all, and will endure beyond all. From eternal cold, dark and silent, the world has flickered. Now it sputters; soon it fades. The hush of an unending winter night is the only true eternity."

"The other primal dragons would argue with that," said Gale. "Certainly the sea is eternal; Abyss is more powerful than Hush."

Purity shook her head. "The sea shall freeze, go silent, and find peace. The oceans are merely restless ice. One day they shall slumber."

"I wouldn't be so cavalier about Rott. Death is forever," I said, aware of the irony that I should make such an argument.

"In the cold, even death loses power. Decay ceases. Entropy grinds to a halt."

"For a little while," said Infidel, raising the Gloryhammer. "But sooner or later, the sun will rise again."

"The sun?" growled Purity. "Glorious, the dragon of the sun, shall be the first to die when the Jagged Heart is in my grasp."

"What?" asked Mako, sounding amused. "You're going to go jab the sun with a harpoon?"

"Killing it forever, yes," said Purity.

Mako no longer looked amused. His brow furrowed as he looked at his mother. "That, uh, can't happen, can it?"

Infidel cleared her throat, "When I was in Greatshadow's realm, he told me that the Jagged Heart was created when Hush fell in love with Glorious and had her advances rebuffed. The bad blood goes back a long way."

"This is stupid," said Mako. "How does one harpoon the sun?"

"You can't," said Sorrow. "Not in the material world. But in the abstract realms?"

I buzzed in with my paper tongue. "Aurora told me the Jagged Heart had the power to open the door to an abstract realm. Something called the Great Sea Above. It's like heaven for ice-ogres."

"I say it can't happen," said Mako, crossing his arms.

"I dunno," said Infidel. "Greatshadow said the harpoon could have killed him. The abstract realms follow the same rules as dreams. Anything's possible."

"No," said Sorrow. "Not anything. It's not dreams that lie beneath the abstract realms; it's myth. Myths are symbolic, resonant truth. Dreams don't have to make sense. Myths must make more sense than actual reality."

"I get that dreams are kind of random," said Infidel. "But I hardly would call the myths I learned as a child sensible. I remember one where a wolf disguised himself as an old woman. Not exactly plausible."

"It's not the details that matter," said Sorrow. "It's the message. Myths are the vessels of great truths. They teach us about justice and love and courage. They help define who we are. Every culture I know of has a myth explaining the creation of the world, and foretelling its destruction. The notion that, before there was heat and light, there was cold and darkness, is a pretty common belief. Simple symmetry predicts that if cold was the beginning, it shall also be the end. Myths follow grand cycles. Everything that is created must one day be destroyed."

Mako threw up his hands, utterly frustrated. "So you're telling me it makes sense that someone can stab the sun with a long, pointy stick and kill it? You and I live in very different realities."

Sorrow nodded. "The thing about myths is they tend to overpower reality. The great truths they carry have the power to push aside the more mundane truths of the material world."

"That's the most absurd thing I've ever heard anyone say," said Mako.

"I agree," Sorrow said, with a shrug. "That doesn't make it false. I'm a materialist. My powers come from seeing through the illusions that limit most people when they interact with the material world. Even though my mind is superbly attuned to recognize reality, I live my life in daily pursuit of things that are not real. I search for justice. I follow a code of honor. I pursue fairness and equality. But justice, honor, fairness, equality… these aren't real. They don't exist as measurable objects. If I had a scale, and on one plate sat a single grain of sand, I could not place a single crumb of honor upon the counter plate to balance it. Yet I value these things more than food, shelter, or any comfort. I've pledged my life to advance these causes. Just because something isn't real doesn't mean it isn't true."

"Truth is stark," said Purity, staring at Sorrow. "Truth is hard. And truth is all that matters."

I scratched my coconut skull. I'd heard these words before, from Father Ver. Was it pure coincidence that I'd hear them again? Or was it just evidence that when you stripped away the quibbling details of the various faiths, all fanatics essentially thought alike?

There were three loud bangs on the boards above us that caused everyone to jump.

"Ma!" Jetsam shouted, sounding as if he were kneeling on the deck directly above.

"What?" Gale shouted back.

"Sage said to let you know it was time," shouted Jetsam.

"Thank you," Gale shouted. She looked Purity in the eyes. "You're a very lucky woman. I'm eager to get back to the material world, so, as tempting as it might be, I'm not going to keelhaul you. As for your fantasies of killing the sun, I think it's best we end this now. I'm tossing both your sword and the Jagged Heart overboard before we leave the Sea of Wine. They'll be lost forever."

"No way!" said Infidel. "The Jagged Heart has to go back to Qikiqtabruk. I've made a vow!"

"On this ship, I'm the final judge and authority," said Gale. "Consider yourself released from your vow. The harpoon goes overboard."

Infidel protested, "But Aurora–"

"–wasn't insane," I said, putting my hand on Infidel's shoulder. "Do you really think if she knew what Purity planned to do with the harpoon, she'd handle things any differently?"

"Stagger!" said Infidel. "I'm doing this for you! You're the one who made the promise to Aurora!"

"She was dying." I shrugged. "Was I supposed to say no?"

"So your vow to her was only a convenient lie?"

I crossed my arms. "There's a difference between lying and changing your mind as new information becomes available."

"What of our wedding vows? Were these also words that can be tossed aside as new information becomes available?"

"What?" I asked, feeling dizzy. How had she made the leap to this?

Captain Romer, sensibly, had no patience for our little spat.

"Mako, meet me on the deck with the harpoon."

Infidel placed herself in front of the stairs. "No one is leaving until I've had my say." The hair around her face began to flutter, as if in a strong breeze.

"We know what you have to say," said Gale. "I admire your sense of devotion, but you cannot prevail."

"Anyone who… anyone who tries… tries to get past this door… will find out… how much I… can prevail." Infidel sounded winded. She looked confused. Suddenly, the Gloryhammer slipped from her grasp and her eyes rolled up into her head. I leapt forward, catching her before she hit the floor.

"What just happened?" I asked.

"As she exhaled, I blocked air from flowing back into her lungs, causing her to faint," said Gale. "She'll be good as new in a minute or so."

Mako slipped past both of us and headed down the hall.

Gale turned to Sorrow. "Is the sword safe to carry?"

"For you? I don't think it's a problem. You obviously have a robust soul. I think Purity can only flow into bodies when the host's soul is weak or absent. That's why her army seems so lifeless. She gathered other women with damaged souls to use in case her current body is compromised."

"She might be able to jump into a body even if the sword doesn't touch it," I said. "The sword was knocked from her grasp by Brand earlier. It fell a few feet away but didn't break the link."

"It didn't quite touch her now," said Sorrow. "Fortunately, all her soulless spares are shackled. There's no one she can jump to, even if she can travel more than a few feet from the blade."

Purity listened to all this talk with a blank expression. If her ghost remained inside this body, she wasn't wasting any energy on manipulating the face. Sorrow retrieved the Ice-Moon Blade carefully and handed it to Gale. They both held their breath for a second, then Gale smiled. "I'm still me."

She left the hold, climbing to the deck. I followed, carrying Infidel in my arms. As we emerged into the permanent sunset, her eyes fluttered open.

"What happened?" she asked weakly.

I paused as I looked down at her face. I didn't want to lie to her. But, if I told the truth, she'd be back on her feet, fighting to stop Gale. "You fainted," I said, which was at least partly true.

"I don't remember… were we arguing?" She lifted her fingers to the knot on the side of her head and winced.

"You've just overexerted yourself," I said, sitting her down beside the door to the forecastle. Menagerie flapped over to us and sat beside her, a concerned look in his hound dog eyes.

"I had trouble breathing?" she said, half statement, half question. "I've never fainted before."

I was glad that my coconut face and paper voice lacked expression. Otherwise, she would have instantly sensed how troubled I was as I said, "It was stuffy in the hold. You've not had much to eat since you got injured. You're breathing for two now. You need to take it easy. When we get back home, our first priority is going to be to find someplace where you can live in peace and quiet."

She sighed. "Peace and quiet. It's going to be…"

"Boring?" I asked.

"A nice change," she said, scratching Menagerie on the back of his neck, where fur and feathers intermingled. "I swear, I really don't wake up in the mornings thinking, 'Boy, I can't wait to fight a dragon today!'"

I laughed, or tried to. She smiled.

Then Mako came onto the deck with the Jagged Heart, still wrapped in its frost-covered sail.

Infidel's whole body went stiff as Mako met his mother at the starboard rail. "What are they–?"

"This is for the best," I said, placing my root-hand against her shoulder, pinning her against the boards. "Aurora would understand."

"You son of a bitch," Infidel growled, as her eyes flashed to anger. She thrust her arm toward the Jagged Heart, and shouted, "Fetch!"

Menagerie shot forward like he'd been sitting on a spring just as Mako flipped the sail over the edge, letting it unfurl, sending the harpoon toward the Sea of Wine. Menagerie's ever changing form shifted, his mouth and wings growing bigger, his body smaller and more streamlined as he flapped to full speed. Gale tossed the sword overboard just as Menagerie's jaws clamped onto the shaft of the harpoon. The weight of the harpoon proved too great for his pelican wings and he dropped like a stone, vanishing from my sight over the rail as the sword, too, disappeared.

I stood, spinning from Infidel, suddenly wishing we'd made more of an effort to find out how far Purity's soul could travel from the sword. Because, whatever faint intelligence might yet linger in Menagerie, there was also the very real possibility that he was a body without a soul.

From off the starboard rail came the laughter of a woman, as the bloody sky above us began to snow.

13 - Last, Best Hope

WITH A FLAPPING sound like the world's largest swan taking to air, an angel rose next to the *Freewind*. I use the term angel only because that's what springs to mind when one is confronted with a human body held aloft on giant, feathered wings. Of course, calling the body human was stretching things a bit. The thing that flew above our ship was shaped like a woman, slender and well-muscled, but the limbs and torso were covered in black and tan fur similar to a hound. The woman's hair was a mass of long platinum curls and as the breeze pushed the hair from her face I was shocked to find that her visage bore a striking resemblance to my wife. Menagerie had some of Infidel's blood in him after all.

In the creature's left hand was the Jagged Heart. In the right was the Ice-Moon Blade. The blended thing before us bent back her head and laughed as she flapped to the level of the crow's nest.

"What a marvelous shell!" she said, growing an extra set of arms from beneath her first two as she spoke. "It's as malleable as false matter!" The black and tan fur rippled as it changed to a downy white. The enormous pelican wings were mostly white save for their black tips, but even these faded to the color of new fallen snow. Purity's pale eyes glowed red with the reflected light of the omnidirectional sunsets as she stared down at Gale and Mako.

"I'm almost grateful enough for this protean gift that I'm tempted to let you live," she laughed. "Almost."

She extended the Jagged Heart toward Captain Romer. I turned, intending to grab Infidel and carry her to safety since the Gloryhammer was downstairs in the hold, but Infidel was gone. In the passageway beneath me I heard running footsteps.

The deck above the main hold splintered as Infidel exploded into the air, flashing toward Purity faster than I could follow. She slammed the head of the Gloryhammer into the woman's jaw with a fury that made me wince. Purity's head snapped backward, tearing at the throat, nearly decapitated by the blow. Infidel's momentum carried her skyward, leaving Purity dangling in mid-air for the microseconds it would take for her wings to realize they were dead.

Only, the wings kept flapping. Even as Purity's head continued to tear from its shoulders, a new head grew in its place. Menagerie had been able to change shapes too swiftly for the eye to follow. Purity had inherited this speed.

"That was unpleasant," Purity's new head grumbled as her old head dropped toward the Sea of Wine. High above, Infidel had managed to halt her upward course and was now turning back down for another pass.

If Purity had delayed even a tenth of a second, Infidel might have stopped her. As it was, the four-armed witch waved the Ice-Moon Blade toward the main mast of the *Freewind* and suddenly there was a full scale iceberg looming above us, the mast caught within its core. Every timber shuddered as the boat began to tilt toward starboard.

Then, with Infidel barely a hundred feet away, Purity swept the Jagged Heart across the sky, cutting open a rip in reality. A black night glittering with stars showed through the gash. Purity flapped her wings to race into this new sky just as Infidel passed through the space where she'd dangled an instant before. Infidel swung her feet down, trying to slow her descent, but I could tell from her speed she was about to smash straight through the deck. Yet before she hit, every rope in sight rose to catch her, forming an impromptu net. She punched through the deck despite this, but it sounded as if she came to a crashing halt below without breaking through the hull.

Not that it much mattered.

The iceberg around the mast weighed at least as much as the ship. The *Freewind* turned completely on its side as the iceberg crashed into the waves of wine. Everyone on deck was thrown toward the sea.

The last thing I noticed, as I tumbled toward the wine, was that the flies had caught up to us once more. I hit the rail with a jolt that flipped me roots over nuts and the world went dark. An instant later I was submerged, unable to see. Ropes tangled me, halting my further descent. For a panicked moment I struggled, certain I would drown, before the fluid washing about within my barrel chest reminded me that I had no lungs.

Calming myself, I searched the darkness for the red glow of the endless sunset. Instead, everything was black as pitch in all directions. Then, in the distance, I saw a light flicker to life. I turned toward it, and saw that it was a lantern held by a red-haired girl who was standing on the main mast at a 90-degree angle, walking along it like a spider. Cinnamon?

I pushed my head above the surface and the puzzle pieces slipped into place. It wasn't Cinnamon who was sideways, it was the ship. The *Freewind* was on its side, the masts parallel with the water. And, judging from its grayish hue, this was indeed water. We were no longer in the Sea of Wine. Captain Romer must have triggered our journey back.

I tried to call out to Cinnamon, but my waterlogged tongue failed to produce even a squeak. Not that my ordinarily faint voice was likely to have been heard over the noise all around. It sounded as if there was a waterfall not ten feet behind me, and every timber of the ship was groaning. Add the pops and cracks coming from the sizeable iceberg that loomed in the darkness, plus the general lapping of waves, and it's a wonder that I was able to hear Mako call out, "We're taking in water! Get the main hatch closed!"

I spun around and found the source of the waterfall. The main hatch was indeed open, and given the perpendicular orientation of the deck, the bottom edge of this gaping hole was a good foot below the waves, sinking deeper by the second. Ordinarily, the double hatch doors lay flat against the deck when open, one toward starboard, one toward port. The port door was the half above water. Jetsam appeared from nowhere, swimming through the air in a series of graceful kicks. He released the pin that secured the hatch door to the deck and darted aside as the giant door swung under its own weight to crash shut. Unfortunately, this did nothing to ease the immediate crisis; the starboard half of the hatch was the part taking on water, and this door was beneath the waves.

I let the current carry me to the edge of the hatch, catching myself before I was pulled into the hold. With my wooden fingers stiff and waterlogged, I groped for the outer edges of the door beneath me. I found them, but the wood wouldn't budge; it was no doubt secured by a pin.

Mako appeared in the water beside me, gasping for air. He'd obviously been beneath the water, trying to move the door. "I can't see the damn pin!" he shouted. "Get the lantern closer, Cinnamon!"

Cinnamon turned from studying the ice-bound upper half of the mast and ran along the thick wooden beam with confidence. A rope swung out as she jumped. She landed at a crouch on the looped rope, dangling the lantern down until the base skimmed the waves. The water glowed, pale and ghostly.

Mako sucked in air and dived. I followed, dragging myself down by following the door's edge. I reached the bottom and found Mako trying to free a wooden pin that ran through a small metal ring, securing the door. It was stuck, resisting even his enviable muscles. I reached for it to give aid, but before I drew near he thrust his mouth to the metal ring and bit it in twain. I'd never seen anyone spit underwater, but he managed to do so, sending the fragmented pin and ring tumbling into the dark depths. Mako strained to move the door, which was heavy even in air. Trying to move it through water required more than strong jaws. I braced myself as best I could and got both hands underneath the edge. Slowly, the heavy wooden door began to move. Mako got beneath it, his muscles straining as he added to my efforts. In half a minute we had the hatch jutting out at a right angle to the deck, at which point it was impossible to move it further while we were in the water.

"Where's Rigger?" Mako shouted as he thrust his head up for air. He glanced at Cinnamon on her rope. "He's obviously recovered."

"Well enough," a faint voiced cried off to our left. Rigger was sitting in the doorway of the forecastle. From above, a block and tackle with a sizeable hook lowered toward us. In seconds, Mako had it secured to the door's edge. He and I pushed from below, but Rigger and his pulleys did the real work, lifting the door until it was free of our grasp. It closed into place and Jetsam flitted around the edges, securing a further series of pins that held it shut.

"S-s-so c-cold," Cinnamon said as she wrapped her arms around herself. Everyone was breathing out great puffs of fog, and ice was starting to form on every moist surface.

"Our course was plotted for the artic," Mako said. "Look at the stars! You can tell from the way the Tallship hangs on the horizon that we're well north of the Silver Isles."

I glanced up. Unfortunately, while I was an expert at finding my way through trackless jungles, I was completely lost trying to fix my location via constellations.

"Where's mother?" Rigger asked.

"I don't know," Mako called back. "She was near the main hatch as we capsized. I saw her crouch to touch the deck and trigger our journey back to the real world, but lost sight of her after that."

"Find her," shouted Mako. "Our only hope of saving the ship is to get wind under the sails to push us upright."

I suspected that was a doomed mission. With the masts dipped down into the waves, the canvas sails were spread out beneath the water, their white forms giant, ghostly jellyfish.

"I know that Poppy was in her bunk," Mako said. "Mother, Sage, Infidel, and Sorrow are unaccounted for."

"Also Brand and the princess," said Jetsam.

"And the ice-maidens!" said Cinnamon.

"Abyss take the ice-maidens," growled Mako. "Unless they've become master locksmiths, we know where they are."

The ship groaned as it sank lower in the water. The sound was both physical, caused by the stress applied to ship's beams as it sat at such an unnatural angle, and also spiritual. The ship's ghost was screaming, an incoherent howl of pain that only I seemed aware of.

I tried to speak, but again found my tongue useless. My wooden body was so tangled in rope there was no chance it would sink into the deep. I abandoned it, crossing the threshold of the golden door in my chest and flying free, a phantom once more. Instantly, my ghostly senses returned and the savage chill of the night sliced through me. The Romer's were dressed for a tropical climate. Freed of the sepia hues of my wooden eyes, I could see the blue cast to their lips.

The ship groaned again and with a thought I was at the figurehead, its carved features now twisted in pain.

"I c-can't hold the t-timbers together much longer," Jasmine's ghost stammered. "S-saw off the main mast if you m-must! It's our only h-hope of r-righting the ship!"

"On it," I said.

I ghosted into the ship's hold, to the captured women in their manacles, now thrown against the ship's hull as if it were a floor. It was pitch dark; I could see them splashing around only thanks to my ghostly senses, and even this was a strain. These women's souls were like ash-covered embers, nearly invisible. Fortunately, they possessed at least some will to live, as most struggled to stand. Failing to stand meant drowning; the water in the hold was now hip deep. Those who'd been knocked unconscious by the ship's tumble were being helped by Sage and Sorrow.

Though it was entirely the wrong moment for such an experiment, I had to know. I reached my phantom fingers into the torso of the nearest woman. Would my still vital spirit fill her nearly soulless body?

Alas, whatever trick Purity used to possess others eluded me. I felt no connection with the woman's physical form. My half-formed notion to control her and tell the others to saw the main mast free was thwarted.

Worse, my faint hope that I might find a new permanent body should I somehow happen upon a soulless male was dashed almost before I'd even fully conceived it.

I shrugged the failure off. There were more pressing problems. Where was Infidel?

At the thought, the braided wedding band on my hand tugged my arm out. I followed, sensing a connection to the band of hair she wore. I ghosted into the galley. Bags of flour had burst, coating everything in a pale white powder. The air smelled of vinegar, lard, and molasses. Dark gore coated the left side of Infidel's scalp; shards of glass stuck from her hair. She was stretched out on the floor, only, as I made sense of the boat's tilt, I realized she was actually standing, and that the floor was now a wall she leaned against. She stood in shin deep water, conscious, though obviously dazed. The glove of the Immaculate Attire brushed the goop from the side of her head, leaving clean skin in its wake. She wasn't bleeding. Instead, a broken jar of molasses had shattered as it bounced around the small space and was dripping down upon her. Infidel groped for the Gloryhammer beneath the wheat-frosted water, lifting it to cast light on a large splintered hole in the wall. Only, it wasn't the wall, it was the ceiling, turned sideways. This was the hole she'd punched in through. She was close to the waterline, but not quite submerged; icy waves sloshed across the broken boards as the ship pitched.

In a flash, she jumped back through the hole and shot into the air.

"Where's Purity?" she shouted.

"Gone!" Mako shouted back. "The ice is pulling the ship under!"

"Not if I can help it," she called out, landing near the crow's nest, buried beneath at least thirty feet of ice. She planted her boots on the slick surface and swung the Gloryhammer overhead in a two handed grip. With a grunt, she struck, hitting the ice with such force her feet lifted into the air. I raised my hand instinctively to protect my eyes from the flying shards, though, of course, they passed through my phantom form harmlessly. The blow sounded like lightning striking mere yards away, and the crackling that followed had the quality of an electrical storm. Deep cracks ran through the ice and also through the frozen main mast.

The ship screamed like a woman in childbirth as the main mast splintered at its base, then snapped completely. Infidel was thrown back as the iceberg tilted, but the hammer lifted her skyward long before her boots hit the water.

The ship shuddered as it lifted slightly, but failed to right itself. All of its sails were waterlogged, and the rooms beneath on the starboard side were filled with water.

A small hatch on the poop deck suddenly banged open. Captain Romer crawled out, completely drenched. She must have been swept into the hold by the rushing water.

Gale wasted no time. She surveyed the chaos around her and began to bark commands. "Cut all the sails! They're dead weight at this point."

Mako dived into the icy ocean, snapping ropes with his teeth. Between his speed in the water and Rigger's powers, the sails wouldn't weigh us down for long.

I flashed back into my wooden body, determined to make myself useful. Unfortunately, I was still tangled in ropes. Instinctively, I reached for my bone-handled knife, but, of course, that was tucked in the belt of my ghostly form, not this clunky wooden shell. I wound up getting a free ride as the boat tilted and slowly rose as the Romer brothers succeeded in their task.

Mere minutes after the peril had seized us, it was over. The boat was upright, or something like it. The ship listed to starboard at least twenty degrees.

"Romers!" a woman's voice called out. I looked toward the foredeck and saw Sorrow. When had she come from below? She was standing by the ship's enormous iron anchor, which had somehow managed not to slip from the deck. She placed her hand upon the painted black iron. "Gather round before you catch your death of cold!"

The iron anchor bent upward as she grabbed it in the center. In seconds, she'd formed it into a rough tripod. She rubbed her hands along the tip of the tripod until the iron glowed a deep cherry red. She snatched her fingers back and said, "This thing's hot as a stove, so be careful."

Cinnamon and Jetsam were beside it an instant later, their hands outstretched, steam pouring off their black sleeves.

"Thank the seven stars," Cinnamon whispered through chattering teeth.

"Hooray for witchcraft!" said Jetsam, riding the warm updraft above the hot metal.

It took a few moments for the rest of the Romers to join us. Captain Romer used her control of the wind to circulate a warm dry breeze heated by the anchor. Even the captives below would get their share of life-saving warmth. The immediate danger of hypothermia was averted. Infidel was the final arrival, landing across from me on the opposite side of the anchor, her gaze not meeting mine.

"You've some nerve to return to the ship," Mako growled.

"I did just free you from a killer iceberg," said Infidel.

"If you hadn't sent your damn monster to catch the harpoon, none of this would have happened!"

"We can't know that," said Sorrow. "Given her experience with possessions, Purity probably sensed Menagerie's soulless shell the second she came on board. She may have timed seizing his body to take advantage of the instant Mako dropped the Jagged Shard. Magical weapons sometimes act to protect their users via enchantments their owners might not even know about. It's possible if she'd attacked while Mako carried the harpoon, she would have wound up frozen, or worse."

"This is nothing but speculation," said Mako.

"Informed speculation," said Sorrow. "The Jagged Heart isn't carved from lifeless ice; it's the very heart of a primal dragon, or a fragment of it, at least. It's more magic than matter. It bonds spiritually with its owner. It's almost a parasitic relationship, as the owner provides the weapon with mobility and purpose while the weapon provides the owner with improved attacks and defenses. It's similar to Infidel's Gloryhammer."

"The Gloryhammer doesn't defend me as much as I'd like," grumbled Infidel.

"Doesn't it?" asked Sorrow. "The bones of your arms should be shattered by the blows you deliver. The weapon should rip from your merely human grasp as it accelerates you into flight faster than an arrow leaves a bowstring. Its enchantments protect you passively; there may be other powers you could utilize if only you knew of them."

"How would I find out about them?" Infidel asked. "For instance, I can make it glow brighter or softer just by thinking, but it seems like it should also be able to put out heat, which would come in useful in times like this. But, no matter how hard I try to make it hot, it stays cool to the touch."

Sorrow nodded. "That's because the sun isn't a source of heat."

Infidel furrowed her brow, confused.

"The monk Inquisitus proved three centuries ago that heat originates within the earth and light originates within the sun. The two are attracted to one another, but have independent sources."

"I can feel heat on my face when I look at the sun," said Infidel.

Sorrow shook her head. "You feel the heat attracted to the light reflecting off your face. Inquisitus proved his theory by documenting temperatures at over nine-hundred locations. His data show that the peaks of mountains are consistently cooler than the land surrounding them. If the sun were the source of heat, mountaintops should be warmer, since they're nearer. Conversely, the bottoms of mines, far removed from the sun, are intensely hot. Thus, he proved that the core of the earth is the true source of warmth."

Captain Romer interrupted. "This is all very interesting, but let's focus on our immediate problem. Putting aside the issue of who's to blame, the fact remains that we're the only people in the world aware that there's a shape-shifting ghost planning to murder the sun, armed with a weapon capable of the crime. How do we stop her?"

"This doesn't have to be our fight," said Mako. "King Brightmoon and the Church of the Book know of the harpoon's power."

"We've got the king's daughter chained to a bunk down below," said Rigger. "We can send her to ask for help."

His voice was so deadpan, I didn't recognize this as a joke until Poppy giggled.

Captain Romer sighed, rubbing her eyes. "Have we checked on the prisoners? Is everyone okay?"

"Bumps and scrapes from being tossed around," said Sage. "They're fine."

Captain Romer nodded and looked around the ship. "Unchain the prisoners," she said. "We've got an enormous amount of work to do to get this ship seaworthy, starting with a bucket brigade to get the water out of the holds. Any prisoner willing to pitch in will be set free at the next port. Anyone not willing to help will be pointed toward the nearest island and allowed to make a swim for it."

"Even Brand and the dwarf?" Mako asked.

Captain Romer nodded.

"Maybe the dwarf really is Princess Innocent," Poppy said.

Mako rolled his eyes. "You're as crazy as she is. *He.* As crazy as he is."

"We deal with crazy every day," said Sage. "Having a long missing princess hiding aboard our ship is almost mundane."

"It doesn't matter," Rigger said, dismissively. "With the ship crippled, it could take weeks to deliver our so-called princess to her so-called father. Meanwhile every time the sun goes down, we'll be wondering if it's coming back up again."

"Infidel can fly her," said Sage.

"Um, no," said Infidel. "I'm a wanted criminal on the Silver Isle. I'd never get near the king."

"It doesn't matter," said Gale. "The dwarf isn't the princess. Next idea?"

Infidel asked, "If we're in the artic, how far are we from Aurora's village? The ice-ogres know more about the Jagged Heart than anyone. We can enlist their help in stopping Purity."

"We're less than three hundred miles," said Sage, looking at the stars.

"I could reach it in four or five hours, maybe," said Infidel. "I can take Sorrow, since she speaks the lingo."

Sorrow shook her head. "I'll be needed here. Wood-weaving is one of the material arts I've mastered. If this ship can be saved, my talents will come in handy."

"There is no 'if,'" said Gale. "We will repair the *Freewind*."

"I'm not as confident," said Sorrow. "I'll do all I can to help, but look around you. Every board on this ship has been twisted. There's not a nail or joint left flush. The *Freewind* may be beyond repair."

"Go with Infidel if such is your attitude," Gale grumbled.

"I'm sorry if you're wanting me to spout optimistic affirmations," said Sorrow. "I'm simply being realistic. But, if optimism is what you are looking for, have you considered that the loss of the *Freewind* might be a positive development for your family?"

Gale's brow furrowed.

"The *Freewind* stands out in any harbor thanks to its burgundy hull. If you had a new ship, it would be harder for your enemies to spot you. You could have something like a normal life once more."

Jetsam laughed. "Normal? Have you paid any attention at all since you met us?"

Infidel interrupted. "We're getting side-tracked again. Who's going with me to the ogre village?"

Sorrow nodded toward me. "Take Stagger."

"I can't talk," I said, pointing at my mouth. Then I realized I'd heard my own words, albeit faintly. The warm breeze was drying out my tongue.

I shrugged as I lowered my hand. "I don't speak the language."

"I can work around this," said Sorrow. She reached up and grabbed the right bean pod that served as my ear, popping it off. Oddly, despite its removal, the backdrop noise of wind and waves didn't lessen.

"You'll be able to hear what this ear hears, no matter how far away you are," she said, fastening the bean pod to her golden earring with a loop of silver. "And, if I listen closely, I'll be able to hear what your other ear hears due to sympathetic vibrations. I can translate for you from afar."

"I want to be a witch when I grow up," said Cinnamon.

"You're a witch now," said Jetsam.

"Can... uh, can Infidel support my weight?" I asked. Despite the drying breeze, I was waterlogged. It wasn't my weight I was worried about, however. I knew she was still mad that I'd lied to her.

Infidel nodded. "Once I'm in the air, the extra weight doesn't really matter. Guess it's one of the powers of the hammer I don't really understand." She wasn't looking directly at me. "I'll need to wait until dawn. I don't know how to navigate via stars. In daylight, if I follow the coast line, I presume I'll be able to find the village from above."

"You might be waiting a while," said Rigger. "At this time of year, this far north, night lasts a long time."

"At winter solstice, the sun doesn't rise at all," said Sorrow, her voice trailing off.

"That's only a day away," said Rigger.

"Then that's all the time we have to stop Purity," said Sorrow.

"How can you be sure?" asked Gale.

"I can't be," said Sorrow. "But Hush is at her most powerful on the winter solstice. According to ice-ogre lore, Glorious, the sun dragon, is afraid to show his face on that day after months of being beaten back by Hush. When he does emerge the next day he's helpless as a newborn babe as he rises into the Great Sea Above. He survives only because he's so feeble Hush pities him. Then, he grows stronger and stronger, until he banishes the night completely. Only, he then takes pity on Hush for the pain he causes her, and in his moment of weakness, she once more begins to build her power."

"Ogres have stupid legends," Mako grumbled.

"Maybe. But their myths also serve as a cultural warning against feeling pity for an enemy. In any case, Purity seems devoid of that particular emotion. What better moment could there be for her to strike than the dawn following the solstice?"

"If daylight's so short, I guess there's no point in waiting," said Infidel. "That fox cloak Purity showed up in looked pretty warm, if anyone knows where it is. I have a feeling I'll need some good insulation once I get up in the air. Also a helmet, if there's one lying around."

If I'd had eyebrows, they'd have shot up.

"What?" she asked, sensing my surprise. "You think I can't learn?"

I shook my head.

Infidel looked at Gale. "Since I don't know how long I'll be gone, I'll carry fresh food and water for a week, if you can spare it." She cast a glance toward me and managed, "I guess I should be grateful you don't need to eat."

I nodded, relieved that she was at least speaking to me again.

"I'll get the cloak," said Sage, heading for the hatch.

"I'll gather provisions," said Cinnamon.

"There's still the question of how I'm going to find this place in the dark," Infidel said.

"I can find it," I announced.

"How?" Infidel sounded skeptical.

"Living things give off an aura. A village should stand out like a torch against the backdrop of a frozen, lifeless landscape."

"Excellent," said Captain Romer. "The two of you will be our primary plan to deal with this threat. I shall explore a second option."

"Which is?"

"There are secrets we Wanderers do not share with outsiders," said Captain Romer. "Suffice it to say, there are channels of communication within the ocean that extend far beyond human senses. It's possible I can get a message to… to my eldest son, Levi."

The Romer children's eyes grew wide at this announcement.

"Don't give me that look," Gale said.

"He'll betray us to the Stormguard," said Mako.

"No he won't," said Sage. "No matter what uniform he's wearing, he's still a Romer."

Gale nodded. "More importantly, his vessel is one of the few that could reach us in time to make a difference. The fate of the world might be at stake. If I have to swallow my pride and ask Levi for help, so be it."

"I like having a second plan," said Infidel. "Anyone got a third?"

Perhaps it was an illusion caused by the fact that one of my ears was now dangling against her cheek, but it sounded as if Sorrow started to speak. Yet, her breath caught in her throat at the last second.

"What?" I asked. "You have a plan?"

"Not a plan, no," said Sorrow. "Nothing so fully formed."

"An idea? A hunch? A gut feeling?" I prodded.

Sorrow shook her head. "It's nothing. Undertake your mission as if you're the world's last, best hope."

14 - BAD BLUBBER

READYING OURSELVES FOR the journey took some time. I needed new clothes so that my inhuman body wouldn't draw unwelcome attention, but even Mako's muscular frame was no match for my own. His pants only came to mid-shin, but his boots were tall enough that it hid the difference. With a little stuffing, his boot even made my peg leg look like a foot again. His shirt wouldn't go around my barrel chest. In the end, I wore it backward. Barrel staves were exposed on my back, but this was covered by a cape we made from old sails.

Unfortunately, as soon as I was dressed, my left arm stopped working. Sorrow was summoned. She discovered the copper wire that held my shoulder joint together was corroded and brittle.

"Sea water isn't good for any metal," she said as she fashioned me a new arm from a broken chair. "Even without your exposure to Rott you'd be falling apart."

"He's been falling apart since the day I met him," said Infidel.

Which was true enough. She'd met me when I was thirty-five. I was at my physical peak, my body hardened by years of jungle explorations. Alas, the problem with being at one's peak is there's no where to go but down. In the next fifteen years, I'd lost hair, teeth, muscle… everything but weight.

Sage had produced Purity's white fox cloak, which fit Infidel perfectly and complemented her Immaculate Armor as if they'd been made for each other. One of the smaller Skelling helmets had been de-horned to fit beneath her hood. It was little more than a steel hat, offering no protection for her face, but it was better than nothing.

Once she had fixed my arm, Sorrow took another Skelling helmet and stretched the metal to form a full faceplate, leaving only a gap for eyes. She placed this over my coconut noggin and wired it on. Sorrow produced a small silver mirror and I had to admit I passed as a human warrior, an intimidating one at that.

"Now the ice-ogres won't rip you apart for being an abomination against nature," said Sorrow.

"They'll just rip me apart for being human," I said. "Aurora made them sound a bit… isolationist."

"Ogres aren't known for their propitious natures," said Infidel.

"Propitious?" I asked.

"It means friendly," she said.

"I know what it means," I said. "It's just that you normally eschew magniloquence."

"I'm secure enough that I don't need to flaunt my vocabulary. You use big words because the monks who raised you made you feel like an idiot. You've spent the last forty years trying to prove that you're smart."

"Ouch," I said, wounded by the penetrating sharpness of her analysis. "I take it you're still mad at me?"

"I can't understand why you didn't back me up. If Gale had just left the Jagged Heart alone, everything would be okay now. Don't you trust me?"

Sorrow cleared her throat as she ran the last of the fresh copper wires through my new arm. "Perhaps this would be a conversation best carried out in private?"

Infidel pressed her lips tightly together and nodded.

Sorrow made a few adjustments on my new arm, then said, "Almost done. Pick up the sea chest so we can test your strength."

The chest was sitting on its side behind the door, where it had come to rest following the upheaval. I grabbed it with my fresh arm and manhandled it back to the foot of the bed.

"Good as new," I reported, but my words we almost drowned out by a low, slow, unearthly wail that came from the other side of the wall, where there should be only ocean.

"What in the name of the primordial paper was that?" I asked.

"Whale song," said Infidel. "I first heard them during the Pirate Wars. The Wanderers try to keep it a secret from outsiders, but they understand the various whale languages."

"Whales talk?" I asked.

"This must be the secret Captain Romer wouldn't share with us," said Sorrow. "Whale songs travel great distances. Wanderers use the whales to pass on messages, allowing ships hundreds of miles distant to communicate."

"So help could be on the way soon," I said.

"Highly unlikely," said Sorrow. "In the summer, these waters are filled with fishing boats due to the abundance of cod. During the winter, there's little to attract ships to these latitudes. I'm doubtful there's another Wanderer within a thousand miles. As she spoke, Sorrow shoved her handcrafted sword into my belt.

"I've been doing better with my fists," I said.

"Let's hope the only tool you really need is your tongue," she said. She gave me one last inspection. "You're as good as you're going to be. Fly safely."

We went above deck. Captain Romer gave Infidel a quick guide to the northern constellations. I noticed an odd shimmering haze in the sky. I slipped from my shell and saw the haze was rainbow colored, dancing about. I'd heard legends of these northern lights, but never expected to see them. They fluttered like an ethereal curtain draping the stars.

"Beautiful," I said the second I'd returned to my body.

"Yes, handsome?" said Infidel.

If my mouth had been mobile I'd have smiled.

THEN WE WERE ALOFT. The *Freewind* quickly became a mere speck amid a sea of specks. Icebergs were everywhere. I hoped the ship regained its maneuverability before it was menaced by one of these crushing behemoths.

Once the ship was out of sight, it became impossible to guess how high we were. There were no familiar features with which to orient myself. The brightness of the Gloryhammer before us washed out most of the stars.

"I'm going to step out," I said.

"What?" Infidel yelled back.

"I'm going to step out of my body. I'll be limp for a moment."

"Go," she said.

I once more leapt from the golden cage and out through the wooden staves, sailing freely into the frigid winds. It occurred to me that if Sorrow was listening to my words, it's possible she now knew I could escape from her cage. She'd been treating me rather fairly since I'd given her the map to the Knight's Castle, but would she try to cage me again? I'd deal with that if and when I saw her.

I slowed, letting Infidel pass on. As the glow of the Gloryhammer faded into the distance I saw that the curtains of light had dimmed, leaving behind stars of stunning crispness. Until now, I'd only seen the sky through the humid, gauzy air of my island home. Here, every last trace of moisture had frozen and dropped from the sky, leaving the stars fully exposed. I felt much the awe and wonder I'd experienced when, as a teen, I'd seen my first naked woman. I was glimpsing something ordinarily hidden from the eyes of man. I sensed that if I could understand what I was gazing upon I would find wisdom.

Of course, the main wisdom I gathered in studying the bodies of women in my youth was that any serious course of education was going to be expensive. But these stars, these stars.... The Sacred Writs are full of tales of men who go into wastelands to find communion with the Divine Author. At this moment, I grasped why. The stars were so numerous that patterns emerged wherever I glanced, as if the celestial canvas was some immense manuscript that a man might one day learn to read.

No wonder the ice-ogres thought of these starry reaches as heaven.

Of course, I'd resisted the call of heaven so far. I shook off my fascination and returned to the task at hand. Looking back, though it had been beyond the gaze of my wooden eyes, I could see the *Freewind* aglow like a distant star against the inky darkness of the sea. To the north and west I could see the sea turning white in the distance. Flying higher, I saw that I was gazing at a shoreline, like the world's smoothest, widest beach, formed of sand white as pure salt. But given the chill that numbed even my ghostly bones, I soon deduced I was looking not at sandy beaches, but at the edge of a vast, unbroken ice sheet.

Infidel flew along the edge of this ice sheet, looking like a shooting star in the distance. With a thought, I was back at her side, animating the driftwood golem once more. She sensed my return and asked, "See anything?"

"The stars are amazing once you're free of the glare of the Gloryhammer."

"Hmm," she said. "You can't see the stars right now?"

"Not much."

"I see them fine," she said. "In fact, now that I think about it, I never get blinded by the hammer's glow. It must be one of those passive powers Sorrow talked about."

"I think I know another power of the hammer," I said.

"What?"

"When you were at the Jawa Fruit village, Tower flew straight to you, and I remember him saying that he'd told the hammer to find you. So the hammer has some kind of ability to track people."

"If that's true, why didn't he find me years earlier? He's had the hammer ever since I vanished, and was obsessed with me the whole time. Why didn't he come looking for me?"

"Maybe the hammer is like a bloodhound," I speculated. "It has to have some reference point to use for tracking?"

Infidel's face went blank at the mention of a bloodhound.

"You're thinking of Menagerie, aren't you?"

"Yeah," she said.

We flew on through the darkness for some time before she asked, "Is this all my fault?"

"I don't see how you can be blamed for the insane plans of a 200 year old witch."

"What if I'd killed Menagerie when the Black Swan told me to? None of this would have happened."

"The Black Swan also told you to kill Greatshadow and you didn't," I said. "I think you made the right call. I think, against all odds, you converted an enemy of mankind into a grudging ally. I heard you explain your reasons to Zetetic. The Isle of Fire should remain untamed. I can't agree more."

"Am I crazy to want to raise our daughter there?"

"No," I said. "It's dangerous, but it's the only place in the world I've ever felt that life makes sense. You saw how happy my grandfather was living with the Jawa Fruit tribe. The island can be paradise if you respect it rather than trying to tame it."

"I know," said Infidel. "I want our daughter to love exploring the jungle just as much as we did. I want her to be able to appreciate nature by getting dirt and blood under her nails as she stalks her own meal. But I don't want her growing up as some naked, unwashed savage like your grandfather. I want her to read the books that you loved. I was bored by operas and museums and cathedrals when I was a girl, but now I want her to see these things, so that she can understand the beauty that man is capable of producing. How do I do this? How do I raise a child to be both wild and refined, civilized and feral all at once?"

"You're describing yourself, you know," I said. "Half forest dragon, half princess. The ultimate blend of beast and beauty. My god, I never stood a chance. You captured my heart the moment I first laid eyes on you."

"Oh, that was just lust," she said, dismissively. "I was pretty hot when I was twenty."

"You're pretty hot now," I said.

"Actually, right now I'm freezing," she said. "My nipples are hard as walnut shells."

"It's lucky you ditched that chrome-plated bra."

She laughed, but then her voice went serious. "I'm scared, Stagger."

"Of being a mother?"

"What do I know about raising a child? What do I know about anything? Other women have mothers, sisters, best friends they can talk to. People who can tell them what to expect, what to worry about and what to shrug off. I don't have any of this. I'm thirty years old and I can rattle off a list of about three hundred people who've vowed to kill me, and precisely two people I count as friends, and they're both dead!."

"Two?" I said, instantly regretting that I sounded surprised she had a second friend.

"There's also Aurora," she said. "I mean, it's dumb. A month ago she was nobody to me. But I really connected with her on the dragon hunt. She told me her secrets, I told her mine, and… I dunno. There was a bond. It was almost like I had a sister. Which is why I feel so strongly about keeping this promise."

"I understand," I said. "But she won't know if you keep the promise or not."

"How do you know? You've managed to keep tabs on me."

"I saw Aurora move on. She went to her heaven… the Great Sea Above." I glanced up. "Maybe she's up there right now, looking down, watching us streak across her sky like a comet."

"If she's watching, she knows what a mess I've made," said Infidel. "Old Infidel would have shrugged this off. New Infidel intends to clean things up."

"Your newfound devotion to cleaning will probably be a big help in motherhood."

"Let's hope so."

"As for advice on childbirth and raising kids, Gale Romer can probably give you some guidance."

"She'll charge me for it," said Infidel. "We're not really friends. I was just a mercenary she employed. I liked her as a boss, but I can't say we were close. And after all the grief I've caused her on this trip, she probably hates me."

I didn't know what to say. Infidel couldn't return to her own family for assistance. My father was a monk and would be of no use; my mother had been a whore who abandoned me at an orphanage. I wasn't her only child, but even though I have a dozen half-siblings out in the world, they're strangers to me. My grandfather would probably be willing to help, but, as noted, he's gone feral. Also, while Judicious seemed remarkably sound in body and mind, it was no trivial matter than he was a whisker away from his hundredth birthday. It was no certain thing he'd be around in nine months.

"I don't know what the future holds," I said at last. "But, if my past is any guide, things always work out."

"Not always," she said.

"Often enough," I said. "My gut tells me everything will be okay. My gut tells me you'll be a great mother."

"You don't have a gut anymore," she said.

"Well, my brains tell me."

"You don't have brains either!"

"True. All that's left is my soul. And if a soul isn't the ultimate judge of the rightness of things, what is?"

"Hmm," she said, before the faintest flicker of a grin crossed her face.

We flew on in silence. I felt as if she were happy for the moment, or at least in a state of relative peace, and I worried that it would be too easy to tip her mood back into worry.

Slowly, a curious thing unfolded. The sky at our backs grew noticeably lighter.

"Everything's turning blue," said Infidel as she slowed, turning back to watch the sky.

I slipped out of my shell to verify that this was so. An eerie twilight had broken through the gloom, distinctly azure in hue. Then, with no fanfare, the bright white upper edge of the sun peeked above the southern horizon. I'd never appreciated seeing the old dragon Glorious quite so much.

I wasn't the only one happy to see the sun. I noticed that the internal glow of the Gloryhammer had intensified. The weapon gave off a slight crackling sound. Infidel held the weapon toward the distant orb.

"Feel this," she said. "Put your hand on the hammer."

I placed my gloved root on the shaft, but felt nothing. "What should I be feeling?"

"The hammer is sort of humming. It's almost like the purr of a kitten when it's being held by someone it knows."

"The Glorystones fell from the sky when Glorious first merged with the sun. Maybe the hammer remembers him. They've been separated for over a day now, since the sun never appeared on the Sea of Wine."

"Maybe," Infidel said.

But if the hammer truly had a memory, it was not allowed to dwell for long on these recollections. After a leisurely stroll across the horizon where it never quite got airborne, the distant sun once more began to recede.

We turned north and flew on, the landscape beneath aglow in the relatively bright twilight. Against this backdrop, anything dark stood out, and far ahead I spotted specks upon the ice, small as fleas. I pointed toward the dark forms with my gloved hand. Infidel nodded and altered our course to investigate.

Quickly we came to see that our targets were moving. As we closed upon them, the specks became two large humanoid figures crouched over a gray mass on the ice. They had their backs to us; the gray smear they were hunched over proved to be a large seal they were butchering. As one of the butchers moved to the side, I spotted tusks jutting from his lower jaw. Ice-ogres!

Infidel came in low. The Gloryhammer caused long shadows to stretch before the ogres. They turned back to look at the source of the light, raising their hands to shield their eyes.

"Sorrow," I said. "Right now would be a fantastic time for you to teach me the ice-ogre word for 'hello.'"

"Awk," she responded almost instantly.

"I can manage that," I said. "Awk! Awk!"

We were several hundred yards away. Between the faintness of my squeaky voice and the rush of wind I can't believe they heard me. But, something triggered them to choose this exact second to abandon their kill. They ran toward a ragged looking patch of ice. This proved to be a deep pool of slush leading to the ocean beneath, or so I deduced as they disappeared into it.

"Damn," said Infidel, landing on the ice where they'd just stood.

"Do ogres swim?" I asked.

"They're excellent swimmers," said Sorrow. "If they had time to fill their lungs they can last almost twenty minutes underwater. Their high body fat helps retain heat. They can travel miles beneath the ice; they use their tusks to bash their way up through thin spots."

"Weird," said Infidel, with her ear almost pressed to mine. "I can hear you, Sorrow. Just barely."

"It's the sympathetic vibration of the other half of the seed pod."

"Have you… have you been listening to everything we said?" Infidel asked.

"I told you before you left that I would hear what Stagger heard. But, don't worry, I haven't been paying attention to your confessions of maternal inadequacy. We've been preoccupied here by the arrival of Levi. The whales messages found their mark."

"Levi? Gale's oldest son? He showed up fast."

"It turns out he has his mother's talent for shortcuts," said Sorrow. "Though that's not really the thing that stands out about him." I waited for a elaboration, but she had said all she had to say on the subject.

Infidel said, "I feel bad that we scared them off. They'd done a lot of work." She was looking at the seal. It was in a relatively advanced state of butchering, the skin flayed from the muscle and stretched out to create a tidy workspace. Neat slabs of meat were spread over the surrounding ice, faintly steaming as the winter air sucked out their moisture. The nutrient rich organs like the heart and liver were laid out as neatly as if they were in a butcher's window. The skull had been worked free from the spine and set aside, the lidless eyes forced to watch the dismemberment of the body. Either the ogres were fast workers or we'd frightened them away from the fruits of several hours' work.

"Maybe they're heading back to the village to sound a warning," I said. "We might be close."

"Maybe," said Infidel. "But I didn't see anything like a village anywhere near."

"Hang tight," I said. "I'm going to slip beneath the ice and figure out which way they're going."

"Go," she said.

I let go of the silver threads and slipped from my shell. I willed myself down through the ice, shuddering from both the chill of my environment and the existential crises that confronted me every time I let go of the illusion of solidity and embraced the advantages of my spectral nature.

In the water, the ice overhead was a pale translucent gray-blue through which the twilight seeped. From above, the ice looked uniform, but from beneath it revealed itself to be riddled with cracks. Since we'd been flying up from the south and hadn't spotted a village, I had a hunch that the ogres were heading north. I pursued and a moment later spotted their faint auras. I flashed toward them just as they reached a gap in the ice. With powerful kicks, they burst upward, doing what can only be described as a reverse dive. Once above, they began to run without so much as a pause to catch their breaths.

I continued to give chase, hoping they'd reach their destination soon. They didn't. I couldn't accurately tell time, but I'm certain I gave chase for at least an hour. The blue twilight that had persisted after the sunset receded once more to black. I had only starlight to see by, but it was sufficient to reveal that the ice the ogres ran across was now bordered by actual land, steep cliffs a half mile high.

At the second hour of their headlong flight through the darkness, I began to wonder if Infidel would give up on waiting for me. I should have committed to a time limit, but planning ahead wasn't something either of us were famous for. The ogres showed no signs of weariness as I floated beside them. Aurora had told me she was a runt among her kind, and assuming that these two random specimens were closer to average, she'd been right. They were each at least ten feet tall, broad shouldered, with arms and legs packed into seal fur tights that fit like second skins. Given the tightness of their pants, I had evidence that these were males of the species. Their faces were the same pale blue white as Aurora's, but squarer. Their brows were dappled with hemi-circular scars that reminded me of overlapping scales. I'd seen similar scarification as decoration among river pygmies, who sometimes marked fish scale patterns along their shoulders and spine.

Just as I'd decided to give up and return to Infidel, I saw a glow on the northern horizon, completely different in nature from the brief sunrise I'd witnessed earlier. I flitted upward and found the cliffs cut back in a sharp V shape a mile across at the open end. Within was a frozen bay decorated by what looked like hundreds of perfect hemi-spheres packed closely together. My lack of perspective made these look small at first, until I saw ogres going in and out of them through seal skin curtains. Drawing closer, I saw that they were hollow domes of ice almost fifty feet across. Most had dark black holes at the tops of the dome from which smoke rose; the fires within lit the structures with a dim yellow light. Black shadows moved menacingly against the backlighting. The atmosphere above the village had the distinct aroma of rotting fish and burnt bacon, a scent reminiscent of the whale oil the Wanderers burned in their lamps, but much stronger.

Having at least a minute's lead on the two startled hunters, I flitted into the nearest dome. The smell within was so foul I reached up to pinch my nostrils, forgetting the intangible nature of both fingers and nose. In the central fire pit they were burning what looked like cow patties, though of course there were no cows within a thousand miles. Perhaps they were ogre turds; at least a dozen of the beasts were packed into this dwelling. They'd shed their clothing and went about naked. The floors of the ice dome where carpeted with thick sheets of skins, and the warmth of the room was surprising; I wondered how the walls survived. A mother ogre was nursing three youngsters simultaneously; she was equipped with four working breasts. I'd never noticed this excess of mammary glands on Aurora, but Aurora had typically dressed in a manner that concealed the true contours of her body. She'd worked for the Black Swan for two years before I realized she was female.

The ogres within the dome all lifted their heads at once. The two hunters were close enough to the village that their shouts could be heard. Flitting back outside, the commotion grew; not only were the two hunters shouting as they covered the last few hundred yards toward the village, news of their arrival was being trumpeted in deep barreled baritones from dome to dome.

I couldn't understand a word, as my link to Sorrow was now several miles distant. Again, I never claimed that some future monument to me would be engraved, "The Man Who Thought Ahead."

The cacophony of voices reached a crescendo as the news reached the furthest edges of the village. From my aerial position I watched as the two hunters were led along what looked to be a well-trodden path to the north. I quickly spotted why. Unlike the jagged, natural looking cliff on the southern half of the V shaped bay, the northern cliffs had been carved into an impressive edifice. The face was sheer granite, polished smooth, and riddled with windows and balconies. Statues of ogres sat within alcoves. I was looking at either a palace or a temple, or some blend of both.

Before I could go within to investigate, a white-clad figure emerged from the torch-lit interior of the highest archway. This was an ogre even larger than the two I'd been chasing. A cheer went through the crowd that gathered beneath. They began to chant, "Tarpok! Tarpok!" I guessed it to be his name, though perhaps it was just a more formal greeting than "awk."

Tarpok stuck out a beefy arm and the crowd fell silent. He called out to the crowd with a voice powerful enough to rattle window glass and startle the horses, if the village had possessed either glass or horses. Though I didn't speak the lingo, I sensed from his tone that he'd asked a question, most likely, "What's all the racket?"

The two hunters were pushed to the front of the crowd and shouted back something. They both waved their hands as they spoke. Given their gestures and inflection my translation was, "A two-headed creature from the stars swooped down and attacked us! We abandoned our catch and ran for our lives!"

Tarpok asked a short question that made the crowd laugh. My hunch: "Maybe you chewed some bad blubber?"

The two hunters bowed, placing their hands over their hearts in the near universal gesture, "I swear it's true."

The ogre in the window responded with an appropriately solemn and studious look. I drew closer. Tarpok was a good twelve feet tall, and solid looking. I mean, none of the ogres would blow away in a stiff wind, but something about their subcutaneous fat gave most ogres a doughy look. Tarpok was chiseled. What I thought had been white clothing was in fact his bare skin, all the better to display the elaborate tapestries of tribal scars that decorated his imposing form. I also noted that he had four dark blue nipples; apparently this *was* standard ogre anatomy.

At last, having posed in dramatic contemplation for a sufficient length of time to build suspense in the crowd, the big ogre thrust out his hand in a stiff salute and screamed, "Hack hack hack hack!" or words to that effect, which, judging from the jubilation that followed must have meant, "I believe you! I will find this star-beast and kick its ass!"

A smaller ogre appeared in the shadows and handed Tarpok a large horn carved from a narwhale's tusk. He blew into the end with a long, tooth-rattling "BLAAAAAAAAT!" As the note trailed off a dozen shooting stars streaked down from the heavens, as if they'd been shaken loose by the call.

Tarpok disappeared into the shadows. I watched the window for his reappearance, since the crowd continued gazing in that general direction. A minute later they cheered with excitement, but I didn't see him. Then I realized he was now on top of the cliff. He was wearing a black cloak I assume was whale hide, with matching pants of the same material. He had a battle-axe with a head the size of a coffee table slung over his back, and in his left hand he carried a harpoon that was more menacing than even the Jagged Heart, a twenty-foot-long shaft of iron with the tip hammered into a flesh-mangling mess of serrated hooks and barbs.

I had to wonder if the Immaculate Attire would stand a chance against a weapon like this. I consoled myself that Infidel could at least escape by taking to the sky. Then I saw the crowd pivot. Something big flew overhead, blotting out stars.

Having lived by the ocean most of my life, I've seen my fair share of whales. Menagerie had one among his tattoos that I'd never actually spotted in our tropical climes, a beast that vaguely resembled a panda in its stark black and white coloring, but was more evocative of a dragon by virtue of a dagger-toothed mouth that could open wide enough to swallow boats. He'd called the thing an orca.

He hadn't told me they could fly.

Or, perhaps they can't, and it was merely some enchantment that kept this beast in the air. Whatever the case, I watched, slack jawed, as a sixty-foot black and white whale sailed up to the cliff, swimming in air as if it were water. The beast cruised with its back just below the top edge of the cliff. Tarpok leapt into the air, the crowd screaming with jubilation as he landed astride the beast. I spotted that the whale was rigged with an elaborate leather harness. Tarpok wrapped his fists into these lines and tugged the beast's head toward the southern horizon. The orca let loose a loud "whuff" from its blowhole and with a flick of its tail surged in that direction.

The crowd gave chase from below, but the whale picked up speed with every wave of its tail. Tarpok raised his harpoon above his head and shouted, "Chakaaaaa!"

"Chakaaaaa!" the crowd screamed in unison.

With Sorrow unavailable, I held out hope the word meant, "Good-bye," and not, "Death to star-monsters!"

I'd seen enough. It was time to get back to Infidel.

15 - BONES AND TEETH

AS THE TRACKLESS ice flashed beneath me, I feared I'd never find Infidel. Had I been limited to ordinary sight, my fears would have been well founded. Fortunately, when I held my left hand before me with its phantom wedding band, I could feel a pressure like the tug of a distant magnet. At last my ghost eyes spotted her by the bright aura she cast as the only living thing for miles around.

It was fortunate I could see her aura, because the Gloryhammer couldn't be seen at all. Infidel had cleared the butchered meat from the seal skin and flipped it fur side up, then stretched out on the ice with her fox cloak curled tightly around her, forming a very tiny tent that hid both her and the hammer.

My wooden body was laid out on the ice next to her, its arms folded neatly across its chest, as if it had been prepped for burial. I jumped inside. My wooden bones clattered as I sat up. She stirred, raising the lip of her hood ever so slightly. A bright beam of light shot over the bloodied ice.

"Was I snoring?" she asked, sounding drowsy, as pale fog rolled out from the gap she'd made.

"You we're sleeping out here? You'll freeze to death!"

"No, no, it's pretty comfy," she said. "The fur traps my body heat really well. I just conked right out. Were you gone long?"

"A couple of hours."

"I needed the nap. Now, I feel ready for anything."

"Trust me, you aren't ready for what's coming. Let's get out of here," I said, standing, looking north. "The two hunters made it to their village and sounded an alarm. Now the village's top warrior is on his way here to do battle with the monster that stole the hunters' seal."

"That's good news, isn't it?" Infidel sat up. The moisture that had been trapped by the fur instantly turned to frost on the silver trim of her armor, and left tiny glittering diamonds of ice on her eyelashes. "We want them to come to us."

"This guy's riding a flying whale and carrying a solid steel harpoon. He looks like the very definition of bad news."

Infidel furrowed her brow. "We came here looking for help against Purity. That means we need to talk to someone important. He sounds important."

"He sounds dangerous! Let's get out of here!"

"Excuse me," said Sorrow in my ear. "Did you just mention someone riding a flying whale?"

"Yeah," I said.

"That would be Tarpok," said Sorrow.

"Is that the whale or the rider?" I asked.

"The rider. The whale is Slor Tonn."

"Is this a private conversation or can I listen in?" Infidel pressed her cheek close to my ear without waiting for an answer.

"So, you've met Tarpok?" asked Sorrow.

"Not really," I said. "He didn't see me, but he's on his way here, and he looked like he was coming for blood. The whole village was shouting him on, yelling, 'Chakaa!'"

It was difficult to hear, but I think Sorrow sighed. She asked, "What did you do to get him angry?"

"Nothing!" said Infidel. "We just startled a few hunters."

"Tarpok is the village champion," said Sorrow. "He'll lose face if he doesn't return with some corpses. He's a very dangerous fighter, but his whale is even worse. When you fight them, target Slor Tonn first."

"What?" I said. "We aren't going to fight. We're going to run!"

"Or," said Infidel, "Pardon me for having a crazy idea, but can't we try to talk to him? The Divine Author knows how many miles we just flew to do that, right?"

"Tarpok is a fight first, ask questions later type," said Sorrow.

"How do you know so much about him?" Infidel asked.

"I told you I'd had difficulty on my trip up north. I escaped the Skellings only to be captured by ice-ogres. Fortunately, they treated me rather well. Their priestesses somehow knew I was a virgin, and they needed my blood for some magic ritual. But, the night of the ritual was months away, so during that time I was kept in the temple, well fed and comfortable. That's when I picked up some of their language. Luckily, I never learned what ritual the priestesses needed me for. Tarpok learned I could manipulate gold and silver, so he wanted to see my talents. I was able to bribe him and gain my freedom by promising to build him an iron harpoon with magical strength and toughness."

"So the harpoon's magic?" I asked.

"No, but he doesn't know that. Most ice-ogre weapons are made of bones and rock. Show them some steel and they think it fell from the heavens. Which, actually, it did, since I pulled the iron from a meteor they kept in the temple. But, despite its heavenly origins, the harpoon doesn't have any special powers."

"So the harpoon isn't dangerous?" Infidel asked.

"It's a twenty-foot shaft of hardened steel with hooked barbs sharp enough to shave with," said Sorrow. "It doesn't need to be magic."

"But you were able to bribe him," said Infidel. "He listened to reason and he kept his end of the bargain in letting you go."

"Actually, he tried to double cross me, but one of the ogresses in the temple helped me escape to spite him. I got the feeling there was a power struggle between Tarpok and the priestesses. Tarpok's something of a bully."

"Then we'll surrender," said Infidel. "Grovel a little. Tell him we're too scared of his reputation to even think of fighting. We'll butter him up with praise, then tell him that Purity called his mother a bad name."

"Hmm," said Sorrow. "That's not a bad plan."

"Here's a better one," I said. "While Tarpok is out here looking for us, we sneak into town and find someone to talk to who isn't riding a monster that can swallow us before we say hello."

"I feel like you're not trusting me again," Infidel said, crossing her arms.

Before we could argue further, there was a faint gurgle at our feet. The hole the ogres had escaped in was frozen over now, but a few cracks in the ice suddenly began to spurt seawater. The fluid washed over the bloody ice where the seal had been butchered, sending little pink rivulets in all directions. The water froze an instant later, locking my boots in place.

Infidel tapped the ice with her hammer, freeing the soles of my boots. The glow of the hammer cast rainbows in the frosted ice beneath us. A fresh stream of water shot up through the cracks.

Infidel bent at the knees, preparing to leap as she raised her hammer and wrapped an arm around my waist. She said, "Hold—"

I think her next word was going to be "tight," but it was rendered moot as a shaft of solid steel punched through the ice beneath my feet. My right leg was instantly torn from my body, sending me spinning backward. There was a loud *CRACK*, as if lighting had struck us. The ice bulged upward as Slor Tonn punched up from the depths, throwing us both head over heels. I fell toward Tarpok, whose feet were wrapped in the leather harness as he used both hands to drive his harpoon through my barrel chest.

"We surrender!" I squeaked.

"Pamiiyok!" Sorrow screamed in my ear.

"Pamiiyok!" I tried again. I'd slid down the shaft of the harpoon far enough that I could have reached out and shaken Tarpok's hand if he'd had one to spare at the moment.

"I accept no surrender," Tarpok growled, in my own language.

He gave the harpoon a sharp jerk to the left and I was thrown back down to the barbed head with such force that my helmet fell loose. I watched it fall away into the icy hole left by Slor Tonn's arrival. As the slats of my chest fell apart, I shook loose of the harpoon and tumbled headfirst toward the water, until my left hand suddenly snagged in the whale's harness, purely by luck. With my fall halted, I grabbed the straps with my right hand and held on.

I felt dizzy as Slor Tonn wheeled in the sky and the stars above us spun. An instant later the sky gave way to ice and I saw Infidel, sprawled on the snow beneath us looking dazed, the Gloryhammer just beyond her grasp. Tarpok drew back his harpoon to hurl it, but hesitated as Infidel looked up toward him. Her cloak had fallen open and her helmet had come off, revealing her face and hair.

"Purity?" Tarpok muttered. Then he barked, "Kisault, Slor Tonn!"

In defiance of all ordinary physics, the whale stopped instantly in mid-flight.

"Purity!" Tarpok shouted. "How did you reach this interloper before me? Why didn't you tell me of your plans? I could have killed you!"

Infidel used Tarpok's hesitation to scramble across the ice and grab the Gloryhammer. She rose on rubbery legs and snarled. "We just wanted to talk, you jerk!"

"Purity?" Tarpok asked, utterly confused.

"Rrrrraaaah!" Infidel cried, in full warrior goddess mode as she launched herself into the sky. I lost sight of her as Slor Tonn wriggled in the sky, either to take evasive action, or to meet her head on.

It proved to be the latter, as Infidel drove the Gloryhammer into the tip of the whale's nose with a wet smack. A wave rippled through the beast's blubber, snapping some of the harness rings, and it took everything I had to hold on as the whale lurched sideways. Up above, Tarpok cried, "Chakaaaa!" and thrust the harpoon with a grunt.

Seconds later, I heard Infidel shout, "Damn it!" She sounded more annoyed than hurt. For the briefest instant, she flashed through my line of sight in a rapid arc; her long white cape was snagged by the barbs of the harpoon.

Tarpok looked perturbed that his throw hadn't resulted in a direct hit.

"Nakkertok, Slor Tonn!" he shouted.

I had no time to ask for a translation as the whale spun to hang perpendicular to the ice a hundred feet below, its body rigid as a plank. Infidel floated beneath us, trying to shed her cape, but the clasp had twisted back over her shoulder.

"Chakaaa!" Tarpok shouted again, and we descended toward the ice like God's own gavel.

Infidel managed to get the Gloryhammer beneath her, so the enchanted mallet took the brunt of the impact, smashing the ice to chips an instant before her body slammed into the freezing ocean and was promptly pushed a hundred feet beneath by Slor Tonn's bulk. Whether from the impact, the shock of the cold, or the crushing effect of descending a hundred feet underwater in the span of a heartbeat, Infidel went completely limp. The Gloryhammer slipped from her fingers and began to float upward, until Tarpok used his ape-like reach to snag it. With his other hand he brought in the harpoon, dragging Infidel's slack body toward him.

She was barely alive. In the pitch darkness beneath the ice her aura flickered, growing dim. Her light became so faint I became aware of a second glow, no bigger than a firefly in the lower half of her belly. Our daughter?

With each second that we lingered beneath the frozen waves, Infidel's aura grew dimmer, like a candle surrendering to the wind.

The bubbles of gas that seeped from my clothes suddenly changed directions. Slor Tonn was pointed toward the surface once more. Seconds ticked by before I could see the shattered ice toward which we swam, then, with a great splash, the mighty whale burst into the air and kept swimming in the sky.

As we leveled off, Tarpok shoved Infidel's body under a harness line, trapping it. Water drained from her mouth and nostrils, quickly turning to ice. She coughed weakly, her eyes closed, and began to breathe shallow teaspoons of air, the faintest puffs imaginable escaping her darkening lips.

Certain that my arms were wrapped in the harnesses, I slipped from my body. I saw the golden cage now dangled by a single silver wire within what was left of my chest. If not for my shirt holding them together, all my chest staves would have fallen away. What would happen if the golden cage were to come completely loose?

I had no time to think of such things. Instead, I let my ghostly form hover next to Infidel. Her lips had turned blue. She'd been sopping wet and now her hair and clothing had frozen solid. Tarpok had shoved the Gloryhammer beneath the harness as well. I remembered how, in her phantom form, Aurora had been able to touch the Jagged Heart to trigger its powers. Could I do the same? If I could place the hammer in Infidel's grasp, would its magical energies revive her?

My spectral fingers sank into the glowing weapon. Instantly, I regretted my action. When I'd touched the hammer previously, it had been with wooden fingers and nothing had happened. When my spectral palm passed through the surface of the weapon, I felt the precise opposite of the surge of power Infidel had described. Instead, there was a terrible suction hungry to devour my spiritual energies. My vision blurred as I struggled to resist the weapon's pull. In my panic, I reached for Infidel's limp hand, which lay outstretched toward me. To my astonishment, my fingers felt solid as they closed around hers. With her as my anchor, I resisted the suction of the hammer and pulled myself free.

I stared at the weapon. What had just happened? It had unfolded so swiftly, I'd had no time to understand the experience. But… there was something inside the hammer, residing in the Glorystone from which it had been carved. It felt… intelligent, ancient, vast, and lonely. So lonely. Unending solitude lay at the core of this weapon, an emptiness that wanted to consume all that it touched. What did this mean? Had I somehow encountered the soul of Glorious within the Gloryhammer? Could I possibly communicate with him if this was so? I shook my head. I dare not expose myself to this terrible emptiness again.

As frightened as I was of the hammer, I was even more frightened that I could touch Infidel's hand. Only once in my phantom form had I experienced the sensation of physical contact… when I'd felt Ivory Blade's phantom blood trickling across my fingers.

Was I now feeling Infidel's soul? Had she slipped so far loose of her mortal shell that she was now in the between realm where I dwelled, half way between life and not-life? I wrapped my arms around her, determined to hold her soul in her body. She stirred at my touch.

"So c-cold," she whispered in my ear, though her blue lips didn't move in the slightest.

"Hug me back," I whispered, tightening my grip on her. "Take my warmth."

She didn't respond. Did she hear me? Did I have any warmth to give? What could I, a ghost, offer in comfort or strength? And yet... Sorrow had treated my soul as a source of energy that her golem could tap. This energy had taken form in my ghost blood. Sorrow had taken my life force without my permission. Could I give it willingly?

With Infidel, giving was so easy.

My hand moved to the bone-handled knife in my belt. I drew the blade across the palm of my left hand. Beads of ghostly blood bubbled up. I took Infidel's hand and made a matching cut across the palm. I rolled the bone-handled knife across my palm until it was wet, then placed it in her grasp.

I wrapped my fingers over Infidel's hand, our woven wedding bands touching. Under other circumstances, this might have been a romantic gesture, even loving. But what did I truly know of romance? What did I know of marriage, beyond the exchange of rings? My own upbringing had been devoid of parents to guide me on such matters. Most married men I met in Commonground had left their wives in distant lands, and gladly so. All I knew of marriage was that it was treated by much of mankind as a burden.

I would gladly bear any burden for this woman.

A sudden warmth flushed over me as I remembered the tropical heat of our last shared night on this earth, fleeing through the jungle, pouring sweat, my heart pounding, but not with fear. There had been such excitement in the air that evening, such a grand pulse of adventure stirring our mutual blood. Had she known then how much I loved her?

Of course, I'd finally told her when we'd met again, on the volcanic slopes of Greatshadow's spirit home in the abstract realms. There we'd held each other naked in the dry, near-blistering heat, our bodies braided into a single knot. It hadn't been imagination... my life energy had flowed into her, creating a spark of new life.

I squeezed her hand with all my strength. Our ghostly bloods mingled as our grasp grew feverishly hot. I began to sweat as I felt the spiritual flame within me gush through my veins. Like water draining from a sink, my life force began to swirl out of me, passing though the enchanted knife to flow into my bride. I raised my spectral hand and saw it age rapidly, the flesh withering, flaking away as sprites of light and heat which engulfed Infidel. As I watched, her cheeks once more took on color. Her breathing grew stronger and steadier.

As quickly as the sensation started, it switched off, and my spectral teeth began to chatter. All my heat had now drained away. There was no flesh or blood left of my hand, only bone.

With a gasp, Infidel opened her eyes. I could see myself reflected against her open pupils, twin black mirrors showing a human skull staring at her.

I squeezed her hand where our rings met, but my fingers found no purchase. She was now safely returned to the material world.

And I? I fell backward, drifting in the artic air, utterly drained. I caught a glimpse of my body as I tumbled, a mere skeleton, translucent and fading in the starlight.

I'd grown too weak to hold onto this world any longer. It saddened me to know that I would never learn how Infidel's story played out, whether she'd survive to give birth to our daughter, whether she'd live a full life long after my band of hair had fallen to dust and my memory was hard to summon.

I closed my eyes, prepared to vanish.

Then, though Slor Tonn had flown on half a mile as I'd drifted, I heard a single whispered word on the wind: "Stagger?"

It was Sorrow's voice, sounding in the bean-case ear.

I opened my eyes. A single silver filament, finer than human hair, snaked through the night sky toward me. It slithered between my jaws and hooked me like a fish, reeling me back into the golden cage.

"Stagger, can you hear me?" asked Sorrow. "What's happening. Is everything okay?"

I didn't feel strong enough to move my arms, but with effort I found my paper tongue. It was frozen solid, but somehow I coaxed from it a sickly, crinkling rattle no one could ever mistake for a human voice: "Save Infidel."

Perhaps Sorrow's attunement with the magic of my wooden body allowed her to understand me, since she answered, "If she needs saving, I take it you're both still alive?"

I felt like this deserved a sarcastic response, but I couldn't find the energy.

"You know what I mean," Sorrow amended a second later, perhaps chastised by my silence.

"Slor Tonn… from below," I crinkle-croaked. "Infidel alive… barely. I'm… used up. Nothing left… but ghost bones and teeth."

"Bones and teeth are rather durable," said Sorrow, sounding clinical. "They can last centuries. Perhaps your rate of disintegration will slow now."

Her words were both a comfort and a curse. Perhaps I could linger for centuries in this condition. But did I want to? All my strength had been stripped away. I felt as if I was in the grip of the most formidable, incapacitating hangover of all time.

"In any case, just hold on," said Sorrow. "There's not much left for me to do with the *Freewind*. Even with my powers, the damaged keel is beyond repair. Levi's trying to convince Gale to abandon ship."

I wondered what this would mean for the ghost of Jasmine Romer, but had no energy to ask the question.

"I'm going to join you once I've made preparations," Sorrow said.

"How?" I asked, or tried, as my voice gave out.

"I'll be out of contact a while as I focus on … on something important," Sorrow said. "Just hold on a little longer!"

I didn't have the strength to ask further questions. I could only watch helplessly as the ogre village appeared on the horizon. Given the stark sameness of the landscape, I hadn't noticed before how low Slor Tonn was flying. With the village providing a fixed reference, I noticed that the whale cut a rather drunken path through the sky. How much damage had Infidel done when she'd hit him?

Seconds later I had my answer, as we reached the edge of the village and Slor Tonn failed to clear one of the ice domes. It shattered beneath his belly. The mighty whale's body trembled as he gave one last push with his tail, trying to gain altitude, but he rose only a few dozen feet before his arc leveled out. He swam through the air another quarter mile toward the cliff temple. Then, despite Tarpok calling out commands urging him onward, the beast's body went slack. We slammed into the ice, sliding a hundred yards across the glassy surface before skidding to a halt.

In seconds, we were surrounded by a throng of ice-ogres. Three of the crowd were ogresses dressed in long, black walrus coats, the same style that Aurora used to wear. I'd always assumed she was merely being stylish, but now I wondered if this was some sacred garb of her priesthood, since the three black-coated ogresses began to shout commands that were instantly obeyed. They also sported the same top-knots of blue hair, and were somewhat shorter than the other ogres in the surrounding crowd.

Once more, I found my lack of actual vocabulary to be less of a hindrance to understanding what was being said than one might suppose. Tarpok freed Infidel from her bindings and tossed her limp form to the nearest priestess, with a gruff statement that certainly amounted to, "Here's your damn monster."

The priestess responded with a question ending in the word, "Purity?"

Tarpok shrugged. He loosened the Gloryhammer and brandished it. His next sentence was short and declarative. I'm pretty sure it translated, "I'm keeping this."

He slid down from the whale, pausing as he caught sight of my limp form tangled in the harness. "How the hell did this get here?" was the gist of his grumble as he ripped me free and tossed me across the ice.

Almost immediately, an ice-ogre ran toward me, only to be knocked aside by another who dove and slid across the ice as he scooped up my component parts in his thick arms. He stood and growled something threatening and the dozen hungry looking ogres staring at him kept their distance. If I could have chuckled, I would have. I think they thought I was edible. Were they in for a disappointment!

The ogre who'd claimed me carried me away, walking past Slor Tonn's mouth. The whale had vomited when it landed and the ice was covered in seal parts and half-chewed cod, which other ogres fought over.

Slor Tonn had what I can only describe as a split lip, a yard long gash running up from a now-toothless segment of his upper jaw, jagging like a raw-pink lightning bolt in an arc back toward his left eye. Tarpok and a priestess stood by the beast's head, their hands upon it as they whispered words of comfort to the wounded whale. I felt a sense of remorse - no one likes to see an animal suffering - mixed with a feeling of satisfaction that Infidel had at least gotten in one good lick.

As for Infidel, I caught one last glimpse as I was carried away, when I spied the priestess carrying her toward the carved cliff-side, cradling her like a baby.

Still unable to lift a limb or even move my tongue, I was helpless as my ogre captor carried me through the village back to his home. He stooped to enter the icy dome. A trio of young ogres looked up as he entered. An ogress with four flabby teats rolled over on a nest of sealskins and asked something. My captor responded by throwing me to the floor. One of my eyes popped off and skittered across the ice as my coconut skull cracked on impact.

The ogress asked something to the effect, "How am I supposed to cook that?"

The ogre seemed to reply, "Don't vex me, woman! I've done my part!"

The ogress stirred from the bed, muttering beneath her breath as she reached to grab the nutshell. She crushed it between her thick fingers, then pulled the rest of my form to her. She quickly stripped free what remained of my cloak and pants. She looked utterly crushed as she found nothing but rotting wood underneath.

If she'd bothered tearing open my chest, she would have found the precious metals inside, and maybe the male ogre could have pretended that the whole wooden body thing was just a way of hiding his real gift, a tiny golden cage with a silver mosquito. But, instead of opening my chest, she looked up at her mate and said a single word that certainly didn't sound like, "Thanks!"

The male responded with a savage growl and a sudden, backhanded slap across the ogress's cheek. He shouted at her, a rapid string of syllables I couldn't begin to pick apart. The three young ogres all huddled together at the farthest side of the room, their eyes wide with terror.

The ogress ran her hand across her mouth. She paused to study the blood on her fingertips. She said something in a calm, firm tone.

The male ogre sagged, his face going slack, his arms dangling uselessly by his side. Whatever she'd said to him had taken all the fight out of him. He turned slowly and slouched away, pausing to look at his children with a mournful gaze, before stooping to crawl from the ice-hut.

Ogre-mom lifted me up, staring at my coconut face with an expression of complete disgust. Without further ado, she tossed my body on the dung-fire.

16 - TONGUE OF FLAME

THE FIRE WAS slow to claim me. At first, I wondered if I might extinguish the flames as the ice that coated my wooden form melted, sending water gushing into the foul slurry of whale oil and dung. The water pooled into shallow circles that hissed and turned to steam.

My paper tongue loosened as the ice crystals that stiffened it melted away.

"Save me," I whispered, but my voice was too faint for the ogres to hear over the sizzle of the flames as they licked the oak staves of my chest.

"Sorrow," I cried out, praying she would hear, not knowing what she could possibly do. Alas, she didn't answer, or if she did, I failed to hear it as my seed pod ear shriveled, crackling in the heat.

I had no choice but to abandon my wooden body. But once I was rid of it, could what remained of my spirit endure? Could I ignore the subtle whisper growing ever louder in my mind to accept that I was dead, that it was time to disperse, to surrender what slight energy remained in me back to the universe?

Within my golden cage, I tried to urge my spiritual body toward the door. I failed to budge. I lacked the energy even to crawl. I could do nothing but smolder and wonder what came next.

The paper at the back of my coconut jaws crinkled and writhed as it baked in the increasing heat. Any second my tongue would burst into flames, silencing me forever. But what was left to say?

Despite the growing heat a chill ran through me as I realized there was only one name one dare not waste if gifted with a tongue of flame. A jet of smoke curled from my ragged jaws as I spoke: "Greatshadow!"

The embers that swirled above my desiccating body suddenly turned. The swirl of sparks paused for an instant into a shape resembling the head of a horse. Twin clusters of sparks on each side coalesced into eyes, studying me.

"Help me," I murmured with my tongue now wreathed with dancing fire.

"You are familiar to me," whispered the smoke and cinders above.

"I'm the husband of Innocent Brightmoon," I said, as my tongue crumbled to ash.

The flames about me danced into a decidedly serpentine appearance. The outline of an equine head filled with more red sparks, thickening to resemble scales. Smoke knifed into the shape of fangs as the creature's mouth parted to speak. "You are Abstemious Merchant. You brought the Jagged Heart to my kingdom to kill me."

"I came to your kingdom to rescue the woman I loved," I said. Though I no longer had a tongue, Greatshadow still looked like he was listening. "She spared your life when you were at your weakest. You owe her."

"I owe her nothing. And you, less than nothing," the dragon said.

"It's a favor I seek, not a reward. Save Infidel. At the very minimum, help me save her."

By now, the boards in my chest had dried sufficiently to catch fire with a sudden *WHOOOMPH.* Jets of flame from my shoulders reached up like a beggar's arms, pleading for Greatshadow's aid. "Infidel reminded you of how well humans have served your purposes," I said, desperate to persuade him. "We feed you daily. Even now, you devour my body. Is it too much to ask for a little help in return?"

Greatshadow said nothing.

There was a sudden pain, sharp and stabbing, where my heart used to be. The gold and silver inside me were melting.

"Please," I whispered.

Greatshadow turned his face away. "Even if I wanted to help you, what makes you believe I have the power?"

"You *are* power," I whispered. "If you cannot aid me, then all hope is lost."

Greatshadow continued to look away. With a sigh, he said, "Your faith is great. What you ask shall be given… for a price. You will give me your body in exchange."

"Anything," I sobbed.

"So be it," he said.

The swirling flames above me took on the shape of a large red claw, reaching for my chest.

About five years ago, I'd bitten into an olive and been careless of the pit. I'd cracked a molar right down the root. Infidel had volunteered to yank the tooth, using iron tongs borrowed from a blacksmith. I downed shot after shot of whiskey until her offer sounded sensible, then let her get to work.

I should have drank a *lot* more whiskey.

This tooth extraction came to mind as the tiny speck of blood inside the mechanical mosquito within me began to boil and bubble free from its tiny cage. It was as if Greatshadow's claws had reached inside and snagged my soul, and now yanked it loose with the same bone-mangling enthusiasm that Infidel had displayed in her amateur dentistry.

Slowly the pain subsided. The ringing in my ears ceased as I stopped screaming. The stars dancing before my eyes faded one by one. I was left staring at my clenched fingers, writhing in the air before me.

I had fingers. I had arms!

I once more had lips, because I smiled. *I was alive!*

Only, as I sat up, I understood that I'd merely returned to my previous phantom existence, with the illusion of life, at least. I glanced down at my spectral body, nothing but dry bones when last I'd gazed upon it, and found my limbs now sheathed with muscles. My legs still glowed with internal heat, faint flames shimmering as they cooled into a new sheath of skin.

I was briefly distracted from my rebirth by a whirlwind of activity around me. The ogress and her children were grabbing their belongings and tripping over themselves as they fled the hut. The raging bonfire that my wooden body had unleashed had thrown sparks onto the sealskins that lined the room. The oily hides now burned with ferocious energy. The icy chamber transformed into a furnace as the last ogre child slipped out the door.

"Abstemious Merchant," Greatshadow roared from smoke that whirled up through the small chimney hole. "This was not your true body I've devoured!"

"Not my original body, no, but I'd gotten comfortable in it, more or less," I said.

"I've breathed life once more into your spiritual body," said Greatshadow. "I demand your physical flesh in exchange."

"I promise to dig up my corpse the first chance I get, though it's probably pretty ripe by now."

"I don't want your old shell," said Greatshadow.

"What else do I have to offer?"

"Your daughter. Her form will contain enough of your physical essence to satisfy me. You must give her freely."

I raised my fist to him. "Over my dead body!"

"Don't be so ungrateful," said Greatshadow. "I've given the aid you sought. You now owe me."

"I'm not going to let you kill my daughter!"

Greatshadow chuckled. "She would be of no use to me dead."

"Then what–"

"The Isle of Fire is my domain. I require that your daughter dwell there as she is raised."

I ground my teeth together. What game was the dragon playing at? Did he know that's what Infidel and I had already wanted for our daughter?

"That's all you ask? That she grow up on the Isle of Fire?"

Greatshadow nodded.

"Have you… have you heard us speak of this?" I asked, thinking of the lanterns aboard the *Freewind*. "It's said that you watch mankind through every flame."

"Every candle, every lantern… and every dung filled hearth in these frozen wastes. From cook-fires on the cliffs surrounding this bay, I watched as a ship from the Silver Isles arrived this summer. I've caught whispers as an alliance was formed between King Brightmoon's men, Tarpok, and Hush's chosen prophet, Purity. I stood witness as the sky above the village tore open and Purity returned in her new body, carrying the Jagged Heart."

"Purity's planning to kill Glorious," I said.

Greatshadow chuckled. "Indeed. But Purity is merely a pawn in a much larger game. There are forces at work that wish to destroy all primal dragons. It's no coincidence that the plot against Glorious follows on the heels of the attempt to slay me. Nor is Glorious the only target."

"King Brightmoon and the Church of the Book are behind all of this," I said.

Greatshadow's chuckle turned into a guffaw. "The primal dragons need fear no mortal king. Were it my will, I could burn his kingdom to bare stone. The king is a mere puppet dancing on the strings of the true threat."

I held my tongue. I couldn't help but think of the Black Swan. She'd openly admitted to working behind the scenes to manipulate world events. Could she be the puppet master? As curious as I was to learn of the greater plot, I pushed aside my questions to focus on my most urgent desire.

"Infidel," I said. "You've got to help me find her. We came here to stop the plot against Glorious. I've seen you create avatars to enforce your will in Commonground. Can you create an avatar from the fuel at hand to help us fight Purity?"

"If I were to openly meddle outside my recognized domain, other dragons would take notice. For now, you alone must aid your spouse. Have faith. Infidel has proven capable of protecting the world from those who seek to alter the balance of power."

"I'll help her however I can," I said. "But–"

Before I could get out my next word, a thunderous *CRACK* rang out from the ice dome above me. Half a second later, the whole dome collapsed and the flames around me were instantly snuffed. I stood amid the wreckage unharmed, my phantom body glowing faint red beneath a coat of fine ash, as if I were metal pulled fresh from a forge. This glow slowly faded, restoring my ghostly shell to its ordinary translucence. Judging from the crowd of ogres that gathered to gawk at the fallen dome, I deduced I remained invisible. None even glanced at me as I waved my hand and said, "Awk!"

My status quo as a phantom wasn't such a horrible thing. I was free to move about again and proceeded to do so. The burnt hair and dead fish stink of burnt seal pelts was a good incentive to move on.

Goal one: Find Infidel.

I felt for the tug of her wedding band. Nothing.

I looked down at my ring finger. My braided ring was gone, consumed by the spiritual flames Greatshadow had used to restore me.

So instead I searched for the pull of the bone-handled knife, once as powerful as gravity. I couldn't sense it. Of course, when it had been in the spirit world with me, it had never felt like anything other than an ordinary knife. It had only affected me when it had been a bridge across dimensions, a gate between life and not-life. What had happened to it when I'd left it in Infidel's grasp? When her spirit had fused once more with her body, had the knife been sucked back into the material world? Or had it simply tumbled from her grasp, an immaterial thing, now lost forever on the artic wind?

I flew toward the temple. The ogres were busy chopping a trench in the ice around Slor Tonn. The whale was still alive; I could see his breath as great puffs of steam from his blowhole. His wound had been stitched up and sealed beneath a poultice of oily jelly with a vibrant green hue. The ogres jumped back as a slab of ice around Slor Tonn's head snapped loose, sending tall fountains of water jetting up through the gaps around it. The whale flopped like a fish on a bank as the water washed over it, sending further cracks through the ice. With a powerful full-body thrash, the whale pulverized the weakened ice beneath it sufficiently to open a hole. Slor Tonn slid into the frigid waters below. I wondered if he'd regain the strength to fly.

I hovered before the cliff, studying it closely. There were at least a dozen possible entrances. The lowest and largest was a cave at the level of the bay; the ice continued inside for as far as I could see. It looked big enough to sail a boat into. I floated down, and found that the entrance was partially blocked by a mound of severed ogre heads, some little more than skulls, others looking freshly frozen. Their dead eyes stared at me with looks of indignation. Far beyond them, I saw faint lights. I decided to begin my investigation here.

Within the chamber, I found a medium-sized schooner lifted from the frozen waters and supported by what can only be described as a dry dock of ice. The ship appeared to be in good condition. Closer inspection showed that the ship was the *Relentless*; having spent my adult years in conversation with sailors from around the world I knew that this ship belonged to King Brightmoon's Judgment Fleet. The king had empowered these ships to serve as floating courts. They enforced the law at sea, with their captains serving as judge, jury, and executioner. The judge-captains kept a commission from the ships they seized to pay for their expenses; the rest was sent to the king. Even minor infractions were enough to justify seizing a ship, cargo and crew, which could only be released after payment of substantial fines.

In Commonground, it was noted that most people who functioned under a similar business model were labeled pirates and hung from gallows in civilized ports. In these same ports, the judges were revered as champions of the law. Of course, a judge would face a fate far less dignified than hanging if he'd dare sail into Commonground. Everywhere you look in this world there's symmetry.

I hadn't come here looking for symmetry, but for my wife. Unfortunately, I felt no connection pulling me. A score of corridors led off from this frozen underground bay. Which to follow?

As I contemplated my next move, I spotted a light from a tunnel near the *Relentless*. Shadows danced out over the frosted wooden surface of the ship. A second later, a robed man emerged from the hall. I recognized him instantly from his drab garb as a friar of the Church of the Book. Unlike the monks I'd been raised among who rarely strayed from the grounds of their cloister, friars were nomadic holy men, traveling the world. I use the term 'holy men' loosely; while they were respected members of the church, they lacked the direct connection to the One True Book demonstrated by Truthspeakers, and, unlike monks, they took no vows of meekness. Most of the assassins who'd shown up in Commonground looking for Infidel had been friars.

This friar carried a bundle wrapped in a large sealskin. He looked quite agitated. While friars did share vows of poverty with monks and priests, this one was sporting a rather eye-catching bit of wealth; a signet ring on the middle finger of his right hand was inset with a facetted glorystone, casting a light bright as a lantern.

The friar headed up a series of gangplanks to the deck of the *Relentless*. His loud footsteps on the beams caused the door of the aftcastle to be thrown open. A large man in a heavy coat stepped out and said, "Be quiet, brother. The judge is already in bed."

"Wake him at once," the friar said, shaking the bundle of skins he carried. "He must see this."

"There's nothing in those pelts that can't wait until tomorrow," said the guard.

The friar dropped to his knees and whipped the sealskin forward, unfurling it like a blanket. Within was the Immaculate Attire, from boots to collar. A lump formed in my throat.

"Blade's armor?" the guard asked, completely befuddled. "What's *he* doing back here?"

"Blade wasn't wearing it," said the friar. "It was taken off a woman. A woman with platinum hair and silver eyes."

The guard's breath caught in his throat. He whispered, "The Infidel?"

"She fought Tarpok using Lord Tower's Gloryhammer," said the friar. "She survived being crushed by Slor Tonn, though she's been injured. The ogresses are tending to her wounds."

"What?" the guard exclaimed. "If she's wounded, she should be finished off!"

"I know!" said the friar. "The ogresses say that her death would be wasteful. They say she's more valuable to them alive."

"Did you warn them of–"

"They've no respect for my words," the friar snapped. "This alliance is madness! Judge Stern must intervene!"

Judge Stern? The judge who'd hung his own mother? Sorrow's father?

The guard shook his head, then said, "Wait here."

I was disinclined to wait. I flew down the tunnel the friar had emerged from, hoping to find Infidel. Instead, ten yards in, the tunnel forked. On a whim, I chose the right branch. It forked again. Flying back, I chose the left branch. It led to polished dome of ice where murals of whale hunts had been painted on the walls with frozen blood. A half dozen corridors led from here.

With a thought, I was back at the ship. My best hope at finding Infidel was that Judge Stern would demand to see her. I'd follow him, and then what? If he tried to execute Infidel, how could I stop him?

Judge Stern emerged from the aftcastle a moment later, dressed in a thick woolen nightgown. He wasn't a terribly imposing figure, of medium height and build, with a wrinkled face that sagged on his skull. His hair was thinning, but enough remained to pull back into a frazzled braid. He had bushy muttonchops and eyebrows so thick they looked like gray caterpillars crawling on his liver-spotted brow.

"Tell me everything you know, Brother Will," said Stern.

I learned nothing new from the testimony that followed.

"What became of the Gloryhammer?" the judge asked.

"The heathen Tarpok claimed it as his prize," said Brother Will.

The judge grunted his disapproval. "This sacred relic of the church cannot remain in the hands of such a beast," he said. "We'll deal with that matter at another time. For now, we need the ogres to guide us across the Great Sea Above if we're to complete our mission."

This would have been a handy time for Brother Will to ask, "And what is our mission, exactly?" so that I could have learned what the hell they were planning. Alas, he'd already been briefed.

"If the Gloryhammer and Immaculate Attire are here, then the quest to kill Greatshadow must have succeeded, since these assets were deployed there," said Judge Stern. "The guiding hand of the Divine Author has brought these items to us on the eve of our final journey."

"Or else the mission failed," said Brother Will. "Could it be that the most sacred champions of the church have been slain by the Infidel and she's come here to stop us?"

Judge Stern scratched his stubbled chin with his neatly trimmed nails. He nodded slowly, drew a deep breath, then said, "At present, all we have is speculation. Perhaps it's a lucky thing the woman was taken alive. I'm greatly interested in hearing her testimony. Brother Will, go inform the ogresses I shall visit the prisoner as soon as I'm dressed."

"At once, sir," the friar said, before spinning around and scuttling back down the gangplank. I followed, frustrated by how slowly he walked, though in truth I suspect his pace would have winded me if I'd still been alive. After following for five minutes, I was grateful to have a guide. The underground passageways were a labyrinth. They were also curiously empty. I had yet to spot an ogress. Instead, I spied a dozen human men in a long hall, who sat eating from bowls filled with gelatinous lumps of whitefish cooked in a thin gray broth. They were a rough looking bunch, no doubt the sailors from the *Relentless*. They looked well fed. I thought about the ogres in the village so hungry that they'd fought over whale vomit.

At length we reached a cavern carved from solid ice. The place was large enough you could have fit the Grand Cathedral of the Silver City inside it. Starlight filtered down from the translucent ice roof, casting ghostly shadows all about. The front and side of the room was ringed with large ice stalagmites matched below by stalactites; the way they jagged together almost reminded me of teeth.

The undulating floor could have passed for a giant tongue. The spiritual hairs on the back of my phantom neck began to tingle.

Brother Will hurried across the cavern, toward a gap in the ice teeth that led once more into a corridor of stone. To reach this, he passed three large boats covered in hide, similar to the ones that had turned up in Commonground, though lacking dragonheads.

I remembered something Aurora had said in passing back during the hunt for Greatshadow, something I'd paid little attention to at the time: "We'd sail from the dragon's jaws into the Great Sea Above."

Despite Brother Will's brisk pace, I felt I had time to check out my hunch without losing him. I tilted my head skyward and bid my spectral body to rise. I shot into the ice, then through it, rising into the starry sky above. I flashed a mile into the air at the speed of thought before looking down.

The landscape beneath me was all white on white; the starlight provided little in the way of contrasting shadows. Off to the west about a mile away, I could make out the top edge of the cliff and, beyond this, the frozen bay studded with the ice-houses.

Directly beneath me was nothing but snow-covered hills leading off to the west in a series of serpentine ridges. As my eyes adjusted, the truth slowly emerged: The ridges of the hills formed the spine of a dragon.

I was flying directly above the motionless body of Hush. Brother Will had just walked through the cavern of her open jaws.

Perhaps I was growing jaded. Since my death, I'd witness four primal dragons — Abyss, Greatshadow, Rott, and now Hush. I was no longer astonished by their sheer size. It was difficult to judge Hush's true length given that she lay with her body curled, but I would roughly calculate that from snout to tail tip she was a good five miles long. Despite her glacial size, I couldn't help but notice that she was frozen stiff and had apparently not moved in a very long time. She was more landscape than lizard.

I'd been gone long enough. I dove back down, passing straight through her snout into her cavernous mouth, quickly spotting the passage Brother Will had been shuffling toward. I flew in that direction, catching up to the friar mere seconds later.

He descended a winding stone stairwell. Frost sparkled on the walls, lit by his glorystone ring. To my surprise, the passageway came to an abrupt dead end at a wall formed of ice. He rapped the ice with his ring. The space beyond was obviously hollow.

An ogress stepped through the ice-wall, passing through its solid surface as if had been merely a sheet of flowing water. She could have been Aurora's sister for all I knew; her walrus coat, hair, and skin tone were identical, though she stood a few inches taller.

"What do you want?" the ogress asked gruffly.

"Judge Stern wants to interview our prisoner. Is she awake?"

"She is," said the ogress. "But she's *our* prisoner, not yours. She attacked our villagers. She was bested by our champion. Your judge has no authority over her."

"She was carrying holy relics of our church," said Brother Will.

"We've already given you the armor. If your judge wants the hammer, I suggest he argue his case with Tarpok. In any event, you've no need to speak to the prisoner."

"I beg to differ," said Brother Will. "We've every reason to think that this woman is a great enemy of our church."

"*We* are great enemies of your church," said the ogress, in an impatient tone one might use speaking to a particularly dull-witted child. "Purity is an even greater threat to all you hold dear. Your argument isn't terribly convincing."

"Listen to me!" Brother Will said, waving his finger in her face. "Your prisoner has devoured the enchanted blood of the primal dragon Verdant! It gives her strength beyond imagining. She can bend steel with her bare hands. The sharpest blades are blunted when they strike her invulnerable skin! You don't know the danger she poses!"

"You're obviously mistaken about the identity of our captive," said the ogress. "We were able to stitch her wounds with a bone needle; her skin is no tougher than any other of your race. And if she can bend steel with her bare hands, why does she struggle so helplessly when we've bound her limbs with mere leather?"

Brother Will furrowed his brow, obviously stumped by this revelation.

I saw no reason to stand in the hall and listen to these two argue. Instead, I ghosted through the ice and found myself in circular stone cell about seven feet across. Infidel was alone, leaning against the wall, her body covered by a seal pelt. Her bare arms lay before her, bound at the wrists by tight loops of leather. To my astonishment, she held my bone-handled hunting knife in her left hand.

The room was stuffy, even warm, despite the wall of ice that sealed the door. Only a few gaps in the stone allowed air to flow; Infidel looked dazed and drowsy, and I wondered if she was suffocating in this nearly air-tight space. On the other hand, despite the glazed look in her eyes, the color had returned to her cheeks. Save for the numerous bruises around her shoulders and a stitched-up gash on her chin, she looked not too shabby for someone who'd been crushed by a whale.

She looked up as I drifted near her.

"Stagger?" she whispered.

"You can see me?" I asked, my ghost heart freezing. Was she so close to death's door?

"And hear you," she said, keeping her voice low as she glanced at the ice wall. The light from Brother Will's glorystone cast the ogresses shadow on the ice in stark outlines. Infidel winced as she rose to meet me. Beneath her sealskin she was wrapped from armpits to upper thigh with tight white bandages. Her feet were bound together by leather loops that let her move her feet only a few inches apart. She leaned back against the wall to steady herself. Her breathing sounded shallow.

"You're not dead?" I asked.

"I'm too sore to be dead."

"Why'd they let you keep my knife?" I asked. It seemed very odd to leave a prisoner with a weapon, and for the life of me I couldn't imagine how she could have hidden it.

"The ogres don't see the knife," she said. "Only I can see it and feel it; it was stuck to my hand by dried blood. But even when they stitched up my palm, it never fell from my grasp. They ran needles through it as if it wasn't even there."

"It must still be halfway between the spirit realm and the real world," I said. "Maybe it's letting you see me."

"I wish it was letting me cut these cords," she said, placing the knife in her teeth and trying to stab the leather at her wrist. The blade slid right through, like vapor.

"You're in the middle of the ice-ogress temple," I said. "You'd have a hard time getting out of here even if you weren't tied up. To make matters worse, one of the Judgment Fleet is here, the *Relentless*. Judge Stern is on his way to interrogate you to find out of you're *the* Infidel."

"Stern?" Infidel said, spitting the knife back into her palm. "Sorrow's father?"

"Maybe," I said.

"That's a pretty big coincidence, isn't it?" she asked.

"The monks used to say that what we think of as coincidences are all part of the Divine Author's master plot."

"And that plot would be?"

I shrugged. "From what I can gather, just as King Brightmoon allied himself with the Black Swan to slay Greatshadow, he must have struck a deal with either Tarpok or Purity to help kill Glorious. Judge Stern is here representing the king's interests. Maybe. There are lots of gaping holes in my information. But, we don't have time to figure things out, because Stern's coming here to see you. You need to figure out a cover story, quick, so he won't learn who you really are."

"Or I tell him who I really am," said Infidel. "Maybe I can convince him that my father will reward him handsomely for my safe return."

"Or he puts you on trial immediately for high crimes against the church and you're dead before the day's out."

As I said this, the ice door cracked, suddenly collapsing beneath its own weight. Rather than revealing the ogress and the friar, a tall woman with four-arms and wings stood in the doorway. Save for being coated with fine silver fur, her face was a perfect match for Infidel.

"I apologize for eavesdropping," Purity said, with a slight grin. "It's the hound in me, I fear; I can hear every word spoken for a hundred yards in any direction."

"You hear me?" I asked.

"Menagerie's animal senses detect you, though faintly," Purity said. "Have you never felt as if dogs were sometimes staring at ghosts? It seems, indeed, they are."

"Can they also *feel* ghosts?" I said, leaping forward, making a fist, putting all I had into a swing at her chin. I had one shot at taking her by surprise. That shot failed as my ghostly arm wafted through her.

"It seems not, now that you're free of your driftwood shell," she said.

"How about this?" Infidel shouted, hopping forward, raising her bound fists in an uppercut punch.

Alas, Purity caught Infidel's arms with her hands and pushed her away. Infidel's back slammed into the wall. Purity was on her a half second later, grabbing her by the neck, lifting her in the air.

"I like your spirit, princess," Purity said. "I suspect your quickness to violence explains how you've managed to retain your virginity to the spinsterly age of thirty. You're exactly who I need to wake Hush. Sacrificing one of my poor ice-maidens will never do when I can have the blood of a virgin princess!"

Infidel clawed at Purity's wrist. "Your information is out of date. I'm not a virgin. I'm pregnant!"

"Pregnant by a ghost, via copulation in an abstract realm. In the material world, your physical form has never been defiled by a man!"

"Hey!" I protested. "She wasn't *defiled*, period. We're married! And wherever and however it happened, she is indeed pregnant. I saw our baby's spirit glowing in her womb. Anyway, how can you possibly know what happened with us?"

Purity drew her face close to Infidel and sniffed the perspiration that now beaded on her brow.

"An ebony bird told me," she said, staring into Infidel's eyes. "You *are* pregnant. I can smell it in your sweat."

"So you won't be sacrificing her," I said.

"So when I sacrifice her, I'll be sacrificing two virgins at once," said Purity.

"Why do you need to sacrifice anyone?" I asked. "What the hell is going on?"

"This world has seen its last sunrise," said Purity, dismissing me with a wave. "There's nothing you can do to stop me. The ogresses have gone to prepare the boats. Tarpok stands ready with the sacred harpoon. Stern even now dons his sacred garb and readies his Writ of Judgment. Leave this place, little ghost. I find your faint murmurs annoying."

"It makes no sense!" I protested. "Killing the sun is insane! What can you possibly hope to gain from such a thing?"

Purity glanced at me. "An end to ceaseless, pointless chatter, to start with. I've been to the Promised Land, little ghost. I've seen the world in its pristine state, before the sky was tainted by the sun. All the world was once in permanent winter, beneath a silent, smooth blanket of white, slumbering like an innocent child until it was raped by noise, by heat, by light. It is time to complete the circle, and return the world to perfection."

"You're out of your frozen mind," I said.

"And you're annoying me," Purity grumbled. "Go away, little ghost."

When the Black Swan had used similar words, I'd been pushed away against my will. Whatever magic she'd used, Purity hadn't mastered it. I felt no force compelling me to leave. So I wonder if she was surprised when I disappeared?

17 - THAT INFIDEL

MY FINAL TEN minutes in the material world were somewhat hurried. Of course, I was unaware that my moments left were so few. Perhaps there were things I could have done differently, though it's too late for second-guessing.

With ten minutes left, I willed myself back to the deck of the *Freewind*, arriving at the speed of thought. The ship had been tidied up somewhat but was still listing. From the bow of the ship looking toward the stern I couldn't help but notice that the mizzenmast and the foremast were tilting in opposite directions.

The other thing I couldn't help but notice was the giant. I blinked, certain that my phantom eyes were confused. There was a naked man at least a mile tall wading in the ocean beside the *Freewind*. The waves broke against his belly button. Above him, the darkest, most menacing storm clouds I'd ever seen churned violently, though for some reason the seas all around us were relatively calm and only the barest breeze stirred the air. Gale's handiwork, perhaps?

"Your eyes do not deceive you," said Jasmine Romer, materializing before me. "This is my eldest grandson, Levi, short for Leviathan. You may guess the magical gift granted him by the Mer-King."

"He gets big?"

"And stays big," said Jasmine. "Once, he was able to return to human size, but he hasn't done so since he fell in love with a young cloud giantess. He's thrived in his new world, and is now a commander aboard a hurricane."

This was interesting, but had nothing to do with my reason for returning to the ship. Before I could tell Jasmine about Infidel's peril, Levi bent over the *Freewind* and used fingers the size of tree trunks to gently scoop up Cinnamon, Sage, and Poppy from the deck. He lifted them toward the swirling clouds high overhead. It made me notice how quiet the ship was. Shouldn't ice-maidens still be working their bucket brigade?

"Levi feels the *Freewind* is beyond repair," Jasmine said, shaking her head sadly. "The keel has been damaged and Sorrow said she'd be unable to mend it unless the ship was in dry dock. Only Gale, Mako, and Rigger remain aboard, vowing to see the ship to port. Their stubbornness may be the death of them."

The mention of Sorrow snapped my focus back to my immediate problem: "Infidel's been captured. From what I can figure out, Purity has been allied with the ice-ogres and the Church of the Book to kill Glorious for some time now. They plan to use Infidel as a human sacrifice to wake Hush. I don't think we have much time to stop them."

"Then let's hope my grandson's aim is as good as he says it is," said Jasmine.

"I need to find Sorrow," I said. "I'm hoping she can... wait, why should we worry about Levi's aim?"

"Because an hour ago, at her request, he threw Sorrow at the ice-ogre's village."

And that's how the first minute of my last ten came to a close.

Nine minutes left: I willed myself back into the sky above the ogre temple. Sorrow was nowhere to be seen. Had she fallen short? Assuming that Leviathan's strength scaled magically, and that Sorrow had been a mere pebble in his hand, was even he big enough to fling her this far?

I glanced down at Hush's mouth atop the cliff. Should I go back and try to find Infidel? What could I do there when I did find her, other than annoy Purity? There had to be a better plan.

I looked south, back in the direction of the *Freewind*. If I went back there, could I convince Leviathan to come up here? He'd gotten to the *Freewind* quickly enough. I had some experience with hurricane force winds; he could probably cover a hundred miles or more in an hour. But, as I looked toward the horizon, I saw a bright speck against the night sky, like a shooting star with no trail, hurtling toward me.

With a thought, I flew closer. As the distance closed, I realized I was looking at a rather sizable bird. But, my sense of scale was thrown off by the difficulty of judging size with only the stars as a backdrop. I drew closer still and found that I wasn't looking at a bird; I was looking at a pair of copper limbs shaped to resemble albatross wings, covered with fine glass feathers that sparkled in the starlight. Judging from the human figure at the center, the wingspan was at least sixty feet across.

At the center of the wings was a suit of jet black iron armor. Behind the helmet's gleaming glass faceplate, I caught a glimpse a woman gazing out. Sorrow?

Who else could it be?

She sailed past, leaving only a soft tinkling sound in her wake, like wind chimes in a gentle breeze. With a quick glance at the ground flashing below, I saw she was flying at a pace that would have left Slor Tonn in the dust. Of course, 'leaving in the dust' is really only an appropriate metaphor for horseback riding; fifty years of earth-bound existence had left me unprepared for good analogies in describing the speed of flight. Suffice to say, she was moving very damn fast. I gave chase, as one moment bled into the next.

With eight minutes to go, I realized I had no way of speaking with Sorrow. My wooden body was now completely gone... save for the one seed pod earring that Sorrow wore. I caught up and peered through the glass visor that protected her from the wind. It was apparent she couldn't see me, and it was difficult to tell given the tightness of her iron helmet if she still wore the earring. I brushed my spectral fingers along her left cheek and found the pod. My fingers tingled as they connected with whatever faint magic remained in the dry vegetation.

I stretched next to her and placed my lips against her cheek.

"Can you hear me?" I shouted.

I heard nothing, but Sorrow jerked her head to the left.

"Stagger?" she said, though I could barely hear her above the rush of wind. "Where have you been? What's wrong with your voice?"

"Body's gone," I said, trying to keep things as simple as possible. "Purity's in the dragon's head on top of the cliff. She's captured Infidel."

Sorrow's eyes scanned the landscape. She gave a quick nod. "I see it."

I looked in the dragon's direction, surprised that Sorrow had found it so easily, and discovered that Hush's head of translucent ice was now aglow with a pale blue light. Sorrow's wings sang out like a thousand tiny bells as she tilted into a dive leading straight for the dragon's skull.

Even with the amazing speed with which Sorrow flew, we were still so far away. Impatient, I zipped back in the cavern of Hush's jaws, with seven minutes left.

The three walrus skin boats had been dragged into the center of the room. In one boat stood Judge Stern, Brother Will, and the bodyguard from the ship, now dressed in the Immaculate Attire. Behind them sat a crew of human oarsmen. Judge Stern held a yard-long tube of rolled up parchment with both hands. This scrolled glowed faintly in my ghostly vision. It was still sealed, but I recognized it at once as a Writ of Judgment.

These sacred documents were issued by the Voice of the Book himself; they were not issued lightly. If the Voice of the Book pronounced you guilty of a crime deserving death and the Writ of Judgment was read in your presence by a duly appointed authority of the Church, you would die.

In the second boat stood Tarpok, holding his cast-iron harpoon straight as a flagpole, his chest thrust out, looking as if he were in command of the world. The Gloryhammer hung across his back, slung on a strap of seal leather. Behind him were three ogresses, all priestesses judging from their garb, and a dozen human sailors from Stern's boat at the oars.

In the final boat loomed Purity, in a boat manned by ice-maidens. She held the Jagged Heart, which proved to be the source of the light I'd seen outside. Due to the brightness of the glow, it was difficult to look at Purity directly, though I had no choice. She was holding Infidel by the throat, dangling her off the front of the boat. Infidel squirmed in her grasp, which was loose enough to allow for some cursing.

"You prehistoric witch!" Infidel shouted, vainly trying to stab Purity with the phantom blade of the bone-handled knife. "You can't be this stupid! The judge will kill you the second you've completed his dirty work! It's probably your name on the scroll!"

"The judge knows this is a one way journey for him," said Purity. "He's willing to die for his cause. How can I not trust a man like that?"

Judge Stern frowned. "If your trust in me is so great, I wish you'd allow me to question your prisoner. I fear, if she is the Infidel, her dragon-tainted blood may ruin your sacrifice. There's no way her spiritual essence can be considered innocent."

Purity chuckled. "There's no dragon blood in this poor girl's veins. I'd be able to smell it. She may be *an* infidel, but she's not *the* Infidel."

I hovered near the roof of the cavern. No one knew I was there. I had to get Infidel free. There was one thing I hadn't yet done as a ghost that sprang to mind, though whether from inspiration or desperation I cannot say.

With six minutes remaining, I dove down from the cavern toward Purity, waving my phantom limbs for all they were worth, thrusting my face inches before the old witch's mug. I screamed at the top of my ghost lungs, *"BOO!"*

To my utter astonishment, it worked. Purity flinched, dropping Infidel to grab the Jagged Heart with all four hands. She looked frightened as she swung the harpoon in a clumsy arc, using it as a battle staff rather than a thrusting weapon. Given my proximity, I was nowhere near the blade. This proved fortunate, since the shaft of the harpoon impacted my ghostly ribs with a sickening thud that knocked me backward. I flitted toward the roof, clutching my chest. The pain was unbelievable. My ghostly bones had been broken. How could ephemeral mist fracture?

Despite my lack of actual lungs, I coughed violently. Dark blood sprayed from my phantom lips.

Purity composed herself as she realized the source of her ambush. She tilted her head back and laughed.

"Little ghost!" she said. "I thought you'd fled! You should use more caution. Don't you know this harpoon is used to hunt the dead?"

Actually, I did know that. Aurora had said that she used the harpoon to hunt phantom whales. Apparently, it could injure phantom men as well. I was glad I hadn't been near the pointy end.

Infidel had landed on the ice and was trying to wriggle away. Judge Stern's bodyguard leapt from his boat and loped toward Infidel to retrieve her. The formfitting Immaculate Attire didn't flatter his rather large gut. Any sense of comedy I might have felt about his appearance vanished the second he drew his sword with his eyes fixed on my wife.

"Before you kill me," I said to Purity, blinking away tears as blood dribbled down my chin, "you should know that Infidel was right. I spied on Judge Stern earlier and he has three Scrolls of Judgment; one for Glorious, one for you, and the last for Hush!"

It was a lie, of course. At least, if it was truth, it was a truth I couldn't verify. I felt lightheaded as I wiped blood from my mouth. It glistened on my ghost fingers, red and wet and warm.

I looked down at the bone-handled knife in Infidel's hand as she made one last desperate, instinctive attempt to use the phantom blade to cut the leather that bound her legs. Blood on the knife had always pulled my ghostly form more fully into the material world. Would the blade still react to blood?

I flew down and closed my bloody fingers around the intangible steel. I shuddered as I felt it drink.

Five minutes left.

I remained a ghost. But the bone-handled knife, coated with my blood, suddenly sliced through the leather that bound Infidel's legs. The guard stood over her, sword drawn. Infidel kicked with her now free left leg, letting loose a loud grunt as she put her full strength into the guard's right knee cap. With a popping sound, his leg bent backward. He toppled toward her, chopping his blade toward her brow.

Infidel raised her bound wrists, straining to pull her hands apart. She caught the falling blade against her leather bindings. It didn't quite cut through. She twisted her arms, and yanked the sword from the guard's grasp. Bracing the sword between her knees, she slid her wrists along the sword's edge and was free.

With a back flip, she sprung to her feet, sword in hand. Before anyone could react, she sprang forward and punched the tip of the blade into the back of guard's skull, in the half-inch gap between his helmet and his collar. His flailing limbs instantly went slack. Everyone on Judge Stern's boat turned pale.

"Yeah," she said, with a glare in their direction. "*That* Infidel."

I wasn't certain she should be boasting, given that she was half-naked, bruised head to toe, and armed only with a sword and a semi-material hunting knife, facing off against a shape-shifting witch and a half-ton ogre carrying weapons crafted from dragons. In fact, as much as I admired her swagger, I really hoped she'd find her inner Stagger and run like hell. Before I could draw a pained breath into my broken chest to offer the advice, the roof caved in.

Four minutes to go.

A chunk of ice the size of an elephant smashed into the floor between Infidel and the three boats. Something dark was atop this, but vanished in a blizzard before my eyes could focus. Infidel reacted with surprising calmness, stepping backward to avoid the gusting snow. Some of the mariners aboard Judge Stern's boat didn't wait for the air to clear before jumping ship and making a break for it. Stern cast a wicked glance backward, the ferocity of his gaze halting the remaining mariners from abandoning their posts.

The snow cleared and revealed Sorrow crouched atop an imposing boulder of bluish ice. Her wings had either been torn away by impact or she'd shed them to improve her freedom of movement. Her iron armor clung to her like a coat of paint. She stood, stretching her left hand. Iron razors six inches long sprang from her fingertips.

Her other gauntlet crumbled, revealing her right hand, blood red with rust. For some reason, her naked hand was far more menacing than the clawed gauntlet.

"I come to this place intending no malice," she announced. "Purity, we're kindred spirits, aware that the world is an unjust place. We seek, in our own fashion, to better it. I'd rather be your friend than your foe, but I cannot let you extinguish the sun. Renounce your plans and join me on a more constructive path. If you refuse, I give my solemn vow that I shall kill everyone in this room."

"You're the crippled materialist," Purity scoffed. "The pathetic failed witch who nearly killed herself with a bone-nail. Despite the drama of your entrance, you've no power to enforce your threats."

The iron and glass helmet that covered Sorrow's features flowed backwards like mercury, revealing her face and scalp. From my hovering vantage point, I counted swiftly: One, iron. Two, copper. Three, glass. Four, gold. Five, silver. Six, wood. And seven… seven was something black as tar, something that made my eyes ache and my stomach turn.

Sorrow said, in low, firm tones, "I've carved a nail from a fragment of tooth belonging to Rott, the all-consuming. I now command the elemental force of decay. I possess the power I've long sought to remake the world. It does not suit me to have the world end just as I gain the ability to save it."

The helmet spread back over her scalp and face. She said, calmly, "I will begin killing when I count down from three. Three."

Which, as fate would have it, were the number of minutes I had left.

Purity glared at Sorrow's red right hand. I had trouble taking my eyes off it myself. We both had to be wondering what Sorrow's new powers might do to ghosts.

Sorrow had her gaze locked on Purity. From the corner of my eye, I saw Tarpok lean back in his boat, hefting his iron harpoon over his shoulder.

"Sorrow!" I wheezed, though of course no one in the room but Infidel and Purity could hear me. Infidel started running toward Tarpok but it was too late. He hurled the massive shaft of steel, which flashed through the gap of air between him and Sorrow. Sorrow proved more attentive than I'd supposed. She stretched out her right hand, palm open like a shield to catch the harpoon's razor tip. The horrible weapon turned into a cloud of reddish dust, swirling to settle on the ice at Sorrow's feet.

"Two," said Sorrow, though I technically had over two and a half minutes left.

The mariners in Judge Stern's boat once more scrambled overboard. Stern spun around and barked, "Any man whose boot touches the ice shall be hanged!"

The sailors didn't even pause.

Sorrow, on the other hand, turned her head slightly.

"Father!" she called out, in astonishment.

This distraction was all that Purity needed. She lunged forward, her vast wings unfolding, as she thrust the Jagged Heart like a pike. The tip barely touched Sorrow's frozen armor before Sorrow caught the shaft with her red right hand.

Instantly, Sorrow's armor spider-webbed with cracks. As she moved, the iron began to flake away, rendered brittle and useless by the Heart's extreme chill. The narwhale horn of the shaft yellowed where Sorrow touched it, but didn't disintegrate.

The momentum of the impact knocked Sorrow backward. She slipped from her icy perch. Her armor shattered into scraps of black shrapnel skittering across the floor as she landed flat on her back. Purity came to rest on the icy boulder where Sorrow had perched a second before.

"Foolish girl," the shapeshifter growled. "You come here and boast that you wield the power of a primal dragon? What of it? I've surrendered myself to Hush for two full centuries. I'm more than her prophet; I am her avatar! You brandish the power of decay? Cold stops decay!"

Sorrow opened her mouth and drew a breath. I knew her next word would finish her countdown.

But Sorrow wasn't my sole focus of attention. In the exact same span of seconds that Sorrow and Purity had fought, Infidel sprang into action. Tarpok had just thrown his harpoon, his right arm still outstretched. Infidel no longer had the dragon strength that had allowed her to leap rivers in a single stride, but she was a well-muscled woman in her prime who could cover the twenty-yard gap between her and Tarpok in heartbeats. Tarpok clenched is fists as Infidel reached his boat. The upper lip of the leather vessel was eight feet off the ice, but Infidel leapt to within inches of the edge, sinking her bloodied knife into the leather, using it as a pivot point as she swung her body up. In the blink of an eye, she was over the rim, leaving the bone-knife dangling in the leather. With a snarl, she placed both hands on the hilt of her long sword, planted her feet firmly, and drove the honed steel tip with all her weight into Tarpok's belly.

The point of the blade skittered along his stomach, tearing a gash in his sealskin coat. Beneath this a tiny line of beaded blood rose on his white hide. Her most powerful blow had only scratched him.

Infidel had no time to prepare a second strike. Tarpok caught her by the hair and snatched her from her feet.

"I'm going to wring your scrawny neck," he boasted, as he brought her face inches from his own.

Infidel reached over his shoulder, her fingers closing around the shaft of the Gloryhammer. The weapon flared as she took command of its power. Tarpok and Infidel shot skyward with the speed of lightning. They were beneath a section of roof that remained intact. Tarpok's head smashed into the ice, sending a spray of crystalline daggers flying in every direction. Infidel curled her body beneath his as they rose. On impact she drove her elbow straight into the ice-ogre's throat.

Unfortunately, the awkwardness of her position caused the Gloryhammer to tear from her grasp, and they both tumbled back to the floor. They slammed to the ice ten feet behind Sorrow just as she said, "One."

I actually had two minutes left.

Sorrow lay on the ice wearing only a modest silk slip. The braces she'd once worn were gone; her limbs looked to be in full health once again. Perhaps she now had the power to reverse entropy as well? She kept her eyes fixed on Purity as she rose.

"You were warned," the young witch said. Then, she opened her mouth wide as her belly swelled. With a violent convulsion, she vomited, sending a jet of oily black fluid spraying toward Purity. The air instantly stank of rotten meat, a foulness that gagged even me.

The spray broke into black droplets in the air, which began to flitter and buzz. What can only be described as a tornado of flies swallowed Purity. The flies swelled forward from the whirlwind, engulfing the three boats. Screams filled the air as the black cloud covered everything.

Meanwhile, on the ice behind Sorrow, free from flies, Infidel had recovered half a second before Tarpok did. On her knees, she ripped the Gloryhammer free of the leather straps that held it on the ogre's back. She rose to stand above the fallen warrior.

Infidel looked rough. Her impact with the ice had torn loose the stitches on her brow, and bright red blood flowed across her cheek and down her throat. If she felt any weakness, she didn't show it. Instead, she lifted the Gloryhammer with both hands high above her head.

Tarpok, flat on his back, had by now recovered enough to recognize his danger. He swung his right arm up to protect his face.

It didn't help. Infidel swung the hammer down with such force that it snapped his forearm, driving flesh and bone down to pancake flatness as it impacted with his face right between his tusks. His head caved in, squeezing his brains out through his ears.

Infidel stumbled backward as she tried to avoid the sudden gush of blood rolling toward her feet. She looked pale and exhausted as she landed on her butt. The impact caused her to drop the hammer. She took a deep breath as she probed the bleeding wound on her brow with her fingers. She pulled away her hand, coated with her own blood.

To balance herself, she placed her bloodied hand upon the ice beneath her. The ice throughout the cavern instantly turned pink.

My final moment:

The cloud of flies turned white as the insects developed a coat of frost. They plummeted from the air, bouncing as they landed with tiny tapping sounds that built to a deafening crescendo, like a billion bits of gray hail striking a tin roof all at once. In the aftermath, Sorrow had proved unable to live up to her boast of killing everyone.

Not that she hadn't given it her all. The human sailors were dead, or nearly so. Half of them were little more than skeletons wreathed in maggots, the other half were still-living men with skins swollen to the bursting point by writhing things within them gorging on their organs.

The only man unaffected was Judge Stern, who hugged the Writ of Judgment tightly to his breast. These documents were often protected with glyphs to ward off damage; these protections must have shielded the judge as well.

The boat of the ice-maidens was none the worse for wear. The ice-armor that coated the women had proven impervious to the flies.

The trio of ogre priestesses on the final boat were also unscathed beneath shells of ice, but the oarsmen who'd shared the boats with them had been utterly maggotized.

Standing on the boulder of ice, Purity looked down at Sorrow. The shape-shifting witch had sheathed herself with icy armor.

Sorrow took a step backward, bringing her fists up, her brow furrowed as if she was pondering how to respond to this turn of events. But if she'd not expected her attack to be thwarted, she was even more surprised when her feet slipped out from under her and she landed on the pink ice with a wet *smack*.

The dragon's frozen tongue was melting, and melting fast.

Sorrow and Infidel struggled to make it to their feet. They were both soaked by the time they stood. The cavern floor was now six inches deep with pinkish water. The cavern was filled with the aroma of spit mixed with a little blood. The fluid was deep enough that the seal skin boats were starting to float.

With a wave of the Jagged Heart, Purity literally froze both Sorrow and Infidel in their tracks, trapping their bodies in ice.

"Hush has tasted virgin blood!" Purity shouted, looking toward the trio of ogresses. "We've only seconds before the dragon awakens and propels us into the Great Sea Above! Secure our prisoners and place them in the center boat!"

The ogresses leapt from their boat and ran to Sorrow and Infidel. One paused before Tarpok long enough to kick him in the gut, before aiding her sisters in lifting the frozen bodies and rushing back toward Purity's boat. The Gloryhammer was retrieved as well, along with the corpse of Stern's bodyguard still spotless in the Immaculate Attire. The ogresses understood the artifacts were too valuable to leave behind.

The old witch looked over her shoulder. "Judge Stern, as your crew has proven inadequate to the task at hand, would you be so kind as to move to my boat?"

The judge looked dazed, but he nodded and climbed out into the knee-deep water. He paused for a moment, looking down at the remains of his men, then reached into the boat to grab something I couldn't see and stick it in a pocket of his robe. The entire cavern shuddered as he sloshed toward the middle boat.

"Hurry!" Purity cried, watching events from her perch on the ice boulder. "Hush wakes!"

In response, there was a groan, soft at first, building to a deafening roar loud enough that Judge Stern covered his ears as the ogresses helped to push him into the center boat. The frozen forms of Infidel and Sorrow were tossed in like stiff baggage, coming to rest in the middle of the vessel.

The dragon's groan faded, ending with what could only be described as a sob. The noise reminded me, for all the world, of the cry of a woman who'd just been told of the death of a lover. It was the sound, on the most primal level, of a broken heart.

And then the blood came, gushing up the dragon's throat in a great carmine flood. It surged through the chamber, lifting the boats. The dragon's jaws opened to let the blood flow out toward the cliff edge in a great river ten feet deep. Purity flitted down from her icy perch as the flood engulfed it, landing in the central boat.

To the right, the boat that Tarpok commanded spun in the current, the bone-handled knife sticking from its bow.

Despite the fact that my broken ribs made me feel as if my torso was full of shattered glass, cutting me with even the feeblest of motions, I stretched my arm out as I flew toward the boat. The knife was now solidly in the material world. Was there enough of it still in the middle realm where I dwelled that I could grasp it?

I almost laughed as my fingers closed around the hilt and yanked the blade free.

The boats raced forward on the river of roiling gore with Purity standing on the bow, harpoon in hand, her eyes scanning the horizon in the direction of a sunrise which might never come.

This witch had to die.

I flew toward her with the fullest speed of my imagination.

She caught me mid-flight with the Jagged Heart, moving faster than I could follow, driving its tip into my chest beneath my left collarbone. With a push and a twist, my ghost heart was torn free from its arteries and forced down to meet my liver.

The bone-handled knife slipped from my fingers to land at the witch's feet. I opened my mouth to curse her, but only a bubble of blood escaped.

My time in the material world had come to an end.

18 - DEAD IN THE WATER

HOW MUCH OF what happened next is memory and how much is dream is difficult to say.

I hung upon the Jagged Heart like a pig upon a spit. Purity grimaced as my ghost blood ran down the narwhale shaft in dark red spirals, staining her hands. She tried to shake me loose, but the barbed head held me tightly. In the end, she was forced to awkwardly manipulate the harpoon close to her so that she could grab the portion of the staff that jutted from my buttocks. I hung upside down in the boat for a moment. I saw Judge Stern remove his heavy black cloak and drape it over his frozen daughter.

"You attempt to warm her in vain," one of the ogresses said with a scowl.

"I merely wish to hide the shame of her unclothed limbs," said the judge.

By then, Purity had shifted her grasp on the harpoon. She shook the shaft over the edge of the boat and I slid, face down, toward the growing river of blood. I splashed into the fluid, blinded for a moment by the opaque tide, before I floated face up to the surface. I felt no pain. I couldn't move, or even blink. I bobbed along in the current, utterly limp. Just as I could no longer reach for one of the oars cutting into the blood mere feet from my shoulder, my mind, too, lost its ability to hold on to reality. I felt as if fog rolled in from the edges of my memories, blotting out all that remained of my consciousness.

And yet… and yet I do have impressions of my journey into the realm beyond. Perhaps some faint spark of personality remained to bear mute witness to my fate. Or, equally plausible, I've imagined details to fill in the gaps.

Be it truth or dream, this is my recollection:

When the river of blood reached the edge of the cliff, rather than spilling over to flood the ogre village below, the river darkened as it spread outward into the air, flowing toward the stars. My corpse was carried by the current far ahead of the boat that carried Infidel. Purity stood on the bow, the harpoon held before her like a battering ram. A pale glow originated from the Jagged Heart and spread across the sky, triggering a magnificent display of the northern lights. Behind the boat, Hush stirred, her icy body rising, her coat of snow and ice falling away to reveal a crystalline dragon the size of a mountain. As she spread her snowy wings, blizzards spun from the tips, dancing outward in ever strengthening waves. Much of the world would wake to a morning covered with snow.

The blood flood continued to rise, though at some point my perceptions flipped and instead of rising, we were falling. The stars above were now the stars below, and we tumbled, one and all, toward the vast black sea of night. As the waters grew closer, I saw that the stars, so small at a distance, were actually bits of ice, brilliant as diamonds. They continued to grow larger as I fell, growing from flea specks to fragments the size of fingernails, to chunks as large as my palm, to floes as big as boats, until they became small islands, hundreds of yards across. I smashed into the waters that separated these icy isles. The sea was awash with light. As I bobbed back toward the surface, I saw that the cold waters were dense with phosphorescent krill, glowing ghostly shades of green and blue. Ghostly was an especially apt adjective, since the krill looked like translucent wisps of light rather than beings of flesh. I understood, at last, the origins of the auroras we'd witnessed in these northern latitudes.

By pure chance, my face turned heavenward as I reached the surface. Purity's boat was nowhere in sight. Snow clouds roiled high above, filling the sky, reflecting the pale glow of the sea.

From these clouds emerged a whale. It was Slor Tonn, his head split open. I could see through his great black and white form as he tumbled through the air. He was as much a phantom now as I'd been. He splashed into the waters some distance away from me. My body was tossed by the waves created by his impact. I found myself upside down, my lifeless eyes staring into infinite blackness, my feet now above water. I could not move to right myself. I don't know how long I drifted, numb and silent.

Dead in the water.

Then, far below, a faint circle of white, like a smoke ring, growing, rising toward me.

It was Slor Tonn. His massive jaws were opened into a toothy circle. His jaws clamped down on my waist, severing my legs. The last thing I remember, or dream I remember, is the pressure of his tongue flattening me against the roof of his mouth before he swallowed.

And then there was nothing.

AND THEN THERE was something. In the dark and silent void, I heard… music. The song was faint, the far away voices of women singing unaccompanied by instruments. I couldn't recognize the words; the language sounded like that of ogres. It didn't matter. The music was the most beautiful thing I'd ever heard, haunting and heart-breaking yet joyful, filling me with loneliness, then promising to take that loneliness away.

My peaceful communion with this ghostly melody came to an abrupt end as I was vomited from the belly of the whale. Imagine a sound like a cat coughing up a hairball, assuming you were inside the cat, and the cat was fifty feet long. This disgusting cacophony served as my trumpet to awaken me to judgment day. I found the will to open my eyes as I was squeezed through the whale's undulating esophagus, my passage illuminated by reeking buckets of half-digested ghost krill. I exploded out upon the whale's great pink tongue, my arms flopping uselessly. My left hand snagged against the whale's saw-like teeth and was severed as I was spat onto an ice floe. The pain of losing my hand was agonizing. The pain of everything was unbearable. My chest was nearly hollow; half my guts had spilled out when Slor Tonn had snapped me off at the legs. My heart was trying to beat, but faced the difficulty of having been chopped to mince-meat by Purity's harpoon.

I squeezed my eyes tightly to hold back the gush of tears. Never had I hurt so badly, not even when I'd died the first time in the material world.

There were voices around me, ogres judging from the deepness of the tones and the harsh, hacking syllables of their vocabulary. Not such a big surprise, I guess. The Great Sea Above was heaven for ogres.

Clenching my teeth to control the pain, I managed, through extreme force of will, to open my eyes. I was flat on my back on the ice. An ogress crouched above me. She was nude save for a necklace of whale teeth, and her pendulous breasts nearly touched my nose. She shifted, giving me a better view of her face, though I wish she hadn't. Her visage was a horrifying mass of blisters and raw flesh, black around the edges, as if she'd been burned. Above her blackened tusks, her pale blue eyes were gentle, even kind. Her hair was pulled back into a severe top-knot, the hair singed and frizzed.

Her half-charred lips were set in what can only be described as a bemused grin.

"I was there the night the fortuneteller predicted the sea would swallow your bones," she said. "She forgot to say you'd get spit back out."

"Aurora?" I gasped.

"Yes," she said. "I'm guessing you're in a world of pain."

Tears streamed down my cheeks as I swallowed hard. "Unbearable."

She reached into a pouch at her side, then pushed something rubbery between my teeth. With her meaty fingers, she worked my jaws, forcing me to chew. The taste was like raw, rotten kidney mixed with licorice. I wanted to spit, but she held my lips shut. I decided to swallow. Given that my stomach had fallen out of my rib cage, it was the fastest path toward getting rid of whatever foul thing she was poisoning me with. However, as I swallowed, my pain eased. It wasn't just a numbing that came over me, but a flush of heat and energy.

"That was a slice of dried adrenal gland from a polar bear," Aurora said. "That gland sits next to the kidney, so your saliva's going to taste like urine, I'm afraid. Give it a minute to kick in and you should feel better."

I nodded. "Not even a minute. That's pretty good stuff."

Aurora shrugged. "Get used to it. Now that you're dead, you'll be eating it by the fistful. It's pretty much the only thing to soothe the pain."

"I've been dead for weeks. Until now, it hasn't really hurt," I said.

"Last I saw you, you hadn't passed on to the afterlife. You were just a pathetic ghost haunting the woman you used to love."

"Still love," I said. "Nothing's pathetic about that. And last I saw you, you'd been fried by Greatshadow, and your ghost was off to the Great Sea Above to find your family."

Aurora picked me up, placing me upright on the ice. We were surrounded by a score of ogres in various states of decay. Most were short a limb or two. Some were missing heads. "I found them."

I raised my remaining hand and said, "Awk." The ogres who could manage it raised their hands to return the greeting. They were a sad looking lot. Most were chewing on rubbery bits of bear gland like gum. Even from a distance, their breath smelled of piss.

"I thought the Great Sea Above was heaven for your people," I said. "Why is everyone in pain?"

"Heaven and hell are myths of your people. For my people, there is life, and beyond. Once you're in the Great Sea Above, you're immortal. Your body no longer ages. This also means that it no longer heals. You remain in the same state you died in, unless you suffer further injuries here, or your corpse decays or is damaged back in the material world. Ordinarily, this isn't a problem. We entomb our dead in ice, where their bodies may remain unchanged for eons. Alas, when I was driven from the temple, conflicts that followed led some ogres to desecrate the bodies of my relatives. The call song I sing extends back thirty generations. I should be surrounded by legions; only this small band remains."

"I'm sorry," I said.

Aurora shrugged. "Eternity is too long to dwell on regrets. For now, I'm grateful for what I have. I'm among those I love. My family needs me. I have a purpose, which makes me happy. And now that my oldest friend has found me, my happiness is increased even more."

"Really?" I asked, trying not to sound shocked. "I was your oldest friend? I always thought you didn't much like me."

"You?" she chuckled. "You were likable enough, but I was speaking of Slor Tonn." She looked up. Slor Tonn floated directly above us. "I'm sorry he's passed on, but happy he found me. I'm not surprised. There was always a bond between us." She looked down at me. "On the other hand, I'm completely befuddled that you're here. Your kind normally passes on to different realms."

"I'm a bit surprised myself."

"I assume there's some logical explanation?"

I shook my head. "I don't think logic has much to do with this."

I told my story, starting with Infidel promising to return the Jagged Heart, all the way up to the point where Purity stabbed me. It took a long time, long enough that I required a second dose of bear gland, but Aurora listened patiently, as if she had nothing but time.

In the end, she nodded, contemplating what I'd told her.

"I'm probably missing some important details," I said. "I don't really know who this Tarpok character is, or why he'd ally himself with someone like Purity."

"Tarpok was my eldest brother," said Aurora. "He was the biggest, strongest, toughest ogre in the village. I was his runt sister, in a family with twenty siblings. As a hunter, Tarpok brought great prestige upon my family. Then I entered the priesthood, and eventually became high priestess. In my youth, the villagers would look upon my father and say, 'there is an ogre who deserves respect, for his semen has produced the mighty hunter Tarpok.' Once I was high priestess, the praise changed, and they said, 'this great ogre's semen has blessed our village with Aksarna the wise.' Aksarna, by the way, being my true name. As you can imagine, this hurt Tarpok's pride."

"I would think it would hurt your mother's pride, hearing your father get all the credit."

"Tarpok and I have different mothers. Father has produced twenty children, by seven different mates."

"Oh. Are ogre's polygamous, or is child birth just that difficult?"

"Ogres are fiercely monogamous. Most of my father's wives were murdered by younger females wanting to catch my father's attention. Only after the old wife was out of the way would father choose a new wife."

"And he'd choose a known murderess?"

"It showed she had passion. It's considered highly flattering if a female is willing to kill to gain access to your semen."

I furrowed my brow. I tried to be open-minded about cultural differences, but this was a bit much.

"Semen is *very* important to my people," Aurora said, sounding worried I hadn't caught on. "Which added to Tarpok's shame. He was a mighty hunter, yet his first bride bore him no children. He murdered her two years later and took a second wife. She, too, bore no children. Then he married Sinnatok, a widow who'd four young children, so she was certain to be fertile. This marriage, alas, produced no offspring. Whispers grew that Tarpok the mighty was really Tarpok the seedless. Women snickered as he passed. His shame was great."

"Tarpok seemed pretty popular when I saw him," I said. "Your people must have gotten over the fact he was sterile."

Aurora shook her head. "Now that I've rejoined my family, I've learned what happened in my absence. With the Jagged Heart gone, the priestesses were weakened. Tarpok announced that we were at war with the Skellings, and that he was to be our warlord. He took up residence in the temple, since it was the most defensible structure. He killed any priestess who objected, but spared the few who broke their vows of chastity in an attempt to, shall we say, sanctify his semen."

"From what I can count, there were only three who agreed."

"Three too many," Aurora grumbled. "There were twenty-five priestesses in various stages of training. All should have chosen death over defilement."

"They might not have had a choice," I said. "He's almost twice their size. You can't blame the victims of a rape."

"I can blame any priestess who hasn't attempted to slit his throat, or failing that, to slit her own. Can you imagine the blasphemy of what he's done? He had the entire village watch as he defiled the priestesses upon the western altar, then had them announce that, by bathing his genitals in their holy blood, he'd healed his infertility. It was further proclaimed that he'd been given a divine vision that he was to build a great army to one day stand against those who had stolen the Jagged Heart. It was essential that the village produce as many offspring as quickly as possible. He announced that he was going to sleep with every ogress in the village, taking a different lover every night, so that his blessed seed might produce a new crop of warriors. This pronouncement didn't go over well, as you may imagine."

"It sounds like he went insane," I said.

Aurora nodded. "Tarpok may have been insane, but he was also unquestionably the greatest warrior in the village. The strongest males declared war on him, and it was during this war that his ancestors, and therefore my ancestors, were desecrated. The fighting lasted years but Tarpok eventually prevailed, and build a monument from the skulls of those who'd opposed him. The remaining males of the village became rather more philosophical about Tarpok sleeping with their spouses. Some of the females resisted at first, but after a few of his early partners became pregnant, most went willingly. Tarpok was the embodiment of male power. The chance to be filled by his semen was a great temptation."

"So was he *was* cured by sleeping with the priestesses?"

Aurora shook her head. "By sleeping with every female in the village, he could claim that any child born the following year was a product of his seed. But he didn't demand chastity on the part of his lovers; most were probably impregnated by their true husbands."

"I have a hard time thinking that a monster like that gets cheered by the crowds I saw."

"Ah, but there's one final, perverse twist. The males who challenged Tarpok were the best hunters in the village. After they died, Tarpok alone accounted for over half of the meat the village fed upon. My people are on the verge of starving, and flattering Tarpok is their best route to being fed."

"But he's the reason they're starving!"

Aurora shrugged. She said something in her native tongue.

"I'm sorry, I didn't catch that," I said.

"It's a proverb of my people. *Wisdom is the first thing devoured by an empty belly.*"

"I'm afraid your people may be even hungrier now, since Infidel caved in Tarpok's face."

"There was a time when this would have concerned me," said Aurora. "But everyone I knew will be dead soon enough."

"Because Purity's going to murder the sun?"

Aurora shook her head. "Because the lifespan of an ogre is but a single beat of a heart when measured against the expanse of forever. Being dead gives one a sense of perspective. What was the point of all the struggle? In the end, death will claim the just and the unjust. For all the harm that Tarpok did to my people, he's here now, another of the dead in the endless sea of death." She stared out over the ice floes. "As blood kin, he will be drawn to our family song. I look forward to assisting him with his pain."

"You'd soothe the pain of a villain who's done such harm?"

"I said assist, not soothe."

"Ah."

"But this will happen in its own time. Now, we've a more pressing matter." She pointed toward the horizon. "In little more than an hour, Glorious will once again rise over the edge of the sky. Purity will no doubt use this moment to strike. If we're going to stop her, we must depart at once."

"I'm very happy to hear you say this," I said. "I was worried that your new-found stoicism might keep you from taking the threat seriously."

Aurora whistled to Slor Tonn. The whale did a cartwheel, then plunged into the water nearby. "I care little about the fate of the world. But, Purity was responsible for robbing me of the Jagged Heart. Even now, she defiles it with her heathen grasp. I cannot let this be."

"Purity's no pushover," I warned. "She's got all of Menagerie's shape-shifting powers, plus ice powers just like you."

"Actually, I don't have those powers anymore," said Aurora, sounding apologetic. "My spiritual connection with Hush was severed when I came here."

"Oh. Then we might be in a rather lopsided fight."

"She's sailing in a walrus skin boat," said Aurora. "We'll be riding a flying whale. This fight may be lopsided in an entirely different direction than you think."

Slor Tonn floated up beside the ice floe and Aurora lifted me, slinging me over her shoulder. "Hold tight," she said as I wrapped my arms around her neck. She shoved another bit of bear gland between my lips. I pushed it between my teeth and cheek and sucked on it to make it last longer. Aurora jumped onto Slor Tonn's back.

"He doesn't have his harness any more," I said. "He's as naked as we are."

"Who needs a harness?" she asked, walking toward the center of the whale, right behind his blow hole. She made a clicking noise with her tongue and the whale slapped his tail against the water, then surged skyward. Aurora crouched, keeping her center of gravity low, her arms spread for balance. I tightened my grip around her neck.

We climbed swiftly, as the dead ogres on the ice floe began to sing their family song to call Aurora back. For a moment it seemed that the higher we climbed, the louder the voices grew, but soon their voices faded, lost to the wind. As Slor Tonn banked in response to Aurora's clucked and grunted commands, I caught a glimpse of her family on the ice below, now small as bugs.

"Aren't you afraid you won't be able to find them again?" I shouted above the rushing wind.

"I can hear my family song no matter where I travel," said Aurora.

"How about the Jagged Heart? You said you used to be able to feel its tug."

"I lost that connection, I fear," said Aurora.

"So how will we find Purity?"

"I don't think we can, unless we get exceedingly lucky. She's on a tiny boat on an infinite ocean. We'll never find where she is now, but we don't need to. We know where she's going. Fortunately, Slor Tonn can carry us to Glorious before he ever rises above the horizon."

"We're just going to fly to the sun?"

"Why not?"

"And what will we do when we reach it?"

"Talk to Glorious," said Aurora. "Ask him not to rise until we've eliminated the threat."

"Oh." I found the directness of her plan a little unsettling. "Do you really think it will be that easy?"

"I'm almost positive it won't be. But we should try a direct approach and deal with complications only if they arise."

And on we flew. Below us, the ocean spread out like a jewelers display case, with glistening gems spilled against a backdrop of black satin. Above was endless darkness, save a floating blue-green ball no larger than a grapefruit.

"What's that?" I asked, pointing with my stump.

"Our old world," she said. "The material world. We lived there."

"It's so small," I said.

"It's far away," she said. "Maybe a thousand miles."

"Wow," I said, surprised I could see anything at that great a distance.

Of course, I'd seen this orb before, when falling back from the realm of the dead where Greatshadow dwelled.

"I've now been in three different realms of the dead," I said.

"What of it?"

"Zetetic, the Deceiver, said that there was no objective reality. He said we were all the authors of our own worlds, and our unconscious collaboration creates what looks like solid reality, but is, in fact, nothing but a malleable fiction. What if the realms of the dead are like this? We spend all our lives imagining what the afterlife will be like, and then, when we die, that's what we get. Doesn't that mean we'd have the power to change things if we wanted to?"

"If we could change things to what we want, I wouldn't have half of my flesh burned away," said Aurora. "I'm guessing you'd still have your legs and your hand."

"But that's not the way I imagined my afterlife. I always assumed that, when I died, I'd just fade away. That's almost what happened, until my soul got sucked into the bone-handled knife."

"Look!" Aurora said, pointing into the distance. I could see nothing but ice floes and black ocean where she pointed. "A boat!"

She used her clucking, snorting commands to steer Slor Tonn down toward the ice. I narrowed my eyes, trying to see what she'd seen. At last, I spotted it: a single walrus skin boat, empty of passengers. A few oars lay in the bottom. I saw a rip in the bow, where Infidel had dug in with her knife.

"This was the boat Tarpok and the priestesses were in before Sorrow unleashed her plague of flies," I said.

Water sprayed over us as Slor Tonn came to rest in the dark water. Aurora leapt from the whale's back into the center of the boat. She grabbed an oar and deftly maneuvered the vessel toward the nearest bit of pack ice. Then she hopped out and dragged the boat onto the ice.

"This boat is a great treasure!" she exclaimed. "Not all of my ancestors retain the bodily integrity needed to swim. This will allow us to extend our hunting range. We should turn back and take it to my family."

"What does a boat matter if the world is on the verge of ending?"

Aurora looked up. "If the world ends, it will become even more crowded here. My family will require resources to remain comfortable."

I had to admire her pragmatism. "If this boat is here, Purity must be near."

"Perhaps. The currents that flow from the material world into the afterlife are chaotic. She could be miles away."

"Then let's stick with the plan," I said. "Let's find Glorious first."

"You weren't this impatient when you were alive," Aurora grumbled. But, I'd won the argument. She left the boat on the ice floe, as she hopped once more onto Slor Tonn, and steered him toward the horizon.

"Hold tight," she said. "We won't stop again until we're within shouting distance of the sun."

19 - Nothing New Under the Sun

"THERE'S ONE THING I don't understand," I said to Aurora as Slor Tonn sailed through the dark sky.

"Only *one* thing?" she asked, in mock astonishment.

"One thing immediately pertinent," I corrected. "When we were hunting Greatshadow, Father Ver sounded confident that killing the dragon would have no effect upon the continued existence of fire. He said that the primal dragons were interlopers who'd merged their spirits with existing elemental forces. Killing the dragon would merely free the element, not destroy it. For instance, the church killed Verdant a long time ago, and trees continue to do okay."

"So you're wondering if this mission is even necessary?" Aurora asked.

"I mean, suppose Purity does kill Glorious. I'm completely at a loss to figure out if she's here to hunt his body or his spirit, but does it matter? Isn't the sun still going to be around? I hate to sound callous, but would our lives be worse in any way if she succeeds?"

Aurora sighed.

"You sound disgusted by my question."

"Not disgusted," she said. "Just a little... weary. The Church of the Book has gone out of its way to hide the true history of our world. Most of the so-called 'civilized' men I've spoken to have been brainwashed by the church's dogma, to the point that they insist their self-evident falsehoods are the only truth. For those of us privy to the actual reality, conversations about the world's origins with the church's faithful are a little tiresome."

"I'd hardly identify myself as one of the faithful."

"But you were raised by the church," she said. "You judge everything you're told my how well it meshes with the myths of your childhood."

"I also judge the myths of my childhood by how well they mesh with reality. For instance, the Church of the Book teaches that the world is precisely 1082 years old, that it sprang into existence fully formed the day the Divine Author finished writing the One True Book. But I earned my living exploring ruins that my grandfather calculated to be at least 3,000 years old. I've gotten my own hands dirty on the roots and rocks of the Vanished Kingdom, and grandfather's math makes much more sense than the church's attempt to explain away the evidence."

"They bother to explain away the evidence?" she asked. "Most believers I speak to aren't even aware there is evidence."

"The monks said that the world looks older than a thousand years because that's the way the Divine Author wanted it to look. A creator can give his creation attributes of a past, even if it was created only moments before."

"That's stupid," said Aurora.

"Maybe. But a lot of smart people buy into it. When I was nine, I was studying literature under a monk named Brother Brown. One day we took a break from reading stories and he asked me to write one. I composed a tale about a knight named Lord Brilliant. Brother Brown kept asking me for details of my character, and my imagination was more than eager to supply them. I remember that when my story began Lord Brilliant was twenty, which seemed old to me at the time. I remember his hair was the color of golden wheat. He was strong enough that he could carry his horse across a dangerous bridge. His parent's names were, um... Honor and Faith, if memory serves. Oh, and his favorite food was snails in mustard sauce."

"I can't believe that would be anyone's favorite food," said Aurora.

I shrugged. "I'd heard that rich people ate such things. At the monastery we mostly ate barley and salt cod. Anyway, in my adventure, Brilliant undertook a ten year quest to hunt down... uh... hmm."

"Hunt down what?"

"Uh... don't be offended, but he hunted down ogres. I was just a kid. I didn't know any personally at the time."

Aurora shrugged. "We tell our children that humans use ogre bones to flavor their soup. Don't worry about it."

"Anyway, my point is, my twenty-year-old knight undertook a ten year quest. So when I was asked by Brother Brown how old he was at the end of the tale, I said he was thirty. But my teacher pointed out that I had created Lord Brilliant only that morning. He was little more than a few hours old. Despite this, Lord Brilliant possessed properties, such as parents, that indicated a much longer existence. Brother Brown explained that our world could also appear to be much older through the same principals. To this day, I really haven't thought of a good argument to challenge this."

Aurora shook her head. "By that logic the world might only be a year old. Even one minute old. Nothing really existed before we started this conversation. There'd be no way of ever knowing the truth."

"Truth isn't as solid for me as it once was," I said. "The way Zetetic's magic worked… it was like he was creating new realities by the second. I saw it with my own eyes. Who am I to judge what's real and what's unreal?"

Aurora sighed. "Human's are so weak-minded. Your kind confuses philosophy for fact. How is it you came to rule most of the known world?"

"We don't make our weapons out of ice, for one thing. It gives us a little more range."

She rolled her eyes. "We're off topic. Let's get back to Glorious. Do you ever wonder why the Vanished Kingdom is three-thousand years old? Why you don't find traces of something older?"

"Sometimes. Was there a civilization before the Vanished Kingdom?"

"No," said Aurora, somewhat emphatically. "There's nothing older than three thousand years. The world existed before then, but we can never know for how long, since three thousand years ago marks the invention of time. Before then, there were no fixed days or years."

"That makes no sense whatsoever."

"It's a human failing that you wish for the world to make sense. You'd rather embrace a sensible lie than an absurd truth. Time was the invention of Glorious. It was his whole reason for merging his spirit with the sun."

"You're losing me," I said.

"Before three thousand years ago, the sun was a wild thing. It followed no set course across the sky. Sometimes it raced across the heavens, other times it loped at a leisurely pace, pausing to nap at the apex of its climb. Some days it rose in the east, other days in the west or north or south. Nor did it always journey across the vault of heaven toward the opposing horizon. Some days, it would lazily roll back down the sky to finish where it had started."

"If there were days, then there was time," I said, having instantly spotted the gaping hole in her logic.

"But now, a day is a fixed measurement. The sun passes through the sky on a schedule. Its path is so steady, we can divide days into hours, minutes and seconds, or lump them together into months or years. Has it never struck you as odd that the sky has an agenda? It's self evident from the regular procession of moon phases, eclipses, and other celestial phenomenon that there is some guiding intelligence imposing order upon them. Glorious is that intelligence."

"I know that in the Vanished Kingdom, Glorious was revered as a god. The ruins are rife with big disks representing the sun."

"With good reason. Glorious made civilization possible. Before he merged with the sun, agriculture couldn't take hold. Of course, this wasn't Glorious' goal when he fixed the sun into a specific course. He had no idea he was creating the conditions needed for humans to thrive."

"Then why did he do it?"

"Who knows? Perhaps you can ask him. Look ahead."

I did so and saw instantly what she was referring to. The black sea beneath us was lightening, taking on hues of pale blue, tinted with pastel pinks. The ice floes beneath us grew ever thinner, until at last there were no stars to be seen. We flew on, and at length the ocean grew still and took on the perfect azure of a calm tropical lagoon. Far in the distance, like a vast white pearl too dazzling to look upon directly, was the sun, floating calmly amid the blue.

Aurora raised her beefy arm to shield her eyes as we grew closer. She said, "It's funny that, in telling of the invention of time, I've so lost track of it. Here's the short answer to your original question: Glorious' body was destroyed when he merged with the sun. You know that Hush loved Glorious, and was willing to betray Greatshadow to mate with him. But Glorious spurned Hush; he was too fixed on his plan to merge his soul with the sun to waste his energies on such a thing as love. Hush, in her anger, attacked him, striking a mortal blow just as he was merging with the sun. Her blow killed his reptilian body, but this proved a boon, since it liberated the spirit of Glorious to freely merge with the sun. Hush threw herself at the sun in her rage, but succeeded only in gouging a large crater. The rubble from this blow fell to earth."

"The glorystones," I said.

"Exactly. And, as the glorystones rained down like fire, they caught Greatshadow's attention. At the time, he was merely an ordinary dragon who specialized in elemental flame magic, and he was curious about this new source of heavenly radiance. He flew to investigate and found Hush standing over the body of Glorious. She confessed that she'd offered herself to Glorious and been rejected. Greatshadow's rage at this revelation was the final push needed to fuse his soul with the elemental flames he'd mastered, marking his birth as the primal dragon of fire. As Hush realized she'd lost both Glorious and Greatshadow, her heart shattered and the chill wind that rushed into the void pushed her across the elemental barrier to become the primal dragon of cold."

"So, if his body is already dead, all that's left of Glorious is his soul," I said.

"Yes. He is, in some ways, the most vulnerable of the primal dragons. We must warn him. If he dies, the sun will no longer be guided by his intelligence. It will once more meander through the sky unpredictably, meaning the end of the world as we know it."

"Purity has a different idea. She thinks the sun will be extinguished. But, it's hard to think that the Church would be going along with this plan if they thought that was right. They must think things will pretty much stay the same."

Aurora fell quiet as she thought this over. Finally, she said, "What will follow the death of Glorious is an open question. Let's hope we never learn the answer."

And on we flew.

Have you ever approached a bonfire on a dark beach? From a distance, the fire is bright white at its core, while everything around is draped in black shadows. Yet, when you are directly beside the fire, the shadows don't seem as stark, and it's possible to gaze into the flames and see the individual logs burning, a hundred glowing hues of yellow and red and white mixed with streaks of dark black soot.

So it proved to be with the sun. The yellow white pearl floating half-submerged in the still blue water could now be gazed upon directly. The pearl was enormous, large enough that the entire Isle of Fire could have been contained within it. If the sun was a giant pearl here in the Great Sea Above, I couldn't help but wonder if, somewhere in the mythology of the ogres, there was a legend of a giant oyster.

Beneath the pearl's translucent surface, I could see the draconic spirit form of Glorious curled into a tight ball. His snout was tucked beneath a wing, and his long tail coiled around his entire form. He dwarfed any of the primal dragons I'd yet witnessed. Abyss had been large enough to swallow a fleet of ships; Glorious was large enough that he could have swallowed Abyss like a grain of corn.

His eyes opened as we approached.

"You're the ones I've waited for," he said, in a surprisingly gentle whisper. There was something curiously familiar about his voice. Then I realized it was my own voice. Glorious was speaking directly in my thoughts.

I assume Aurora received the same message. She grunted a command and Slor Tonn slid to a hovering halt. Aurora dropped to her knees and bowed on the whale's broad back. Since I was clinging to her neck, this left me staring right at the sun.

"We're sorry to disturb your slumber, oh Glorious!" Aurora cried. "We recognize that we've not cleansed ourselves with the proper rituals. We ask that you—"

"There's no need for these formalities," Glorious said, shifting his face within the pearl to look upon us more directly with eyes as large as the Commonground bay. "Do you think me ignorant of earthly plots? You've come to murder me, to release my soul to oblivion."

"No!" said Aurora. "Hush and her minions await your return to the northern reaches of the Great Sea Above. It is they who wish you harm. We've come to warn you. But... you already know of this plot?"

"The Church of the Book is not so clever as they believe," said Glorious. "They shun the use of candles and torches since they fear that Greatshadow may gaze out of the tiniest flame. But they light their most private sanctums with glorystones. My soul fills all solar material, even these remote fragments. I'm witness to the church's every scheme."

"Then you know that the Church has produced a Writ of Judgment that can destroy you," I said.

"Yes. And I've heard their tedious debates as they convinced themselves this will not matter. They believe the sun will continue its current path through pure momentum. They shall learn the truth, I suppose. Even without the scroll, I cannot survive an encounter with the Jagged Heart. Its hateful bitterness will poison my soul and I will, at last, find welcome relief in oblivion."

"You welcome this fate?" Aurora asked, sounding confused.

"For three thousand years I've guided the sun across the skies in a never-changing path, utterly alone in my journeys. When I began my task, I was driven by pure intellectual hunger: was it possible to impose order upon a chaotic world? I believed it was, and I believed I was the only being who had the intellect and strength of will to force such a change. When I first traveled to these abstract realms, I welcomed my solitude. The material world is violent and cacophonous. I could barely hear my own thoughts. I dreamed of a better place, a domain of peace, order, and silence, where I might at last organize my thoughts and realize the true potential of my intellect."

Peace, order, and silence. I wonder if Glorious knew how much his personal agenda overlapped with Purity's dream?

"When I first merged my soul with the sun, all was blissful," Glorious said. "I invented days, which gave birth to years, then to centuries. I was free at last to sequentially organize my thoughts and memories. From my vantage point above the world, I saw the changes my works had made possible. Mankind embraced time, measuring it out with sundials and hourglasses, with calendars and clocks. They sang my praises and carved my image from stone, the better to worship me."

He sounded wistful as he relayed his story, though perhaps 'sounded' isn't the correct word for a message conveyed through telepathy. Still, I was certain Glorious held the memory of this time to be bittersweet. What followed, however, was only bitter.

"My brethren dragon, alas, were slower to see the advantages of time. They were wiped out by the explosive growth of human civilization, slowly fading from history, until only the primal dragons remained. Then I watched even the primal dragons succumb, losing their intelligence and identities to the elemental forces they commanded, until only a handful of my kind endures. Alas, the survivors are the dragons who despise and resent me most. Never in all of existence has any creature ever been as alone as I am."

"But you aren't alone," I said. "If you can see through the glorystones, you're connected with the world! You must experience the lives of thousands each day."

"It is so. And, long ago, this was good. The first men to create agriculture worshipped the sun. They sang my praises and offered sacrifices. While I no longer needed to eat, my pride fed upon their deeds. I felt… loved."

"Men still love you," I said.

"No," said Glorious. "Men now take me for granted, at best. Today, most men bemoan my great gift, time. They curse the relentless pulse of seconds, they rail against my ceaseless crawl across the vault of the heavens, and treat the years as something I steal from them rather than as a gift given freely."

"People are fickle," I said. "That's hardly a reason to want to die. Give them another thousand years and they'll be back to worshipping you again."

"You cannot judge me," said Glorious. "My loneliness increases with each year. Time has become my curse. If my loneliness is unbearable after thirty centuries, imagine the agony of another hundred, or thousand, or ten thousand. I do not possess the courage to face eternity; no being could. The cycles and patterns of life I observe once delighted me; now they bore me. There is nothing new under the sun. Thirty centuries is enough. I am done."

"What will happen when you die?" asked Aurora. "Who's right? Will the sun carry on without you guiding it? Will it meander as it once did? Or will it be extinguished?"

"What does this matter to me?" he asked. "It was never my intention to give birth to the world you know. Should I care if my choices now end it?"

"Yes!" Aurora said. "You can't condemn a world to death just because you're bored and lonely."

"I believe I can," said Glorious. "And I believe I will."

As he spoke, he uncurled his body. He was a being made of pure light, but the pearl of the sun rocked and bobbed as he spread his limbs, disrupting its internal balance. His body passed though the glassy surface and he stretched his golden wings to span the horizon.

Slor Tonn wheeled unexpectedly. I clung tightly to Aurora as she struggled to keep her balance.

"What's happening?" I cried.

"That gloomy idiot has spooked my whale," Aurora shouted, as Slor Tonn fled toward the darker waters we'd come from. I glanced back to see Glorious rising ever higher above the pearl. The waters beneath us churned as the sun's orb bounced and twisted, moved by the dragon's struggle to free himself. I looked up, toward the distant globe of the physical world, and wondered what the sky must look like at this moment.

We were putting quite a bit of distance between us and Glorious. I shouted, "Slor Tonn can really move."

"It won't matter," Aurora shouted back. "Glorious will overtake us in the blink of an eye once he gets underway. The only thing we have going for us is that this is the first time he's been outside the sun in three thousand years. Maybe we have a minute or two while he catches his bearings."

"Then that's a minute or two for us to find Hush."

"Agreed," said Aurora. "We can stop Purity and Judge Stern. We can save Glorious whether he wants to be saved or not. Then we can talk him back into the sun… I hope."

"I'll handle the talking," I said. "I won't be much help in a fight."

"That was true in life as well."

She said this humorously, but I sensed an undercurrent of resentment that her only ally in saving the world was a legless, one-handed ghost. I sucked the bear gland nestled in my cheek and said nothing. My brain raced as I struggled to find an argument that might convince Glorious to carry on. I doubted there was anything I might say that would ease his loneliness.

But maybe I was focusing on convincing the wrong dragon. Glorious wouldn't listen to me. Would Hush?

20 - TOO LATE

THE WAVES BELOW churned into white caps. Glorious caused the pearl of the sun to bob and spin violently as he continued to rise, shaking his spirit free of its shell. His radiance cast Slor Tonn's shadow on the water before us like a long dark arrow. I cannot guess our speed, but at least several minutes passed while the waters beneath us grew ever darker. At last, Glorious was merely a glow on the horizon. Sparkling ice floes once more speckled the velvet black waters of the Great Sea Above.

As the turbulent waves from the thrashing sun reached the ice floes, some bobbed, while others shot into the air and hurtled towards the material world, high above. Many a night had I gazed into the dark sky and contemplated shooting stars. Had this always been their origin? Great blocks of ice breaking free from the celestial ocean to fall toward earth? It seemed so unlikely.

But I had little time to contemplate heavenly mechanics before Aurora shouted, "There!" Her arm was outstretched toward the largest iceberg I'd ever seen.

Only, it wasn't an iceberg. It was Hush, walking along the surface of the ocean, which froze into thick ice sheets to support her weight. Waves crashed against the advancing ice wall and bobbing atop these waves was a tiny boat. It stayed barely a hundred yards ahead of Hush's advance by virtue of the enslaved ice-maidens rowing furiously. Purity stood at the bow, her wings spread for balance. Even from this distance, I could tell by the tilt of her head she had spotted Slor Tonn. She thrust the harpoon in our direction. A pale blue beam filled the frozen air with bright sparkles as it crackled toward us. Slor Tonn banked hard to the left to avoid the attack.

"Can the harpoon hurt you?" I shouted to Aurora.

Aurora nodded. "Ordinary cold doesn't bother ogres, but the Jagged Heart isn't ordinary cold."

Slor Tonn turned back toward the boat. From our vantagepoint, I spotted two long bundles in the floor of the boat, one with platinum blonde hair. "I think I see Infidel."

"Good," said Aurora. "She can help even the odds once we capsize their boat."

"Infidel's lost her powers," I said. "Capsizing the boat might kill her!"

"Doing nothing means that she dies along with everyone else."

I nodded, knowing she was right.

A second beam shot toward us. Again Slor Tonn banked to avoid it, then turned his nose straight down. Aurora said, "Hold on tight. Things are about to get rough."

"I'm ready," I said, chewing the bear gland in my cheek furiously as we plunged toward the black water.

I wasn't ready. Even though Slor Tonn took the brunt of our impact with the waves, the cold that washed over me numbed both body and mind. In the frozen darkness, I struggled to remember where I was or even who I was. My arms went slack and I lost my grip on Aurora.

Fortunately, she had the coolness of thought to keep hold of me. We exploded from the water a moment later, with Purity's boat caught in Slor Tonn's mighty jaws. With a loud crunch, he bit off the front end where Purity had stood. Fear instantly wiped away my cold induced lethargy as I thought of Infidel getting chewed by the whale's attack.

My fear was short lived as the back half of the boat tore away and fell to the ice, sliding to a halt before Hush. Infidel was there amid the tangle of stunned ice-maidens, as well as Sorrow and Judge Stern. I could see this all plainly by the light of the Gloryhammer, which danced across the ice, free from anyone's grip.

From the corner of my vision, I saw Judge Stern rise and gaze toward the hammer. I couldn't let him get hold of it. But, how could I stop him? Did I dare touch the Gloryhammer again? Before, I had been overwhelmed by the bottomless loneliness of Glorious. Now, in theory, he'd severed his connection with the sun.

"I need to get the Gloryhammer! Throw me!" I shouted. I didn't have time to weigh the pros and cons of the plan.

Aurora needed no further prompting. She grabbed me by my left elbow and flung me toward the weapon. My spinning flight, as you can imagine, was rather disorienting. I hit the ice with force enough to shatter what remained of my ribs. I was going to need a lot more bear gland to deal with my pain when all this was over. I skittered across the ice toward the hammer, my good arm outstretched, just as Judge Stern broke into a sprint for the same target.

I reached it first.

To my great relief, the overwhelming loneliness that had threatened my naked spirit earlier was gone as my fingers closed around the shaft. The surge of power Infidel had described as being filled with pure sunlight swept through me. With half my body torn away, I saw the full effect rather vividly. It was as if the hammer understood where the true outlines of my body should be and filled this shell with radiant energy. I rose on legs of light. I flexed my severed left hand, now composed of fingers of dazzling luminance.

Judge Stern skittered on the ice as he tried to stop before he collided with me. He wound up with his feet out from under him, hitting the ice butt first.

He waved his fist at me as he shouted, "Devil! You defile a sacred weapon! Surrender it at once!"

"Finders, keepers," I argued. I was surprised a legal scholar such as himself had been unaware of this fine point of the law.

Stern rose to his knees, then lunged with what might have been an impressive tackle at my shins if they'd been actual shins. Instead, he passed right through my limbs of light, crashing chin first onto the ice. I waited a few seconds, but he didn't get up. I was finally ready for some action and my first opponent goes and knocks himself out. Typical.

With Purity swallowed by Slor Tonn and Judge Stern unconscious, my top priority was to speak to Hush.

Unfortunately, when I gazed at the lumbering dragon, I saw that she was about to crush the frozen bodies of Infidel and Sorrow beneath her giant claw. Conversation would have to wait. I swung my hammer toward the women and willed myself to fly. I flashed toward them as Hush's massive talon fell. I didn't know if my light hand could grab the women, so I willingly crashed into the ice, sliding into Sorrow's frosty form, using it as a cue ball in a game of body billiards. She caromed into Infidel and they both skipped across the frozen sea. I closed my eyes as the gap between Hush's claw and the ice quickly vanished, but opened my eyes a fraction of a second later when the impact didn't come. Behind me was a thunderous sound. I'd made it clear, though if I'd had physical legs I'm certain that wouldn't have been the case.

I spun around, searching for Infidel. I saw her splayed on the ice, limp, her body free of the frozen shell that had enwreathed her. My pool shot had shattered her icy cage. Was she even still alive?

As I flew toward her, she stirred, raising her hand instinctively to shield her eyes. In my panic, I'd stoked the Gloryhammer to high-noon intensity. I thrust the weapon into her grasp. My face was inches from hers as her eyes snapped open, glowing as the energy of the hammer surged through her.

"Stagger!" she exclaimed, before grabbing me by the back of my neck and pulling me to her for a powerful kiss. The kiss proved briefer than I would have liked. Perhaps she was aware of the urgency of our situation, though her haste might also be explained by the bear piss aroma filling my mouth.

Using the power of the hammer, she spiraled up into the air. I clung to her shoulders to keep from falling. Apparently, the hammer's energy could only flow into one of us. My limbs of light were gone. She looked down and turned pale.

"Oh, Stagger," she said, sadly.

"I've been in better shape," I admitted.

"Does it hurt?" she asked.

"Yeah," I said. "But Aurora has fixed me up."

"Aurora?" She looked around, and spotted her old friend perched on Slor Tonn's back.

I took a deep breath. "We're in the Great Sea Above. Slor Tonn's eaten Purity, I've knocked out Judge Stern, but any second Glorious is going to come over the horizon intent on suicide. We have to stop Hush before she kills him and ends life as we know it."

Infidel closed her eyes and rubbed them with her free hand as we drifted higher into the sky. She shook her head and grumbled, "Can't I have one freaking day when I'm not having to prevent the imminent destruction of the world?"

"There's always tomorrow, baby," I said. "Unless, you know, there isn't. We should get to work on that."

We were now a good quarter mile above the battlefield, not that there was much battling going on. Sorrow had bounced back with remarkable speed and had dispatched most of the survivors from the spilled boat with a rather gruesome efficiency. I watched as she leapt onto an ogress struggling to her feet. Sorrow placed her bare hand upon the ogress as she rose. Instantly dark red veins of infection spread across the ogress's skin. In seconds, her victim collapsed, coughing up blood.

Sorrow moved on to the next person rising to her feet, one of the ice-maidens, her armor cracked and missing along her left shoulder. Despite the fact that the woman had been mentally enslaved, Sorrow showed no mercy, dispatching her with the same cold efficiency.

"I wonder if she can kill Hush," said Infidel. Her voice sounded doubtful, a doubt, I suspect, both about Sorrow's offensive capacity and Infidel's own. Hush was an imposing figure as she crawled beneath us, freezing the ocean half a mile before her with each step forward. In scale, we were like fleas contemplating an attack upon a dog. No doubt we'd draw blood hitting her with the Gloryhammer, but would Hush even notice?

"Fly down!" I shouted. "Get in her face!"

Infidel obeyed. In seconds, we hovered before the dragon's left eye. I could see our reflection in the dark iris. Hush had green eyes, the shade of fir boughs. Save for her pink tongue, it was the only thing about her not snowy white.

But, I'd not come here to contemplate the pigments necessary to complete her portrait. Aware that time was running out, I shouted, "Hush! Please stop and listen! You don't need to kill Glorious! He's lonely! He knows he was foolish to reject you! You have a second chance at winning his heart!"

Hush didn't even pause as she marched forward. Infidel kept us flying one step ahead.

"Stop, please!" I shouted. But I couldn't tell if Hush was even focused on us. Sometimes, a gnat inches from ones face is more difficult to see than one a yard away. I don't know if she even heard us.

Slor Tonn approached. Even the whale proved tiny in comparison to the dragon, though if we were fleas, the whale was at least a fair-sized beetle.

"She can't hear you," Aurora called out. "Her ear drums are dozens of yards across. Your voices are too tiny to register. Also, I don't know if she understands your language. I always spoke to her in my native tongue."

"But you can still talk to her?" Infidel said, her voice filled with hope.

Aurora shook her head. "I could only communicate with her via a direct spiritual connection when I held the Jagged Heart. Right now, that's in Slor Tonn's stomach."

I sighed. "I guess I'll have to go in and get it. I've made this trip before." I glanced toward the horizon. It was a pale pink. Any second, Glorious would rise above the edge of the water.

"I don't have a better plan," Aurora said, with a nervous glance at the brightening sky. "Slor Tonn, open wide!" But, rather than opening his jaws, Slor Tonn chose that moment to twitch violently. Aurora was thrown into the air as if she'd been caught by surprise astride a bucking bull. She landed on the whale's back with a thud as the beast arched his spine. A gush of dark blood sprayed from his blowhole, spattering Aurora in a psychedelic shade of purple.

"What—," escaped her lips before the whale suddenly froze stiff, coated with a thick rind of frost from jaws to tail. Without warning, the great beast dropped from the sky. Aurora tumbled from his back as he fell, and only

Infidel's keen reflexes saved her as she swooped down and caught the ogress by her topknot.

"Slor Tonn!" Aurora shouted as the whale hit the ice below and shattered into a million pink and gray fragments.

Purity stood in the midst of the frozen chunks, still in her winged woman configuration, coated with ice, only seemingly much larger. In fact, there was no question: the Jagged Heart harpoon was eighteen feet long, and she quickly grew to that height, then doubled it. Her skin color changed until she had a white belly and a black back... Slor Tonn's colors.

"Wonderful," I sighed, as I adjusted my grip on Infidel's shoulders. "Looks like Menagerie's body has added whale's blood to the mix."

"Nothing can kill me in this body!" Purity shouted, eyeing us with a taunting gaze. "I can adapt to any assault! Thanks to your futile efforts, I'm more powerful than ever!"

"The only thing I hate worse than someone trying to destroy the world is a braggart," Infidel grumbled.

"Wait," said Aurora. "You're sure this is Menagerie's body?"

"At the core," said Infidel. "It's had some additions."

"As high priestess I can summon the spirits of the dead," said Aurora. "Ordinarily, I can only call forward the shades of my own tribe. But Menagerie and I worked side by side for years. He and the rest of the Goons became my new tribe once I reached Commonground. He might respond if I called out to him."

"Do it!" said Infidel.

"There's one catch," said Aurora.

"Let me guess," I said. "You need the Jagged Heart."

"Give me ten seconds," said Infidel. Without warning, she dove toward the ground, dropping me and Aurora on the ice. With a *whoosh*, she shot toward Sorrow, who had just finished off the last ogre priestess and was turning to her father. Judge Stern was conscious once more. He skittered backward on the ice as she approached.

"Away from me, you abomination!" he cried out, closing his eyes as Sorrow's hand reached for his face.

In what had to be the most surprising answer to prayer on record, Infidel stretched out her free arm and caught Sorrow by the waist at exactly that second. Sorrow screamed a very bad word as Infidel swooped her skyward.

"I need you to do that rotting trick on Purity," Infidel shouted as she swung back around.

"Ice neutralizes my powers!" Sorrow cried back.

"That won't be a problem," Infidel said as she shot toward the winged giantess.

Purity stood braced for the attack. She fired one of the thin blue rays at Infidel, but Infidel banked down at the last possible second to avoid it. Skimming along just inches above the ice, she plowed into Purity at the ankles, flipping her head over heels.

Aurora broke out in a hard run, trying to reach the shape-shifting witch before she could get back to her feet. Purity proved more resilient that we hoped, however, and in seconds she was on her knees, using the Jagged Heart as a staff to help her rise the rest of the way. But, as she stood, Infidel raced up from behind and struck a powerful blow with the Gloryhammer directly on the back of Purity's wrist. The frozen gauntlet that coated her hand shattered. Before she could even think of reworking the ice Sorrow struck, leaping from Infidel's back to cling to Purity's log-sized forearm.

Purity screamed as red and blue veins of infection raced up her arm. Sorrow dug her fingers deeper into the putrefying flesh on the back of the witch's hand, the skin sloughing away in ragged strips, the bones visibly twisting and warping with advanced arthritis. The Jagged Heart dropped from Purity's withering fingers. Aurora was there to catch it.

Unfortunately, by now Purity had grasped the nature of the combined sneak attack. She swung her arm with all her remaining strength, smashing Sorrow into Infidel as she prepared another hammer strike. The two women tumbled through the sky, dizzy from the impact. Sorrow crashed into the ice from a dozen feet up, while Infidel managed to halt herself in mid-air, a grimace on her face as she fought to regain her aerial footing.

Purity stared at her damaged hand. She furrowed her brow as she willed the flesh to knit itself back together. Menagerie's powers proved up to the task of reversing the damage. She capped her new fingers with a fresh coat of ice. I wondered how she had the power, since we'd robbed her of the harpoon, before seeing that she still carried the Icemoon Blade in one of her lower hands, now barely the size of a dagger in her oversized grasp.

Aurora shouted toward the sky in a language I didn't understand. Though she had the harpoon in her grasp, she wasn't wielding it in any sort of defensive maneuver I could recognize. Instead, she waved it around in erratic loops like a woman trying to swat a fly with a broom.

"Is this supposed to be menacing?" Purity growled, reaching for the harpoon.

Aurora switched from her ogre speech into the Silver Tongue. "In your own language, old friend, I call to you," she shouted. "Menagerie, I summon your shade, that you may reclaim what has been taken from you!"

Purity snatched the harpoon away. She was now thirty feet tall. Aurora, the largest person I normally dealt with on a daily basis, looked like a toddler compared to her. Purity kicked her, sending the ogress bouncing across the ice.

"If you'll excuse me, I have a sun to slay," Purity said, turning toward Glorious as he hung above the horizon. She flapped her wings and lifted toward the heavens. High above, I could see the material world floating like a blue-green grapefruit, but it was obscured by wispy tendrils of black smoke. The black smoke writhed and whirled as it descended toward us. Purity jerked her head up, gazing at the approaching smoke with a look of terror. An instant later, I heard the sounds of wolves and lions and chimpanzees howling and roaring and screaming, above the trumpets of elephants and the shrieks of eagles. It was as if someone had rattled the cages of every zoo in the world at once.

The cloud whirled straight toward Purity. She brought the harpoon up to defend herself as the smoke took on a shape I recognized. Menagerie had been a tall man, covered with black tattoos from his scalp to his toe tips, a bestiary of the animals of the material world. The cloud coalesced into this tapestry of tattoos, but only the tattoos, with no underlying flesh or bone. You could see through the gaps in his chest the tattoos that covered his back. The tattoos looked wet, like fresh ink, and now that they were barely a hundred feet above I could see that they weren't truly black, but a deep, deep shade of red, like congealed blood.

Purity opened her mouth to scream. Before any sound came out, the tattoo swarm formed a tight vortex and spun between her lips. Her throat bulged as the torrent of blood forced itself inside her.

Purity went limp as a rag doll. The harpoon and the Ice-Moon Blade slipped from her fingers as she shrank. Her wings vanished, along with her fur and killer whale markings. In less than a second, all her animal traits had disappeared and she looked exactly like Infidel. She dropped from the sky, falling twenty feet to hit the ice with a horrible *smack*.

Any concern I felt about watching this false Infidel fall was instantly pushed away by the real Infidel swooping down and grabbing me. We flew toward Aurora, who ran to grab the Jagged Heart, which stood tip first in the ice like an empty signpost.

Aurora's fingers closed around the harpoon. She turned to face our approach and held out her hand. "Ready to talk to Hush?" she asked.

Infidel and I placed our hands in Aurora's huge palm.

"Do it," we said in unison.

A slow whirlwind built around us, flaking ice into snow, swirling in a gentle flurry, before building to a blizzard. The last thing I saw before the white washed away everything was Glorious flapping his wings and flying toward us.

And then... we'd already moved beyond the material world, into the realms abstract. What lay beyond? Was reality like an onion, composed of layer upon layer upon layer?

I can only report that as the snow fell away, we found ourselves standing in a place that was neither the Great Sea Above nor the material world. Instead, we were in a vast, empty void, where the entirety of creation was the trio formed by Infidel, Aurora, and myself. Our physical bodies vanished and we stood revealed as beings of pure light, no longer human in shape, more like rainbows shimmering in the darkness.

Stripped of our bodies, I had no trouble recognizing Infidel or Aurora. Infidel was a nearly pure white flame, intense and focused. She had nothing that could be described as a belly, but at the core of her light a tiny white candle burned even more brightly. Our daughter? Aurora was a calmer, cooler shaft of blue. I couldn't see myself; I wondered what the others saw?

In the center of the triangle formed by our energies the Jagged Heart hovered. The blue shaft that was Aurora trembled and I heard her voice. "Hush," she said. "It is Aksarna, your humble servant. I've brought two guests who wish to speak with you." I was surprised that she wasn't speaking the ogre tongue. Or, perhaps she was, but we were in a place where all languages were one and the same.

"You violate the sanctity of this place," the Jagged Heart answered. "You've not performed the required rites. You dishonor me."

"I beg forgiveness," said Aurora. "But time is of the essence. As we speak, the dragon of the sun approaches. Purity came to the Great Sea Above to slay Glorious. But Purity was bonded with you; if she wills that Glorious should die, it's because you wish that fate upon him."

"This is not my wish," Hush answered through the harpoon. "This is my need. Glorious must die so that I may go to my final rest. While he visits my realm, I can never know true peace. You, my priestess, know of the paradise I speak of. It is the pure silent darkness of the frozen night. It is the great calm that existed before the creation of light. It is the only hope of relief for my shattered heart. In the eternal peace of winter, I will forget all pain, all longing and loneliness."

"How about all selfishness?" Infidel asked.

"Forgive her," said Aurora. "She speaks out of fear."

"I speak out of honesty!" At these words, I swear that the shaft of white flame threw up what looked like arms in frustration. "This frigid lizard is willing to destroy the world because she's suffered a broken heart. *Boo hoo.* Every day, people suffer loss. I watched the only man I ever loved die before my eyes. Did I think about killing myself? Did I feel like the world needed to be punished because I was alone and scared? No. I sucked up my pain, pulled on my boots, and tried to find a new path for my life. People do it every damn day. Why should this frozen cry-baby feel that her suffering is any different?"

Aurora's pale column flickered, looking afraid. But, the Jagged Heart floated unchanged, as the dragon spoke once more. "You cannot understand. Human lives are too short. You've no time to truly feel anything. You flash through existence like shooting stars, vanishing as swiftly as you appear. You cannot judge the pain of timeless beings."

"Then you can't judge our pain," said Infidel. "You can't understand how precious time is to us, how few hours we're given to share with those we love."

"Do not speak to me of love and sharing," Hush growled. "Your time may be brief, but while you live you're surrounded by throngs of your kindred humans. We primal dragons exist as unique beings in our own realms. There is no one to share the burden of our solitude."

"Have you tried?" I asked. "Because I heard a very similar argument from Glorious. He's lonely as well, lonely enough that death looks like a welcome alternative. Maybe neither of you needs to die. Maybe you need to go to one another and talk. The legends say that you loved Glorious once. When he arrives, tell him how you feel!"

"How I feel?" Hush said bitterly. "Glorious rejected my love. The shame and humiliation of that moment can never be forgotten. I shall never show such weakness again."

"Are all dragons such cowards?" Infidel asked. "Or is it just you?"

"Have a care, human," said Hush. "You stand in the antechamber of my mind. With a thought, I can erase you from existence."

"You would punish her when she's right?" I asked. "I spent ten years in the company of the woman I loved without confessing my feelings. I've no excuse for these wasted years other than my own cowardice. I, too, was afraid of exposing myself to rejection and isolation. I dealt with my pain in pretty much the same fashion you do. You want the world to be so quiet and dark that you can go into a slumber that's like death. You want to just stop feeling anything. I did the same thing with booze. I'd drink until I couldn't remember my own name. I'd drink until I couldn't remember why I was drinking. Self-obliteration is the coward's path."

The flat blade of the Jagged Heart turned toward me. I swear I could see a dark green eye peer at me through the ice.

I said, "If you want to feel alive, you have to take the bad with the good. You can't feel joy unless you open your heart to sadness. You can't feel love unless you're willing to bear loneliness. When Glorious arrives, tell him how you truly feel. Confess that you love him. What do you have to lose?"

"It's too late for conversation," said Hush.

"Infidel and I are proof that it's never too late," I said.

"You don't understand. It is, indeed, too late," said Hush. "Now leave."

Suddenly we were back on the ice, standing exactly as we'd stood when the blizzard had surrounded us. Well, two of us were standing. Deprived of legs once more, I hit the ice with a loud *splat!* I clawed the frosty surface to hold on as it suddenly tilted beneath me. All around us, the once solid sheet of ice had shattered into a thousand ice floes, bobbing on violent waves.

My eyes widened as I saw that Glorious had arrived while we'd been talking to Hush. He was pushed to the ice, wings down, his throat exposed, his body limp. His eyes were open, full of fear, wet with tears that ran down his golden cheeks to freeze on the ice beneath him. Hush sat upon his chest, her jaws clamped around his throat, ready to rip through this windpipe.

"We're too late," Aurora cried, dropping to her knees, sounding beaten.

"Like hell we are." Infidel cracked her knuckles, loud enough that even Hush's green eyes shifted toward the noise.

21 - COLDER EVERY SECOND

I BLINKED AND Infidel was gone, leaving a swirl of snow in her wake. I turned my head in time to see her punch into the side of Hush's jaw with the Gloryhammer. The thunderous blow spread in waves from the tip of the dragon's snout all the way down her serpentine neck, causing an avalanche to fall from her scales. Hush craned her head to snap at Infidel as she zoomed skyward. Infidel surprised Hush by making a mid-air u-turn and darting between the dragon's closing jaws, into the vast chasm of her mouth.

With a sudden explosion of blinding light, the tree-sized teeth near the back of Hush's jaws burst outward as Infidel hammered through them. Hush roared with pain as Infidel spiraled back into the sky.

Glorious lifted his head to see what had halted his planned suicide. Blood trickled from his throat, but it didn't seem to be a mortal wound. As large as Hush was, Glorious was even larger, and her initial attempt at tearing out his throat had resulted in little more than an extra-nasty hickey.

"Now that I've got your attention," Infidel shouted down at the dragons, "stop fighting! If you don't, I'll tear out your teeth and claws until you're too mangled to misbehave!"

"You dare threaten us?" Glorious growled, rising to all four legs. He glared at her with a look of elemental contempt.

"This isn't a threat, it's a promise," Infidel shouted. "Everyone acts like primal dragons are one step removed from gods. You're more like one step removed from spoiled teenagers, and trust me, I know about spoiled teenagers. I'm not going to sit by and watch the world get destroyed by a pair of self-important brats too childish to discuss their feelings!"

"I feel only hate!" Hush screamed.

"And I deserve your hate," Glorious screamed back. "I was a fool to spurn you, too vain and arrogant to see that I might one day long for your company. I can no longer stand the suffering! End me!"

Hush's eyes widened. "You long for my company?"

"My loneliness is unbearable," Glorious whimpered. "The pain of knowing that you once offered to save me from my self-inflicted fate doubles my suffering. As I gaze down upon the world, I see the polar regions, white and dazzling like a pearly crown upon the globe, and I think of you. You were so open when you came to me, so courageous, risking your heart. My hunger to tame the sun blinded me. It was not worth the cost of your love."

"Was it not?" Hush asked, her voice calmer now. "With each passing century I've watched you as you traveled through the sky. I've hated you more with each passing year, but also envied you, and admired you. You've truly changed the world by taming the sun. If you'd not rejected me, you would never have accomplished this great task. "

"But I knew it must cause you pain," said Glorious, his voice on the verge of sobbing. "It hurts you still. My sunlight drives away frost from much of the world. I knew I was keeping you from your full potential. This is why, as I abandoned the sun, I sent it hurtling away. Even now, it slowly fades from the sky of the material world. In a month, it will be only a speck, indistinguishable from the faintest planets that travel across the night sky. Then, at last, the world will be forever dark, and you can know your final peace."

"Oh, Glorious," Hush said. "This is such a beautiful gift."

"But it's going to be an even better gift if he puts the sun back into its rightful path, right?" shouted Infidel. "That way the two of you can see each other every day. You don't have to be lonely any more!"

Hush sighed. "The annoying creature is right. If you don't rejoin the sun, you shall wither and perish. You cannot survive as a spirit untethered to matter. I… I would rather the world remain in light than lose you forever."

Glorious clenched his jaws together tightly for a moment. I couldn't read the emotions in his luminous eyes. At last, he said, "So be it. Perhaps my thirst for oblivion has proven… premature. I shall return to the sun. We will continue our conversation, come the dawn."

"I look forward to it," Hush said. Then, her body fell apart into a great mound of snow.

"What just happened?" Infidel asked, sounding worried as she looked down upon the collapsing white mountain beneath her.

Glorious stretched his wings. "Hush has abandoned her abstract form and returned to her true body in the material world." He gazed at Infidel and said, "Do not in any way think that your threats have altered our actions. Either of us could have crushed you with no more effort than you would put into crushing a bug."

"Yeah, whatever," said Infidel. "You just run along and jump back into the sun."

"You speak to us with such insolence! You fail to respect our power," Glorious growled as he turned away, his eyes narrowed. Then, he paused, and glanced back over his shoulder. "And for this… thank you."

"No problem." Infidel smiled as she brushed the hair back from her eyes.

"Son of a bitch," Aurora whispered, as she glanced down at me. I'd grabbed hold of her ankle to keep from sliding around on the bobbing ice. "Did Infidel just save the world?"

"Isn't she going to be a great mother?" I said.

Glorious flapped his wings and rose into the air. This created an instant blizzard as all the snow from Hush's body roared around us in hurricane winds. The air cleared as Glorious rose higher, radiant as noon. He was looking down at the ice. I followed his gaze and saw what he was looking at, a man in stark black robes standing amid the white snow, an unfurled scroll before him. Judge Stern was nearly a hundred yards away, but his deep, authoritative voice could be heard even at this distance as he shouted the verdict toward Glorious: "By the power of the Divine Author, the Voice of the Book has judged you, Glorious and found you guilty of crimes against nature itself. You have trespassed upon the sun, claiming it as your own when the Divine Author gave it freely as a gift to all. The enormity of this crime is unforgivable."

"Infidel!" I shouted.

"This judgment is final and cannot be appealed," said Stern.

"Don't let him finish reading—"

Infidel started moving before I finished my sentence. She'd barely flown a yard before Stern read, "The sentence is death, carried out by the utterance of this truthful statement."

Infidel reached Stern, flattening him with a punch that sent him skidding across the ice on his back.

It was too late. Glorious shuddered in mid-flap. The internal luminance that filled his form instantly snuffed out, leaving his spiritual form a pale ashen gray. With a soft sigh, he fell, but never reached the ice. Instead, his body changed into a fine powder that crumbled, billowing out as a dense cloud.

I stared, mouth agape, as the dust swept toward me. What was there to say? The world had just been condemned to death.

Infidel drifted down from the sky next to Aurora. We gave each other worried looks seconds before the dust engulfed us. Infidel leaned over and scooped up my legless torso, holding me tightly against her side. I wrapped my arm around her and squeezed.

No one spoke a word. Perhaps we each were hoping someone else would be the first to speak, to offer some clever, last second plan to save everything. Instead, the minutes simply ticked by as the dust slowly settled, revealing our grimy faces one by one. We looked like miners, covered in grit.

Infidel sighed. "Maybe the Black Swan is already traveling back in time to give us another shot."

"That's not really how her powers work," said Aurora.

"So what are you saying?" asked Infidel. "That we're screwed?"

Aurora shrugged. "I'm not sure I'd use the word 'we.' I don't see how things are going to change much for me. The material world is going to freeze, but I don't know that things will change for the dead."

I thought this was a slightly selfish stance to take, but I didn't feel like picking a fight by saying so.

At this moment, there was a cough from the dust cloud behind us and we all nearly jumped out of our skins. Sorrow stumbled out of the fog, hacking up dusty spittle. She was wrapped in the coat her father had draped over her. She carried a black walrus coat taken from one of the ogresses. In her other hand she held some oversized boots. She tossed the coat to Infidel. "Figured you'd be pretty chilled by now."

"Getting colder every second," Infidel said, softly.

"What happened?" Sorrow asked, through chattering teeth. "After Purity knocked us for a loop, I was running back to join you when the ice in front of me split open. I was trying to work my way around it when I heard a lot of shouting. Then, poof, dust everywhere. I've been jumping from floe to floe, completely lost, until I saw the light of the Gloryhammer."

"Your father succeeded in killing Glorious," I said. "Dust was all that was left."

"Oh," she said.

"To complicate matters, Glorious said he'd sent the sun away," said Infidel. "He said it would take about a month to turn into a speck in the sky. After that, permanent winter."

"I see," said Sorrow. She sat down on the ice. Her lips were completely blue. She stared out into the distance, not looking at any of us. After a moment, she sighed and shook her head. "Two minutes ago, my biggest worry was that I was going to lose my toes to frostbite."

Her toes were dark black and shiny. She started to put on the boots, which were about three times bigger than her feet, when Aurora knelt before her and said, "Now that I have the Jagged Heart once more, I can treat your frostbite."

She took Sorrow's right foot in her huge hands, rubbing them, then paused.

"Um," she said, "this isn't frostbite."

"What do you mean?" asked Sorrow.

"For some reason, your toes are covered in black scales. It's like snake skin."

Sorrow's eyes grew wide as she stared at her toes.

I said, "Maybe Rott is somehow—"

She held up her hand, cutting me off. "I don't want to talk about it. I'll deal with it. Somehow." She quickly pulled on both boots and stood up. She said, "A more pressing question is, where's my father?"

"Somewhere out in the dust," said Infidel, waving in the general direction she'd left him. "I punched his lights out."

I thought this was an unfortunate choice of words.

"Do you want me to go find him?" Infidel asked.

Sorrow shook her head. "If I saw him again, I'd kill him."

"I'd be okay with that," said Infidel.

"I wouldn't," said Sorrow. "The greatest curse I could place on my father is to let him live with the full weight of his actions upon his conscience. Death would be too merciful."

Before we could further debate the appropriate fate for Judge Stern, I heard a distant cough. I spotted what looked like a naked woman stumbling towards us on an adjoining ice floe. I squinted, and could see that the woman looked exactly like Infidel.

I asked, "Is that—"

"Purity!" Sorrow growled.

Aurora placed a beefy hand on the young witch's shoulder. "Hold on. It's not her."

The woman who looked like Infidel coughed again, and rubbed soot from her eyes as she reached the edge of her ice floe. She stared at us as if we were ghosts. Which, I guess, we were.

"Aurora?" she asked, utterly confused. "I thought you were dead!"

"Menagerie?" Aurora asked.

"Yeah," she said, frowning. "What the hell's wrong with my voice?"

The woman looked down, her eyes going wide.

"This wasn't one of my tattoos," she said, scratching her head.

"You're alive again," said Infidel. "Don't complain."

"Again?" asked Menagerie. "I was dead?"

"We're all dead," said Aurora.

"I'm pretty certain I'm alive," said Infidel.

Sorrow nodded. "My heart's beating as well."

Aurora sighed. "Fine. If you want to be picky, I suppose that only Stagger and I are truly dead. The rest of you have living bodies that came to the Great Sea Above via the Jagged Heart. I can send you back if you'd like. Then you can freeze along with the rest the world."

"I feel like there's a lot I'm missing," said Menagerie.

Aurora recounted our adventures, filling Menagerie in on all that had happened since he died. As Aurora spoke, Infidel sat down next to Sorrow. We had our arms wrapped around each other. She sat the Gloryhammer in front of us. It glowed like a heatless campfire as we listened to Aurora tell the most horrible ghost story ever.

The hair on the back of my neck rose as I thought more about what I was doing. I was staring at a hammer. I was staring at a hammer that was glowing. The hammer glowed because it had been carved out of the sun.

"I know how to save the world," I said.

"You know I married you for your brains, right?" said Infidel.

"The Gloryhammer's part of the sun," I said. "Earlier, when I touched it in the material world, I felt waves of horrible loneliness wash over me. As a spirit, I could sense the soul of Glorious inside the hammer. But, when I grabbed the hammer here, I didn't feel anything. Glorious was no longer inside the sun at this point."

Sorrow's eyes opened wide. "The sun has been primed to hold a soul..."

"And now it's empty," I said. "I, on the other hand, am a spirit with barely even a phantom body to cling to any more. What if I could merge my spirit with the sun? I could guide it back to its proper path!"

"Give me a second to figure out if that's brilliant or stupid," said Infidel.

Sorrow frowned, shaking her head. "This wouldn't be something you could do for an hour or two and be done with it. Glorious had to guide the sun constantly, for three thousand years. If you could be joined with the sun, its material form would supply your spirit with the energy to endure for eons. You'd have to maintain vigilance on a scale human minds cannot grasp. Can you be trusted with such a task?"

"I can if it means that Infidel has a world to go back to where she can raise our daughter," I said. "I accept the task gladly."

"Stagger," said Infidel. "You can't!"

"Why not? What's the flaw in this plan?"

"Living inside the sun drove Glorious crazy," she said. "It's bad enough that you're dead. Now you want to be insane as well?"

"Glorious went insane because he was alone," I said. "But I'll never be alone. I'll always have you. I'll know that as I move the sun through the sky that my light is shining upon you. One day it will shine on our daughter, then her daughters, and if I have to keep rolling the sun across the sky from now until the end of time, I'll do so. How many men can say that their actions will truly be important a thousand years from now? I want to do this. I must do this. Not to leave you. But to be with you forever."

Infidel kissed me hard. When she pulled away, her eyes were glistening with tears. "You old fool. You were always too damn good at talking. Do what you have to do. No matter what, I'll never, ever stop loving you."

"This is all very touching," said Sorrow. "And all completely moot. Menagerie here can occupy his new body because there's a tiny portion of his original blood within it. I was able to bind Stagger to his driftwood shell with the essence of his spiritual blood. But there's nothing here that we can use to bind him to the body of the sun. It's not just a matter of him flying inside the sun and wishing it to move. He's got to have some link, a blood-bridge between the material and spiritual worlds."

"The bone-handled knife!" I said. "Its hilt is made of dragon bone. It held my blood after I was killed. If there's still a trace left within it..."

Sorrow perked up. "This could work. Where's the knife?"

"It was in Purity's boat."

"So it could be anywhere," said Sorrow, looking around at all the carnage. "It's probably at the bottom of the sea."

"The Great Sea Above doesn't really have a bottom," said Aurora. "If something sinks, it sinks forever."

"Let's hope it didn't sink," I said.

Menagerie said, "If I had my old powers, I could change into a wolf and sniff it out. Tracing down Stagger's scent would be a breeze."

"Purity was able to shape-shift even without tattoos," said Infidel. "She was better at it that you, in fact; she could do hybrid forms."

Menagerie looked deeply offended. "Hybrid forms are decidedly *not* better shape-shifting. Animal bodies have been honed into perfect tools by natural forces. Blended forms are for amateurs. I became the whole animal because I was a true master of the craft."

"No need to get snippy," said Infidel. "In any case, when Nowowon killed you, part of your body survived as a tick. Purity could shift into any creature from which your body had drank blood. There was me, obviously, then a hound dog, a pelican, and now a whale."

"Hmm," said Menagerie, rubbing his chin. He closed his eyes as a look of concentration passed over his feminine features. His face elongated as fur sprouted from his body. He dropped to all fours and a moment later he was in the form of a bloodhound.

"Excellent," the hound dog said gruffly. "First of all, I've never been so happy to have fur. Second, if the knife is near, I'll find it."

He loped off, sniffing the ice, leaping from floe to floe.

"There's one last problem," I said. "Let's say this works. I've got a pretty good idea of what path the sun follows through the sky. I mean, it rises in the east and sets in the west. But, up here, how do I know east from west? How do I judge if the length of a day is enough? I don't want to screw up the world with a half ass job."

"If only we could contact my father's astrologers," said Infidel. "He's got an entire squadron of scholars whose whole job is to watch the sky. They can tell you the exact time of every eclipse for the next dozen centuries."

Sorrow tilted her head as she studied Infidel. "I'm sorry, but who, exactly, is your father?"

"Oh. I forgot you didn't know. I'm the real Princess Innocent Brightmoon."

Sorrow chuckled, until she realized the rest of us weren't laughing. "Really? You're not making fun of the dwarf?"

"Nope. I'm the genuine article. Of course, I'm not really welcome company in my father's throne room. It's not like I can ask him to get his astrologers to help out."

"Maybe you won't need to," I said. "Glorious said he could see and hear people through the Glorystones, the same way that Greatshadow can spy on people through candles. If I were merged with the sun, maybe the astrologers could communicate with me and help guide my movements."

Sorrow sighed. "Looks like I can't let the old bastard die after all."

"What? Who?" I asked.

"My father," she said. "Infidel might not be able to ask a favor of the king, but my father can. We need to send him back to the material world with the mission to get the king's astrologers to work with you, assuming Menagerie can find the knife."

"Good plan," said Infidel, standing up. "Give me a minute."

She leapt into the air, rising a few hundred yards. She slowly rotated, surveying the landscape, then darted off, vanishing behind the remnants of the dust cloud. Not thirty seconds later she was back in view, dropping down beside us with an unconscious Judge Stern draped over her shoulder.

"He was coming too when I found him. Had to give him a little tap to make him cooperative," she said as she laid his limp body before us. "He should be up and about any second."

"Let's bind his hands and feet," said Sorrow, tearing off strips from his robes. "Gag him as well." She grabbed a pocket and ripped it. A glowing ring fell out and danced across the ice. It was the glorystone ring Brother Will had worn. Had this been the unseen object he'd paused to take when his shipmates had been devoured by maggots?

When Sorrow showed no sign of grabbing the ring, I snatched it up. As she finished tying up her father, Menagerie returned, still a hound, jumping back across the cracked sea ice, the bone-handled knife held in his slobbering jaws. He dropped the blade before me.

"Sorry about the spit," he said. "It's impossible to put a bone in a dog's mouth and not get a little slobber."

"Apologies aren't necessary," I said. "Good dog."

"Don't make me bite you," Menagerie growled.

"Give me the knife and the hammer," said Sorrow. "I'll need a moment with each to attune myself to their magical resonance. If you and Infidel have any last words to say to one another, now is the time."

Infidel handed over the hammer, then picked me up, rather clumsily now that she wasn't filled with magical energy. I can't guess how heavy I was devoid of legs and guts. She carried me about fifty yards away before setting me down. We were near a second ogress Sorrow had reduced to a skeleton. Infidel liberated her walrus skin coat, spreading it gore side down on the ice. We lay upon it, wrapping it around us for warmth.

"I wish I had some body heat to contribute," I said.

"You're like a damn ice cube," Infidel said with a sigh. "At least I can't complain about your cold feet."

I laughed, but only briefly. "I'm sorry."

"That you're cold?"

"That your last memories of me will be as a semi-frozen, half-devoured corpse. I wish you could remember me the way I was."

"Who says I can't?"

"Gruesome memories have a way of sticking," I said.

"Baby, I've been a mercenary for all my adult life. Hardly a day goes by that I don't decapitate or disembowel someone. Any nightmares I used to have about blood and gore faded away a long time ago. My nightmares have matured considerably. What they've lost in grossness they've gained in unnerving plausibility."

"Do you have nightmares often?" I asked.

"More than I let on," she said. "As my feelings for you grew stronger over the years, I used to have nightmares about hurting you. I had this one nightmare where I'd kiss you and break your teeth, and wind up with blood in my mouth. And, now… well. There's a new one."

"What?"

"I've been dreaming about our baby," she said. "Wondering if she's going to be normal. She was conceived in the land of the dead. You weren't… you weren't in your real body. You were just a kind of imitation life. Will our baby really be alive? Or will she be half alive, half dead?"

I brushed the hair from her cheek. Ordinarily, this would have been a move intended to comfort her. But, I couldn't help but notice that the fingers I moved her hair with were pale white and puffy. Even against the ivory tone of her delicate skin, my flesh looked dead and bloodless. The iciness of my touch couldn't have been a pleasant sensation.

"She'll be fine," I said, dropping my hand to my side.

"How can you know that?"

"First of all, when you were almost dead, I could see our baby's aura. It was bright and clean, like a little white star in your belly. Nothing corrupted by death could have shone so beautifully."

Infidel nodded, looking thoughtful.

"Second, the Black Swan said she's met our daughter. That old witch never misses an opportunity to dig her claws into you. If our daughter were some kind of monster, she would have said something."

"That's kind of a negative logic, isn't it?" Infidel asked. "Drawing a conclusion based on something that wasn't said?"

"Then here's number three," I said. "I didn't take it seriously when I was a child, but I grew up in a religion that believes that a Divine Author has written out all of our lives. I spent most of my life thinking this was bullshit, but now… well, I didn't believe in ghosts, either. I've seen too many amazing things since I died to dismiss any possibility. Maybe there really is some guiding force out there with the job of making sure that everything works out for the good. Our lives sometimes feel like ships without a captain, at the mercy of the wind and the waves. But maybe there's someone with his hands on the wheel after all, guiding us toward our destinies. If Zetetic is right, then maybe just believing makes it true. You've had a tough life, Infidel. But, I can't help thinking that you've become who you were always meant to be, and that there are even better things in store. You're going to be a mother, and you're going to be amazing."

Infidel blushed slightly. "Aw," she said, as she hugged me tightly.

"So the pep talk worked?" I asked.

"Not in the least," she sighed. "But I love you for trying. This is the Stagger I'll always remember. You're the guy who never stopped trying to make me happy. Hell, you even died and remain more of an optimist than me."

"I do these things because I love you," I said.

"And I love you," she said. "And nightmares are only nightmares. What happens in my sleep doesn't matter in the least. When I'm awake, I remember your courage. When I'm awake, I fight off all my fears just by remembering your smile."

I reached into my pocket and produced the glorystone ring. "Here's something else to remember me by."

I tried to slip it on her left hand, but it was too large for her slender fingers. We finally discovered it fit her thumb.

"It's sweet," she said. "But I liked your hair ring better. It was so much more personal."

"This is personal too. I just stole this ring. We spent our lives together as thieves. What could be more appropriate than a stolen ring? As a bonus, if Glorious really could see the world through Glorystones, perhaps I'll be able to see you. I can be there as our daughter grows up."

Infidel kissed me. It felt as if the power of the Gloryhammer were surging through me once more as I hugged her tightly. Then, something cold and wet pressed itself into the back of my neck. I opened my left eye. In my peripheral vision, I spotted furry dog legs. I broke from the kiss and turned to face Menagerie.

"Sorry to bother you," he said, his dog-breath washing over me. "Sorrow says she's ready."

22 - Straight and Narrow

We followed Menagerie back to Aurora and Sorrow. The air had gone eerily silent. The waves caused by the bobbing sun had died off, and the ice floes had come to rest, no longer cracking and grinding against one another. The two women's voices carried over the ice. Aurora was explaining that, from the abstract realms, the Jagged Heart could return a living being to anywhere in the material world. Judge Stern would be sent back to the Silver City. Sorrow said she wanted to return to the *Freewind.*

"I'm surprised you want to go back to the boat," I said. "It wasn't in the best condition when you left it."

Sorrow shrugged. "I can't simply abandon Gale."

Judge Stern was awake now, his face turned away from us, but from the tilt of his head I could tell he was listening. I decided it was best not to ask questions that would lead to further discussion of the *Freewind*, given that Stern was part of the navy hunting the ship.

"Ready?" Sorrow asked, holding up the hammer and the knife.

"Let's do it," I said.

Infidel gave me one last kiss and placed my legless torso on the ice before Sorrow. She loomed over me as she began her improvised ritual. The binding was surprisingly simple. The dragon bone of the knife's blade served a function similar to the silver mosquito, as its porous surface formed natural cages to trap the essence of my blood required to bond my soul to matter. As for the Gloryhammer, solar matter, like all matter, proved vulnerable to decay. Sorrow weakened the head of the hammer with her new command over entropy, then plunged the knife into the softened crystal. I watched with fascination as she kneaded the head of the hammer around the knife. The knife itself became malleable as clay, mixing with the crystalline matter.

I didn't feel anything happening.

I looked toward Infidel. She looked stoic, but her eyes glistened.

Tears filled my own eyes. The outlines of her body blurred.

I blinked and she was gone. Everything was gone.

I was in a world of pure white.

Only, it wasn't a world, and there wasn't an 'I.' I tried to look down to see what form my spirit had taken now, but there was no down. I had no eyes, no neck, no physical sensation at all.

Was I now in the sun?

How was I supposed to move it if I couldn't even move myself?

Despair seized me. I felt even more trapped than I had in the golden cage inside the golem. In that cage, I'd at least had the hope that, if I understood myself, I might gain some magical gift. I now understood the fundamental flaw of Staggermancy. Because, stripped down to my barest essence, I had no magic. I had nothing at all.

I'd been rejected by my mother and father. The adults who raised me had not loved me. I'd become a thief and a drunkard before I even had pubic hair. I'd spent my adult life cowardly hiding my feelings from the woman I lusted after and made my living chiefly by robbing the dead. I'd made fortunes, then squandered them on booze, in constant pursuit of oblivion. Now I'd finally caught it. Oblivion was my ultimate fate.

I'd failed the world.

I'd failed...

Infidel.

Despite my failings, Infidel had cared for me. A princess with the blood of dragons in her veins, and she'd loved me, and now carried my daughter. I never understood how a woman like her could love a loser like me.

But what if she didn't love a loser? What if she'd seen the true me, when even I couldn't?

She loved a poet, a scholar, a joker and, yes, a thief. She loved a man who'd lived his life leaping from tall cliffs and crawling headlong into dark tunnels in search of wonder. I like to say I've done it all for her.

It's a lie.

I'd lived on the edge before I ever met her, not because I pursued self-destruction, but because I loved discovering something new each day. I was besotted by the world, in all its gritty, stinky, sweaty glory. I'd bitten into the apple of life and drank the tart nectar. I'd loved every moment I spent on our crazy whirling planet.

Love may lead you down strange and twisting paths, but it can never lead you astray. You may follow blindly, across dangerous ground, and never quite reach your destination. But the destination never mattered anyway. Love was always the journey.

And now, it was time for me to undertake a new journey, a trip that no man had ever dared before. Glorious had moved the sun with his mind, but I would move it with my heart. Understanding this, a calmness washed through me, and I fell into restful sleep.

I woke on a white sand beach, to the sound of gulls and the soft sigh of sea foam fizzing near my feet. I raised my left hand to shield my eyes from the intense brightness that surrounded me. I sat up, squinting, unable to remember how I'd arrived here.

As the warm sand shifted beneath me, I realized I was naked. I looked down at my toes and gave them a wiggle. For reasons I couldn't quite put my fingers on, I felt happy to see them. They seemed like old friends who'd been absent for some time.

How much had I drank last night? Where was I? What had happened to my pants?

I grinned. It's both a drunkard's gift and curse that his best memories are the ones he can't remember.

Looking around, I was on a long ribbon of white sand. The ocean before me was black as night, with waves topped by milky foam that reminded me of scattered stars. Behind me, the jungle was dark green, bordered with an impenetrable wall of spiky vines. Try as I might, I had no memory of how I'd come to be here.

The sky above was pure white; I couldn't spot the sun amid the burning haze. The light came from all directions at once, reflecting off the white sand with a ferocity that left me squinting.

Assuming I was on the Isle of Fire, most beaches with white sand lay to the west of Commonground. I rose on unsteady legs and spun to my right. I had no idea how far I needed to go to reach the Black Swan, but knew that the sooner I started walking, the sooner I would get there. I began to walk, stumbling and staggering in the soft sand.

Despite the intense brightness that surrounded me, I was grateful for the haze that rendered the sky a uniform white. If the sun had been fully exposed, my bare skin would have burnt to a crisp. As an added bonus, the sand, while warm, didn't burn my feet. But, all it would take would be a shift in the clouds and both of these convenient truths would vanish. Feeling renewed urgency, I stumbled on.

And kept walking.

And kept walking.

My eyes adjusted to the luminance. I had no way of measuring time, but I began to have the curious feeling that I had been meandering along this same stretch of white beach for hours. Or had it been even longer? For a brief moment I felt I should stop and think about my situation, but when I slowed my pace a sense of dread gnawed at the back of my skull and kept me moving forward. I began to count my steps, and grew lost in the unfolding ribbon of numbers, counting, ever counting, until I'd forgotten why I was keeping track. Only as I was reaching one hundred thousand did the size of the number strike me as peculiar. Assuming I was averaging a step a second, I'd been walking for twenty-seven hours. How could that be possible? I hadn't paused to eat or drink; understandable, considering I had neither food nor beverage, but where was my hunger? Where was my thirst? Assuming I drank gallons the night before, why didn't I feel the urge to piss? If I'd been walking so long, why did the sky never darken? Where was the night? Would this day never end?

Eventually, I found footprints in the sand. My heart surged with relief at the thought that I'd soon find someone who could help guide me home. Onward I staggered, picking up my pace, my feet meandering as I crossed the path of the footsteps I followed. Yet, despite the freshness of the trail, I never caught sight of the stranger I pursued. The hours wore on. At length, I came to a second set of prints. Many hours later, a third set was added. I paused to study them. My feet fit nicely within the outlines. Whoever I was following, they must have been similar to me in height; the length of my stride fairly mirrored theirs.

Much later, a fourth pair added to the growing crowd I chased. Then a fifth, and a sixth.

At about the time my internal clock advised that I should start looking for a seventh set of prints, I finally spotted a man, far in the distance. He was dressed in red robes, with black hair in a long ponytail. I ran toward him. As I drew closer, I saw that he had a large red "D" tattooed in the center of his forehead.

Zetetic?

"Zetetic!" I cried out.

The Deceiver's eyes went wide. He stretched his hands toward me and shouted, "Stop!" Then, without pausing to breathe he cried, "Wait, don't stop, just walk!"

Confused, I halted.

Zetetic bounded across the sand and grabbed my hand, jerking me forward.

"One, two, three, four," he said, pulling me into a steady pace. He was carrying a small triangular box with slits in the side. In craftsmanship, it resembled a clock, but it didn't have any numbers or hands. All it seemed to do was produce a steady, rhythmic click. Zetetic's feet fell in rhythm with each beat, and soon mine did as well as I kept pace beside him.

"What's going on?" I asked, confused. "What's that in your hand? What are you doing here? For that matter, where the hell are we?"

"I'll answer all your questions, I promise," said Zetetic, who now reached into his robes to produce a long walking stick. He began to drag the stick behind him, leaving a straight line as we journeyed. "Promise me that you'll keep walking forward, and match the pace of your stride to those of this metronome."

"Metronome?" I asked.

He handed me the box. "It's spring operated. Slide the panel along the back to find the winding mechanism."

"Aren't these something musicians use?" I asked.

"Yes," he said. "Feel free to break into song if you wish. Anything you need to keep your pace steady. You've been staggering rather badly."

"How do you know?" I asked.

"Look at how your footprints keep crisscrossing," he said, nodding toward the sand before me.

"These are all my footprints? How? How did I make it around the island without finding Commonground?"

"You aren't on the Isle of Fire," Zetetic said. "I take it you don't remember what happened?"

I shook my head. "My best guess is I drank myself under a table and some punks robbed me of everything including my socks, then dumped my body on the beach. I've been pushing myself forward until I reach home. I can't wait to tell this story to… to… oh."

Suddenly I remembered Infidel.

Suddenly I remembered everything.

"This is not a beach," I said.

"No," said Zetetic. "This is not, technically, anywhere at all. You're dealing with concepts too large for human senses to fully process so your mind has constructed this symbolic tableau. The infinite ocean represents the void filled with stars. The green forest is the material world. The beach represents the path of the sun. As long as you travel this path keeping the forest to your right, the sun still rises in the east and sets in the west."

"You mean… you mean I'm doing it right?" I scratched my head, or the symbolic equivalent of my head.

"Ha!" said Zetetic. "Not even close! You're appropriately nicknamed, Stagger. The sun has been meandering in an eccentric orbit for the last week. The length of a day hasn't been the same twice since you started. This seems to have thrown the weather off, as I've heard reports of blizzards as far south as the Isle of Apes. As you can imagine, this has led to quite a bit of consternation below. Which is why I'm here."

"Why *are* you here?" I asked.

"Thanks to the information they got from Judge Stern, the king's astronomers have done a wonderful job of analyzing the problem with the sun. But, they didn't possess the power to do anything to put the sun back into its correct path. For that, someone with a more specialized skill set was required. I presented myself to King Brightmoon yesterday. His kingdom is in turmoil; farmers from across the Silver Isles are at his gates, brandishing pitchforks and demanding he take action."

"You're that action," I said.

"Indeed. Through my contacts I'd heard that Glorious had been slain and a new ghost now drove the sun. I assured the king that I possessed the ability to speak to this ghost and put him on a straight and constant path. In exchange, I've been granted a pardon and one of the king's remote island fortresses, plus all the gold, soldiers, and servants necessary to outfit it. I've always wanted a modest place of my own."

I looked at the box in my hand. "So, this is all I need to keep me on pace?"

"Almost," he said. "Once we complete an orbit, we'll find the line I'm now tracing. If you follow this line faithfully, the sun will be back on the correct path."

"And you'll stay with me as I walk?"

"This first time through. After this, I've prepped a glorystone in the Royal Observatory to serve as a channel through which you may speak and be spoken to. The chief of the Observatory, Father Luciferous, is quite eager to talk to you and learn your story."

I smiled. "I like telling stories." I looked at the stretch of sand before me. "And I like walking on the beach. But, I feel like there's a lot I left unfinished in the material world."

"Every dead man I've ever spoken with felt the same way," said Zetetic.

"Fair enough. But, I'm probably the first dead man to actually have some leverage. I'm willing to keep the sun moving through the sky at a constant pace. I'd like you to explain to the king that I feel a little gratitude is in order. I think I can concentrate on my pace a little easier if he'll do me a couple of favors."

"Are you speaking of blackmail?" Zetetic said.

"I think I might be. The king is going to get a lot of love from his subjects once word gets out that he's fixed the sun. I hope that he'll share his good fortune by issuing a few pardons. There's a family of Wanderers called the Romers. I'd like for him to leave them alone. Even more importantly, I want him to issue a full pardon for Infidel. I don't want her to have to hide from assassins while she's raising our daughter."

Zetetic's face went blank.

"What?" I asked.

"Nothing," he said. "I was... I think these are reasonable requests. I'm certain the king can accommodate you."

"I'll want proof," I said. "Glorious said he could see through the glorystones. I obviously haven't picked up that trick yet. But if there's a stone where this Luciferous guy can talk to me, I want you to promise me that you'll bring Infidel to it so I can speak to her."

Zetetic nodded. His face was completely calm and expressionless. "I'll do what I can. Of course, it might take some time to locate her."

"For you? Just tell someone you have the power to find missing people by jumping into the air and landing beside them."

He furrowed his brow.

"What's the problem?"

He shook his head. "No problem. I'm just worried we might have gotten out of step with the metronome. Let's walk in silence for a while."

"For someone called Deceiver, you're surprisingly bad at lying," I said.

Zetetic shook his head. "I'm simply concerned, is all. You must keep moving forward. You must not change your pace."

"You know something, don't you? About Infidel?"

Zetetic said, "Of course not."

I stopped moving. "I'm not taking another damn step until you tell me what's going on."

Zetetic grabbed my arm and yanked me forward.

"No!" I shouted, taking a step backward.

"Keep walking!" he cried. "Think of the chaos you cause on earth when you pause even for a moment, let alone move backwards!"

"Tell me what you know!" I shouted.

"Infidel's dead!" he screamed at me.

I fell to my knees.

Zetetic sighed, and bent down on his knees before me. He said, softly, "I'm sorry. I don't know the full story, just bits and pieces of court gossip. Judge Stern was briefly captured by Infidel and a witch named Sorrow while they were in the Great Sea Above. Stern heard Sorrow and Infidel request to be sent to the *Freewind,* which was damaged and adrift in the artic, just north of the Isle of Grass. They wanted to help the Romers get the ship back to port."

I clenched my hands in the warm sand beneath me. I'd known Judge Stern was listening. Why hadn't I said anything?

"King Brightmoon messaged his flagship, the *Raptor*, to find the *Freewind*. The *Raptor* is capable of flight and covered the distance to the *Freewind's* location in less than a day. One of the old, normal days, not the thirty hour specials you've been serving up. "

"What did they find?" I asked.

Zetetic said, "I really need for you to stand up and start walking again."

"What did they find?"

Zetetic sighed. "The Storm Guard had beaten the *Raptor* to the punch with one of their hurricanes. When the *Raptor* arrived, they found timbers from the *Freewind* scattered across the sea. The Storm Guard had crushed the ship between two icebergs. Ordinarily, the Storm Guard are eager to take prisoners to sell as slaves, but through diplomatic channels we've learned that the crew of the *Freewind* fought to the last man. Their dead and wounded went down with the ship. Presumably, Infidel and Sorrow perished with them."

I nodded. "There were no bodies?" I asked.

"Not that I'm aware of," said Zetetic. "Please get up."

I rose, brushing sand off my legs.

"Infidel's the main reason I'm doing this," I said, stepping forward.

"I understand," he said. "But she was just one person. There's a whole world that depends on you now. It's not just people at stake. Every last blade of grass on the planet needs you to keep walking. Every tree, every bird flitting between their branches, every last fish in the sea depends on you now for survival. The magnitude of your responsibility is incomprehensible."

I looked straight ahead as I walked. "I comprehend."

I matched my pace to the ticking metronome, thinking of all those blades of grass, thinking about flowers, and fields of corn, and all the farmers that worked those fields, and their cows and chickens and children. All of mankind now stared up to watch the sky, needing me to be something I'd never been: dependable, predictable, following a straight and narrow path.

And so I walked. I do it still. I'll do it until every bit of white foam on the ocean around me vanishes as the final stars burn out.

I do not fear eternity.

I have my memories. I have the promise of telling my story for generations to come.

And I have the knowledge that I'm helping Infidel. She isn't dead. Somehow, Levi convinced Gale to abandon ship. Infidel, Sorrow, the Romers... all could use the breathing space that comes from the world thinking them dead. For the time being, they'll no longer be hunted.

One day I'll learn to gaze through the glorystones, and perhaps learn the fate of those I've left behind. Already when I gaze at the luminous paper-white sky I detect all-but-invisible swirls of motion and hear distant, barely perceptible murmurs. I'm on the verge of a new sense awakening. But I don't need to see the material world to be certain that Infidel is still in it.

I know she's alive because she's not here.

If Infidel's dead, she knows where to find me. She's had an unusual amount of practice in navigating the realms beyond life. When her soul finally departs her body, I'm certain she'll battle and bargain and blast her way across whatever abstract realms lie between us.

I can wait. I'm a patient man. The day will come when I see her on this shore. She'll smile and give me a kiss, then place her hand in mine as we walk along this beach. She can tell me what really happened when she made it back, what happened to Sorrow and Gale and even poor Bigsby. She can tell me about my daughter. I wonder what she'll name her?

It's these thoughts that give me the strength to place one foot before the other. In the end, neither of us will walk into eternity alone.

WITCHBREAKER
BOOK THREE OF THE DRAGON APOCALYPSE

"I sometimes think
that what the world
accepts as sanity
is merely the capacity
to grow numb to outrage."

1 - A CONVERGENCE OF DRAGONS

SORROW SHIVERED as she opened the blanket clasped around her shoulders long enough to feed the last shards of the kitchen table into the stove. Commonground was a tropical port, which meant that Menagerie's houseboat had been ill-stocked to deal with the blizzard that had settled over the city for the last week. The small stove had been designed for cooking, not for heating, and Sorrow had quickly exhausted the stocked firewood. When Menagerie failed to return after leaving to speak to the Black Swan a few days earlier, Sorrow had started burning his furniture. This perhaps crossed a boundary as a houseguest, but the shape-shifter struck her as practical. She was certain he'd understand.

The room was pitch-black save for the glowing red square of the open oven door. Yellow flames danced as she slid the table-legs onto the coals. She paused a moment in the improved light to study her feet. She'd returned from the Great Sea Above with her ankles covered in hard black scales. These had grown and spread in the intervening days, leaving her shins covered in overlapping diamond-shaped plates that felt hard as iron.

Despite this unexpected physical change, she didn't regret her decision to hammer a fragment of Rott's tooth into her brain. Doing so had opened a portal within her that allowed her to tap the primal dragon's power of decay. She'd made generous use of his abilities when she'd fought to keep Hush, the dragon of cold, from killing Glorious, the dragon of the sun. For most of her life, she'd pursued the power she needed to change the world more to her liking. Gaining control of a fundamental force of nature was more than she'd dare to dream.

Of course, none of this was going to matter if she froze to death. She wanted to be anyplace other than here, in a snow-covered floating shack miles from civilization. Her desire to be someplace else felt physical, as if an invisible rope was wrapped around her soul, with a team of horses dragging her elsewhere.

She reached to close the oven door. A red claw thrust out of the flame and grabbed her by the wrist. She jerked her hand back, gasping, her eyes growing wide as the red claw retreated back into the dancing flames.

As she stared into the fire, twin yellow eyes formed in the swirling plasma to stare back. The last table leg she'd added split along its length, resembling opening jaws lined with teeth of jagged blue-white jets.

The crackling fire spoke to her: "Rott has been summoned to the convergence. It's rude that you keep him from answering the call."

Sorrow swallowed hard. "But, I —"

The red claw once more shot from the open door. She tried to scramble backward but the talons closed around her face. She felt something tear and suddenly she floated above herself, watching her limp body collapse on the floor. She felt shocked to see herself from this perspective. She wasn't unfamiliar with her own face; she shaved her scalp daily, and was used to seeing herself in a mirror. But, the body that lay upon the floor looked quite different now that it was soulless. The body still breathed, but Sorrow felt repulsed by how much her shell looked like an ill-kept doll made of skin and bones and meat. She was only twenty-five, but the frown lines and furrowed brow of the meat-mask that covered the skull before her looked much older.

"There's no time to study your human aspect," the flames crackled. "It's the dragon within you that's required. Come."

The sensation of a rope tugging her soul became fantastically real. Only, instead of a rope, it was a cord of braided silver. The silver stretched down through the floor of the houseboat. The material world faded before her spiritual eyes and she found herself falling through a cloudless blue sky.

She now saw that the silver cord stretched taut beneath her for what looked like miles. At the other end, Rott tumbled lifelessly toward a green ocean far below. When she'd encountered Rott in the Sea of Wine his body had been half submerged, and all that she'd seen was his serpentine spine, miles in length. She hadn't realized he had limbs, or tattered wings that fluttered uselessly as they fell.

At last, he splashed into the emerald waves. She was dragged down until she was nearly submerged herself. The huge corpse floated back to the surface. The water around him turned white with what she assumed was foam, until she realized it was maggots boiling from beneath his scales.

Repulsed, she willed herself to fly away. She was high in the sky before the silver cord snapped tight, whipping her around to look back at the scene below.

A chain of islands formed into a rough circle directly below her. Though mostly equal in size, the topography and climate of each island was radically different.

The northernmost island was a deep blue mountain of crystalline ice, surrounded by gusting snow. The upper edge of the ice was a saw-tooth ridge that looked like a dragon's spine. Avalanches spilled down the slopes as the mountain lifted her head. This was Hush, the primal dragon of cold, and she looked out toward the other islands with unveiled contempt.

A rapidly churning circle of storm clouds wreathed the island to the east. The hurricane swirled into a serpentine form. A dragon's head emerged, opening its massive jaws to lick the land beneath with a tongue of lightning. Thunder rolled across the green waves, forming a voice: "Who summons Tempest, Lord of Storms?"

To his side was an island of granite. The earth grumbled and cracked and quaked as the dragon stirred from his repose. Dirt slid from a hill-face to expose two enormous diamonds, which narrowed into angry eyes. Sorrow knew enough dragon lore to recognize Kragg, the dragon of stone.

On the island beside Kragg, lava spilled down the slopes of a steep volcano until all the land was ablaze. The smoke and flame snaked together as it stretched into the sky, curling into a dragon's neck and face

"I issued the call," roared Greatshadow, the primal dragon of fire.

The bone-white cliffs of the island next to Greatshadow cracked, releasing rivers of blood. A thousand animals jumped free of the red torrent, multitudes of beasts, from common house cats to lumbering elephants, from swarming ants to slithering boa constrictors. The menagerie marched together, sinking their teeth into the flanks of their neighboring beast, digging their claws deep into flesh, until the writhing, shrieking mass formed a dragon, a towering creature part lion, part snake, and part eagle. This was Abundant, the dragon of animal life. She shrugged her long back as she looked out upon her brethren.

She was beside Rott, who floated belly up in the water, looking like a long chain of black tar covered islets that smelled like a city dump. Rott's unblinking eyes were half submerged, his jaws agape, his yellow teeth cracked and broken.

The dragons glowered at one another, then one by one glanced toward the heavens. Sorrow wondered if they were looking at her, until she looked up to see the sun high in the sky, looking for all the world like a huge disk of gold floating above them.

"What's he doing here?" Abundant asked, with a voice formed by wolf-howls and baboon yowls and the chorus of a thousand robins.

"The sun still respects the pact we made long ago," Greatshadow said. "No primal dragon may ignore the summoning."

"He's not a dragon," Kragg rumbled. "He's an interloper."

"He's here," said Tempest. "This is more than I can say for Abyss."

"It's unlike our brother to be tardy," said Abundant. "I sense he draws near."

The water of the sea in the center of the islands began to boil. From the depths a giant turtle rose, as large as any of the islands surrounding it. Waves spread across the green sea, crashing onto the shores of the other dragons.

"You dishonor us with your delay, brother," Hush growled. "I expect Rott to be late, but you've no excuse."

The turtle turned its head toward the north. With a voice formed by crashing waves, it spoke: "You know the reason for my sluggishness. The cold you've unleashed has frozen my form further south than you've ever before encroached. I normally keep silent about your intrusion into my domain, but this is inexcusable."

"Your domain?" Hush asked with a scoff.

"All here recognize the sea as my abode," said Abyss.

"The sea is nothing but molten ice," said Hush. "You borrow it at my pleasure."

"I would argue that the reverse is true," growled Abyss.

"His is not the only domain you've invaded," Greatshadow said as the pillar of crackling flames that formed his body swirled to face Hush. "You dare blanket my earthly home with snow? How can you justify this insult?"

"It's more than an insult," howled Abundant. "It's an assault! Your blizzards have killed countless tropical beasts who've never known winter. If Greatshadow had not summoned us to the convergence, I would have. We understand you have reason to be angry, but this doesn't excuse the magnitude of your sins."

"You dare to speak of me of sins?" Hush answered with a trembling voice. It sounded as if she was on the verge of tears. "I'm the one who cries for justice! I shall not call back my blizzards until one particularly vile beast is wiped from the earth: man!"

Tempest let loose with rumbling thunder. "We understand your grief, sister. However –"

"You understand nothing! Men killed Glorious! At the moment of my greatest happiness, when my one true love had finally opened his heart to me, he was cruelly slain by a human!"

"You would punish all mankind for this crime?" asked Kragg, with a voice like vast stones grinding together.

"It was not the act of a lone man. These creatures have banded together and declared war upon us all." She stretched an icy claw toward the volcanic island. "Greatshadow! You barely survived when the Church of the Book sent men to hunt you! Surely you must share my thirst for revenge!"

"I think not," the dragon of flame answered. "You've thrown your blizzards throughout the earthly realms. Men have responded by building fires and lighting lanterns. Why should I think ill of those who feed me so faithfully? The time has come for your tantrum to end."

"But the threat the humans pose —"

"– can be contained," said Greatshadow. "I survived the best that mankind could throw against me. The only reason they wounded me at all is that they came bearing a weapon carved from the spiteful ice that once was *your* heart. In failing to kill me, they've left me stronger. I admit, I'd grown complacent. Now, I keep a watchful eye for their schemes."

"You admit there is a threat?" said Hush.

"Yes," said Greatshadow. "Though I'm not certain that humans are the ultimate source."

"What do you mean, brother?" Tempest thundered. "Speak, if you know something."

"I'm hesitant to sully this sacred space with mere speculation," said Greatshadow. "I simply find it curious that the Jagged Heart was stolen from the ice-ogres by members of the Storm Guard, only to wind up in the possession of the Church of the Book. The Storm Guard wouldn't invade the domain of another dragon without your permission, nor would they be so careless with their treasure."

"You say you will not engage in speculation," Tempest grumbled. "But you offer only opinions, not evidence. The Story Guard had nothing to do with the theft of the Jagged Heart."

Greatshadow nodded. "My apologies." He turned his attention once more to Hush. "If I confine myself to statements of simple fact, here is one that is indisputable. The only reason that Judge Adamant Stern, the murderer of Glorious, had reached the Great Sea Above was that you gave him passage there."

"Lies!" said Hush.

"I watch mankind through every candle flame," said Greatshadow. "And I listen to the conversations of ice-ogres through their cook-fires. You personally accompanied Stern on the hunt for Glorious. I accept that you had a change of heart, and would have spared our brother. But what does that matter? Stern was your murder weapon. You fired a bow, and now blame the arrow because your feeling toward the target changed while the missile was in flight."

"You've hated me for centuries!" Hush screamed. "Can anyone ever expect a fire to give honest testimony about the cold?"

"Do you have proof of your accusations, brother?" asked Abundant.

"I've spoken with an eye-witness," he said. "You may trust my testimony."

"Such grave accusations must be backed up by more than hearsay," said Abundant.

Greatshadow turned toward Tempest. "Perhaps there are others among us who may shed light upon these recent events."

"Again you speak to me with veiled accusations," said Tempest. "I do not like your tone, brother."

"I've simply asked myself, who would benefit most from the death of other primal dragons?"

"Obviously, the Church of the Book," the storm dragon answered.

"A church you've a record of manipulating."

"I've been a target of their plots as well," said Tempest. "I've merely been alert enough to thwart them before they endanger me."

Greatshadow kept his jaws shut as he glared at the storm dragon with eyes of flame.

Hush shook her head, sending tornadoes of snow swirling about her. "Greatshadow, you've grown too used to being fed by mankind. It's left you soft. What's more, your smoldering hatred toward me distorts your judgment.

Do you think your kindred dragons will sit idly by while mankind schemes against them?" She looked around the isles. "Or will the rest of you join with me to end their threat once and for all?"

Abundant was the first to speak. "Men are arrogant beasts, foolishly believing they are superior to other animals. Yet, they are still beasts, and all living creatures are dear to me. I cannot allow you to harm them."

"Even though these monsters killed Glorious? Even though they killed Verdant? How many more of us must die?"

"We dragons have killed far more of our fellows than men have," Kragg answered.

Thunder rumbled as Tempest responded, "It's true that men are dangerous. Yet, I've learned a great deal by studying them. Men built their civilization by taming wolves and boars and oxen. Animals that once threatened them now do their bidding. I've taken inspiration and cultivated a breed of man to my liking. I cannot permit you to harm my livestock."

Abyss lifted his head from the water and said, "I care nothing for what happens to men who dwell on land, but there are still Wanderers who respect the pact they made with me long ago. I will not let you harm them."

"You're fools, the lot of you," growled Hush. She turned to Kragg. "You cannot love these animals. They riddle your body with mines and steal your precious gems and metals!"

Kragg writhed, stretching his back. There was a rumbling that echoed long after as boulders larger than houses tumbled down his slopes. "With a shrug, I've plunged an entire city into a vast cleft in the earth. Men are little more than annoying fleas. I can hardly be blamed for scratching them. I care nothing if they all die, but I also care nothing if they live. They aren't worthy of my sustained attention."

"It's five to four in favor of the death of mankind," said Hush. "The rest of you must respect the will of the majority!"

"I fear that the cold has frozen the part of your mind capable of math," said Tempest. "Greatshadow, Abundant, Abyss, and myself all vote that mankind shall live. Kragg's position seems to be one of neutrality. This leaves you alone in wishing the extinction of mankind."

"We must count the votes of our fallen brethren!" Hush howled. "Verdant, slain by humans, votes for vengeance! Glorious, slain by humans, votes for vengeance! And Rott, though his mind is too long gone to give voice to his wishes, is the embodiment of destruction! Is there any doubt how he would vote?"

"The Rott I remember was more complicated than you give him credit for," said Abundant. "For him, life and death were part of a unified whole. He might argue that the deaths of Verdant and Glorious were inevitable. Despite our great powers, we're not gods. We're living creatures who've risen to dominate our chosen environments, but this does not make us immortal. Dragons die just as surely as men. You cannot count Rott's vote for your side."

"You can't count any vote as being on your side other than your own," said Tempest.

"I don't need your approval to destroy mankind. This isn't a democracy!"

"You're the one who brought up voting!" roared Greatshadow.

"The rest of you can't stop me," growled Hush.

"I could," said Kragg. "I could shatter the earth beneath your feet and plunge your frozen lands into the raging flames within the heart of the world. Greatshadow would no doubt welcome you with open claws."

"This will not be needed," said Tempest. "Hush, we've tolerated your invasions of our abodes for a little time, and are not without sympathy for your grief. But you must withdraw to the ordinary boundaries of your domain. It would cause me great anguish if, when we dragons converge once more, you failed to answer the call."

"Is this supposed to be some sort of threat?" sneered Hush.

"It is my promise," said Tempest. "If you continue your campaign of global destruction, I will take whatever actions I must to defend my domain."

"It will not come to this," said Greatshadow. "Hush, you're angry. You've already killed thousands of men with your actions. But this is true each year; never does the human race emerge unscathed by winter. If you spare mankind now, think of the suffering you may inflict for centuries to come. Will this not satisfy your thirst for vengeance?"

The great snow-dragon ground her teeth as she glared at her brethren. She answered them after a moment of silence, her breath rolling out in a great fog. "Very well. I will not darken the memory of our fallen companions by turning my wrath against other dragons. For now, I shall withdraw my blizzards. My cold will follow the normal order of seasons. But know this: when the day comes that humans turn against you, Abyss, or you, Tempest, and rip you body and soul from the earth, I will shed no tears. I will instead savor the cold satisfaction of knowing you were warned."

"I'll take that chance," said Abyss.

"We're decided," said Greatshadow. "Mankind shall be spared."

Greatshadow turned his face upward, gazing directly at Sorrow. He bared his teeth. Sorrow wondered if he was trying to smile.

Abyss sank back into his sea, disappearing beneath the waves. The storms forming Tempest slowed their churn, dissipating into fluffy white clouds. Abundant fell apart, the various animals that formed her disappearing from sight beneath a black cloud of cawing ravens.

Rott began to sink beneath the waves, pulling Sorrow closer and closer to the water. As the other dragons vanished, she looked up at the yellow disk of the sun and shouted, "Stagger! Stagger, are you there?"

She thought, perhaps, that a faint voice answered, just on the edge of her hearing, but it was drowned out by the sloshing, maggot-tipped waves beneath her. She was dragged into the water, sinking into the calm silence beneath the surface, with curtains of light shimmering around her. She sank beyond the light, and there was nothing but darkness, and the cold.

"SORROW?" A WOMAN asked.

Sorrow sat up with a gasp. Though she was drenched in sweat, her teeth were chattering. She stared at the open oven door before her and saw that the fire had gone out. She snapped her head to the left as she realized she wasn't alone. A blonde woman in a long fur coat stood by her side.

"Infidel?" she said. "You came back?"

The warrior woman had lit out for the jungle the second they'd returned to Commonground. Sorrow had assumed she'd never see her again.

"Guess again," said the woman.

"Menagerie?" asked Sorrow. The shape-shifter had left the boat in the form of a hound-dog. She'd known that he'd consumed Infidel's blood and could now shape-shift into her double, but she hadn't seen him do so since returning to the material world.

The woman nodded. Her eyes fixed on Sorrow's throat. "That's a nasty burn."

Sorrow lifted her fingers to her neck and winced. Blisters covered the flesh.

"What happened? Did you fall against the stove?"

"Something like that," she said softly.

Menagerie glanced around the room and sighed. "It's bad enough you burned the furniture. Did you have to take the doors off the cabinets?"

"I burned them early on. They seemed extraneous," she said as she wrapped the blankets around her.

"Burning the boat itself seems like a dead-end plan," Menagerie said. The shape-shifter nodded toward Sorrow's sea-chest in the corner. The lid was open, exposing Sorrow's books, journals, and maps. "Bound parchment burns rather nicely in my experience."

"I've been keeping journals since I was ten," said Sorrow. "But I didn't spare them solely due to sentimentality. I suspect historians may one day find my diaries of value."

"Ah," Menagerie said with a smile. "Still planning on ruling the world?"

"Quite the opposite," she said. "I'm planning to free the world from tyranny."

Menagerie stooped in front of the chest and thumbed through one of the journals without asking permission. "Nice handwriting. Precise and tidy. Nothing immediately tips a reader off that you're insane."

"Just because you're mad that I've burned your furnishings is no need to be insulting."

Menagerie closed the book and stood. "I mean no insult. But, I've earned my living as a mercenary since before you were even born. I'm a good judge of people." The shape-shifter stared at her face with a penetrating gaze. "Mentally, you're one of the most dangerous people I've ever met."

Sorrow smiled.

"I didn't mean that as a compliment."

"I've spent a great deal of my life in pursuit of the goal of becoming more dangerous. As have you, if the stories about you are true."

"My goal wasn't to be dangerous," said Menagerie. "My goal was to be effective. I always knew what I was fighting for, and I always knew the steps I would take to reach my end game."

"As do I?"

"Do you?"

"My end game is a more just world," she said.

Menagerie nodded. "And step one toward achieving this is to gain power. That's why you've got a head full of nails and scales all over your legs."

"Correct."

Menagerie crossed his arms over his breasts. "And what, exactly, is phase two of your plan?"

"I… I'm still in pursuit of the first phase. Once I have the power I need, I'm confident the path forward will be clear. One thing I do know about my path is that I'll need allies. Infidel rebuffed me. Will you consider my offer? You know I can pay your wages."

Menagerie shook his head. He asked, "Did you know there's a hell?"

"So the church teaches."

"I just spent what I felt was eternity there," he said. He pressed his lips tightly together and took a long breath through his nose. "It's… not a place I'm eager to return to."

"Don't tell me the legendary Menagerie has lost his nerve?"

"Menagerie died when an angry god tore his soul into a thousand tiny shreds," he said. "Whoever I am now, I have a clean slate. I've got a chance to make a new life."

"As a woman," Sorrow said. "If you return to the civilized world, I suspect you'll find that people treat you much less equitably than they did when you were a man."

Menagerie shrugged. "I guess I'll find out. I've sold this boat to the Black Swan. I'm using the funds to head for the Silver Isles for a taste of civilian life."

"You won't last a week in that city of hypocrites," Sorrow said. "You've lived too long in Commonground. People here are thieves and murderers and scoundrels, but at least they're open and honest about it. The so-called civilization of the Silver City is nothing but a den of vipers."

"I guess I'll find out. If it's not too much of a burden, could you try not to destroy civilization while I'm still using it?"

"I can make no promises," said Sorrow.

2 - GRAVEDIGGERS

SORROW'S KNUCKLES GREW white as she gripped the sides of the dugout canoe. The Dragon's Mouth, the river that fed into the bay at Commonground, was normally a broad, placid body of water, but snowmelt had swollen the river beyond its banks. Ancient trees felled by the snow bobbed in the current, forming an ever-shifting maze.

The river pygmies she'd hired to ferry her to the Knight's Castle navigated silently through the treacherous waters. When the four canoes had first departed Commonground, the river pygmies had chatted and laughed with one another. Now they paddled without saying a word, their eyes barely blinking as they studied the roiling river, their faces hard, stoic masks.

There were eight pygmies, two in each canoe. She was their only living passenger; the rest of the canoes held her gear, plus Trunk. She'd left him inert for the moment. She didn't want to alarm the pygmies with his unusual appearance. Of course, the pygmies struck her as difficult to alarm. She'd allowed her hood to slip as she boarded the canoe and they hadn't even taken a second glance at her head. River pygmies dyed their shaved bodies blue and cut fish scale scars along their shoulders and backs. Her scalp studded with nails probably struck them as banal.

The terrain around the river grew more rugged and rocky. She wondered if the pygmies would be up to the task of carting her gear to her destination. She'd made her needs quite clear to the pygmy leader, Eddy. (His full name, translated, was White Foam Curling Past an Eddy, which she found rather mellifluous). He'd assured her that his men were the strongest of their tribe, but the tallest of pygmies barely reached the bottom of her ribs, and she'd not packed lightly. She'd come into the jungle seeking the lost Witches Graveyard, and was prepared for an extensive dig when she found it. The canoes were heaped with picks, shovels, wheelbarrows, ropes, tents, and enough food for a six-month expedition.

After several hours of paddling against the fierce current, their immediate destination came into view, the towering, vine-draped walls of the ruins known as the Knight's Castle. She'd lost Stagger's map in the rush to abandon the *Freewind,* but his directions were simple enough. Locate the Knight's Castle and head east. Here, she'd find rows of evenly spaced depressions in the ground. Stagger had been certain the place was a graveyard but had always assumed, since the graves weren't marked, that it had been used to bury people of little importance. No treasure hunter had ever done the hard work of digging there because it seemed unpromising. But, she'd come seeking knowledge, not treasure, and the thought of the waiting graves filled her with an almost childlike excitement.

The pygmies guided the canoes between two enormous walls. In the flooded gap was a broad avenue, draped by shadows. Sorrow strained to see in the dim light. At the end of the avenue steep stone steps rose from the water, leading to the top of the walls. Her canoe shuddered as it scraped unseen rocks beneath the coffee-colored river.

Eddy leapt from the tip of the canoe, his feet splashing loudly as he landed in knee-deep water, his muscles bulging as he pulled the canoe to rest on one of the broad steps hidden just inches below the surface. Eddy wasn't a young man, but his muscles were well-sculpted beneath his leathery blue hide. Sorrow felt embarrassed that she'd doubted the pygmies' capacity to cart her gear. Despite their small stature, these men needed immense physical strength to survive this savage land.

Sorrow rose from her canoe as the other pygmies brought their vessels to rest on the steps. The pygmies still looked nervous, but she felt relieved to be away from the worst of the river.

She said, "Well done, Eddy. You've earned your moons today."

Eddy frowned as his men gathered around Sorrow.

"We must discuss our payment," said Eddy.

"You'll be paid when we reach the graveyard. Three moons each. We were clear on this subject."

"At the market, my brother saw you pay for provisions with a purse full of moons."

"Perhaps he did," said Sorrow. "I don't see how that matters."

"It matters because we're eight warriors," said Eddy. "You're a lone woman, far removed from any long-men who could hear your cries."

Sorrow crossed her arms. "It's bad enough that you would renege on an agreement. I can't believe you're trying to threaten me."

"No, no, no," Eddy said, laughing gently. "You misunderstand. I make no threat. I'm merely saying that, in such a hazardous landscape, you'll give us all your coins. You can hand them over willingly, or we can take them after we are done amusing ourselves with your corpse."

He raised his hand and brought his thumb and little finger together. At this signal, all seven of his companions drew knives from their belts.

Sorrow sighed. "I see. Fortunately for you, I abhor settling disputes with violence, and wish to avoid doing so now. Here's my counterproposal: your men will drop their weapons. You'll unload the canoes in a neat and professional fashion. After this, we shall part ways. In exchange, none of you will die in unimaginable agony. At least, not today."

Eddy drew his own knife. "You've a bold tongue, witch. We'll see if you're still as arrogant when I cut it from your mouth."

Sorrow stepped back as Eddy ran toward her. She snapped her fingers, then extended her hand as Eddy leapt high in the air, swinging his knife at her torso. She caught him by the arm just as a second pygmy attempted to stab her in the back of her thigh. She felt his blade tear through her pants and skitter along the hard scales beneath as she toppled backward.

Meanwhile, Trunk had heard the snap of her fingers and stirred. Her last golem had been built of driftwood, but she'd had no patience for rooting around on a snow-covered beach looking for appropriate timber. Trunk's torso was a heavy cedar chest; his limbs were thick and sturdy boards. Oak dowels formed his fingers and toes. For a head, she'd used a bucket so new it had never been touched by a mop.

As expected, most of the pygmies turned toward the wooden man as he rose with a clatter. She had only to deal with Eddy, who straddled her torso, attempting to press his knife to her throat, and the thigh-stabbing pygmy she'd fallen upon.

Dealing with Eddy was simplest. She relaxed her arm and allowed him to press his iron blade to her throat. The second it touched her flesh, she willed the knife to crumble and it did so, rusting instantly to the core and snapping as Eddy pressed down.

The pygmy she'd fallen on had managed to untangle himself from her legs and rose on his hands and knees directly in front of the soles of her boots. This was an unfortunate place for him. While she wasn't happy about the scales covering her legs, she'd discovered that the external changes were accompanied by internal changes, leaving her with superhuman strength in her lower limbs. She kicked the pygmy squarely in the chest and he went flying, smacking into the vine-draped wall twenty feet away.

"Now, Eddy," she said as she grabbed the diminutive robber's face in both hands, "It's time for me to teach you a lesson in keeping promises."

She could have been merciful and killed the man. Instead, she closed her eyes and focused on the dragon's tooth in her skull. In her mind's eye, it was like a tiny black doorway. She opened the door a crack, allowing the smallest fraction of Rott's power to surge from her bare palms.

Eddy howled as his flesh sagged on his face. She pushed him away and he fell on his back, writhing in agony. He wailed as his teeth turned black, falling from their sockets. His muscles shrank as his skin grew paper-thin. He raised his hands before his face as they twisted into arthritic claws. Mercifully, he didn't have long to stare at his deformity. Thick cataracts fogged his eyes, turning them into twin white marbles.

She rose on trembling legs. As before, when she'd used Rott's power, she found the after-affects unpleasant. Rott's energy hadn't flowed from her cleanly. Her whole body tingled. She nearly gagged as she exhaled. The odor of her lungs was like rotten meat.

Eddy's mewling whimpers of pain drew her focus back to her immediate surroundings. When pressed into violence, she killed as efficiently and coolly as possible. She despised those who took pleasure at inflicting pain. Yet a smile crossed her lips as she looked down at the man who'd threatened her with such swaggering confidence. She fought back the urge to taunt him, but not the urge to educate him.

"You called me a witch," she said, standing over the now ancient man. "It's a term commonly used to describe women inadequately subservient to men. I, however, embrace the word's true meaning. I command forces you can never hope to comprehend. I'm heir to an ancient and awesome power. You should not have betrayed me."

She glanced behind her and found Trunk standing in ankle deep water surrounded by six headless corpses. She shook her head slowly. She'd hoped at least one survivor would bear witness, to spare her further trouble from the locals.

There was always Eddy, weeping at her feet, splayed out like a rag doll, covered in his own bodily waste. She doubted there was enough left of his mind to pass on her warning.

"What's the point in teaching lessons if there's no one around to learn?"

Then, because she was disturbed by the satisfaction she was taking from his feeble, wet sobs, she placed her boot upon his throat and pressed until his suffering ended.

She had Trunk dispose of the corpses in the river while she sorted through her supplies. They would have to cart her gear in one load at a time. Fortunately, the dug-out canoes would prove handy for storing what they left behind. Trunk turned over one canoe and placed it atop another. She used her power over wood to weave the two halves together, forming a sealed container that held most of her provisions. For now, Trunk would cart only tools and a few days' worth of meals.

She led Trunk up the stairs to the top of the wall. She shielded her eyes from the fierce noon sun as she studied the jungle, gray and withered, devastated by the cold. From her vantage point, she could see a slope of black beyond the trees, evidence of the recent lava flow. If Stagger's description was correct, it looked as if the lava hadn't covered the area of the graveyard.

Two hours later, she'd barely made it a hundred yards into the jungle. The ground was mushy, and Trunk kept sinking up to his knees. Sorrow grew coated in mud herself as she worked to free him and drag their supplies forward. She lost one of her boots in the sucking mire. She pressed her lips tightly together as she stared at her now bare foot.

She wasn't overly sentimental, but she missed her toes. After her strange dream of witnessing dragons debating the fate of mankind, the changes in her legs had gotten worse. Her feet were now covered in overlapping bands of scale that tapered to points. If she pressed hard, she could barely feel the bones of her toes still present beneath the surface.

The uncertainty over whether her physical changes had halted added a sense of urgency to her quest to find the Witches Graveyard. The few remaining practitioners of the art of weaving placed great value in their privacy. The handful she'd tracked down seldom gave Sorrow a warm welcome. Sorrow's pursuit of power had earned her more than a few enemies. No living weavers wanted to make themselves a target of the forces allied against her.

Her hope of pushing her education further now lay with dead weavers. She was certain that if she could study the skulls of witches, she could learn a great deal by documenting how they'd placed nails into their brains. With any luck, she wasn't the first weaver to tap the power of a primal dragon. She might yet discover the secret to using Rott's power without corrupting her body.

It was nearly sunset when she finally found the hilly slope covered with rows of long narrow depressions that Stagger had described. Her nostrils twitched as she hacked her way through the spiky vines that draped the area. Did she smell fire? Or was it just a lingering odor from the volcanic eruption?

She sliced her way through a curtain of dying vines and found herself in an area relatively free of undergrowth. The canopy of trees here was particularly thick, blanketing the area in a perpetual gloom that suppressed smaller plants. She looked up the hill and saw a granite boulder, nearly the size of a house, shaped something like a heart. It looked top heavy and a bit out of place despite being girded with thick vines. She suspected it had rolled down the mountain many years ago. Next to the boulder, she saw a small makeshift tent, little more than a large blanket stretched over some branches. Near this was a smoldering fire pit.

She cocked her head. She could hear voices from the other side of the boulder.

She looked toward Trunk and motioned for him to drop his pack. She opened a bundle of tools and supplied him with an axe, then nodded for him to follow. Armed with her machete, she crept silently up the hill. Stagger had warned her that treasure seekers often tried their luck around the Knight's Castle. From what she knew, these were desperate men of low morals who might not behave honorably. She had no fear that they were an actual danger to her. Still, if they did look problematic, she saw no reason to waste the advantage of surprise.

She pressed herself against the heart-shaped boulder and listened to the voices from the other side.

"Here's another one!" said a man in a curiously high-pitched, falsetto tone.

"Gold?" a second man asked, sounding hopeful.

"No. It's green. Maybe more glass? The light's getting bad."

"Let me see," said the second man.

Sorrow furrowed her brow. She'd heard these voices before. What were they doing out here? Then she realized why she hadn't been able to find her map when she abandoned the *Freewind*.

She marched around the boulder and saw a mound of damp earth piled a few dozen feet away. A tall blond man was standing in the pit beside the mound, visible only from his bare shoulders up.

"Brand!" she shouted, stomping toward him.

The blond man looked up. His eyes grew wide. "Sorrow? I didn't expect to see you out here."

"I'm sure you didn't!"

He grabbed a root near the edge of the pit and started to pull himself up. He was half out of the hole when she placed her boot on his shoulder and knocked him back in. He landed next to the second figure in the pit, a pot-bellied dwarf wearing a platinum blonde wig.

"Villain!" the dwarf shrieked, shaking his fist. "You'll pay dearly for striking the scion of King Brightmoon!"

"It's okay," said Brand, rising to his knees. "I think there's been a misunderstanding."

"You stole my map!" said Sorrow.

"Technically, I found a map in the rubble when we were hastily packing. How was I to know it was yours?"

"It was in my cabin!"

"Things got sloshed around when the ship capsized. There's no telling where it originally came from."

"You knew it wasn't yours!"

Brand nodded. "Okay, sure, that's true. But, honestly, when I found it, I saw the word 'treasure' in large letters, underlined, and thought it was a joke. I doubt that most people who hide buried treasure do that."

"You took it seriously enough to come out into the jungle."

"Also true," said Brand. "But after Gale fired me, all the princess and I had were the clothes on our backs. We need to raise some scratch to get back to the Silver Isle. What did we have to lose?"

"The princess?" Sorrow rolled her eyes. "Bigsby still thinks he's Innocent Brightmoon? And you're still humoring him?"

"Him?" asked Bigsby. "Who's she talking about."

Brand shrugged.

"I should just fill in this hole with both of you in it," grumbled Sorrow. "The world has more than enough thieves."

"Have a care, commoner," said Bigsby, wiping a muddy strand of blonde hair from his face. "We don't care for your tone or your accusations."

"I'm not a thief," said Brand. "I'm just lucky at finding stuff."

"Like those shovels and pickaxes? Since you're broke, you obviously didn't acquire them honestly."

"It depends on how you define honest. We bought them. We holed up on the *Black Swan* for a few days during the worst of the blizzard. I earned a few moons reading palms for the patrons."

"You read palms?"

"To the extent that anyone reads palms, sure," said Brand. "It's a talent I picked up traveling with the circus."

"He's very good," said Bigsby.

Sorrow clenched her fists. "You've no magical powers. I'd spot it in your aura if you did."

"I didn't say I knew magic," said Brand. "Fortune telling is ninety per cent listening to your clients, and ten per cent repeating their words back to them with a twist."

"So you swindle fools," said Sorrow. "All the more reason the world won't miss you if I fill in this pit."

"I didn't swindle anyone. My clients are very happy with my work. Let me do you."

"I think not," said Sorrow. "You've nothing to tell me about myself I don't already know."

"I can tell you you're not going to bury us," said Brand.

Sorrow sighed. "No, I suppose I'm not. I'll let you out if you promise to leave peacefully. If you refuse, you know what I'm capable of."

"How about this?" asked Brand. "We get out of the pit, we all eat dinner together, and tomorrow we work as a team to look for the treasure, whatever it is."

Sorrow studied Brand's face. He smiled at her, but this didn't help his cause. She hadn't much liked him when they traveled together on the *Freewind*. Brand was little more than a prostitute, a pretty young man who served as the sexual toy of Captain Gale Romer, a woman old enough to be his mother. On the other hand, one reason that Gale had been so smitten with him was that Brand was a rather impressive physical specimen. Having a gravedigger with broad shoulders and a strong back could speed up her search.

"Fine," said Sorrow. "But you'll work as my employees, not my partners. I'll pay you a set fee to dig graves. What we find will be mine alone. At least you won't be digging blindly with the chance of winding up empty-handed. I'll compensate you and Bigsby a moon for each grave you excavate."

"I'm not Bigsby!" the dwarf shrieked. "Why does everyone keep calling me that? Has the whole world gone mad?"

Sorrow closed her eyes and rubbed them. The prospect of spending an extended time dealing with the dwarf was unpleasant. It wasn't too late to have Trunk dismember them with his axe.

She sighed. She'd always thought of herself as a defender of those outside of the mainstream of society. An insane cross-dressing dwarf certainly fell into that category. How much did she truly believe in her own cause if, when confronted by a person who was an even more of an outcast than her, her first instinct was to bury him in an unmarked grave?

"Sorry, Innocent," she said softly. "I'm just tired. I got confused."

"You're still confused if you think you can address me in such a familiar fashion," Bigsby said huffily.

"Sorry, your highness," she said.

"The apology is accepted," said Bigsby. "But we reject your offer. Any treasure we find is rightfully ours."

"Hold on," said Brand. "We only need enough money to get passage back to the Silver Isle. We'll be rich once we're home. Why be greedy?"

"That's quite rational of you," said Sorrow. "You wouldn't be trying to trick me?"

"Nope," said Brand. He grinned. "If you can't trust royalty, who can you trust?"

"By the pure metals," Sorrow said, shaking her head. "I'm probably going to regret this."

She turned toward Trunk. "Help them out."

Brand helped Bigsby steady himself as Trunk lifted him to the surface. Brand didn't wait for Trunk to bend back again, but once more grabbed a root and scrambled out.

"If it was your map, do you have any idea of what it is we're looking for?"

"Some," said Sorrow.

"I don't suppose we're looking for very fancy knitting needles, are we?" Brand asked, holding up a slender jade shaft.

"You found one!" said Sorrow. "Where's the skull that held it?"

"There wasn't a skull," said Brand. "If these pits used to be graves, any human remains rotted away a long time ago." He pulled two more of the shafts from his pocket. "We also found these rods of onyx and glass."

Sorrow took the glass rod, feeling both excited and disappointed. She already had a nail of glass, and saw no benefit to adding a nail of jade or onyx. "How much do you know about my abilities?"

"We know you're a witch," said Bigsby.

Sorrow nodded. "More precisely, I'm a materialist. By using these nails, I can gain mastery over objects made from the same base materials."

"How?" asked Bigsby.

"You really don't want to know."

"I do! I command you to tell me how to use these items!"

Sorrow drew back her hood, revealing her shaved scalp. "Fine. You take a hammer and nail these into your head."

"Really?" Bigsby asked. "It's that simple?"

"I wouldn't call it simple. A misplaced nail can kill a weaver. If you're lucky enough to live, you're marked forever as a dangerous heretic who can be legally put to death on sight. All power comes with a price."

"But you could show me how to place one of the nails in my scalp?" asked Bigsby. "I could gain your powers?"

"Only women can do it. For reasons I'm not sure of, men always cripple themselves if they try."

"Why should that be a problem for me?" Bigsby asked.

"It's a problem because we're royalty, sister," said Brand. "We represent not just our people, but our religion. Since the Church of the Book says that witches are sinful, imagine the scandal if a princess showed up in court with a nail in her head."

"Good point," said Bigsby.

Sorrow had to admire the calm tone Brand used in addressing Bigsby. She wasn't certain he was doing the right thing by manipulating the dwarf's delusions, but he seemed good at it.

She said, "You can keep these nails. They'll be of interest to collectors. The jade nail might be worth a hundred moons. What I'm looking for are nails I've never seen before. And skulls. Especially skulls." She looked around the darkening jungle. There were hundreds of depressions. She shook her head. "Why did you choose to dig here?"

Brand pointed down the hill. "This is pretty much the highest point among the graves, so I didn't think we'd have to deal with a lot of groundwater. The graves further down would probably fill up with water faster than we could dig."

"Probably," she said. "Still, I hate to think that our search is going to be so… random. This could take a long time."

"Do you know anything that might help us pick the best targets?" Brand asked.

Sorrow shook her head. She glanced at the smoldering fire of their pathetic campsite. She said, "Why don't the two of you get that fire going again while Trunk and I unpack? No point digging further tonight. We can eat dinner, get some sleep, then figure out the best way to tackle this in the morning."

Bigsby looked the golem up and down. "I confess, I've not been as good a student of theology as I should have been. Why does the church hate witches? Being able to build a helper like this seems rather useful."

"Indeed," said Sorrow, giving Trunk hand signals to clear ground to pitch their tent. "Perhaps a bit too useful. Weavers lived in peace for a long time among the rest of humanity until Avaris, Queen of Witches, used her powers to carve out her own kingdom. She upset the existing order of the world by crafting a society in which women were held in higher esteem than men. The church's hatred of witches has more to do with politics than theology."

Trunk tossed aside a small boulder nearly a yard across that had to weigh several hundred pounds. Bigsby looked impressed as the rock rolled down the hill.

"This thing's as strong as Infidel," he said.

"Probably," said Sorrow. "And much more cooperative. I don't know why I wasted my time trying to persuade Infidel to join my cause. If there's one thing I've learned from life, if I'm to truly have companions I can rely on, I must build them myself."

SORROW LAY AWAKE through the night. Though she had pitched her tent twenty yards distant from the brothers, she could still hear Bigsby snoring. But, that wasn't the main reason she couldn't sleep. Partially, there was a sense of anticipation. She'd first heard about the Witches Graveyard almost seven years ago, and it felt unreal that she'd found something she'd been searching for after all this time. The fact that three nails had been discovered in the first grave was a good omen. Honestly, she hadn't expected to find any nails. If these were the graves of victims of Lord Tower, the Witchbreaker, she would have guessed the nails would have been removed either before or after execution. Perhaps only valuable nails had been treated this way. Jade and onyx resembled colored glass; perhaps they'd been left in the grave by mistake.

Underlying her excitement was dread. There had been no skull, or any bones at all. What if she'd come all this way in vain? What if she spent the next year of her life digging for secrets and found none?

She was almost tempted to put Brand's fortune-telling talents to the test. Almost. He'd as much as admitted his skills were mere trickery. But perhaps there was some value in having someone listen attentively as she spoke. She'd kept her talks with the Romer family short and professional. They'd been employees, not friends. She'd opened up a bit with Infidel, but, in the end, they'd had little to say to one another.

She found it interesting that Brand might be a good enough listener that other people paid for the service. Perhaps it was worth spending a moon or two for a demonstration.

Still unable to sleep, she turned on her side, lowering her hand to scratch her left ankle. Her nails slid along the hard, glassy surface of the scales without managing in the least to relieve the itch. She scratched with more pressure, and succeeded only in slicing open the tip of her finger along the edge of one of the scales. She sat up in her tent and reached for her belt. She used the hard surface of the buckle to scrape her ankle vigorously.

She stopped scraping as she heard someone laugh directly behind her.

She spun around and found a pygmy standing not a yard away. How had he gotten into the tent? At least he didn't appear menacing. For starters, he was elderly, his face looking like wrinkled leather over his skull. He was so thin she could have counted his ribs. He was bald, devoid of any of scars that most pygmies sported. He was also missing the pygmy dyes that rendered river pygmies blue. He was white as cotton, save for his eyes, black and empty sockets in the dark tent. The skull-like quality of his face was enhanced by the way he grinned, showing his teeth.

She reached out to grab him as she said, "How did you get in here?" He stepped backward and her fingers closed on empty air. He laughed softly, then sighed, shaking his head.

She lunged, this time trying to grab him with both hands. He jumped backwards. He laughed as he watched her hands flail uselessly in the space he'd stood a heartbeat earlier. But, his back was now pressed against the wall of the tent. There was no more room to retreat.

"You aren't going to think this is funny when I'm through with you," she said, reaching for his throat.

He stepped backward, fading through the tent as if it were made of fog instead of heavy oilcloth. Her hands smacked into it with a thump. She stared at the empty wall. Was she dreaming again? Admittedly, she was exhausted, and had been drifting in and out of the antechamber of sleep. But she was definitely awake now. Wasn't she?

From outside the wall, the pygmy giggled.

She scrambled to the door of the tent, wearing only her cotton slip. She ran around the canvas walls and found the pale pygmy glowing in the moonlight. He was standing a few feet in front of the heart-shaped boulder. He laughed harder as he saw her, tears running down his cheeks.

"What's so funny?" she asked.

"You," the pygmy gasped, pointing at her. He spoke in the Silver Tongue, but she didn't recognize his accent. "The demons in the Forest of Torment told me I should bear witness to the return of the Destroyer." He wiped his wrinkled cheeks. "I can't believe they mistook you for something so dangerous."

"Demons? Forest of Torment? What the hell are you talking about?"

The pygmy shook his head. "There's no point in explaining. You're nothing but a desperate and foolish girl." He sighed. "Demons. I should have known they were trying to trick me. The dragon will devour you and return to his slumber."

"The dragon?" she asked. "Are you talking about Rott? What do you mean, he'll devour me?"

"You're nothing but a tick, clinging to Rott's flesh. You may feast upon him only a little while before he catches you between his teeth."

"Who are you? How do you know this?"

He turned away, facing the boulder. He glanced over his shoulder and said, in a serious tone, "I've had my fill of conversation with the dead this day. At least those other souls accepted their fate." He took another step toward the boulder before looking back again. "Struggle if it amuses you. In the end, this is all there is of life. Take some comfort in the notion that your death may serve as a cautionary tale for others. Now, I must depart. I'm late for the Inquisition."

There was the sound of leaves crunching from the left side of the boulder. Brand appeared around the corner and asked, "Who are you talking to, Sorrow?"

Sorrow glanced at him, then back to the pygmy. Only, the pygmy was gone.

She ran forward and placed her hands on the rock. "Did you see him?"

"See who?"

"A pygmy. He was albino."

"They're all albino, I think," said Brand. "They just dye themselves different colors."

"Did you see him?"

"No."

"But you heard us talking?"

"I heard you talking, sure," said Brand. "But I never heard the other half of the conversation. I thought you might be sleepwalking."

She shook her head. "I think I saw a ghost."

"Really?"

"Don't sound so skeptical," she said. "You've been to the Sea of Wine. You know that souls survive death."

"I don't doubt the existence of ghosts," said Brand. "But I've never met one. I have, on the other hand, met sleepwalkers. And crazy people."

"I'm neither."

"Just throwing out some theories." He stretched his back and yawned. "What time is it?"

"Time for us to dig," said Sorrow, heading back to her tent.

"Can't we wait until dawn?"

"You can go back to sleep if you wish. I've got things to do."

"Like what?"

"For starters, I've got to move this boulder."

"What? Why?"

"Because I'm pretty sure the pygmy just walked into it."

"You think it's hollow?"

"I don't know. But it occurs to me if it really did roll down the mountain and came to rest here, it's probably sitting on top of more graves. Maybe no treasure hunters have ever dug here. With a house-sized rock on top of them, on this high ground, maybe these graves have been protected from rain. Maybe the skeletons haven't rotted."

"That's a lot of maybes. While you strike me as a person who generally gets what she wants, I highly doubt that golem of yours is strong enough to move this boulder."

"I have more tricks up my sleeve than mere brute force," she said, looking back at him as she reached her tent.

"Fine," he said, scratching his head. "You can show me your tricks in daylight. Right now, I'm going back to… to…"

His voice faded off as he stared at her. She followed his gaze and realized he was staring at her feet.

"Are you… are you wearing…"

"These aren't boots," she said. "I think… I think I might be turning into a dragon. I'm hoping I can find something in one of these graves that will help me avoid that. Perhaps you can grasp my sense of urgency."

"I see," said Brand. He nodded, then headed back toward his tent. "Let me grab my shovel."

3 - CLATTER

AS BRAND WENT to wake Bigsby, Sorrow ran her hands along the boulder. The surface was heavily weathered and cracked. Vines had dug deep into crevices in the rock. Sorrow closed her eyes and leaned her forehead against the stone. She took a deep breath and calmly expanded her senses. Since tapping into Rott's power, she been more aware of the decay that surrounded her. She'd noticed it first when she'd returned to the *Freewind* from the Great Sea Above. The second she'd stepped onto the ship, she'd felt the torn and broken wood fibers in the timbers beneath her feet and been keenly aware that the ship was doomed.

Worse, when she'd looked at Gale Romer, the ship's captain, she'd been able to see that Gale was dying. Not in an immediate, urgent sense, but Gale was well along the path of her inevitable fate. Gale was only forty, robust and active, strengthened by life at sea, but Sorrow's new awareness had focused on the woman's gray hairs and weathered skin. It was as if she could watch Gale's life slowly but inexorably seeping away.

Save for dealing with Eddy, she'd barely used her powers since returning to the material world. Her hyper-awareness of the creeping decay had faded. But, it was time to summon that sense once more. Just as humans didn't last forever, this imposing mound of stone before her was on a one way trip toward becoming sand. She spread her arms across the rock and could feel the veins of weakness that radiated through the seemingly solid surface.

She closed her hands around the vines that corseted the rock. The roots and tendrils had weakened the stone over the centuries, but now the thick vines did as much to hold the boulder together as tear it apart. Fortunately, they were easily removed. She closed her eyes and found the dark doorway inside her, carefully opening it. The vines in her grasp crumbled to dust. She opened her eyes as the rot spread through the remaining vines, which twisted and crackled as they withered. In moments, the last of the vegetation peeled away, leaving a ring of dirt around the boulder. She took a deep breath and willed the portal to close. It wasn't so difficult, when things were quiet and calm. But could she ever control the force during the heat of combat?

"Not bad," said Brand, who stood behind her holding his shovel.

"I'm just getting started," she said. She motioned for Trunk. He was now armed with a large sledgehammer. Sorrow pointed toward the top of the stone, where it dipped down into a narrow depression that formed the indentation of the heart-shape. "Climb," she said.

Trunk's inhuman limbs had no trouble scrambling up the cracked surface. Sorrow guided him with a series of commands to what she sensed was the boulder's weakest spot.

By now Bigsby had left his tent and found his brother. He looked like he was still half-asleep. He mumbled, "Whash going on?"

"Sorrow's hunting for ghosts," said Brand.

"Ghosts?" asked Bigsby, rubbing his eyes. "That's crazy."

Sorrow bit her lip to avoid responding. She couldn't let the dwarf distract her. She finally had Trunk right where she needed him.

"Strike the crack before you!" she shouted. "Use your full strength!"

Trunk swung the hammer back behind him. It cut through the air with a loud *WHOOSH* and smacked into the rock with a deafening *BANG*. All throughout the waking jungle, monkeys and birds screeched in alarm.

Sorrow turned and said, "Gentlemen, I'm fairly certain I know how the stone will fall, but I suggest you take a few steps back as a precaution."

Bigsby's eyes narrowed. Sorrow could tell she was about to be scolded for addressing the two men as 'gentlemen.' She quickly added, "You also, your highness."

Behind her, the stone popped and trembled as the shock of the impact continued to reverberate. She stepped away as the loudest crack yet made her flinch. She looked back in time to see the two halves of the heart-shaped boulder split, then tumble away from each other. Both of the top-heavy pieces flipped as they tumbled down the respective halves of the hill they'd been perched upon.

Trunk had been straddling the crack and he tumbled into the hollow pit of black earth left by the departing stones. He landed on his feet, looking none the worse for the experience. She was deeply satisfied by the performance of this golem. The moons she's spent on top quality lumber were an excellent investment.

"That was a lucky break," said Brand. "What would you have done if the stone had split, but just sat there?"

"That wasn't going to happen. I could sense the tension between the two halves of the stone. Each half was held in balance by the other, but doomed to fall once split. Once you know how to look at the material world, it's not that difficult to understand."

Brand shook his head as he looked down the hill to where half of the boulder had come to rest. "I think there's a metaphor here about broken hearts, but I'm too deprived of coffee to piece it together."

"I shall record in my journal that on this day you were at a loss for words," said Sorrow.

Brand laughed. "I don't think I've heard you make a joke before."

Sorrow shrugged. "I'm not certain why you think I've made one now."

She grabbed a shovel and carried it to Trunk, swapping it for the sledgehammer. The ground beneath the boulder was broken and jumbled from the movement of the stone. There were no clues to guide her to a likely place to start digging, other than the fact that the other graves seemed to be laid out in predictable rows. Following from the row that led up the hill, the stone possibly covered a half dozen graves. She eyeballed the nearest grave and used it to locate what might be the first grave in from the edge. Brand used the same strategy to find a grave on the opposite side.

"Shall we race?" Brand asked as he pushed his shovel into the soil.

"It really wouldn't be a fair contest. Trunk is far stronger and never tires."

"You're on," Brand said, as dirt flew over his shoulder. Bigsby grabbed a shovel and joined his brother.

"Dig," she said to Trunk, feeling a slight urge to complain that the brothers had a head start. But she'd never agreed to a contest. Why should she be concerned about who would win?

Ten minutes later, when Trunk's shovel struck something hard, she couldn't resist the urge to shout, "Victory!" Brand and Bigsby had barely dug a pit four feet deep, while Trunk was already in a hole down to his shoulders.

"Congrats," said Brand. "What did you find?"

Sorrow knelt to see better. What *had* she found? Trunk continued to remove dirt, revealing a layer of flat black slates, looking for all the world like roofing shingles. The boulder had been as big as a house, but she hadn't expected to find an actual structure under it.

Brand climbed out of his hole and wandered over.

"It looks like a roof," Sorrow said.

The shingles were rectangles two feet long and a foot wide, with rough edges. Once Trunk had made the hole wide enough, Brand dropped in to help clear the dirt. It soon became apparent the slates were stacked into an arch. The structure was about five feet across, but she couldn't guess how long because they hadn't found either end yet. So far, about six feet of the arch was exposed.

Brand knelt and tested his luck at lifting one of the shingles. He let out a little grunt as he lifted it to his chest, then stood and pushed it out of the hole.

"Are those heavy?" she asked.

"They ain't light," he said.

"Climb out. Let Trunk remove the stones."

Brand did so. Trunk lifted the stones with no hint of effort, revealing another layer of stones beneath. Beneath this, they found glass. Sorrow leaned low to be certain. As one by one the stones were pulled away, she could see that they were exposing what looked to be a coffin made of solid glass.

That wasn't the only thing being exposed, however. For as Trunk stood to lift out a slate tile, a shaft of sunlight fell upon the first rectangle of open glass, illuminating the contents. While Sorrow had little personal experience with male anatomy, she couldn't help but think that what the light revealed strongly resembled the naked crotch of a hairy man.

Brand and Bigsby apparently noticed as well.

Bigsby asked, softly, "Is that... what I think it is?"

"I'm almost certain it is," said Brand.

Of course, there was more beneath the glass than preserved genitalia. As Trunk continued uncovering the glass coffin, he revealed the man's torso. The figure being revealed was covered in kinky black hair over skin white as cotton. Despite his deathly pallor, the man was an impressive physical specimen. He was muscular almost to the point of grotesquerie. Sorrow wondered if he might be a half-seed of some kind, perhaps a man blended with a bear. His shoulders were far broader than any she'd ever seen on a living man. His beastly appearance was compounded by fingernails at least four inches long, thick and gnarled.

Yet when his face was at last revealed, she abandoned any thought that the figure before her was anything other than human. Though his face was mostly concealed by a thick black beard, and despite the long hair draping around his head having the fullness of a lion's mane, there was something deeply human about the man's face. There was a gentleness to it, a look of peace that reminded her of a sleeping child.

"Is he breathing?" Bigsby asked.

Sorrow furrowed her brow as she stared intently at the man's chest. It was perfectly still. She also noted the man didn't possess an aura. All living things carried a faint glow of energy she'd been trained to detect. This man was completely devoid of inner light. "I'm almost certain he's dead."

"Quite well preserved, isn't he?" Brand asked.

"Perhaps he isn't even real," said Sorrow. "You can craft a figure out of wax that looks eerily lifelike. It's difficult to believe anything that once lived has been buried for centuries without rotting."

"He's in glass," said Bigsby. "Maybe he's pickled."

Sorrow suspected the light would refract differently if the coffin had been filled with fluid. But she did notice that the coffin didn't appear to have any seams. Since she knew the art of glass weaving, she knew it was possible to craft a container, heat it to drive out air, then seal it before it could refill, creating a vacuum. The weaver who'd taught her this trick many years ago had used it to preserve flowers. Could the effect be scaled up to preserve a body? Were walls of thick glass enough to hide this corpse from Rott's gaze?

"As treasure goes, this is something of a dud. He's not even wearing any jewelry," said Brand.

"Really?" Sorrow asked. "We encounter something this mysterious and all you can think about is the lack of loot?"

"The Black Swan might buy him," said Bigsby, now speaking in his normal, male voice. "She used to buy all kinds of weird stuff from Stagger."

"I'm here for knowledge, not wealth," said Sorrow. "Somebody went to a lot of trouble to preserve his body. Aren't you curious who cast the spell? For that matter, aren't you even more curious who he is?"

Bigsby nodded. He said, once more in his annoying, fake female voice, "Maybe it's the knight."

"What knight?" she asked.

"You know. The knight from Knight's Castle."

"Stark Tower? The Witchbreaker?"

"Why not?" Bigsby squeaked.

Sorrow sighed. "You know, real women don't sound like that. Just use your normal voice."

Bigsby put his hands on his hips and pushed his voice even higher as he said, "This is my normal voice."

Sorrow was sorry she'd brought the subject up. She returned to the topic at hand. "I can't imagine it's Stark Tower. He was a hero to the church. They wouldn't bury him naked in the middle of nowhere."

"Do you want me to smash open the coffin?" asked Brand.

"No," said Sorrow. "I can weave glass, so opening the coffin isn't a problem. But I don't want to tamper with anything before I get the chance to do some research. We'll need to pull this coffin out and take it back to Commonground. I'm not selling anything to the Black Swan, but she might have some information as to who he is."

"That sounds like a lot of work," said Brand.

"I'll see that you're well compensated for your efforts. For now, let's continue digging the hole you started. Perhaps our mystery man has a brother."

The second grave went quickly, thanks to the combined efforts of both Brand and Trunk. They were aided by the fact that the soil of this grave was bone dry starting a few feet below the surface. It crumbled easily beneath the assault of the shovels. Sorrow stood near the edge of the grave, chewing her nails. What if this grave held another preserved body? Of all the things she'd imagined digging up, a naked man had never entered her list of possibilities.

At the same depth as the first grave, they again hit a stone arch. The structure soon proved to be much larger. They spent hours clearing out an area twice the size of the original grave, and still had failed to find the final shape of the building.

Impatient that their efforts weren't yielding results more quickly, Brand dropped to his knees and pulled away a layer of slate tiles. His efforts only revealed more stones. He was completely drenched in sweat as he kept pulling aside fresh layers. Finally, two feet down, he reached the last of the slate. Glass glinted in the now dimming light. He leaned in close to stare into the dark interior.

"What do you see?" asked Sorrow.

"Nothing," Brand said, sitting up and pushing aside more stones. "I need more light."

As he cleared away more stones, it soon became obvious that insufficient light wasn't the problem. Instead, the coffin beneath the stones was made of smoked glass, almost tar black, hiding the contents.

Brand brushed aside dirt, cupping his hands to block reflections on the dark glass, but shook his head when this failed to produce results. He blew on the edges of his hands where they'd touched the glass. "Ouch. That's kind of hot."

"Hot?" asked Sorrow.

"Everything feels hot to me right now," said Brand. "A side-effect of digging holes. But this glass is like an oven."

"Climb out," Sorrow said. She grabbed Trunk by the hand and said, "Lower me."

"What are you going to do?" asked Brand.

"I'm a glass weaver," said Sorrow. "I'm going to alter the glass to be transparent."

"Nice trick," said Brand as he pulled himself out of the hole.

Sorrow dangled from Trunk's grasp until she was a few inches above the stones. She dropped down and knelt over the glass. She touched it carefully. Brand had exaggerated its heat. It was far shy of an oven, more like a freshly poured cup of hot tea.

She placed both palms on the glass. Pulses of energy flowed up into her shoulders, feeling almost like ants crawling just beneath her skin. "There's extraordinary power here," she whispered. "I've never felt anything quite like it."

"That would have been a very funny thing to say when we first exposed the contents of the other grave," Brand said as he sat on the edge of the pit.

Sorrow ignored him. She concentrated on the substance beneath her fingers. Glass was easy to manipulate. Ordinarily, it would yield to her fingers as if it were a slightly sticky dough. But she didn't want to change the shape of the substance, only its color. There must be foreign material in the glass to create the smoky hue. Could she isolate this and draw it out?

Her brow furrowed as she found that the foreign material was caked mostly on the interior of the glass. The exterior parts of the glass she was touching were transparent, but backed with a dark substance that swallowed all light.

She gave the glass a slight push, hoping to dislodge the darkness. She was pleased when it worked and a chunk of inch thick, sooty blackness fell away. Unfortunately, all this revealed was gray smoke swirling in the interior.

Suddenly, she was tossed a foot into the air as the stones around her jumped, as if they'd been struck from beneath. She landed as black smoke billowed up from the cracks in the stone.

She tried to call out to Trunk, but wound up coughing violently as the black smoke filled her lungs. Her eyes clamped shut as the acrid fumes burned them. The ground beneath her surged again, throwing her onto her back.

A man's hands closed on her forearm. With a tug that felt as if it would pull her arm from its socket the unseen man lifted her, rudely throwing her over his shoulders.

"Hold tight!" Brand called out, though not to her. She managed to crack her eyes open ever so slightly and saw that she was thrown over Brand's shoulder. She twisted to see that he had one hand on a shovel thrust down into the hole. At the edge of the grave, Bigsby lay with his head and shoulders out over the pit, holding the handle of the shovel down. Brand grabbed the shovel and used it to climb. This resulted in an ungraceful tangle of limbs as Brand pushed Sorrow from his shoulder onto Bigsby's back as he crawled out over both of them.

She was too weakened by her inhalation of smoke to protest as she was sandwiched between the two men. They were all tossed into the air by a powerful shock wave that sent huge stones flying straight up from the grave. Another jolt followed swiftly. There was a loud *SNAP* and a chunk of smoky glass that must have weighed a hundred pounds shot fifty feet skyward before falling back into the grave and shattering with a loud crash.

"Trunk, get us to safer ground," Sorrow croaked as she wiped her stinging eyes. She didn't even see where her golem was, but he proved to be within range of her commands. His gloved fingers closed around the belt of her pants and lifted her butt-first from the trembling earth. It was apparently too much to expect to be rescued with any hint of dignity today.

Trunk paused to keep his balance as the earth shuddered again. Bigsby lay near the golem's feet, flat on his back. Sorrow reached out to him. As Trunk started running, her hand closed around the dwarf's fingers and she dragged him as they dashed for safety.

Brand was left behind, but by now he had managed to make it to his feet, nimbly dodging the heavy stones that fell to earth around him. He danced across the shuddering landscape, leaping up to grab a low hanging vine. He used this makeshift rope to pull himself up into the branches of a swaying tree, then leaned out to peer into the smoking grave. The plume was so thick Sorrow wondered if they'd somehow dug into an active volcano vent.

A bony black claw rose from the pit, digging into the earth. This was followed seconds later by an ebony reptilian skull snaking through the billowing fumes. The eye sockets were lit by flickering embers.

"Greatshadow?" she whispered.

The beast opened its jaws and jets of black smoke poured out. It looked as if were roaring, but no noise came from the beast save for the clatter of bone against bone and the sizzle of the damp earth as it dragged its skeletal body to the surface.

The creature now stood revealed as a skeletal dragon, as tall as a warhorse, perhaps thirty feet in length from the tip of its snout to the last smoldering vertebra of its serpentine tail. Within its blackened rib cage roiled organs of smoke and flame. The beast spread its bone wings and flapped, a futile gesture as it had no flesh to catch the air.

Brand was almost directly above the dragon, stretched between branches, now utterly still.

Before the beast could gaze in their direction, Sorrow shouted, "Trunk! Stop!" The wooden man instantly froze. She froze as well. She wasn't certain, but there was a strong possibility the dragon was an expertly constructed bone-golem. In the absence of their creator, these mindless beasts would obey predetermined criteria as to whom and what it should attack. "Anything that moves" was one likely criteria, so until the beast turned its gaze elsewhere, she wasn't twitching an eyebrow.

Unfortunately, Bigsby didn't share her caution. He twisted free from her grasp and ran for a pickaxe that had fallen nearby. He brandished the tool overhead and cried, "For the glory of King Brightmoon, I smite thee!" The "thee" trailed off into a high-pitched battle siren of "eeeeee" as he charged the dragon.

The beast whipped its head toward the dwarf, extended its neck, and let out a whirlwind of smoke. Bigsby disappeared in the swirling smog, but his cry continued undiminished. To Sorrow's surprise, Bigsby leapt up from the smoke a yard away from the beast's snout, swinging the pickaxe with both hands to drive the tip into the monster's nose. Sparks flew as iron bit into bone. The creature jerked its head sideways, throwing Bigsby in a spinning arc through the air. He landed with a bounce, bounced again, and wound up tumbling into the grave where the naked man had been uncovered.

The dragon turned toward the grave, apparently intending to give chase. Sorrow ground her teeth. As tempting as it was to not hear Bigsby's voice again, she couldn't sit by and watch him get slaughtered. "Trunk, stop that thing!"

Her golem lumbered forward, but she could see he would never cover the distance in time before the bone-dragon dove into the pit and finished off Bigsby. As the beast reared back to lunge, Brand swung down on a length of vine and kicked the creature's right hind leg out from under it. The beast stumbled, craning its neck around to see who had attacked it. Brand somersaulted backward as the beast snapped at him, then scrambled up into the trees with the speed of a hyperactive monkey as the bone-dragon's jaws bit into the bark where his feet had rested half a second before.

The dragon dug it's claws into the tree and gave chase. Brand eyed the surrounding vines, planning his next leap. But before the beast could force him from his perch, Trunk reached the bone dragon and grabbed the creature by the tail, yanking it from the tree with a loud clatter.

The dragon spun around with its jaws spread and neatly clipped off Trunk's right arm. The golem swung with his left, delivering a blow to the side of the beast's skull that send a cloud of soot flying from the creature's bones. The dragon responded with a swipe of its dagger like fore-claws, tearing Trunk's wooden-bucket head from his torso.

Sorrow circled through the trees, then darted toward the bone-dragon from behind. She had no direct command over some other witch's golem, and her power of decay would have little effect on smoke-cured bones. Her one hope was that the beast's skeleton had been fixed together with iron or copper wires. She could command these metals to corrode, reducing the beast to a pile of disconnected bones.

The dragon's bony tail whipped unpredictably as it continued to tear Trunk apart. Despite her best efforts at dodging, the tail caught Sorrow in the gut, knocking her backward. Her fingers briefly closed around a vertebrae, but she sensed no metal at all within the creature. The smoky bones were held together with enchanted sinews. She fell to her hands and knees, unsure of what she would do if the dragon turned its jaws toward her.

Fortunately, the dragon was distracted as Brand leapt from the trees and rolled in front of it. He darted away from the beast, waving his arms and screaming, "Over here!"

Sorrow wondered if this was to save her, then saw Brand glance toward the open grave where Bigsby had fallen. The dwarf was climbing from the pit, in full sight of the dragon. The dragon crouched, eyeing the struggling dwarf like a cat stalking a mouse. Brand waved his arms even more vigorously, and the beast's glowering eyes turned to study him.

For a few seconds, the dragon paused, its arcane programming unable to choose between two inviting targets. Sorrow struggled to her feet, running toward the tall tree Brand had climbed earlier. Her powers of rot might not be able to affect the dragon directly, but with luck she might yet be able to strike a blow. The beast had gouged thick claw marks into the wood as it had chased Brand. With a grunt, she drove her hands and boots into the splintered wood and climbed, scrambling to reach the thick branch Brand had stood on, a good thirty feet off the ground. The dragon's hips were almost directly beneath the branch. Breathlessly, she stretched her right arm up until her fingers touched the thick branch, almost a tree in its own right. She felt the dark energy of Rott flow through her into the tree. In seconds, there was a loud *CRACK* as the branch snapped from the tree.

Unfortunately, the beast had by now decided between its targets as Bigsby reached the top of the grave and stood, shaking the dirt from his tangled wig. Something about the shimmering locks triggered the dragon's instincts to strike. The dragon leapt in a graceful arc like a tiger, his jaws opened to consume the dwarf. Luckily, the falling branch caught the last few vertebrae of his tail as it fell, robbing the creature of momentum. Instead of landing on the dwarf, the bone-beast tumbled snout first into the open grave. There was a crash as the glass casket shattered beneath the dragon's weight.

Brand ran and grabbed Bigsby, tossing his diminutive sibling over his shoulder like a sack of potatoes. Bigsby waved his fist at the dragon flailing in the grave and shouted, "We must not retreat! The honor of the Brightmoon name demands victory!"

Brand probably wasn't persuaded by this argument, but it proved not to matter. Graceful as he was, he stumbled on the uneven ground, thrown off balance by his flailing brother. They both slid down the leafy hillside just as the dragon fully emerged from the grave. Sorrow scrambled down the tree, planting both her feet firmly on the ground.

She placed one hand on the tree trunk. She knew that if this didn't work, she was dead. She waved with her free hand and cried out, "Dragon! Face me! I've come to steal your treasures!"

She felt a curious thrill as the monster turned toward her.

"Come and get me," she growled, as she sank her fingers into the thick tree trunk. The entropic force flowed from her and she tore out chunks of crumbling wood by the fistful as the dragon charged. The tree began to creak. She reached into the core, up to her shoulder now, and the tree groaned as it leaned in the direction of the dragon. At last, the wood splintered, snapped, and fell. She nearly laughed that her plan had worked, until its upper branches tangled in the branches of its neighbor, bringing it to a shuddering halt.

By now, the dragon was mere yards away. She stared into the beast's open jaws. What exquisite irony that her quest to restore the weavers to their full glory was to be brought to a premature end by this unthinking relic crafted by her predecessors.

The creature jerked to a shuddering halt, its jaws snapping half an inch from her nose. Soot and cinders washed over her face. She fell to her knees, blind and gasping. The beast sounded like a thousand castanets clacking as it wheeled away from her.

Low to the ground, she forced her eyes opened. Through tears, she could barely make out a large, naked man standing in the first grave, his muscles straining as he held the dragon by the tail. The man let go as the dragon turned in its tracks, its open jaws aimed for the warrior's head.

Sorrow blinked. Her vision improved slightly in time for her to see that the man was definitely the person who'd been buried in the glass coffin. His long hair whipped behind him as he leapt from the grave to meet the dragon's charge. He held a slab of slate the size of a shield in his hand, one of the roofing stones she'd barely been able to move.

The man thrust the slab into the dragon's snapping jaws. The stone shattered, but took with it several of the dragon's teeth. The beast's mouth opened again, and the grave-man thrust his hands into the gap, grasping the upper and lower jaws. His face contorted as he forced the dragon's jaws open wider, then wider still. The warrior showed no sign of pain as the beast's fore-claws slashed out and tore bright red ribbons across his chest. With a *SNAP*, the right half of the beast's lower jaw broke free, leaving the warrior holding a long, toothy club of bone.

Sorrow made it back to her feet, wiping her eyes for a better view, only to be frustrated as the dragon unleashed another torrent of black vapors, completely engulfing the warrior. From the black cloud came a series of grunts and bangs and cracks. Suddenly, what was left of the beast's skull spiraled into the air, landing thirty feet away.

Unfortunately, decapitating a golem wouldn't kill it. As impressive as the warrior had been so far, the fact that he'd bled when cut hinted to her that the dragon would likely emerge the victor. She looked around and couldn't see Brand and Bigsby anywhere. Sorrow wondered if it might not be time for her to make a strategic retreat.

A voice called from above, "Get out of the way!"

She looked up and found Brand in the vines above her, with Bigsby struggling to climb to his level. They both had knives, and were slashing at the vines and branches that held the tree she'd attempted to topple. The dragon was still well-positioned to be crushed. Unfortunately, so was the warrior, even though she couldn't see his exact location within the smoke.

"You'll crush the man!" she yelled, as Brand sawed through the sturdiest vine holding the tree.

"These things happen!" Brand cried.

Sorrow had no time to argue, as the vine snapped and the tree lurched down, gaining momentum as more and more of the smaller branches holding it broke. She ran clear as the massive tree slammed to the earth behind her. She spun, and saw a tornado of smoke rising. Shards of black bones bounced in every direction across the broken ground. The tree had been dead on in crushing the beast's rib cage.

Off to one side, a black claw twitched as the magic that animated it drained away. She ran to the fallen trunk and clambered over it, searching for the warrior.

To her relief, he hadn't been crushed. He was on his feet, looking down at the jawbone in his hand with glazed eyes. His chest and arms were striped with blood from dozens of gashes. His once white flesh was now black with soot. Perhaps the loss of blood had weakened him, for he swayed on his feet, his legs trembling.

"Are you all right?" she asked, standing on the tree, looking down at him.

He didn't look at her. He looked down at his arms, coated with soot and blood. He lifted his hands, and silently stared at his long, curling nails. His brow furrowed in confusion.

She felt confusion all her own. Even though the man was plainly alive and breathing, she still couldn't detect any hint of a life aura. It was as if she were looking at a walking corpse. Hesitantly, she asked again, "Are you all right?"

"Aye," he whispered, then collapsed, landing face down in the leaves.

4 - CHAMBER OF SECRETS

"OKAY, WHAT JUST happened?" Brand asked as he dropped from the tree.

Sorrow shook her head as she climbed down to the fallen warrior. "You know everything I do."

She knelt over the man. He was still alive despite his wounds and missing aura. She could see down to bone through the neatly parallel slices across his ribs. Blood gushed freely from a deep gash on his left arm.

"Give me your shirt," she said. "We need to stop the bleeding."

Brand obeyed, though his shirt was sweaty and covered with dirt. "He'll get infections unless we use clean cloth."

"I think the more urgent problem is his imminent exsanguination," said Sorrow, tearing the shirt into strips. "Once we staunch the bleeding, I can clean and stitch his injuries."

Brand dropped to his knees and wadded up one of the shirt rags, applying pressure to the gushing wound on the man's thigh.

The man began to shiver violently.

"Is he cold?" asked Bigsby, looking over her shoulder.

"He's hot as a furnace," said Sorrow, placing her hand on the man's brow.

"We should feed him," said Bigsby.

"What?" Sorrow asked.

"If he has a fever," said Bigsby. "Feed a fever, starve a cold."

Sorrow started to point out that the man was bleeding to death, not fighting the flu, but pressed her lips tightly together, determined not to get drawn into the dwarf's madness.

"It's starve a fever, feed a cold," said Brand.

Bigsby crossed his arms. "You don't know what you're talking about."

"Which is it, Sorrow?" asked Brand.

"How should I know?" she asked.

"Women learn that kind of stuff from their mothers," said Brand.

"My mother died in childbirth," said Sorrow. Fortunately, this left her companions silent, allowing her to focus on the task at hand.

"I think we've got the worst of his limbs," Sorrow said to Brand. "See if you can lift him so I can work on his ribs." Brand shifted around, placing both hands beneath the man's shoulders. The man groaned as he was lifted. His eyes fluttered open, but were unfocused.

"Can you understand me?" Sorrow asked. "We're trying to help."

The man's eyes fixed on her. Perhaps it was her imagination, but the faintest hint of a smile flashed across his lips before he fainted once more.

She wrapped his chest and ribs with the longest strips of the shirt, putting as much pressure as possible to close the wounds. The dragon's claws had been sharp as razors, resulting in wounds that meshed together quite nicely with a little pressure. A cut with a duller instrument would have left torn and ragged edges that would have resisted such hurried attempts to close them.

"Bigs — I mean, your highness, run to my tent and bring us blankets," said Sorrow, as she helped Brand lay the warrior back down.

"I'm not some common servant," said Bigsby.

"I'll go get them," Brand said wearily. He glanced at Sorrow and gave an apologetic shrug.

Dusk dimmed into night as she continued working on the fallen warrior's wounds. Brand built a fire and boiled water, then constructed an impromptu shelter of blankets, since Sorrow didn't want to risk transporting the man to her tent. As she carefully cleaned each wound, she stitched them using fine silver wires no thicker than a hair. The man's fever abated as she worked. Indeed, he was now cold and clammy to the touch. Despite their best efforts, he'd lost a lot of blood.

The man slept through most of her treatment, though from time to time his eyes would flicker open. Once, he arched his back, gritting his teeth as he sucked in air. She'd grabbed his hand and he'd squeezed until she was certain her fingers would snap before his spasm passed and he lapsed into stillness.

"You're good at this," Brand said as he inspected the zig-zag stitches along the man's ribs.

"I wish I were better," Sorrow said. "If I was a bone-weaver, I could manipulate bodies as if they were clay. Alas, I've never tracked down a living bone-weaver to learn the art. Still, I've learned a great deal about human anatomy. I was fortunate enough to study with Mama Knuckle, who has no peer as a necromancer."

"You studied necromancy?" She could tell from Brand's tone that he equated necromancy with evil.

Sorrow shrugged. "If she hadn't taught me the art of soul catching, I couldn't animate my golems."

Brand leaned over to the fire and poked at the logs with a stick. "Trapping the spirits of the dead seems, um, not nice."

"You were about to use a stronger word."

"I like to be diplomatic."

"You're entitled to your opinion. The souls I capture are doomed spirits who would eventually fade from existence. It's not as if I'm snatching souls off clouds in heaven."

"You believe in heaven?"

"How can you not? You've been to the Sea of Wine. You have the evidence of your own senses to know that our world is surrounded by numerous abstract realms where the dead dwell for a time. Why shouldn't heaven be among them?"

"I didn't think you believed in the teachings of the Church of the Book."

"What I believe is of no importance. The abstract realms are shaped from human collective consciousness. Hundreds of thousands of people believe in heaven, so they've no doubt created it by now."

"By that logic, shouldn't the Divine Author exist as well? The same number of people believe in him."

"Perhaps he does exist."

"And you'd wage war against a god not noted for his tolerance of sinners?"

"If there is a Divine Author, he's the creation of men, reflecting all their flaws and weaknesses. He's the embodiment of hatred and fear and injustice, and I shall fight to my dying breath to oppose him. If I have the courage to overthrow earthly kings, I can muster the will to battle a heavenly one."

Brand chuckled and said, "Wow."

"What's funny?"

"I just haven't met many people, male or female, ballsy enough to take on gods."

Sorrow kept quiet as she finished stitching the last wound on the warrior. She was determined not to respond to Brand's insulting choice of words. In the end, she couldn't hold her tongue. "I'm decidedly not 'ballsy.' Courage isn't dependant on male anatomy."

"All I'm saying is that you're amazingly bold. I meant it as a compliment."

"Yet you managed to turn it into a slight against the entire female sex."

"In addition to being bold, you're also more than a little brittle," Brand said with a frown.

"I'm paying you to dig graves, not judge me."

"That I'll do for free," he said, grinning. "Ever since I learned the art of reading people's hidden natures, I've been unable to turn it off."

"Nothing about my nature is hidden," said Sorrow. "I pride myself on being open in my goals and motives."

Brand laughed.

Sorrow scowled at him.

"You honestly believe that?" Brand asked.

"You've no reason to doubt my word."

"Maybe you should try a little doubt. I would say there's a very good chance you've been deceiving yourself."

"By what right do you think that you know me better than I do?"

"Let's put it to a test. I'll ask you three questions. You answer me as honestly as you can, and I'll tell you what you truly mean."

"I won't engage in such an absurd exercise," she said, with a dismissive wave.

"You just said you were proud to be open. I think we've exposed the first false notion you have about yourself."

She fixed her eyes upon him with a fierce glare. She didn't like having her own words thrown back in her face. Worse, he was smirking. He regarded this conversation as an amusing way to pass the time, while she found it to be an unwelcome intrusion. She owed him no answers.

On the other hand, what did she have to hide? She felt certain she could wipe that smug expression from his face.

"Fine," she said, crossing her arms. "You may ask what you wish."

"Okay," he said. "But don't make it so easy."

"I assure you, it will be easy to disprove your delusions."

"Not with such transparent body language," said Brand. "Crossing your arms like that is like trying to build a little wall between the two of us. You're entering into this as a hostile witness, rather than an open-minded seeker of truth."

"Just ask your first question."

"Why did you tell us your mother died in childbirth?"

"It's factual," she said. "It explained why I didn't feel like answering Bigsby's insane babbling."

"But if you've studied healing well enough to stitch this man back together, I'm guessing you probably know how to treat a fever."

"Yes," she said. "But he was bleeding to death. The fact he was hot was the least of his problems."

"You could have said that. Instead, you played the dead mother card."

She frowned. "This wasn't a poker hand. My mother's death is not a card."

"That's no doubt true, but you brought it up at a very odd time for no other reason than to shock us."

She shrugged. "It brought that ridiculous discussion to a halt."

"True. But it also revealed to me your mother's death has left you feeling entitled."

"Entitled?" she scoffed.

"Perhaps your father overcompensated for your mother's death. Doted on you a bit more than he should have. You could probably play upon his sense of guilt to get your way by invoking your dead mother. As an adult, in times of tension, you still resort to pleading that your loss in childhood should give you special privileges."

Sorrow shook her head and laughed ruefully. "That's your analysis? It's so pathetically wrong I don't know where to begin. No one who knows my father thinks of him as doting. Our family name is Stern. He's the living embodiment of the word."

"Wait… you wouldn't happen to be the daughter of Judge Adamant Stern?"

"I am. Was that your second question?"

"Is it true your father hung his own mother for being a witch?"

"Is that your third question?"

Brand looked lost in thought. "So, I'm guessing you think you hate your father?"

"I don't think I hate him. I know I hate him with every fiber of my being. His sins against mankind, all women, and his own family are beyond forgiveness."

"He's a captain in the king's Judgment Fleet. He has a duty to be tough."

"Did he have a duty to hang his own mother? I was ten years old when my housekeeper snuck me into the public square to witness the execution. As they pulled the hood over her head, my grandmother shouted, 'How can you betray your mother?'" She shook her head, as the memory burned fresh within her. "My father answered, 'How could you betray your god?' Then he gave the command to open the gallows door. I tried to scream, but my housekeeper clamped her hand over my mouth. That unborn scream… it's still inside me. It drives me to this day. All that I do, I do to destroy the institutions and laws that gave birth to a monster so vile as my father."

Brand rubbed his chin. He opened his mouth, about to speak, then fell silent.

"Is there something you wish to say?"

"I suspect I'd deeply regret saying it. I don't know how open you'd be to understanding your true motives."

"I won't be bothered by anything you say. Your supposed insights are merely part of a circus act. The pattern so far is that I tell you something in perfect honesty, then you tell me I meant the opposite of what I just said. Now that I've explained how much I hate my father, I imagine you'll tell me that means I truly love him."

"Oh, it's something much more powerful than love," said Brand. "Don't you see? Your father has provided your template for adulthood. Your whole life has been a quest to become him."

Sorrow rolled her eyes. "You're as insane as Bigsby."

"Your father's a judge. His daily life is devoted to deciding who's right and who's wrong. Now, you've fashioned yourself into a judge. But you've gone one step further. Your father pronounces witches and heretics and common criminals worthy of death. You've decided that all of civilization is guilty and must be destroyed."

"All people are judges," said Sorrow. "To say I'm like my father in this respect is unremarkable. We both eat bread and drink water. It's too trivial to be noteworthy."

"It's not just that you're both judgmental," said Brand. "You're both so certain of your cause it pushes you to do the unthinkable. Your father hanged his own mother. You've hammered nails into your brain."

"I do what I must," said Sorrow. "I've witnessed the true source of evil. Now that I can see what is wrong with the world, I cannot shut my eyes. My father's blind belief in the law has turned him into a monster."

"An interesting choice of words from someone half covered in dragon scales," said Brand.

His voice was calm as he said this, but Sorrow felt as if he'd grabbed her by the throat and shouted into her face. She rose. "I'm tired. It's late. This conversation is over."

"I haven't asked my third question."

"Your senseless speculations following your previous questions haven't left me eager to continue speaking. Besides, it's absurd talking to you about truth when you so openly live a lie. Bigsby isn't the missing Princess Innocent. The king has no son named Brand. I wouldn't believe you were brothers at all if it weren't for your eyes."

Brand nodded. "They are similar, aren't they? I'm certain that Bigsby truly is my brother. But, you're right. I'm no prince. I'm Brand Cooper, son of Grand Cooper."

"Of the Cooper Barrelworks?"

"The same."

"Forgive me for being dubious. Grand Cooper is one of the wealthiest men alive. Why would his children be wandering the world as coinless vagabonds?"

Brand chuckled. "That's kind of a long story. But, who needs coins when we have dragon bones?" He held up a blackened rib.

Sorrow's eyes opened wide. She hadn't even thought of the fortune scattered around them. Dragon bones were worth their weight in gold at blood houses. Even bones burnt black would bring a good price.

"Since we all worked together to kill this dragon, I assume we split this treasure three ways?" he asked.

Yesterday, she would have argued. Their verbal contract said that anything they dug up would belong to her. But Brand had delivered the final killing blow. The division seemed fair. She nodded in agreement.

"This will buy us passage back to the Silver City," he said. "Hell, it will buy our own ship."

"If you're Grand Cooper's son, I'm surprised you don't already own a whole fleet."

Brand shrugged. "I do, technically. But it's been a long time since I've been back home to enjoy any of the trappings of my wealth. My father… he's something of a perfectionist. When Bigsby was born, he couldn't bear the thought of his first son having stunted, malformed limbs. So he commanded the mid-wife to take the baby away and kill it. He buried the body in a closed coffin so no one could see the freak he'd produced, and told the world the child had been stillborn."

"That's awful," said Sorrow.

"Fortunately, the midwife didn't kill the baby. Freaks are a valuable commodity. She sold the child to a circus."

Sorrow shook her head. "It's a sign of this world's corruption that such things can happen. How did you learn of his fate?"

Brand fed a new log into the fire, coughing at the smoke it stirred up. When he caught his breath, he said, "The mid-wife spent her money a bit too freely. My father thought she was stealing from him, but soon learned the truth of what had happened. He kept the secret for almost thirty years. During this time, I was born." He sighed. "I tried to be a good son, but sometimes he just seemed so unhappy. I didn't know that every time he looked at me he was almost paralyzed with guilt."

"He deserved his guilt," said Sorrow. "Though he failed, he'd conspired to commit infanticide. I can only imagine how much you hate him."

"No. I don't hate him. He made a mistake, but he's not evil. Four years ago, he suffered a stroke. His body was half-paralyzed. On his sick bed, he confessed everything to me. Said he'd been a fool to expect perfection from mere human flesh. He begged me to find his lost son and bring him home."

He looked at the sparks that rose from the fire. "The ensuing years have been a pretty wild adventure. I'm a different person that the naïve kid who left home. It's going to be strange going back. Stranger still when I tell Dad that his long lost son isn't only a dwarf, but also completely flipping insane."

"You could…" Sorrow shook her head.

"What?"

Sorrow ground her teeth together. "It causes me almost physical pain to say this, but a truthspeaker might be able to help you."

Brand's face brightened. "You're right. They could command Bigsby to remember who he truly was. It's an excellent idea."

He rose, picking up a branch from the fire. He used his makeshift torch to aid him as he gathered up dragon bones into a pile next to the warrior. "Maybe we'll run into a truthspeaker on the journey home who'll be amenable to a bribe."

"I think they prefer their compensation to be referred to as offerings."

As Brand turned his back to her, Sorrow allowed herself the luxury of scratching her itching thighs. Her stomach tightened as she felt how hard and stiff her skin was beneath the fabric of her britches.

Brand wound up near the pit the dragon had first erupted from. He crouched down, and held out his torch.

"Look at this," he said, sounding excited.

Sorrow welcomed the distraction and walked to the pit. To her surprise, Brand doused his torch on the broken ground as she neared. She held her hands before her as her eyes adjusted to the sudden darkness.

Now she saw what Brand saw. The pit glowed faintly. She carefully crept across the uneven ground to gaze into it. Thin beams of pale light seeped up through cracks in the slate that lined the bottom of the grave.

"I got so swept up in the fight and saving the mystery man's life that I never stopped to think there might be something else in the hole," said Brand. "I mean, I glanced in here while I was gathering firewood, but all I saw was rock. What if that thing was meant to guard something?"

Sorrow slid down the dirt wall into the pit. She grunted as she pushed one of the large flat stones aside. More light seeped up from below. She kept moving stones until she nearly fell through as she opened up a gap. Carefully removing more stones, she revealed the opening to a set of spiral stairs. She was looking down the center of the spiral, and though this was the source of the glow, she couldn't make out anything beyond the stairs.

Brand asked, "Should we wait until daylight to —"

Sorrow didn't wait for him to finish. She swung her feet forward, then slid into the gap.

"Let's think this through," said Brand. "We're both exhausted. I don't have it in me to fight another dragon."

"I'm just going to peek," said Sorrow, placing a hand on the stone wall as she stepped gingerly down the stairs. She knew Brand was right. The smart move would be to wait until she could build a new golem and use it to explore the space. But she'd come to the Witches Graveyard expecting her life to change forever. She felt certain she'd arrived at a pivotal moment of her quest.

The steps opened into a circular chamber twenty feet across and six feet tall, the walls, ceiling and floor hewn from a single piece of slate. A glorystone was set into the center of the slate floor, no bigger than a pea yet sufficient to fill the chamber with light. Alas, the chamber appeared to be completely empty. There wasn't even any dust. Her heart sank, disappointed that such a promising lead had come to nothing.

She clenched her fists. This couldn't be all there was. There must be some hidden passage. She moved to the nearest wall and rapped the stone with her fingers. She turned when she heard footsteps on the stairs. Brand crept down, with a dagger drawn.

"It's safe," she said. "Give me your knife."

"This was worth guarding with a dragon?" he said, crouching as he entered the room to hand her the dagger. "I mean, the glorystone is worth a little, but —"

"This isn't about treasure," she said, tapping the wall with the hilt of the dagger as she held her ear close to the stone.

"What are you doing?"

"Checking for hollow spaces," she said.

"Right," he said, drawing another blade. He started tapping the ceiling as she worked the walls.

They worked for ten minutes, not speaking, just tapping.

"Wait," she said, holding up her hand.

"You got something?" he asked.

She tapped the wall, pressing her ear to it. There was a definite hollowness to the sound. "I think so." She ran her fingers across the slate. "This stone is perfectly smooth. No mason could have finished it to this precision. It has to be the work of a weaver with command over stone."

"How do we open it?"

"I don't know. I've never even heard of a slate weaver. It must be a lost art. A witch with power over slate could simply will the stone to move aside."

"Where there's a will, there's a way," said Brand. "Wait here."

He darted up the stairs. Sorrow scraped at the slate with her dagger blade, marring the finish, then began to hunt for another space behind the stone. Three minutes later, Brand panted back down the stairs with a pick-axe in hand.

"Where was it?" he asked.

She pointed toward the mark she'd made.

He lined himself up. Due to the height of the ceiling, he had to swing sideways. The pick-axe struck sparks and bounced off the wall. The force of the blow caused Brand's back to straighten and his head bumped the ceiling.

"Ow, ow, ow," he said, rubbing the top of his scalp. He ran his fingers over where he'd struck the wall. "Barely even a scratch." He sighed. "The pick is more of a digging tool than a smashing tool. We need a sledgehammer."

"Go get one."

"I couldn't find it. Your golem was carrying it when the dragon tore him apart. Maybe it's under the tree."

"Give me," she said, grabbing the pick-axe. "I can't mold stone, but I'm an artist with iron." The rigid metal turned as soft as clay between her fingers. Brand looked impressed as she squished, squashed, and sculpted the relatively slender arms of the pick-axe into a sturdy hammer-head.

When she handed the hammer back to him, he said, "This should do the job."

This time, he got on his knees, choking up on the hammer to allow for an overhead swing. The hammer hit with a thunderous *CRACK* and the slate splintered into a dozen shards.

The space revealed was no bigger than a breadbox. Within was a glass bottle, lidless and seamless, inside which was a rolled up sheet of vellum.

"A message in a bottle," said Brand.

"A message only a witch can open, as there's no stopper," said Sorrow as she carried the jar into the light.

Brand snatched it away from her. "I think you may be overlooking a more direct approach." Before she could react, he smashed it on the ground, then bent down to pick up the vellum.

"Give me that," she grumbled. He offered it to her with a grin on his face. It was closed with a small band of silver. She could have used her powers to remove it, but decided to simply slide it off the end.

She unrolled the thin leather sheet. From its color and texture, she had the uneasy feeling the scroll might have been made from human flesh. Brand looked over her shoulder at the looping script written upon it.

"I can't read a word of it," he said.

Sorrow frowned. "It's weaver script. Unfortunately, I can only read a little."

"They didn't teach you the secret code in weaver school?"

"I'm mostly self-taught," she said. "I've picked up bits and pieces of the script here and there, but never studied with anyone fluent in the language."

"Can you make out anything?"

"I recognize this symbol," she said, tapping on a small mark that looked like a sword or dagger. "It's the symbol of the Witchbreaker."

"The knight?"

"Either the knight or his sword. His sword was almost more feared than the man."

"Why?"

"Legend has it that the sword was forged from iron stolen from the gates of hell. Supposedly, this gave the sword the ability to open a direct path to the underworld for the soul of anyone it killed."

"That's worthy of a legend, I guess."

She traced her fingers over the symbols adjacent to the sword. "This is the symbol for death. I think… this symbol here is rejoice, or celebrate. And… hmm. I think this reads, Rejoice, sister, the Witchbreaker is dead."

"Maybe that was him buried in the grave," said Brand. "You might have spent the better part of six hours saving the life of your greatest enemy."

"Maybe. But probably not. I can't understand why they would have saved his body." She furrowed her brow as she tried to puzzle out more symbols. "In the midst of defeat, we have, um, cooked? Tasted? Feasted on victory? I think it says we have feasted on victory." She ran her finger further down the page. "But... they must abandon... uh, abandon the... weapon?"

"The sword?"

She shook her head. "No, I know that symbol. This is kind of a blend of the symbol for tool and the symbol for war. I'm reading war-tool as weapon. The symbol after it stands for man, so maybe war-tool man is the way they wrote warrior?"

"Keep reading," he said. "Maybe it will make sense in context.

"The... um. Hmm." She scratched her scalp. "The first one? The original is ours?"

"The original?" he asked. "The original what?"

She sighed and shrugged her shoulders. "I'm lost. I got off to a good start, but I'm guessing at three out of four words. I think these are instructions to leave the war-tool, whatever that is, and meet up at the dancing castle, wherever that is."

"Dancing castle?" asked Brand. "That sounds kind of fun."

"I'm probably reading it wrong. But one thing I'm sure of is that I know I know this mark." She touched a skull like symbol at the bottom of the parchment. "This was signed by Avaris herself."

"The old Queen of Witches?"

"Maybe the current queen," said Sorrow. "It's common folklore that Avaris is still alive, made immortal by her powers, living in a hidden castle until her enemies eventually perish. I guess if you're immortal, you can just wait people out."

"Immortal or not, she's got a long wait. The Church of the Book is still anti-witch, and it's not going anywhere soon."

"It will if I have a say in it."

"Right."

"But my task would be easier if I could find Avaris and have her teach me the full arts of weaving."

"Maybe the dancing castle in the letter is her secret hideout," said Brand.

"Maybe. And maybe some of these symbols I can't read are directions. I think this might be the symbol for east." She tapped the page. "On the other hand, it might be the symbol for star. A lot of these glyphs look alike."

Brand chuckled.

"What's funny?" she asked.

"You weren't happy with the idea that the church could help my brother. What if I told you the church could help you?"

Sorrow frowned.

"There are monks who spend their whole lives studying dead languages and copying ancient documents," said Brand. "I'm guessing somewhere in the church there's a monk who could read this letter."

"I can hardly stroll into a monastery and ask," she said.

"I could," he said. "My father is a great patron of the church. I'm guessing a little name dropping and a few coins in the poor box would have this thing translated in no time."

"An interesting theory," she said, keeping her voice neutral. Would it be that easy? Could she risk placing such a potentially valuable document into the hands of her enemies?

"I need to think about what to do," she said.

"Whatever." Brand shrugged. "It's past my bedtime. I'm dead on my feet."

"There might be more hidden chambers," she said.

"Holding letters we can't read? That's totally worth staying up all night."

"There's no need for sarcasm."

"See you in the morning," he said, going up the stairs.

As soon as he was gone, Sorrow scratched her thighs beneath her buttocks vigorously. She listened carefully at the stairs to make sure he wasn't coming back, then undid the buttons on her pants. Slipping her britches down her hips, her heart froze when she found both her legs now oily black, covered with smooth scales. Her genitals were still untouched, but only just barely.

Had the changes stopped? Her skin itched almost to her belly button. Worse, the bones of her legs ached, as if invisible vises were clamping down, slowly warping them, the way her toes had been fused and reshaped into a tapering point.

She pulled up her pants and sat down on the stone floor. She took a deep breath. She'd always known that her quest for power would involve sacrifices. She'd forever scarred her own scalp, reworking her very brain with self-inflicted surgery. If she wound up covered in scales, well, what of it? She would pay any price.

Just as her father would have paid any price for what he believed in.

Was Brand right? Her father still had the physical form of a man, but at some point he'd turned into a monster. Had he felt the change? Had he understood the moment when humanity slipped away from him? Would she know if she herself neared such a threshold?

She swallowed hard. Her vision blurred as she looked down at the letter. She wiped tears from her cheeks. "Don't be silly, girl," she whispered to herself, her voice trembling. "You're stronger than this."

She didn't feel it. Brand was right. She was exhausted. She lay flat upon the stone floor, staring up at the flawless black of the slate roof. It was like an endless void, and she felt as if she were perched upon a precipice, ready to fall into the dark.

She turned her head, staring at the glorystone, a small fragment of the sun. She idly reached out and ran her fingers along its faceted surface. She wondered what had become of Stagger. During the height of the blizzards, she hadn't been able to tell if the sun was following its normal path, though now that the storms had withdrawn the length of a day felt right to her.

She sat up as she heard a faint voice say her name. Craning her neck, she saw she was still alone. Had it only been her imagination?

Stranger still, she recognized the voice. She placed her fingers on the glorystone once more. She said, quietly, "Stagger?"

And then she fell.

5 - ART THOU A DEVIL?

THE SLATE CHAMBER vanished as Sorrow once more found herself falling through blue sky toward a vast green ocean. Before, she'd been only a disembodied spirit affixed to Rott by an ethereal silver cord. Now, she felt wind rushing across her skin and a strong sense of dizziness as she tumbled. She landed with a splash in the warm ocean, gasping for breath as she floundered to the surface. She shuddered in horror as she looked down.

Her legs were gone. Her hips now flowed into a black, serpentine neck leading to Rott's body. Her still human torso served as the primal dragon's head. She had little to judge scale by in the trackless ocean, but she felt as if the human portions of her conjoined body had grown to giant size to better mesh with her draconian half.

She looked around and found the ocean empty. None of the other islands were present. Above, the golden disk of the sun hung motionless.

"Stagger!" she shouted.

A giant face appeared in the disk of the sun, with a scraggly beard and a mostly bald scalp. The face opened its eyes in a look of surprise. "Sorrow?"

"Where are we?" she shouted. "How did we get here?"

"I don't know!" Stagger said. "Something happened like this a few days ago, but I thought I was daydreaming. Things are a little boring up here. My mind wanders."

"I had the same dream!" she said. "The primal dragons were debating whether or not to destroy mankind!"

"The Black Swan told me she was trying to stop the dragons from wiping out mankind," Stagger said. "But, except for Hush and maybe Kragg, the dragons didn't seem keen on the idea."

Before they could speak further, the sea erupted in the distance as steam and stone shot into the air. In seconds, a mound of glowing stone rose from the boiling ocean. Flame spewed from the tip of the still growing mountain, curling and coiling into a giant serpent of fire.

"Greatshadow!" Stagger shouted.

The flame-dragon nodded. "I see you've learned to journey to the convergence on your own."

"The convergence?" Sorrow asked. "What is this place?"

"This is neutral ground," said Greatshadow. "Here, we dragons may meet in private without doing great harm to the world. If we met in the material realm, our combined might could shatter the earth beneath us."

"How did we get here?" asked Stagger.

"You must have called one another," said Greatshadow. "You must not do so again. When the other dragons learn that the two human interlopers have met in private to scheme against them, they will not be happy."

"We're not scheming against anything," said Sorrow. "I don't even know what I did to come here, or why I look like this."

"Your form reflects your truth," said Greatshadow. "When you first joined your spirit with Rott, only the faintest trace of your soul seeped into his elemental form. But as you've continued to use his power, more and more of his essence bleeds into your world, finding purchase in your body. In exchange, more and more of your spirit flows into his form. Rott's mind perished long ago. He survives only as a bundle of instincts; his chief drive is hunger. As he consumes you, Sorrow Stern, your mind will flow into the vacuum of his now absent will. For a time, you will be the intelligence in command of his power, until the entropy destroys your mind as well."

"There must be some way to stop that." she said. "Help me avoid that fate!"

"If a thing can be avoided, it was not truly fate," said Greatshadow. "For now, I bid you both to depart. You've each stumbled onto the discovery that, like other primal dragons, you're no longer bound to a single physical body. I recommend that you master your new abilities quickly. You may need to defend yourselves sooner than you guess."

"From what?" asked Stagger.

"Return to whence you came," Greatshadow said, turning his back to them.

Sorrow's eyes snapped open. At first, she thought she was blind, until she realized she was simply staring up at featureless black stone. She sat up and banged her head against the rock.

She looked down and began to scream.

SORROW SLID THROUGH the hole that led from the top of the stairs into the grave. Already she could hear Brand's footsteps as he ran toward the pit. She pulled the flat slate slabs surrounding the hole closer, concealing her body from the waist down. She finished just in time. Brand skidded to a halt at the edge of the pit half a second later, his body a dark silhouette against the pink morning clouds.

"Are you all right?" he asked, panting.

"Of course," she said, faintly. She swallowed hard, then said, in a louder, raspy voice, "Why wouldn't I be?"

"We heard screams. We thought it was you."

"Oh, that," she said. She did her best to force a feeble smile. "I had a nightmare. I'm fine now."

"It sounded like you were being murdered!"

"Obviously, I wasn't."

Brand looked skeptical. "Are you sure you're okay? You're voice is kind of quavering."

"I slept all night on cold stone," she said. "I'm a little congested."

Brand nodded. "Come on out and we'll warm you up with some breakfast."

"I'm not hungry," she said. "And I don't want you spending any more time at my camp. Pack your things and go."

"Your camp? Aren't you being kind of possessive?"

"Nothing of the sort," she said. "But… having thought further about our discussion last night, I've decided that I no longer care for the company of a person who thinks that I am in any way like my father."

Brand squatted at the edge of the hole as he said, "Oh. That. I guess I did cross a line. But, honestly, you shouldn't take what I said too seriously. The whole art of fortune telling is maintaining a straight face while spouting bullshit."

"I don't accept your apology. Take the dragon bones and go. You came here looking for wealth. You've found it. You've no further reason to stay."

"You came here looking for knowledge," said Brand. "Have you learned what you needed to learn?"

Sorrow shook her head. "I believe I know less now than I did when I came here. But, mapping the contours of my ignorance has its own value."

"I'm not going to argue myself into more digging," said Brand, standing up and stretching his back. "I'm sore as hell." He looked around and said, "So, how do you want to divide up these bones? Are there any parts you —"

"Take them all," she said.

"But —"

"Take them all and go!"

Brand furrowed his brow. Finally, he turned away. She could hear him moving around. Less than a minute later, he was back at the edge of the pit.

"Your kicking us out wouldn't have something to do with our missing patient, would it?"

"Who?"

"What do you mean, who? The guy we dug up."

"He's missing?"

"You didn't know?"

"I haven't left this chamber," she said. "How could I know?"

"Climb out and let's look for him," said Brand. "He might be wandering around in delirium."

"What do I care?"

"He saved your life!"

"And I saved his. He was free to leave anytime he wished. Just because we saved him doesn't make him our property."

Brand scratched his head. "Are you sure you're okay? You just seem —"

"Leave!" Sorrow said, clenching her fists. "Stop wasting my time with your prattle!"

Brand grumbled something she couldn't make out as he turned away. Time slowed to a crawl as she listened to Brand and Bigsby gathering bones around the grave. The sun grew ever higher in the sky. She adjusted the slate tiles around her to better support the weight of her elbows as she leaned forward. She couldn't believe how much time the two men were taking.

At last, Brand and Bigsby both returned to the edge of the pit.

"We've packed all we can carry," said Brand. "Are you sure you don't want us to stick around? It's dangerous out here alone."

"I believe I've shown myself capable of handling any threats," said Sorrow.

"I bet she's found a bigger treasure," said Bigsby. "She doesn't want to share, so she's getting rid of us."

"Or maybe I'm just sick of the company of a brain-damaged dwarf!" Sorrow snarled. "Get out of here, you little freak!"

Brand shook his head woefully as he and Bigsby turned away. "You weren't exactly friendly before, but I didn't think you were flat-out mean."

"This just proves how bad you are at reading people," she grumbled.

Brand and Bigsby left. She could hear their voices for a little while, growing ever more distant. She waited until they would have had time to move far beyond the graveyard. Then she waited another hour.

Sorrow knew she couldn't sit in the hole forever. Despite her… handicap, she'd obviously had the power to make it to the top of the stairs. She just needed the courage to push on a little further and make it back to her tent. She placed her hands upon the edges of one of the stones, prepared to push it aside. She stared for a long time as her arms refused to move the slate.

Finally she set her jaw, took a deep breath, and pushed the rock away. She moved the other stones that concealed the lower half of her body one by one, studiously keeping her eyes fixed upon her hands, avoiding what lay beneath.

She stared up into the canopy, at the patches of blue she glimpsed beyond the trees. She wiped her brow, wet with sweat, perhaps from the effort of moving the stones, or perhaps due to the rising heat of the day, or perhaps from the undertow of terror that had accelerated her heart since waking.

"I can do this," she said, clenching her fists, gathering her courage. She swallowed hard, then looked down.

From the top ridge of her hipbones, the pants she'd worn had decayed into a fringe of tatters. Her boots had also experienced a similar rapid degradation, devoured by mildew and mold until they'd fallen apart at the seams.

Some other time, the loss of control of her entropic magic would be quite worrisome. But now, she was focused on the all but vanished clothing because it provided a welcome distraction from a much larger and more deeply existential trouble.

The truth was, she didn't need to worry about trousers or boots any more. She finally allowed her eyes to focus on the reason her heart was beating with a speed to rival the wings of a hummingbird.

Her legs were gone. From her hips down, she now possessed an enormous black serpent's tail. She stared at her scales for only a moment before she had to turn her face away and stare at the walls of the pit.

"You're already in a grave," she said out loud. "Why waste the effort of crawling out?" She choked back tears. Never before had she contemplated suicide. She held nothing but contempt for those who threw their lives away. But did she even have a life as a human now? She was more snake than woman. If the changes continued, and she lost her arms… she shuddered at the thought.

Should the day come when she lost her arms, she'd curse herself for not ending her life when she had had the chance. She cast about the broken ground with her hands until she found a shard of glass from the dragon's coffin.

She placed the sharp edge against her wrist. She studied the blue veins beneath her pale skin and set her jaw.

After a moment, she threw the glass away. She wasn't afraid of death. But she couldn't bear the thought of her long war against the church coming to an end due to a moment of weakness. If her life had lost so much value that she found death an acceptable option, wasn't this a liberation? She had nothing left to lose. She could throw herself into her quest to destroy the church without fearing for her own survival. Perhaps she'd been too concerned for herself, too cautious. Now, this timidity no longer stood in her way.

"I'm a monster," she whispered. She found that the words didn't hurt. She said, in half a shout, "I'm a monster!"

The thought calmed her. She'd been a freak and an outcast since the day she'd shaved her head and driven in her first nail. Brand had perhaps been right after all. Her father was a moral monster. It had been only a matter of time before his blood pulsing through her veins drove her to the same inhuman extremes. Let the world see what she had become. If she was to be a monster, better it be in body than in soul.

"I hereby promise myself that I shall never surrender," she said. "Let my enemies gaze upon me and know fear!" She raised her fists in defiance. She was certain she was more ready than ever to take the fight to her enemies, if not for the non-trivial problem that she had no idea how to climb out of this hole. Her mind, trained in the art of placing one foot in front of the other, couldn't quite make sense of the sensations that came from beneath her hips. She could feel the length of her serpentine form spiraling down the stairs, and sensed the weight of her new body pressed against the edges of the stone.

But how to move? She had no memory at all of crawling to the top of the stairs, but she'd obviously done so, with enough precision that only her human half had reached the surface. Her new body was obeying her will, at least on an unconscious level.

Perhaps the key was not to even think of moving. Her body had responded to her fear of being seen by Brand. Now, what she wanted more than anything was something to drink. She'd not had even a sip of water since before they'd fought the bone-dragon. She imagined the canteen in her tent, fixing the image of it in her mind, hoping her body would carry her there.

To her delight and horror, her serpent body began to undulate. Her torso was pushed into the air, until she had risen above the lip of the grave. She looked down. Her serpentine length was now fully exposed. Before, she'd stood five foot, five inches in her boots. Now, her legs had been replaced by a tree-trunk thick expanse of black coils almost twenty feet long. She was standing — if standing was the right word — on the lower ten feet of her serpent tail, which was looped into a rough circle. This left ten feet of her scaly trunk rising into the air, with her human torso balanced atop it. She was suddenly thirteen feet tall. It was oddly empowering to look upon the world from such a vantage point.

As she crawled from the grave, a large fragment of black glass left caught her eye and she momentarily forgot about her thirst. She stretched out her hand toward a particularly large remnant and her body obeyed her unspoken will to lower her toward it. She picked up the glass, a good fifty pound smoke-blackened chunk.

Glass was one of her favorite materials to manipulate. She had only to touch it and think and it would flow to whatever form she imagined, unlike iron or copper which she had to physically sculpt. In seconds, she coaxed the glass into a long flat plane, which she rested against a tree trunk.

She willed herself before it. The midday sun that pierced the leafy canopy was bright enough that it turned the dark glass into a mirror. She stared at herself for a long time. The scales of her tail glistened as if they were wet, though when she touched them, they were dry, smooth as polished wood, slightly warm, and hard as bone. But, despite the hardness, she could feel the pressure of her fingers in the muscles below. Sliding her hands around, she even found that she could feel a pulse. She wondered how her heart found the strength to push blood such a length. And where had she gained all of the new mass? While she could shape glass and wood and other materials, she couldn't create these from thin air. Nothing new was added or subtracted from the total mass of the objects she sculpted. Why should this new nail giving her command of decay suddenly allow her to magically create matter?

She thought about Greatshadow's words. She wasn't creating mass. She was channeling it. Rott manifested himself as a giant black dragon. Her new body hadn't come out of thin air. Somehow, she'd opened a gate. Her own body was now a door that the dragon was slipping through. Why? And, more urgently, would he continue to do so? Had the changes stopped?

Pressing her lips together, she untied her blouse. She shed it, and stood naked before the mirror. From her pubic mound up, she was still completely human, with no hint of scales. She turned and peered back over her shoulders. Her buttocks blended into the serpent body. The line of transformation seemed to mirror the shape of her pelvis.

Frowning, she pondered the gross yet practical matter of how she now went to the bathroom. The loss of her reproductive organs was tragic, yes, but it wasn't as if she'd been using them. But even if she never planned on having children, she did still plan to eat and drink, and these actions had consequences.

With a sense of both revulsion and curiosity, she ran her fingers along her front. The scales of her back and side were the shape and size of the heads of garden spades, but her front scales were more like ringed bands. She explored the length of her body until, three feet from the tip of her tail, she found a gap between the bands that her fingers slipped into. She withdrew her fingers at once, as the flesh within the gap was tender. She furrowed her brow. This was a very long way for food to travel. And there seemed to be only the one hole. When she returned to civilization, she would have to seek out a naturalist who could explain the intricacies of snake anatomy.

Ah, yes. Returning to civilization. That might prove to be a challenge. Even in as wild a port as Commonground, full of half-seeds and the most jaded of humanity, she couldn't imagine she would get a warm reception. She bent down and picked up her blouse. She slithered once more toward her tent, paying little attention to her surroundings as she tied her clothes shut once more.

Twenty feet from the tent she stopped, looking up. She heard something. She stared at the silk walls. Was there someone moving inside? Had Brand and Bigsby tricked her?

In answer, the tent flaps opened and two forest pygmies walked out, carrying a basket filled with dried meats and cheeses, provisions she'd packed for her expedition. The two forest pygmies had dark green skin the color of moss and were naked except for bright red gourds they wore over their penises. Their green hair was pulled back into braids. Each carried a short spear tipped with a stone point. They moved as quietly as cats, craning their necks around to make sure no one had seen them.

They both looked right at Sorrow as if she wasn't even there. They turned their backs to her and began to walk away, then, in unison, they froze and slowly looked back over their shoulders. Both of their mouths fell open at exactly the same second.

Sorrow felt like being tall and she became so, rising up on her tail until she loomed above them by several body lengths.

"Drop the basket and no one gets hurt," she said.

They dropped the basket, though whether they understood her words was debatable. They began to shout in a language she didn't recognize, their voices deep and booming despite their diminutive stature. Both reared back and threw their spears. Sorrow swayed out of the path of one missile, but the second spear struck her on one of the scaly bands where her knees had once been. She flinched, but the spear bounced off.

Sorrow ran her fingers along the impact point to make certain she was okay. She couldn't even feel a scratch. In addition to being tall, she was also spear-proof, it seemed. At least, parts of her were.

When she looked up, she found that the two pygmies were at least a hundred yards away, leaves and dirt flying as they fled headlong over the graves before finally vanishing in the underbrush.

Sorrow picked up the basket and removed a hunk of beef jerky. She chewed it slowly as she contemplated what would've happened if the spear had flown a yard higher. She suspected that, unless she could find a way to reverse the changes to her body, she would have to get used to people's first reaction being to throw things at her.

After washing the jerky down with the water from her canteen, she slithered back to the hilltop. Despite the massiveness of her new form, her motions proved surprisingly silent. The whisper of her smooth scales sliding across one another was much quieter than her footsteps had been. She also took note of her speed. Though she didn't feel like she was moving terribly fast, she made it back up the hill as swiftly as if she'd sprinted. She would have preferred not to be a hideous reptilian abomination, but she tried to take some comfort that her new body had its strong points.

Of course, while the new parts of her physical form were stronger and tougher, she was still greatly concerned about the safety of her old, non-spear-proof human parts. Fortunately, the dragon's shattered coffin provided plentiful raw material to ameliorate her vulnerabilities. Glass had a reputation for brittleness, but during her years of working with the substance she'd learned it could be spun into long, thin, interweaving fibers that could be sealed inside a matrix of smoother glass. This woven glass was practically shatterproof, much lighter than iron, and quite tough.

She found a large chunk of black glass and held it above her head. Her fingers sank into it as it liquefied, turning into slow moving black molasses that seeped down her arms and flowed over her shoulders. Inspired by the diamond pattern of her lower half, she willed the threads to form overlapping scales of black glass. In a few moments, she had turned the glass into a suit of jet black scale armor that matched her bodily scales in gloss and shape. There was just barely enough material left to form a dark, gleaming helmet to conceal her face. Only her hands remained bare; her magical abilities required her to touch the substances she commanded.

She returned to the mirror she'd made earlier. It was almost impossible to tell where her armor ended and her scales began. With her face hidden, she looked even less human. For some reason, this was a relief. Before, she'd been a freak, a woman sewn onto a snake. Now, she looked like some ancient demi-god who'd crawled out of hell. Despite the existential discomfort of her inhuman form, she was quietly pleased to look so formidable.

For the greatest part of her life, she'd been nearly invisible. There had been advantages of being a young woman of petite build. Concealing her shaved scalp beneath a cloak, she'd been able to walk down city streets unnoticed. Hiding in plain site was no longer an option. Brand had laughed at her boldness. At last, she looked as dangerous as she felt.

She decided to increase her air of menace by crafting a pair of curved swords from the picks and shovels she'd brought to the site. She had no training in fighting with such blades, but anticipated she might need to learn swiftly. In all her recent fights, she'd relied on Rott's power to vanquish her foes. Wielding such power had almost become addictive. But it was plain that there was a connection between using this power and losing her legs. She wanted to hold onto what remained of her humanity. She dared not use Rott's abilities again.

She packed the few belongings she thought she might need into a large satchel that she slung over her shoulder. She decided to travel lightly; she would create a case from the leftover glass and bury all but her current journal for later retrieval. She wished to make it back to Commonground as swiftly as possible. She felt certain that a complete translation of the letter she'd found would provide clues to finding Avaris, if she was still alive. Brand's suggestion of finding a monk to translate was definitely not an option. But a more likely translator was nearby — the Black Swan. The unofficial empress of Commonground's underworld, the Black Swan had a reputation for uncovering secrets. Sorrow felt it likely that the Black Swan could read the ancient script, or employ someone who might be able to.

She set off as the sun was low in the sky. Soon the forest was a maze of shadows. Her difficulty in seeing her path made the feel of her serpentine body slithering over roots and rocks and slimy leaves more unsettling. She wouldn't have enjoyed walking through the jungle barefoot, and now she was effectively crawling through it on her belly. On the other hand, if she'd navigated this root-filled wilderness on foot in such poor light, she couldn't have gone twenty feet without tripping. Her new body moved across the dark terrain with confidence.

At last, she made it to the river and crawled out onto a long sandy bank. Now that she was out from under the trees, the night was awash with moonlight. She wondered what to do now. Should she swim? Could she, given that she was wearing armor?

She looked down river and spotted the hulking remains of the Knight's Castle. She wondered if the canoes were still there. Her body was now longer than a canoe, but perhaps if she lashed two together with poles, she could create a craft that might support her weight. She slithered toward the dark ruins. If nothing else, she could take shelter and wait out the night before deciding her next move.

She reached the fortress wall and leaned back to look at its upper edge, at least eighty feet above. She wondered if she could find a path to the top now that she had only starlight to guide her. As she thought about reaching the top of the wall, her body slithered forward with a mind of its own. Her torso slammed into the stone. She barely managed to push herself back as she was forced higher up the rock. In seconds, her body was moving vertically along the wall, as her belly scales grasped the imperfections in the rock face. Before she could really focus on how she was moving, her head popped over the top of the wall. There was a small tree here growing from a crack in the stone. She grabbed it with both hands, steadying herself as her body continued to snake upwards.

Realizing she was now fully atop the wall, she let go, and slithered to the center of a ten foot wide pathway that ran the length of the ruins.

"That was interesting," she said, swaying back out over the edge of the wall, looking down at the ground far below her. Interesting and unnerving. Was she actually in control? Or did her serpent tail genuinely have a mind of its own, listening to her thoughts, but acting independently? Was there a second intelligence inside her?

"Stop scaring yourself, Sorrow," she whispered.

She turned, and was scared by someone else. Standing directly behind her, covered in tattered and muddy bandages, was the man they'd found in the grave, his wild mane of hair tangled with twigs and vines. His eyes narrowed into slits as he lunged toward her.

She swayed back, avoiding his arms, but discovered that it hadn't been his intention to tackle her. Instead, as he leapt past her, he grabbed both of the iron swords affixed to her belt and tore them free. He rolled as he landed and sprung back to his feet before whirling around and placing the tip of one blade atop the glass scale directly over her heart.

In a thunderous voice, he barked, "Art thou a devil?"

"No." Sorrow's hand flashed to the blade. She calmly bent the iron tip into a u-shape. "I'm a pissed-off witch who's going to teach you some manners."

6 - SLATE

THE SHAGGY WARRIOR responded as Sorrow knew he would, driving his unbent iron blade into her serpent coils. Her command over this metal meant that he might just have well attacked her with a wad of damp clay. The metal folded like an accordion against her scales.

The warrior spent no time dwelling on the loss of his weapon. He spread his arms and unleashed a savage growl, driving forward on his powerful legs to tackle her. His arms wrapped tightly around her body in roughly the area where her feet would once have been. He squeezed her in a bear hug that caused jangling pain to dance along her extensive spine. She fell backward, writhing uncontrollably as she felt two of her new ribs snap.

Though she was too rattled to think clearly, her tail possessed its own battle tactics. Her body looped into great coils around the man, crushing him as he crushed her. Unfortunately, she failed to catch his legs. To her great surprise he managed to rise, lifting her easily despite her new mass. To her greater surprise, he charged toward the edge of the wall.

They plummeted toward the earth below. She barely had time to think before she slammed into the wet sand at the base of the fortress. Her body slackened as the impact stunned her. The warrior hadn't even been winded by the fall. Her crushing coils had the unanticipated effect of cushioning him.

He kicked himself free of her limp form as he clawed up the length of her body.

"Foul devil!" he growled as he straddled her human torso. "Thou shall trouble the human world no more!"

He raised both his fists together over his head and swung them with a loud grunt, delivering a strike to the faceplate of her helmet as powerful as if he'd been swinging a sledgehammer. Spots danced before her eyes as she clawed at the bandages covering his chest with her bare fingers. She knew she could save herself if she unleashed Rott's powers, but, try as she might, she couldn't summon the dark energy. If she released the entropic force again, the dragon might swallow all that remained of her humanity. Perhaps she would die because of this fear, but at least she would die with her own face.

While Rott's powers couldn't save her, her dragon half came to the rescue anyway as the tip of her tail whipped up and slapped the warrior in the side of his neck as he was preparing a second blow. The force knocked him sideways. With her vision blurred, she couldn't see where he'd gone, but it was enough that his weight no longer pinned her down. She was lifted into the air by her tail until she stood at her ordinary human height. She clenched her fists as she craned her neck, trying to see where the man had fallen.

Her head jerked to the left as a sudden motion caught her eye. The warrior leapt toward her, swinging a branch as long and thick as his arm. She tried to raise her hands but was too slow. The club slammed into the lower edge of her helmet and her world exploded into showers of bright sparks. She was vaguely aware of her helmet flying from her head as she fell backward into the muck.

The glowing sprites before her grew in intensity, becoming a uniform white light that blotted out the jungle. All she could hear was a loud whistle, rising in shrillness, building as a great wave of pressure in her skull. When the sound stopped, the world went dark.

SHE WOKE WITH the worst headache of her life, a significant milestone given the numerous times she'd voluntarily hammered nails into her own skull. Her eyes snapped open, then immediately clamped shut due to the intensity of the light before her. Her nose wrinkled as she breathed in smoke. She turned her head, coughing. She opened her eyes once more and found she was sprawled on a dark, sandy beach. The left side of her body was considerably warmer than her right side. From the sound of crackling nearby, she deduced she was near a fire.

Who'd built it? Why? Where was she?

She turned toward the fire, squinting against the glare, feeling nauseated by the sensation of her brain sloshing around. She could barely make out a dark, vaguely human shape beyond the flames.

Suddenly, she remembered what had happened. Her body whipped into the air, balanced atop her tail. She felt certain she would vomit, but managed to suppress the urge long enough to demand, "Who are you?" of the shaggy-haired warrior who sat on the opposite side of the fire.

The man slowly shook his head, and said, in a soft voice, "I don't know."

"Excuse me," she said as she spun away. She could no longer hold in the contents of her stomach. Green bile erupted as she collapsed to the ground, supporting herself on her hands. She continued to throw up much longer than she would have thought humanly possible. Of course, she wasn't human anymore. She had no way of knowing how large her stomach was now. The quantity of fluid that spilled from her seemed enough to fill a bathtub.

In the aftermath, she slithered into the river. She was still wearing her armor, though she had no idea where her helmet had wound up. She plunged her face beneath the surface. The water was chilled by snowmelt. Under ordinary circumstances, the cold would have been unbearable and she would have exited the water with utmost haste. Now, she left her head and shoulders immersed, allowing the icy river to numb her throbbing skull. She noted that, just as her stomach seemed larger than it had once been, her lungs had apparently also been altered. Several minutes passed with her head beneath the surface, yet she felt no great urgency to rise for air.

Finally, the frigid waters froze the sloshing contents of her skull into something less soupy. She rose from the river and sucked in air in a long gasp. She wiped her face with her hands, then slowly turned back toward the fire.

"Why didn't you kill me?" she asked.

"Thou art the woman who tended my wounds. I did not recognize thee at first."

"You remember fighting the dragon? You remember me stitching you up?"

"Aye. And nothing before."

"Nothing?"

He shook his head.

"You must have some memories," she said. "You remember how to fight, obviously. You seem to have a grasp of traditional theology judging by all the devil talk. You must have learned this somewhere."

"Aye. I must."

"But you don't remember who you were before you climbed…" She let her voice trail off. She decided not to tell him she'd found him in a grave. "I mean, before you attacked the dragon?"

He scratched his shaggy mane. "My first memory is the bone dragon rattling above me. I acted to save thee from the beast. Are we… are we not companions?"

She shook her head. "I'm sorry. You just sort of, um, showed up. I don't know anything at all about who you were before you jumped in to save my life."

Or did she? The ghost pygmy said he'd come to witness the birth of the Destroyer. He'd not been impressed with her. Maybe he'd been looking at the wrong person.

She asked, "Does the name Stark Tower mean anything to you?"

He shook his head.

"Avaris?"

He furrowed his brow. "She is… a queen?"

"Yes. Queen of what?"

He looked lost as he sadly shook his head.

"Do you know what a weaver is?"

"Aye," he said. "A witch. Thou art one."

"Why do you say that?"

He tapped his fingers against his scalp.

"Right. The nails. You know what I am."

"A woman. Not a devil."

"Not everyone thinks kindly of weavers," she said.

He shrugged. "I've no cause to hate thee."

"Right. But, if you know what a weaver is, you had to learn it somewhere. Forget about remembering yesterday or last week. What about your childhood? Who was your father?"

He didn't answer.

"Your mother? Do you have any siblings?"

He shook his head.

"No siblings? Or you don't remember."

"I've no memories of anything before fighting the dragon."

"You knew how to build a fire. How did you learn?"

He looked toward her leather satchel. "I found a flint and steel within. I know how to use them, but don't remember where I learned."

"You can't be a completely blank slate."

He shrugged, looking apologetic.

She crossed her arms, tapping her glass-covered biceps with her fingernails as her mind raced. Maybe this man was brain-damaged, but, as a fighter, he put any golem she'd ever built to shame. Infidel and Menagerie hadn't been interested in joining her mission, but this hairy brute didn't seem like he had anything better to do with his time.

But what if his memories returned? What if this was Stark Tower, the Witchbreaker, somehow returned from the dead? Shouldn't she end his miserable life here and now, in payment for his crimes? If he was Tower, and his memories returned, he'd almost certainly attempt to kill her.

On the other hand, what if he wasn't Tower? The letter had a symbol that blended together the glyphs for war, tool, and man. Was the man before her some sort of living weapon?

She squinted as she looked at him. Though some auras burned more faintly than others, she was certain that the man before her had no inner-light. She'd met such people before. The Skelling ice-maidens had been abused to the point that their spirits were extinguished, though their bodies stubbornly carried on. Could lost memories produce a similar effect?

A more fantastic possibility was that she was in the presence of an elaborate flesh golem. She'd discovered with Stagger that the remnant souls that animated golems could retain aspects of their former personalities. Short of tearing open this man's chest and seeing if it held a golden cage instead of a heart, she was unsure how to test her theory. When cut, he'd bled. Would this be true of a flesh golem?

She uncrossed her arms. "Did you find the food in my pack? Have you eaten already?"

"I found the food," he said. "But I'm no thief."

"It's good that you know that about yourself."

"I was greatly tempted," he said. "I was delirious when I first woke. I felt… I felt a pull that drew me to this place. I didn't think of food, or clothing. Thou must think me quite the savage, wandering through the jungle nude, little more than a beast."

"You've more manners than a beast," she said, slithering over to the pack. She dug out a package bound with string and tossed it to him. "Here's some jerky."

"Aren't thou also hungry?"

She shook her head. She felt hollowed out inside, but could still taste snake bile on her tongue. "It might take a while to recover my appetite."

She watched as he untied the string and her heart froze as he laid the open package on his lap, lowered his head, and clasped his hands together. He closed his eyes and sat a moment in silence.

"Are you… praying?" she asked.

He looked confused. "I don't know. I just… if I'm praying, I can't remember who I'm praying to. But the motions… felt natural."

She looked up at the ruins beside them. "Like coming here felt natural?"

He shrugged. "I… was delirious. I was dreaming as I walked. I imagined a fortress, resplendent with banners. I found only these ruins."

She pressed her lips tightly together. That was certainly tilting the scales toward him being Lord Tower.

"Are you a knight?"

He tilted his head, looking slightly surprised by her question. He nodded slowly. "Aye," he said. "Aye. I believe I am."

She resisted the temptation to say a bad word out loud. Just because he was a knight didn't mean he was the Witchbreaker. A knight who couldn't remember the god he served might be a valuable commodity.

"If you're a knight, I happen to be a damsel in distress," she said. She felt cheap describing herself in this fashion, but she knew it was the truth. "As you may have noticed, I've got a bit of a problem." She waved her hand along the length of her body.

"Once I saw your scalp, I assumed you were a bone weaver. They often alter their forms."

She wondered how he knew this, but decided not to press the issue. "I didn't voluntarily choose this form," she said. "I'm dealing with a little bit of a curse right now." Neither statement was completely true, but neither was completely false. "I'm hoping to find Avaris, Queen of the Weavers, so she can help restore my human form. Will you aid me in this quest?"

"Aye," he said. "I cannot deny a damsel in distress. I pledge my strength and my sword to thee, my lady."

She smiled, almost despite herself. "Thank you." She extended her open hand to him for a handshake. "All this serious talk without a proper introduction. My name is Sorrow."

He surprised her by taking her outstretched hand in his and kissing the back of her fingers. Ordinarily, she would have been repulsed by a gesture with such romantic undertones. But, his face seemed so innocent, she couldn't find it in herself to be offended.

"I fear I'm at a loss," he said, as he released her hand. "I don't know what you shall call me."

"Slate," she said, looking into his dark gray eyes. "In honor of your eyes."

Though, in truth, it was because, if his mind was a blank slate, it would be her hand that filled that empty void with knowledge, until he became the ally she needed him to be.

IT WAS WELL past sunset the following evening before Sorrow slithered once more into Commonground. Slate was at her side, dressed in glass armor similar to her own. She'd returned with him to the Witches Graveyard, telling him she needed to gather the raw materials to outfit him. In truth, she'd wondered if the sight of the grave where he'd been buried might stir further memories. The hunt for memories had proven unsuccessful, but she'd cut up the fabric of her tent to fashion undergarments for Slate, molded glass to fit his form, and equipped him with a fresh sword. He looked quite formidable in his black armor.

When she'd last walked these docks, no one had given her a second glance. Now all eyes were upon her and her muscular companion. But unlike a town in more civilized parts of the world, no one seemed afraid or repulsed by their appearance. They were being sized up as competition. They were rough customers in a city of rough customers.

They arrived at length at the floating saloon known as the *Black Swan*. She'd spent several weeks dwelling here not long ago, designing and building a body for the eponymous owner of the bar. The Black Swan was the unofficial queen of Commonground, a woman so wealthy she could purchase the loyalty of anyone she wished. She also had a reputation as a powerful sorceress, a reputation only enhanced by the fact that she continued to oversee her business concerns after death as an animated skeleton. It had been rumored that the Black Swan was a weaver, but Sorrow had held the woman's skull in her hands and saw no signs that it had ever been punctured by nails. Despite the rather intimate connection she'd had with the Black Swan while fitting her skeleton into a new iron shell, she'd been unable to learn the true nature of the woman's abilities.

Sorrow pushed open the doors of the saloon and slithered into the room. Few people even looked up from their cards as she entered. She wrinkled her nose at the cigar smoke combined with the strong perfumes of the painted women who accompanied the men at the tables.

The fact that no one found a woman blended with an enormous serpent more interesting than their cards was partly the blame of the man tending bar. Battle Ox was a half-seed, an eight-foot-tall minotaur with broad shoulders and iron-clad horns. Despite his fearsome aspect, during her time at the bar she'd discovered that Battle was actually a rather gentle soul.

"Battle," Sorrow said, drawing up to the bar, her head just above the level of his own. "Good to see you again."

He looked up, his brow furrowed. She could see her black helmet reflected in his eyes. She pulled her helmet off and his expression changed.

"Sorrow! This is a new look for you. Are you on stilts or something?"

"Something," she said, realizing that most of her lower body was hidden by the bar. "My additional height is one reason I'm here. I need to see the Black Swan."

"Are you sure?" he asked.

"Pretty sure. Why wouldn't I be?"

"Ever since you left, the boss has been griping that you cheated her."

"What gall! She complained about a thousand completely fictional defaults in my workmanship and tried to avoid paying my wages. She was the one who attempted to cheat me!"

"But she did pay you. And now that she's had time to adjust to her new body, she hates her voice."

"She's lucky to have any voice at all," Sorrow said. "She has no lungs or throat. That I was able restore her power of speech using bellows and reeds borders on the miraculous."

"In any case, when you see her, you'll get an earful."

"I'll risk it."

"Fine. But don't laugh when she's chewing you out. She hates that. It's just… she does kind of sound like a duck."

"If people think that, I'm hardly to blame," said Sorrow. "She's the one who chose to name herself after a waterfowl."

Battle cast his gaze toward Slate. "Who's the big guy?"

"I'm called Slate, *half-seed*."

"He's agreed to help me with a problem I'm trying to solve," said Sorrow.

Battle nodded. "Let me go tell the boss you're here." He disappeared behind a curtain that covered a door behind the bar.

Sorrow turned to Slate and said, "Try not to sound so contemptuous."

"Contemptuous?"

"The way you said 'half-seed.' It sounded judgmental."

Slate shrugged. "His mother sullied herself with animal seed. His inhuman soul was fated for damnation from before his birth. How can you not judge such a beast?"

"Considering you don't remember who your own parents are, you might want to keep an open mind."

"I may not remember them, but the evidence of my own eyes testifies that they were human."

Battle returned a moment later and said, "She'll see you. But your bodyguard stays here."

Sorrow had expected as much and made no protest as she slithered around the bar.

"So," he said, as he finally saw her full form. "You've, uh, got an interesting new look."

"Indeed," she said. "It's given me a new appreciation for the plight of your kind."

Battle tilted his head. "Plight?"

"You didn't ask to be born half human," she said. "It's a cruel fate, and it disgusts me that you're treated with contempt by thoughtless fools."

"You know what I hate more than contempt?" Battle asked. "Condescension. I happen to be proud of who and what I am. I'm bigger and stronger than any of the pathetic pink-skins who think they're better than me. And, I'd wager I'm better hung than anyone else in this port."

"There's no need to be crude," she said as she felt her cheeks go red. "I'm sorry if I've offended you. I just … I'm certain you've had a difficult life. I was trying to convey my empathy."

"You don't feel empathy. You feel pity. That's just another form of judgment."

Sorrow started to say that it was possible that a lifetime of poor treatment had left him unable to realize when someone was actually being nice but decided to hold her tongue.

Battle opened the door at the end of the hall. "Madam, Sorrow is here to see you."

"How delightfully ominous," said a reedy, squawking voice.

Battle stepped aside and Sorrow slithered past. The room beyond was lit by lanterns. When last she'd been here, the room had been stripped bare, but now it was crowded and cluttered with old dusty furniture that must have been quite lovely in its day. On a low velvet couch, the Black Swan waited, stretched out in what might have been a relaxed pose, if her body were still capable of looking relaxed.

Sorrow had been hired by the Black Swan to build an iron shell to encase her old bones. Any fair-minded person would have judged Sorrow's handiwork to be a masterpiece of sculpture. The Black Swan's new skin was, of necessity, much less flexible than a body of flesh. The lacy black dress that the Black Swan wore over her iron limbs somehow made her look even stiffer. She brought to mind a manikin that had toppled over. Still, with her slender limbs and long fingers, the old witch possessed pleasant echoes of the female form. Indeed, her face might even be thought beautiful, though her eyes were now made of glass and her eyelashes fine wires. But one had to admire the symmetry and proportions of her visage. The plates that formed her cheeks slid silently as the Black Swan's iron lips parted. Her polished teeth chopped the squeaking notes produced by the bellows and reeds inside her chest into a voice that was eerily musical.

"I know why you've come," the Black Swan sang. "You've found a letter."

Sorrow raised her eyebrows. "How could you know that?"

"Because Brand arrived yesterday. Only I had the resources to negotiate a fair price for such a large hoard of dragon bones. When he recounted the story of their discovery, he mentioned that you'd found a letter signed by Avaris herself."

"Oh," she said. "Right. Brand. Do you know if he's still in port?"

The Black Swan shrugged. "He seemed eager to depart for the Silver City. Perhaps you'll meet him there."

"Doubtful. I was merely curious as to his whereabouts. I'm hardly going to follow him to a city full of my worst enemies."

"You will if you wish to have the letter translated."

"You can't translate it?"

The Black Swan shook her head. "Why would I know the lost script of the weavers? For this, you need an authority on dead tongues. The person best fitting this description is Equity Tremblepoint, who resides in the Silver City."

"Tremblepoint? Why do I know that name?"

"Given your upbringing, my dear, I'm surprised by your ignorance. Lord Tremblepoint was the author of a dozen of the world's most beloved plays."

"Oh," said Sorrow. "You'll have to forgive me. I fear I've neglected my education in the fine arts."

The Black Swan released a series of squawks that might have been intended as laughter. "I would hardly describe Tremblepoint's work as fine art. He was a horrid playwright, possibly the most dreadful of all time. He acquired his family name because, in each scene, his stage directions require the actors to tremble and point as they deliver their melodramatic soliloquies."

"I thought you said his plays were beloved?"

"Indeed. While his works are meandering, long, and riddled with inconsistencies, they're also rife with the lowest forms of humor. The public has a hunger for jokes involving bodily output and the most shameful forms of sexual congress. His works have been popular for centuries. Equity Tremblepoint, his sole living descendant, makes a healthy living as a thespian due mainly to the fame attached to the Tremblepoint name."

"And this actor is also an authority on dead languages?"

"Indeed. The Tremblepoint family has collected a library of literary manuscripts that date back centuries. It is only natural that Equity would learn to read them."

"And you're certain you can't read the letter?"

"Why would you doubt me?"

"Because, despite your denials, the world believes you to be a weaver. It's fair to say you might even be the most famous weaver alive today."

"This would not be the first time that a thing commonly believed has proven baseless. I've not a single nail in my skull," the Black Swan said, tapping the solid dome of her forehead with a razor-sharp fingernail. "You know this."

"True. But I recently encountered a ghost named Purity. She hinted that the nails were only one crude method of becoming a weaver. She said emotions could be as powerful as physical spikes, and that hatred and the thirst for revenge had opened channels in her mind to grant her powers."

"Interesting. Might I suggest you discuss this matter with her?"

"Unfortunately, Purity was intent on murdering the sun. Stopping her required killing her."

"And in the course of stopping her, you took the drastic step of merging your soul with that of Rott."

Sorrow frowned. "Brand couldn't have told you that. I never explained my powers to him."

"My dear, you crawled into the room on a serpent's belly. You're covered in dragon scales. There's a nail in your scalp of a matching ebony hue."

"Fine. You've diagnosed my problem correctly. Is there nothing you can do to help me?"

"You drove that nail into your scalp seeking great power. Why did you do so if you weren't willing to pay the price?"

"I had no idea my body would change like this. I want it to stop."

The Black Swan shook her head slowly. "It won't stop. I'm sorry, Sorrow, but your fate was sealed when you chose to access Rott's powers. As a dragon, Rott had centuries to study the elemental force he blended his soul with, and still his mind was decayed by entropy."

"Perhaps my mind is stronger," said Sorrow. "Life has toughened me, if nothing else."

The Black Swan shook her head. "You risk the world if you approach your current problem with arrogance. You've been given a great opportunity to change the fate of mankind, but doing so will require that you alter your goals."

"But my goal *is* to change the fate of mankind."

"By waging a pointless war against the church, when the true threat to humanity lies with the primal dragons. What use will it be to overthrow fellow men if humanity is wiped from the world by the collective power of these beasts?"

"I'll deal with the dragons when and if they're a problem," said Sorrow. "For now, I know who my enemies are. It's just my friends I'm having trouble identifying."

The Black Swan nodded. "We may not be friends, but I feel I owe you at least the courtesy of a warning."

"A warning against what?"

"Despite your confidence, Rott is an ancient power whose will far exceeds your own."

"I met Rott in the Sea of Wine. He's dead. I don't think he has any will at all."

"You saw his physical body intact in the Sea of Wine. His form would only persist if some flickering hunger for survival were left within him. By blending your soul with his own, you may stir this hunger enough to wake the dragon.

If the beast awakes while he shares your form, the dragon will devour your spirit and digest your intelligence to nourish his own quiescent mind."

Sorrow found that she'd unconsciously begun to chew her nails. She pulled her hand away from her lips. "You can't know that. You're like all prophets, speaking in vagaries."

"Let me say this as directly as possible. I believe that Rott's powers are too powerful for you to control. You can halt your slide toward total domination by the beast by removing the nail you carved from him and giving it to me for safe-keeping."

"That's not going to happen," said Sorrow. "I finally have the power I've sought for all these years. I'm going to learn to control it."

"How?"

"I don't know, but that's never stopped me. I've become an expert at defining my most dangerous areas of ignorance, then learning what I must to survive. I know it's possible to tap a primal dragon's power without losing one's intelligence because Purity did it. I saw it with my own eyes. If a thing can be done, it can be duplicated."

"You're a fool," said the Black Swan. Her iron fingers clanked as she clamped them to her chest. "If you have such command and control over your abilities, why did you produce such poor work on my breasts?"

"By the vacant moon," said Sorrow, closing her eyes and rubbing them. "They're made of iron! They're never going to look real!"

"So you admit you've delivered an inferior product," the Black Swan said. "I insist you remain here until they've been remade to my satisfaction."

"You've lost your mind," Sorrow muttered. "When the worms ate your brains, they shat out your sanity."

"I was a fool to have faith in you," the Black Swan said in a low squawking tone that might have been intended to convey disappointment, though she sounded more like a duck with a sore throat.

Sorrow curled around to face the door, resisting the urge to curse. She slithered down the hall and found Battle and Slate leaning on opposite sides of the bar, engaged in an arm wrestling contest. A score of gamblers had gathered around them, staring intently at the match. Slate had removed his helmet, and his face showed signs of strain. The cut on his neck she'd stitched shut was bleeding freely again.

With a thud, Slate's arm went down and the crowd erupted in cheers. Battle pumped his fists in the air. Slate rose, rubbing his wrist, then extended his open hand.

"An honorable victory," he said. "Well fought, my friend."

Battle shook his hand. "You had me worried for a minute, buddy. Thought we'd break the damn bar. The Swan would take that out of my pay."

Slate chuckled as he nodded. Sorrow slithered around the bar and grabbed him by the arm.

"We're leaving," she said.

Slate allowed himself to be pulled toward the door. "Must we depart in haste?"

"I don't need you rough-housing in here. Battle's right. The Black Swan will bill us for any damage."

"No harm was done," said Slate as they stepped outside.

"I suppose I should be happy you just arm wrestled instead of getting into a brawl."

"We had no cause for combat," said Slate. "Ours was a friendly contest."

"Fifteen minutes ago you thought he was an unholy abomination. Suddenly he's your friend?"

Slate shrugged. "We talked as we waited. Beneath his beastly exterior, he's a good soul." He sighed, and leaned against a piling on the dock. He removed his glass gauntlet. His arm was covered in blood. "I could have bested him if my stitches hadn't torn."

Sorrow shook her head. "Was it so important to find out who was stronger that you'd risk hurting yourself?"

He grinned. "A day isn't well lived until I've spilt a little blood, even if it's my own."

"You don't have much extra to spare," she said. She removed her helmet and took his arm to examine her torn handiwork. "Let's find a room for the night. I need to fix you up again."

Slate chuckled. "How is it, if thou art the damsel in distress, I'm the one who requires mending?"

Before she could answer, a voice called out, "Sorrow?"

The curious thing about the voice was that it came from directly overhead.

7 - CIRCUS

SORROW LOOKED STRAIGHT up. A teenage boy with curly black hair floated above her. She raised her hand and cried, "Jetsam!"

Jetsam smiled broadly as he kicked his legs to swim down through the air. When she'd parted company with the Romers, the family had been the most miserable creatures in all of creation, Wanderers without a ship. The *Freewind* had been transportation for Sorrow, but for the Romers it had been home. They'd escaped with little more than the clothes on their back. Now, Jetsam was outfitted in a crisp white uniform of cotton breeches and vest, with a bright green sash for a belt and a matching bandana serving as a cap.

"Zounds!" Slate cried as he spotted the flying teenager.

"Zounds?" Jetsam asked. "What are you, an actor?"

"An actor?"

"The only place I've heard that word was in the Tremblepoint play, *The Merchant of Monkeys*."

"When would you have seen a play?" Sorrow asked. "You've lived your whole life on a ship."

Jetsam's head reached the level of her own when he stopped swimming down through the air. He spread his arms and brought himself to a halt, his feet still sticking straight up. "I've done more than seen the play. I performed in it. I played the role of second monkey when I was eight. The show was staged on the fo'c'sle of the *Horizon*."

"I had no idea Wanderer's had thespians among them," said Sorrow.

"We're sailors, not barbarians. One of the reasons Commonground even exists is so we can get together and enjoy plays, concerts, dancing, etc."

"How is it that thou dost fly?" Slate asked.

"'*Thou dost?*'" Jetsam responded, eyebrows raised. Then he shrugged and said, "My family rescued a mermaid princess. As a reward, each member of my family got to blow a note on the mer-king's magical conch. We all wound up with different powers based on our names, more or less." He performed a loop in mid-air, righting himself so his feet were pointing down. "I got the best power, if I do say so myself."

"Aye. 'Tis quite a talent."

Sorrow said, "Forgive me. I was so surprised to see you, I haven't made the proper introductions. Jetsam, this is Slate. Slate, Jetsam."

The two men shook hands.

"Speaking of surprises," Jetsam said, glancing at her serpent tail. "You, uh, look... different... somehow." A few awkward seconds passed, before he asked, cheerfully, "Have you lost weight?"

She sighed. "I'm surprised you recognized me, to be honest."

He laughed. "I have an unusual level of experience with looking at the tops of people's heads. Believe me, even from fifty feet up, the second you took off your helmet I knew who you were."

"I take it from the uniform you've found work on a new ship? Was your family able to remain together?"

"Yep and yep. You'll never guess who we're working for now."

"Brand Cooper," she said.

"You're a better guesser than I gave you credit for."

"I happen to know that Brand recently came into some money, and a ship was one of the things he mentioned buying. Your mother must have mixed feelings about working for him."

"Nah. Ma's fine. It's Mako who's pitching a fit."

"And Brand's going back to the Silver City?"

"Yep."

"Might he be interested in taking on passengers?"

"I can't answer for him, but I know Ma wants you back on board."

"Really? Why?"

Jetsam shrugged. "I just heard her telling Sage that there's never a witch around when you need one."

"What do they need a witch for?"

"Who knows? But come on back to the ship. Everyone's asleep, but I'll wake Brand and let him know I'm bringing you aboard."

"We're most grateful," said Sorrow. "Where's your ship?"

"Right here!" Jetsam pointed to a clipper docked next to the *Black Swan*. The name on the bow was *Circus*. The figurehead beneath the bowsprit was a buxom woman painted to look like a clown. "Used to belong to some wealthy gambler. Well, wealthy before he came to Commonground. When he tried to skip town on his debts, the Black Swan sent her enforcers after him. They were kind of messy. It smelled like hell when we came aboard. We've spent our whole first day cleaning up dried blood and worse from all the nooks and crannies."

Jetsam led them up the gangplank. The timbers creaked as Sorrow slithered onto deck. The ship smelled strongly of soap, with only a hint of rotting meat. Yet even that masked whiff made her stomach growl. She'd not had a thing to eat since she'd been sick at the Knight's Castle, and she was now undeniably famished. When she realized it was the scent of putrefied human remains triggering her hunger, her appetite fled once more.

Jetsam led them to the aftcastle and softly rapped on the door. They waited in silence for a moment, and just as he was about to knock again, the door creaked open and Brand looked out. Sorrow's eyebrows shot up.

"You've cut your hair!" she said.

Brand ran his hands along his closely cropped scalp. With his long locks gone, he looked older. His face seemed squarer, less feminine. "I'm a business man now. I figured I should clean up a little." His eyes focused on Sorrow. She could see his whole body tense up.

"Let's play fortune teller," she said. "I can tell you what you're about to ask."

"What happened to your legs?"

"You said it too fast."

"But –"

She held up her hand. "It's a long story."

He looked at Slate. "Is he part of the story?"

"This is Slate," said Sorrow. "He's agreed to help me find Avaris."

Brand wiped the sleep from his eyes, then silently contemplated Slate. "Does he… I mean…"

"Can we talk privately?" Sorrow asked. "We'd like to book passage to the Silver City, and I dislike discussing money in public."

"Come in," said Brand.

"I'll be out in just a moment," Sorrow said to Slate and Jetsam.

She slithered into Brand's cabin. It was pitch black when he closed the door. There was a soft click and the room filled with light. Blinking, she saw that Brand was now sitting on his bunk, holding a small open locket in his hands. The pearl-sized glorystone inside produced enough light to rival a large lantern.

"The big guy looks like he's survived his injuries well enough," Brand said. "I guess the next question is, who is he? Or maybe, what is he?"

"Excellent questions," said Sorrow. "He has no memories. At least, no memories of a personal nature."

"Is it safe for him to be on board?"

"Why wouldn't it be?"

"Buck naked, he beat a dragon half to death with its own jawbone. I hesitate to think what he might do now that you've armed him."

"He seems friendly enough. And the fact I made his armor means I can keep him on a short leash. All I need to do is touch him and I can cause the armor to fuse into a single piece, trapping him. I'm surprised you're worried. You've never struck me as possessing an excess of caution."

"Things have changed a lot in the last day. I own a ship now. I have responsibilities. I don't want to do anything to place my crew in danger."

"Slate won't be a danger to them. But I have to wonder about you."

"Me?"

"You buy a ship, then conveniently hire the woman who's the object of your unrequited love as your captain?"

"Gale's experienced. And, on a purely economic level, hiring the Romers is a bargain. When Rigger's on deck, he's like twenty men working, but only one mouth to feed."

"So you admit you're exploiting Rigger. What about Gale?"

"What about Gale? Her family needed a ship. I needed a crew."

"You've placed yourself in a position of power over her," said Sorrow, crossing her arms. "You now feed and clothe her and her entire family. If you invite her back into your bed, can she refuse you?"

"I should be insulted that you think I'm some sort of manipulative pseudo-rapist. But, I'm more bugged that you think so little of Gale. She's not a whore who's going to crawl into my bed because I throw a few coins her way."

"You crawled into her bed when the tables were turned."

He raised his eyebrows. "You think I was sleeping with her because she used to be my boss?"

Sorrow shrugged. "Not many men wind up involved with women old enough to be their mother."

"But the reverse is so common it barely merits mention," he said. "My father has wed three times, each time to a younger woman. His latest wife is only two years older than me."

"This is one of the things I despise about the world," said Sorrow. "There cannot be equality in such a marriage."

"Equality is a vastly overrated commodity. I didn't enter into a relationship with Gale because I thought she would be my equal. I expected her to be my superior. I wasn't disappointed. The things I learned in her bed opened my eyes to –"

Sorrow raised her hand. "Just stop. I really don't want to know. I will point out, however, that a woman who sought out lovers to increase her experience would be shamed and branded a slut. As a man, you're free to openly boast of your experience."

"I suppose it's a bit of a double standard," said Brand. "But it's all behind me. I'm changing my ways now that I've found the only woman who could ever complete me."

Sorrow stared at him, wondering if he was trying to fool her, wondering even more if he was fooling himself.

He ran his fingers through his hair, looking confused. "How the hell did this conversation become about me? You're turning into a giant snake, and this isn't the main topic of discussion?"

"What's there to discuss? I've lost control over some aspects of my magic. Regaining control is my immediate priority. The next person who might be able to help me is Equity Tremblepoint, who resides in the Silver City. Will you give us passage there?"

"Of course," he said. He furrowed his brow. "Tremblepoint? Like the playwright?"

"Am I the only person who's never heard of him?"

"I don't think Equity Tremblepoint is a him. I think she's a she. Maybe."

"You're not sure?"

"I've seen her, or maybe him, in a couple of plays. In a *Midwinter's Fantasy*, Equity played the Fairy Queen. But in *Brightmoon the Eighth*, she played the king. Amazing performances in each role, by the way."

"If she's adept at playing both genders, perhaps she can give Bigsby a few tips," said Sorrow, though she instantly regretted the words. It was cruel to mock a person who was genuinely mad.

"Maybe," said Brand, apparently having taken no offense. He stretched his arms and yawned. "It's still a long ways until dawn. We can let Slate bunk with the boys. With your, uh, different configuration, I'm not sure you'll fit anywhere but the cargo hold."

"I won't be choosy," she said. "I'm sorry if I sounded scolding earlier. I know you're a good person at heart."

"That goes both ways. For a person with a head full of nails, you're nowhere near as mean as you look."

Sorrow glanced down at her tail. "My head is now the least frightening part of my body. I hope my appearance won't prove alarming for the younger Romers."

Brand chuckled. "The Romers used to routinely take shortcuts through the Sea of Wine. From what Gale told me, nearly getting chewed by Rott on their last trip was one of their less eventful journeys. I don't think any of the Romers are that easy to shock."

THE CARGO HOLD was mostly empty save for a few barrels and large sacks of grain in the corner. Jetsam turned the space into a makeshift bedroom by supplying pillows and blankets, along with a jug of fresh water and a basin.

"Not fancy," he said.

"It's fine," she said.

Slate was already in the bunkroom shared by Mako, Rigger, and Jetsam. It had only three bunks, but one of them was always on duty, so no one was inconvenienced.

Jetsam closed the door, leaving Sorrow alone. She was weary down to the center of her bones. She quickly shed her glass armor. Despite the fact the suit fit her like a second skin, the hard edges chaffed beneath her armpits and especially around her hips, where her human flesh turned dark gray before blending with the ink-black scales.

She ran her fingers along the band of transitional flesh. The chafed, scraped skin that her armor had rubbed proved to be a surprising source of encouragement. The raw flesh formed a rough band around her belly, providing a visible limit of where her human skin had ended when she'd first donned the armor. While wearing the suit, she'd been paranoid that her itching midsection might be changing further. Fortunately, the scales had not advanced. Had she halted the changes by refraining from further use of her powers?

She poured water in the basin and washed herself. She was especially careful around her face. There was a knot on her temple that felt like an egg under her skin where Slate had clocked her. She wondered how long it would be before the swelling went down.

Once she was cleansed of jungle grime and sweat, she lowered herself to the blankets. She normally slept on her back, but this was all but impossible now. She crossed her arms beneath her head, wondering if she would ever get to sleep like this.

She soon had her answer, as the sound of waves lapping against the hull lulled her into slumber. She'd not even had to extinguish the lantern Jetsam had left behind.

Her eyes snapped open. She lay perfectly still, listening.

Scritch. Scritch. Scritch.

The sound was coming from behind the sacks stacked in the corner.

Scritch. Scritch. Scritch.

She knew it was rats. She had no particular fear of rats, nor was she overly fond of them. Under ordinary circumstances, she might have thrown a shoe in the direction of the noise, scared off the pest, then gone back to sleep.

Of course, she no longer had shoes.

She rose, her head nearly touching the beams. The noise stopped suddenly as her shadow shifted across the wall. She held her breath, waiting. She felt paralyzed. It wasn't fear that stilled her, however. It was something else. Not for the first time, she had the sensation that there was a second intelligence within her body, and it was now exerting its will.

Scritch.

Her ears precisely fixed the sound of the rat clawing into the sack. Her body whipped forward. In less than a second she arced over the sacks and shot down, arms outstretched. The rat jumped as her fingers brushed its fur.

Mindlessly, she crammed the squealing rat between her jaws and snapped its head off. The hot blood filling her mouth sent a wash of electric ecstasy through the length of her body. She swallowed the head whole, the whiskers still twitching, then crammed the rat into her mouth, pushing, shoving, cramming the bloodied flesh between her teeth. She wanted to scream, but couldn't, as her throat was distended by the rat's torso. She wanted to vomit, but swallowed instead, then swallowed again, and again, until the rat's slender tail slipped between her lips.

As she shoved the last of the rat into her mouth, she once more gained control of her hands. She held them before her face and discovered them covered with blood and fur and feces.

Despite the horror, she continued to swallow.

She raced back to the basin to wash the blood from her hands. As she loomed above it, she could see herself from the shoulders up, reflected in the water. Her neck was bulging and contracting, swollen so that it distended out past her chin. Her clavicles felt as if they would break as the mass in her throat pressed outward. She still couldn't breathe.

With one last gulp, the rat cleared her windpipe, and her breathe returned with a gasp. She started to scream, but clamped her hands over her mouth, stifling her cries. She couldn't bear the thought of anyone rushing into the hold and finding her in this condition.

She plunged her face into the wash basin, scrubbing it roughly, then rubbed her hands in the water until they felt raw. She was acutely aware of the hot lump now swelling her stomach. She grabbed the pitcher and poured water into her mouth, but didn't dare swallow the foul hair and ooze that it washed off her tongue and teeth. She spat out gray sludge, then rinsed again.

At length, there was no more water, and nothing left to scrub off.

She leaned against the door to be certain it would not open. After a moment, a spasm ran the length of her body, and she began to weep.

SHE WAS STILL awake many hours later when there was a knock on the door.

"I'm not decent," she whispered. "Come back later."

"It's Gale," said the voice on the other side. "Open up."

"I'll be out in a little while," said Sorrow.

To her consternation, Gale tried to open the door.

"Can't I have a little privacy?" she asked, throwing her weight against the wood so that it only opened a crack.

"Privacy is exactly why we must talk now," said Gale, her voice little more than a whisper through the gap. "Jetsam just went to bed. Mako has gone to the crow's nest. Everyone else is asleep. This is a conversation that must not be overheard by prying ears."

Sorrow sighed. "Fine. Just give me thirty seconds."

"Agreed."

Sorrow grabbed a blanket and wrapped it around herself. Her belly still seemed grossly distorted, but perhaps it was only her imagination. She said, "Enter."

When the door opened, she discovered that Gale wasn't alone. Sage Romer was with her, dragging the wooden figurehead that had once decorated the *Freewind*. Sage was Gale's oldest daughter, a serious-minded fifteen-year-old who shared her mother's curly black hair and athletic build. She was a talented clairvoyant, and Sorrow had witnessed her ability to boss around her older brothers with the same forcefulness as her mother.

Gale closed the door behind her. Sage placed the figurehead against the wall, then removed the spyglass she carried in a holster on her hip. She stared into the spyglass even though the end was capped, then announced, "Jetsam's sound asleep. Mako's got his spyglass out and is watching the *Maelstrom*, probably hoping Sandy will come above deck. Poppy's awake, but she's reading that book about knights. We're clear."

"You can see in any room?" Sorrow asked. She wondered if Sage could possibly have seen what had happened earlier. Were they here to discuss the danger she posed to their family?

Sage nodded. "I do my best not to invade the privacy of others. Alas, some of my siblings don't feel the same way."

"Jetsam eavesdrops at every opportunity," said Gale. "Mako can hear things much better than an ordinary man. It's difficult to keep secrets from them."

"What secret do you think I need to keep?" Sorrow asked.

"You?" Gale asked. "I imagine that is between you and your conscience."

"Jetsam warned us about your condition," said Sage. "I don't see how you could keep it secret if you wanted."

"Then what —"

"Can we trust that nothing we say will leave this room?" asked Gale.

"You have my word," said Sorrow.

Gale motioned toward the figurehead. "This is all that's left of the *Freewind*. I've saved it not because I'm sentimental. I rescued it because my mother's soul is trapped inside."

Sorrow looked at the wood. "I fear you may be mistaken. I would see an aura."

"I see the aura," said Sage. "But it would be concealed from you. When grandmother's soul was bound to the ship, steps were taken to conceal her spirit from Rott's gaze. Otherwise, the *Freewind* couldn't sail the Sea of Wine unmolested. This same spell of concealment hides her from the gaze of other magically aware individuals such as yourself."

"Okay," said Sorrow. "What do you need me to do?"

"We can't leave her trapped in this figurehead," said Gale. "Before, my mother's ghost could roam the *Freewind*. Watching her family carry on was her own personal heaven. Now the magic that sustained her has been damaged. We don't know if she can see us or hear us. If she's withering away, deaf and dumb, she may be in her own private hell."

"How long has your mother been dead?" Sorrow asked, tracking the lines of the figurehead's face.

"Eighteen years," said Gale.

"Are you certain her soul is still in the wood? Souls don't last forever in the material world. They're like the residual heat from a fireplace. Once the fire dies out, the heat may linger a long time in the stones, but it isn't infinite."

"I know this," said Gale. "But mother's soul drew power from the Sea of Wine every time we crossed it. The Sea of Wine embodies the dreams and myths of all Wanderers. It sustains our souls for all eternity."

"Can you not return to the Sea of Wine? I was under the impression this was one of your magical talents."

Gale shook her head. "I could trigger the transition, but mother was the true cause. When she bargained with Avaris to bind her soul to the ship, she didn't know that her state of bridging the gap between life and death would weaken the fabric of reality around her, to the point that the *Freewind* could tear through."

"Wait. Avaris? Your mother knew her?"

"So I've been told," said Gale. "Truthfully, my mother's life story is a complicated matter. She lived a life of grand adventure. Alas, she was also prone to, shall we say, fabricate certain elements of her history."

"If we found Avaris, she could explain the spell she used to bind your mother to the ship."

"We know a good deal about the process," said Sage. "Grandmother was quite ill when she made her bargain with Avaris. She knew she had very little time left. So, she allowed Avaris to kill her. All blood was drained from her body. This blood was diluted in wine, then soaked into to the *Freewind* board by board."

"This is why our former ship had such a distinctive hue," said Gale.

"Right," said Sorrow. "But problematic. Since your mother doesn't have any blood now, we couldn't duplicate the original binding."

"If we can't place her spirit into a ship once more, can we release her? Better to swim on alone into the Sea of Wine than to live in a prison of wood."

Sorrow nodded. "I agree. But we shouldn't give up hope. As it happens, I'm on a quest to find Avaris. I think she can help me with my, um, skin condition. If your mother's soul can last until then, Avaris may know some new trick to save her. Right now, my best hope of finding her lies in the Silver City, so it's fortunate you were heading there, yes?"

"Good fortune indeed," said Gale. "We're departing later in the day. We can —"

Gale was interrupted by a knock on the door.

Sage whipped out her spyglass. "No one's there," she whispered, confused.

There was a second knock.

"Who is it?" Sorrow asked.

"Slate," a deep voice answered.

Sage lowered her spyglass as her mouth went slack.

"I'm getting dressed," Sorrow said. "Go find the galley and get some breakfast. I'll join you later."

"May I prepare something for you?" he asked.

"I'm not even a little bit hungry," Sorrow said, doing her best to ignore the feeling of fullness in her abdomen.

She heard Slate's heavy feet as he climbed the stairs up to the deck.

"You look spooked," Gale said to Sage.

"I didn't see him!" Sage said. "I mean, once he started talking I realized I could see him, but I hadn't seen him the way I normally see people. He's like a big, walking sack of meat. He has no aura at all!"

"Is he undead?" asked Gale.

"He breathes, he sweats, he bleeds," said Sorrow. "He's alive in every way I've thought of testing."

"Sounds like you were pretty thorough in your testing," Gale said with a sly grin. "I don't blame you. Jetsam makes him sound like quite a feast for the eyes. Is there any sort of agreement between the two of you? A partnership that it would be impolite to intrude upon?"

"What? Are you… are you asking if we're lovers?"

"You said you'd tested him in every way you could think of. I know the first thing I'd test."

"By the pure metals, no! It's nothing like that."

"Good. I had thought that, since you slept alone, you might not be possessive of him."

"I'm not, but, really, I don't think you should, um, test him yourself."

"I agree!" said Sage. "I'm not even certain he's human!"

"Also, you would drive Brand absolutely insane," said Sorrow.

"Brand employs me," said Gale. "He's not my husband. He has no say as to whom I share my bed with."

"You know he's in love with you."

"I know he thinks he's in love with me."

"You're not worried he's trying to manipulate you by providing you with a new ship?"

"I'm certain he is. But, no matter. Brand may make any attempt he wishes to seduce me. I can see through his every action. When we share each other's bed again, it will be due to my actions, not his."

"When?" Sorrow asked. "Why would you…"

Gale shrugged. "Since we can no longer shorten our journeys via the Sea of Wine, we'll be between ports for weeks at a time. In times of boredom, a woman can be forgiven for seeking… amusement."

"When I tried to find amusement with Will Fortune aboard the *Monsoon,* you practically broke my arm," grumbled Sage.

"You'll thank me later. He wasn't the right man for your first time."

"It wasn't going to be my first time. We were going to just fool around a little."

"Fooling around a little is how I wound up pregnant with Levi when I was sixteen," said Gale.

Sorrow folded her arms across her chest. "I'm not really comfortable with this discussion."

Gale nodded. "My apology. I forgot that you were raised to follow the tenants of the Church of the Book. It's no wonder they've become the most populous faith in the world, considering how they discourage the discussion of sex."

"Wouldn't refraining from discussing sex have the effect of reducing the population?" asked Sorrow. "The less the mind is focused on the topic, the less feverish it becomes."

"So the church teaches. But all their efforts lead only to ignorance. Men and women among the faithful are left to rut like animals on pure instinct. The men know nothing of seduction, and the women know very little about how to entertain themselves without spilling out babies."

Sorrow thought this was an odd attitude for a woman who had seven children, but let the matter pass.

Gale wasn't through, however. "In most other cultures, sex is an act of the body. Wanderers, by being free to discuss the act, have turned it into an act of the mind. Until you've experienced the difference between the approaches, you can never understand how one is superior to the other. Perhaps you can speak to Brand about it. He was an enthusiastic student."

"It's not a topic that's ever interested me," said Sorrow. She looked down at her tail. "For obvious reasons, it interests me even less now."

She led them toward the door. "If you'll give me a moment, I'd like to get dressed. I'm sure you both must have a million things to do before this ship can leave port."

"True," said Gale. Sage lifted the figurehead.

"You know that Mako sneaks out to see Sandy and you never say a word," Sage muttered as she passed her mother.

"Mako doesn't stand a chance with Sandy," said Gale. "She doesn't like his teeth."

"How can you know that?" asked Sage.

"A mother knows," said Gale, as Sorrow closed the door behind them.

Sorrow dressed, finding her armor no tighter than it had been before. The sensation that her belly was bloated to twice its normal size was all in her mind. She ran her hands along the remnants of her pelvic bone, letting her fingers pause where her crotch had once been.

She sighed. "I wasn't using it anyway."

8 - CHILD'S PLAY

SORROW SPENT THE following day in the hold. The ship had departed at dawn, and when Sage had come below to bring breakfast, Sorrow claimed to be suffering from sea-sickness. In truth, she wasn't, but she suspected it wouldn't take much to nauseate her considering her most recent meal. As horrible as the rat had been going down, she couldn't bear the thought of having it come back up. She felt her best course to avoid this was just to remain in the dimly lit hold and try to sleep until she was certain her unanticipated late night snack was completely digested.

She attempted to distract herself by updating her journal. Writing always took her from the realm of emotion into the realm of objective analysis:

> *It was only meat. For most living creatures, my meal was a completely natural event, barely worth note. Lions and wolves and housecats survive on raw meat; certainly humans can tolerate the diet. In some respects, the convention of gutting and skinning a beast, draining it of blood, cutting out the bones, then cooking only the muscles seems wasteful.*
>
> *I should feel proud to have moved beyond such unnatural prissiness. Civilization has done all it can to suppress the hunting instinct that lies within us all. To have this instinct reawakened is an improvement, not a curse.*

She closed her journal with a sigh, not convinced of a word she'd written. She began to think that her self-confinement was keeping her from moving past the incident. If she would only go up on deck, she could be distracted by the activities of the Romers.

If all the Romers had been adults, her decision would have been simple. She could hear Poppy and Cinnamon on deck, and they were ten and twelve, respectively. It had been one thing to slither into Commonground and face the stares of scoundrels and ruffians. If they were given nightmares by her appearance, she felt no pity for them. But Sorrow had seen things no child should see at Poppy's age, and didn't want to give the girls nightmares. Still, she couldn't hide below deck for the entire voyage, could she?

Her self-imposed exile in the hold came to an end with a knock on the door. The hold was dark save for the lantern. She threw her blanket around her shoulders to conceal herself before opening the door.

It was Brand, looking concerned as he slipped into the hold.

"Can I help you?" Sorrow asked.

"You've been hiding out down here since we left port. I was wondering if perhaps you needed help."

"I'm just feeling… queasy. I have more stomach to upset than I used to."

Brand held up a gnarled, tan root. "Ginger. Chew on this and you can handle rough seas. Gale's powers do push a ship across the waves faster than most people are used to."

Sorrow took the root. It looked tough and fibrous. She had doubts about putting it into her mouth.

"So what's the real reason you're hiding?" Brand asked.

"Why do you doubt that I'm sea-sick? On my previous travels aboard the *Freewind* I spent most of my time in my cabin."

"Some company would be good for you."

"I've been too busy for company," said Sorrow. "I've been updating my journal."

"Is there a section about how I killed the dragon?" Brand asked with a grin.

"You've been mentioned, yes. As an aide in my successful gambit to stop the beast."

"Do you also talk about me being a good listener with interesting insights into your true feelings and motives?"

"No." She rolled her eyes.

"I think you're hiding down here because you're ashamed of your appearance."

She crossed her arms. "I've been seen by half the Romers already. What do I have to hide?"

"It's the only explanation I can think of for why you're letting Slate run around the ship without you watching his every move. Considering you went to that graveyard digging for answers, I can't believe you don't have the biggest question you found under constant surveillance."

"Slate's… running around the ship?"

"He's playing with Poppy and Cinnamon on deck right now."

Sorrow frowned. What had she expected? That he would spend his journey lying in his bunk immobile as a corpse? She shouldn't have been surprised to discover that Slate was interacting with the crew. He'd been quick enough to make friends with Battle Ox. But, somehow, after she'd eaten the rat, all thoughts of trying to figure out who and what Slate might be had faded in importance.

Sorrow sighed. "Let me get dressed and I'll come up top. In truth, I'm feeling better adapted to the waves now that we've been under way for so many hours. I'd reached the decision to go to the deck on my own just before you knocked."

"Right," said Brand.

She dressed in her full armor. She knew that this was pointless attire aboard the ship, but she felt stronger when she wore it. She did modify the helmet, opening the faceplate to reveal her features from eyebrow to chin. When she was done, she slithered from the hold up the stairs to the deck.

When her torso rose above the edge of the hold she ducked, as she found herself in the midst of battle. Poppy was wearing a bucket on her head and lunging at Slate with a mop handle. Slate parried her blow with a mop handle of his own. Slate had shed his armor and was dressed in the same white cotton uniforms sported by the Romers.

The mock sword battle between Poppy and Slate was being watched from the aftcastle by Cinnamon and some short woman that Sorrow didn't recognize. She did a double take and realized that the woman was Bigsby. The dwarf had his platinum blonde wig piled on his head where it was held in place by a dazzling silver crown studded with emeralds. He was wearing a cream colored silk dress adorned with abundant frills. His face was powdered to the point that it almost resembled a white mask, with bright red lips, pink cheeks, and thin arched eyebrows penciled on.

"Glad to see you've joined us," Brand said from behind.

She turned around and asked, "Where does he keep getting these outfits?"

Brand shrugged. "He knows a seamstress in Commonground named Rose Thirteen. She apparently has a whole wardrobe full of outfits his size."

Sorrow was confused.

Brand shrugged and said, "I didn't ask questions. I had a million things to do to get the *Circus* ready. Plus, Rose was a little too friendly for my taste."

"You found a woman to be too friendly?"

"I didn't think it was possible either, but she asked if I wanted to marry her about five minutes after we met."

"That's too friendly."

Brand nodded.

Sorrow turned back to the sword fight between Poppy and Slate. Slate obviously had the upper hand, but Poppy was making up for her lack of experience with speed and agility. Slate parried every blow, but she easily tumbled and rolled away from any attack he launched. She ducked beneath his latest swing, jumping forward, rolling into a ball, then springing back to her feet only inches in front of Sorrow.

"Sorrow!" Poppy said. "Slate's teaching me to be a knight!"

"Girls can't be knights!" Cinnamon shouted from her seat on the aftcastle.

"Not true," Bigsby answered. "Like my ancestor Queen Alabaster Brightmoon, I'm also a famous knight of the church."

"Then why aren't you down here training?" Poppy asked, placing her hands on her hips.

"My abilities are innate in my royal blood. Before I could even walk, my father placed me in the saddle atop his finest steed and I bested twenty men at jousting. I need no training."

Poppy fixed her eyes on Sorrow. The girl circled her finger next to her skull as she silently mouthed, "He's crazy."

"Be that as it may," Sorrow said, "your sister is correct that you can't be a knight."

"Ma says that a Wanderer can be anything she wants to be."

"But being a knight isn't merely a profession," said Sorrow. "It comes with a lot of religious baggage. Wanderers can't be knights because they don't believe in the Divine Author."

"I'll convert," said Poppy.

"Please don't let your mother hear you say that," said Brand. "She'll skin me alive for giving you that book."

"What book?" Sorrow asked.

"When I took possession of the ship, I found a dog-eared copy of *Champions of the Book* tucked in behind the mattress in the captain's cabin. It's a history, sort of. Mostly its blood-drenched legends of knights battling monsters, witches, and dragons. I immediately thought of Poppy."

"Why?"

"Did you ever see the books she read on the *Freewind?*"

"No."

Poppy said, "I like reading about battles. The bloodier, the better."

"Is this appropriate reading material for a child?" Sorrow asked.

"No!" said Cinnamon. "It makes her mean. She's always hitting people!"

"I'm not mean," Poppy grumbled. "You're just a —"

"Poppy is rambunctious," said Slate. "Full of energy and daring, but lacking formal training. She would make a fine warrior."

Sorrow raised an eyebrow. "So… you believe it's okay for women to fight? That's not exactly a tenet of chivalry."

Slate shrugged. "I suppose it's not. But, somehow, it feels right to me that women should engage in combat. You certainly held your own in battle."

"By the seven stars!" Poppy exclaimed as she bent over to look down into the hold at Sorrow's serpent form. "It's true!"

"Don't be alarmed by my appearance," Sorrow said. "I'm still the same woman you knew."

"Alarmed?" Poppy said, dropping to her chest and stretching her arm down. "This is amazing!" She ran her fingers along Sorrow's scales. "You're like a dragon!"

Cinnamon was suddenly at the hold as well, bending over to stare at Sorrow's tail.

"Come out into the light!" she said.

Sorrow was surprised by the reaction, but complied by slithering up the steps until she was completely on deck.

"I thought Jetsam was lying," said Cinnamon.

"You look just like Avaris!" said Poppy.

"What?" Sorrow was bewildered. What could this girl know about Avaris?

Poppy ran across the deck and grabbed a bag lying next to the mast. As she ran back, she thrust her hand into the bag and pulled out a book. The tome was leather bound and thick, with dog-eared pages and a spine that had seen better days. She flipped through the yellowed paper until she found the page she was seeking. "This is Avaris!"

She held the book towards her and Sorrow's stomach clenched.

An old woodcut portrayed Avaris as a demon with a serpent's body from the waist down. Avaris also had fangs, and fins for ears, not to mention menacing talons in place of hands.

"Beyond the obvious, I don't see the resemblance," said Sorrow.

"Your scales are so smooth," Cinnamon said, lightly running her fingers along Sorrow's tail.

"It's impolite to touch others without permission," Sorrow said.

Cinnamon drew her hand back, looking hurt.

"They're children," said Slate. "It's natural they'd be curious."

"My scales are sharp," said Sorrow. "She could injure herself."

"You have to play with us!" said Poppy. "You can be a dragon, and Slate and I will be the knights that slay you!"

"I'm uncertain why I would find that entertaining."

"It's merely play," said Slate.

Sorrow furrowed her brow. She hadn't expected the dragon-slayer she'd allied herself with to play well with children. To possibly be a destroyer worthy of discussion in hell, Slate was proving to be unexpectedly… *nice.*

"Is something bothering you?" Slate asked.

"You?" she said, noting the change in his grammar. "What happened to the thous and thees?"

"No one else speaks that way," Slate said with a shrug. "I've adapted."

Sorrow regretted wasting so much time below deck sulking. If Slate was a magical creation, it's possible he was programmed to adopt the mannerisms of those surrounding him to better fit in. She should be the one shaping his personality rather than leaving him in the hands of children.

"If you need a sparring partner to hone your skills in combat, you shouldn't battle these girls," she said. "As it happens, I've spent much of my life avoiding hand to hand combat, but suspect that will be more difficult from now on. I can craft swords of unnatural sharpness. You can teach me to use them effectively."

"It would be my honor," he said, bowing toward her. "But I shall continue training Poppy, as she continues to teach me."

"He's forgotten a lot about being a knight," said Poppy. "He didn't remember the code."

"The code?" Sorrow asked, thinking of the letter she couldn't read.

"The Code of Knighthood," said Slate. He straightened his spine and pulled back his shoulders, placing his hand over his heart. "A knight shall be brave, courteous, and kind, obedient to his king, a defender of his faith, and a champion to all men of virtue."

Sorrow crossed her arms. "That might mean more if you could remember your king or your faith."

"Aye," he said, wistfully. "I mean, yes."

"Even if he's lost his memory, he's still brave, courteous, and kind," said Poppy. "You can see it in his eyes."

Sorrow looked at his face. His dark eyes still reminded her of cold, hard stone. Despite his newly revealed gentleness, she could still see in his visage that Slate was a man capable of remorseless violence. Perhaps Poppy saw in his eyes only what she wished to see.

"I think his eyes are dreamy," Bigsby chimed in. He gave Slate a dainty wave with his gloved hand.

Slate looked uncomfortable as he turned his back to the dwarf and said to Sorrow, "Let's go below and examine your swords. If you wish advice on how best to use them, I should be familiar with your weapons."

They headed down the stairs. Once they were out of sight of Bigsby, Slate whispered, "I'm told that the short, portly woman is a princess. But I'm beginning to suspect she may not even be female!"

Slate looked bewildered as Sorrow laughed so hard that tears came to her eyes. It was a relief, of sort, to discover she still had the capacity to find something funny. When she wiped the last of the tears from her cheeks and caught her breath, she found her ribs were sore. She had a lot of ribs.

HER RIBS CONTINUED to suffer abuse in the coming days as Slate made good on his promise to train her. Her strength and speed were better than ever, but he still had no trouble slipping past her best defenses and whacking her flanks with the flat of his wooden sparring sword. After nearly a week of training, she grew frustrated, and threw down her blades.

"I give up!" she said. "I don't know why I thought I could do this."

"You can do it," he said. "You've learned a great deal in the last week. Once or twice you've actually turned my sword aside."

"My ribs are black and blue. I thought that one of the virtues of a knight was to be kind. What's kind about beating me to a pulp?"

"Do you enjoy pain?"

"No!"

"Then you definitely wouldn't enjoy having a real sword cut into your flesh. I tap you just enough to provide you with an incentive not to get hit."

"But the problem is that this isn't real combat," she said. "When I do engage in violence, I always strike to kill. I've never been in a fight that lasted more than thirty seconds. I can't really attack you with the full force of my powers. I've no desire to hurt you."

"Perhaps I need to hit you harder. You need not hold back against me."

Sorrow clenched her fists, thinking of the entropic forces she'd managed to suppress so well for the last week. Her body hadn't changed since she'd stopped using those powers. She said, "Let us hope, for both our sakes, I continue to hold back."

Before their conversation could go further, Sage shouted from the crow's nest, "Ship!"

Sorrow rose to twice Slate's height and scanned the surrounding sea. She saw no ship, but Sage's abilities let her spot ships many miles away.

"Where? How many?" Gale shouted from her position at the wheel.

"Only the one. Just beyond the horizon, dead ahead."

"What flag do they fly?"

"The flag of King Brightmoon, but it's probably a deception," said Sage. "I know this ship. It's the *Seahorse!*"

"Wonderful," said Gale, with a sigh.

Sorrow slithered back toward the wheel where Gale stood. "Is there a problem?"

"The *Seahorse* is a pirate ship," said Gale. She shook her head. "A real pirate ship, I mean."

Sorrow understood why Gale had felt the need to explain this. Her entire family had been branded pirates after they'd freed slaves from a fellow Wanderer's ship. The Wanderers had recently engaged in a civil war over whether it was against the values of the Wanderers to accept slaves as cargo. Gale's family had been on the losing side.

"So the *Seahorse* might try to board us?" Sorrow asked.

Gale shook her head. "We won't be getting anywhere near them. Between my control of the wind and Sage's ability to see them before they see us, we'll just slip around them."

"Of course. It's just that you sounded bothered when you learned it was the *Seahorse*."

"To be honest, the only good news I heard during the length of the pirate wars was a report that the *Seahorse* had been sunk by Brightmoon's fleet. Captain Stallion and I have something of a history."

"A romantic history?" asked Sorrow.

Gale looked genuinely offended. "No. Eight years ago, he raided my cousin's ship, the *Stormfront*. Piracy is just a day-to-day part of the business when you make your living on the sea, and my cousin attempted to dissuade Stallion from harming her ship or crew with a sizable bribe. Many pirates are merely businessmen, but Captain Stallion is motivated by sadism even more than greed. I'll spare you the details of what unfolded on the *Stormfront*, and say only that he occupied the ship for three days, misusing and abusing the crew in the most horrific fashion. Under other circumstances, I wouldn't steer away. I'd race right toward him for the chance to hang his head from my bowsprit. Alas, I may be captain of the *Circus*, but I'm not the owner. My first duty is to keep the ship and its passengers safe. My revenge against Stallion must wait."

"We need not endanger this ship," said Mako, coming back to join the conversation. Mako was the eldest child aboard at twenty-one. He was tall and sleek-muscled, with long ink-black hair that hung down his back in a perfect glistening stripe. Despite the near perfection of his body, his face was disturbing to look upon. His mouth was twice as wide as an ordinary man's, and when he spoke he revealed row upon row of saw-like teeth in his muscular jaws. "It was sheer luck Stallion escaped when we ran into him near the Isle of Apes. I've nothing to fear from him. I'll just swim over to his vessel and bore a hole in the bottom. When his crew hits the water, I can easily finish them off."

"No," said Gale. "We've been hired to sail to the Silver Isles. We aren't being paid to settle old grudges. Also, we don't even know if Captain Stallion's still alive. Just because he once captained the *Seahorse* doesn't mean he's still in charge."

"Oh, he's still alive," said Sage, looking down from the crow's nest. "I see him on the deck. Even if I didn't have my magic, he's not a tough figure to spot."

Sorrow wondered what that comment meant, and apparently Gale read the question in her face.

"Stallion is only human from the waist up," she explained. "From the waist down, he has the body of a jackass."

"Inhuman scum," Mako cursed, the syllables spilling without a hint of irony from his shark-like jaws.

"He's a half-seed?" asked Sorrow.

"No," said Gale. "Ten years ago he was human. But, as I mentioned, he has a sadistic streak. Unfortunately for him, he got rough in the sack with the wrong woman. One of his victims proved to be a bone-weaver. She used her power over flesh to graft his torso onto a donkey. She told him if he was intent on behaving as a jackass, she would make him look like one as well."

"Maybe we should stop chit-chatting and start taking some evasive action," Sage called down. "They're heading directly toward us."

"Do they see us?" asked Gale.

"I don't see how," said Sage. "We're still over their horizon. But, if I didn't know better, I'd say they were adjusting their course to intercept us."

"Luckily, they don't know who they're dealing with," said Gale, turning the wheel hard to starboard. "Mako, go wake Rigger and Jetsam. I want all hands on deck until we're well clear."

"Sure, Ma."

"Sure, *Captain*. We're employees now. We must be more professional."

"Right," Mako said tersely. "Captain."

The ship lurched as the wind shifted and the *Circus* turned due north. They sailed on this course for about five minutes before Sage reported, "They're turning. They're on a course that will intersect ours."

"That can't be a coincidence," said Rigger as he came back to the wheel. Rigger was a few years younger than Mako, a thin and lanky figure who always had bags under his eyes. "There's no reason for them to change direction out here on the high seas."

Gale said, "How are they seeing us?"

"Another clairvoyant?" asked Mako.

"Look up," said Rigger.

All eyes turned toward a sky mottled with clouds. A small dark speck drifted across an expanse of blue between the white puffs.

Sage stared into her spyglass. "Crap," she said. "It's another half-animal like Stallion. This is an old woman with wings like a vulture. She's looking straight at us, and pointing in our direction with her toes. Stallion is watching her with his spyglass."

"Get Brand," Gale said to Mako.

Brand had gone below deck to have breakfast with the Princess in her cabin and had yet to come back. Mako ran to get them and five minutes later everyone aboard the ship stood on the deck.

Sage pointed toward the horizon with her spyglass. "They're getting closer."

Indeed. Sorrow could see the white sails as specks bobbing on the horizon. They were still quite distant. She squinted, but the ships were still too far apart for her to see Captain Stallion. If he really had run afoul of a bone-weaver with sufficient talent to weave together a man and a donkey, she wanted to learn that weaver's identity.

"Here's our first option, sir," Gale said to Brand. "We keep heading toward the Silver Isles. I'm fairly confident I can outmaneuver them, but can't guarantee it. I may hate Stallion's guts, but he wouldn't still be alive if he weren't a damn good sailor."

"What's the second option?" asked Brand.

"We turn tail. They're only getting closer because we're heading in converging directions. If we turn, I'm certain I can outrun them. I know nothing about their aerial spy, but she can't stay aloft forever. Assuming she can't see us at night, we turn back toward the Silver Isles at sunset and slip past them in the dark."

Brand stroked his chin. "Effectively, we'd lose a day of travel. That doesn't seem such a high price to pay."

"Why should we pay any price?" asked Mako. "Option three: we take the fight to them. Stallion has a price on his head. We can come out of this with a profit."

"Mako!" Gale said. "We don't kill people for profit. If I've sacrificed everything to not trade in live bodies, I'll be damned if I'll sully myself by trading in dead ones. If we kill Stallion, we do it for justice, not to collect a chest full of moons."

"Yes, *Captain*," said Mako. "But you don't have the final word on this matter. Brand does."

Brand looked thoughtful as he said, "So, we'd be ridding the world of a known pirate and earning a nice reward?"

"If rewards are your only motive," Gale said, "how do we know you won't one day turn us in? The gold on our heads spends just as well."

"Oh, that won't be a problem," said Bigsby, drawing back his shoulders and thrusting out his stuffed cleavage. He took a deep breath and stretched out his hands, as if encompassing the whole of the ship, as he said, in formal tones, "In the name of the Brightmoon throne, I hereby grant all members of the Romer family an immediate and unconditional pardon!"

"Well, that's a weight off my shoulders," said Rigger.

Brand sighed. "Mako, I'm sure you could take these jokers out by yourself, but I don't see any reason to risk it. I've been gone from the Silver City a long time. I'm returning home with a new fortune and long-lost family." He placed his hand on Bigsby's shoulder. "I'm not going to risk it all just to teach some pirate a lesson."

"Well reasoned, sir," said a voice from the bow.

Everyone looked up. A young boy, no older than ten, stood on the bowsprit. Water beaded on his golden-tanned skin and seeped from his white cotton breeches. He was skinny; you could count the ribs on his shirtless torso. His black hair was cropped close to his scalp, and his eyes were dark and intense as he looked at them.

"Who the devil are you?" Brand asked.

"An interesting choice of words," said the boy. "For it seems my role in life is to be the eternal adversary. Once, I believed I was the savior of mankind. Now, I suspect, I'm the death of it. But, today, I'm merely enjoying the carefree life of a seafaring scoundrel. We've come to take your ship, your treasure, and your women."

"Oh, heavens," gasped Bigsby, placing the back of his palm against his forehead.

Gale put her hands on her hips. "Aren't you a little young, boy? Why do you need women? To have your diaper changed?"

"Amusing." The boy chuckled, hopping to the deck next to the anchor.

"Grab this idiot before he hurts himself," Gale said to Mako.

"Idiot?" said the boy. "You wound me. I assure you, I'm the most educated person on this ship."

"Certainly the most talkative," said Mako, stalking forward.

The boy waited patiently. He was unarmed. Mako was at least two feet taller. Yet the boy's spiky red aura radiated out several yards around him, making him look like a giant in Sorrow's eyes. "Be careful," she warned.

"Yes," said the boy, with a grin. "Be careful. You don't know who it is you face."

"In fairness, Brand did ask your name," said Mako, reaching for the boy's arm.

As he leaned forward, the boy took him by the wrist and spun his shoulder into Mako's guts. Half a second later, Mako toppled heels over head across the railing. "What the…" he cried, before a loud splash muffled his voice.

"You! Down below!" the boy shouted toward Mako as he grabbed the anchor. "Be a friend and hold this for me, will you?" Though the anchor had to weigh more than he did, the boy tossed it overboard.

The chain went *clackety clackety clackety* as the weight dropped.

"Luckily, the sea's too deep for the anchor to catch," said Rigger.

"I would have thought an experienced sailor such as yourself could deduce from the color of the water that there's a sea mount directly beneath us," said the boy.

Just then, the ship whipped to a halt, dipping forward and throwing everyone from their feet.

Sorrow, lacking feet, remained upright, her tail wrapped around a mast to keep her stable. Not that her stability helped much. The boy somersaulted across the pitching deck faster than Sorrow's eyes could follow. There was a loud smack to her right and when she turned her head she saw that both Rigger and Gale were flat on their backs, unconscious.

Sorrow looked up. The boy was in the rigging directly above her, grinning down.

"Want a job?" he asked. "I've been staffing my pirate empire with half-seeds and braided-beings. You'd fit right in."

Suddenly, there was a grunt off to Sorrow's side. The boy reached out his hand almost casually and caught a belaying pin that had just been thrown at him by Slate, who'd made it back to his feet. The boy flicked his arm like a whip and the small wooden club flew back at his attacker, bouncing off the center of Slate's forehead. The big man winced, but seemed unharmed. With a growl, he leapt into the rigging and began to climb after the child.

"Sorry for the interruption," the boy said to Sorrow as he climbed higher. "By now, it should be apparent that I'm winning. Care to join my crew?"

"Who are you again?" Sorrow asked, utterly befuddled.

"My name is Numinous Pilgrim. You may have heard of me as the Golden Child, or perhaps the Omega Reader."

Sorrow's eyebrows shot up. She *had* heard of him. "You're the perfect being that the Church of the Book has been waiting for?" The words sounded odd as they came from her lips. The book that the church was founded upon was far too sacred for any ordinary man to dare open. For the last thousand years, the church had been awaiting the arrival of the Omega Reader, the flawless human who could open the book without its holy purity burning out his sinful soul. She'd never believed in such a being, but she'd never seen an aura like this before.

Numinous leapt to the mast, then bounced to another set of ropes, easily avoiding Slate's outstretched arm.

"I didn't expect the Omega Reader to be a common pirate," Sorrow said, as Jetsam rose in the air behind him. Jetsam was carrying the light rapier that she'd seen him use to great effect. If she kept the boy's attention, maybe Jetsam could finish him.

"I would hardly call myself common," said Numinous. He shifted sideways as Jetsam lunged. The tip of the thin blade poked through the air where his belly button had been a half-second before. Numinous snatched the rapier away, then kicked Jetsam in the throat, sending him to crash on the deck below, gagging.

Numinous stretched the rapier toward the rigging Slate climbed and made two fast slices. Slate frowned as he found that the rope supporting his weight was no longer attached to anything. He fell to the deck, his head smacking hard on the wood.

Sorrow asked, "Why, exactly, if you're the savior that the church has been waiting for, are you out here robbing boats and threatening women?"

"It's a curious truth that the Omega Reader is at once both a savior and destroyer," said Numinous. "If it's my fate to bring an end to this wicked world, I thought I should first investigate the true nature of sin. So far, the *Seahorse* has been an entertaining classroom."

Numinous dropped from the rigging as Brand started to rise. He'd been knocked unconscious earlier when the ship slammed to a halt and had been sprawled face down. Numinous drove his foot into the back of Brand's skull, smashing his face into the deck, rendering him still once more. By now, Poppy had recovered. She grabbed a belaying pin and pressed it against the mast. When she let go, it shot toward Numinous. Her mermaid gift was the power to 'pop' anything she touched, turning anything she placed her hands on into an impromptu missile.

The boy made a show of yawning as he leaned three inches to the left so that the pin flew past his ear.

He cast a quick glance toward Sage in the rigging, then his eyes darted back to Poppy, who was fishing about for something else to fire at him, and Cinnamon, who was hiding behind the hatch that led to the cabins below. He looked back to Sorrow. "Your only remaining allies are three unarmed girls. Ready to switch sides?"

Sorrow rose, riding her serpent body ever higher, until she loomed over Numinous by a good ten feet.

"You seek an education in wickedness?" she asked, drawing her swords, "You've just met your final teacher."

9 - SPOILS OF WAR

BEFORE SORROW COULD act, Poppy somersaulted toward Numinous, bouncing high enough that she could land perched upon his shoulders. Numinous grinned as he stood frozen, almost as if he was looking forward to the attack.

Poppy's hands pressed down on his shoulders just as Slate rose from the deck barely two yards away, shaking his head. He wasted no time in spotting the boy and lunged, attempting to tackle Numinous by driving his shoulder into his gut.

Only Slate's tackle came just as Poppy bounced off and Numinous shot straight up with the speed of a cork popping from a champagne bottle. Instead of Slate hitting Numinous, he wound up slamming into Poppy as she dropped back to the deck. The force of his blow was powerful enough to send the girl flying. Her head banged against the ship's rail with a loud *WHACK* and she tumbled limp into the sea.

"That was unfortunate," Numinous said from above. He was standing on one the yardarms of the foresail. He'd apparently escaped being launched completely off the ship by grabbing a rope. "I know that legends say that Wanderers can't drown, but I wonder how they fare unconscious in shark infested waters while bleeding from a head wound?"

Sorrow knew Numinous was trying to taunt her into jumping into the sea to rescue Poppy. But if she rescued the girl, she would leave everyone else aboard to the mercy of this boy.

She'd already made her choice when Slate jumped to the railing, scanned the waters beneath him, then dived in.

"Noble, isn't he?" Numinous asked. "I wasn't certain which way he'd go. Something is masking his aura." He squinted as he stared at Sorrow. "Either that, or he has no soul. While you, intriguingly, seem to have two."

"Then you're outnumbered!" Sorrow cried out, brandishing her swords as her serpentine body uncoiled to launch her heavenward. Numinous smiled as he jumped to meet her attack. His feet flashed over her face and an instant later he landed on her back. He slid along her smooth scales, zipping along her spine to reach the deck.

Sorrow twisted around and the boy lunged toward her torso. He trailed a long length of rope that had been coiled near the main mast. He kicked hard and sailed over her head, the rope spiraling behind him. The hemp wrapped around Sorrow's forearms. Her wrists clapped together forcefully enough to knock her swords from her grip, which was fortunate since her bound fists smacked against her throat as the line went taut. Despite her supernatural strength, she was helpless as the boy formed a makeshift pulley by running the rope through the base of the anchor chain. He reeled her in, until the back of her helmet smashed against the large iron loop. As she struggled, she felt something tighten around the tip of her tail. The lower half of her body began to rise into the air. She caught a glimpse of a rope whirring through a pulley high in the riggings. In seconds, she was completely upended, stretched with the tip of her tail high in the air and her bound neck and wrists fastened to the deck in such a fashion that her armored shoulders were pressed hard against the polished wood.

Numinous crouched beside her, "I apologize for the rough treatment. I hope you'll take a moment to calmly contemplate your circumstances. It should be obvious that I can anticipate your every move. I see your truths quite plainly. Your predominant narrative is that you crave power. This has led you to make use of forces beyond your control. I'm the living embodiment of control. Serve me, and I'll teach you how to see past your own lies. Only in truth will you find mastery."

"I'll serve no one," she growled. "Least of all a brat like you!"

Numinous chuckled. "You'll remain defiant for a while longer. But your surrender is inevitable. I see it quite clearly."

Sorrow bit her lower lip. Was the boy onto something? Perhaps she could simply pretend to surrender. Could she bargain joining his crew in exchange for sparing the Romers?

She grimaced. Whatever the boy thought he knew about her, the one thing she knew beyond doubt was that she'd never surrender. She had only to tap into a fraction of Rott's power and the ropes that bound her would crumble to dust. She could open the gate to Rott's full power and the boy would be devoured by flies. But, if she did so, would she lose even more of her humanity?

"You're afraid of something," he said. "Something you believe is more terrible than me. What is it that troubles you?"

"You honestly don't want to find out," Sorrow whispered.

At that moment, the hatch to the cabins beneath banged open. Sorrow's eyes darted toward the noise.

Bigsby stood in the opening, wearing a full breastplate and helmet, his limbs draped in chain mail. He brandished a large mace with both hands as he cried, "Face me, villain! You may have bested these common sailors but you now face Princess Innocent Brightmoon, champion of the oppressed!"

Numinous burst out laughing.

Bigsby clanked and clattered as he advanced across the deck at a pace more akin to a tortoise than a hare. Numinous yawned loudly, crossing his arms as the dwarf approached. He said, "Could you pick up the pace, 'princess?' I'd like to get back to making a deal with the snake-woman."

Bigsby responded by bounding forward and swinging his mace. Numinous leaned back to avoid the blow. To Sorrow's surprise, a loud *WHACK* followed. Numinous fell to his back, clutching his right cheek with his hand.

His eyes were wide as he spat out blood and mumbled, "How did you —"

Bigsby answered by shuffling forward and swinging the mace over his head. Numinous rolled to keep his brains from being bashed in, but Bigsby still managed to strike a glancing blow to the boy's shoulder. Numinous made it to his hands and knees and tried to crawl away, but Bigsby pursued him, driving the mace into the boy's ribs.

Numinous sucked in air through clenched teeth as he rolled across the deck. He stared at the dwarf with terror in his eyes.

"Your reality… it's fractured," he whimpered, his voice trembling. "You exist outside the truth!"

Bigsby swung his mace again and Numinous rolled away barely in time. Sorrow was surprised the blows were even close. Despite her poor skills with weapons, she was certain she could have avoided Bigsby's blows, given that he was weighed down by armor and swinging a weapon twice as heavy as he could effectively handle. Perhaps Numinous wasn't quite as in control of events as he'd like to believe.

Just then, soft footsteps whispered across the deck toward Sorrow. She turned her eyes toward the sound and found Cinnamon Romer dashing from her hiding place with a knife in her grasp. The red-headed girl dropped to her knees in front of Sorrow and whispered, "Hold still." She began to saw at the ropes binding Sorrow.

At the same instant, Sorrow felt vibrations near her tail. The second her wrists were free she turned her gaze upward and saw Sage Romer hanging upside down from a rope in the crow's nest, grasping the cord that bound Sorrow's tail. With a slash of a dagger, Sorrow was free. Her tail fell against the main mast and instinctively coiled around it.

"Mind if I borrow this?" she asked as she took the butcher knife from Cinnamon.

With her tail braced high above on the mast, her torso flew into the air to get a better view of the fight between Bigsby and Numinous. The boy was now near the back of the ship, with a fresh cut above his left eyebrow. Bigsby had apparently gotten in another lick.

Bigsby had the mace swung back over his shoulders with both hands and was lumbering forward to deliver another blow. Numinous furrowed his brow as he studied the dwarf's motions.

Bigsby swung. Numinous jumped aside at the last possible second before bouncing forward and grasping Bigsby's shining helmet with both hands. He snatched it from the dwarf's head, revealing the platinum blonde wig.

Numinous clasped the dwarf by the cheeks, stared into his eyes, and shouted, "Your madness shall lift! Be healed!"

He let go of Bigsby's face. The dwarf staggered backwards, tripping and falling on his butt. He reached up and pulled the blonde locks from his head and stared at them with a look of terror. He looked around and saw Sorrow, Sage, and Cinnamon staring at him.

"Oh god," he whispered.

Numinous picked up Bigsby's mace from where it had fallen.

He limped toward the dwarf, lifting the mace high. He spat out blood as he grumbled, "Enjoy your moment of clarity, 'princess.' It will end when I splatter your brains across this deck."

Sorrow flashed toward Numinous. The boy saw her coming and leapt aside, but his actions were plainly impaired by his injuries. She failed to grab him, but her fingers did close upon the shaft of the mace. He released it, dancing across the deck to land on the railing near the anchor chain. He looked back over his shoulder and grinned.

Sorrow's heart sank. The *Seahorse* was now barely a hundred yards away. Fifty men stood upon the deck, many holding grappling hooks. Most were bestial blends of man and animal. A single ten-year-old boy had left the *Circus* all but defenseless against this crew of monsters.

"You win, kid!" Sage Romer shouted from high in the riggings. "As the most senior officer still conscious, I'd like to talk surrender!"

Numinous looked up. He frowned as he said, "You're lying. You're trying to distract me so –"

At that moment, Cinnamon Romer rose from behind an overturned barrel and dashed toward Numinous. He turned, facing her, and jumped for a rope overhead. Her fingers barely brushed the tips of his toes as he climbed into the rigging.

The small contact proved sufficient. Cinnamon had the power to control a person's taste buds. The boy's face contorted in a mask of horrified disgust. His body convulsed as he began to violently vomit. His trembling fingers lost their grip on the rope and he fell to the deck, landing hard. Any hope he would be knocked out by the fall was quashed as he rose to his hands and knees, his body heaving as he threw up once more.

Sorrow assumed that Numinous was too busy trying to purge the foul taste from his mouth to pay attention to her. She lunged toward him, the knife in one hand, the mace in the other, prepared to put him out of his misery.

Alas, her blows bit into the vomit covered deck as the boy again displayed inhuman reflexes in rolling aside. Spitting with each motion, he jumped to the rails.

Wiping his lips, he whispered, "My troops can finish you!" He spat again, and flipped backward into the sea.

"Mako!" Cinnamon shouted, leaning over the rail. "Mako! Catch him!"

"Mako can't hear you," Sage shouted down. "He's at the *Seahorse*. He headed there the second Numinous threw him overboard."

"He left us even though we were under attack?"

Sage shrugged. "I doubt he thought we'd have a problem beating a little kid. You know he'd rather tear into a ship full of bloodthirsty pirates than climb back on board and fight a boy half his age. How much longer before the kid stops feeling sick?"

Cinnamon shook her head. "I only had contact for less than a second, but I hit him with weeping cheese."

"Weeping cheese?" asked Sorrow.

"Sometimes cheese aboard ships gets infested with a kind of translucent, gelatinous maggot," said Sage. "When they break through the rind, it looks like the cheese is crying."

"It's the worst thing I've ever put in my mouth," said Cinnamon. "Believe it or not, some rich people consider it a delicacy."

"Let's hope there are no rich people among these half-seeds," Sorrow said as she watched the *Seahorse* draw to within a hundred feet. "We're about to be overrun."

"I can assure you that we aren't," said Sage, pointing toward the stern of the *Seahorse*.

Sorrow spotted Mako climbing the massive rudder. He was biting through the heavy iron bands that held the beams together. The *Seahorse* lurched as her rudder suddenly tore loose. Even from a hundred feet away, Sorrow heard Captain Stallion curse, "What the devil?"

A dozen pirates ran to the stern and peered over. Mako reached up and flung the closest few into the waves, then leapt to the stern rail and shouted, "Fight for your lives, you scurvy dogs! I take no prisoners!"

Cinnamon ran past Sorrow on her way toward her mother. She grabbed Gale by the shoulders. The older woman's face contorted, her nose wrinkling, and she suddenly sat up, spitting.

"Sorry," Cinnamon said. "I had to wake you fast. You should be tasting mint now."

Gale wiped her mouth on her sleeve. "That's much better." She looked around. "What's going on?"

Sage shouted down the current battle status as Cinnamon moved to revive Rigger.

Sorrow wondered what had happened to Poppy and Slate, and moved to the rail to see if she could spot them. She found the big man climbing the anchor chain with the now conscious Poppy clinging to his shoulders.

"Are you both okay?" she shouted.

"I'm fine!" Poppy cried.

"I'm eager to hit someone," said Slate. "Where's the boy?"

"He went into the water," said Sage. "For some reason, I can't see him. But if you need a little violence, we have a whole ship at the ready."

"You can't touch Stallion," Gale cried. "He's mine!"

"I'm not sure that got explained to Mako," said Sage.

"Jetsam and Brand are awake!" Cinnamon shouted.

"Where's Bigs — the princess?" Brand asked groggily.

Bigsby stumbled past, his wig in his hand, the kohl around his eyes running down his cheeks. "She's going below to find a bottle of rum," he said softly as he unclasped his breastplate, which clattered to the deck.

Gale paid the dwarf no mind as she readied her twin cutlasses and jumped to the railing.

"Ready, Rigger?" she asked.

"Bring the wind, Captain," the young man answered as he took the wheel.

On the *Seahorse*, chaos had broken loose. A half dozen pirates now flailed in the waves behind the ship. Mako had liberated a cutlass from one of the cutthroats and was busily cutting throats. Sorrow couldn't guess how many dead bodies lay around him. Suddenly, a short, shirtless pirate covered with quills broke from the pack and flicked his arms toward Mako, unleashing a hail of barbed darts. Mako flinched as the tiny missiles turned his face into a pincushion. His eyes scrunched shut from the pain. Blinded, he dropped his cutlass and dove back into the sea.

The *Circus* turned toward the *Seahorse* and closed fast. Brand intercepted Bigsby before he went below deck.

"Don't take off your armor just yet, Princess," Brand advised. "There's about to be a big fight. Time to bring a little Brightmoon justice to these pirates!"

"I'm not a princess," Bigsby said with a sigh. "I'm a fishmonger. You know that."

Brand raised an eyebrow. "I'm just happy to hear that you know it!"

"Happy? Now that my secret's out, I'm ruined," Bigsby moaned. "It's hard enough being a dwarf among the ruffians of Commonground. Now that everyone knows about my... other wardrobe... I'm doomed."

Sorrow's attention turned to a discarded element of Bigsby's wardrobe. She slithered over and picked up the gleaming breastplate from the deck. The front and back halves of the armor clanged together on their leather straps as she lifted them, taking a closer look to see if they'd work for the plan she had in mind. Despite the smallness of his limbs, Bigsby's torso was as large as most men. "If you don't need this any more, I've got a use for it."

"Take it," Bigsby said, shaking his head. "I can't fight. I'm nothing but a coward."

"I don't believe that," said Brand. "I've watched you charge at a dragon without batting an eye. If Princess Innocent was brave, you're brave."

Sorrow had no time to listen to Brand's attempt to cheer his despondent brother. She snaked around and headed for Slate, who stood at the rail with his fists clenched as the space narrowed between the two ships.

She held Bigsby's mace toward him. "I'm sure you can bang some heads together with your bare hands, but you might do more damage with this."

"Aye," he said, taking it from her.

"I thought you might also benefit from a little armor," she said, presenting him the breast plate.

"It's too small," he said.

"I can adapt it," she said, lining the iron plate up to his chest. "Hold still."

She bent the edges of the plate outward, stretching them to fit over Slate's impressive musculature. She spun him around and worked on the back, molding and sculpting the metal to his form. She tightened the leather straps, then spun him back around. She glanced back toward where Bigsby's helmet had fallen. She flicked it with the end of her tail, sending it bouncing across the deck toward her. She caught it and plopped it onto Slate's head. Satisfied that it fit without any further adjustment, she ran her hands along Slate's chest to smooth out her handiwork. Slate stared at her intently as she worked.

A little too intently.

She suddenly felt awkward. Was she really trying to perfect his armor? Or were her fingers lingering on his muscles for reasons she was unwilling to admit?

"That should be good enough," she said.

"Your eyes," he whispered. "I… remember them."

"We've seen each other every day for over a week. You've not had much of a chance to forget them," she said.

"No…" His face sagged as he shook his head. "It's… it's like a memory from… long ago. Of you outfitting me for battle. But now… it's gone."

Sorrow pressed her lips tightly together. Was he merely remembering when she'd fitted him with his glass armor?

But there was no more time to ponder such things, because the *Circus* was now within grappling range of the pirate vessel.

Captain Romer leapt beside Slate and Sorrow. "The three of us lead the charge," she said. "Mako's already in the water and Jetsam's heading down now. Knock everyone you can into the drink. My sons will make swift work of them."

Cinnamon ran up, with Sorrow's swords in her grasp. "I figured you might need these."

Sorrow grabbed the blades. She looked across the narrow gap to the assembled pirates. Despite Mako's attack, there were still at least three dozen. Among the pirate ranks she spotted a half-bear, a half-boar, and a long-jawed monstrosity that might have been half-crocodile. This wasn't going to be an easy fight.

Gale cried, "Poppy! Clear a path!"

Gale stepped aside as a barrel shot past her, splintering against the horns of a goat-man at the rail of the *Seahorse*, knocking him backwards. Gale raised both her cutlasses and leapt across the six-foot gap dividing the ships, shouting, "The moment you chose to be pirates is the moment you chose to die!" She landed where the goat-man had stood and severed the head of a dog-faced boy who'd had the misfortune of standing too close.

Slate followed Gale's lead, easily crossing the gap between the rolling ships despite his new burden of armor. He plowed into the crowd, swinging his mace in wide arcs that sent pirates flying.

Sorrow stretched across the gap. She had the misfortune of facing off with the half-bear, who slapped away the blade she drove toward his left shoulder and swatted her face with his massive right hand, full of claws. Her helmet spared her any cuts as the man-bear's nails slid along the glass, but the impact left her seeing stars.

He opened jaws full of ugly teeth and made a thrust for her neck. The pirate's charge was halted by Slate's mace, which drove his snout-like nose back into his brains.

She had no time to thank him. Her serpent half had now slithered fully on board and was being attacked by a dozen swords at once. Her scales proved impervious to the combined assault. As if it had a mind of its own, her muscular tail whipped back and forth, knocking pirates overboard.

Sorrow turned to face the alligator-man as Gale Romer flew past, swinging over the battle on a rope, to land on the upper deck where Captain Stallion watched the fight unfolding in the company of the porcupine half-seed. The quill covered creature bristled as it readied an attack on Gale, but with a flash of steel its head tumbled from its shoulders.

Stallion turned, looking at first as if he might be getting ready to flee, but instead he kicked out with his back hooves catching Gale in the chest. She went flying, falling to the lower deck, where a mob of pirates jostled for the chance to finish her off.

None reached her. Instead, the rigging unknotted and snaked to life, catching each of the pirates who attacked Gale by the neck. All were jerked from their feet by impromptu nooses. Sorrow glanced over her shoulder to find that Rigger had come aboard and was standing on the rail, his hand upon a line leading up to the main mast.

A few of the remaining pirates on the deck turned pale as they looked at their brethren kicking overhead. They had no need to fear death by hanging, however, as Slate plowed through their ranks, bashing skulls and breaking limbs.

Gale bounced back to her feet and again leapt for Captain Stallion. The half-horse cursed as hurricane winds whipped his hair and carried Gale toward him. But, fast as Gale moved, she was no match for his equine legs. He chose flight over fight, making a magnificent leap over the railing. He hung in the air with a look of defiance, before dropping, legs kicking, arms flailing, toward the shark-infested water.

Sorrow lingered for half a second as she tossed a pig-man into the drink, studying the water below. She never saw Stallion surface. The waves were crimson with blood and countless shark fins churned the water. Mako was climbing up the anchor chain and Jetsam had jumped into the air and was swimming up to the level of the deck.

Sorrow turned back toward the action, only to find there was none. The only two animal men still alive were rather pathetic. A half-rabbit was curled into a fetal ball by the mainmast, tugging his ears.

"I-I-I-I s-s-surrender!" he shrieked.

"We both surrender," a turtle man said in a thick, slurred voice as he slowly raised his fat, wrinkled hands.

"The b-b-boy made us d-do it!" the rabbit man cried. "I n-never wanted to be a p-p-pirate!"

Mako advanced on the cowering figure, drawing his bloodied lips wide as he growled, "I said we'd take no prisoners!"

Gale placed her hand on Mako's shoulder. "Hold! I gave no such command."

"We dare not show mercy!" Mako screamed as he spun to face his mother. "These crud aren't even fully human!"

Jetsam laughed. "That just seems funny when you've still got bits of pirate stuck between your teeth."

Mako frowned as he glared at his brother. He ran his fingers between his lips and dug around, producing an earring, and what once might have been an ear.

"There's no need to hurt us," the turtle man said. "Hopper is right. We were kidnapped by the others, but the only dirty work we ever did was swab the deck."

Mako shook his head. "If you've eaten their food, you've shared in the spoils of their plunder. Honest men would have fought their captors!"

"They w-would have k-killed us!" said Hopper.

"Better to die an honest man than to be moved by fear to wallow in a life of sin," said Slate.

"Let's just put them out of their misery," said Mako.

Gale shook her head. "We gain nothing by killing these two. If they give us no trouble, we'll spare them."

Mako crossed his arms and slunk away, sulking.

"I suppose you're not going to let us keep any of the good stuff we find, either?" Jetsam asked as he crouched over the body of a dead cat-man who had a beautifully crafted rapier in his now limp grasp.

"A Wanderer must never kill in order to enrich himself or herself," said Gale. "But we did initially attempt to avoid this fight. They brought this battle upon themselves. We may claim the spoils of a justly fought war."

She made a hand gesture toward Sage, still in the crow's nest of the *Circus*. The girl pressed her eye to her spyglass. Sorrow deduced she was searching the ship for any lurking dangers.

"Will we take possession the ship?" asked Rigger.

"I don't see the wisdom of laying claim to the only ship on the ocean more hunted than the *Freewind* was," said Gale.

"W-will you g-give us s-safe passage?" asked Hopper.

"No," said Gale.

"But the two of us aren't enough to sail this ship," said the turtle man.

"You couldn't steer if we'd left all the crew alive, what with your rudder torn to splinters," said Gale. "You're at the mercy of Abyss now. Perhaps his currents will guide you to land before you run out of food and water."

Before the half-men could beg for a different fate, Sage shouted, "You won't believe what I just found!"

"I'm almost certain I will," said Rigger, leaning against the foremast. "I've lost all capacity for surprise."

"Is it treasure?" Jetsam called out. "The proverbial pirate chest of gold?"

"It's a painting," said Sage.

Rigger furrowed his brow. "I retract my statement. I can't believe you're excited about finding a painting."

Jetsam scratched his head. "Is it… you know… a naked lady?"

Gale smacked the back of his head.

"I really think you should take a look at it," said Sage. "It's in Captain Stallion's cabin."

Sorrow was nearest to the door. She grasped the tarnished brass handle and turned it. The room stank worse than a horse stall. She covered her mouth to cut the stench, and still couldn't quite bring herself to slither into the filthy chamber. But, in the dim light, she could see a painting bolted to the wall. It was a large canvas in a gilded frame. The painting was difficult to make out; the varnish had darkened, leaving only shadowy figures. Yet, there was something about the colors and the poses she could make out that reminded her of paintings that had adorned the wall of her father's mansion. If this was the work of an old master, it could be a far more valuable prize than any gold or jewelry.

"It doesn't look like much," Mako grumbled as he pushed past Sorrow. If the stench of the room bothered him he gave no indication. He tore the frame off the wall, more roughly than Sorrow thought necessary. If it was valuable, why damage it?

Mako carried the painting into sunlight. Now the colors were brighter, the shapes clearer, though it was also more apparent that much of the painting had been splattered with various forms of filth over the years, obscuring the images. Sorrow recoiled as she understood the subject matter.

Jetsam, now floating overhead, well out of Gale's reach, said, "I was right! A naked lady!"

Indeed, one of the foreground figures was an unclothed female. But the painting didn't portray her as a figure of beauty set against some pastoral setting. Instead, the woman was bound with her wrists stretched overhead, fastened to a hook on a wooden pole. Kindling was stacked around her legs to the midpoint of her thighs. The woman's face was a mask of terror. Her head was shaved and bleeding from numerous holes in her scalp.

This was a painting of a witch being put to death.

Judging from the apparent age, the canvas could possibly have been painted during the war against the witches those long centuries ago. A trio of men stood near the woman. A truthspeaker was present, reading from a scroll. Beside him was a large man in ebony armor, carrying a sword that was painted charcoal black. He was pointing toward the woman's feet, seemingly issuing a command to the third man, a ghostly white pygmy who stood by the piled kindling with a torch in his hand.

"Isn't it amazing?" Sage asked.

Sorrow jumped. At some point, Sage had left the *Circus* and was now standing right beside her.

"I'm not amazed," said Sorrow. "My father had an extensive collection of similar art. I heard him say that one painting he most wanted for his collection had been stolen. The painting was called *The Witchbreaker*."

"The guy with the sword that could send you straight to hell?" said Jetsam.

"I suppose, if the sword did have that power, then death by flames was an act of mercy," said Slate.

Sorrow frowned at him.

"If you were to be put to death by fire, you would have time to repent your sins while the flames were building," Slate explained.

"So you think the painting's worth something?" asked Jetsam.

The painting wasn't in the best of shape, given the way the varnish had colored and cracked. Nor had Captain Stallion taken care with it. What looked like mustard hid the face of the truthspeaker, and what was almost certainly manure was smeared across the face of Stark Tower, which gave Sorrow a certain grim satisfaction. Despite the painting's poor condition, she knew it would easily find a buyer. "My father would no doubt pay to have this in his collection. The halls of our family home are adorned with similar atrocities. To keep it from his hands, I'll negotiate whatever price you consider fair. Then I shall destroy it."

"What?" Sage said. "You can't destroy this!"

"Why not?" asked Mako.

"You stumble onto a mystery like this and your first instinct is to destroy it?" asked Sage.

"What mystery?" asked Sorrow. "The Silver Isles are rife with such paintings. The Church of the Book is ever eager to celebrate the torturers of women. Entire cities are named for these ancient witch slayers."

"But —" Sage shook her head and chuckled softly. "Sorry. I'm an idiot. I sometimes forget that not everyone sees the things I see. Look." She licked her thumb and rubbed the grime obscuring the truthspeaker's features. Details of his face emerged. He was a dark-haired man with his hair pulled back into a severe ponytail. Oddly, a large red 'D' was painted on his forehead. "Don't you know who that is?"

"I can't say that I do," said Sorrow.

"That's Zetetic the Deceiver! He came to us a few years back seeking passage to the Sea of Wine."

"We didn't do business with him," Gale said. "He offered good money, but how can you enter a contract with someone who openly calls himself a Deceiver?"

"It does kind of look like him," said Jetsam. "But it can't be. Zetetic is, what, maybe 40? This painting's got to be hundreds of years old."

"I'm positive it's him," said Sage.

"I admit there's a resemblance," said Gale. "But I'm sure it's just a coincidence."

"Maybe," said Sage. "But what do you make of this?" She pulled down the sleeve of her blouse and spat on it, then scrubbed away the filth that covered Stark Tower's face.

Gale's eyes widened. Jetsam let out a low whistle. Mako's monstrous jaws gaped. Sorrow's breath caught in her throat.

In unison, they all turned to stare at Slate.

Slate cocked his head as he realized he was the target of their combined gaze. "Does something trouble thee … I mean, you?"

"I think we have a clue as to why you talk like you've walked out of a previous century," said Jetsam.

10 - SUCH A BAD THING

The Romers were still sorting through the items found aboard the *Seahorse*. Sage could identify some of the rightful owners of the stolen objects, and there was a great deal of political goodwill they could purchase among their fellow Wanderers by reuniting them with property taken by Stallion.

Slate had grown quiet after discovering his resemblance to Stark Tower. Sorrow had been speaking with Sage about the possible fate of Numinous when she'd noticed Slate discarding his armor and returning to the *Circus*. Her initial instinct had been to let him have time to think things over. Perhaps his memories would be jogged further. But she noticed that Poppy was also absent, and wondered if the girl might be trying to cheer him up. The girl's romantic notion of knights bore little resemblance to their real world cruelty, and she worried that Slate might receive false impressions from her.

Sorrow found Slate and Poppy in the galley.

"You should be excited," Poppy said to Slate as Sorrow slithered silently through the door. "Stark Tower is one of the best knights ever. He saved the whole world from evil witches!"

"Your book tells you this?" Sorrow asked.

Poppy turned her head swiftly, looking startled that Sorrow was right behind her. She swallowed, then said, "I know that not all witches are bad."

"Your book tells you that?"

Poppy shrugged. "The book really only has one kind of witch. But you're a nice witch. Aren't you?"

Sorrow frowned. It was a simple enough question. Why couldn't she bring herself to say, "Yes, I'm nice?" Instead, she said, "Can I speak to Slate in private?"

"I guess," said Poppy, who looked a little worried as she glanced at the big man. He was normally cheerful in her company, but now his expression was completely neutral.

"Leave us," he said.

Poppy left the table, leaving her book of knights resting where she'd been sitting.

The door closed behind her. Slate and Sorrow eyed each other without speaking. It had been a long day. The daylight was fading. Neither made a move to light the lantern.

"You knew who I was," he said.

"No," she said. "I didn't. And I don't. So what if you look like him? I know nothing about who you really are, or who you were before we met."

"Tell me again how we met."

"You know. You were there. I was attacked by a dragon's skeleton and you jumped up to save me."

"Jumped up."

She pressed her lips tightly together.

"Tell me everything," he said.

She sighed. "This is everything. Brand and I found you buried in the Witches Graveyard. You were in a glass coffin. We thought you were dead, but you made a remarkable recovery after the bone-dragon smashed open your casket."

Slate placed his hands upon the table and stared at them. "My nails… my hair…."

"Were rather long, yes," she said. "You may have been underground for a while."

"Then… I am Tower? Returned from the grave? Due to your magic?"

"I can assure you that I don't have the power to raise the dead. If I did, I can also assure you that I wouldn't use that power on the Witchbreaker. He deserves to rot in whatever hell may hold him."

Slate pulled the book toward him. He ran his beefy thumb along the edge of the cover.

"According to this book, the man was a hero," said Slate. "He abandoned his comfort and fortune in the Silver Isles to lead the battle against the greatest threat ever faced by the Church of the Book. He literally traveled to hell and back to acquire the weapon that turned the tide of history."

"Don't believe everything you read," said Sorrow, crossing her arms. "You saw the damn painting. The witches didn't have a traditional army. They mostly lived in peace among all the different kingdoms of the time. Tower's war didn't involve him testing his might against hordes of armed warriors in battle. It mainly involved him kidnapping women from their own homes and torturing them into confessions. That's not heroism."

"According to the book, Avaris commanded an army of devils and beasts that threatened all of mankind."

"History is written by the victors. Her only crime was building a following of women and offering them an alternative to the oppression they faced elsewhere. If she threatened anything, it was to improve the lives of half of humanity."

"Why should I believe you? You hid the full truth of how you discovered me. I was a fool to trust you."

"You're right. I should have told you everything." She shook her head slowly. "In perfect honesty, I seldom have people's trust. It leaves me a poor steward of the commodity when I stumble upon it. Can you forgive me?"

"Let me turn the question upon you," he said. "If I am Stark Tower, would you forgive me? Or are we enemies by blood, forever? A witch and a witchbreaker?"

"Whoever you used to be, as far as I'm concerned you crawled out of that grave a new man. There's no need for us to be enemies."

"Even if I'm a champion of the Church of the Book?"

"But you're not!" She slammed her fist onto the table. "You don't remember anything about the church. Your mind's a damned blank slate! How can you want to be a champion of something you know nothing about?"

Slate grinned slightly, looking bemused.

"Did I say something funny?"

"I fear I'm a slow learner at times. Until just now, I didn't comprehend why you decided to call me Slate. What is it that you wish to write upon me, Sorrow?"

"What do I wish to write?" she said. "Only the truth."

"Indeed? And you hoped to bring me to the truth by lying about my origins? By stringing me along by your claim to be a damsel in distress?"

"I didn't want to confuse you. I was going to tell you more when the time was right."

"I'm ready to hear what you wish to tell me."

She sighed. "Fine. All cards on the table. Maybe I have been stringing you along. I've even been trying to manipulate you. I don't have a lot of friends, Slate. I've been fighting most of my battles alone for a long time. I thought… it would me nice to have an ally."

"An ally against what?"

She took a long, slow breath. "Against the Church of the Book. My life's goal is to destroy it."

His eyebrow's raised.

"Forget what Poppy's fairy tales have told you. You may not have any memories, but I have a lifetime of moments I can never forget. My father was a judge. I watched him hang his own mother after she was accused of being a witch."

"Was she?" asked Slate.

"How can that possibly matter?" Sorrow asked. "He. Hung. His. Mother. He killed her because he loved his church more than he loved his own flesh and blood. I was ten years old when I witnessed this. I learned the truth of the world that day. My father wasn't wicked; he was the product of an entire society of wickedness. The supposed laws of a supposed god had been warped and twisted to make evil seem like good and good seem like evil."

Slate looked thoughtful. He said, "But if she was a witch?"

"If she was a witch, she was like the vast majority of those who practice weaving, and used her powers in secret for the good of those around her. Weavers don't seek glory or fortune. We seek knowledge and live to help our friends and neighbors. Weavers are sought out by mothers for potions to cure sick infants. They're consulted by farmers who wish to learn the best nights to plant. Unlike the church, which tells men that they'll have a better life in some distant, spiritual kingdom, we teach men to make the most of their time in the material world. We make life better here and now. How can anyone be put to death for such a thing?"

Slate didn't answer.

"Now you know my true intentions. I want to change the world. I want to rescue it from the cruel ideology that has corrupted it. Will you join me?"

He shook his head. "A knight shall be brave, courteous, and kind, obedient to his king, a defender of his faith, and a champion to all men of virtue." He sighed. "If I were to go against this code, I doubt I could look Poppy in the eyes."

"You can't make the sole guide for your life the opinions of a ten-year-old girl."

He looked at her, his head tilted slightly to the side, studying her before he asked, "Haven't you?"

FOR THE REMAINDER of their journey to the Silver City, Slate barely spoke to Sorrow. Nor could she think of a good way to once more initiate conversation. It wasn't that the air between them was hostile. Instead, Slate's formerly jaunty nature had been replaced by a haunted sullenness. Sorrow had no idea what to say that might console him.

She chose to stay below deck as they sailed into Salvation Bay. From her porthole, she could see the vast walls that lined the bay. The Silver City was a fortress encompassing several square miles with walls taller than the trees on the Isle of Fire and towers that vanished into the clouds. The whole of the city sparkled in the morning sun. She felt a curious swell of sentimentality as she returned to her childhood home. But the warmth quickly faded as she glimpsed the mirrored spires of the Cathedral of the Book looming above the massive walls.

Brand, Bigsby, and Slate were on deck directly above her cabin. If she focused, she could just make out their conversation.

"Cheer up, gentlemen," Brand said. "You seem so glum when you're each about to start a new life in the most wonderful city ever built."

"If it's so wonderful," Bigsby grumbled, "why do so many of its inhabitants come to Commonground looking for happiness?"

"I would argue they come to Commonground looking for booze and loose women," said Brand. "Which, admittedly, are in short supply here. But, there are parks and theatres and opera halls and museums. Something wonderful to see every day, if you're high-minded."

Bigsby replied, "I'm a fishmonger whose sole pleasure in life is wearing women's clothing. Is that 'high-minded?'"

"You were almost killed by Greatshadow. People do crazy things after almost dying."

Bigsby sighed. "I can't blame the dragon for my insanity. I started stealing women's underwear from clotheslines when I was still in the circus. I'm wearing Sorrow's pantaloons right now."

Sorrow started to say something, but held her tongue.

"When on earth did you get your hands on those?"

"I rummaged through her bags before we left camp," said Bigsby. "As luck would have it, she's had no reason since to spot their absence."

Brand chuckled. Then, in a voice barely audible, "When you meet father, don't break the ice with this topic."

"Why not?" Bigsby asked. "Will it embarrass him? Will it make him disown me? He's ignored my existence for thirty years. Why should I care what he thinks of me?"

"You've every right to feel aggrieved," said Brand. "But, take a look at those docks. Do you see the ships being loaded with cargo?"

Bigsby's weight shifted on the planks above. "So?"

"What's that cargo packed in?"

Bigsby sounded puzzled. "Crates? Barrels?"

"Precisely. And our father has a near monopoly on their manufacture. He's a very wealthy man. You, dear Bigsby, are his eldest son, and rightful heir. I'm throwing away a grand inheritance by bringing you here. Is it too much to ask that you at least pretend to be happy about this?"

"Why?"

"Because it's better to be a wealthy dwarf in stolen underwear than a poor one?"

"I mean, why did you come and find me? Why throw away your inheritance?"

Brand didn't hesitate with his answer. "I've seen how father's silent guilt has hollowed him out over the years. If I'd gone on a false quest, and returned and reported you dead, I would have inherited only shame. It's in my own self-interest to do what is right, my brother. It lets me sleep soundly at night."

Bigsby said, "I can live with that."

"Nice speech, Brand." It was Gale's voice, at some distance. "If I didn't know better, I'd say you said it just loud enough that you'd be sure I overheard and thought better of you."

"Did it work?"

Gale laughed. Sorrow thought the laugh sounded derisive, but perhaps it was flirty. She was a poor judge of such things.

"We approach a city of marvels," Brand said, sounding as if he was once more speaking to Bigsby. "Anything can happen." There was a pause and Brand asked, "Has it changed much since you were last here?"

Sorrow thought this was an odd question to ask of Bigsby, who'd only been in the city as an infant.

It was Slate who answered. "I've no memory of this place."

"If you really are Stark Tower, you've arrived at an interesting time," said Brand. "The current Lord Tower got himself killed fighting Greatshadow. He has no heir, so the family fortune is currently being fought over by various cousins. If you can find a truthspeaker to verify your identity, you might have the best claim to the estate."

"I've no interest in wealth. What I crave more than anything is purpose. Having no past has robbed me of any future."

Sorrow bit her lip to keep from shouting out that she'd offered him a purpose.

"If you're the Witchbreaker, you might find things kind of boring. There aren't many witches left these days."

"If you were the Witchbreaker, would you kill Sorrow?" Bigsby asked.

The ship turned. Through the porthole, Sorrow could see Slate's shadow stretching over the water. "I'm choosing not to dwell on the prospect," said Slate.

"It would be a shame to rid the world of a pair of such beautiful eyes," said Bigsby.

"Aye," said Slate, sounding dreamy. "Like emeralds."

Sorrow's jaw went slack. She'd never before heard men describe even a portion of her appearance as attractive. It was unsettling.

"She's bald and covered with scales," Brand said. "You guys need better taste in women."

"Says the man who's moon-eyed over a woman old enough to be his mother," said Bigsby.

"As far as I'm concerned," Brand said loudly, "she's the only woman in the world."

"I'm not," Gale called out.

SORROW WATCHED THE bustle of the docks from the porthole in the master cabin. She found it distasteful to be hiding, but there were simpler ways to contact Equity Tremblepoint that didn't require her catching the attention of guards.

She'd had Jetsam hire a messenger to deliver a letter requesting that Tremblepoint come to the ship to verify the authenticity of an ancient manuscript. She'd thought of offering a fee for the service, but decided against it. A genuine scholar would be drawn by the sheer intellectual curiosity of reading a newly discovered manuscript.

Hours later, when the messenger reappeared at the gates and began to walk toward the docks alone, she wondered if she'd made a mistake. Where was Tremblepoint? Perhaps Jetsam had made a poor choice of a courier.

Judging by his unruly hair and soiled clothing, the messenger was from a family of low character, if indeed he had a family at all.

Sorrow frowned as she felt the prejudices of her youth bubbling up inside her. Her father had been disdainful of the poor, viewing them as too slovenly and weak-minded to improve their lot. A person's greatness in life was determined solely by talent and ambition. Strip a wealthy man's fortune away, and he would make another within the year. Perhaps there was a little truth in this, as she had been without a coin to her name many times in her travels, but always seemed to have an easy enough time getting her hands on whatever funds she needed.

She held her breath as she listened to the conversation above deck.

"Why did you bring the letter back?" Jetsam asked.

"Sorry, sir," the courier answered. "But Equity Tremblepoint has left the city. Just last week, in fact."

"Where has he gone?"

"If you want to know, you have to pay me first."

"You don't get paid. You didn't deliver the letter!"

"I ran five miles across the city. I deserve remuneration."

"I bet you didn't even go, you liar."

Sorrow banged on the ceiling of the cabin. She shouted, "Just pay him so we can find out where Tremblepoint is now."

She listened, but Jetsam was now talking so quietly she couldn't make out what he was saying.

Five minutes later, there was a rap on the cabin door. She opened it and Jetsam handed her the letter.

"I was going to haggle to pay half to find out Tremblepoint's new address before you butted in."

"You were insulting him," said Sorrow. "He would have just left."

"You don't know a thing about haggling," said Jetsam. "I'm a natural. I could have talked until he wound up paying me for the privilege of listening to the new address."

Sorrow rolled her eyes.

"Anyway," said Jetsam, "I'm told that Zetetic the Deceiver recently saved the world and has been rewarded with his own private island. He's paying scholars to come live there so he can have sparkling dinner conversations."

"Really?"

"The messenger told me Zetetic is bringing scholars to his island. I'm just guessing about the dinner part."

Sorrow brought her nails to her lips, but caught herself before she chewed them. She'd not given a great deal of thought to Zetetic's presence in the same painting as the Witchbreaker. Hearing he was involved with Tremblepoint, even tangentially, made her feel as if she was catching glimpses of larger forces at work. She was only looking for Tremblepoint because the Black Swan had told her she should. The Black Swan claimed to be a time traveler. Did she have something to do with the painting?

"I guess Zetetic has really earned the title of Deceiver," she said. "If he's claiming to have saved the world from Greatshadow, I heard the real story from Stagger and Infidel, and it was mostly their doing."

Jetsam shook his head. "According to the kid, Zetetic put the sun back on course after it started slipping backward in the sky."

"No he didn't!" said Sorrow. "That was me! And, you know, Infidel and Stagger."

"Maybe you can explain things to the king and wind up with your own island fortress."

Sorrow chuckled ruefully. "Did you learn where we can find Zetetic's island?"

"Sure thing. It's in the Spittles. That's a string of tiny islands halfway between here and the Isle of Storm."

"I know where they are." She reached for her purse. "I'm going to need you to hire another messenger.

We need to get word to Brand to see if we can take the *Circus* to –"

She never completed her thought. Sage shouted above, "All hands on deck! Release the moorings! Hurry!"

Jetsam went to the hatch and called out, "What's the emergency?"

Gale Romer looked into the hatch and said, "You weren't ordered to ask questions, you were ordered to report to the deck."

"Yes, Ma," Jetsam said, heading up the steps.

"Captain," said Gale.

"Captain, Ma," mumbled Jetsam as he flew up the stairs.

Sorrow started to follow, but had to slip back into her cabin to avoid Poppy and Cinnamon running past to report for duty. Once they passed, she started out again, only to pull back as Mako jumped down the steps into the hall, charging toward a door near the end.

"Rigger!" he shouted as he banged on the door. "Wake up!"

"What's going on?" Sorrow asked.

"Don't know yet," said Mako. "But this port is the home base of Brightmoon's navy. We knew the second we sailed into this bay that we might have to leave in a hurry."

He pounded the door again, so hard that Sorrow wondered if it would come off its hinges.

A sleepy voice came from the other side. "Whassa…? Huh?"

"Get out of bed, you layabout!"

The door opened. Rigger was unclothed saved for a pair of briefs. Dark bags lined his eyes as he hoarsely protested, "It's still light. I'm not on watch until sunset."

"Get to the wheel," Mako said. "Sage says we need to get to open water."

Rigger sighed. "Let me get some clothes on."

"We may not have time," Mako said, grabbing his brother by the arm and yanking him bodily down the hall. Sorrow followed, blinking as she emerged into full sunlight. She left most of her serpentine form below deck to avoid drawing attention.

Her efforts at caution were perhaps unnecessary. Despite the activity aboard the *Circus*, it quickly became apparent that most people along the docks had their eyes turned toward a commotion at the main gate in the wall leading into the Silver City. Though the gate was at least 100 yards away, the shouting could be heard from here.

Suddenly, three uniformed guards went flying from the gate. A second later, Slate leapt over their limp bodies with Bigsby slung over his shoulders. Brand followed close on his heels, running as if an army were chasing him.

And, indeed, an instant later a sizeable army of guards surged through the gate only a few yards behind the fleeing men. Slate and Brand had their eyes fixed upon the *Circus*, which already had sails rattling up the pulleys.

As they neared the ship, a score of archers appeared on the city walls. Sage cried, "Incoming!" as the volley of arrows rained down.

Fortunately, the three men avoided injury as strong winds suddenly whipped over their heads, deflecting the missiles. Brand outpaced Slate and leapt onto the ship. Slate threw Bigsby onto the deck, then spun around, fists clenched, and growled at the onrushing squadron of guards.

Though he was unarmed and they were outfitted with mail and armed with spears, the guards slid to a halt. Sorrow noticed that Slate's knuckles and sleeves were splattered with blood.

A barrel shot past Slate and smashed into the legs of the closest guards, upending them. Slate spun and leapt for the *Circus* as Poppy readied another barrel.

"Stay alert!" Gale shouted as wind filled the sails with a thunderous *WHUMPH!* The ship lurched as arrows began to pepper the deck. "I can't deflect arrows while I'm pushing the ship."

Poppy launched another barrel, but missed the bravest of the guards who ran along the dock and leapt for the *Circus*. His heroic efforts came to naught as Mako leapt to the railing and caught the man square in the face with a punch, dropping him into the water. Mako leapt back as an arrow jutted from the wood where he'd just stood.

"We're sitting ducks," Mako grumbled.

"Only if you're idiot enough to be a target," Sage called down. "Take cover!"

Mako looked around to find that all of his family, plus Brand and the others, were crouched low behind bulkheads. Only Sage was exposed, but she swayed her body back and forth, avoiding the barrage of arrows with ease. Mako jumped to Sorrow's side, pressing his back to the doorframe of the stairs leading into the hold.

Bigsby made a dash from his hiding place, shouting, "Out of the way!" as he charged toward Sorrow.

Sorrow retreated below deck as Bigsby tumbled down the stairs. Mako swiftly followed. The sound of arrows biting into wood, *thunk thunk thunk,* echoed in the confined hall.

"I didn't ask for this!" Bigsby screamed, rising to his feet with a clatter of metal on metal. It was only now that Sorrow noticed the dwarf's wrists were bound with manacles. "I was happy in my old life! Happy!"

"I take it things didn't go well with your father?" Sorrow asked, snipping the iron links with her fingers.

"He's dead!" Bigsby said. "And apparently our mom's a real bitch!"

Brand bounded down the steps. "She's not our mother. She's a step-mother, and not one I've met before."

"She's an evil witch!" growled Bigsby. He looked sheepish as he glanced toward Sorrow. "Metaphorically. No offense."

"None taken."

"I may have mentioned that my father had outlived several wives," said Brand, looking at Sorrow. "Apparently, before he died, he married wife number five. She's younger than me!"

"You disapprove of such age differences between couples?" Mako asked, sounding smug.

"I don't give a damn about the age difference," said Brand.

"Why bring it up?" asked Mako.

Brand shook his head. "It's not important. What's important is that she accused me of being an imposter, and ordered the town guard to arrest us."

"But you're his true son," said Sorrow. "As much as I hate to say this, couldn't a truthspeaker vouch for your identity?"

"She had a truthspeaker present. But he never got around to testing me. He started off on Bigsby, accusing him of murdering the ringleader of the circus who'd once employed him. And Bigsby confessed!"

"Once owned me, you mean," said Bigsby. "I was nothing but property to him! I'd stab the bastard again if I had the chance."

"But we were outnumbered ten to one. Why did you attack the guards?"

"They were shackling me!" Bigsby shouted, rattling the links still cuffed to his forearms. "I swore I'd die rather than wear chains again!"

"You almost got to do both," said Brand.

At this point, Slate walked down the stairs. He was covered in an alarming amount of blood, but didn't seem to be in any pain. "Things may have gotten out of hand," he said.

"You tore that guard's head off," Brand said, sounding mournful as he ran his hands through his hair.

"In my defense, he had an unusually slender neck," said Slate.

"You fought the city guard?" Sorrow asked. "Even though there was a truthspeaker present?"

"He bashed out the truthspeaker's teeth!" said Brand.

"I was put off by the way he shrieked as I approached him," said Slate. He shook his head. "I'm sorry. I don't mean to be flippant. The situation quickly grew out of control. Bigsby's life was in danger. I grabbed him and ran, laying low anyone who stood in my way."

"Why?" asked Sorrow. "If he's a confessed criminal and you're a knight, shouldn't you have sided with the guards?"

Slate shrugged. "If I'd thought about it, perhaps. But for most of the life I remember, the people aboard this ship have been my companions. When Bigsby believed he was a princess, he was playmate of Cinnamon and Poppy. A knight is loyal. In my heart, this ship is the kingdom I serve."

The ship lurched hard to starboard. Sorrow glanced at Mako.

"You seem calm."

"We've done this before. Things happened so fast they won't have time to blockade the harbor. We'll escape."

"Back to Commonground?" asked Bigsby.

"To the Spittles," said Sorrow.

"The what?" asked Bigsby.

"It's a chain of damp pebbles dead in the center of nowhere," said Brand. "Why there?"

"It's where Zetetic the Deceiver hangs his hat these days. He might be able to answer our questions about the painting."

Before Brand could ask any further questions Cinnamon bounded down the steps and said, "You can come out now. We're out of arrow range and none of the navy has even hoisted sails yet."

Brand and Bigsby followed Mako back above deck. Sorrow placed her hand on Slate's shoulder before he could leave. He turned to her with a quizzical look in his eyes.

"You're not going anywhere until I tend to your wounds."

"I believe I'm uninjured," he said.

"You're covered in blood."

"Little of it's mine."

"Humor me. Let's at least get you washed up."

She led him back into the master cabin. A porcelain pitcher of fresh water sat next to a small white basin. She poured water into the basin, then grabbed a towel and moistened the tip of it.

"Wash your hands," she said.

Slate did so as Sorrow pushed the door shut with her tail. She dabbed away the flecks of blood on his face. He certainly had no injuries there.

His hands were not as pristine. The skin of his knuckles was bleeding and bruised. She examined them closely, then said, "I don't think I'll need to stitch you up again. Take off your shirt."

She washed away the blood that had soaked through his sleeves. She inspected his old wounds, the ones he'd suffered from the dragon, and saw that they were still healing well.

She didn't look at his face as she said, softly, "I may know why you found it easy to attack a truthspeaker."

"I acted in the heat of the moment."

"Perhaps. But perhaps you acted as you were meant to act."

"What do you mean?"

She pressed her lips together, certain that what she was about to say was a mistake.

And then she told him everything. Told him about the mysterious man-weapon referenced in the letter. Told him about the pygmy ghost who claimed he'd journeyed from Hell to witness the birth of the Destroyer. Finally, she revealed the information that she most wanted to hide from him.

"You have no aura," she said.

"What does that mean?"

"I don't know for certain. But, I want to be honest with you. It's possible that you aren't human. You might be some elaborate magical construction, created to defend witches, not kill them."

He shook his head. He held up his bruised fists. "I bruise. I bleed. I breathe. I laugh when I play with Poppy. I'm a living man, I've no doubt."

"I have to admit there are many holes in my theory," she said. "But I heard you on the deck. Talking about how you would like to have a purpose. It may be that you already have one. You've been created to make the world a better place by helping me fight the church."

Slate shook his head. "I refuse to believe that I've been created solely as a weapon. I must have a past. It's only my memory that's missing, not my humanity."

Sorrow nodded. "You don't have to be only a weapon. Try to think of your lack of yesterdays as a gift. You've no shackles chaining you to the way things are. You've the freedom to make the world anew. Not having a past gives you an open path to the future."

Slate stared at his bruised hands, lost in thought.

At last, he rose and walked for the door.

"Thank you for telling me this," he said.

As he was halfway out the door, she said, softly, "And thank you."

She was surprised when he turned back and asked, "For what?"

She blushed. But honesty had worked out pretty well over the last few moments. "I heard you compliment my eyes." She looked down at her serpentine body. "I wake up most mornings feeling inhuman. It was… welcome… to discover that someone could still see past this. It's not such a bad thing, to be human."

"Aye," said Slate.

11 - THE MUNDANE DESTRUCTION OF ORDINARY LIFE

SORROW'S NOSE WRINKLED as she slithered from the launch onto a gray pebble beach filthy with bird droppings. Her body felt stiff as she slid along the cold earth. The Spittles were a decidedly bleak stretch of real estate, cloaked this morning with clouds. Her breath came out in fog amidst a drizzle that was half rain, half snow.

Sorrow pulled her cape tightly about her. She'd left Commonground with little in the way of a wardrobe beyond her glass armor, and was grateful to have a cloak to protect her from the elements. Since regaining his sanity, Bigsby had avoided outright depression by keeping himself busy with sewing. Bolts of cloth had been among the booty of the *Seahorse*, and Bigsby had been somewhat obsessive in attacking the raw fabric with scissors, needle, and thread. Sorrow's cloak had been cut large enough that when standing still, it was just barely possible for her to coil her tail beneath her and have it completely hidden by the fabric. Of course, this left her standing nearly nine feet tall, so it wasn't as if she was inconspicuous. Further drawing attention was the fact that Bigsby had crafted the hood in such a fashion that, in profile, her head now resembled that of a cobra. She was certain the dwarf had meant well with his design choices.

She surveyed the cliff of jagged rock that ran the length of the beach. She saw no obvious way to climb it. She looked back to the launch. Slate was pulling the small vessel further up the stony strand, overturning it so it wouldn't fill with rain. Brand was struggling to find a convenient way of holding the canvas-wrapped painting he carried. Bigsby didn't offer to help, but instead stood with his hands in the pockets, looking sullen.

"This doesn't seem like the sort of place a king would build a palace," Bigsby said as he contemplated the inhospitable scenery.

"This isn't a palace," said Brand. "It's a fortress. For centuries the Silver Kingdom and the Isle of Storm fought wars over who would control these islands."

"What's so valuable about them?" Bigsby asked.

"Damn near nothing," said Brand. "After the last war firmly established the land as belonging to the Brightmoon family, there were a few feeble attempts to colonize the place, but the settlements kept dying off. Eventually, the Silver Kingdom abandoned the islands entirely. It was expected that the Isle of Storm would try to claim them, but, apparently, the only reason they ever wanted them was to keep the Brightmoons from having them. Now, all that's left is a few ghost towns and the graveyards of all the soldiers who died trying to hold on to the place."

Sorrow rose up on her tail as high as she could and strained to see over the cliff tops. "Are we certain this is the right island?"

"Sage assures me there's a fortress up there," said Brand. "We couldn't see it from the ship because of the mist, but I've learned to trust what she tells me."

Sorrow looked at Slate and said, "Toss me the rope. My snake half can climb almost anything. I'll go up and throw you a line down."

"That won't be necessary," said a voice from above. If Sorrow had been forced to guess, she would have said the voice sounded like that of an old man. "If you journey a quarter mile to the west, there are steps carved into the rock. They lead to one of the entrances of our modest little shelter."

"Who are you?" Slate shouted.

"An excellent question," the unseen voice answered. "It's perhaps the sole topic I find of interest these days. But we need not stand here in the rain and debate my identity. I'm certain it will be a topic of conversation at dinner. It usually is."

"You're inviting us to dinner?" Brand asked.

"Everyone on this island is invited to dinner," said the voice. "Whether they wish to be or not."

Bigsby shook his head. "I should have stayed on the ship."

"Excuse me," Sorrow called out. "But we've come looking for Equity Tremblepoint. Do you –

"Equity will join us at dinner," said the voice.

"How about Zetetic?" Brand called up. "Will he be there? There's a painting we're wanting him to look at."

The voice didn't answer.

"Hello?" Brand asked.

"Let's go find the stairs," said Sorrow.

They did so, though the steps didn't lead to the top of the cliff. Instead, they led to the mid-point of the rock face, where they opened into a tunnel. Large oak doors stood ajar, their iron hinges locked with rust. Slate took the lead, advancing a few yards into the opening before turning quickly. He leapt back out into the drizzle, coughing violently.

"Sorry," he gasped. "I wasn't prepared for the smell."

Now that he'd stirred the dank air of the guano filled tunnel, ammonia-laden fumes rolled out in eye-stinging waves.

They fashioned makeshift masks from the silk handkerchiefs Brand and Bigsby had in their pockets and pressed ahead in silence. No one dared breathe deeply enough to initiate conversation. A few yards beyond the door the tunnel, it became too dark for Sorrow to see her hand before her face. There was a soft *click* at her back and shadows were cast before her as Brand opened his glorystone locket. As Sorrow slithered forward, she found she would have preferred the tunnel to remain dark. The roof was black with sleeping bats. The floor was covered with a carpet of thick white filth, fuzzy with mold. Sorrow wouldn't have wanted to walk through this with boots on, and now she was crawling across it on her belly. Footprints in the muck showed that they weren't the only ones to pass this way in recent days, though it didn't seem that Zetetic had very many guests. Breathing as shallowly as possible, she followed Slate.

At the end of the tunnel they found another oak door. Tacked to it was a hand-painted wooden sign that read, 'Welcome to the Inquisition.'

"It's not too late to turn back," Bigsby whispered.

"I believe it is," Slate said, pressing his shoulder against the heavy door, his feet slipping in the mire.

The door opened into a vast room filled with casks and crates. Brand's light did little to illuminate the outlines of the space, save for rows of stone columns rising to vaulted ceilings twenty feet above. The play of light and dark created by the glorystone left Sorrow imagining she was seeing movements in every shadow.

Slate closed the door behind them.

Bigsby lowered his handkerchief. After a few breaths, he said, "It's just as bad in here."

"We've got gunk all over our boots," said Brand. "You'd think they'd at least have a door mat."

"Feel free to wash your feet with the contents of the casks," said the same unseen voice who'd greeted them from the cliffs. "The wine's long since turned to vinegar."

Sorrow's ears pin-pointed the patch of darkness where the voice originated. Whoever the speaker was, he seemed to be clinging to the ceiling.

"Come into the light," Sorrow said.

"It's best for everyone that I don't," came the answer. "My appearance can be somewhat alarming."

Sorrow pulled back her cloak, revealing her nail-studded scalp. She coiled up on her tail and said, "We may be more open-minded than you give us credit for."

"Some of you are indeed open-minded." Sorrow heard a faint rustling as the voice spoke. The speaker seemed to be moving. "Once, all minds were open to me. It was as if I was surrounded by men shouting their most sacred secrets. Now I hear barely intelligible murmurs, save for the dwarf. His mind sounds like an old, familiar song."

"I've had my fill of mind-readers!" Bigsby said, shaking his fist. "Get out of my head!"

"Perhaps you should learn to keep your thoughts inside you." There was a further rustling in the shadows. "Your fear amplifies your inner voice into a scream."

"I-I'm not the one afraid," said Bigsby. "You're the one hiding in shadows."

"Ah, but you are afraid. You felt a swell of panic when you saw that our host has labeled this fortress the Inquisition."

"It's an unpleasant name," said Bigsby. "The only time I ever hear the word is when the church is seeking to root out heretics."

"We're all heretics here," the voice answered with a chuckle. "That doesn't mean we welcome fugitives."

"Why would you think we're fugitives?" Bigsby asked.

"You fled the Silver City as wanted men, did you not? Bigsby, you stand accused of murder. The man with no memories killed at least three of the city guard, and maimed uncounted others. Brand is accused of fraud. I see he's innocent, but that will matter little as long as juries can be swayed with bribes and his stepmother controls his family fortune. And Sorrow… I don't care to spend the time it would take to catalogue her crimes."

"If you know our names, tell us yours," said Sorrow.

"Ah. This is an easier question to answer than your original query. If I know nothing else of myself, I at least know what my father called me. My name is Brokenwing."

"That's an odd name," said Bigsby.

"Perhaps. But it is my one precious possession."

Bigsby crossed his arms. "I hardly see how a name can be precious."

"There's one among you who does not know the name given to him by his father," said Brokenwing. "Or, indeed, if he even had a father. Ask him how precious he would consider a name."

Everyone looked toward Slate. Slate shrugged.

"I fear that the hours grow short," said Brokenwing. "Our host is rather insistent that everyone arrive for dinner promptly and in appropriate attire. It will take some time to make yourselves presentable. You look like vagabonds from the sea, and smell even worse."

"If we offend your nose, might I suggest you find a shovel and muck out the path to your front door?" said Brand.

"This is a back door," said Brokenwing. "The other side of the island has a more pleasant approach. For now, if you continue moving forward, you'll find the exit to the cellar. Turn right in the hall and follow it to the third staircase on the left. This will lead you to our guest quarters. By now the servants should have your rooms prepared. Hot baths are being drawn. Dinner is served at sunset. I'll see you there."

"But will we see you?" asked Bigsby.

Brand said, "We really don't want to be rude, but we came here seeking answers, not dinner. Is there no chance we can see Zetetic now?"

There was no answer.

"Nothing is stopping us from going back to the ship," said Bigsby.

"We're staying. There's something here that I want more than anything else in the world right now," said Sorrow.

"Aye," said Slate. "Answers."

"Those too," said Sorrow. "But I was talking about the hot bath."

THE DINING HALL was lined with fireplaces large enough for a grown man to stand up in. Firewood being in short supply in the Spittles, the flames were fueled by small mountains of coal. The fires did an admirable job of chasing away the chill, but the coal gave the room a rotten egg miasma.

While the hall was large enough to seat hundreds, the handful of current guests were seated at three long wooden tables arranged in a triangle so that everyone could easily see each other. Servants led Bigsby, Brand, Slate and Sorrow to seats along one side of the triangle. At the next table sat a liver-spotted old man, two empty chairs, and a person Sorrow suspected was a woman, given the shape of her face and the slenderness of her build. But she was wearing a man's suit and had a mustache, which confused the matter somewhat.

"I don't suppose you're Brokenwing," Brand asked as he eyed the old man.

The old man grinned as he scratched his bald head. "I knew my skin was getting a bit scaly in my later years, but certainly I've not gone that far."

The person at the end of the table said, "I've told you, Vigor, there's something reptilian about your mannerisms."

The old man nodded. "I've spent seventy years studying the beasts, Equity. It's only natural I've picked up a few of their traits."

"Equity?" Sorrow asked. "You're Equity Tremblepoint?"

"Indeed. And the old reptile is Vigor. I'm glad to see that Zetetic has finally arranged for other scholars to join our little party. Though, I fear, I don't recognize any of you from my normal circles."

"We aren't scholars," said Brand. "I'm Brand Cooper. This is my brother, Bigsby, and my friends Sorrow and Slate."

"If you aren't scholars, what are you?" asked Vigor.

"A weaver, a warrior, a fish baron and a retired circus performer," said Brand.

"Indeed," said Equity, with thinly disguised disappointment.

There was a moment of awkward silence until Vigor cleared his throat. "I can't help but notice, my dear Sorrow, that you're a rather impressive blend of serpent and human. I'm the word's foremost authority on reptiles, from the common skink to the mightiest dragon. Perhaps later we can meet in private? I would find it most interesting to examine you unclothed."

"I think not," she said.

"She's on to you," said Equity.

Vigor's wrinkled cheeks flushed red. "My dear, my curiosity is entirely scholarly."

"He's nothing but an old letch," said Equity. "He propositions me five times a day."

"I most certainly do not," Vigor grumbled. "I wouldn't risk you saying yes. I've been in your company for over a week and still haven't deduced if you're a man or a woman."

Sorrow had been wondering about that as well. Equity was the most androgynous person she'd ever encountered. He or she was tall for a woman, a little short for a man, and thin for either sex. Equity's hair was cropped in a severe, mannish cut, but her or his face was feminine, with eyes shadowed blue-green and lips painted crimson. Above these lips sat a thin, curly mustache that may or may not have been woven from horsehair. Equity's throat, which might have solved the mystery with the presence or absence of an Adam's apple, was hidden by a high collar. The rest of Equity's wardrobe proved equally confounding, consisting of pants and a jacket of a masculine styling, but trimmed with frills of crimson lace.

"Actually," Bigsby said, looking at Equity. "I'm a little confused myself."

"You shall remain confused," said Equity. "I'm all sexes, and none. My only gender is thespian. If the world knew the configuration of my genitalia, they would have prejudice in regards to the roles I play on stage. I will not allow my biology to shackle me."

"I'm surprised you haven't been thrown in shackles, period," said Vigor. "I've never been to the Silver City, but from what I know of it, the people there don't think kindly of deviants."

"Then it's wise you've avoided the place," said Equity. "As for my survival in such a conservative enclave, my talent in the theatre places me beyond reproach. I'm honest enough to admit that my family fortune may also play some small role in my relative freedom. When the poor make people uncomfortable by refusing to comply with the prevailing morality, they're imprisoned. Similar transgressive behavior among the wealthy is tolerated as mere eccentricity."

"It must be nice to dress however you want and not worry about it," Bigsby said.

"I wouldn't know," said Equity. "I worry over the finest details of my appearance with what must surely be an unhealthy obsession. Today, I changed my undergarments nine times before settling on the correct pair, despite my certainty that none but myself will ever see them."

"I just meant it would be nice to have the freedom to look however you want in public," said Bigsby.

"We're all born with such freedom," said Equity. "If you lack the inspiration and audacity to live as you wish, you've no one to blame but yourself."

Sorrow left her spot at the table, gliding toward Equity with her undulating motion as she retrieved from her pocket the scroll that had launched her on this journey. "I haven't come to discuss clothing. I'm informed you're the world's foremost authority on dead languages."

"I dabble," said Equity. "My ancestors bequeathed me a voluminous collection of ancient plays. It would have been wasteful not to read them."

Sorrow unrolled the scroll. "I found this on the Isle of Fire. I believe it may have been written by Avaris, Queen of the Weavers."

Equity picked up the aged parchment. "Hmm. This is the old weaver's script. I'm a bit rusty. There are no plays written by witches, I fear."

"So you can't read it?"

"I didn't say that. I'll need to investigate a few of the words, but the gist of the manuscript is obvious. 'Dear Sisters, our struggle has been a long and difficult one, etcetera, etcetera.'"

"It's the etcetera part I'm interested in," said Sorrow.

Equity nodded. "Very well. It goes on to say that the great persecutor is in our possession. There's something about the man-weapon having been hollowed and needing to be refilled. These lines here explain the wisdom of retreat. The author says she will travel to the eastern isle to regain her strength, and encourages her sisters to go into hiding."

"Does it say which eastern isle?"

"If it did, I would have told you."

"Does it say who or what the man-weapon is?" asked Slate.

"No, but —"

At this moment everyone grew silent as a dragon the size of a small pony limped into the room on misshapen, bandaged limbs. Slate leapt up, sending his chair skittering across the floor. They'd come to dinner unarmed, but Slate wasted little time in changing that situation, bounding to the nearest fireplace and grabbing a heavy poker.

He spun around to face the dragon, brandishing the makeshift weapon.

"I told you my appearance was alarming," said the dragon. "Please put that down, sir, before I'm forced to defend myself."

"Brokenwing?" Sorrow asked.

"An appropriate appellation, no?" the dragon asked, glancing toward his back where his wings were braced with wooden splints. "Vigor is doing what he can to restore my limbs."

"We were talking to a dragon?" Bigsby said, his eyes nearly popping from his skull.

"This isn't the first time we've spoken, Bigsby," Brokenwing said. "I paid you a visit in Commonground. You knew me then as Relic."

"You're the guy who wanted to kill Greatshadow!" Bigsby's brow furrowed. "But if you're a dragon, why did you want to kill another dragon?"

"Do men not kill men?" asked Brokenwing. He kept his gaze on Slate, who still brandished the poker. "I'll ask you again, sir, to assume a less threatening pose. Not to mention it's unwise of you to linger so close to the flames. It unsafe to stand between me and my father."

"Your father's Greatshadow?" asked Sorrow.

"And you want to kill him?" Bigsby said.

"Our relationship is complicated," said Brokenwing.

"Stand down, Slate," said Sorrow.

"But... but... dragon," said Slate.

"How eloquent," said Equity.

Slate placed the poker back on its stand. "I suppose I've no cause to hate thee. I mean, you."

Brokenwing removed the chair beside Vigor and drew up to the table. "After I informed our guests of the importance of promptness, I see that Walker and our host have failed to show up."

"Perhaps I've been here all along." All eyes turned to an albino face that rose above the edge of the table next to Brokenwing. It was a pygmy, who climbed up in his chair and walked across the table. He hopped to the main table. He walked to the throne that sat beside the table and looked down. "As for Zetetic, it's possible he's too small to be seen. I led him to the mathematical realms earlier. He insisted on pressing on alone to explore past the zero, though I warned him he might return as only a fraction of himself."

He knelt for a closer look and shook his head. "I sense no trace of him."

Sorrow could hold her tongue no longer. "It's you! You're the pygmy who came to my tent!"

Walker nodded. "Indeed. I thought I recognized you. You've engaged in some interesting addition and subtraction of your own."

"You're the one who was looking for the Destroyer?" asked Slate.

"Yes. And you're wondering if you're him."

"Am I?"

Walker shrugged. "I confess I've not thought much of the Destroyer of late. It's been, what, seventeen years since I last visited hell to discuss the matter with the demons."

"It's not even a month since I met you," said Sorrow.

Walker chuckled and shook his head. "No my poor witch. Eternities have passed. Admittedly, not locally. But I'm seldom in one place for long."

"Let's get back to the Destroyer," said Slate. "Who was he? What was he?"

Walker shrugged. "In the grand design, we're all destroyers. We trample unseen kingdoms of insects beneath our heels, oblivious to their hopes and dreams, their wars and gods. We destroy nature, enslaving fields to do our bidding, robbing the ocean to steal food from the mouths of sharks. Even seated alone in a room, holding our breath, we grind the past to dust by perceiving the present. Destruction is a synonym for life."

"I suppose that's true, but the mundane destruction of ordinary life hardly seems like the type of destruction discussed in hell," said Sorrow.

"I assure you that ordinary life is a topic of great interest among the damned."

"I mean, demons would probably focus more on a Destroyer that burns cities and topples empires."

"Or one who erects cities and builds empires," the pygmy said.

"You're not really answering our questions," Sorrow grumbled.

"Perhaps you're not really asking them," said Walker, with a broad smile.

"Pay no mind to our pale associate," said Vigor. "He's completely in… sane…"

Vigor's voice trailed off as he stared at the door. A tall man with a black ponytail had just walked backward into the room, completely naked, drenched in sweat and bleeding from a thousand small scratches. The blood was smeared into patterns of lines and squiggles. Sorrow squinted. Were these all numbers?

The man walked backward to his throne and sat, turning his face toward his guests. The large red 'D' tattooed in the middle of his forehead burned with a faint, pulsing glow. His mouth opened. ".reverof no tnew tsuj taht rebmun lanoitarri na htiw tnemugra na otni tog I .gnitiaw uoy peek ot yrroS"

Walker laughed so hard he fell off the table.

"?ynnuf os s'tahW" asked Zetetic.

Walker wiped tears from his eyes, unable to breathe.

".etunim a tiaW. ?ereh klat elpoep od noitcerid hcihW" He stood up and walked around his throne backwards. When he sat down he said, "Is this better? Do you understand me now?"

"I don't think I've understood anything since I got off the damned boat," said Bigsby.

"You're Zetetic?" asked Brand.

"I certainly hope so," the man answered. "I'm sorry if I've kept you waiting. I'm sure you all must be hungry. Fortunately, I have the power to summon a feast from thin air merely by scratching my nose."

He did so. Nothing happened. Sorrow blinked and suddenly all the tables were heaped with large platters of roasted birds, steaming cauldrons of soup, and bowls stacked high with fruit representing every color of the rainbow.

Bigsby stared at the platter of flaky white cod stacked before him. "I'm glad you didn't live in Commonground," he said. "It's tough enough making a living selling fish."

Zetetic waved his hand dismissively. "Your industry is safe. I never, never repeat myself." He grabbed a quail and tore it in two, shoving the breast into his mouth. With his mouth full, he said, "Forgive me. I'm famished." He glanced at Walker. "Next time, we should pack a lunch. I haven't eaten in three days."

"We just had dinner last night," said Vigor.

"Time moves at different rates in some realms. It can get confusing. When Walker led me through the abode of dreams undreamt, we returned nineteen minutes before departing. I met myself as I was preparing to leave. Those nineteen minutes alone with myself were very educational." He shook his head as a wistful smile settled upon his lips. "Very educational indeed."

"Speaking of things that are confusing," said Brand, "there's a painting in my room I'd like you to look at."

"The one with me, Walker, and the Witchbreaker?"

"You've seen it?"

"It was in my possession for a while. It used to hang in the Monastery of the Book until I stole it. When the church caught me and killed me for a little while last year, I lost track of it.

"Do you know why you and I appear in the painting?" Slate asked.

"I have two theories," said Zetetic. "The first is that, at some point in the future, I'll travel into the past. Walker's in the painting, so I assume he comes along."

"I'm not in the painting," said Walker.

"It certainly looks like —"

"I assure you, I'm not in the painting. Neither are you."

"Are you arguing for the sake of argument here?" Zetetic asked. "Because I know what I've seen with my own eyes."

"Do you?" asked Walker. "Or have your eyes been deceived by a falsehood? The representation of a thing is not the thing."

Zetetic sighed and poured himself a glass of wine. "Some other time I'll puzzle out what the hell it is you're trying to say. Right now, I've got too much of a headache to focus on your riddles." He took a long drink, emptying his glass, then poured himself another.

"What's your second theory?" asked Sorrow.

"About what?"

"The painting. How you got into it."

"Oh. Right. My second guess is that I'm a lunatic." He downed the second glass of wine. "Do you know that a few weeks ago I walked into the interior of the sun and talked to the ghost who lives inside?" He ran his finger along the rim of the now empty glass. "I've a dragon for a houseguest. I've danced across stone stripped of all truths to stare into the eyes of dead gods and witness the end of the world." He let out a long sigh. "Now I'm drinking wine that I've lied into existence. Does any of this sound sensible?"

"I can think of few situations where drinking wine isn't exquisitely sensible," said Equity, raising a glass.

"True. But what if my sanity is so far gone that everything and everyone I experience are merely figments of my imagination. For all I know, I could be a brain in a jar dreaming of a more interesting life. I can't devise any possible test that could determine what's real and what isn't." He threw his glass against the wall, where it shattered into shards. "Did that just break? Did I dream it broke? Was there a glass at all? Perhaps if I clapped my hands forcefully enough, I'd wake myself. Everyone here would vanish, fading as my true life returned."

Sorrow inhaled sharply as Zetetic swung his hands toward one another. With his palms an inch apart, he snapped to a halt. He sat for several seconds, staring at his barely separated fingers. At last, he lowered his arms, and everyone let out their breath.

He grabbed an apple from a nearby bowl. "Now would be a poor time to test my theory. I detest dining alone."

"If you're done scaring us," said Bigsby, "what about Slate?"

"What about him?"

"You said you thought you might go back in time to wind up in the painting. Why's Slate in it?"

"Oh." Zetetic chewed his apple thoughtfully. "I suppose he could also travel through time with me, and become Stark Tower. Or perhaps he's the original Stark Tower, and has somehow managed to sleep all the way into our time."

"Why don't I have any of Stark Tower's memories?" asked Slate.

Zetetic shrugged. "Perhaps you aren't him after all. Avaris was a master bone-weaver. If she ever got so much as a hair from the true Tower, she could have grown an exact duplicate."

"How can I discover the truth?" Slate asked.

Zetetic shrugged. "Today I carved equations into my bare flesh with the thorn of a screaming cactus while sipping wormwood steeped in dragon's urine. It tasted like doubt and despair, but I swallowed every drop so that I might glimpse one hair-thin aspect of truth."

Brokenwing narrowed his eyes. "You've been collecting the contents of my chamber pot?"

Zetetic waved away his query. "Anyway, Slate, I'm sure Walker would be happy to ply you with various pharmaceuticals that would lift you above the confines of ordinary life in order to look down and see the larger patterns. Or if you want to know what Avaris has done, you could stop bothering me and just go ask her."

"That's easier said than done," said Sorrow. "I've been searching for her for years. The letter that brought me here says she retreated to an eastern island, but beyond this I know nothing of where she might be, or if she's even alive."

"Of course she's still alive," said Zetetic. "At least, she was alive three years ago. I studied a full month in her walking castle."

"You know her?" Sorrow asked.

"In every sense of the word," said Zetetic. "She required I make love to her three times every night between the span of two full moons." He eyed Slate. "I recommend a diet high in protein before you seek her out. You look like her type."

Sorrow slowly lowered her fork to her plate.

Equity studied her face and said, "You look absolutely mortified."

"Avaris was a great champion of women. I can't believe she'd trade knowledge for sex."

"Sexual energy is a vital component of bone-weaving," said Zetetic. "Without capturing procreative energies to animate her creations, Avaris would just be sewing meat together."

Sorrow felt the blood drain from her face. "I suppose I won't be learning bone-weaving."

"Why not, dear?" asked Vigor.

"I learned the truth of what lies in the hearts of men when I watched my father hang my grandmother. I've never felt the slightest inkling of physical desire for a man."

Equity nodded. "I have my own father-issues. But you needn't turn to men for sexual energy. You have other options."

Sorrow crossed her arms. "This discussion is pointless. At the moment, I don't even have genitals."

"Not human genitals," said Vigor. "But reptiles aren't lacking in reproductive organs. I can train you on their function."

Sorrow grimaced, feeling an urgent need to change the subject.

"How would we find this walking castle?"

"It's on Podredumbre, but you can't find it," said Zetetic. "It finds you. Luckily, once you know that the castle feeds on souls, it's not difficult to trick it into appearing. I murdered an old woman from a village on the edge of the swamp to summon it."

"That's reprehensible!" said Sorrow.

"She wasn't long for this world," Zetetic said. "She was too weak even to scream when I stole her from her bed."

Sorrow stared at him, her jaw slack.

"Human sacrifice seems a bit extreme," said Brand. "Is there no other way?"

"There is a way that doesn't require you to harm another," said Walker. "If you're bold enough to risk it."

"I've my failings, but a lack of boldness isn't among them," said Brand.

Bigsby looked puzzled. "Why do you care if Sorrow finds Avaris? Shouldn't we be more focused on clearing our names?"

Brand shrugged. "When we sailed into the Silver City, I thought I was about to be trapped in a life I didn't truly desire. I've learned to enjoy my time as an adventurer. Hunting for an ancient witch seems like a more entertaining goal than waging a war with our-step mother over who is going to oversee the manufacturing of barrels."

"I admire that you understand your priorities." Walker chuckled as he stared into the young man's eyes. "I shall meet you all on Podredumbre. Who am I to stand in the way of your goals?"

12 - Mama Knuckle

PORT HALLELUJAH WAS much as Sorrow remembered it. She'd been fifteen when she came here, a young witch hungry for knowledge, impatient for power. The bay was surrounded by rolling hills where white brick houses with red tile roofs stood atop one another in a chaotic jumble. It was evening and the tropical air was thick with the haze of a thousand lit stoves as the town prepared dinner. The wind smelled like charcoal, bringing with it the sweet scent of plantains roasting and the savory aroma of oysters cooked in their shells.

The Isle of Podredumbre had been conquered by the Brightmoons two centuries ago. Everywhere she looked Sorrow saw the spires marking places of worship for the Church of the Book. In the Silver City, grand cathedrals could welcome tens of thousands of worshippers under a single roof. Of course, the religion had been dominant there for a long time, and most people were united in their faith. Here, two hundred years of colonization hadn't quashed the lingering tribalism of the populace. You couldn't gather a hundred people under a roof without at least some of the members attempting to kill each other over ancient grudges. Thus, the hundreds of smaller chapels, each offering services to a select few families.

"We've got company," Sage announced as a launch approached the *Circus*.

"Tax collectors," Gale explained. "They'll make a show of searching our ship, then slap a tax on our cargo.

"We don't really have cargo," said Brand.

"That won't matter. They'll inform us there's a tax on the wasted space in our hold, or fine us for having excess barnacles on the hull. No ship escapes free of charge."

"Should we be nervous that these are representatives of the king?" asked Brand. "There's been time for word to spread to be on the look out for us."

Gale shook her head. "The only law here is the law of the greased palm. After we make a show of protest over their fees, we'll slip the inspectors a few moons and a bottle of rum and they'll be on their way. There's an art to these things."

Sorrow interrupted their conversation and said, "While I'm certain that bribes can handle this situation, before they board I'm going to slip off the ship. I've got an old friend to visit."

"You have a friend?" Brand asked. He winced as soon as he said it. "Sorry. I didn't mean to sound so surprised."

Sorrow ignored the slight. "After you buy provisions, leave the city along the western road. When you arrive in the village of Two-Mile Ditch, ask for Mama Knuckle. I'll be waiting for you there."

"Got it," said Brand.

By now, the inspectors had pulled along side the *Circus*. Sorrow slipped over the other rail, which was on the shadow side in relation to the sunset. She'd not gone swimming yet with her new body, but instinct kicked in once she hit the water. Even weighted down with her glass armor, her powerful tail had no difficulty propelling her across the calm bay. The setting sun painted the ripples spreading out from her in colors of flame. If anyone spotted her monstrous body swimming toward the river that fed the bay, they failed to call out an alarm. By the time it was dark, she was well up river and able to slither out of open water into a long, marshy field of reeds.

Even though the moon was only a sliver, she had little problem finding her way among the canals that cut the landscape into a neat patchwork. In most farmlands, the canals would be for irrigation, bringing water to parched crops, but in Podredumbre the canals were used to drain water from swamps, leaving behind spongy black soil. Most of the cotton traded in the Shining Lands came from these fertile fields, and other parts of the island were famous for rice. All dry land was officially the property of King Brightmoon, meaning the workers here were trapped in permanent poverty, eternal squatters living on shacks build atop stilts in marshes and other marginal lands unfit for producing profit. The king made a show of generosity, keeping any able-bodied person who wanted work busy on the farms or toiling to reclaim new land. He paid just enough to avoid the abject misery that might stir his subjects to rebellion, but not enough for them to have excess money they might save to escape to a better life.

It was well past midnight when she slithered into Two Mile Ditch. The landscape seemed unchanged from a decade ago. A few shacks lined the western road, next to the ferry that crossed the eponymous ditch, nearly two hundred feet across. She followed the ditch toward the oaks in the distance. Such old, tall trees were a rarity in Podredumbre outside the treacherous depths of the swamps. Most trees that could easily be reached had been felled to provide firewood and building materials. Only a few thickets stood here and there, protected by various quirks of geography, fate, and luck. This particular patch of trees was lucky enough to be home to Mama Knuckle. No one who knew that name would ever touch this timber.

Sorrow squinted as she looked into the shadows of the gnarled old oaks. There were corpses sitting against the tree trunks, their arms limp by their sides, their crow-picked eyes turned in her direction. Sorrow bowed and said, "Uncles, I'm grateful you watch over this weary traveler. Do not rise from your rest; I'm a friend."

The corpses said nothing.

Sorrow slipped past unmolested, which was a much less interesting arrival than her first visit here, when she'd barely escaped the clutches of Mama Knuckle's guardians.

Though it was late at night, there was a soft glow from the window of the shack sheltered by the trees. Mama Knuckle kept nocturnal hours, working throughout the night, sleeping through the day.

Sorrow slithered up to the house, preparing to knock, but the door swung open on her approach. She crouched to slip through the doorframe.

"Come in girl. As much of you as will fit anyway." Mama Knuckle stood in front of a wood stove, stirring a large black pot. A monkey skull bobbed in the bubbling broth, until Mama pushed it under with a heavy wooden spoon.

She wiped her hands on her cotton apron and turned to Sorrow. Her dress looked out of place amid the spooky hut, with its furniture all formed of twisted wood and wired bones. The fabric was a pattern of bright red flowers against a field of blue, threadbare, but clean and well mended. Mama had lost much of her hair in the last decade. Only a few threads of pure white lay across her leathery scalp. Her eyes, failing when Sorrow had trained here, were now twin white moons. Though the cataracts had certainly robbed her of all ordinary sight, she smiled and said, "I never thought I'd be so happy to have Sorrow cross my doorstep."

"Did you know I was coming?" Sorrow asked.

"Girl, you're crawling around on Rott's own tail. Ghosts are gonna talk." Mama's dead eyes scanned the length of Sorrow's body. "I wasn't sure I believed 'em. The dead get a little stupid after their brains fall out. But it's true. You've got two souls inside you now. You're half-dragon. It's what you always wanted, I guess."

Sorrow shook her head. "I never wanted this."

Mama smiled faintly. "The day you first came here, girl, you were all about power, power, power. You were gonna overthrow kings and topple churches. If you're only goal is to make things fall down, it's only natural that you partnered with Rott."

"I don't consider this a partnership," said Sorrow. "I consider it an unpleasant side-effect. I was hoping you might know how to reverse it."

"Have you considered taking that sliver of Rott's tooth out of your brain? I've got a good salve you can put on afterward. Armadillo fat. Seals up any wound."

"If I remove the nail, I lose the power," said Sorrow. "There's no guarantee my body will return to normal."

"No, but you won't lose any more of your human bits, that's for sure."

"Those I have lost will have been lost in vain. I'll be no closer to saving the rest of you from the systems that oppress you."

Mama Knuckle shook her head as she placed a lid on the pot. "Girl, I'd hoped you'd outgrow such talk by now." She took a cane from beside the stove and used it to steady herself as she crossed the small room to a rickety rocking chair. The chair creaked as she lowered her bony frame into it. "It's natural to be angry at the world when you're young. Anger's just part of the blood then. But it should have boiled out of you by now."

"How can you not be angry? You live in a country where a foreign king has stolen your land and reduced your kin to little more than slaves. A church that no one truly believes in imposes its tithes and forces women into lives of subservience."

Mama Knuckle shook her head. "Girl, ain't no church did that to women."

"I've seen how free women are among the Wanderers. They're treated as equals, not house servants."

"Wanderers are different," said Mama. "The men and women are stuck together on the same ship along with their kids. It's easy to divide up the duties. But in the rest of the world, the men labor outside the house all day, or are sent to the ends of the earth as soldiers. Women stay at home to raise the children not because they're oppressed, but because they are the only ones who can be trusted to do it right."

"There's no reason it has to be this way."

"Once you carry a baby around inside you for nine months, you see things different. That child is your flesh and your future. It's no burden to dedicate yourself to being a mother."

"But —"

"It's nature girl. Haven't you opened your eyes a single day in this world? It's not a human invention that mothers care for their children. The lion, the eagle, the alligator… the females take care of the babies. It's the great wheel of life, girl. I'm sad for you that you haven't decided to ride it."

"This conversation isn't going at all like I expected," Sorrow said, crossing her arms.

"I suppose not," said Mama. "Sorry to be scolding you. I just thought you'd learn your lesson after all these years."

"Why didn't you tell me these things when I was here the first time?"

"I did, girl. Every day! But you only hear the things you want to hear."

Sorrow shook her head. "I didn't know you thought so little of me. Am I truly such an awful person?"

Mama sighed. "Oh child, you ain't so bad. You're just a little turned around. Your father got you all twisted up long before I got hold of you. You went out into the world thinking you knew something about the truth, and you did. You did. But there's more than one truth, girl. And if you don't understand that, then the one truth you do know will turn into a lie."

"My one truth is that my father and the system he represents are wicked," said Sorrow. "Is this a lie? Is it?"

"Not always."

"I thought you of all people would understand."

Mama nodded. "I do understand. The world could be a better place. Maybe you can make it so."

"I have to try."

"You didn't come here to see me. To the island, I mean."

"Avaris is here. Somewhere in the swamps. Why didn't you tell me? You knew ten years ago I wanted to find her."

"Avaris is dangerous, child. She's got bad things in her heart. Hate and bitterness and pride, poisons of the soul."

"She has reasons to be bitter," said Sorrow. "She was once a queen. She was beloved by thousands of women. The church killed almost everyone who was loyal to her, because they couldn't stand the thought that there was someone offering a better way of life."

"She was a queen, yes. But she ruled by fear. Maybe she started with good in her heart, but she made pacts with terrible powers that turned her spiteful and cruel."

"Those are the lies the church tells," said Sorrow. "You can't believe everything the victors of war say about their enemy."

Mama Knuckle lowered her head, looking weary. "When you came to me, girl, I knew I had to train you. I could see in your eyes that nothing would stop you from finding the answers you sought. I taught you many things, but you never learned mercy. You never learned love."

"I show mercy constantly," Sorrow said, thinking of how she'd spared Eddy, the river pygmy who'd betrayed her, from suffering a moment more than necessary. "As for love, I don't know that you can teach something that may not even exist."

"Oh child," Mama sighed.

"Love is just a mumbo jumbo word used to hide our animal natures," said Sorrow. "Between men and women, it sanitizes lust. Between a mother and child, it's a pretty word for an instinct that, as you say, even wild animals possess. We romanticize these feelings, blend them together, and label them love. We attempt to make something noble out of mere biology."

Mama Knuckle rose and hobbled back to her stove. She lifted the lid and a cloud of steam rolled out. The fat from the marrow of the monkey bones had turned the broth a dull yellow. Mama Knuckle pulled down a bundle of dried chilies that hung near the stove and tossed them into the pot without bothering to chop them. After stirring the concoction in silence for a few moments, she said, "I took you into my home, girl, when you were nothing but a hungry little runaway with a scalp full of oozing wounds. I nursed you to health and taught you my secrets. I cared for you even though the guardian spirits told me to kill you. They said you were sharp with anger, the way a porcupine is prickly with quills. Touch that girl, they told me, and you'll bleed."

"I don't deny I'm angry. What I've never understood is why everyone else isn't. Why is the world so blind?"

Mama Knuckle fixed her unseeing gaze on Sorrow's face. "Because the rest of the world can't see the things you see, do you think they maybe don't exist?"

"Don't be absurd. The cruelty, the injustice, the hatred… they're the facts of the world even if no one else has the courage to see it."

"But because you're blind to love, you think it doesn't exist."

Sorrow grimaced. "Fine. I'm honest enough to admit I may have a few blind spots. What does it matter?"

"It matters because the world is in balance, Sorrow. You see only the bad things. I remember how you would walk through the cotton fields and come home to tell me how you saw workers sagging under the weight of their burdens. You'd tell me how hungry the children looked. You never told me about walking through the village in the evening and seeing the men and women dancing. You never talked about the children running around like wild things in the alleys, laughing with their friends. There's good in this world. Ordinary people can bear their heartaches because they're lifted by their joys."

"You think I can't feel joy?" Sorrow asked.

"Can you?"

Could she? She'd felt excitement, obviously, like the anticipation she'd experienced finding the Witches Graveyard. She could feel satisfaction, like the sense of accomplishment she felt when she constructed a particularly useful golem. And, she could certainly feel amusement. She'd been able to laugh when Slate had been confused about Bigsby's gender. Weren't these things joy?

Thinking about Slate, she said, "We've talked about me long enough. I've some questions of a more practical nature."

"Yes?"

"I've met… a man. Who has no aura."

"Is he lethargic? Sad? Sometimes the soul perishes before the body."

"He's anything but lethargic. And, while he's a bit moody, he certainly smiles more often than I do."

"Perhaps some magic masks his soul?"

"Maybe," said Sorrow. "Do you know how to create such a mask? Would you know how to remove it?"

"I've not had much reason to mask souls," said Mama Knuckle. "But, I know it can be done."

"So do I," said Sorrow. "Apparently, there was an animating spirit locked into the woodwork of the *Freewind*. I spent weeks on the ship and never suspected. I was told the soul had been masked to hide it from Rott. That ship was destroyed, but the soul lingers on inside the figurehead. The family is wanting me to help move the spirit into a new ship. I've no clue how to do this."

"Blood, child. Spirits flow with blood."

"I know this. But, there's no body, only wood."

Mama nodded. "Then someone from the family would have to supply the blood."

"I'm sure there would be volunteers," said Sorrow. "How much blood would we need?"

"Enough to soak each board of the new ship."

"That would take gallons! No one has that much blood."

"The blood could be diluted in wine. Still, to remain potent spread across an entire ship, you would probably need all the blood from an adult."

"I doubt that's going to happen. I imagine any of the Romers would be happy to bleed a little for the cause, but it makes no sense for one of them to sacrifice their life just to free one ghost."

"Without understanding love, it's impossible for you to judge these things," said Mama Knuckle.

Sorrow stretched her arms out to the side and yawned. "You've given me a lot to think about. Maybe some of it will make sense to me in the morning."

"Will you stay the night here?"

"We both know I won't."

"Why not?"

"Because if you don't want me going to see Avaris, you have a hundred different tricks to stop me. You once showed me the recipe for that paste you put on sleeping men's tongues to destroy their will and render them obedient. Going to sleep in your presence wouldn't be very smart."

"Sorrow! You trust me so little? I would never harm you. Though you'll never understand it, I love you, girl."

"Even though I scare you? Even though you think I'm corrupted by ambition?"

"Everything in balance, child. You may be blind to the good in life, but I see the good in you. The ghosts tell me you helped save the sun. The world would be a cold, dark place without you."

"I played some small part in ensuring that we'd still have daylight, yes. I can't pretend that was a particularly difficult moral choice."

"If not for your ambition, you would never have had the power to do this important thing. If not for the coldness in your heart, you wouldn't be able to stay clear-headed and focused in the face of danger. You're as close to fearless as anyone I've ever met."

"Not so fearless. If you offered me a cup of tea, I wouldn't have the courage to bring it to my lips."

Mama Knuckle laughed. "That's wisdom, not fear."

"I've seen what you've put in your teapots," Sorrow said, also laughing.

SORROW SPENT THE remainder of the night and much of the morning sleeping in an old barn on the edge of Two-Mile Ditch. Perhaps it came from seeing Mama Knuckle, but she felt a wave of nostalgia sweep across her as she curled up in the loft, away from prying eyes. In recent years, she'd had the money needed to live in relative ease. She lived as a vagabond, but a comfortable one, able to afford the best rooms in the best inns, or her choice of cabins aboard ships. But for most of the first few years following running away from home, she'd slept any place that kept rain off her head - under bridges, hiding in cellars, haunting old houses half-way fallen down. She'd fed herself by stealing from gardens and, when hungry enough, from the scrap heaps of taverns. A wriggling rat had been a horrifying meal, but it wasn't at the top of the list of the ten worst things she'd put in her mouth.

She rolled her eyes, thinking of those starvation meals, amazed at the things one could feel sentimental about.

She spent most of the day watching the main road through a gap in the boards. At last, she saw Brand, Slate, and Bigsby approaching town in an ox-wagon. Most surprising of all, Jetsam was with them, sitting next to Brand on the bench.

Sorrow slithered out of the barn. Though it was getting late in the day, the light was still strong enough that there were men working the fields. They fled as she undulated toward the road, most heading in the direction of Mama Knuckle's hut. Hopefully the necromancer would calm them down.

As she reached the road, Brand called out, "Sorry we're a little late. Arranging to have the *Circus* restocked took longer than I planned."

"What are you doing here, Jetsam?" Sorrow asked. "Wanderers can't come onto land!"

"Technically, I'm not on land. I'm on a wagon. Abyss doesn't have a problem with us walking around on boats or docks. A wagon is kind of a land-boat."

"But what if someone knocks you off?"

Jetsam shrugged. "Hopefully I'll have time to get airborne and make it to water. But, if I lost the protection against drowning offered by Abyss, I know it would break Ma's heart, but I really don't think I'd be worried. I can walk on water. I'm more likely to break my neck tripping over a wave than I am to drown."

"But why risk coming here at all?"

"Ma has a letter she wants me to give Avaris."

"I could deliver the letter."

"Ma says she can only trust a family member."

Sorrow frowned. She didn't like that Gale was doing things involving magic without consulting with her.

Slate stood up in the back of the wagon. He was dressed in the form-fitting, black glass scale-armor Sorrow had crafted for him, though he wasn't wearing his helmet. "Have you found Avaris yet?"

Sorrow shook her head.

"Any sign of Walker?" Brand asked.

"No."

"Perhaps we should have asked him to explain his plan in more detail," said Brand.

"What's the point?" said Bigsby, clanking as he stood. "The more he talks, the more confused I get." He was once again dressed in the chain mail he'd worn when he'd thought he was a princess, only without his breast plate. It also looked as if he had lined his eyes with black make-up. At least he wasn't wearing his wig.

"We're still a few miles from where the road ends in the swamp," Sorrow said. "My understanding is we'd find him there."

"Lead on," said Brand.

Sorrow led them to the ferry. The riverman fled as she approached, but left his pole behind. Jetsam flitted ahead to grab it. Seconds after the wagon was secured, he had the ferry free from its moorings and pushed off from shore.

"I'm a little surprised to see you geared up for battle," Sorrow said as she glanced at Bigsby.

The dwarf looked at his mace as if he was also surprised to find it in his hands. "I've been thinking a lot about what Equity said. About having the courage to be who you want to be, no matter what the world thinks. There was something deep inside me that wanted to be a warrior. I mean, I had my armor made up long before I went crazy. The legend of the missing Princess Brightmoon has been going around for a while, and it was fun to daydream crazy scenarios where I might be her."

"I can assure you that you're not," said Sorrow. "Infidel was the true Princess Brightmoon." As soon as she said it, she wondered if that was the sort of thing she was supposed to keep secret.

"Hah!" Jetsam said.

"You don't believe me?" asked Sorrow.

"Of course I believe you!" Jetsam laughed. "It makes perfect sense."

Sorrow couldn't tell if she was being mocked.

Bigsby said, "I was used to being bullied in Commonground. For release, late a night, when I was alone in my shop, I'd dress up in my armor and wig and beat the living crap out of strawmen with my mace. But the odd thing is, when I went crazy and got into some real fights, I did okay. Maybe I'm more of a natural fighter than I thought. Maybe Equity was right. All I've been lacking is courage."

"I think Equity was talking about the courage to wear whatever clothes you wanted," said Sorrow.

"I'll start with testing myself in combat. That's less daunting than going out in public wearing my wig."

"But I notice you didn't throw that mop overboard like I suggested," said Brand.

"It's an expensive wig," said Bigsby.

They continued to follow the road on the other side of the creek. They soon left behind cultivated fields and before long the road was flanked on both sides by marshes. Twisted trees rose from the water here and there. Blue herons perched in their branches, huge, ungainly birds that turned into graceful ballerinas once they took flight. Trunks fallen into the river were thick with black turtles, still catching the last rays of the vanishing sun.

As the sun disappeared, so did the road. It came to an end with a row of pilings stretching off into black water, looking like the foundation of a bridge or a dock that had never been finished. Across the water stood a thick forest of tangled trees. The air was cacophonous with frogs.

"I'm guessing this is where Walker will meet us," said Sorrow.

Jetsam jumped from the wagon and kicked up into the air. "What do we need him for? From what I know, Avaris lives in a walking castle taller than these trees. It seems like she should be easy enough to spot. At least, if the light was better."

"If her castle only walked this world, that would be true." They all turned toward the voice and found Walker sitting on the bench where Jetsam had just been.

"You seem to know a thing or two about walking between worlds," said Sorrow. "When I saw you on the Isle of Fire, I thought you were a ghost. Now you look solid enough. Are you a spirit, or a living man?"

Walker grinned. "Aren't we all ghosts?"

"I'm reasonably sure I'm not," said Jetsam, hovering above.

"Living men are merely bewildered ghosts, oblivious to their true nature," Walker said. "Were you not dead before you were born?"

Bigsby smiled. "I like having him around. It means I'm no longer the craziest person here."

Sorrow studied Walker. "I don't think you're crazy. I've been to the Sea of Wine and the Great Sea Above. I know that our reality is like the heart of an onion, surrounded by other layers. How is it that you move between them so easily?"

Walker's face suddenly turned serious. "I've paid a great price. Nothing of my existence is easy."

"What price?" asked Sorrow. "Who exactly are you? Why are you helping us? For that matter, the first thing you said to me was that you'd come from hell where you'd been chatting with demons. Why should we trust you at all?"

Walker shook his head. "I speak to demons for the same reason I speak to men. Infinity is a lonesome burden. Conversation offers a moment of relief. As for who I am, I was once called —" He suddenly let out a string of whistles that sounded like a bird call. "I was the shaman of the Spike Bark tribe. I was taught by my father to grind roots into a paste that I rubbed in my eyes. This allowed me to see the true nature of the world. For a long time I served my tribe, helping guide the spirits of my dead brethren to the Realm of Roots."

"That's another afterlife?" asked Sorrow.

"I would not use the word 'after,'" said Walker. "Though even I made the mistake in assuming there was a distinction between the material world and the spirit world. I did not learn the truth until my wife died. In my grief, I tried to follow her spirit. But she was already tangled in the roots, being sucked back into what I thought of as the living realms. When I tried to follow her back, to discover how she would be reborn, I found myself… elsewhere."

"Elsewhere?"

Walker looked wistful. "It looked the same, my village in the trees, my children, my brothers, my sisters. But, all was changed. I saw the truth for the first time. What I thought of as the 'real' world was only a waking dream, neither more nor less substantial than the Realm of Roots. The treasure I thought of as life was only a facet of the larger jewel of death. I was certain that I misunderstood what I saw, so I left my village to seek the wisdom of others. Eventually, as I was led through more and more abstract realms by my guides, all barriers between the worlds became visible to me. They're thin as tissue, and easily torn."

Sorrow had more questions, but Brand interrupted. "I'm sure that this would be a fascinating conversation under other circumstances, but I'm having a little trouble focusing while I'm being devoured by mosquitoes. Why don't we set up camp and get a fire going?"

"You didn't come here to camp," said Walker. "You came seeking Avaris."

"Any chance we'll find her while I still have some blood left?" Brand asked, slapping a bug that had alighted on the side of his neck.

"Her castle is near," said Walker. "I came here last night and sang for it. It enjoys music. It will return once more for my serenade."

"Start singing. That sounds a hell of a lot easier than the human sacrifice Zetetic was talking about. I'm not sure why you thought that required a lot of boldness, however."

"Sacrifice will be required. The castle will listen to my song, but it will not leave the Black Bog unless it can feed."

"The Black Bog is the swamp?" asked Jetsam.

"The Black Bog is another realm of the dead," said Sorrow. "It's part of the local mythology."

"What kind of sacrifice?" Brand asked Walker.

"You must die, of course," the pygmy said. "But not for long. I'll guide your spirit back into your body once the castle crosses into this world to feed."

"So… what? I slit my wrists and trust you to handle the rest?"

"The castle dislikes the taste of suicide," said Walker. "It prefers the flavor of murder."

"If we kill Brand, what guarantee do we have that the castle will notice?" asked Sorrow.

"It's here right now, watching us."

Everyone craned their necks toward the forest, searching the shadowy treetops.

"Come here," Walker said, motioning for Sorrow. "I'll help you see past the veil."

Sorrow leaned toward the pygmy. Without warning, he grabbed her by the back of her neck and pulled her forward. A shard of obsidian appeared in his hand, seemingly from nowhere. She cried in pain as he sliced the sharp stone across her eyebrows.

She punched him in the chest and jerked away. She grabbed her face with both hands. The wound across her brow didn't feel deep, but it hurt like hell. She wiped at the blood dripping into her eyes.

"Why did you do that?" she grumbled.

"Look to the trees," he said.

She did so. She grew still. Looming above the forest was a huge shadow, oval in shape, like a turtle shell large enough to encompass a village. Unlike a turtle, it was held aloft by four spindly insect legs, at least a hundred yards tall. At the front of the oval was a second, smaller oval, almost like a head. On that head were two narrow slits, glowing pale red, like eyes formed of embers.

She swallowed hard as she realized the eyes looked directly at her.

13 - DARK MIRROR

"WHAT IS IT you see?" Slate asked, hopping down from the wagon.

Sorrow said softly, "It's here. Her walking palace. I see it."

"Cut me," Slate said to Walker.

The pygmy stood on the seat of the wagon to comply.

Slate sucked in air through his teeth as he pressed his hands against the wound. He shook off his pain and looked up. His jaw went slack.

"Is it… a structure? Or a living thing?" he asked.

"Whatever it is, it's staring at me," Sorrow whispered. "I feel… I feel the way a mouse must feel when there's an owl on the branch above."

"I guess someone needs to kill me," said Brand. He looked at Walker. "Should they stab me?"

"Strangling would be best," said Walker. "Your body remains mostly undamaged, making it easier to return."

"Slate, you've got good strangling hands," said Brand.

"I'll not kill an innocent man, even if asked," said Slate.

"Me neither," said Jetsam.

Brand looked surprised. "You kill people all the time, Jetsam! You sing while doing it!"

"Yeah, but only to defend my family. Killing for any other reason means that when you make that final trip to the Sea of Wine, the Joyful Isles will forever retreat on the horizon."

"How about you, Bigsby? Do you have an appetite for fratricide?"

"No," said the dwarf. "How can you be so flippant about this? I know this is important to Sorrow, but why would you do something so stupid?"

Brand raised an eyebrow. "Stupid? I'm being offered a chance to experience death with the promise it won't be permanent. How can anyone with a healthy level of curiosity not be intrigued at the thought?" He turned to Sorrow and said, "Since you're the one wanting to see Avaris, I guess it's up to you to do the deed."

Sorrow heard a crashing, splashing noise as Brand spoke. She looked to the shadows and saw that the walking castle had turned tail and was running away.

"There's no point in anyone dying now," said Walker, shaking his head. "The castle has been spooked. It will not return, even if we offered it a dozen souls."

"No!" Sorrow screamed, slithering forward into the murky water of the swamp.

Slate splashed into the water beside her.

"There's no point in chasing it," said Walker. "It retreats further into the Black Bog."

"You can cross between worlds," said Sorrow. "You've taught Zetetic! Lead us!"

Walker laughed. "Zetetic practices seven disciplines of insanity each morning before breakfast. His mind is hardened against the blending of the real and the unreal. Untrained minds fall prey to nightmares and never escape."

Sorrow whipped back to the shore with the speed of a rattlesnake striking. She grabbed Walker by his shoulders and shook him. "Don't talk to me about falling prey to nightmares! I've seen things that would frighten your damned demon friends and I've come out stronger for it! Take me over!"

"If she goes, I go," said Slate.

Sorrow's hands suddenly lost their grip on Walker as his body turned to fog.

As he faded away, his laughter lingered in the air, along with his final words, "How can you go when you're already there?"

Sorrow drew back. To her horror, Brand, Jetsam, and Bigsby were dead, reduced to skeletons fallen across the ox-wagon. The ox, too, had become a pile of jumbled bones.

"We've crossed the veil," Slate said softly as he turned slowly to study the landscape. The swamp, once abundant with life, was reduced to dead trees amid oil black pools. Not a single frog chirp disturbed the still air.

Sorrow glanced back toward the walking palace. It was a mile away by now, only a gray silhouette against a starless night sky black as ink. Slate started to jump into the water once more, but Sorrow caught him.

"Careful," she said. "If the legends are correct, once you swim in these dark channels, you lose all memories of your mortal life."

"That would mean I would forget that I don't remember who I am," said Slate. "It sounds almost like a fate I'd welcome. If we don't enter the water, how are we to give chase?"

Sorrow sighed. "I wish I'd grown some damned dragon wings instead of this dumb tail."

As the words left her lips, she cried out in agony. It felt as if someone had just driven a sword into her back. She fell to the dusty ground, her body trembling.

"Sorrow!" Slate cried, kneeling beside her. "What's wrong?"

"Can't... breathe," she said through clenched teeth. It felt as if her armor was shrinking, crushing her torso. In desperation, she willed her glass armor to fall away, returning it to the sand from which it came.

Sorrow sucked in air as she sat up. She covered her bare breasts as she looked at Slate, who was staring at her with wide eyes. She nearly fell backwards. A terrible weight had settled on her shoulders. Throwing modesty to the wind, she reached both hands over her shoulders and discovered a giant bulge on her back, like a watermelon between her shoulder blades. The skin was so taut it felt as if it would tear open any second.

And then it did, with a sickening wet rip. She screamed, but the pain was followed instantly by relief. She looked over her shoulders and found black, bat-like wings spreading from her spine, large as sails. They were wet and slimy, like a newborn baby, and as they moved the cool air felt soothing.

She stood up, stretching her wings, wondering if they would be as simple to master as her tail had been. Then she realized she'd just stood up. She stared down at her bare legs, now restored to full humanity.

"You wished it," said Slate, "and it came true."

"So it would seem," said Sorrow, once again having the presence of mind to drape an arm across her breasts.

"I wish I could remember who I was," said Slate.

He stood silently for a moment, his face devoid of emotion.

"Did it... did it work?" she asked.

He shook his head.

"Maybe you have no memories to restore," she said. "I don't think my wings came out of nowhere. Instead, it's like I have a certain amount of dragon in me, and I was able to move it around due to the dream-like nature of this place."

"Can you fly?" Slate asked.

"That's kind of the obvious question, isn't it?" Sorrow said, managing to muster a feeble grin.

She turned her head toward the skies, spread her wings, and, in a sensation that filled her with indescribable pleasure, she bent her knees and ankles to crouch. It felt good to have legs again. The muscles in her thighs and calves felt warm and powerful. She tested their strength as she jumped with all her might.

Her wings beat down, striking the earth, lifting her higher. She flapped again and shot up a dozen yards, leveling off, feeling the wind beneath her wings as she glided in a wide circle around Slate, who gawked at her. It was an unwelcome sensation to have a man stare so openly at her nude body. On the other hand, if Slate had suddenly shed his clothes and grown dragon wings, would she have been able to turn her eyes away?

She scanned the skies. The palace could no longer be seen, but she knew which direction it had been heading. It would be simple to give chase.

"Will you be able to carry me?" Slate shouted.

Did she want to carry him? She'd always imagined she would be making the journey to see Avaris alone. She didn't even know why Slate was here. Yes, she understood his primary motive. Avaris might be able to explain who he was and why he had no memories. But then what? Would Slate swear allegiance to Avaris, grateful that her magic had given him life? Or would he attempt to kill her, reverting to the witch-breaking cruelty that she'd seen in the painting?

On the other hand, she'd been keeping journals for almost fifteen years and the one constant theme was that no one ever chose to stand by her side in her battles. She was in a nightmare landscape full of unknown dangers and Slate wanted to be here with her.

It wasn't a difficult choice.

"Spread your arms," she yelled. "I'm going to swoop down and grab you from behind."

He did so. She wheeled through the air, then adjusted her flight with numerous small movements to keep herself on target. The horror she'd felt waking up with her legs replaced by a serpent's tail was replaced by a casual, matter-of-fact acceptance that she now had wings. Perhaps it was the dream-like nature of the abstract realms that explained how natural her new limbs felt. Here the impossible became the mundane.

The second she slammed into Slate the absurdity of what she was doing was knocked back into her. She lost most of her speed on impact, with the wind knocked both from her wings and her lungs. Worse, while she'd managed to wrap her arms tightly around his chest, momentum carried them both toward the swamp. She had only seconds before she discovered if the mind-numbing properties of the water were true.

Of their own accord, her wings beat a mighty downstroke that altered her trajectory. Slate's boots left ripples as he danced across the water, dangling from her grasp. Her wings beat again and they rose, barely clearing the trees. He brought his hands to her wrists and grasped them with a death grip. She couldn't drop him now if she wanted to.

They continued to climb. The dead forest lay in shadows beneath them, a jumble of jagged trunks and limbs, twisted so that they looked like men frozen as they writhed in agony.

"I see it!" Slate shouted, pointing in the darkness.

His eyes proved superior to hers. She flew in the direction indicated for a full thirty seconds before she could distinguish the moving shadow.

The castle's back was to them. As they drew closer, she could see that her initial hunch that the structure resembled a turtle was accurate, assuming turtles grew to be a quarter mile across. She saw no obvious windows or doors on the bone white shell.

"We'll have to go around to the front," she said. "Maybe we can enter through the mouth."

As she spoke, the castle shuddered. With startling speed the beast whirled on its spindly legs until its glowing eyes faced her. It opened toothy jaws that would have been more at home on a shark than a turtle. Without warning, a jet of puss-colored fluid arced toward them. She banked hard, wincing as droplets of the yellow liquid splattered her wings, burning holes. Fortunately, her human skin was shielded by Slate. His glass armor proved well suited to defend against an attack of acid. Still, as she climbed higher, she said, "Okay, maybe not the mouth."

"Drop us on the center of the shell," said Slate. "The creature's head can't possibly turn to cover its own back."

Sorrow wasn't certain that was true in a place like this, but had no better strategy. She tilted her wings and they slowly dropped onto the apex of the beast's shell. She wasn't surprised to discover that this area was defended as well. As soon as Slate's boots hit the bone, the roof splintered for a dozen yards in every direction. Human skeletons rose from their bony matrix, their eye sockets turning to face the two interlopers, their jaws open wide in silent, outraged battle-cries.

"Let's try closer to the —"

Before she could compete her thought Slate broke free from her grasp. Following the battle with the pirates, he'd expressed satisfaction with the results he'd gotten from Bigsby's mace, so she'd crafted one for him with a longer shaft and larger head that took advantage of his unusual size and strength. He tore into the nearest skeletons with a fury, reducing them to splinters with each blow.

Sorrow realized she would only get in Slate's way, so she leapt into the air before the remaining horde could reach her and patiently flew in circles for the handful of minutes it took Slate to pound his way through the last of the undead. She landed amid a cloud of chalky dust and said, "Sorry I wasn't more help. You looked like you were having fun."

Slate shook his head as he picked up a fallen skull. "These were men once. It's tyranny to enslave the living. How much greater is the crime of enslaving the dead?"

Sorrow didn't feel like debating the matter. Instead, she studied the roof they stood on. Her Rott-informed sense of the decay in all things kicked in as she studied the joints of the bone plates.

"It's weakest here," she said, running her fingers along a seam. "One good whack will split this wide open."

"Stand back," Slate said, bringing the mace overhead with both hands.

Sorrow shielded her eyes as he swung. There was a loud cracking sound, followed by a *WHUMP*. She lowered her arms to find Slate missing. Her toes were at the edge of an octagonal hole large enough for an elephant to fall through. She peered into the room below.

Slate was on his butt in the middle of the collapsed roof. He'd fallen into what looked to be a library, with long rows of shelves lit by orbs of glass filled with what looked like fireflies. From her training in soul-catching, she suspected the lights were actually the souls of unborn children. They gave off a particularly gentle light when restrained.

She dropped into the library and looked around at the rows of leather-bound books.

"It would take a lifetime to read all of these," she said.

A single book near her feet said, "Read me before you read the others. My unread words burn within me, like a breath held burns the lungs. Release my words! Free them!"

Sorrow's eyebrows rose as she took a second look at the book, which plainly had a face. The leather binding, it seemed, had come from a man. His eyes were sewn shut, and his lips had once suffered a similar treatment, but the thread that closed the mouth had frayed, perhaps torn loose when the ceiling fell.

She turned away, pointing toward a door at the far end of the room. Slate nodded as he headed toward it.

"You can't leave me," the book cried, loudly enough that other books on the shelf awakened. Most of their lips were stitched together, reducing their pleading to incoherent whimpers. A fresh voice broke free of its binding, shouting, "There's no hell so dark as an unopened page! Read me! Restore my purpose!"

Slate paused, looking worried as he asked Sorrow, "Should we —"

"Ignore them. You could be trapped here for all eternity trying to satisfy them. The unread books of the world will always demand more of the living than can be given."

"But these aren't ordinary books."

"More ordinary than you think," said Sorrow, grabbing him by the wrist and pulling him toward the door.

She pushed it open. She wished she'd looked for another door.

Beyond was a chamber of horrors. There were double the shelves of the previous space, but rather than being filled with books, the space was filled with jars. And if the dancing fireflies in the lights were the souls of unborn children, the jars most certainly held their bodies. Pickled babies in various stages of development floated in pale gray alcohol. She'd seen such things before, curiously enough, in the collection of her father, who had a room of his mansion devoted to such oddities as embryonic calves with two heads and human babies with flippers instead of limbs. But this room contained thousands of the unborn. At least, she assumed they were unborn. Some looked rather large and well developed.

"Who would possess something like this?" Slate whispered.

"Try not to judge. It's disturbing to look upon, true. But physicians learn the skills they need to help the living by dissecting the bodies of the dead. I'm certain these bodies have some educational purpose."

Slate looked around. "Which way should we go?"

Sorrow shrugged. "It's not like I have a map. Just keep moving until we see a door. What's the worst that can happen?"

She regretted the question the instant it left her lips.

The next room was the kitchen. Sitting on the butcher's block was a child's head. It looked fresh. Slate looked as if he was going to be sick.

"You've seen decapitated heads before," Sorrow said, trying not to stare at the cutting board. Poppy's book had said that Avaris ate babies. This was definitely not a baby. It looked like a girl six or seven years of age. Why that mattered, Sorrow couldn't say. But could she even trust her eyes in a place like this? Or was she seeing a butchered child only because she'd been told she'd see them?

Slate covered the head with a towel, looking pale.

"We really can't know what happened here," said Sorrow.

"A young girl was killed, butchered, and eaten?"

"Maybe she died of natural causes. Or some accident that severed her head. Maybe she's been brought here to be cleaned up before burial."

"To a kitchen."

"Kitchens get used for lots of things."

"You cannot excuse this."

"I'm just saying we may not understand everything we're seeing. This isn't the world we know. We're in no position to judge the inhabitants."

"I believe I *am* in a position to judge," said Slate. "I'm a tolerant, patient man. But I've no mercy for those who would harm a child."

Sorrow ground her teeth together. She, too, thought of herself as a protector of children. Was she so hungry to learn from Avaris that she was ignoring plain evidence that Mama Knuckle had been right?

Slate marched from the kitchen, opening a door into a long hall.

"I may be turned around, but I think this leads toward the head," Sorrow said.

Slate moved down the hall with his mace at the ready. The door at the end of the hall was far more ornate than any they'd yet encountered.

"It would be nice if Sage were here to tell us what's behind the door," Sorrow whispered.

"After what we've seen, I'm ready for anything," Slate said. He leaned back and kicked the door open.

They'd found the throne room. A red carpet led toward a throne of black bones. Perched upon it was a woman of breathtaking beauty. She wore a jeweled red gown that glistened like fresh blood on her ivory skin. Her hair was black as coal, held in place by a crown of teeth. She was fifty feet away, behind a crystalline orb nearly a yard wide. A black, bat-like creature could be seen in the light moving within the crystal. It took Sorrow a few heartbeats to realize that the image in the orb was her own.

The woman clapped her hands together in an exaggerated fashion as a large man in plate armor stepped from behind the throne.

"Bravo," she said. "A magnificent performance from both of you. Kicking in the door of my throne room was satisfyingly dramatic. I imagine it must have been quite cathartic for you as well. You came looking for Avaris, Queen of Weavers. You've found her. Now that the dramatic opening is behind us, may I summarize the rest of the plot? You'll growl a few threats. I'll respond with witty banter. We'll bargain. In the end, we'll all get something we want, and I'll spare the lives of your friends."

"Our friends?" Sorrow asked.

"The three you left behind," said Avaris. "The three who can't see my palace. I've turned us around so we can kill them. They'll die without ever knowing why."

"No one needs to die," said Sorrow. "I've come looking for answers, not to fight you."

"I'm not sure your companion agrees," said Avaris. "He's positively trembling with rage."

"We found a girl in the kitchen," Slate said.

"Part of one, at least," said Avaris.

"Did you kill her?" Sorrow asked.

"Heavens no," Avaris answered. "Her body was given to me in exchange for favors."

"Favors?" asked Sorrow.

"Why would you traffic in the body of a child?" Slate asked.

"To eat them of course," said Avaris. "I'm six hundred years old. Without a steady diet of youth, I imagine I'd be quite the fright."

Slate growled, brandishing his mace and charging. The large, armored man stepped forward, drawing his sword. The blade was pitch black, and as it left its scabbard the air was filled with the distant howls of souls in agony. Sorrow recognized the sword at once from the painting they'd found on the ship.

"Slate!" Sorrow cried. "It's the Witchbreaker!"

Slate showed no caution, however, charging the man and swinging his mace with both hands. Sparks flew as Avaris's defender caught the shaft of the mace against his blade. The iron in both weapons rang as they slid against one another, bringing the two men's faces inches apart. Slate wasn't wearing his helmet. His opponent was wearing a helm that hid his face. Which was why everyone was surprised when Slate head-butted his opponent. The swordsman staggered back by the blow. As the gap between them opened, Slate drew back his mace. But he didn't aim his blow at the warrior. Instead, he threw his weapon at Avaris, still thirty feet away. She was caught off guard by the attack, dodging at the last second. The mace missed, smashing into the back of the throne where her head had just been. But the heavy iron handle slammed into the side of her head just above her ear, knocking off her crown.

Avaris tumbled to the floor, landing on one knee. She rose shakily, beating a hasty retreat toward the velvet curtains on the rear wall. Sorrow gave chase. She was furious at Slate for losing his temper and attacking, and furious at herself for knowing that the crimes Avaris had just confessed to didn't change Sorrow's desire to talk to the woman. If Avaris had become a parody of evil, it was only because her enemies had made her thus.

Avaris slipped behind one of the curtains. Sorrow heard iron bars rattle down. She glanced back and saw Slate and the warrior still grappling. Slate kept close, where a two-handed sword like the Witchbreaker was nearly useless. Slate had managed to slip his hands beneath the warrior's helmet and squeezed his foe's throat with all his might.

Sorrow pushed aside the curtain and reached out to touch the iron bars that blocked the doorway. With a thought, they crumbled to rust. She pushed through, her wings scraping against the edges of the doorframe.

She found herself in a luxurious bedchamber. A canopy bed sat in the center of the room, with gilded bedposts and satin bedding. All around the room were mirrors in frames of gold. Beside the bed was another crystal sphere, as large as the one outside. She could see the two warriors in the throne room struggling. Could hear them, too, the clinks and clangs of their armor echoing faintly from the crystalline surface. The room was almost silent other than this.

Almost.

There was an open door at the back of the room. The obvious path was to go through it. But in the relative silence of the room, she heard a noise. Her ears fixed upon a large wardrobe on the far wall. She moved before it, holding her breath to hear better. She furrowed her brow. Someone was definitely inside. And they were sobbing?

She yanked the door open. Avaris fell at her feet, her hands clasped around her bleeding temple, as she whimpered, "Please! Don't kill me! I'll give you anything you want!"

Sorrow raised her eyebrows. The woman seemed genuinely terrified.

"You were a queen once," Sorrow said. "Now you grovel at the feet of an unarmed woman?"

Avaris snorted. "You don't need to be armed. You've blended your spirit with Rott. You're destruction incarnate."

"I just expected... someone a little..."

"Braver? I fear death so much I've hid from it for six centuries. I live in shadows because I fear the scorn of those who remain in light."

Sorrow didn't know what to say to this. As she silently stared at the woman, she heard laughter from the crystal at her back.

A man's voice said, "Your hands grow weary. I see you've inherited none of my cleverness. How stupid must you be to try to strangle a dead man?"

Sorrow blocked this from her mind. If Slate bested his foe, he could burst through the door any moment and kill Avaris. If the swordsman bested Slate, he might prove more courageous than the queen. In any case, she needed to speak quickly.

"I may be blended with Rott," said Sorrow. "But I'm having difficulty controlling my power. I'm hoping you can help. If anyone knows how to command the powers of a primal dragon, it's you."

Avaris shook her head. She ran her fingers through her black hair, pulling locks away to reveal an ugly bubble of scar tissue on the pale flesh beneath. "This is all that remains of my one attempt to master the powers of Rott. In the end, I gladly plucked the nail from my skull."

"You had the same powers?" Sorrow asked, unable to take her eyes off the scar. "And you threw them away?"

"I had lost an even greater power," said Avaris. "Since I was young, men have done my bidding, seduced by my beauty. I lost that power when I blended my soul with Rott. No matter how I tried to blend the dragon's body with my own, I wound up repulsive, covered with scales. My once perfect mouth was ruined by fangs." She glanced up at Sorrow's nude body. "You've kept your figure better than I did. If you found a man who didn't mind the wings, you might still seduce him."

"I'd rather be part dragon than seduce men," said Sorrow.

"Truly? Then you squander your greatest natural gift. Women need no magic to enslave men. After I gave up on the false path of controlling the primal force of decay, I rediscovered the primal force of womanhood. I restored by body with bone-weaving and went on to seduce my greatest tormentor."

Sorrow almost asked who that was. She turned her gaze toward the crystal ball as a loud clang rang out. Slate had recovered his mace. He'd just knocked the warrior's helmet from his head.

The two men stared at each other in the aftermath. Save for the swordsman's deathly pallor and gray hair, they were as alike as twins.

"Stark Tower," Sorrow whispered.

"The Witchbreaker," said Avaris. "My mortal foe, now my undead champion. Once I seduced him, perverting what little good remained in him, it was a simple matter to enslave his body and ferry his soul to hell. I keep his corpse healthy with a daily supply of virgin blood."

Sorrow started to ask if Avaris meant that Stark drank the blood, but decided she didn't want to know.

Avaris looked puzzled as she stared at Sorrow, "If you don't seduce men, how do you summon the procreative energies required for bone-weaving?"

"I don't," said Sorrow. "I've never learned the art. That's why I've been hunting for you all these years."

"Ah. Then we can make a bargain. I give you knowledge. You spare my life."

"We spare all lives," said Sorrow. "Call off your castle's attack on my companions. Tell Tower to spare Slate."

"You've asked just in time. The castle has found your friends and stands above them now, unseen. It shall not strike unless I will it. As for Tower, he may be my slave, but his cruel streak exceeds my control. He'll play with Slate until he grows weary. Slate will die in terrible pain. It would be tragic, I suppose, if he were truly a living thing."

"Slate isn't alive?"

"For all physical purposes, Slate's indistinguishable from a living man. But he's my creation, an exact duplicate of Stark Tower, woven from the original's blood. I magically endowed him with all of the original's prowess in battle, but warped other aspects of his mind so that he would be Tower's dark mirror. Tower swaggered around the world claiming to be the champion of good. I created Slate to be the champion of evil. Only, I had made the mistake of believing Tower's own myth. When my creation woke, he was not the scourge I had hoped for. Instead, in his mirror nature, he proved kind where Tower was cruel. He was selfless where Tower was vain. While Tower hated mankind, Slate was quick to form friends, even with those who should have been his worst foes. In the end, I was forced to give the useless dolt a potion that destroyed his memories. I intended to find a wicked spirit in the realms of the dead more suited to my needs and offer him Slate's impressive shell. Alas, these events unfolded in chaotic times. Though I soon made the true Witchbreaker my slave, his army still overpowered my own and I was forced to flee. Slate was left in stasis, neither alive nor dead, until such time that I could return for him. Of course, in my exile, I decided to change my tactics."

"How?"

"The kingdoms of the world rejected my rule. I came to understand they were never worthy of my time. Let the masses suffer under their false churches. What they believe was a victory against me was the beginning of their long doom. I'm immortal. What does it matter to me if it takes my enemies centuries to fall?"

There was more laughter from the globe. Sorrow looked back to see Slate clutching his side, bleeding. Much of his armor was shattered. Save for his missing helmet, Lord Tower looked none the worse for wear.

"You're younger," Tower said. "Faster. Perhaps even a bit stronger. A benefit of still having a heartbeat, I suppose. What a shame that a living body so quickly grows weary. I do not miss pain. I do not miss the burning in my chest when breath grows short." He swung his sword overhead with both hands and chopped down. His blow didn't seem aimed to kill, but to maim, targeted on Slate's legs. At the last possible instant, Slate rolled aside, and the sword bit deep into the bone floor.

Sorrow looked back at Avaris. "How long will it take you to give me a nail of bone? I still wish to learn this art. It's said that bone-weavers can alter their forms. Can I not restore my humanity with it?"

Avaris shook her head. "The dragon spirit is stronger than mere flesh. You may rearrange your body, but only if you sever all ties with Rott can you be fully human. As for the bone nail, have the weaver arts decayed so far that you don't see the simple truth?"

"There aren't many witches left."

"But all should be bone-weavers."

"But I've never found a bone nail. I've never even discovered a bone-weaver's skull to study!"

"Fool! Peel away your scalp and what would you find?"

"My skull?"

"Made of?"

"Oh," said Sorrow.

"You were born with the tools. You merely lack the teaching."

"How long will I have to train?"

"A lifetime. I still discover new aspects to the magic. But there is a short cut."

"What?"

"You've already shown a willingness to blend your soul with a dragon. Would you be open to blending your mind with mine?"

"How?"

Avaris ran her fingers along Sorrow cheek. "I will take your left eye. I will give you one of mine in exchange."

Sorrow stared at the woman's face. Avaris looked serious. Her eyes were a perfect match for Sorrow's own emerald green.

Sensing Sorrow's hesitation, Avaris said, "It is only painful for a short time. After this, I will see all that you see. We can converse by thought though separated by miles and dimensions as easily as we speak now. I can guide you in the art of bone weaving, and improve your mastery of other skills. I may even be able to guide you in dealing with the dragon spirit. I held the power for over a decade before rejecting it. I know a thing or two about control."

"And sparing your life is the only price?"

Avaris laughed. "No. No, I think not. Of course, you've already dedicated yourself to the thing I would find most pleasing."

"The destruction of the church?"

Avaris nodded. "My price cannot be something you would do on your own. So, I will make it simple. You will kill someone of my choosing."

"Who?"

Avaris shrugged. "I don't know yet. It may take me many years to decide."

Sorrow frowned. She thought about the decapitated girl in the kitchen. There were people in this world she couldn't and wouldn't hurt. She turned away. "I cannot accept your bargain. If you were to demand I kill a child, I could not obey you."

"Even if the child were Numinous Pilgrim?"

Sorrow pressed her lips together.

She was still thinking the offer over when Avaris said, "Fine. No children. Nor anyone you would consider innocent, though no such creatures exists. I promise when I name my target, you will agree that they have committed the most flagrant sins."

Sorrow nodded. "Agreed." She turned to shake the elder witch's hand. Instead, she found Avaris standing behind her. The woman's left eye was a barren socket. The woman grabbed Sorrow's face, bringing her mouth toward Sorrow's eye. The witch's teeth warped and grew into long blades. Sorrow screamed as the fangs gouged into her flesh.

14 - JUST MAN

"SORROW!" A VOICE cried out. It was Slate from the other room, still alive despite all the odds. She couldn't look at the crystal ball, however. She couldn't look at anything. There was nothing but a veil of perfect blackness before her. Avaris' fingernail dug around within her left eye socket, removing dangling bits of flesh. The pain was so great that she reflexively clamped her right eye shut, effectively blinding herself.

There was a terrible pressure in her skull as Avaris jammed something hot and wet into her bleeding eye socket. Suddenly the veil of black was full of dancing white stars. Avaris removed her hand and Sorrow jammed her palms over her face. She probed as gently as she could and felt that she once more had two eyeballs.

With sheer force of will, she pulled her hands away and opened her eyes.

Everything in the room was doubled. She blinked, but it did little to improve her overlapping vision. She craned her neck. Avaris was nowhere to be seen. She rose on trembling legs, steadying herself on the bed frame. She glanced into the crystal ball. Through her doubled vision, she could see Slate still on the floor before the Witchbreaker. Judging from the chopped up nature of the floor, he'd rolled out of the path of dozens of blows.

"You're getting slower," Tower taunted as he raised his sword once more. "I can keep this up for all eternity."

Sorrow stumbled back toward the door she'd entered, placing her hand on the wall as she fought for balance. Her heartbeat pounded in her temples as she squeezed her eyes shut, fighting dizziness. The weight of the wings upon her back threatened to bring her to her knees. Just how much blood had she lost?

Taking a deep breath, she forced her eyes open once more. Her doubled vision snapped into focus as she stared at the bloodied handprint she'd left on the wall. Outside the room, she heard Lord Tower erupt into powerful laughter.

She stumbled into the doorway in time to see Slate once more roll aside as the Witchbreaker bit into the floor of the throne room. Slate's efforts at avoiding the enchanted blade had left an almost perfect circle chopped into the pale white bone that both combatants stood upon.

Slate was bleeding from a gash in his forehead and a slice across his right shoulder. He was drenched in sweat, his limbs rubbery as he managed to rise into a crouch.

"Don't you understand the futility of struggle?" Tower asked with a sneer. "Look upon my face. You're nothing but my reflection, a redundancy, a pathetic doppelganger stubbornly clinging to the illusion of life."

"Bold words," Slate wheezed, wiping sweat from his eyes, "from a man without a heartbeat."

Tower shook his head. "Hearts are a tremendous liability. Allow me to demonstrate!"

The knight swung the Witchbreaker high overhead. Sorrow leapt forward, spreading her wings, but in her weakened condition succeeded only in crashing to the floor.

Her flailing wings distracted Lord Tower enough to allow Slate to roll aside before the Witchbreaker once more sliced into bone. The knight looked at Sorrow as she tried to rise. He smiled as he said, "Gravity is not your friend."

"Nor yours!" Slate cried as he rose to his knees, wrapping both his arms around Tower's armored waist. With a gurgling grunt, he bent the undead knight backward, until Tower's leather boots lost their grip and the knight's heavy frame slammed into the center of the weakened circle of bone.

A loud *POP* echoed from the few inches of bone that remained intact around the circle. Cracks formed and broadened. Just as Sorrow made it back to her knees, the floor beneath the two warriors gave way and they dropped from view.

"Slate!" she cried, leaping forward, landing so that her body dangled out over the gaping hole.

The two men tumbled toward the earth a hundred yards distant. There was no time for her to even move.

From nowhere, a smaller airborne man dodged around the falling circle of bone, spreading his arms as he kicked toward Slate. It was Jetsam! From the smell of the humid swamp beneath, Sorrow realized that they'd crossed once more into the material world.

Jetsam wrapped his arms around Slate's belly, kicking furiously to push toward the waters of the swamp. They disappeared an instant later into the ink-black waters.

The bone floor turned on edge and landed upright, punching into the ground immediately behind the wagon where Bigsby and Brand were sitting. The ox harnessed to the cart bolted like a startled rabbit, plunging them all into the swamp. Lord Tower's armored form landed in the rut of the cart's wheel and lay very still.

Sorrow rose from the hole, feeling too weak to risk flying. She turned and found two overlapping images of Avaris directly behind her. The two raven-haired witches quickly resolved into one as Avaris drew back and delivered a powerful kick to Sorrow's gut. Sorrow fell backward into the open hole.

As she dropped, she heard Avaris say, "Fledglings need a little nudge from the nest."

Sorrow twisted in midair, spreading her wings, her fall slowing as she caught the air. She wound up in a dizzying spiral as the dark ground rushed toward her. Fortunately, her wings slowed her fall enough that, when she landed in the marsh grass, she sank in the muck to her knees but was otherwise unharmed.

She craned her neck toward the star-filled sky and watched as the walking castle lumbered back into the swamp, fading deeper into shadows with each step. In seconds, its feet no longer splashed in the waters of the material world.

She tried to will herself back across the veil to give chase. She had many more questions for Avaris. But her body remained stubbornly stuck in the realm of mud. With a loud *SLUCK* she pulled herself from the mire and stumbled back to drier ground.

"Walker!" she shouted. "Walker!"

"He's gone," Brand said. "Just faded away, until nothing was left but a grin. Then even that vanished."

With some effort, she focused her eyes on him. Brand was still dry, apparently having jumped from the cart just before it hit the water. He said, "Walker told us to be patient before he vanished. Jetsam was keeping watch while Bigsby and I caught a little shut-eye. Next thing I know I'm waking up with the damn castle directly overhead, people are falling from the sky, plus you've got wings, and, oh yeah, legs. Care to explain what's going on?"

Sorrow didn't answer. What was she to say?

"Are you all right?" he asked stepping closer. Suddenly his expression changed from consternation to concern. He placed his fingers on her chin and turned her head to get a better look at her eye. "By the sacred quill. I thought you just had mud on your face. I didn't realize you were injured."

"It's just a head wound," she said with a feeble smile. "I collect them to fill my idle hours."

"New body parts also seem to be a hobby," said Brand. "Wings?"

She shrugged. "My body was a bit more flexible in the Black Bog. I'm still halfway to dragonhood, but at least I can wear shoes again."

Brand took off his shirt and offered it to her. "You might have more urgent things to cover than your feet," he said, glancing toward the swamp, where Slate and Bigsby were crawling up the bank. Jetsam was balanced on the surface of the water, kneeling before the ox thrashing in the mud, using his sword to cut away the beast's harness.

Sorrow looked at the shirt, baffled by how it would possibly work with her wings. In the end, she tied it around her hips to serve as an impromptu skirt, then crossed her arms over her breasts.

The dripping wet ox thundered past an instant later, galloping off across the field in a panic. From above, Jetsam said, "Sorry. Lost my grip on his lead as I guided him back to land. I couldn't just let him drown."

"It's okay," said Brand.

"I'm not okay with it," said Bigsby, shaking mud from his limbs as he walked back up between the ruts left by the ox cart. "It's a long hike back to town." He came to a sudden halt as he encountered the armor sunk into the ground before him.

"Careful," said Sorrow. "He might not be dead!"

"From that height?" Jetsam said. "He's dead."

"Okay, yes, but he was dead before and it didn't slow him much."

Slate approached the fallen knight and dropped to his knees. He grabbed the knight's left shoulder and tried to turn Tower over onto his back. The man's arm came loose in his hands. Maggots writhed in the exposed tissue inside the iron sleeve.

Jetsam and Brand gagged as the stench of rotten meat billowed into the air. Sorrow wrinkled her nose reflexively, but realized that the stink didn't strike her as particularly foul. Perhaps sharing body parts with Rott had deadened her revulsion to such smells.

Bigsby also seemed oddly oblivious to the odor as he walked up to the body and stared at the face, which had been partially revealed by Slate's efforts.

"He looks… familiar," Bigsby said.

Brand pinched his nose shut and covered his mouth with his hand as he asked, "How can you stand so close to that stench, brother?"

Bigsby shrugged. "I ran a fish market for almost twenty years. I guess even nostrils can develop calluses." Looking back at the corpse, he asked, "Who was he?"

"He was me," said Slate, shaking his head mournfully.

"Explain," said Brand.

Slate told them what he'd learned, which meshed pretty well with what Avaris had told her. Apparently, Tower had been chatty during battle.

Everyone stared at Slate quietly after his tale. His expression was completely unreadable.

Finally, Brand said, glancing at Tower, "I suppose the decent thing to do would be to go borrow a shovel and bury him."

"That sounds like work," said Jetsam. "Can't we just toss him into the swamp?"

"No," said Slate. "He may have been turned into a monster in death by Avaris, but in life he was a great champion of the church. He deserves better than to have his body tossed into some nameless swamp."

"I'll bet actual money the locals have a name for this place," said Jetsam.

"I'll build a coffin," Slate said. "I need to take his remains to a respectful resting place."

Sorrow couldn't hold her tongue. "Are you out of your mind? He tried to kill you! He was laughing as he tore new holes in your flesh!"

"You mistake the corpse for the man," Slate said. "Avaris perverted his remains. You witnessed her atrocities. You heard her casual boasts of wickedness." He glanced at her. "Or can it be, even with one eye nearly missing, you're still blind to her evil?"

Sorrow touched her face. With all the blood, Slate must have assumed that Avaris had attacked her. No one needed to know of the bargain made.

"You're right," she said. "I may have had, perhaps, an overly optimistic idea of the kind of person she was. But don't you see the same is true of Lord Tower? He was a cruel monster in life as well as death. Disposing of him in the swamp is almost an insult to the swamp."

Slate pulled Tower's body completely free of the soft earth. The Witchbreaker was revealed in the dirt beneath. Faint howls of agony filled the night as Slate lifted the ebony blade. They fell silent as Slate slid the weapon back into its scabbard.

"A blade that that sends the souls of its victims to hell," said Sorrow. "Is that the weapon of a hero?"

"It is now," said Slate, slinging the scabbard over his shoulder.

"You're keeping the blade?" Bigsby asked. "I think having to hear those screams every time I used it would give me nightmares."

"A just man need not be disturbed by hell," said Slate. "After the events of this night, I understand the need for such a place, and the justice of it."

"Slate, listen to yourself!" Sorrow said, throwing her hands into the air. She quickly clamped them back over her breasts when she saw Jetsam's eyes bulge. She returned her focus to Slate, marching up and shouting, "You aren't a champion of the church! You're just a bit of magic that looks like a man. The church despises things like you and is dedicated to wiping them from existence!"

"However odd my origins, I'm a man," said Slate, remaining calm. "I breathe. I feel. I think. I may lack memories, but I have a conscience."

Sorrow sighed. She was confounded by Slate's reaction. But what would she want? That he would be outraged by his origins? Wouldn't that just make him hate witches? Did she desire that he be filled with despair? Of what use would he be if he were despondent, or suicidal?

"I'm sorry," she said. "You're right. You're a man, and a good one at that. I shouldn't have said that you weren't. I'm merely asking you to consider that, possibly, the real Lord Tower didn't quite live up to the ideals laid out in Poppy's book."

"That doesn't mean I can't," said Slate. "Whatever Lord Tower's sins may have been, I'm his second chance. I can live as the hero the world believed him to be."

"Is this settled?" Brand asked. "If we're going to build a coffin, that might take a while. I guess we can use wood from the cart, but we don't really have the right tools."

Sorrow shrugged. "If he must have a coffin, I can make one. With my wood weaving abilities, it won't take long."

She waded into the water to tear boards off the cart. The dark water was warm as a bathtub. She dipped beneath the surface to clean the blood from her face.

"And where exactly are we hauling him off to?" Bigsby asked.

"There's a vault for highly honored knights in the Cathedral of the Book," said Brand. "But, going back to the Silver City is out of the question any time soon."

"Saints get air burials at the Temple of the Book," said Jetsam.

"Air burials?" asked Bigsby.

"The temple is high in the mountains of Raitingu," said Jetsam. "There's no real soil there, just rock, so bodies are left out for birds to devour. The left-over bones are put into an ossuary beneath the temple."

"It looks like the maggots aren't leaving anything for the birds," said Bigsby.

"The Temple of the Book," Slate said, as if he was trying to remember something. "That's where the One True Book was discovered? The birthplace of the church?"

"Yep," said Jetsam. "Kind of ironic, since now the place is surrounded by Stormies."

"Stormies?" asked Slate.

"The Isle of Storm is where Tempest dwells," said Brand. "For the last couple of centuries, the dragon has been worshipped as a god by the locals. Stormies isn't the most respectful way of addressing them."

Slate looked confused. "Why would men worship a dragon?"

"Why would men worship a book?" Jetsam asked.

"They don't worship a book. They worship its author," said Slate.

Jetsam held up four fingers, tapping them one by one as he said, "Church. Of. The..." He let the last word go unspoken as he stared at Slate.

SORROW TOSSED THE last of the boards she'd need onto the bank. She left the water, shaking her wings to dry them. Her strength had returned somewhat after her bath.

She began the work of fusing the coffin together. She took care to close the cracks in the old boards and smooth out any splinters. The cart had been in use for years, giving the wood a natural patina that sealed the pores. Once the body was inside, smell wouldn't be an issue.

Sorrow straightened up when her job was done, using her wings to shield herself from Jetsam's gaze from above as she stretched her back. "Once you gentlemen are done discussing religion, you can load the body. I trust you'll figure out how to get it back to the ship. I'm going to fly on ahead and rustle up some proper clothing."

She jumped, flapping her wings. She clenched her teeth, surprised by the effort required. It had definitely been easier to fly in the Black Bog. Back in the material world, climbing a hundred feet into the sky took almost as much energy as sprinting up a flight of stairs of equal height. She only made it to two hundred feet before she was forced to lock her wings as wide as she could and glide while she caught her breath. Her wings seemed to have the necessary power, but now that the rest of her body had returned to human proportions, her lungs felt inadequate to the task.

"People think flying's easy," Jetsam said, his voice just beneath her. She looked down and found he was doing a backstroke about fifty feet below. "But it's more like swimming. It wears you out fast if you aren't careful."

"I'll get better with practice," she said.

"You keeping the wings?" Jetsam asked. "I thought your whole reason for looking for Avaris was to return your body to normal."

"You saw how bloodied I was," said Sorrow. "Avaris wasn't exactly helpful."

"I hope you can explain that to Ma. She'll be upset I didn't deliver her letter."

"I'll talk to her," said Sorrow. "I'm sure she'll understand."

They passed over a freshly plowed field. Jetsam spun in the air until his back was facing her. He spread his arms and rose, just as air lifted her own wings.

"Follow me," Jetsam called out. "I know the types of land to watch for that produce updrafts. The air is full of currents. I can teach you how to ride them. You can cover twice the distance with half the effort."

"Lead on," she answered, as they swam among the stars.

IT WAS DAYBREAK when they returned to the *Circus*. Sage met them on deck. The second Jetsam's feet touched the planks, she said, "You still have the letter."

"You noticed."

"This surprises you?"

"Not in the least. Does Ma know yet?"

Sage shook her head. "She went to bed a little while ago. Run below and wake her."

As Jetsam ran below deck, Sage knelt and opened a satchel sitting beside her. "I noticed you've returned a bit altered. I hope you don't mind that I took the liberty of securing you some clothing."

"Mind? I'm unspeakably grateful!"

"Here are some pants. And I've cut the back from this blouse. You can slip it on from the front, then tie it around your neck and waist," said Sage.

"A seer and a tailor," said Sorrow, taking the clothes. "You're quite talented."

Sage shrugged. She said, in a neutral tone, "I count lip reading among my talents."

Sorrow froze for half a heartbeat as she pulled on the pants. She asked, "So, can you… can you see into the abstract realms?"

"Alas, no," said Sage. "You and Slate vanished from my sight the second you left the material world."

"Ah," Sorrow said, nodding. She smiled wistfully. "Too bad. You missed quite an adventure."

"I must have. It's not often that people leave this ship and return with entirely new body parts."

Sorrow looked up at her wings. "I don't think of these as new, so much as rearranged. I think my body still has the same amount of dragon mass. I was just able to move it into a more useful configuration."

"With the help of Avaris?"

"No, I pretty much did it just by wishing for it, but don't ask me how."

"So how did your meeting with Avaris go?"

Sorrow considered her answer as she tied her blouse shut behind her neck. "If you were watching, you saw that I returned from her palace with a rather nasty facial injury."

"True enough," said Sage. "But what's even more interesting is, you've returned with someone else's eye."

"What?" Sorrow asked, trying her best to scoff.

"Your left eye. It's different. Like it belongs to someone else entirely. You left with two auras and you've come back with three."

"Strange things happen in the abstract realms," said Sorrow.

"Strange things happen here as well," said Sage. "People my family trust have been known to betray us."

Sorrow didn't say anything.

"And I've been known to do very bad things to those who willingly place my family in danger."

"You've no reason to be worried about me. I can't explain what you think you're seeing, but, trust me, I'm perfectly fine. Everything's alright."

"No, it's not," a woman answered from behind. Sorrow turned to find Gale and Jetsam behind her. "Since we couldn't appeal to Avaris for aid, my mother is still trapped."

Sorrow nodded. "I'm sorry. But before I left for the Black Bog, I investigated a solution to this problem on my own. I explained things to Mama Knuckle, a highly skilled necromancer."

Gale's face brightened. "And she had an answer?"

"An answer, yes. A solution, probably not. Blood is ordinarily required to sustain souls. The *Freewind* had been prepared to house your mother's soul by having her blood dissolved in wine, which was used to soak the timbers. Unfortunately, while there may be some residue of your mother's blood in the figurehead, we'd never be able to soak a whole ship with it."

"Then there's no hope?" Gale asked.

Sorrow sighed. "I don't… I don't think so. Mama Knuckle said that it was possible for a family member to supply the blood. But it would require all the blood from an adult. Someone would have to die to restore your mother."

Gale shook her head. "A life is too high a price. It's over. All hope is lost."

"Perhaps your mother's soul can still travel on to the Sea of Wine. You may see her again one day."

Gale looked crestfallen. "I've failed."

"Grandmother had a good life, and was able to watch her grandchildren grow for many years after her natural death," said Sage. "You haven't failed her."

"I've failed everyone," said Gale.

"You've never struck me as someone prone to wallowing in self-pity," said Sorrow.

"This isn't self-pity. This is realism. The ship that was my family home has been lost. My family would have been broken up long ago if not for the *Freewind's* ability to sail the Sea of Wine. It kept us beyond the reaches of our enemies. Our supernatural speed meant that we could keep clients even as the oceans became increasingly dangerous to sail."

"We don't really need clients now," said Sage. "Brand's willing to foot the bills with his dragon-bone money."

"That's charity, not business," said Gale. She looked at Sorrow. "It's time to admit the larger truth. Even if the *Freewind* hadn't been lost, my family would have been broken apart soon enough. Most Wanderer ships are crewed by forty or fifty people, with the core family supplemented by spouses and cousins and close friends who've outgrown the confines of other ships. I've extended a hundred offers to other Wanderer ships to provide homes for excess crew, and been rebuffed each time."

"The pirate wars are still fresh in people's minds," Sorrow said. "In a few years, things will calm down."

Gale nodded. "But the calm won't lead others to join us. Instead, they'll accept us, one by one. Levi left our ship and married soon after. Sage, you've caught the eye of many a young man. How long before you're seduced away?"

"I wouldn't abandon you," said Sage.

"But don't you see? It wouldn't be abandonment. It wouldn't be betrayal. I've not created a ship where you can forge a future. I want you to be happy. I want you to know love, to form a family. If I'm honest with myself, I know that means you'll have to leave me. It breaks my heart, but it hurts more to think that you might not leave to pursue your own happiness."

"You certainly didn't take that attitude with Levi," Jetsam said, sounding skeptical.

Gale frowned. "I know I'm bitter. It's not as if the circumstances of Levi's departure were simple. He killed a man, then fled, then joined forces with some of our worst enemies."

"But only because he fell in love," said Sage. "And you know he thought he was defending you when he killed our dryman."

"You're not telling me anything I don't already know," said Gale. She sighed. "When he left, I still had hope that our friends and relatives would make peace with us. I felt like he left before I could really work things out. Now, I see I'll never work things out. All I can do is help each of you prepare for the day when you leave this ship to start your life anew."

"Is this why you keep making us call you Captain?" Jetsam asked.

Gale nodded. "I want you to have good habits for the day you serve on another ship."

"I don't think that's going to happen with me," said Jetsam.

"You say that now. But sooner or later, the lure of another ship will be irresistible."

"No," said Jetsam. "I mean, when I go, I don't think I'm going to live on another ship. The rest of you only see the world from its shorelines. I've been lucky enough to explore the landscapes of the islands we visit from above. I've got to tell you, the land looks a hell of a lot more interesting than the sea."

"Jetsam!" Sage said, sounding shocked.

"You would betray your culture?" Gale asked, her voice trembling.

"What's so special about our culture?" Jetsam asked. "I've been told since I was a toddler that Wanderers value individuality and freedom, but it seems to me like most of the other Wanderers look down on us because we're different. There's more than one way to live a life."

"If you feel that way, then go," Gale said. "Be like Levi. What's keeping you here?"

"Love," said Jetsam. "You mean the world to me. Everyone in this messed up family of ours is more important to me than all the stuff I've seen on land. Maybe one day our family will be scattered over a half dozen ships, pursuing different lives. But until that day comes, as long as the Romers man a ship, I plan to be part of that crew. That's just the way I feel, Captain."

He stepped forward and wrapped his arms around his mother. Gale hugged him back, tears in her eyes. "Ma," she said.

"Captain Ma," said Sage, as she wrapped her arms around the both of them.

Sorrow turned away, wiping her eyes. For some reason they were watering. At least, her right eye was. Her left eye was clenched into a contemptuous little slit and despite all of her willpower she was unable to open it.

AFTER SLEEPING MUCH of the day, she went above deck in mid-afternoon. She knew that a winged woman walking around in plain sight might draw unwelcome attention to the *Circus*, but she and Jetsam had flown onto the ship together that morning when the docks had been bustling with fishermen preparing to leave port. By now, word that the *Circus* held monsters had to have spread to the far ends of the town.

What she didn't expect was to climb out of the hold and find the air cloying with the aroma of flowers and incense. Mako stood at the gangplank, arms crossed, looking annoyed as he stared at her.

"What?" she asked.

He nodded for her to look down the gangplank. The whole of the dock below was filled with vases of flowers, baskets of bright fruit, and hundreds of lit candles. Smoke wafted from incense burners scattered amid the colorful clutter.

"You've made an impression on the locals," said Mako. "They've been leaving offerings for you all day. A few have tried to get on the ship, but turn tail when I show my teeth."

"Offerings?" she asked, not sure she'd heard him correctly.

"Another name for Podredumbre is the Decaying Isles. Before he stopped manifesting bodily in the material world, Rott used to make his home here. Most of the locals publicly worship the Church of the Book, but in private they still live as if Rott is the lord of this place. Did you know that every year on the winter solstice, they dig up the bodies of their departed relatives and bring them back inside to sit at the table as part of a winter feast?"

"I've heard that," Sorrow said.

"Nice wings," said Mako.

Sorrow shrugged. "I haven't really had much of a chance to look at them." She walked down the gangplank. Some of the vases were made of blown glass, and a few of the incense burners were silver. She grabbed them and returned to the deck to make mirrors.

"You never struck me as the vain type," Mako said as he watched her turn to study herself in the looking glasses.

"This isn't vanity. It's curiosity." She ran her fingers along the inner folds of her wings. The scaleless flesh was smooth and soft as her inner thighs. "You'd understand if you ever grew a new body part over night."

Mako opened his massive jaws, his head tilting back so that his face effectively disappeared, leaving nothing but a gaping maw filled with rows of arrowhead teeth perched upon his shoulders. He closed his mouth and said, "I wasn't born like this, you know."

"You can't pretend you didn't spend a great deal of time studying your new mouth in the mirror," she said, as she stretched her wings to their fullest extent. Light seeped through the flesh at its thinnest spots, revealing dark veins.

"I don't need to pretend," said Mako. "I don't look at myself in the mirror. Ever. The others may have gotten rewards from the Mer-King, but I've been given a curse."

"It can't all be bad," said Sorrow. "You seem to be a lot stronger than a normal man. I'm under the impression you can stay underwater a long time as well."

Mako shrugged. "Being strong and a good swimmer are normally things that girls find attractive. But girls stay far away from me. The few that do talk to me never stop staring at my teeth."

"I'm not a good person to talk to about romantic frustrations," said Sorrow, looking over her shoulder to study her back in the mirror. "I find the subject entirely uninteresting."

"You aren't interested in children?"

"In what way?" As she said this, the image of the head they'd found on the butcher block flashed into her mind.

"In having them."

"Oh. No. I think not."

"But you're estranged from your father," said Mako. "Don't you want a family of your own?"

She chuckled. "For now, I'll just keep borrowing yours."

15 - STORMCALLER

BY MIDNIGHT, THE dock next to the *Circus* glowed as bright as noon from all the candles. Along the waterfront, crowds had gathered, singing in a language Sorrow didn't understand.

At this point, all the Romers were awake and on deck. Mako seemed especially high strung as he paced along the railing.

"Calm down," Sage said as she stared into her spyglass. "There's no point in getting worked up. I'll see if anyone tries to board, but I don't think anyone's going to bother us. Listen to the music. This isn't some battle anthem. It's a hymn. They aren't here to hurt us."

"It's still spooky," Cinnamon said from her perch in the rigging. "Look at all the coffins."

Sorrow had made note of this herself. The local mausoleums had apparently been emptied out. For every living person in the crowd, there were just as many coffins, lids open, their skeletal contents lifted for a better view of the ship.

Poppy was balanced on the rail near the gangplank, steadying herself with a hand on the rigging. "If anyone tries to bring a coffin on board, I'm popping it to the moon."

"This might be a good time to talk about Slate," Jetsam said to Sorrow.

"Right," said Sorrow. Then, addressing the rest of the Romers, "Slate and the others are bringing back a coffin."

"I know," said Sage. "They're almost here. The crowds are slowing them down."

"I see them too!" Jetsam cried out.

Sorrow's eyes followed Jetsam's pointing finger. She couldn't make much sense of the jumble of humanity before her. Finally, she saw a coffin held higher than the others. She recognized this as the coffin she'd made, and watched as Slate and Brand pushed their way through the crowd to the dock. Each was holding up one end of the casket. Bigsby walked between them. He broke free as they neared the gangplank and rushed back aboard the ship.

"I thought I was going to be trampled to death," he said, gasping.

Slate and Brand marched up the gangplank and laid the closed coffin carefully onto the deck. Brand glanced at Sorrow. "So," he said. "You seem… popular."

"How can you be sure they're here to see me?"

"Because street venders are selling little winged dolls woven from marsh grass and cornhusks." He produced one of the dolls from his pocket. The cornhusk wings had been dyed black with squid ink. "They're saying the Death Angel has come to free them from their oppressors."

Sorrow eyed the spires of the nearest church.

"Don't," said Brand.

"Give me one reason why I shouldn't," said Sorrow.

"Because if you lead this mob on a church burning rampage, you'll only be setting the stage for tragedy."

"I'll be helping to lift the colonial boot from their neck," said Sorrow.

Brand slowly shook his head. "Let's say you spark a rebellion. Once news reaches the Silver City, the king will simply launch his navy to retake this town. Or maybe the Isle of Storm will hear about the rebellion and decide that now's a good time for them to stage an invasion. Maybe you'll get a thrill from watching these churches burn. Will you get an equal thrill when tens of thousands of people die from the war you trigger?"

Sorrow clenched her fists. "How am I at fault if there's war? The blame falls upon the king who claimed land not his own in the first place! For too long in this world, we've accepted that might makes right. Is it not better to die free than to live in fear?"

"That philosophy is the foundation of my life," said Gale. "But if these people long for freedom, they must seize it themselves. They have the power to set fire to a church or a jail. Instead, they light candles beseeching you to save them."

"If I have the power to save them, shouldn't I use it?"

"If you lead them to war tonight, are you willing to remain here for the years required to lead them into peace?" Gale asked. "Are you a builder? Or only a destroyer?"

Sorrow turned her back to the crowd. Her body felt like a spring that had been wound for fifteen years. Now was the time to release a lifetime of tension and achieve her first important victory against the church.

She took a deep breath, opening her hands, staring into them. She knew Brand had a point. The king would only send his navy. With all the wealth and worshippers commanded by the Church of the Book, any church she watched burn tonight would be rebuilt within a year. Leading these people might win a fleeting battle, but would do nothing toward winning her war.

"You're right," she said, tersely. "It's not worth the price. Let's depart for Raitingu before I change my mind."

"Raitingu?" Rigger asked. "Why, exactly, are we going to the Isle of Storm?"

Slate answered. "This coffin holds the mortal remains of Stark Tower. It's my duty to deliver them to the Temple of the Book."

"Stark Tower?" Rigger asked. "The Witchbreaker? Are you sure?"

Slate drew the ebony sword from the scabbard across his back. The howls of the damned gibbered around him as he held the blade before him. "I'm reasonably sure."

"That is so windswept!" Poppy said, jumping down and running up to stare at the blade.

"Windswept?" asked Slate.

"It means amazing! Wonderful! Excellent!" said Poppy. "Can I hold it?"

"I don't think that's wise," said Slate as he slid the blade back into the scabbard. "Carrying the sword is a great responsibility. For now, its burden must be mine alone."

"Still, wow, we've got a magic sword and a quest to travel to a legendary temple," said Poppy. "This is just like the stories!"

Rigger cleared his throat. "Excuse me, but may I be the voice of reason and point out that Raitingu is an insanely dangerous place for us to visit?"

"When has that ever stopped us?" asked Jetsam.

"Our biggest advantage at sea is Ma's ability to control winds," said Rigger. "Maybe you're unaware the priestesses who serve Tempest are known as stormcallers? They not only control wind, they also command rain and lightning."

"And we control kicking butts," said Jetsam. "Let them try to mess with us."

"What about Levi?" Rigger asked.

That brought looks of concern to the faces of all the Romers.

"What about Levi?" asked Sorrow. "He was helpful when his hurricane came to our rescue north of Skell."

"If we meet him near Raitingu, he'll be defending the island," said Rigger. "Are we really going to go there and possibly fight our own brother?"

Gale walked toward the wheel. "If we face Levi in battle, it's because of choices he made, not us." She took the wheel in hand. "In the meantime, we're sailors. We go where the owner of the ship commands. So, Brand, what say you?"

"Sorry, Rigger," said Brand. "Going to Raitingu makes sense to me as well."

"Why? To bury some dead knight?"

"No. Because my father had business contacts there. I know several of them from a trip I took with my father when I was a teenager. Going there gives me a chance to make my case to them that my father's little empire should belong to me and Bigsby, not that gold-digger living in his mansion."

"I thought you didn't want to run your father's business," said Sorrow. "I thought you were happy to start a new life where you could make your own fame and fortune."

"I am," said Brand. "But that doesn't mean I want some woman I don't even know to enjoy the fruits of my father's labor. She can't do what she's done to me and not expect to face the most horrible revenge I can dream of."

"You're going to kill her?" asked Sorrow.

"I'm going to sue her," said Brand. "There are hundreds of lawyers in the Silver City who would like a piece of the Cooper fortune. With a few letters and the testimony of my father's business partners, I'm going to wage a legal battle against my stepmother that will strip her of every last moon. She wants to use the law against me? Two people can play at this game."

"I didn't know you had a vengeful streak," said Sorrow, nodding. "I like it."

WEEKS LATER, EIGHTY miles out from Raitingu, the sea grew rough and choppy. Jetsam had been training Sorrow with daily practice flights since they left port, but the winds were so strong this morning that she kept being forced back into the rigging.

Jetsam stood in the ropes next her. She shouted, "It's getting too dangerous. We should just go back down."

"Oh?" He grinned. "You only want to fly in good weather?"

"Could you fly in this?"

"Sort of. It's more like body surfing. Only the waves are invisible. Once the wind gets this bad, you ride where it takes you."

"When your mother wakes up, will she calm things down?"

"Maybe a little. But we're close to the city of Kaikou, at the mouth of the Ookawa river. That's where the cloud giants' hurricane ships anchor when they need to take on supplies. They slow their winds when they're over the city, but even at their lowest speed it's like being caught in a tropical storm."

"Hurricane ships?" Sorrow said. "Do you think Levi will be there?"

"Maybe."

"I didn't really get to talk to him much, but he seemed nice enough. How did he wind up getting involved with the Storm Guard?"

"It's really more a matter of getting involved with a cloud giantess. Tempest forces all the cloud giants to serve in his military, even though they're by nature gentle creatures. But when you live on clouds, and the dragon who has absolute control over clouds asks you to do something, you do it."

Cold rain began to spatter against Sorrow's wings. Worse, Sorrow had gotten used to Gale keeping the ship reasonable steady. Up here in the rigging, the pitching and swaying of the ship left her stomach lurching.

"It might be time to go below deck," she said.

"Aw, it's just a little water," said Jetsam. "I need to stay on watch until Sage wakes up, but you go on down."

Sorrow climbed carefully to the deck. The rigging grew increasingly slick as the rain set in with a vengeance. She wasn't completely vulnerable to the elements. Bigsby had modified the cloak he'd made for her. It no longer fit over her wings, but it served as a hooded shawl that protected her shoulders and head. Still, even with her head covered, her body was quickly drenched.

She saw Rigger at the wheel, standing beneath a canopy made of a loose sail stretched between taut ropes that shielded him from the rain.

He shrugged as he watched her shivering and said, "There's room for two."

She tried to shield herself with her wings as she traversed the rolling deck, but the wetter they got the colder she felt. Her teeth were chattering by the time she made it under the canopy.

"Who says you don't have sense enough to come in from the rain?" Rigger said.

She studied his face, unable to tell if she was being insulted. Though Rigger was only two years older than Jetsam, his thin face was marked by worry lines. He held out a steel flask. "Take a swig of this to warm yourself."

"I don't drink alcohol."

"It's only tea. I can't keep it in a cup since it would slosh out."

She took the flask, grateful for the warmth as she wrapped her fingers around it. She took a sip and nearly spit it out. It was unbearably bitter. "What is that?" she managed to ask despite the numbness spreading across her tongue.

"Just tea. A few cloves as well."

"It doesn't taste like tea."

"You've probably had the dainty version where you steep the leaves then drink the runoff. I crush the dried leaves into a fine powder before mixing it with the water. It gives it a little kick."

"Kick is right. My mouth feels numb."

"That's the cloves. They deaden my ability to taste anything."

"If you don't like the taste, then why —"

"Because it keeps me alert. When I'm hooked into the ropes, it's like my fingers are hundreds of yards long. I'm touching every part of the ship. I feel so much that it's easy to get distracted. The tea helps me focus."

Sorrow nodded. She had to admit, a single mouthful had certainly made her feel more awake. Sorrow gave the flask back to Rigger, who took a long swig before slipping it back into his pocket. His face showed signs of strain as he pulled the ropes wrapped around his arms.

"Is it tough sailing in weather like this?"

"Are you just making small talk?" he asked. "You can't possibly think that there's anything easy about sailing a ship this size by myself. It's difficult even in good weather."

"Maybe I am just making small talk. We've been at sea together for months since I first met you aboard the *Freewind*, but I don't think we've even talked for ten minutes."

"That's because I'm always working or sleeping. Did you know when I was born, the *Freewind* had forty-three people running the ship? My aunt Rosemary's family lived on board then. She has eleven children, and four of them were married by the time I came along."

"And the war drove them away?"

Rigger shook his head. "Ma tells people it was the war, but, really, it was me. Once she discovered I was all the crew she needed, she quit having to compromise and cooperate with other Wanderers in order to keep her ship in business. I kept taking on more and more responsibility, wrapping myself in more and more ropes, not completely understanding how tied up I was becoming. Everyone else on this ship gets to dream about one day leaving and starting a life their own. I'm tied to this ship until Ma quits, and that's not going to happen."

"You might be surprised."

"Nothing surprises me any more," said Rigger.

"Haven't I heard you proven wrong after saying that?"

"On the small scale. But on the large scale, my life is depressingly predictable."

"If you feel that way, why don't you quit? I understand how another ship might not be eager to take on Mako, but any captain would have to instantly recognize your worth."

"I wouldn't go to any ship that wouldn't hire Mako," said Rigger. "And, while I gripe about mother's unwillingness to compromise, I also couldn't work aboard a ship that transported slaves. Also, while another Captain might welcome me, would another crew? I suspect my presence aboard a ship might cause some resentment. My magical gift might be useful, but I don't pretend that I'm not a freak. Everyone aboard this ship is. So, my perfect job would be upon a ship that was anti-slave, welcoming to freaks, and where no one resented my talents." He managed a grim smile. "I know of only one ship that meets these criteria, and I already have a bunk there."

SORROW RETURNED TO the hold and sat in the dark and relative quiet, to be alone with her thoughts. Of course, her hope was for the exact opposite, which was to find company in her thoughts, via the link Avaris had told her would be established once they traded eyes. Since embarking for the Isle of Storm, she'd tried meditating several times daily in hopes of quieting her own thoughts enough that Avaris could be heard. It hadn't worked yet.

It wasn't working now.

Hours passed before Gale and Mako could be heard as they returned to the deck. Sorrow gave up on her futile attempt at finding Avaris within her own skull and decided to join them above.

"Can I go get some sleep now?" Rigger asked as his mother approached. "I should get a little rest before we hit the eye. We'll be needing to adjust the sails then."

"I'm afraid there's no time for that now," Sage said, calling down from the crows nest. "You don't need magic to see that we're coming toward the eye of the storm."

Sorrow looked forward and could see that the sky brightened in the distance. Gale guided the buffeting winds to the tail of the ship and pushed it toward the light. A few minutes later, the wind calmed and the rain gave way to sunlight. The eye of the hurricane was an almost perfect circle of calm several miles across. Ahead were two steep stone mountains rising at steep angles toward the heavens. In between the two mountains was a valley cut through by a broad river. The banks of this river were thick with thousands of almost perfectly square buildings with roofs of woven bamboo. Roads rose up from this city, winding along the steep mountain cliffs, disappearing among the clouds. To Sorrow's surprise, rope bridges ran from the mountains out into seemingly thin air. Men moved along the bridges, guiding large goats harnessed to carts piled high with barrels and baskets. They vanished into a dense bank of roiling clouds that seemed to hang in a stationary position above the city.

"By the winds!" Rigger said, his eyes growing wide. "That's Levi's ship! *The Thunder!*"

"Wonderful," Gale muttered.

Sorrow stared at the heavens. "How can you tell? They look no different from any other clouds."

Sage traced her fingers in the air. "See those wispy white clouds? Kind of like little squiggles? They're the ship's markings."

Sorrow tried to follow Sage's gaze, but it was hopeless. All she could see were clouds.

By now, word had somehow spread below deck that Levi's ship had been sighted and all the Romer children came up top. Brand and Bigsby followed close behind.

Slate was the last to come on deck, shielding his eyes as he studied the city. They were close enough now that Sorrow could make out individual people. The city resembled an anthill in its level of activity. Every street and alley was thick with men and women carrying loads back and forth.

"Why do they all look alike?" Slate asked.

"By law, all the citizens dress identically," said Rigger. "Male or female, they all wear gray pants, gray shirts, sandals and straw hats. And both sexes wear their hair in the same ugly bowl cut."

"It's worse than just clothing," said Gale. "Everyone here looks alike, at least within age groups. They practice infanticide against any child born with any visible flaw, even harmless birthmarks."

"Thank the Divine Author that I come from a more civilized society, where flawed babies are sold to carnivals instead of being killed," said Bigsby.

"Why would people live like this?" Slate asked.

"The infanticide is obviously unacceptable, but other than that, is this truly such a bad way to live?" asked Sorrow. "All the citizens are provided with matching clothes, identical houses, and equal shares of food. It's a society without wealth or poverty. It seems far more fair than the feudal system of the Silver Isles, where a handful of families control the majority of the wealth."

"They may be equal, but they have no individuality or freedom," said Jetsam, hanging upside down in the rigging. "They're kind of anti-Wanderers."

"And Tempest is their king? They're ruled by a dragon?" Slate asked, sounding distressed.

"Tempest is their god," said Rigger. "From birth, they're ingrained with his philosophy. *The lone raindrop is powerless, but a storm can wash away mountains.* The people believe their lives only have meaning as tiny parts of a larger whole."

"But, to have no hope of advancement or growth...," Slate said, letting his thoughts trail off.

Rigger said, "They aren't completely without hope. Men can increase their status by joining the Storm Guard and rising in military rank. Women can serve in the shrines built to Tempest, and some go on to great honor as stormcallers."

"Speaking of which," said Sage, who was listening in above, "we're about to have company."

Two ships were approaching, both packed with armed men. Unlike the gray, loose-fitting clothing worn by the townsmen, these men were dressed in tight black coats lined with brass buttons. Golden lightning bolts decorated their shoulders. They wore leather bucklers on their forearms and swords that hung from their waists to their ankles.

"Are we in for a fight?" Sorrow asked.

"I'm sure this is just a routine inspection like we faced in Port Hallelujah," said Brand. "Despite the uniformity imposed on the citizens, Kaikou is a relatively cosmopolitan port. Most of the world's iron passes through this port, so they're welcoming toward people coming here for business. Even among dragon worshipers, money trumps philosophy."

Gale nodded in agreement. "Also, the city makes a lot of money from the steady stream of pilgrims visiting the Temple of the Book. We'll tell them that's why we're here. They'll name a docking fee, we'll pay it, and that should be the end of their interest in us."

"I should get below deck," said Sorrow.

"That would have been an excellent idea about thirty seconds ago," said Sage. "I can tell from the way the stormcaller on the lead ship is holding her spyglass that she's just spotted you. We'll have to tell them that you're a half-seed."

"Not that they're fond of half-seeds," said Mako.

"Things will work out," said Gale. "Everyone keep their mouths shut and let me do the talking and we'll be done with this in moments."

Slate crossed his arms and glared as Gale ordered Rigger to trim the sails, allowing the ships to pull alongside. Gale had Poppy and Cinnamon lower rope ladders to give the boarding parties easier access. She donned her Captain's hat and buttoned her coat, standing beside Rigger with her arms clasped behind her.

Eight soldiers climbed aboard, four from each ship. They stood at attention beside the ladders as a woman climbed up from the ship on the starboard side and a man who was obviously an officer boarded from the port. The officer's uniform was identical to those of his men, save for three golden lightning bolts on each shoulder and a sword with a decorative scabbard, inlaid with blue stones forming a stylized dragon. The stormcaller wore black robes, and if Gale hadn't informed her that stormcallers were women, she wouldn't have known. The black robes hid the shape of her body, and her face was concealed behind an azure dragon's mask. She carried a three-foot rod carved from clear quartz crystal that glowed with a magical aura separate from that of the woman.

"Captain," the uniformed man said, bowing toward Gale. "Welcome to Raitingu. I am Inspector Rim. My companion is Stormcaller Lotus. Please order all your crew and passengers to the deck."

"We're all accounted for," said Gale. "No one is below."

"Truly?" Rim asked, his eyebrows raised. "Such a small crew for a ship this size?"

"Our crew was once larger," Gale said. "We're doing what we can until I recruit more."

"What is the purpose of your visit?" Rim asked.

"This man is on a pilgrimage," said Gale, nodding toward Slate. "He carries the mortal remains of his father to the Temple of the Book."

Rim looked at Slate. "You would sail all this way to dispose of a corpse? He must have been a very important man."

"Important to me," said Slate.

Rim walked closer to Slate. Slate was once again dressed in his glass armor, which Sorrow had repaired after they returned to the ship.

"This is unusual armor," he said. "Are you a soldier?"

"A knight," said Slate.

Rim ran his fingers along the glass scales. "Is it dragon hide?" he asked.

"Just glass," said Slate.

Rim looked skeptical. He turned back toward Gale. "Unfortunately, it's illegal to transport a corpse to our land. We must confiscate the body."

"Illegal?" said Gale. "Since when?"

"Kaikou is a city of half a million people," said Rim. "Corpses can spread illness."

"Getting your drinking water from the same river you dump your sewage into might also cause a few sniffles," said Rigger.

Gale cut her eyes toward him.

Rigger shrugged. "Sorry, that just came out."

Gale sighed. "We are but humble Wanderers, Inspector, ignorant of your laws. If there are permits required to transport a coffin to the Temple, we understand. Would a fee of 50 moons acquire the necessary permissions?"

Rim chuckled. "50 moons? This man's dragon-hide armor is worth a hundred times that. A thousand."

"What if we give you the armor?" Gale asked, aware of its relatively humble origins.

Lotus interrupted, shaking her head. "Inspector, the knight speaks the truth. The armor is not dragon hide."

"You're certain?" he asked, sounding disappointed.

"The claw of Tempest caressed my cheek at our wedding," said Lotus. "I'm intimately familiar with dragon skin. This man does not possess it." Her masked face turned toward Sorrow. "This woman, however, does. Look at her wings."

Rim looked at Sorrow. "What manner of beast are you?"

"Just a half-seed," she said.

"There are no dragon half-seeds," Rim said. "The fetus would be fatal to any mother."

"What if my father was human and my mother was a dragon?" Sorrow asked, knowing Rim would probably find the answer insulting. She respected Gale's desire to talk and bribe their way past these guards, but her gut level hatred of men trying to exercise authority over her was nearly impossible to suppress.

He nodded toward his men. Two of them flanked him as they approached Sorrow. On an unseen signal, all three men drew their swords.

"I apologize for the woman," Gale said. "Her half-animal nature has left her dimwitted. Please ignore her babbling."

"Remove your hood," Rim said, as he fixed his eyes on Sorrow's face.

Sorrow smiled as she obeyed. The look on Rim's face as he spotted the nails on her scalp was quite satisfying.

"Witch!" Rim shouted. In unison, he and his men drove their swords into her belly. Luckily, her command over iron meant her skin was even better than dragon hide against their blades. The swords folded limply against her stomach.

"Down!" Lotus cried as the three men stood gawking at their ruined weapons. At her command, they threw themselves to the deck. Lotus pointed her crystal rod at Sorrow and shouted, "Khong!"

Sorrow spread her wings as brightness flared within the crystal, but suspected she wasn't going to get out of the way in time.

Slate threw himself in front of her as a loud *CRACK* filled the air. An arc of brilliant white light sliced into Slate's armored chest, vanishing as quickly as it struck. In the aftermath, Slate looked none the worse for wear. The stormcaller raised the glass rod toward the sky and began screaming out a prayer. Poppy dropped down from the riggings, balanced on the woman's shoulders for half a second, then vaulted to the deck as the woman shot toward the clouds, her prayer changing to a shriek. Her azure mask and the crystal rod clattered as they fell to the deck.

Sorrow blinked and suddenly there were dozens of Storm Guard spilling over the rails. Rigger grimaced as a score of ropes snaked toward them. The soldiers proved remarkably coolheaded in the face of such a strange assault and deftly leapt over the dancing hemp, slicing ropes with their swords as they charged toward Slate and Sorrow.

The air around the *Circus* sounded like an orchestra of harps being plucked as soldiers climbed the rigging of their ships and began to shower arrows toward the *Circus*. A whirling wind knocked the missiles off their path as Gale cried, "Don't kill anyone!"

Mako froze with his jaws half an inch away from Rim's throat. "Are you serious?" he growled.

"If no one dies, we might still bribe our way out of this," Gale shouted. "If we kill anyone, we're going to have to flee this port. That's not what Brand hired us for."

Brand said, "I also didn't hire you to be pin-cushions. Do what you must to defend yourselves!"

"Storm Guard!" a voice thundered from above, so loud it sounded as if a giant had shouted it. "Stand down!"

Sorrow looked up. A giant *had* shouted it. A man one hundred feet tall was walking down a staircase of wispy clouds. He was dressed in a uniform similar to the one worn by Rim, but with so many lightning bolts they jagged together to form a chain all the way around his shoulders. In his open palm he carried the stormcaller launched by Poppy. The front of her robes were flecked with vomit.

"Levi!" Jetsam shouted, as the storm guard lowered their weapons.

"That's Commander Leviathan to you," Levi said, as he stepped onto threads of fog that rose up from the sea. He lowered Lotus carefully back to the deck of her ship, then drew a crystalline battle-axe that sparked with static from a holster on his back. The head of the axe was the size of a mainsail. He gripped the weapon with both hands as his eyes narrowed. "Did you really believe you could strike a beloved bride of Tempest and not face my righteous wrath? Surrender at once, or face destruction!"

16 - PATH OF THE PILGRIM

LEVI RAISED HIS weapon overhead to strike. Sorrow bounded across the deck and grabbed the crystalline lightning rod. She raised it toward Levi, prepared to shout, "Khong!" Before she could finish inhaling, Mako tackled her, knocking the breath from her lungs. He pinned her to the deck, her wings folded beneath her in a painful fashion.

"We surrender!" Mako shouted, craning his neck toward the sky.

Sorrow was almost as shocked by these words as she was by the tackle. Mako wasn't known for avoiding fights.

"We most certainly do not surrender!" Gale shouted, raising her hands toward Levi, whose hair began to flutter in the wind.

"Brand!" Sage shouted. "It's your ship! Order Ma to give up!"

"Gale," said Brand, "Give up."

Gale clenched her jaw, her lips pressed tightly together.

Brand cupped his hands together and called out, "I own this ship and I surrender!"

Gale turned her back to Brand, folding her arms across her chest. The wind that stirred Levi's locks vanished.

"A wise choice," Levi said as he sheathed his ax. He looked down at Inspector Rim's ship. "Carry on with your duties," he said. "I personally will take these foreign heathens into custody."

Rim frowned.

"Is something displeasing you, Inspector?" asked Levi. "Speak freely."

Rim looked like he was in pain as he said, "Should we trust these foreigners into the custody of someone who is himself a foreigner?"

Levi ran his fingers along the chain of lightning bolts encircling his shoulders. "That's Commander Foreigner to you, Inspector. Your trust is not required, only your obedience."

Rim bowed deeply. "As you say, Commander."

Mako rose, freeing Sorrow, as Rim barked out orders for the two ships to leave.

"I'm sorry if I hurt you," Mako said.

Sorrow said nothing, ignoring the hand he held out to help her rise. There was a cold pit in the center of her belly. She worried that if she opened her mouth, dark energy would spew out and reduce Mako to bone.

A woman's voice screamed in her left ear, *Don't fear this power! Master it! You'll never learn to control Rott's power if you shun all opportunities to unleash it!*

Sorrow turned her head. No one stood beside her. Perhaps sitting quietly in the dark had been the wrong strategy for inducing Avaris to teach her. But this lesson would have to wait for another time. She breathed deeply, calming herself. The tension in her stomach seeped away. She took Mako's outstretched hand.

"Are you alright?" he asked.

You're a weakling and a coward!

Mako showed no reaction to the angry voice, though it was so loud Sorrow was surprised other people couldn't hear it.

"I'm fine," she answered softly.

As the two ships departed, Levi knelt next to the *Circus*. He smiled broadly and said, "Rescuing you guys is turning into a full-time job."

He placed his fingers on the deck of the boat and Poppy and Cinnamon ran up to hug them.

Jetsam swam through the air to hover in front of his brother's face. "I knew you wouldn't hurt us!"

"I needed to put on a show, though," said Levi. "Most of the ordinary Storm Guard members are suspicious of me due to my foreign origins. They hate that I've become commander of a hurricane in such a short time."

"We knew you were a good sailor, but it's impressive that you've risen in the ranks so quickly," said Jetsam.

Levi shook his head. "It's all dumb luck. When I met Flutter and fell in love, I had no idea she was the daughter of Commander Rumble. He only accepted me as part of his crew because Flutter threatened to live out the remainder of her life on land with me if he didn't."

"That's romantic," said Poppy. "Like something from a story book."

"The story books skip over the hard parts, I'm afraid," said Levi.

"Like betraying your family by joining the armed forces of their enemy?" Gale asked, still not looking back at him.

"You're not seeing the story from my perspective," said Levi. "At the time, I'd lost my power to shrink back to human size. I'd been forced to leave behind my life as a Wanderer simply because there were no ships I could board without capsizing them. I thought I was fated to live out my life alone, on a desert island, until Flutter looked down and spotted me. My choice to join the Storm Guard had nothing to do with politics. It was my only chance to live a normal life."

"You live in a cloud," said Jetsam.

"Which feels curiously normal after a while."

Gale shook her head. "It's one thing to join their crew. Now you command their forces?"

Levi shrugged. "Again, dumb luck. What I didn't know about cloud giants when I went to live among them is that they might be huge as clouds, but they're also just as fleeting. They go from babies to adulthood in about six months. The average cloud giant lives only seven years. A few truly ancient specimens make it to ten. This means there's a lot of churn in the ranks aboard any cloud ship. In the human world, I'm still wet behind the ears. Among the giants, I'm practically an immortal, and treated like I'm in possession of some special age-imbued wisdom."

"Are you?" asked Jetsam.

"Only if heartbreak is wisdom," said Levi. "I live in a world where anyone who becomes important in my life passes away almost before I get to know them. I was seventeen when I met Flutter. She wasn't even a year old, but already considered something of an old maid among the giants. She passed away last year, just after her fifth birthday."

"Oh Levi," Sage said. "I'm so sorry."

Levi smiled wistfully. "She had a good life. I've learned a lot about living for the moment. You have to drink every bit of life that flows into your cup today, because the cup might fall from your hand tomorrow."

"Why didn't you tell us this when you helped rescue us when the *Freewind* was sinking?" asked Sage.

"You guys had your own problems. I knew Ma's heart was breaking to lose that ship. I didn't want you to worry about me just because I'd lost someone I loved."

Gale's shoulders sagged. "I'm sorry for your loss," she said, turning to look at him. "But, what about the loss of all those Wanderers who fought on our side during the pirate wars? Every day, we received reports of some new ship lost at sea to the Storm Guard's hurricane fleet. How did the lives of Wanderers become so cheap to you?"

Levi shook his head. "It's not that simple. I didn't start the war. Cloud giants don't even keep slaves. Pygmies just fall through the clouds. Even after you drink the zephyr elixir, you still need really big feet to get any traction on mist."

"We Wanderers didn't start the war either," Gale said.

"I'm almost entirely certain you did," said Levi. "And you had good reason to. Every time I return to this port, I watch Wanderer ships hired by slavers unload their human cargo at the pygmy market. It turns my stomach to see people in chains, sold to the highest bidder. If I'd already been commander when the war started, I would have done anything I could to tip the battles in your favor. Alas, I wasn't in command of the ships."

"You still could have changed things."

Levi nodded. "The question of what I should have done burns in my mind every single day. Unfortunately, what I should have done has to be weighed against what I could have done. Giants have learned the art of steering the winds and shepherding clouds together into semi-stable structures to live upon. But they don't actually make clouds. If they ever earned the wrath of Tempest, he could simply blink his eyes and the clouds we live upon would evaporate. The dragon holds the power of life and death over every last giant. As long as there are giants in my life that I cherish, that means Tempest controls me."

Sage asked, "Did you have children?"

Levi shook his head. "No. I don't know if humans and giants can't interbreed, or if there was just something about the two of us. But even though we had no kids of our own, her brothers and sisters were quite prolific. There's about three hundred cloud giants who call me uncle. If I were to openly defy Tempest, it would be bad for all of them."

"Giants need not live on clouds," said Gale. "As a race, you could free yourself from Tempest's power just by moving back to land. It's where giants lived long ago, before discovering the zephyr potion."

"True enough," said Levi. "And Wanderers could avoid the whole slaving controversy just by giving up the sea."

Gale didn't respond to that.

Levi said, "Just because my new family is important to me doesn't mean I don't still love you guys. Why have you come here? What can I do to help?"

Brand stepped forward to explain his situation and tell Levi about Slate's quest.

Levi answered, "I'll tow the *Circus* to the slave market. There's a dock next to it reserved for ships under quarantine. We can anchor you there and no one will mess with you. I can arrange the proper travel permits so a few of you can leave the ship. I suppose we need two for Brand and Bigsby and one for Slate?"

Two! Avaris shouted, so loud that Sorrow flinched.

Her sudden motion caught Levi's eye. "Yes?"

"I need a permit as well," Sorrow said. "I'm going to the Temple of the Book."

Slate looked at her with an expression of extreme suspicion.

"What?" she asked. "If I wouldn't burn churches at Port Hallelujah, do you think I'm dumb enough to walk into the most sacred sanctuary of the church and try to pick a fight?"

"Then why would you come?" asked Slate.

Tell him you love him and cannot bear the thought of not being at his side.

"I most certainly will not," said Sorrow.

"I'm confused," Bigsby said. "Are you going or aren't you?"

Men are simple creatures. You'll gain great power over him if he thinks you desire him.

"Shut up," Sorrow said.

"I'm just asking," said Bigsby.

"I just... I guess I'm still a little scatterbrained from where Mako banged my head into the deck."

"I said I was sorry," said Mako.

"Apology accepted," said Sorrow. "So, let me be clear, I'm not going with Slate because I in anyway find him attractive."

Eyebrows shot up around the deck. Slate looked especially surprised.

"I'm going because I've spent my whole life hating people who worship a stupid book. And I've never even seen this book. I mean, what if there's something about this religion that I'm just not getting because I haven't taken the time to really try to understand?"

"This is... open-minded of you," said Brand.

Sorrow shrugged. "A lot of things changed in the swamps of Podredumbre. It's not just my body that got rearranged. I'm starting to see I might have the same vulnerability to blind faith that I accuse my enemies of. I give you my word I'm not going to this temple looking for trouble."

"That's twice you've mentioned Podredumbre," said Levi. "You wouldn't have anything to do with the uprising there, would you?"

"What uprising?" Sorrow asked.

"We've gotten reports that the residents killed King Brightmoon's governor two weeks ago. The whole island is in a state of anarchy."

"We left Port Hallelujah two weeks and one day ago," said Jetsam.

"But we didn't start a revolution," said Sorrow. "Not directly at least. And, I promise, I'm not going to start anything here."

Slate still looked skeptical, but said, "The path of the pilgrim is open to anyone who cares to walk it. I cannot tell you to remain on the ship."

They believe your words, said Avaris. *We both know you're going to the temple with malice in your heart.*

"I'm going because you told me to!" whispered Sorrow.

"What's that?" said Bigsby.

"Nothing," said Sorrow.

As Levi grabbed the jibboom in his massive hand to tow the *Circus*, Sorrow turned and ran below deck, whacking her wings against the edge of the hatch as she descended. Once she was out of earshot of the others, she said, "Now is a fine time for you do decide to speak to me. You've been inside my head for two weeks. Why haven't you said anything?"

I saw no purpose. By now you must have noticed that Rott's power tries to enter your body during moments of stress. You've spent the last two weeks in calm meditation. And out at sea, if you'd summoned Rott's powers, there was no one to harm but your shipmates. Now that you're in a city of enemies, you'll have more suitable targets to focus your power upon.

"Fine," said Sorrow. "But couldn't you have explained things before now? Have you been watching and hearing me this whole time? Why haven't I seen or heard things you've experienced?"

You haven't experienced my senses because I do not wish you to. As for whether I've been watching you continuously, I've actually given you little thought. As you've just learned, events in my corner of the material world have been turbulent. Many have sought my aid. No evening goes by when the child of some colonial master isn't presented to me as an offering. My castle has engorged itself with their fat souls.

"Are you trying to provoke me?" Sorrow asked. "Are you purposefully boasting of such evil deeds as some sort of test?"

It would be convenient for me if you believed that it was only a test, wouldn't it?

Sorrow clenched her jaw. Just what kind of creature had she made her bargain with? But knowledge was knowledge, and Avaris obviously knew more about magic than anyone else Sorrow had ever met. A man who trained in the use of a sword could use that skill either for murder or for the defense of his family. Just because Sorrow would learn from a person with corrupted morals didn't mean that she herself would follow the same path into darkness.

The first thing you must do is protect the rod you've stolen.

Sorrow had almost forgotten about the lightning rod. She looked at the yard long crystal she carried. Here in the shadowy hold, its inner light was quite brilliant.

Stormcallers can sense the weapon and will soon send enforcers to recover it. You must mask it at once with bands of negation. Since you weave iron, I assume you know how to make these?

"Yes," said Sorrow. She found one of the swords she'd used when training with Slate. She tore off fist-sized wads of metal and molded them into rings around the shaft. Most energetic magics were baffled by iron barriers.

Excellent. The lightning rod is more than just a powerful attack. It absorbs any lightning directed toward it. Even Tempest could not harm you with his electrical bite.

"Will the rod work even with the negating bands?"

No. But you can remove them with only a touch.

Which was true enough. Of course, she hadn't come here to fight stormcallers or Tempest.

"I assume you want me to make use of Rott's powers when I go to the Temple of the Book?"

"Why be timid? You command the power to decimate armies. You've spent your whole life wishing to strike a blow against the church. Wouldn't destroying the sacred book itself bring you satisfaction?"

Sorrow felt her heartbeat quicken. The thought of tearing through the temple on a rampage of destruction certainly appealed to her. But she felt unprepared for the aftermath. She didn't know how the world might change once the book was gone. Would she be opening a path to a golden age, or would she only be inviting anarchy?

Don't concern yourself with the effects of your destruction. You're now a force of nature. Greatshadow devours stands of trees with insatiable hunger, leaving only barren land in his wake. Yet new growth sprouts in earth made fertile by his rampage. If you burn through all of civilization, leaving ashes in your wake, you will create fresh soil for a new world to grow.

"I know you're right. I still feel unprepared. If you'd only spoken to me earlier, we could have formulated a better plan for me to enter the temple." A board creaked overhead. From the weight, it had to be Slate. "I'd rather fly ahead and leave Slate behind. If things turn violent, I'd as soon not have to fight him as well."

So you do have feelings for him.

"Yes. I feel like he practically knocked my damn head off the first time I fought him. Also, he didn't do a bad job of taking down your unstoppable bodyguard. It's wise to keep him at a respectful distance. The only problem is, if I fly toward the temple, I'm bound to be seen. I'll have a whole army of knights and truthspeakers waiting for me by the time I arrive."

You need not fear armies.

"I'm glad you're so confident in my abilities. I'd feel more encouraged by your words if the army you want me go fight didn't scare you so badly you live in another reality now."

Fine. If you fear being spotted in the air, walk.

"That doesn't help," said Sorrow. "It's not like my wings disappear when I'm walking. They're too damn big to hide with just a cloak."

Then change your body to something that can be concealed.

"How? I was able to alter my form in the Black Bog, but I can't just wish away my wings in the material world."

True. The body of Rott that bleeds through from the abstract realms can't be gotten rid of. But with bone-weaving, you could still alter your form.

"What? And go back to the tail?"

You could spread the dragon mass evenly across your body. I did so briefly. It was monstrous. Even your face will be covered with scales. Your hands will be hideous talons. You'll be much larger than your current stature, but not inhuman in size. You could conceal your body beneath a cloak and a veil, and hide your talons with gauntlets.

"Trade my wings for full body disfigurement? You really know how to sell a plan."

You're the one who came to me to learn the art of bone-weaving. Now you reject the very tool that would help you reach your goals? Slate's lack of memories and confusion over his origins leave him vulnerable to emotional manipulation. You could bed him this evening. Given his enviable physical attributes, you'll no doubt find the experience to your liking. As your body fills with procreative energies, I can guide you in the transformation of your form.

"I was just thinking that, if I did decide to experiment with physical contact with a man, there's nothing I'd want more than to have a disembodied bystander watching the whole thing and shouting out advice."

If you reject all my suggestions, I've nothing to teach you.

Sorrow hid the lightning rod amid her blankets. "I know," she said. "Just... give me a little while to think about this."

As you wish.

BY NIGHTFALL, THE *Circus* was in quarantine and Levi had gone to secure the necessary papers. He wouldn't be back until the morning. The Romer children were in good spirits after seeing their brother, but Gale was still pensive as she stood vigil near the wheel, staring at the docks nearby.

Sorrow joined her. She followed Gale's gaze and saw that she was staring at the slave market, barely fifty yards away. The place was a long dock with a warehouse upon it, with iron bars over every window. A lone ship was unloading, with a string of thirty pygmies walking down the gangplank, their legs in shackles.

Gale shook her head. "I thought I'd raised him better."

"Levi isn't to blame for this," said Sorrow. "Slavery is as old as mankind. We live in a world designed to corrupt. He's as much a victim of the system as those poor pygmies."

"I risked everything to oppose that system."

"As have I. Don't despair, Gale. The world that exists today is built upon a foundation of lies and oppression. Place the right weight upon it and that foundation will crumble, as it has in Podredumbre. Change is coming, faster than you think."

Gale glanced at Sorrow. "I've heard your speeches before. You're fighting for a cause larger than yourself."

"I'd like to think so."

"And your battle places you in great danger. Just by allowing you on my ship, I'm placing my family at risk."

"I won't deny it. But you're tough enough to bear the burden of associating with me. You've spent the money I've paid in the past to charter your ship happily enough."

"Happily isn't exactly the sentiment," said Gale. "But it's not that far off either. I'd rather be ferrying a revolutionary dreamer around these isles than another load of cotton or booze. I like you, Sorrow. I hope I can help you reach your destination."

Sorrow tilted her head, not sure if she'd heard Gale correctly.

"Don't look so surprised. We're both people who act as if our beliefs matter, even as the world around us tries to make us abandon our most deeply held values. No matter how hard the headwinds become, no matter how rough the sea, you push forward. I've no patience for the poor souls of this world who get driven off course the moment they encounter a patch of bad weather. You're never going to turn away from your goals because the going gets rough."

As Gale's words sunk in, Sorrow smiled.

"This isn't something you should smile about," said Gale. "Having the courage to stand up for what's right when the rest of the world is determined to drag you down is a terrible burden."

Sorrow smiled even more broadly. "I know. But I didn't know you felt this way. I just... I never meet anyone who approves of my goals. I'm used to people telling me I should let go of my anger. I'm used to people looking at me as if I'm crazy!"

Gale shrugged. "Perhaps we're both crazy. I sometime think that what the world accepts as sanity is merely the capacity to grow numb to outrage. I find sanity to be a depressingly common commodity. Your anger exists for a reason, Sorrow. I admire that you still have the capacity to feel it. I admire that you're willing to risk everything in order to try to put the world right."

Sorrow couldn't control herself. She threw her arms around Gale and hugged her with all her might. Gale hugged her back, and whispered, "You're more my daughter than Levi is my son."

"Oh, Ma," Sorrow answered, as she choked back tears.

IT WAS LATE at night when Sorrow knocked on Brand's door. Sage had gone to sleep. Mako was on watch in the crows nest.

"Risk everything," she whispered. "Don't be afraid of a patch of rough water." She took a deep breath as she heard Brand's footsteps approach.

Brand's hair was wet when he opened the door, his face pink and freshly shaven. Before he could speak she pushed him back into his cabin and closed the door behind them.

"I suppose it was a bit optimistic to imagine it might finally be Gale paying a visit," Brand said with a sigh. "What can I help you with, Sorrow?"

Sorrow swallowed hard. She didn't look him directly in the face as she said, "The... the same thing you were hoping Gale would want from you."

Brand laughed softly. "I don't think you know what you've just asked of me."

"I believe I do."

Brand stopped smiling. "This is... an unusual request."

"Is it? I was under the impression you'd had multiple sexual partners."

"I was under the impression you hadn't," said Brand.

"Your impression is correct," she said. "But circumstances have changed. You were present at dinner with Zetetic. He told me that sexual release was an important source of magical energy. I've decided I can no longer afford myself the luxury of ignoring it."

"I can tell you that I've felt something very much like magic during, uh, the requested activity. So maybe there's an energy in the act that you'll know how to use. But I really can't help you."

"Why not? I'm willing to pay you."

"I'm not a prostitute, Sorrow."

"I ask as a favor from a friend."

"There's a lot you need to learn about friendship." Brand crossed his arms.

"If you overlook the wings, am I not attractive?"

"For what it's worth, the wings make you even more interesting. There's also an appealing honesty about your look. You don't go out of your way to fool men with make-up or fancy clothes. There's an innocence about you that is almost irresistible."

"Then, why —"

"I'm in love with Gale," he said, shaking his head. "You know this."

"But she's not in love with you."

"She feels what she feels. It doesn't alter what I feel. I gave her reason to mistrust me by sneaking a stowaway aboard the *Freewind*. I'd love to win her heart with some big gesture, but I also accept that it may take me years to earn back her trust. I'm willing to wait."

"Gale never needs to know anything happened between us," said Sorrow.

"I would know. If you ever loved anyone, you'd understand."

Sorrow shook her head. "What I'm asking has nothing to do with love. It need not involve any emotion at all. I'm asking only for physical assistance. It need be no more a betrayal of Gale than if you were to scratch my back."

"Emotionless sex isn't anything I'm interested in. One day you'll understand it's not what you're interested in either."

Sorrow's shoulders sagged. She'd been certain that Brand would help her.

"Ordinarily, I'd give you a hug and tell you things will be okay," Brand said as he sat on the edge of his bed. "But I'm worried you might misinterpret any physical contact. You've denied your sexuality for so long you probably have a very steep learning curve ahead of you."

"I was hoping you would be a good teacher."

"Sex is one of the few things where your first lessons are probably best learned from other beginners. Have you approached Slate?"

"No!"

"That's surprisingly emphatic."

She waved her hand as if she were swatting away his words. "He's not my type."

"Tall, dark, and handsome isn't your type?"

"He's so empty it frightens me. He's so desperate to fill himself with something. He's trying to serve a religion he doesn't even understand. I'm certain he would find sex outside of marriage to be a sin."

"The original Tower didn't."

"And he's Tower's opposite."

"And you don't want to corrupt him."

"Corrupting him is very high on my agenda," she said. "I'd hoped to turn him into an ally against the church, but he seems to be going in the opposite direction. He'll probably be a saint one day."

"Why… oh, wait. I get it. Since Slate has no memories, you've been able to project all your hopes and dreams onto him. Despite your protests, you imagine him to be perfect. He's the man of virtue your father failed to be. Having sex with him would shatter that illusion, and make him merely human."

"Is this more of your carnival act? Just take anything I say and tell me I meant the opposite?"

"How's it worked so far?"

Sorrow turned to the door. "I'm sorry to have wasted your time." She paused as she took the latch in her hand. "Brand, can I ask —"

"I won't say a word about this. Good luck with your lessons."

Sorrow left Brand's cabin. Her arms were wrapped tightly across her breasts. The night air was cold enough that her breath came out as fog. Pale moonlight filtered through the clouds, painting the deck a ghostly gray. A shadow moved before her. Her body tensed as it drew closer. She looked up and found Mako in the rigging directly above.

"I… underestimated Brand," he said, softly. "I thought he was only toying with my mother's affections. I didn't realize how deeply he felt about her."

"You heard us?" she asked, mortified.

"Sight isn't a terribly important sense for a shark. But they can hear a wounded fish flopping on the surface from many miles away. Usually there's so much sound in the world I have difficulty making sense of everything. But, late at night, on a sleeping ship, a single hushed conversation is difficult to ignore."

"Did you also —"

"— hear when Sage and Mother spoke to you about Grandmother's ghost? I did. Why they don't simply include me in their confidence is no mystery. How did mother phrase it? That I have freakish hearing? That no girl would ever want me because of my teeth? She's seen the thing I become when I smell blood in the water. It's hard enough to know that no girl will ever trust me. It's harder still to know that my own mother fears me."

"She still loves you. As do all your siblings."

"And I love them. Still, the love of my family only serves to remind me that I will never have a family of my own. It's a lonely thing, to be a monster."

Sorrow folded her wings about her, and ran her fingers along the fine scales that covered the leading edge. "I know how you feel."

Mako dropped to the deck before Sorrow. He said, "Ma would lash me if she knew I'd left my post."

"We can't have that," Sorrow said, turning her back to him.

He placed his sharp-nailed hand between her shoulder blades. His fingers were rough and callused as he lightly scratched her back. "This need not involve any emotion at all," he murmured, inches from her ear.

She shuddered as his inhuman mouth pressed against the nape of her neck. She could feel his saw-toothed jaws beneath his cold lips as he kissed her. His hands moved to rest lightly upon her hips.

She placed her hands upon his, feeling the soft webbing between his fingers. She turned to face him. His eyes were dark as the ocean's depths.

"Some things are best learned from other beginners," he said, as he brought his lips toward hers.

17 - SAFE PASSAGE

THE FOLLOWING MORNING, Sorrow waited on the dock in front of the *Circus*. Slate appeared on deck dressed in his black armor, standing patiently as Rigger helped outfit the coffin with a rope harness. Slate wrestled the coffin onto his back and headed down the gangplank. Through the holes in his helm, she could see his eyes fixed upon her. She knew he didn't recognize her. She was outfitted in a suit of full iron plate mail complete with a jousting helm. Mirrored glass shaded her eyes. She now stood nearly as tall as Slate, and carried an iron mace almost as large as the one she'd crafted for him. He watched her closely as he approached, seeming more wary of her than he was of the trio of Storm Guard next to her.

Of course, the Storm Guard weren't terribly impressive. None stood even as tall as Sorrow's shoulders. She also noticed this morning how uniformly thin the residents of Raitingu appeared. Apparently, Tempest believed in keeping his worshipers a bit hungry.

One of the guards bowed toward Slate. He held out a scroll, similar to the one he'd already given Sorrow. He said, "Good morning. I'm Agent Nori. I've orders to guide you to the city gates. Beyond, this permit will provide you safe passage as a pilgrim."

Slate took the scroll, but his eyes were still fixed on Sorrow.

She cleared her throat and said, "You seem fascinated by my new armor."

"Sorrow?"

She nodded. She could tell from his eyes he had a thousand questions, but he wisely held his tongue as he turned to Agent Nori and said, "We're honored to have you serve as our guide. Lead on."

The three guards formed a triangle around the two as they passed through the bustling city streets. The roads were paved with gray gravel and were remarkably clean. Old men with rakes smoothed out the gravel in the wake of passing carts. The same attention to maintenance showed in the buildings. Unlike the worn, shabby atmosphere of Port Hallelujah, each building in Kaikou looked freshly painted, albeit in unappealing shades of cloudy gray. Small gardens graced the fronts of each house, but were devoid of flowers. Instead, each was a merely a box of raked sand sporting a few round stones of random size and placement. A few boxes also featured a single gnarled juniper tree, severely cropped to stand no more than a few inches tall. The gardens reminded her of sand-boxes where children played in the Silver City, but she saw no one playing. What children she spotted were all engaged in labor, mending thatched roofs, sweeping doorsteps, and running chamber pots down the steep streets to the river.

At length they reached the city gates. The frame of the main gate was carved in the fashion of a giant dragon's head, requiring them to enter the jaws in order to reach the barred doors at the back of the throat.

"This is where we must part," Agent Nori said as he bowed. "I hope you find safe passage beyond these walls."

"Why would we not?" asked Slate. "We've been granted permission, yes?"

"Bandits don't bother with permits," Nori said.

"Bandits would be fools to bother with us," said Sorrow.

"As you say," Nori replied, with a bow. He turned to depart, with a final blessing: "May the clouds always protect you from the oppression of the sun."

Slate and Sorrow passed through the iron gates as they slid open. As they walked through the tunnel of the dragon's mouth on the other side, Slate whispered, "What happened to your wings?"

"It hurts like hell, but I was able to fold them beneath my arms and around the front of my chest. It's why my armor is so barrel-chested."

"Your voice sounds different," he said. "Deeper. Gruffer."

"It's probably just my helm that makes it sound different. There's an echo in here."

"I can't help but notice that you're taller as well. And apparently much stronger, given how swiftly you walk in that armor and how lightly you carry that mace."

She chuckled as she tossed the mace back and forth between her iron gauntlets. "The mace is hollow; it's mainly for looks. As for my height, it's a simple thing to add a few additional inches in my boots and to the top of my helm. The weight of the armor doesn't matter because I'm wearing almost nothing beneath. My magical control over any iron I touch means I'm moving the armor with my magic, not my muscles. Going on this pilgrimage as a winged witch was only going to cause us both a lot of grief. Going as another knight, I'll barely draw attention."

They stepped through the gate as she spoke these words. Immediately a mob of filthy men and women in ragged clothes rushed toward them and threw themselves groveling at their feet.

"Knights!" a woman cried as she stared up at them with tears in her eyes. "Please! We're humble pilgrims seeking to reach the temple! Have mercy!"

Sorrow sighed, reaching for the purse on her belt. The woman's left arm was nothing but a bandaged stump. She felt pity enough to spare a few moons.

The woman shook her head as Sorrow produced the coins. "It's not moons we want. It's protection. We've all attempted the journey and been turned back by violence. We've lost everything but our lives."

Slate nodded. "We were warned of bandits."

"Bandits?" the woman said, shaking her head. "There are no bandits on this road. The Storm Guard shows no mercy to their ilk."

"Who has reduced you to this state?" asked Slate.

"The Storm Guard themselves! They place barriers in the most narrow gap of the mountain pass and demand a toll to pass. Even if you pay the price they demand, they still take from you anything of value."

"They took my daughter and stripped her bare before me," said a man with an empty eye-socket. "She was only eleven. I tried to protect her honor but they beat me, tossing me into a ravine, leaving me for dead. I almost wish I had died when I hear her terrified cries in my dreams."

"You may journey with us," Slate said, his voice trembling. "We'll protect you from such atrocities!"

"Hold on," said Sorrow. "We aren't the only warriors to travel this road. From what I understand, the temple is defended by hundreds of knights. Why don't they protect the pilgrims?"

The one-eyed man shook his head mournfully. "Tempest forbids them to intervene. If the knights were to take action against the Storm Guard, Tempest would direct his wrath against the temple itself. The first priority of the knights is to protect the One True Book from harm."

"The code of the knight requires him to be a defender of all men of virtue," said Slate. "Protecting a book is no excuse for turning a blind eye to the suffering of fellow men."

This is why I buried the poor fool.

Sorrow jerked her head to the left, but, of course, Avaris was nowhere to be seen. Sorrow grimaced. She had thought that her iron helmet might hide her senses from the elder witch.

Of what use is a warrior who takes pity on the suffering of others? He lacks the hardness required to do all that is needed to achieve victory.

Sorrow didn't answer, partially because she'd learned her lesson about talking to herself, and partially because the opinions of Avaris didn't matter. What Avaris took for Slate's weakness, Sorrow saw as his strength. She'd worried he would stand in the way of her goals. Now, she realized, he'd be key to achieving them.

She looked up the mountain. "We've many miles to go," she said, placing the coins back into her pouch. "Together we shall reach the temple, and no thug with a barricade is going to stand in our way."

"Forward," Slate cried, his voice a strange mix of optimism and outrage. Sorrow smiled. If Gale was right, and sanity was merely the capacity to grow numb to outrage, Slate might prove crazy enough for her needs after all.

THE FIRST THIEVES they encountered were shopkeepers along the way. Bamboo shacks selling noodles and barbequed rock lizards were scattered along the route. In most of the world, such a simple meal would require the exchange of a few coppers. Here, a single bowl of noodles cost an entire moon. Sorrow was tempted to test Slate's temper, to find out if she could provoke him into stealing to feed the score of hungry pilgrims who traveled with them. Instead, while she contemplated what she might say that wouldn't seem like outright manipulation, he surprised her by producing a bag of coins and buying food for everyone.

"You shouldn't pay these thieves such prices," she said, as the pilgrims hungrily slurped down noodles.

Slate shrugged. "Brand gave me a purse before I departed and insisted I keep it, just in case I found myself in a situation where I'd need a few coins. I won't miss money that wasn't truly mine to begin with."

"So you're merely going to pay the toll when we encounter the Storm Guard?"

Slate nodded toward the old woman stirring the pot of noodles. "These people didn't threaten us to gain our money. They had something we wanted and offered it to us for a price. Perhaps an unfair price, but we had the option to move on."

"But the Storm Guard have something we want as well," said Sorrow. "If this is your attitude, why shouldn't they be allowed to set a price?"

The one-eyed man wiped his mouth on his sleeve and said, "There's the treaty. King Brightmoon granted Tempest control of a few islands south of here in exchange for a promise that the path of the pilgrims would remain open. The Storm Guard ignores the law because no one dares to punish them."

Slate had his helmet off, looking lost in thought as he nibbled absent-mindedly on a lizard thigh. He glanced at Sorrow, who still had her helmet on, and asked, "Aren't you going to eat?"

"I'll do it later. You know why I don't want to reveal my head in front of others," she whispered.

"Right," he said. "Sorry."

THE MOUNTAIN PATH they followed was barren of vegetation. When night arrived, they had nothing to use to build a fire. The pilgrims huddled together beneath an outcropping of stone, shivering as the wind howled up the steep path.

Slate lowered the coffin he carried to the ground and sat beside it, pulling off his helmet with a weary shake of his head. Sorrow stood before him.

"Aren't you weary?" he asked.

"Not as much as you might think," she said. "My armor has done most of the walking. I'm just kind of along for the ride. Except for my wings feeling bruised, I'm still pretty fresh."

He nodded. After a moment of silence, he asked, "Why are you here, Sorrow?"

"I told you on the ship. I've been rethinking a lot of assumptions in my life."

Slate stared at her. "It would be easier to judge your words if I could see your face."

"Who appointed you as the judge of my words?"

"I fear… I fear that you may not be undertaking this pilgrimage with the best of intentions."

"Allow me to try Brand's little trick. When you say you mistrust my intentions, you mean you mistrust your own."

Slate cocked his head to the side as he puzzled over her response.

"I saw your expression when that pilgrim told you that the knights didn't defend pilgrims. You're wondering if I'm right, and if the code of the knight in Poppy's book isn't just a romantic fiction. The body you're carrying in that box belongs to a knight who certainly failed to live up to Poppy's standards."

"What do the actions of others have to do with my intentions?"

"Because, at heart, you share the same basic emotional attribute that defines Gale and myself. You still have the capacity for righteous anger. You might be mad that the Storm Guard abuses pilgrims, but you expect evil from them. However, the idea that supposedly good men stand by and do nothing… that outrages you."

"And what if it does?" he asked.

"You find yourself in the same position I've been in ever since my grandmother stood on those gallows. You'll come to see that the true problem with the world isn't the wickedness of a few, it's the unthinking acceptance of the many. You either surrender in the face of their apathy, or you let the anger build inside you until you have no choice but to fight."

"Fight who? Brother knights whose only sin is inaction?"

"What makes them your brothers? The fact they pay lip service to a faith you imagine you believe in? Or will you wake up and realize that you're more kin to the Romers? Your true family is found among those who would give everything in defense of what they believe."

Slate lowered his head. He sighed. "We can't know that it's apathy that holds back the knights of the temple. It would be unfair to judge them based on the testimony of others."

"Fine," she said. "I just ask that you maintain the courage to accept what you see, instead of what you wish to see."

"Who are you to demand this of me?"

She removed her helmet. In the moonlight, her still human face reflected in the polished steel.

"I'm your friend, Slate," she said. She glanced toward the pilgrims. From the sound of their collective snores, they'd fallen asleep quickly. She slid her finger along her breastplate and peeled it open, shrugging it free, then lifted her arms to spread her wings. She willed the legs of her armor to open and stepped out barefoot on the cold ground. Goose bumps quickly covered her body. Her arms were bare. She wore only a simple cotton slip that hung to the upper part of her thighs.

"You've no idea how good it feels to be out of that suit," she said, stretching her aching wings, savoring the soothing cold.

"The transformation is remarkable. You looked quite mannish in that armor. I much prefer this look."

She sat beside him and pulled her breastplate near. She ran her fingers along it, stoking the metal into a red-hot glow. He scooted closer to her, until their legs were touching, as he stretched his hands out over the glowing metal.

"So, you prefer me this way?" she asked. "Wings and all?"

Perhaps it was the red glow of the iron, but it looked as if Slate were blushing as she looked into his face.

He smiled softly and said, "Aye."

"The wings don't bother Mako either," she said. "He kissed me last night."

Slate's eyebrows shot up.

"Don't be jealous. Nothing happened. There was just a... momentary misunderstanding."

"What cause have I to be jealous?" he asked, tersely.

"Oh. I just thought... there have been moments...."

"Aye. There have been moments."

"Under different circumstance, I think... if I were to ever feel for a man, it would be a man like you." She sighed. "But these aren't different circumstances. My life has been the only life I've lived, and my heart is the only heart I have. It shattered a long time ago. I don't think I'll ever be able to feel anything like ordinary love."

Slate shrugged. "Is there anything ordinary about love?" He stared at his hands as he rubbed them together. They were covered with thin white scars from where he'd fought the bone dragon. "I think about you stitching me up after battle, the tenderness in your touch, the concern in your eyes, and I sometimes believe you're an angel sent by the Divine Author to grant me happiness. Then I listen to you make excuses for monsters like Avaris, and I wonder if you aren't a devil. Perhaps the warmth I feel in your presence presages the fires of hell."

"Hellfire?" Sorrow chuckled. "That's harsh."

"Aye," he said, managing half a smile. "Perhaps I exaggerate. I get a bit addled in your presence. You're a very confusing woman, Sorrow."

"Aye," she said. "And a confused one as well."

He placed his hand upon hers where it lay on her bare thigh. She shivered.

"Art thou still cold?" he asked.

She grinned and said, "A little too warm, actually."

She pushed his hand aside and stood, stretching her wings once more. She stepped back into her iron pants and willed them shut.

Coward. Bad enough you rebuffed the boy. Now you miss the chance to enslave the heart of a man who may yet prove to be your greatest enemy?

"I'm an honorary Romer," said Sorrow. "I don't believe in slavery."

"What does slavery have to do with anything?" Slate asked, completely befuddled.

"I was merely thinking that I couldn't shackle anyone, without feeling shackled myself."

You try to frame your avoidance of sex as a matter of independence, but we both know you merely lack the courage.

"I think I'm displaying courage by following my own path," Sorrow said softly as she placed her hands on her iron-clad hips.

Your words would be more convincing if you weren't wearing what must certainly be the world's largest chastity belt.

THEY SPENT MOST of the next day struggling up the steep mountain path. Progress was slow, as the pilgrims had to stop and rest often. The cold was getting worse, and Sorrow worried that frostbite awaited many of the pilgrims. She felt guilty in the comfort of her armor, whose temperature she controlled with only a thought. Looking behind her, the city they'd left the day before was still visible, though the white sails of the ships in the harbor were no larger than snowflakes.

Looking up at the thick clouds directly overhead, she wondered if she wouldn't soon have actual snowflakes on hand for comparison. The trail ahead led directly into the cloudbanks.

They pressed on, the visibility growing worse with each step. Soon the fog was so thick she couldn't see her hand when she held it before her face. The pilgrims all locked arms to move forward, with Slate in the lead, sure-footedly finding his way along the all but invisible rocks. Sorrow brought up the rear of the group. Partially this was to defend against anything that might try to attack unseen, and partially because the mass of her armor provided an impassible barrier if any of the pilgrims slipped and fell.

Suddenly, there was a blinding flash, followed by a loud rumble, and the wails of the pilgrims before her. Gravity lost its hold on Sorrow as she fell. The sensation was very much like falling to sleep. An electric blue swirled in front of her, blotting out the snow.

When her vision cleared she sensed that she was no longer on the mountain, but was once more falling toward the waters of the convergence. She spread her wings and soared above the waves. Looking back along the length of her body, she found she retained her now familiar dragon-winged but otherwise human form. Unlike before, the convergence was dark and sunless. The sky above was filled with clouds, the lightning within providing the only light.

"You're the interloper the others whisper about," a deep voice rumbled. "The human who usurped the power of Rott."

"And you, I presume, are Tempest," she said.

"Rott's elemental essence is omnipresent," said Tempest. "I cannot exclude him from my earthly domain. But, Rott's intelligence has been absent for centuries. I'm not happy to see the human mind that now directs his powers finds my earthly empire worthy of her attention. Why have you invaded my home, usurper?"

"I mean no disrespect. I'm not here to confront you. I accompany a companion on his quest to the Temple of the Book. Once we're done, I'll leave this land as fast as humanly possible."

"That is not much of a promise from one who can walk through the realms immaterial. You could leave in the space of a heartbeat. And before coming, you could have summoned me to the convergence to ask permission to walk through my domain. Instead, you forced me to bring you here."

"There's a lot of this dragon stuff I'm figuring out," said Sorrow. "If you have any suggestions on how I can learn more, I'm willing to listen."

"Bah. I wouldn't waste such knowledge upon you. I see now that, while your mind has touched Rott, you are not yet the sole vessel of his essence. You're still merely a mortal. It would be a simple thing to kill you."

Sorrow's heart skipped a beat. Could one dragon attack another in the convergence? She suddenly felt very alone, and wished that Stagger was here to refresh her memory of the rules.

As she thought this, the dark waters below began to brighten. She looked up and saw a pink glow breaking through the clouds above her. The storm parted and a shaft of golden sunshine burst down through the clouds.

"Sorry to interrupt," a voice said.

"Stagger!" Sorrow shouted.

"The second usurper," the thunder grumbled.

Stagger's voice came from high above the clouds "I felt a tug to come here, so I did. I've been practicing looking into other realms, and even tried my hand at crafting avatars. Perhaps now that I'm here, Tempest, you could offer a few pointers?"

"I think not," growled Tempest. A draconic head formed from the roiling clouds and fixed its gaze upon Sorrow. "I believe that you visit my kingdom intending no malice toward me. I will overlook this insult… this time. Complete your journey with haste, then depart. We shall not speak again."

There was a flash of light that washed away Sorrow's sight and a clap of thunder that deafened her. She blinked and shook her head and the white persisted. Her body felt strangely heavy. She turned her head and the white shifted. She suddenly realized the lenses of her helmet were covered with snow. Somehow Tempest had pushed her back to the real world.

"Sorrow!" Slate was shouting from above. "Sorrow!"

She wiped the snow away from her visor and managed to sit up. Her legs were wedged between two massive rocks at the bottom of a steep slope. She pulled herself free with a grunt.

"Sorrow!" Slate shouted again, his voice slightly further away.

"I'm down here," she yelled back.

"Are you alright?"

"I think so," she said, examining the slope. She could see dark splotches among the fresh snow where she'd tumbled down. "I must have slipped and knocked myself out."

Slate came sliding down the slope through the swirling snow. He was carrying a stout rope, one he'd had wrapped around the coffin.

"I've been looking for you for ten minutes! I worried you were dead, like the others."

"Dead? What others?"

"The three pilgrims ahead of you. They were killed when the lightning struck!"

"Lightning?" she said. She shook her head. Her visit to the convergence seemed so unreal. Had Tempest really just paid her a visit that had proved fatal to bystanders? Or had she gotten jolted into unconsciousness by standing too close to a lightning strike and merely dreamed the whole conversation?

"Grab the rope!" Slate said as he reached her. "We can't waste more time. I've sent the surviving pilgrims on ahead. If they stop moving in this storm, they'll freeze..." His voice trailed off.

"What?" she asked.

"Your chest."

To see what he was staring at, she removed her gauntlet and placed her hand on his helmet, willing the glass to form a mirror finish. The light was dim, but good enough to make sense of what she saw.

Her breastplate was scorched in three jagged parallel slashes. It looked for all the world as if a dragon had raked its claws across her chest.

THEY RECOVERED TOWER'S coffin after they climbed out of the ravine, each lifting an end rather than wasting time wrapping it with ropes once more. They pressed forward at the quickest pace they could muster, their feet slipping in the mounting snow. Yet despite the misery of their condition, the light was definitely getting brighter. Had they climbed so far in the last few hours that they were now rising above the clouds?

This proved to be the case, as the snow faded into drizzle that changed to ice as it misted over them. The coffin grew increasingly heavy as the ice built.

The clouds came to an abrupt end as the path they traveled led into a long gap between two steep cliffs. The span between the cliffs was no more than fifty feet across. The sun was red as it sank into the ocean of clouds at their back, painting the cliff walls a deep crimson. Ahead, they saw the pilgrims on their knees, huddled before a wall of men in heavy fur coats who stood as a living barrier to their passage.

"Storm Guard?" Sorrow asked.

"Who else could it be?" answered Slate. They moved forward. Sorrow counted thirteen guards. She couldn't tell if they wore armor beneath their coats, but could see that they were armed with heavy hammers and battleaxes. In contrast to the clean-shaven, slender soldiers of the city, these were large, burly men with thick black beards and bushy eyebrows. Their coats were silver and brown, pieced together from the hides of wolves.

Slate lowered his end of the coffin. Sorrow set her end down. They marched through the kneeling pilgrims, who had their hands clasped before them in prayer.

The largest of the armed men stepped forward and shouted in short, guttural syllables.

"Do you not speak the Silver Tongue?" asked Slate.

The pilgrim who was missing an eye said, "They demand twenty moons for safe passage, and that you surrender your weapons."

"Tell him my weapon is a sacred relic that will not be relinquished."

The man frowned. "If I tell them that, they definitely won't let us pass unmolested. They'll steal the relic and hold it for ransom."

"So be it," said Slate. "Tell them."

The man swallowed hard. With a look of pain, he choked out a string of syllables.

The leader smiled as he barked back a response.

"It's as I feared," the one-eyed man said. "He now demands we turn over the relic in exchange for safe passage."

"Tell him…"

Before Slate could finish, the leader barked out a new jumble of sounds.

"He says that if you cause trouble, his men will kill all of us. He asks that you weigh your answer carefully."

Slate looked at Sorrow. "Are you ready to give our answer?"

"I'm ready if you're ready," said Sorrow.

Slate removed the Witchbreaker from its scabbard. The walls of the narrow canyon echoed with the howls of the damned.

Sorrow dropped her mace and allowed her gauntlets to crumble to rust.

"Anything you want to teach me, now's the moment," she said.

Slate replied, "Just follow my lead," not guessing that she hadn't been talking to him. He said to the translator, "Tell them to clear our path, or face destruction."

"There are thirteen of them," the man answered weakly. "There are only two of you. You're gambling with our lives!"

"You're the ones who begged to join us," Sorrow snapped. "Just tell him what Slate said."

The man turned pale as the looked back at the warriors and gave his answer.

The thirteen warriors roared in unison, raising their axes and hammers. Before they could finish inhaling, Slate leapt forward and drove the Witchbreaker deep into the belly of the leader. A soulful wail of terror filled the air, though nothing but bloody gurgles escaped the dead man's lips.

A half dozen of the warriors leapt toward Slate as he kicked the leader free of his blade. The rest of the men charged the kneeling pilgrims, with only Sorrow standing in their path.

Breathe flies, Avaris commanded. *You will feel a door open within your belly. Do not let go of this door!*

Sorrow was familiar with the sensation, having used this power to dispatch a band of warriors she'd faced in Hush's lair. She pulled her helmet free as the pressure built within her stomach. In her mind's eye, she saw the small black portal in her center, wobbling and warping as flies boiled into her belly.

She was vaguely aware that a warrior was three strides away from smashing a warhammer down on her bare scalp. She opened her lips and the man's face disappeared in a tornado of flies that erupted from inside her. The hammer dropped as his fingers went limp and he fell to his knees before her, his body collapsing against her legs. She looked down and found his face was nothing but a skull writhing with maggots.

Don't allow yourself to be distracted! Do not lose the door!

Sorrow found the disembodied voice screaming at her far more distracting than the dead man rapidly falling to bits around her feet. The boundaries of the black gate grew fuzzy. Suddenly, she lost all sense of where its edges lay.

Fool! You've just allowed more of Rott's essence to bleed into your physical body. When you open a door, you must have the discipline to close it properly!

"Good advice," Sorrow said as she watched the other warriors near her fall to the ground, tearing at the maggots writhing under their skin. "Maybe if you hadn't waited until one second before I needed to know to tell me, I might have found it useful."

She was snapped back from her argument with Avaris to her present danger by a head bouncing past her.

Slate had finished off four of the Storm Guard and was currently driving his blade into the fifth. Unfortunately, the sixth had bolted, and had run quite some distance up the path. She couldn't allow him to bring reinforcements.

She glanced back at the pilgrims, whose mouths gaped in horror at the maggot-ridden body before her. She felt something tickling her lip and brushed a fly away. If they'd witnessed this, there was no reason to hold back. With a thought, her armor fell away and she leapt into the air, still carrying her mace. The guard made it another hundred feet before she dropped onto his back, driving the mace into his neck with all her strength. Unfortunately, she hadn't been lying when she'd said the mace was hollow. Her victim still struggled beneath her, and if he made it to his back and freed his arms, he might yet cause her grief.

She placed her hand upon the nape of his neck. She imagined the black portal once more, this time opening in her shoulder. She focused as dark energy flowed down her arm and the man's flesh liquefied in her grasp. She never took her mind's eye off the portal. Clenching her jaw, she willed the pulsing black circle to grow smaller, then smaller still. With a final gasp, she closed it completely.

She raised her hand, wrinkling her nose at the pink gore that coated it.

Well done. If you maintain such discipline in the future, you may grow powerful indeed.

"And if I don't?"

You'll lose the last of your humanity as Rott consumes you.

Sorrow nodded. The risks were clearly laid out. Before, she'd been frightened by the uncertainty of what dangers she faced. Now she knew what the risks were, and could push through the fuzzy veil of fear into the firm embrace of pure terror.

18 - A Bit of Clever Magic

THE WIND HOWLED through the narrow stone gap as Sorrow stared at her gore-covered hand. She knelt and wiped her fingers on the man's wolf coat, then headed back down the pass to retrieve her armor before she froze to death.

Slate stood over the maggot-ridden bodies of the men she'd killed. The pilgrims were all huddled together, still on their knees, their eyes wide as they stared at Sorrow. At least most of them were staring at her. Quite a few eyes were focused instead on Slate, who still held the ebony sword in his grasp, filling the air with faint cries of agony.

"What magic is this?" Slate asked as she drew close. "These men have been reduced to skeletons!"

"You knew I had tapped into Rott's power," she said.

"When we fought the pirates together, your methods were less… disturbing."

Sorrow arranged the components of her discarded armor and molded her now ice-cold iron shell back into position. She commanded the metal to warm, but her teeth were still chattering as she said, "I don't think you're in any position to declare my methods disturbing. You just sent your enemies' souls directly to hell."

As if to prove her point, the screams of torment that echoed from the sword grew rather loud at that moment.

"Is this not an appropriate fate for the wicked?"

"I'm not certain it is," she said. "First, the Storm Guard have a very different conception of the afterlife than the Church of the Book. I'm not up on my theology, but I'm pretty sure they didn't feel like their actions were going to earn them an eternity in a fiery pit tormented by demons."

"The failings of their belief system are unfortunate," said Slate. "Without the fear of hell, how are men of weak morals to be brought to the path of righteousness?"

"So you admit that this church you're so enamored of uses fear and the threat of torture to ensure obedience?"

Slate frowned. "It's not as simple as that. Men who behave in compliance with the Divine Author's will are rewarded with paradise. The possibility of hell is merely…"

When he seemed at a loss for words, she said, "It's merely a threat to catch the few poor souls who aren't swayed by bribery?" She nodded toward the blade. "I'll never worship a god who built a place that sounds like that."

He said nothing as he slid the Witchbreaker back into its scabbard, silencing the cries.

She tucked her wings under her arms and closed her armor. "Besides, I thought everything that will ever happen is already recorded in the One True Book. Why have this whole system of punishment and bribes to control men when every last choice they're given has been decided by the Divine Author? By the very tenants of your faith, these men were only in our way because it was His will that we kill them." She pointed to the huddled pilgrims. "These poor fools have lost possessions, loved ones, and limbs because your god thought it would make a good story."

Slate crossed his arms. "I'm a knight, not a theologian. I'm sure there are others at the temple who can explain our beliefs more eloquently than I can."

Sorrow donned her helmet once more and moved to stand beside Slate as he stood before the shivering pilgrims.

"It's almost nightfall," he said to the pilgrims. "But these guards must have a camp nearby. If any guards remain there, we'll take it by force. Tonight, you'll sleep in the beds of those who caused you such grief."

The one-eyed man cleared his throat. "We've decided to turn back. We'll complete our journey another time."

Slate glanced over his shoulder at the corpses behind him. "Have we… frightened you?"

"We… we didn't understand… what manner of creatures… we journeyed with. We'd heard stories of demons who disguise themselves as men —"

"We're not demons," said Slate. "I'm a knight. My companion is… unusual in appearance, but human."

"He's right," said Sorrow. "We're both human. Which means we're even more dangerous than demons. If you want to turn back, turn back. You wanted a roadblock removed and we removed it. What direction you go from this moment is entirely up to you."

"You all have reasons for being here," said Slate. "Your faith has brought you this far. You can't turn back now."

And yet, one by one, the pilgrims stood and began to walk back down the path, toward the churning clouds at the mouth of the gap, linking hands as they vanished into the storm.

"They were slowing us down," said Sorrow. "Don't look so dejected."

"It was as if they feared me as much as you," Slate said, shaking his head. "We fought to save them and they hate us for it?"

"Welcome to every damn day of my life."

NIGHT HAD FALLEN when they discovered the camp of the Storm Guard, a tight cluster of stone huts with hide roofs. Someone shouted out an alarm as they approached, and a moment later they were attacked by five warriors.

The fight was brief.

They spent the remainder of the night in the largest of the huts, warming themselves in front of a stone furnace fueled by coal. Sorrow stared into the flickering flames, wondering if she might dream of Greatshadow once more. Slate looked glum, and even though the hut was well stocked with dried meats and fruits, he ate nothing. He silently removed his armor and stretched out on the ground beside the stove, covering his massive form with a heavy blanket pulled from one of the bunks. His eyes were locked on the Witchbreaker, which rested atop his armor.

Sorrow welcomed his silence. She had worries of her own. The familiar itchiness had returned to her skin, this time concentrated in her arms and hands. She'd shoveled a load of coal into the furnace when they'd arrived, leaving her hands black with dust. Now, as she watched, the blackness hardened on fingers, growing shiny. Her nails grew longer and thinner, turning into hard claws.

Seduce him and I'll teach you bone weaving. You cannot rid yourself of the dragon's essence, but you can push it to less visible parts of your body.

"I know," she whispered. "But, it's not going to happen."

Why not? I see the way you glance at him. You're not immune to his charms.

Sorrow rose and walked to the far side of the hut. "I want to end our agreement. I'm sorry if I've inconvenienced you, but I don't feel that you're the best teacher for me."

You've more than inconvenienced me. You invaded my home, assaulted me, and destroyed my companion. You cannot turn away from my teachings now.

"Are you teaching me? Or punishing me?"

There may be some overlap. It doesn't change anything. You promised me you would take a life at my request. Until this promise is kept, our bargain remains in place.

"What if I tell you I don't intend to kill anyone just because you ask me too? Can we end our bargain then?"

If you betray me, you forfeit all the power I've taught you to use.

Sorrow started to argue that wasn't very much, but thought better of it as she contemplated the possible ways Avaris might remove the knowledge. The old witch probably knew exactly what parts of Sorrow's brain to probe with a long fingernail in order to scrape away her memories. For now, she was still trapped in her bargain.

Why the doubts now? You were the picture of confidence when you battled your way into my castle.

"I don't have doubts. I have... finality. There's no real time left to learn anything before tomorrow."

Tomorrow you will reach the Temple of the Book.

Sorrow nodded. "Tomorrow, I'm going to cripple my enemies with a blow they can never recover from. I… I intend to win tomorrow's battles, but I'm not kidding myself. There's a strong possibility that tonight is my last night alive."

All the more reason to seduce him.

Sorrow shook her head. "No. If I'm to die, I intend to die true to myself. I've lived with the certainty I had no need of men. It's the wrong moment for second guesses. But if there is anything you have to tell me about Rott's power that I don't yet know, now is the time to reveal it. You have to want the church to feel pain as much as I do. Now's your chance to turn me into your ultimate weapon for revenge."

Your father has already done that work for me.

Avaris began to laugh inside Sorrow's skull. It wasn't a pleasant sound.

DURING THE NIGHT, Sorrow had held out some slender hope that the changes to her hands weren't as bad as they seemed. The coal dust and the darkness of the hut perhaps make her skin appear darker and rougher than it truly was.

In the pale light of morning, she had no reason for hope. She melted snow in the iron bowl of her helmet and washed her hands, if they could still be called hands. Her pinkies had fused with her ring fingers and all of her digits had become longer and banded by scales. Her nails were now claws, tapering to razor-sharp hooks.

When she heard Slate stirring, she hastily pulled on her iron gauntlets, willing the metal to stretch to hide her deformity. She folded the now empty pinkies of the gauntlets closed and fused them, hoping no one would notice their lack of motion.

Slate looked even more exhausted than he had when he went to sleep.

"Rough night?" she asked.

He shook his head. "Climbing this mountain with a coffin balanced on my back has drained me. From what the pilgrims told me, the temple is only a few hours walk. I look forward to divesting myself of my burden."

"It's a burden you placed upon yourself," said Sorrow. "We could have buried Tower in the swamp."

"Tower had already suffered the abuse of having his corpse reanimated as a slave of Avaris. The hero of Poppy's storybook deserves a better ending."

"He's dead no matter where his body winds up," she said. "His ending is already written."

Tower didn't look directly at her as he rose to dress. He buckled his armor without saying a word.

"I guess this conversation is over?" she asked.

"This conversation is impossible."

"What does that mean?"

He sighed. "Only that I will never be able to explain myself." He walked to the coffin and knelt beside it, placing his hands upon the wooden surface. His voice was soft as he said, "I was created from Tower's blood. I'm like a branch snapped from a tree that's taken root in new soil. Is the new tree a different entity than the old tree, or merely an extension of it? I'm not Tower's duplicate. I'm his continuation. Who else in all of history has borne the burden of having to bury himself?"

SORROW HAD EXPECTED the Temple of the Book to be a more imposing structure. In fact, it wasn't a structure at all, just a series of dark holes chiseled into a cliff of solid white quartz. The landscape surrounding it was windswept and barren, nothing but rough gravel over frozen gray soil.

The dark holes led into the mountain, and she could see shadows flickering across the well-lit interiors. They were still several hundred yards away, but from the flurry of activity, she gathered they'd been spotted.

A horse galloped out of one of the uppermost holes, bearing a rider upon his back. The horse was a pure black mare, well-muscled to support the heavily armored knight upon her back. Glorystone horseshoes shot beams of bright light down from the mare's hooves, and the horse raced across the sky upon these columns of radiance. The knight was armed with a crystalline lance, which had a pale blue glow similar to the lightning rod Sorrow had stolen. He wore a flowing purple cape trimmed with golden silk. There were words embroidered within this trim, but Sorrow couldn't make them out at this distance.

The horse charged toward them in eerie silence, coming to a stop roughly a hundred feet up in the sky.

"Halt!" the knight shouted.

Slate halted. Sorrow felt an almost uncontrollable urge to step forward, so she did.

"I said, halt!"

"What right do you have to prevent anyone from walking the path of the pilgrim?" she asked.

The knight flipped up the visor of his helmet, revealing his face. He was a square-headed man with bright blue eyes and a thick gray mustache that hung several inches below his jaw. "Don't pretend you don't know who I am," the knight answered. "I'm Sir Forthright Castlebridge, the Fist of the Book, the rightful protector of Utmost Humble, the Voice of the Book. For thirty years I've defended this sacred place with the power of my mighty steed, Sunracer, my legendary lightning lance, and my unflagging faith."

"Horses don't live thirty years," said Sorrow.

"This is Sunracer VI, though that doesn't matter," said Castlebridge. "What matters is that the Voice of the Book is the sole authority to decide who may enter the temple, and I am the enforcer of his will. I command you both to lay down your arms and surrender."

"We command you to take your lance and shove it up —"

"Sorrow!" Slate snapped. "Is there a reason you're being so disrespectful of a duly appointed defender of the temple?"

Sorrow clenched her fists, then relaxed them. "I don't like men bossing me around. You talk now."

Slate lowered his coffin to the ground. He knelt and said, "Good sir, we come on a mission of peace. This coffin holds the mortal remains of Stark Tower, the famed Witchbreaker. He was a great hero of the church. I've delivered him so that his bones may rest in a place of honor surrounded by his fellow saints."

"Whatever your intentions," said Castlebridge, "you killed an entire camp of Storm Guard yesterday. We received word of your crimes this morning. The Voice of the Book has decreed that you will be turned over to representatives of the Storm Guard to face punishment."

Slate rose. "We killed only thugs who were molesting pilgrims unjustly. Is it not the duty of any knight to defend the followers of the Book?"

"The first duty is to defend the Book," said Castlebridge. "This is a dangerous land. We are but an island amid a vast ocean of enemies. Our peace with Tempest is a fragile one. In seeking to punish a handful of greedy men, you place the most sacred ground of your faith in danger of invasion."

"This is madness!" Slate cried. "Are there no men among you willing to stand up to evil?"

"Standing up to evil is a vice if it harms the greater good," said Castlebridge. His eyes lifted from Slate to look down the road. Sorrow turned and saw a large group of men on shaggy horses loping up the trail.

"Grant me permission to speak to the Voice of the Book," Slate said.

"Permission denied," said Castlebridge, pointing his lance at Slate. "The only matter left for debate is whether the Storm Guard will take living men into their custody, or corpses. If you wish to make a show of defying me in order to provoke my attack, I understand. Storm Guard justice is known for its brutality. The death I unleash shall be swift and merciful."

"How do you want to handle this?" Sorrow asked. "Should I devour him with flies, or do you just want me knock him off his horse so you can chop off his head and condemn his soul to hell?"

"I'll not use the Witchbreaker upon a fellow knight," said Slate.

"So, flies?"

"I haven't come here to harm the defenders of the temple!"

"Have you come to surrender to the Storm Guard?" she said, looking at the approaching horses. "Because you've got maybe two minutes left to make a decision."

"I'm going to speak to the Voice of the Book!" Slate shouted at Castlebridge. "Do not stand in my way!"

He stepped forward. Castlebridge lowered his lance. Sorrow willed the iron sheathe of her mace to crumble away, revealing the lighting rod within. There was a loud *CRACK* and a flash that left her blinking her eyes. The crystal rod she held was hot and brightly glowing. In the sky, Castlebridge was frowning.

"I don't need my lance to deal with you," he bellowed, flipping his visor down as he dropped his lance and drew his sword. The sword was blood red and had an aura separate from that of Castlebridge. As the knight charged down from the sky brandishing the blade, she had the flicker of an idea that perhaps she should delay her attack in order to learn what enchantments the blade might possess. But the idea vanished as she felt the familiar pressure in her belly of Rott's power bubbling up from the abstract realms. She quickly found the edges of the portal and focused as she widened the gap. Her body convulsed as she threw her helmet aside and snapped her jaws open. A black whirlwind swirled into the air, engulfing Castlebridge and the horse he rode in on.

To her great consternation, Castlebridge and Sunracer VI emerged from the whirlwind unscathed. Castlebridge leaned in his saddle and swung his blade toward her. She jumped aside, but the tip of his sword sliced through her armor as if it were mere fabric, slicing a three-inch gash along her right bicep. She clamped her hand upon the wound as she sucked air through her teeth. The pain was nearly blinding as the blood gushed between her fingers. Worse, the shock of the blow had once more distracted her from properly closing the energy gate. The dose of dark portal dissipating through her set her nerves jangling from scalp to toes.

Sunracer VI turned swiftly, targeting Slate. Slate stood with his legs spread to steady his stance. The horse seemed aimed to collide with Slate's chest, veering at the last possible instant to allow Castlebridge to aim his slashing sword at Slate's neck. Slate's hand shot out and grabbed Castlebridge by the wrist, halting the blow, knocking the older knight off balance. Slate yanked Castlebridge from his saddle and threw him to the ground. Castlebridge's helmet tore free from its clasps as the knight rolled across the rocky earth. He wound up on his back, looking dazed, his arms spread to his side. The red sword was still in his grasp. Slate jumped toward the fallen knight, driving his boot into the wrist that held the blade.

"Yield, and face no further harm," Slate said.

"Fool!" Castlebridge's face twisted with fury. "You don't know what you're doing! It's you who must yield! Your companion's already dead!"

"Wrong," said Sorrow, walking toward them. "Still alive."

"A fleeting condition, witch!" Castlebridge said as he stared at her scalp. "The wounds inflicted by the blood blade never heal. You'll bleed to death soon enough."

Sorrow looked toward the approaching horsemen. She wasn't feeling confident about trying to use Rott's power again, and twenty men on horseback seemed like a lot even for Slate to handle.

"Let's get inside the temple," she said.

"I'll fight to my dying breath to stop you!" growled Castlebridge as he rolled to his side, struggling to free him arm. Fortunately, he was in full plate armor. On the ground, his movements were somewhat reminiscent of a turtle.

Sorrow knelt. She still had one hand clamped onto her arm to slow her blood loss, but she placed the hand of her wounded arm upon Castlebridge's armor. She could feel enchantment within the casing, perhaps a protective spell that had spared him from her power earlier. Enchantment or no, the armor was made from iron, so it was a simple matter to force Castlebridge once more to his back. She ran her hand from joint to joint, crimping the metal, swiftly turning his armor into a prison.

She tore his cape free. Now that it wasn't flapping, she could see the embroidered letters spelled out 'Castlebridge.' For some reason, this increased her pleasure in tearing the cape into shreds.

She willed her own armor to fall into rust. She wouldn't be needing it anymore. She handed Slate the strips of cloth and said, "Bandage me. Make it tight."

"Your hands…" he said, staring at her talons.

"I know. You can stare at them later. Just bandage me."

He tied the strips around her arm, pulling the cloth so tight it was painful. But the pressure had the desired effect, as the blood loss slowed to a seep.

By now, the horsemen were in full gallop toward them, no more than half a mile away and closing quickly. She looked back and saw an army of knights pouring out of the Temple of the Book. She noticed Sunracer VI returning to the hole she'd originally seen him launch from. Apparently, the steed didn't like Castlebridge anymore than she did.

She turned Slate away from her and wrapped her arms around his chest. "Hold tight!" she shouted as she spread her wings. Her most powerful flap failed to lift them. For her to carry him, she'd need to already have some momentum.

"Run down hill!" she cried as she pushed him. "Keep your arms out to your side!"

He did so, even though this meant he was now charging directly at the mounted Storm Guard. She waited until he was thirty yards away before running after him, then kicking off with all the strength she could muster. She could feel the weariness of her sleepless night draping over her like a heavy blanket, weighing her down as she flapped as furiously as she could manage. It was enough for her to catch air beneath her wings. By now, Slate was a hundred yards down the slope from her. She glided toward him, building speed, the ground flashing by mere inches beneath the tips of her wings. Slate and the horsemen were only yards apart when he caught him and jerked him into the sky. His left foot caught the lead horseman in the face, knocking him from his saddle and stripping Sorrow of a bit of momentum. Gritting her teeth, she flapped so hard she feared her wings would tear from her shoulders. The effort paid off, and soon she was soaring well above the heads of the thundering Storm Guard.

"The coffin!" Slate shouted. "We can't just leave it!"

"I can't carry it and you," she said, her voice strained. "We'll get it later."

Slate said nothing as she banked and cut a long arc through the air. Drawing on Jetsam's lessons, she found the edge of a steep slope exposed to the rising sun and caught the wind that pushed up from it. She spiraled higher on the updraft, her sweat turning to beads of ice upon her skin. At last she climbed higher than the temple. She tilted toward it, intending to glide the remaining distance. Unfortunately, as she approached, she saw archers in every window. She wasn't certain she could dodge missiles while carrying Slate.

A curious thing happened as she came within range. All the archers lowered their bows in unison. They vacated the windows of the temple, leaving her a choice of landing sites. She aimed for the largest opening, filled with the brightest lights. It was the only one wide enough to accommodate her wingspan.

"This might get rough!" she called out to Slate. They were flying too fast. Landing at this speed was going to be painful, but if she tried to slow her flight they would drop below the window and crash into the face of the cliff. She would have to turn her wings into parachutes the second they were safely inside. She'd practiced rapid landings with Jetsam, but never carrying an armored knight.

But it wasn't her lack of practice that endangered her as she flashed through the window. Instead, the second she entered the room beyond, her left eye went blind. She crashed into a chandelier comprised of hundreds of tiny glorystones linked together by fine silver chains. This unexpected net entangled her wings and she crashed to the stone floor. Slate tore from her grasp as she bounced upon the white quartz. The glorystones beneath her tore into her like glass shards.

The world swirled slowly as spots danced before her. No matter how hard she blinked, she had no sight at all in her left eye. She tried to rise on her hands and knees, but failed, collapsing to the floor, weak as a baby. It was more than just exhaustion or blood loss. It was as if half the life had been sucked from her body.

Slate had fared better. He was already on his feet, studying their surroundings. As near as Sorrow could gather, they were in a long hall lined with doors. At the end of the hall, she saw a large iron door swing open. A man in black robes stepped through, pausing to lock the door behind him. He walked toward them, his hands clasped behind his back. He was old and thin, with thick curls of snow-white hair that hung about his shoulders like a lion's mane. His expression was a curious mix of sternness and serenity as he approached them.

"I apologize for telling the archers to stand down," the man said. "I saw no need for them to get hurt."

"Apologize?" asked Slate.

"I'm certain you were eager for battle. The two of you have a thirst for attacking lawful authorities," the man said. "A man of your description killed several guards in the Silver City only weeks ago. You're obviously the same ruffians who abused the port inspectors earlier this week, and I heard you confess to Forthright that you killed the Storm Guards who camped at the pass."

"You heard… how?"

The man shrugged. "I've lived in this place a very long time. I'm spiritually attuned with the very rocks you stand upon. There is nothing that takes place upon this mountain of which I'm not aware."

"Then, you must be —"

"Utmost Humble, the Voice of the Book," he said.

Slate knelt before the man. "Sir, I've come on a sacred mission to inter —"

"Inter the body of a damned man?" Utmost said, with a scoff. "Stand up."

Slate stood.

"Your journey has been in vain. Whatever he may have been in life, Stark Tower is undeserving of a place among the saints."

"Please," said Slate. "As a Knight of the Book, I ask you to—"

Utmost shook his head. "You're not a knight. You're not even human. You're an abominable imitation of a man, a bit of clever magic that has broken free of the control of its caster."

"The blood of Stark Tower beats within my veins," said Slate. "His soul is my soul."

"You should be grateful that statement is untrue. Avaris killed Tower with his own sword. The poor man's soul has burned in the deepest pits of hell for nearly five centuries," said Utmost, shaking his head as if recounting this was distasteful. "Take comfort that, when you die, you'll face no such torments. Nothing but oblivion awaits you. It's almost a peaceful fate, if you contemplate it."

"It's not a fate I accept," said Slate.

Utmost sighed. "I understand. You're not to blame for the travesty of your own existence. I'm sure you would prefer to live a life that had some semblance of meaning. And perhaps you will."

Sorrow's head had cleared somewhat by now. She rose to her hands and knees, contemplating the blood on the stone beneath her. Utmost turned his face toward her and said, "You will lie back down."

She did so, though she fought with all her will to rise.

"What meaning?" Slate asked. "What meaning can my life have if I am soulless?"

Utmost gave a feeble smile. "When I turn you over to the Storm Guard, your torture and torment will occupy them for days, if not weeks. It will give tensions time to ebb. Nearly daily, I'm faced with the emissaries of Tempest, threatening to invade this sanctuary and destroy the One True Book. Ordinarily, I would lend no credence to his threats. But after our mission to kill Greatshadow ended in failure, and our plan to kill Glorious left a human intelligence in command of an elemental power, Tempest has become quite anxious."

"Because he believes he's your next target?"

Utmost laughed. "No. He's not our target. He's our ally. He approached us with a plan to eliminate the other primal dragons. His Storm Guard were the raiders who stole the Jagged Heart. He gave us advice as to which abstract realms would provide the most advantageous battlegrounds. Now that our first two assassinations have gone awry, he's blaming us for the failures."

"What? Why would Tempest ally himself with you? Why would you ally yourself with him?"

Utmost shrugged. "This island has been the birthplace of many religions. Tempest knows that even primal dragons may be slain. He wishes to escape death by transcending his draconic nature and becoming a god."

"And why would you assist him in this?"

"If we trust the truth of our faith, then we trust the truth he will fail. But, for now, he's helping us target other primal dragons. Also, there's the not inconsequential matter that he does hold this temple hostage. The Storm Guard society doesn't function well. It's corrupt, built upon an unsustainable economy of slaves, and fails even to feed its own people. The Silver Isles would have conquered this land long ago, if not for Tempest's threat to destroy this sacred place." He nodded toward the door he'd entered. "The One True Book lies beyond that door. This holy ground is protected by wards that bar elemental spirits, but, even so, the dragon would only have to extend his power a few hundred feet to destroy it forever."

"Then move the book!" Slate said, sounding completely exasperated.

"The book is too holy for human hands to ever touch," said Utmost. "Until the Omega Reader arrives, men's souls are too sullied by sin to survive a brush with the divine power the book contains. They would burn like a leaf placed upon a red-hot forge."

"But —"

Before Slate could argue further, Sorrow finally regained some control of her limbs. She rolled to her side, then sat up.

"You will lay down," said Utmost.

She did so, then, taking a shuddering breath, she asked, "Any advice?"

"What advice do you seek?" asked Slate.

"Avaris can't hear you here," said Utmost. "As a dweller of the Black Bog, her dark soul withers when exposed to the radiance of the glorystones."

Sorrow furrowed her brow. "You know about Avaris?"

"And of her plot to reclaim Rott's power."

"You may have some mistaken information," she whispered as she strained to lift herself from the floor.

"You're the one who's been deceived. Avaris once before attempted to steal Rott's power. Of course, Rott's intelligence was far more active then. He resisted her control, and began to control her. She cut herself free from his power before her personality was completely devoured. Now she's watching you to see if Rott's will has decayed sufficiently that her mind could dominate."

"The flaw in that theory is that I'll be one controlling Rott's power."

"Avaris could crush your spirit with no more effort than it would take me to crush a snail. You're no obstacle to her plans, girl, only a stepping stone. At least, you were going to be, before you embarked on your pathetic plan to barge onto this sacred ground and attempt to destroy the One True Book. It's a pity your intelligence doesn't match your audacity."

Sorrow had tucked the lighting rod into a cotton sash around her waist. She felt it beneath her hip. If she could move only a few inches, she could aim it toward Utmost and release its power.

"I can almost hear the gears whirring in your head, witch," said Utmost. "Instead of thinking of desperate schemes of escape, might I suggest this would be a good time to contemplate repentance?"

"I have nothing to repent," she said through clenched teeth as her talons strained to touch the rod.

"You will go limp," said Utmost, shaking his head.

Every muscle in Sorrow's body fell slack.

Utmost sighed. "You can't say I didn't give you the opportunity to confess your sins and plead for the Divine Author's mercy." Utmost turned toward Slate. "Draw your sword."

The now familiar howls swirled through the air as the blade left its scabbard.

"You imagine yourself to be a continuation of the famed Witchbreaker?" Utmost asked. He didn't wait for Slate to answer. "For one brief moment, allow me to indulge your fantasy." He pointed toward Sorrow.

"There's a witch. *Break her*."

19 - RUMBLE

SORROW HELD HER breath as Slate turned toward her. She managed to lift her head half an inch from the floor before Utmost cried, "You will remain still, witch!"

Sorrow's head banged onto the stone floor. She couldn't even move her jaw to speak. If she opened the dark portal within her to channel flies, would she be able to release them safely, or would they simply tear through her face? But she had to try. Only, despite the full force of her will calling it, the black portal failed to open. The wards that protected this place were too strong for Rott to overcome.

Slate's boots drew closer. From her vantage point of having her cheek pressed to the floor, she could only see the two men's feet. Then, unexpectedly, Slate's boots turned from her.

"Don't turn back," Utmost said. "Kill her!"

Slate walked toward the Voice of the Book. The Witchbreaker fell silent as Slate slid it into its scabbard.

Utmost stammered, "Wh-what are you —"

He was silenced by a sudden *WHACK*. Sorrow couldn't see the source of the noise, but half a second later Utmost crumpled to the floor with blood streaming from his mouth. Sorrow jerked her face off the floor as her body returned to her control.

"You've no authority over me," Slate said, standing over the old man with his fists clenched. "You've no authority over anything!"

"How can you defy me? I'm the highest of the truthspeakers!" Utmost shouted, blood spraying from his torn lips.

"I defy you because you're the lowest of liars," Slate said. "You've confessed as much with your own lips. The true Voice of the Book would defend his faith with all his body and soul. You've thrown away your authority through bargains with false gods."

"For the greater good, you fool!" Utmost cried. "Our bargain with Tempest is ultimately a trap for him! When his usefulness to us exhausted, he, too, shall die!"

"So you deceive him?" said Slate. "You befriend him with the intention of stabbing him in the back? These are not the actions of an honest man."

"Who are you to judge me?" Utmost spat out bright red spittle. "You're nothing but a motherless abomination."

"Whatever my origins," Slate said, "I strive to be an honest man. As Poppy's book teaches, a single honest man outnumbers a legion of liars."

"We'll find out!" Utmost said, before screaming, "Help! Help!"

Slate grabbed Utmost by the back of his robes and pulled him to his feet. "Silence! I'll let you live if you open the door to the One True Book."

"I'll do no such thing!"

"I saw you place the key within your robes. We may both preserve a bit of dignity if I'm not forced to strip you bare to find them."

"What are you doing, Slate?" Sorrow asked as she limped toward him, still pulling shards of glorystone from her skin.

"I'm setting things right," he said. He glanced at her. "Perhaps there was truth to your words. The church has become corrupt, willing to accept evil in the name of maintaining the status quo. But you're wrong to think that the church deserves to be destroyed. It needs instead to be cleansed. We must drive the false prophets from the temple and return the One True Book to the hands of righteous men."

By now, Utmost had his keys in his hand. "You simple-minded fool. The One True Book must remain in this temple."

Slate pushed him forward.

Utmost continued, "No man may touch the book without destroying his soul. We know the truths within only through prayer and meditation. No man has prayed longer and more intently than I have!"

"Just open the door," Slate said, pushing the aged cleric up to the heavy iron portal.

Utmost toyed with the lone key on the ring. It was a small key for such an imposing door, no longer than a man's thumb. The head of the key was rather simple, merely three stubs sticking out from the shaft.

"Stop playing with your key and open the door," said Slate.

Without warning, the key ring fell from Utmost's grasp and clattered on the floor. Sorrow glanced at the iron ring and realized it was empty. Before she could act, Utmost tilted his head backwards as he shoved the key into his mouth.

He fell, choking, both hands upon his throat.

Slate shook his head as he reached for the hilt of the Witchbreaker. "I'd hoped this could be done without any further decapitations."

"That won't be necessary," Sorrow said, placing her hand on the iron door. She willed it to crumble to rust. She was thrown back as a jolt of energy crackled through her, landing hard on the floor, cutting her lip open.

Utmost laughed wetly as he finished swallowing the key. His eyes were filled with something like delight as he watched her writhe in pain. He said, with a raspy voice, "These doors are forged from the same hell gate iron as the Witchbreaker. Your witchcraft is useless against its abstract nature."

Sorrow crawled back toward the door. Tears ran down her cheeks. Each inch she moved was agonizing, but Utmost's taunts spurred her on. When he died, it wouldn't be with a smile on his face.

Her hands fell upon the iron key ring. She rose on rubbery legs as she crushed the ring between her palms and rolled it into a shaft. Despite the claw-like nature of her hands, she still retained her gift for sculpting. It took only seconds to pinch and pull and snip the metal into a duplicate of the key she'd seen.

She slid the key into the lock and turned it. There was a soft, but satisfying, *click*.

Utmost fell silent, as his face turned ashen gray.

"You don't look like you're feeling well," she said, as she pushed the door open. "Was it something you ate?"

Utmost didn't answer. Sorrow grew quiet herself as she turned her eyes to the chamber beyond, a simple oval of rough cut white quartz with a low ceiling. The floor was smooth and polished from centuries of use. A ring ten foot around the central pedestal had a groove worn into the stone from the actions of innumerable truthspeakers who had over the years knelt there and pressed their heads against the stone in prayer.

Upon the pedestal of quartz was the One True Book.

The tome failed to impress her. She'd heard the book was as tall as a man, but this was only the size of an atlas, still large for a book, but small for a legend. Rather than being bound in hide so black you could see stars twinkling in the void as you stared at it, the book's cover was merely a dark brown, the leather seeming to be from a creature no more exotic than a cow. The pages, rumored to be trimmed with gold, were merely wrinkled parchment, yellow with age. The cover and spine were wordless.

"This is it?" she said, placing her hand upon the wall to steady herself. "This is what caused all the suffering for so many centuries?"

"This hasn't caused suffering," said Utmost. "Suffering is the natural state of mankind. This book is the source of hope. It's the promise that all our earthly travails have meaning, that everything that happens unfolds for a reason."

Sorrow took a stumbling step toward it.

"Go no further," said Slate.

She glanced at him.

"You came here to destroy the book. I will not allow this."

"I don't need your permission," she said. "You should want this as much as I do! Can't you see the mere existence of this book is to blame for Utmost's making deals with dragons? He loves this pile of parchment so much he cherishes its survival more than he values the lives of pilgrims. Ridding mankind of this vile tome is the only hope of creating a just world."

"You cannot speak to me about making deals with evil," said Slate. "Just what happened when you chased Avaris into the farther room? How many of your nonsensical mutterings have been private conversations with the Queen of Witches?"

"What do you think happened? I made a deal with her. She would teach me to use Rott's powers safely and instruct me in bone-weaving."

"What did you give her in exchange?"

"Nothing. Yet. Just a promise."

"Was destroying the One True Book the promise made?"

"No."

"She couldn't destroy it if she tried," said Utmost. "The second she touches it, her soul with perish!"

Slate tossed Utmost to the floor and walked toward the pedestal.

"What are *your* plans, Slate?" she asked.

"I'm going to do what should have been done centuries ago. I'm going to carry this sacred book from this land of dangers and deliver it to the Cathedral of the Book in the Silver City. There it may be defended by men of greater character than those who dwell here."

Slate held his hands over the book.

"D-don't," whispered Utmost. "The divine power within will surely destroy you."

"I'm an abomination not born of woman," said Slate. "I've no soul to risk."

He placed his hands upon the book. Sorrow's heart skipped a beat as he lifted it. Despite her hatred of the book, she half expected Slate to fall over dead. Instead, it was Utmost who clenched his chest with both hands, his face twisting in pain as Slate lifted the tome from its pedestal. The old man's eyes rolled back in his head as his body went limp.

Slate turned toward the door and said, "I'll send anyone who attempts to stop me straight to hell."

Sorrow sighed, her shoulders sagging. "I won't try to stop you. You asked what price I promised Avaris. I promised her I would kill anyone she asked me to kill. But, I won't harm you. You may be a motherless abomination, but you're also the first honest man I've ever met. I won't have your blood on my hands."

Slate nodded toward the door. "I was talking to them."

Sorrow turned and found the chamber beyond filled with knights. Slate walked toward them, despite being outnumbered at least fifty-to-one. Sorrow tried to summon flies to help clear his path, but still felt no connection to the dark energy.

As Slate approached the knights, one by one they lowered themselves to their knees and took off their helmets, staring at Slate with an expression best described as awe.

"Are you the Omega Reader?" the nearest knight asked.

"No," said Slate.

"But you disobeyed the truths spoken by the Voice of the Book. You could not do so unless your truths were greater than his."

"The Omega Reader is said to be flawless, devoid of sin. I am not that man. These sacred words must wait for their final reader. I'm taking the book to the Silver City. With the book safe, Tempest will no longer be able to corrupt the church."

"You'll not travel alone," said the knight. "My name is Steadfast Plowman, a knight of the book. I didn't take up arms for my faith with the intention of living like a coward. For years, my brother knights and I have seethed in silent anger as our superiors commanded us to ignore the wickedness of the Storm Guard. We're men of true hearts willing to give our lives for your cause."

"Then rise and take arms. The road before us is long and steep. I don't expect our journey to the sea to go unopposed."

"We need not take the road," said Steadfast. "Follow us."

"Give me one more minute to catch my breath," said Sorrow.

Slate shook his head.

"I fought beside you believing you were my friend, when all along you plotted with Avaris behind my back. I... do not hate you. I believe that, like Utmost, you possessed good intentions. In the name of a greater good, you've allowed yourself to embrace evil. I won't kill you. You still have hope of redemption. Perhaps one day you can turn from the dark path you've chosen. For now, we must part ways."

Sorrow slid down the wall to rest upon the floor as Slate left the chamber. She couldn't find the strength to chase him and lacked the will to argue with him. She'd spared his life because of his innate honesty. Because of that honesty, his words had been hammers driving nails of truth into her aching skull. As she sat with her wings pinned beneath her, staring at her clawed hands, she understood that it wasn't her body that had become a monster. She was just as corrupt and compromised as Utmost. She thought her eyes had been forever tuned to see the evil that others were blind to.

In the end, she was the one who'd been most blind. Like her father, she held her principles so dearly, so tightly, that she'd smothered them.

She still had the key she'd used to open the door. She pressed it between her fingers until it became a razor sharp scalpel. She brought the knife toward the left side of her face, until she could no longer see it. In this temple of truth, her left eye was already blind.

In this temple of truth, there was more than one way to undo a bad bargain.

SHE USED THE silver threads from the fallen chandelier to stitch her wounds shut. The wound inflicted by the blood blade continued to ooze despite her efforts, painting her arms in red tendrils. She used the lightning rod as a cane as she hobbled toward the large window they'd flown through.

She steadied herself with a hand on the wall as she looked down. The cliff face below her was sheer. She jerked her head up as battle cries broke out above her. Horses erupted from an unseen window, leaping out into open space and landing on the beams of light that shot from their glowing horseshoes. The horses continued to jump until there were more than she could count, each bearing a knight upon its back. She called out, "Slate!" as she spotted him in the middle of the pack astride a magnificent black stallion. Whether he heard her or not, he didn't look back.

She looked down at the ground once more. With only one eye, her depth perception was too poor for her judge the distance, but, in the end, what would it matter? She would either leap and find the strength to fly, or fail and plummet. Whether the distance to the ground was fifty feet or five hundred, she'd be dead.

She tucked the lightning rod back into the cotton sash she'd tied around her waist, then held her arms clasped together before her, preparing to dive. She spread her wings and fell forward. The second her toes left the white quartz floor, she felt a surge of strength flow through her. Her connection with Rott had returned! Draconic power pulsed through her veins, feeding her wings. They caught the rushing wind and threw her across the sky, in hot pursuit of the galloping horses.

What foolish thing have you done, girl?

"Avaris!" she cried in dismay.

Did you think that eyes alone sealed our contract? You may pluck out an eye, but you cannot pluck out a soul. I'm part of you until you've fulfilled your vow!

"Fine," said Sorrow. "For the time being, all I want you to do is shut up. I've got my hands full at the moment." Which was true enough, as she reached for the lightning rod. She paused for a heartbeat as she found a patch of rough scales along her hip. The return of Rott's power had brought further changes to her body, it seemed. She had no time to inspect herself, however. The knights were galloping directly toward the bank of clouds beneath them. Flickers of lightning lit the churning gray mass. She dissolved the iron rings around the rod to protect her from any stray bolts.

Her prescience paid off, as a gray-skinned cloud giant rose from the storm below with a quiver full of glowing javelins strapped to his back. He hurled one at the closest knight, who was thrown from his saddle as a bolt of lightning cut his horse from beneath him. The giant drew a second bolt, but before he could strike, Steadfast Plowman, whom she recognized from his coat of arms, broke free from the pack of knights and charged with blinding speed toward the giant, his lance set to strike. Sorrow winced as Steadfast drove his weapon into the giant's eye. The giant toppled, ripping the lance from Steadfast's grasp, disarming him just as three other giants climbed atop the clouds, javelins at the ready.

Half the knights peeled off to engage in combat while the core of knights surrounding Slate closed even tighter as together they plunged into the clouds. Thunder rumbled as lighting crackled across the sky. Sorrow aimed toward the area of greatest intensity, the lightning rod held before her. Its glow flared as it sucked power from the charged air. Sorrow's wings were quickly soaked by the torrential rain within the cloud, and the winds spun her about like a chicken caught in a tornado. Suddenly her momentum came to a bone-jarring halt as a giant hand wrapped around her, squeezing her torso until she felt ribs snap. A pair of enormous fingers approached her head, looking ready to pinch it from her shoulders.

Her body was already ruined. She opened the dark door inside her letting the entropic force flow into the giant that held her. Flesh sloughed from the digits, leaving only fingers of bone, which loosened their grasp.

Sorrow fell, sucking in wet air, shivering as rain mixed with snow froze on her exposed skin. She managed to spread her wings just as she tumbled out of the clouds. She was mere yards from a snow-covered slope, and it was more luck than skill that allowed her to swerve out of the path of the largest boulder before she slammed into it.

She flapped her wings with all her might, shaking free the ice that coated her, and flew on beneath the rumbling storm. She craned her neck from side to side but couldn't see Slate or the knights anywhere. Had they met their end inside the cloud? Somehow, she doubted it.

She hurtled down the mountainside at speeds she'd never before dared. The wind froze her arms as she held them before her, turning her skin gray. Or were her limbs turning dark for other reasons?

At last she broke free from the worst of the rain. Before her, she could see the port, and her eyes scanned the rim of the bay looking for the *Circus*. Her heart sank when she found towers of flame rising from that very area. But as she drew closer, she saw that the *Circus* was half a mile out in the bay, all sails set, smashing through the waves.

The flames came from the slave market. The whole of the complex was ablaze. A bucket brigade had been formed, but its efforts were too late. The pitch-soaked pilings that supported the dock were the source of the most energetic flames. The firefighters threw down their buckets and ran as the docks groaned, tilting and twisting beneath the weight of the structures upon them. Seconds later, the last half of the dock collapsed, sending great whirlwinds of embers roaring into the sky.

Sorrow flew around the columns of sparks, gritting her teeth as the winds tossed her side to side. Closing on the *Circus* was slow going until she caught the gusts that Gale had summoned to drive to boat to full speed. She rode this wind toward the deck, tilting her legs down to land on the aft-castle.

Gale, Sage, and Rigger were at the wheel, along with Brand. Most of the other Romers plus Bigsby were occupied with what looked to be a hundred pygmies, helping them steady themselves as they descended the stairs to below deck. Mako was the only one not visible.

"Get ready for full speed!" Gale called out as she held he hands above her head, fingers spread wide.

"This isn't full speed?" Sorrow cried as her feet touched the pitching deck.

"Sage saw you coming. I slowed down so you could catch us."

Brand turned pale as he looked at her. "What happened?" he asked, studying her face.

She touched the crusted stitches over her empty eye. "I feel like I should have a witty reply, but I don't."

"This has something to do with our conversation?" Sage asked.

"Something, yes."

"Oh. I didn't even notice the eye," said Brand. "I was talking about the scales."

Sorrow let her talons fall to her cheeks. She found her skin was now covered with smooth, hard beads.

"These things happen," she said. She glanced toward the pygmies. "And apparently, a lot of other stuff has happened as well. How did your business meetings go?"

Brand steadied himself against the rail as the wind lashing the ship grew even stronger. He shouted, "One of dad's associates was a slave-trader named Price. I spoke to him for about five minutes before I realized that the only favor I wanted from the sleazy bastard was to watch him suffer and die. But he was thrilled enough to meet me that he gave me a tour of the slave market. From one of the windows, I could see the *Circus*. After that, one thing led to another."

"Where's Mako?" Sorrow asked.

"I'm right here," Mako said as he pulled himself up over the railing, dripping wet. He tossed an augur to the deck. He whipped his head to fling his long, slick hair out of his face. "While Jetsam and Ma got the fire going, I was making certain any ships that might pursue us had holes in their hull."

"What about cloudships?" Sorrow asked.

Gale said, "I'll take Levi at his word that if he'd been commander during the thick of the pirate wars, he would have taken actions to tilt the battles in our favor."

Sorrow looked up. The sky directly above them had patches of blue.

Amid this blue, a trio of horseman could be seen in silhouette, galloping toward the *Circus*.

"They're attacking from above!" Jetsam shouted.

"It's Slate!" Sage called out. "Ma, calm the deck so the horses can land!"

Gale lowered her arms.

"Another delay," grumbled Rigger. "Am I the only one in a hurry to get onto the high sea before Tempest intervenes?"

"Tempest isn't going to pay attention to a few missing slaves," Mako said. He had his eyes fixed on Sorrow. She turned away, feeling awkward. His feelings had been so hurt when she'd spurned his advances. But after her conversation with Gale the other night, she wasn't going to betray the woman's trust by engaging in loveless sex with her son.

"What will it matter if we're on the high seas?" asked Brand. "There are storms at sea as well."

"True," said Gale. "But that's also the domain of Abyss. We could ask for his protection."

Slate and the trio of knights reached the deck. The horse's hooves clomped loudly on the wood as they tried to steady themselves.

"Windswept!" Poppy shouted as she ran toward the horses. "I've never gotten to touch a real horse!"

"Stay back," said the knight on Slate's right, who wore a green tunic over his armor. "Our steeds are agitated after what we've just been through." He dismounted, stroking his horse's neck. "I wouldn't want you risking injury."

"I've always dreamed of riding a horse!" said Poppy.

"The experience isn't as pleasant as you might think," Slate said as he dismounted, standing on rubbery legs. He had the One True Book clasped beneath his left arm. It looked a bit waterlogged.

"I can teach you to ride sometime," said Bigsby. "I'm an excellent equestrian."

Everyone looked at him.

"Um," said Brand, "that was the princess who was jousting as a toddler, not you."

"I know," Bigsby said. "But I learned to ride while I was with the circus. I was so good I could stand on horseback and juggle knives as I rode around the tent."

"Wasn't the owner of your carnival killed with a thrown knife?" Brand asked.

"And I made my escape on horseback," said Bigsby. "There's probably a lesson to be learned there." He glanced back at the now distant city, toward the smoke rising to mix with the churning storm front. "Having been an unwilling employee, it does my heart good to see a place like that burn. I only hope Price didn't make it out alive."

"He didn't," said Jetsam, as he guided the last of the pygmies to the stairs.

The pale green pygmy looked forlorn and frightened until Bigsby clicked, clucked, and whistled something to him. The pygmy smiled gently as he went below deck.

"What did you say?" asked Jetsam.

"The smallest men walk away from the longest falls," said Bigsby. "It's an aphorism forest pygmies use to cheer themselves up when faced with hard times."

By now the knight to Slate's right, who wore a tunic of gold embroidered with a large red lion, had dismounted. He said, "I thought the cloud giants had the best of us. I can't understand why they suddenly retreated when we were so outnumbered."

"Indeed," said a thundering voice that rolled across the bay. "It's quite the mystery. I look forward to learning who issued such a command once I'm finished retrieving my property."

The thunderhead above the burning docks writhed as a whirlwind spun out to form a long, serpentine neck. Sheets of clouds spread across the sky, shaping themselves into wings. Shadows fell across the *Circus* as Gale raised her hands to summon winds. The sails caught air with a loud *SNAP* and smashed into the rising waves as Tempest emerged from the clouds, a massive gray dragon far larger than their ship. The great beast easily outpaced the *Circus*, looping around before it with the grace of a creature that had dwelled for centuries in the skies.

Tempest's mouth was full of lightning as he said, "You've stolen something from me. I would like it back."

"We'll never give you the slaves!" Brand said, leaping onto the bowsprit and shaking his fist at the sky-monster. Before waiting for the dragon's reply, Brand glanced back at Gale and grinned. "Any of this turning you on?"

Gale smiled. "I'd answer, but I don't want my children to blush."

"Oh, Ma," said Sage.

"The slaves are of no concern," rumbled Tempest. "You've stolen the One True Book. Its presence in my kingdom brings me a great deal of power."

"You've no right to this sacred tome!" the green knight shouted, drawing his sword. Sorrow was puzzled as a soprano voice suddenly filled the air, singing a rousing battle-hymn. "My singing sword and I shall defend this holy book to our dying —"

There was a flash. A mound of molten slag burned into the black circle on the deck where the knight had stood as flecks of green fabric drifted through the air. The singing sword landed on the deck, still calling out its battle-hymn, until it was drowned out by the wave of thunder that washed across the lurching ship. Sorrow was thrown to the deck. The impact knocked the lightning rod from her hands. It rolled across the planks, bouncing as it went, until she was certain it would fall into the sea. As luck would have it, Bigsby fell in front of the rod and caught it, though Sorrow couldn't tell if he'd leapt to make this catch, or merely lost his footing on the pitching deck.

Tempest whirled around the boat once more, giving everyone time to study the burnt spot that had once been a man. His voice again thundered through the rigging. "Place the book upon the spot I've marked, turn away, and I shall spare you."

Gale shouted, "Hold steady for the mouth of the bay!"

"Have we thought about giving him the damn book?" Rigger asked. "What's it to us?"

"If he wants the book badly enough to chase us, he can't capsize the ship without losing it! If we turn the book over, we've nothing to shield us!"

"You've nothing to shield you now," Tempest said, as he turned his gaze toward Gale and opened his jaws wide. Sorrow could see straight down his gullet as the lightning arced toward them.

20 - FLESH AND BONE

BIGSBY MADE IT to his feet a few yards in front of Gale just as lighting erupted from Tempest's jaws. The lighting rod flared as thunder cracked so loud it rattled Sorrow's teeth. In the aftermath, no one was harmed.

Tempest's eyes narrowed as he glared at the dwarf. He flapped his wings forward and waves rose in towering whitecaps, crashing across the deck. The wall of water swept Sorrow from her feet. As she was washed over the rail, ropes snaked through the surf to wrap around her arms and legs. She jerked to a halt, yelping as her stitches tore, and wound up choking on a mouthful of brine.

As Rigger dragged her back aboard, she saw Slate was gone. Had he been washed overboard, or had he gone below to place the One True Book in a safer location? Two of the horses skittered in the air a yard above the pitching deck. The third horse charged toward Tempest with the red-lion knight in the saddle. A tight shaft of brilliant ruby light beamed from the tip of his lance and left a path of burnt scales across Tempest's face. The dragon roared, punctuating his pain by spitting lightning. Knight and horse fell toward the water, trailing smoke.

"I gave you a fair chance to surrender the tome!" Tempest cried. "You shall pay the ultimate price for your defiance!" Lightning arced from his jaws once more, targeting the front of the boat, well clear of Bigsby's rod. The top half of the foremast toppled into the crashing waves, the sails in flame.

Tempest circled the ship, whipping his tail, leaving waterspouts in his wake. Hail pelted Sorrow like shot from a sling. She was too rattled by the assault to think clearly. She could feel the dark energy building in the center of her being, but didn't dare attempt to release it while she was so muddled.

A chunk of hail the size of a fist slammed into her forehead, knocking her flat. She blinked stars from her eyes as she stared up at the churning clouds. Without warning, the clouds tore in twain and a giant man dropped from them. It was Levi, grown to half a mile in length, splashing into the bay with a wave that threatened to turn the *Circus* on its side. Levi wrapped his arms around Tempest's neck, dragging the massive reptile down into the sea.

Instantly, the waterspouts collapsed upon themselves. Sorrow grabbed the railing and struggled back to her feet as the wind lessened and the hail stopped pounding her. Tempest was apparently as susceptible to distraction as any other living thing.

"Go!" Levi shouted as the backwash swirled the *Circus* past his thighs. "I can't hold him for long!"

"You can't hold me at all!" cried Tempest as an enormous claw closed around Levi's throat. With a rapid slash, he slit Levi's jugular.

"Levi!" Gale cried as her son fell toward the *Circus*, clutching his windpipe.

Levi's eyes were unfocused, but with his last flicker of thought he lurched to the side to avoid crushing the ship. Blood sprayed across the *Circus* as he fell, speckling the sails with crimson as his enormous body splashed into the water. The *Circus* rose atop a wave that lifted the ship to the clouds.

At last the wave broke, dropping the ship into the brine red with blood. Sorrow held her breath as the ship plunged beneath the surface. She couldn't see a thing for half a minute, until the *Circus* popped above the bloodied water like a cork.

"That son of a bitch!" Rigger cried, turning the wheel hard. Every rope on deck rose, until the ship resembled an inverted jellyfish, its tendrils probing for a meal of dragon.

"What are you doing?" Brand shouted.

"I'm going to drown that bastard!" Rigger answered. "The waves are the domain of Abyss! Tempest will be weakened if he doesn't make it back to the sky!"

Rigger's hope of revenge came to a rapid end as Tempest swam away from the *Circus*, his body whipping through the water. When he finally spread his wings, they caught the wind and lifted him from the whitecaps. Tempest flew nearly a mile away from the ship before turning. His mouth glowed as he opened his jaws once more. There was a loud crack, but again his lightning failed to rake the deck. Instead, Sorrow saw the arc stop a few hundred feet before the dragon's gaping mouth. She narrowed her eyes, squinting through the squall, cursing her half-blindness.

She spotted the thin columns of light cast by a knight's horseshoes. Only, it wasn't a knight in the saddle. It was Bigsby, lashing the steed forward, holding the glowing lightning rod above the long, flowing locks of his bright blonde wig.

"Is he committing suicide?" Sorrow shouted.

"When the hell did he get the wig?" Brand asked.

Rigger fought the wheel as the ship slid down a mountain of water. "He said he was going to shove the rod down the dragon's throat! If he can rob the beast of his lightning, we stand a chance!"

The dragon assisted Bigsby in his mission by thrusting his neck forward and snapping his jaws shut, swallowing the horse in a single gulp.

"Now!" Cinnamon shouted.

Sorrow turned in time to see Poppy balanced on her sister's shoulders. The girl jumped off and Cinnamon shot into the air, tracing a perfect arc toward the dragon's nose.

"No!" Gale cried as she watched her daughter fly.

"Yes," Sage shouted from beside Poppy. "I helped them aim! She's going to hit her target!"

"It was Cinnamon's idea," Poppy said, defensively. "She's going to make the dragon so sick he can't fight!"

"Have you both lost your minds?" Gale cried.

Sage knelt and ran her fingers along the deck. It looked as if the planks were awash with wine. "I've never seen things more clearly." She turned and ran for the hold just as Slate emerged from below deck, Witchbreaker in hand.

Sorrow had no time to follow what was happening on the ship. Instead, she watched Cinnamon land dead center of Tempest's snout. The dragon's eyes grew wide. His jaws snapped open as his tongue shot from his mouth as if it were trying to escape. Bigsby tumbled out of the dragon's mouth, plummeting toward the sea, leaving his wig fluttering in mid-air. He looked to still be alive to judge from his flailing limbs, but he was falling from a quarter mile up. His odds of surviving the impact weren't favorable.

Just before Bigsby hit, Mako shot from the waves like a dolphin, wrapping his arms around the dwarf, absorbing some of his momentum as they splashed into the froth.

Tempest whipped his head back and forth, his body convulsing as he gagged. Cinnamon lost her grasp on his scales and was tossed aside. Sorrow hoped Mako saw her as the girl plummeted. Instead, it was Jetsam who came to her rescue, jumping from wave to wave, sprinting and vaulting until he neared her. He used the momentum of a cresting wave to kick into the air, spreading his arms to catch his sister before they both disappeared.

Tempest cut a long, slow arc through the air as he probed his jaws with his claws, plucking free the lightning rod.

"Poppy!" Slate shouted. "Pop me!"

The girl leapt into the riggings and jumped onto his shoulders. Half a second later, Slate zoomed into the sky, brandishing the Witchbreaker. Tempest turned his back toward the knight and lashed out with his tail, batting Slate back toward the ship. Rigger snared him in ropes as he fell, but Slate still hit the deck hard enough that Sorrow felt the impact.

Sage came back from the hold, dragging the masthead of the *Freewind*.

"Levi hasn't died in vain," she announced. "His life energy is soaking every board! It's the same aura that used to envelop the *Freewind* when we'd cross into the abstract realms! We have to get Grandmother in place on the bow! If we free her, we can escape to the Sea of Wine!"

"Give her to me!" Rigger shouted, wrapping his ropes around the wooden figure. "I can lash her to the hull in seconds!"

Sorrow headed toward the front of the ship. "Contact with the blood may be enough to free her, but I'll use my powers to blend the figurehead to the ship!"

The figurehead was directly above Sorrow, carried forward by ropes. Without warning, a reptilian claw stretched from the clouds and tore the wooden bust from Rigger's grasp.

"Was this precious to you?" Tempest snarled as he whirled above them. The sea began to swirl as he swept around them, sending the *Circus* in a dizzying spin. "As precious as the book was to me?"

"Where's Jetsam?" Mako asked as he leapt over the rail, dragging Bigsby by the collar. The dwarf gasped loudly as he hugged the deck.

"He brought Cinnamon on board then went back into the air," said Sage, "but he can't fight the dragon alone!"

"He's not alone," said Sorrow, clenching her talons. She spread her wings, allowing the hurricane winds to snatch her from the deck. She didn't want to be touching the *Circus* for what came next.

Tempest turned his jaws toward her. Lightning glowed in his mouth.

She opened her jaws and a jet of flies shot forth. They quickly burnt to ash as Tempest unleashed his lightning. Sorrow's human skin felt as if it was boiling away.

But not from the lightning.

Because the second her feet had left the deck, she'd focused on the nexus of the dark energy, seeing it clearly in her mind's eye like a wobbling black disk. She grabbed the portal with the fingers of her mind and stretched it as wide as possible. Her blood turned to ice as she stared into the void beyond.

The void stared back, with eyes devoid of all emotion other than hunger.

"Come out," she'd whispered.

And it came.

Every time she'd killed by releasing flies, she'd wondered in morbid curiosity what it must feel like for those caught on the edges of her assault. These poor souls survived the initial wave of acid spewing insects only to have the few that burrowed into their skin multiply and devour them from within. Now, she understood as a billion unseen teeth chewed her muscles and gnawed her bones, erupting from her skin in black boils, until the whole of her body was covered in a shell of flies, gleaming black and chitinous. Her body swelled, doubling in size, then doubling again. She flapped her wings out of pure instinct, keeping airborne as she recovered her wits enough to scream.

Only, as the air rushed through a windpipe now several yards long, it erupted from her toothy jaws as a roar. All pain vanished as unearthly strength flowed through her new muscles. During her transformation, she'd lost sight of Tempest. She banked, curving her serpentine neck enough that she could see her new draconian form.

Pain returned suddenly as the plate-like scales along her ribs began to burn. Thunder nearly deafened her as it crashed into her eardrums, now larger than dinner plates. Tempest spit another gob of lightning, blowing a hole in her thigh. The damage would have disintegrated her human body, but she was now more massive than a whale, and the burnt crater in her side felt like nothing more than a solid punch.

There was no blood. She felt a flicker of panic as she realized that she had no heartbeat, but the panic quickly changed to understanding. Rott's body was already dead, and had been for centuries. The strength she felt in her limbs was not the power of life, but the unstoppable elemental force of decay.

She blinked as she turned back toward Tempest and realized she was now seeing him through two eyes. Had she finally broken her connection with Avaris? She had no time to contemplate this, or anything, as she sailed through the sky toward the dragon.

Tempest's jaws again glowed. She belched out a cone of swirling flies that met the lightning, the survivors flitting onward to speckle the storm-dragon's blue gray hide. Sorrow glanced down to make sure the *Circus* wasn't directly beneath them. She saw Poppy balanced on Slate's shoulders, but the ship was in the clear if she or Tempest fell.

In seconds, the distance between her and Tempest closed. Before she could understand what was happening, Tempest's jaws snapped around her throat. If she'd still needed to breathe, the blow might have been fatal. Her fear that they would crash into the sea proved unfounded as a powerful whirlwind swept around them both, pushing them higher in the sky. She wrapped her tail around the storm-dragon and raked at his belly with her hind claws. Rott's power flowed through her limbs and the storm-dragon's scaly flesh sloughed away in massive strips of putrid meat. Her mind went clear, all thoughts silent as lightning boiled her blood from snout to tail. But as her human mind faltered, Rott's draconian hunger came to the fore and she sank her jaws into the meaty flesh of Tempest's powerful shoulders. Tempest's jaws loosened on her neck from the shock of the blow and she vomited flies into his gaping wounds. Maggots bubbled up along the length of Tempest's spine as he writhed in agony.

Sorrow was vaguely aware of something slamming onto her back, near her hips. She ignored the blow, focusing on the entropic energy surging through her jaws into her struggling victim. They lurched through the sky as one of Tempest's wings suddenly tore from his shoulders, spiraling off, leaving a trail of engorged worms. The storm-dragon's howls suddenly went silent as a loud, wet, gurgle came from his back. The maggots had eaten through his skin to open his lungs to the air. Tempest went still as Sorrow released his now skeletal form, and watched it fall lifelessly to the sea.

The bust of Jasmine Romer also plunged into the waves. She caught a glimpse of Mako leaping into the chaotic water. She spread her wings wide in the buffeting wind to keep from joining him. She climbed toward the roiling clouds. The weight that had slammed into her hips now shifted to the center of her back and clung there.

Then, to her dismay, the clouds bulged downward, as a dragon's face took shape from the billowing vapors.

"Fool!" Tempest thundered as the clouds turned into jaws large enough to swallow Sorrow whole. His eyes glowed like twin suns as he turned his gaze upon her. "I am the will of the whirlwind! The soul of the storm! I am the lord of wind itself, a god of this world! Do you think you can stop me by destroying mere flesh?"

His new jaws shot toward Sorrow. She opened her mouth to release more flies, but to what end? If she destroyed Tempest's body yet again, he would merely grow another one. Her touch could destroy all material things, but how could she attack his soul?

As she hesitated, the weight upon her back lifted and what felt like tiny footsteps ran the length of her neck. As Tempest closed his jaws around her, ready to bite her in half, Slate suddenly ran between her eyes and along her snout, the Witchbreaker held above his head with both hands.

He leapt, shouting, "It's not your flesh my blade thirsts for, monster!"

He landed upon the creature's gray tongue and plunged his blade into the roof of the dragon's mouth as it closed. She heard the blade bite through bone, plunging into the gray matter beyond.

Tempest's teeth turned to mist as they sank through the scales on Sorrow's back. She could see nothing around her but gray haze as the interior of the storm-dragon's mouth changed once more to clouds.

Her body dove almost before she understood why it was doing so. She emerged from the clouds and spotted Slate falling toward the ocean. She flapped her wings to overtake him, snatching the knight from the air with her hind claws, leveling off as she charged toward the *Circus*. Ropes still snaked into the air around the ship. Did they understand that the black dragon approaching them was her?

She dropped Slate as she passed over the ship, counting on Rigger's reflexes to catch the knight. She spun around and tried to call out, "I'm Sorrow! I won't hurt you!" but no sound escaped her lungs. She'd forgotten to breathe since exhausting her lungs earlier.

Needing a moment of stillness to ponder her new condition, she landed in the sea. When she'd first encountered Rott, he'd been swimming through the Sea of Wine, so she didn't fear sinking. The sea was calming as the clouds began to dissipate. It felt like mere minutes had passed since she'd leapt from the Temple of the Book, but the sun had merely been low on the horizon then. Now, the moon slowly emerged from the thinning haze. The enormity of what she'd just done slowly sank into her.

The *Circus* pulled alongside her. The clown figurehead was gone, and Mako and Jetsam were at work with hammers, fastening the bust of Jasmine Romer beneath the bowsprit, guided by Sage, who balanced on a rope beside them. Gale and Brand stood at the wheel. Brand's arms were wrapped around Gale, who sagged into his embrace, tears in her eyes. Bigsby was up in the riggings, stretching his stunted arms as far as he could manage, his fingers spread wide, as he snatched his fluttering wig from the air.

Cinnamon, Poppy, and Slate stood at the rail, staring down at Sorrow.

"You saved us!" Cinnamon shouted.

"I thought the horses were windswept!" Poppy called out. "I didn't know you could turn into a dragon! By the seven stars, you have to give me a ride!"

"You'd ride her even smelling like that?" Cinnamon asked.

Sorrow wondered what was wrong with the way Poppy smelled, until she realized that Cinnamon was talking about her. Her sense of smell and taste were mercifully absent. She remembered Rott's putrid aroma from the Sea of Wine and was grateful for her missing senses.

Sorrow lifted her head from the waves and made the conscious choice to breathe. "Perhaps another time," she answered with a deep, guttural voice she didn't recognize as her own.

Slate removed his helmet. He looked heartbroken as he asked, "Can you… can you change back?"

"I don't know how. I think… I think I may be spending the rest of my life this way." Assuming life was the correct word.

Her voice caught in her throat as she thought of it. She'd lived so long consumed by anger and grief that she'd never noticed the wonder of her mere human life. But as she looked at Slate and the others, she understood that her humanity was the most precious thing she'd ever possessed. She now had all the power she'd ever wanted, and more. She'd become the Destroyer that Walker had come to witness. She now had the strength to topple churches and crush kingdoms. She possessed the pure force to put an end to everything she hated.

She would have traded it all to be once more standing on the ship on human legs, with the music of a heartbeat pulsing through her.

"What will you do now?" Slate asked.

"I don't know," Sorrow whispered, or at least as close to a whisper as she could manage from her gargantuan throat.

I know.

"No!" Sorrow cried in anguish.

"What's wrong?" Slate asked.

"It's Avaris! She's still in my head!"

We made a bargain, girl. Until you kill the person of my choosing, I'm part of you. But don't despair. It's time for me to name my chosen target. Obey, and you shall be free.

"It cannot be anyone upon this ship! Our bargain was that it would be a person I agreed to be guilty! Someone worthy of death! All aboard this ship are innocent!"

But what of those who swim beside it?

Sorrow swallowed hard, a very long and dramatic gesture given that her neck was nearly as long as the *Circus*.

Kill yourself, Sorrow.

Sorrow didn't answer.

You've nothing left to live for. You've lost the last of your humanity. You've become the monster of flesh that you long ago became of the soul. Death will be a sweet release from the torment of the sins that burn inside you.

"How can I die?" she screamed. "This body is already dead!"

Slate could end your misery. He wouldn't deny your request.

Sorrow stared at the clearing sky, toward the stars above, which took on halos from the dampness of her eyes. Avaris had chosen her victim well. Sorrow couldn't dispute that she was deserving of punishment for all the things she'd done. But as she looked back at the *Circus,* and saw Slate studying her with tears in his eyes, she thought of his reaction on learning of his inhumanity. He'd left the Black Bog not in despair, but with an attitude of atonement. He'd chosen to fight for redemption.

She couldn't surrender all hope. Whatever had happened to her body, her soul was still her own. Perhaps she'd trapped herself in this strange half-life, but she still could think. As long as she had free will, there was hope. Slate wouldn't have given up, nor would any of the Romers.

Kill yourself now, or forfeit all!

"No!" Sorrow shouted. "I defy you!"

Once again, laughter filled her skull from the inside. She lost all sensation from her tail, then her limbs, then her torso. Her eyes lost all sight as she found herself gagging breathlessly in the foulest atmosphere imaginable. Despite herself, she filled her lungs in amazement as she realized that she once more had human arms and legs… even if they were encased in quivering acrid slime.

Suddenly, she found herself flying at great speed. Her sight returned as she passed between massive black teeth and emerged into the night sky. She tumbled head over heels, slime flying from her limbs as she skipped across the ocean, until at last she sank beneath the water.

She gasped as she kicked back to the surface. She ran her hands along her scalp and found that Rott's nail was gone. There wasn't even a scar. The whole of her head was smooth as she probed it frantically. All her nails were gone! Her reborn body at least had two eyes, and all her many wounds were healed, even the one left by the blood blade. But she was utterly powerless as Avaris rose from the waves in Rott's body, her hind claws finding the bottom many leagues below. The ancient witch stood like a tower, her mighty lungs sounding like giant bellows as she inhaled, before setting the sea shuddering with her laughter.

"It's mine once more!" she cried. "Rott's will is completely absent! At long last I have the power to avenge the indignities I've suffered!"

Slate rocketed into the air toward the dragon-witch, propelled by Poppy. Avaris reacted with the speed of thought, snatching him from the air with one claw, plucking the Witchbreaker from his grasp with the other.

"Your glass armor insulates you well from my touch," she said. "A pity it won't spare you from your own blade!"

But as she fumbled with the relatively tiny weapon in her massive claws, it slipped from her grasp. Before she could snatch it back, a rope whipped out from the *Circus* and wrapped around the hilt. A dozen other lines knotted themselves around her claws, straining to pull Slate free.

Sorrow spat out seawater as she bobbed in the waves caused by the thrashing dragon. A muscular arm wrapped around her waist as a Mako shouted in her ear, "Don't struggle!"

In a dozen powerful kicks, he dragged her back to the *Circus*. He grabbed a rope and they lifted toward the deck.

He didn't look at her directly as he softly said, "I'm sorry… the other night when I kissed you –"

"It's okay," she said. "You've nothing to apologize for. It was a confusing night for both of us."

Then they were both back on the deck, which lurched sharply as Avaris tugged at the ropes that tangled her.

"I can't free Slate!" Rigger shouted. "The dragon's too strong!"

"We'll have to depart without him!" Sage answered.

"We can't leave him!" Poppy screamed as she ran toward Sorrow and draped a blanket over her naked shoulders.

"Leave for where?" Sorrow asked as she pulled the blanket around her. "What's going on?"

"Levi's blood has soaked every inch of the hull," Sage said. "He died to save us, and in his sacrifice he's given new life to grandmother as well. We can travel once more to the Sea of Wine!"

"You seem remarkably cool-headed to think of freeing your grandmother after the shock of watching your brother die," said Sorrow.

Sage nodded. "We'll all grieve later. The important thing at the moment is to make sure no other Romers die today."

The main mast creaked and groaned as it bent like a fishing pole. Avaris had stopped thrashing randomly against the ropes and was now coolly pulling the ship toward her.

"We can't wait any longer!" Gale cried as she knelt on the deck. "Whatever Sage did, I can sense mother's spirit spreading through the hull once more. We have to cross into the Sea of Wine before the *Circus* is torn apart! I'm sorry!"

"No!" Sorrow shouted. "We can't flee to the abstract realms! Rott already swims the Sea of Wine. Avaris might be even more powerful!"

"We have to try!" Gale shouted, placing her hand upon the wine-colored wood. The whole of the ship gleamed in the moonlight. The glow encompassed Avaris as well.

Avaris suddenly turned her head to the sky and shouted, "No! I cannot leave now! I defy your summons!"

"Release the ropes!" Sage screamed. "She's crossing over with us!"

But it wasn't the *Circus* that tugged the witch-dragon toward the abstract realms. Instead, the sea boiled as Abyss, the dragon of the sea, rose from the depths behind the black dragon.

"No dragon may refuse the call," he growled as he clamped his turtle-beak onto her wing.

The material world grew ghostlike around Sorrow. She raised her hand and found she could see through her flesh to her bones.

21 - CONVERGENCE

"SOMETHING'S GONE WRONG!" Sage shouted. "We aren't passing cleanly to the Sea of Wine! It's like we're caught in some vortex!"

The sea churned as Abyss's island-sized body changed suddenly to churning whitecaps. Rott's body trembled, then collapsed, changing into a dragon sized mass of writhing maggots that fell toward the frothing waves.

The night vanished, replaced by bright, dazzling sunlight. Sorrow clamped her eyes shut. She blinked and saw Slate tumbling through sky toward the deck. Rigger was apparently blinded as well, as no ropes moved to catch the knight. He slapped into the mainsail, his armor tearing the fabric as he slid down it, before dropping ten feet to the deck with a *THUMP*.

Sorrow ran to see if he'd survived the fall, but was distracted as her vision cleared and she recognized her surroundings. "This is the convergence!" Sorrow shouted as she looked around at the tropical seas. "It's where the primal dragons meet to talk to one another!"

Sorrow craned her neck to see which dragons were present. Greatshadow's smoke poured up from the sea, as did Kragg's stony spine. A massive iceberg lifted from the northern waves, as a tropical jungle screaming with the cries of a million animals rose to the south.

The ship groaned as it shuddered to a sudden halt, run aground on an island of wriggling maggots that clotted beneath them. Beside the ship, a larger mass of maggots climbed skyward, hatching into black flies that took on the form of Rott.

The central sea bulged upward as Abyss rose from the depths, lifting his head to stare in the direction of the *Circus*. "This is not your first time here, witch. You cannot claim ignorance of the rules. When you are summoned to the convergence, you answer."

Sorrow thought Abyss was speaking to her, but before she could think of a response, Avaris roared, "Don't speak to me of rules, sea-dragon! I'm destruction and ruin! The death of all who displease me is now the only law!"

Hush rose from the iceberg to the north and turned her face toward Avaris. "Destruction and ruin are the order of the day, witch! Tempest has been slain!" The ice-dragon's eyes narrowed as she looked around at her kindred. "I warned you all of the dangers! I warned you that mankind was a threat to each of us! With Tempest slain, can you still be blind to the consequences of inaction?"

"I witnessed his death," said Abyss. "Tempest could have avoided his destruction simply by ignoring the humans. He brought his end upon himself by meddling too deeply in the affairs of men."

"Believe as you wish," said Hush. "But your voice is only one among many. I bring you all here to ask again, shall we destroy mankind? I say yes!"

"No!" Greatshadow roared as he rose in a whirlwind of smoke and sparks from his volcanic home. "Tempest brought his fate upon himself. We cannot punish mankind for his hubris!"

"Agreed," said Abyss.

"I vote for death!" rumbled Kragg. His mountainous form shifted, sending rocks sliding from his limbs into the sea. "First Verdant, then Glorious, now Tempest? I would be done with this danger that I might slumber in peace."

"Abundant!" Hush demanded. "What say you?"

"Men are still beasts," she said, folding her arms across her chest. "I cannot condone their extinction. But, can we not be satisfied with destroying all they have built? Let us tear down their cities and burn their fields. Let us strip the clothes from their backs and force them naked into the forests, where they may root and forage to survive. These arrogant beasts have forgotten their animal nature. It would be satisfying to remind them."

"No!" shouted Hush. "Humiliation is not enough! Destruction is the only solution!"

"Agreed," said Kragg.

"Then we are deadlocked," said Greatshadow. "No opinion has the majority!"

"I vote for destruction!" Avaris said, rising up on an island of maggots. "The men who dwell within the world are corrupt and pitiful creatures, worthy only of disdain! Let us wipe them from creation! In my home within the Black Bog, I've labored for centuries to perfect a new breed of men. These are superior to their predecessors in every way, and completely obedient to my will. Under my guidance, these new men shall never endanger another dragon!"

"You get no vote!" Abundant growled. "Rott's mind is still silent. You're only a human puppet master, making his jaws move. And you've brought other men! You sully these sacred seas with their presence!"

Avaris turned her gaze upon toward the *Circus*. "These pests? They will bother us no longer."

Avaris inhaled deeply, her torso swelling. With a buzzing roar, a wave of flies churned from her jaws and shot toward the ship.

Sorrow's eyes turned toward the golden disk above. "Stagger!" she yelled. "Now would be a good time to help!"

"I was just thinking that myself," a voice said from the heavens. Fingers of golden light beamed down, shaping into a hand that closed around the flies. When the hand opened, the cloud of pestilence had vanished.

Sorrow shielded her eyes as Stagger knelt upon the island of light above the convergence, smiling as he leaned over the edge to look down. Avaris turned away from his outstretched arm, shrieking. Stagger caught the dragon by the tail. In scale, he was like a man catching a cat.

"No!" Avaris sobbed as she clawed the maggots beneath her. "No! Let go! Let me go!"

"You're the one holding onto something that isn't yours," Stagger said.

Rott fell silent, his body collapsing limp upon the worm island as black smoke bubbled from his nostrils. The smoke shrieked as it coalesced into the shape of a woman before flying off over the waves.

"She gone!" Sorrow cried. "Utmost told me Avaris couldn't stand the light of glorystones. Stagger's whole body is a glorystone!"

"Her vote still counts!" Hush cried.

"No," Kragg grumbled. "It would be base hypocrisy to pretend that the witch spoke for Rott. We continue to be deadlocked."

Stagger sat on the edge of the sun island, dangling his feet as he looked down. "Permit me to undeadlock you. Allow me to introduce myself. My name is Stagger, and I'm the new sun. It's a pleasure to meet you."

"You're just another interloper," Kragg said.

"And you violate the sanctity of this place by attacking a dragon!" Hush screamed.

"Rott's none the worse for wear," said Stagger. "I just helped rid him of a parasite."

"Using power that you've stolen," said Abundant. "The stink of humans is on everything these days."

Stagger stepped down from the sun to stand amid the dragons, a glowing giant with skin too bright for Sorrow to look at directly.

Stagger crossed his arms and said, "I know that none of you are happy I'm here, but I suggest you get used to it. I've been practicing this avatar trick. I know how to get into your little clubhouse any time I want."

"You shouldn't speak to us so boldly, human," said Kragg. "It's not so long ago you were a living man. There are still things in this world that are precious to you. Things that dwell in our domains."

Stagger nodded. "Agreed. I don't deny you have the power to hurt me. I even acknowledge that, collectively or alone, you have the power to wipe mankind from the planet. I know I couldn't stop you. But I also know, if you decide to do so, I could make things very uncomfortable for all of you."

"Was that a veiled threat?" asked Hush.

"Allow me to unveil it. This convergence seems like a pretty nice place, the green waters warm and sparkling in the sunshine. And guess who owns that sunshine? I have the power to turn my back on you all. I can simply leave the sky and make the world a very dark, unpleasant place in the aftermath. The seas will freeze. The trees and animals will wither and die. You'll win a world free of men. You'll simply lose daylight, forever."

"Eternal winter is what Hush desires!" Abyss bellowed.

"So she's happy. What about the rest of you?"

"I'm not happy being threatened, human," said Kragg.

"Nor am I," said Abundant. "I recognize you have the power to carry out your threat, but you cannot protect humanity forever. You've seen by now that no dragon is immortal. Why do you believe you will outlive us?"

"I'll worry about how this ends another time," said Stagger. "For now, the only thing I ask in exchange for sunrises and sunsets is that men be left to live however they wish."

"Very well. I vote with Greatshadow and Abyss," said Abundant. "Mankind shall be spared. For now."

"We're concluded here," said Abyss. He swam toward the island of maggots that the *Circus* was beached upon, sending a bulging wall of water onto the shore to lift the ship. The waves crashed upon the hull, forming an inhuman voice that gurgled, "Leave and do not return!"

"Hold tight!" Gale shouted as the *Circus* rocked upon the tide, the hull bumping along Rott's submerged and lifeless body. "Let's get to the Sea of Wine before we lose our bottom!"

"We've only made the journey by moonlight," Rigger said. "What's going to happen if we try to make the jump in sunlight? Do we even know that we can get there from here?"

"Do we have a choice?" asked Mako. "Do it!"

Gale knelt and placed her hands on the boards.

Instantly, daylight changed to darkness. Sorrow couldn't even see her hand before her face. Everything was quiet until Brand flicked open his glorystone pendant.

"Where are we?" he asked.

"Nowhere," said Sage, staring into her spyglass. "We... we've crossed into a place beyond all dreams or myths." Her face turned pale. "This is limbo."

Sorrow looked over the rail. The ship wasn't floating in water. It hung in mid-air, supported by nothing. Nor was it falling; there was no hint of any breeze or motion.

"I've got an idea," said Bigsby. "Let's go somewhere."

Gale still knelt on the deck, her shoulders trembling as she pressed her hands against the boards. "I'm trying to push the ship across the abstract barriers, but this place... it has no edges! It has no barriers to cross."

"We got in," said Mako. "There must be a way out."

"Those poor pygmies in the hold," said Cinnamon. "They've kept so quiet through all of this. They must be terrified."

"You're not?" asked Bigsby.

The girl shrugged. "We're all still together. Romers can figure out anything."

"But can we figure out nothing?" asked Jetsam, scratching his head as he studied the surrounding void.

Sorrow suddenly remembered Slate. She ran back to the main mast and found him sprawled there, face down, completely limp. She knelt and turned him onto his back.

"Is he alright?" asked Rigger. "I didn't even know he'd made it back onboard."

"Avaris dropped him as we passed between realms," said Sorrow. "I can't tell if he's breathing!"

She pulled off Slate's helmet. He had a knot on his forehead the size of an egg. Blood was caked around his nose. She held her fingers over his lips and felt no air.

She pressed her cheek to his chest, but couldn't hear a heartbeat through the thick glass. She tried to will the glass to dust, but it didn't respond. She was truly powerless.

Except...

She'd always had the power of bone-weaving. She didn't know exactly how to access these powers. But perhaps there was a reason why, in storybooks, curses were always lifted with a kiss.

And so she kissed him, placing her lips tentatively against his at first, then more firmly. Long seconds passed as she felt heat grow where their faces touched.

And yet... with their lips pressed together, there was no mistaking the fact that he wasn't breathing. She placed both hands upon his cheeks and opened his mouth, breathing into him as her tears flowed.

The air she filled him with left his lungs as a soft groan. She pulled her face away, uncertain if she'd heard the sound at all. At last he inhaled on his own. His eyes fluttered open as he lifted his fingers to touch where Sorrow's tears trickled down his cheek.

His eyes focused on her face, still only inches from his. To her great shock, he placed his hand on the back of her neck and pulled her lips to his once more. Her eyes grew wide.

He opened his eyes as well and she pulled away. "Forgive me," he said. "I'm just overjoyed to see that you're human once more!"

"No apology necessary. I'm happy to see you too. But... we perhaps should celebrate our mutual joy someplace a bit more private?"

She looked around to find all the Romers gathered round them, illuminated by the light from Brand's locket. Brand and Gale were holding hands; was it just to comfort each other, or had Brand finally won Gale over?

"Don't stop on account of us," said Jetsam.

Gale slapped him on the back of the head.

Mako turned and walked off into the shadows.

Slate rose to his elbows and looked around. "It's quiet. I take it we defeated Avaris?"

Sorrow nodded. "We sent her running home with her tail between her legs."

"I'm not sure *we* did much of anything," said Rigger. "Stagger did all the work. I guess it pays to have friends in high places."

"Stagger's in a high place because I put him there," said Sorrow. "We wouldn't have won if not for steps I've taken in the past."

"You can't pretend that Stagger's intervention was part of some master plan you had," said Rigger.

Sorrow shrugged. "I planted the seed that brought us victory. I don't see why I can't take credit for the harvest."

"Good to see your ego hasn't taken a hit just because you're powerless," said Brand, staring at Sorrow's scalp.

"I'm hardly powerless," said Sorrow. She ran her fingers along Slate's stubbled cheeks and said, with a gentle smile, "I've everything I need to take up bone-weaving."

Brand's eyebrows shot up.

"And what's more," she said, standing and helping Slate to his feet. "I'm human again. I've a sound body and a keen mind and that makes me one of the most powerful forces of nature imaginable. I'm ready to take whatever life throws at me." She held a clenched fist before her face to illustrate her words. She lowered her hand as her eyes drank in the unending blackness that engulfed them. "Not that this does me any good in limbo."

"Limbo?" asked Slate, looking around at the surrounding dark.

"We didn't make the leap between realms cleanly," said Sage. "We've wound up literally nowhere."

Slate shook his head, looking forlorn. His shoulders sagged. "In seeking to protect the One True Book, I've placed it in even greater danger."

"We'll think of something," said Poppy. "We're Romers! We get out of tight spots for a living."

"But we're not in a tight spot," said Sage. "We're in no spot at all. I didn't see things ending like this." She sighed. "I'm so sorry."

"I'm the one who made the jump," said Gale. "Long ago, mother warned me she could only find her way across to the spirit realms at night. Sunlight blinds her to the path. I pushed her anyway."

Sorrow snapped her fingers. "Sunlight!"

She marched toward Brand and grabbed the locket at his throat. She thrust her lips inches from the glorystone and shouted, "Stagger! We're in limbo! Help!"

Brand looked at her as if she'd gone insane.

"The glorystone is part of the sun," she explained. "Just as Greatshadow can see through every candle, Stagger, in theory, can see through every glorystone. But, there are thousands of little fragments like this. I just want to be sure we catch his attention."

"There's only one sure way to catch Stagger's attention," said Bigsby. He tugged on Brand's shirt. "Bend over."

Brand did so, and the dwarf cupped the locket in both hands and shouted at the top of his lungs, "Battle Ox has just tapped a fresh keg and I'm buying 'til it's dry!"

Bigsby looked around. Everyone was quiet. The dwarf sighed. "I thought for sure that would work. Anytime similar words were spoken at the Black Swan, he'd fly through the doors so fast he'd knock tables over."

Everyone jumped as wood banged against wood all around the deck. The ropes overhead began to rattle in the pulleys.

"Rigger?" Gale asked.

"It's not me!" he called out, spinning around to see who had hold of the ropes.

Sorrow's jaw dropped as she saw horned demons flying in from the edges of limbo to light upon the deck of the *Circus* where they grabbed at the rigging. They were monstrous creatures, with skeletal human bodies and animal heads. They were dressed, curiously enough, in sailor uniforms identical to the ones worn by the Romers.

"You might need this," Rigger said as he thrust the Witchbreaker into Slate's hands.

"Someone's at the wheel!" Gale shouted, racing into the shadows. Sorrow gave chase, though Mako beat them both to the wheel, cursing as he tried to grasp the pale, wraithlike form he found there. Sorrow squinted in the darkness, seeing a short, light-colored head just behind the wheel. Bigsby? As Brand approached, the light fell upon an albino pygmy who smiled at Sorrow with a familiar grin.

"Walker!"

"Sorrow. I'm happy to have found you at last. Stagger's guidance was most helpful. It's a shame you waited so long to call to him."

"Not that we're ungrateful, but why were you looking for us?" Brand asked.

"Because you've created an atrocious mess," said Walker. "It would be unfair to task others with cleaning up your mistakes, not that many haven't tried."

"What mistakes? What are you talking about?"

"Twenty years ago, you robbed most of the world of their faith in the One True Book. The Silver Isles have sunk into outright despotism in their attempt to maintain order. War, famine, and pestilence are daily life for most men now. But as bad as the material world has become, your greater error was to provide Tempest a doorway to a place he did not belong. The dragon has used the intervening decades to craft a new empire, one with a far larger population than his old one. I'm weary of hearing my demon friends grumble about the new management, and have persuaded a few of the more rebellious ones to join me in rescuing you."

"Wait, wait, wait, wait," Brand said. "Twenty years? We've barely been gone twenty minutes!"

"I informed you earlier that time isn't constant between the various realms," said Walker. He spun the wheel hard to the left.

"Where are we going?" shouted Gale.

They splashed into a broad river between smoking black banks of gravel. For an instant, given the horrid heat that wrapped around her, Sorrow thought they were riding on a lava flow back on the Isle of Fire, and expected the boat to burst into flames. The sky above was a writhing mass of angry clouds, crackling with lightning.

"The river!" Jetsam called out as he leaned overboard. "It's pure blood!"

"Nonsense," Walker said with a giggle. "Nothing here is pure."

"This isn't blood," Sage said as she looked around the landscape. "It's memories!"

"You've good eyes," said Walker. "What else would fill the rivers here? Nothing burns its way down a parched throat like memories."

Sorrow went to Slate's side and took his hand. He squeezed her fingers gently as he stared down into the red currents lapping the hull.

"I've never felt such thirst," he whispered. "Even knowing all that I now know of my origins, I still ache for memories."

She placed her fingers on his chin and turned his face toward her. She stood on tiptoes to kiss him gently. "We both have a fresh chance to make new memories." She looked across the wasteland. "Though, I admit, making good ones in a place like this might prove to be a challenge."

Bigsby climbed up the rigging for a better look. "I give up," he said. "Where the hell are we?"

Walker's fingers slipped from the wheel as he fell to the deck, laughing as tears ran down his cheeks.

CINDER

BOOK FOUR OF THE DRAGON APOCALYPSE

"Blind, as one who falls into a swoon,
she stumbled in the darkness and went down."

1 - THE FINAL CHAPTER

WIND LASHED THE BLACK SWAN as she straddled the massive killer whale that flew through the howling blizzard. The night was utterly dark, the stars lost behind storm clouds, but her gaze extended beyond the material world. In the faint glow of the spiritual realms, she could see the Keep of the Inquisition rising before them.

"We're close enough to land," she shouted above the cry of the wind.

The whale tilted, diving down. With her inhuman eyes, she saw the frozen surface of the sea rushing toward them and wondered if Menagerie was about to crash. At the last second, the whale shifted shape, taking on the form of a polar bear inches above the ice, landing with a jolt. The Black Swan dug her iron fingers into the beast's fur to keep from being thrown.

"Ow," said Menagerie, rising on her hind legs as the Black Swan dropped to the ice. "Pulled fur doesn't feel any better than pulled hair."

"I can't remember what that's like," said the Black Swan. "It's been centuries since I last had hair."

Still standing, the bear sniffed the air. The beast wore a gray silk cape that flapped in the wind, the ends threadbare and tattered. Menagerie's nose twitched as she turned her head first to the left, then the right, before releasing her breath in a great cloud of steam.

"Be ready," said Menagerie, her voice a gruff growl. "Someone's near. I smell them."

"Alive or dead?" asked the Black Swan.

"Alive," said Menagerie. "Whoever it is, they're wearing way too much perfume. Bears have better noses than bloodhounds. This much concentrated lavender is obnoxious."

"I'll take your word for it. I haven't had a working nose in a long time, either," said the Black Swan.

The Black Swan climbed to the peak of a frozen swell, the spikes in her iron feet skittering on the gray ice. Her diamond eyes whirred as she adjusted their focus, until at last she spotted the purple-robed figure standing atop jagged rocks on the nearby shore.

No, not standing. Dancing, arms lifted, toes barely touching as the figure gracefully leapt from rock to rock.

"Zetetic?" Menagerie asked as she climbed up the swell.

The Black Swan shook her head. "Equity Tremblepoint."

"Is she a lunatic? She'll freeze in this wind."

"No one who lives here can be called sane," said the Black Swan, as she slid down the swell and continued toward the Keep.

White flowers of frost crunched beneath the Black Swan's steel toes as she ascended the pebble beach toward the front gate. She glanced back across the trackless ice.

"I hope we've had enough of a head start," she said.

"I didn't mind flying here as Slor Tonn," said the bear. "It helped clear the scent of burning flesh from my lungs."

Hours had passed they fled the Silver City. The last of King Brightmoon's elite guard had tried to push back Tempest's unliving armies by pumping burning oil from massive jets atop the palace walls. The endless hordes of marching corpses had kept advancing as they burned, crushing against the heavy oak of the barred doors until the wood finally gave way. The burning army had surged into the palace, bringing death to the last defenders of civilization.

Reaching the main gate of the Keep of the Inquisition, the Black Swan pounded on the iron bars, hoping her knocking could be heard above the storm. Her hope was rewarded as chains clattered within the walls and the gate rose. Beyond the gate, massive iron doors slowly opened.

After weeks without seeing the sun, she had to raise her hand to block the radiance that flowed from within the castle. She stepped into the great hall, brightly lit with a thousand glory stones floating in silver cages that filled the torch sconces. After the chill of the frozen ocean, the warmth of the hall felt like a furnace.

The bear stood once more on her hind legs, then shrank until it took the form of a woman with gray hair. For an instant, the frost that had tipped the bear's fur glittered like diamonds against her nude skin until her gray cloak fell around her. She took a step forward, stumbling slightly.

"Are you okay?" asked the Black Swan.

"I'm fine," said Menagerie. "A little out of practice. First time I've walked on human legs in weeks."

The Black Swan moved further into the hall, gazing at the paintings and sculptures covering the space. It was difficult to discern a theme among the artwork. Paintings depicting church-like piety hung above marble nudes posed in acts of depravity.

Menagerie paused before a painting of a platinum-haired woman wearing pure white armor. The resemblance between the faces of the viewer and the subject was striking.

"Queen Alabaster Brightmoon," the Black Swan said. "Your current body's distant ancestor."

"With paintings like this around, it's surprising it took us all so long to realize Infidel was a Brightmoon."

The Black Swan shrugged. "I knew it all along. I recognized the value of keeping her secret."

Menagerie shook her head. "Does anything have value now? Both of us spent our lives in pursuit of wealth. My estate on the Silver Isles makes this fortress look like a cottage. You've got enough treasure stashed away to purchase kingdoms if you wished. Now, what's it all worth? Absolutely nothing."

"So I don't need to pay you when this is over?" asked the Black Swan.

"A contract's a contract," said Menagerie.

"Of course," the Black Swan said. "It's good to see that some things remain true even in these—" The Black Swan stopped in mid-thought as a drawing in a glass frame caught her attention. It was a likeness of herself, naked, or at least unclothed. She didn't know if the bareness of her iron shell constituted nudity or not. In any case, she now wore britches and a jacket of leather to conceal her metallic form. A broad-brimmed hat concealed her hairless scalp. Only her iron feet, fingers, and face remained bare.

She picked up the frame, studying the intricate detail of the drawing, carefully inked with crisp black lines. Beside the depiction of her outer form, dozens of gears, pulleys, and braided iron wires were sketched out, along with a pair of bellows. These comprised her internal organs. A human skeleton was drawn next to the objects. The stark depiction of her naked bones felt like the ultimate invasion of privacy.

"When did you pose for that?" asked Menagerie.

"I didn't," she said, the lenses in her eyes clicking into ever sharper focus, until she could be certain that the black lines weren't soaked into the paper as ink, but instead sat slightly raised upon the surface, crafted of pure, rustless iron filaments fine as hair. "Sorrow's been here. She sculpted my current body. These were her final plans, the ones I approved." She shook her head slowly. "The breasts look better on paper."

"Please don't get started on that again," Menagerie said with a sigh.

"Yes," said a faint voice behind the two women. "Please don't start a discussion of breasts until I'm close enough to participate. I've strong opinions on the subject."

They turned and found an ancient man hobbling toward them, supported by a stave decorated with carved serpents. The old man was toothless, his right eye a yellow, sightless moon. His good eye sparkled as he regarded the two women.

"I'm so pleased you're here!" he said, smiling. "I'd given up hope of seeing an actual woman again before the world ended."

"What of the woman dancing outside?" asked Menagerie.

"Equity? She's no woman. At least, I don't think she is. Or he is." He scratched his scaly scalp. "Pronouns get muddled when Equity takes the stage."

"Why's she dancing?" asked the Black Swan.

"To say goodbye to the world, of course," said the old man. "Zetetic tells us it's ending within the hour. If we make haste and disrobe along the way, we can still reach my chambers in time to—"

"If you finish that sentence I'll disembowel you," said Menagerie.

The old man frowned.

"We've no time to waste," said the Black Swan. "We must see Zetetic at once."

"Zetetic isn't taking visitors.

"Tell him the Black Swan must see him."

"And Menagerie. He knows me. We were companions during the quest to slay Greatshadow."

The old man smiled. "As long as we're doing introductions, I'm Vigor."

"I know who you are," said the Black Swan. "You're an authority on reptiles."

"Yes," he said. "Though my specialty is dragons."

"If you know about dragons, do you have any clue how we can stop Tempest?" she asked.

Vigor shook his head. "Tempest is something much worse than a dragon these days. Nothing can save us, I fear."

"I can't accept that," said the Black Swan. "Zetetic's powers are almost without limit. Why hasn't he acted? He has the power to stop this with any of a thousand different lies."

"Zetetic would agree with you," said Vigor. "But he says things will happen as they happen. He says that lies are but shadows cast by truth, and that truth has vanished from the world."

"What does *that* mean?" asked Menagerie.

Vigor shrugged. "It's been a long time since I had a conversation with Zetetic where I understood a single thing he was talking about."

"Then let us talk to him," said the Black Swan.

"As I said, he's not taking visitors."

The Black Swan's arm sprung out with spring-driven force and clamped iron fingers around Vigor's throat. "Take us to him or I'll throttle you."

Vigor smiled weakly, gasping, "Threats aren't… terribly effective… with the end… so near."

The Black Swan opened her fingers. "There won't be an end if Zetetic acts. With a single utterance, he could undo all of this! He could send Tempest's armies back to Hell. He could free Abyss from Hush's control. He could at least tell us what Tempest did to the sun, and how we might put it back into the sky!"

Vigor rubbed his throat. "I hold out the faint hope that Equity's sense of stagecraft has rubbed off on our host. Perhaps he's waiting for the moment of greatest peril to make a grand entrance and turn back all the horror."

"It's hard to imagine things getting any worse than they are at this exact moment," said Menagerie.

From outside the open gate, above the howl of the wind, came a bone-shivering, high-pitched shriek. The Black Swan cut her eyes toward Menagerie, her iron eyebrows knitting together.

"I regretted saying it before the last word left my lips," said Menagerie.

Equity Tremblepoint stumbled through the open gate into the hall. Her purple robes were torn to tatters. When she spotted Vigor, she raised the back of her hand to her forehead, shuddered, and collapsed against the door, her figure framed by the darkness behind her. She arched her back, extended her hand with its long, red nails, pointing into the darkness, trembling, as she exclaimed, "The damned! They've found us!"

The Black Swan ran to the gate. A trio of dead soldiers stood in the darkness barely a yard away, with shreds of Equity's robes still dangling from their skeletal fingers. One carried a black blade that stank of sulfur as he raised it overhead, preparing to chop the Black Swan in twain.

There was a slight tap on the Black Swan's shoulder as a squirrel used her for a launching pad to fling itself toward the sword-wielding corpse. By the time it reached the warrior, the squirrel had changed into an enormous silverback gorilla. The beast grabbed the lead corpse by the wrist and swiftly disarmed it, in the most literal meaning of the word. Using the dismembered limbs as clubs, the gorilla knocked the skulls free from the shambling forms flanking the first skeleton.

Menagerie turned to the Black Swan. "Find the Deceiver! I'll hold them off!"

The Black Swan peered into the darkness, spotting the ragged forms lurching over the frozen swells. Their numbers were uncountable, as if Hell had thrown up all of its damned souls. Which, of course, was precisely what was happening. The damned had been promised the world once the last of the living perished. As far as the Black Swan knew, the last men still alive were the inhabitants of this small island.

"Why hasn't he stopped this?" whimpered Equity. "I thought he would stop this!"

"Fall back!" the Black Swan shouted to Menagerie. "There's too many of them! Get inside the gate!"

"You've seen how quickly they can penetrate a fortress," Menagerie growled. "I can hold out far longer than iron bars."

"Not alone," said the Black Swan.

"He won't be alone," said Vigor, hobbling forward.

The gorilla's eyebrows shot up. "No offense, but I'm not sure how much help you're going to be."

Vigor began to undress, struggling to pull his robe over his head, revealing his boney, wrinkled body.

Equity's sobbing despair turned into a rueful chuckle. "There was no chance the world could come to an end without Vigor taking one last opportunity to display his genitalia."

But it wasn't Vigor's crotch that caught the Black Swan's attention. An elaborately inked tattoo completely engulfed Vigor's torso, depicting a dragon in minute detail. The dark lines pulsed and glowed as Vigor pulled a small flask of powder from a pocket before he tossed his robe aside.

On wobbly legs thin as sticks, he shouted to Menagerie, "You think you're the only person who ever studied blood magic? For three long years I lived with the scion of Greatshadow. I collected blood frequently while he was under my care. He had no reason to suspect I intended to study draconic biology from a vastly improved perspective."

He popped open the cork on the vial and tilted his head back, shaking the powdery contents into his gaping mouth. The wind snatched away much of the dark powder, giving the air the scent of blood. Vigor coughed as he strained to swallow the dusty mouthful. Red spittle flew from between his lips. He coughed again, more violently, and a jet of flame shot ten feet from his open mouth. The flames melted his face, which grew longer, more narrow, as the heat covered his skin with vivid red blisters, crusted with black. His body bulged as he dropped to all fours. With a horrible rip, his paper-thin skin split along his spine and two long red wings unfolded from between his shoulder blades.

In ten seconds, the transformation was complete, and a dragon larger than a bull with wings the size of mainsails stood facing the armies of the damned. He opened his crocodilian jaws and roared. An inferno billowed over the waves, incinerating the front ranks of the shambling dead.

Menagerie grabbed the Black Swan by the shoulders, refocusing her attention.

"Go!" the gorilla shouted. "Make Zetetic stop this!"

The Black Swan nodded, turning, grabbing Equity by the waist and slinging her over her shoulder as she ran into the hall.

"Where can I find him?" she shouted.

"Put me down before I throw up!" Equity shouted back.

The Black Swan put the aged thespian back on her feet. Equity responded by pointing at a stairway at the back of the hall. "Zetetic dwells in the uppermost chamber of the main tower!"

"You're sure he's there?" asked the Black Swan.

"Of course not. He's probably long gone into an abstract realm. Even if you find his body, I don't know that his mind will be with it. But what choice do you have but to try?"

"I've been asking myself that for over two hundred years," grumbled the Black Swan as she ran toward the stairs, her feet clanging like hammer blows on the marble floor. She took some comfort from her certainty that Equity was wrong. Zetetic hadn't fled to another reality. If a portal to an abstract realm had been opened here on the island, she'd know it. As a traveler of those realms, she could feel a pressure in the roof of her mouth, faint but unmistakable, whenever she was near a dimensional veil that had been breached.

She raced up the steps to the floor above. The light of a great fire flickered through an open window. She glanced out to see Vigor nearly a quarter mile out on the ice, spewing flames, spinning as he blasted the armies massed against him. Unfortunately, from her higher vantage point, the vastness of the army stood revealed. As large as the dragon was, he couldn't protect the Keep from being overrun.

She ran on. Her only hope lay at the top of the stairs. Her tireless legs moved with machine precision to propel her upwards, leaping three steps at a time.

At last she reached a locked door. She hoped beyond this she'd find Zetetic. She pounded on the door with her fist. "Open up! It's the Black Swan! You owe your life to me!"

When no reply came, she threw herself against the door. The thick wood cracked, but held. She threw herself again, then again, until the door came apart and she stumbled into the chamber beyond. Instantly, she felt the familiar sensation in the roof of her mouth. In passing through the door, she'd left the material world behind.

She found herself in a room lined with paper, in large sheets pasted roughly to stone walls. The paper had been painted white, though here and there some faint traces of words seeped through the chalky wash. The edges of the room were difficult to pinpoint, but the space felt cavernous. In the center of the space, dressed in red robes, sat Zetetic, cross-legged, his head in his hands, staring at objects before him.

She stepped closer, and saw a can of white paint before him, a worn and ragged brush balanced on the lip of the open container. Beside this was an inkwell, with a simple goose quill next to it, the tip black as soot. On the paper before Zetetic a few hundred words had been jotted, in a language she couldn't read.

"Zetetic?" she said, softly.

He said nothing.

"Zetetic, it's me. The Black Swan. I paid King Brightmoon to spare your life when you were captured by the Church of the Book all those years ago. I greased the palms required to let the king trust you with teaching Stagger how to guide the sun, and paid the necessary fees to have you take possession of this island. You owe me."

Zetetic didn't even look up.

She moved to a few feet away. She crouched, her iron joints creaking. Studying his face, she confirmed he was awake. He blinked, but never lifted his eyes to acknowledge her.

She reached for the quill, the focus of his attention.

The Deceiver's hand shot forward and grabbed her wrist.

"I owe you nothing," he said in a calm, measured tone.

"Zetetic, listen to me. I know that out here in the Spittles, news may be slow to reach you. The Dragon Apocalypse is upon us."

"It know what lies beyond these walls. Nothing at all, or very nearly nothing. All that remains of our world are echoes and shadows, soon to fade."

"That can't be true!" she said. "Yes, Stagger has vanished, and the sun has been torn from the sky. In the endless night, Tempest has thrown open the gates of Hell and the destruction wrought by his army of the damned is unimaginable in scope. Hush has enslaved Abyss, his mind frozen by her elemental chill, so that nothing prevents her from turning the whole world into a frigid wasteland. But it's not too late! We have to hope that pockets of humanity yet survive. If we stop the dragons, enough remains of the world that we can rebuild!"

"I know all of this," said Zetetic, lifting the quill, running his finger along the edge. "I've known it before it happened, thanks to your careful reporting from the future. Everything is happening, just as you said. You have the ultimate opportunity to say, fully, profoundly, 'Told you so.' This must provide you a great deal of satisfaction.' "

"Don't be absurd!" she cried. "I've devoted numerous lifetimes to preventing this day. You swore you'd help me stop it!"

He smiled, ever so faintly. "Certainly you knew better than to take the word of the Deceiver."

"Why would you lie when it means your own death?"

"Why should I fear death? It's nothing but a door."

"A door I've passed through many times," the Black Swan said. "Trust me, the living world is far better."

"You've traveled to the abstract realms, as have I. They are mere shadows of the living world. When life is gone, and they fade away, what will we discover beyond?"

"What if it's nothing?" she asked. "Certainly it's best to fight to save the world we know."

"I don't believe that at all," said Zetetic. "I'm certain that the reality we know is nothing but a fiction created for the entertainment of beings unfathomable. We're puppets. I would rid myself of strings."

The Black Swan stared into his face, unable to fathom the placidity of his eyes. She whispered, her voice breaking into despair, "You're mad."

"Perhaps." Zetetic focused his gaze on the tip of the quill, as if inspecting its quality as a writing instrument. "But insulting me is a poor strategy for getting me to change my mind."

"What will change your mind?" she asked.

"The more valuable secret for me would be to discover how to stop it from changing."

If she'd still had hair, she'd have torn it out. She'd never enjoyed any of her previous conversations with Zetetic, but she had no patience at all for his babble now. She stretched out her arms, seeing no choice but to take him by the throat and throttle him into obedience.

"That will end very badly for you," he said as her hands approached him. "Besides, you've other concerns at the moment. Stagger's back."

"What?"

"Stagger's back. I know you've been searching for him. He's approaching the Keep even now."

The Black Swan drew her hands back. She knew he was telling the truth, or else had told a lie that had become the truth. The pressure in the roof of her mouth became a stabbing sensation. A being of enormous power had just entered into the real world.

"Stagger?" she whispered, then ran back to the stairway and the nearest tower window.

Walking along the ocean toward the Keep was a flare of light vaguely the size and shape of a man. His radiance disintegrated the undead hordes as he passed.

Pressing a button on the side of her temple, the Black Swan dropped lenses of smoked glass over her eyes. The radiance dimmed, allowing her to see a man at the center of the light, wearing a suit of yellow silk, his long hair tied back neatly into a ponytail.

Bright sunlight lit the frozen waves surrounding the Keep. On the sea below, the dragon gazed up at the light, smoke rising from his nostrils. In a circle several hundred yards around him charred corpses were heaped high.

Menagerie, still in gorilla form, stood atop the wall of corpses, her fur completely matted with dark blood.

Stagger reached the mound of bodies. Extending his arms to his side, he drifted into the air, rising above the corpses, until he was eye level with the gorilla.

"Who are you?" Vigor demanded from inside the circle of bodies, his voice loud enough to be heard from the top of the tower.

"Once I was Abstemious Merchant," said Stagger. "A solar gentleman. Now, I am a loyal servant of Tempest. If you'll please step aside, I'm here to kill Zetetic before he completes the palimpsest."

"Kill Zetetic?" asked Menagerie. "I thought the two of you were buddies."

"Menagerie," said Stagger, turning his gaze toward the shapeshifter. "I'm genuinely sorry." A flash followed. The Black Swan blinked to clear her vision. All that remained of Menagerie was a black streak of ash.

Vigor roared, flames belching from his serpentine neck as he blasted Stagger. As the flames died, Stagger proved unharmed. Vigor lunged toward him, his toothy jaws clamping on Stagger's head. Stagger calmly lifted his hands and pried the dragon's jaws open, freeing himself.

"You have the same aura as Brokenwing, but you're obviously not him," said Stagger.

"Urah muh daggoo," answered Vigor, his speech rendered unintelligible by Stagger's grip.

"Whoever you are, farewell," said Stagger. The Black Swan shielded her eyes from the flash she knew was coming. When she lowered her hand, Vigor was gone. His ashes drifted down to the ice like black snow.

Stagger walked closer to the tower, ascending with each step as if he climbed an unseen staircase.

The Black Swan hesitated. Stagger was here to kill Zetetic? Why? Should she go warn the Deceiver? Was it possible that he didn't already know?

As the living embodiment of the sun, there was little hope of stopping Stagger by force. Fortunately, she knew one important thing about the man. He loved to talk.

The Black Swan leaned her iron body against the wall and locked her joints. She loosened her grip on her physical shell, stepping outside its confines, connected only by a slender silver thread. She floated out the window to meet Stagger as he drew closer.

"Stagger," she called out.

"I expected to find you here," he said.

"I most certainly didn't expect to find you here," she said. "Where have you been?"

"In Hell," he said. "Just another damned soul."

"No," she whispered.

"Yes," he said. "Tempest is my master now. He's achieved his dream of total dominion over the world. At least, he will once Zetetic has been vaporized."

"I can't let you do this," said the Black Swan. "Zetetic is our last hope of undoing all the destruction."

"You cannot possibly stop me," said Stagger.

"Return to your bones," said the Black Swan, pointing her wraithlike fingers toward the man.

Stagger smirked. "Necromancy isn't as effective as it once was. Life no longer holds power over death. Now, be a good girl and step aside, won't you? I can vaporize your spirit as well as your body, but we both know I'd rather not harm you."

The Black Swan closed her eyes as the silver thread pulled her back into her iron shell. It was time to leave. She'd again failed to stop the end of the world. It was time to go back and try once more.

She opened her eyes. She frowned. She was still in Zetetic's tower. The winds still howled above the frozen sea outside the window. The toe of Stagger's boot fell upon the window ledge. He stepped down to the floor beside her.

"You won't be going anywhere," he said.

"How?" she asked. "How are you stopping me?"

"The Church of the Book used to draw magical glyphs that protected their holy sanctuaries from assaults from the abstract realm. In coming here, I've traced the outline of one of these glyphs to encompass the island. Tempest doesn't want Zetetic to flee into a different reality."

"I wouldn't dream of it," said Zetetic, his voice coming from the paper-lined room. "We've reached the last words of the last page of the final chapter. We're all precisely where we must be."

Stagger stepped into the room. The Black Swan followed, her mind racing. How could she hope to stop Stagger?

Zetetic no longer held the quill. He now held the paint brush. The words that had filled the paper directly in front of him were mostly gone, lost beneath a sheen of glistening paint. Somehow, in the seconds since the Black Swan had last seen him, he'd worked up a sweat. Huge beads of perspiration stood against the large red "D" tattooed in the center of his brow.

"Goodbye, Zetetic," said Stagger.

Zetetic drew his brush across the words before him. They vanished beneath the white.

Stagger silently faded away. The Black Swan blinked.

"Where?" she whispered.

Zetetic put down the brush and picked up the pen. As he dipped the tip into the inkwell, the inkwell vanished. He frowned as the dry tip of the quill hit the paper. Then, the quill disappeared.

"My calculations were off a few seconds, I see," he said with a heavy sigh, studying his empty fingers.

The Black Swan lifted her own hands, confused as to why she could see through them.

In the roof of her mouth, she felt something pop. She didn't know why, she didn't know how, but she sensed that the glyphs Stagger had drawn around the island were no longer there.

By instinct, the Black Swan leapt, jumping from the world of the living into the nearest adjacent realm. She tumbled into darkness, falling, falling. Since she'd been on an island, she expected to pass through the Sea of Wine, but it was gone. The Realm of Roots had always held a special magnetism for her ethereal self. She could no longer feel its tug. Stagger had arrived from Hell. The dimensional gateway should still be easy to pass through. Yet… nothing. She felt nothing. Hell itself had been swallowed by an all-encompassing vacancy.

She tumbled through the timeless dark, her mind blank, incapable of conscious thought, as a memory, exceedingly faint and long, long lost, crept into her awareness. She'd experienced this void before. When Numinous had read the One True Book, and ended the world. It seemed like the sort of thing that would be impossible to forget. But how can a mind keep a grasp on nothing?

She closed her eyes and stretched out her arms. The sensation of falling, she understood, was merely a remnant of her last physical sensation. It was impossible to fall in a place with no up or down, no side to side, where width and depth and breadth weren't even concepts. She was in a place that was not a place. Which meant she couldn't be here. She had to be somewhere else.

She no longer felt as if she were falling. She opened her eyes, finding impenetrable darkness above. She sat up and discovered herself surrounded by an endless plain of white paper covered in dark scratchings. She'd never been able to understand these symbols before, but realized suddenly that they bore a strong resemblance to the letters Zetetic had scrawled before him.

She stood, gazing over the final realm, the foundation that all of reality rested upon. She'd come once again to the Primordial Pages. Once, the pages had stretched out unblemished for as far as she could see. Now, she saw horrible rips in the paper, long gashes where she'd fallen through on her previous journeys back along the narrative stream of reality. Once, she'd been able to travel back decades with ease. Now, her repeated journeys had left the pages in tatters. Rips had grown and merged, leaving only thin and fragile bridges of intact paper for her to navigate.

Fortunately, she needn't travel back far. A single step across the lines could carry her back days, even weeks. A few hours of careful treading on the fragile pages might yet take her back a few years. The limbo she'd fallen through provided her an important clue. Numinous Pilgrim had somehow survived her ambush on the Sea of Wine. Only the Omega Reader could have destroyed the abstract realms so completely.

Twenty years ago, Infidel had nearly killed Numinous while he was still a child. How difficult would it be to finish the job? With her destination in mind, she stepped forward.

Her body tensed as she heard the ripping caused by the single step.

When she'd traveled to the Keep, to gain traction on the frozen waves, she'd extended the spikes in her feet. She'd never retracted them.

"No," she cried, but denying what was happening didn't stop it. With a loud tearing sound, she plummeted through the page. She grasped at a dangling shard of paper, desperate to climb back. The paper tore from her iron grip and she fell, tumbling toward a recent yesterday.

2 - THE DEAD MAN

"MOTHER," CINDER SAID softly as she climbed onto the platform of woven branches. "Mother, wake up."

There was no sound from inside the small thatched hut where her mother slept. Daylight was still an hour away. Most of the pygmies of the Jawa Fruit tribe slept soundly in the closely packed tree houses that filled the upper branches of the village. Save for the warriors who patrolled the territory at night, ever vigilant for attacks from the hated river-pygmies, Cinder was the only member of the tribe awake at this hour. She took care not to raise her voice and earn the wrath of the village elders.

She knelt before her mother's hut and pushed aside the curtain of leaves to peer inside. Her night-acclimated eyes quickly made sense of the darker shadows within the hut. The hammock her mother normally slept in was empty.

Cinder looked out over the moonlit jungle canopy. Her mother had probably gone hunting. The fact that she hadn't invited Cinder along hinted at the territory she'd selected for her hunting grounds.

Grabbing her spear, Cinder leapt from the platform, dropping from branch to branch to reach the ground far below. The pygmies could cover miles in the canopy without ever touching earth, but Cinder had grown too large to travel across the more slender branches. At nineteen, she was twice the height of any of the pygmies, a few inches taller even than her mother, who the pygmies called "Nagana," which meant "the giant."

She ran swiftly through the inky gloom. The thick foliage blotted out the moon and stars, but every rock and root in her path was familiar to her.

The stars reappeared when she reached the eastern slope. Before she was born, a magma flow from the volcano had scoured away the forest, leaving a frozen river of black rock. When she was little, the black rock had been barren, but over the years weeds and vines had found purchase in the cracked surface, and now berry bushes covered the area. As dawn approached, the bushes sang with the music of a million birds gathered for breakfast.

Boars often came to this area to feed, their fat bodies and heavy hooves clearing pathways through the thorns. Cinder raced through the maze of bushes, moving ever further down the slope.

Dawn glowed on the horizon when she reached the cliff. At some point, the importance of finding her mother to tell her about the visitor had faded as a priority and reaching this cliff had become the true reason she'd kept running.

Perched on the high rocks, she studied the rolling hills far below. In the faint light, she saw the long-men had been busy since she'd last spied on them. They'd added a wooden palisade around the village, and she could see several new houses, with many more partially constructed. Five battered ships sat anchored beyond the breaker, joining the small fleet that had brought the previous settlers. As always, there was a flame dancing in mid-air directly above the largest building at the center of town. The wooden structure was taller than the surrounding trees, with a tear-drop shaped roof. Painted in deep reds, warm oranges, and vivid yellows, the building resembled a frozen bonfire. Smoke rose from the tip of the teardrop, and the dancing flame floated several yards above the smoke, its bright light casting a glow over the area. She still couldn't guess what fuel fed the flame. She wondered how the long-men ever got any sleep, when they never allowed their night to be truly dark.

She crouched when she spotted the sentries patrolling the outer walls of the settlement. She doubted they could see her. With her black skin the same color as the volcanic rock, she was well camouflaged, even if the sun had been above the horizon.

She would have liked nothing more than to sit and watch the town of the long-men wake up, to watch them come out of their strange houses and resume the work of building their settlement. She found long-men fascinating, their habits so inexplicable and bizarre, that she imagined she'd never grow bored watching them. Long ago, these had been her mother's people, which meant they were her people despite the difference in their skin tones. She'd grown up among pygmies as a freak, too large and clumsy. Her eyes had also been a source of much teasing when she was younger. Where other people had irises of varying shades, her eyes were a uniform black. The teasing had only stopped when the pygmies realized that her eyes could see far more than their own. Now, most pygmies kept out of her path, and when interactions with her were unavoidable, they never looked directly at her. When they spoke of her behind her back, she could hear the fear in their voices.

When her grandfather, Tenoba, had still lived, the villagers had at least been polite to her, out of respect for the old man. But that was years ago, and now she often went days without speaking to anyone but her mother. By necessity, she'd taught herself to enjoy her solitude, and most of the time she managed not to feel lonely. Still, looking upon the village, she couldn't help but wonder, would the long-men be more accepting of her odd physique? They'd come from over the ocean. Certainly, they'd seen so many different things that she wouldn't be that unusual. She sighed. What a pointless thing to contemplate. Her mother had forbidden her from going near long-men. Even coming to this cliff to study their settlement was breaking her mother's rules.

Cinder turned away and headed back into the maze of brush. Her mother would soon be returning from her hunt. Perhaps Cinder could still catch her before she reached their home village.

By now, the song of the morning birds in the brush was cacophonous as a waterfall. She didn't hear the huge boar rustling along the pathway until she turned a corner and found the beast less than ten feet away. The boar was one of the largest she'd ever seen, six feet long from tusks to tail, its powerful muscles bulging beneath a rust-colored hide. She skittered to a halt, startled. The boar looked as surprised as she was. Half the time, a startled boar would bolt and run. This was not one of those times.

The boar lowered its head, its tusks pointed like twin spears, and lunged. Cinder met its charge by lowering her spear, planting the tip into the beast's shoulder. The spear caught in the mound of thickened skin that protected the creature's neck, failing to hurt it. The boar's momentum ripped the spear from her hands. At the last possible second she leapt, lifting her legs above the slashing tusks, using the creature's back as a springboard. She landed on the path behind it and ran.

Around her, a million birds took to the air as the boar spun in its tracks, let out a bellowing squeal, and raced after her. Its heavy hooves thundered on the volcanic rock.

Cinder was the fastest runner among the Jawa Fruit tribe, but the boar was soon at her heels. She could hear it panting behind her, but dare not look back. She still had a hundred yards to cover before she reached the edge of the forest. There, she could leap for a branch to clamber to safety.

When she felt the boar's hot breath wash over the backs of her legs, she knew she had no choice. Though her mother had forbidden it, she would have to escape to the other place. She leapt, stretching her arms before her. When her feet left the ground, she was in the living world. When she landed, she'd passed through to the Realm of Roots.

She stopped as the now ghostly boar ran through her, its snorting, panting breath muffled and distant. All around her, the berry bushes lay dead and withered, their leaves fallen. The berries still clinging to the thorny branches were shriveled and dry. The sky, pink with morning light only seconds before, was dark and starless. The air stank of dead flesh, and the ground beneath her writhed with worms and beetles.

She could still see into the living world. The shapes there were wraithlike, more shadow than substance. She saw the boar charge on a few more yards before spinning around, rage changing to bewilderment. The shadows of birds flitted into the air to the left of the boar, their cries of alarm muted by the dimensional barrier.

The source of the birds' distress quickly revealed itself as Cinder's mother leapt from the bushes beside the boar. Her mother was the tribe's greatest warrior, a titan five and a half feet tall. At fifty, she was one of the oldest members of the tribe, though her body was still athletic, chiseled by years of constant use. Like other members of the Jawa Fruit tribe, her skin was dyed green, with her hair a lighter shade of lime. Unlike other members of the tribe, she wore more than just a loincloth, concealing her torso with a vest of leather.

She carried a spear like the one still stuck in the boar's shoulder, but her mother had far more expertise with the weapon. With a grunt, her mother drove the obsidian tip between the beast's ribs. With a howl of pain the boar twisted around, its tusks slashing the air, as Cinder's mother leapt from their path. She then calmly reached out and grabbed Cinder's spear, plucking it free. As the boar jabbed its tusks toward her once more, she thrust the spear into the beast's left eye. Bringing all her weight to bear, she drove the tip deep into its skull. The creature's body fell dead.

For half a second the creature's spirit stood before Cinder. The ghost glared at her with its one intact eye, shuddering with fury. Before Cinder could take any action to defend herself, the spirit turned and bolted. Before it had gone even ten yards, it stumbled on a root, crashing heavy to the ground. Its tusks became stuck under a low root. It shook, trying to pull free, but only succeeded in ripping more of the roots from the ground. The roots fell across the writhing beast like heavy ropes. The boar's breathing grew more labored as it sank deeper into the earth. It let out a squeal, short and sharp, then fell silent, growing still, as if understanding its final fate. In the end, all things surrendered to the roots.

"Until now, I never knew pigs had a hell of their own," said a voice from behind.

"Oh," she said, turning around. She found the dead man who'd visited her earlier in the night, insisting he needed to speak to her mother. Now that she was in the Realm of Roots, she could see and hear him plainly. Before, his shape had been nothing but fog, his voice only a murmur. "You followed me? Why didn't I see you?"

The man standing before her shook his head. "I didn't follow you. I followed Infidel." He nodded toward Cinder's mother, who squatted over the fallen boar, freeing Cinder's spear. Infidel frowned as she studied the mangled leather strapping that held the obsidian tip in place. Cinder knew her mother would recognize the spear as one of her own and deduce who had to have planted in the boar's shoulder. Other members of the Jawa Fruit tribe used spears much shorter than those she and her mother preferred.

"Tell her I must speak to her at once," the man said.

"She'll kill me if she finds out I came to look at the long-men," Cinder said. "She'll kill me if she finds out I fled to the Realm of Roots!"

"You engage in hyperbole," the man said. "She'll scold you, no doubt, nothing more."

"We should wait," said Cinder.

The man scowled, though his scowl wasn't much different than his normal expression. Dead men seldom looked happy, but this one's face seemed permanently set to a look of disgust, as if merely speaking to Cinder was a loathsome task.

The man was a good deal taller than she was. He held his body in an unnatural posture, his spine straight and stiff as bamboo. His nose and lips were thin, his eyebrows white and bushy, his scalp bald and dabbled with dark spots. His forehead was covered in a thick mass of scars. He wore long black robes, with white gloves and boots, unlike most other dead men she'd met, who were normally unclothed. He differed also from other dead men in his gaze. Most of dead she'd met had wandering eyes, confused expressions, as if they couldn't quite comprehend where they were or why they were there.

This man's expression was focused, unblinking. He appeared to have no doubt as to the where or why of his existence.

In the living world, Cinder's mother stood up and shouted, "Cinder! Cinder!"

"She thinks the boar has killed you," the man said. "It would be cruel not to tell her you're unharmed."

Cinder sighed and nodded. "Wait here."

"Where else am I to go?" the man asked.

Cinder reached out, parting the dimensional veil as if it were a curtain, and stepped through. The humid jungle air washed over her, rich with a thousand scents, flowers, berries, bird droppings, and, above all, the odor of blood as the boar bled out from the slit her mother had carved in its throat with her obsidian knife.

"Cinder!" her mother cried out again, facing away as her daughter emerged from the land of the dead. The worry in her voice could be plainly heard now that it was no longer muffled by the dimensional veil.

"I'm here," said Cinder, softly. "I'm okay."

Her mother ran to her, grabbing her shoulders. She looked ready to hug Cinder, her face a mask of joy. Then, her face took a sterner cast, and she kept Cinder at arm's length. "Are you trying to scare me to death? I found your spear! I thought… I thought you had… what on earth were you doing out here? Don't you know how dangerous it is?"

"I'm fine," said Cinder. "I was looking for you."

"Looking for… why? What was so urgent it couldn't wait until I got back?"

Cinder placed her arms behind her back. "There's… there's a dead man who's come to see you. He says he knows you from a long time ago."

"Stagger?" her mother whispered, her eyes growing wide.

"It's not father," said Cinder. "He says his name is Ver."

Her mother's face fell. She wiped her bloody knife against her loincloth, shaking her head slightly.

"You've been to the Realm of Roots."

"I had to go there to escape the boar."

"And you've been spying on the long-men," her mother said. "You say you came here looking for me, but you really came to watch the settlement. This is the third time! Why do you insist on disobeying me?"

Cinder felt both guilty and relieved to discover that her mother didn't know her actual visits here numbered in the dozens. "Since you hadn't told me you were going out, I knew you must have come hunting here, on the edge of the settlement."

Her mother looked even angrier. "So you knew I didn't want you to come, but you still followed me?"

"I only came because Ver says his business is urgent."

"He's dead," her mother said, sheathing her blade. "How urgent can anything be?"

"Tell her I come with news of an old friend," said Ver.

"He says he's come with news of an old friend," said Cinder.

"Not Tower, I hope," she said.

"It's not Tower," said Ver. "Tell her I swear it."

"He swears it's not Tower."

Infidel crossed her arms, frowning, looking lost in thought. "I suppose the bastard isn't going to give you any peace until I say yes. Fine. Let me talk to him."

Cinder held out her hand. Her mother hesitated, then took her offered grasp. She looked around, seeking the visitor. Infidel's eyes locked on a nearby form, invisible in the material world, but revealed now that she shared Cinder's connection with the Realm of Roots.

"Ver," said Infidel. "I can't say I'm happy to see you."

"Infidel," said the dead priest. "It would be a dark day in Hell before I came to you for help. A dark day indeed, but that day that has come."

"Hell's had a lot of dark days lately, hasn't it?" asked Infidel. "Even among the pygmies, the news has reached us. Those long-men settled here because every night the Silver Isles are being overrun with armies of the damned."

Ver nodded. "Tempest long ago completed his conquest of Hell. With the land of the dead conquered, he's turned his eyes toward the living world, tearing down the very Gates of Hell to clear the path for his accursed army."

"You don't sound like you approve."

"Approve?" Ver looked incredulous. "Allowing the damned to return to the land of the living is a sin against the Divine Author. Hell exists to punish the wicked. According to the sacred text of the One True Book, that punishment was to be eternal."

"Maybe Tempest never bothered to read the book," said Infidel. "And, I guess it's too late now even if he wanted too."

"True," said Ver. "Wicked times have fallen upon the world of the living since the One True Book was stolen twenty years past. Men have lost faith in the truth. They degenerate into depraved beasts with no spiritual guidance to point them toward divine virtues. To make matters worse, your father's attempts to tame his rebellious subjects have transformed him into a brutal dictator. Many of his subjects prefer anarchy to life beneath his iron fist."

Infidel nodded. "I voted for anarchy a long time ago."

"So you did," said Ver. "Which is why I find it so distasteful to turn to you for help. You, whose soul is untamed chaos, are now my only hope of restoring order."

"What exactly do you want?"

"I want the world set right. I want the living world to be unmolested by the damned, and I want the damned back in their rightful place, suffering as justice demands."

"That sounds like a job better suited for priests. Certainly there are at least a few members of the Church of the Book holding on to their faith."

"Perhaps. But, though it galls me, no other person alive has fared as well as you when it comes to battling primal dragons."

"Ah. And just because you ask nice, you think I'm going to gear up and go fight Tempest?"

"No," said Ver. "You're too small-minded to take such grand action."

"I think my mind is plenty large," said Infidel. "Large enough to know more about the afterworld than you can ever hope to, Ver. I know that the Church of the Book is mistaken in thinking all unrepentant souls go to Hell. I've sailed the Sea of Wine. I've trudged across ice floes in the Great Sea Above."

"And you've copulated on the forested slopes above the Bay of Blood," said Ver. He glowered at Cinder. "You've given birth to a child trapped between life and death. Given the magnitude of your sins, do you feel no obligation at all to seek redemption?"

"We're done, Ver," said Infidel. "Go to Hell, or wherever you're calling home these days."

"Wait," said Ver, placing his hand on Infidel's wrist before she released her grasp on Cinder. "I haven't told you about Sorrow. You remember Sorrow, don't you?"

"I've known more sorrow than I care to recall."

"I speak of Sorrow, the witch. Your friend."

Infidel furrowed her brow. "My friend… the witch?" She didn't sound as if she had a clue of who he was talking about.

"She had nails in her scalp," said Ver.

"Right," said Infidel. "I remember her now. I don't dwell much on that time of my life. I haven't heard anything about her in twenty years. She's in Hell now?"

"Yes."

"That's not a big surprise. She seemed dead set on fighting the world. Eventually, the world was going to win. How did she die?"

"She didn't," said Ver.

Infidel looked confused.

"Sorrow has arrived in Hell via a journey through limbo. She and her companions are still alive, though I doubt they'll remain so long in such a treacherous landscape. I need you to rescue them."

Infidel shook her head. "My adventuring days are behind me, Ver. Certainly there's some valiant Knight of the Book who's up to the task."

"It pains me to say so, but the remnants of my church contain no men of true valor. It galls me further to admit that there is a man among the heretics in the settlement nearby who does, indeed, possess a virtuous heart, despite the folly of his beliefs. Alas, I've no way of speaking to him."

"That's too bad," said Infidel. "But it also confirms what I suspected."

"Which is?"

"For me to get to Hell, you need Cinder to take me there."

"If she must be born with a curse, shouldn't at least try to use it for good?"

"It's not a curse," said Cinder.

"Stay out of this," said Infidel. Then, addressing Ver, "You're crazy. Go away. I'm not letting you lead my daughter to Hell."

"You have no choice!" cried Ver. "Just as the damned have no place in the land of the living, the living don't belong in the realm of the dead."

"Completely agree, which is why we're not going."

"You don't understand the implications!" the priest said, his voice trembling. "If living men remain too long in Hell, it will unravel the truth of that place. All of reality will fray and tear. The world that we know will come undone!"

"I've no doubt you believe that," said Infidel. "But I'll take my chances that you're as wrong in death as you were in life. This conversation is over."

Infidel tore her hand from Cinder's grasp.

"Mother," said Cinder, "what if he's telling the truth?"

"Then I suppose reality will unravel," said Infidel, crouching next to the boar. "Until it does, we've got work to do. I'm going to start cutting up this boar. Run back to the village and tell Kanopi to send men to help carry the meat."

"Mother, the dead man is screaming. He says you're condemning your friends to death."

Infidel shrugged. "He's trying to trick us. Ignore him."

"Trick us? Why?"

"I don't know and I honestly don't care."

Cinder found the dead man's shouting distracting. But it wasn't what he was saying now that found purchase in Cinder's mind. It was something he'd already said. "This person called Sorrow? Isn't she the weaver who put Father inside the sun?"

"That's her," said Infidel, working her knife along the boar's belly.

"Don't you want to save her?"

"It's not that. It's just… Sorrow's not really the kind of person who needs saving," said Infidel as the guts spilled out. "When I last saw her, she'd given herself the powers of Rott, the primal dragon of decay. She was insanely powerful. Scary powerful."

"You're not going to rescue her because you're scared of her?"

Infidel didn't look up as she cut the intestines free of the body. In the jungle heat, meat could spoil quickly if a hunter didn't work fast.

"I'm not scared of her, or for her," said Infidel, tossing the intestines into the bushes. "It's you I'm worried about."

"Me? Nothing can hurt me as long as I can flee to the Realm of Roots with but a thought."

"You don't think there's monsters in the Realm of Roots?"

"Not that I've seen. It's mostly empty whenever I visit. The dead aren't able to hold on for long there. They get tangled in the roots and fade away. Ver has stuck around longer than any spirit I've encountered."

Infidel wiped her cheek, leaving a smear of blood against her emerald skin. "The bastard was the most stubborn man I ever met. Hopefully he'll go away if you ignore him."

"He's not making himself easy to ignore," said Cinder. Even though she was now fully in the material world, she could still see his shadowy form before her, arms lifted as he raged. His voice seemed so loud even from the other side of the veil it was difficult to believe her mother couldn't hear him.

Though, in another sense, it wasn't difficult at all to think that there were things her mother couldn't hear. It wasn't only the dead she could turn a deaf ear to. Cinder herself fared no better. Her mother might have technically listened to her as she spoke, but she seldom gave anything Cinder said any serious consideration.

"This meat isn't going to carry itself," said Infidel, looking toward the jungle. "Go get help before the day gets hot."

Cinder jogged off toward the village. The dead man floated beside her, his hands clasped behind his back, his legs not moving. He looked calm now, lost in thought.

"You should go away," Cinder said, finding his silence more unnerving than when he'd been shouting at her. "My mother's not going to help you."

"Your mother doesn't have the power to help me," said Ver. "Now that the false hope has been eliminated, the true solution is clear. You're the one who possesses the power to traverse to the realms of the dead. You're the one who must save the world."

"Um," said Cinder. "I don't think that's going to happen."

"Why not?"

"First, mother would kill me if I did. Second, while my mother has taught me a thing or two about defending myself, I'm nowhere near the fighter she is. I'm certainly not ready to fight dragons."

"You won't need to fight at all, should you help. As I said, in the village nearby, there's a man of valiant spirit. He's well trained in combat, and, more importantly, possesses a spotless conscience, having lived his life in obedience to his faith, albeit a faith based on falsehoods. Still, the truth of his beliefs matter little. A pure heart is the ultimate armor in Hell. No evil shall be able to touch him."

"You'll have to find someone else," said Cinder. "There's no way my mother would give me permission to go to the long-men's village, let along make the journey to Hell."

"You're no child," said Ver. "Your mother didn't ask the permission of her mother when she went to fight Greatshadow. She didn't consult with her father before travelling to the Great Sea Above and battling Hush and Glorious. You're nineteen, an adult in anyone's eyes. You may do as please."

They were nearing the Jawa Fruit village. She slowed her jog to a walk, looking skyward to make sure no one was watching her. If the other villagers heard her speaking with no one around, they'd assume she was talking with a ghost.

Ver's eyes followed her gaze up to the houses and walkways spread throughout the canopy. He said, "You don't belong here."

"It's my home," she said.

"Your mother has told you of her adventures?"

"Yes. But only after the village children told me tales of her past. She said most of the stories were exaggerations, and wanted me to know the truth."

"Truth is a precious thing. Did she tell you the title I possessed in life?"

"She said… you were a Truthspeaker."

Ver nodded. "It's a title I hold precious even in death. I'm incapable of deceit. I speak the truth when I say you don't belong here. The tribesmen have never accepted you."

"That's not true. My great grandfather, Tenoba, was chieftain of the tribe," said Cinder. "He took in my mother when she was pregnant. At first, she says the pygmies didn't accept her, especially since she was a woman who hunt and fought. Then, when I was still an infant, she single-handedly slew eleven members of the Spike Branch people when they tried to raid our village. The tribe holds my mother in the deepest reverence."

"Yes. But they fear you. You've never truly belonged."

This was truth. She looked down at her hands, black as soot. Her mother was taller than the pygmies, it was true, but she dyed her skin the same color, and with her prowess as a warrior, she'd earned her place of honor within the tribe. The pygmy dyes merely made Cinder's skin a shade darker. The village midwife said it looked as if she'd been burnt in the womb and named her Sakoni, the charred one. Her mother had liked the name, though she translated it into the tongue of the long-men as Cinder. When Cinder had been old enough to understand the intimacies between a man and a woman, Infidel had explained that there was truth to her being burnt in the womb. She'd been conceived on the slopes of the volcano above the Bay of Blood, the spiritual realm where Greatshadow's soul had hidden when his physical body had been slain. Her sooty skin was no doubt a side effect of her unusual origins, having been conceived in a dead land by a dead father and given birth by a living mother in the realm of life.

If it had just been her skin that was different, perhaps the tribe would have eventually have accepted her. But, from the earliest age, she'd had conversations with people no one else could see. Everyone assumed she was crazy. Sometimes, she'd vanish for hours, even days, and when she'd return she'd explain how she'd been in a place of shadows. She couldn't explain how she'd gotten there, or how she came back. When she was finally old enough to grasp the concept of death, and could explain to the village elders that her imaginary friends were actually the spirits of the dead, it had made matters worse. No longer was she called crazy. Now, she was called unclean. Children said she stank like a rotten corpse, though her mother said she smelled just fine. Children also said her touch would make them sick, and that the sound of her laughter was a sure sign that someone in the village was about to die. She'd stopped laughing. People died all the same.

"You're not one of them," said Ver.

She placed her arm against a tree to steady herself. Her run to the cliff and back had left her weary. She needed a moment to find the strength to climb up to the village.

She ran her fingers through her hair. "Perhaps. But I don't belong with the long-men, either."

"Your mother and father were, as you say, long-men. You won't know happiness until you live among your own kind."

"Do you think I've never went among the long-men?" she asked. "I have. They were far, far worse than my tribesmen."

"Among the long-men? In the settlement?"

She shook her head. "In Commonground."

"Ah," said Ver. "A city of rogues and half-seeds. I assure you, you didn't find the best examples of long-men in that horrid place."

"Didn't I?" asked Cinder. "Mother told me that what happened there might have happened anywhere in the world, save for here among the pygmies."

"Truly? And what happened?"

"It's a long story."

"I'm willing to listen." Ver smiled. It proved a chilling expression on his cadaverous face.

3 - CALAMITY

"HELL?" BIGSBY ASKED, bewildered. "I mean… I always kind of knew I'd wind up here, but… are we dead? I don't feel dead."

"We're not dead," Sorrow said emphatically as she glanced around at her fellow travelers. "We still have living auras."

Keeping the blanket that hid her body clasped tightly around her, she walked toward Walker, the albino pygmy who stood at the wheel, who watched her with a sly, knowing grin. She said, "I don't know how you did it, or why, but this is your fault. I'll give you ten seconds to take us back to the material world or—"

"Yes?" asked Walker, sounding genuinely curious as to how she would finish her threat.

She frowned. "I'll be very, very cross with you."

"I'm already cross with you," Gale Romer said, stomping toward the pygmy. She pointed to the riggings, where a trio of demons busied themselves with the sails. "Tell these things to get their hands off my ship! Let loose of that wheel at once. No one pilots the *Circus* but me and my family."

"The rivers of Hell are not easily navigated," said Walker. "Inexperienced hands swiftly run aground."

"We'll take that risk," said Gale. "I'd rather have my family's safety in my hands than in the claws of these… these—" Her voice trailed off as she glanced up at the creatures.

"You may call them monsters," said Walker. "Demons; devils; unholy scum… their feelings aren't easily damaged."

Walker stepped aside to let Gale take the wheel. The pygmy placed his fingers between his lips and let loose a shrill whistle. The trio of demons in the rigging dropped to the deck.

All three stood taller than Slate, heavily muscled, with large black wings and bright red tails that swung from holes in their sailor's britches. One had the head of a vulture, another the head of a lion whose skin had been peeled off, and the last, where a head should be, had a hornet's nest, complete with swarming hornets.

"May I introduce Fester, Fume, and Foment," said Walker. "They're my truest friends in Hell, and are now your friends as well."

"I'll call no devil friend," said Slate, clutching the Witchbreaker tightly in both hands. "Begone, the lot of you, before I show you the power of my blade."

"They know well the power of your blade," said Walker. "It sends the souls of those you slay to Hell. Which, of course, is where we already are."

"So, if he stabs someone here, will they go back to the living world?" asked Bigsby. "If so, I volunteer to be stabbed at once."

"There's no need to volunteer for a violent death," said Walker. "You won't need to wait long for such an end in this wretched landscape."

"All the more reason to leave this place," said Gale. "Sage! Can you see a clear path out of here?"

Sorrow glanced up to the crow's nest. Sage, Gale's eldest daughter, swept her spyglass across the fiery landscape. "I... I don't think it's safe for us to jump," she called down. "I'm not certain we can transition back to the Sea of Wine without risking getting caught in Limbo."

"There are other paths to the Sea of Wine," said Walker. "This very river empties into it."

"How can that be?" asked Gale. "The Sea of Wine is the afterlife for Wanderers. Hell is the afterlife for wicked followers of the Church of the Book. They're two completely different abstract realms."

Walker shook his head. "Nonsense." He turned to Sorrow. "You've been to at least four abstract realms. The Sea of Wine, the Great Sea Above, the Black Bog, and the Convergence. You must have taken note that all share an aquatic nature."

"You told us you were from the Realm of Roots," said Sorrow. "Is there water there?"

Walker nodded. "The Dark and Winding Stream feeds the Realm of Roots, before flowing on to the great unknown. Of course, I know the unknown. All of these deathly waters share the same source. They all flow to the same ocean."

"So... we can sail this river to the Sea of Wine? Then we can transition from there to the living realms," said Gale. "Sage, can you plot a course?"

Sage shook her head. "Every direction I look, the horizon is hidden by storms."

"Yes," said Walker. "Storms in every direction. By now, no doubt you've seen something else odd about the landscape."

"Hell is more than odd," Sage said. "The terrain... it's... creeping. The land looks to be in constant motion."

"Do you notice anything strange about those who walk upon the land?" asked Walker.

"I can't say that I do," said Sage. "Honestly, I don't see anyone here but us."

"Ah," said Walker, sounding pleased with her answer. "Curious, isn't it? Where are the damned?"

"What do you mean, where are the damned?" asked Sorrow. "I would assume they're here, in Hell."

Walker shook his head. "The banks of this river once teemed with damned souls pressed shoulder to shoulder, crying out to slake their thirst. Look about. The shores are vacant."

"Has... has Hell been emptied?" asked Slate. "How is such a thing possible? The Divine Author would never allow such injustice."

Walker let loose a sharp laugh, almost a bark. "The mere existence of Hell is proof the Divine Author cared nothing for justice."

"This place exists that the wicked may suffer for their sins," said Slate.

"As your progenitor, Stark Tower, suffers?" asked Walker.

Slate frowned. "The man I was copied from fell prey to his temptations. If his soul is here, it's justice. He allowed the desires of his flesh to overcome the moral judgment of his soul."

"Are you truly so simpleminded?" Walker asked. "You believe he's here because he gave in to his lusts?"

"His sins are well known to me. Though, I suppose justice has been denied. He's not here, is he?" asked Slate. "You said Hell was vacant."

"I said these shores are vacant. In the darker valleys, in the deeper pits, there are souls too crippled to heed Tempest's summons."

"Tempest?" asked Sorrow. "What does he have to do with any of this? We killed him."

"Yes," said Walker. "With the Witchbreaker. A sword forged from metal stolen from the Gates of Hell. A sword with the power to send the soul of any creature directly to this place of torment."

"Tempest is here?" asked Slate. "No wonder there are storms everywhere."

Walker nodded. "Indeed. When you killed him with the Witchbreaker, his soul journeyed to this place. Devils fell upon him at once, preparing to drag him to eternal torment. Alas, a primal dragon is not a power to be trifled with, even when his soul has been ripped from his body. Tempest easily overpowered the devils who came to plague him. After he'd slain a few hundred, the remaining demons begged for mercy. He had them swear fealty to him. Then, he launched a war of conquest, slaying any devils who opposed him, until most joined him willingly. Demons are weak-minded beasts, eager for subjugation by a more dominant spirit. It took him several years, but eventually he made himself master of this accursed place, taking his seat upon Hell's empty throne."

"Empty?" asked Slate. "Why was Hell's throne empty? The church teaches that the Master Deceiver sits upon the throne, the eternal foe of the Author of Truth."

"He sat upon the throne many, many centuries ago," said Walker. "Then he grew bored and left."

"How do you know all of this?" asked Sorrow.

Walker shrugged. "I listen. I learn."

"What does Tempest being Lord of Hell have to do with the shores being empty?" asked Sorrow. "You said Tempest sent out a summons?"

"Indeed," said Walker. He glanced at the black blade in Slate's grasp. "Having felt the bite of the Witchbreaker, he took inspiration. He gathered the spirits of every blacksmith dwelling within this domain and built a forge, a pit of flame more fearsome than any that had ever raged before. Then, he had his army of devils tear down the Gates of Hell, so that they might be smelted into weaponry. For seven years, his damned blacksmiths hammered hell steel in the dragon's forge. In the end, they produced an armory of the most fearsome weapons imaginable. Once, the Witchbreaker was unique. Now, thousands of blades with the same power exist. Tempest then offered the most fearsome warriors ever to fall into Hell one more chance to walk the living world, one more chance to seek glory in battle. He sent them forth armed with the hell-blades, knowing that all they killed would be sent to the dark kingdom. As his army spread across the surface of the earth, the population of this place increased. To keep it from becoming unpleasantly crowded, he spread his offer to all the damned. They could leave through the gap where the gates once stood, and seize the living world for Tempest."

"This is horrible," said Slate. "How could the Divine Author allow it?"

"The Divine Author?" asked Walker. "Why blame him? Weren't you listening? *You* are the author of this calamity."

"Me?" asked Slate.

"You sent Tempest's soul here."

Sorrow stepped forward. "Slate can't be blamed for that. Tempest attacked us. We had to defend ourselves."

"If Slate isn't to blame, who is?" asked Walker. "You, perhaps?"

"How could she possibly be to blame?" asked Slate.

"Sorrow was warned repeatedly that her heedless pursuit of power would lead to ruin."

"People said it would lead to my ruin," said Sorrow. "I was hardly warned that I might be bringing on the end of the world."

"Weren't you? I told you the devils believed you were the Destroyer. I didn't see it, but I've been wrong before."

Sorrow crossed her arms. "I've made some mistakes. I'll even admit I was blinded by my hunger for power. Still, I had nothing but the best of intentions."

"Look upon the dark rocks that pave the shores of this river," said Walker. "The waters are memories. What might the stones be composed of?"

Sorrow didn't answer.

Slate spoke up. "You said… you said that the soul of Stark Tower still dwelled in this place? Is that true?"

"When have I ever said things to you that weren't true?"

"Can I… can I see him?"

"I don't believe you would find the experience pleasant," said Walker.

"I don't want this because I think it would be pleasurable," said Slate. "But… the Voice of the Book told me I'm a body without a soul. I would… I would like to look upon the soul that was once my own."

"Stark Tower's soul is trapped within a prison built from the bones of those he killed with his cruelty," said Walker. "The journey to find it would be dangerous. To actually enter the place would be unimaginably perilous."

"I don't fear danger," said Slate.

"Then let me be afraid for you," said Sorrow, placing her hand on his arm. "There's no point in seeking out Stark Tower's soul. You know he grew corrupt in life. Let him rest in the prison he built for himself."

Slate frowned, looking lost in thought.

The deck shuddered as the hull dragged on something unseen on the dark water. Walker turned to Gale and said, "This would have been a good moment to have me at the wheel. I fear you've stirred up the mud."

"We're clear of it now," she said.

"True. But the sediment will flow down the river before us. It will alert others of our travel. There are forces here who do not wish us to reach the Sea of Wine."

"Why not?" asked Gale. "I don't see what we have to do with any of this. We're Wanderers. We don't belong here, living or dead. We'll reach the Sea of Wine and be free of this place."

"Then you'll return to the living world?" asked Walker.

"Of course."

Walker grinned. "And how will you make your living in the living world?"

"After twenty years, I imagine the world has forgotten the price upon my family's head," said Gail. "We'll manage."

"Haven't you been listening?" asked Walker. "The armies of Hell have spilled across the living lands. Each night, they expand their empire. Mankind attempts to regroup during the day, when the dead dare not stir, but there's never enough time to undo the horror before night comes once more. Unless Tempest's legions are halted, there will be no safe harbor. There will be no ports where you may seek trade. All the cities of the world will be populated by the damned."

"The world's a big place," said Gale.

"Hell is a much larger place," said Walker. "There are far more dead souls than living ones."

"We've faced tough odds before and come through safe and sound," said Gale. "I refuse to think there's no hope."

"I never said there was no hope," said Walker. "You, Gale Romer, are that hope. You and your family may yet set things right in the world."

"Don't speak in riddles," said Gale. "What do you want from us?"

"I want you to reach the Sea of Wine and find the Happy Isles. There were many great warriors among the Wanderers. As residents of the Happy Isles, they've not succumbed to Tempest's temptations. Your task shall be to return with an army, that we might pull the usurper from the throne."

"You can't ask this of me," said Gale. "Those who dwell upon the Happy Isles are at peace. I won't disturb them."

"Even if their happiness is threatened by Tempest? A Wanderer slain by one of the hell-forged blades is sent to Hell as surely as a believer of the Book. The Happy Islanders won't be so happy when a generation of Wanderers who share their heritage no longer find their way to those blessed shores."

Gale looked out over the hellscape, trusting the evidence before her that Walker was telling at least a partial truth, but uncertain if she could trust him. The idea that they'd been thrown forward in time twenty years was difficult to swallow. The idea that the world could be on the verge of total destruction was even harder to believe. Yet, somehow, the sheer impossibility of the claims gave them weight. If Walker was trying to manipulate her, certainly he could easily have crafted more plausible lies. Her sons stood nearby, studying her closely.

"We'll do whatever you want, Ma," said Jetsam, floating in the air above Mako's head.

"But we shouldn't do what this pale bastard is telling us," said Mako.

"Agreed," said Rigger, moving to his mother's side. "I don't trust him. What if these demons want us to show them the way to the Happy Isles? We'd be crazy to listen to him."

"Any sane person should find everything I've said completely absurd," said Walker. "Unfortunately, sanity is poor tool for coping with the madness of these times."

Gale tightened her grip on the wheel as she studied the pygmy's face. "You swear you can guide us to the Sea of Wine?"

"I would not have told you this if it were not true."

Gale released the wheel. "Take it. Steer us there."

"Ma!" said Rigger and Mako in unison.

"I don't trust him either," she said to her sons. "But, you have eyes. We're in a place we shouldn't be. He says he can guide us from here. I'll take that chance."

"You'll have to make the voyage without me," said Slate.

"What?" asked Sorrow.

"I... I can't leave. Knowing his soul is out there... it's... it's a hunger I can't describe. I have to find it. I have to know."

"Know what?" asked Sorrow.

"Can it be redeemed? A living man may repent of his sins up to the moment of his death. I'm a continuation of Stark Tower's living flesh. If I walk the narrow path he failed to keep, might I yet save him?"

"Slate, think about what you're saying," said Sorrow. "Tower died five centuries ago. His soul has been tormented all this time, seared and scarred and picked at by devils. Would you even recognize it if you found it? There's no point in taking this risk."

Slate's face remained calm as he weighed Sorrow's words. "Until a few hours ago, you had willingly blended your body and soul with that of Rott. You, of all people, know that there are some rewards worth any risk."

"Fine," said Sorrow. "Let's go below deck and get packed."

"Packed?"

"We aren't going traipsing across Hell without at least a few supplies, are we?"

"We?" said Slate. "Why would you take this risk?"

"You just answered that two seconds ago," she said.

He crossed his arms. "I can't allow this."

"I don't recall asking your permission. I hate to get all possessive, but not even half an hour ago, you'd stopped breathing. I brought you back to life."

"Aye," said Slate. "With a kiss. And I'm grateful."

"Then show your gratitude by shutting your mouth."

Slate shut his mouth, then nodded and followed her below deck.

SORROW AND SLATE entered the hold that had served as her quarters since she'd boarded the *Circus* several weeks prior. The room was packed with the pygmies they'd rescued from the slave markets in Raitingu. Cinnamon and Poppy, Gale's youngest daughters, moved among the crowd of frightened refugees, handing out food. Brand Cooper waited just inside the door, kneeling next to a sack of dried fruit, scooping out small portions into bowls with a measuring cup.

"I noticed you'd disappeared from deck," said Sorrow.

"Being in Hell is bad," said Brand. "Being in Hell with a hundred panicking pygmies screaming at the top of their lungs would be worse. I decided they might take the news of where we're at better on a full stomach."

"That's noble of you," she said.

"I suppose. Anyway, I couldn't stay on deck. I was getting seasick."

"Seasick?" Sorrow asked. "The river's fairly calm."

"It's not the water. It's the land. Didn't you notice it was moving? The hills were rolling slowly like swells on the sea."

"I noticed," she said. "Though it didn't make me feel sick. Just terrified."

"If you're terrified, you don't need to accompany me," said Slate, who now knelt next to the pack that held his few earthly possessions.

"At least one of us should have the good sense to be afraid if we want to make it out alive," said Sorrow.

"What are you talking about?" asked Brand.

"Slate wants to search Hell to find the soul of Stark Tower."

Brand stared at her, his mouth slightly agape.

"That was my initial reaction as well," she said.

"Are you both crazy?" asked Brand.

"I think that's been established beyond all debate by this point," said Sorrow. "I don't suppose you've seen my sea chest in here, have you?"

"We put it over there," said Poppy, nodding toward the corner.

Slate retrieved the large chest, carrying it as if it weighed next to nothing. They retreated back to the hall. She had Slate put the chest into the bunk room where the Romer brothers normally slept, then told him to wait outside.

She shed the blanket that Sage had covered her with when they'd fished her naked out of the sea and knelt before the chest. She was similar in size to Sage, who'd given her a few pairs of old canvas pants weeks ago when she'd lost her serpent's tail. The worn, patched, snow white canvas contrasted with the finely tailored black silk blouse she retrieved from the chest. She dressed quickly, completing the outfit with a pair of boots Sage had given her. The chest still held a sword she'd crafted when she had power over iron, and a scabbard. She strapped these to her hip, then opened the door. Slate stood there, waiting patiently.

"I'm decent now," she said. "Come in."

"I was tempted to leave while the door was closed," he confessed. "I still doubt the wisdom of you joining me on my quest."

"Why'd you stick around?"

Slate moved toward the bunks. He dug beneath the mattress to produce a large book. "When Tempest attacked, I ran below deck to hide the One True Book. I dared not leave it behind."

"Hmm," she said, eyeing the tome. "I'm fairly certain it will fit in my leather backpack. That's all that will fit, however. Doesn't leave us a lot of room for provisions, and I'm not certain we can live off the land in Hell."

"Knights must fast from time to time," said Slate. "I'll endure."

"I've no doubt you will. I think I can go quite a while without eating as well, now that I'm getting the hang of bone magic."

"This is how you healed me?"

She nodded.

"But your other powers, over iron, glass, silver… these are gone?"

She nodded again.

"Don't you see the madness of leaving the relative safety of this ship while you are powerless?"

She placed her hands on her hip. "First, I'm not powerless. I still know a little necromancy I learned from Mama Knuckle. And bone magic is one of the most valued of the weaver arts. I'm not only good at healing wounds. I can inflict them as well. At least, I'm pretty sure I can. I admit, there may be a learning curve."

"Perhaps you could defend yourself from foes of flesh and blood, but in Hell we'll face devils… and a dragon."

"Ah," she said knowingly.

"Ah?" He sounded confused by her tone.

"You're not just hunting for Tower's soul. You're planning to go fight Tempest all by yourself."

He set his jaw, looking at her sternly.

"Don't deny it," she said. "This is exactly like you. You think you're to blame for Tempest arriving in Hell—"

"It's certain that I am."

"—so now you think it's up to you to fix it, and kill him without getting me or the Romers into danger."

"You... are correct," he said, softly. "Though you're mistaken in believing I don't intend to find the soul of Stark Tower. Before his seduction by Avaris, he was a warrior without peer. He may prove to be a powerful ally in this terrible place."

"Tower was mainly famous for killing unarmed women," Sorrow said. "I don't recall him slaying any dragons."

Slate opened his mouth to argue, but Sorrow placed a single finger lightly upon his lips to silence him. She whispered, "We can quibble about the details once we're off the boat. Mako is probably listening to us. His hearing is superhuman."

"So what if he is?" asked Slate.

"It's... I suppose it doesn't really matter. I'm sure I'm just being paranoid. Honestly, he'll probably be more than happy to see me leave the ship."

"Why?"

She looked at her feet, wondering how much to tell him. "Things... things didn't go well between Mako and myself the last time we were in private." She took a deep breath. "He made... advances."

Slate nodded. "You said he kissed you."

"I told you? Oh, right. Before we reached the Temple of the Book. Things got so crazy after that, I completely forgot I mentioned it."

"I didn't," Slate said, somewhat tersely.

"It's really nothing but a misunderstanding," said Sorrow. "I mean... I'd given him reason to think that I might be, um, receptive." She shook her head. "I didn't turn him away as tactfully as I should have. I haven't had much experience rebuffing the advances of men. I wasn't someone men found even remotely attractive."

"I assure you that isn't true," Slate said, his eyes locked upon her face.

She turned away, finding the intensity of his gaze disquieting.

"It wasn't just the fact my head was covered in nails and scars," she said. "Before you knew me, I spent over a year with half my body paralyzed. My arm and leg were withered, given motion only by the iron bracing I wore. My facial muscles on that side had atrophied. From one side, I looked like a teenager. From the other, I looked like an old woman who'd had a stroke. I was able to reverse a lot of that damage after I tapped into Rott's power, but I was still... asymmetrical. Unbalanced."

"I never noticed it," said Slate.

"I did. I stared at myself in a mirror every morning while I shaved my scalp." She ran her fingers along the baby-smooth skin of her head. "I guess I won't be needing my razor now. I wonder what I'll look like with hair. I've been bald since I was twelve."

Slate smiled. "I'm curious to learn what color your hair is."

"Me too," said Sorrow. "I've honestly forgotten."

"I must remain curious, I fear. Listen carefully to me, Sorrow. This journey before me is one I must make. Please don't endanger yourself by—"

She poked his chest with a finger, hard. "This isn't up for debate. You've fought one primal dragon, and he nearly killed you. I dealt with Hush, Glorious, Rott, and Tempest, and survived every encounter."

"But—"

"But shut up. You and I have been partners ever since I dug you out of the ground. You'd still be sleeping in a glass coffin if I hadn't found you. That means you're my responsibility. Anyway, I'm more to blame for Tempest's death than you are. You might have struck the blow that sent his soul here, but I'd torn him to pieces before that."

"With Rott's power, which you no longer have."

"I still have my wits. I still have my will. I may no longer be a dragon, but I'm still a force of nature. Do you honestly think Tempest stands a chance against me?"

Slate opened his mouth, then closed it.

"I see I have no choice," he said. "I've no doubt you would follow me at a distance if I didn't agree to your company. It's best you remain close, under my protection."

"You've got that backward. I'm staying close in order to protect you."

"Yes, ma'am," said Slate.

He offered her his large, calloused hand. She placed her small, baby-soft, newly restored palm against his and gave the firmest handshake she could muster.

4 - BAY OF BLOOD

CINDER CLIMBED THE tree and found Konoko, a village elder, and told him of the boar her mother had slain. Konoko placed his fingers between his lips and gave out three shrill bird cries, waking any members of the tribe who still slumbered. Moments later, the men set out for the berry fields, scampering across the treetops like green monkeys.

Cinder waited until they were gone, then went into her mother's hut. Ver sat in the shadows. Here in the dim light, he looked almost like a living man save for his unnatural paleness. She'd noticed that he wore white gloves, pristine as a sun-bleached shell. The flesh of his face was whiter still, adding contrast to the darkness of his eyes.

He said, in a gentle tone, "If you're ready to talk about what happened in Commonground, I'm willing to listen."

"I never said I'd tell you," she said.

"Only I can help you see the truth," said Ver. "You no doubt witnessed things in that pagan city that forever poisoned you against long-men. Commonground is not a proper place by which to judge the civilized world."

"Mother said what happened was the ultimate truth about civilization."

"Tell me the story," said Ver. "I'll gladly acknowledge if your mother is correct."

Cinder sat on the hammock that her mother slept on each night. Cinder had never mastered the art of sleeping. As far as she could tell, other people went to the edge of death each night, their minds silent, their bodies still, only to come back to life each dawn. Since she already straddled the boundary between life and death, sleep had no hold upon her.

"It happened a long time ago," said Cinder. "When my great-grandfather, Tenoba, lay near death."

"How old were you?" asked Ver.

"Twelve, I think, as a long-man would say it," said Cinder. "Pygmies don't use numbers to measure age. We would say only that I was the age where a girl transitions into a woman."

Ver nodded, listening, as Cinder told her story.

IT WAS AFTER *the season of summer storms, when the air grows cool at night. The sun was low when Tenoba called Mother to his bedside. I came with her. He told her he would die before the next full moon. He said we shouldn't mourn, for he'd lived a full life. He told her he had no regrets about leaving behind the cities of the long-men to live with the Jawa Fruit tribe.*

"No regrets?" my mother asked, perhaps sensing a tone in his voice that my young ears missed.

Grandfather chuckled at her question. "One," he admitted. "Without fire, the pygmies have never learned the art of distillation. The fruit wine they make is sweet and quenching, but I sometimes miss the harder stuff. The warmth of a good rum spreading through my chest… there are few pleasures left for a man my age. I wish I had a bottle to carry me through these dwindling days."

Mother smiled. "You really are related to Stagger, aren't you? Get some rest, Tenoba. Promise to live for three more days and you shall have your bottle."

"I'll do my best," he said, before slipping into slumber.

My mother left Tenoba's hut. I followed her and asked, "What's rum? What's a bottle?"

She gave me a wistful look. "Rum is something long-men drink. It makes them feel less pain. Bottles are… well, they're like empty gourds, only made of glass."

I opened my mouth to ask a question, but mother interrupted. "Glass is something like the shiny volcanic rocks, only clear." She shook her head slowly. "Your father would be appalled at the holes I've left in your vocabulary."

"I don't understand why I need the long-men's words at all," I said. "Who am I to speak to other than you and Tenoba?"

"You might not always live here in the jungle," she said. "Believe it or not, few people in this world speak forest-pygmy. Millions speak the silver tongue."

I was confused by her words. Though she had taught me the numbers of the long-men, I couldn't grasp how the concept of millions.

She studied my face, seeing my bewilderment. She smiled at me with wistful eyes. "I guess now's as good a time as any. I think you're ready."

"Ready for what?"

"To go to Commonground."

My eyes grew wide. "That's… that's the bad place. Why would we go there?"

"The bad place?" she asked.

"They say the forest-pygmies who disappear are taken there. They say the river-pygmies sell them to long-men. They're taken to distant lands, where they die without ever seeing their homes again."

"Ah," said Mother. "Yes. That does happen."

"Why would we go to such a terrible place?"

Mother sighed. "The world is complicated. Yes, bad things happen to forest-pygmies. Bad things happen to everyone, from long-men to ogres, even to dragons. It's just that different categories of bad things happen in Commonground than what happens here. And, it's not all bad. I knew some good people in Commonground."

"Then why did you leave?"

"Way, way, way too many people wanted to kill me," she said with a shrug. "It got a little tedious. But, hey, everyone probably thinks I'm dead."

"What if some of these people recognize you?"

"How likely is that?" she asked, holding up her hand and studying the back of it. "I'm as green as an unripe banana. No one's going to recognize me if I pop back into the city for a little visit. And if anyone tried to start trouble..." She cracked her knuckles. "I've won a fight or two in my day."

"We'd risk this for a bottle of rum? Is it truly such a magical drink?"

My mother shrugged. "I never cared for the stuff myself. But, I do care for Tenoba. We're not going there for rum. We're going there for him."

With these words I put aside my fear, and resolved to make the journey by her side.

We left an hour later, as sunset gave way to stars. My mother was dressed in strange attire, something she'd pulled from the old trunk she kept hidden in the hollow tree by the creek. I'd never seen anyone wear pants before, or a blouse, and the leather coverings on her feet, boots they were called, looked dangerous to me. How could you grasp slender branches with your toes covered? She'd left behind her hunting spear and now carried a sword in a black scabbard. Her long, flowing hair was tied back, mostly concealed by a square of black cloth she called a scarf.

She'd outfitted me as well for the trip to the city. For most of my life, I'd gone naked, like other pygmy children. As I reached the age where I was to become a woman, I'd begun to wear a loincloth, as other women do. Mother had me don one of her old leather vests, though I found it itchy and confining. She gave me a pair of her old pants as well. I was almost as tall as she was even then, but the pants were baggy. They had to be cinched up with a tight belt, which felt as if it would cut me in two if it were to snag on a branch. At least she didn't insist that I wear boots.

We made good time along well-worn paths through the jungle. I was frightened by the very ground we tread upon, for I knew that the paths were the work of river-pygmies. From time to time, I'd see their shadowy forms far off in the brush, but none approached us.

Mother sensed my fear.

"It's okay," she said. "I've got a reputation among the surrounding tribes. No one's going to mess with us. And if they do, just remember your training."

I tried to take comfort in her words, but failed. Mother had taught me to defend myself even if I was unarmed. I often pinned her when we wrestled, but I suspected she only let me win so I would feel confident. But, no matter how aggressive my mother might be with my training, I knew she'd never truly hurt me, let alone kill me. Could I really handle an opponent intent on doing me harm?

By the end of the night, I'd never been so far from home. When my mother paused to sleep in the heat of the day, I slipped into the Realm of Roots, preferring its barren silence to the buzzing, chirping, creaking and crunching jungle.

Night had fallen again by the time we reached the edge of the bay. We stood on a low bluff, looking at the city before us. I had never seen so many lights! There were uncountable ships rocking gently on the waves, all festooned with lanterns. Even from a mile away, I heard the murmur of hundreds of voices, some shouting, some singing, and the wind carried with it a multitude of new and mysterious smells. Mother said we'd arrived at high tide, which meant I was spared the worst smells the city had to offer. Instead I caught hints of pastries fresh from the oven, of meats roasting over charcoal, and of exotic spices packed in the holds of ships. Along the docks, hundreds of vendors hawked various foods that could be shoved onto a stick and fried in bubbling vats of oil.

I followed Mother along the shore to the nearest dock, then out to the city. "There's a lot here to see," she said. "But looking is all you should do. Promise me you won't touch anything."

I nodded in agreement.

Looking would be more than enough, I felt. I'd never seen such strange creatures as the long-men stumbling along the docks. I'd thought the flowers and birds of my jungle home must surely represent every combination of color possible, but there were men dressed in vests woven from threads of a dozen different colors, and women who painted their skin not in a single shade, as is the custom of pygmies, but in multitudes of hues, with crimson lips and dark green powders around sparkling blue eyes, topped with long flowing hair the color of sunshine. And the dresses they wore! I'd never imagined there could be so many kinds of fabric.

We approached a large boat festooned with flags, fields of white that sported the dark silhouette of some sort of bird I didn't recognize.

"That's a swan," said Mother. "A black swan. We had them back in the Silver City. Except they were white."

We went up a gangplank onto the huge boat. Music played on instruments I'd never before heard spilled from the swinging doors as we approached. Mother walked boldly into the room beyond without hesitating. I followed closely behind, never more than an arm's length away. The air inside was foul with acrid smoke. I feared something had caught fire, until I saw that men were placing burning rolls of dried leaves into their mouths, drawing in the smoke, then puffing it out. I had little time to be bewildered by the custom before I was confused by other things, like men sitting at tables staring at handfuls of colorful cards, and other men leaning over tables and throwing small cubes of bone. The women here made me especially uncomfortable. I'd grown up in a land where no woman other than my mother concealed their breasts. Here, all the women were clothed, but in such a way as to push their breasts up into the faces of the men who surrounded them. Their breasts were large and full, as if they were all overdue to be suckled by their babies, but there wasn't an infant anywhere to be seen. It was unthinkable that a collection of more than three or four women in the Jawa Fruit tribe could be gathered without at least one holding a child.

As strange as the long-men were, the creature behind the bar was stranger still. My mother might be called a giant by our tribe, but the beast serving drinks truly was a giant, and not a human one. His head was like that of a water buffalo, only not as shaggy, and his horns curled less. My mother walked toward the creature without hesitation.

"Hello, Battle Ox," my mother said to the beast. "It's been a while."

The beast stared at the green woman before him, then said in a deep voice, "Do I know you?"

"Let's say you don't," she said. "It's simpler that way. I'm only here do a quick transaction then get out of your hair. I need a bottle of your finest rum."

"I'm sure I've seen you before," he said, sounding distracted. "Are you that lady pirate who sailed with the South Shore Savages?"

My mother winked at the beast. "Battle Ox, what happens outside Commonground, stays outside Commonground."

"Right, right," the beast said. "Sorry." He turned and pulled down a bottle of dark fluid. "Five moons."

"Five!" my mother sounded shocked. "It used to cost only a single moon!"

"Yeah, like ten years ago," said Battle Ox. "But ever since things went to hell in the Silver Kingdom, the supply lines have tightened up."

"Things have gone to hell in the Silver Kingdom?" Mother asked. "Is… is Brightmoon still the king?"

"Last I heard. But… you know the One True Book's gone, right? The Church of the Book has collapsed. The kingdom's falling apart now that no one's afraid of Truthspeakers anymore."

"The One True Book is gone?" Mother scratched the back of her neck as she contemplated this revelation. "I wonder if Sorrow had anything to do with that?"

"How do you know Sorr– wait a minute," he said, his eyes going wide. "I knew I knew you! You're Infidel!"

"Shhhh," she said, holding her fingers to her lips.

"I thought you were dead."

"And I'd like for the rest of the world to keep thinking that."

"I can keep a secret," said Battle Ox. "But… where have you been? Why are you back? And… my memory's not what it used to be, but were you always green?"

"I'll help you keep those secrets safe by not sharing them with you," said Mother. "But look, we've always treated each other fairly. I need to buy a bottle of rum, but I don't have five moons."

"You don't have… I figured your finances would have improved now that you're not hanging out with Stagger."

Mother managed a forced half smile. "When I got back to the Isle of Fire, I only had two moons in my pocket. I haven't spent them in all these years. Can't you do an old friend a favor? The bottle for two moons?"

Battle Ox shook his head. "You know how the Black Swan watches inventory. I guess I could extend you credit…"

Mother shook her head. "I'm not coming back to Commonground for a long time. Maybe never. I don't want credit. I just want to pay a fair price and be on my way."

Battle Ox turned back to the wall of bottles behind him. He retrieved a bottle that was more than half empty. "This one's half gone. I guess I can let you have it for two moons. I feel bad about taking your last moons, though."

"No need to feel bad," said Mother. "I'm offering them to you. I'll take the open bottle. The man I'm buying for probably couldn't finish the whole thing anyway."

"I mean… well, if you're broke, I know where you can find work. The new goons aren't working out. The Black Swan has sent messengers out to look for Menagerie, but who knows if he's even still alive? She'd hire you in a second."

"Yeah, thanks for the offer, but no. I'll be fine."

Mother placed two small disks of metal on the bar. The giant slowly handed her the bottle, looking as if he was contemplating more questions. Mother took the bottle, turned, and said, tersely, "Thanks." She grabbed my hand and headed for the door.

"He recognized you," I said as we walked off the boat onto the docks. "Is he one of the people who wants to kill you?"

"No," she said. "Don't worry. I shouldn't have said anything. The kind of enemies I used to make tend to have short lives. Everything's fine. Relax. Try to think of this trip as a fun adventure."

I nodded. We headed away from the barge, down the docks back toward the shore. Gazing at the waiting jungle, I could feel the tension in my belly slacken, instantly replaced by hunger. We'd traveled a long way with little rest. While my mother had brought along dried meat and a few Jawa Fruit for rations, I'd been too nervous to have an appetite.

As we walked along the docks, we passed by rows of small shacks along the boardwalk where people were holding up food of all sorts, including one with skewers of friend monkey, bright red with spices.

All my life, my mother had told me how delicious these delicacies were, so I reached out and took one from a gray-haired, toothless man holding it toward me. I kept walking as I tore the meat from the bamboo and placed it between my teeth.

Behind me, the man started shouting. I turned to see what the commotion was and saw he was hobbling toward me, shouting, "Thief! Thief!"

He was an old man with a cane, one eye blind with cataracts. He lifted his cane as if to strike me, but as he swung, my mother's hand shot out and caught the makeshift club.

"Whoa!" she shouted. "What's your problem?"

"Thief!" the man cried, his good eye fixed on me.

My mother glanced at the red meat still dangling from my lips and cringed.

"Cinder!" she said. "What are you doing?"

"Eating?" I said, confused by the question.

"She didn't pay for that!" the man said.

A fat woman from across the dock came up and said, "It's true! I saw her steal it!" She was followed closely by a large, heavily muscled youth with the faintest wisp of a beard.

I didn't understand what the fuss was about. In my home village, there was no such thing as money. Food was food for whoever was hungry.

"She didn't know better," my mother said. "I'm sorry."

"Sorry don't pay for it," said the old man.

"Yeah," said the fat woman.

I held out the skewer to the old man, wanting to give it back. This only made him angrier.

"You've already eaten half of it!" he cried. "Payment! Now!"

"We've no money," said Mother. "Please, she meant no harm."

"No money!" the fat woman scoffed. She eyed the scabbard on my mother's belt. "That blade is worth a few coins, at least."

"The blade isn't up for barter," said my mother, crossing her arms.

"The blade!" the old man said. "She's already eaten the meal. I'll take the blade as payment!"

Mother rolled her eyes. "There's no possible economic theory where this sword and that little stick of meat have equal value."

"You should have considered that before you took something that wasn't yours." It was the large youth who spoke, stepping forward, fists clenched.

"Let's all take a deep breath," my mother said. "I'm sure we can – "

The youth lunged, grabbing for the hilt of the sword. Before my eyes could properly focus on what was going on, there was a loud SMACK and the boy was flat on his black, his nose bloodied.

My mother rubbed her knuckles and said, "Now, can we just talk? I'm willing to make a bargain. How about my boots? Where I'm heading, I don't use 'em much."

A crowd was starting to form around us. Two men even larger than the youth mother had just knocked down pushed their way through to the front of the crowd. One of them carried a large knife, still wet with blood from where he'd been butchering monkeys. The other one was unarmed, but far more menacing, shirtless and muscular, his head shaved and covered with scars. The bald one said, in a slurred voice, "What's the problem, Ma?"

"This thief stole meat from your uncle," the fat lady said. "The woman said she was going to trade her sword for the meat, but now she's trying to welsh on the deal. On top of everything else, she just broke Buck's nose for no reason!"

"I made no such trade, and Buck's nose would be fine if he kept his hands off stuff that wasn't his."

"Oh," the old man said. "So, you're saying we're in our rights to break the girl's nose? She did more than touch my monkey. She ate it!"

My mother positioned herself between me and the men. "Everyone just back off. I didn't come here looking for a fight."

"Grab them!" the fat woman screamed.

The bald man leapt toward my mother. She met his advance with a solid punch to the mouth, but his sheer mass carried him forward. They slammed down hard on the dock, with him on top. I jumped out of the way of their flailing limbs, only to have the second man grab me by the hair. I scratched at his wrist, screaming, struggling to break free. He pulled me closer to him, and brought the knife to my throat.

"I got her, Ma!" he screamed, right in my ear.

Instinctively, I went to the other place. To my shock, he came with me. He instantly released his grasp, spinning around, disoriented by the ghostly shadows that surrounded him. The once green slopes of the jungle were covered with dry and withered trees, the branches stretching up like the arms of beggars. The water around the dock was black and stank of blood.

"Where?" he asked, bewildered, stumbling as he tried to make sense of his surroundings.

I felt similar confusion. Never in my journeys to the Realm of Roots had I ever seen it look like this. It wasn't just the bay of blood that was different. The Realm of Roots was almost always vacant. Here, scores of shadowy, naked figures, men and women, young and old, stumbled along the docks, their eyes vacant, their faces slack. Some moaned, some murmured, some sobbed softly. It was nothing like the silence found in the Realm of Roots.

One of the ghostly figures, holding his hands before his face as if he were studying cards, staggered toward us, mumbling, "Fold, fold, fold." He passed through the faint forms of my mother and her bulky attacker as if they were made of fog.

The knife-wielding man shrieked as the man drew near. He swung his knife at the ghost, the blade passing through the man's torso without resistance. Off balance, he flailed his arms as he found himself at the edge of the dock. With a cry, he toppled into the blood.

I stepped back into the living world to find the second man straddling my mother, his hands around her neck. Her left arm was pinned beneath his bulk. Her face was bright red as she struggled to break his grip with her free hand.

"Get off her!" I shouted, jumping forward to punch the brute in his ear. He shifted his weight to swat me away. I tried to dodge, but even the glancing blow he landed was like being struck by a heavy rock. I fell to the dock.

Fortunately, his shifted weight freed my mother's arm. She grabbed the hilt of her sword and pulled the blade free. No one was more startled than I when the sword burst into bright orange flame with a loud WHOOSH! She struck the brute straddling her across the eyes with the flat of the burning blade. He rolled away, yipping at the pain.

Springing to her feet, my mother screamed, "Back off! Everyone back the hell off! If anyone is within ten feet of me or my daughter two seconds from now, I swear I'll gut you."

Nearly everyone ran, save for the fat woman who screamed, "Where's Newt? Where's Newt?"

Since the man who grabbed me was still missing, I guessed who she was looking for. I looked at my mother. She looked at me, and instantly guessed what I'd done.

"You can take people to the Realm of Roots?" she asked. "Why didn't you ever tell me this?"

"I didn't know!" I protested. "And… it's not the Realm of Roots. It's… someplace worse."

"The bastard deserved it," she said.

I frowned, not knowing if he did. Yes, he probably would have hurt me, but if I left him in the other place… wasn't that the same as killing him? I'd caused this whole mess by taking the meat. I didn't fully understand why it was wrong, but I did grasp that I'd broken some rule.

"I'll be back," I said, grabbing a coil of rope that lay near a mooring, then stepping back into the realm of the dead. Distantly, I heard my mother call for me to stop.

I knelt at the edge of the dock where Newt had fallen. I saw him floating in the water on his back, not struggling. His eyes were wide open. I worried he was dead. "Newt?" I asked.

I saw his eyes turn toward me.

I threw the rope to him. The coil landed on his chest. He sunk down into the red fluid that surrounded him, moving his arms lazily. More by chance than deliberate action, the rope wrapped around his wrist. I heaved with all my might to pull him toward me, dragging him close to the dock pilings.

"Can you climb?" I asked.

He didn't answer. He made no motion to try to grab the dock.

Dropping to my chest, I stretched my arm to grab his hand. There was no way I could lift him. Hopefully, his brother could.

I shifted us both back into the land of the living.

The bald man my mother had struck had tears streaming down his cheek, but his expression was one of rage rather than pain. He glared at my mother, blinking hard, his fists clenched.

"You think I'm going to let you live after this?" he said with a snarl.

"It's Newt!" I shouted, leaping to my feet and pointing toward the water. "He's drowning!"

"Newt!" the fat woman cried, running to look into the water. "Ham! Get over here!"

"Not now, Ma!" the bald man screamed.

"Newt's drowning! You gotta save him!"

"Listen to your mama, Ham," said my mother, moving to my side and grabbing me by the upper arm, squeezing so hard I winced.

"You're not going anywhere, bitch," said Ham. But instead of advancing toward us, he stepped back, to the other side of the dock. He reached down and picked up a long pole tipped with a giant hook. "I'll gut you like a damned fish!"

Mother sighed as she let go of my arm. Ham lunged, swinging the pole. Mother easily ducked beneath the hook. She rose from her crouch sliding the blazing sword between Ham's thighs. She didn't thrust hard enough to cut him, but when she pulled the blade away, Ham's crotch was on fire. He yelped and rushed to the edge of the dock, leaping into the bay.

"Save Newt while you're down there!" the fat woman yelled.

Mother gave the onlookers surrounding us a hard glower. "Anyone else want to try their luck?"

Nobody had the courage to answer that, or even to look directly at her.

The crowd parted as mother walked toward the shack where the skewers of meat were on display. She grabbed a handful, then announced, "We're leaving now."

Mother nodded for me to follow her down the dock, not bothering to look back, the burning blade still crackling in her grasp.

"Taking stuff that doesn't belong to you is wrong," she said as we put distance between us and the scene of the altercation.

"But… but you took those skewers," I said, staring at the meat in her hands.

"This is an idiot tax," she said. "It's the price they pay for me letting them live. I mean, what the hell did they think I was going to do? Just hand over the sword?"

I furrowed my brow, trying to process the wisdom she was trying to impart.

She stopped walking, sheathing the sword. She shook her head, her lips pressed tightly together. "Fine. I shouldn't have taken the skewers. I've never been able to tolerate bullies. I mean, they were just looking for an excuse to rob us."

"Should we take the skewers back?"

"Nah," she said, glancing over her shoulder. "I'm sure I didn't do any real damage to either of the guys I fought. They're dumb enough to start something if we went back. I've gone a really long time without disemboweling anyone. I'd hate to break my streak." Her eyes narrowed as she looked at the distant figures. "The guy who grabbed you. You brought him back?"

"Yes. I… I think."

"You think?"

"There was, um, something was wrong with him. He fell into the blood – "

"What blood?"

"In the other place."

Mother nodded. "The Bay of Blood," she said. "It's sort of a Hell for the lost souls of Commonground who have no place else to go."

"I saw a lot of ghosts," I said. "They did seem lost."

"The old-timer's say that if you fall into the bay, you lose your memories. You don't even remember that you're dead."

"Newt… he couldn't understand me anymore. His eyes were blank. I think… I think his mind was gone."

Mother shrugged. "He probably won't miss it."

Glancing at the black hilt by her side, I couldn't help but ask the obvious question.

"Where did you get a flaming sword?"

"This?" She patted the hilt. "Found it."

That felt like a very short origin story for such a wondrous object, but there was something in her tone that told me further questions would be useless.

"I can't believe that man got so angry that I took that skewer," I said. "People have to pay for food? The way you paid for that rum?"

"Yes."

"But… what if you don't have money?"

"You go hungry."

"Even if others have more food than they can eat? They had enough monkey to feed half our tribe."

"That's pretty much how it works in every part of the world that proudly calls itself civilized."

"Oh," I said. "I don't think that's something I would be proud of."

My mother smiled. We left the dock and climbed back up the jungle slope. When we were a good way into the jungle, my mother stripped off her clothes, starting with her boots. I took off my leather vest, my whole torso feeling raw and chafed. She cut our pants into strips to fashion fresh loincloths for us. She tossed the remnants of our clothes into the bushes. We walked on, never looking back.

AS PROMISED, VER had listened patiently to the story. His face gave no indication that he found the story remarkable, or even interesting.

He said, "I still say that Commonground is a poor representation of civilized life."

"Then… mother was wrong? In other cities, I might have eaten my fill, even though I had no money?"

Ver frowned. "No," he said. "While there are houses of charity in the Silver City, if you'd taken food from a street vendor without paying, you would be arrested as a thief. Your punishment would likely be mild, however. Perhaps nothing more than a public flogging."

"Then mother is correct when she tells me I'll be happiest here in the jungle."

Ver's eyebrows lifted, ever so slightly. "Most likely. Now that we've established that, will you come with me to the village that I may speak to the knight?"

"No," said Cinder. "If he's part of the civilized world, I want nothing to do with him. You just admitted I'll be happier if I remain here!"

"Ah," said Ver. "I understand now. You're suffering from a rather common delusion."

"And what would that be?"

"That happiness matters anything at all in this world. It's far better to bear the unpleasant burden of a truth than to be lifted by the buoyant pleasure of a lie. The truth is, you have the power to save others in need. This is now your burden. You must lift it."

"In truth," said Cinder, "I don't like you and I don't trust you. I'm not going to change my mind. Go away."

Ver nodded. "As you wish. When the world crumbles around you, and all that you love perishes, remember this as the moment when you chose not to prevent such tragedy."

With that he turned, his white-gloved hands crossed behind his back, and walked away through the wall of the hut.

5 - A PENCHANT FOR VERSE

FESTER, FUME, AND FOMENT stood on the forecastle, arms crossed, glowering at Slate and Sorrow as they returned to the deck. Slate glowered back. He tightened the straps that held the heavy pack on his back, then placed his hand upon the hilt of the Witchbreaker. The three demons crouched slightly, looking ready to pounce.

"Don't provoke them," Sorrow whispered.

"The presence of these monsters is an abomination," Slate whispered back. "I feel fury any time I gaze upon them."

"There's no need to murmur," said Walker from his position at the wheel. "The devils can read your thoughts. Whispers do nothing to protect your privacy. As for the growing rage you feel, it's only natural. These demons are flaws in the great tapestry of reality. They're things that should not be. Look upon them too long and you'll go mad."

"Then we should depart at once," said Slate. "I don't know how much longer I can stay my hand."

"Hopefully you'll manage to control your temper long enough to reach your destination," said Walker. "You'll not travel far in Hell without one of these three guiding you."

"Why do we need a guide?" asked Sorrow.

"Hell is the terrain of nightmares. The landscape here is not as obedient as it is in the waking world. A step forward might leave you behind the point where you started. You might set out to climb a hill, only to find yourself at the bottom of a canyon."

"My faith will guide us," said Slate.

Walker gave the faintest hint of a smile, then turned to Sorrow. "Perhaps you will be more receptive to reason."

"It doesn't sound as if reason is going to be of a lot of use down here," she answered.

"That is a most reasonable attitude," said Walker. "But, you've yet to answer the question. Will you accept help, freely offered? You, of all people, shouldn't fear Fester, Foment, and Fume merely because of their hideous countenances. When last we met, you were half covered in dragon skin."

"If merely looking at them would drive us mad, it sounds dangerous to have them along."

Walker chuckled. "On the contrary. A touch of madness is required to traverse this treacherous terrain. A sane man would never take a single step in this place."

Sorrow nodded. "Very well. We'll take the one that's part bird."

Slate frowned, but said nothing.

"That's Fester," said Walker. "An excellent choice."

The vulture-headed devil stepped forward. It bowed respectfully before Sorrow.

"If my looks don't unnerve you," the beast said, in a surprisingly gentle and well-mannered tone, "it's an honor to serve you."

"I didn't expect a demon to be so polite," she said.

"My brothers will envy me when I tell them your name. Your war against the Book has brought you great fame."

Sorrow looked toward Walker. "Does he always rhyme?"

"A penchant for verse is part of his curse," said Walker.

"Is it too late to pick another demon?"

"Certainly not," said Walker. He nodded toward the one with hornets for a head. "Since Fume has no mouth, he speaks via expelling gas from his bowels. With close attention, you'll soon enough understand his speech. The odor, alas, is noteworthy. As for Foment," he said, motioning toward the lion-headed demon, "he doesn't so much speak as shriek like a wounded rabbit."

"Fester it is, then," said Sorrow.

By now, the Romers had gathered round them, save for Mako, who was nowhere to be seen.

"This is incredibly dangerous," said Gale. "Suppose you do find Stark Tower's soul. Then what? How will you ever escape this place?"

"You're coming back with an army, right?" asked Sorrow.

"Who knows how long that will take?" Gale threw up her hands. "When I ask Walker how long we'll be sailing this river, he tells us, quote, 'long enough to arrive.'"

Cinnamon, Gale's youngest daughter, ran up and embraced Sorrow's legs.

"Don't go," Cinnamon said softly. "It's too scary out there."

"Don't listen to her!" said Poppy, stepping forward, plainly excited. "Slate, this is just like in the book about knights! You have to do this!"

"They might get killed!" said Cinnamon.

"You can do this, Slate," said Poppy, placing her fist in her palm. "You're a brave knight with a pure heart. Nothing can stop you!" She concluded with a crisp salute.

Slate returned the salute, then embraced the child. "I'll tell you all about my adventures when we meet again."

One by one, the Romers said their goodbyes. There were hugs and handshakes, but no tears. Wanderers never shed tears at parting; to do so was bad luck. Brand and Bigsby, however, weren't bound by the Wanderer's code. Bigsby walked away from his parting hug with Sorrow, wiping his eyes.

Brand looked into Sorrow's face long enough for her to grow uncomfortable. She took him by the arm and pulled him away from Slate, who was still talking with Poppy and Jetsam.

"I know this look," she grumbled. "You're getting ready to tell me I'm doing something stupid."

He shook his head. "I don't need to tell you. You know it already. I almost–*almost*–understand why Slate is doing this. I can't understand what's in this for you."

She glanced at Slate. "He's in it for me."

"Ah," Brand said. "Finally admitting to yourself that you're in love?"

"I honestly don't know." She crossed her arms. "I haven't had much experience with the emotion. But… back in the Temple of the Book, the Voice of the Book told Slate to kill me. Slate disobeyed."

"Isn't the Voice of the Book, like, the head Truthspeaker? How could Slate disobey?"

"One of the knights we met said that Slate possessed a greater truth. The truth is that it was more important to protect me than to obey the Voice of the Book. Then, later, when we stood before the One True Book…" Her voice trailed off.

"Yes?"

"You have to understand. I went to the Temple with every intention of destroying the Book. I wanted to tear apart everything Slate believed he was fighting to defend."

"Why wouldn't I understand that? You don't exactly keep it secret."

"Opposing the church wasn't some idle whim. It was part of my identity. When I looked in the mirror each day, I saw the face of a destroyer, and I liked it."

"Everybody needs a hobby," said Brand.

"Don't be flippant," she said. "I'm trying to tell you something important."

"Sorry," he said.

"When Slate picked up the Book and vowed he intended to save it… I couldn't harm the Book without harming him."

"Oh." he said, his eyes widening slightly, as if he suddenly understood something. He glanced over his shoulder to make sure Slate wasn't listening, then whispered, "Don't tell me you're just sticking around him until you get a second chance at the Book. I assume that's what he's carrying in his backpack?"

She shook her head. "You really don't understand. At the moment Slate took up the book, I might have killed him, and fulfilled my destiny. Yet, I couldn't harm him. He's somehow… precious to me. More precious than my dreams of destruction."

Brand nodded. "So you don't plan to destroy the One True Book?"

"I won't go that far," she said. She raised her hand to her lips and bit at her nails before catching herself, and putting her hands back to her side. "But… if what Walker says is true… is there a Church left to destroy?"

"If there isn't, that leaves you with a lot of free time on your hands."

"Walker says we were in Limbo for twenty years. Twenty! Think of all the people we knew who've died during that time."

Brand shook his head. "I intend not to think of that at all. For now, all the people I care about most are here on this ship. After my father died, I didn't feel much of a connection to my old life."

Sorrow crossed her arms. "My father may still be alive. He was over sixty when I last saw him, yes, but some men live to see a century. Perhaps… perhaps there's hope he yet lives."

"Hope? You always wanted him dead."

"No. I wanted to kill him. I wanted him to suffer for his sins, *at my hands.* Anything else would be unjust."

Brand looked around the hellscape, with its black gravel hills and pools of bubbling lava. "Hmm. I think I'm finally starting to get your true motive here."

"Caring for Slate isn't enough of a motive? Keeping close to the One True Book to ensure it doesn't return to the Church isn't enough of a motive?"

"You might hope your father's alive, but you're betting he's dead."

She didn't respond.

"And you think he's here," he said, in a tone half statement, half question.

"Is it too much to dream that he be damned to the very Hell to which he condemned witches, outlaws, and heretics?" asked Sorrow. "Perhaps hypocrites suffer greatly in this place… except this place is broken, is it not? Apparently, the damned can simply walk right out the gate." She waved her hand toward an imagery door in the distance. "I can't allow that. If my father *is* dead, he should be here, not out wandering the land of the living doing further harm."

"You have a gift for making metaphysical matters somehow personal. I do believe you'd overthrow Tempest just to ensure your father suffers eternal torment."

"Yes," she said. "I believe I would."

"And… you do see that, in a way, you'd be defending one of the central teachings of the Church of the Book? A teaching you once told me was unfair and cruel? The notion that a brief life of sin earns one an eternity of torment?"

Sorrow frowned. "Brand… you don't… I mean… I should go. You've got your own problems, helping Gale and Walker find an army. I need to get on with Slate's quest, and mine."

Brand gave her a firm hug. "Sorrow, the world would be a much duller place without you. Swear to me you'll stay alive."

"I swear."

"And promise that you won't pick a fight with Tempest in order to get your dad back into Hell," he whispered in her ear.

"I can't promise that," she whispered back.

She walked toward Slate as the knight broke free from the embrace of the younger Romers. Surveying the deck, she noticed Mako was still absent. In a way, she was relieved. She felt no hard feelings toward Mako for making advances upon her. Indeed, she felt nothing but sympathy and affection toward him. Still, it did spare her the awkwardness of having to look him in the eyes as she said goodbye.

Of course, the universe had little interest in sparing Sorrow any discomfort. As she reached Slate's side, Mako climbed up the stairs from the hold. He carried a wine bottle in his hand. The bottle was broken, the bottom neatly sheared off.

He cleared his throat as he came closer. "Leaving this ship would be suicide for most people. But, if anyone's going to survive out there, it will be the two of you."

"Thank you," she said.

"You make a surprisingly good team, considering you're natural enemies."

"Slate's not my… well I mean…" Sorrow's voice trailed off.

Slate nodded. "I know what you mean."

Mako held out the wine bottle. "I've had this for a long time. I've been below filling barrels, but now I want you to have it."

Sorrow furrowed her brow, wondering if giving a broken bottle was some sort of obscure Wanderer insult.

"Mako," said Gale. "If you give them the bottle, you might never see it again."

"I know. But, without it, we might never see them again. I doubt there's fresh water anywhere here to drink, and, unlike us, they can't carry barrels."

"What's so special about this bottle?" Sorrow asked.

Mako uncorked the bottle and tilted it. Water spilled from the mouth, splashing on the deck, and kept spilling far beyond the capacity of the bottle, even if it hadn't been broken.

"It's a bottomless bottle," said Mako.

"When we had to abandon the *Freewind*, this was one of the first items we secured," Gale explained. "It's something Mako found in the wreckage of the *Wave Wolf*. The bottle will pour any liquid you wish, and can never be emptied. For years, we've used it to keep our ship supplied with fresh water."

"Oh," said Sorrow. "Mako, this is too precious for you to give away. Your family needs it."

Mako looked directly into Sorrow's eyes. "I'm the one who found it. By the law of salvage, I may dispose of it as I wish. My family will be fine. As I say, I've filled every barrel in our hold with fresh water."

"We've a lot of thirsty mouths," said Gale. "Has anyone even got an actual count of the pygmies?"

"Rigger, you're the one good at math," said Mako. "With our stocks full, even with a hundred bellies to fill, we can be at sea for three months if we're not wasteful. Are my calculations correct?"

Rigger shrugged. "Sounds close enough. In truth, we're more likely to starve before we run out of water. We didn't stock provisions for such a crowd, and these unnatural waters can't be safe to fish."

"You always know how to put a positive spin on things," said Jetsam, floating just above Rigger.

Mako clasped his webbed fingers around Sorrow's hands, forcing her to take the bottle. "The bottle is yours. I give it freely. Your need is more immediate than ours."

Sorrow nodded, turning her gaze away from his dark eyes. Was he trying to make her feel guilty? She suspected not. She knew Mako had a fierce temper, even a touch of bloodlust, but she'd never detected any trace of cruelty, or the capacity for deceit.

She tried to put the bottle into Slate's pack, jamming it next to the One True Book. She took care not to let her fingers brush against the cover. All her life, she'd been told that the book was so holy that no living person could touch the book without being destroyed, as the purity the book would burn away their unclean flesh. She wasn't certain she believed this, but decided that she'd wait until a later time to test it. Alas, the bottle wouldn't fit. She placed it in her own pack, though the seemingly empty vessel proved unnaturally heavy, as if it held gallons.

They lightened their load by leaving behind the wineskins and canteens they'd filled to prepare for their journey, then, with a final wave goodbye, they leapt from the deck of the *Circus* as it pulled within a few feet of a steep bank. Sorrow made the leap easily, but the black soil crumbled as Slate landed in his full armor, the bank collapsing, threatening to send him into the treacherous river.

Fester, the demon, flapped his wings, lifting from the deck, swooping toward Slate. He grabbed the knight's flailing arm and carried him safely to the bank. Slate stumbled as Fester dropped him to his feet, then spun around, his hand on the hilt of his sword.

"Even though my death you'd cherish, I promise not to let you perish," said Fester.

Slate stared at the devil for a long second, then removed his hand from the sword. "Thank you."

"We shall be the best of friends, fighting to our bitter ends," said Fester.

"This rhyming is going to get tedious really fast," Sorrow grumbled, rubbing her temples. "Is it too late to take the demon who speaks by farting?"

"It is," shouted Walker, as the *Circus* pulled away from the bank. "Welcome to Hell!"

THEY WATCHED AS the *Circus* vanished around a bend in the river.

"There's no turning back now," said Sorrow.

"As any demon will plainly tell, there's never turning back in Hell," said Fester.

"I had no intention of turning back," said Slate. The muscles of his face twitched as he forced himself to keep his eyes on the devil. "Walker said you'd guide us. He also said you could read our minds. You know where I wish to go. Take us."

"Stark Tower's soul I'll help you find," said Fester. "But your lover has a different soul in mind."

"First of all, we're not lovers," said Sorrow. "Second, if Slate wants to find Stark Tower, I want to help him."

"You would find that quest a bother," said Fester. "The soul you search for is your father."

"I don't even know if he's here," she said.

"You need not fear. Of course he's here."

Sorrow felt the blood drain from her face. It was the news she'd wanted to hear, but, now that she heard it, she felt no satisfaction. "Where is he?"

"In the foul, dark valley of despair, where he chokes on poison air."

She nodded slowly. "How did he die?"

"This news, perhaps, will make you weep," said Fester. "He passed quietly in his sleep."

"After the Church of the Book collapsed? After he watched all the thought was true crumble?"

"I'm sorry, he didn't survive that long. He died before he learned the Book was gone."

"But he's still here? Why didn't he leave when Tempest opened the gates?"

"Your father has faith that sinners burn," said Fester. "He won't relent when it's his turn."

"If you want to find him first, Stark Tower can wait," said Slate.

She turned her back to the demon, wondering how he could possibly read her mind at the moment, since she herself wasn't understanding all the conflicting fragments of thought scattered through her brain. "I don't know what I would say to him that would do me any good. It sounds as if he's finally getting taught the lesson I wanted to teach him. I can only imagine his shock at going to sleep thinking himself a saint and waking up in Hell."

Fester shook his head. "Of this fact, your father knew the truth. His soul was black, and each man he hung was proof."

"He knew?" Sorrow ran her hands along her scalp, feeling as if this revelation didn't quite fit inside her skull. "If he knew, why didn't he change?"

"He traded his soul for a greater good, as you also think you should."

Sorrow turned back to Fester.

"I… I don't need to see him. I don't want to see him. Slate's mission should come first."

"I suspect this decision is one that won't rest," said Fester. "But, as you wish, we'll do your lover's quest."

Sorrow started to protest the second use of the word 'lover,' but held her tongue. It could simply be in the demon's nature to try to get a rise out of her. She wouldn't give him the satisfaction.

"Which way should we go?" asked Slate, surveying the hills around them. Sorrow looked around as well, realizing that landmarks she'd been unconsciously cataloging were already gone. The hills were moving, too slowly for the naked eye to track, but rapidly enough to rob her off all sense of direction.

"Toward the snow, we all shall go" said Fester.

"There's snow in Hell?" Slate asked, surprised.

"Since Tempest's allied himself with Hush, half his kingdom is cursed with slush."

"We really should stop asking him questions," said Sorrow. "If I listen to one more rhyme, I think I'm going to scream."

Fester said, "Screaming here would be—"

"Ahh! Just stop talking!" she cried.

"—unwise," finished Fester. "It would draw the gaze of dangerous eyes."

"Oh," she said. "Fine. I'll keep my voice down."

"Too late for that now, I fear," said Fester, gazing toward the ridge of a nearby hill. "A gibbering guardian now draws near. If we're to survive this endless night, draw your blades, for now, we fight!"

Slate had the Witchbreaker drawn before Fester finished speaking. In the living realms, whenever he drew the blade, the air was filled with the moans of the damned. Now, the weapon left its scabbard with a more earthly sing-song of metal scraping metal. Yet, as the blade's vibrations fell silent, Sorrow heard voices in the air, not from the Witchbreaker, but coming from over the hill that Fester faced.

Sorrow drew her own blade, deeply regretting her outburst. It sounded as if an army of thousands crept up the far side of the ridge. Still, while Avaris hadn't been terribly helpful in teaching Sorrow the secrets of bone magic, she knew, in theory, she could alter her body to better prepare for a fight. Bone magic focused the procreative energies of life itself. Simply by moving the energy within her body, she could will her limbs to possess ten times their normal strength and speed. With focus, she could heal any wound mere seconds after a foe struck her. But the only clue Avaris had given her to tapping the magic of her body was that the energy would build with sexual contact. This didn't seem helpful under the circumstances. Why had she ever trusted Avaris to teach her?

She set her jaw. This was no time for self-pity. She'd had no teacher for most of the magics she'd mastered. She'd figure it out. As for sexual contact… simply by kissing Slate, she'd found the power to heal his wounds following their battle with Tempest.

The crowd of voices grew louder. At any moment, their attackers would rise over the ridge.

"Slate," she said firmly. "Look at me."

He turned his head.

Before she had time to second guess herself she stood on her tiptoes, grabbed the back of his neck, and drew his face toward hers. As their lips pressed together, she felt nothing but pressure. Her lips lingered for several seconds, with each second growing more awkward. If this was supposed to spark some magical energy within her, it had failed.

Then, Slate wrapped an arm around the small of her back, and his lips, unprepared for her initial assault, moved to match hers. What had been little more than a collision of lips swiftly transformed into a genuine kiss. A pleasant warmth spread through her.

Slate drew his face away, loosening his grip on her waist. He was smiling, plainly pleased with her actions, but with more than a trace of confusion in his eyes.

"Can't a lady kiss her knight to wish him luck?" asked Sorrow.

"Aye," said Slate, as he turned his eyes back toward the ridge, to the legion of voices. "For luck."

Sorrow focused on the warmth still filling her, then, despite herself, she shivered. The energy swirled within her, almost impossible to hold. She closed her eyes, thinking of Slate's face. She focused on the way his arm had brushed against her back, of how strong he'd seemed, of how right it had felt for his arm to be there. Still, the energy faded, sputtering, nearly gone.

Though she made no conscious choice to do so, her memory shifted, not to the kiss that had occurred only seconds ago, but to the first time she'd touched Slate, when he'd crawled naked from his glass coffin and fought a dragon with his bare hands. In the aftermath, she'd cleansed his wounds, and stitched them, her fingers exploring every inch of his perfectly-muscled body. Her eyes had lingered a long time on his face, all covered in long whiskers, his hair like a lion's mane. He'd looked like a wild beast, and, though she'd never have admitted it, his masculine scent had stirred an animal hunger within her.

She opened her eyes. The warmth was back. Her sword felt light in her hand. She felt swift and strong and tough, ready for anything.

Then the gibbering guardian crested the ridge. She learned that one is never quite prepared for Hell.

6 - Immaterial Material

THE DEAD MAN was back, floating beside her, his gloved hands clasped behind him.

Cinder ignored him, focusing instead on the thorny blood-tangle vines she slowly climbed. With careful movements and a little luck, she could reach the beehive in the hollow of the trunk above her without needing to pluck barbs from her feet and hands for the rest of day.

Ver cleared his throat. "There's an urgent situation that requires your attention."

Cinder said nothing, continuing her climb. Until a few years ago, raiding hives had been the work of older boys. Enduring the stings was a test of manhood. But, Cinder's ebony skin gave off a slight smoky scent. Insects never lighted upon her. Since she'd been old enough to climb the highest trees, she'd become the chief honey gatherer for the Jawa Fruit tribe. Whenever she returned to the village with loads of fresh honey, even the girls her age who hated her most would greet her with a smile.

Cinder carefully stepped from the vine onto a thick limb jutting from the tree. Ordinarily, a limb like this would easily support her weight, but the bees had chosen this tree because it was hollow. The branch might be connected by mere inches of healthy wood. A few extra pounds might cause the branch to tear free.

She stood still, her arms spread for balance, as she focused on the bark beneath her toes. It felt solid enough.

"It's rude to pretend you don't hear me," said Ver.

"It's ruder to keep bothering me after I told you to go away," she said, inching closer to the hive. The vibrations of her movements traveled through the branch and sent a tornado of angry insects swirling from the black hole in the trunk. The bees darted toward her, then veered off sharply, as if bouncing off some invisible wall.

"I understand you won't help set things right in Hell," said Ver. "I've no illusions you'll change your mind. Your mother possessed legendary stubbornness. You've inherited this trait."

"Can't you see I'm busy?" she asked, pressing her ear against the trunk. From the sound of the buzzing within, the hive extended down several feet from the hole. This would keep her tribe supplied for weeks.

"There are more urgent matters than collecting honey," said Ver.

"Have you ever had honey?" she asked, gripping the bark and scooting up to the hole.

"As a child," said Ver. "Truthspeakers are forbidden to eat such things. Sweets are one of the seventy-seven false pleasures that lead men to ruin."

She thrust her arm into the trunk and dug her hand into the hot honeycomb. The wax squished between her fingers.

She pulled out her hand, flicked away the few bees stuck to the surface, and took a bite.

"False pleasure? Mother said your religion was crazy." She spoke with her mouth full as she chewed the honeycomb. "If this isn't genuine pleasure, I don't know what is."

Ver shook his head. "The seven genuine pleasures are prayer, study, service, charity, fidelity, obedience, and truthfulness. Pleasures of the senses lead men to their doom."

She took another bite. "Honey will lead to doom." She rolled her eyes. "I'll never doubt my mother again."

"Yet, it's never truer than at this moment. As you stand here licking your fingers, you bring a good and innocent soul closer to death."

Cinder smirked. "I can't imagine how my enjoying a little honey can possibly hurt anyone."

"As we speak, a knight from the nearby settlement fights for each breath. I alone am aware of his peril. You alone have the power to save him."

"What are you talking about?" Cinder asked, bewildered.

"When last we spoke, I told you there was a knight of pure heart who lived in the settlement. His name is Luminous Mantle. This morning, Mantle ventured into the forest with a band of hunters, searching for game to help stock the larders of the settlement."

"Mother says that knights avoid useful work whenever possible. Are you sure this one's helping feed his village?"

"Your mother again has given you a false view of the world. In previous forays into the forest, hunters have faced harassment from your tribesmen. Mantle is along to protect them."

"Perhaps these hunters deserve harassment, or worse," said Cinder. "They intrude upon hunting grounds pygmies have carefully cultivated over centuries. However, it's not my tribe that's fighting the long-men. Jawa Tribe territory ends at the berry fields. The long-men are encroaching on the Spike Branch tribe. The Spikers are terrible people, but they can't be blamed for defending their territory from poachers."

Ver gave the faintest hint of a smile. "Then your claim pygmies share their food freely was a lie?"

"No," she said, wiping her sticky fingers against the bark. "The Jawa Fruit tribe takes care of its people, and the Spike Branch tribe takes care of their people, and… look, it's not the same as what the long-men do. In any case, don't blame my people for what the Spikers do. Our tribes have been at war since long before I was born."

Ver nodded. "I haven't come to place blame for Mantle's current peril. I wish only to save him."

"From what?"

"Since the hunters would be ineffective if they remained too close together, they split into teams of three, with Mantle remaining at a central camp. One of the trios was led deep into the jungle by the clucking of tree hens. From my spiritual vantage point, I could see the sounds they followed were made not by birds, but by pygmies. The small men were camouflaged among the greenery. The hunters never suspected their peril."

"That's unfortunate for the long-men," said Cinder, shaking her head. "The elders say that the Spikers are cannibals. Mother told me it wasn't true. She says every tribe in the jungle thinks their neighbors eat men, while their own tribes are too virtuous to do so."

"Which do you believe?"

Cinder shrugged. "My mother says she's traveled all over the island, but the elders have lived in the jungle a long, long time. Maybe the Spikers don't really eat people, but I still keep clear of them."

Ver nodded. "I cannot state with any certainty that the Spike Branch tribe are cannibals," he said. "I can testify that they led the hunters into a clearing filled with snares and nets, capturing two of them. Only one escaped, though grievously wounded by a spear. He fled to the camp to warn Mantle of the attack. The knight boldly set forth to rescue them."

"By himself?"

"Mantle has few peers when it comes to speed. No one can match him in a sprint, and his enemies seldom land even a glancing blow in battle. Alas, with his speed, he sometimes acts before thinking about consequences. When he abandoned the hunters who'd returned to camp at the sound of the wounded man's alarm, Mantle left them vulnerable to capture. He was too far away to hear their cries of surprise, and too focused on the path he'd discovered, a muddy track along which the first captives had been dragged, kicking and struggling, into the dark reaches of a ruined temple."

"A temple?" Cinder asked. "Forest-pygmies never go into those ruins. Mother says the old places are harmless, but on this, I agree with my tribesmen. It's an unnatural thing to voluntarily go beneath a roof of stone. Stone belongs beneath one's feet, not above one's head."

"The Spike Branch tribesmen do not share your taboos," said Ver. "They'd no qualms about using the ruins to trap the long-men sure to come looking for their captured brothers. The pitch black interior of the temple concealed an ancient cistern, very deep, with sheer and slippery walls. The pygmies crossed the cistern with the aid of a bamboo ladder that spanned the gap. But after crossing, they positioned the ends of the makeshift bridge directly on the lip of the pit. When the knight followed, the bamboo bent, dropping him into the cistern. As we speak, he floats within the dark, deep waters. His fingers find no purchase on the smooth stones that line the pit. He's shed his armor and weapons to be able to float, but it's only a matter of time before he drowns."

Cinder put her hands on her hips. "What does this matter to me?"

Ver stared into her face. She felt her left eye twitch.

"I mean, the long-men would be safe if they didn't go where they weren't wanted," she said.

Ver continued to stare at her.

She shifted her weight from one foot to the other, then back again, unnerved by his silence. "Aren't you going to say something?"

"What is there to say?" he asked. "Your brusque protests against caring reflect what you've learned from your mother. However, I've been a judge of men's souls for a very long time. You don't need me to tell you right from wrong. In your heart, you know you have the power to save a fellow man from unnecessary death. You believe yourself to be a good person. Now, we shall both discover if that is true."

"Fine." Cinder said, throwing up her hands. "I'll go tell Mother. She'll know what to do."

"That would be unwise," said Ver.

"No it wouldn't. The Spikers are terrified of Mother. She'll be able to reach the temple safely."

"They fear your mother because she's slaughtered dozens of their brethren. But, as you say, the Spikers are merely defending their territory. You could reach the temple safely on your own, without any blood being spilt," said Ver.

"She'll never let me go. She tells me to stay away from Spikers and long-men. I don't see why she'd change her mind now." Cinder shook her head. "Of course, she does things all the time that she tells me I shouldn't do."

"When I traveled at your mother's side, for most of our journey she wore a disguise. If she says one thing then does another, her words are a disguise for her true values. If you save this knight, she'll hold you in high regard within her heart, no matter what she might say about it."

Cinder bit her lip, weighing his words. If her mother was seen crossing into Spiker territory, it might provoke skirmishes that would lead to the deaths of warriors from both tribes. Still, she didn't share Ver's faith that her mother would secretly approve of her saving the knight.

She glanced at the sun. If she left for Spiker territory now, it would be dark when she arrived. At night, her black skin made her all but invisible. Rescuing the knight sounded simple. All she needed to do was lower a vine into the cistern, make sure he climbed out, then slip away. He would never even see her. She could return home without her mother knowing what she'd done.

"I'll do it," she said softly, looking around as if expecting her mother to be hiding just out of sight. "But only if you swear you'll leave me alone afterward."

"I give you my word," said Ver.

IN THE MOONLESS dark, Cinder followed Ver along the game paths that wound beneath the tree top villages of the Spike Branch tribe. She could hear the Spikers in the canopy, their conversation little more than murmurs punctuated by short chuckles.

She cringed, pressing her back against a trunk, as a shriek like a wild animal came from overhead. The cry died off, replaced with raucous laughter.

"What's so funny?" she whispered to her ghostly companion.

Ver looked up, studied the shadows, then shook his head. "The pygmies amuse themselves by tormenting the long-men they've captured."

Cinder held her breath, listening closely. She could hear weeping, the deep-throated sobs of long-men. One babbled, begging for mercy. His weakness was met with more laughter.

"Savages don't show the respect for prisoners that is the custom of civilized men," Ver said, his voice dripping with disgust. "They live so far beyond the truth that the pain of a fellow man amuses them."

She clenched her fists. "My people would never be so cruel."

"Perhaps. But they tolerate the cruelty of their neighbors. The Church of the Book never turned a blind eye to wickedness. We sought to bring the truth to the far reaches of the world."

"Let's keep moving," she whispered, wanting to get beyond the horrible sounds from above. "How much further?"

"Not far," said Ver. "Come."

They ascended a steep hill to reach a landscape of vine-draped boulders. She took note of the blockish shapes of the stones and realized they moved among one of the countless ancient ruins hidden within the thick vegetation of the Isle of Fire. Tenoba had told her tales of the Vanished Kingdom, and she sometimes imagined what the island must have looked like long ago. Once, the forests had been trimmed and tamed, the land thick with cities from the highest ridges of the mountain all the way down to the shores.

Ver's ghost walked through a veil of vines. Taking a deep breath, she slipped through into the dark interior of an ancient building. She eyed the stone ceiling carefully, worried it might collapse at any second. After a moment, she accepted that it wasn't likely to fall and allowed herself to look around the rest of the interior. Ver had called the place a temple, but Tenoba had told her that no one really knew the true purpose of the old buildings. What modern men might label a temple could perhaps have been a granary. In the darkness, she had no way of judging the function of the place, or even its full size. The only thing she could see clearly was Ver's pale form, glowing faintly with spiritual light.

He moved forward a few dozen yards, then turned.

"The lip of the cistern is directly beneath me. Take care as you approach. The drop is nearly one hundred feet."

"Do I even need to approach?" she asked. "Is the knight still alive?"

"Hello?" a voice called out from the darkness. The word echoed, as if rising from a deep pit. "Is someone there?"

She didn't answer. She'd been careless, forgetting that while no one but her could hear Ver, anyone in the living realm could hear her.

"Can hear me?" the voice cried out, "Beware! There's a deep pit before you!"

She glanced through the veil of vines at her back. If the knight kept shouting, the Spikers might hear him. But, she'd come too far to run away now. Using her spear to tap the stone before her, she crept forward, stopping before she reached Ver's floating form.

"I've come to help," she said into the pit, her voice barely a whisper.

"Who are you?" the voice asked, now clearly coming from below. "You speak the silver tongue, but strangely."

"Who I am isn't important," she said. "Now, please, stop shouting. The Spikers will hear you."

The voice below chuckled. "I'd rather die in a hail of spears than freeze to death."

She noticed for the first time the shiver in the man's voice. It was cool within the cave, but hardly freezing.

"The water below is untouched by sunlight," said Ver. "It soon drains a man all warmth. You must act swiftly."

She nodded, the said into the pit, "I'm going to go cut vines. We'll get you out in a moment."

"We? Is someone with you? Who are you?"

"Hold on," she said. "I'll be back."

She moved to the veil of vines. Freeing her obsidian knife from the pouch on her loincloth, she cut loose several strands. Working as quickly as she could in the darkness with her sharp blade, she trimmed the thorns from the vines, then knotted the ends together. Having lived her whole life in trees, tying knots that wouldn't slip was a fundamental survival skill.

She crept back to the pit, pausing when her tapping spear fell upon open air. She crouched, feeling the edge with her fingers. Assuming Ver was right about the drop being one hundred feet, she had more than enough vine for the job. She'd anchored the far end around a sturdy boulder just beyond the doorway.

"Watch out," she whispered. "I'm throwing down a rope."

Without waiting for his reply, she tossed the looped vine. It whispered through the air, then splashed in the unseen water. The echoes seemed loud as thunder in her stony surroundings. If the Spikers heard, her rescue would be in vain.

She felt the line grow taut.

"I'm ready," the man below said, sounding weary. "Pull."

"Pull?" she said. "You'll have to climb."

"The cold has robbed me of strength," the man said. "It took all I had to wrap the rope round me. You must pull."

Cinder set her jaw. Among the pygmies, she was considered quite strong, but she had little hope of lifting a grown man on her own.

"We should have told mother," she said to Ver. "Between the two of us, we might lift him."

"Certainly you're not giving up when you're so close to saving him?"

Cinder looked around. In the darkness, she couldn't spot anything she might loop the vine around for better leverage. Perhaps, come morning, there would be sufficient light to work by. Would the man survive that long?

Ver still floated in the thin air above the pit. He cleared his throat, which struck her as strange, seeing that he didn't actually breathe.

"What?" she asked.

"You possess a gift far better than a mere rope. Why not use it to save him?"

She frowned.

"You have the power to take others with you as you cross between the lands of the living and the dead."

She still wasn't following him.

He looked down at his feet. His white boots rested on nothing at all.

"What are you saying?" she asked. "That I can float like you?"

"Some souls within the spirit realm remain earthbound, but only by force of habit. You may freely walk anywhere you wish, whether deep below ground, or high in the clouds."

She furrowed her brow. The whole idea seemed absurd. On the journeys she'd made to the Realm of Roots, she'd always stood upon what felt like solid ground. Still, Ver wasn't the first ghost she'd ever witnessed who could walk upon the air.

"Take my hand," he said, holding it toward her. "I'll teach you."

She stared at his bony fingers. Was this a trick? But a trick to what end?

"What's happening?" asked the voice from below. "Are you still there?"

"Hold on," she said.

"Please hurry," he said, his voice sounding weaker even than it had a moment ago.

"His inner fires grow cooler with each breath," said Ver. "If you don't choose to save him now, you may find yourself explaining your delay directly to his phantom."

She stretched out her hand. She closed her eyes on the material world and opened them in the Realm of Roots. Ver's hand closed around her fingers. His grip was the coldest thing she'd ever felt.

She looked around. Ordinarily, the Realm of Roots was much darker than the living world. But in the tomb-like darkness, the stone surrounding her possessed a ghostly radiance. She saw her surroundings clearly for the first time. The pit before her was twenty feet across and quite deep. She hesitated as she reached the edge, leaning over only slightly, still fearing she would topple. A bright glow rose from the depths, as if a fire burned on the water. With her free hand, she shielded her eyes as she gazed down.

The fire proved to be a man. Until now, her mother's spirit had been the brightest soul she'd ever seen. It was a mere candle compared to the bonfire spirit of the man below.

"He's so ... I've never..." Her voice trailed off, the wondrous light robbing her of words.

"What you look upon is a virtuous soul," said Ver. "They're rare and precious things. If he'd been a Knight of the Book, Mantle might have turned back the tide of darkness that washes over this world."

She furrowed her brow. "Doesn't the purity of his soul prove your church wasn't in possession of the only truth?"

Ver shook his head. "Pure souls may exist even among pagans and schismatics. His mind may embrace a falsehood, but his heart leads him along a righteous path."

Cinder still had her feet on the stone floor. It felt solid. She felt solid. She looked at the open air beneath Ver's sandals and shook her head.

"I can't do this," she said.

"Certainly you can, my child," he said. "Here, all that you see or feel or touch is pure spirit. The stone and the air, my body and yours, are all the same immaterial material. Step forward, and have faith."

She took a deep breath, held his hand, and moved her foot over the open space. Exhaling, she stepped forward, to stand upon nothing.

She looked down, grasping the implications of her new power immediately. "This is certainly going to be helpful when I'm gathering honey."

"How practical of you," said Ver, still holding her hand. "Now, follow." Hand in hand, they walked down toward the water as if descending an unseen staircase. They stopped when they reached the water of the cistern. The dark liquid felt like yielding sand between her toes.

The knight still clung to the vine she'd tossed down, his wrist entwined in the vegetation. His eyes were closed, his teeth chattering, his head resting on his shoulder as if he no longer had the strength to lift it. Though his internal light still burned brightly, she could see his skin was pale, almost blue.

She stepped forward, letting go of Ver, and willed herself back into the living world. She gasped as she splashed into the cold water.

Though she knew the knight was mere feet before her, she could no longer see him. The darkness disoriented her, and she took a gulp of water as she tried to breathe. She coughed violently, then went still as icy fingers closed around her wrist.

"Don't tell me you fell in," the knight said through chattering teeth. "I can't bear the thought that I've led you to your death."

"We're not dead yet," she said, pulling him closer. She shifted back into the spirit world, carrying the knight with her.

His eyes grew wide. "I see you." He looked around, at the faintly glowing walls, until his eyes fixed upon Ver's ghostly form.

He stared at his own glowing fingers. In the faintest of whispers, he asked, "Am I… dead?"

"No," said Cinder. "Come. Walk."

She climbed from the spirit waters, her feet finding purchase where her mind wished. Less than a minute after discovering her power, if felt perfectly natural, as if she'd known how to do this all her life. But the knight wouldn't move his legs and he proved difficult to lift. Spirits might be weightless, but it didn't mean they couldn't be heavy.

Ver came to her side and draped the knight's arm across his shoulder. Together, he and Cinder climbed back up the invisible steps. The knight didn't struggle, saying nothing, his head turning from side to side, his eyes unfocused. Perhaps he imagined he was dreaming.

They reached the stone floor above and laid him down. With a thought, she and the knight moved back into the living world. Darkness embraced her once more.

"You still alive?" she asked, shaking the knight's shoulder.

"I d-don't know," he said with a groan.

"Think you can walk?" she asked, as he shivered violently beneath her fingers. "It's warmer outside."

"I'll t-t-try," he whispered.

Her eyes had adjusted sufficiently to the darkness that she could see the entrance to the structure as a rectangle of dark gray against a background of pure black. She helped the knight rise. With his arm draped over her shoulder, they stumbled forward.

The jungle night proved warmer than the damp air of the ruins, but the breeze set the knight's teeth chattering louder than ever. She helped him sit on a rock. After only a second he fell to his back, completely limp. If not for his chattering teeth, she might have thought him dead.

She wished she had pelts to drape over him. He wore no clothes save for a pair of thin cotton britches. If he'd come out here with boots, they'd apparently been shed.

She'd lived her life in a village where clothes consisted of nothing more than the loincloths worn by women and the gourds worn by men. Nudity held little interest for her, but she'd never been able to study a long-man in such a state of undress. He was well-muscled and impossibly tall, easily six foot, if not taller. His skin was white as foam upon the waves.

Still disoriented by his ordeal, he had yet to fix his gaze upon her for any length of time. He moved his arms feebly without opening his eyes, until his finger closed around a dried, dead vine. The leaves crunched as he pulled it free from the rock. With a grunt, he struggled to sit up, succeeding at last and crossing his legs. Opening his eyes, he gathered every leaf and twig within reach, gathering them into a mound before him.

"What are you doing?" she asked.

"Starting a fire," he answered.

"With what?" she asked. Her mother had taught her how to start fires with a bow, but the man had no cord.

"Prayer," he said. He lowered his head, cupping the driest leaves in his hands, and whispered, softly, "Dear Lord of the Flame, Bringer of Heat, Guardian of the Foundry, you are hallowed in my heart. If it be your will, oh Lord, grant me a spark, that your Sacred Flame my warm my limbs once more."

Cinder's eyes grew wide as tendrils of smoke rose from the dried leaves. A pale flame flickered, then spread, like a delicate yellow butterfly opening its wings. The knight lowered the flame down onto the bed of leaves, then began to feed it twigs.

"It's a pity," Ver said, shaking his head. "Such a good man, seduced by a false faith."

Cinder had bigger worries than the man's religion.

"The Spikers will smell the smoke," she whispered. "Put it out."

The knight shook his head, rubbing his water-puckered fingers over the small fire. "Let them come. I don't fear them."

"You should," said Cinder. "They're torturing your fellow long-men. We need to leave as soon as you can get to your feet."

The knight frowned. "If my brethren are being tortured, this is all the more reason to stay."

"They'll kill you," she said.

He gave a grim smile. "They can try. I'm a Knight of the Flame, in the presence of a fire. Though greatly weakened by my time in the water, I won't dishonor the Lord of Flame by retreating now that he has graced me with his spark. We're in no danger. Those who dwell in darkness fear the fire."

She gazed up into the surrounding trees, feeling distraught. Had she saved him from the cistern only to witness him commit suicide?

He looked at her, studying her closely, as if seeing her for the first time.

"You speak with the accent of a forest-pygmy," he said. "Yet, plainly, you're human, though oddly colored. Why have you dyed your skin this shade?"

"It's not dyed." She found his presumption somewhat rude. "And of course I'm human. So are pygmies."

"Some people have this opinion," he said, nodding. "I've no basis for arguing it, I suppose. But, if they're fellow men, they've proven unreasonably hostile to our presence."

"Does that surprise you?" she asked. "If river-pygmies paddled their canoes across the great waters and built homes at the edge of the Silver City, would they be welcomed with open arms?"

He shook his head. "I suppose they wouldn't, though the question is now moot. From what the most recent arrivals tell me, that once great city has fallen to Tempest's legions of the damned. Save for the Wanderers, the people of my village may be the last living men."

Cinder suspected this news would be of interest to her mother, though how she'd ever tell it without revealing she'd spoken with a long-man she couldn't imagine. She continued to study the surrounding trees, looking for any moving shadows, listening hard for any rustle that might betray approaching Spikers.

"I may know of your mother," said the knight. She looked at him, and found he was staring at her with an unblinking gaze. She crossed her arms over her breasts, though they didn't seem to be his focus. He studied her face carefully, then asked, "There's a woman who once lived in Commonground. A mighty warrior, and infamous heretic. Her name was once a curse on the lips of every worshiper of the Church of the Book. She was called Infidel."

Cinder said nothing.

"It's said she went to live among the pygmies," he said. "And that she was pregnant, with a child conceived in Greatshadow's spiritual presence."

"She sounds like an interesting woman," said Cinder.

"You're her child?" the knight asked, in a tone balanced between a question and a statement.

Cinder didn't answer.

"You may tell me without fear," said the man. "Infidel may be a heretic to the Church of the Book, but within the Church of Sacred Flame, she's honored as a saint. Our Great Lord lives because of her mercy."

Cinder's mouth opened slowly as she finally grasped exactly who the Lord of Flames had to be. "You worship Greatshadow?"

The man held his finger against his lips. "His divine name shouldn't be uttered idly. It's to be used only in a house of worship, or within a foundry. But, you're Infidel's daughter, aren't you? I didn't dream that you and a ghost carried me from that pit. I passed through the land of the dead to return to the living realm, did I not?"

"If you know so much, I don't see why you need me around to answer questions," said Cinder, looking at the fire he'd stoked into a sizable flame. "I should go. You should go too. If you linger here, you'll be dead before dawn."

He grinned. "I appreciate your concern." Then, to her surprise, he shifted his weight onto his knees and used his bare hands to extinguish the fire.

"Because I believe you're Infidel's child, I obey," he said. "You're the daughter of a saint. You may regard me as your faithful servant." He kept his eyes on her feet now, as if it would be an offense to look into her face. He asked, "Will you grant me the honor of telling me your name?"

She looked at the last glowing remnants of the fire, at the black lines among the pale red embers.

"Cinder," she said. She saw no reason to hide her name. If word got back to her mother that a young woman with ebony skin had rescued a knight by carrying him through the Realm of Roots, she could hardly hope to be mistaken for someone else.

"Since becoming a Knight of the Sacred Flame, I've taken the name Luminous Mantle. I'm yours to command, Cinder."

"Fine. I command you to leave here at once," she said. "We're lucky the Spikers haven't seen us yet."

"Not so lucky," said Ver, his eyes scanning the treetops. "With the fire gone, they've no reason to hide any longer."

Cinder looked up, saw the moving shadows, and knew it was too late to flee through the forest. She'd have to go once more into the Realm of Roots.

Before she could grab hold of Mantle, she heard a whisper in the air.

"Spear!" cried Ver.

She phased from the living world an instant before the spear sliced through the space where she stood.

There was a cry behind her. She spun around to see Ver struggling as black vines, writhing like snakes, rose from the stones he stood upon to entrap him.

She drew her knife, stepping forward to cut him free, when a pygmy stepped in front of her. He was covered in scars in the shapes of leaves and wore a headdress made of parrot feathers. He held the thighbone of a long-man in his right hand, pointing it toward her.

"You're the child shaman of the Jawa Fruit tribe," he said, in his harsh, barking Spiker accent. "I hope you breathed deeply before leaving the living world. You shall return there no more."

7 - BROTHER WING

CINDER'S OWN TRIBE had a shaman, of course, Ganak, the Silent One. It was said he, too, could traverse between the lands of life and death, but she'd never encountered him during her visits to the Realm of Roots. Nor did she often see him in the living world; Ganak lived in a hollow tree on the furthest edge of the village, and seldom mingled with the other members of the tribe.

This Spike Tree shaman looked much younger than Ganak and far more muscular as he waved the thigh bone at her, chanting deeply in a language she'd never heard. The black roots that covered the rocks snaked up her legs with alarming speed, squeezing like a boa. In seconds, she'd be as trapped as Ver.

Unlike Ver, she had an escape route. With a thought, she left the Realm of Roots for the living lands. The entangling vines faded like smoke. Of course, now she had other concerns, like the score of pygmy warriors swarming toward the boulder where she stood next to Mantle. In the brief seconds she'd been gone, the ground had sprouted several dozen spears. Somehow, all had missed Mantle. Did all Spikers have such bad aim?

She formed a second theory as to how the spears had missed an instant later, as Mantle leapt from the boulder toward the onrushing pygmies, fists clenched. He moved with a swiftness she'd never witnessed, showing no sign of weakness. Either the fire had revived him more than she would have thought, or the call to battle gave him new strength.

A pair of pygmies met his charge, swinging clubs spiked with jagged shards of obsidian. Mantle grabbed a low vine, lifted himself above the swinging bludgeons, then kicked out, catching both attackers in the face. He dropped to the ground as they fell, snatching their clubs in each hand.

By now, more pygmies had closed in. Mantle moved gracefully through his attackers, avoiding their blows. With every swing of his clubs, pygmies fell with caved in skulls and crushed ribs. He wasted no motion, with each foe falling from a single impact.

Cinder stood with her jaw agape. Not even her mother fought this well.

Nor, she remembered, could she, as a trio of Spikers ran toward her. She dared not slip back into the Realm of Roots while the shaman lay in wait.

Setting her jaw, she plucked up a spear embedded in a root by her foot and hurled it at the closest pygmy. He swatted it away with his club, but before he could recover from his swing she lunged, her obsidian knife in hand, and sliced across his throat with all her strength, just as her mother had trained her.

Her first foe fell, but now the second was upon her, swinging his club. Cinder tried to dodge but he struck her in the hip. The stone spikes dug into her flesh, knocking her from her feet. As she fell, by pure luck her legs tangled in his and he tripped. Off balance herself, she slashed out with her knife, catching him in ribs, the knife biting deep. He screamed and rolled away, taking her knife with him, but leaving his fallen club at her fingertips. She grabbed it and lifted it just in time to block the blow of the third pygmy. He raised his weapon to strike again but she swung first, catching him in the knee, the obsidian spike punching down to bone. He gave a yelp as he fell sideways, writhing in agony. Cinder put an end to his pain with a sharp, hard blow to his nose.

She lay back, panting, her eyes searching for the next attack. She spotted no one but Mantle, a club in both hands, bodies scattered in a circle around him. He panted hard, his eyes probing the shadows as he tracked the remaining pygmies who now fled for their lives.

"Are you all right?" he asked, cutting his eyes toward her.

She bit her lip to keep from crying as she looked at the blood running from the gashes in her hip. Mantle ran to her side, kneeling, pushing aside her bloodied loincloth to examine the wound. His fingers, so cold when she'd pulled him from the water, felt like hot coals upon her flesh.

He tore off a strip of cotton from his own leggings and wiped the blood from her skin. He probed her flesh, pressing hard, causing her to gasp.

"It doesn't feel as if any of the stone remained inside," he said. "Nor are any bones broken. Do you think you can stand?

She nodded. With a grimace, she rose, holding his hand for balance. She took a step forward, feeling dizzy. The forest spun around her. Mantle caught her as she fell and helped her sit again.

"How far is it to the territory of your people?" he asked.

"Several miles," she said. "Why?"

"I should take you there at once. They can tend to your injuries."

She shook her head. "I don't think that would be a good idea."

"Why?"

Showing up wounded was already going to lead to a difficult conversation with her mother. Showing up carried by a knight would compound the unpleasantness of that conversation. Still, she felt embarrassed to tell this man that she was afraid of her mother.

"Uh," she said. "My people are cannibals."

Mantle looked skeptical, but didn't argue. "Then we must hide you while I rescue the hunters."

"Rescue them? Do you have a plan?"

He nodded. "Now that they know I'm not to be trifled with, I'm hoping they'll listen to reason."

"I'm not sure the Spikers are all that reasonable," she said. "Do you even speak forest-pygmy?"

He shook his head. "Perhaps one among them will speak my language."

"Take me. I can translate."

Mantle looked surprised by her offer. Cinder felt surprised herself. But, despite her injuries, the battle had left her feeling strangely invigorated. She could see why her mother had once been addicted to such dangers.

"I can't accept your offer," he said. "You'd be in great danger."

"I can't possibly get into deeper danger than I already am," she said, still thinking of her mother.

"Very well. Perhaps keeping you in my sight is a surer way to guarantee your safety than trying to hide you on enemy territory." Without asking permission, he slid his hands beneath her knees and back and picked her up as if she were a small child. She instinctively wrapped her arm around his shoulder to balance herself.

He glanced up at the trees. "You got me out of a pit with your magic. Can you take me up into their village?"

"I don't think it's safe to go back into the Realm of Roots," she said. "There's a shaman—"

"No," said Ver, looking over Mantle's shoulder. "The shaman is no longer a threat."

"You're alive?" asked Cinder, surprised that Ver hadn't been dragged permanently into the roots.

"I'm not sure why you would doubt this," said Mantle, not understanding that she wasn't talking to him.

"Of course I'm not alive," said Ver. "That pathetic shaman posed no threat to me after the initial surprise of his ambush. I had only to explain the errors of his flawed faith. He vanished as he came to understand the impossibility of his continued existence."

"You talked a man out of existence?" she asked, incredulous.

"What are you talking about?" asked Mantle. "Oh, wait. I remember, there was a man who helped carry me from the well. He was… more ghostly than you."

"His name is Ver," said Cinder. "He's right behind you, though you can't see him."

"Ver?" Mantle said, his eyebrows lifting. "The Truthspeaker slain by our Lord's sacred flame?"

"I think that's how he died, yes," said Cinder.

"Hmph," said Ver. "The dragon struck while we were distracted. It was a dishonorable and cowardly attack. There was nothing sacred about it."

"Yes," Cinder said to Mantle. "He says that's exactly how he died."

"His spirit still lingers so long after his death?"

Ver shook his head. "I've not lingered. I've journeyed through distant realms. Tell him I need to speak to him."

"If you're afraid to return to the Realm of Roots, it doesn't matter," said Mantle, taking off running without warning. The movement jostled her. She clenched her jaw to keep from crying out in pain.

He reached a thick vine, placed both her arms around his neck and said, "Hold tight."

"You'll climb with both of us? You couldn't even get out of the pit on your own."

"Not after such a long immersion in water, no," he said. "But the flame has restored my strength."

She clung tightly as he scrambled up the vine as skillfully as a monkey. Reaching the branches, they climbed higher, until they reached a platform of woven bark. She dropped from his neck, wincing, but found that she could stand on her own. She limped after him as he strode across the woven branches toward a thicket of huts faintly visible in starlight. He walked into the midst of a seemingly abandoned village.

"Call out to them," he said. "Tell them no one else need die tonight. Return the hunters I seek, and we'll leave peacefully."

She said, quietly, "We're in the heart of their territory. I don't know if this is the safest place to be shouting out demands."

"I can't imagine any place better," he said.

Before Cinder could decide whether to obey him or not, a single pygmy slowly crept across a branch from a nearby tree, his hands raised, looking frightened.

He said, in a trembling voice, "You are free to go. We shall hunt long-men no longer."

She relayed the message. Mantle shook his head.

"Those aren't my terms. They'll hunt us no longer, yes, but they'll also give back the hunters they kidnapped."

Cinder repeated his words in the pygmy tongue. The pygmy they spoke to swallowed hard and said, "You killed many of our warriors tonight. Meat will be needed for their funeral feasts. The hunters are already dead to you. Leave them."

Mantle nodded as Cinder translated, then said, "The way he phrased it, it sounds like they're still alive."

"I think so," said Cinder. "Plus, I heard the long-men crying out not even an hour ago."

"It's so," said Ver, floating to the side of the platform. "While you climbed, I explored. The men yet live."

"Ver says they're alive," she said.

"Tell our friend the hunters must be returned in five minutes," said Mantle.

She at first thought Mantle meant Ver, before realizing she was to convey her message to the pygmy. The pygmy answered instantly, with a single word.

"Or?" she asked.

"Or I'll burn this village to the ground," said Mantle.

She shuddered at the coolness with which he spoke. It was one thing to kill warriors in the heat of self-defense. But burning the village would kill women and children, or at least leave them homeless.

"Tell him," he said, when she remained silent.

She took a deep breath, then repeated his message.

The pygmy turned a paler shade of green, then darted back across the branch.

Mantle let out his breath slowly, then showed the faintest grin as he said, "All that's left to do now is stand here until we die in a hail of spears."

"You should have thought of that before making threats."

"I did think of it," he said. "But this is no time to show doubt."

The pygmy returned a moment later.

"You'll find the hunters on the ground below," he said. "Leave this place, and never darken our forests with your shadow again."

Mantle shook his head when the message was translated. "I've every intention of returning. Tell him I'm aware that the warriors his tribe lost tonight were important, just as our hunters are important. To honor them, I'll return tomorrow with items of great value. We've no fresh meat to give for the memorial feast, but we can give a full barrel of salted cod, and iron knives, one for each warrior they lost. Tell them our people haven't come to conquer this land, but to live in peace as neighbors. We understand the game we must hunt is game that could fill their bellies. Tell them we can pay them for the rights to hunt here."

"They don't really have a word for 'pay,'" said Cinder. "No matter. I'll figure out some way to explain the concept."

The pygmy listened intently as she explained Mantle's offer, then ran back across the branch to deliver the message. They waited several minutes. When he returned, they quickly arranged for a time and place for representatives of the tribe to meet with representatives of the settlers. The iron knives were of great interest to the Spike Tree tribe. They'd seen such things used by the river-pygmies, who frequently traded with long-men.

When they were done talking, Mantle asked if she needed help climbing down. She felt steadier on her feet than she had, but still agreed to be carried on his back. She felt conflicted by what she'd just done. The Spike Tree tribe might well use their iron knives against the Jawa Fruit people. As terrible as this would be, she also found herself strangely worried for the Spikers. Going to meet the long-men seemed risky, given the ordinary fate of forest-pygmies.

As he placed her on the ground, she could hold her tongue no longer. "Are you tricking them?"

"Tricking them?"

"To trap them. Do you intend to make slaves of them?"

Mantle shook his head. "My faith regards slavery as an abomination. Even if we didn't, they'd still be in no danger. The slave trade has no purpose now that the mines on the Isle of Storm are no longer being worked. I promise, when we restore civilization, slavery will be forbidden."

"Restore civilization?'

"Yes. That's why we're here. As I said, Tempest's armies have brought ruin to the rest of the world. One day, we intend to take back what was lost, and rid the world of its present darkness."

"What if that darkness comes here?" asked Cinder, wondering what her mother would make of this news.

Mantle shook his head. "Our Lord is allied with the Heavenly Light."

"The sun?" asked Cinder.

Mantle nodded. "The Sun provides the illumination that all creatures see by. The Sun has chosen to bend the light around this island, hiding it from those who would do it harm."

Cinder had been told that her father was the ghost who guided the sun. Perhaps he was hiding the island to save her. But the thought chilled her. Why should she be spared while millions of innocents died?

Mantle continued: "The Isle of Fire will be untouched by this war. In the end, when Tempest and Hush believe they've vanquished all, our Great Lord will emerge from hiding and sear the face of the earth, driving Hush back to the frozen wastes, robbing Tempest of the armies that give him power. The Church of the Sacred Flame will send out ships to the ash covered wastelands, plant fields and forests in the enriched soils, and build cities once more. Civilization will be restored, in an era more just and peaceful than any yet known."

Ver sighed so loudly, Cinder almost expected Mantle to hear him.

Ver said, "The plans of his people are doomed to failure. It's plain to me that the dragon they worship is only fattening them up to devour them at the time of his choosing."

Mantle noticed the tilt of her head, the way that her eyes seemed fixed on something he couldn't see. "Is Ver still here? Is he talking to you?"

"Yes," she said. "He's... offering opinions on your church."

"I don't imagine they're favorable ones," said Mantle. "I suppose if he'd understood the truth of my faith, he'd never have helped you save me from the cistern."

"Actually, saving you was his idea," she said. "He told me where to find you."

"Truly?" asked Mantle. "How curious."

"The simplest way to satisfy his curiosity is to let me speak to him," said Ver.

Cinder said, "He wants to talk to you. Do you want to talk to him?"

Mantle stroked his chin. "I'm not certain that's wise. Many members of the Church of the Sacred Flame are former members of the Church of the Book. The remnants of the Church regard us as heretics. Member of that faith are under orders to kill us on sight."

"Ver claims he killed the Spiker shaman just by talking to him," said Cinder. "Your caution is justified. Still... he did rescue you."

"And you don't know why?"

"Actually, I do, even if I don't fully understand all of it. He says that there are living people trapped in Hell. He says if we don't help guide them out, it could cause reality to unravel."

"Unravel?" asked Mantle, scratching his head.

Cinder felt confused as well. Maybe she wasn't using the right word? It wasn't like she got to practice the long-men's language often.

Mantle looked around, his eyes surveying the darkness. "I believe I hear the hunters beyond that ridge. Let's join them and see to their wounds."

He started moving toward them, but she didn't follow. He glanced over his shoulder. "Aren't you coming?"

"I don't think that's wise." The more people who saw her, the greater the danger that her adventures would reach the ears of her mother.

"You should reconsider," he said. "Now that I have to care for the hunters, I can't accompany you to your village. Trying to cover so much territory on your own while you're injured is risky. You should return with me to the settlement."

She shook her head. "I'm forbidden to go there."

"I understand," he said. "Still, I'd consider it a great honor to introduce you to our leader, Brother Wing. He can tend to your wounds."

"When I get back into my home territory, I'll gather herbs to make a poultice that will speed my healing," she said. "I'll be fine."

"I don't doubt you can care for yourself. But Brother Wing has magical gifts far greater than the medical properties of plants. With his touch, he can restore your flesh. It will be as if you'd never been injured."

Cinder pondered this news. Returning home uninjured was an appealing prospect, but it came at the price of being gone even longer from her village. If she wasn't home by dawn, she knew her mother would come looking for her.

Sensing her indecision, Mantle added a further incentive. "Brother Wing will also know what to do about the ghost who haunts you. His gaze reaches into the spirit realms."

Ver frowned. "I see no need for Brother Wing's involvement. Let me speak directly to Mantle. He will see the truth of my words."

"Going to see Brother Wing sounds like an excellent idea," said Cinder.

"Are you intentionally vexing me?" asked Ver.

Cinder nodded. The ghost scowled.

They crept through the jungle darkness cautiously until they found the captured hunters, their arms and legs bound, sitting at the base of a dead tree. Her stomach turned as she got close enough to see them clearly. All were stripped naked and covered in gore.

Mantle crouched and used her obsidian knife to slice their bonds. Most proved able to stand on their own. The wounds they'd suffered had been designed to inflict pain and humiliation rather than mortal injury. Teeth had been broken, nostrils slit, and fingernails torn out by the root. Still, only one hunter had broken legs.

Working in silence, aware of the Spikers watching in the trees above, Cinder helped fashion a litter from branches and vines to carry the hunter who couldn't walk. As Mantle positioned the wounded man on the litter, she found that it was no longer the Spikers' gaze that worried her. Mantle's eyes had never lingered on her naked breasts, nor had he seemed put off by the darkness of her skin. The hunters proved less polite. Some glared at her with disdain, others stared in confusion, and a few leered at her near-nudity. She crossed her arms over her breasts, feeling awkward, before thinking of how her mother would handle such things. She lowered her arms, straightened her shoulders, and defiantly met the gazes of the men. All turned their eyes away.

It took hours to move through the jungle, descending slowly along twisted roots and slippery rocks. As dawn brought color to the sky, they reached a cliffside path leading down to the settlement. When they neared the palisade, Mantle called out, "Open the gates! We've injured men!"

Instantly, the silhouettes of numerous heads rose above the walls. Shouts rang out and the gates swung open as their party approached. As they passed inside the walls, women ran toward them, throwing arms around the returned hunters, weeping with joy. Other women ran up carrying blankets, which they draped over the shoulders of the naked men. A young woman dressed in a white nightgown moved toward Cinder with a blanket in hand, then stopped short a few feet away, her eyes opening wider as she studied Cinder's face.

"Thank you," said Mantle, stepping forward to take the blanket. He turned and draped it over Cinder's shoulders, then said, softly, "I know it's not the custom of your people to conceal your flesh. This is merely to take the edge off the chill of the morning air."

"There's no need to lie," she said. "My nakedness causes discomfort here."

"Yes," he said. Then, with a gentle smile. "And, quite likely, a good deal of jealousy among the women."

His eyes lingered on her face. Before, when he'd looked at her, it had always been with a utilitarian purpose. Now, he seemed to be studying her in a new light. As she looked back into his eyes, she also felt as if she was seeing him for the first time. Often, when she caught glimpses of the faces of long-men, their visages seemed distorted, even monstrous. In addition to the corpse-like paleness of their skin, their noses were too sharp, as if the bones beneath might push through. Their mouths were too wide and their lips too thin.

Mantle shared these hideous features, but she was also struck by the symmetry of his face, the way the sharp lines and the gentle curves merged. Stubble had darkened his chin, and his skin proved tan in the morning light, quite far from corpse flesh.

She turned her eyes away, feeling uncomfortable. Mantle took her by the hand and led her through the gathering crowd. He gave quick, polite acknowledgements to the countless folk who ran up to greet him, and kept moving forward without breaking his stride.

She quickly realized he was leading her to the largest building in the settlement. The teardrop shaped structure had caught her eyes many times. It rose much higher than the walls that protected the settlement, and was painted in bright shades of red, orange, and yellow that glowed in the morning light, as if the building were built of unmoving flame. Smoke rose from the uppermost tip of the structure leaving a black, serpentine trail across the sky. High above the smoke hovered a dancing flame, forever burning with no apparent fuel.

The throngs that followed them fell back as Mantle reached the steps of the structure. Only Ver remained at their side as they approached the door.

"The fools regard this temple as sacred ground," said Ver. "The masses only enter on feast days."

The doors to the temple opened as Mantle reached them. They moved into the cavernous space beyond. In the center of the room was a raging fire. She hesitated, filled with an instinctual fear of large fires that only someone raised in a forest could truly understand. She quickly realized, however, that the flame was contained within an iron cauldron at least fifty feet in diameter. While it glowed dull red, the heat within the room proved no worse than the heat of a midday sun. The tall chimney did an admirable job of leaving the room free of smoke.

Mantle dropped to one knee before the inferno and lowered his head. In a soft voice, he said, "Brother Wing, forgive me for entering this holy space unannounced. The woman by my side is—"

"I know who she is," said the fire, in a voice that nearly deafened her. She cringed, drawing back, but Mantle still held her hand.

"There's no need to be afraid," said Ver, his voice unexpectedly comforting. "The one who speaks will not harm you."

"Are you so certain of that, little ghost?"

"You know me," said Ver. "Certainty is a commodity I possess in abundance."

"Bold words," said the flame, "for a priest who found his eternal reward in Hell."

"Even in Hell, there is truth," said Ver. "Indeed, in Hell there is nothing but truth."

The flame laughed, a frightening sound that caused Cinder to try to break from Mantle's grasp. Then it stopped laughing and said, "Don't be afraid, girl. The dead man speaks truthfully. I mean you no harm."

At these words, the flame shuddered and swayed. Sparks shot from the center of the flame, then spiraled up the rising smoke toward the chimney. A shadow moved within the inferno, a dark red form that rose, and kept rising, until it loomed over them.

The red thing stepped forward. A scaly leg sporting long, black talons clamped onto the edge of the cauldron. Enormous wings spread from the flame, stretching from wall to wall, as dark ash and bright embers rained from glowing scales.

A long serpentine neck snaked from the center of the flames, topped with a reptilian head covered with horns. Eyes that seemed filled with liquid gold fixed upon her. The toothy jaws opened, revealing a cavernous maw that could have swallowed her in a single gulp.

In a gentle voice, the dragon spoke. "You're welcome here, Cinder Merchant. Though we've never met, I'm a friend of your parents."

"I doubt that *friend* is the word they would use," said Ver.

"Twenty years in Hell haven't taken the sting from your tongue, I see," said the dragon.

"And twenty years among the living haven't removed the fork from yours," said Ver. "It took a skilled liar to deceive me those long years ago, Relic. I'm not surprised to see you've found a new life leading men astray with a religion built upon lies."

"Relic?" the dragon sounded a bit bewildered. "Oh, yes, that was the name you knew me by. You were already dead when my father gave me the name Brokenwing."

"And now you call yourself Brother Wing," said Ver. "You weave deceit into your very name. No dragon may ever be a brother to men."

Cinder could hold her tongue no longer. Her mother had told her the story of Brokenwing.

"You're Greatshadow's son," she said.

Brother Wing nodded.

"But… but mother said that Greatshadow hated you. She said he maimed you, tormented you, and vowed to kill you. Why would you risk returning to the Isle of Fire?"

"Because I am his son," said Brother Wing. "But not his only son. My eyes have been opened to the larger reality. Fire is the foundation of civilization. Without it, there would be no law, no art, and no science. My father is the hidden architect of the highest achievements of mankind, and I am his prophet, revealing his sacred plans. I've returned to the Isle of Fire to save the world. And you, my dear Cinder, belong at my side."

8 - Nobody Gets the Girl

FESTER REACHED OVER his shoulder and grabbed a spiky protrusion jutting from between his wings. With a tearing, slurping sound, the skin over the protrusion pulled free. Using both hands to draw out the object he'd freed, the spike became a rod, then a staff, then a shaft much longer than Fester's body. With a final tug that sent a shudder through the demon's form (and a wave of nausea through Sorrow), the shaft came free, revealing a trident dripping with gore.

"To die in Hell is the final death," said Fester, panting. "Fight fiercely if you cherish breath!"

Slate, as was his nature, hadn't waited to hear Fester's admonition. Brandishing the Witchbreaker, he unleashed a savage battle cry and charged up the slope toward the figures that continued to rise over the hillcrest.

At first, the gibbering guardian had appeared to be three men jammed together, their bodies bent and distorted into a single horrific form. The three mouths jabbered and babbled, their voices forming a cacophony from which only a few individual words could be discerned. "Pervert! Lamprey. Ox! Indigo. Helmet? Smell."

As Slate drew closer, the gibbering guardian climbed higher up the ridge and Sorrow saw it wasn't three bodies melded together, but a dozen, then a hundred. By the time Slate reached the guardian and struck with his hell-forged blade, it was apparent an entire army had been mashed into this single form. A thousand legs all kicked and stumbled and shuffled to bear the mob-thing's hideous weight, their seemingly random motions somehow driving it forward.

Slate hacked again and again, slicing heads free of the mass, digging deep gouges into the maze of torsos. Some of the heads cursed, others wept like brokenhearted women, but most continued their ceaseless, mindless babble: "Umbrage. History! Scissors. Bar. Negation? Spine! Penance."

Despite Slate's superb skill with the blade, a single arm slipped past his parry, the grimy fingers slipping into Slate's chest plate at the neck. A second hand clamped onto his wrist, jerking him forward, so that more hands took him by the throat, the ankle, the elbow, and lifted him. Some of the voices gave shuddering cries of delight, others moans of hunger, and the sound of teeth clacking and clicking against Slate's glass armor filled the air as the remaining voices changed from random babble into a single chant: "Feed! Feed! Feed!"

With a flap of wings, Fester darted into the sky, landing atop the writhing mass. He jabbed his trident into the limbs that entrapped Slate. Slate tore his right arm free, then his left. With swift slices of the Witchbreaker, he cut loose the hand that gripped his throat, then made short work of the limbs trapping his legs. He fell before the writhing mass, rolling down the steep slope an instant before the countless legs would have trampled him into paste.

Sorrow ran to Slate's side and helped him rise. "Are you all right?"

"No," Slate said, sounding shaken.

"What's hurt?" she said, seeing no place the gibbering guardian's teeth had broken through his armor.

"My pride," he said, with the ghost of a smile.

Meanwhile, Fester attempted to pull his trident free from the wriggling mass, but a score of hands had gotten a grip upon the weapon. Letting go of the shaft, he spread his wings to fly free, but a hundred grasping hands now had hold of his legs and tail. Fester tilted his beak toward the cloudy skies and uttered an animalistic squawk of despair.

"We must save him!" Slate shouted, darting up the hill.

Sorrow agreed. Losing Fester would mean they'd never find their way through this ever-changing landscape. She suspected Slate's motives weren't so pragmatic, however. Though he'd been willing to kill Fester on sight not even an hour ago, now that they were brothers in combat, Slate's honor would require him to fight to the death to rescue the devil.

Slate fought more strategically on this second charge, using the length of the Witchbreaker to keep him beyond the reach of the grasping hands. With each sweep of his blade he severed two, three, four limbs, but it made no difference. The wall of writhing limbs never showed any sign of pain.

Sorrow still held the energy of Slate's kiss in the center of her torso. She felt stronger, faster, tougher than ever before, and was certain her own blade could make short work of a hundred limbs before her energy waned. But what would be the point of such an attack? In the end, the gibbering guardian would simply wear her down.

She furrowed her brow as she studied the beast. In her years of study under Mama Knuckle, she'd learned a thing or two about anatomy. The gibbering guardian appeared to be nothing but the bodies of damned men jammed together randomly, but genuine random placement of muscle and bone would have produced a quivering mass incapable of movement.

She also knew that master bone weavers were capable of blending bodies. Not long ago she'd encountered Captain Stallion, who possessed a man's torso grafted onto the body of an ass, supposedly the work of a vengeful bone weaver he'd romantically betrayed. If bone weavers could put bodies together, couldn't she tear them apart?

Though she knew it meant losing her enhanced strength, she shifted the magical energy from her muscles to her eyes. Instantly, the logic of the gibbering guardian became plain. Ten thousand muscles braided together in a fashion that enhanced strength rather than destroyed it. Bone melded with bone in such a way that it provided the solid framework that allowed the mob-thing to move without collapsing beneath its own weight. Most importantly, she could see the nerves. Her witch eyes made each spinal column glow with a pale blue aura. From the base of each spine, a tendril of nerve dangled, threading together into a network of rhythmic signals that caused limbs to move in concert. At the center of it all, encased in a single orb fashioned from hundreds of skulls, she saw a brain, large and throbbing, pulsing with dark black thoughts.

"Moonlight! Hush. Net! Entropy? Cubic," jabbered the mouths as she ran toward the gibbering guardian.

Now that the guardian had pulled Fester down, a thousand mouths gnawed on his flesh, but most took only one bite before spitting in disgust. Demons apparently didn't taste all that great, though Fester looked a great deal worse for wear from the test nibbles. In its feeding frenzy, the gibbering guardian had dropped Fester's trident. Sorrow snatched it up. With her strength back to normal, the weight of the weapon nearly caused her to stumble, which would likely prove fatal so close to the grasping arms. Steeling herself, she focused on the nearest bodies. With her enhanced vision, the jumble of shoulders and hips behind the limbs seemed almost like a staircase. With the shaft of the trident she knocked an arm aside then leapt, landing on a shoulder, climbing swiftly, using the trident to keep her balance on the writhing bodies beneath her. With her new knowledge of the creature's anatomy, she kept safely out of the grasp of the straining hands, though she did nearly place her foot in a gaping mouth before catching herself.

She moved past Fester, not daring to let her eyes linger. He was bleeding from a thousand wounds, though perhaps bleeding wasn't the correct verb. Instead of blood, fat white maggots poured from his lacerations.

The chaotic whirlwind of words seemed to settle on a single theme as she leapt across the melded bodies, a thousand tongues crying, "Bitch! Mother! Whore! Slattern! Weaver!" The words goaded her to greater speed, and gave her confidence that her plan was going to work.

Five seconds later, she reached the center of the mass. The dull glow of the braincase lay beneath a further shield of intertwined torsos. A black-nailed hand reached for her and she grabbed it, wrapping her fingers around the wrist. With a loud grunt, she pulled, and a skeletal, gray-haired man pulled free of the tangled bodies, shouting, "No! No! Yes! Yes! No! Please!"

Free of the mass, he stumbled away from her, before arms caught him by the ankles and pulled him down. He cried in terror, then went silent. She didn't look back to see his final fate, as she tore loose another damned soul, this time a woman, no older than herself, yet horribly scarred, covered in scabs and stretchmarks. The woman collapsed instantly, weeping tears tinted yellow with pus, her shrieks of grief as loud as the alarm bell of a town sentry.

A third body came free, a pale, petite thing that might have been a child or a small woman. She saw only its back before it fled, skipping across the flailing arms for a good twenty feet before being caught and pulled down to the mouths. It met its fate in utter silence.

By now, hands had gotten hold of her ankles. Nails dug into her thighs, clawing higher, pulling her britches low on her hips. A mouth dug into her shin, but the teeth couldn't break through her leather boots.

With a loud gasp, she filled her lungs and raised the trident over her head with both hands. "Die!" she screamed, as she brought the shaft down with all her might. Though she lacked magical strength, she was far from frail, and the tines of the trident were sharp as well-honed knives. She tore through the entrails of the torso she stood upon, broke through the woven skulls, then drove her weapon into the surface of the pulsing brain below her. The organ proved spongy, yielding, and at first she feared her weapon would merely bruise it. Then, with a gush of black blood, the membrane surrounding the brain split beneath the trident. She drove the shaft deeper, twisting it, and the mouth that gnawed her boot opened, crying, "Mercy!" The word was echoed by the next mouth, then the next, until it seemed a million voices begged her to pull back.

Sorrow pressed deeper, using the full weight of her body to drive the shaft to the very center of the quivering brain. One by one, the voice's that cried for mercy fell silent. A few whispered words of confusion—"What? Where? Why? How? Why? Why? Why?"—before the roving eyes above the mouths glazed over, then moved no more.

With a loud *schluck*, she pulled the trident free. Though the limbs no longer clawed at her, she decided that a second blow was merited, then a third, until the organ beneath her felt well-minced and the last limb stopped twitching.

She straightened up, instinctively wiping her sweaty brow with the back of her hand. This only made her discomfort worse, considering the gore that dripped from her fingers.

"Slate!" she called out, unable to see him from her vantage point.

"Here!" he called back, not so far away.

She climbed over bodies to reach the crest of the fallen guardian. Below her, Slate crouched over what remained of Fester. He had his hands on Fester's beak, looking into his face. Fester's eyes were unfocused, full of haze. The demon coughed and pale, writhing maggots flew from his nostrils.

"He's dying," said Slate. "Can your magic...?"

"One... never born... cannot perish," Fester whispered, his chest heaving with the effort. "I m-merely vanish ... from this half-life I ...ch-cher..."

His voice trailed off as his eyes slowly shut. He drew one last, ragged breath, then fell still.

Sorrow knelt, pressing her fingers against his neck, searching for a pulse. His body was hot as a stove. She jerked her hand away before her fingers blistered. In her few seconds of contact, she'd found no trace of a heartbeat, but did that mean anything? Did he even have a heart?

With the last remnants of magic still in her eyes, she tried to make sense of Fester's injuries, or even of his anatomy, but it was too late. His body fell apart, turning into worms and bugs that wriggled down through gaps in the fallen guardian. In seconds, all that remained of the devil were the britches he'd worn.

"He died that I might live," Slate said, his voice choked.

"You threw yourself back into combat to save him," she said. "You've no cause to feel guilt."

Slate rose, looking around. "Don't I?"

"You did all you could," she said, picking up Fester's pants and shaking them to remove the maggots and beetles. She wiped her hands on the tattered cloth to remove the worst of the foulness still coating them.

"Perhaps I did too much," said Slate. With his arm, he directed her gaze across the tortured landscape. "How many men have I sent to this place?"

"I really couldn't count," she said.

"I thought this was a place of divine justice. But… how could the Divine Author allow such a place? What possible sins could a man commit in life to deserve… *this*?" He shuddered as he looked down at the mass of faces and limbs he stood upon.

Satisfied her hands were as clean as they were going to get in this filthy place, she used the few dry spots left on the ragged pants to wipe the shaft of the trident. "I'm not the right person to ask," she said. "Your religion would condemn me here a dozen times over. If your church ever captured me, my eternal torture would be preceded by weeks of agony upon a rack. I'd be starved and beaten in some dank cell, before the mercy of being burned at the stake. If the judge was feeling especially kind, perhaps I'd be hung."

Slate frowned, but said nothing.

"You know I'm right," she said.

He took a deep breath. "Yes. Given your actions, I suppose you couldn't expect much in the way of mercy."

"My actions?"

"You've waged war against the church for years. I know you have your reasons, but you can't deny you have blood on your hands." He glanced at the gore-smeared rag in her grasp. "Metaphorically speaking."

Sorrow threw the rag aside, feeling rage building inside her. But, as she looked over the mass of bodies she stood upon, her rage sputtered, then vanished.

"I won't pretend I'm innocent," she said. "I've made bargains with terrible, dark forces in pursuit of power. I've never felt the slightest flicker of remorse. Perhaps the Divine Author believes that fear of a place such as this is the only thing that has any hope at all of causing me to abandon my wicked ways."

"Would you?" he asked. "Could you?"

She leaned on the trident, allowing herself a second to consider his question. Now that she was a witness to Hell, she finally understood a falsehood she'd embraced for far too long. "Before I came here, I thought my enemy was your church. In my heart, I believed men had corrupted the truth of a larger, more benevolent god. But… what if I've been wrong? The Truthspeakers, the judges, the Knights of the Book… what if you're all following the plan of the Divine Author to the last letter?"

Slate didn't answer. He couldn't even meet her gaze.

"Perhaps it was cowardice on my part," she said.

"Cowardice?" he asked.

"To think that my enemies were mere men. The truth has been before my eyes a long time. I've lacked the courage to see it." She lifted the trident, holding it steady, planting her feet on the firmest bones beneath her, bracing herself for Slate's reactions to what she was about to say.

"My true enemy isn't the Church of the Book. My true enemy is the Divine Author."

He looked up, at last meeting her gaze. "I cannot imagine a more blasphemous statement."

"Neither can I," she said. "Nor can I imagine I'll ever regret uttering the words. I'm an enemy of all you stand for, Slate."

He lifted the Witchbreaker as she spoke, gazing into the dark void of its surface.

"What now?" she asked. "We fight?"

He didn't answer, continuing to stare at the blade.

"Circumstances have pushed us together," she said. "We've been allies out of necessity, but I don't think either of us is under any illusions about the fundamental facts. I'm a witch. You're a witchbreaker. In the end, one of us is going to have to kill the other."

Slate lifted his face toward hers and dropped his sword. His cheeks were wet with tears.

"Then kill me," he whispered.

"What?" she asked, shocked by the look in his eyes.

"Kill me," he said. "Do it now. If one of us must perish at the hands of the other… I offer myself to you."

"Damn it," she said. "Not like this! I don't… I can't just…"

"It wouldn't even be murder," he said, looking at his open hands. "I'm not truly a man. You know this well. I'm a doppelganger, an empty shell. I'm a clever bit of magic wrapped in flesh. I'm not your equal."

"Oh Slate," she said, stepping forward, forgetting that mere seconds ago she'd been prepared to kill him if he'd raised his blade against her. "You're more than my equal. Since the day you've come into my life, you've surprised me, even shocked me, with your kindness, your courage, your devotion to doing what's right. If I'd met even one man like you in my childhood, my life might have taken a very different course. You've changed me, Slate, in ways I can't even express."

Sorrow cast her gaze over the hellscape. "This place could never make me change for the better. But you… I've changed in a thousand small ways since the day I met you. I care nothing for the judgement of the Divine Author. I despise his opinion, should he have any notice of me at all. But you… I want to be a better person because of you."

Slate looked skeptical as he met her gaze.

"It's true," she said. "Until I met you, I hadn't felt… hadn't felt a single positive emotion in so long. I couldn't remember what it was like to not be angry all the time. I couldn't imagine what it was like to look upon my fellow men and not feel scorn, or outright hatred. But with you, I've discovered I can still feel tenderness. Just hearing you speak is like listening to music. And when I look into your eyes… I feel something profound. It's… like safety. Like hope, and joy, and… fear, somehow."

"Fear?" he whispered.

"Not fear of you. A fear… of a world without you." She turned away, shaking her head. "I'm sorry. I know this isn't the best time or place to tell you this."

"There's no place where you should tell me this," he whispered. She could tell he'd turned away from her as well.

"Then… you don't feel the same way?" she said softly. She set her jaw, having expected the reaction. Yes, he'd shown signs of affection, but just as often, he'd reacted to her with horror. She'd betrayed him in the Black Bog. She'd manipulated and used him to reach the Temple of the Book. And he'd seen not only the darkness of her soul, but her very body distorted, covered in scales, sporting tail and wings, her hands monstrous talons. She might once again look human, but he'd seen her at her worst. To expect him to summon any emotion more substantial than simple kindness towards her was too much to ask.

His hand fell upon her shoulder. She turned her to face him, the trident dropping from her trembling fingers.

"You shouldn't tell me this because… because I'm not a thing worthy of such feelings. If… if I were a man, I… I would love you," he said, gazing deeply into her eyes. "I cannot imagine a woman anywhere in all of reality more driven than you, more courageous, and certainly none more beautiful."

She'd always rolled her eyes at such statements in romantic tales, believing them to be duplicitous, lust-driven drivel. But now her eyes were fixed on his, and she found she believed every word he uttered.

"But I'm not a man," he said, turning his face away. "I'm an abomination."

"No! Don't say that. Nobody I know has more humanity than you."

"But I am nobody," he said, forlorn. "Less than nobody. I'm no more alive than Fester was. Don't you understand? How can you not understand? *I have no soul.*"

"That's not true," she said, placing her fingers on his chin and turning his gaze toward hers. "You have half of mine."

She pressed his lips to his. He hesitated, one second, two, his lips devoid of warmth or movement, like the lips of a corpse. Then he seized her by the arms and pulled her tightly against him. His lips warmed, then parted, and her tongue slipped between his teeth.

Their shared breath flowed from lung to lung, making her dizzy. If he was truly an empty vessel, she wanted nothing more than to fill him, to pour all the joy and pain and hope and regret within her heart into him.

Heedless of where they were, he loosened the clasp at her neck that held her cloak. He spread it over the twisted limbs, forming what might have been the most terrifying bed in all of creation. Still locked in an embrace, they lowered themselves to the velvet cloak. She moved her fingers skillfully along the clasps of his glass armor. Having forged it herself, she knew how to free him from it with the required alacrity, revealing his magnificent bare chest. At some point, her blouse had come undone, whether by his fingers or her own she couldn't recall.

She pressed her breasts against his skin, his warmth filling her. She felt as if her body were awakening from a long slumber. For the first time, she understood how men and women had survived in the world so long without killing one another. She'd thought she'd experienced pleasure before, thought she'd felt it contemplating a lovely sunset, or listening to old fisherman singing by the docks, thought she'd found pleasure in the tart sweetness of strawberries, in the richness of cream. But she'd never truly felt pleasure until now, never known how divine the touch of a man she loved would be. As his fingers ran along the length of her spine, her mind filled with a pure white light that erased all hope of conscious thought.

Lost amid the barren wastes of Hell, they found each other. In the furthest reaches of the land, even the most wretched souls of the damned fell silent. For the first time since the creation of eternity, love flickered to life in Hell, a pale white candle that, for a moment, held back the darkness.

9 - INHUMAN FREAKS

RIGGER STEADIED HIMSELF with a hand against the wall as he moved down the narrow steps leading below deck. At the end of the short hall, in the cabin reserved for Bigsby, he heard murmuring voices. He'd been controlling the sails for the last ten hours, following Walker's guidance to navigate the winding river. Every muscle in his body felt spent. The winds in Hell were ever-changing, and Walker had advised Gale against controlling them since it might draw Tempest's attention. The effort needed to keep the *Circus* from running aground had exhausted Rigger. They'd anchored in a deep bend in the river where there was little current. A few hours' sleep and he'd be back at work.

Rigger slouched into the bunk room he shared with Mako and Jetsam, pleased to find it empty. He wasn't in the mood for mindless chitchat. He collapsed onto his bunk, his eyes closed, eager for sleep to claim him.

His eyes opened. The murmuring from Bigsby's room... he was certain he'd heard Mako's voice, and that of his mother.

Rigger closed his eyes again, settling deeper into his bunk. He then sat up. What were they talking about? What else could they be talking about? Maybe they were trying to answer the question he'd been too busy focus on, but a question gnawing at him all the same.

"Sleep. Talk later," he mumbled to himself, leaning once more toward his pillow, until his body swayed and he found himself on his feet.

"No one on this damn ship ever follows my advice," he grumbled, opening the door. "Not even me."

He went to Bigsby's room. He paused as the voices from the other side went quiet. He raised his fist to knock, but before he could the door opened. Mako grabbed him by the arm and pulled him inside. Though it was Bigsby's room, the dwarf wasn't present. Brand, Mako and his mother stood in the small room. Sage sat cross-legged on the bunk, gazing into her spyglass.

"Glad you could make it to our little family meeting," said Mako, keeping his voice just above a whisper.

"I might have been here sooner if anyone had bothered to mention it to me," Rigger grumbled. He eyed Brand, then asked Mako, "If it's a family meeting, what's he doing here?"

"He does own the ship," Sage said, not looking up from the spyglass.

"Brand will be part of any discussion of our future," said Gale, giving Brand's hand a squeeze.

"Well this stinks of low tide," said Rigger, shaking his head. "You two are a couple again?"

"Try not to sound so enthusiastic," said Brand.

"I thought you were never going to forgive him for bringing on a stowaway?" Rigger said to his mother.

"Brand has since proved his loyalty to our family many times over," said Gale. "Without him, we couldn't have freed the slaves on Raitingu."

"Ah, yes, the pygmies. That's a lot of mouths to feed, when the *Circus* only took on supplies for eleven people back at Port Hallelujah."

"We'll manage," said Gale. "Bigsby and the girls are taking a full inventory and drawing up a plan for rationing. Bigsby's run a successful business for years, so I've faith he'll be able to manage the stock. As a bonus, Bigsby's fluent in several of the pygmy dialects. Without him, we'd never have kept them calm."

"Maybe we should make them nervous," said Rigger. "Get them too worried to eat."

"You don't mean that," said Brand.

Rigger sighed. "I suppose I don't. It would just be nice to feel like anyone else on this ship is as worried as I am." He looked at Mako. "It certainly didn't help that you've given away the bottomless bottle. We can't even count on fresh water."

"The bottle was mine to give," said Mako.

"You think that the bottle is going to make Sorrow love you?" Rigger asked.

"Rigger!" said Sage, her voice soft but scolding. "Don't be cruel."

"I'm only saying what we all know. Everyone can see how he feels about her."

"My feelings had nothing to do with my gift," said Mako. "I simply want to help Sorrow and Slate survive their quest."

"I didn't want them to make that stupid journey at all," said Rigger. "Why the hell did we let them go?"

"What authority did we have to stop them?" asked Gale. "They can take care of themselves."

"All the more reason they should have stayed with the *Circus*," said Rigger. "I can't believe we're going to make it through Hell without something trying to stop us. There's strength in numbers."

"I've been defending this ship since I was old enough to swim," said Mako. "If trouble comes, you can hide behind me."

Rigger smirked. "You'd be dead a dozen times over if I didn't have your back."

"It's only natural you'd have my back, since I'm always out in front," said Mako.

"Seems to me you're usually two steps behind Jetsam," said Rigger. "Speaking of which…"

"He's gone up to talk to Walker," said Sage.

"Alone?" asked Rigger.

"You've been talking to him by yourself," she said.

"Yeah, but I'm not the type to fall for Walker's mumbo jumbo mysticism. Aren't you worried that Jetsam is a little impressionable?"

"Not in the least. That's why we sent Jetsam up to talk to him," said Gale. "He'll be fine."

"Sent him? Why?"

"Because as long as Walker's talking to him, he's not spying on us," said Sage. "At least, I hope he's not. If he's telepathic, who knows how far his range is?"

"Are we hiding something from Walker?" asked Rigger. "If we are, is it safe to send Jetsam up to talk to him? If he's telepathic, he'll know we're trying to distract him."

"Jetsam doesn't know the purpose of his mission," said Sage. "I told him to go tell Walker all the dirty jokes he knows."

"That's… that's a lot of jokes. And hardly any of them are actually funny. Why have we decided Walker deserves this kind of torture?"

Sage kept looking in her spyglass as she said, "I just think it's important to figure out the truth about him before he leads us into something even worse than where we are now."

"Worse than Hell?"

"There was Limbo," said Brand.

"Sure. And he got us out of there. I mean… look, I'm the biggest skeptic on the ship. But, if Walker wanted to do us harm, I can think of a hundred different ways he could have killed all of us by now."

"I don't think he wants to kill us," said Sage. "Not while we're useful."

"Useful for what?"

"I have no idea. I don't know his true goals. I honestly don't even know what Walker is. He's definitely not a pygmy."

"Are you sure?" said Rigger. "According to what he told Jetsam back on Podredumbre, he used to be a shaman."

"I'm sure," said Sage. "His aura isn't remotely human, at least not when I study him in my glass. Somehow, he manipulates his aura to look human when I look at him directly, but whatever he's doing doesn't affect what I see in the spyglass. Walker's aura has a lot in common with the demons."

"Okay," said Rigger. "Let's assume he's a demon. I still don't see how he could possibly be leading us anyplace worse. I'm not up on the theology of the Church of the Book, but is there some super-Hell I'm unaware of, Brand?"

Brand shrugged. "Why are you asking me?"

"Didn't you grow up in the Church?"

"I mean, sure. But it's not like I paid attention to the sermons."

"I think he's told us the truth about where he's taking us," said Gale. "My gut tells me that he really is guiding us to the Sea of Wine."

Rigger nodded. "I'm not as reliant on my gut, but, yeah, I can't think of reason he's trying to trick us."

"I think the trick is coming later," said Mako. "He wants us to go to the Happy Isles and bring back an army to overthrow Tempest. Why?"

"To save the world?" said Rigger.

"Sure. But what's he going to do with the world afterward?" asked Mako. "When Tempest is no longer ruling Hell… who will be?"

Rigger scratched his head. "You think this is some kind of bid for power? Walker wants to be king of Hell?"

"I'm saying we should consider all possibilities," said Mako.

"Oh, I totally agree," said Rigger. "I'm more than happy to accept that Walker has a secret agenda. But… so what? Do we have a better plan than to get to the Sea of Wine and look for help?"

"Maybe," said Sage. "When we get to the Happy Isles… we stay there."

"That doesn't sound like a good option to me," said Rigger.

"Only because the word Happy is involved," said Sage. "You'd be miserable."

"I mean… what? We abandon the rest of the world to its fate?"

"Why does this have to be our fight?" asked Sage. "Don't forget, the *Circus* now holds the souls of two fallen Romers, both Grandmother and Levi. Don't we owe it to them to get them to the Happy Isles once and for all?"

"Hold on," said Brand, lifting his hands. "I understand you want the best for your departed family members, but everyone else on this ship is still alive. We can't seriously give up on getting back to the living world, can we?"

"The way Walker describes it, there might not be a living world to return to," said Mako, shaking his head. "Can it be true? Has Abyss really fallen to Hush?"

"If so, there will be Wanderers in the Happy Isles who can verify it," said Sage.

"If all the oceans are frozen, what's the point in going back?" asked Mako.

"What's wrong with you?" asked Rigger, studying Mako's face. "I would normally expect you to be the one arguing we should go back and fight no matter what the odds."

Mako frowned, an almost clownish expression given his inhumanly large mouth. "Who are we fighting for? Everyone I care about is on this ship."

"I'm with Rigger," said Brand. "I can't believe any of you would seriously consider not going back."

"Then why are we even discussing this?" asked Rigger. "It's your damn ship. You give the orders. Tell Ma we're going back."

"I'm not giving her orders," said Brand. "We need to make a mutual decision." He looked toward Gale. "I have to say, you've been awfully quiet."

"Indeed," she said. "Listening to you all has given voice to the conflicting thoughts in my own mind. When we fought against the slaving Wanderers, I sometimes felt as if our ship was alone against the world. In truth, we weren't. We still had a safe haven in Commonground. There were friendly ships upon the sea crewed with Wanderers who supported our cause. But even if we had been utterly alone, we've never allowed this to keep us from doing what's right."

"That's the question though, isn't it?" asked Rigger. "What's right? How do we answer that question when it sounds as if the apocalypse is already underway?"

Gale nodded thoughtfully. She took a breath, preparing to speak, when a shout sounded from the deck above.

"That's Jetsam," said Mako.

"Is he in trouble?" asked Brand.

"We may all be in trouble," said Sage, peering into her spyglass. "There's another ship approaching us."

"Maybe it's friendly?" asked Brand. He tilted his head the second he said it, looking incredulous at his own words.

Loud bangs sounded on the timbers overhead as Jetsam stomped to get their attention. "All hands on deck! It's the *Seahorse!*"

"The *Seahorse*?" asked Brand as they rushed through the door. "Captain Stallion's ship?"

"I wondered if he'd survived his leap into the sea after our last encounter," said Gale. "If he's in Hell, I guess I have my answer."

They reached the deck. Jetsam was now high above the ship, swimming through the air. Sage leapt into the ropes and climbed to the crow's nest, swift as a squirrel. Rigger moved toward the wheel by instinct, though it wasn't likely there was steering to be done. They'd lowered the sails when they'd dropped anchor in the still water. The ship coming for them was fully rigged, closing fast, and, while the river was broad, it wasn't so broad that they could outmaneuver their attackers in order to avoid being boarded.

Wrapping his hands in the ropes that hung near the wheel, he glanced back at the approaching vessel. It was the *Seahorse* alright, though much worse for wear than when they'd last seen it. The black sails flapped in tatters and seaweed hung from the rigging, as if the vessel had spent time in the briny depths.

The ship was now close enough that he could see skeletal figures climbing the ropes. Most were humanoid, but with the skulls of beasts. When last they'd encountered the *Seahorse*, it had been crewed by half-seeds. They'd killed three score of the human-animal hybrids in that fight, leaving only two survivors aboard the rudderless ship. From the angle of approach, he couldn't tell if the rudder had been repaired, not that it mattered much with the wind propelling the ship straight toward them.

Rigger wondered where Walker had gone, and when he looked around he found the pygmy standing directly beside him.

"It seems the memories we stirred up when we struck bottom have found their rightful owners," said Walker.

"I'm not surprised that Stallion wound up here," said Rigger. "He was a fallen Wanderer, and would never reach the Sea of Wine. I guess his crew of half-seeds wound up in the appropriate afterlife as well. But how did the *Seahorse* wind up here? Do ships have souls?"

Walker nodded. "The *Freewind* did, and now, so does the *Circus*. Stallion may not have been a good Wanderer, but he loved his ship. The ship, it seems, returned his love, and went down with its captain."

Jetsam drifted above their heads. "I can't believe they're crazy enough to attack us. We kicked their butts last time."

"You spilt their blood to end their lives," said Walker. "Now, they have no blood. You do."

Mako stood on the rail, staring down at the water. "There's still time for me to rip a hole in their hull. Walker, what will happen to me if I dive in the river?"

"You'll survive," said Walker. "But when you emerge, you'll no longer have your own memories. The thoughts of others will have filled you. Your own mind will float bodiless along the currents, lost forever."

"So, no swimming," said Mako. "We'll do this the hard way."

"Are your demon friends any good in a fight?" asked Rigger.

"They're quite ferocious, though not necessarily efficient," said Walker. "They take a bit too much pleasure in tormenting their foes."

As Walker spoke, Bigsby poked his head above deck. "Is something going on?" he asked.

Cinnamon and Poppy appeared beside him. "Is it a fight?" asked Poppy. "If it's a fight, let me get my weights."

"No," said Gale. "Get back below deck. Keep the pygmies calm, no matter what you hear happening."

"Ma, I can take care of myself," said Poppy.

"Those are orders!" snapped Gale.

"Yes, Captain," Poppy grumbled.

As the three disappeared below deck, Rigger said, "You know, Ma, Poppy's powers might actually come in handy."

"Don't question me," Gale said. "You heard Walker. We can't stab or strangle these enemies. If we hope to survive this fight, I'm going to need to focus. I can't be distracted by worrying about the girls."

"What?" asked Jetsam. "You're not worried about us?"

"You should come down from the sky now," said Gale.

"Why?" asked Jetsam. "You plan to smack me?"

"I'm about to make it very, very difficult for you to ride the winds."

Jetsam kicked through the air to the nearest rope and secured himself in the riggings.

"If you use your powers, Tempest will likely notice us," said Walker.

"We'll fight that fight when it happens," said Gale. "Right now, shut up, and let me save my ship."

By now, the *Seahorse* was less than a hundred yards away. Rigger thought the deck of the ship looked more crowded than he remembered. Stallion and his half-seeds weren't the only men they'd ever sent to Hell. Perhaps the ranks of his crew had grown on these dark waters.

"Ma, if you're going to do something, do it now," said Sage. "In another minute, even your strongest winds won't keep us out of the range of their grappling hooks."

Gail nodded and climbed onto the bowsprit, lifting both hands. "Sage, you've never seen the strongest winds I can summon." She held her hands before her, her fingers caressing the breeze. "I've always used my control over the winds to push our ship as fast as the sails could stand, but I've also known that I could push them faster. Much, much faster."

She pushed her hands forward. Instantly, every sail on the *Seahorse* snapped backward, slapping against masts and ropes. Waves rose from the previously calm water as the bow of the ship lifted from the force of the gust.

Gale pushed again, then again, and the deck of the *Seahorse* turned into a scene of chaos as the skeletal sailors in the rigging lost their grip and fell among the dead men below. Few of the attackers kept their feet beneath them as the deck pitched violently.

The *Circus* began to roll in the ensuing waves. Rigger hoped the pygmies below weren't prone to seasickness. All the Romers, plus Brand, wrapped their arms in ropes to keep from getting tossed about. The two demons, Foment and Fume, leapt into the air, clear of the pitching masts. Walker simply stood where he'd been standing, his hands clasped behind him, looking unperturbed.

The *Seahorse* spun to the side. Rigger could see the rudder was still missing, leaving the ship all but defenseless against the wind. The tattered black sails ripped further, flying away in a flurry of loose rags that resembled a murder of crows. In under a minute, the ship was stripped of all canvas.

"You're doing it, Ma!" Jetsam shouted from above. "Don't let up! You're going to send them to the bottom!"

For half a second, Rigger thought he was right. With the *Seahorse* broadside to the wind, it listed to such a degree that much of its crew tumbled overboard, vanishing in the waves. If its hull sank any further, water would pour in through any open hatches and the ship would go down.

Then the lightning struck. Rigger was blinded, then deafened as thunder slammed his whole body like a giant's fist. In the aftermath, he smelled burning wood. He screamed, "Ma!" but his ears rang so loudly he couldn't hear his own voice. All he could see before him was a field of white sparks.

With his sight and hearing gone, he was left to rely on his sense of touch. His power let his mind flow through every rope on the ship. He could feel anything touching the rigging. He could tell that Jetsam and Mako were still clinging to their ropes. Brand had let go of his and might be anywhere. His mother hadn't been touching a rope, and his heart sank as he detected a slackness before him. The ropes stretching out to the bowsprit had snapped. The burning wood he smelled came from that direction. Had lightning struck his mother?

"Ma!" he yelled again, this time faintly hearing the word. "Ma! Are you alright?"

"A little help, please!" someone yelled from in front of him. Brand?

He blinked, trying to make sense of the fragmented images that began to bleed through his snowy vision. The bowsprit was aflame. The lightning had apparently struck right where his mother had been standing. Where she'd stood, Brand now had one knee hooked around a broken post from the guardrail, with his torso bent over the damaged front of the ship.

"Rigger!" Brand yelled again, his voice on the edge of panic. "Rigger, I can't hold on much longer!"

Rigger instantly understood the man's peril and every rope in reach snaked out and wrapped around Brand's legs. He tried to lift the man, but was surprised when Brand weighed more than he should have.

With a grunt, he pulled harder, lifting Brand free of danger. To his relief, he discovered the reason that Brand weighed so much was that his hands were wrapped around Gale's wrist. To his even greater relief, he saw that his mother was not only alive, but seemed not even singed by the lighting strike that had torn apart her perch.

He lowered them to the deck.

"Ma!" Mako yelled, leaping from his perch to run to her side. "Ma what happened?"

"I guess we caught Tempest's attention," she said. She reached to her belt, where her cutlass hung. Rigger noticed for the first time the cloth bag just behind it. She opened the bag and pulled out a glowing glass rod.

"Good thing I picked this up when it fell to the deck after our last fight with Tempest. I held onto it for safekeeping."

Rigger had forgotten all about the lightning rod they'd taken from the Stormcaller. It had protected his mother from the lightning, though the protection must not have spread to the wood she stood upon.

Rigger glanced up at the sky. "What chance do we have if Tempest can just blast our ship out from under us?"

"He won't," said Walker. He glanced at the *Seahorse*, which settled upright now that Gale was too rattled to summon winds. In the chaotic current, the ship had drifted closer. Rigger felt a sinking sensation as he saw skeletal warriors climbing onto the railings, grappling hooks in hand, preparing to board.

"Finish them off," said Walker, nodding toward the invaders. "Then sail as fast as you can to reach the end of the river. I'll have to trust that Sage can navigate, though I'd rather not have put that to the test. I'll return before you reach the Sea of Wine, if I can."

"Where are you going?" asked Gale.

"To give Tempest a more enticing target," said Walker. He looked up at Fume and Foment and said, "Come."

Rigger blinked, still trying to clear the last of the sparks from his vision. When he opened his eyes, Walker and the demons were gone. He had no time to ponder the vanishing act, however. By now, the grappling hooks from the *Seahorse* were lashing onto the *Circus*. Rigger's command over ropes only extended to ropes he touched, or ropes that touched ropes he touched. He had a half dozen coils of ropes linked together along the rails and he used these to snake out and tangle the grappling hooks, lifting them free and tossing the skeletons climbing them into the drink. Unfortunately, for every grappling hook he removed, three more found purchase, and already the two ships were close enough that the boldest skeletons from the *Seahorse* made the leap to the deck of the *Circus*.

With the two ships so close, Gale couldn't use her control of the winds to separate them. Instead, she drew her cutlass and leapt toward the rails. Mako and Jetsam joined her. Gale fought with cool-headed precision, her blows aimed at the leathery ligaments that held the skeletal limbs together, freeing arms from shoulders and legs from hips. Mako showed his usual bloodlust despite his enemies' lack of blood. Finding that decapitating his opponents didn't slow them, he tossed aside his sword and grabbed a foe by the rib cage, using it as a battering ram to knock the invaders overboard.

Jetsam normally entered combat with either a quip or a song, but now he fought in utter silence, his face grim as his rapier failed to do real damage to the skeletons. He kept being pushed back, focusing on parrying their attacks. Rigger tried to help, using his ropes to trip and tangle the skeletons surrounding Jetsam, but it was no use. Jetsam vanished beneath an ever-growing mass of thrashing bones.

"Jetsam!" Sage cried from above. To Rigger's great surprise, she dropped onto the skeletons that had buried Jetsam, a belaying pin in each hand. Sage seldom engaged in hand-to-hand combat, but not from lack of skill. Her supernatural eyes could spot the weakest point in any foe and keep her safely away from every blow aimed at her. For a moment, she danced over the wriggling heap of dead men, breaking arms and spines, bashing in skulls, but, in the end, there were just too many. Skeletal fingers closed around her ankles and she vanished into the scrum.

Rigger continued to pluck away skeletons to free his siblings, though in his heart he was certain they were already dead. With his focus on saving Jetsam and Sage, he didn't notice the clacking of skeletal feet on the wood behind him until a half second before the attack. He ducked, then spun around to find himself face to face with a huge, horse-headed skeleton wielding a mace. The creature swung at him again and Rigger rolled away, abandoning the guidelines that connected him to the rest of the ship. Holding onto them wouldn't do him any good if his skull was bashed in.

He bounced back to his feet, looking around for a weapon. Unfortunately, he saw plenty of weapons, all in the hands of skeletons that charged toward him from all sides. He crouched to leap, praying he could get high enough to brush his fingers against the lines overhead. But, as his feet left the deck, skeletal fingers grabbed him by the belt. He was thrown down with enough force to leave him seeing stars. Before he could recover his wits, a skeleton fell on him, then three more and in seconds he was completely pinned. Yet, curiously, none of the skeletons delivered a final blow. He heard cursing to his left and turned his head to see Mako fall, pushed down by countless bludgeoning arms and legs. Mako disappeared under his attackers, yet he too continued to live, judging from his abundant cursing.

Rigger scanned the deck, looking to see if anyone could aid him. He spotted Brand balanced on the rail, dodging the blows of a trio of skeletons armed with halberds. Brand kicked away the skull of his nearest attacker, but was clipped behind the ankle by the shaft of a halberd as his leg came down. He waved his arms for balance, to no avail. He vanished over the rail, plunging toward the river.

Now, only his mother was free. Her opponents were packed in so thickly around her that she was able to leap atop them, dancing across the flailing mob, until she reached the rigging and climbed. The skeletons followed, but from her higher vantage point they had no hope of reaching her as she coolly leaned over and sliced free the fingers of any skeleton who tried to climb toward her.

"That should do," called a voice from the other ship. "Bring them all together."

The skeletons manhandled Rigger to his feet, with his arms pinned against his back. They dragged him toward the middle of the deck, where he found Jetsam and Sage already waiting, their limbs held by skeletal fingers.

Mako was the last to arrive in the center of the skeletal mob. Everyone was scratched and bruised, but Mako definitely had taken the worst beating. His nose had been broken, one eye was swollen shut, and his hands dripped with blood.

Now that he was standing, Rigger could see over the heads of most of the skeletons. On the deck of the *Seahorse*, Captain Stallion had finally made his appearance. Unlike his crew, he still had flesh, though that didn't seem to be a gift. His skin was corpse-white and spongy, the flesh of a drowned man. On the flanks of his horse half, the hide had peeled away, revealing gray, putrid meat crawling with pale worms.

Stallion looked at Gale, still free in the riggings, and said, "I've waited a long time for this day. You and your bloody family are to blame for my being here. For twenty years, I've dreamed of making you suffer for your crimes."

"Crimes?" said Gale. "We defended our ship when you attacked us! You've only yourself to blame for being here. You died a coward's death, diving into the sea rather than facing me in combat."

"It would hardly have been a fair fight," said Captain Stallion. "You and your family are inhuman freaks."

"Says the man who's half horse," said Jetsam.

A skeleton punched Jetsam in the gut, silencing him.

Captain Stallion came to the rail, then leapt to the deck of the *Circus*. "Gale, you should come down from the rigging now. If you don't, I'll kill one of your children."

"Don't listen to him, Ma!" yelled Sage, before skeletal fingers clamped over her lips, muffling her.

"I see we have a volunteer for who'll go first," said Stallion, drawing his saber as the skeletons parted to give him a clear path to Sage.

Gale dropped from the ropes, landing between Stallion and her daughter, cutlass at the ready.

"Are you so eager to die again?" Gale asked.

"Oh yes," said Stallion, his voice suddenly soft. "Yes, indeed, I'd welcome death. A final oblivion, sweet as sleep… I want this more than you can ever know. It's why I'm here, instead of in the lands above, helping Tempest's armies. I don't want to continue as a dead man, above or below. I want to be finished. To be free."

"Take another step forward and you'll have your freedom," said Gale.

Stallion shook his head. "You haven't the power to end this. Stab me, drown me, burn me to ash… always, my essence will endure. We're all immortals, Gale. A thousand deaths will never end us."

"If it's all so futile," said Gale, "why bother with any of this?"

"Because the priest tells me this ship carries the one thing that can bring an end to eternity," said Stallion. "He sent me here to recover the artifact. I've come for the One True Book, Gale. Hand it over, and I'll spare the life of one of your children. I'll even let you choose which one."

10 - Hell's Outer Wastes

CINDER'S HEART SLOWED back to a normal beat after the initial spike of fear she'd felt when Brother Wing had emerged from the flame. Her mother had fought numerous dragons in her day, and Cinder had imagined them as monsters the size of mountains, with wingspans wide enough to blot out the sun. Brother Wing was the largest living thing she'd ever seen, yes, but he fit comfortably into the temple. As for the rest of his appearance, his jaws were no toothier than those of the crocodiles who lurked in the deep rivers. Reminiscent of the boas that slithered among the treetops, his scales glinted like smooth jewels, in a hundred shades of ruby and orange. His catlike eyes were a golden hue, and when he looked upon her she felt no fear. Though his inhuman face couldn't convey emotions, she sensed deep down the creature meant her no harm.

"You're correct," said Brother Wing. "I wouldn't hurt you. I can, in fact, help you, if you allow it."

"You… you're reading my mind?" she said, remembering that her mother had told her that dragons had this power.

Brother Wing nodded. "Forgive the invasion of privacy. I cannot turn off this sense, any more than you could turn off your hearing. You may trust, however, that I'll never share what I might overhear. Now, let's return to the matter of your wound."

"Had we even talked about the matter of my wound?" she asked.

"Oh," he said. "I suppose we hadn't. Not out loud. But Mantle would like me to heal you."

"You possess the gift of healing now?" Ver asked.

"Indeed," said Brother Wing. "During the time I lived with Zetetic, I dined with many of the most talented mystics from throughout the Shining Lands. Zetetic was obsessed with all the conflicting, yet functional, systems of magic that existed in the world, and continually searched for a grand unified theory of magic that might incorporate all of them."

"He already knew the explanation," said Ver. "Truth is finite, while lies are boundless."

"Perhaps," said Brother Wing. "Zetetic would no doubt debate the assertion, but I feel no obligation to defend his opinions. I parted ways with Zetetic primarily to protect my own sanity. When I first went to dwell with him, my telepathy had yet to recover from my father's mental assault. As my mind healed, I found it harder and harder to ignore Zetetic's thoughts. His willingness to accept everything as truth bewildered me. His thirst for ever more knowledge frightened me. One day, in his quest to know all, he hopes to discover some hidden thread of reality. It frightens me to know that he would willingly pull this thread and unravel the entire universe."

"Indeed," said Ver. "That's very much what I've come to speak to you about."

"In a moment, ghost," said Brother Wing. He turned his gaze once more on Cinder. "My apologies. It's easy to ramble off topic anytime one discusses Zetetic. The point I intended to make is that I learned many secrets of magic from his guests, including the art of healing. If you'll permit me to touch you, I can repair your damaged hip."

Cinder nodded her assent.

His talons were sinewy and hard looking, his claws black and sharp as obsidian flakes, but his touch proved gentle as he brushed his claws lightly across her bloodied hip. His eyes fixed intently upon the wound. His nostrils twitched.

"It's good that Mantle brought you," he said. "I smell infection. Spikers never clean their weapons. By tomorrow, you would be feverish. A week from now, you'd be dead. Fortunately, I can draw out the puss."

He cupped his talon over her hip. She felt a strange, negative pressure, then a burning sensation that grew ever hotter until she involuntarily cried out.

Brother Wing released her. She staggered away, her hip aching, feeling more injured than she had when he'd first touched her. She looked down to examine how much harm he'd done, and found, to her shock, fresh, unblemished flesh. The jangling, burning sensation of her newly knitted nerves throbbed with each heartbeat, but as the seconds passed the pain grew fainter, fading from agony to mere tingling, before no longer being detectable at all.

"You did it!" she said, putting her full weight on the leg. She felt completely recovered.

The dragon shrugged. "Like any skill, I've grown better with practice. Building this settlement has been dangerous work. I've treated wounds far more serious than this. There are few within the town walls I haven't healed." He looked at Mantle. "Save for you, of course. I see you've once more returned from battle unscathed."

"As you say," said Mantle, "everything becomes easier with practice. I've trained for combat since I was old enough to walk."

"Mantle's prowess is why I've come to you," said Ver. "Though many things in the living world are hidden from my dead eyes, his soul gleams like a beacon. Mantle's a man of virtue and courage, a pure soul who, alone of all the men left in the world, may undertake the terrible task I must lay upon his shoulders."

As the dead priest spoke, Cinder took Mantle's hand into her own, so that he could hear the ghost's words.

The dragon studied Ver's face. "I see. There are innocent souls in Hell."

"I wouldn't call them innocent," said Ver. "The Romers are Wanderers, the pygmies are animists. Sorrow's a witch, and would wind up in Hell soon enough. Slate isn't even a man, merely a bit of magic too stubborn to stop breathing. Yet, none of them arrived in Hell due to the judgment of the Divine Author. They must be rescued, returned to the realm of the living at once."

"You fear that, the longer they remain there, there's a chance that Hell might come undone?" Brother Wing sounded skeptical. "I hardly think this likely."

"Which of us is the theologian?" asked Ver. "You can see my mind. You know I believe it to be true. You also know I've studied this matter in far greater depth than you."

"I don't dispute that you believe the threat is real," said Brother Wing. "I simply feel the problem is somewhat remote from our immediate troubles. The problems this settlement faces are far more acute. The world beyond these shores grows less inhabitable by the hour. The bay at Commonground is a mass of ships now, as Wanderers are driven there by the sea ice that grows ever closer. They carry with them refugees from other lands. Some are upon the ships because the Wanderers felt mercy, others because, even in the face of doomsday, there were still Wanderers willing to let wealthy men purchase passage."

"Which is why our first priority must be to fortify our settlement," said Mantle. "It's only a matter of time before the refugees leave Commonground to find new homes upon the Isle of Fire. We'll welcome with open arms anyone who comes in peace to help us build. But, we also know that many of these men will see our humble settlement as ripe territory for conquest."

"You see why I'm reluctant to have Mantle join your quest," said Brother Wing. "Reluctant… but not completely unwilling."

"I'll go where you wish me to go," said Mantle. "But, why do these people trapped in hell matter to us?"

Brother Wing sighed. "Because I know them. Some of them, anyway. Bigsby was one of the first humans I encountered when I came to Commonground. I fear I didn't treat him well. Later, at the Keep of the Inquisition, I dined with Slate, Sorrow, and Brand, and found them interesting. While I've never met the Romers personally, in the time I lived in Commonground, I learned of them from the minds of their fellow Wanderers. They're people of great integrity. The world will be poorer for their absence."

The dragon paused, looked as if he were weighing something further, then said, "I should also add that I know Sorrow much more intimately than from a single dinner."

"My mother knew Sorrow," said Cinder. "I'm told she was very driven, and very angry."

Brother Wing nodded. "Traits I shared, in my younger days." His eyes seemed less focused, as if he was lost in memories. "My father cast me aside as a fledgling, my wings broken, with every expectation I would die. But I killed the lava-pygmies who came to collect my body. From their minds, I caught the faintest glimmers that there was a larger world beyond the jungle. I filled my belly with the bodies of the lava-pygmies, but they couldn't satisfy my intellectual hunger. Driven by a desire to understand more of the world, and more of myself, I descended the mountain and made my way to Commonground."

"Even in a city of half-seeds, I can't imagine they welcomed a dragon with open arms," said Ver.

"No," said Brother Wing. "I was met with hostility and violence, driven back into the wilds weeping and wounded. However, as a telepath, I quickly learned to hide myself from the gaze of men. At first I merely hid in shadows, but soon I learned the art of disguising myself in rags. Moving among the crowds of the city unmolested, I drank in the minds of those around me, and soon mastered human languages. I'd left the jungle feeling deep emotions, emotions I had no words for. But soon after I arrived in Commonground, a woman in a cloak of fine green silk walked past me. Instantly, she caught my full attention, for here was the first human I'd encountered who felt precisely the same emotions that I'd known since being discarded. She was filled with hatred of her own father, and a deep and abiding desire for revenge against him. In her, I'd found a kindred spirit."

"And how did she feel about you?" asked Ver.

"She never knew me. She was too intently focused on revenge against her father, and the religion that had shaped him, for me to ever hope of winning her over to my cause. Plus, she'd come to Commonground at the summons of the Black Swan, who'd hired her to make use of her talent as a sculptor. I stayed near her, careful to remain beyond her range of vision. At night, I'd slink into her sleeping chambers and stand by her bedside, exploring all she'd learned. It was from her I learned the basics of necromancy and soul catching that allowed me to craft my first golem, Patch. Alas, he proved to be a flawed creation, not even lasting through his first fight."

"I find it disturbing that you would read her mind as she slept," said Cinder.

"It was inexcusable," said Brother Wing. "I'd never engage in such a thing now. My years of study at the Keep of the Inquisition exposed me to many arguments about morality. My most steadfast companions were, I fear, somewhat hedonistic. They'd argue I'd done no wrong to Sorrow. You don't harm a flower by gazing at its colors or smelling its scent. I didn't harm Sorrow by studying her thoughts."

"But you don't agree with this?" asked Cinder.

Brother Wing nodded. "Now, I inform everyone I meet that I can see into their minds. It's their choice if they wish to stay near me. I gave Sorrow no choice. What's more, with the wisdom of twenty years of hindsight, I understand that the emotional bond that drew me to her, her unquenchable anger, was a poison to my own soul. It took me many years to forgive my father and learn to love him."

"Does he love you back?" asked Cinder.

"He hasn't killed me yet," said Brother Wing. "Perhaps that's all the love he's capable of expressing. But, if you'll pardon my insight, I see a hidden layer of depth in your question. You're wondering if your own father loved you."

Cinder crossed her arms. "I don't see how he could. He was dead before I was born."

"Yes. But his spirit lingers on, guiding the sun. I'm sure he watches over you constantly."

"Does he?" asked Cinder. "My mother explained his choices to me. He did what he had to do. But, I get no more sunshine than anyone else in the jungle. Not that I would expect this. Does he even know I was born?"

"I'm afraid I don't know. But, during our journey to slay Greatshadow, I was intimately connected with your father's spirit. His love for your mother was genuine and profound. I'm certain he would have loved you."

Ver cleared his throat. "This discussion is heartwarming, but I fear we're wasting time. Will you allow Mantle to journey with me to Hell to rescue Sorrow and the others?"

Brother Wing took a deep breath. He studied Mantle's face and said, "I see you would embrace the quest if I asked you to go. There's no place you fear to tread, not even Hell itself."

"If this Sorrow was important to you, she's important to me," said Mantle, crossing his arms. "I won't turn my back on a soul in danger."

"I never imagined you would." Brother Wing turned his gaze toward Cinder. "You understand what's being asked of you?"

"Maybe?"

"You alone have the power to guide living men into the realms of death. You alone have the power to return them. If Mantle is to undertake this quest, you must go with him."

"That's what I thought," she said. She frowned. "This seems like the sort of thing I should discuss with my mother."

"Your mother would forbid it," said Ver. "But there's no need to ask her. You're a woman, Cinder, not a child."

"I still have to live with her when I get back," said Cinder.

"It may be that your mother wouldn't forbid it," said Brother Wing. "Infidel's traveled to many abstract realms and lived to tell the tale. When I knew her, she was fearless."

"So I've heard," said Cinder. "But the woman I've known seems afraid of everything, at least where I'm concerned."

"It's a mother's duty to have such concerns," said Ver. "It's an equal duty to accept when a child is no longer a child."

Cinder bit her fingernails, torn with indecision. This was precisely the sort of adventure her mother used to have. It could be a chance to prove to her mother that she was ready to go off on her own. It could also be an excellent way to die in some far off realm, and never be heard from again.

Before she could arrive at a decision, shouts sounded from outside. Metal clanged against metal and men cried out in pain as the sound of someone heavily armored moved up the steps to the temple.

"An attack!" said Mantle, racing toward the door. "But who?"

Brother Wing furrowed his brow as Mantle neared the door. He called out, "Wait!"

Too late. The door splintered as Mantle reached it, the heavy fragments knocking him backward. A woman covered head to toe in black iron armor marched into the room, wielding a massive mace.

"Cinder!" the woman yelled, in a peculiar squawking voice that sounded almost like a goose honking. "Don't listen to these fools!"

Her forward march was halted as Mantle clawed free of the debris and clasped his hand around her ankle. She craned her torso to look at him. As her metallic ribs slipped and twisted, Cinder realized that the woman wasn't wearing armor at all. Somehow, her entire body was made of iron.

"You!" the metal woman cried, raising her mace over Mantle, who still lay on his back amid the debris. "With your death, this all comes to an end!"

"No!" Cinder cried, leaping toward the woman. She slammed into her back, with about the same effect as slamming into a wall. Still, she jarred the woman just enough that Mantle rolled out of the path of her blow. The mace shattered the stone where he'd been, missing by inches.

"Cinder, move!" Brother Wing cried.

Cinder leapt aside as the iron woman spun toward the dragon's voice. Cinder shielded her eyes as white hot flame shot from the dragon's mouth. In the aftermath, the woman glowed a dull cherry red. This didn't slow her as she sprang forward and attacked Brother Wing with a savage, two-handed swing of her mace. The weapon crunched into the side of the dragon's jaw. Bloodied, broken teeth clattered across the floor.

Brother Wing drew back on his hind legs, his wings spread, so that he seemed to fill the whole of the temple. With his tail he reached out and swept Mantle, still on knees, behind him. "Black Swan!" he growled. "You dare? You dare defile the sacred temple of my father?"

"There's nothing sacred about your father," the Black Swan answered. "I know where his true loyalties lie. Stand aside. This man must die."

"You're the Black Swan?" Cinder asked, stepping backward. "My mother always said you were dangerous."

"Dangerous, yes, and in the right. Listen to me, all of you. I'm here to save the world. Cinder, go home at once. You don't need to witness what comes next."

"You intend to slay Mantle," said Brother Wing. "But…why? Your mind… I can't make sense of your thoughts. Memories overlay memories, until all is chaos. Why would you—"

"I don't have time to explain," said the Black Swan. "I'm sorry, but I can't let you stop me." As she spoke, long needles grew from the tips of her left hand. She lunged toward Mantle. Brother Wing extended a talon into her path, seeking to block her. But perhaps her attack had merely been a ruse, since she ran straight toward the open talon and jammed her finger-needles into the dragon's wrist.

Brother Wing hissed in pain, drawing his talon toward his face. His eyes fixed on his wound, mere pin pricks, before his gaze shifted once more toward the Black Swan. Then, his eyes rolled backward, his body convulsing. Sorrow watched his body collapse, utterly limp, while his spirit lingered above, looking down on his fallen form in confusion.

The Black Swan leapt to avoid being crushed by the falling dragon. Though inhumanly strong, her iron body proved too slow to make it to freedom. She vanished under Brother Wing's torso, her mace clattering across the floor.

"Flee!" Ver shouted to Cinder. "You must take Mantle and flee the living lands. In Hell, the Black Swan cannot touch you."

By now, Mantle had made it to his feet. He ran and recovered the mace, then turned to face the Black Swan.

"I don't think the Black Swan will be bothering anyone once Mantle's done with her," said Cinder.

"Fool! She's far more dangerous than your mother has warned you. Mantle's attack will be countered with more trickery!"

This proved to be true. As the Black Swan pulled herself free of the dragon's body, she pressed a button on her forearm and was instantly hidden by a cloud of inky smoke.

"Go!" said Ver. "Her diamond eyes allow her to see clearly through the smoke. Don't wait for her to make another attack!"

"I'm going," said Cinder, running to Mantle's side. She reached him just as the smoke enveloped them both. In the darkness, she heard the Black Swan's metallic footsteps.

"Stay back," said Mantle. "It's dangerous for you to be near me."

"No," said Cinder grabbing his arm. "It's dangerous for you to be without me."

As she willed it, their bodies turned to spirit. The Black Swan's poisoned fingers sliced into the space where Mantle's neck had been. As the material world faded around them, all she could hear was the muted, distant sound of the Black Swan squawking in rage.

BROTHER WING LOOKED down on his body, disbelieving the sight. From his spiritual vantage point, his physical shell seemed translucent, and he could see the black threads of poison that had stilled his heart and silenced his brain in only a single heartbeat. With his training in necromancy, he recognized the substance as the legendary bad blood, a poison that took seven years to distill, refined from the heart-blood of a hundred murderers. A single drop could kill a man. She'd injected him with nearly half a cup.

The room vanished around him, the walls of the temple fading away. Since birth, he'd been able to see into the lands of the dead immediately adjacent to the living world, and grown familiar with the varied terrain. Since most of the members of his community had been recruited from former believers of the Church of the Book, the spiritual realm next to the village had been the outer reaches of the church's traditional Hell, intermingled a bit with the Realm of Roots encroaching from the faith of the nearby pygmies.

As each second carried him further from the realm of the living, he expected to find himself in these familiar surroundings. Instead, he found himself falling freely through an open sky. Far below was a shimmering green ocean. There was no land in sight, and no way of knowing how far he would fall before hitting the water.

He clenched his jaw tightly, feeling old resentments rising within him. Any other dragon could simply spread his wings and fly to escape the fate of falling. But, though Vigor had made his best attempts to heal Brother Wing's childhood injuries, his damaged wings had never been strong enough to bear his weight in flight.

He closed his eyes, as the stinging wind rushed past his face. He spread his wings, feeling the wind catch the sails of his skin. When he'd lived at the Keep of the Inquisition, the island had been constantly buffeted by storms. He'd often climbed to the roof of the highest tower, spreading his wings, catching the wind, closing his eyes and imagining what it would be like to fly, to claim the birthright of any creature born with wings.

In the living world, due to his ill-knitted bones, even his make-believe flights had caused knifelike pain to run through his shoulders and down his back. Here, with his spiritual body, there was no pain.

No pain.

And wind beneath his wings.

He opened his eyes. Instinctively, he'd stretched his wings to their fullest. In the time his eyes had been closed, he'd fallen close enough to the sea that he could now see whitecaps atop the waves. Yet, the whitecaps grew no closer. He was no longer falling toward the water. He was moving forward, in a smooth, painless glide.

With a cry of joy, he flapped his wings, and climbed higher in the sky. He flapped again, and again, feeling the power of an unbroken body. The wind whispered along his scales in a sensual caress. He was flying!

Tears again filled his eyes, but no longer from the stinging wind. Since his birth, he'd walked the living world, with various Hells always haunting him from the shadows. He'd always assumed these dark landscapes would be his eternal home one day.

With a sob that became a laugh, and a laugh that became a song, he beat his wings with all his strength as he joyfully flew through the sky of Heaven.

CINDER'S TRANSITION INTO the spirit world was unlike any previous journey she'd made. The atmosphere of the Realm of Roots was steamy, smelling of dank decay mixed with a cloying sweetness of rotting fruit. Now, the air surrounding her was hot as a furnace, desiccating, with a volcanic stench of sulfur. The ground beneath her felt like fine, loose powder, sloped into a steep dune, yielding, threatening to engulf her. Unlike the ghostly glow of other spiritual realms, here she was surrounded by unbroken darkness. She couldn't see her own hand before her face, though her spiritual body normally possessed its own internal light.

Nor could she see Mantle, though she still grasped his arm with one hand.

"What's happened?" asked Mantle, still unseen in the darkness. "Why have you brought me to this place?"

"That metal woman was going to kill you," said Cinder. She coughed violently after she said this, as dry dust blew into her mouth.

"She was certainly going to try," said Mantle. "We must go back. We have to defend Brother Wing."

From the darkness ahead of them, Ver, unseen, spoke. "Brother Wing is dead."

"Then I must return to avenge him!"

"I understand your pain," said Ver. "But, I'm afraid we've landed upon shifting sands. Climbing back to the living world from here will be all but impossible. To reach firmer ground, we must move forward."

Cinder finally managed to stop coughing, taking shallow breaths through her nose. She craned her neck to see around her.

"Have I gone blind?" she whispered. "Even in total darkness, I should be able to see you, Ver."

"Your eyes still work. It's your mind that's failed. This happens to many new arrivals to Hell. Their eyes see the horror around them, but their minds deny what they see. I'm a moment or two, your sight will return. Soon after, our mission here will be complete. The ones we seek aren't far at all."

"I see fine," said Mantle. "This place is bleak, certainly. Barren. But, far from horrific."

"You cannot see the world the way Cinder sees it. The sand you walk upon? It's not made of crushed stone. In life, all men carry a great cargo of hope. For some men, hope is their most priceless treasure. For others, it's their heaviest burden. But in Hell, all hope is lifted from men's shoulders. The hopes are crushed, then scattered on the winds. The dust eventually settles here, on Hell's outer wastes. You see only powdery soil. Sorrow's spiritual vision sees the truth of what she walks upon, and rejects it."

"I don't want to be here," said Cinder. "You never told me... you never told me it would be so horrible."

"It's Hell, my dear," said Ver. "What were you were expecting? No matter. You wish to leave. I want your swift departure as well. We've only to gather those we've come for. Follow me. Mantle, you'll have to guide her."

Now it was Mantle who took her by the arm. "I have you," he said, in a calm voice. "We'll get through this together."

"Follow!" Ver said, his voice growing more distant.

Mantle moved forward and she followed only to immediately lose her footing in the dust. He lost his grip on her as she flailed for balance. As she struggled to remain upright, she wound up taking a deeper breath that she should have. Dust filled her lungs. Suddenly, she felt the crushed hopes of a thousand dead souls weighing heavy on her shoulders. She gave a choked cry as her legs gave out beneath her. Blind, as one of falls into a swoon, she stumbled in the darkness and went down.

11 - A Map of Hell

GALE SILENTLY CURSED the day that the One True Book had come aboard her ship. Trying to take the book from the Isle of Storm had caused Tempest to attack them, which led directly to the death of her eldest son. Levi had given his life to save the rest of his family, even though he'd been estranged from Gale for years. Gale's grief was still fresh, and bound tightly with guilt. If she'd had possession of the book at this moment she'd gladly tossed it overboard to be rid of the cursed thing. But, if she did have the book, there was one thing she most definitely wouldn't do, and that was turn it over under pressure of blackmail, even if she'd thought a villain like Stallion had any intention of keeping his word.

Still, this was the wrong moment to tell him that. With all eyes fixed on her, she saw a figure moving behind the skeletal mob. It was Brand, climbing back to the deck. It looked as if he'd grabbed a rope as he fell and saved himself from the river.

She focused her gaze on Stallion, hoping he'd not seen her eyes wander. From her peripheral vision she saw Brand slink silently along the deck, then go over the rail once more, climbing down toward the porthole in the master cabin.

So far, the skeletal army had made no move to go below deck. Gale knew, as sure as she knew her own mind, what Brand's next move would be. She had to buy him time.

She threw down her sword and raised her hands. "Is that what this is all about? The book? You didn't need to attack us at all," she said, in a laughing tone. "I'll turn it over gladly. The book means nothing to me."

"The priest said there'd be a knight guarding it," said Stallion. "That big fellow, the one who helped you attack my ship." He glanced around. "Where is he?"

"Slate?" she said, trying to convey a mixture of surprise and sadness. "He's dead. Drowned in the bay at Raitingu."

Stallion shook his head. "Don't lie to me Gale. I was told the knight was aboard your ship by a Truthspeaker."

"A Truthspeaker?" asked Gale. "If he was in Hell, he must not have been very good at his job."

Stallion chuckled. "It turns out that Hell is full of their ilk. But this one was right in everything he told me so far. He said that Tempest would pull down the gates of Hell, and forge the iron into weapons for an army to invade the living realms." He pulled a small pocket compass from his vest. "He also gave me this."

"A magic compass?" she said, eyeing the object.

"No! Something better! A real compass! Even here in Hell, it points toward true north. Ver said that even this trivial bit of truth would tame Hell enough to let me navigate. I only had to patrol until you came, then finally have my revenge against you. He also swore that, if I brought him the One True Book, he'd help me escape Hell forever, not as some shambling skeleton in the living realm, but through permanent, final oblivion."

"Then let's not waste more time," said Gale. "Free my children, all of them, and you'll have the book. If what you want is oblivion, I don't see what value you'll find in taking revenge against me."

Stallion shook his head. "I'm not negotiating, Gale. I'm offering fair terms. I'd dreamed of many, shall we say, *exotic* ways of making you suffer. The Truthspeaker assured me that the only true way to hurt you would be to hurt your children. But won't it be a fine thing that one will still live?"

"Speaking of children," said Gale, not knowing if Brand had yet got into position. "What happened to that boy who was pushing you around? What was his name?"

"Numinous?" Stallion said. "The priest told me the bastard made it to shore."

"We were three hundred miles from land," said Mako. "Even I can't swim that far."

Mako was swiftly silenced by a blow to the gut from a club-wielding skeleton.

"I always thought the boy was lucky," said Stallion. "Not to me—he was a plague from the day I laid eyes on him—but he always boasted it wasn't luck that kept him alive. He said it was destiny, said he couldn't die until he accomplished his great deed. I thought he was crazy, but the Truthspeaker told me the boy really was what he said he was… the Omega Reader."

Gale furrowed her brow. "The Omega Reader?"

"Aye, you're probably not much better versed on the Church of the Book than I was. The Omega Reader will read the One True Book on the Day of Judgment. When the book is read, all the false, sinful things in the world will be wiped away. That includes you, that includes me, and most assuredly it includes this accursed place!" With the hand that held the compass, he motioned toward the dark, twisted landscape.

"That kid wasn't the Omega Reader," said a voice from outside the circle of skeletons. Gale's eyes were drawn toward the voice, and found Bigsby standing by the stairs that led below deck. He wore a helmet, beneath which hung the long blonde curls of his wig. He carried a mace that looked too large and heavy for him, and was weighed down further by a vest of chainmail. As the skeletons turned toward him, Bigsby said, "The Omega Reader is supposed to be perfect in everything. But when I fought that punk, I kicked his butt."

Stallion looked at the dwarf with an expression somewhere between amusement and bewilderment. He asked, "Who the devil are—"

He never finished his sentence. At that exact second, Poppy dropped from the rigging onto Stallion's equine back. She wore her belt studded with large lead fishing weights, letting her land a good, solid blow that caused his legs to buckle. She bounced off to the side the second she made contact. Stallion launched into the sky. Gale's gaze followed as he whizzed straight up. In the ropes above, she was thrilled to find Brand, with a long coil of rope in his hand. Brand's hand darted out, as if he was attempting to punch Stallion as he whizzed past, but he never made contact.

Looking down, a strange smile on his lips, Brand shouted, "Rigger!" then threw the rope.

Gale had no time to ponder how Brand had gotten above her. Instead, she snatched up her cutlass and whirled toward the skeleton who held a blade to Sage's throat. With a swift and precise jab, she cut the sinews at the creature's elbow. Its sword fell, only to be caught by Sage before it hit the deck. She spun around and severed the skull from the neck of the skeleton that had menaced her, then launched an attack on the next one.

From the corner of Gale's eye, she saw that her sons made good use of the fraction of the second in which the skeletons had watched their captain fly away. With a savage growl, Mako did a reverse head-butt to the skeleton that held the blade to his throat, knocking its face in. In seconds, he was free of the grasping limbs and once more in possession of a sword.

Rigger, meanwhile, had turned the rope Brand had thrown him into a writhing serpent that pulled away the blade against his throat and entangled Jetsam's attackers as well.

At the same time, Bigsby had charged forward and shattered the knee-cap of the skeleton nearest to him. The blow left Bigsby off balance, and he might have been overrun by the undead warriors who lunged for him, except that three pale green pygmies darted up the stairs bearing makeshift weapons of iron skillets and a large butcher knife from the ship's galley. They ran to defend Bigsby, only to be followed by three more, then a dozen, then an entire army of small green men armed with anything heavy that could be turned into a bludgeon. With jungle battle cries from their various tribes, they yipped and yelped and jabbered their way through the confusion of skeletal warriors, shattering thigh bones and knee caps, before bashing in the skulls of falling opponents.

"Watch out below!" Brand yelled from the rigging.

Before Gale could look up, Sage wrapped her arms around her mother's waist and pulled her forcefully to the side. The two of them fell to the deck just as there was a horrible sound, a mix of a splash and a thump, directly behind them. Cold, dark, foul-smelling fluid spattered her. She turned and saw Stallion had fallen back to the deck where she'd been standing. The impact had reduced him to a mass of broken bones jutting up from an oozing puddle of pulverized meat.

Before she and Sage could make it to their feet, a skeleton armed with an axe charged toward them, brandishing his weapon. She rolled to her back, raising her cutlass to block the coming blow, when Brand swung down on a rope and kicked the skeleton in the chest with enough force to carry the creature back over the rail.

The splash of it hitting the water was indistinguishable from the sound of a countless other skeletons being tossed overboard. By the time Gale rose, the battle was all but over. The only reason the skeletons had posed any threat at all was their overwhelming advantage in numbers, and the pygmies had proven to be even more numerous.

"Gale!" Brand called out as the rope swung him back toward her. He dropped off to land by her side. "Are you alright?"

"Except for being spattered in goo," she said, wiping the flecks of gore on the back of her hand against Brand's silk shirt. "Where's Cinnamon?"

"I'm here!" the girl called out from the stairs. She came above deck carrying a saw and a hammer. "I'm afraid I've had to cut up all the furniture to give the pygmies weapons."

"We'll make do," said Gale.

Brand turned to Sage and held out his hand. "I got a present for you."

He turned up his palm to reveal the compass Stallion had held earlier.

"When did you get your hands on that?" she asked.

"It was flying into the air with him."

"You saw it? And grabbed it that fast?"

"You know I'm good with my hands."

Gale put her hands on her hips and opened her mouth to speak.

Sage cut her an evil glance. "Ma, don't say anything that will embarrass me."

Sage took the compass from Brand and examined it.

"Is it magic?" he asked.

"Just the opposite," she said. "If it was magic, I'd see the aura. Stallion was telling the truth. This is something even more precious. It's completely mundane."

Brand scratched the back of his head. "Um, one of us apparently doesn't know the meaning of the word precious."

"Don't you see?" said Sage. "Hell is an ever changing place of magic, devoid of the normal reference points that make reality manageable. The landscape is fluid, so that hills become valleys, swamps become deserts, and there's no way of knowing where you are. But, underneath it all, there must be some physical truths. Gravity still seems operational, at least." She glanced at the mashed mess that used to be Captain Stallion. "Apparently, there's also a north here. The needle holds true as I move it."

"And we didn't have a compass of our own?" Brand asked.

"Of course we did," said Gale. "But, until now, what good did it do us to know which way's north?"

"I guess it doesn't help, does it?" asked Brand. "It's not like we have a map of this place. We don't know if the Sea of Wine is north or south, east or west."

"We don't need the compass to reach the Sea of Wine," said Gale. "It's always night here. I can feel mother's spirit stirring within the boards. I only need to give the order and she can take us there."

"But, you said… I heard you ask Sage if—"

Sage shrugged. "I saw the path immediately. But I read the look in Ma's face and knew she didn't want me to reveal that."

"I'm more confused than ever," said Brand. "Why aren't we already there? Why go through the bother of sailing this accursed river?"

"Because I wasn't ready to trust Walker," Gale said. "I'm less ready to trust him now."

"Then it's a good thing he's not here, right? We can make our move before he gets back," said Brand.

"Not yet," said Gale. "You're right about the compass being useless without a map. My guess is we'll find something useful if we search the *Seahorse*."

Before Brand could question her further, Gale turned to Bigsby, who was surrounded by a cluster of pygmies. "Excellent work," she said. "Tell the pygmies they've earned double rations tonight."

"Ma," said Rigger, who stood nearby. "We don't know how long we'll—"

She narrowed her eyes at him, stopping him in mid-sentence. "Instead of standing there complaining, grab a mop and get this deck cleaned."

Rigger frowned, but said, "Yes, Captain."

Gale barked out further orders, telling Poppy and Cinnamon to get Mako and Jetsam stitched up. She had Bigsby assemble a crew of pygmies to repair the damage to the ship, using parts from the *Seahorse* if needed. She took it as an article of faith that the forest-pygmies, who spent their whole lives living among trees, would prove to be gifted carpenters.

She then had Sage, Brand and Bigsby follow her to the rails, where they hopped onto the now abandoned *Seahorse*. The deck was slippery with slime, but the boards beneath still seemed solid enough. If the ship hadn't been structurally sound, her earlier attack with hurricane winds would have torn it to splinters. She took a minute to tell Bigsby what structural components they would need for repairs. When he left to relay his orders to the pygmies, she had Sage and Brand follow her toward the back of the ship in search of the captain's quarters.

The found a single crewman left aboard the ship. It was the rabbit man, one of only two survivors when they'd fought the *Seahorse* in the living world. The rabbit man seemed not to have moved at all from where she'd left him, cowering and weeping, terrified of the fate awaiting him. Now, though he'd been dead twenty years, he still cowered, his body emaciated, his rabbit fur riddled with holes. His hands were over his face and his back trembled as he noiselessly sobbed.

"What's he so afraid of?" Brand asked as they walked past. "How much worse can things get?"

"How much better can they get?" asked Sage. "It must be a terrible thing, to have all hope stripped away."

"A coward in life has no hope of courage in Hell," said Gale. As she said it, the words struck her as somewhat militant, and for the briefest moment she thought of the times when it had been her own young children sobbing in fear. They'd never received any kinder words than she'd uttered just now. Her own mother had been kinder, more patient and petting, but the earliest skirmishes of the slave wars had come when Gale was only fourteen. She'd caught fire then, convinced that courage, discipline, and a good steel blade might somehow carve the world into a better place. When her own children came along, she'd taught them never to back down, never to show fear, or even to admit you felt it. Save for Levi, her teachings had kept her children alive and clearheaded through a host of dangers that would have left weaker people on the verge of madness. She would never, ever, say she'd done them wrong, raising them as she had. But the thought that there might be a place where one day she could weep, could say she was afraid, could feel all that her heart wished to feel… was that Hell? Or Heaven?

She quickly pushed the musings from her consciousness as they reached the captain's quarters. With Brand's glorystone locket bringing daylight to the gloom, she instantly spotted what she'd expected to find. A map was stretched open on a rough-hewn table, the four corners weighted down with skulls, and a large, gold-rimmed magnifying glass sitting in the center. Drawing nearer, she saw that the parchment was made from cured human flesh, covered with tattooed mountains and valleys, as well as the winding, twisted river they sailed upon. Like the land itself, the whole of the map was in motion, the features slowly shifting, reflecting the ever-changing contours of Hell.

"A compass wouldn't be enough by itself to navigate," said Gale. "But with this, we've got a chance."

"A chance for what?" Brand asked. "If you can get us to the Sea of Wine, why don't we just go there? Walker's not here, so he won't know what's happened."

"Walker's only half our problem," said Gale. "We have to find Slate and Sorrow, and quickly."

Brand cocked his head to the side. "Why? They seemed pretty insistent on striking out alone."

Sage seemed to instantly understand. "Stallion said he was looking for the One True Book. Slate has it."

"Whoever this priest was that sent Stallion to find it, I don't want him getting his hands on it," said Gale.

"You take it seriously?" asked Brand. "The idea that, somewhere, somehow, there's an Omega Reader who'll read the book and bring reality as we know it to an end?"

Gale pressed her lips together and took a long, slow breath, which was something of a mistake given the charnel atmosphere of Stallion's quarters. Still, it gave her time to weigh the matter.

"Yes," she said. "All my life, I've been content to let others believe as they wished to believe. We Wanderers had our faith, the Church of the Book had theirs, and even the fact that the poor fools on Raitingu worshiped a dragon didn't bother me. It's a big world, with room for a lot of ideas. But, right now, there's one ideology dedicated to bringing an end to everything. I don't think we can shrug off the threat they represent."

"It's a shame Sorrow isn't here," said Brand. "She'd give you a hug right now that you wouldn't believe."

"I'll be happy to repeat the words when I find her," said Gale. "Though I doubt Slate will be happy to hear what I have to say. When we find them, we have to destroy the book."

"Destroy it?" Brand said. "That seems… seems…"

"You were raised to respect the teachings of the church," said Gale.

"I was raised to respect a lot of stuff that I figured out wasn't worthy of respect," said Brand. "I haven't been inside a church in ages, and can't fathom what circumstances would take me back inside one. But that book matters to a lot of people. Despite what Sorrow thinks, the church brings good to the world as well as bad. It encourages charity. It encourages loving your fellow men."

"We Wanderers are charitable, and love just as much as any person, without need of a book to tell us right from wrong. The world can survive without this text."

"Besides," said Sage, "if I understand correctly, no one really reads the book. The Truthspeakers say what's in it without ever looking at its pages. I don't see how the absence of the book will interfere with their ministry at all."

Brand nodded. "I can't think of an actual objection. Whenever religion comes up as a topic, I'm so used to telling Sorrow she's not thinking straight that I'm arguing out of instinct."

There was a single knock on the cabin door. They turned to see Jetsam sticking his head into the room. "Ma, there's something you should see."

Taking the magnifying glass and rolling up the map, Gale and the others followed Jetsam. He swam through the air back to the *Circus*. Gale felt a sense of relief as she jumped from the rails of the *Seahorse* back to her own ship. The atmosphere changed instantly. Despite the nearness of the two ships, the stench of death gave way to the clean, sharp odor of pine soap. The deck was spotless, freshly mopped. The pygmies had cleared away all traces of the skeletons who'd menaced the ship, and were already at work prepping the damaged bowsprit for the replacement that Rigger was helping to pull free from the *Seahorse*.

Mako stood in the now clean spot where Stallion had fallen. Mako's wounds had been expertly stitched by Cinnamon, whose small and steady hands made her quite adept at the task. Behind Mako was a barrel. He stepped aside as Gale approached, revealing square of canvas draped over something roughly the size of a cantaloupe atop the barrel. Jetsam flitted down beside Mako. "I heard it, Ma. Rigger was about to throw it overboard, but I heard it."

"I heard it first," said Mako. "I was the one who stopped Rigger. Don't take credit for stuff I did."

"I didn't say you didn't do those things," said Jetsam.

Gale sighed. "Boys, what are you—"

Before she could finish, Jetsam pulled away the canvas with a flourish. Beneath it was Stallion's head, relatively intact despite the fall.

Gale turned her eyes away, her stomach tightening. "Why on the waves would you think I'd want that as a trophy?"

"No!" said Mako. "That's not our intent. Stallion's still alive!"

Stallion's eyes opened halfway at the sound of his name. His jaws moved, his lips forming words, nearly soundless. Gale couldn't tell if he was trying to speak but Mako said, "He says, 'Not alive.' He's still as dead as ever, I guess. But that hasn't shut him up."

"Good," said Gale, stepping closer. "I've got questions for him."

The jaws opened wide, the pale tongue trembling.

"He's laughing," said Mako.

"I gathered," said Gale. She crossed her arms. "Stallion, I don't see much use in threatening you. You're as beaten as any man could ever be beaten."

Stallion gave a grim smile, then spoke again, with Mako translating, "If I were in your shoes I'd threaten to pluck out my eyes, shove hot irons into my ears and nostrils."

"You'd like that," said Gale. "You probably don't enjoy seeing, hearing, or even smelling what's become of you."

Stallion frowned, then said, "I'll never tell you a damn thing you want to know."

"Since I can't threaten you," said Gale, "I've no choice but to bribe you."

Stallion laughed again, his face twitching for a long time.

When he calmed at last, Gale said, "I can take you to the Sea of Wine."

Stallion's eyes opened wide.

"I'll never take you to the Happy Isles, but I'll throw you into the wine. You'll spend your eternity in drunken bliss, unless Rott devours you. The price of passage is only a few answers."

"What do you want to know?" he asked.

"Who's the priest who sent you on this mission? What's his name?"

"Ver," said Stallion.

Brand scratched his head. "Where have I heard that name?"

"From Infidel," said Gale. "When she told us about the failed quest to slay Greatshadow. Ver was the Truthspeaker who led the expedition."

"Right," said Brand.

"Ask him how he uses the map," said Sage.

Gale did so. Stallion told her that the magnifying glass could be used to study the tiniest details of the map, even the location of individual souls. Then, with the guidance of the compass, you could simply will the terrain around you to change until it gave you a clear path to whoever it was you wished to reach.

"How do you know where to look on the map to find the soul you want?" asked Sage.

"I didn't say it was easy to use, or fast," said Stallion. "You search by studying the map inch by inch, until you find what you want, or go mad. Few things in Hell are easy to look upon."

"One more question," said Gale. "We've been travelling with a pygmy named Walker, and a couple of demons named Fume and Foment. We think there's more to Walker than he's letting on. What do you know about him?"

"Walker?" Stallion said, looking confused. "Never heard of him. But Fume and Foment… they used to hang out with a devil named Fester. Together, the three of them were the last devils to remain loyal to the Alpha."

"The Alpha?" asked Gale.

"The first ruler of Hell," said Stallion.

"So, the guy Tempest overthrew when he got here?" asked Brand.

"No," said Stallion. "The throne of Hell was empty when Tempest arrived. The Alpha simply walked away from his job centuries ago, or so I'm told. Said he was tired of the role the Divine Author had written for him, and was quitting to seek a different fate."

"I had no idea that was allowed," said Brand.

"But it meshes with what we know of Walker," said Sage. "First, if he walked off the job, it might explain his name. Second, it would explain why Tempest would focus his attention on Walker and leave us alone. Third, it would explain why Walker is so knowledgeable about Hell, and why the devils seem so deferential to him."

"Why would he come back?" asked Brand, looking around. "Once you escape a place like this, it doesn't make sense you'd come here voluntarily."

"You couldn't be more wrong," said Stallion, with the faintest trace of a bittersweet smile. "Everyone comes here voluntarily. There's not a soul born who isn't warned that Hell awaits if he doesn't mend his ways. We all plunge headlong toward damnation just the same."

"Speak for yourself," said Gale. "Some of us try to live a virtuous life."

"Aye," said Stallion. "And your kind are thick as fleas here."

"Put him back under the tarp," Gale said to Jetsam. "Get him below deck, someplace safe."

"We should just toss him overboard," said Mako. "His stink is unbearable."

"I made a deal," said Gale. "We'll drop him in the Sea of Wine. Until then, breathe through your mouth."

12 - BITTER WOODS

SORROW WOKE SLOWLY, luxuriating in the warmth that ran through every muscle. Until now, she'd only toyed with magic, only caught glimpses and hints of what it was like to wield true power. Yes, she'd experienced the raw elemental magic of Rott, a destructive, nihilistic force that had almost devoured her. But in Slate's arms, together they'd awakened something new and powerful within her, a force of creation, a power of life instead of death.

With her eyes still closed, she frowned. Where was Slate? She'd fallen asleep in his arms, his chest glued to her back by sweat. Now, he wasn't touching her.

Sorrow sat up. She instantly placed an arm across her naked breasts as she found that she wasn't alone. In a tightly packed circle around the silk cloak they'd fallen asleep on, a score of old men and women stood shoulder to shoulder, glaring at them with judgmental eyes.

Slate sat next to her, pulling on his pants with one hand, holding onto the Witchbreaker with the other.

"I don't think the sword is necessary," she said softly. "They look too old and toothless to hurt us."

"Appearances can be deceiving in Hell," said Slate. "It's not their teeth I fear, nor their limbs. It's their eyes that tear into me. I've never felt so… *naked*."

Sorrow put her hand on Slate's back to comfort him. He instantly tensed up, and said, "Don't touch me while they watch."

She pulled her hand away, watching the faces of the assembled crowd take on an even deeper look of disapproval following her touch. One of the old women whispered, barely audible, "Whore." A man on the opposite side of the circle murmured, "Sinner." A third voice behind her, too weak and trembling for Sorrow to determine the sex of the speaker, hissed, "Shameful!" The word was taken up, passing among the crowd. "Shameful! Shameful! Shameful!"

"No!" Slate cried, pulling on his shirt. "You don't understand!"

"Slate, calm down," she said, noting the panic in his voice. She'd never heard anything vaguely resembling this emotion come from him before.

He turned to her, tears welling in his eyes. "We should have waited," he said, his voice choked. "We—"

"Hussy. Tramp. Fornicator. Dirty, dirty, dirty," murmured the crowd.

"Please," said Slate. "It was only a moment of weakness."

Sorrow stood, her fists clenched. She made no effort to conceal her nudity. She stared into the eyes of the woman nearest to her. "You're wasting your time."

"Shame!" scolded the woman.

Sorrow shook her head. "I feel no shame. You've no power over me. Go away."

The woman flickered, turning halfway to smoke, before solidifying again. Her eyes now focused on Slate, completely ignoring Sorrow. "Seducer," she said, clucking her tongue. "Shame! Shame!"

Slate clamped both hands over his eyes, shaking his head. Sorrow grabbed him by the wrist and pulled him to his feet. "Snap out of it!" she said. "Don't you see? These things are feeding off your shame."

"What have we done?" he asked, his voice trembling.

She slapped him, hard, much harder than she intended. He was nearly knocked from his feet, and remained standing only because she still had hold of his wrist.

"What's wrong with you?" she said. "How can you possibly be ashamed of what we did? It was wonderful. We're in love, Slate! We made love! Don't you understand the beauty of what we did?"

He swallowed hard. "There are… there are *rules*."

She struggled to resist slapping him again, took a deep breath, and said, "Love has no rules."

"Love cannot be anarchy," he said. "If so, it's meaningless, capricious and fleeting."

She poked a finger into his chest. "Love isn't anarchy. But we don't have to follow anyone's script, not even the Divine Author's. If our love turns out to be fleeting, so be it. Last night was still precious to me. You're the first man I've ever given myself to, and it meant something to me." She crossed her arms, feeling a chill run through her. "It meant… everything to me. I love you, Slate. Do you know how impossible those words sound to my ears? Do you not understand how much of myself I had to let go of in order to embrace you? Now, to find out you're filled with… with regret… I… I…" She couldn't finish her sentence. Tears welled in her eyes, blurring his figure.

She closed her eyes, fighting back her tears, when his arms closed around her. He kissed her softly on the forehead. "I'm sorry," he whispered. "You're right. You're absolutely right. I love you. What happened between us was precious and pure. There can be no shame attached to it."

She turned her face upward, until their lips met.

Around them, the crowd hissed, then groaned, then wept. She opened her eyes to find them slinking away, one by one.

"They were scolds in life," she said, understanding the truth. "Scolds incapable of love, hating the very sight of the genuine emotion. They only have power over us if we give it to them."

"Aye," said Slate. "I see that now. I don't know why I… I said what I did. Why I felt ashamed. There was no trace of shame within me when we fell asleep."

"A lot of people who feel confident of their actions in private crumble when they know they're being watched. Though, in your case, perhaps there are… other issues."

"What do you mean?"

"I'm talking about the whole reason we're out here in the first place. Your unhealthy obsession with Stark Tower."

"Unhealthy?" Slate asked, sounding confused. "Your whole life has been guided by your obsession with your father."

"What does that have to do with anything?"

"Stark Tower is more than my father. I was crafted from his blood. I'm the continuation of his body, the same person on a fundamental level."

"You think that, yes," she said. "And that's probably why you felt such guilt. Stark Tower became the lover of the queen of witches. He let himself be seduced by the very thing he'd sworn to destroy."

"Yes," said Slate. "And his weakness led to his being here."

"But not the weakness you imagine," said Sorrow. "You think he's here because he gave in to his lust. You think he's here because he betrayed his church."

"These are the sins we know of."

"His greater sin was hypocrisy. If he grew to love Avaris, he hid his love from the world during his lifetime. He could have sworn off his war against the witches, made amends for what he'd done. Instead, he chose to wear one face in public, and another in private."

Slate nodded, looking as if he were weighing her words carefully.

"Do you still want to find him?" she asked.

He didn't answer. He studied the distant hills with a vacant gaze.

"You do," she said, seeing his face settle into certainty.

"Yes. I have to talk to him. I have to know. Why did he fall? Where did he go wrong?"

"So you can avoid his fate?"

"I don't believe I'm in any risk of his fate," said Slate. "I'm nothing but a body, devoid of spirit. When I meet death, it shall be final. There will be no eternal punishment, and no hope of reward."

"If you could only understand how much I envy that," she said, kneeling to retrieve her clothes. As she picked up her boots, she noticed a clawed hand at the edge of her cape. With three fingers and the thumb, it grasped the cloth. The other finger pointed straight out.

"Is this Fester's arm?" she asked, nudging the thing away from her cape with her foot.

"I believe it is," said Slate. "There's his other arm." She followed his gaze toward a mangled limb atop a mound of bodies they stood upon. It, too, had the fingers tightly curled, save for the first one, which pointed toward the horizon. Was it her imagination, or was it pointing toward the same spot the first one had indicated? She dressed quickly, keeping her eyes on the limb she'd pushed away, watching as the fingers clawed to move it back into alignment with the other limb, then extend a lone finger, pointing into the distance.

"This is crazy," said Sorrow. "I think Fester is still trying to tell us where to go."

Slate by now had his armor half-donned. She moved to his side to help him finish buckling up.

"I say we follow it," said Slate. "We've no better guide."

"What if it's not really pointing at anything?" she said. "It could lead us nowhere."

"Then it's no worse than simply striking out on our own," he said.

"Good point." She bent over and picked up first one arm, then the other. As she moved them from side to side, the fingers bent to keep pointing in the same direction. "I guess we'll know where we're going when we get there."

As she dressed, she looked around the landscape, finding it completely unfamiliar. The hill where they fought the gibbering guardian had been utterly barren. Now, they were surrounded by woods, dark and tangled with vines. An acrid, bitter stench rose from fallen, rotting fruit that covered the ground. Craning her neck, she saw no trace of the river, though it had still been in sight when they'd fallen asleep. Upon realizing the absence of the river, she felt suddenly thirsty. She found the bottomless bottle Mako had given her and took a long, cool drink.

She passed the bottle to Slate, but found her thoughts focused on Mako. She didn't regret rebuffing his advances, but she did feel bad about hurting his feelings. She worried most of all that he might think her rejection had been due his physical oddities, like his saw-toothed mouth. She would never have turned him away for a reason so shallow, especially since, at the time, she'd had wings and more than a few scales. She hoped that one day Mako would grow to see the wisdom of her choice and they could be friends.

Slate wiped his lips and handed the bottle back to her. He looked as if he were about to say something important, but said only, "We should go." She suspected these weren't the words that he'd contemplated speaking.

They each took one of Fester's arms and navigated through the tangled, gloomy, bitter woods, breathing shallow breaths. At times, she sank shin deep in the muck of rotting fruit. The acidic mush burned as it seeped through her canvas britches. At last, they cleared the worst of the thickets, emerging onto a plain of jagged rocks. It looked as if all the arrowheads, spear points and stone knives ever chipped out by mankind had been dumped here. Her boots proved durable enough to tread upon the surface, but she moved slowly, using Fester's trident as a staff. To fall here would prove painful.

They walked across the field of stone knives for what felt like hours. In the distance was a mountain range half obscured by storm clouds, the lower slopes white with snow. Both of Fester's arms pointed toward a single peak. Slate took the lead, and she found it was easier to keep her orientation if she focused on his back rather than on the land around her. The energy generated by their lovemaking was still powerful within her. Even through Slate's armor, she could see the structure of his body plainly, the scaffolding of bone bound together with sinew and set in motion by muscles. Slate was very close to masculine perfection, but even as she admired the symmetry and balance of his form, she also saw the design flaws he shared with all other men. She felt as if she could simply reach out, grab a tendon in his neck, and peel him apart if she so wished. It was only the magic, she knew. Back when she'd first gained power over iron, she couldn't pass by a table held together with nails without an almost irresistible urge to make the nails disintegrate into rust. Hopefully, the novelty of her powers would soon wear off and she'd be able to see people as a whole once more, instead of seeing a collection of components to be manipulated.

From time to time in the distance, shadowy forms stumbled across the landscape, human in size. Their shuffling movements reminded her of Mama Knuckle's "uncles," men whose bodies continued to serve the old necromancer long after their souls had departed. She wondered if Mama Knuckle was still alive after all these years.

Lost in reverie, she almost walked into Slate when he came to a halt.

"Listen," he said.

She listened. A child screamed in the distance, the voice coming from behind a crumbling wall. She'd noticed the remnants of structures before. She'd yet to see an intact building in Hell.

Slate took a step toward the screams. Sorrow placed her hand on his arm. "It could be a trick."

He nodded. "There… there couldn't be children here, could they?"

"Why not?" she asked.

"Children are incapable of falsehood. They've no reason to be condemned here if they die young."

"How many young children have you met?" asked Sorrow. "In my somewhat limited experience, children learn to lie almost as quickly as they learn to talk."

"It's probably a devil, trying to draw us nearer," Slate murmured, echoing her original objection.

Somehow, his agreement stirred her to a contrary emotion. She suddenly knew, beyond all doubt, that Hell was full of children. Her rage against the Divine Author surged so powerfully she felt herself tremble. She couldn't bear the thought of walking away from a child suffering from his cruel, so-called justice.

"Let's at least see what's making the sound," she said. "It's going to haunt you just as much as it haunts me if we walk away."

Slate nodded and set off for the wall at a brisk jog. She kept pace, feeling as if she could easily run rings around him. Her magical awareness of her body made her feel as if she hadn't really known how to use her legs to their fullest extent until this moment.

Slate slowed as they reached the edge of the crumbling wall. He stuck his head slowly around the corner, then pulled back.

"It's a child," he whispered, his face pale. "A boy, I believe, though so emaciated it's difficult to tell."

"What's happening?" she asked. "Is he being tortured?"

Slate nodded. "He's in the grasp of a giant hand."

Sorrow clenched her fists. "We've fought giants before."

"Yes, but there isn't a giant," said Slate. "Only a giant hand, thrusting up from the ground."

She moved past him to look for herself. Slate had assumed the child was a boy, perhaps because the child had no hair. Having been bald herself for so many years, she thought the child looked more like a girl. The girl was held in a huge, filthy fist, blood caking in the knuckles and nails. The girl was nearly skeletal, her ribs prominent. She was held from the waist down, but her torso and arms were free. She writhed, her expression more fear than pain, scratching at the hand with her twig-like fingers, beating it with her tiny fists, twisting and pushing and fighting to get free. Her mouth was open wide as she wailed in terror.

Sorrow pressed her back to the wall and swallowed hard. "I… I shouldn't have looked."

"Aye," said Slate. "'Tis a horrible thing."

"We can't just leave her," said Sorrow.

"Even if we free her… then what?" asked Slate. "She'll still be in Hell."

Sorrow pressed her lips together tightly as she contemplated what to do. Rationally, she knew that taking action to free the girl would be unlikely to bring any permanent relief in a place like this. Still, on a gut level, she knew she had no choice but to act.

"Let's hit it hard and fast," she said, not waiting for Slate to respond before charging around the wall.

Her suspicion that she could now run much, much faster proved true. She was at the hand mere seconds later, jamming the trident into the tendons on the back of the fist, rendering the forefinger useless. Again and again, she struck. In mere seconds, the fist relaxed, every tendon severed.

The ground trembled, then cracked. She skittered backward, certain that the giant buried beneath the ground was about to emerge. Instead, she saw the wrist sinking slowly, withdrawing with the child still entangled in the limp fingers.

Slate had reached the hand by now, grabbing one of the huge fingers to pull it away from the child. The child continued screaming.

"It's okay!" Sorrow called out as she sprang forward to help free the girl. "We're going to save you!"

The girl didn't seem aware of her words. It continued to claw and scratch at the finger that pressed against her hip.

Only, as Sorrow drew nearer, she saw that the girl wasn't trying to free herself of the giant's loosened grasp. Instead, she now dug her nails into the flesh and pulled, as if trying to keep the finger wrapped around her.

With a grunt, Slate pulled the creature's uppermost finger fully open, revealing part of the palm.

Sorrow gasped. The girl had no body from the hips down. Her torso merged with the flesh of the giant's palm. She grabbed the girl by the wrist, yelling, "Hold on! Hold on!" as the giant hand sank further into the earth.

"No!" the girl screamed, in the first coherent word Sorrow had heard her utter. "No no no no no no no!" She squirmed, twisting her arm, desperate to break Sorrow's grip.

Sorrow kept hold, trying to ignore the screaming and focus on the area where the girl and the giant merged. Perhaps her magical awareness of bodily structures might let her see a way to cut the girl free of the giant. Even if the girl lost her legs, wouldn't that be preferable to getting dragged underground? What she saw vexed her. The girl didn't seem to be a separate body embedded in the giant's hand. The two appeared to be a single entity. The tormenter and the tormented were of one flesh, and she couldn't spot an easy way to tear them apart without killing the girl.

Before she could study further to see if a more complicated surgery might accomplish her goal, the girl struck her, slapping her hard across the cheek. Sorrow at first assumed the blow was unintentional, an accident of the girl's flailing arms. But the slap was followed by the girl snarling, locking both hands on Sorrow's throat, and pulling Sorrow's face toward her own. The girl's jaw's opened as wide as they could and she bit down on Sorrow's left eyebrow, her chin jammed into Sorrow's eye.

Reflexively, Sorrow defended herself with bone magic. By instinct, she snapped the bones in the girl's fingers, freeing her neck, and caused the girl's teeth to crumble wherever they touched her. The girl squealed and drew away. Sorrow fell backward. Gauntleted fingers wrapped around her upper arm. She looked up and saw Slate on his knees above her. She was now in a pit formed by the retreating hand.

Slate dragged her to the lip of the pit as the hand continued to sink. The girl wailed, blood streaming from her damaged mouth, her eyes fixed on her mangled fingers. Then the giant fingers closed over the girl once more. Her screams trailed away. A placid look crossed her face as the giant hand once more formed a crushing fist. The dirt of the pit fell in upon her, and she was gone.

For a moment, it seemed as if their journey would end here, as the pit walls grew deeper, collapsing as they tried to climb free. Slate sank the Witchbreaker deep into the earth to anchor himself and shouted, "Climb over me!"

She did so, her fingers finding easy purchase in the gaps in his armor. As she clawed her way up his body to the edge of the pit, she found that the barren, jagged landscape had once more changed into a tangled forest of trees. The scent of rotten fruit made her stomach turn, left her feeling weak, but she had no time for weakness. With the trident still in her grasp, she jabbed the tines into a nearby root, making an anchor on the surface to pull herself once more onto relatively level ground. She spread her limbs wide on the edge of the pit, which still shuddered and rained dirt down on Slate. She tossed down the edge of her cloak. Slate grabbed hold, tugged the Witchbreaker free, then climbed.

They lay together panting, limbs entwined, as the shaking earth slowly calmed. In the silence that followed, the only sound was their panting. Then, from deep, deep beneath the earth, the girl began to scream once more, her muffled cries more forlorn than ever.

Sorrow closed her eyes. The vision of the girl's bloodied mouth came to her mind. The thought of the additional pain she'd caused hurt more than nails driven into her skull.

"I only wanted to help her," she whispered, her voice on the edge of a sob.

"You're bleeding," Slate said.

She opened her eyes to find him staring at her, his face a mask of concern. The vision of her left eye was tinted red. She rubbed her brow and found the girl had broken the skin with her bite. Closing the wound proved effortless, nothing more than rubbing her finger across the cut to push the damaged tissue back into place. The blood in her eyes was washed away by tears, which came freely now.

Slate took her into his arms, comforting her. "You did your best. You didn't mean to hurt the child."

"They were one," she said, her voice trembling. "The girl, the giant, both the same. Attacking one did damage to the other."

"It's this place," he whispered. "Nothing but horrors."

"No." She wiped her cheeks, sniffling, and pulled away from him. "It's not Hell where such entanglements are formed." She felt a hollowness in her gut, a void as terrifying as the darkness that had dwelled inside her when she'd been merged with Rott. "It's life. It's my life. I fought so hard to be free of my father. I thought him a monster, a beast to not only escape, but to vanquish. But... he was part of me. His blood fills my veins. My thoughts... my very soul... are forever bound with his." She gazed around at the entangling vines that choked the twisted trees, seeing how perfectly they reflected her soul. She shook her head, drawing a deep breath. "If I'd ever succeeded in destroying him, I would only have destroyed myself."

Slate looked at her with an expression that bordered on skepticism.

"What?" she asked.

"That seems like a vast change of heart," he said. "You've never said a kind word about the man. Now you credit him for what you've become."

"Credit?" she scoffed, astonished he could misunderstand her so. "I blame him! I hate him for it!"

"But... if you are one and the same... that would leave you hating yourself."

She wrapped her arms across her chest and looked at the pit the girl had vanished into, hearing the cries from far below. She would never be free of her father's grasp. The revelation smothered her thoughts and filled her body with tremendous torpor. The urge to lie down and never again rise overwhelmed her.

Slate removed his gauntlet. His warm fingers fell lightly on her chin as he turned her gaze toward him.

"Can it be that you don't love yourself?" he asked. "You're so precious. A unique soul, so beautiful, so worthy."

She sniffled, then murmured, "If only I could believe it."

"I've never lied to you," he said. "You are loved. I swear it."

He leaned forward and kissed her tenderly. Gently, he wiped the tears from her cheeks. She wrapped her arms around him and felt her strength return. He loved her. He truly loved her. A sweet, floral aroma filled her nostrils, taking the edge off the acrid bitterness of the atmosphere.

Opening her eyes, she found a thousand small, blood red blossoms freshly opened on the branches that bent toward them.

13 - DEEP IN THE DUST

THE BLACK SWAN SQUAWKED with rage as Cinder and Mantle faded from sight. In desperation, she leapt over Brother Wing's lifeless body, her arms outstretched. Her iron fingers clacked together, closing on empty air where Mantle had just stood. She slipped through the dimensional veil in pursuit, hoping it wasn't too late.

It was too late. Her feet sank into the soft dust of the outer dunes of Hell. She'd traveled to this realm enough not to be blinded by the bleakness of it, but her keen vision did her no good. Cinder and Mantle couldn't be seen. Ver knew how to navigate the paths between Hell and the living world better than anyone, and could have brought them out at the place of his choosing. Given Hell's protean landscape, they might be anywhere.

"Well, well, well," said a familiar voice from behind her. "Looks like Ver knew what he was talking about. It's been a long time, Swan."

The Black Swan had sank knee deep in the dust. She twisted around as best she could, knowing who she would find. High on the dune above her stood Reeker, a mercenary she'd once employed, a member of the legendary Three Goons. He'd been dead for twenty years.

"You've talked to Ver?" she asked. "Is he near? I must speak to him."

"He doesn't have anything to say to you," said Reeker. "Which is why he's paid me a tidy sum to kill you."

"Paid you? You're dead! Where are you going to spend it?"

"Haven't you heard?" asked Reeker. "The damned can leave anytime they want these days."

"True," she said. "And I've met my share of withered corpses stumbling through the wasteland Tempest and Hush have created. I can't say it's qualitatively different from what you have here."

"This is just the early stages of the invasion," said Reeker. He moved closer as he talked, treading lightly on the dust. Usually, any damned souls that tried to cross the outer dunes wound up buried, forever choking on the acrid powder. Reeker seemed buoyed by something. He was dressed surprising well for a damned soul, in a nice suit and leather boots polished to a mirror finish. Did the boots have some sort of enchantment?

Reeker kept talking. "Once we've killed the last of the living, the world will be ours. Then we'll divvy up the spoils. Ver understands I'm a man used to luxuries. He's promised me the palace of King Brightmoon himself!"

The Black Swan nodded, understanding. Reeker wasn't held up by magic boots. He wasn't sinking into the dunes because Ver had filled him with hope. His dreams of glory made him buoyant.

The Black Swan bent her wrists sharply, causing the blades stored in her forearms to spring out. "I wouldn't come any closer if I were you," she said. "Your powers are useless against me."

"I know," he said, pausing to take a cigar out of his vest. "Which is why it was my job to distract you."

She spun around, a second too slow. Something hard and heavy smashed in the side of her head with a deafening CLANG! The impact lifted her from the dust and threw her tumbling down the slope. When she landed, the world to her left was completely dark. She raised her hand and found that her brow on that side had a sizeable dent. Her eye had completely popped from its socket. Her head tilted on her shoulder at an odd angle and she couldn't straighten it. She shook off the shock of the damage and looked up in time to see a huge man running down the slope toward her, swinging a large iron ball and chain over his head.

"No-Face!" she called out, lifting her arms to protect herself. "Stop!"

He didn't stop. The iron ball smashed into the slender blades extending from her wrists, shattering them. The ball banged against her forehead, but had lost enough momentum to keep from denting her further.

No-Face planted his feet wide to steady himself as he drew back his ball once more.

"Goodbye, Swan," said Reeker, placing the cigar between his lips.

"My thoughts exactly," she said, as No-Face grunted, swinging with all his might.

His blow struck only empty dust. With a thought, the Black Swan returned to the living world.

She was flat on her back in the Temple of the Flame. She sat up, still unable to hold her head upright. She probed her left eye-socket. Though she knew the damage could be repaired, her asymmetry caused her mental pain. When she'd first taken up residence in her iron shell, the construct had felt like a machine, something she operated. Over the years, she'd gotten so used to it that it felt as if it were the body into which she'd been born. Any reminder of its artifice caused her discomfort.

She became aware of a soft ripping sound to her left. She turned and found a buzzard perched atop Brother Wing's neck, tearing at the dragon's tongue. How had the creature found the body so swiftly? Or even gotten inside the temple?

"I see you decided to start without me," said the buzzard.

"Menagerie?" she asked.

"You know many other talking birds around here?"

"Yes, actually. Commonground's full of parrots."

"Right," said the buzzard. "That was a dumb question." The buzzard lifted her bloodied beak and studied the Black Swan's face. "I take it this knight I'm supposed to kill fights with a mace?"

"He didn't do this to me," said the Black Swan, touching her damaged brow. "I ran into some of our former associates."

Menagerie nodded. "But you got the knight?"

"No," she said. "When you didn't show up on time, I had to act on my own. They got away, slipping into Hell."

"I got here as fast as I could," said Menagerie. "And, now that I'm here, we can follow them. I can turn into a bloodhound."

"Hell's the last place you'd want to be with a superb sense of smell," said the Black Swan. "No, it's on to plan Z."

"Plan Z? You mean Zetetic?"

"No, I mean it's the last plan I've yet to try."

"So… no Zetetic? Couldn't he fix all of this with a single lie?"

The Black Swan attempted to shake her head, but her limited movement made this difficult. "I've tried a dozen times to get Zetetic to help. He's gone completely mad."

"He wasn't exactly sane when I knew him. But, if you still have one good plan, why haven't you used it before?"

The Black Swan took her head in her hands and tried to carefully shove it back into position. She managed it, but when she let go, her head slipped sideways once more. "I never said it was a good plan. I've exhausted all the good plans. Sometimes, more than once."

"But you can keep trying," the buzzard said, her voice garbled a bit as she swallowed a large chunk of fatty tongue. "That's the advantage of being a time traveler."

"It's an advantage I've lost," she said. "Each time I've returned along my storyline, I've returned closer and closer to the final days. Now, at best, I could travel back a few hours."

"We could try this ambush again."

"It won't work," she said. "Something always goes wrong. This time, you showed up late. The time before, Brother Wing didn't get a full dose of my poison and I wasted precious minutes struggling with him. The time before that, Cinder and Mantle never even returned to the temple before Ver led them into Hell. I feel like this moment is… unlucky."

"I never knew you to rely on luck," said Menagerie.

"I'm not relying on it. I'm blaming it."

"So, plan Z," said Menagerie, hopping from the dragon's skull onto the floor.

"Yes," said the Black Swan. "Though I've done everything I could to keep her out of this."

As she spoke, Menagerie changed into a cat. "Keep who out of it?" With a faint *shlup shlup shlup,* the little beast lapped at the blood that had spilled onto the floor. The Black Swan waited patiently. Long ago, Menagerie gained his shapeshifting powers from magical tattoos. Ever since a remnant of his magic had gotten trapped inside a tick, however, he added new forms to his arsenal by ingesting blood. The cat lifted her head, licking her whiskers. "Oh, wait. I know who you're talking about." Menagerie gave a feline shrug. "She's a big girl. She can take care of herself."

A spasm ran through the cat's body, from tip to tail, to be replaced by a dragon, identical to the dead one it towered over. Menagerie unleashed two small jets of flame from her nostrils. She look pleased, until she stretched her wings and found one significantly shorter than the other. Menagerie sighed. "Great. I can finally turn into a dragon, and it's broken."

"So, fix it," said the Black Swan. "You're a shapeshifter. You can't alter a few parts?"

"In theory I could," said Menagerie. "But it would be artless."

"Artless?" said the Black Swan. "Art is in the eye of the beholder. If you fixed your wings, who would know? For that matter, I don't know why you still insist on changing into Infidel when you return to your human form. Couldn't you change in to a man? Why not look like who you used to be?"

Menagerie changed back into her human body. The gray cloak reappeared and fell around her shoulders. The Black Swan wasn't certain why the cloak appeared on some of Menagerie's bodies, but not on others.

Menagerie held out her arm, staring at the back of her hand. "I'm not as sentimental about my old body as you might imagine," she said. "I often wear a dozen different bodies a day. I don't get terribly attached."

"If you aren't that attached to them, it makes even less sense that you won't tweak them a little."

Menagerie shook her head, then asked, "How many old practitioners of blood magic have you met?"

"Just you, I suppose."

Menagerie nodded. "The temptation to alter the forms you've borrowed from the blood of others is quite powerful. Few blood magicians can resist making at least a few alterations. At first, they're minor. You change into a lion, and give it stronger muscles, sharper teeth, and longer claws. Then, you decide it would be advantageous if the lion had wings, or maybe gills. You start to mix and match parts from different creatures in a never-ending quest to create the perfect beast for the job at hand."

"What's so terrible about perfection?" asked the Black Swan.

"Nothing, other than it can never be attained," said Menagerie. "And once a shapeshifter starts making compromises to his physical integrity, his moral and mental integrity are sure to follow. If a blood magician is fortunate, maybe he'll one day become a hideous, terrifying monster, a chimera blended from a hundred different beasts."

"That's fortunate?" asked the Black Swan.

"Compared to the alternative," said Menagerie. "A far more common fate facing shapeshifters who lose their integrity is that they lose control of all their forms, and wind up stuck as quivering, gelatinous blobs unable to maintain any constant form."

"So the monster is the more fortunate fate," said the Black Swan.

Menagerie smiled faintly. "Or one can follow my path. Never cheat. Never be unfaithful to the forms you copy. With constant vigilance, it's possible to still hold onto some last, lingering shred of my core humanity."

"Very well," said the Black Swan. "Then I guess the wing stays stunted."

Menagerie rolled her eyes. "You sound disappointed. A flightless dragon is still a damn powerful thing. You did see me snort fire, right?"

"Right," said the Black Swan. "I apologize if I've sounded dismissive of your choices. You're still my most reliable ally, and I can think of no one I'd rather have by my side in these final hours."

"Don't say final," said Menagerie. "We'll win. We have to."

"Of course," said the Black Swan, "though, for the plan I have in mind, I'm going to need you to turn into something much, much smaller than a dragon."

THE SEA STRETCHED on forever beneath Brother Wing, a glistening sheet of emerald. He knew that time must be passing, but the sun remained constantly overhead, its orb concealed behind thin clouds. Brother Wing still felt the exultation of flight, and experimented with loop-de-loops and barrel rolls, high climbs and steep dives, thrilled at his newfound mastery of the air.

Behind the joyous beating of his heart, however, a second emotion set in, a gnawing, barely sensed anxiety. For a long time, he avoided letting this distant, tiny concern creep far enough into his consciousness that it might latch onto words and make itself heard. Unfortunately, the beauty of the endless seascape could only hold his attention for so long. With a wince of remorse, he allowed the miniscule worry to find a voice.

If this was Heaven, why was it so empty?

He attempted to reason the question into submission. He'd been born a telepath. For as long as he could remember, whenever he was around another living thing, their thoughts had intruded upon him. When his father had crippled him and tossed him down the slope, the thoughts of the lava-pygmies who'd come to claim his body had given him warning of their intentions. Through their eyes, he'd witnessed his body, broken and bleeding. Through their eyes, he'd seen himself struggle, rising, nipping and scratching. They'd persisted in their efforts to kill him, to no avail. Knowing their thoughts, even his injured frame had been able to avoid every attack. He'd felt their pain as he crushed their bones with his jaws. He'd shared their terror as his hind claws opened their bellies and the smell of blood and excrement grew thick in the jungle air.

He'd long since gotten used to being surrounded by others. Even mice creeping through the walls at night had desires and plans, however primitive. He'd long imagined the true heaven of one day being alone with his thoughts.

What if he'd been wrong? What if an eternity of being alone with your thoughts was actually Hell?

THE HEAT OF AFTERNOON had settled upon the Jawa Fruit village. This was normally the quietest time of day, when all the villagers would retreat to shade to sleep until evening. Infidel was waking as her tribesmen were settling in. She'd spent all night hunting, journeying to the great river in pursuit of a troop of howler monkeys. The beasts possessed a seemingly supernatural gift for staying one tree too far away for her to get a good shot with her spear, at least until they'd run out of trees at the river's edge. Even then, she'd only managed to kill two, both runts. The one good thing about killing them near the river was she'd had the luxury of a long swim after she'd cleaned her prizes. She'd returned home at dawn, bone tired, and collapsed into her hammock the second she'd walked into her hut, not even bothering to see if Cinder had enjoyed success with the beehive she'd discovered the day before.

Upon waking, she took a long drink from a gourd fill with cool water, then crawled out into the sunlight. Rising, she stretched her limbs to shake off her torpor. One of the village women had left a plate of fresh jawa fruit and sun-dried beetles in a wooden bowl beside the entrance to her hut. She knelt, rustling her fingers through the bugs in search of a meaty one.

As she lifted the beetle toward her lips, she heard the harsh, raspy cry of a macaw from the south. She turned her head toward the noise, recognizing it as a warning signal from a sentry.

Infidel grabbed her spear. The macaw sounded again from the south, then changed in mid-call into a battle cry. The voice was swiftly joined by a second cry, then a third, as the southern sentries attacked whatever was causing them trouble.

She leapt from branch to branch to reach the sentries, wondering what the problem might be. It couldn't be an incursion of Spike Branch warriors—they'd be shouting their battle cries just as loudly as her tribesmen.

As she scrambled through the treetops, she was soon outpaced by a half dozen male pygmies racing through the trees, spears at the ready, yipping their high-pitched war calls. She could hear when they reached whatever was attacking. Their shouts lost their initial ferocity and became tinged with confusion and fear. The *clink, clink, clink* of stone spear points striking iron rang out from ahead.

Long-men, she deduced, equipped with armor and shields. It had only been a matter of time before the settlers pushed to expand their range.

She tossed aside her spear, knowing it would be useless, and reached for the magical sword that hung by her side. If she was about to engage with armored long-men, she'd need to even the odds. She pulled the sword free of its scabbard. She frowned as the sword sputtered to life. Once, it had ignited before it even cleared the sheath. Of late, its flame was slower and less bright. Why?

She'd been in possession of the sword for a long time, but it wasn't as if she'd been given any instructions on how to use it. She'd still been pregnant with Cinder, only a few weeks after she'd gone to live with the pygmies, when she'd had a vivid dream of walking up the slope of the volcano and finding the sword jutting from black lava. In her dreams, she'd pulled the sword free and it had burst into flame. She she'd awakened, she'd found the sheathed sword by her side. Wisely, she'd waited until she was outside the wooden hut to first draw it. She'd used it sparingly over the years. But, perhaps after two decades, its magic was simply fading?

Up ahead, the sound of stone on metal grew silent. The tribesmen had thrown away their spears. A second later they began to pass her, fleeing silently in the opposite direction. Pygmies weren't cowards, but they understood the value of a strategic retreat.

One of the warriors almost ran into her. She grabbed his arm as he darted past, stopping his flight.

"Brother," she said. "What attacks us?"

"A metal woman," he said, with fear in his tone, though whether it was fear of the intruder or fear of her flaming sword Infidel couldn't guess.

"A woman?" she asked. In her spying on the settlement, she'd seen only men bearing arms and armor.

"Our spears can't hurt her," he said. "She walks toward our village with impudence. We plan to lead her into one of the traps."

Infidel nodded. The village was ringed with pits, deadfalls, and snares, so the strategy was sound. Still, something wasn't adding up.

"A woman in armor? And she comes alone?"

"Yes."

"On foot or on horseback?"

"On foot."

"What weapons does she carry?"

"None that I saw," the warrior answered.

"Then… why do we think she's attacking us?"

"The sentries called out to her to halt. She answered in our own tongue, saying she wouldn't stop until she reached the village. So they attacked her with spears. She ignored them, and continues marching toward our home."

Infidel let him go, saying, "Go make sure the traps are ready."

She sheathed her sword as she leapt to a nearby vine and climbed down to the forest floor. She took note of the unearthly silence that surrounded her. All the birds, frogs and insects had gone quiet. Ahead in the shadows, she heard the soft, squishy sound of footsteps in spongy jungle soil.

She pressed her back against a large tree and waited for the intruder to pass. She didn't have to wait long before a figure she'd seen before walked by, close enough to touch. It was the Black Swan. When Infidel had last spoken with the old witch, Sorrow was putting the finishing touches on the Black Swan's new iron body. That had been twenty years ago, and the Black Swan seemed little changed by the passage of time, save for the fact that her head was dented, and sitting at an odd angle on her shoulders. The rest of her body seemed in excellent condition. Sorrow's craftsmanship was such that the woman moved through the jungle with little more noise than she would if she'd been made of flesh. Infidel had to listen carefully to hear the faintest whisper of springs coiling and stretching within the woman's iron limbs, and the barely perceptible ratcheting of cogs.

"You can stop right there," said Infidel, still leaning against the tree, her arms crossed.

The Black Swan turned toward her.

"I would have guessed you'd still be asleep," the iron woman said in her reedy, musical voice. "You've become more nocturnal of late."

"I'm not sure where you're getting your information," said Infidel. "Honestly, I don't care. Whatever you've come here to ask me to do, the answer is no. Nope. Never. It won't happen."

"Why such hostility?" the Black Swan asked. It was difficult to judge with her inhuman voice and the limited range of expression in her metal face, but she sounded as if her feelings were hurt.

"When have we ever talked to one another without hostility?" asked Infidel. "You've hated me from the day I first came to Commonground."

"No," said the Black Swan. "I never hated you. Quite the contrary. I always did all I could to keep you alive, and discourage you from risky adventures."

"Why would my survival matter to you even a little bit?"

The Black Swan hesitated a moment, then said, "You... you've been precious to me a long time."

Infidel rolled her eyes. "Flattery is a welcome change of strategy for you, I suppose, though you don't seem very good at it. I guess you didn't get a lot of practice, all those times you tried to get me to do what you wanted with insults, threats, and blackmail."

"I did what I had to do because you're so hardheaded. I'm trying to save the world and you—"

"Not this again," Infidel said, closing her eyes and rubbing her temples. "You told me twenty years ago the world faced a dragon apocalypse. But, guess what? The world's still here."

"You might think so, from the vantage point of your village. But in the rest of the world—"

Infidel sighed. "Yeah, yeah. I've heard. Some kind of alliance between Hush and Tempest."

"And Hush has enslaved Abyss," said the Black Swan. "Now, three dragons are united to destroy mankind."

"Is it mankind they're after?" asked Infidel, not hiding her skepticism. "So far, they've mainly been attacking the Silver Isles. Since the Church of the Book killed Verdant, who once made his home there, I figure it's some kind of revenge thing. They won't mess with the Isle of Fire."

"Can you truly be so selfish?" asked the Black Swan.

"There you go," said Infidel, with a satisfied smirk. "I knew you'd get back to insults soon enough."

"Just because you aren't immediately threatened, you think nothing about the millions of people who face their death elsewhere in the world?"

"Listen to yourself," said Infidel. "Let's pretend I believe everything you're saying. I'm just one person. I'm not going to make a difference in a battle on this kind of scale. From what I've learned from the Wanderers I've talked to, Tempest has opened the doors to Hell. Even back in my prime, I did my best fighting one on one. I'm not some kind of strategic genius, a great commander waiting to whip what's left of mankind into a well-honed fighting force. This isn't my kind of fight."

"You might not have been effective against an army, but you've certainly battled your share of dragons."

"And I've made peace with them," said Infidel. "I didn't kill Greatshadow or Hush when I fought them."

"In the battle between mankind and dragons, aren't you on mankind's side?"

Infidel shrugged. "The dragons are aspects of nature. Aurora's people live peacefully with Hush, the Wanderers thrive by cooperating with Abyss, and the pygmies manage to be happy living right under Greatshadow's nose. I say live and let live."

"Except Hush and Tempest aren't letting people live," said the Black Swan. "You know this! You just said you knew about the armies of Hell!"

Infidel frowned. The stories she'd heard were pretty gruesome, but also pretty distant. They'd been easy enough to push out her mind.

"The undead armies can't really win, can they?" she asked, hoping the Black Swan wouldn't hear the lack of confidence in her voice. "I mean... I've heard that the dead avoid sunlight. How hard can it be to fight an army that can only be active at night? Living men would have the advantage of fighting any time, day or night."

"But the dead have advantages over living men," said the Black Swan.

"They don't need food or water," said Infidel, knowing what the Black Swan was about to tell her. "They don't get tired, or have to worry about diseases thinning their ranks. Still, I can think of a hundred ways to take apart an undead warrior. I know the Church of the Book has seen better days, but it seems like a band of a few hundred knights and Truthspeakers could end this war pretty quickly."

"Perhaps. But, following the loss of the One True Book, the schisms that wracked the church have meant that even a modest force of knights can't be assembled. As for Truthspeakers, with the book gone, all have lost their faith. No longer do they have the power to police what is real and what is unreal."

Infidel had heard these rumors as well. Despite her isolation in the pygmy village, she occasionally made trips to the edge of Commonground to hear the latest scuttlebutt. She sighed, thinking of her father, the king, of all his advisors, the priests and generals and bankers who whispered their so-called wisdom into his ear. She'd heard he was dead now. She hadn't mourned the news. The family of her birth had been dead to her a long, long time.

She pulled herself from her reverie. "I'm sorry that the Silver City has gone to Hell, or that Hell has come to it. But, I've got other things to worry about. Other people I'm responsible for now."

"Cinder," said the Black Swan. "Your daughter."

Infidel rested her hand on the hilt of her blade. "How did you learn her name?"

"I've known her name before you conceived her."

"Oh, great. More of your cryptic time travel bullshit."

"Why disbelieve me? You witnessed it yourself! Surely you remember how I knew beforehand of Greatshadow's attack on Commonground. With your own eyes, you saw history rewritten."

"I… only remember… a lot of confusion," said Infidel. "I jumped down a dragon's throat that day. That's the sort of memory that crowds out a lot of other stuff."

"Your confusion is common for those who experience my time jumps only rarely. Aurora and Menagerie were they only ones close enough to me to perceive the alterations in time. They both informed you of my powers, and I know you trusted them."

"Sure, I trusted them. But I've never trusted you."

The Black Swan's shoulders sagged. Her inhuman voice was little more than a hum as she said, "It hurts me to hear you say this, though I've always known it."

"Forget the whole time travel thing," said Infidel. "You ran Commonground with an iron fist long before you had, you know, iron fists. Your goons killed anyone who crossed you. And if there was money to be had, you made sure you got a take. You made your living by selling booze to men who couldn't afford it, by killing anyone with enemies willing to shell out a high enough bounty, off slaves—"

"Never!" the Black Swan squawked. "Never did I take a dime from the slave trade!"

"Okay. But you certainly turned a blind eye to it."

"No! You don't know what Commonground was like before you arrived. If the slave trade had continued at the pace established by Ambitious Merchant a century ago, the Isle of Fire would be empty by now. He left a business plan for Judicious Merchant to follow. Once the last of the forest-pygmies had been enslaved, the river-pygmies were to empty the island of the lava tribes. Then, the river-pygmies, addicted to long-men's wealth, would turn tribe against tribe and sell their neighbors."

"Fortunately, Judicious didn't follow this model."

"No. But he didn't stay behind to actively thwart the avarice of the slave traders who filled the vacuum when he quit the industry. That fight was left to me. I financed the civil war that sprang up among the Wanderers. I saw to it that the most efficient and effective of the slave merchants came to bloody ends. It's true, I never eliminated the slave trade. The more difficult I made it to traffic in pygmies, the more valuable such slaves became, which only meant that new slavers flowed into the business as swiftly as I eliminated the old ones. Still, I did all I could to stem the tide of humanity that flowed out from these shores."

"Fine," said Infidel with a sigh. "So you weren't a slaver. Hooray. You've got one redeeming feature. I still don't trust you."

The Black Swan's dented face shifted in a way that almost conveyed remorse. "I know. You didn't trust me even before I became the Black Swan."

"Before you became the Black Swan? You were called the Black Swan from the first day I came to Commonground. From what I understood, you'd been a force in town since long before I was even born. I never knew you before."

"But you did," the Black Swan said. "You were the first person ever to know me."

Infidel rolled her eyes. "What is it with you? Is there some invisible accountant somewhere who gives you a moon every time you say something that doesn't make sense?"

"What I say always makes sense," said the Black Swan. "You just never make the effort to understand me."

"That must be true," said Infidel. "You've been jabbering at me for ten minutes now and I still don't have a clue what you've come here to say."

"I've hidden this from you for a very long time," said the Black Swan. "And I don't expect you'll believe me immediately. But, before I was called the Black Swan, I had another name. A name you gave me."

14 - CAGE OF BONE

"YOUR HAIR IS growing fast," Slate said, running his fingers across the top of Sorrow's head. She raised her hand to feel the fuzz, soft as baby hair. She looked at herself in the smooth surface of Slate's glass armor. It looked almost as if she wore a dark skull cap.

"I guess this is the closest thing we have to a clock," she said, rising. She didn't know how far they'd walked after their encounter with the child. It had felt like many hours, but in this sunless, moonless place, devoid even of a consistent horizon, there was no way to keep track of time. They'd walked until they were weary, moving ever closer to the mountain peaks, then rested. She'd fallen asleep with her head on Slate's lap.

"Did you sleep any?" she asked.

He shook his head.

"Why not catch a nap while I keep watch? You must be exhausted."

"I'm fine," said Slate.

He didn't look fine. He looked like he'd aged ten years since they'd been here. Still, she knew it would be pointless to argue.

She dug through her pack for the dried cod and the bottomless bottle. She pulled out the meat, then wrinkled her nose in disgust. The leathery, salt white flesh writhed with maggots. She tossed it away, then emptied her bag. All their rations were spoiled.

"Looks like were on a liquid diet," she said, removing the cork from the bottle. She took a deep swig. As her thirst vanished, she grew more keenly aware of her hunger. She tried to ignore it, but any time she pushed it from her mind it came back instantly. Her enhanced awareness of her body had one downside, it seemed.

Slate took a long draught from the bottle, then lifted the demon hand. He asked, "Ready?"

She nodded as she stuffed the wine bottle back into her pack. She fastened her cloak as Slate marched off. She had to walk swiftly to catch up to him. She understood his sense of urgency. As her hair and her hunger testified, time still passed for them. Perhaps they wouldn't die of thirst, but death by hunger was now a real possibility. It struck her as poignant, the notion that she would have survived armies, giants and dragons only to be brought down because she had nothing to eat. She'd long assumed she'd perish through violence, dying in the thick of battle, or perhaps finally caught by the church and burned at the stake. Starvation had never been a concern.

They walked, kept walking, then walked some more. By now, the magic of their lovemaking had ebbed. She still carried a small spark of energy, cradled next to her heart, saved for a moment she would truly need it. She didn't want to waste it on simply making her walk easier. Her weariness was great, but as long as Slate had the strength to move, she swore to herself she'd stay on her feet. He seemed so driven, so focused. She was certain that, should she collapse, he would simply pick her up and carry her. She couldn't bear the thought of becoming a burden when he needed his strength for whatever was to come.

Of course, she was still unclear on what was to come. She didn't know what Slate hoped to accomplish by finding the soul of Stark Tower. She suspected that Slate was still under the impression that he was part of Stark, and Stark a part of him. She hoped that, when they did find Stark's soul, it would be so loathsome that Slate would turn his back upon the thing, and finally be free of the ghost that haunted him.

Slate paused as they came to the crest of a hill crawling with centipedes. Sorrow gingerly followed, keeping her eyes toward the ground. The crunch of insect shells wasn't the worst thing she'd heard in hell, but still unnerved her. She didn't look up until she reached Slate's side. He took her hand to steady her.

In the distance was the first intact structure they'd seen, a palace, gleaming white against a landscape black as tar. She didn't need enchanted eyes to recognize the building material. The whole structure was formed of skeletons. Judging from the pelvises, the bones were mostly those of women.

The demon claw pointed directly toward the palace.

"He's inside," said Slate.

"What?"

"Stark Tower. His soul. He's inside that building. I know it."

Sorrow turned his face toward hers. "You don't have to do this."

"Yes," he said. "I do."

He moved forward. She followed. Her sense of hunger gave way to a sense of dread. What if Slate's quest wasn't in vain? What if he really could rescue the soul of Stark Tower? What if rescue, in this instance, meant that Stark's soul would take up residence in Slate's body?

She shuddered at the thought. The man she loved would be transformed in a twinkling into the greatest enemy she could imagine. She tried to think of anything she might say that would change his mind and keep him from entering the place, but knew it was futile. They'd come too far, endured too many dangers, and there was nowhere to go by turning back. The only way forward was forward.

As they closed in on the white walls, her eyes searched for any sign of a door. She found nothing. They circled the structure, looking for a way inside, but found no openings.

When they circled the building completely, Slate moved to the nearest wall. The skeletons weren't wired together. Instead, all the skeletal fingers clasped the limbs of their nearest neighbor in a matrix of bone.

"Perhaps there's a way in from above," said Slate, sheathing his sword and climbing, his boots finding easy purchase upon the ladder-like structure of the limbs. Before Sorrow followed, she stopped to stare at a nearby skull, at a dull red speck a few inches up from where an ear had once been. It was a nail, a witch nail, made of iron. She drew it free, finding it intact despite the rust. Brushing the rust off with her cloak, she spotted the arcane inscriptions on the surface.

She ran her fingers over her fine, silky hair. She'd lost all of her nails when she'd been reborn in a fresh body after Avaris had kicked her out of Rott. She was happy to have at last grasped the potential for bone magic, but she missed her old power over iron. Still... what would Slate think if she filled her head once more with such things? She gave a slight jerk as the ramifications of her thought became clear. She'd never before hesitated to alter her form as she saw fit. Should Slate have any say in what she did with her body? Once, this would have been the most repugnant thought imaginable. Now, she felt as if her choice was partly his as well.

Knowing that she'd need to discuss restoring her old powers with Slate didn't prevent her from gathering the materials she'd need. She put the iron nail in her bag and began to climb. Along the way she spotted a nail of glass, and another of silver. She plucked them free, then a nail of rough granite, and another of green copper. She took careful mental note of the placement of each nail. She had extensive notes on the placement of many already, but these were still in her chest aboard the *Circus*.

When she reached the top, she found Slate with the Witchbreaker drawn, standing near the center of the vast roof. There was still no sign of a door. Before she could speak, he chopped into the bones beneath him.

She braced herself. The last time he'd hacked into a roof, they'd been atop Avaris's walking palace and they'd fallen inside. This time, the shattered bones revealed another layer of bones beneath.

"The demon claw points straight down," he said, explaining his strategy, raising his sword to strike again. He grunted as his sword dug into the bones below him.

"The absences of doors hints that whatever's inside is dangerous," she said. "Do you really want to let what's inside the cage out?"

Slate let his actions answer her as he chopped again. He paused after the blow, kneeling to pick up fragments of bone and toss them aside. He'd carved out a shallow pit, only a few feet deep. On his knees, he struck again, then again.

The next time he paused to clear his path of shattered bone, he tossed aside a nearly intact skull with a trio of nails jutting from it. She retrieved the skull and found a nail of dark gray iron, with no hint of rust, its surface protected by a clear, hard patina. A nail of wood showed similar craftsmanship, as did a nail of pure black slate. She'd known slate nails must have existed, having seen a chamber of slate that could only have been formed by a weaver skilled in such magic, but she'd never before seen one. As Slate worked, she pulled her journal from her pack and took detailed notes.

When she looked up again, Stagger was shoulder deep in an pit of jagged bone. He'd removed his helmet. Sweat streamed from his face. He struck again, and when he lifted his sword something bright and glowing shot up from the pit. Instead of falling like the fragments of bone, it continued to rise. The second she recognized the substance, she was on her feet, running, loosening her cloak so it wouldn't slow her movements. She leapt as high as she possibly could, her fingers just barely making contact with the hovering nail. It was enough. She caught the object between her fingers and pulled it down.

"Stop!" she cried out.

"Why?" asked Slate, who'd knelt to scoop out more bone.

"We need to find the skull this came from," said Sorrow. "This is a nail carved from a glorystone! I've never seen such a thing!"

"I'm certain that's interesting," said Slate, wiping his brow. "Why do I need to stop? We're a long way from the center of this place."

"I need to find the skull this came out of," she said.

"Why?"

"To see how it was placed! I can't even begin to guess what part of the brain this should penetrate."

"Is this important?" asked Slate. "You aren't planning to mutilate yourself again, are you?"

"Mutilate?" asked Sorrow. "I preferred to think of it as self-improvement. And… why not? Why limit myself to bone magic?"

"It's just… I thought, since you were back to normal—"

"Normal?" she asked, her hands on her hips. "I wasn't normal before?"

"You had no legs when I first met you," said Slate. "Then you had wings. Is it wrong of me to say I prefer your current look?'

"No," she said. "I wasn't a fan of those looks either. But, those only came about because I tried to make use of the powers of a primal dragon. Before that, I looked much as I do now. Only, you know, bald. With nails in my head."

Slate stared at her.

"Look, just find me the skull, okay?"

Slate frowned, staring at the fragments of bone in his hand. "I suspect it's already shattered. That's probably why it flew free. I think this is part of a skull." His hand moved, and picked up another bone. "Aye, and this as well. Oh, and here's more, an upper jaw." He handed her the bones, then bent to retrieve others. In a few moments, it became clear that she had not only the shattered bones of a single skull, but fragments from at least three different women. She placed them in her pack, along with the glorystone nail. Perhaps in better circumstances, she'd be able to reconstruct the skulls.

Slate resumed his work. He descended another twenty feet before he climbed out of the pit to drink from the magic bottle.

"How's your strength holding up?" she asked.

"I endure," he said. "Knights train for such tribulation. Hunger, weariness, loneliness… these burdens we bear willingly in the service of our cause."

"I don't know why you included loneliness on that list," she said.

"I meant nothing," he said with a smile. "I cherish your company."

"Would you still cherish me if I was bald again, with more nails than ever?"

He pressed his lips together. "I love you, Sorrow. I'll love you even if that is the path you choose."

"But you wish I wouldn't choose that path."

"Aye," he said. "When we leave this place… I'd hoped we could leave behind our life of combat. It sounds as if the church you hated, and the one I sought to serve, is no more. We should find some distant, quiet vale and retire there, to live the rest of our days in peace."

Sorrow considered this option. It felt unsatisfying, but she couldn't bring herself to tell him that. "Let me dig some," she said.

She climbed into the pit. Unlike Slate, she didn't need brute force to remove the bone. With a brush of her fingers and the slightest release of her bone magic, she could command any skeletal form she touched to untangle itself from its neighbor. But, though the energy cost was small, if multiplied by a dozen commands, or a hundred, she might expend the last of her energy. She took a moment to contemplate the surrounding skeletons. She began to make sense of the pattern, the way the skeletons were woven together. Closing her eyes and grasping a skeletal hand, she let her magic explore the entirety of the structure. A picture of the bone matrix formed in her mind, save for a void in the bone directly beneath her, perhaps fifty feet down. This, she suspected, was where they'd find Stark Tower.

"We've been doing this the hard way," she said, looking up at Slate. "Let's go back to the ground."

"And give up on the progress we've made?"

"Trust me," she said. "Now that I'm immersed in these bones, I understand the true nature of this cage. I know how to open it."

"Very well," said Slate, sounding weary. He stretched his arms to his side. "My back will be quite grateful not to chop any further."

"I promise a massage later," she said, climbing up the skeletons to his side. "Come on."

Slate followed as she went to the edge of the roof and climbed down. When he was clear of the structure, she placed her hands upon a skeleton directly before her. She stared into the empty eye-sockets, waiting patiently. After a moment, the skulls of the skeletons beside the one she gaze at slowly turned their faces toward her. Soon, she felt the eyeless stare of all the skeletons in the outer wall.

"Sisters," she said, in the respectful tone Mama Knuckle had used whenever she'd addressed the uncles. "I know who dwells within this cage of bone. I know who you were, and why he is entombed, and the justice of such a prison. Your service is an honor to me. I'm your sister, a fellow weaver. Please open a path that I may see the one you embrace."

The wall clattered as the skulls nodded in unison. The clatter grew into a cacophony as the entangle skeletons shifted position, pushing and pulling into a new configuration, a tunnel opening before her.

They entered cautiously, as the rattling of bone still sounded from all directions. Ten feet inside, the gloom was impenetrable. Cut off from the dull gray light of the cloudy sky outside, she couldn't see her hand before her face, even as she willed her pupils to their widest.

She remembered the glorystone nail in her bag. Even without hammering it into her skull, it would prove useful.

Slate raised his hand to shield his eyes from the light. She reached back and took him by the wrist and guided him forward, toward a thin figure she could see at the far end of the tunnel.

It was a man. A man of flesh, unlike the chalky skeletons that embraced him from all sides. He bled from innumerable wounds, as countless nails of various substances pierced his skin. The man's eyes were wide, with tears of blood flowing down his cheeks, but his expression wasn't one of fear. Instead, as he saw Sorrow, his visage became one of abject hatred.

"Witch!" he hissed. "Thou shalt answer for your sins! Hell's eternal torments await thee!"

"Really," said Sorrow. "Don't you know where you are?"

"Dost thou think me unaware?" he asked, his voice trembling with naked rage. "This is Hell! I'm surrounded by the bones of all the witches I've slain, caught in their embrace until the final page of the One True Book is turned! But thou I would see perish before that day!"

"Since killing witches landed you here, maybe you could be a little less aggressive?" asked Sorrow.

"It wasn't killing witches that led to my imprisonment," said Tower. "It was loving them! The foul slatterns seduced me, desperate to save themselves from the pain of death. Again and again, my carnal desires brought me into their embrace, to my great and everlasting shame!"

Slate stepped forward. "But some witches were spared? After they made such a wretched bargain?"

Tower laughed scornfully. "Don't be a fool. I did my duty. All were put to death. I watched many burn while the taste of their kisses still lingered upon my lips. Their deaths did not redeem my weak…" His voice trailed off. His gaze moved from Sorrow to fix fully upon Slate.

"Step… step closer," he whispered.

Slate did so.

"It's you," he said, his voice a bare whisper. "The doppelganger."

"Aye," said Slate.

"Free me," Tower said, swallowing hard. "Take my hand. Let me inside you."

"Hold on," said Sorrow, grabbing Slate by the shoulders and pulling him back. "Touching him would be a very, very bad idea."

"Don't listen to that whore!" cried Tower. "Touching me would be the greatest thing you've ever done. You're nothing but an empty shell, a soulless parody of a living man. With but a touch, my soul will find a home in life once more. Together, we'll be whole."

"Whole," said Slate, raising his hand.

"Stop!" Sorrow said, moving between him and Tower. "You can't let him take control of you."

"Is that what you fear?" asked Slate. "Can't you see that I shall take control of him? His presence here is proof that flesh may overpower a soul."

"Slate, no!" Sorrow said, putting her hands on his chest and shoving him back a step. "Don't take that chance. This wasn't a man, but a monster. A monster! He's nothing like you. You should want to be nothing like him!"

"But... but this is my soul," he whispered. "My rightful soul."

"Souls are vastly overrated if you ask me," she grumbled. Then she sighed. "Please don't do this, Slate. Please. I'm begging you. I love you. I love you more than I ever knew I could love anyone. I don't want to lose you."

"You won't," he said. "I know it. I love you as well. My love is powerful. He cannot corrupt it."

"Why even take the risk?" said Sorrow.

"Because I love you," he said. "Because I want to be complete, to be a man for you."

"What? You think you aren't a man?"

"I know you think of me as such," he said. "But... don't you see he's right? Without him, I'll forever have this void within me. "

"Oh Slate," she said, pressing her head against his chest. "You still feel empty? So did I, before I met you. But together... together we can be whole."

"Don't listen to her lies!" screamed Tower. "Slit her blasphemous throat!"

Slate put his hands on her neck. Then he pulled her to him, kissing her softly, gently. The magical spark she held next to her heart grew more powerful, becoming a flame. She pressed her lips tightly against his, their mouths opening. She breathed out, letting the magic in her heart seep into her lungs. The magic flowed into Slate, filling him.

She pulled away, studying his face. His eyes were unfocused, wet with tears.

"What... what is this?" he whispered. "What is this I feel?"

She could see it. See the change within him as the magic flowed into his blood. She'd long had the power to see the auras of living things. When she'd first met Slate, he'd had no aura. Now, though faint, the pale light of an aura surrounded him.

"You ... you have an aura Slate. It's just as I said. You don't need his soul. You can share mine."

"No!" Tower howled, struggling at the skeletons that held him. "Fool! Cut out her tongue! Don't let her seduce you!"

"I will not harm her," said Slate.

Tower's face fell. "But... but... "

Slate knelt before the bleeding man. "You've done me a great service. Thank you."

"Don't thank me! Save me! Take my hand!"

Slate rose.

Sorrow gasped as Slate extended his arm, taking Tower's fingers into his grasp.

Tower's tortured face took on an expression of rapture. He twisted his face toward the unseen sky and cried, "At last! At last! At... last..."

He went silent. His expression changed from joy to confusion.

"I… I'm not free. I'm not part of you."

"No," said Slate. "You never were. You're a man of hatred and anger, a man of lust and regret. I was never that man. I never will be."

Slate let go of Tower's hand. "Farewell," he said. "In a way you will never understand, it was good to finally meet you.

"B-but… what… don't… I-I can't… please…"

Slate turned from the sputtering spirit and walked away. He didn't look back.

Sorrow lingered for a moment as Slate moved outside. Tower wept tears of blood as he silently sobbed, his face turned toward hers.

At last she turned away, and said, calmly, "Sisters, don't be gentle."

Tower's sobs changed to screams as the skeletons closed in upon him. Sorrow hastened her steps, though the skeletons let her pass unmolested before closing ranks behind her. Soon, Tower's voice faded to only a murmur. By the time the last of the bones clattered shut behind her, the knight could no longer be heard.

Slate waited for her, his hands resting on the hilt of the Witchbreaker.

"That was quite a gamble, taking his hand," she grumbled.

"No. After you kissed me, I knew. I knew there was no room within me for his broken spirit. You're right, Sorrow. I'm whole, thanks to you. I'm grateful."

"I'm glad, but you still scared me. I thought my heart was going to stop when you touched him.""

"I had no choice," said Slate. He looked back at the cage of bone. "If I hadn't touched his soul directly, I would always have wondered. I would never have been certain that I wasn't truly him. I had to know. I had to prove to myself that I'm my own man." He gave her a smile. "Your man, actually."

"I'm happy to have you," she said, returning his smile. "Now, we've only got one trivial problem facing us. How do we get out of Hell and back to the realm of the living?"

"We stay alive until the Romers find us."

"I'm afraid the Romers won't be coming back," said a deep voice from above. They looked to the top of skeleton cage and found a tall, gaunt man standing there, dressed in dark robes, save for his gloves, which where whiter than the bones he stood upon. "By now, the Romers have fallen into the hands of their enemies. They're either dead, or desperately wishing to be so."

"Who the devil are you?" asked Sorrow.

"My name is Ver," said the thin man. "I'm a Truthspeaker. In truth, your journey comes to an end here."

15 - PILGRIM

SORROW GRIPPED HER trident tightly at finding herself in the presence of a Truthspeaker. These powerful priests of the Church of the Book had tried time and again to kill her. Over the years she'd thinned their ranks quite a bit. She didn't remember killing this one, but had to assume he wasn't here to wish her good health.

Slate held the Witchbreaker at the ready, looking skeptical as he studied Ver atop the cage of bone. "A Truthspeaker? Why would a Truthspeaker be in Hell?"

"Because of the greatest truth of all, Slate," said Ver. "All men are born into a world corrupted by falsehood. Before a babe ever leaves the womb, the lies of the world have already poisoned his soul. No one is born innocent. No one dies redeemed. I once believe that Hell was the separation of man from truth. Now, I've learned that Hell is the ultimate, final truth. Hell is home to all. Heaven stands vacant."

"That's blasphemy," said Slate.

"In a universe of a falsehood, all truth is blasphemy," said Ver, spreading his arms as he gazed toward the nightmarish horizon.

"It's self-evidently false!" Slate protested. "If all men are damned, and there's no hope of eternal reward—"

"Then nothing divides good from evil," Ver said gravely. "The sacred becomes indistinguishable from the profane."

"I'm starting to understand how he wound up here," Sorrow said to Slate. Then she looked back to the Truthspeaker. "What do you want with us? How do you know my name?"

"When other souls arrive in Hell and learn the truth, that they never had hope of an eternal reward, they succumb to despair, or burn with impotent rage. I trained a lifetime to accept truth, no matter how harsh. By embracing the truth, I freed myself from the miseries inflicted upon other souls. Instead of despair, I found wisdom. Hell has proven an excellent textbook, teaching me things I could never had learned in the living world. In seeking truth, I have the power to wander where I will, speak to whom I wish, and see things hidden from others."

"You sound like Walker," said Sorrow.

Ver shook his head. "He and I are nothing alike. Walker does his best to reject the truth of who he is."

"Wait," she said. "You know him?"

"Of course. Who in Hell wouldn't know him?"

"Why would he be famous here?" asked Slate.

"You truly don't know?" asked Ver. "Walker once was king of this realm."

"Are we talking about the same guy?" asked Sorrow. "The Walker I know is a pygmy shaman who answers every question with more questions."

Ver let out a dry, rasping chuckle. "It seems you do not know the Walker you know. You know only his mask. His true aspect would drive a mortal to pluck out his own eyes."

Sorrow didn't know what to believe. She'd often found Walker annoying, but he'd never struck her as evil. On the other hand, he did seem to know his way around Hell.

"You still haven't said why you were looking for us," said Slate. "You claim to be a Truthspeaker. Answer plainly."

Ver looked over his shoulder, then glanced back, fixing his gaze on Sorrow instead of Slate. "I've recruited two assassins to kill the both of you. I fear I've literally left them in the dust, though they seem to be finally catching up."

From the left side of the cage, Sorrow heard voices.

"I think Ver went around here," a man said. "Are you sure you can see okay now?"

"Yes," answered a young woman. "Though I almost wish I couldn't."

From their tone, Sorrow gathered that they didn't know they were only yards away the people they'd come here to kill. She saw no reason to waste the element of surprise. Raising her trident, she charged toward the voices. She turned the corner and found a tall man and a slender, dark skinned young woman barely ten feet away. The woman jumped back, startled. The man crouched. Sorrow leapt toward him, thrusting her trident with both hands to drive the tines deep into his chest.

With a fluidity of motion so smooth it was as if they'd both rehearsed this dance, the man dove forward, his shoulders passing less than an inch from the trident tips. He rolled once and rose, driving up the heel of his right palm beneath Sorrow's chin. Stars exploded before her and she fell backward, her mouth full of blood.

"Sorrow!" Slate cried. She heard his heavy feet rush toward the man, the clatter of his armor as he drew back the Witchbreaker to strike.

"Wait!" a girl cried out in an odd accent. "We've come to—"

The girl didn't get to finish her sentence before there was a loud CRACK and Slate's breath exploded from him in a grunt.

"Demons!" Ver shouted from atop the cage of bone. "We're too late! They're already possessed by demons! Kill them if you hope to save yourselves!"

On her back, Sorrow swallowed the blood in her mouth. She took a deep breath through her nose to clear her head. With a thought, she leapt back to her feet, in time to see Slate once more swing the Witchbreaker. Somehow, though his opponent was unarmed, Slate's breastplate had been completely shattered.

The dark haired man sprang into the air, the Witchbreaker slicing through the space where he'd once stood. With a loud, sharp cry he kicked out with both feet, catching Slate full in the face. Slate's helmet flew apart in a spray of gleaming black shards and he fell backward, his body limp, the Witchbreaker falling from his grasp.

Before the dark haired man hit the ground he caught the Witchbreaker by the hilt. He landed, turning his gaze toward Sorrow.

"You," she whispered, suddenly recognizing his aura. Though he was now twenty years older, she'd fought him before. "You're the boy who attacked the *Circus!*"

"Yes," he said. "I remember you, witch."

"You know her, Mantle?" The young woman stepped out from behind the man. Sorrow's mouth dropped as she saw past the woman's unusual appearance to recognize the woman's aura.

"Black Swan?" she asked, bewildered by the change. Having spent weeks in the Black Swan's presence, there was no mistaking her aura. But what had happened to the iron body Sorrow had crafted for her? Somehow, she was once more a creature of flesh and blood, and a young one at that. The Black Swan had always dressed in heavy gowns and dresses that revealed little of her skin, but now she wore no more clothes than a pygmy. Odder still, her skin was black as cast iron, as if the metal shell Sorrow had sculpted for her had turned to flesh.

"You've mistaken me for someone else," said the young woman. "My name is Cinder. Why did you attack us? We've come here to save you!"

"We're too late," said Ver. "You saw how they attacked without question. They've been possessed by demons. Don't believe a word she utters! She'll say anything to catch you off guard."

Sorrow frowned. Was Ver warning them, or her? With her enhanced senses, she could see that both Cinder and Mantle were living beings. They no more belonged in Hell than she did. Further, she heard no guile in the girl's voice. Cinder truly believed she'd come here on a rescue mission.

Sorrow dropped her trident and raised her hands. "I believe you didn't come here to fight. Let's talk."

"No! Her tongue is her most dangerous weapon," said Ver.

"Possessed or not, I recall you clearly now," said Mantle, shifting the Witchbreaker from hand to hand, testing its weight. "You killed all my shipmates. I alone survived to tell the tale. I've no reason to think you any less wicked in Hell than you were in the living world."

"But you knew we'd come to save her," said Cinder. "We said her name a dozen times."

"I didn't realize we were talking about the woman who tried to kill me when I was only a boy," said Mantle.

"As I recall it, I was only defending myself from your attack," said Sorrow. "And... you didn't call yourself Mantle. Your name was Numinous. Numinous Pilgrim. You said you were... were..." All blood drained from her face as she recalled the full truth of the boy's identity. "You said you were the Omega Reader."

As she spoke, Slate rose to his knees. Blood streamed from his broken nose. She looked at the leather pack on his back, thought about what lay inside, and understood at once the true danger.

"You didn't come here to save us," Sorrow said, clenching her fists. "You've come for the book."

"What book?" asked Cinder, sounding genuinely perplexed.

"Cover your ears, Cinder! Don't let her fog your mind with confusion," said Ver.

Slate rose to his feet. He looked up at Ver and said, "If you're truly a priest of the Divine Author, heed my words. I possess a priceless treasure of the church, and vow to protect it with my life until I at last bring it to the Grand Cathedral in the Silver City. Help us reach this place."

Ver shook his head. "The Grand Cathedral is no more. It burned years ago, in the vicious war that rent the church when the One True Book vanished. The harm you've done is immeasurable."

"Then help me set things right!" said Slate. "It's never too late for a man to make amends for the harm he's done."

"Even if that were true," said Ver, "you never were a man."

"And what role do you play in all this, Black Swan?" Sorrow asked, not caring to go along with the woman's pretense of having a different name. "You've always played the long game, threaded scheme into scheme. Are you here to save the book? Or to destroy it?"

"I don't know what you're talking about," said the woman.

Sorrow frowned. The Black Swan was no friend of the Church of the Book. She had to be deceiving the Truthspeaker. This must be a plot to seize the One True Book for herself. To destroy it? More likely, to ransom it. Whatever else she knew about the Black Swan, she knew most of all that, somehow, she planned to come out of this richer than ever. If the remnants of the church offered her enough money for the book, it would be theirs.

Her eyes glanced down and spotted where the trident had fallen. The tines lifted a few inches off the ground, resting on a skeletal pelvis they'd knocked free earlier when attempting to bash their way into the cage.

"Slate," she said, stepping on the center tine forcefully. "Catch."

The shaft flew into the air. Slate caught it.

"We're not giving you the book," said Sorrow.

"No," said Numinous. "Of course not. A demon would never do the right thing willingly."

As he spoke, Sorrow concentrated her magical energies within her eyes. It proved a wise move, as Numinous sprang forward with a speed that she would never have followed otherwise. He held the Witchbreaker in a two-handed grasp, pulled back over his shoulder, his eyes fixed on Slate's neck. Though she couldn't match his speed, she threw herself forward, hands raised, and caught Numinous by the wrist as he chopped at Slate. This slowed the blow enough that Slate parried the blade with the shaft of the trident. While Sorrow had contact, her magic flowed from her fingertips into his skin. Numinous broke away with a hiss, his whole forearm covered in bruises.

Slate thrust with the trident, in what should have been a killing blow, but with supernatural speed Numinous twisted his torso away. Then, in a flurry of motion, he slammed the pommel of the Witchbreaker into the back of Slate's hand, causing Slate to lose his grasp on the trident. As part of the same motion, Numinous jammed his elbow hard into Sorrow's throat. She stumbled backward, struggling to breathe.

Numinous, meanwhile, once more threw Slate to the ground with a kick to the warrior's left knee. Slate rolled to his back, raising his arm as Numinous lifted the Witchbreaker for a final strike, his hair fluttering around his face as a sudden, violent wind swept across the landscape.

Before the blade could fall, a long, slender rope snaked from behind Numinous and coiled around the shaft of the blade. Numinous spun around, eyes wide, to discover a fully rigged sailing ship rolling toward him along a river that hadn't been there a few seconds before. The rope that held the Witchbreaker came from the deck of this ship.

With Numinous distracted, Sorrow forced herself to draw a deep breath, though it felt as if her throat had closed to the size of a needle. She raced toward Numinous, arms outstretched, her eyes dancing over his form as she searched out the best muscles to rip from his back. With her focus on attack, she gave no thought to stealth, and at the last second Numinous released his grasp on the Witchbreaker and spun around with a high kick that caught her in the temple.

For an unknown time, everything was black. She forced her eyes open, her skull throbbing, gazing at bloodied mud before her as she slowly raised her head. Mere seconds had passed since she'd fallen. Numinous now had an obsidian knife in his grasp and had sliced free the ropes entangling the Witchbreaker. Strong winds buffeted him, but he kept on his feet. Slate had risen to one knee, shaking his head to clear it.

Numinous spun around to face Slate.

Sorrow cried out, "No!"

Her words counted for nothing. Numinous drove the Witchbreaker into Slate's torso, the blade slipping between Slate's ribs. With the stone knife, he slashed the straps that held Slate's pack. Releasing both blades, he caught the pack before it hit the ground.

A look of serene joy passed over his features as he lifted the leather flap and glanced at the book inside. Slate shuddered violently. Blood sprayed from his lips as he slumped to his side.

Sorrow felt as if the life had drained out of her own body. She had no will to rise, no power to stop the horrible thing about to happen as Numinous cast his gaze toward her. With the pack in one hand and the Witchbreaker in the other, he stalked toward her, slicing away the ropes that reached toward him from the deck of the *Circus* without bothering to even glance back at the ship. The gale force wind that tore at him ruffled his hair, but did little to slow him.

Behind him, she saw Brand swing down from the deck. He darted toward Numinous, a dagger in each hand, keeping directly behind his target. With the wind so loud, there was no way Numinous could hear him coming. Yet, an instant before Brand could complete his attack, Numinous whirled, swinging the pack. He caught Brand in the face, knocking him sideways. Numinous completed his spin, once more facing Sorrow, and kept walking as if the attack had never happened.

He stood before her and said, in a voice barely audible above the wind, "Now you see the truth. I'm the perfection of mankind. My senses are so finely tuned I felt the footsteps of your latest defender as he drew near. He had no hope of striking me."

He raised his right arm. The dark outlines of her fingers showed where she'd grabbed his wrist, painted in dark shades of purple and yellow. "Not many people have hurt me, witch. Few who've done so lived to tell the tale. I'm tempted to drag you with me to the pulpit, so that you can feel the ultimate despair as I fulfil my destiny. But, the simpler, wiser course is simply to slit your throat."

He drew back the Witchbreaker. Over his shoulder, she saw something big and dark fly through the air. There were no footsteps to warn Numinous, yet some subtle shift in the wind was enough to make him spin around. Mako had leapt from the deck of the *Circus*, his toothy jaws opened wide. Numinous jumped aside, but didn't count on Mako's own inhuman speed as the shark-man flipped in midair to land on his feet, then sprang once more at Numinous. Mako's body was tuned to swim swiftly in the ocean's depths. In mere air, he moved like lightning.

Numinous howled in pain as Mako sank his teeth into his shoulder. The blow crippled the arm that held the Witchbreaker, which dropped from his now limp grasp.

Any hope that pain would cripple Numinous proved fleeting. He drove his knee hard into Mako's groin. At the same time, he dropped Slate's pack, and used his now free hand to drive his fingers hard into Mako's left eye. The pain loosened Mako's bite, and Numinous leapt away, before charging forward to kick Mako in the chest, knocking him from his feet.

Mako's shoulders hit the ground but he kept rolling, springing back to a fighting stance. With a snarl, he charged toward Numinous. Numinous leapt straight up, letting Mako pass beneath him, then kicked down hard into the base of Mako's spine with both heels. Mako skid along the ground, his limbs sprawled, his legs feebly kicking.

Numinous didn't press his attack. Instead he dashed back to where Slate's pack had fallen and grabbed it. Once more a rope snaked toward him, and once more he ducked beneath it, then snatched up the Witchbreaker. He ran toward Cinder, who stood watching the combat, looking confused. Brand made it back to his feet and hurled one dagger, then the other. Numinous side-stepped the first, then swatted the second from the air with the flat of his blade. He jumped high as a barrel flew from the deck of the *Circus*, smashing to splinters on the ground where he'd just stood.

He reached Cinder as a hundred pale green pygmies began leaping from the deck of the *Circus*, yipping out their battle cries as they charged toward the pair.

"Let's go!" he shouted.

"Where?" she responded.

"Not here!"

She nodded, accepting the wisdom of his advice as the pygmy army closed upon them. She placed an arm around his back, stepped forward, and both vanished into thin air. The pygmies stopped short, their war cries trailing off into confused murmurs.

Sorrow rose, rubbing her throat, willing the swelling to go down. She took a deep breath, then ran to Slate's side. Dark blood still pulsed from the gash between his ribs. *Alive!* she thought, though she knew he had mere seconds left.

A shadow fell over her. She looked up to see Brand, his face pale and grave.

"I need a dagger!" she said.

Wordlessly, he handed her one.

Not pausing to explain her actions, she sank the dagger into Slate's wound, then twisted it, prying the gap in his ribs into an opening large enough for her to insert her fingers. His interior felt hot as an oven as she probed the depths his chest cavity. Judging from the darkness of the blood, the sword had pierced one of the major veins carrying blood to Slate's right lung. A surge of heat around her fingers told her she was near. She felt the vein, sliced cleanly in two. Desperately, she tried to piece the two ends back together, a feat that proved impossible with only one hand.

"Pull his ribs apart," she said to Brand.

"Sorrow," he said softly, shaking his head. She could see he'd already accepted that Slate was dead.

"Pull his ribs apart!" she demanded.

But it wasn't Brand whose hands moved next to her own. Webbed fingers grabbed Slate's ribs and levered them apart. She turned her head to find herself looking into Mako's eyes.

"Hurry," Mako said, the strain evident upon his face.

She hurried, digging both hands into the wound. She closed the major vein that had been severed, then smoothed shut a large artery that had merely been sliced open. As she moved her hands back toward the surface, she paused again and again to stick together blood vessels. The pulsing blood slowed to a trickle as she pulled her hands free.

"I... I've done what I can," she said, wiping her brow with a bloodied hand.

"He's lost so much blood," whispered Brand.

"He's a fighter," said Mako, moving his hands so that Sorrow could piece together the external gash.

"He has a chance," said Sorrow, pressing her fingers against Slate's throat to feel his pulse, weak and racing. "When Numinous struck, he didn't push the blade all the way through Slate's torso. He may have been worried about cutting into the One True Book."

"It would still have been a fatal blow if you hadn't acted," said Mako. He lowered his ear to Slate's chest. "There's not much air getting into his lungs. Still, there's some."

Sorrow nodded. Then, she looked again at Mako, her eyes widening.

"You're on land," she said.

He shrugged, keeping his eyes on Slate's face. "I don't know if the Wanderer pact with Abyss extends to Hell." Then he met her gaze. "If I've damned myself, so be it. I couldn't stand by and watch that bastard gut you."

"Oh, Mako," she whispered, the weight of his sacrifice falling heavy upon her.

"So that was Numinous?" asked Brand. "The kid who attacked us in the middle of the damned ocean? The self-proclaimed Omega Reader?"

She nodded, running her fingers along Slate's chest, wondering what else she could do. All the energy she'd commanded earlier was now exhausted.

"And he has the book?" asked Brand.

She nodded again, though only distantly aware of his questions.

"I would really, really like to cuss right now, but I honestly don't know any words quite strong enough," said Brand.

"Now isn't the time for joking," said Mako, once more pressing his ears to Slate's chest. "I… I'm having a hard time hearing his heart."

Brand frowned, turning away from Slate, looking at the bone cage. Then, he turned back.

"Look, I'm as worried about Slate as anyone," he said.

Sorrow knew that couldn't possibly be true.

"But," he continued, "the goddamned Omega Reader just ran off with the One True Book! This has to be a priority. Is it safe for Rigger to move Slate back onto the ship?"

"Can you give me five minutes?" Sorrow asked, running her bloodied hand across her head. "Let me think. I need to think."

Silence followed, save for faint, ragged, irregular wheezes coming from Slate.

Brand shifted uncomfortably, placing his weight on one foot, then the other, before actively pacing.

"Sage!" Brand called out, looking up at the deck. "Did you see where they went?"

"Sort of," she said. "The way the air folded around them… I think they fled across a dimensional membrane."

"Like, back to the living world?"

"Maybe. But they were close enough to the *Circus* they could have touched the hull. My hunch is, wherever they thought they were going, they wound up in the Sea of Wine."

"That might be a lucky break," said Brand. "Maybe they'll drown."

"We won't be lucky," said Sorrow, annoyed by the chatter around her but unable to ignore it. With Slate so precariously balanced on the edge of death, she wanted the luxury of being allowed to worry, of being allowed to feel her own heart pierced with needles of fear, of grief, of guilt. Maybe if she hadn't attacked so rashly before knowing who they faced...?

She clenched her fists, forcing her mind to grow still.

"When Numinous was about to kill me, he made an offhand remark about heading for a pulpit. That's where we'll have to stop him."

"That doesn't really tell us much about the location," said Mako. "He didn't say a city? Even an island?"

Sorrow shook her head.

"It guess we'd couldn't expect him to simply spout out longitude and latitude, could we?" said Brand.

She cut him a nasty glance. Did he ever take anything seriously? But, she had no time for anger with him now. "I may have a second lead."

"What?"

"The girl who was with him. I don't know why she's here, and I don't know how she changed into flesh and blood, but that was the Black Swan."

"Are you sure?" asked Brand. "I met her when I purchased the *Circus*. I didn't see much resemblance."

"I recognized her aura."

Before Brand could ask another question, a soft groan escaped Slate's lips. He didn't inhale after this. The pale, half light of the soul she'd shared with him faded to black. Mako once more pressed his ear to Slate's chest, first one side, then the other. He looked at Sorrow, but couldn't find any words.

"I know," she said quietly, looking at the blood pooled onto the ground around her. She knew. She'd known. She'd known all along. Everything she'd ever touched turned to ruin. She'd sealed Slate's fate the second she'd allowed herself to love him. Soul or no soul, to die in Hell was a final death.

"Take him onto the ship," she whispered. "I'd like… I'd like to bury him where we found him, back on the Isle of Fire."

Mako nodded.

Brand said, "I'm so sorry."

"I know," she said, her voice devoid of emotion.

He looked as if he were about to say something else. Then, he motioned toward Rigger to lift him back to the deck. As the rope wrapped around his waist, he said, "Take as much time as you need."

She nodded. "I won't be long."

In the course of the fight, the pouch in which she'd gathered the witch nails had been torn. In the blood around her sat nails of jade, of glass, of gold. One by one, she found them and wiped them clean. The final nail hovered in the air, glowing like a tiny sun. She closed her fingers around it, then stood. She took one long, last glance at the cage of bone.

Then she turned away. She had no time for grief or regret. The One True Book had to be dealt with. It was time to finish what she'd begun all those long years ago.

16 - He and We

CINDER SENSED SOMETHING was wrong the second she stepped through the dimensional veil. Ordinarily, her surroundings took on a translucent, muted-color as she walked between worlds. Now, the ship that had attacked them seemed more solid than ever, as if it were the center of a spiritual realm all its own. It was so solid it possessed its own gravity, and she felt herself pulled toward it. The river it rested upon surged within its banks. Suddenly, the ground gave way beneath her and she plunged with a cry into burgundy waves, losing her grip on Mantle. By instinct, she held her breath, though not before the dark, sweet fluid splashed across her tongue. She closed her eyes as momentum carried her beneath the surface. Weightless in warm liquid, she had no sense of up or down. She flailed her limbs, finding nothing solid near her. She forced her eyes open, regretting it instantly. Whatever she'd fallen into, the fluid burned her eyes. Fortunately, she saw light above and darkness beneath stretching into unknown depths. She kicked hard, swimming toward light.

She emerged beneath a fiery sky. Hell's sky had been an unbroken storm cloud, but here the clouds were wisps, painted brilliant red and orange by a sun barely beneath the horizon.

"Mantle!" she called out, looking around. In every direction there was only trackless ocean, the color of blood, and the overwhelming stink of wine. The ship which had pulled her here was nowhere to be seen. She called again, "Mantle!"

With a splash, Mantle's head and shoulders popped above the surface. The oiled leather of the pack held air, turning it into a makeshift buoy. "Cinder!" he called out as he spotted her. "Grab hold!"

She swam to his side, grabbing hold of the pack, feeling far more exhausted from the short swim than she would have expected. She normally swam in placid pools beneath the falls of the river. The bobbing motions of the waves left her feeling slightly ill and more than a little disoriented.

"Where are we?" she asked.

"The Sea of Wine," said a voice from above. She craned her neck to find Ver hovering above them, his form pale and translucent against the red sky. Despite the wraithlike nature of his body in the waning light, he carried the Witchbreaker in one hand. She hadn't paid attention to it before, but she saw that the soles of his boots were white as his gloves. Her own feet felt filthy after walking across Hell.

Ver said, "The ship that attacked you was crewed by Wanderers. They apparently brought their abstract realm along with them. Take care not to swallow the wine. It will dampen your ability to tell dreams from reality."

Cinder wondered if she'd already swallowed some. The floral, fermented scent was heavy in the air, making her feel as if the world was slowly spinning. She clung to the bag, wanting to summon the strength to leave, but couldn't concentrate due to her growing nausea.

"I see you saved the sword," Mantle said, looking up at the priest. "I lost my grip when we hit the water."

"It seemed like something you might wish to save," said Ver.

Mantle studied Cinder's face. "Are you alright?" he asked. "You look... pale. More gray than black."

"It's the fumes," she whispered. "They're making me dizzy."

"Then rise above them," said Ver. "This is a realm of spirits. You may walk upon the air."

She tried to remember how she'd done it before in the Realm of Roots. It had felt effortless then. Now, every time she moved her legs to find purchase on the spiritual substance engulfing her, she wound up off balance, her struggles pushing her beneath the waves.

"I can't stand," she said. "The world... it's spinning too hard. I think... I think I'm going to be sick."

"Bobbing in the waves isn't helping," said Mantle, looking around, his eyes fixing on gulls wheeling high overhead. "Ver, from your vantage point, can you see land? Gulls only go so far out to sea."

"Not land," said Ver. "But a solid place that will serve. Follow."

Ver began to walk along the air toward something she couldn't see. Mantle wrapped an arm around Cinder's torso and paddled in pursuit. Even though she could barely move her legs, he proved up to the task of propelling them both across the surface. Her stomach lurched as they swam into waves heaving higher and higher. They swam so long she was certain hours had passed, but the sunset had yet to give way to night. Her nausea was compounded as the wine-stench gave way to an overpowering miasma of rotting meat. As a particularly violent wave carried them up, she caught a glimpse of red waves breaking into pink foam on a nearby spit of black gravel. She lost sight of it as they fell into the trough of the wave, then fixed her eyes on it again as the swell carried them up. The beach they swam for curved in a serpentine fashion.

"Oh no," she whispered, remembering her mother's adventure in the Sea of Wine.

"What?" asked Mantle.

"It's Rott," she said, softly.

"Indeed," said Ver. "There's nothing to fear. He's quite dead. His back will serve well as a place for you to get your bearings."

As the stench grew more powerful, Cinder almost told Mantle she'd rather stay floating in the wine. Before she could speak, her toes bumped against something smooth and hard. Mantle's legs stopped kicking and the position of his body changed as he found footing in the pink surf. He dragged her up the dragon's back, across a field of loose scales the size of banana leaves. White bones showed through gaps in the scales. She shuddered with revulsion as Mantle lowered her onto a broad, flat rib of bleached bone.

Mantle let loose his grip on her, waving his hand swat away the flies that swarmed him. Even here, however, her smoky scent kept the insects at bay. Mantle quickly realized this and moved to her side.

"Take a moment to get your bearings," he said.

"I feel worse here than I did in the wine," she whispered. "The stench…"

Her voice trailed off as her stomach staged a full-scale rebellion. She rolled to her side and spewed the contents of her guts onto a deep, dark hole beside the rib she lay upon. She heaved until she was empty, then heaved some more. She rolled to her back, trembling, as Mantle knelt before her. With a tender smile, he wiped flecks of vomit from her chin.

"You'll feel better now," he said.

She doubted this. She felt completely hollowed out, devoid of the strength even to sit up.

Mantle rose, facing Ver. "You guided us into Hell. Can you guide us back into the living world?"

"Of course," said the priest. "The two of you fled Hell too swiftly for me to offer guidance. From here, we may chart a more deliberate course to the living world. We need only wait for Cinder to regain her strength."

Cinder closed her eyes. "Why did we come here?"

Ver said, "The presence of Wanderers caused the Sea of Wine to be the closest spiritual realm adjacent—"

"No," she said. "I mean, what was the point of all this? You brought us to Hell on a rescue mission, then insisted we attack the people we'd come to save."

"You saw for yourself that they'd been possessed by demons."

"And this wasn't something you'd assumed would be a possibility?"

"There was always the risk," said Ver.

"You said if we left living souls in hell, all of reality might unravel. Even possessed by demons, don't they need to be taken from Hell?"

"I understand your confusion," said Ver. "But, while their bodies may yet survive, they are living souls no longer. The demons have devoured their souls, removing the threat."

Cinder frowned. She felt certain he was lying. Yet, her own mother had said that Ver couldn't lie. She wished she didn't feel so dizzy. She felt like, if her head would only clear, she might grasp clearly whether or not he was tricking her.

"Does this have something to do with that book?" she asked, opening her eyes and studying the leather pack Mantle carried. "Was finding Sorrow and Slate not the true goal?"

"How could I have known it they carried the One True Book?" Ver answered. "The tome vanished nearly twenty years ago. Everyone assumed it had been destroyed."

"Perhaps it should be destroyed," said Mantle.

"Don't speak foolishly," said Ver.

"Look at the misery this book has brought the world," said Mantle.

"You seem ignorant of the proper usage of the word 'misery,'" said Ver. "When the One True Book was present in the temple, its timeless truths were the foundation of centuries of peace and prosperity."

"If the truths were timeless," said Mantle, "the church wouldn't have collapsed the second the book vanished. The truths would have endured in men's hearts, even if they weren't written down."

"The One True Book gave the weight of authority to these truths," said Ver. "Without respect for authority, how is one to judge truth from falsehood?"

"But corrupt authority can pass falsehoods off as truth," said Mantle.

"A corrupt authority is no authority at all," scoffed Ver.

Mantle looked at Cinder, his face showing his irritation with Ver's circular logic. She felt glad he shared her skepticism.

"Some of the color has returned to your face," he said.

She nodded. Now that she'd grown numb to the smell, her illness had ebbed. Holding his hand, she rose on unsteady legs and said, "I think I can make the jump."

As she stood, her foot landed on a black scale. It slid against its neighbor. She pulled her foot away and it clattered down the slope of the dragon's rib cage. Pale light seeped up from the gap in the bone she'd uncovered.

"What's this?" Mantle said softly, lowering himself to one knee. To Cinder's surprise, he dropped onto his belly and shoved his hand between the dragon's ribs, digging down until his arm was buried the beast. A look of intense concentration was replaced by a look of pleasure as the pulled his hand free, revealing a cutlass, its blade glowing a soft, pale green.

"It's the Sword of Phosphors," said Ver. "It once belonged to the notorious pirate, Gale Romer. I wonder how it came to be lodged here?"

"Pirate?" said Cinder. "She was my mother's friend."

"You mother's employer, more accurately," said Ver. "Before you were born, Infidel earned her living as a mercenary. It mattered nothing to her who paid her fee. She killed who she was hired to kill."

Mantle slipped the blade into his belt. "This may come in handy in defending our settlement."

"I've no doubt it will," said Ver. "It's good to know that enduring the stench of this place hasn't been in vain."

Mantle raised his eyebrow. "I didn't know ghosts had a sense of smell."

Ver took a deep breath through his nostrils, holding in the stench a long time, then exhaling. "Hell would hold less sting if even one of the senses were dulled. Now, if you're ready, let's leave this place."

Ver held his hand toward Cinder. She took it, as Mantle took Cinder's other hand. Together, they stepped forward. The air shimmered before them...

... and they emerged someplace far darker than the Sea of Wine. A wave of cold washed over her, so intense she heard crackles as the moisture in her still damp hair instantly froze. Her teeth chattered as she looked around, crossing her arms over her breasts. Mantle lifted the Sword of Phosphors, letting its soft light spill over their surroundings. They were in the shell of a vandalized building, a church judging from the overturned pews, or perhaps a cathedral, given the grand scale of the place. Empty window frames in the arched walls looming overhead showed heavy clouds lit by faint flickers of lightning. Snow blew through the open windows, filling the air with drifting jewels. Beneath them, shards of stained glass glittered beneath a carpet of frost.

Tapestries that had once decorated the walls lay in crumpled heaps at the base. With customary swiftness, Mantle moved toward the tapestries. Seconds later he draped a heavy, makeshift cloak over Cinder's shivering shoulders. She pulled it tightly about her, though the cloth was as cold as the surrounding air.

"Where are we now?" Mantle asked. He looked over his shoulder, then craned his neck around the room. "Ver's gone?"

"He's still here," said Cinder. "You can't see him without my help, now that we're back in the land of the living."

She took his hand. He turned until he spotted their ghostly guide, and said, "This has to be the Grand Cathedral of the Silver City."

Ver nodded. "It was. Speak softly. Tempest's armies are massed here in great numbers. Voices carry far in the still of a winter's night."

As did footsteps, Cinder realized, as she heard heavy crunches on the snow along the wall outside. Whoever approached the open door was soon joined by a companion, then another. She held her breath as a skull-faced warrior peered around the corner. His torso was draped in chain mail, and his fleshless hands grasped a gore-encrusted battle ax.

The dead man's empty eye sockets fixed instantly upon the Sword of Phosphors. Raising his ax, he lumbered forward.

"Stay back," Mantle said coolly, moving at a casual pace, until he was close enough for the dead warrior to strike. As the axe sliced toward him, Mantle stepped to the side and with one swift slice of his blade severed his attacker's wrists. The ax clattered to the floor, leaving the dead warrior staring at his stumps. Mantle's blade sliced a second time, lopping off the skull, then twice more, driving into joints in the armored knees. He stepped aside as his crippled opponent fell forward, then took two rapid steps toward the door and drove his blade deep into the eyes of the next undead warrior to come around the corner. The light flickered as the blade plunged again and again into the bodies of dead men lumbering toward the door. Several moments passed before the wave of invaders was exhausted, and Mantle had a moment to fall back and catch his breath.

"Why have you brought us to this wretched place?" he demanded of Ver as he grabbed Cinder's hand once more.

"So you could see the world your god has created."

"My god?"

"Greatshadow turned his back on mankind, letting the other dragons destroy the world."

"Greatshadow protects the chosen," said Mantle. "By his grace, we shall rebuild."

Ver shook his head. "Look around. All is dead. All is frozen. There will be no rebuilding. You've fallen for a grand deception. Greatshadow grows weaker with each day that passes without the flames of the civilized world. It's only a matter of time before the Isle of Fire falls."

"We can't simply give up. Is there nothing we can do to save what's left of mankind?" asked Mantle.

"The One True Book," said Ver. "Read it."

"What?" asked Cinder. "That makes no sense. Mantle's not of your faith. He doesn't believe in the book."

"He's pure of heart," said Ver. "And he's seen the truth. He believes."

"What will happen when I read the book?" asked Mantle.

"All falsehood will be removed from the world, including the greatest falsehoods of all, the primal dragons. You'll free the world from the grip of their terror."

"This… this is what you've been planning all along," said Cinder. She looked toward the overturned pew where Mantle had placed the bag before defending against the undead attackers. Dropping her cloak and letting go of Mantle's hand she leapt toward it, snatching it up. "I can't let you do this."

"Why not?" asked Mantle. "Look around you! All of mankind faces death if we don't act to save them."

"I don't trust Ver," she said.

"I'm incapable of lies," said Ver. As he spoke, he shifted the Witchbreaker to hold it with both hands.

"Any liar could make that claim," said Cinder.

"True," said Mantle. "Perhaps he is capable of lying. But… why would he? What would he have to gain?'

Cinder frowned. Something was off about Mantle's statement. What?

Mantle stepped closer to her. "I don't blame you for doubting Ver. But, though we've only met a little while ago, we've been through a lot together. You've saved my life, and I've saved yours. Can you trust me?"

She didn't answer, staring at his hands as he held them toward her, palms up, asking for the pack. Suddenly, she realized what was wrong.

"You heard him," she whispered.

"What?" he asked.

"When he said he was incapable of lies, I wasn't touching you. But you heard him all the same."

"Oh." Mantle's expression turned completely blank. Then, his whole body relaxed and he broke into a subtle smile. "I suppose I did."

Ver said, "The veils between the worlds grow thin—"

Mantle raised his hand to cut off the priest, "Further deception won't be necessary. She's onto us."

"Have you… have you been lying to me since we first met?" Cinder asked.

"I've been lying since long before we met," said Mantle. "Brother Wing could read minds. Preparing myself for this role required believing my own lies so completely he'd never suspect a thing. Step by step, I've done what was needed to bring myself closer to you. You've a rare gift, Cinder. You wouldn't have willingly helped us if you'd known the truth."

Cinder leaned forward, preparing to leap back into the spirit world, when suddenly the world exploded into stars. She landed on her back, unable to focus her eyes. Her whole face felt numb. She tried to breathe and wound up coughing violently. The warm metal tang of blood filled her mouth. Had Mantle just punched her? She hadn't even seen him move!

A foot fell onto her chest, pressing down between her breasts, pinning her. She squinted, trying to clear her vision, and found herself looking up at Mantle, who held the book in one hand, the glowing sword in the other.

"Why are you doing this?" she gasped, straining to breathe.

"To fulfill my destiny," said Mantle. "A proper introduction has yet to be made. My name is Numinous Pilgrim. I'm the Omega Reader. I'm going to save the world."

"Save it?"

"By reading the One True Book. From the first syllable, the falsehoods of this world shall be erased. I suppose it would be an act of mercy to kill you now."

Still fighting to breathe, she sank her nails into his legs, digging in with all the strength she could muster. The attack didn't even cause him to flinch. He bent over, his face placid, and placed the tip of the sword slightly to the right of her windpipe.

"We'd never have done this without you," he said as he flicked the sword, slicing her throat. "Thank you."

He stepped away. She snapped her hands to her throat, pressing against the surging blood. She felt lightheaded, feverish, but she wasn't dead yet. In an act of pure will she sat up, the world whirling around her. From the corner of her eye, she saw Numinous ascend the stairs into the pulpit of the cathedral.

"Don't," she whispered, her voice gurgling.

"Give up, child," said Ver, standing over her, the Witchbreaker raised as if ready to strike. "You've played your part. Go to the eternal darkness. When he reads, there will be no Heaven, no Hell, only oblivion. When nothing is true, the only truth is nothingness. This is my gift to all of existence. At long last, an end to struggling, to suffering, and pain. At long last, an end to the ultimate falsehood, the sad, sick delusion that anything ever existed at all."

With trembling limbs, she made it to her knees. Numinous jabbed the tip of the Sword of Phosphors into the podium he stood before, creating a makeshift reading lamp. He opened the leather pack and pulled out the One True Book. His eyes were full of reverence as he gently traced his fingers over the binding.

"Don't," she whispered again, as blood spilled from her lips.

Numinous placed the book upon the podium. He closed his eyes and mouthed a prayer she couldn't hear. She staggered toward him, the frosted glass crunching beneath her bare feet. He didn't look toward her.

Numinous opened the book. He began to read, in a tongue she'd never heard before, in a voice not his own.

"No!" she cried.

"Yes!" said Ver, in a tone of pure rapture. He turned his face toward the heavens. He dropped the Witchbreaker and spread his arms, as if ready to embrace all the sky. A bright light spread from the podium. Keeping one hand on her neck, she raised her other to block the light. She could see no sign of Numinous, not even a shadow. The bubble of light rolled toward her. She turned, took a step forward, and stumbled from the living world. She found herself in a place she'd never been before, a vast, verdant field of green, rolling hills in a valley ringed by snow-tipped mountains. Wild ponies munched lazily on fresh spring growth. Then, to her shock, the distant mountains vanished, boiling away in the pure white light that followed her from the cathedral. The light flowed from the mountains like a flood, washing toward the hills. The ponies looked up, tried to gallop, and vanished as the light overtook them. At the last possible second, she turned, leaping, passing once more into a new realm.

She landed on an ice floe in a vast, dark ocean. Blue ogres on the floe next to her turned their heads at the sound of her wet, gurgling gasps. She sank to one knee, certain that death was near. A trio of ogres walked toward her, harpoons in hand, oblivious to the growing white wall behind them. As they vanished into the light, she rose with a groan, and took another stumbling step into the unknown.

From the shadows that surrounded her, she assumed at first she'd reached the Realm of Root. Instead, she found herself sinking into foul, black mire. Black serpents slithered through branches above her. She tried to run, but the mire sucked at her, and before she knew it her head sank beneath the black muck.

Though it would only hasten her bleeding to death, she let go of her throat and grabbed for a vine that had been dangling overhead. Her fingers found their target and she pulled herself free of the mire. With superhuman effort, she dragged herself onto a fallen tree half-submerged in the muck. Looking around, she found herself in a misty swamp, with darkness on every horizon. Then, there was light. Looking to her left, she saw once more the wall of white sweeping toward her.

She sobbed, understanding the futility of flight. She'd be dead in seconds whether she ran or not. She turned to face the light. Then clenching her jaw, she leapt toward it, once more passing through a dimensional veil. She found herself inside a large cavern, with spikes of stone hanging from the ceiling and rising from the floor like the teeth of some great beast. All was dark save for the faint glow of the spirit light that manifested in such places.

A voice, so deep and low she felt it in her bones, grumbled, "You aren't welcome here." The ground beneath her shook. With loud cracks, the stone spikes above her snapped free and fell toward her. She jumped from their path, passing through yet another veil, and kept jumping. Her senses barely had time to register as she fled between worlds. She fell through a land of clouds, landing on the thigh of a gray-skinned giant lounging on mist, before leaping once more, to find herself far beneath the sea, in a kingdom built of coral, as mermaids veiled with seaweed red and brown swam toward her, eyes wide with curiosity, before the pursuing light devoured. She plunged onward, to a bright sandy beach covered in footprints, the white light at her back. She kept running, jumping again and again, her lungs aflame, through valleys of darkness, across deserts burning beneath a throbbing sun, through frost and through smoke, across glowing fields of lava and marshes drenched by rain.

The burning in her lungs faded. Her heartbeat no longer sounded in her ears. She kept running. She kept leaping.

In the end, every leap took her to the same place. She tried a hundred times to jump away, but there were no veils any more. There was nothing but the surface she stood upon, and the black void above.

She looked down, trying to make sense of her surroundings. The ground looked almost like paper. She knelt, running her fingers along it. It *was* paper, pristine, unmarked, save for the lines of dark blood traced by her fingers. It extended in all directions, toward endless horizons.

"Where am I?" she mumbled.

"The Primordial Pages," answered someone behind her.

She turned to find an old pygmy staring at her. He had no dyes to identify his tribe. He was white as a corpse, save for his dark eyes and yellow teeth. He wore no clothes, and his long white beard hung far below his waist.

"Who are you?" she asked.

"That's a question I've spent a great deal of time pondering," said the pygmy. "Some people know me as Walker. It will serve. Who are you?"

"I..." she froze. She frowned. "That seems like it should be a simple question."

He nodded as he looked at the mud drying on her body. "You've been swimming in the Black Bog. Your name is the first thing it takes from you."

She ran her fingers through her mud-caked hair. "I don't... I don't remember how I got here. I was... running from something?"

"That's likely," said Walker. "Everyone's running from something."

"Where did you say we were?" she asked.

"The Primordial Pages," he said. "The very foundation of reality."

She held her fingers to her throat. No blood flowed from her wound. She pressed her fingers firmly against her neck. She found no trace of a pulse. "Am I... am I dead?"

"That's probable," he said. "Most people are alive for only the briefest blink of eternity. Death tends to last longer." Then, he narrowed his eyes, studying her more closely. "I think I've heard of you. Cinder, the girl who walks between the worlds. From the Jawa Fruit tribe."

Her own name seemed unfamiliar, but she could dimly remember growing up among such a tribe. Her memory of jawa fruit itself was clear. She could remember the smell and taste, remember the soft but firm flesh of a bright pink, fully ripened globe.

Her mouth watered at the memory. She swallowed. The pain in her throat caused the reality of her present circumstances to once more move to the front of her mind.

"Don't be afraid," said Walker.

"I am afraid," she whispered, touching the gash in her throat. "But not because… because I'm dead. I remember… there was a book… and there was snow, and glass beneath my feet, and…" Her voice trailed off.

"Go on," said Walker.

"I think… I think I saw the end of the world."

"Yes," said Walker. "The final words have been read. I watched from Hell as the Omega Reader closed the covers on all of creation. When Hell faded away, I came here." He crossed his arms. "I found the ending… unsatisfying."

"What?" she asked.

"Unsatisfying," he said.

"I heard you," she said. "I don't understand you. Under what circumstances could the end of the world possibly be satisfying?"

Walker chuckled. "I gather you haven't read many books. It's a great paradox that the books with the most satisfying endings are the ones you wish the author had continued writing."

"Then the Church of the Book was right all along?" she asked. "The world was only a book? Reality was nothing but a lie?"

"But if reality itself was a lie, then wouldn't that mean that lies are real?" he asked, scratching his belly beneath his long beard.

She looked at him, as if seeing him for the first time. The darkness of his eyes haunted her. She whispered, "Are you… are you the Divine Author?"

"We all were," he said, with a soft smile. "Everyone who ever lived, everything that ever was, we were all aspects of the Author. Our stories were His stories, His stories were our own. He and We are synonymous in this understanding of creation."

"If I were the Divine Author, I wouldn't let the book end this way," she said. She shuddered as a chill ran along her spine. "It's… I can't remember why clearly, or how, but… it's my fault. It's all my fault!" She fell to her knees, too weak to stand. "This can't be all there is."

"The book is closed. The final words lie over the horizon. It's too late to alter them."

She looked around. "The final words?"

He nodded. "The book is closed. That doesn't mean it was never written. Everything still dwells within the sacred ink. Perhaps some future reader will find these words, and bring our world to life once more."

She turned slowly, her eyes scanning the horizon. "Where? Where can I find these words?"

"All the best stories are circles," said Walker. "One measures a circle beginning anywhere."

She rose to her feet, stumbling forward. Slowly her hesitant, staggered pace gave way to a steady walk. Fighting off her weariness, she managed a slow jog. The white paper seemed infinite. Was she even moving? She glanced over her shoulder and saw Walker in the distance, little more than a speck as he waved at her.

If she was moving away from something she must be moving toward something. Turning her face forward, she started to run. She kept running, feeling no hunger, no thirst, no weariness, as her dead limbs let go of the shackling necessities of life. She ran until she couldn't remember why she was running.

Then she found herself passing along slender, dark squiggles running in parallel lines along the paper and remembered what she'd been looking for. She'd found the story! She came to a halt, her eyes running over the marks. Her heart sank. She couldn't read the script.

"Am I… am I back far enough?" Even without looking behind her, she somehow knew Walker would be there.

"Far enough for what?" he asked.

She held her fingers before her, touching the air. "I… I feel… veils. The words are making worlds come into existence. The world still exists!"

"Your world will always exist. The absence of a future doesn't negate the past."

"I know the world ends," she whispered, doubting herself as she said the words. The details eluded her but, just as the Jawa Fruit had been clear in her mind, she could recall small, discreet images. The snow, yes, that was clear. And there had been a dragon, a dragon rising from a cauldron of flame. And… a temple. She frowned. Had the dragon been in the temple with the snow, or a someplace else? But what did it matter if she couldn't remember the full details. She knew that the world faced a final day. "I have to stop it," she said. "I can't let it end."

"You seek to edit the story from within?" Walker asked, sounding amused. "It can't be done."

"How do you know?" she asked. "Have you tried?"

"Why would I try?" he asked. "It's impossible."

"You said… you said we were all the Divine Author." She turned to him, grabbing him by the shoulders. "Can you read this script? If I go back to the world here, will I have time to save it? Have I gone back far enough?"

He shook his head. "You can never go back far enough to undo what is written."

She pushed him away. "Watch me."

Once more she ran. The dark squiggles passed beneath her, a ceaseless narrative guiding her ever further into the past. Her natural body clocks of hunger and thirst had vanished. She tried to remember how long she'd been running. A day? A week? Was it enough?

"I'll admit," said Walker, suddenly at her side. "It will be interesting to see you try."

Cinder turned to look at him, losing her balance as she took her eyes from the path. With no time to brace herself, she fell. When she hit the paper, it ripped, revealing only void beneath it. For a moment, she dangled on the edge of the tear, trying to claw her way back to the surface.

Walker waved at her and said, "Good luck."

The paper she clung to tore free. With a cry of despair, she dropped into the unknowable.

17 - Merchant

CINDER LANDED ON her hands and knees. Sharp, volcanic rock sliced into her hand. She winced as she sat up, staring at the bloodless wound. She looked around the shadowy landscape. Was this the Realm of Roots?

Through the gap in the canopy overhead, she could see stars. A cool ocean breeze ruffled the foliage as it wound its way up the slopes. She stood, sniffing the air, recognizing the scent of the jungle. A thousand blossoms competing for the attention of insects, filling the air with sweet floral notes. As she filled her lungs, she realized she hadn't been breathing only a moment before. She repeated the action, feeling as if the air was restoring her to life. Her hand throbbed. Tiny beads of blood gathered on the gash in her palm where she'd fallen on the volcanic rock.

"I'm alive?" she asked, her voice little more than a squeak. She remembered the reason she'd died, and pressed her fingers to her neck, finding a scar.

Despite the fractured state of her memories, she knew she'd returned to the Isle of Fire. She grabbed a vine and climbed into the branches of the tallest tree she could find. It was a moonless, cloudless night. In a large bay far in the distance she spotted the lanterns of hundreds of ships. That had to be Commonground. With this reference point, she felt memories of the geography of her home returning. Walker had said she belong to the Jawa Fruit tribe. At a gut level, she felt as if the muscles of her legs would lead her there even if her mind remained fogged.

Her confidence in her ability to navigate to the village proved misplaced. As the hours progressed she found herself increasingly lost in the dark jungle. Some landmarks along her journey proved familiar. She remembered the large stone head draped with vines, the half-crumbled wall decorated with tiles made of shells, and the waterfall that led to a pool that looked like the outstretched wings of a giant bird. But, along the edges of the pool she felt she should have found the shell border tokens of the Blue Mussel people. Instead, she found perforated bark threaded with dried palm fronds. As best she could remember, this marked the territory of the Bug-Wood folk. She hadn't seen these marking since her childhood. The Bug-Wood folk had been almost completely wiped out by slavers.

By dawn, Cinder was well into what should have been Jawa Fruit territory, but still found only Bug-Wood totems. The trees looked familiar, towering giants that had stood for centuries. She felt certain she was nearly home. As the sky lightened, she scanned the canopy above for signs of the woven platforms, listening closely for the murmur of voices. She saw nothing but branches, and heard only the cries of birds. She scrambled into the treetops, panting as she leapt from branch to branch. She furrowed her brow in confusion. Some trees she didn't recognize at all, but others brought back a strong sensation of familiarity. The hair on the back of her neck rose as she ran her hand along a pattern of knots in a tree that looked almost like a cat's face. She knew this place. This was the tree where she'd lived with her mother.

At the thought, she could see her mother's face, remembered her long hair, her towering height, the sharp, hard lines of her shoulders. What she couldn't recall was her mother's name.

"Mother!" she cried out. "Mother!"

She succeeded only in silencing the birds around her. For several seconds, the stillness lingered. As the birdsongs rose again, from far down the slope she heard the faint, almost imperceptible scream of a woman.

Knowing it might have only been her imagination, she set off in the direction of the noise, moving with reckless speed through a canopy that kept throwing her surprises. Vines she expected at her fingertips had vanished, while thick branches she'd never seen provided fresh routes among the leaves. The morning jungle came to life. Parrots and parakeets danced around her as she ran, and vibrant green snakes slinked along vines, their eyes fixed on the small gray monkeys that leapt from her headlong run.

In the sunlight, she covered in minutes the distance she'd traveled in an hour during the moonless night. She paused in front of a dangling bit of bark and realized she was mere yards from a Bug Wood village. As confirmation, a shout came from just ahead, followed by a grunt. She pushed through a leafy wall to find a trio of blue-skinned pygmies. They were wrestling with a dark green woman entangled in a net in the center of a large woven platform. To the side of the scene, an old man with green skin lay on his back, his belly sliced open, his entrails sliding from the wound. The old man's eyes blinked slowly as he stared into the sky.

"Let her go!" Cinder shouted.

The trio of river-pygmies turned their faces toward her, their eyes growing wide. She must have looked like some jungle spirit, with her ebony skin and relatively imposing height.

If she'd hoped that her appearance might startle the river-pygmies into flight, her hopes were dashed when they all drew swords. She frowned as she saw the metal blades. No pygmies crafted such weapons. They were only found in the hands of river-pygmies who sold forest-pygmies to the long-men.

Cinder clenched her fists and said, in a low growl, "I am the wrath of the forest. Flee me, or face destruction!"

To her great relief, the two pygmies furthest from her lost their nerve and sprang away, leaping from the platform to dangling vines. The pygmy closest to her charged with a savage cry.

Cinder stood her ground, then, as her attacker came within striking distance, she reached for the branch above and pulled herself up. Her attacker's blade sliced through empty air before she dropped onto his back. As he collapsed, she straddled him. Though he was wiry and strong, she had the advantage of size and leverage. She needed only a second to pry the sword from his grasp. Before he could try to grab it back, she hit him hard in his temple with the pommel of the weapon. He went limp immediately.

Cinder ran to help the woman the pygmies had been capturing. She'd crawled to the side of the fallen man, not bothering to disentangle herself from the net. The woman held the man's hand and wept. Cinder reached out, intending to touch the woman's shoulder and ask what was happening, but stopped short.

There was nothing she could say that would lessen the woman's grief, and nothing the woman needed to explain about what had happened. Cinder deduced all she needed to know. Slavers had raided the village at dawn. They would now be marching their captives to the river, a good three miles away. They'd travel along the ground. River-pygmies lacked the skills to travel through the canopy while managing a band of captives.

She set off for the river, sword in hand. If slavers were active in the area, could they be the reason she couldn't find the Jawa Fruit tribe? It made no sense. Even if they'd taken the people, the platforms and huts would have been left behind. Unless…

She came to a stop. When she'd fallen through the Primordial Pages, how far back in the story had she come? The Jawa Fruit people had migrated into the territory she'd grown up in after the Bug Wood people disappeared. That had been long before she was born. It was impossible that she'd come back so far. Was she still disoriented from her immersion in the Black Bog?

Resuming her pursuit through the canopy, she overtook a group of river-pygmies winding along a rocky path below. There were five of them, adult warriors armed with swords, prodding and poking about twenty forest-pygmies, mostly women and children.

Once more, a vision of her mother appeared in her mind. This time, her mother's face and hands were red with blood, as she stood over a gutted boar. Though her mother's name still eluded her grasp, she remembered her mother's prowess as a hunter and a warrior. In her gut, he knew exactly what her mother would do in this situation.

Cinder leapt from the branch onto the rear-most river-pygmy, plunging her blade deep into his back. His sword clattered on the rocks as he fell. As the others turned toward her she'd already reached the next in line. He had no time to raise his blade before she impaled him, driving her blade between his ribs. As he fell, the twist of his body tore her blade from her grasp, but without pause she caught his blade as it slipped from his dying fingers. She charged the next pygmy in line. He turned to flee, screaming in terror. She struck low across his thighs, dropping him, then leapt to reach the next slaver. Unfortunately, as her element of surprise faded, that slaver bolted like a frightened hare, joined by the last river-pygmy, who'd also decided he valued his life more than his prisoners.

Cinder paused to finish off the ham-strung pygmy, then used her blade to free one of the captives, a boy perhaps ten years old. He looked at her with stoic eyes as she cut through the vines that bound his wrists.

"Are you a hoorga?" he asked as she placed the blade into his hands.

She wasn't familiar with the term. Every pygmy tribe had its own band of forest spirits, good and evil. Perhaps he'd mistaken her for such a creature.

"What's a hoorga?" she asked.

"The black bird who flies through the Realm of Roots," he said. "The black bird who takes the shape a woman when she comes for the dead."

"I'm not here for you," she said, handing him one of the fallen blades. "Use this sword to free the others. How many more have been captured?"

"All of them," he said. Unfortunately, some pygmy tribes had no words to express numbers.

"Then I'm going to free all of them," she said, leaping to a nearby tree and climbing once more.

It took only a little while to reach the river. The water was swollen from recent rains. Her heart sank when she saw several dugout canoes far down the river, moving rapidly despite being laden with huddled captives. The river-pygmies skillfully navigated through the whitewater boiling around boulders. A half dozen canoes still rested at the water's edge, with at least twenty blue warriors gathered into a band to listen to their jabbering brethren, the two river-pygmies who'd escaped her.

Cinder clenched the branch tightly as she contemplated her options. Diving headlong into twenty men was crazy. Crazy seemed like her best strategy. If most of the group fled, she was confident she was more than a match for any single pygmy, or even a band of two or three.

Before she could talk herself out of it, she grabbed a hanging vine, cut one end free, and swung toward the slavers. A sane approach would be to strike from the back of the group. Instead, she dropped directly into the center and spun, not bothering to aim for killing blows. She swiftly sliced into as many faces as she could while screaming at the top of her lungs.

The pygmies exploded away from her. She caught one by the hair as he fled and threw him to his back. Before the others had time to catch their wits, she pinned him to the ground and placed her sword against his throat.

"The Jawa Fruit tribe," she demanded. "Where are they?"

His terrified eyes were wide as he stammered, "J-ja-jawa? Jawa fruit?"

He plainly didn't know what she was talking about. With his potential usefulness exhausted, she slid her blade into his neck, finishing him. She stood up, studying the forest around her. The frightened river-pygmies had abandoned their canoes and their captives. To her relief, some of the prisoners were adult men. Many were badly beaten, half-blind with swollen eyes, but a few still looked strong enough to stand if their bonds were severed. She freed them, handing them swords left behind when the slavers had fled.

"Free the others and get back to your village," she said as she cut their bonds. "If you catch sight of a river-pygmy, attack without mercy!"

She went to the river, contemplating the whitewater. She'd never used a canoe before. Getting herself drowned wasn't going to get her any closer to the slavers, or to answers about what had happened to her tribe. Fortunately, she knew where the slavers were heading. They'd sell their captives in Commonground. The thought of going to the city filled her with nameless dread. She felt that something bad had happened to her there, but couldn't remember what it was. Still, if it was where she must go, so be it.

BEFORE CINDER SET out for Commonground, she raided the canoes for supplies, finding dried fish and fermented mango paste wrapped in banana leaves, along with gourds of fresh water. She also equipped herself with an iron knife and a second sword. A large and elaborate cape of brightly colored feathers may have once belonged to a tribal chief. She took it, vaguely remembering it would be important to cover her nudity in the city. As a final supply, the last river-pygmy she'd killed had worn a belt with a leather pouch filled with small silver coins. She'd no idea if the few dozen coins constituted a pittance or a fortune, but sensed they might come in handy in when she reached the city.

Cinder moved along the river, her weariness increasing with each step. She'd never before felt any desire to sleep, but she'd also never felt such exhaustion. She'd been running since returning to the living world, and running across countless dimensions for an unknowable time before that. She climbed into a tree, stretching out on a long, broad branch. With a distant, half-memory of having seen her mother fall asleep, she closed her eyes, not knowing if she would be able to fully succumb to slumber.

She woke hours later, in the heat of the afternoon, with every muscle aching. She sat up with a groan. Her exhaustion had diminished, but her whole body hurt. Life in the jungle had kept her fit, but she wasn't used to so much fighting.

Now that she'd slept, her mind felt slightly less fogged. She still had only shards of memory, but she finally felt ready to grapple with the thought that had earlier crossed her mind. What if she'd come back to the world before she'd even been born? If she did find her mother, now young… what could she to say to her?

She shook her head. It was madness to contemplate such things.

After a brief bath in the river, washing off sweat and dried blood, she gathered up her belongings and made her way along the canopy at the river's edge. She kept moving when the day gave way to night, with the barest sliver of a new moon providing light. By dawn, she'd traveled many miles, finally reaching a place where she smelled the strong stink of human feces wafting from below. Dropping to the lower branches, she found a sandy riverbank marked with deep trenches where river-pygmies had pulled their canoes ashore. The remnants of a fire had turned gray with ash. Judging from the footprints, the captives had been tied together into a single group. The broken ground where they'd been kept provided the toilet stench that tainted the morning air. Judging from the ashes, the pygmies must have stayed here for most of the night, departing at first light. They couldn't be far.

With renewed strength she pushed on. The river grew broader. She caught glimpses of canoes floating upon the wide, placid waters. Unfortunately, she saw no signs of the slavers. All the canoes she spotted were manned by fishermen.

Hours later, she reached the edge of the forest and saw Commonground in the distance. Pulling her feathered cape tightly around her shoulders, she dropped from the trees and advanced toward the town, sliding her swords into the leather string of her loincloth.

Like the forest, the city was both familiar and unrecognizable. She vaguely remembered the last time she'd been here, how the city seemed to radiate from a huge black barge at the center. Now, the city had no center. Boats were clustered in more or less random clumps around the bay. Street vendors no longer gathered along the docks. Instead, huge sailing ships guarded by large men seemed to house most of the commerce. Keeping her head down, she passed by the ships, ignoring the sounds of drunken laughter that sang out from some, not turning to look at the angry shouts of brawling rising from others. On her last visit, Commonground had stank, the way any city sitting in its own wastewater would stink. Yet, while the waters had been foul, the boardwalks had been mostly clean, free of litter. Now, the jumbled plankways were covered with trash. Everything, piers, ships, the water, even the people, seemed painted with a palette of gray. The first bright color to catch her eyes belonged to a pair of long-women, their lips a crimson hue. They wore dresses of blue silk. Their tight-fitting clothes made their hips swell out beneath impossibly thin waists.

"Look at this one," one of the women said in the silver tongue, her gaze fixed on Cinder. The woman had yellow hair, and there was something unnatural about the way it sat coiled upon her scalp, almost as if it were a hat.

"Aren't you exotic," the other woman said, running her eyes along Cinder's lanky form. Her hair was cropped short and dyed to the same shade of red as her lips. "Looking for work?"

Cinder shook her head. "I'm looking for the Bug Wood folk."

The two women looked at her with blank expressions, as if they hadn't understood her.

"Forest-pygmies. They were brought here to be sold as slaves."

"Everyone's buying or selling something," said the red-headed woman. "You don't look like the typical slave buyer."

"I'll take that as a compliment."

The blonde woman smiled, then asked, "You got money, girl?"

"Enough for my needs," Cinder answered.

"Then, for a quarter moon, I might know something about those pygmies."

Cinder hesitated, then reached for her bag of coins. She had no idea if she had a quarter moon within or not. She pulled out a coin and tossed it to the woman.

The woman said, dryly, "Aren't you a big tipper?" Then, with a nod of her head, "You're looking for the *Maelstrom*. That's the big Wanderer ship down in the eastern bay. Heard they're loading fresh cargo this morning."

"Thank you," Cinder said.

She wound her way eastward along the docks, aware of all the eyes following her. She noticed, for the first time, that the eyes belonged almost exclusively to full-blooded men and women. In her hazy visions of her previous visit, she remembered seeing more half-seeds and partially civilized pygmies.

She had little trouble finding the *Maelstrom*. The ship stank from all the bodies cramped within its hold, an aroma that filled her nostrils more powerfully than the competing stench of the bay. She saw activity on deck, and heard voices speaking to one another. She started up the gangplank. A large man moved to block her.

"Buyers and sellers only," he said.

She produced the purse and jingled it.

He nodded and stepped aside. "Better hurry. The guy who just came aboard says he's making an offer on the whole inventory."

She brushed past him. Five men stood near the entrance of the hold. One wore a tricorn hat decorated with feathers. She assumed this would be the captain. He was flanked by three large men in matching uniforms. Crewmen? Before these four stood a tall, slender man in a linen suit. He was talking, though with his back to her she couldn't make out his words. As she approached, the captain saw her. His crew fixed their gaze upon her.

Turning to see the source of their distraction, the man in the suit looked behind him. She felt a vague sense of unease as he saw his face. Had she met him somewhere before?

"Which one of you is selling slaves?" she asked, her voice firm, her hands loose at her side, giving no hint that she might be ready to move for her swords.

"I am," said the captain. Something in the tone of his voice rankled her, causing her jaw to clench. The way he owned the fact, his utter lack of shame, struck her like a hand across her face. She might as well have asked if he'd been selling bananas.

She'd arrived with no plan. Slitting this man's throat seemed like a pretty direct route to her goal of freeing the pygmies. Before her hands found her swords, however, the man in the linen suit spoke. "I'm sorry, miss, but the captain doesn't have anything to sell."

The captain frowned. "We've not yet signed a deal."

"We've agreed to the terms," the man said. "Isn't a Wanderer's word as good as a signed contract?"

"It used to be," the captain said. "But those were simpler times, and simpler cargoes. We're living in the world your father made. If this girl has an offer, let's hear her out."

"There will be no transaction," said Cinder, fixing a cold stare upon his eyes. "The people of the Bug Wood tribe aren't yours to buy and sell."

"I've already bought them," said the captain.

"And you've already sold them," the man in the suit said, before turning to Cinder. He studied her with a scholarly gaze. "You're no pygmy," he observed. "Are you a half-seed?"

She shook her head, thinking of what the pygmy in the forest had called her. "I'm a hoorga."

The man nodded. "That's Bug Wood dialect. It means, um… a large dark bird, I think? A black heron? An ebony swan?"

His words didn't interest her as much as his voice. She'd heard it before. She knew this man, even though his face had no place in what was left of her memory.

"Who are you?" she asked.

"How rude of me." He gave a slight bow. "My name is Judicious Merchant."

"Judicious..." Her voice trailed off as she stared at him, slack jawed. She remembered knowing him by another name. *Tenoba.* This was her grandfather, only young.

"You look like you've heard of me," he said. "I suppose I'm something of a big deal in this town."

The captain chuckled. "Your father was a big deal. Not many people can boast of getting so rich so fast. But you... have you ever earned an honest moon in your life? You squander your father's fortunes digging around in the jungle. Now this craziness with the slaves. Why do you even need them? Why would you throw your money away like this?"

"It's my money," said Judicious. "Do we have a deal or not?"

"If this girl's not here to shop, I suppose we do. Saves me the expense of feeding the cargo all the way to the Isle of Storm."

Judicious shook the man's hand. "Excellent. My representatives will be along within the hour to finalize the arrangements. We'll take possession of the cargo the second the contract is signed."

"Suits me," said the captain.

Judicious walked away, passing by Cinder and said, in a firm, low voice, "Come."

She followed, confused by his tone. Had he recognized her? How could he? Her grandfather had been a very old man when she'd been born. While she wasn't experienced with judging the ages of long-men, the Judicious Merchant who stood before her still had all of his hair, though there were a few threads of gray along his temple. His face was weathered, but nothing like the mask of wrinkled leather her grandfather had worn. If she had to guess, Judicious was in his late thirties, maybe his mid-forties. A shudder ran through her. She really was in the past. Sixty years at least, perhaps seventy. It might be decades before she was born. Her mother wasn't even born yet! She followed Judicious in a daze, barely able to think.

He led her to a sailboat. For a man of his wealth, the boat was modest in size, though well outfitted, and gleamed as if it had been built the day before. An absolute giant of a man stood at the gangplank leading to the sailboat, adorned in leather armor, with a full metal helmet covering his face.

"They make the deal?" the man asked in a gruff, grunting voice.

Cinder looked up as he spoke, and saw thick brown fur jutting from beneath the helmet. Inhuman eyes glared out through the visor, and she knew she was looking at a half-seed.

"For all the good it does," Judicious answered, shaking his head as he led her onto the boat.

She entered into a luxurious, though cluttered, cabin. Shelves of books lined the wall, the spines decorated with gilded lettering. A desk filled the other side of the room, covered with crudely drawn maps and several open notebooks, the pages full of scribbles.

Judicious closed the door behind her and asked, "What were you thinking?"

"What do you mean?" she asked.

"I saw your hands moving toward your swords. Were you desperate to get yourself killed?"

"I'm a better fighter than you imagine," she said.

"Not so good you noticed the sentry in the crow's nest with the crossbow," said Judicious. "You'd have been dead if your fingers had reached the blades."

She frowned.

"So tell me, Dark Duck, Black Swan, whoever you are... what's your interest in the Bug Wood tribe?"

"I was present when the river-pygmies raided their village. I saved some; I don't like leaving a job unfinished."

"If you've come to free them, know that I've accomplished this without risking life or limb. I purchased not only the members of the Bug Wood folk, but every pygmy aboard the *Maelstrom*. By this evening, they'll be free to return to their homes."

She scratched her head. "With an empty cargo hold, what's the keep the *Maelstrom* from taking on more slaves?"

Judicious sat down on the chair before the desk. He ran his hands through his hair, looking sad. "I've asked myself that question a lot." He gave a weak smile. "I don't have an answer." He shook his head. "For now, I've a better question. You gave your name with a Bug Wood word. But your accent tells me you come from a different area of the forest."

"Perhaps," she said. She didn't want to tell him too much about herself. If he learned she was from the future, who knew what problems that might lead to?

"I recently returned from an expedition into the Vanished Kingdom. I found a marvelous temple complex near the caldera, right beneath Greatshadow's nose. Hah! That's an adventure I'll have to write down some day."

"I've no doubt you will," she said.

"My guide was a forest-pygmy named Parrot. At least, that's how his name translates. I can't quite do the tongue clicking needed to say his name in his native tongue." He gave a crude attempt and she was startled to find him speaking Jawa Fruit dialect.

"You... you know the Jawa Fruit people?" she asked.

"A lovely people," said Judicious. "It's a pity they're so hounded by their neighbors." Judicious looked at his hands, rubbing them as if there was some stain on them she couldn't see. "Parrot went his own way after I came back to the city. But he came back last night to tell me that, when he'd gotten home, his wife and children were gone, captured by raiders of the Fish Bone tribe. With a little research, I discovered they were aboard the *Maelstrom*. I supposed I could have negotiated only their release but... " He sighed deeply. "If you know who I am, you know who my father was. You know how he made his fortune." He tapped his fingers nervously on the map before him. "If I could stop this damned trade by giving up every last moon I've inherited, I would."

She nodded, certain this was true. A great sadness filled her as she thought of the future. In her time, slaves would still be a commodity bought and sold in Commonground. Judicious wouldn't come up with a plan to stop it. Perhaps individuals could be saved, either with violence or with coins, but in the long run, there was money to be made. If there was one thing she remembered about the world of the long-men, it was that nothing took priority over money.

Judicious shook off his angst, summoning a smile when he looked back at her. "You're connected to the Jawa Fruit people, are you? I'm surprised Parrot didn't mention someone with your, uh, striking appearance."

"The word you're looking for is inhuman," she said.

"Nonsense," he said. "You saw Paw-Paw out front. Half man, half bear. I employ many half-seeds. I find their lot in life to be a cruel one. I take what small actions I can to ease their burden."

"That's admirable," she said. "And no... I'm... I'm not associated with the Jawa Fruit people." She almost added, "not anymore," but stopped herself. It would have been more accurate to say, "not yet," but even this felt wrong. Separated in time by at least half a century, she suspected she'd never go home again.

"So, what tribe are you from?" he asked.

"None," she said. "I have no home. My future... lies here in Commonground."

"Good luck with that," he said. "I'm tied up here for a long time as well. I swear by the sacred quill, there are days when I'm tempted to toss my money in the bay, strip off my clothes, and go live out my days in the trees."

"I might have a more use of your money than the bay would," she said.

"Of course, my little Black Swan," said Judicious. "If you find yourself in need of funds, know that my purse is always open."

They shook hands. He studied her face, looking puzzled by her expression. She was lost in thought She knew so much of the future, and yet so little. She alone knew, years from now, that the world would face total destruction. Perhaps with her grandfather's fortune and the better part of a century to prepare, she had the resources she'd need to stop it.

18 - Strange Alliances

"THIS IS YOUR craziest lie yet," said Infidel.

The Black Swan studied her mother's face. She wasn't surprised by her incredulity.

"I know this isn't easy to accept," said the Black Swan. "I apologize for hiding the truth from you all these years."

Infidel looked back through the trees. "My daughter's back in the village right now."

"Truly? You saw her this morning?"

Infidel frowned. "I didn't have a chance to look for her."

"Go," said the Black Swan. "Find her."

Infidel's face showed her worry as she darted into the shadows of the dense forest. The Black Swan followed, taking care to avoid the traps that lay in her path. When she reached the ground beneath the village, Infidel leapt down, landing in a crouch. She sprung up with a growl, driving her full weight into the Black Swan's torso, slamming her against a tree.

"Where is she?" Infidel demanded.

"Right about now? Probably still in Hell. Though maybe she's reached the Sea of Wine. I need you to help me find her."

"I swear to the Divine Author that if you've hurt her—"

"I am her," said the Black Swan. "Think back. I've always known your every secret."

"So you've got telepaths on your payroll."

"The last time you saw me as Cinder, I was going to gather honey. You were going to find a troop of monkeys that had been playing at the edge of our territory."

"Information you could have gotten from Cinder if you've kidnapped her."

"I suppose that's true. And, I suppose you'll be skeptical when I tell you that Ver never really went away. He came back at sunset yesterday, and persuaded me to go with him."

"Cinder wouldn't be that foolish. I warned her he was dangerous."

"You warned me of lots of things," said the Black Swan. "You treated me like a child. Ver played off my resentment toward you. He kept telling me I was an adult who could make my own decisions."

"Really?" Infidel said, sounding amused. "How'd that work out for you, if you're her and she's in Hell right now?"

"I'm not saying I made the right choice."

Infidel let go of the Black Swan and stepped back.

"I don't believe you," she said.

"Nor would I expect you to, given our history. Fortunately, you have the ability to verify my story. Draw your sword."

"How do you know about the sword?" Infidel looked at her fiercely, on the verge of anger, then her face softened. "Okay, don't answer that. I know what you're going to tell me. Big deal. You know I have a sword given to me by Greatshadow."

"A sword of flame, through which we can talk to him."

"Talk to him?" Infidel asked. "The sword just burns stuff."

"He hears whispers through every candle flame," said the Black Swan. "Our voices through the sword will be a shout."

Infidel nodded, then placed her hand upon the hilt. The Black Swan watched closely as Infidel drew the sword. It wasn't her imagination; fire filled Infidel's eyes as the sword cleared the hilt, not mere reflection, but a deep, internal flame.

"Do you feel different when you hold the blade?" she asked.

Infidel nodded. "Hot, mostly. There's also a feeling of, I don't know, lightness? Like my body weighs less than it should. It's like I've got some of my old strength back. And look…" She ran her fingers through the crackling flames, turning her hand to and fro, letting it linger in the yellow intensity of the blaze. "Fire doesn't hurt me."

"Are you invulnerable?"

Infidel shrugged. "I honestly don't want to know."

"Don't want to know?" the Black Swan asked.

"Life out here in the jungle can be a little, um, monotonous. If I had my old powers again, I might be tempted to make life more exciting. That wouldn't set a very good example for my daughter."

"Cinder wouldn't begrudge you an exciting life," said the Black Swan.

"No. But she might try to emulate it."

"Would that truly have been so bad, letting her pursue the sort of adventures you undertook when you were young?"

Infidel sighed. "Look, I didn't exactly choose a life of adventure. I was trying to get out of an arranged marriage, and next thing I know I'm running for my life with armies of religious zealots hot of my heels. I didn't come to the Isle of Fire looking for excitement. I came here to save my skin. Then I met Stagger and, well, stuff happened. Some stuff was good. Other stuff was terrible beyond all words. I want to spare Cinder some of the grief I've known."

"You didn't succeed," said the Black Swan.

Infidel looked hurt. The Black Swan felt old anger stir within her. She'd always wondered if her life might have turned out differently if her mother hadn't kept her so ignorant of the larger world. It was as if her mother had groomed her to be the perfect target for Numinous and Ver.

She didn't give voice to these feelings. Instead, she looked deeply into her mother's eyes, into the flames that danced within them.

"What?" Infidel asked.

"Greatshadow," said the Black Swan. "He's already here."

The twin flames within Infidel's eyes flickered.

"Dragon!" said the Black Swan. "We must speak. You know why."

Infidel opened her mouth. But, when she spoke, it wasn't her voice that came from her throat. Instead, her voice was a crackling roar, like a bonfire.

"I know you," the fire voice said.

"Yes," said the Black Swan. "You've known me since before I was born."

Infidel nodded.

"Mother said you'd made a bargain with my father. I was to be raised on the Isle of Fire. Why?"

"You know why," answered Greatshadow.

"No," she said. "I don't. Tell me."

"As you wish. I knew that, as the child of a living mother and a dead father, you'd be born with the power to travel between the realms of life and death. If Infidel had returned to raise you in more civilized lands, your early trips to the abstract realms would have taken you to Hell. The wicked things that dwell there would have devoured an innocent soul that came among them. By growing up among pygmies, you made your early journeys to the Realm of Roots, a much less dangerous landscape."

"Why was it important to you that I survive? What did you see in my future?"

Infidel shook her head. "I'm a dragon, not a prophet. I didn't know your fate. But, I know a thing or two about keeping a fire burning. Only a fool waits until a snowy night to hunt for fuel."

"So… I'm firewood. Something placed in store, to await a time when I might be useful."

"A time of cold and darkness," said Greatshadow. "And now, that time is upon us."

"A cold and darkness you've allowed. Why did you withdraw your protection from the civilized world? Why allow Hush and Tempest to ravish the earth?"

"With the Church of the Book in disarray, civilization was destined to crumble. As it's done so, the number of tended fires around the world has dwindled. Tempest has tempted me many times, promising to use his lighting to keep forests constantly ablaze should I help him. I've resisted his advances."

"This isn't always the case," said the Black Swan. "Once, I managed to have Infidel kill Numinous Pilgrim when he was still twelve. I thought the world was safe, but in that timeline Stagger never joined his soul with the sun. When Glorious was slain by Abyss, you allied yourself with Tempest to turn the world into a place of permanent flame."

"You must judge me as I am, not as I may have been in other histories."

"I'd feel better if you'd put up more of fight against your fellow dragons."

"As I weaken, I've little choice but to let Tempest and Hush cleanse the world of the old kingdoms. From the ruins, I hope the humans I've sheltered may build a new and better world."

"Why do you think Hush and Tempest will allow this?" asked the Black Swan.

"I've allies of my own, who will work to drive back the cold and the storm once they've vented their fury," said Greatshadow. Then, Infidel shook her head. "Though… with one less ally than I'd planned."

"Abyss," said the Black Swan. "You didn't count on him falling under the control of Hush."

"Abundant and Stagger remain committed to my cause. Kragg remains neutral; whether men live or die matters nothing to him. I don't believe he'll interfere with my plans. And, though time grows short, I've taken steps to ensure we shall have one more ally."

"It's not just you who must be weaker. With so many animals perishing, doesn't Abundant suffer as well?"

"Yes. Fortunately, Stagger remains strong."

"Stagger isn't a warrior at heart," said the Black Swan.

"True. But Tempest's army of the damned falls back from his radiance."

"Don't you think Tempest is aware of this vulnerability to his armies?" asked the Black Swan. "He must be planning to somehow neutralize Stagger's threat."

"I'm certain this is true," said Greatshadow. "It's important to our plan, in fact. As long as Tempest remains in Hell, we cannot harm him. But if he leaves Hell to strike a blow against Stagger, he'll be vulnerable."

"I hope you're right," the Black Swan said. "But I'm here to talk to you about an even greater danger. All your plans won't matter in the end, once the One True Book is read."

"The One True Book is gone," said Greatshadow. "Lost forever in limbo."

"Forever turned out to be shorter than you imagined," said the Black Swan. "The book is no longer in limbo. The Omega Reader has it. If we don't stop him, there will be no world at all to rebuild."

"If a candle or lantern is lit to read the One True Book, I'll see it," said Greatshadow. "If read in sunlight, or in the presence of a glorystone, Stagger will see it."

The Black Swan pressed her iron lips tightly together. She'd witnessed the reading of the book. She remembered a pale green light. A candle within a lantern of tinted glass? If so, why hadn't Greatshadow intervened? If only she could remember where the light had come from.

Light.

Suddenly, hope flickered within her.

Infidel's stance changed. Her eyes focused on the flaming sword in her grasp.

"Okay," she said, in her normal voice. "What just happened?"

"Greatshadow possessed you. We had a little talk. You don't remember?"

Infidel shook her head.

"I'll fill you in on what he told me later," said the Black Swan. "But, he did explain why he wanted me raised on the Isle of Fire, confirming that I'm your daughter."

"In a conversation I don't remember," said Infidel with a smirk. "Convenient."

"It doesn't matter if you believe me or not. All that matters is that you let me speak to Stagger."

"What?"

"The key," said the Black Swan, "is Brand Cooper. Wherever he is, Stagger can see him!"

Infidel's brow wrinkled. "Brand? I know that name. Gale Romer's boyfriend?"

The Black Swan nodded. "Though, when I last did business with Brand, they apparently were no longer romantically involved. Still, when the Romers showed up in Hell to confront Numinous Pilgrim, Brand was with them."

"This helps us how?"

"This helps because Brand has a glorystone set into a locket. This means, no matter where he's at, Stagger can find him if he focuses on the stone. You must let me speak to him."

Infidel looked confused.

"You are… on speaking terms?" asked the Black Swan.

"Not for a long time," said Infidel.

"When I was little, whenever I played in the sun, you told me he was always present in the light, watching us."

Infidel sighed, running her fingers along the back of her neck. "Maybe. I honestly don't know. I don't know if he watches me anymore."

"But… his love for you was so powerful, so pure…."

"That was a long time ago. And, sure, we swore that our love was eternal. The same sweet, heartfelt promises that lovers throughout the ages have whispered to each other." Infidel sheathed her flaming sword as she spoke. "But then he died, and I kept living."

"He didn't die, he went to live—"

"—inside the sun. Whatever. Other dead people go to the Realm of Roots, or the Sea of Wine. Stagger's moved on." She looked up at the sparkling rays of light that filtered through the canopy. "The past is past. The future is the only way forward."

"There'll be no future without Stagger's help," said the Black Swan.

"So… what? I'm supposed to yell at the sun and ask for help?"

"Do you have another plan?"

"That seems suspiciously like praying."

"I suppose it does."

"I was Stagger's wife," said Infidel, crossing her arms. "Not his worshipper."

"The entire world rests on you seeking his help."

A hand fell onto the Black Swan's shoulder.

"She doesn't need to ask for help," said a masculine voice. "I was her worshiper, not the other way around."

"Stagger," Infidel whispered, her face growing pale.

The Black Swan turned to find her father standing beside her. He looked just as she remembered from the years she'd known him in Commonground, only a good deal cleaner. He wore a suit of luminous white fabric, much finer than silk. In life, he'd always been scruffy, but now he was clean shaven, with his hair pulled back into a white ponytail. He wore dark glasses, seemingly forged of solid iron. She didn't know how he saw around them, then realized he didn't need his eyes to see. Anything and everything touched by sunlight was in his vision.

Infidel stepped forward and wrapped her arms around him. "Oh Stagger," she whispered. "You were listening?"

"More like lip-reading. Part of me is always watching you, at least by day." He hugged her tightly as he spoke.

"Why have you been away for so long?" she whispered. "If you could come back…?"

He shook his head. "It's… it's hard for me to be here. I've gotten better at forming avatars over the years, but it's still… unsettling. I'm here before you, but I'm also inside the sun. The price I pay for looking like a man is to increase my awareness that I'm no longer human."

Infidel nodded, pulling away, but still holding his hand. "Thank you for coming. I know this isn't easy."

Stagger turned to the Black Swan. "You're Cinder, huh?"

"You believe me?"

"It's obvious, in retrospect."

"I wish I'd never had to reveal this to you."

"Why?" asked Stagger.

"I'm not proud to be the cause of so much death and destruction. I'm the—"

"Hold on," said Infidel. "Don't blame yourself for what's happening with Hush and Tempest. You're trying to stop it." Then she turned and jabbed her finger into Stagger's chest. "But you. You! Why are you letting them destroy everything?"

Stagger floated backward in the air, beyond the reach of another chest jabbing. "It's not that simple."

"Then give me a complicated answer," she said. "How could you let this happen?"

"Because I love you," he said.

"What does that have to do with anything?"

"I've hidden the Isle of Fire by shifting the light around it. Tempest and Hush can't find it. But Kragg doesn't need light to know you're here. Kragg hates me, viewing me as an interloper, a fraud wielding an elemental power that should belong to a dragon. He isn't fully aligned with Hush and Tempest, but he's warned me that if I ever raise my hand against another dragon, he'll shrug and plunge the Isle of Fire into the sea. This threat meant nothing when Greatshadow was strong, but now I don't know if he could defend the island."

"So you're letting Kragg bully you?"

"I'm playing strategically. I'm surrendering territory in the short term, but plan to take it back later. Only, if I've lip read your conversation correctly, there isn't going to be a later because the Omega Reader is going to end the world."

"But you can help us stop him," said the Black Swan. "You can find Brand Cooper."

"And then?"

"And then he's on Gale Romer's ship, which is either in Hell or in the Sea of Wine. When I fled Hell with Numinous, we wound up in the Sea of Wine. I nearly drowned. We had to rest before we came back to the material world."

Stagger nodded. "I could get to the Sea of Wine without needing the Romers. It's as easy for me to travel to an abstract realm as to the living world. Unfortunately, I'm practically blind in the Sea of Wine. The sun is permanently below the horizon. I won't have any way of seeing Numinous unless I'm pretty close to him. A few miles, at least."

"Once we find the *Circus*, Sage can spot Numinous," said the Black Swan.

Stagger raised his eyebrows. "That's brilliant. So we ambush Numinous—"

"—and destroy the book," said Infidel.

"Um... no," said Stagger.

"Why not?"

"In theory, everything that's ever been and ever will be are inside that book. We can't know the full ramifications of destroying it."

"We'll worry about that after we find it," said the Black Swan. "Right now, time grows short." She offered her hands to both Stagger and Infidel. "Are you ready?"

"Ready," they said in unison, as they took their daughter's hands.

ALL THE PYGMIES had returned to the ship by the time Sorrow got Slate's body secured in the hold. She walked past them, deaf to their murmurs. She was vaguely aware of walking past Jetsam.

"Sorrow," he said.

She didn't look at him, didn't acknowledge him. She knew all that he had to say. All the Romers would find time in the coming hours to tell her they were sorry for her loss. She didn't want or need their sympathy. People died. Those left behind mourned. There was nothing noteworthy about her grief. It was a common, valueless thing, unworthy of her time. The only thing remaining in the world that held any importance at all was revenge.

As she went up the stairs to the deck, she saw the storm clouds of Hell roiling overhead. She saw in them a reflection of her own mind, dark, angry, and ready to throw lightning. She opened the bag of nails she'd collected from the cage of bone. The bright glow that lit her face gave her hope. She'd need every advantage when next they encountered Numinous. When she'd first set out to become a weaver, it often took her months to fully tap into the power of a new nail. She had only hours. Fortunately, she had three advantages. First, she wasn't a novice. She very likely knew more about the art of weaving than any other living witch. Second, she now knew bone magic. If the placement of the nail wasn't perfect, she could heal more quickly than she used to. As for her third and most important advantage....

"Sage!" she called out as she looked around the deck.

"Up here," Sage called down from the crow's nest.

Sorrow climbed the riggings, moving as swiftly as her exhaustion would allow.

"It's just as well you're up here," she said as she reached the crow's nest. "I want to speak to you in private."

"In that case, we should wait until Mako's asleep."

"The matter's too urgent to wait," said Sorrow. She emptied the bag of nails into her hand, trapping the glorystone nail between her fingers so it wouldn't float away. "I need you to hammer these into my head."

"Uh," said Sage.

"When we fight Numinous again, I need to have all my powers."

"You fought him before with all your powers, plus the power of Rott. He beat you without breaking a sweat."

"We didn't know who we were up against when we first fought him. Even though he's achieved something close to human perfection, he's still only a man. We've seen him slip up. Rigger caught him off guard, and Mako got in a good hit, and—"

"And the second the element of surprise was lost, Numinous got away."

"Exactly. He ran. He's afraid. If he faces me at full power, he doesn't stand a chance,"

Sage picked up an iron nail. "I suppose, if I don't help you, you'll try to do it yourself."

Sorrow nodded.

Before they could discuss the matter further, Jetsam called out from below, "By the tides!"

"Company," said Sage, looking into her spyglass.

Sorrow looked down on a trio of figures. Even though she saw only the tops of their heads, she recognized the darkest of the three forms instantly. "It's the Black Swan!"

"Her aura resembles that of the girl who was with Numinous," said Sage. "And the woman who's with her... it's Infidel! The man... I can't see clearly. His aura's too bright to look at directly."

"Stagger," said Sorrow. "It's Stagger, back in human form."

"I think you're right," said Sage. She stood and called out, "Rigger!" Instantly, a rope swung from below. Sage leapt to it without hesitation. Sorrow felt this would be a foolish way to die, but jumped for the rope anyway. The rope carried them swiftly to the deck, where the trio of new arrivals found themselves surrounded by the Romers.

"Wow," Infidel said, looking from face to face. "You guys haven't aged a day in twenty years."

"Being trapped in limbo does wonders for your skin," said Jetsam.

"I'm glad to see Walker helped guide you out," said Stagger.

"Right. That guy," said Bigsby. "How exactly do you know him?"

Stagger shrugged. "I don't get a lot of visitors in the sun. Walker shows up occasionally. We chat. In general, I don't understand a damn thing he says."

"Yeah, that's him," said Bigsby. "Been a long time, Stagger. Good to see you."

"You did say you were buying, right?" Stagger grinned. Then his face took on a harder look. "We need you to take us to the Sea of Wine, so that Sage can find Numinous Pilgrim. I plan to blast him to smithereens."

"You can blast people to smithereens?" asked Infidel.

"The part that impressed me was that he managed to say it in so few words," said Bigsby.

Stagger shrugged. "This might be the first time we've talked when I was sober. I'm less prone to sesquipedalianism when I'm not drinking. And, yes, I can disintegrate things just by glaring at them."

"Make sure you don't disintegrate our daughter by accident," said Infidel.

"Your daughter?" asked Sorrow. "The girl with Numinous? The one with ebony skin?"

"Cinder," said Infidel.

"Cinder is your younger self?" Sage asked the Black Swan.

"That's something of a leap, isn't it?" asked Rigger.

"Not if you can see auras," said Sage.

"That can't be true. The Black Swan was doing business in Commonground before I was born," said Bigsby.

The Black Swan said, "My life isn't easy to explain. The short answer is I've discovered a way to travel back in time."

"But how can you and Cinder exist at the same time?" asked Sorrow, eying the Black Swan carefully. There was no question this was the body she'd built, despite the damage to the face. "I mean, if you've been in Commonground while Cinder was living only a few miles away... the paradoxes..."

"The paradoxes exist," said the Black Swan with a shrug. "Usually, when I go back in time, I take the place of my old self. But I think that, until Cinder makes her first trip back in time, her personal timeline doesn't create conflicts with mine. That said, I've taken care not to have direct contact with her before now, since I wasn't sure what the ramifications might be."

"So finding her might be dangerous?" asked Infidel.

"We have to take the chance. I've seen death and destruction play out before my eyes more times than I can count. I'll risk anything to finally stop it."

Gale had been listening silently. Now, she spoke. "I don't think there's anything further to debate. Numinous killed our friend. He intends to destroy the world. We'll do anything in our power to stop him."

"Take us to the Sea of Wine at once," said the Black Swan. "We may be nearly out of time.

Gale knelt and placed her hand on the deck. The planks glowed faintly as a red light swept across the *Circus*. There was a blast of wind and a powerful, heady smell of wine. Stagger stumbled as the boat rocked, nearly falling over, until Infidel grabbed him by the arm.

"What's wrong?" she asked.

He turned his face toward the sky. "The eternal sunset ... it drains me."

"Then Hell should have killed you," said Rigger. "It's permanently night there."

Stagger nodded. "I didn't feel great there, either, but the ship wasn't pitching in the waves. Don't worry. Even at a fraction of my strength, I'm more than a match for Numinous."

Infidel grabbed a rope to steady herself then took Stagger by the arm. "My sea legs aren't much better. It's been a long time since I was on a ship."

"Fortunately, I can help both of us," said Stagger, wrapping his arm around her waist. His glow intensified slightly and they rose off the deck.

"Much better," said Infidel, smiling. "It feels exactly like flying with the Gloryhammer."

"My whole body is a glorystone," said Stagger.

"You look fleshy enough," she said.

He shook his head. "I'm manipulating the light around me to present a human appearance. My true form is more crystalline."

Infidel squeezed his biceps. "You're not kidding. I noticed it when I poked your chest, but thought you'd been exercising. You're hard as a rock."

"Harder than rock by a significant degree," he said.

"Found them!" Sage said, gazing into her spyglass. She pointed away from the reddest part of the horizon, toward the darkest part of the sky. "That way. Unfortunately, they're hundreds of miles away. Even with the fastest wind mother can summon, we might not reach them in time."

"I can reach them," said Stagger.

"I'm coming with you," said Infidel.

"Me too," said Sorrow.

Stagger shook his head, studying Sorrow's bruised face. "I can carry two people, but I don't know if you're the best choice. Numinous beat you pretty badly."

The Black Swan stepped forward. "I know you're hungry for vengeance, Sorrow, but I should go."

"No offense, but you don't stand a chance against him," said Sorrow. "You're already damaged."

"Only my face. My body's intact."

"I know your limits better than you probably do," said Sorrow. "You can't begin to match his speed and agility."

"Let him strike me as many times as he wishes," said the Black Swan. "He can't harm me with his fists. Plus, over the years, I've made improvements." She held up her long fingernails. "Poison needles in my fingers, for instance."

"Sorry, Sorrow," said Stagger. "The Black Swan's right. Facing him with the most powerful fighters we have is our best chance."

"Then why take Infidel?" asked Sorrow. "She has no powers at all anymore."

"I've got a kick-ass flaming sword and more experience killing people than the rest of you combined," said Infidel.

"If she wants to go, she goes," Stagger said, sounding apologetic. "I'm not crazy enough to say no to her."

"It's true," said Infidel. "It's the main reason I fell in love with him."

Sorrow crossed her arms and turned away, making no effort to hide her seething anger as she stomped toward the hold leading below deck.

Stagger rook the Black Swan's outstretched hand and they all rose into the air. "Point me toward them, Sage. In this dim light, I can't make out anything beyond a few miles. Once I'm close, I should be able to spot him."

Sage pointed, Stagger turned, and they zoomed off.

19 - Animal Spirits

"CAN YOU BREATHE?" Stagger shouted over the rushing wind.

The Black Swan tried to answer, but her vocal reeds lacked the volume to be heard above the roar. Certainly he knew she didn't need to breathe anymore. The query must have been directed toward Infidel.

Infidel nodded, but her cheeks glistened with tears.

"I'm fine," she said, as Stagger slowed his flight. "The wind's just stinging my eyes."

The Black Swan tried once more to speak. She could barely hear the squeaking of her voice. "We need a strategy."

"I'm listening," said Stagger.

"Our first target should be me," she said.

"I could drop you right now."

"I mean the younger me, Cinder. When we first reached Rott, I was disoriented. Numinous gave me time to clear my head. But, if we'd been attacked, I could probably have made a leap between worlds, though I don't know where we might have wound up with my head spinning."

"But you can follow her, right?" asked Stagger.

"Even if I could guess which realm she leaping to, a few steps difference when passing into the veil can lead to our emerging hundreds of miles apart. We can't let her leap."

"She not going to run from me," said Infidel.

"I'm not sure of that," said the Black Swan.

Infidel frowned. "My daughter trusts me."

"Yes," said the Black Swan. "And she loves you very much. But, at this time in her life… in my life… our feelings toward you weren't entirely positive."

"She's never said anything to indicate she has a problem with how I'm raising her."

"The fact that you still think you're raising her is at the heart of the problem. She's nineteen, and you treat her as if she were nine," said the Black Swan.

"You don't know what you're talking about," said Infidel. "I let her go hunting alone. I don't watch her from the shadows when she goes to collect honey, the way I did when she was younger. She's well on her way to being an independent woman."

"Hunting and honey gathering only get you so far in this world," said the Black Swan.

"They're skills you need to thrive in the jungle."

"There's more to the world than the jungle."

"Technically," said Stagger, "at this exact moment, there really isn't much world left outside the jungle. Everywhere else is a frozen wasteland under siege by the vengeful dead."

Infidel smirked. "My parenting strategy looks pretty good right now."

"You did what you thought was best," said the Black Swan. "But I found my education lacking when I went to live in the long-man's world."

"What was she supposed to do?" said Stagger. "I mean, what sort of advice could she have given you on how to become the unofficial queen of Commonground?"

"Yeah," said Infidel. "I think I should get some credit for never teaching you the skills you'd need to one day run a brothel."

"I can't expect you to approve of my choices," said the Black Swan. "Mere survival in the long-man's world wasn't an option. I needed the power to change the future. I had to thrive. In Commonground, you rule either by having people fear you, or by having people dependent upon you to supply their darkest vices."

"So you did both," said Stagger. "Speaking of being afraid, why in the world did you threaten to kill me all those times I didn't pay my tab?"

"A bluff, obviously," said the Black Swan. "I treated both of you as well as I dared. I couldn't show a hint of affection toward either of you. If my enemies suspected I valued your lives, you'd have become targets. Just know that another man who betrayed me repeatedly would have wound up in the bay with an anchor around his neck."

"I always made good eventually," said Stagger. He turned his face toward hers. "I may be misjudging your facial expressions, since I'm not used to looking at iron lips. Are you frowning?"

"I don't like talking about your years in Commonground," said the Black Swan.

"Why not?" asked Stagger. "Those were pretty good years."

The Black Swan groaned, though her vocal reeds produced only a light squawk.

"What was that?" Stagger asked.

"That," the Black Swan said, "was my frustration seeping through."

"Frustration?" asked Stagger. "Why?"

"Why?" she asked, incredulous. "You obviously disapprove of my behavior as the Black Swan."

"It's just… I don't…" Stagger's voice trailed off.

"If he won't say it, I will," said Infidel. "I know you were faced with terrible choices. I believe you really are trying to save the world. But it's still hard to reconcile that you're my child. I did everything I could to make sure Cinder would never care about wealth or power. Now you're boasting about dumping bodies in the damn bay? If you're my daughter… I wish you'd found a better way."

"Perhaps you should have set better examples."

Infidel said, "In the jungle, I raised you to—"

The Black Swan cut her off. "When I was a child, you played the role of mother as well as you could. You forget that I also know of all those years you lived in Commonground. You're unhappy that I've dumped people into the bay? I watched you return from mercenary assignments wearing necklaces of human teeth. And the people you killed got off lucky. I can name a hundred men you maimed and mangled. If I'm ruthless, mother, it runs in my blood."

Infidel pressed her lips together, plainly angry, but holding her tongue.

"As for you, father—" said the Black Swan.

"I know," he said.

"Do you?"

Stagger nodded. "You knew me as a drunk, with, shall we say, a lackadaisical attitude toward honest employment. You've heard me lie. You've heard me beg. You paid me for loot that I freely admitted to stealing. I can't imagine you were proud of me."

"Then you lack imagination," she said. "It's true, your excesses often pained me. Still, I admired that you were a man of keen intelligence in a city of brutes, a man more comfortable holding a book than a knife. More importantly, I saw your unfailing kindness in a city where cruelty was the most common commodity. Yes, it grieved me to see you drowning your demons with liquor, but, more often than you'll believe, I was proud. And, mother, for all your violence, for all your swaggering roughness, I stood in awe of your unbreakable spirit. Despite your public show of recklessness, I admired your restraint. You had the strength to topple kingdoms, but never gave into the seduction of becoming a conqueror."

"I never felt the slightest temptation," said Infidel. "Who would want to rule the world?"

"I've tried to do so from the shadows," said the Black Swan. "You know my reasons."

"As do I," said Infidel. "And they're good ones. It's lucky you didn't take after me. My cynicism about the world led me to withdraw from it. I heard rumors of the world falling apart and shrugged them off. You didn't have that luxury. Whether we win this fight or not, I'm proud of you."

"We have to win this fight," said the Black Swan.

Infidel cracked her knuckles. "If I understand things correctly, here in the Sea of Wine, I can punch Ver?"

"Yes," said the Black Swan.

"Excellent," said Infidel with a smile.

"There's the warrior I knew," said the Black Swan. She paused. "We have to be the world's strangest family.

Stagger's forward momentum suddenly halted. They hung still in the air.

"Found them," he said. "I see them. They're on Rott's back. Cinder's lying on her side, her eyes closed. Numinous is sitting next to her. And there's Ver, hovering next to him. I thought you said he'd be solid here?"

"Ver knows a few tricks about navigating the abstract realms, but he should still be punchable. Mother, you take him. Stagger, Numinous might be the perfect human, but he's still flesh and blood. You should finish him easily. I'll make sure Cinder can't help them."

"Sounds like we have a plan," said Stagger.

"Let's do it," said Infidel.

"Take a deep breath," Stagger said to Infidel. "Press your face into my chest to protect it. We're going to move fast."

The Black Swan scanned the horizon. At this distance, from this height, she could see perhaps twenty miles or more. She couldn't make out Rott's form upon the distant waves. Could Stagger fly fast enough to cover so many miles in the time Infidel could hold her breath?

The pink sky and the red sea blurred. A loud boom rattled every joint in her iron body. Then, though only a second had passed, she found herself standing on an island of dull black scales, with clouds of flies swirling around her as she stumbled to keep her footing.

She saw Numinous lift his face toward the flash of light that accompanied Stagger's movements. He reached his hand toward Cinder, touching her shoulder.

"Stand away from her," Stagger barked.

Cinder stirred, rubbing her eyes.

"Blast him," Infidel said as she pulled her face from Stagger's chest and turned to see what was happening.

"I can't while he's so close to Cinder," Stagger whispered.

"Let me put a little distance between them," said Infidel, lunging forward, drawing her flaming sword.

"This isn't the plan!" said the Black Swan.

Infidel shouted, "Hey! Golden Child! Remember me?"

Numinous grinned. "The woman who pretended to be a machine!" He glanced at the Black Swan. "In the company of a machine who pretends to be a woman." With his hand still on Cinder's shoulder, he hissed, "We need to leave!"

"Don't listen to him!" Infidel shouted, now only a few yards away.

"Mother?" Cinder asked, furrowing her brow.

Infidel swung her blade with both hands, slicing the air above Cinder's head. Numinous, alas, was nowhere near the path of the sword. He ducked beneath the blow, diving past Infidel. He planted both hands on the ground and kicked back, driving his heels hard into her back. The blow knocked her from her feet, sending her sliding across the slimy scales.

Numinous bounced to his feet. He glanced back to Cinder, who rose on trembling legs.

"Get ready to get us out of here," he growled, eyeing the bag that held the One True Book, sitting a few yards away.

"But, my mother," said Cinder, completely bewildered.

"Yet another demon, child," said Ver, floating in the air above her. "Flee at once!"

"Don't listen to him," the Black Swan shouted.

"You!" Cinder said, her eyes growing wide as she recognized the woman who'd attacked her in the Temple of Flame. She ran toward Numinous, stretching her arm to grab him.

Before she reached him, Stagger removed his dark iron glasses. Cinder skid to a halt, raising her hand to block the blinding ray of light that stabbed the ground where Numinous had just stood. The ground crackled and hissed as foul fumes filled the air.

Stagger slid his glasses back on. The radiance faded, revealing a large hole in the ground, leading into the dark cavity within Rott's rib cage. Twenty feet behind the pit, untouched by the blast, stood Numinous, who'd jumped away at the last second, landing where the Witchbreaker sat next to the backpack that held the One True Book. He grabbed the sword as Stagger once more raised his glasses. A second flash of light vaporized the ground. When the flash cleared, Numinous had jumped clear, leaping toward the first hole Stagger had blasted in Rott's hide. With a final somersault he vanished into the darkness.

"Fast little bugger, isn't he?" said Stagger.

"I thought you were faster!" said the Black Swan.

"Is he telepathic?" asked Stagger. "It's like he sees what I'm going to do before I do it."

"He's watching your body language," said the Black Swan. "He sees where you're going to strike."

"That can be rectified," said Stagger as he drifted over the pit where Numinous had disappeared. The light shimmered around him and he vanished. His disembodied voice said, "I can bend light around me, though the precaution's probably not necessary. I've held back so I wouldn't hurt anyone else. I can hit him with a broader blast if the rest of you aren't near. He won't be able to dodge that." His voice sank into the dark interior as he spoke.

"Cinder," Infidel said as she made it back to her feet and ran toward her daughter. "Are you all right?"

"Run, Cinder. Run away!" cried Ver, still hovering in the air. "She's not who she appears to be!"

Cinder didn't run away. She instead ran toward her mother. The two of them threw their arms around each other.

"Mother," Cinder said, "it's really you!"

"It's not!" screamed Ver. "It's a devil who's taken her form!"

"I see her aura," said Cinder to the Truthspeaker, sounding annoyed. "You think I don't recognize my own mother?"

"You little fool," said Ver. "Listen to me—"

"It's time for you to shut up," said the Black Swan, stepping forward. She held her hand out, opening her iron fingers to reveal a tiny glittering object.

"No," whispered Ver as his eyes fixed on the delicately made silver mosquito that rose from her palm.

"I take it you're familiar with soul catchers," said the Black Swan. "A master necromancer named Mama Knuckle crafted this one for me. I've been waiting a long time to get it close to you, Ver."

Ver didn't answer. Instead, he turned his gaze toward the red clouds above and shot upward swifter than an arrow from a bow. The mosquito's golden wings buzzed as it took off in pursuit.

"That's one problem dealt with," said the Black Swan. "The soul catcher will either capture him, or keep him running for eternity."

"What's going on?" Cinder asked, staring at the Black Swan. "Mother, who is this woman?"

"A friend," said Infidel. "The Black Swan."

"A friend? I thought you hated her!"

"We've reconciled," said Infidel. "We're here save you."

"Save me?" asked Cinder. "What danger was I in?"

"For starters, you nearly drowned in the Sea of Wine and your boyfriend is the Omega Reader."

Cinder crossed her arms. "He's decidedly not my boyfriend. He was in danger of drowning. I saved his life. Then this woman attacked us, killed Brother Wing, and we had to run."

"You killed Brother Wing?" asked Infidel, looking sideways at the Black Swan.

"You can't take half measures with a dragon," said the Black Swan. "Cinder, I wasn't there to hurt you. I was there to stop Numinous from talking you into going to Hell."

"Numinous? You mean Luminous?"

"He's lied to you this whole time," said Infidel.

"That's impossible," said Cinder. "I've seen his aura. There's not a hint of evil within it."

"You're right," said a voice behind them. "Nothing I do can be evil."

They turned to find Numinous climbing from the hole Stagger had blasted. He wore the backpack, but his hands were empty. Then, he knelt at the edge of the hole and leaned down. When he rose, a light followed him. It was Stagger's body, glowing dimly, save for a spike of pure darkness that jutted through the center of his chest, emerging from the spine. Numinous grabbed the hilt of the Witchbreaker and pulled it free, pushing Stagger's limp and lifeless body away. It drifted in the air, with all illusion of flesh gone, revealing the crystalline structure of the face and hands. His eyes, no longer hidden by the iron glasses, were empty sockets.

"Stagger!" Infidel cried, releasing her grip on Cinder.

"He can't hear you," said Numinous, glancing at the blade. "If I understand the workings of this thing, I've sent his soul to Hell. He's Tempest's toy now."

As he spoke, the endless sunset of the Sea of Wine faded to black. For the first time in eternity, the sky above it twinkled with stars.

"No!" Infidel cried, brandishing her flaming sword.

"Stop!" the Black Swan said, grabbing Infidel by the arm. "He'll kill you!"

Numinous nodded. "I'll kill her whether she attacks or not, unless Cinder agrees to take me back to the material realm."

"What?" asked Cinder. "Why? Why are you doing this?"

"Because, as you say, there's no hint of evil within me. I'm pure of heart, and pure of purpose. I exist to bring an end to falsehood and wickedness, to turn the final page on iniquity."

"To bring an end to falsehood?" Cinder scoffed. "You've lied to me this whole time!"

"It would be poor strategy to unilaterally disarm when doing battle with the lies of the world," said Numinous. "Now that you know who I am, let's be reasonable. We can make an honest bargain, devoid of any falsehood. Take me and the book back to the material world, and I won't kill your mother and send her soul to Hell."

"You can try," said Infidel, tearing her arm free of the Black Swan's grasp.

"You can't fight him," the Black Swan said firmly. "Especially not while he carries the Witchbreaker!"

"I've fought men with big swords before," said Infidel. "They don't impress me."

The Black Swan moved to grab Infidel once more, but the warrior woman moved faster than a jungle cat. She lunged at Numinous, swinging the sword of flames with her right hand. He parried her blade, then, as if he'd understood all along that her sword attack had been only a feint, he easily twisted his body from the path of a small knife she thrust toward his ribs with her left hand. He brought his elbow down hard on the back of her skull, but she rolled with the blow as she hit the ground. She was back on her feet in seconds, raising her blade to block the Witchbreaker. Unfortunately, Numinous also proved well-versed in the art of the feint. He drove his knee hard into Infidel's gut. Her face went pale as she stumbled backward, unable to breathe.

"Mother!" cried Cinder, rushing toward her side.

"Hands off," Numinous said, leaping up and kicking Cinder in the jaw. She fell backward, landing hard on the black scales. "When we leave, we leave together."

Cinder tried to rise, but he kicked her in the face once more. Her eyes fluttered shut as the blow robbed her of consciousness.

Infidel took advantage of his momentary focus on Cinder to once more charge Numinous. He turned to face her with time to spare. With his speed, he could easily have run her through with the Witchbreaker. Instead, he delivered a swift, sharp blow straight to her nose. Her sword flew from her grasp as she fell, completely limp.

Numinous turned to face the Black Swan. "I can't kill Infidel just yet. I need to carve her up until Cinder cooperates. But you? I don't see why I need you at all, whoever the hell you are."

"You don't know my identity?" the Black Swan asked, genuinely surprised. "I thought you could see the truth of anything."

"There are some poor souls so submerged in lies there's no longer any truth for me to see," said Numinous. "But you… you're a puzzle. Your aura is like nothing I've ever seen, chaotic and indistinct. There's something inhuman within you as well. Animal spirits, thousands of them. Curious."

The Black Swan held her hands to her side and let her razor sharp nails extend. "Curious and dangerous. You'll never defeat me, Numinous. I've had lifetimes to prepare to fight you. You don't even know who I am."

"I know you have a soul, however distorted it might be," said Numinous. "And I know I have the power to send it to Hell."

He raced toward her, raising the Witchbreaker overhead. He chopped it toward her. She raised her left hand and caught it. The force of the blow sent her thumb flying and dented the plate that formed her palm.

She swung her right hand toward him, her nails raking empty air as he ducked. He gave a loud cry and drove his shoulder into her iron belly, the force knocking her backward. She staggered, her feet skittering on the slick scales as she fought to keep her balance.

"That blow might have knocked the breath out of me, if I had lungs," she said.

Numinous kept his distance for the moment, rubbing his shoulder. His eyes narrowed as he studied her. She knew he was looking for any point of weakness, in either body or soul.

He tossed the Witchbreaker aside. "An edged blade isn't the best weapon for a bloodless foe," he said. "And with your overlapping souls, who can say how much of you would be sent to Hell?"

"Hell holds no terror for me," said the Black Swan. As she said this she crouched, her spring-driven legs propelling her forward, her right hand outstretched, her nails dripping poison. He leaned from her path, reaching out to grab her wrist. He added his momentum to her and threw her face first on the scales. She slid down Rott's ribs, gaining speed as the slope grew deeper. Before her lay the Sea of Wine, and certain oblivion were she to vanish beneath its waves.

Fortunately, her fingernails weren't her only body part spring-loaded with sharp things. With a thought, spikes sprung from her knees and elbows, digging through Rott's flesh, scraping on bone. Her momentum halted and she rose, only to find Numinous standing before her. He now carried the small dagger Infidel had used. With an almost casual motion he reached out and jammed the tip into the joint of her right shoulder. He twisted and she lost all ability to move the arm. She swung her left hand toward him, nails extended, and he ducked beneath them, then rose and grabbed the arm by the wrist and threw his full weight against the joint of her elbow, taking care to avoid the long spike. There was a crack as her arm bent too far backward. The spring-loaded spike popped out of its mounting, and Numinous caught it before it fell. He danced to her side faster than she could turn her head. The next thing she knew she lost all command of her left leg as he drove the spike deep into the joint of her hip, popping the iron cable within free of the pulley it rode upon.

With a clatter, she fell to her side.

Numinous stood over her, a smile on his lips. "For someone who claims to have spent lifetimes preparing to fight me, you certainly haven't proven very good at it."

"Listen to me!" she said with a desperate squawk. "I've seen the end of the world! I know what happens when you read the One True Book. It's not falsehood that comes to an end. It's everything! You erase reality itself!"

"If that's the will of the Divine Author, so be it," said Numinous. He placed his foot on her torso and gave her a little nudge. She started sliding once more toward the Sea of Wine, with only her right leg still functioning. She tried desperately to halt herself, but it was luck alone that stopped her, as her hip dropped into a particularly large hole in Rott's decayed flesh.

Numinous loped down the slope toward her.

"Do you truly hate the world so much you'd end it?" she asked.

He placed his foot on her chest once more.

"I don't do this out of hate. It's my destiny to bring the story to an end." He eyed the waves, mere yards away. "Your story, it seems, ends here."

"Please!" she begged. "Listen to reason!"

"What's more reasonable that doing the thing I was born to do?" he asked. "Defying the will of the Divine Author is pointless. Farewell, my curious foe."

As he flexed his muscles to send her once more toward the waves she cried, "Wait! Are you really curious? Don't you want to know why there's more than one soul in my body?"

"Not really," he said. "It happens to the mad sometimes."

"But the animal spirits! Don't you want to understand how they got inside me?"

He smiled. "Anything worth understanding will be found within the pages of the One True Book."

Yet, despite his professed lack of curiosity, he didn't kick her into the wine. His eyes fixed on her face as he spotted the movement in her mouth. He furrowed his brow as a small brown head poked out from between her iron lips.

"A mouse?" he whispered. "That's your true form? A mouse?"

Then the mouse changed into a tiger. Numinous grew pale as he leapt backward. With the maximum speed that his perfect human legs could muster, he ran up the slope, putting distance between himself and the huge jungle cat.

Human speed, even maximum human speed, proved inadequate to the task. The tiger easily caught up in a single bound. Numinous rolled aside, scrambling on his hands and knees to reach the discarded Witchbreaker. He let out a cry of triumph as his fingers closed around the blade.

The tiger crushed him to the ground as it leapt onto his back. The beast's fore-claws hooked deeply into the man's ribs as glistening canine teeth sank into the man's neck. Numinous shrieked like a dying rabbit as the tiger twisted its mighty head. Numinous fell silent as his neck bent at an unnatural angle. The tiger dug its claws into the man's throat and raked, then raked again. With one final, savage jerk, it tore the man's head free. The tiger spat the head away. The head splashed into the waves and disappeared.

"Perfect man, meet average tiger," the tiger said, through bloodied jaws. The tiger rose onto its hind legs and turned into a chimp. The chimp clambered down the slippery slope to reach the Black Swan.

"He wasn't so tough," said Menagerie.

"Why'd you wait so long to attack?" she asked.

"When Stagger accelerated with such insane speed to get here, the shockwave rang your body like a bell. It proved a bit much for a mouse to endure, I fear. I must have been unconscious for a few minutes."

"You woke just in time," she said.

Menagerie dragged her up the slope, helping her sit next to the unconscious forms of Infidel and Cinder. The chimp's eyes carefully surveyed her dented and damaged arms. "What the hell did he hit you with? A sledgehammer?"

"His fists, mostly," she said. "I warned you we couldn't trifle with him."

"I took your warning seriously," Menagerie said. "Once I got into the fight, it was over in, what? Ten seconds? Fifteen, tops?"

"It felt like eternity to me. And why the tiger? You can turn into a dragon!"

"This didn't seem like a good moment to be trying new stuff. I've got decades of practice as a tiger."

"If you'd failed, the world would have fallen."

"Then it's a good thing I didn't fail," the chimp said, frowning. "What's it take to get a 'thank you, good job' out of you?"

"Thank you," she said. "Good job."

"So," said Menagerie, looking at Cinder. "This is her? The young you?"

The Black Swan nodded.

"And if we've stopped the end of the world, she's never going to run back in time and become you, right?"

"I suppose not."

"Then why the hell are you here?"

The Black Swan shrugged. "My entire history is a sequence of unresolved paradoxes. I don't dwell upon them. From my perspective, my continuity remains intact. It's only everyone else's reality I've altered. I've spared this timeline from destruction. At least, destruction by Numinous."

"We still have a dragon problem," said Menagerie.

"Yes. We need to free Abyss from Hush's grip and drive Tempest's army back into Hell," She glanced up at the stars. "And we'll be doing in in the dark, it seems. Stagger's a slave of Tempest now. We have to save him."

"So," said Menagerie. "Just another day at work, then."

Infidel groaned as she lifted her hands to her nose. She mumbled, "What hit me?" She sat up, looking toward Menagerie. She scratched her head. "A chimp? Why did I pick a fight with a chimp?"

"Hello, Infidel," said Menagerie.

"Okay. I'm not really awake." She cradled her head in her hands, then looked back at the chimp. "Wait. I get it. Hello, Menagerie. Where the hell did you come from?"

"He's been with us the whole time," said the Black Swan. "I didn't dare reveal his presence to you. There are too many mind-readers we might have encountered."

Infidel studied the chimp's face. "I thought you'd given up the mercenary business?"

"I did, for a while," said Menagerie. "But, don't forget that my human form is now a copy of you."

"I remember that pretty well," said Infidel. "I have a hard time forgetting it, in fact. It's a bit unnerving to think there's a perfect copy of me out there somewhere."

"Trust me, it's not much fun being your doppelganger," said Menagerie. "I thought I had a lot of enemies. But you! Every other day I was fighting some assassin out for your head. I had to move back to Commonground to keep my family in the Silver City out of danger." The chimp sighed. "Not that it did any good in the end. Tempest's armies have killed everyone there."

"We've all paid a price," said the Black Swan. "But, at least we've removed the threat of the Omega Reader once and for all."

Infidel furrowed her brow. "He's the one who hit me? Man, it feels like he punched the memories right out of my skull. You guys beat him?"

The chimp tilted his head toward the headless body further down the slope. For the first time, the Black Swan noticed that the man's hands were missing as well. Odd. She hadn't noticed the tiger tear them off.

"Right," said Infidel. "He looks pretty beaten." She stood and went to her daughter. She touched her lightly on the cheek and Cinder's eyes fluttered open.

"Mother?" she whispered.

"It's okay," said Infidel. "We're safe now. Everything's all..." Her voice faded as her face grew pale.

She rose and turned, until she spotted the faintly glowing crystalline form hovering a few feet above the black pit. "Stagger!"

Infidel ran to his side, pulling his body to her, clasping it in her arms. The crystalline limbs hung limp. "No," she whispered. "No!"

"Stagger's soul's been sent to Hell," said the Black Swan.

"Then we're going to Hell," said Infidel, firmly. "We've got to rescue him."

"I've been to Hell," said Menagerie. "I'm not going back."

"We'll find work for you elsewhere," said the Black Swan. "Rescuing Stagger is only one of a long list of things we must accomplish."

"This was... this was my father?" asked Cinder.

Infidel nodded.

Cinder rose to step toward him, then stopped as her eyes spotted the mangled body down the slope.

"Luminous," she whispered.

"We told you his real name," said the Black Swan.

"It doesn't... I still can't believe..." Cinder shook her head. "Why did he lie to me?"

"It's all because of this damn book," Menagerie said, knuckle-walking toward Numinous and the leather backpack he still wore that held the cause of so much misery.

Just as the chimp reached the body, the Black Swan saw a dark shadow move toward him, almost invisible in the starlight. From the other side of the chimp's body, a burst of intense light cast a shadow in her direction. The light suddenly diminished as a sizzling sound filled the air. The chimp fell backward, then vanished, and the light flared again. As the Black Swan's vision adjusted to the glare, she saw a man in black robes grasping a flaming sword standing over the body of Numinous.

"Ver!" The Black Swan couldn't believe he'd returned.

Infidel craned her neck, searching the ground near her.

"This is indeed your sword," said Ver, holding the blazing blade before him.

"Greatshadow!" Infidel shouted. "Don't let him—"

"Don't waste your breath," said Ver. "The dragon's spirit moves within the blade, but lacks the power to dominate my will."

"How did you escape the soul catcher?" asked the Black Swan.

Ver held out his free hand. Between the fingers of his white glove, he ground something that fell in glittering silver flakes. "If this thing had reached my spiritual flesh, it might have been unfortunate. Luckily, it blunted its nose against the Immaculate Attire."

"The Immaculate Attire?" asked Infidel. "My old armor? It was lost in the Great Sea Above."

"And then it was found," said Ver. "Certainly you've noticed my gloves? I've been in possession of the Attire for years."

Ver knelt over the Numinous. With a swift motion, he cut the straps of the backpack.

"This isn't over," said Ver, lifting the pack. "If Numinous wasn't the Omega Reader, there must be another. In the end, the will of the Divine Author shall be done."

20 - RULE ONE

THE BLACK SWAN'S MIND whirled as she weighed how to attack Ver. She hadn't had time to refill her smokescreen, and, with her arms disabled, she couldn't aim the poison darts spring-loaded in her forearms. With his powerful will, Ver was probably immune to the handful of necromantic commands she knew. If she abandoned her physical form, she could face Ver ghost to ghost, but since he was armed with a flaming sword and wearing impervious armor, her odds of besting him seemed slim.

Before the Black Swan could decide how to proceed, Infidel rose on rubbery legs and said, "Drop the pack, Ver."

"You can barely stand," said Ver. "I've nothing to fear from you."

"Then you'll need to handle me," Cinder said as she stood, holding one of the steel spikes that Numinous had torn from the Black Swan's body.

"You won't be able to get through his armor," Infidel said in a calm tone. "Go for his head."

"He has a big enough mouth," said Cinder. "I'll aim for that."

"You'd send your child to fight me, Infidel?" asked Ver. "Are you so eager to see her die?"

"Surviving day to day in the jungle isn't a job for wimps," said Infidel. "She'll take you down. Wearing armor and carrying a sword doesn't make you a fighter."

Ver's eyes narrowed. Thanks to the sword, he could see clearly within the circle of light immediately around him, but Cinder eluded his gaze by stepping backward, crouching down. With her dark skin against Rott's black hide, she was all but invisible. Ver looked from side to side, searching for any sign of movement.

On the lookout for Cinder, he completely failed to see Infidel sprinting toward him until the last second. He swung his blade toward her but she easily ducked beneath it, rising to grab his arm. He twisted the blade toward her. She gasped as the flames scorched her face, but he couldn't break her grasp.

Without warning, Cinder flew from the shadows, holding the spike overhead with both hands, slashing toward the Truthspeaker's head. Ver's reflexes proved better that the Black Swan would have guessed as he raised the backpack up in time to protect himself. The spike dug into the leather, ripping downward. Ver pushed Cinder away before she could get her balance, but the motion caused the One True Book to topple out of the torn backpack.

"No!" Ver cried, releasing his grip on the sword of flame and jerking his arm free from Infidel's clutches. He lunged, using both hands to catch the One True Book before it hit Rott's slimy scales.

For an instant, a look of triumph crossed his face as he stared at the tome he'd rescued from the filth. His face went slack as he realized the truth of what he'd done. Gloves, even magic ones, weren't enough to negate the blasphemy of his action. He'd laid hands upon the One True Book, an object so sacred it would burn away the sinful soul of any flawed being who touched it.

"No," he whispered, as white light burned through his spiritual flesh.

The One True Book dropped the final inches to the ground.

Ver's robes collapsed into a flat heap as his final cry of despair vanished into the night.

BROTHER WING HAD GROWN to hate the endless noon of the afterlife. Had he been dead hours? Days? Years? Whatever the span of time, the thrill of flight had become a tedious chore, and the once-welcome silence of being along with his thoughts had turned into unfathomable loneliness. What would he feel after a hundred years? A thousand? He contemplated the unbroken sea below, wondering if he should throw himself into its depths. To what end? Was there a death after death? He didn't have the courage to find out. He wasn't tired or hungry, and felt no physical pain. He'd known all of these things in his infancy. As terrible as his loneliness was, he knew full well there might be worse hells than this.

Oh, what he would give for any hint of the passage of time. How he would rejoice to see a sunset!

Then there was night.

Brother Wing blinked, wondering if he'd gone blind. He hadn't. He could see stars overhead, their reflections twinkling on the water below. The sun hadn't sank below the horizon. It had simply stopped shining. Had his desire for change in his surroundings caused this somehow?

Before he could ponder the implications of a landscape molded by his unconscious will, he spotted a tiny, faint, red light on the horizon. Veering toward it, he could see the light was different from the stars or their reflections. As he flew onward, the light grew larger. When he first spotted it, the light had been no brighter than a candle flame seen at a distance. Soon, it grew to resemble a ship's lantern far out in the harbor, then a torch perhaps a mile away. Breathing deep, he tasted smoke on the night air.

In the starlight it was difficult to be certain, but it seemed to him that the sea ahead gave way to a vast dark shape. A shoreline? As he glided toward the light, he heard the sound of breaking waves.

He spread his wings, slowing his flight, gliding lower and lower, his eyes fixed on the flame. He could now see it was a bonfire on a beach. A signal fire? Who would be signaling whom in this land of the dead? He'd always possessed a strong instinct for survival. The prudent course would be to keep his distance, watch and learn. After the tedium of flying so long without a landmark, however, he couldn't resist the lure of the bonfire. He'd built a church around the worship of flame. After all, within every flame dwelt Greatshadow.

Brother Wing landed on the black shore. The stench of smoke nearly choked him. The land all around him was black and burnt, with here and there the dull, rounded shape of a tree stump hidden beneath ash. He could see that what he'd taken for a bonfire was, in fact, a thorn tree, the only tree still standing within his sight, though it wouldn't stand for long, given how violently it burned.

Brother Wing walked to its edge, then lowered his head in the pose of prayer he'd stolen from the minds of human faithful.

"Father," he whispered.

"My child," the flame answered, as a hot wind caused the branches of the thorn tree to tremble.

"Why have you summoned me here, Father?" asked Brother Wing.

"Darkness has fallen upon the world," said Greatshadow.

"What has happened to the sun?"

"The spirit that dwelled within it has been enslaved by Tempest. Tempest wills darkness that his armies may freely move upon the earth. The sun obeys."

Brother Wing rose. "How can the world survive this?"

"It can't," answered the flame.

"There must be some hope," said Brother Wing. "The sanctuary I founded houses hundreds of people faithful to you, waiting for the day you and your allies will overpower Tempest and Hush. They're willing and ready to rebuild. Their faith cannot be in vain."

"Faith?" Greatshadow scoffed. The thorn tree threw off sparks as the smaller branches crumbled. "Faith is nothing but the stubborn refusal to let go of hope in the face of all contrary evidence. Faith cannot save the world, only action."

"Then why haven't you taken action?" asked Brother Wing. "Why haven't you fought back against Tempest and Hush?"

"I am weakened, my child," said Greatshadow. "There are fewer flames in the world today than ever before. In a direct confrontation with another dragon, I would surely perish."

"Are you saying all is lost?"

"I said I couldn't survive a direct confrontation," said Greatshadow. "What my opponents don't yet know is that I launched oblique attacks upon them long ago. Whether these attacks succeed we shall soon learn."

"Then the world may yet be saved?"

"Perhaps," said Greatshadow. As he spoke, more branches fell away from the tree. "I've no direct knowledge of the future. But there has long been one who dwelled on the Isle of Fire who believed she did: the Black Swan. Through her mind, I've witnessed the end of the world. At first, I thought she was mad. But, as she rose to power in Commonground, I took note of how often events she prepared for came to pass. I decided it would be wise to take precautions. Perhaps those long ago actions on my part may yet save us all."

"The Black Swan is the woman who killed me," said Brother Wing.

"I know. You were standing next to the cauldron's flames within the temple. I witnessed it firsthand."

"If you witnessed it, why didn't you stop her?" asked Brother Wing.

"Your death was a necessary part of my plan." The larger branches of the thorn tree broke off, leaving only the twisted, central trunk still burning. "The Black Swan knew she would one day fight you. I judged that her poison would bring you a swift, painless death."

Brother Wing furrowed his brow. "How could my death possibly save the world?"

"Because there are places only the dead may easily go," said Greatshadow. "Follow."

With a final shudder, the remnants of the thorn tree collapsed, sending glowing embers dancing into the air. The embers swirled together, taking on a shape that vaguely resembled a dragon as the wind swept it away from the shore, over the blackened hills of the island. Brother Wing flapped his wings, sending ash flying as he rose into the air to give chase.

"OKAY," SAID INFIDEL, taking a few steps back, the flaming sword now in her grasp. She eyed Ver's empty robes carefully, then turned her gaze to the black tome that rested on the gloves of the Immaculate Attire, before looking toward Cinder and saying, "Rule one: Don't touch the book."

"Noted," said Cinder, backing away.

"Agreed," said a woman's voice from the shadows behind her mother.

Cinder looked toward the voice. Her eyes filled with confusion when she found a perfect duplicate of her mother standing there, nude save for a ragged cloak.

"We've never met," the woman in the cloak said. "I'm Menagerie."

"His original body got destroyed by an old god," said Infidel, sensing the need for an explanation. "He turned into a tick and sucked my blood so now he can turn into me." She frowned as she said this. "Does anyone else ever have moments where perfectly accurate statements leave them questioning their sanity?"

"Yes," said the Black Swan.

"All the time," said Menagerie. "I'm alive because I changed into a starfish. They're champs at regeneration."

"You have the weirdest friends," Cinder said to her mother.

"We have to figure out how to get the One True Book back into the backpack," said the Black Swan. "We can't just leave it lying there."

Cinder didn't pay attention to this as she went closer to her mother. The right side of Infidel's face was covered with blisters, and her hair near her ear was singed down to stubble. "You're hurt."

"I've lived through worse," Infidel said, taking carefully placed steps toward Ver's robes. She knelt near the boots and began untangling the Immaculate Attire from the robes. "We can worry about the One True Book later. We have to get to Hell to rescue Stagger."

"I think I can find my way back to Hell," said Cinder.

"We can't ignore the book," said the Black Swan. "We can't risk it falling into the Sea of Wine if Rott sinks beneath the waves."

"What's the big deal?" asked Menagerie. "Let's nudge it back into the backpack with a sword. It didn't hurt anyone while it was in the pack."

"It was put into the pack by Slate, a man with no soul," said the Black Swan. "I'm not even sure it's safe for us to touch it indirectly."

As the Black Swan spoke, Infidel grabbed the edges of the white gloves, then yanked them from beneath the book.

"What are you doing?" asked the Black Swan, exasperated. "Just by touching the gloves you might have been erased!"

"I wasn't," said Infidel, shrugging as she inspected the inner lining of the Immaculate Attire. Finding no trace of Ver within it, she began to strip off her old clothes.

"Mother," said Cinder, covering her eyes.

"What?" she asked. "Menagerie knows what I look like naked. And you've seen me naked before, which means the Black Swan has seen me."

"How does that follow?" asked Cinder.

"Oh, right," said Infidel. "You don't know. The Black Swan is you, from the future."

Cinder's jaw grew slack as she stared at the iron woman.

"It's true," said the Black Swan. "Though I would have preferred to break the news more gently."

"But... but how can..." Cinder couldn't grasp the idea enough to even question it properly.

"It's a long story," said the Black Swan. "And it may no longer be true. You don't have to become me anymore, Cinder. You can chart your own destiny."

Infidel pulled on the armor's leggings. "With the Immaculate Attire, the Witchbreaker, and the Sword of Flame, I feel pretty good about heading to hell to fight Tempest."

"You do have more experience at fighting dragons than anyone," said the Black Swan. "Which is why you'll need to leave rescuing Stagger to Cinder and myself. You need to get back to the Isle of Fire."

"The Isle of Fire can wait," said Infidel."

"No it can't," said the Black Swan. "With Stagger in Hell, he's no longer bending the light around the island. It's in full view of Tempest, Hush, and the enslaved Abyss. I've no doubt they're already moving to wipe out the last traces of mankind sheltered there."

"Greatshadow and Abundant will fight them," said Infidel.

"They're both weakened. They'll need all the help they can get."

"All the more reason to free Stagger first," said Infidel.

"If Stagger intervenes, Kragg will plunge the whole island into the sea," said the Black Swan.

Infidel fastened the clasps of the leather breastplate. "You have an answer for everything, don't you?"

"No," said the Black Swan. "Only desperate guesses."

"I've lived in a dozen cities, but Commonground's the only place that felt like home," said Menagerie. "I'll be happy to defend it."

"I'm sure you would," said the Black Swan. "But this isn't the best use of your talents. I'll need you in Hell."

Menagerie shook her head. "I can't go back. I won't. Besides, Infidel should have some backup."

"I'm not sure a tiger is going to help against dragons," said Infidel.

"You know better than to underestimate me," Menagerie said. "I have a few tricks up my sleeve."

"You don't wear sleeves," said Infidel, pulling on her boots.

"Enough squabbling," said the Black Swan. "I need you all to follow my plan."

"First, my plan, which is to ignore you," said Infidel. "I'm going to save Stagger. And you are out of your iron skull if you think I'm going to allow Cinder to go to Hell without me watching out for her."

"Mother, I can take care of myself," said Cinder.

"And she'll have my help," said the Black Swan.

"Numinous crippled you!" said Infidel. "You can't even stand."

"Remove my head. That way, I can guide Cinder. We've no time to wait for the *Circus* to reach us so that Sorrow can repair me, assuming she even has the power to do so."

"Um..." said Menagerie, looking toward the horizon, "I don't think we'll have to wait long."

They all followed her gaze toward a renewed sunrise in the east.

Infidel shielded her eyes as the light grew ever brighter. She whispered, "Stagger?"

"It's not Stagger," said Menagerie in a screeching voice. Cinder glanced up to see a large eagle flying over them. The eagle said, "I can see shapes within the light. It's a ship."

"A ship?" asked Cinder. "In the sky?"

"A cloud ship?" the Black Swan asked, confused. "Has Tempest sent the Storm Guard after us?"

"No," said Menagerie. "It's a Wanderer vessel. And there's a woman carrying it."

Infidel squinted as the small sun grew closer. "I... I do see a boat-like shadow in the light. But what do you mean, a woman's carrying it?"

"Which words don't you understand?" asked the eagle. "A woman's holding the boat above her head with both hands. And she's flying."

As the light grew closer, the Black Swan saw that his words were accurate. There was a shadow in the light exactly the size and shape of a fully rigged ship. She could even make out silhouettes of people on the deck. Below the ship, in a pillar of light, a distinctly feminine form could be discerned as the source of the radiance.

The ship moved with such speed that it reached the island in under a minute. The ship sank down toward the waves. The woman dropped the ship into the wine, darting backward behind the bobbing vessel. For a moment the light was dim.

"It's the *Circus*!" said the Black Swan.

A second later, the glowing woman shot up over the deck, streaking toward them like a bolt of lightning, only to come to a halt before them. The light faded, revealing the woman at the center of the light, her head studded with nails.

"Sorrow!" exclaimed Infidel.

"The sun's gone dark. What happened to Stagger?" Sorrow asked.

"Numinous ran him through with the Witchbreaker," said Infidel.

"Sending his soul to Hell," said Sorrow, nodding. "I felt something happen only seconds after Sage hammered the glorystone into my scalp. The elemental energy that filled me had an intelligence behind it at first. I sensed something gazing at me, then, suddenly, the intelligence vanished. The elemental power flowed without resistance."

"The glorystone lets you fly," said Infidel. "But, how could you pick up the ship? When I flew with the Gloryhammer, I couldn't move such a heavy mass."

"The Gloryhammer was external. My power is internal. However, the glorystone alone wouldn't have done the trick. Fortunately, I once again have a nail of wood. For me, solid oak feels as light as balsa, and I could mentally hold the hull together as I lifted it."

"You couldn't have recovered your powers at a better time," said the Black Swan. "With Stagger gone, Hush and Abyss will attack the Isle of Fire."

"First things first," said Sorrow. "Since Cinder's here, I assume you captured Numinous?"

The eagle landed on the Black Swan's shoulder. With a wing, Menagerie pointed down the slope toward the headless body. "Captured is an understatement."

The inner light that flowed from Sorrow dimmed for a moment. She took a deep breath, clenching then unclenching her fists. "It... it would have been selfish to ask you to take him alive." She frowned, and looked back at the eagle. "Does no one else find it odd that this bird just spoke?"

"Sorry," said the eagle. "You didn't know I was tagging along. We met before, years ago."

"Menagerie?" she asked.

"At your service."

"Since Numinous is beyond your vengeance, may I have you focus instead on repairing my body?" asked the Black Swan.

Sorrow sighed. "For the millionth time, your breasts are fine."

"No, they aren't," the Black Swan grumbled. "But I meant I need my limbs repaired. Certainly you noticed they're damaged?"

"Oh," said Sorrow. "I didn't. You'll forgive me if I'm a bit distracted. Let me take a look."

"Look quickly," said Infidel. "Now that you've got your powers back, the course is clear. I'll go to Hell to rescue Stagger. You and the Romers go to Commonground and stop Tempest and Hush."

"Excuse me," said Rigger, calling down from the deck of the *Circus*. "Did you just volunteer us to fight two primal dragons without asking if we agreed to the plan?"

"We both know you'll agree to the plan," said Infidel.

"Well, yes," said Rigger. "But it would have been nice to be consulted before you start barking out orders."

"She's not barking out orders," said the Black Swan as Sorrow dug her fingers into the socket of her iron shoulder. "I've more experience than any of you in how this day must unfold. And, on this, I agree with Infidel. The Romers must return to Commonground. Then, they need to set the whole city aflame."

"You want them to burn Commonground?" asked Infidel.

"Greatshadow's weak. Once, he was fed by millions of flames. Now, only a few lanterns and stoves in Commonground sustain him." She eyed Gale Romer, standing at the rail. "Burn the city. Burn the forests if you have to. We have to make Greatshadow strong again. While he's weakened, Infidel's sword of flame isn't powerful enough to finish off Hush. If we slay Hush, there's hope that Abyss might be freed."

"What about Kragg?" asked Infidel. "He threatened to destroy the island if Stagger intervened. You think he'll sit back and let them take out Hush?"

"I'll take care of Kragg," said Sorrow, bending the Black Swan's elbow back into shape. "Move your fingers for me."

The Black Swan wiggled her fingers, pleased to find the mobility in that limb restored.

"You can't fight Kragg alone," said Mako, now beside Gale. "I'll come with you."

"Not where I'm going," said Sorrow. "I'm going to confront him in the Convergence."

"Only dragons can reach that abstract realm," said the Black Swan.

"I know," said Sorrow.

"No," said Sage, joining Mako and Gale at the rail. "You can't seriously be thinking what I think you're thinking."

"I think you're thinking exactly what I'm thinking," said Sorrow, as she focused her attention on the Black Swan's neck.

"Don't expect me to help you," said Sage. "It's too great of a price. You lost your humanity the last time you tried this! How can you throw it away again?"

"When that blade slid into Slate's chest, every last bit of my humanity died with him," said Sorrow. "I'll give up nothing I cherish."

"This is a great sacrifice you're making, Sorrow," said the Black Swan.

"Will you stop being so cryptic?" Mako growled. "What sacrifice? What are you going to do?"

Sorrow glanced down at the black scales beneath her feet. "I'm going to merge with Rott once more."

"No," whispered Mako.

"It's the only way," said Sorrow. "The dragons allied against mankind are at the peak of their power. Our only allies are weakened. But if I command Rott's might once more, I'll be more than a match for any dragon. Kragg will agree to leave the Isle of Fire alone or I'll turn him into a pile of gravel."

"We can't let her do this," said Mako.

Gale put her hand on his shoulder. "Son, what right have we to stop her? She's a free woman."

Sage crossed her arms. "I'm a free woman as well. I refuse to help her."

"Please, Sage," said Sorrow, as she adjusted the tension of the Black Swan's leg cables. "The precision that comes with your mystic vision allowed me to absorb the power of these new nails at a speed I never dreamed possible. With your help, I can control Rott's power to the fullest."

Sage shook her head. "Sorrow, I know you came aboard our ship as a passenger, but after all we've been through together, you're a friend. You're practically family. Please don't do this. I know it hurts to lose Slate. We all miss him. But, can't you see? You're not alone. You still have us."

"We'll all discover what true loneliness is if Tempest and Hush destroy Commonground," said Gale. "The remaining Wanderers are sheltered in that port. How can we not give our all to save them?"

"It's not only the Wanderers," said the Black Swan as she rose, holding Sorrow's hand. "All that's left of living men are sheltered on the island. Sorrow may lose her humanity, but, without her, we may lose mankind."

"Not to mention animalkind," said Menagerie.

Sage turned her back to everyone as a shudder ran through her. When she turned back, she eyes glistened with tears. "Very well," she whispered. She glared at Sorrow. "But only if you swear—swear!—when this is over, you'll let me remove the nail."

"We… we can try," said Sorrow. "I swear to let you try."

"Do what you must to ready the nail," said Sage, through gritted teeth.

"I will," said Sorrow. "But there's other business I must attend to first."

"Do we have time for other business?" asked Gale.

"I'm not even taking time to use the bathroom," said Jetsam, popping his head over the rail.

"First, there's the matter of the One True Book," Sorrow said, kneeling next to it. She reached into a pouch on her belt and pulled out two silver moons. "It will destroy the soul of anyone who touches it, but souls can't pass through a barrier of silver." The coins turned to puddles in her palm, then dripped down onto the tome. The silver flowed, guided by Sorrow's will, until it completely encased the book. Taking a deep breath, she touched it with a single finger.

She exhaled slowly. "Good. That worked."

"You weren't certain?" asked the Black Swan.

"I was pretty certain," said Sorrow, picking up the book.

The Black Swan stepped forward and held her open hands toward the book. "May I? I think the book is best left in my protection."

"I suppose it's as safe with you as anyone," said Sorrow, handing it over. "I've got other things to worry about at the moment." She walked to where Stagger's crystalline corpse still hung in the air. As she approached, its dull light began to glow more brightly. Sorrow put her hands upon the chest. "I can plainly see the matrix of the crystal. I understand how to shape it. Stagger's left us a great treasure indeed."

"Hold on," said Infidel, grasping the hilt of her blade. "You're not selling Stagger's body."

"Who's left to buy it?" asked Jetsam.

"Of course I'm not going to sell it," said Sorrow, as her fingers sank into the crystalline surface. "I'm going to sculpt it."

"Stop!" said Infidel, grabbing Sorrow by the shoulders and pulling her away. "I'm not going to stand by and watch you mangle my husband's corpse."

"This is only an avatar," said Sorrow. "It's no more his body than those lava dragons you killed in Commonground twenty years ago were Greatshadow's body. It's a tool he used to visit you. Now, it's a tool we can use against the dragons."

"What do you have in mind?" asked the Black Swan.

"Weapons," said Sorrow. "I can reconfigure the raw material of the head into a helmet for the Immaculate Attire. This will give Infidel even more protection, and, as a bonus, she'll be able to fly, just as she could with the Gloryhammer." She looked at Infidel. "Assuming you agree. There's not much use in making a helmet if you won't wear it."

Infidel took a deep breath as she thought this over. "You're absolutely sure this won't somehow hurt Stagger?"

"Positive. All traces of his spirit are gone from this glorystone."

"And when we free his soul from Tempest, he'll return to the sun," said the Black Swan.

"Are you sure?" asked Infidel. "Or is that wishful thinking?"

"Wishful thinking is pretty much the plan, I'm guessing," said Menagerie.

"The only thing preventing it from being a solid plan is Hell itself," said the Black Swan. "The terrain is nearly impossible to navigate. I'm hoping I can provoke Tempest into attacking us. Otherwise, we might search for eternity and not find him."

"Another reason to take me along," said Infidel. "I've got no peers when it picking fights."

"I might debate that if we had more time," said Sorrow. "But the time for debate is over. The Black Swan's delegation of duties is our best option. You must go to Commonground, Infidel.

Infidel opened her mouth to argue, but Sorrow cut her off. "This how it must be. We're all fighting for something bigger than our own personal interests. Rescuing Stagger will make for a bittersweet victory if the Isle of Fire is a dead, frozen wasteland when he returns to the living world."

"Fine," Infidel said, though her expression indicated arguments were still running through her mind. "But how will—"

Gale Romer interrupted before Infidel could ask her question. "I've you're worried about how Cinder and the Black Swan can find Stagger in Hell, we've got something that will help."

"What's that?" asked the Black Swan.

"A compass," said Gale. "And, more importantly, a map."

"You won't be unarmed in Hell, Swan," Sorrow said, turning Stagger's torso around as she studied it. "I've more glorystone here than I have time to fully exploit. It shouldn't take too long to craft a few swords for you and Cinder. They're the perfect weapons. Demons and the damned can't stand sunlight."

"Actually," said Cinder, "I'd prefer a spear."

"That can be arranged," said Sorrow. "We have our missions, but before anything can be done, I need to focus. I require perhaps an hour to craft the glorystone into new configurations, then another hour to properly prepare a fresh nail from Rott's scales. Until this is ready, there's little more the rest of you can do. I advise that you return to the *Circus*. Sage, please tend to Infidel's wounds."

"It's just a few blisters," said Infidel."

"It won't hurt to let Sage look you over," said the Black Swan. "As for the rest of you, I advise a hearty meal and a few moments of rest. The battle that follows will be the toughest you've ever fought. Summon what strength you can in these fleeting moments."

"Excellent," said Jetsam. "I've got time to use the bathroom after all."

21 - PRAYER OF BUBBLES

THE TRANSITION FROM the sultry tropical heat of the Sea of Wine to the freezing hurricane winds of Commonground was instantaneous. A tall wave instantly broke over the bow of the *Circus*, drenching everyone on deck with a cold spray that swiftly turned to ice.

Mako stood in the rigging, raising his hand to spare his eyes from the wind-driven snow. There were flashes of light high above, and rumbling thunder could be heard through the howling gusts. As the flashes faded, darkness engulfed them, as gloomy as the deepest sea. Fortunately, Mako's eyes could plumb such depths. He spotted lanterns off starboard, not too far distant.

"Go!" Sage shouted from the crow's nest.

"Are you talking to me, or Infidel?" he shouted back.

"Both of you! Hurry!"

Before Mako could leap into the water, the door of the forecastle opened and intense light spilled across the deck, turning the snow into a veil of shimmering diamonds. Infidel emerged from the forecastle, her helmet glowing like a small sun. Save for slits around her eyes, none of her face could be seen. She drew her sword from its scabbard. The snow hissed as it met the dancing flame.

Scanning the sky, she called out to Sage, "Which way to Hush?"

"Her aura is everywhere," Sage shouted. "I don't know which direction to send you. Just start flying around. Hopefully, she'll target you."

"So I'm bait," said Infidel. She gave a thumbs up. "Great plan."

She bent her knees, then rocketed skyward.

"Why are you still here?" Sage called out to Mako.

"I'm not," said Mako, doing a backflip into the waves. The water of the bay was still relatively warm, at least in comparison to the blizzard above. Once he was below the water, the roaring wind faded, replaced by the body-shaking rumble of waves crashing on the shore. As he swam in the direction of the lanterns, he noticed the bay was packed with fish, everything from minnows to great white sharks, and, judging from the low, keening songs echoing across the bay, more than a few whales. He listened to the message of their song, his heart sinking. Could it possibly be true that the full surface of the ocean beyond the bay of Commonground was now frozen?

Darting up through a shoal of herring, he shot from the water to grab the anchor chain of the first ship he reached. He noticed the figurehead and recognized the ship at once as the *Blue Maiden*. It was just his luck to be pleading his case to slavers, Wanderers who'd once made every effort to remove his head from his shoulders. Still, the war was twenty years distant. Certainly old grudges would be put aside in times like this.

The second he poked his head above the rail, a shout of alarm went out. A large man with a cutlass charged toward him and shouted, "Die again, you cursed devil!"

Mako dropped back down the chain as the cutlass bit into the rail where his head had been. With his depth-honed speed, he leapt up before the man could pull his blade free, swinging over the rail, driving his feet into the chest of his attacker. The cutlass clattered to the deck. The man staggered backward, but managed to keep his feet.

The Wanderer's eyes were full of hate as he studied Mako. "I know you," he said. "One of those blasted Romers. Some said you'd gone to sail the Sea of Wine, but I knew your kind would be rotting in Hell." He pulled a dagger out of his belt and assumed a defensive stance. "Come on, dead man. Time to send you back to eternal darkness."

"Dead man?" asked Mako. "I'm as alive as you."

The man frowned.

"Put down your blade. I need to speak to Mariner Conch at once," said Mako.

The man looked confused. "Mariner passed away almost fifteen years ago. His daughter's captain these days"

"Coral?" asked Mako. In the years before the Pirate Wars, he'd played with Coral when they'd both been children. Once, in the third year of the War, they'd both met on the docks at Commonground. She'd changed from child to young woman, and he'd changed from a normal boy into a freakish shark-man. He'd been too ashamed to speak to her then, and had jumped into the waves when she'd called out his name.

Before the man could answer, a short figure in a heavy coat and large hat approached. From the build, Mako knew it was a woman, though her face was hidden by her upturned collar, held in place by a gloved hand. She drew closer, revealing her face, her eyes wide with shock.

"Mako?" she asked.

"Hello, Coral," he said, recognizing her through twenty years of aging.

"You... you look so young," she whispered.

"It would take too long to explain why," he said. "For now, I've come to tell you the plan."

"Plan?" asked Coral. "What plan?"

"For fighting Hush and freeing Abyss," said Mako.

"How?" asked Coral.

The sailor beside her picked up his blade as a pale, half-rotten hand closed onto the rail. He gave a cry and lunged forward, severing the fingers, dropping the intruder into the waves. "Blasted dead men," he growled. "That's the twentieth one I've dropped in the last hour."

"Tempest's armies of the damned have been on the march ever since the sun went dark and the bay began to freeze. It won't be long before we're overrun," said Coral. "We were in Raitingu when the gates of Hell first opened. We saw that city fall in a single night. For years, freezing seas have kept pushing us further and further south, until Commonground was the only port remaining. When this place falls…" her voice trailed off.

"Then it can't fall," said Mako. "To make sure it doesn't, light every lantern and stove aboard your ship. Then, go onto the docks, drench everything in oil, and set this whole city on fire!"

"So we can burn instead of freeze?" asked Coral.

"So we can feed Greatshadow," said Mako. "Make him strong enough to fight Hush."

"Greatshadow will be powerless against Abyss," said Coral. "Ever since Hush froze his mind, he's been a puppet to her will. Ordinarily, seawater wouldn't freeze this quickly. The ice advances because Abyss allows Hush power over his domain. Even if we awaken Greatshadow, it's hopeless."

"Bite your tongue," said Mako. "Let every last dragon oppose us. Let all the armies of Hell rise against us! We're Wanderers, damn it! We fight until we fall! We die as free as we lived!"

Coral's eyes brightened. "You're right. Forgive my moment of doubt. I'll relay your orders to my crew at once."

"Good," said Mako. "I'll spread the word to other ships. We need to move quickly, to give Infidel her best chance to—"

"Infidel?" asked Coral. "There's a name I haven't heard in years. She's still alive?"

Almost in answer, a loud curse came from overhead. They glanced up as a glowing form tumbled through the curtain of snow, shielding their eyes as the light grew brighter. They'd raised their hands to cover their eyes just in time, as a blast of hail swept over the ship, the wind-driven ice as sharp as a thousand needles.

Infidel smashed into the upper mast, then tumbled toward the deck. She still carried the sword of flame, though it appeared to be held only loosely in her grasp. Suddenly, her limp form snapped straight and her grip tightened around the hilt of the blade. Her descent came to an instantaneous halt a few feet above their heads.

"Hello, Mako," she said.

"You alright?" he asked.

"Hush noticed me. Part one of the plan is a success!"

She spun around until she faced up, then zoomed off into the clouds.

"Yes," said Mako to Coral, "still alive. Let's keep her that way. Light the fires!"

With a backflip, he dove into the icy waves.

INFIDEL ZOOMED INTO the sky. Between her helmet and her sword, she had all the light she could possibly want, but she still couldn't see more than a foot in front of her face through the snow. Fortunately, though he'd been gone from her life for twenty years, Stagger's encyclopedic knowledge, freely shared when he was drunk, now came back to her. Once, they'd been high on the slopes of the central volcano, and watched as storm clouds passed beneath them. He'd told her the volcano was roughly four miles high, so the clouds were about three miles high.

At full speed, Infidel shot above the clouds in under a minute. She glanced around, not seeing the top of the volcano. She must have been higher than four miles, and her shortness of breath testified she'd risen to a point where the air was quite thin. Fortunately, the trip accomplished her purpose. From above, the storm clouds spread out in an endless blanket in every direction. Directly beneath her there was an unmistakable sinewy curve that marked Hush's spine and neck. Twin layers of clouds spreading above the others marked the primal dragon's wings.

Infidel hesitated, taking in just how vast Hush had become. She'd been mountainous when they'd last fought. She'd stood inside Hush's mouth and assumed she'd been inside a vast cavern. But now? Hush's scale was unfathomable, her wings and tail tip stretching to the horizon.

Infidel still wasn't sure that she'd done the right thing by coming here instead of joining Cinder in Hell. The sooner she finished off Hush, the sooner she could take on the mission closest to her heart. But, the importance of her fight was now clearer than ever. She thought of the Jawa Fruit tribe, facing the blizzard huddled and shivering. Their tree huts, built to welcome cooling breezes, would provide no meaningful shelter. The Black Swan was right. If Hush won here, all that remained of humanity was lost.

"Let's get her attention," Infidel said to the sword. The flames grew brighter, then brighter still, until she held a bonfire in her hand. Yet she remembered the dragons she'd fought in Commonground long ago, how their jets of flame had shot out hundreds of yards. In comparison, this flame was but a small torch. Was Greatshadow truly so weakened?

She had no time to ponder the matter, however. As she'd hoped, a section of cloud directly beneath her rose up, taking on the shape of a dragon's head.

An impossibly loud voice called out, "This is your champion, Greatshadow? This is all you can throw against me?"

Infidel focused on the origin of the sound, spotting the whirlwind of ice that formed Hush's throat. Clenching her jaw, Infidel dove straight down Hush's gullet. Unfortunately, though she was buffeted by wind, and pounded by hail the size of coconuts, she found nothing solid to slash with her sword as she raced through the churning clouds.

Suddenly, the clouds vanished. She found herself mere yards above the frozen sea. She tried to pull out of her dive, but there was no time. With an impact that not even the Immaculate Attire could spare her from, she slammed into the ice.

RIGGER FOUND HIMSELF unexpectedly busy repelling an invasion of dead men attempting to claw their way onto the ship.

"Did I miss something during the planning?" he shouted. "I don't remember being told we'd need to fight the undead!"

"Quit your whining," said Jetsam, running along the rails and using his rapier to pop the eyes of any dead man who made it past the flailing ropes. They howled with pain and rage as they fell back into the sea. "At least we don't have to sit here twiddling our thumbs while Mako and Infidel have all the fun."

"This isn't fun," Gale said, as she and Brand slashed at the dead men trying to clamber up the gangplank. "Get over here! We need to get a path clear for the pygmies."

"On it," said Jetsam, flying low down the gangplank, tripping the walking corpses in his path.

On deck, Bigsby and Cinnamon busily handed out makeshift torches to the small army of pygmies who'd climbed out of the hold. Rigger took note of the utter stoicism in their faces as Poppy ran among them with her own torch. They'd been kidnapped, sold into slavery, witnessed a fight between primal dragons, then dragged into Hell. After all this, having orders shouted at them by a wig-wearing dwarf in the middle of a blizzard must have felt completely normal.

The pygmies ran down the gangplank to the docks. Jetsam flew before them, slashing and stabbing to clear their path. The pygmies reached the shore and ran into the forest. As they vanished into the thick foliage of the slopes, their torches disappeared one by one.

Rigger pressed his lips together, not surprised that the torches had gone out. The torches they carried were nothing but shattered bits of furniture topped with rags dipped in lamp oil. They were never going to burn for more than a few minutes, and unlikely to be hot enough to light the underbrush in a jungle that was already wet with snow.

From above, Sage shouted, "It's working!"

Rigger squinted, trying to see through the windblown veil of white. He couldn't see what Sage was seeing, which was par for the course. Then, suddenly, he spotted it: A line of fire, perhaps fifty feet wide, climbing up the slope, driven by the wind.

As he watched, a second wall of fire appeared a hundred yards further up the mountainside. Then, another, and another.

"They're doing it!" he cried out.

"Hush only got here a little while ago," Sage said. "It's the dry season. There's still a lot of fuel to burn. Let's hope Infidel can hold out long enough for Greatshadow to recover."

INFIDEL GROANED AS she rolled to her back. Hitting the ice hadn't knocked her out, but she almost wished it had. The Immaculate Attire couldn't be cut or marred, and did a pretty good job of keeping her physically intact, but all magic had limits. She'd hit the ice with her left shoulder and now she couldn't move that arm at all. Her ribs on that side felt as if a dozen knives had been jammed into them. She took the shallowest of breaths and wound up coughing violently. When she swallowed afterward, she tasted blood. She closed her eyes. If she could only take a short nap…

"You still alive?" a familiar voice asked.

She forced her eyes open to find a large white bear looming over her.

"Alive and kicking," she murmured.

The polar bear furrowed its brow. "Let's see you kick."

"After a nap," she mumbled.

"You go to sleep out here, you won't be waking up," said the bear, nudging her with a giant paw. "Get on your feet. Walk this off."

Infidel took the deepest breath she could manage and rose into the air, hovering before the bear. "Walking is for chumps, Menagerie."

"So's crash landing," said the bear.

"The last time I fought Hush, she was more solid. Now, she's nothing but wind and snow. How do you fight wind and snow?"

"The same way people have been fighting it since the dawn of time," said Menagerie. "With fire."

The bear grew larger, then larger still, sprouting wings and dark red scales.

"I had no idea you could turn into a dragon," said Infidel.

"New trick. Unfortunately, it's a dragon with mangled wings. You'll forgive me if I take your quip about walking personally."

"Then let's get you airborne!" said Infidel, flying over Menagerie's back. She grabbed hold of a large, spikey scale jutting from the dragon's spine. The power of her glorystone helmet flowed into the dragon's mass. Menagerie spread her wings to their fullest extent, letting the wind catch them.

"I can fly! What did you do?"

"I shared a little of the glorystone's power with you," she said, straddling his neck. "You breathe fire, right?"

In response, the dragon upchucked a gout of flame that shot forward a hundred feet.

Infidel brandished her sword. Its flames grew brighter than before. Through gaps in the snow, she could see hundreds, perhaps thousands of bright flames dancing below her as the docks of Commonground caught flame. The frigid wind took on the scent of smoke.

"The sword's gotten stronger," she said. "The flames below are feeding Greatshadow."

"Yes," said Menagerie. "In this form, I feel… I feel…" The dragon's voice dropped several octaves. "I feel restored."

"Menagerie?" she asked.

"Greatshadow," answered Menagerie. "My spirit dwells in every flickering candle. This dragon has flame coursing through its veins."

Infidel was thrown off as the dragon's body shuddered. The stunted, broken wings spread wide, then wider, becoming wings of fire. Menagerie's draconic body had been as big as a bull, but now the dragon grew to the size of an elephant, then the size of a whale.

"Hush!" Greatshadow roared. "Face me!"

The snow responded by swirling into a shape like a giant eye. As big as Greatshadow was, he was a mote in Hush's gaze.

"How sad!" The words came on the howling winds from every direction. "You once possessed a flame which rivaled the sun. Now, you're nothing but a match in the face of a hurricane."

Infidel flew toward the center of the eye, a black void. She drew to a sudden halt and willed her flaming sword to nova brightness.

The wind laughed at her efforts. Greatshadow opened his jaws wide and unleashed a river of flame. The flames engulfed Infidel, but didn't burn her. The wind howled, a sound like pain, as the snow caught by the flames turned to steam.

"You cannot win!" the wind cried out as Greatshadow's jet of flame died out. "Cold is eternal! Flame is a flickering, fleeting thing, existing only a moment before it's lost to eternity."

"Perhaps," said Greatshadow. "But this moment belongs to me!" He unleashed another torrent of fire.

Infidel raised her hand to keep from being blinded. She flew higher, hoping to make sense of what was going on. She punched through the clouds, emerging in starlight. The serpentine neck of clouds curved beneath her. She could make out where the clouds that formed Hush's head met the neck.

This would hardly be the first foe she'd ever decapitated. She dove toward the neck, slowing as she entered the snow. She hoped she was in the right place.

"Greatshadow!" she called out. "Pour your flame through the sword!"

There was a ferocious roar, and a deafening thunderclap that echoed from the nearby mountain like a scream.

"We hurt her!" Infidel cried.

Suddenly, the clouds drew back, leaving her and Greatshadow in the eye of a tremendous hurricane. Infidel looked at the retreating clouds and shouted, "That's right! Run!"

"I'm not running," the chill winds answered. "I'm letting my new lover deal with this."

Infidel heard a thundering sound beneath her. She looked down in time to see the frozen bay cracking. Suddenly, an enormous mouth, like the world's largest turtle, shot from the ice. Infidel darted upward before its jaws could close on her, but Greatshadow proved less maneuverable. The turtle jaws closed around the dragon, then plunged back beneath the ice floes.

Infidel's sword instantly went dark, or nearly so. Only the faintest wisp of flame remained around her blade.

"Snow may yield to flame," cried the wind, "but no fire ever burned so bright as to survive the sea."

Infidel didn't stick around to argue. She had only seconds before Greatshadow's flames were completely extinguished. Folding her arms to her side, she raced toward the broken surface of the ocean, aiming for a gap in the ice. No longer protected by the warmth of the flaming blade, the icy sea shocked her as she dove within, leaving her dizzy and disoriented.

She had no time for weakness. She shook her head, fighting back to full awareness. Below her, she could make out the enormous skull of Abyss. She willed herself to fly through the water and found it could be done, though she strained against the resistance. She passed by Abyss's giant, dark eye, and saw ice crystals within it. He looked more solid than Hush had, but she suspected there was little point in attacking him directly.

She found the edge of his turtle beak and flew along the rim, hoping the light of her helmet would reveal a gap between the upper and lower jaw. Her heart raced as she found an opening just big enough for her to squeeze through, in a motion that caused her cracked ribs to feel as if they were cutting into her lungs. Within the dragon's mouth, she saw a faintly glowing ember fading in the distance. She flew toward it and found a tiny dragon, no bigger than a mouse, black as a lump of coal save for the dull red glow of its eyes.

She still had no strength in her left hand. Sheathing her sword, she took the tiny dragon and shoved it under her helmet. She let out a gulp of air, hoping to give the small dragon a few more seconds of life.

Infidel spun around, seeking the gap she'd come entered through. Unfortunately, the narrow space between the dragon's tongue and the roof of its mouth looked the same in every direction. Her lungs ached as her pounding heart burned through her remaining air.

THE TERRAIN BROTHER WING flew over in pursuit of the dancing ember stretched in all directions as an unbroken, uniform black. The wind that carried the ember whipped up fine ash, gathering it into drifts. Brother Wing had seen this landscape before, in the nightmares of his human followers, former members of the Church of the Book.

"Hell is much like the humans imagined it," he thought.

"Yes," the ember answered, the voice faint on the breeze. "As it should be, since each human crafts his own Hell during life. The land beneath you, however, is not Hell. At least, not a human Hell."

"Then… where are we?"

"The Convergence," answered Greatshadow, as the ember's light pulsed between a dull orange and a dim red. Its heat seemed to be waning, and the voice became even fainter. "The Convergence is the nexus of elemental realms. The primal dragons meet here. Its neutral ground, and it spares the material world the full impact of our… debates. So much pure elemental energy placed in conflict in the living world would be catastrophic."

"Or apocalyptic," said Brother Wing. "Is it true the dragons intend to destroy the world?"

"The world will endure no matter what we choose to do," said Greatshadow. "The living things of the world, be they ants or oaks, hummingbirds or humans, are far more fragile."

"It's said that Abundant keeps watch over the ants and hummingbirds," said Brother Wing.

"She does," said Greatshadow. "But Hush, Kragg, and Tempest care nothing for life. Hush and Tempest would gladly reshape the world to their tastes."

Brother Wing, though born with an angry heart, still couldn't grasp why any dragon would desire such destruction. "What do these dragons gain from causing so much harm?"

"Each has a goal that to them seems priceless." The ember faded further as Greatshadow spoke, going black for a brief instant before flickering back. "For Hush, the eternal silence of winter's night is the ultimate peace. She fights to make the world into Heaven, though a Heaven only she will love."

"And Tempest?"

"Tempest's goal is, perhaps, more fundamental, and more comprehensible. He seeks to ensure his own survival."

"But… he's dead."

"No. Tempest's body was destroyed. His soul was sent to Hell. As long as a dragon's soul survives, he can make a new body if needed."

"Then what does he fear?"

"The destruction of his soul, of course."

"Is such a thing even possible?"

"It is," said Greatshadow. "As I know full well, to my eternal shame."

The last words were difficult to make out on the breeze as once more the ember went black. Brother Wing strained his eyes, searching for it, before the dim red speck pulsed with heat once more.

"Did you say you feel shame?" asked Brother Wing. "What do you mean?"

"I said the land beneath us is not a human Hell. It is, instead, a Hell of my creation."

Brother Wing considered the hills of ash below him. "Because you burn things? Because you leave behind ash?"

"Because of what I burned. Because of who I burned."

"I don't understand."

"You do understand. You've absorbed enough minds that you have all the information you need. In time, the answer will become plain."

Brother Wing sighed. "Given that I'm dead, I suppose I have ages before me to unravel this mystery. But I'd prefer you speak plainly. What is it you wish me to know?"

"When we elemental dragons emerge in the Convergence, we take the forms of islands."

"What of it?" Brother Wing said, his tone no longer concealing his impatience.

"The island you fly over was once a primal dragon. A dragon I selfishly helped destroy."

FROM THE DECK of the *Circus*, Gale watched as the clouds above pulled away, leaving a circle of calm air over the bay. In the center of the circle flew a fiery dragon larger than the ship, and beside this was a dazzling star, which she guessed to be Infidel's helmet.

Without warning, the ice further out in the bay split apart, as the vast head of Abyss rose to close his jaws around the fire dragon. Abyss splashed back into the sea, sending huge waves toward the *Circus*.

"Hold tight!" Gale shouted.

Seconds later, the waves washed over the deck. Fortunately, her family had a great deal of experience with rough seas. As the water washed away, all were present and accounted for, save Mako, out somewhere among the Wanderers, and Jetsam, who'd gone with the pygmies.

She looked back toward the sky just in time to see the white form of Infidel plunge into the sea.

"Sage," shouted Gale, climbing into the rigging. "Can you see Infidel? What's she doing?"

Sage didn't answer.

"Sage?" Gale asked, climbing faster. She poked her head over the edge of the crow's nest. Sage sat with her hands over her eyes, her spyglass at her feet.

"Daughter, what's wrong," asked Gale.

"Everything," Sage whispered.

"What?" asked Gale.

"It's... it's over," Sage whispered. "I... I've seen more than I can tell you. The whole world..."

"Sage, be strong," said Gale. "Pick up your spyglass. Tell me what's happening to Infidel."

Sage shook her head. "I can't. It's too late. We must return to the Sea of Wine."

Gale scowled. "This isn't like you, Sage. I've never heard you give in to despair."

Sage wiped her cheek. "I'm sorry," she whispered. "I... I don't know why I... it's just... before the left the Sea of Wine. When I placed the final nail into Sorrow's skull, the nail of Rott..." Her voice trailed off.

"What does that have to do with anything?" asked Gale.

"Because I was looking in Sorrow's eyes as I did it and I saw... I saw Rott take hold of her. I gazed into the infinite depth of his eyes and saw..." She swallowed hard. "There will be no victory. There's no hope, in the end. Death and decay were always the fate of the world. We fight in vain."

Gale grabbed the spyglass and shoved it back into her daughter's hand. "Excellent. You can still feel despair. That means you're sane. So do the sane thing, and look into your spyglass."

Sage wiped her cheeks. "I've... I've never felt this lost before."

"I have," said Gale. "When my mother died. When your father died. When Levi betrayed us, then when he gave his life to save us. If I'd allowed myself tears for all I've grieved, I'd weep a new sea."

"I've never seen you cry," said Sage, sniffling.

"You never will," said Gale, standing straight. "I may not escape Rott in the end, but at this moment I'm alive. As long as I'm alive, I'll fight to save my family, my ship, and my world, in that order. Now wipe your damned eyes and look into your glass and tell me what's happening to Infidel!"

As she spoke, the eye of the hurricane filled back in with clouds. Snow and sleet spattered against the mast. Sage wiped her eyes, picked up the glass, and stared at something she plainly did not want to see.

"Infidel's trapped," she whispered. "She's inside Abyss's mouth and… and she's lost. Her aura's fading. She's running out of air."

Gale pressed her lips tightly together, then leapt from the crow's nest.

"Rigger! Catch me!"

"Maybe shout that before you jump next time!" Rigger called back, but not before sending a rope her way. Seconds later, she was on the deck, sprinting toward the anchor.

"Lash me to the anchor," said Gale. "Then throw me into the sea."

"Mother!" Sage shouted as she climbed down the rigging. "Are you trying to teach me some sort of lesson? I had a moment of weakness, but I'm not suicidal!"

"Neither am I," said Gale. "I'm a Wanderer of pure blood. Since the day of my birth I've not set foot on dry land. I've kept the pact. Abyss won't let me drown!"

"Abyss no longer has free will!" said Sage. "He's been enslaved by Hush!"

"And we've spent our lives fighting to free slaves," said Gale.

Brand ran toward them. "Gale, you can't do this!"

Gale took a step toward him, formed a fist, and knocked him cold with a single punch to the jaw. She rubbed her knuckles and said, "Anyone else want to tell me what I can't do?"

Sage turned to Rigger. "Lash her."

"You're both officially out of your minds," he screamed, throwing his hands in the air.

"Do it!" said Sage.

Rigger muttered something beneath his breath, but the ropes on the deck rose to wrap around Gale and the anchor. Then, with tears filling his eyes, he raised his hands. The ropes carried the anchor into the air. He pushed his hands forward. The anchor went over the edge of the *Circus*. He opened his hands, and turned away as his mother splashed into the waves.

As Gale fell toward the waves, she had the faintest, fleeting doubt. Despite this, she took a deep breath an instant before she plunged into the sea. The cold nearly shocked the breath from her, but instinct kept her lips closed tight. She sank swiftly through the water. Silver fish swirled around her like tiny mirrors in which she saw the desperation in her own eyes. The rumble of thunder and the roar of wind faded as she settled into the black mire at the bottom of the bay.

In the silent darkness, she opened her mouth and spoke a prayer of bubbles.

"Abyss," she said with her last breath, "You have my faith."

Her heart beat like a taut drum but her body slackened. With all her will, she fought back the desire to cut free the ropes that held her.

Gale closed her eyes, inhaled deeply to fill her lungs with saltwater, and held tight her faith.

22 - THE DRAGON SEED

INFIDEL STABBED AT the tongue, trying to cause Abyss to open his jaws, to no avail. She was now so turned around, she couldn't begin to guess which direction she should go to find the edge of the mouth. She kicked and crawled, but for all she knew she might have been heading down the beast's gullet. The lack of air fogged her mind. It took all her will to keep her jaws clenched tightly, as her body screamed for her to open her mouth, to draw in a breath, despite the complete absence of air.

"Greatshadow," she thought. "Are you still alive?"

The tiny dragon pressed against her cheek didn't answer. Her sword had no flames here in the icy fluid, but still possessed a faint red shimmer, like steel fresh from a forge. She tried to pour her will into, tried to stoke the heat to a brighter glow, to no avail. Rapidly, the light within the sword grew duller, until, finally, it was black, and she could no longer feel the small, scaly dragon beside her skin.

"ARE YOU SAYING that the island we fly over was once the manifestation of Verdant in this realm?" asked Brother Wing.

"Yes." Greatshadow's voice on the wind was fainter than ever.

"She was the primal dragon of the forest," said Brother Wing, recalling all he could of her history. "The first king Brightmoon worked with the Church of the Book to destroy her."

"Correct," said Greatshadow. "As the dragon of the forest, Verdant fought back against men when they cleared the wilderness to build their cities, or cleared fields to plant their crops. Today, all the plants covered in thorns, all the plants whose leaves drip poison, and all the plants whose pollens choke and sting men's lungs, are remnants of her battle against mankind."

"Even covered in scales, my youthful encounters with blood-tangle vines were most unpleasant," said Brother Wing.

"And yet, the most dangerous plants that endure today are but docile relics compared to the dark and deadly woods men faced. Alone, mankind would never have been able to conquer the forests. Unfortunately for Verdant, mankind possessed a powerful ally."

"You," said Brother Wing.

"Yes," said Greatshadow. "The fires of the natural world are sporadic, the product of lightning strikes and volcanos. My very existence depended on the whims of Kragg and Tempest. The civilization sought by Brightmoon promised to be a more dependable source of sustenance. They stoked their forges to heats that rivaled the fiercest volcanoes. They cooked their food in ovens, warmed their homes with fireplaces, prayed at night by candlelight, and tamed the dark with lanterns."

"Men thrived due to your benevolence."

"Benevolence?" The voice on the wind gave the faintest bitter laugh. "Hunger drove me. Mankind has long tamed beasts by feeding them. Before I understood what had happened, I found myself… domesticated."

"Domesticated? Men fear you like a god!"

"I've known gods," said Greatshadow. "As the Lost Kingdom fell, I tamed them. You think men fear gods? No doubt they do. But never to the degree that gods fear men."

"Why would a god fear a man?"

"Because without men, they are lost," The ember sank lower in the air as Greatshadow spoke. "They need men's fear and men's faith. But men are fickle, and shockingly temporary."

Brother Wing knew this to be true. Though he'd only been alive two decades, this had been more than enough time for him to understand mankind's innate fragility.

"I'd already seen a great civilization fail," said Greatshadow. "The people of the Vanished Kingdom mastered arts and sciences lost to mankind today, and still their world fell to ruin in the span of a few generations. Having seen civilization fail once, I was understandably interested in helping sustain it when I saw it gain a foothold on the Silver Isles."

By now, the ember and Brother Wing wafted along only a few yards above the ground. A shudder ran through Brother Wing as he saw, among the mounds of ash beneath him, the remnants of a long line of stumps fallen on their sides, resembling vast vertebrae. He finally grasped the full implications of what Greatshadow was telling him.

"You killed Verdant here. You killed her soul in the Convergence."

"There are subtleties and nuances that this assertion doesn't capture," said Greatshadow. "But, yes. Ultimately, I'm to blame for her death."

Brother Wing felt a lump form in his throat. "Father, for many years, I hated you for what you did to me as a fledgling. As I grew, I let go of that hate. I admired you. I worshipped you! Now you tell me this?"

"You're free to hate me if you wish. You've every cause."

Brother Wing's mind raced. He now knew why Tempest would welcome the end of mankind. "Tempest fears the destruction of his soul because he's seen another dragon perish! He wages war, but the destruction of man is only a means to an end. His true target is you!"

"Yes," said Greatshadow.

Brother Wing tilted his wings up, bringing his feet forward. He was suddenly very weary. He didn't know what to say to his father. Greatshadow's harm to him had been so personal. Ultimately, he'd been able to forgive a sin that only he had suffered. But how could he judge his father now? The magnitude of his crime was beyond comprehension.

Brother Wing landed, ash rising around him

"You're thoughts are tangled," said the dim ember as it danced before him. "I'm unsure what you think of my news."

Brother Wing didn't know what he thought either, and gave no response.

After a long moment, the voice on the wind asked, "Have you ever wondered why I am called Greatshadow?"

Brother Wing furrowed his brow.

"The other dragon's names reflect their nature. Men might have called me Blaze, perhaps, or Inferno. I chose the name Greatshadow, and made sure others used it."

Brother Wing dismissively waved the words away with his talon. "How can this be of any importance?"

"In seeking to light the world with flame, I cast darkness upon it," said Greatshadow, "Mine was the original sin that forever bred distrust among the primal dragons. Because of my actions, the other dragons have formed their strategies for dealing with the dangers represented by mankind. Abyss made a pact with humans who would be loyal to him. Tempest enslaved the men who dwelled on lands under his control. Hush made sure her realm was barren, devoid of men. My own alliance with mankind has taken a dangerous turn, as the Church of the Book has tried repeatedly to kill me, and not a single fellow dragon has come to my aid."

Brother Wing hung his head low, feeling as if his thoughts were too heavy for his skull. Greatshadow had been right about one thing. Everything his father now confessed could have been deduced by Brother Wing. He'd read the minds of men from all over the world and known their myths. In his years at the Keep of the Inquisition, he'd dined with historians and scholars and philosophers, all of whom brought pieces of the puzzle. How had he failed to see the truth?

"You wanted to believe I was, at heart, more great than shadow." The ember drifted only inches from him now. The voice was barely audible.

"I'd forgiven you for what you'd done to me," said Brother Wing. "I thought I understood you. I could see how integral you were to the world, how men would be nothing more than beasts without you. If you killed some men, and maimed others, your motivations were beyond my comprehension. Now, to learn you were motivated by simple hunger…"

"By gluttony," said Greatshadow. "And vanity, and arrogance. And, in the end, by shame, and by hope."

Brother Wing looked over the black, ruined land. "This is a poor place to speak of hope."

"This is the only place to truly speak of it," said Greatshadow. "And you, my son, are the source of my hope."

"How?"

"Because of your thirst for revenge," said Greatshadow. "Because you brought Infidel to me."

"Ah, Infidel," said Brother Wing. "I haven't seen her in many years, not directly, at least. Some of the men of my settlement have caught sight of a green woman, too tall to be pygmy. From their memories, I've recognized her. I'm pleased she's still alive, though I doubt she would feel the same about me."

"She isn't one to hold grudges," said Greatshadow.

"Are we discussing the same woman?"

"Yes, though she's changed somewhat since you knew her. You studied her thoughts. Tell me: What was the source of her strength?"

"The blood of Verdant, saved by the Church of the Book in a cask at the Grand Cathedral. She stole it, and devoured it all."

"Yes. The blood of a dead dragon, pulsing through the veins of a living woman. Later, you witnessed Nowowon, the old god I'd enslaved, as he split the woman and the dragon into two beings."

"The she-dragon… it was alive," said Brother Wing. "Did Verdant's blood circulating within Infidel somehow revive Verdant's spirit?"

"Perhaps. When I aided Brightmoon and the church in killing Verdant, I couldn't imagine how completely they would tame the wilderness of the Silver Isles. Nothing wild grows there now beyond weeds and a few twisted thickets of stunted pines. With Verdant gone, nothing prevented men from destroying the primeval forest. I decided I would never allow the Isle of Fire to share this fate. I'd like to think that, by preserving one last patch of pristine wilderness, I helped the dragon spirit within Infidel stir to life."

Brother Wing shook his head remorsefully. "Perhaps you did. But, though I didn't personally witness it, I believe that Infidel killed the dragon spirit while she was in the land of death."

"She killed it and devoured a small piece of the beast. But the remainder of the corpse was left practically at my feet. So, I brought it here, twenty years ago, and gave it a proper burial."

"If Verdant is dead and buried, why did you speak to me of hope?" asked Brother Wing, as he followed the drifting ember up the side of a steep slope.

The ember came to a halt at the top of the hill. Brother Wing trudged toward it, his talons slipping in the ash. He shifted his gaze from the ember to a tangled silhouette beneath it. He drew closer and found it was a thorn bush identical to the one on the shore, only alive, unburnt, fresh and green, its leafy branches thrusting into the air like a grasping claw.

"What is this?" asked Brother Wing.

"This is what grew from the corpse," said Greatshadow. "Though it took twenty years, last spring, a single flower blossomed. It was like no flower I'd ever seen before, the head broad and thick, the size of a sunflower, with petals of white, the edges rimmed with emerald. The flower thrived all summer, then withered, leaving behind—"

"A seed," whispered Brother Wing, spotting the pod at the end of a long stem. He raised his claws and gently plucked it. "What would grow from such a seed?"

"A primal dragon, I suspect, given the right soil."

"Where could we find such soil?"

"You are the soil," said Greatshadow.

"Me?" Brother Wing was utterly bewildered.

"Once, you were part of me, my son," said Greatshadow. "But you became a separate being, independent and strong. Long ago, the elemental spirits of the world bonded with dragons. We primal dragons became the lords and protectors of our various domains. But by the time Verdant perished, there were no dragons left to bond once more with the elemental power of the forest."

"There are no dragons now," said Brother Wing. "I've died. This is why I'm here."

"All fires must fade, leaving only embers. Yet, a single ember may set an entire city ablaze. Death doesn't have to be the end. It can be a new beginning. Swallow the seed, my son. Become the dragon of the forest."

"Will I still be myself?" asked Brother Wing. "Or will Verdant's spirit erase my own?"

"We cannot know," said Greatshadow, his voice fainter than ever, the ember so dark as to be nearly invisible in the night. "Never before has a dragon been created this way."

"I paid a great price to become myself," said Brother Wing. "You cannot know the pain I've felt."

"We b-both know I can. I-I know everything about you," said Greatshadow.

"Except for whether or not I'll swallow this seed," said Brother Wing, taking note of the growing weakness in his father's voice.

"You m-must," said Greatshadow. "H-hurry."

"Your voice grows faint, Father. Is something happening to you in the material world?"

Greatshadow didn't answer. The ember give up the last of its heat, and floated down toward the black soil. Brother Wing caught it at the last instant, before it was forever lost among the ash.

"Father?" he asked.

All around him was silence, save for the whisper of ash stirring in the night breeze.

GALE'S BODY FELT light as the silver fish shoaled around her. An unexpected peace settled over her mind. This wasn't the first time she'd been so close to death. Every time before, she'd fought, body and soul, to live on. She had too much to live for to surrender willingly. Her family, first and foremost, but also her values, her cause. From her earliest age, she'd seen how the world had gone wrong and swore she'd give all to set it right. Always before, in the face of death, she'd refused to stop fighting while her tasks were yet undone.

The small silver fish shimmered and danced around her like starlight on midnight waves. All her anger, her outrage, her righteous indignation, meant nothing now. Dying, she at last saw the world as it truly was. Beautiful. Life was beautiful. And not just life, but all things, from the most distant stars to the tiniest grain of sand upon a beach. In this vast, variegated cosmos, all things had their place, all things their perfection. Her life, her struggle, her family and friends and foes, all she'd loved and all she'd hated, all had fit into the universe with wondrous precision.

The fight was over. Her death had found its moment and its place. She didn't go to death as a surrender to a foe. She spread her arms to embrace it as a long lost love.

Before her, the silver fish flickered away, leaving behind a wall of darkness. Only, not a perfect darkness. Within her, some faint remnant of consciousness stirred. Her mind came alive enough to make out that the void before her wasn't a void at all. It was, instead, the iris of an enormous eye, rimed over with ice.

The unblinking eye studied her, dull and distant, uncomprehending.

Without will, without force, simply because the perfection of the moment allowed it, her body tilted toward the frozen eye. Her hands pressed lightly against the ice. She leaned forward, her lips puckered. She kissed the face of the being she'd served her whole life.

The ice shattered as the vast eye blinked.

Strong arms wrapped around her waist. She turned her head over her shoulder to see a dark outline behind her, caught a glimpse of sharp white teeth biting through the ropes that bound her to the anchor.

Now free of the ropes, she shot up through the water, smashing through a thin layer of ice covering the bay above her. Momentum carried her high into the air, rising almost to the level of the deck of the *Circus*.

"Gale!" Brand shouted, though her eyes couldn't find the source of his voice.

"Mako!" shouted Sage.

"Got them!" shouted Rigger.

As Gale reached the apex of her flight from the water, a dozen ropes coiled around her limbs. She coughed violently, forcing water from her lungs, as the ropes carried her to the deck. She held herself on her knees and elbows as she continued to spit up water, taking deep, painful gasps of air between convulsions. From the side of her eye, she saw Mako's sinewy, webbed feet.

"What the hell is going on?" Mako demanded as he charged toward Rigger. He gave his brother a shove. "Were you trying to kill her?"

"It was her idea!" Rigger protested.

Mako drew back his fist, looking ready to floor Rigger. Brand leapt forward and caught Mako's arm. "He's right! Gale wanted this!"

"I can't believe you found her with all the commotion in the bay," said Sage. "Even I can't follow everything that's happening."

Mako frowned. "The fish told me where to find her."

Rigger laughed. "So now you talk to fish?"

"I know it sounds strange but there were voices, voices all around me, telling me where I should swim. Luckily, I wasn't far away."

"It's Abyss," whispered Gale.

"What?" asked Mako.

"It's Abyss." Gale raised her head. She held out her hand, and Brand took it, helping her rise. "It's Abyss. He called you. He kept the pact. He wouldn't let me drown."

"Then Abyss is free?" asked Rigger.

"Look!" shouted Sage.

All around them, the once violent sea settled into an unnatural calm. There was not a single ripple upon the water. The only sound was the creaking, crunching, cracking sound of the ice upon the bay breaking apart.

High overhead, the snow clouds boiled together into the shape of a dragon's head. Hush opened her jaws and bellowed, "You can't defy me!"

The water of the bay suddenly bulged. The *Circus* tilted nearly sideways upon a swell unlike any Gale had encountered in all her years at sea. From the surface of the swell, the head of a giant turtle emerged, rising upward to meet Hush, as a roar of rage echoed across the waters.

INFIDEL CLOSED HER eyes. This wasn't the first fight she'd lost, but it seemed certain to be the last. She'd failed. She didn't fear death, but the knowledge that she'd failed her friends, failed Cinder and Stagger, made her heart feel torn in two.

She had no strength to fight as a woman's hands pulled her helmet from her head. She found herself bewildered to be staring into a mirror. No, not a mirror. The face in front of her was her own, but the face as she'd used to look, before she'd joined the Jawa Fruit tribe and her complexion had become a permanent green. The woman before her was pale as snow. Her lips were tinted blue as she tilted her face toward Infidel, locking their mouths together in a deep kiss. Infidel had resisted the urge to inhale as long as she could. She breathed deeply as the air in her double's lungs flowed into her own.

The new air was hot and stale, but revived her from her torpor. The woman pulled away, and placed Infidel's helmet back onto her head. As the eyeholes slipped back into place, the woman was gone, replaced by the largest octopus Infidel had ever seen. Tentacles wrapped around her wrist. The beast dragged her across the smooth surface of the tongue.

She was relieved to discover Greatshadow's sword was still in her grasp. She wasn't certain how she'd held onto it during the worst of her airless swoon. The sword looked black and lifeless. Greatshadow's spirit was gone from it, and, it seemed, from Menagerie. Infidel wondered if her old friend had any idea which direction would lead them to freedom. The air Menagerie had shared with her wouldn't last long.

The giant tongue they traveled along slammed her into the hard roof of the mouth without warning. Despite herself, the jolt forced precious gulps of air from between her lips. She felt disoriented, feeling her center of gravity shifting rapidly despite her being pinned motionless.

An instant later, she was free, as the mouth yawned opened. She tumbled toward the open gullet beneath her. As she spun, she saw the face of Hush above. The octopus let go of her wrist and changed into a sparrow, darting free of the open jaws. Infidel contemplated the gaping throat she fell toward for only a fraction of a second before laughing. "Right! I can fly!"

Folding her arms to the side, she shot free of the impossibly large jaws of the turtle as they clamped shut onto the throat of the snowy dragon above them. Both dragons let out deafening screeches as the island-sized turtle dragged its aerial foe down toward the sea just outside of the mouth of the bay.

From her vantage point high in the sky, Infidel could see by starlight that the once solid ice of the sea had broken into a field of giant, jagged islands of slush.

"It looks like the Great Sea Above," said the sparrow as it flitted past her right ear.

"Abyss is fighting Hush?" Infidel asked as the two dragons vanished beneath the churning sea.

"Something must have freed him," said Menagerie.

A swell of unfathomable size rose from where the two dragons fell, rolling toward the bay. Infidel watched the lanterns on the Wanderers' ships beneath her sink as the waters of the bay retreated far from the shore, gathering into a monstrous tidal wave. For a few seconds, she could see all the fires that had been lit along the dock. Every shack of every plank seemed to be burning. Along the shore, hundreds, if not thousands of fires roared among the undergrowth.

The wave roared back toward shore and the fires vanished one by one.

"Greatshadow!" she yelled, hoping some trace of his spirit in remained in the sword.

"I don't think he'll answer," said Menagerie. "When I turned into a dragon, I felt his spirit enter me, and—"

"Turn back into a dragon!" said Infidel.

"I can't!" said Menagerie. "While under the water, I felt his spirit struggle, then fade, then vanish. He's gone."

"No," she whispered.

"Yes!" a voice thundered from the sea.

Rising from the waves, her body scaled to such size that it vanished over the horizon, the crystalline form of Hush lifted into the sky. Her head alone seemed as large as the Isle of Fire. Within her icy jaws she carried a turtle, flipped on its back, its limbs struggling in vain.

"You cannot win," her voice cried, speaking to Abyss, though Infidel felt the sting of her words. "All the world is frozen! Your own domain now feeds my strength! Struggle all you wish. In the end, the cold conquers all!"

"I hate braggarts," said Menagerie.

"And I hate bullies," said Infidel. "Hitting her when she was a cloud was like trying to hit, um, a cloud." She cracked her knuckles. "She looks punchable now."

"In the same way a mountain is punchable," said Menagerie. "Hitting her will probably prove just as effective."

"Most mountains don't have brains," said Infidel.

"Most brains aren't surrounded by a skull dozens of yards thick," Menagerie protested.

"When Lord Tower fought Greatshadow, he was like a mouse going up against a man. But, he flew high, and he flew fast, and was able to punch through Greatshadow's scaly hide."

"Tower was surrounded by the armor of faith," said Menagerie. "The impact couldn't hurt him. And, it still wasn't enough to kill Greatshadow, only wound him."

"Maybe Tower didn't fly high enough, or fast enough." She frowned. "Why are you arguing this?"

"Because there's no point in getting yourself killed doing something dumb. As Aurora explained it, Tower could never have won no matter how hard he hit Greatshadow. Only the Jagged Shard could truly kill Greatshadow, since it was formed from the heart of the dragon he'd once loved."

Abyss stopped kicking his limbs. Ice once more spread over his form.

"I can't just watch this," said Infidel. "I have to at least try to break through her skull."

"It's suicide!" said Menagerie. "There has to be another way."

"You can't talk me out of this," she grumbled.

"Don't be so hardheaded!"

"With a glorystone helmet, my head's as hard as it's ever been," she said with a grim smile. She snapped her fingers.

"What?" asked the sparrow.

"The glorystone! Before it was part of Stagger, it was part of Glorious. And Glorious is the dragon who broke Hush's heart. If Greatshadow was vulnerable to the fragments of Hush, then Hush might be vulnerable to a piece of Glorious."

"Hmm," said Menagerie. Infidel had never imagined what a thoughtful expression on a bird might look like before this moment, but recognized it when she saw it. The sparrow said, "Okay. But, your helmet might not be enough. What if you—"

Infidel didn't wait for him to complete his sentence. She folded her arms to her side and zoomed down toward the still churning bay. Amid the chaos, it would have been almost impossible to make out which of the ships bouncing upon the waves was the *Circus,* save for one thing. While other ships sported yellow lanterns and torches, the portholes of the Circus glowed a pure, even white.

Sorrow had made use of Stagger's limbs to craft weapons for Cinder and the Black Swan. But Stagger's torso was still in the hold. She had no time to speak to the Romers as she flashed past them to land with a crouch on the deck. She threw open the door to the stairs leading into the hold. The air beneath was rank, the product of a hundred unwashed slaves having been quartered in the enclosed space. But when she spotted Stagger's torso floating in the middle of the hold, the air suddenly tasted sweet.

Stripped of limbs and head, the torso no longer resembled something that had belonged to a living being. Instead, it was a large gemstone filled with light. She studied the facets within it. Clenching her jaw, she assured herself that Stagger wasn't here anymore, that the stone before her was only a stone.

It was a stone far, far harder than a diamond. Sheathing her sword, she grabbed the torso in both hands. She held it overhead, then leapt. She punched through the thick planks of the deck like a sheet of paper. She heard the shouts of Romers calling her name, but never looked back. She took a deep breath, expanding her chest despite the pain, filling every last crevice of her lungs. Then, wrapping her arms around the torso, she let the power of the glorystone fill her and she flew higher, then higher still. The wind rushing past her ears sounded like every waterfall in the world pouring by her at once. In seconds, she was above the clouds. In another second, the water that still soaked her hair and skin crackled as it turned to ice. She wondered if Hush could see her through this ice. She wondered if the dragon could hear her.

"I let you live once," she whispered. "I'm correcting that mistake."

Infidel could no longer hear air rushing past her ears. She couldn't hear anything at all save for the pounding of her heart. She looked down. She was so high, when she stretched out her hand, she could cover both Hush and the Isle of Fire.

She dove, pushing the glorystone torso before her. The wind threatened to rip it from her grasp, but she clung to it with every last ounce of her strength. The air around her erupted into flame as she flew at unimaginable speed toward a foe she could no longer see beyond the radiance of the glorystone. Hopefully, her aim was good. It helped that her target was a good deal larger than the broad side of a barn.

At this speed, despite her armor, despite her shield of glorystone, Infidel knew she wasn't going to survive the impact. She smiled broadly. She'd always wanted to go out taking down someone a lot bigger than herself.

SAGE CLUNG TO the rigging as the *Circus* tossed and spun in the violent sea. Rigger cursed like the sailor he was as he fought to keep the ship from sinking. Above the chaos of the waves, she spotted a familiar form swimming through the air back to the ship. It was Jetsam!

"Good to see you alive," she shouted.

"For all the good it will do us," he called back. She could see now that he was drenched. "The waves put out all the fires on the slopes. All the pygmies I was leading, the waves caught them. I can't imagine many survived."

Jetsam drifted in the air above Sage and suddenly threw up his hand. A bright light blazed across the sky, as a shooting star bright as a comet tore loose from the heavens and roared toward the towering form of the ice dragon that loomed out at sea.

"What the hell is that?" he shouted.

"That," said Sage, "is our last hope."

The dragon of ice looked up as the comet blazed toward her. She opened her jaws, allowing Abyss to fall. The turtle splashed into the waves. The entire sea looked made of flame as the burning comet spread its light over the waters.

With a crack that sounded as if the world had split in half, the comet smashed into the top of Hush's head. The shockwave that followed knocked Jetsam from the air, bouncing him across the deck. Sage was pushed into the rigging by the blast, but the net of ropes kept her from falling. It felt as if every tooth in her jaw was loosened by the hammer strike of frigid air. She raised her arm just in time to spare her eyes from the darts of ice that suddenly filled the air.

She lowered her arm, her bare hand numb and bleeding. In the distance she watched Hush stumble sideways. Between the ice-dragon's eyes was a crater as large as any she'd ever seen when studying the moon with her spyglass. Hush spread her wings as if to flee from the pain of the blow. With a final shudder, her body fell apart, disintegrating into snow.

"NOOOO!" HUSH HOWLED in pain and outrage. She'd been so close to victory! In all the world, only the Isle of Fire had remained unfrozen. She looked around at the frigid sea surrounding her, seeing shattered ice flows in every direction. It looked very much like the landscape of her final battle, save for the sky, which danced with ghostly green hues. Her physical form had been destroyed. Her spirit had been forced back to the Great Sea Above.

Hush ground her teeth together, mad enough to spit blizzards. Then, she inhaled deeply, fighting to cool her rage. What did it benefit her to feel such hot emotions? She'd killed Greatshadow. She'd felt his spirit go out like a candle in the face of a gale. This victory, at least, had been won.

With the death of her body, Abyss would be free once more. But, what of it? Tempest had enslaved Stagger. The sun would never rise upon the seas again. Let Abyss have his kingdom of darkness. Let Abyss watch what was left of his precious Wanderers perish in the gloom. While his forces withered, the ice ogre priestesses that served her would build her a new body. She'd return to the living world to claim a final, lasting victory.

"I will not rest until every warm thing has perished," Hush vowed to the silent sea surrounding her. To her surprise, the sea answered her.

"This shall come to pass," whispered the waveless sea.

"What?" Hush asked, baffled.

"All life is warmth. All warmth shall perish," the sea answered.

Hush furrowed her brow. The only time she'd ever heard the sea speak, it had been Abyss who spoke through the water. But this wasn't Abyss. The voice possessed a feminine tone.

"Who speaks?" she demanded. "Who dares follow into my sacred domain?"

"I am found in all domains," the voice replied. "Where I swim, nothing is sacred."

At these words, the ice floes spread apart before Hush, revealing open water, black as ink. The water rippled, serpentine, stretching before her like a vast serpent.

"Rott," Hush whispered.

"No more," said the serpent, its black, empty eye sockets rising from the water. Its jaws moved slowly as the serpent said, "Forevermore, I am Sorrow."

"The... the interloper," Hush said, her voice dying in her throat. "The false dragon!"

"The final truth," said Sorrow, as the black cavern of her mouth grew wider. Hush turned, spreading her wings to flee from the dark maw. But as she turned, the horizon grew nearer, then nearer still, until the jaws of the universe closed upon her. With a final choked cry, Hush tumbled into the dark, eternal peace she'd so long desired.

SORROW FELT THE jagged cold claw its way down her mile long gullet. The numb pain that followed was almost welcome. It reminded her of the pain she'd felt as Slate had died in her arms. It reminded her of how her heart had numbed, witnessing her grandmother hung by her own father. It reminded her of the hurt that forever circulated in her mind with the regularity of blood pulsing through her veins. When last she'd possessed Rott's elemental powers over entropy, she'd feared the loss of her humanity. What had been the essence of her humanity? Her pain. Her numbness. Her sorrow. Despite her draconic body, she felt more human than ever.

When she could no longer feel Hush struggling within her, she swished her tail and swam forward, passing with a thought from the chill depths of the Great Sea Above into the tropical warmth of the Convergence. She found it dark and starlit, a welcome change from its former brightness.

"Kragg," she said calmly. "I call you."

"I'm already here," answered a voice like a landslide.

Sorrow swum around lazily to face him, finding an island of barren stone looming above her.

Boulders tumbled down from the heights of the mountain, their scrapes and thuds forming sounds resembling words. "You've come to kill me."

"I won't let you destroy the Isle of Fire."

"What do you care?" asked Kragg. "If I don't push the island into the sea, you will."

"In time," Sorrow confessed, surprised to discover how at peace she was with that notion.

"There's no need for a confrontation between us," said Kragg. "I've watched Hush and Tempest and all the others play their petty games. I've watched as humans grew in power with the aid of my brethren. They all ignored my advice that the very humans who made sacrifices to them would one day bring about their doom. They didn't listen to me. But what if they had? In the long view, nothing at all would change. All will meet an ending. Even you, interloper. Have you ever wondered what will become of you after you've devoured everyone and everything? A whole universe, devoid of stars and stones, empty even of dust and light. All that shall be left are unfathomable silence, and darkness beyond imagination. This will be the kingdom you one day inherit. In the end, your reward will be insufferable loneliness."

"I have claimed this reward," whispered Sorrow. "Do not harm the Isle of Fire."

"Very well. It costs me nothing to ignore that wretched rock," said Kragg. "Now leave me, cursed one."

Sorrow nodded, sinking slowly into the waves.

23 - THE WHEEL

CINDER AND THE BLACK SWAN hovered above the outer dunes of Hell, held aloft by their weapons of glorystone. In her centuries of life, the Black Swan had mastered nearly every weapon imaginable, but ever since she'd worn her iron body she'd found that her own hands—supplemented with razor nails and steel spikes—had been her most reliable defense. So, instead of the sword Sorrow had initially proposed, the Black Swan now wore two spiked gauntlets of glorystone.

Cinder carried a long spear and large shield of glorystone, plus her obsidian knife tucked into her loincloth. Her mother had offered her the Immaculate Attire, insisted upon it in fact, but Cinder had successfully argued that her life of near nudity would make the outfit an unwelcome distraction. In the end, she'd agreed to the shield. She'd trained with one from time to time in sparring matches with her mother, though she suspected that, should she actually see combat, she'd wind up tossing the shield aside to fight in her more practiced style of knife and spear.

The Black Swan motioned for Cinder to follow. Together they flew over black dunes. Cinder found flying to be surprisingly natural. Having lived her life in the trees, she had no fear of heights. She was used to leaping between slender branches hundreds of feet above the forest floor. She had muscle memory to balance herself against the resistance of the wind and the inertia of her body.

They swiftly left the black dunes behind, arriving at a landscape of large boulders. The Black Swan touched down lightly on one of the bigger rocks. Cinder followed, landing in a crouch, the hair rising on the back of her neck. Despite the barren nature of the land, she was certain they were being watched.

The Black Swan took note of her eyes, and said, "The unease you feel is perfectly natural. Your mind is protecting you from the full horrors of this place, but on an unconscious level, you still perceive the truth. For instance, you probably permit yourself to see a field of boulders around us.

"What else is there to see?" asked Cinder.

"The boulders aren't made of stone. They're made of guilt. Underneath every rock, there's a damned soul struggling against the burden. That's why the stones are moving."

Cinder felt the stone beneath them shift ever so slightly. Now that she was aware of the subtle motion, she could see the large boulders all across the plain jerking and falling in tiny movements, rising perhaps an inch for a moment or two before dropping back into place.

The Black Swan opened the map given to her by Sage and held the magnifying glass over it.

"Sage had the advantage of her supernaturally gifted sight in knowing exactly where to look on the map to find her destination," said the Black Swan. "Fortunately, we aren't looking for something as small as an individual soul. Tempest's plans to conquer the living world required him to gather all the blacksmiths in Hell in order to hammer the iron gates into weapons for his army. Given how many of the weapons I've encountered in various timelines, I imagine the dragon's forge is quite a prominent feature upon the landscape."

Cinder took note of the authoritative tone in the Black Swan's oddly musical voice. She couldn't imagine ever projecting such confidence, especially in a place as terrible as this.

"You're who I become?"

"Not in the new timeline we're creating."

"But you? You used to be me?"

The Black Swan nodded.

"You… you seem so commanding," said Cinder. "Like you're used to people listening to you."

The Black Swan nodded. "I'm used to being obeyed."

"I don't care about being obeyed," said Cinder. "I'd just like to talk to other people without them either ignoring me or being afraid to look directly at me."

"You'll have that one day. At least, you will once you leave home."

"My previous trips outside my village haven't gone well," said Cinder.

"No. But, ultimately, that's to your benefit."

Cinder tilted her head, not sure what the Black Swan meant.

"Suppose you wanted to become a master lock picker," said the Black Swan. "How good could you get if every door you encountered was unlocked? In the long term, every success you'll achieve in life is built upon a foundation of failure."

Cinder managed a faint grin. "Then I have the potential to be very successful."

"I'm certain you will be," said the Black Swan. The magnifying glass paused in its travels over the map. She tilted her head closer. "And at this moment, however, failure isn't an option. I've found the forge. And, there's an even bigger building beside it. This has to be Tempest's palace."

Cinder studied the distorted image in the glass. Within the glass, storm clouds churned around a gigantic iron spike that pierced the sky. Lighting danced over the dark surface.

"This is the plan," said the Black Swan. "As long as Stagger is Tempest's slave, the living world has no defense against the undead armies. We have to free him."

"That's really more of a goal than a plan," said Cinder.

"True. So we'll use our mother's plan for anytime she and Stagger wanted to rob a place."

"Smash and grab?"

"Smash and grab," said the Black Swan. "I'm not certain we can beat Tempest alone, but I'm guessing I can get his attention. While he's focused on me, you find Stagger and free him."

"I feel like this plan is missing important details," said Cinder.

"That's because we're missing important details," said the Black Swan. "We don't even know for certain that Stagger's in the palace."

"Then isn't a direct attack a huge gamble?"

The Black Swan shrugged. "I own a casino. I know a thing or two about odds. Our odds of saving the world with this plan are low. Our odds of saving the world by standing here and trying to make a better plan in the complete absence of information are nil. Everything I've done for centuries has been a gamble. You'll never win your bet if you don't spin the wheel."

Cinder gripped her spear and shield tightly as she rose into the air. "Smash and grab it is, then."

The Black Swan opened her backpack, sliding the rolled up map down beside the One True Book, still encased in silver. She slipped the backpack over her shoulders and rose into the air beside Cinder. "Take my hand."

Cinder took it. They rose higher over the field of boulders. The Black Swan leaned forward.

The landscape beneath them began to shift and twist, the terrain blurring as if they were flying at impossible speed, but Cinder's internal sense of balance told her they weren't actually moving. Somehow, the Black Swan's knowledge of the palace's location was causing the landscape to shift. Rain and hail began to pelt against them as the storm clouds above them grew darker. Lightning struck the earth all around them. Still holding Cinder's hand, the Black Swan flew straight up. Visibility within the clouds was non-existent. Everything was black except when lightning arced, then everything was white. The only thing that could be heard over the howling wind was the crashing of thunder. Cinder held the glorystone shield close to protect her from the worst of the lashing sleet, but was still soaked. Her teeth chattered as they finally broke through the worst of the clouds, rising into a starless sky, with the storm clouds churning below like a turbulent sea. A mile or so ahead was the iron spire. They flew closer, and the smooth surface of the tower proved to be ornately decorated with iron sculptures shaped like giants writhing in agony. The lightning continually striking the spire created a net of glowing plasma. As they drew closer, a stream of the bright white energy peeled free and flashed toward them. Fortunately, it struck her glorystone shield and fizzled to nothing. The impact had been nothing worse than the kick of a goat.

Now that they were only a few hundred yards distant, she saw that the mouths of the iron giants were open in permanent screams. Through their open mouths, she could see a pale bluish light flickering within. The interior of the tower looked to be hollow, with the mouths forming windows.

"Ready?" the Black Swan shouted.

"Not even a little bit," Cinder shouted back. "But that's never stopped our mother!"

They released each other's hands and flew toward a gaping mouth. Another tendril of plasma whipped toward them. Cinder took the blunt of the blow, but a thread of the blue light bent around and hit the Black Swan's back with a crackling sound. The Black Swan didn't seem injured, but the leather straps of her backpack were burnt clean through. The Black Swan tried to spin to catch the tumbling pack, but proved too slow. Cinder folded her arms and dived, catching the tumbling parcel between her shield and her hip.

The Black Swan gave her the thumbs up, then darted into the mouth of the nearest giant. Cinder followed. Once inside, she was relieved to find the sleet came to a halt, though the wind through the mouths created a skull-piercing howl. From a distance, the spire had seemed needle thin at its highest point, but now that they were inside it was cavernous, opening onto a base that must easily have been a mile across.

In the center of the vast space sat a dragon, its scales made of iron. The huge beast didn't look up. Had they really taken Tempest by surprise?

The Black Swan evidently thought so. Clenching her fists, she dove straight down the center of the shaft. Tempest still hadn't looked up. Cinder hesitated. Should she attack as well? The plan was for her to find Stagger. But where would she even look?

Far below, the Black Swan was now a tiny figure, her dark body invisible against the iron scales of the dragon, her glowing gauntlets like twin fireflies. Without warning, the fireflies veered sharply away from their straight downward line. An instant later, the Black Swan slammed into the side of the spire, ringing the entire structure like a bell.

In the relative quiet that followed, a low, rolling thunder resolved into a chuckle.

"Fool. You come to me wearing iron skin? I am the lord of lightning. When I run my energies through iron, I become a powerful lodestone. I don't even need to add your soul to my ring to make you a puppet."

The dragon lifted his claw. His talons were adorned with golden rings, capped with diamonds as large as a man. Inside each of the diamonds, Cinder could see a vaguely human shape writhing within the facets. Was this where her father was kept?

The dragon moved his claw toward the Black Swan, who was pinned to the wall. He gave a sudden jerk and the Black Swan shot straight up the shaft, her glowing gauntlets blurring into streaks of light.

Cinder raised her shield. The Black Swan smashed into her. The glorystone absorbed most of the impact, but the blow still knocked the wind out of her.

"Run!" the Black Swan squawked. "I can't control myself!" She kept swinging her arms in viscous punches. Cinder hid behind her shield, but the impact of glorystone against glorystone felt as if her forearm was getting smashed with a large rock. The backpack holding the One True Book slipped on one of the blows. She raised her leg to pin it against the shield once more, but the distraction allowed the Black Swan to punch the top edge of the shield, driving it into her forehead. Dark spot danced against her eyes as she flew backward, up the shaft, trying to get away. The Black Swan pursued with unflagging intensity.

"Flee," the Black Swan begged. "He'll keep hitting you until you fall. You can't defend against me forever!"

She was right. Cinder couldn't defend forever. So she did what her mother would do, and attacked. She threw her shield aside and thrust with her spear, driving the glorystone shaft straight through the center of the Black Swan's breast. The Black Swan swung hard, the gauntlet flashing a hair's width away from Cinder's nose. Clenching her jaw, Cinder channeled the full power of the glorystone spear into forward flight. With a clang, she pinned the Black Swan into the nearest wall, then leapt back, drawing her knife.

She fell the second she no longer held the shaft of glorystone. Fortunately, she'd tossed her shield down, and could twist her body toward it. The second her fingers grasped the edge, she was weightless again. But instead of flying up, she doubled the speed of her dive, aiming for the tumbling backpack several dozen yards below her. She slashed at the leather bag with her knife, slicing it open. The silver clad book broke free of the leather. She slowed her pace to match its fall and cried, in the best imitation of her mother's voice, "Tempest! I've come for you!"

"Then you've come to die!" the dragon roared, opening his jaws as he looked directly up the shaft.

Cinder drew up her legs, curling into a ball completely hidden behind the shield. Something smacked against it and arcs of lighting shot sideways, as sparks traced bright patterns upon the iron walls. She peeked over the edge of the shield. The silver coating the book had been boiled away by the blast of lighting. The One True Book fell freely, its pages flapping in the rushing air.

Tempest's eyes narrowed to focus on the relatively tiny object, perhaps thinking it was a weapon. There was the subtlest change in posture when he realized it was only a book. Then, his eyes grew wide, as if he recognized the tome.

Tempest opened his jaws as if to blast the book, but by now the book had reached his snout. It fell into his gaping mouth and landed on his tongue. A low, guttural whimper burst from his throat for the barest second as light filled the entirety of his body.

Cinder blinked. When she opened her eyes, the dragon was gone. The large book fell to the floor where he'd been standing, landing closed, looking completely unharmed by its fall.

Cinder shot back up the shaft. The Black Swan was still pinned to the wall.

"Are you back in control of your body?" she asked.

The Black Swan nodded. "How did you know he'd blast you with lightning? How'd you know the lighting would melt the silver from the One True Book, but not destroy the book?"

Cinder shrugged. "Sometimes, you have to spin the wheel."

She grabbed the spear and placed her feet against the Black Swan's torso. With a yank, she pulled the shaft free.

"Doesn't that hurt?" she asked, staring through the hole in the Black Swan's chest. She could see through to the wall on the other side.

"I haven't felt physical pain in a long time," said the Black Swan. "Now, let's hope those rings contain who I think they contain."

Cinder followed the Black Swan back down to the floor of the spire. Tempest was gone, but the giant rings he'd worn now lay scattered about. When they landed, the ring hoops were large enough for Cinder to walk through, with the diamonds nearly as big as a pygmy hut.

There were nine rings. The Black Swan studied their facets closely.

"We should be careful," she said. "We can't know what other souls are trapped in these rings. We don't want to free something horrible."

Cinder walked straight to one of the diamonds. The light flickering in its facets seemed to speak to her.

"This one," she said.

"Are you sure?" asked the Black Swan.

Cinder nodded, running her hands along the surface. "The glow feels like sunlight on my face. It feels like I've known it all my life. Stagger's inside."

"Then let's get him outside," said the Black Swan, leaning back, her arm outstretched. She swung her glorystone gauntlet with tremendous force against the corner of one of the planes of the diamond. With a snap, the diamond split into two halves, dropping its prisoner to the floor. It wasn't Stagger.

"Walker!" cried the Black Swan as a pale white pygmy rose on trembling legs.

"I was so sure!" said Cinder.

"You were deceived," said Walker. "I've some experience with lies, as the former lord of Hell."

"Current lord of Hell, you mean," said the Black Swan. "Tempest is dead."

Walker shook his head. "The Divine Author wrote me into the book to rule over the damned. As any author can attest, some characters have a mind of their own. Let Hell rule itself."

"That's all fine and good until someone like Tempest comes along to take over the place," said the Black Swan. "The living world's in ruin thanks to him. None of this would have happened if you'd not abdicated your responsibilities."

"You feel someone should have the task of running Hell in a way that protects the living world?" asked Walker.

"I most certainly do," said the Black Swan.

Walker bent down and placed his hand upon the golden ring he'd been trapped inside. The ring shrunk at his touch, until it was small enough to fit a human hand. Putting his tongue into the corner of his lip, he pressed together the two halves of the diamond, now the size of a quail's egg. The pieces stayed together as he set them back into the ring.

"What are you doing?" asked the Black Swan.

"Preparing a symbol of office, of course. Human kings have crowns. The Voice of the Law had a stave. The ruler of Hell has rings."

"Then, you'll rule Hell once more?"

"No," said Walker. "You will."

"Me?" squeaked the Black Swan.

"Her?" asked Cinder.

"She's got centuries of administrative experience," said Walker. "She's well practiced at managing cutthroats, thieves, and scoundrels." He handed the Black Swan the ring. "You'll be perfect for the job."

The pygmy walked toward another of the diamonds. He placed his hands upon it. "Stagger's in here. I wouldn't recommend opening the rest."

Walker kept walking, moving to the back of the huge diamond. Cinder followed him, wanting to ask more questions about Stagger's presence in the gem. She had no reason to trust Walker, given that he'd just admitted to lying to her.

She kept walking around the gem until she got back to the Black Swan.

"Where'd he go?" she asked.

"Leaving mysteriously is a habit of his," said the Black Swan, looking at the diamond in her palm.

"Can we trust him? Is he trying to trick us into opening the wrong diamond?"

"I don't think so," said the Black Swan. "I haven't had much dealing with Walker personally, but he's always seemed more of a philosopher than a troublemaker." She glanced at the One True Book, still sitting nearby. "Not that philosophers don't cause plenty of trouble."

"Then let's free Father and leave this place," said Cinder. "Mother may still be fighting Hush in Commonground. We should get back and help her if we can."

As she said this, Cinder thrust her knife at the edge of a facet. It bounced off without even scratching the stone.

"Let me help," said the Black Swan. "My mechanical eyes can see the subtle flaws in the crystal." She punched the diamond, which fell in two parts. A tall, thin human with long gray hair toppled out, landing limp on the floor.

"Stagger!" said the Black Swan.

"Is he alive?" Cinder asked, kneeling next to the withered figure. She could see his ribs through his skin. She turned him over. His face was skeletal, his eyes sunken. He moaned softly as she touched his throat to find a pulse. If he had one, it was too faint for her to feel.

"Give him the spear," said the Black Swan.

Cinder placed the spear into Stagger's palm. His fingers closed around it. The bright crystal turned black, then crumbled to sand. The Black Swan grabbed Cinder's shield and placed it into Stagger's grasping fingers. He still hadn't opened his eyes, but his face looked less pale as he drew the light out of the glorystone shield until it too went dark and crumbled away.

By now, the Black Swan had removed her gauntlets. Stagger's eyes flickered open as she brought them near. He raised his hands to touch them. Their energy flowed into him and his chest heaved as he drew a sudden breath.

He sat up, still gaunt, but his eyes now possessed an internal glow. "The sun," he whispered. "Tempest had me bend its light away from the world, then had me guide it toward the distant darkness."

"Can you bring it back?" asked Sorrow.

Stagger nodded. "I've already summoned it. Now that I'm free of the diamond, my soul is once more part of all glorystones, everywhere. I'll grow stronger as the sun draws nearer. Help me rise."

Cinder wrapped Stagger's arm across her shoulder. In the Sea of Wine, after his death, his body had reverted to crystal. Now, he felt like a living man, warm, slick with sweat, his breath stinking as if all his teeth were rotten.

"Where's Infidel?" Stagger asked.

"Back in Commonground. She's gone to save it from Hush."

"Alone?" asked Stagger, the lines on his face deepening.

"With the Romers, and Menagerie."

"Hush will slaughter them," said Stagger. "We have to get back."

"You're too weak to fight," said Cinder.

Stagger placed more of his weight on his own feet, standing straighter. "I'll revive once the rays of the sun reach me. But that won't happen in Hell. We have to get back to the living world."

"Take him to Commonground," said the Black Swan.

"Aren't you coming?" asked Cinder.

"I've got loose ends to tie up," she said.

Cinder nodded, then, feeling no need for further discussion, she and her father stepped forward, climbing through the spectral lands, passing from Hell to the Realm of Roots, and from there to the Bay of Blood. She paused, horrified. Ghosts were everywhere. It was as if all the city had died at once.

"Oh no," she whispered.

Stagger gazed out to sea. "I can see the shadows of the living world from here. I don't see Hush. I don't even feel her spirit."

"She's already killed everyone," said Cinder, unable to hide her despair.

"No," said Stagger. "You can see across the veil. Look around. Beyond all the dead, there are still hundreds of living souls. Thousands, perhaps."

Cinder took a calming breath. It was true. The sight of so many recently dead ghosts had shocked her, but now she could see living souls everywhere. Wanderer ships still bobbed upon the waves, their crews alive. Along the hills, she spotted dozens of pygmies who'd made it to safe heights.

"I sense a glorystone out there, just beyond the mouth of the bay," said Stagger. "It's your mother's helmet. Let's go."

With Stagger's arm still over her shoulder, they walked across the surface of the water. It was over a mile out to the mouth of the bay, and the terrain was ever shifting. The waters of the bay were full of corpses, broken ships, and uprooted trees, floating among huge chunks of ice. She saw the spirits of the dead wandering along the surface of the water, and others just beneath it. But she also saw strange shadows crawling up onto the ice floes, dark forms neither living nor dead.

"It's Tempest's army of the damned," said Stagger. "Just because he's gone doesn't mean they'll be eager to return to Hell. No living thing is safe until we drive them back."

"Maybe mother will have a plan," said Cinder.

"Smash and grab won't improve this situation," said Stagger.

They kept walking, leaving the bay. The glow of the glorystone became apparent, rising and falling on the deck of a ship that bobbed on the rolling sea.

"It's the *Circus*," said Stagger.

They quickened their pace. Stagger didn't say a word as they neared the ship. His face looked grim. They walked up through the air to the deck of the ship, then stepped through into the living world.

"Stagger!" a voice called out as they appeared from thin air.

Stagger turned to see a dwarf running toward him, his long blond hair hanging about his face in tangled ropes. "Hello, Bigsby."

The dwarf threw his arms around Stagger's thighs and gave him a big hug. "You're alive again!"

"Still technically dead," said Stagger. "But I appreciate the sentiment."

Cinder turned from the dwarf to find all the other Romers standing in a circle. They looked back toward her with sad eyes. The oldest girl, Sage, cradled the glorystone helmet against her chest.

Bigsby broke his grip on Stagger's legs and said, softly, "They say you see through every glorystone. So you know. You know. I'm sorry."

Stagger nodded.

Cinder marched toward the circle of Romers. "Sorry for what? What's happened?"

One by one, the Romers stepped aside. In the center of their circle, her arms folded neatly across her chest, was the still form of her mother on her back, looking as if she were sleeping.

But she wasn't sleeping.

21 - THE DRAGON FORGE

THE BLACK SWAN WATCHED Stagger and Cinder walk out of Hell. For a moment, she contemplated calling out to Cinder, but fought the impulse. She had a deep sense of dissatisfaction from her encounter with her younger self. This version of Cinder would forge her own path. She would never become the Black Swan. Still, the Black Swan couldn't help but feel that there was something she should have said, some bit of advice or wisdom to pass on, that might have made Cinder's life easier moving forward. She knew so much more now than she knew then, but, were there any lessons that could be learned without the pain of experience? Would her wisest advice be mere platitudes, seeds sowed upon the wind that would find no purchase in the soil of a soul lacking her experience?

As she thought of her own experiences, she looked down at the ring still in her palm. Queen of Hell. She wasn't exactly sure what she was going to do with her days now that they'd halted the dragon apocalypse, but the notion of spending eternity in this place held little appeal.

The Black Swan turned away from the point in space where Cinder had vanished, shaking off her reverie. Stagger could deal with Hush, if Hush was still a problem. She had a bigger challenge. How could she hide the One True Book someplace it would never, ever be found?

She froze as she studied the iron floor where the book had fallen. The space where it had sat seconds before was now bare. The book was gone.

She ground her iron teeth, suddenly knowing the one thing she should have told Cinder, though the girl would learn it on her own soon enough: *Nothing is ever easy.*

"NO," CINDER WHISPERED, dropping to her knees. "She can't be dead. She can't be!"

Her mother's helmet had been removed, but she still wore the Immaculate Attire. The mystical armor looked pristine, and her mother's body showed no hint of injury. Cinder lowered her ear to her mother's lips, listening closely for the faintest breath.

Gale knelt beside her and put a hand on her shoulder.

"I'm sorry," she said.

"How did it happen?" asked Stagger, taking the glorystone helmet from Sage, who held it toward him.

"She flew at full speed into Hush," said Sage. "The blow killed them both. I saw Hush's spirit spiral up toward the stars, drawn to the Great Sea Above."

"Did you see Infidel's spirit?" asked Stagger.

Sage nodded. "She wandered off across the water, back toward the island."

Cinder rose. "I have to find her!" She ran toward the rail of the ship and leapt, letting her body shift from the living world into the Bay of Blood. She landed on the water and began to run.

The spiritual realm was still crowded with the spirits of the recently dead. She ran among them, looking at the lost and forlorn faces, hoping against hope she might find her mother. It proved futile. It was like hunting for a single leaf in the canopy of the jungle.

She gazed up the steep, forested slope of the volcano. Her eyes widened as she saw a light, flickering like a torch, climbing the slope, disappearing and reappearing as it moved among the trees. Cinder hadn't noticed the flaming sword with her mother's body. Could her mother's spirit still be carrying the blade?

She set off in pursuit of the light, running with all the speed she could muster.

"WE'VE GOT A PROBLEM," said Mako, looking over the waves, still thick with large ice floes.

"Sage, get into the crow's nest," said Gail. "Rigger, to the wheel. We need to put some distance between us and the larger ice blocks before they stave us in."

"That's not the problem I was referring to," said Mako, pointing toward the waves. "The undead. Just because Hush is gone doesn't mean Tempest's army has given up. They've apparently got our scent. There are hundreds of them converging on the ship, swimming beneath the surface."

"I didn't know the undead could swim," said Bigsby.

"But you find it plausible that they walk around and get into swordfights?" asked Jetsam.

"I'll take care of the undead," said Stagger. "At least, I will in about an hour. I'm already guiding the sun back into its proper path. Once the sun comes up, the damned will retreat into the shadows of Hell.""

"Then we'd better get ready to fight," said Sage, scanning the waters with her spyglass. "It's not hundreds that have our scent. It's more like thousands. It's going to be a very long hour."

"It would make more sense not to fight," said Gale. "I'll guide us back to the Sea of Wine."

"We don't need to be afraid of waterlogged corpses," said Jetsam. "I can fight an army of them with one hand behind my back."

"We've nothing to gain by the fight," said Gale. "We're leaving."

"A wise strategy," said Stagger. He knelt over Infidel's body. "Leave once I've cleared the ship."

He studied the glorystone helmet in his grasp. In Hell, he'd drawn power from the glorystones to revive his soul. Now, he absorbed the physical structure of the stone, changing his body back into its crystalline state. He placed his hands under Infidel's shoulder and beneath her knees and lifted her, his eyes fixed on her pale, lifeless face. He pressed his lips tightly together. He wasn't in the habit of breathing anymore, but, without thinking, he took a long, deep breath and exhaled slowly.

Stagger rose into the air, looked back at Gale Romer and said, "When the sun rises once more on the horizon of the Sea of Wine, it will be safe to return."

"Not that there's much to return to," Rigger grumbled.

"There's everything to return to," said Gale, looking over the waves toward the ruins of Commonground.

"We must be looking at different things," said Rigger. "Sure, we've beaten Hush and Tempest. But the whole dragon apocalypse thing that the Black Swan was trying to stop? Open your eyes. It's already happened."

"I still see ships floating in the bay," said Gale. "The jungles of the high slopes are still full of life. Abyss is free, and I've faith he'll restore the oceans to their former health. This isn't the end of the world, Rigger. It's a fresh start. It's a chance to build things even better than they were before."

"It's always darkest before the dawn," said Bigsby.

"I'm working on that," said Stagger. "Goodbye, old friend."

Bigsby returned the parting words as Stagger walked across the air toward the Isle of Fire. In the trees along the shoreline, he spotted a large, tattered sail tangled among the limbs. The canvas practically glowed in the starlight. Still holding Infidel in his arms, he willed a fist-sized chunk of glorystone to break free from the small of his back. The smaller stone reconfigured into a hand, floating independently. With this free hand, he tugged the canvas loose. It followed him as he walked on.

Twenty years ago, when he'd first become part of the sun, the idea of modifying his body in such an unnatural fashion would have caused him a great deal of unease. He'd spent most of his living years thinking of his body as his true self. Being human seemed like the most wonderful thing imaginable. Twenty years later, he accepted how limited his imagination had been.

Stagger found himself lost in memories as he walked along the shore, his eyes flickering over the dark jungle. Directly up the slope, he recalled, was one of the larger towns of the Vanished Kingdom, draped beneath vines. He and Infidel had spent weeks there, going at the ruins with picks and shovels, drenched in sweat in the tropical heat. In the end, all they'd gotten from their hard work had been a handful of jade beads and a clay tile glazed in bright purple and yellow, a fragment from some larger piece of art they'd never located.

In the evenings, they'd wash off in a nearby stream, then sit around a campfire eating mangoes. One evening they'd found a turtle and cooked it in its own shell. He remembered how bland and stringy the meat had been, and the off-putting, damp-boot smell it gave off while it cooked.

At night, they'd slept fitfully, plagued by mosquitoes and ants. The bugs couldn't hurt Infidel, of course, but she still swat them away when they'd crawl on her lips or ears.

Such misery. But they'd been miserable together. Such paradise.

Stagger crossed the very stream he'd just been thinking of. He followed it up the slope until he reached a small pool. He lowered Infidel's body onto the shore. Slowly, he undressed her. Given his own past as a tomb raider, he knew if he buried her in the Immaculate Attire, it would only be an invitation for some treasure hunter to disturb her final rest.

Once she was disrobed, he lowered her into the water and gently washed her, echoing the movements she'd gone through twenty years before as she readied his corpse for burial. Once he was done, he placed her body in the center of the sail and wrapped her carefully within the makeshift shroud. He lifted her once more and proceeded on his journey.

Minutes later, he reached the high, sandy bluff that had been his destination. He stepped down onto the turf. Looking at the scraggly grass that covered the area, there was no hint that, a few feet below the surface, his bones slumbered in their final rest.

He held Infidel tightly to his chest as more chunks of his body pulled free, taking on the shapes of picks and spades. He turned away to look at the starlit ocean as the grave was dug. The sky above was utterly dark, the stars crisp and vivid. She'd picked a wonderful place to bury him.

When the hole was finished, he whispered, "Sleep well, my love."

He pressed his crystalline lips against the shroud, feeling her cold lips beneath. After this final kiss, he lowered her gently into the grave. He threw in a handful of sandy soil, then turned away to allow his various tool selves to complete the burial.

He would never see her body again.

But her soul? As Gale had said, this wasn't an end, but a beginning.

Stagger crossed his arms behind his back, waiting patiently as the sky lightened. The orb of the sun rose above the horizon, turning the waves into gleaming jewels. He spread his arms to embrace the morning light.

CINDER DRIPPED SWEAT as she climbed along the air to reach the volcano's rim. Though she didn't need to actually touch ground to move in the spiritual realm, rising up the entire length of the volcano had still been an effort. Despite her exhaustion, she couldn't stop to rest. She'd seen her mother's spirit cross the rim of the caldera only a moment before, moving at a slow but steady pace, like a sleepwalker.

As Cinder reached the rim, a blast of hot wind set her hair fluttering. Below her, the surface of the caldera was paved with dark stone, laced with cracks showing red. Perhaps a quarter mile away, her mother walked steadily along the black stones, showing no sign of discomfort from the blistering heat. Cinder ran toward her, panting loudly, her heart pounding in her ears.

When she was a few dozen yards away, she cried out, "Mother!"

Infidel looked over her shoulder. Her spiritual flesh was white as ivory, lacking the green hue of the pygmy dyes that that stained her physical form. The flickering flames of the burning sword highlighted her face and hair in shades of yellow and orange.

"Cinder," Infidel said, with a gentle smile. "I'd hoped to see you before I left."

"Where are you going?" asked Cinder.

Infidel stopped, looking puzzled. "You know I'm dead, right?"

Cinder caught up to her mother, placing her hands on her knees as she bent over, gasping for breath. "I know. But… this isn't the Realm of Roots. You don't belong in this place."

"No," said Infidel. She raised the flaming sword. "This does. When I woke up dead, the sword was in my grasp, aflame once more. Greatshadow must be back. I'm returning the blade to its rightful owner. Did you save Stagger?"

Cinder nodded. "He's safe. But, I wish I had been in Commonground with you. Maybe you—"

"Maybe we'd both be dead," said Infidel. "Things worked out for the best."

"No!" said Cinder. "Having you dead isn't for the best. There has to be a way to save you."

"It's too late for that," said Infidel. "I'm at peace with what has happened. I had a good run. I died like I lived, fighting something bigger than myself. Leaving you is my only regret."

Cinder shook her head. "It's never too late. The Black Swan... she said she could run back through time. That means I could go back a few hours, I could—"

Infidel placed the tip of the sword into a crack on the stone, then walked toward Cinder. Infidel placed her arms around Cinder, drawing her tightly against her. Cinder returned the hug, clinging to her mother fiercely, determined never to let her go.

But her mother finally broke the embrace, pushing away, but keeping her hands on Cinder's shoulders. They gazed into each other's eyes, and Infidel said, firmly, "The only way forward is forward."

"But—"

"Listen to me," said Infidel. "There never has been, and never will be, any event too tragic to endure, no matter what the scale. You've grown up in the ruins of the Vanished Kingdom. Would your life have been better if you could somehow go back and keep that empire from falling apart?"

"No," said Cinder, sniffling. "But I'm not talking about saving the world. I'm talking about saving *you*. You are my world."

"Oh, honey," said Infidel. "You'll build a new world. I've started over again and again. I used to be a princess. I put an end to that and became an outcast for a time, wearing my loneliness and anger like a suit of armor to scare away anyone who even thought of messing with me. Then I came to Commonground, met Stagger, and my life changed again, to something weirder and wilder than I'd ever imagined. Then Stagger died, and I thought I had nothing to live for, and I've never been more wrong. You were still in my future. Life is like a raging river. It sweeps you along, and sometimes it will slam you into rocks. But, if you stay afloat, it always brings you back to calm waters. The only way out is forward. Promise me you won't make the same mistakes the Black Swan made."

Cinder wiped tears from her cheeks. "I promise," she whispered. "Will I... will I see you again, in the Realm of Roots?"

"I don't think so," said Infidel. "When Stagger first died, he told me he felt his spirit disperse, spreading out into the infinite, not so much going anywhere as going everywhere. Despite all the supernatural things I've witnessed, I'm not really a believer in one afterlife. I've seen the Sea of Wine, the Great Sea Above, the Bay of Blood... I know there's more than one truth. Ultimately, I don't really believe any of them are the final truth. There's something bigger than the afterlife, something stranger, maybe, or something grander. I suppose, once I return this sword to Greatshadow, I'll finally learn what's really out there."

"You'll never return the sword to Greatshadow," said a low, rumbling voice.

Infidel spun around, her hand outstretched to snatch up the sword, but the sword was gone, vanished into a widening crack in the volcanic rock. Flames licked up from the crack. Cinder grabbed her mother and pulled her back, dragging her into the air, putting distance between them and the growing flames.

"Wait," Infidel cried out. "It's okay. He's not going to harm us."

Cinder wasn't sure what "he" her mother was referring to, until she saw the flames condensing, coalescing into a form that was almost solid, spreading wings of orange flame as it took the shape of a dragon.

"You're not Greatshadow," said Infidel, her eyes narrowing. "Yet, I still feel as if I know you."

"You know me well," said the dragon. "First as Relic, then as Brokenwing."

"Where's your father?" asked Infidel.

"Gone," said the dragon. "He used the last of his spiritual power to lead me to a place where I could assume the mantle of a new primal dragon. I was to be the new spirit of the forest."

"Then shouldn't you be green and leafy?" asked Infidel.

The dragon shook his head. "My father's spirit was distilled into a single remaining ember. I watched the ember fade, as my father's spirit perished. I breathed the ember into my own body, where the flames inherent in my blood flowed into it, opening the gateway for his elemental power to flow into me. I'm the rightful heir to Greatshadow, the new primal dragon of flame. My father had an uneasy relationship with mankind. He helped build cities, and he helped devour them. I've learned from his mistakes. I intend to be a benevolent partner of mankind, helping humanity reach new heights. I shall be known from this day forward as Forge."

"It's important to have goals," said Infidel. "Speaking of which, if you've got the sword back, I suppose my time here is done."

"Let's hope not," said Forge. "You see, before he died, my father led me to this." He held out a claw. Unlike the rest of his body flame, the claw looked to be made of scaly flesh. He opened his talons, palm up, to reveal a bright green ovoid the size of an almond.

"A nut?" asked Infidel.

"A seed," said Forge. "The distilled essence of Verdant."

"Verdant's been dead a long time," said Infidel.

"Until you blended her blood with yours. Your life gave her soul a renewed spark. You were the incubator. Now, you can be the vessel."

"The vessel?"

"Take the seed," said Forge. "Devour it. Become the new dragon of the forest."

"I've lived long enough in the jungle to know that the forests don't really need a dragon to survive."

"Perhaps. But beyond this island, the world has been scoured by ice. Restoring the world to health will not be an easy task. The forests have a better chance to thrive once more if there's guiding will behind them."

"Will you still be you if you eat the seed?" Cinder asked her mother. "Or will Verdant's personality overpower yours?"

Infidel shrugged. "I stayed in control for a long time with dragon blood in my veins. I'm not easy to overpower."

"Then you'll do it?" asked Forge. "You'll devour the seed?"

Infidel stretched out her hand, her fingers lingering for a few seconds above the green pod. She grinned. "The only way forward is forward."

GALE SAT ON the forecastle, wrapped in a blanket, sipping the warm drink laced with rum Brand had gotten for her. Her dive into the icy water had taken more out of her than she cared to admit. Ten years ago, perhaps even five, she could have shrugged off her chill quickly enough. Now, an hour later, her teeth still chattered.

Brand had his arm draped around her as they watched the horizon of the Sea of Wine grow steadily brighter. They sat in silence. What was there to say after a day like the one they'd witnessed? But it was more than that. Yes, she'd softened to Brand, felt her former attraction to him rekindle with his derring-do and confidence in recent days. But, long term? She was still old enough to be his mother. Would her infatuation with him survive in ten years? In twenty? She'd once regarded him as little more than an amusing toy. She now knew that behind his charm and good looks he possessed intellect, wisdom, and courage. Would these traits prove enduring in the trying days of rebuilding before them?

Brand finally spoke, as the horizon turned a fiery red. "Every other time I've been to the Sea of Wine, I thought I was looking at a sunset," he said. "From now on, we'll know we're looking at a sunrise."

"An eternal dawn," said Gale, feeling the optimism of those words draw her out of her funk. She turned and kissed him on the cheek. "A pity we can't stay to watch it." She stood, tossing aside her blanket. "Rigger! Get to the wheel! Time to get back to Commonground."

"Not yet," Sage called out. From the crow's nest, she pointed north. Gale followed her gaze, until she spotted black gulls flitting in the distance. "It's Sorrow. She's returned to the Sea of Wine."

"Is she still merged with Rott?" asked Mako, climbing into the rigging to get a better view.

"Yes," said Sage. "It's her aura within the dragon."

"What's she waiting for?" asked Mako. "Why doesn't she change back into her human form?"

"Do we even know if she knows how?" asked Brand.

"She only has to remove the nail," said Sage.

"If she became human now, she'd drown in the Sea of Wine," said Gale. She summoned a southern wind, and said, "Set the sails. We're going to her side."

Seconds later, the sails caught the wind and they smashed through the waves, at speeds that left the hull of the *Circus* groaning. The ropes creaked as the ship climbed up swells and slid down them once more. The birds in the distance grew ever closer.

Gale stilled the winds and the sails fluttered slack as they pulled alongside the black, serpentine spine that crested the waves. The cacophony of sea birds whirling overhead was deafening.

"Sorrow!" Mako shouted, his voice booming from his oversized jaws. "Sorrow, we're here. You can change back!"

The dragon drifted silently, with no sign of awareness.

"Sorrow!" Mako bellowed again. This time, he was joined in the riggings by Jetsam, who added, "Wake up, sleepy head!"

Again, silence was the only response.

Now Cinnamon and Poppy came into the rigging beside Mako and Jetsam. They all began to call her name, and were soon joined at the rail by Brand and Bigsby. Gail didn't follow them to the rail. She suspected she knew more about Sorrow's heart than anyone else on board. She alone had lost beloved partners to death. Gale knew full well the heavy burden of grief, of how it could easily pull a soul down with its weight. She'd been fortunate, as her family had always been at her side to share her burden. No matter how depressed Gale had felt waking in bed all alone, sensing the vacancy on the pillow beside her, she'd always been pulled from beneath the covers by the needs of her children.

From what she knew of Sorrow, now that Slate was gone there was no one left to pull her back from the depths of grief. Before she loved Slate, Sorrow's only purpose in life had been revenge against the father and his church. With her father dead and the church destroyed, was there anything left for her?

"No," a woman's voice whispered in Gale's mind. "There's nothing left."

"Did anyone else hear that?" asked Jetsam, craning his neck from side to side. "It sounded like Sorrow, but I can't tell where her voice was coming from."

"We all heard it, I'm guessing," said Sage. "The voice came from inside us. Dragons are telepathic."

"So you can hear us," said Brand. By now, the ship had pulled even with Rott's milky, unblinking eye. He gazed into the moonlike orb and said, "Hush and Tempest have been beaten. Stagger's free. You can let go of Rott's power now."

"I am where I am meant to be," the voiceless voice replied. "I am what I always was. Death. Destruction. *Sorrow*."

"Sorrow, we've always talked straight with each other," said Brand. "You've never sugarcoated a single thing you've said to me, and I've respected you enough to return that bluntness. Listen to me. I know you're hurting. We all share your grief that Slate is gone. But you can't surrender to despair. You're stronger than that."

"Despair always wins," the voice whispered. "In the end, sorrow claims all."

For the first time, the corpse-like body of Rott showed signs of movement as its head submerged into the water. Its back humped up for a moment, then, with a flick of its tail, it dove beneath the waves.

"No!" cried Mako, crouching, preparing to leap in to give chase.

"What are you doing?" Jetsam cried, grabbing his brother's arm. "You can't dive in the wine! Swallow a single drop and you'll go mad!"

Gale shook her head. "Sorrow's made her choice. We have to respect it."

"I respectfully disagree," Sage cried out, sliding down the ropes to the deck. "Sorrow gave me her word. We had a verbal contract! You don't break a contract with a Wanderer lightly."

"I'm not sure convening a sea court back in Commonground is going to help resolve this," said Brand.

Sage didn't answer, instead darting down the stairs into the ship's hold. Gale moved to the rail, watching the oily slick left by Rott's passing as it spread across the burgundy waves. She could still see Rott's form swimming beneath the surface, diving ever deeper.

Sage ran back up the steps to the deck. She carried a wine bottle with its bottom broken off. "Catch!" she yelled, tossing the bottle to Mako.

Mako snatched the bottle from the air and shoved it between his teeth. Then he tore free of Jetsam's grasp, leapt out from the ship, and plummeted into the waves.

"Mako!" Gale cried, stunned by her son's recklessness. She whirled to face Sage. "What did you do?"

"When Sorrow returned to the *Circus* in Hell, she brought back the bottomless bottle. If Mako keeps it in his mouth, he can fill himself with fresh water instead of letting any of the wine through his lips!"

"Awesome," said Jetsam. "I should have thought of that."

"No one should have thought of this!" Gale said. "Sorrow's made her own choice. There's no reason Mako should risk his life to save someone who doesn't want to be saved."

"Mako can make his own choices, too," said Sage, putting her hands on her hips. "And Sorrow doesn't have a choice here. Verbal contract, remember?"

"You're as crazy as Mako," Gale said, tossing her hands in the air. "I've been in the Sea of Wine. It nearly broke me. Mako's never going to—"

She stopped, as everyone's eyes turned toward the wine, which began to churn.

SORROW SWISHED HER tail once more, her limbs and wings pulled tightly against her body as she dove into the unending darkness. She felt no remorse, no sense of loss or surrender. In the silent darkness of the endless sea, she'd sleep without dreams in the cradle of oblivion.

Before her mind could settle into permanent peace, however, she felt the smallest tickle at the far tip of her tail. In scale, it was similar to when she'd worn a human shell and had an ant crawl across her toe. Reflexively, she twitched to shake off the annoyance. To her consternation, the insect that touched her held on and began to crawl along the length of her tail.

With her draconic senses, she didn't need to turn her neck to see that it was Mako who clawed his way along her scales. All dragons could hear the thoughts of others, and Mako's mind was like a shout. She could hear his fears, couldn't ignore his compassion, and recoiled at his anger. Anger? More like rage. What right did he have to rage against her? Who was he to feel betrayed or wronged by her choices?

She writhed, contorting her body violently, and still Mako held on. She fixed her jaws. Very well. He mattered nothing. He could ride her all the way into eternity for all she cared. Let him cling to her until hunger claimed him, let his body fail, then fall, then rot. Sooner or later, her victory would be complete.

She swallowed hard, staring into the unfathomable depths below. Once before, she'd stared into this void. As before, she found that something stared back, something beyond thought, a force beyond emotion, a primal thing, the primal truth, in fact. Before her lay nothing at all, the ultimate fate of all men, of all animals, all plants, the final sum of stones and stars, the complete value of all love, all hate, all fear, all hope. Everything was nothing. The void devoured all.

She was that void. It was her fate to devour Mako. Why delay? With but a thought, she could direct her nihilistic energies through the scales he clung to, could reduce him to gelatinous muck dissolving within the wine.

Sorrow closed her eyes. A single thought and she'd be free. A single thought. He climbed further, advancing along her spine. His persistence galled her. The courage that radiated from him, his refusal to respect her choice, his defiance in the face of complete defeat, jabbed into her conscience like needles. Or nails.

Sorrow recognized this courage. She knew this defiant rage. It had been part of her for most of her life, as constant as her heartbeat, as essential as breath.

Perhaps, at heart, she was the avatar of something primal. But at her core, stripped of everything else, her central truth bore no resemblance to the silent acceptance of oblivion and surrender.

The thing that stared at her from the void below knew this as well. In silence it judged her, then cast her out.

"I SEE THEM!" Poppy and Cinnamon cried out in unison, pointing toward the waves. Gale ran back to the rail. Ten feet down she saw a dark shape, much smaller than Rott. It rose swiftly through the waves, changing form, looking something like a misshapen octopus with limbs pointing in all directions. With a splash, Mako broke the surface of the wine. A second later the bald, nail-studded head of Sorrow emerged from the waves beside him, clinging to his back. She had a bloody, festering wound where the nail of Rott had once pierced her scalp, but the nail was gone.

Ropes snaked down from the deck and plucked Mako and Sorrow from the drink, setting them gently onto the deck. Sorrow was nude and Gale moved swiftly to her side to drape her blanket over her shoulders.

"You came back!" Sage cried.

"I thought for sure we'd lost you," Brand said, walking to Sorrow's side. "Did Mako pull out the nail?"

Sorrow shook her head. "I… I let go of the power. Or perhaps the power let go of me."

"What changed your mind?" asked Brand.

"This idiot," Sorrow grumbled, nodding toward Mako. "He would have killed himself trying to pull a dragon back to the surface. What a stubborn, hard-headed…" Her voice caught in her throat. She took a shuddering breath and said, softly, "Thank you."

"You'd have done the same for any of us," said Mako.

Sorrow nodded, pulling the blanket tightly around her as she looked toward the other Romers. "He's right, you know. I'm sorry to give you such a scare. But, if there's one thing I learned just now, with Mako ready to swim all the way to damnation to save me, it's that all of you are precious to me. You're the family I never had."

As she spoke, Cinnamon and Poppy ran up to hug her, joined swiftly by Sage and Gale. Mako came up behind his mother and sister and embraced them, and Jetsam drifted down to place his arms across the shoulders of his younger siblings.

"I guess we have a happy ending after all," said Brand, motioning toward Rigger. He spread his arms wide as he approached the others. "Care to join the group hug?"

Rigger smirked and rolled his eyes. "I'm not really the hugging type."

But a rope wrapped around the gathered family all the same.

25 - THE FIRST CHAPTER

THE BLACK SWAN EMERGED from the icy ocean, walking through waves of slush up the dark beach toward the Keep of the Inquisition. Like the last time she made this journey, she found Equity Tremblepoint standing on a high rock amid the waves, waving her arms in wild gesticulations, shouting at the top of her lungs, though her words were washed away by the wind.

The Black Swan marched without pause toward the door of the keep. With her iron fist, she banged on the heavy oak. It proved no surprise at all when Vigor opened the door and leered at her iron body, his eyes lingering at her iron breasts.

"I have it on good authority the world will end in a matter of minutes," said Vigor. "What if I told you I could make those minutes the best of your life?"

"I'm a skeleton sheathed in iron," said the Black Swan, somewhat exasperated. "I can't even imagine what you think you might possibly do that would cause me pleasure."

"If you have imagination, nothing stands in our way," said Vigor. "All the physical sensations we associate with the body are, in fact, products of the mind. It's never too late to learn new tricks."

"I suppose it isn't," said the Black Swan, extending her hand to brush her fingers along the gray hair of his cheek. "Like this trick, for instance." With a snick, the poison needles beneath her fingernails sprung into his flesh. His eyes grew wide, then turned glassy. He fell to the floor, limp, foam flecking on his lips.

The Black Swan stepped over Vigor, his limbs still twitching. "Sorry. I'm on a deadline, and didn't have time to deal with you if you'd decided to turn into a dragon to keep me from reaching Zetetic."

She wasn't sure if he could hear her. In theory, the poison she'd given him wasn't lethal, but she'd never tested the dosage on a man his age. No matter. If she didn't reach Zetetic in time, Vigor and everyone else would be dead in a few minutes anyway. Worse than dead. Erased.

Her iron feet rang against the stone as she ran up the stairs, not pausing to look through windows. This time, there would be no armies of the dead storming the castle. This time, she wasn't here to save Zetetic from the damned, nor to plead for his aid against them. This time, at last, she finally grasped the truth of what she'd witnessed when last the world had reached its final chapter.

She reached the heavy oak door at the top of the chamber. Bracing herself with her arms spread across the passageway, she kicked the door again and again, until it splintered.

She marched into the room beyond. As before, it was covered in paper. This time, however, the paper was covered in squiggles. She'd seen these squiggles before, many times.

She paused. Though she'd stood on these pages before, was it safe to enter? Might she meet the same fate as Tempest and Ver if she tread upon the pages of the One True Book?

"Don't be afraid to come in," said Zetetic, from a point in the room she couldn't see. "These words aren't sacred here. Nothing is sacred here. This chamber is beyond the gaze of the Divine Author. I like my privacy."

The Black Swan entered the room. Though they were at the top of a tower, theoretically the smallest room, the space was vast, much bigger than she remembered. She turned and found the door she entered hanging in empty space. Beyond it, she saw Zetetic standing at a wall, contemplating the words before him, a paint can in one hand, a brush in the other.

"I've been expecting you," said Zetetic. "When I snatched the book from behind your back, I suspected you'd come looking for it."

"How could you touch the book without it killing you?"

Zetetic held up his hands. They looked a little too large when compared to his arms, and their tone didn't match the hues of his face. "I snatched the Omega Reader's hands after Menagerie killed him. It's taken a few hours to get used to using them." He wiggled his fingers. "Where is Menagerie, by the way? Hidden away as a mouse inside you?" He gave her a closer look. "Ah. I hear a hornet buzzing around inside your torso. Did you know that I have the power to keep Menagerie from changing form just by snapping my fingers?" He snapped his fingers.

He turned his gaze back to the paper before him. He dipped his brush in the can of white paint he carried and lifted the tip to the page.

"Don't," she said.

"Don't worry," said Zetetic. "I'm not erasing you. Not yet." He drew the paint along the script, leaving a pristine line of gleaming white. "All of history is created by these words. On one of my journeys into the past with Walker, I witnessed a woman burned at the stake by Stark Tower, the Witchbreaker. I've seen many unpleasant things in my time, as you might imagine. But there's something about the way her body writhed, the way she struggled against her bonds, that haunts me. Sometimes, when I'm on the verge of sleep, I see those movements as shadows at the edge of my sight. I always sit bolt upright, my heart racing. My bedroom seems to echo with her screams. The smell of burning hair takes forever to leave my lungs. And now…" He drew the brush along another line of text, "Now she's gone. Never born. Never burned."

"What are you planning to do?" asked the Black Swan. "Erase everything you found unpleasant? Wipe away any bad memory that torments you?"

Zetetic chuckled. "My dear Black Swan, you must know how impossible it would be to limit the erasures to only that. What if this poor witch had a child before she was burned? They're gone now. If we searched the pages, I've no doubt we'd find a hundred gaps in the prose created by this simple erasure of a single life. How many lines will I need to erase before the book is blank? I've done the math several times. One calculation has me erasing the world in a mere ninety-three strokes. But who knows? Perhaps some things will persist until the last word is erased."

"You know I can't let you do this," said the Black Swan, walking toward him.

"You know I have the power to stop you where you stand with just a glance," he said, glancing in her direction.

She stopped, dead in her tracks, unable to move forward.

"You also know I'm impervious to any of the various weapons you've got stashed in that hollow shell of yours," he said. "You can't hurt me. But having lived your life outside a fixed timeline, I imagine you'll be almost impossible to erase from history until the last words are blotted out. So, please, relax, and watch patiently as I rid the world of the past."

"Why would you do this?" asked the Black Swan. "What can you possibly gain by wiping out the past?"

"The future, of course," said Zetetic, running his fingers along the lines of text as he searched for the next point in time and space to paint over. "You know I'm a dreamer. I've got big plans for what's to come. Once I have a blank slate, I can write the world anew. Ah, such tales I'll tell. Aren't you eager to see what I put into the first chapter? "

He dipped his brush once more.

"You've no right to do this," she said.

"There's only one essential right in this world," said Zetetic, his fingers stopping on a line dense with cramped writing, as if the author had been in a hurry to convey something important. "The right to do as you wish until someone comes along to stop you. As we've established, you are not that someone."

"How can you hate the world so much you'd want to erase it?" she asked.

"This has nothing to do with hatred." Zetetic gave a gentle smile. "I've never seen my lies as an instrument of harm or destruction. Lies are the ultimate tool of creation. Without lies, life would be impossible."

The Black Swan weighed his words carefully. When last she'd been here, she'd thought he was insane. It was now important to discover whether or not this was so.

"I don't follow your logic," she said.

He nodded. "Few do. I've seen the world from a different perspective for a long time."

"Why?" she asked. "What changed you?"

Zetetic pressed his lips together as he walked to a different section of the paper, eying the words carefully. He drew his brush across a line of words, blotting them out. When he turned to her, the red D on his forehead was gone. "I don't know if you ever had any tattoos, but, I assure you, having one needled into your face while you're chained to a rack doesn't make for a pleasant evening. I just erased the Truthspeaker who, three hundred years ago, decreed that Deceivers were to be marked to warn others." He smiled. "He was, ironically, a very kind man, believing Deceivers could be redeemed. Before him, my kind was routinely put to death."

"Which might be a good idea," said the Black Swan. "It was a mistake to save you when the church tried to hang you."

He chuckled. "I appreciate that I owe my survival then to a lie. You asked how I came to see the world differently." He paused before a section of writing. "I've already located that part of the book. Would you like to hear the story?"

He'd gotten closer. She tried once more to move her limbs, but found she was still powerless to move in his direction.

"Tell me," she said.

"It's a simple tale. My father was a faithful adherent of the Church of the Book. Like many members of his faith, he desired to make the pilgrimage to the Temple of the Book on the Isle of Storm. He was a nobleman, a man of some wealth. So, unlike most pilgrims who make the journey on foot, he was able to hire a wagon, as well as a bevy of guards to protect it from bandits."

"A guarded wagon would make a tempting target compared to a pilgrim on foot with nothing but the clothes on his back," said the Black Swan.

"You've lived long enough in Commonground to think like a thief, I see," said Zetetic. "You're correct. Three days into our journey, our guards were cut down by arrows fired from higher rocks. When the bandits had killed our protectors, they seized my father, and demanded to know who else was in the wagon. He told them he traveled alone, that his wife and child had died of fever during the sea voyage. They searched the wagon, emptying every chest and satchel, taking anything of value, including the oxen that drew the wagon. When they were done, they slit my father's throat."

"But they spared you?"

"They never found me," said Zetetic. "The wagon had a false bottom, where my mother and I hid during the attack. Though the bandits found clothing belonging to a child and a woman, they must have believed my father when he said we were dead."

"So," said the Black Swan. "You owe your life to a lie."

"Two lies," said Zetetic. "The false bottom of the wagon also counts. My mother and I were found by other pilgrims. We completed our journey to the Temple of the Book. The Voice of the Law must have seen some hint of potential, because he asked my mother to leave me in his care, that I might become a Truthspeaker. For many years I wrestled with the truths taught by the church. In the end, I saw that everything they thought of as truth was simply a lie that couldn't be disproven. This simple revelation led me to become a Deceiver. Once I started down that path…" he gazed at the brush in his hand. "You must see how believing that there's no difference between lies and truth can be something of a slippery slope. You can see how logical it is that I'd want to wipe away this horrible perversion of reality that we all exist in and start afresh with something a bit more… rational."

"So, you're not insane," said the Black Swan.

"Not in the least," said Zetetic.

"Which means you're morally culpable for your actions."

"I suppose so," he said. "Though it's pointless to make me try to feel guilty. I thrive in the magnitude of the sins I've committed, and the greater sins still to come."

"Excellent," said the Black Swan. She raised her hand to the space between her breasts. She pressed a rivet there, popping open a secret panel.

"I told you no weapon you have can harm me," said Zetetic, noticing her movements, pausing with his brush held above the line he targeted.

"This isn't a weapon," said the Black Swan, as the hornet Zetetic had heard within her torso flew free. She reached into the compartment and pulled out a ring bearing a large, glittering diamond. She slid the ring onto her left hand, where it sat like a wedding band.

"Where have I seen that ring before?" Zetetic asked, his brow furrowing.

"In Hell, most likely," said the Black Swan. "It's where you'll be seeing it again."

Zetetic eyed the hornet as it landed on the paper beside his foot. He raised his boot to stomp it. "Menagerie isn't all that scary when I can squash him like a bug."

"That's not Menagerie," said the Black Swan, as the hornet darted from beneath Zetetic's stomping foot. It rose to a level above Zetetic's head. Suddenly, the hornet became two, then twenty, then a thousand hornets, then a million, coalescing into the muscular form of a winged demon with a hornet's nest for a head.

Zetetic shouted, "I'm immune—" but couldn't complete his sentence as hornets swarmed onto his tongue, sinking their stingers deep into the muscle. Zetetic howled in wordless agony. His eyes grew wide as the demon seized him by his shoulders. The creature squeezed hard, causing Zetetic to physically shrink beneath the pressure, first to the size of a child, then the size of a doll, before being squeezed to the size of an insect in the demon's palm.

"Excellent work, Foment," said the Black Swan, holding her hand toward him.

Foment held the struggling Deceiver carefully between his claws. Zetetic made squeaking, chirping sounds, his voice unintelligible thanks to his swollen tongue and miniscule lungs. Foment placed the Deceiver against the diamond set into the Black Swan's ring. The Deceiver sank into the stone.

The Black Swan studied the facets of the gem, seeing Zetetic's agonized face reflected in a tiny hall of mirrors. No hint of his voice escaped the ring.

She pointed to the doorway hanging in the center of the room. "Foment, this door leads back to the living world. I know Walker showed you the path in and out of Limbo when he had you rescue the Romers. Once I leave, take this door to Limbo. We can't risk anyone ever finding this room again."

"As you wish, my queen," said Foment, in a wet, fart-like voice.

That will get old quickly, she thought as she left the room. But, Walker had trusted Foment, so she hadn't wanted to take a chance giving this mission to any of the other demons. No doubt, there were quite a few demons unhappy that she'd stayed on to rule over Hell. She was certain they'd test her strength in the coming days. But she'd tamed Commonground, more or less. Hell wasn't going to be any problem at all.

IT WAS A YEAR to the day since the end of the dragon apocalypse that the *Circus* sailed into the bay of the Silver City. Cinder stood at the bow, looking over the jumble of broken buildings. It was just before dawn, with the horizon softly aglow. Bird songs rang out from the young trees sprouting in thick clumps along the ruined city walls.

Brand stood next to her. He pointed toward a dome half hidden by vines. Glints of metal reflected in the faint light.

"That used to be the Grand Cathedral," he said. "It will make a decent spot to set up a base camp."

Cinder looked back over the crowd of people gathered on the deck. These were brothers and sisters of the Church of the Flame, the exiles who'd fled to the Isle of Fire to live in the settlement founded by Brother Wing. The exiles were returning home, to rebuild from the ruins.

Cinder had been tasked with carrying the flaming sword given to her by Forge back to the settlement. Once there, she'd found herself regarded as a figure of authority, both because she carried the sword and because she wore the Immaculate Attire, the garb once worn by her distant ancestor, Queen Immaculate Brightmoon. She'd discovered the armor on her journey to the settlement, after stopping by the Jawa Fruit village to see that all was well with them in the aftermath of the storm. As she'd travelled through the jungle, she'd spotted an unusually bright beam of light piercing the canopy and followed it, half expecting to find her father. Instead, she'd found the Immaculate Attire neatly laid out. She'd known it was a gift from her father and tried it on despite her initial reservations about being so fully clothed. Fortunately, the armor fit like a second skin.

"I wish you all the best," said Brand, as Rigger lashed the ship to what was left of a mangled dock. "I'd like to see the city restored for sentimental reasons. Plus, it's a little rough to manage a trade ship like the *Circus* when the only open port in the world is Commonground."

"We'll make it two ports soon enough," said Cinder. "When we've rebuilt here, we'll move on. There's a lot of the world I'd like to see."

"You might be bogged down here for quite a while," said Brand. "Some of the Wanderers that came here earlier told me their dry men were besieged by feral dogs in the ruins, not to mention rats as long as their arms. Also, there are still a few resourceful undead lurking in the sewers and catacombs."

"Stray dogs and dead men aren't something I'm worried about," said Cinder. "With this sword and this armor, I can clear the area swiftly."

"You've got your mother's confidence," said Brand.

"More than her confidence," said Cinder. "I have her blessing."

She pointed forward, and Brand's eyes moved toward the city walls. Cinder smiled as the sun crested the horizon, its gentle light caressing the honeysuckle that draped the walls. A million delicate yellow flowers opened slowly to embrace in the day. In the virginal glow of morning, all the world looked freshly born, and innocent.

BONUS NOVELLA
GREATSHADOW: ORIGINS

Author's Note: Before there was Greatshadow, the novel, there was Greatshadow, the novella, which originally appeared in an anthology called Blood and Devotion edited by W.H. Horner. I'm including it here out of a sense of historical completeness. You'll find several familiar characters here, sometimes under different names, and the plot of the novella provided the basic framework for the plot of the novel. I liked the novella when I wrote it, but felt there were missed opportunities for developing the themes and characters with more depth. It's likely that I would never have written the Dragon Apocalypse if I hadn't first given the ideas a test run in the novella.

""It confirms all I've heard about Commonground, that the best man you could find for the job is a woman."

FOR TWENTY ODD years, Bigsby the Dwarf had run a little seafood shop near the docks of Commonground. The years had been odd indeed, given the cast of scoundrels that frequented his establishment. Commonground was a lawless city, haven of pirates, abode of goblins, home to thieves and thugs. Bigsby hadn't grown wealthy serving such a clientele. Still, he scraped by, and over the years had accumulated a treasure of interesting stories to share with friends over a pint of ale.

By reputation, Bigsby was a mirthful sort, good company in a bad city. Lately, Bigsby was rarely seen at his favorite bars. He spent his evenings in his shop, sullenly chopping at blocks of ice. His lantern burned late into the night. His face took on a pale tone, his eyes lined with red.

One evening, after he'd shuttered the windows and started to work on the ice, Bigsby heard a knock. He stopped chopping.

"It can't be him," he muttered.

The knock came again, more firmly.

"Go away," he shouted. "We're closed!"

He looked at the flat surface of the ice. With his ice-pick, he drew a line across the block. Even with good winds, it took three days to sail from the Silver City. If they left on the Feast's Eve, two days ago, they couldn't have arrived yet.

Again, the knocks came, swiftly followed by a thump, then a crash, as the door came off its hinges.

In the doorway was a giant of a man. The intruder was heavily muscled and horribly scarred, with a face that looked sewn together with bits from several different people.

Bigsby opened his mouth. A squeak issued forth.

He cleared his throat.

"F-Fish?" he said. "Are you here for…?"

"I'm here for you, traitor."

Someone else had answered. Bigsby glanced away from the monster. In the doorway stood another man, hardly any taller than himself. This stranger was hunched over beneath his tattered cloak, his body bent until his head was even with his waist. The hunched man leaned on a gnarled wooden staff. Rags tightly entwined his body, concealing every inch of skin. His eyes glowed like embers beneath his dingy hood.

Bigsby wiped away the sweat stinging his eyes.

"D-Did you say… t-trader?" he asked. "T-that I am. A humble trader in--."

The hooded stranger chuckled. "You have no secrets, dear Bigsby. I call you traitor with precision. You were a traitor twenty years ago when you cruelly poisoned Lord Brightmoon. Now you contemplate the betrayal of a friend. I know of the letter."

Bigsby hadn't heard the name Brightmoon in years. He'd all but forgotten the enormous price placed on his head. Countless souls in Commonground would betray him for the money, if they knew the truth.

Bigsby narrowed his eyes. He'd killed before. It was time to kill again. With desperate speed, he flung the icepick at the brute's throat as he dove from his chair. He swiftly pulled open the drawer that held his knives. It fell to the floor in a clatter. He grabbed his sharpest, longest blade and spun to face his attackers.

He was met with a bemused chuckle from the hooded hunchback. The icepick was buried to the hilt in the brute's throat, but the brute seemed unaware of this.

"You don't know who you face," the crooked man said.

"Then enlighten me, stranger," snarled Bigsby, holding his blade so that lantern light gleamed from its razor edge.

"Hmm." The hunchback nodded. "Stranger. That will do. My silent friend goes by Patch."

Bigsby stared at Patch and at the hilt of the icepick. The man wasn't even bleeding.

Stranger stepped forward. With a terrible groan he reached his spindly arm high and grabbed the icepick, freeing it with a grunt. He lay the pick on the block of ice.

"I'm not here for the reward," said Stranger.

"You'd be disappointed," Bigsby said. "I've never poisoned anyone."

"But you did receive a letter, yes? From a man named Jack Blade. You're meeting him as early as tomorrow. He's requested you lead him and his companions to the lair of the dragon, Greatshadow."

"Don't be absurd," Bigsby said. "I-I wouldn't know how to find Greatshadow. Why would anyone think that?"

"Because you drunkenly boasted of it one night. You said you'd stumbled upon the place and found it filled with riches. You wisely fled, of course."

"Ah," said Bigsby. "Perhaps I said such a thing, once, years ago, while drunk. It isn't true."

"Just another lie in a life of lies, then? But I see you speak the truth. You don't know how to find the dragon. But you won't admit this to Jack Blade. Instead, you plan to lead him on a wild goose chase into the Blackwater Swamp."

Bigsby felt limp hearing these words. When Stranger had spouted the truth about his distant past, Bigsby assumed the man had done some careful sleuthing. When Stranger had spoken about Jack's letter, he guessed the letter had been intercepted and read. But to know about his plans to lead the others into the swamp... he'd shared this with no one. Stranger was obviously a wizard. Bigsby swallowed hard.

"It's true," he said. "But this isn't betrayal. I've heard rumors that Greatshadow lives in the swamp. We might find him."

"You might meet your death by quicksand. But you'll never find Greatshadow in the swamp. Greatshadow lives in the mountain wastelands. The path to his abode is within my very blood. I shall lead you."

"Oh," said Bigsby, biting his nails. "Good."

"You'd as soon face the swamps," said Stranger.

"I saw Greatshadow once," whispered Bigsby. "Ten years ago, when the Armada of the Silver Kingdom sailed into this bay. I was watching from the window when night seemed to suddenly fall. My shop had fallen into the dragon's shadow. He passed over the water and breathed flames. It was horrible. The whole of the ocean was ablaze. Not a ship survived. Charred, bloated bodies washed ashore for days. I'm not eager to face the beast in his lair."

"My poor Bigsby," said Stranger. "What you are eager to do is unimportant. You'll do as I tell you, or I will reveal the price on your head to every soul in this accursed city."

Bigsby stared at his knife. He'd survived some terrible scraps over the years. But what chance did he have against a wizard? He let the knife fall from his grasp.

"Curse you," he mumbled. "I'll do as you tell me."

"It's not such a bad thing," said Stranger. "I promise you Bigsby, this is no journey of self-destruction. Greatshadow will meet his end. When he does, you may leave with all the treasure you can carry. Even with your small stature, that's immeasurable wealth. The dragon has more diamonds than the mer-king has pearls."

Bigsby rubbed his chin. Certainly, a trip to Greatshadow's lair was suicide. But, just in case, he would wear pants with really big pockets.

"Let us hasten," said Stranger. "You aren't the only ally I seek tonight."

Bigsby followed the wizard through the busted doorway. Patch picked up the door and leaned it into place. Bigsby shook his head with a sigh. The broken door was the least of his worries, but he dreaded the thought of haggling with Jardon the carpenter to get it repaired. The little goblin charged as if each nail was made of gold.

STRANGER LED BIGSBY to Blackstone's Barge. The squat ship glowed upon the dark water with the light of a hundred lanterns. The drunken men shouted and women squealed as they crossed the swaying plank. Stranger pushed open the door. Thick smoke rolled forth.

Inside, Bigsby hung close to Patch. Bigsby had been tripped over by more than a few drunken fools with foul tempers. But, drunk or sober, people got out of Patch's way. They moved through the crowd without brushing against a single body.

In the far corner of the room was a rough-hewn wooden booth. Sitting in this booth was a woman Bigsby knew by reputation. Everyone called her Infidel. She was a muscular woman, with dark eyes beneath a stern brow. Her red hair was cropped close to her scalp, and black tattoos ran the length of her arms. A scar ran down her left cheek, from eye to lip.

She sat alone, carving letters into the thick oak table with a dagger as she sipped a large flagon of mead. Bigsby was a good judge of body language. This woman wasn't in the mood for company.

"Infidel," Stranger said. "Well met this evening."

She glared at him.

"What the devil are you?" she asked.

"A humble traveler, in need of your assistance."

"Right. No, seriously, what are you beneath those rags? You sure as hell ain't human. You're not a goblin, neither."

"Madam, I suffer many deformities. How unkind of you to draw attention to them."

"Bullshit," Infidel said, reaching toward Stranger's hood.

Patch caught her wrist. It looked almost accidental, as if Patch had been moving his arm in her direction on a whim and happened to meet her hand. With his fingers clamped around her wrist, her arm was immobile. She strained to pull free, but Patch didn't budge.

"Let's forget about my face, *Isadora*," said Stranger.

Infidel responded by using her free hand to drive her dagger deep into Patch's elbow. With a twist of the blade, Patch's hand sprung open. In an instant, Infidel flew from the booth and tackled Stranger, the dagger pressed to his throat. His hood slipped back, revealing only rags that enshrouded his face.

"Where did you learn that name?" Infidel hissed.

Before Stranger could respond, Patch leaned over and grabbed the woman by her ears. She shrieked as Patch lifted her from the floor. If Patch felt any pain from the injury to his elbow, it failed to show on his impassive face.

"A bargain, Infidel," growled Stranger, struggling to his feet. "I don't speak that name again. You don't look beneath my hood."

Infidel responded by chopping down with the dagger, burying it deep into

Patch's thigh. She pulled it free and struck again, and again. Patch didn't even flinch.

Stranger chuckled.

"There's another name you'll be interested in hearing," he ventured. "Tristram Castlebridge."

Infidel raised an eyebrow as she thrust the dagger toward Stranger, who stood just beyond its tip.

"You're one of *his* men?"

"Hardly," said Stranger. "We plot his demise."

"You certainly know the words a woman wants to hear," she said, a sudden smile upon her lips. "Drop me."

Patch let loose of her ears and she dropped to the floor, staggering to keep her feet.

"Goddammit," she grumbled, rubbing her ears. "Where'd you pick up the big guy?"

"Patch is an old friend," said Stranger. "Several, actually."

She pulled the bent remains of a gold ring from a particularly bloody spot on her upper ear.

"You owe me a new earring," she said.

"Treasures aplenty await you," said Stranger.

"Sure. Whatever. What's with the dwarf?"

Bigsby bowed politely. "Bigsby's the name. I'm—"

"You're that fish guy," she said.

Bigsby was surprised she had ever noticed him.

"If it makes you feel any better, I didn't fare any better against Patch than you did."

"That's freaking great. Wait until word gets out I'm no better than a dwarf fishmonger in a brawl."

"Killing Tristram Castlebridge will more than assure your reputation," said Stranger.

Infidel nodded. "Let's talk more about this killing thing."

She looked around the silent room. Everyone, man, woman, and goblin, stared at them.

"Hey!" she shouted. "Mind your business! Me and my buddies are plotting a murder!"

A few of the larger men laughed, while most of the goblins in the room turned a paler blue than usual. All turned away, and soon the room was awash in voices.

"Have a seat," she said.

Stranger twisted his bent body at awkward angles, grunting as he slipped along the bench. Bigsby climbed in beside him.

"You both look like you could use a little ear-hanging from the big guy," said Infidel. "Put a few inches on you, Shorty. Maybe take the kinks out of your back, Rag-face." She raised her arms above her head and stretched, her sinews popping. "Does wonders for the spine."

"Tomorrow, or in the days soon after, a ship will arrive," said Stranger.

"Ships arrive every day," said Infidel.

"This one carries a band of adventurers."

"Tristram's one of them?"

"He leads them," answered Stranger.

"He's the bossy sort."

"They've come to kill Greatshadow."

Infidel perked up. "And we tag along to watch them die? Could be fun."

"I think they will succeed," said Stranger.

"Shyeah. Right."

"Tristram carries Frostbite."

Infidel raised an eyebrow.

Bigsby thought "carries" was a strange verb to place before the noun. What was significant about some knight missing a few toes anyway?

"Frostbite's been missing for years," said Infidel. "How'd Tristram get it?"

"Unimportant. The sword will protect Tristram from Greatshadow's flames. The dragon's skin will have no resistance to its cold bite. A single cut will freeze the dragon's blood."

"So Tristram might actually beat Greatshadow."

"He'll claim this land in the name of the Silver Kingdom," said Stranger. "I would rather this island remain under… local control. So after Tristram and his friends exhaust themselves besting the dragon—"

"We take them out," said Infidel. "Gotcha."

"Excuse me," said Bigsby. "But if this Tristram fellow is tough enough to best Greatshadow, what makes you think we're tough enough to fight him?"

"We?" said Infidel. "Don't flatter yourself. Frostbite's a good sword, yeah, but it doesn't worry me. What do you bring to the party, fishmonger?"

"Bigsby has a friend among Tristram's party."

"Jack Blade," said Bigsby. "He was kind to me when I lived in the Silver City. He helped me escape."

"Escape what?"

Bigsby clenched his fists. *Stupid!* Twenty years of caution thrown to the wolves.

"Taxes," said Bigsby. He grinned sheepishly.

"Yeah," said Infidel. "Taxes are a bitch."

THE SHIP SAILED into the harbor the following evening, under a Northsea flag.

"That's not a Northsea ship," said Infidel, as she, Bigsby, Stranger and Patch watched from a hill above the harbor. "Who's he fooling?"

"The dragon, possibly," said Stranger. "Ships of the Silver Armada don't have a lucky history in this port."

"It has three lanterns hanging from starboard," said Bigsby. "That's the signal."

"We'd better get a move on, then," said Infidel. "Slow as you three move, they'll be old and gray before we get down there. That'll scare Greatshadow. A bunch of toothless old men limping into his lair, waving their canes."

Bigsby thought a bunch of toothless old men would probably fare as well as anyone. He chased after Infidel as she loped down the hill. Despite her cruel humor, Bigsby felt safer near her than he did alone in the presence of Patch and Stranger.

Bigsby was out of breath by the time they made it to the docks. He looked behind him. Stranger and Patch were nowhere to be seen.

"Infidel," he called out.

She stopped and looked toward him.

"Yeah?" she asked.

"Stranger," said Bigsby, between gasps. "You trust him?"

"This some joke?"

Bigsby shook his head. "I have a rowboat. We could escape in it before Stranger finds us."

"Sounds like a plan. Go for it. But I'm sticking around. There's killing to be done."

She headed toward the ship. Bigsby looked back. Stranger could now be seen at the far end of the docks. There was still time to run. But once he made it to the boat, where would he go? He'd lived in Commonground most of his adult life. Plus, there was still Jack to consider. Bigsby could care less if Stranger and Infidel murdered Tristram, but Jack had once been his friend. It seemed only fair to warn him. Of course, if he did warn him, Stranger would know it. The bastard could read minds.

"Don't forget that," Stranger called out, now a dozen yards away.

Bigsby shook his head. Could things get any worse?

"Oh look," said Stranger, drawing beside Bigsby, his eyes fixed on the deck of the ship. "They have a Truthspeaker among them."

"Great," said Bigsby, staring at the black-robed figure on the deck. "They're even worse than mind-readers."

"Don't forget *that,* either," said Stranger.

FORTUNATELY, THE TRUTHSPEAKER remained on the deck of the ship as Jack Blade bounded from the gangplank to the dock. He raced forward and grabbed Bigsby by the shoulders, lifting him in the air with his embrace.

"Old friend!" he said.

"Ixnay on the endfray," whispered Bigsby. "People don't know I used to live in the Silver City."

"Understood," said Jack, setting Bigsby back on his feet. "My, the years have been, uh, years since I've seen you. Put on a little weight, I see."

"The years have been kind to you," said Bigsby. And they had. Jack had aged in twenty years. He still had the same long flowing tresses, and sported the same fancy silk cloak over his immaculate black leather armor. Bigsby could see his face reflected in Jack's polished thigh-high boots.

"Wearing clothes like that around here's asking for trouble," said Bigsby.

"Let trouble come," said Jack. "It's important to look good in public."

"You look like you're on your way to a ball instead of a dragon hunt," said Infidel.

Jack smiled. "Bigsby. You've brought friends."

"Um. Yeah. This is, uh, In—"

"Ingred," said Infidel.

"Charmed," said Jack.

"Whatever," Infidel replied.

"And this," said Bigsby, "is Patch."

Jack looked at the hulking figure, and managed a smile. "A pleasure," he offered.

"Finally," said Bigsby, motioning toward the robed hunchback, "this is, uh, Stranger."

Jack's smile wavered a little as he studied Stranger's ragged form.

"I'm not a leper, if that's what you're thinking," said Stranger.

"Jack!" A voice thundered down from the deck. A silver-haired man clanked down the gangplank, his armor gleaming red in the fading sunlight. Without introduction, Bigsby knew this to be the famed knight Tristram Castlebridge. It was clear from the steely gleam in his eyes, the noble thrust of his chin, and the frost-encrusted scabbard that hung from his waist. Plus the name "Castlebridge" was stitched in gold thread around the hem of his flowing purple cloak.

"Is this the fellow you spoke of?" asked Tristram.

"May I introduce you to Bigsby, the Fish Baron of Commonground."

Infidel snickered.

Tristram cast his gaze upon her. She stared back. He looked down at Bigsby.

"Is she with you?"

"Yes," Bigsby said. "I thought an extra blade might come in handy."

"It confirms all I've heard about Commonground," said Tristram, "that the best man you could find for the job is a woman."

Bigsby dared a glance toward Infidel. She didn't have her hand upon her sword.

"I also brought Patch." He gestured toward the monster behind him.

"Beefy fellow, aren't you?" said Tristram.

Patch stared silently, as flies crawled about his face.

The hunchback stepped forward. "And I am Stranger."

"I see," said Tristram.

Stranger said, "Bigsby has told me of your desire to rid the land of Greatshadow. I share your desire. I know I am nothing but a withered old man, but I beg you to allow me to accompany you. I speak the language of every tribe upon this island, even the Dragontongue."

"Hmm," said Tristram. "That could be useful."

"Tristram!"

It was a deep, booming voice that called out the knight's name. It was like the voice of thunder, the voice of the heavens. Down the gangplank strode a man in a black cotton robe, a thick, gilt-edged book held in his right hand, a jagged, rust-spotted scythe carried in his left.

"Thomas," said Tristram. "Good of you to join us. This is Jack's friend Bigs—"

"Can you think of any reason for me to know the names of this lot?" interrupted Thomas.

Tristram seemed to flinch at the question.

"You there." Thomas the Truthspeaker extended a long, bony finger toward Bigsby.

The dwarf looked into the man's dark eyes, like pools of ink with little pearls gleaming in them. He felt faint.

"Yes, sir?" he asked.

"Why do you offer your services to us? Answer truthfully!"

Bigsby tried to lie. *Because I humbly wish to be of service to your noble cause.* His heart skipped a beat. *Because I can think of no greater duty*... he couldn't complete the thought. It felt as if the Truthspeaker's bony fingers had reached into his chest and gripped his heart.

"Because we seek to enrich ourselves with the dragon's treasure when you perish!" Bigsby blurted out.

"Hah!" laughed Tristram. "This quest will not end with our deaths, but with the dragon's! You have too little faith in us, dwarf."

The Truthspeaker smiled. The expression didn't suit him. "Let us have an understanding. We will tolerate your heathen presence, as well as this band of rabble you've gathered, because we need your knowledge. In return, we shall provide you a modest share of the dragon's wealth. There is no need for you to like us, and no need for us to like you."

"Wow," said Infidel. "It's like I think it and you say it."

"In our kingdom," said the Truthspeaker, "women speak only when spoken to."

"Not your kingdom," said Infidel.

"Since you choose to dress like a man, you can help unload the ship. You also," Thomas commanded, pointing toward Patch.

Stranger nodded. Patch lumbered forward. Infidel stood silent for a moment, her hand edging closer to her sword. Then, with a shrug, she headed up the gangplank.

THE CARAVAN OF ADVENTURERS left at dawn, while the cutthroats of Commonground were still sleeping off the previous night's revelries. This was Bigsby's favorite time of day. Usually by now he'd been working for a few hours, and would take a moment at daybreak to step outside his shop and watch the sun come up at the mouth of the bay. He would smoke his pipe and listen to the gulls and be filled with a tremendous sense that all was right with his world. He wondered if he would ever feel that way again.

Commonground was a long city, but a narrow one. It stretched for miles along the hilly shores of the bay, but once one ventured over those hills, even the half-hearted pretense of civilization was left behind. Commonground was located on the southeastern shore of a large island marked on most maps as the Isle of Fear. Bigsby had never much worried about what lay beyond the hills of Commonground. Now, he was being forced to think about it by another one of Jack's companions, a man named Magidance, who'd made his appearance only moments before they'd departed.

"...Wildcats, wolves, and wyverns," finished Magidance, who'd spent the last several minutes counting off the various threats that lay before them, starting with, "Ants: giant, man-eating."

The band of treasure seekers marched at a vigorous pace. Bigsby struggled to keep stride with Infidel, but kept slipping behind, to find himself once more within earshot of Magidance at the rear of the party.

"Seventy-three species capable of killing a man," said Magidance.

"If you're so worried, why are you here?" Bigsby asked.

Magidance shrugged. "I may have been drinking a little when Jack talked me into this."

Bigsby couldn't guess why Jack had recruited such a sickly looking fellow. Magidance was a pale, scrawny man, with bags under his eyes and thinning hair. He was armed only with a dagger, and Bigsby wondered if even the dagger was too much for him to handle.

The rest of the Jack's companions looked brawnier, consisting of a half dozen men-at-arms with well-kept weapons, and another ten burly men brought along to carry gear.

"Shame we can't have horses," sighed Magidance. "How long did you say this would take? Are we close?"

"We haven't traveled an hour!" said Bigsby.

"Horses *are* particularly favored by dragons," said Magidance. "Domestic animals are plump and slow compared with a dragon's normal fare. That's the real reason people haven't settled here. Dragon's don't give a damn about people as food, but civilization is built on livestock. I'll bet there are no cheese shops in Commonground."

"The goblins make a kind of cheese from the milk of cave goats," said Bigsby. "It's seasoned with the husks of firespiders."

"Sounds intriguing. I suppose I'd try it. I'll put anything in my mouth at least once. When I was up north, I had some fantastic cheese in a village of the snowmen. It was made from whale's milk of all things, and was half-transparent, like ice riddled with air. Master Solodon wouldn't touch the stuff. Said it smelled like rotten teeth. It did, I suppose. But it was salty on the tongue, like anchovies."

"Solo ... did you say Solodon?" asked Bigsby.

"As in 'the Great and Wondrous Master of Mysteries Solodon,'" said Magidance. "Formerly master of me, as well. I apprenticed with him."

"You? You're a wizard?"

"Not according to Thomas the Truthspeaker. He says I'm a thrice-damned liar who shouldn't be suffered to live. Fortunately, he gave Tristram his word he wouldn't kill me."

"Why does he think you're a liar? Aren't you a real wizard?"

"Magic is nothing but a lie you tell the universe," said Magidance. "The trick is to make the universe believe it. Truthspeakers and wizards are eternal enemies. But dragon hunts make for strange alliances."

"Thomas seems like a very mean man," said Bigsby. By now he and Magidance had fallen far enough behind that they could speak freely, though not so far back that they couldn't dash for the safety of the group should a strange growl come from the bushes.

"Thomas is a very righteous man," said Magidance. "As was Solodon. Only someone with weak morals could see them as mean."

Bigsby frowned. He had expected a sympathetic ear, not a scolding.

"Perhaps it's true," said Magidance, with a shrug. "There may be a Hell, and it may be my fate. Better than sharing Heaven with that bastard, eh?"

A scream came from the trail ahead.

Bigsby ran toward the safety of the larger party. He could see one of the carriers thrashing about on the ground, as Infidel dove into the tall grass.

"Snakebite!" someone shouted.

Magidance ran past Bigsby, trailing a stream of obscenities.

"Got it!" yelled Infidel. She stood. On the end of her dagger writhed a yard long white snake with black stripes.

"I didn't hear 'zebra snakes' in your list," Jack said to Magidance.

Magidance fell to his knees beside the snakebite victim. He produced a small sack from his cape. The bitten man thrashed about, screaming between gasps.

"Hold him!" Magidance shouted.

Jack and two other men grabbed the man's flailing limbs, pinning them.

Magidance pulled the tiny, toothful jawbone of a snake from his pouch. He pressed this into the man's flesh above the wound, then below, all the while humming rhythmically. He then blew a pinch of white powder into the man's eyes. The man cried in pain, then fell still and silent.

"Not even noon and we've lost a man," complained Tristram.

"He'll live," said Magidance. "I've cured worse."

"Will he be able to travel?" asked Thomas.

"Not soon. He'll sleep the rest of the day. Tomorrow, he'll be too weak to walk. But in a week, he should be good as new. If we take him back to the ship—"

"No," said Tristram. "We'll set up a tent here. Leave him food and water. We journey on."

"Leave him? Alone?"

"He won't stand a chance out here," said Bigsby. "There are monsters about. Man-eaters!"

"All the more reason for haste," said Tristram. "It would slow us to carry him."

"Sir," said Magidance. "Perhaps we could -"

"Enough!" said Thomas, in a tone that silenced even Tristram. He knelt beside the now peaceful form of the victim. "This isn't open to debate. I've known this man since he was a boy. His name is Pious, and he is a good and faithful servant. He deserves the best possible fate."

Thomas cradled Pious in his arms. Bigsby could see better now. Pious was a young man, barely old enough to shave. His face was angelic in slumber.

"Wake," said Thomas.

Pious stirred, his eyelids fluttering open.

"You have lived well," said Thomas, bending to place a kiss upon the young man's brow. "You are welcomed home."

As he said this, a breeze stirred the tall grass and wispy clouds dimmed the sun. A chill ran down Bigsby's spine. Pious closed his eyes. His chest fell still. Thomas looked up with a dreamy smile.

Magidance swayed as if about to faint.

"You …," whispered Magidance. "You killed him."

"I *saved* him," said Thomas.

Magidance started to speak, then stopped. He stood trembling, his hands in tight fists. He turned, his face red, and stomped away. As he passed by Bigsby he mumbled, in continuation of his list, "Zealots."

IN THE FOLLOWING DAYS, the pretense that Bigsby was guiding the party grew thin. Whenever directions were asked, Stranger would be the one to jump in with an answer. Bigsby never even approached the front with Stranger, Tristram, and Thomas. Instead, he stayed as far away from them as possible, at the rear of the party, usually in the company of Magidance, and now Infidel, who seemed to enjoy Magidance's dry humor. If she did enjoy it, she was in luck, for Magidance seldom shut up.

Magidance carried a folded leather map that he made notes on as they traveled.

"Most maps in refer to this as the Isle of Fear, though some still call it the Isle of Fire. The coast is mapped reasonably well, but the interior is all guesswork. I did find a five-hundred-hundred-year old atlas that called this place Myhryrha, which is an oldtongue word for wine. It showed several fair-sized cities on this island. That's the real reason I agreed to come. The thought of finding the ruins of a lost civilization. That's the sort of stuff that gets your name remembered through the ages."

"I've heard goblins speak of hidden cities," said Bigsby.

"Hell, I've been to three of them," said Infidel. "Me and Boggy McBee used to do a little tomb scavenging. I gave it up, though. Too much digging, not enough gold."

The talk of lost cities caught Bigsby's imagination. Every shadow in the forest, every strangely shaped rock, hinted that they passed through ancient ruins.

The land gave his imagination plenty to work with. This was rocky ground, with huge stones the size of houses all around. Ahead, low mountains loomed, their round peaks gleaming domes of white stone.

On the evening of their ninth day of travel, as they journeyed around the base of a stony mountain, the air filled with an incredible stench. Stranger led them to the source of the smell. It was an enormous turd, the size of a small horse, black with flies.

"We're near," said Stranger.

Magidance stepped closer to the dragon dropping, carrying a small glass dish.

"My God," he said, brushing away flies and scooping some of the brown-green excrement into the dish. "On the mage markets dragon's dung sells for its weight in gold. It's useful for an invisibility spell. This alone covers the cost of our trip."

"We've not come this distance to content ourselves with dung," said Tristram.

"We should leave," said Stranger. "The goblins who live nearby will be drawn to the smell. They use the dung for—Aanh!"

Stranger fell forward, a small, rough-hewn arrow jutting from his back.

Suddenly, the air was filled with high-pitched trills and the whistling of hundreds of arrows. All around Bigsby, men began to fall. Fortunately,

Tristram stood between him and the brunt of the attack. The arrows bounced harmlessly from Tristram's gleaming armor. Magidance, meanwhile, had taken shelter behind Patch, who stood stoically as arrows sank into his broad chest. Magidance shouted words in a language Bigsby had never heard. A strong wind swept up behind them, blowing the poorly made arrows back in the direction they had come. Tristram ran forward, sword drawn.

From behind rocks and shrubs, Bigsby could now see the dirty blue faces of dozens of goblins. Bows were thrown to the ground and jagged blades drawn as the goblins readied for hand-to-hand combat.

Tristram, Jack, and Infidel were upon them in seconds, their swords biting into goblin bone with each hack. Thomas joined in, swinging his scythe in a wide arc, liberating heads from their torsos.

In less than a minute the battle ended, with a score of goblins dead on the ground and the rest vanished into the sheltering brush.

Jack knelt over one of the bodies left behind.

"Look at this," he said, holding up a small shield.

"Dragon hide," said Magidance when he saw the finely scaled skin that covered the shield. "Where would—"

"The dragon keeps a harem of young female dragons," said Stranger, through teeth gritted with pain. Patch stood by him now, helping him back to his feet. The bloody arrow yanked from Stranger's back was still in Patch's hand. "Greatshadow kills them after they first give birth, before they grow old and powerful enough to challenge him. He tosses their bodies, and the helpless male chicks, into a deep gorge not far from here. Female chicks are allowed to live, for his future pleasure. The goblins must raid the gorge for the bodies."

"Then we're near," said Tristram.

"With a brisk march, we could be at his lair in less than an hour," said Stranger.

"Stay away from him!" shouted Infidel.

All eyes turned to see the female warrior with dagger drawn, standing between the Thomas the Truthspeaker and one of the carriers, who lay bleeding on the ground.

"I'll not stand by and witness another act of mercy on your part," Infidel said, her eyes narrow slits.

"You will not stand at all," Thomas said. He stretched his arm toward her and commanded in a rumbling voice, "On your knees!"

Infidel's body swayed drunkenly. Her knees bent, her legs trembled, but she did not kneel.

"Your resistance prolongs the inevitable," said Thomas.

Infidel staggered forward, her dagger rising toward the holy man's throat.

"Halt!" Thomas thundered.

Infidel jerked like a dog reaching the end of its leash. Sweat poured down her face.

"You cannot win this fight," Thomas said. "I see into your very soul."

Infidel growled, as she moved her limbs in spastic jerks. A trickle of blood flowed from her mouth.

"Your bravado masks the heart of a frightened girl," Thomas said, his voice calm. "I see a great shame within you. There have been times when you've contemplated taking a dagger to your own throat. No doubt, that would be for the best."

Infidel grunted as her dagger moved toward to her throat.

"No!" Bigsby cried out. He ran forward, his knife drawn, and plunged his blade into the Truthspeaker's thigh.

Thomas fell backwards, knocking Bigsby to the ground.

Infidel fell, limp as a puppet with its strings cut.

Bigsby struggled from beneath Thomas, only to find a hand on the back of his neck. He was lifted from the ground, dangling in the grip of Tristram.

"Traitorous wretch," Tristram snarled. "You cannot strike a holy man in my presence and live!"

Thomas struggled back to his feet with the help of one of the men-at-arms. He faced Bigsby. His eyes once more looked like inky pools of night.

"I can see into you now," said Thomas. "Your cowardly attack has revealed your true nature. There is a terrible sin in your past. Confess!"

"Ahhhn!" Bigsby bit his lip to silence himself, but it was to no avail. His mouth moved against his will.

"It's true! Ahhhhhhh! Oh, God. I poisoned Lord Brightmoon! Nnnnah!"

"Truly?" said Tristram. He tossed Bigsby roughly to the ground. "Then I won't break your neck after all. It would be rude to deprive Brightmoon's son of the pleasure."

Tristram looked toward one of the henchmen. "Tie him up. And the woman."

But when they looked to where Infidel had fallen, she was gone.

"How shocking to learn the truth about one's companions," said Stranger with a sigh.

Jack Blade turned his face away as Thomas looked in his direction.

"Three hours," said Tristram, looking toward the darkening sky. "Very well. We make camp here. The goblins should be too frightened to return, and the stench of his own dung should keep the dragon from catching our scent. We'll leave for our assault on the dragon come daylight, with every able-bodied man. And Thomas?"

"Yes?"

"Allow Magidance to tend to the wounded. Your wound as well."

"As you wish," said Thomas with a nod and a scowl.

THAT NIGHT, BIGSBY sweltered in the heat of his tent. The stench of the nearby dung stung his eyes until tears rolled down his cheeks. He couldn't wipe them away. His hands were bound behind his back with a stout rope, making it impossible to lay comfortably. He couldn't have slept anyway. After all these years, his secret was out. His future led to the gallows.

From outside the tent, there was a faint groan. The flap of the tent was lifted, allowing cool air to flow over Bigsby.

"Stay quiet," whispered Infidel. She crawled forward and cut the ropes that bound him.

He rolled onto his back, rubbing his wrists. Infidel was already slipping from the tent. Bigsby hurried after her.

Outside, he couldn't see her. At his feet lay one of Tristram's men, his throat slit.

Infidel's hand fell upon his shoulder. She dragged him into the bushes. They traveled for several minutes across the rocky ground, before Infidel motioned for him to stop.

"I won't lie to you," she said. "We're probably going to die."

"I'm a dead man anyway, if I fall into their hands."

"I have to go back," Infidel said. "Steal what I can. We won't make it far with only the clothes on our backs."

Bigsby nodded. Then he asked, "Why did you save me?"

"Did you really kill Lord Brightmoon?"

"Yes," said Bigsby quietly. "My father was his cook. Lord Brightmoon was a cruel man. He would have my father beaten for the smallest trifles. 'This soup scalded my tongue! Have the chef beaten.' 'This ham is too salty! Have the chef lashed.'"

Bigsby looked down at his hands. "My father was younger than I am now, but his hair was gray, and his face lined with wrinkles. Lord Brightmoon was killing him one day at a time. When I began my apprenticeship, I returned the favor, and poisoned the bastard."

Bigsby began to weep.

Infidel lowered her head.

"My father paid the price for my sin," said Bigsby. "When I fled, I left a note confessing… no, *boasting* of my crime. I later learned they executed my father anyway. I… maybe I do deserve to hang."

"No," said Infidel. "I witnessed Tristram's reaction to the news. He was gleeful, laughing. Lord Brightmoon's death brought Tristram closer to the throne. But the hypocrite was all tears and sobs at the funeral. God, even then he was a bastard."

Bigsby wiped his cheeks. "You knew Tristram?"

"Worse," Infidel said. "I loved him."

Bigsby sniffled, and stared at the muscular, tattooed woman before him. He didn't know what to say.

"I was born into wealth," Infidel said. "My father was an advisor in Tristram's court. I was a stupid little girl who imagined that when I grew up, I would win Tristram's heart."

Infidel sighed.

"When I was thirteen, Tristram returned from battle. After the death of Brightmoon, there had been a minor uprising in the southern provinces. Tristram had been gone for a year, helping to suppress the uprising.

"I was warned," said Infidel. "Some of the older girls told me that when Tristram returned from battle he carried a terrible temper, that he could fly into brutal rages.

"I was pleased by this. If the other women avoided Tristram, I would have a chance. I'd let him see that I was different, that I would love him even in his darkest moments."

Infidel rose from the rock she was sitting on. She stalked to a nearby tree, and sunk her dagger into it with an overhand thrust.

"I waited in his chambers, only to talk. And the bastard attacked me," she said, her face turned from Bigsby. "He beat me with his fists, kicked me when I fell, and laughed at my tears. The servants pulled me from the room more dead than alive. When my father learned of the attack, he was furious. Not at Tristram, but at me. He said I deserved it for startling Tristram in the privacy of his quarters. He banished me to a nunnery."

She looked at Bigsby, shrugging. "It didn't take. I fled the nunnery. I've spent the rest of my life on the road."

"I'm sorry," said Bigsby.

"Don't be," said Infidel. "I understand Tristram now. I understand the deep satisfaction of violence. That rush of power that comes when the sword leaves my scabbard. That electric thrill when I see my opponent's blood. It's better than sex. Tristram made me who I am. I can't wait to thank him properly."

Bigsby didn't know what to say to this.

"A touching tale," said a voice from the darkness.

Two shadows moved toward them, resolving into Stranger and Patch.

Patch tossed two packs onto the ground.

"You'll never make it back to Commonground without supplies," said Stranger. "Not that reaching Commonground will do you much good. You'll both be fugitives, and where will you go when even Commonground can't hide you?"

"We'll survive," said Infidel.

"You can do much more than survive," said Stranger. "You can triumph. You can perform the duties you agreed to, and kill Tristram once he kills the dragon."

"I used to stay up nights dreaming about killing Tristram," said Infidel. "But now…? Now I'd really like to kill that damn Truthspeaker."

"I don't want to kill anybody," said Bigsby. "I just want my life back."

"If none of Tristram's party survives, your secret is safe," said Stranger.

"But Jack… and Magidance…"

"They stood by you earlier, eh?" said Stranger.

"I'm in," said Infidel.

"I guess I have no choice," said Bigsby.

"Follow me," said Stranger.

They marched through the darkness for an hour. Stranger led them to a small cave and told them to rest while they could.

"From here, you can watch the entrance to Greatshadow's lair. Once Tristram's party enters, you must follow swiftly. Have no fear of being seen. Tristram and his men will be too focused on what's before them to worry about what's behind them."

"Patch and I will be with Tristram. After the battle, his men should be no match for Patch. Tristram himself may be another matter. But I have faith in you, Infidel."

"What about Thomas and Magidance?" asked Infidel. "How do we counter their magic?"

"Should they survive Greatshadow, I will handle them," said Stranger.

"What about me?" asked Bigsby. "I'm no match for any of them."

"You did well enough striking Thomas from behind," said Stranger.

BIGSBY WAS WIDE-AWAKE when dawn came. Infidel had slept a little, but stirred as light seeped into the cave. Across a rocky valley they could see a huge gash in the mountain's face. Bones lay in great heaps at the entrance.

Before the mists of morning burned away, Tristram and his men appeared. Tristram led the way, followed by five men-at-arms bearing spears and shields. Thomas, Stranger, and Magidance followed with Patch shuffling behind.

Searching the shadows, Bigsby spotted Jack Blade, well in front of the others, creeping among the bone mounds at the lair's mouth.

Stranger cast a single glance their way, and nodded. Infidel slipped from the small cave and crouched behind a boulder. Bigsby followed.

A moment later, Infidel peeked around the rock.

"They're almost there," she whispered. "Can't see Jack. Must be inside. C'mon."

Infidel scrambled across the rocky ground, keeping low. Bigsby breathed deep to gather his courage and chased after her. Quicker than he would have liked, they reached the bone field. Up close, the jagged rock revealed itself to be covered with intricately carved demons. Stairs were cut into the rock, leading into darkness.

"I've seen carvings like this before, when we robbed the tomb of Kuranath," said Infidel. "This place was a temple."

Without waiting for Bigsby's reply, she raced up the steps, staying close to the wall. She motioned for him to follow.

As he reached the top step, Bigsby caught his breath. He could see himself reflected in the floor. For as far as he could see, the floor was made of seamless, gleaming silver. The room was enormous, hundreds of yards deep with a ceiling that vanished into shadows high overhead. From cracks in the rock, shafts of light pierced the darkness.

In the distance, the room held more stairs, rising into an immense, shadowy chamber. Tristram and his men gathered at the foot of the steps. Jack was near the top step, moving cautiously.

Infidel grabbed Bigsby and dragged him into a niche in the wall. She held a finger to her lips.

Jack crept forward into shadows.

Then a scream, abruptly halted, echoed through the chamber. Tristram and his men readied their weapons. Jack's head came bouncing down the stairs.

From the shadows emerged a strange creature, almost human, but taller than Patch. It had four arms, each carrying a sword of flame. It wore armor that glowed red as if fresh from the forge.

"Run!" shouted Magidance.

Tristram's men hurled their spears. One missed, clattering on the gleaming steps. The other four spears crumbled to ash as they touched the glowing armor.

"Halt!" cried Thomas, motioning toward Magidance. The wizard's legs stiffened and he tumbled, skidding across the polished floor.

"Fool!" screamed Magidance. "That's a *godslayer*! A soldier of the wars between Heaven and Hell! We cannot best it."

Tristram's men looked like they had doubts as well. They drew swords, but crept backwards as the godslayer stepped toward them.

Thomas alone held his ground.

"I fear thee not, Devil!"

The godslayer raised a sword overhead, preparing to strike the Truthspeaker who strode boldly forward.

"You are an abomination," cried Thomas, holding his holy book before him.

The godslayer staggered backwards, as if struck a powerful blow.

"An obscenity!" shouted Thomas.

Again, the Godslayer was thrust backwards. It spun about, and fell to one knee.

"Accursed soul!" Thomas raised his scythe over his head. His body glowed with brilliant blue light. He brought the scythe down with all his might, into the center to the godslayer's breastplate.

A crack of thunder shook the chamber. The godslayer's armor and weapons shattered, falling in jagged shards. Naked now, the godslayer was revealed as a bronzed-skinned, well-muscled youth, with golden hair and a serene smile. Bigsby couldn't help but notice the creature also had the longest penis he'd ever seen.

The tip of Thomas' scythe rested against the creature's chest, but had not scratched it. With a grunt, Thomas raised his scythe to strike again.

Still smiling serenely, the godslayer grabbed the fallen spear from the steps. With a single motion, he brought the tip of the spear up to the Truthspeaker's belly. Thomas cried out, his body rising from the floor, his scythe clattering to the ground.

"Now!" cried Tristram.

His five men charged, swords raised against the godslayer. The smiling devil kicked out at the first to reach him, catching him firmly in the chest. The man's sword flew from his grasp as he fell. With a graceful sweep of his lower left arm, the godslayer plucked the sword from the air and used it to sever the head of the second man-at-arms. As the man fell, his sword, too was captured. In a blur of motion, the four-armed youth waded forward, killing two more men before Bigsby could blink, and arming himself with their swords. The final man gave a panicked cry and fell forward, his sword thrust with both hands toward the godslayer's chest. The godslayer danced aside, slow by a second. The man's sword drew a thin red gash across the devil's ribs. The godslayer repaid the scratch with a dozen savage blows that tore the man to bits.

Bigsby limbs felt like lead. He watched helplessly as the godslayer descended the steps.

Only Tristram, Stranger, and Patch remained standing. Magidance tried desperately to regain his footing, slipping and sliding across the gleaming floor in his panic.

Tristram pulled Frostbite from its scabbard. Impossibly, a gentle snow began to fall inside the chamber. Bigsby's breath suddenly came out in clouds.

"I see you can bleed," said Tristram, addressing the godslayer while tightening his grip on his shield.

The four-armed devil leapt forward in a whirl of blades. Tristram grunted as two of the blades fell against his shield, while another slipped harmlessly across his breastplate. The godslayer's final sword was parried by Frostbite. The blade iced over. The godslayer struck again, and again Tristram blocked the blows. This time, the impact of the godslayer's attack caused the blade touched by Frostbite to shatter.

The godslayer's brow furrowed as he glanced at the now bladeless hilt held in his upper right arm.

Tristram attacked, driving Frostbite's tip into the creature's chest. The godslayer drew a sharp breath of pain and raised his lower right arm, bringing his blade up under Tristram's armpit, slipping it between the joints in his armor.

Tristram cried out and fell back, his sword-arm useless at his side. Frostbite hung for a second in the godslayer's chest, then slipped out and clattered noisily at his feet. A crust of red ice quickly sealed over the wound.

Stranger motioned toward Patch.

"Goddammit," grumbled Infidel, rushing from the shadows.

The godslayer struck at Tristram, more savagely than before. Tristram's shield splintered, and one of the beast's blades cut a deep gash into Tristram's neck. Tristram staggered backwards, his hand over the gash. He turned to flee, but the godslayer kicked out, tripping him.

The godslayer readied to deliver the killing blow. Before he could strike, Patch reached him, landing a solid punch to his nose.

The creature looked bewildered, as if he hadn't noticed the huge man. Patch struck him once more, causing a trickle of blood to run from his nose.

The godslayer struck with his remaining blades, piercing the patchwork man, then twisting the swords with a growl.

Patch's torso came free of his legs. He fell forward, locking his hands around the godslayer's neck as his legs stumbled away.

The godslayer began to spin around, hacking at Patch's arms. On his third rotation, Patch's torso and left arm flew free, leaving only his right hand around the godslayer's neck.

And then Infidel reached the godslayer.

She used her momentum to slide forward, between the godslayer's legs. As she passed, she grabbed his manhood with both hands. She stood suddenly, yanking with all her might, and the four-armed devil fell forward.

Infidel released her grip on the godslayer's member and drew a sword in one hand, a dagger in the other. As the godslayer hit the ground, she struck, drawing each blade across the creature's hamstrings. The godslayer rolled to his back, his legs useless as he raised himself on two arms. He still carried a sword in each of his free hands, and used these to strike at Infidel, the blades flashing in silvery arcs.

Infidel easily avoided the blades, then leapt forward, dropping her dagger, thrusting her sword with both hands into the godslayer's throat. She used her momentum to vault over the creature, as the tip of her blade dug ever deeper, nearly twisting his neck from his body.

The godslayer fell limp, a bubble of red blood rising from his lips. Infidel kicked at his head, then kicked again, and again. The head tore free, rolling across the floor to where Magidance had fallen. The mage was now nowhere to be seen.

"Heh," snickered Infidel, wiping her mouth. "Heh heh heh."

She walked to Tristram. He was alive, still conscious, but his life seeped between his fingers with each heartbeat.

Infidel knelt over him.

"Hey," she said, touching his cheek. "The name Isadora mean anything to you?"

Tristram stared at her, his eyes wide with confusion.

"No?" she said. "Hell, why should it?"

Then Tristum stiffened. His lips moved, forming the words, "My God."

"I've hated you for so long," she said, her voice trembling. "So do I kill you now? Or do I sit and watch the life drain from you? What will give me the most satisfaction?"

The decision was never made. A roar rumbled through the chamber. Infidel vanished in a rolling wall of flame. Bigsby felt himself pushed from his feet by an unseen hand. The weight of a man fell upon him, as flame roared above his head. Strangely, he felt no heat. Indeed, he felt as if he'd been plunged into ice water.

"Remain silent," whispered Magidance, unseen. The weight rolled from Bigsby's chest.

As the flames receded, Bigsby could see the smoldering remains of Infidel, still kneeling over the blackened corpse of Tristram. Stranger alone survived, standing calmly as his robes burned.

From the chamber beyond came Greatshadow.

Bibsy wet himself.

The dragon was impossibly large, having to crouch in order to slither into the enormous room. Greatshadow's skin was black with soot. The stench of sulfur filled the air. The dragon spoke, in a language Bigsby had never heard, yet understood instantly.

"Bold fool," Greatshadow growled, drawing his head near Stranger. "Do you know what you've cost me? Centuries. Three centuries of incantations are needed to enslave a godslayer. I'm pleased you survived. Your crime deserves a long, painful punishment."

Stranger pulled away the last of his charred rags and padding. He stood revealed, a dragon seven feet long from snout to tail, with a red scaly hide and a pair of wings upon his back, one twisted at an unnatural angle.

"You made my life a long, painful punishment," said Stranger. "From the day you plucked me from my mother's womb and threw me still wet into the gorge."

"Bigsby," whispered Magidance. Bigsby glanced over his shoulder to see the wizard, Frostbite in his grasp. "We can still snatch victory from the jaws of defeat. This land shall belong to the Silver Kingdom. Our fate rests in your hands."

Magidance held the enchanted blade toward him.

"Take this. While Stranger distracts Greatshadow, you must strike swiftly."

"But—"

"There is no time for debate," said Magidance. "I have transferred my invisibility and can hide you as you approach. You must do this, Bigsby."

"But—"

"Hurry. At this distance, dragons read thoughts. Shielding our minds weakens me with each second. Hurry!"

Bigsby took the sword. Instantly, he realized Magidance was right. The sword filled him with power, gave him strength and courage. *A single blow*, it whispered to him, *and I will rob Greatshadow of his fire*.

Bigsby stalked forward, the sword gripped in both hands.

"You amuse me, little Brokenwing," said Greatshadow. He pushed Stranger to the ground and pinned him with a single claw. Stranger kicked and bit, to no avail.

Bigsby reached Greatshadow. The dragon crouched in such a way that Bigsby could strike at the beast's throat just above the chest.

The sword whispered to him, filling him with cold resolve. He would kill Greatshadow, and liberate the land from his fiery rule.

With a gasp, Bigsby dropped the sword, and cried out, "Greatshadow!"

Across the room, Magidance toppled to the ground, unable to shield Bigsby further.

The enormous dragon snaked its head around. Now that he no longer held Frostbite, Bigsby could feel the furnace-like heat of Greatshadow's breath.

Greatshadow stared right through him.

"Hmmm," Greatshadow said. "Perhaps the blade would have killed me after all. You believed it could, at least."

"Take it," said Bigsby. "Destroy it. It's the only threat you face. All I ask is that you allow us to leave."

"You are in no position to ask anything of me," said the dragon.

"No," said Bigsby.

"But you don't have enough meat on you to be worth eating," said Greatshadow. "Go. Take this failure with you."

He rolled Stranger over on his belly, and twisted the disfigured wing, breaking the bones with a sickening snap. Stranger squealed. Greatshadow flicked his claw, sending the small dragon skidding.

"Little Brokenwing," Greatshadow growled. "A life of pain awaits you, if you flee this island. But should you choose to remain here beyond the dawn of the third day, I will find you, and grant you swift death."

Bigsby ran to help Stranger to his feet.

"Yes, Father," said Stranger, between gasps of pain as he rose.

Bigsby helped support Stranger as they limped from the ancient temple. On the steps, drenched in sweat, Magidance waited.

"Well, that was just great," he said. He spat in Bigsby's direction. "We were so close, and you chickened out."

"I found my courage," said Bigsby. "I won't ask you to understand my reasons. Now, will you help me? We have three days to get Stranger off this island."

"Not Stranger," the small dragon said. "He gave me my name. I am Brokenwing."

Magidance looked the dragon over.

"Hmm," he said, gently touching the damaged wing.

Brokenwing winced.

"I think I can set this to heal properly," said Magidance. "And I know places to hide you until you grow stronger."

"You would help me?" asked Brokenwing.

"How many chances will I get to study a live dragon up close? We'll never make it back to Commonground in three days, though."

"We can make it to the Red River by nightfall," said Brokenwing. "We can build a raft and let it carry us to the sea."

"What about the men we left in camp?"

"They're too far away to reach and still make it. They're on their own," said Brokenwing.

Magidance scratched his chin. "Ah, what the hell. It's not like any of them owe me money."

NIGHT FOUND THEM on the Red River, afloat on a crude raft. The moon turned the water to a silvery sheet as smooth and gleaming as the floor of Greatshadow's lair. Bigsby was skeptical that the raft would survive the night, given the haste with which they had assembled it. But, even with his concerns, he couldn't keep his eyes open. He stretched out beside Brokenwing, who was already sleeping, as Magidance stood over them, using a long stout pole to move the raft around obstacles.

"So, try me," said Magidance. "I'm dying to hear."

"What?" Bigsby asked, drowsily.

"Your reasons. Why didn't you kill him?"

"Greatshadow keeps this land wild," said Bigsby. "When he falls, this place will be overrun with farms and churches and men like Tristram."

Magidance nodded. "That *was* the plan."

"It wasn't my plan," said Bigsby. "I like this place as it is, untamed and untamable. I think the world still needs a place where the wicked can hide from the righteous."

Magidance raised an eyebrow.

"Damn," he said. "That's not a bad reason at all."

ABOUT THE AUTHOR

James Maxey's mother warned him that reading all those comic books would warp his mind. She was right! Now an adult who can't stop daydreaming, James is unsuited for decent work and ekes out a pittance writing down demented fantasies about masked women, fiery dragons, and monkeys.

Among his more infamous scribblings are the post-apocalyptic *Bitterwood* series, superhero novels like *Nobody Gets the Girl* and the *Lawless* series, the secondary world fantasy of the *Dragon Apocalypse*, and the steam-punk visions of *Bad Wizard.*

In 2015, in what is surely a sign of the approaching end times, James was named by the arts councils of the Triangle area of North Carolina as the Piedmont Laureate.

James lives in Hillsborough, North Carolina with his lovely and patient wife Cheryl and too many cats. For more information about James and his writing, visit jamesmaxey.net. Or, if you want a more direct communication or to sign up for news of future releases, email him at james@jamesmaxey.net.

www.ingramcontent.com/pod-product-compliance
Lightning Source LLC
Chambersburg PA
CBHW060542310726
48982CB00009B/1347/J

* 9 7 8 1 7 3 2 5 5 3 7 3 6 *